January 1, 1985

The Watchtower

Announcing Jehovah's Kingdom

ARMAGEDDON —WHAT IT IS NOT

January 1, 1985
Vol. 106 No. 1

The Watchtower

Announcing Jehovah's Kingdom

THE PURPOSE OF "THE WATCHTOWER" is to exalt Jehovah God as the Sovereign of the universe. It keeps watch on world events as they fulfill Bible prophecy. It comforts all peoples with the good news that God's Kingdom will soon destroy those who oppress their fellowmen and that it will turn the earth into a Paradise. It encourages faith in the now-reigning King, Jesus Christ, whose shed blood opens the way for mankind to gain eternal life. "The Watchtower," published by Jehovah's Witnesses continuously since 1879, is nonpolitical. It adheres to the Bible as its authority.

"WATCHTOWER" STUDIES FOR THE WEEKS

Average Printing Each Issue: 11,150,000

Now Published in 102 Languages

SEMIMONTHLY EDITIONS AVAILABLE BY MAIL
Afrikaans, Arabic, Cebuano, Chichewa, Chinese, Cibemba, Danish, Dutch, Efik, English*, Finnish, French, German, Greek, Hiligaynon, Igbo, Iloko, Italian, Japanese, Korean, Lingala, Malagasy, Maltese, Norwegian, Portuguese, Sepedi, Sesotho, Shona, Spanish, Swahili, Swedish, Tagalog, Thai, Tswana, Xhosa, Yoruba, Zulu

MONTHLY EDITIONS AVAILABLE BY MAIL
Armenian, Bengali, Bicol, Bulgarian, Croatian, Czech, Ewe, Fijian, Ga, Greenlandic, Gujarati, Gun, Hausa, Hebrew, Hindi, Hiri Motu, Hungarian, Icelandic, Kannada, Kikuyu, Kiluba, Malayalam, Marathi, New Guinea Pidgin, Pangasinan, Papiamento, Polish, Rarotongan, Romanian, Russian, Samar-Leyte, Samoan, Sango, Serbian, Silozi, Sinhalese, Slovenian, Solomon Islands-Pidgin, Tahitian, Tamil, Telugu, Tshiluba, Tsonga, Turkish, Twi, Ukrainian, Urdu, Venda, Vietnamese
*Study articles also available in large-print edition at same cost.

The Bible translation used is the "New World Translation of the Holy Scriptures," unless otherwise indicated.

Twenty cents (U.S.) a copy

	Yearly subscription rates
Watch Tower Society offices	*Semimonthly*
America, U.S., Watchtower, Wallkill, N.Y. 12589	$4.00
Australia, Box 280, Ingleburn, N.S.W. 2565	A$6.00
Canada, Box 4100, Halton Hills (Georgetown), Ontario L7G 4Y4	$4.50
England, The Ridgeway, London NW7 1RN	£5.00
Ireland, 29A Jamestown Road, Finglas, Dublin 11	£5.00
New Zealand, 6-A Western Springs Rd., Auckland 3	$7.00
Nigeria, P.O. Box 194, Yaba, Lagos State	₦3.50
Philippines, P.O. Box 2044, Manila 2800	₱50.00
South Africa, Private Bag 2, Elandsfontein, 1406	R5.60

Remittances should be sent to the office in your country or to Watchtower, Wallkill, N.Y. 12589, U.S.A.

Changes of address should reach us 30 days before your moving date. Give us your old and new address (if possible, your old address label).

The Watchtower (ISSN 0043-1087) is published semimonthly for $4.00 (U.S.) per year by Watch Tower Bible and Tract Society of Pennsylvania, 25 Columbia Heights, Brooklyn, N.Y. 11201. Second-class postage paid at Brooklyn, N.Y., and at additional mailing offices.

Postmaster: Send address changes to Watchtower, *Wallkill, N.Y. 12589.*

Published by
**Watch Tower Bible and Tract Society
of Pennsylvania**
25 Columbia Heights, Brooklyn, N.Y. 11201, U.S.A.
Frederick W. Franz, President

Why So Much Talk About

ARMAGEDDON?

"You know, I turn back to your ancient prophets in the Old Testament and the signs foretelling Armageddon, and I find myself wondering if—if we're the generation that is going to see that come about."—Ronald W. Reagan, president of the United States, October 18, 1983.

"Apocalypse is today not merely a biblical depiction but it has become a very real possibility. Never before in human experience have we been placed on the narrow edge between catastrophe and survival."—Javier Perez de Cuellar, secretary-general of the United Nations, June 8, 1982.

"ARMAGEDDON" has become the talk of the world. The ominous-sounding word is heard more and more frequently from the lips of clergymen, politicians, statesmen, military generals, scientists, and even economists. In the United States alone, the word Armageddon is found in the titles of at least 15 books in circulation during 1983. It has become the subject matter of numerous other books, some of which have sold into the millions of copies.

It may seem strange that this word has skyrocketed to popularity, for the first recorded use of the word Armageddon is found in the Bible—and there it is used only once. (Revelation 16:16, *King James Version*) Yet the clergy have not had the sole claim on use of the word. In the 1800's the word Armageddon began to be used in a non-Biblical sense as well. However, it was not until the early 1900's that "Armageddon" became synonymous with "any great slaughter" or "final conflict." Since then the word Armageddon has slowly crept into the vocabulary of diverse

groups of professions, each one coloring it with a different shade of meaning. In 1912, Theodore Roosevelt, campaigning for a further term as president of the United States, gave the word a political twist. He boasted: "With unflinching heart and undimmed eye, we stand at Armageddon and we battle for the Lord." Roosevelt lost that political battle for reelection.

Nowadays it is a bad case of world jitters that is causing all this talk about Armageddon: threats of global nuclear annihilation, a long nuclear winter due to detonating those fearsome weapons, a great war in the Middle East, or a sudden collapse of the world's economic foundation. The word Armageddon is thus popping up today even in the most unexpected places:

♦ A full-length Japanese animated feature cartoon film entitled "Armageddon in Kichijoji" depicts cartoon figures that represent good and evil in a battle to the finish.

♦ The expected 1986 reappearance of Halley's Comet caused the *Frankfurter Neue*

Presse to say that it "could well again presage Armageddon" for the superstitious.

But not one of these is *the* Armageddon. Today another voice proclaiming Armageddon is being heard—one soaring in intensity and sounded by more than two and a-half million people. Have you heard it? By listening to this voice, you will be able to learn not only what Armageddon is not but, more importantly, what it really is.

ARMAGEDDON
—What It Is Not

Your destination is only a short ride from Haifa. Under the blaze of the Middle Eastern sun, your car speeds along south of the meandering Kishon River until the valley tapers. Through the narrow gap between the towering Carmel range and the Galilee hills you go, until suddenly the valley opens out before you like a wide, flat saucer—the Plain of Esdraelon. You are motoring on the south side of the plain when your eye catches sight of one hill with an unnaturally level plateaulike top. This is what you are looking for! The tell, or mound, of Megiddo, the source of the word Armageddon.

ARMAGEDDON is shrouded in mystery and misconceptions. Ideas as to its meaning abound. The word Armageddon, though, is derived from *Har–Magedon,* or Mountain of Megiddo.* It is a Bible word found at Revelation 16:16, which states:

---

* Kittel, also McClintock and Strong, Biblical language scholars, are uncertain as to the meaning of the word "Megiddo," but make reference to the fact that the word could mean "assembly" or "place of troops."

"And they gathered them together to the place that is called in Hebrew Har-Magedon [or, Armageddon]."

Who are gathered to Armageddon and why? Revelation 16:14 answers: "The *kings* of the entire inhabited earth" muster "to the *war* of the great day of God the Almighty."

Those answers raise a host of other questions. With whom do "the kings" battle, and over what issue? Where will they fight? Will they use nuclear weapons? Can the war be prevented? Really, what *is* Armageddon?

Not a Geographic Spot

Armageddon could not be a geographic location. No mountain by that name actually exists—though a mound called Megiddo remains to this day. The real meaning of Armageddon casts its shadow back in history to warfare that centered in that area of Megiddo.

Megiddo has been the site of some of the most fierce and decisive battles in Middle Eastern history. It all began during the second millennium B.C.E. with Egyptian ruler Thutmose III's smashing victory over Palestinian and Syrian rulers, and stretched through the centuries to the year 1918 when British field marshal Viscount Allenby inflicted a stinging defeat on the Turks.

But more important to Bible students, Megiddo witnessed the magnificent victory of the Israelite forces under the command of Judge Barak over King Jabin's mighty Canaanite army led by war chief Sisera. Jehovah God intervened and provided the Israelites with a resounding triumph.—Judges 4:7, 12-16, 23; 5:19-21.

Therefore, Armageddon begins to take the form of a crucial battle, with only one clear victor.

Not a War Between Earthly Nations

The issue surrounding the battle of Armageddon—world rulership—is the great issue of today. But, although two opposing superpowers are now grappling for world domination, Armageddon will not be a world war, pitting one of these against the other. True, the world is in the most expensive and frenzied arms race in all history, prompting this comment from *India Today:* "All this is pushing the planet grimly to the edge of Armageddon—the ultimate war among nations." But Revelation 16:14 indicates that "the kings of the *entire* inhabited earth" mobilize a united front at "the war of the great day of God the Almighty."

Therefore, Armageddon is not man's war. It is God's war. Armageddon will find all earthly nations united in battling 'the armies of heaven' under the military command of the "King of kings and Lord of lords," Christ Jesus. He is the rightful ruler of the world because God also "subjected all things under his [Christ's] feet." —Revelation 19:14, 16; Ephesians 1:22.

Not a Nuclear Holocaust

For many people, nuclear war is too chilling to think about. A 1983 joint study by 40 scientists estimates that in an all-out nuclear war *one third to one half* of the total world population would suffer immediate death. Their report, published in *Science* magazine, predicts a grim future for the survivors. It warns: "In any large-scale nuclear exchange between the superpowers, global environmental changes sufficient to cause the extinction of a major fraction of the plant and animal species on the Earth are likely. In that event, the possibility of the extinction of *Homo sapiens* cannot be excluded."

Would Almighty God Jehovah allow such a horror? No! He did not create the earth "simply for nothing," but as he reassures us, he "formed it even to be inhabited." (Isaiah 45:18) At Armageddon God will "bring to ruin those ruining the earth," not scorch it in a nuclear holocaust.—Revelation 11:18.

Not a Continuous Battle Between Good and Evil

Some religious leaders believe Armageddon to be a running struggle between the forces of good and evil, whether worldwide or in the mind. "Armageddon is occurring in some part of the world every day," notes one Bible commentary. How could this be when the Bible promises that Armageddon will bring swift doom for all evil nations and people? Christ, as God's anointed King at Armageddon, "will break them with an iron scepter, as though a potter's vessel [he] will dash them to pieces."—Psalm 2:9; see also Proverbs 2: 21, 22; Revelation 19:11-21.

Not a World Economic Collapse

The world's most powerful governments fear that a Third World default on debt would propel the global economic situation into what *Business Life* magazine calls an "Economic Armageddon." A collapse of the world's banking institutions would truly be tragic, but it would not be Armageddon. The Bible Armageddon is a worldwide situation involving war, not economics. The prophet Jeremiah describes it in these graphic terms: "There is a controversy that Jehovah has with the nations. He must personally put himself in judgment with all flesh. As regards the wicked ones, he must give them to the sword." —Jeremiah 25:31.

Not a War in the Middle East

"Somewhere in time, the last conflagration will take place in the Middle East," preaches world-renowned evangelist Billy Graham. On this matter, he echoes the views of many of his religious colleagues. Graham also believes that Armageddon can be delayed. "I think that the world is heading right now toward Armageddon," he says, "and that unless there is a spiritual awakening and we turn to God, the world may face its Armageddon in this decade."

The region of Megiddo could not begin to hold all "the kings of the earth and their armies." (Revelation 19:19) Therefore, would this not rule out any fundamentalist teaching that Armageddon will be a world war squeezed into the literal plain of Megiddo? The prophet Jeremiah indicates that Armageddon will encompass "the remotest parts of the earth" and that the casualties will be seen "from one

---

What Is Armageddon?

Armageddon IS NOT. . .

♦ a geographic location
♦ a battle between nations
♦ a nuclear holocaust
♦ a global economic collapse
♦ a struggle between good and evil
♦ a Middle Eastern conflict

Armageddon IS. . .

♦ the worldwide situation where all earthly nations will battle against God's Son, Christ Jesus, and his angelic army in "the war of the great day of God the Almighty"

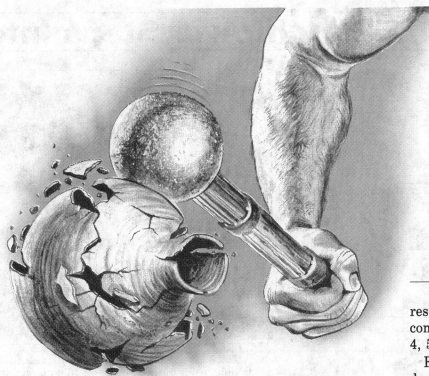

At Armageddon God's King, Jesus Christ, 'will break all evil nations with an iron scepter, as though a potter's vessel he will dash them to pieces.'—Psalm 2:9.

end of the earth clear to the other end of the earth."—Jeremiah 25:32, 33.

And since Armageddon means "the war of the great day of God the Almighty," no one can prevent it. There is nothing that humans can do that will delay it. Jehovah has set an "appointed time" for the battle to start. "It will not be late."—Revelation 16:14; 11:18; Habakkuk 2:3.

Basis for Hope

Armageddon is not to be feared by people who love righteousness. To the contrary, it can be a basis for hope. The Bible says: "And I saw the heaven opened, and, look! a white horse. And the one seated upon it is called Faithful and True, and he judges and *carries on war in righteousness.*" (Revelation 19:11) The battle of Armageddon will wipe the earth clean of all wickedness and pave the way for the restoration of righteous conditions.—Isaiah 11: 4, 5.

For more than a hundred years, the voice of Jehovah's Witnesses has been heard proclaiming God's future victory over the corrupt, unyielding rulers of this system. Especially since the year 1925 the Witnesses have had a clear view of what Armageddon is and they refuse to keep silent about it. Their desire is to help people to become Armageddon survivors, not casualties. So they urge all who listen to follow the advice of Joel 2:31, 32, which speaks of "the coming of the great and fear-inspiring day of Jehovah," and adds: *"Everyone who calls on the name of Jehovah will get away safe."*

Some, though, may still wonder: Although Armageddon is global in scope, will it start in the Middle East? How could a God of love allow an Armageddon? Will true peace follow Armageddon? Read the next three issues of *The Watchtower,* for they will address those questions.

The Watchtower Steps Into

Swedish

Danish

Norwegian

Finnish

Portuguese

German

In July 1879 the first issue of this magazine stated: "As its name indicates, it aims to be the lookout from whence matters of interest and profit may be announced to the 'little flock.'" Today, *The Watchtower* serves spiritual food also to "a great crowd" of sincere persons who look forward to gaining everlasting life here on earth.—Luke 12:32; Revelation 7:9-17.

As the circulation of *The Watchtower* increased so did the number of languages in which it appeared. Today, these languages total 102. Reports show that new subscriptions to *The Watchtower* and its companion magazine, *Awake!,* have increased remarkably over

Sepedi	Tsonga
Sesotho	Zulu

Simultaneous Publication

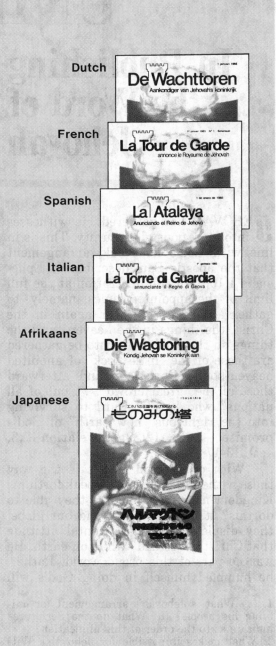

Dutch — De Wachttoren — Aankondiger van Jehovah's koninkrijk

French — La Tour de Garde — annonce le Royaume de Jéhovah

Spanish — La Atalaya — Anunciando el Reino de Jehová

Italian — La Torre di Guardia — annunciante il Regno di Geova

Afrikaans — Die Wagtoring — Kondig Jehovah se Koninkryk aan

Japanese — ものみの塔

the past 70 years. So also has the field placement of individual copies. Here are some available figures:

Year	New Subscriptions	Magazines Placed
1914	2,746	95,973
1944	292,258	9,293,913
1964	1,551,436	127,055,165
1984	1,812,221	287,358,064

Now we reach another milestone in the 105-year history of *The Watchtower*—its simultaneous publication in 20-and-more languages. A joyful development indeed! May Jehovah continue to use this magazine mightily in announcing his Kingdom by Christ Jesus!

Tswana — Tora ya Tebelo — E Itsise Bogosi jwa ga Jehofa

Venda — Tshiingamo — Tshi Divhadzaho Muvhuso wa Yehova

Xhosa — IMboniselo — Evakalisa Ubukumkani BukaYehova

Cibemba — Ulupungu lwa kwa Kalinda — Ulusabankanya Ubufumu bwa kwa Yehova

UNIFIED

In Publishing the Word of Jehovah

"Have among yourselves the same mental attitude that Christ Jesus had, that with one accord you may with one mouth glorify the God and Father of our Lord Jesus Christ."
—ROMANS 15:5, 6.

JEHOVAH has gathered his witnesses into a precious global unity. This is in line with God's household arrangement that the apostle Paul describes at Ephesians 1:10: "An administration at the full limit of the appointed times, namely, to gather all things together again in the Christ, the things in the heavens and the things on the earth." First to be gathered are those of the "little flock" of anointed heaven-bound Christians and afterward those of the "great crowd . . . out of all nations" who look forward to surviving into the righteous "new earth" of God's promise.—Luke 12:32; Revelation 7:3, 4, 9, 13-17; 21:1, 5.

2 "With one accord"—that is the way these witnesses of Jehovah speak forth his Kingdom message. Why are they able to do this? It is because, around our globe, they display "the same mental attitude that Christ Jesus had" while on earth. He was no part of this proud world. Rather, he humbled himself in doing God's will and in building up a warm, loving unity among his disciples. This was the start of a global unification that distinguished true Christians during the centuries to follow.—Philippians 2:5-8; John 13:34, 35; 17:14.

3 This unity of organization has reached its most wonderful expression during these "last days," standing out in sharp contrast with the divisions afflicting Satan's system of things, where hatred and lawlessness are rampant. (2 Timothy 3: 1-5, 13; Matthew 24:3, 12) Never before in the history of mankind has there existed around our earth, in 203 lands, an organization that is in full accord as to belief, purpose and activity. This global society of Jesus' disciples may be recognized by the fruit that it bears.—John 15:8; Hebrews 13:15; Galatians 5:22, 23.

Unity of Action

4 Unity of action in Jehovah's organiza-

---

1. (a) What is Jehovah's arrangement for unifying his people? (b) What do the Scriptures indicate as to the order of this unification?
2. What makes it possible for Jehovah's Witnesses to speak "with one accord"?

3. (a) What sharp contrast is to be seen on earth today? (b) How do the Scriptures help in identifying the global society of true Christians?
4. (a) What controversy arose in the first-century congregation? (b) According to Acts 15: 1-6, what theocratic action was initiated?

tion is illustrated for us at Acts chapter 15. Picture in your mind's eye a gathering of mature witnesses of Jehovah—the 12 apostles, other older men of the Jerusalem congregation and Paul and Barnabas, elders from the Antioch congregation. In Antioch, and also in Jerusalem, some converts from among the Jews have been insisting that people of the nations must be circumcised and must observe the Law of Moses in order to be saved. So the apostles and the older men have "gathered together to see about this affair."—Acts 15:1-6.

5 There is open-minded discussion of the problem, with those devoted men airing all the pros and cons. They do not have their minds made up ahead of time. They are willing to examine the matter from all angles. There is "much disputing," but obviously they maintain good order and listen respectfully to one another's views. The apostle Peter bears witness to the fact that God has given holy spirit to uncircumcised people of the nations—surely powerful testimony that physical circumcision is no longer a requirement for those being saved. Barnabas and Paul add to this testimony, describing the many wonderful things that God has accomplished through their ministry to the nations. —Acts 15:7-12.

6 Next, James quotes the Scriptures in support of the argument that has just been presented. He explains that Amos 9: 11, 12 points forward to the restoration of divine favor under the Greater David, Jesus Christ, and to Jehovah's extending undeserved kindness to "all the nations upon whom [his] name has been called."

James sees no need to trouble converts from the nations by insisting that they be circumcised and observe all the rules embodied in the Law of Moses. However, a few things are necessary: They must abstain from idolatry, from partaking of blood in any form and from sexual immorality.—Acts 15:13-21.

7 The governing body in Jerusalem comes to a unanimous decision. It dispatches messengers to the Antioch congregation with a letter that concludes with the encouragement: "If you carefully keep yourselves from these things, you will prosper. Good health to you!"—Acts 15:22-29.

Theocratic Procedure

8 In modern times, the Governing Body of Jehovah's Witnesses, representing the Master's "faithful and discreet slave" on earth, follows the same apostolic pattern. (Matthew 24:45-47) Thus, Christian experience, guidance from the Bible, and the leadings of Jehovah's spirit direct this group of anointed Witnesses to theocratic conclusions on matters of great concern to the congregation. For example, in recent years the Governing Body has followed the Scriptural procedure in clarifying such matters as the Bible's view of "ministers," the God-given conscience, the carrying of lethal weapons, and the extent to which features of Isaiah's prophecy apply to the future Paradise on earth.—Compare John 14:26; 1 Corinthians 2:10.

9 The procedure of Acts chapter 15 must be followed also by congregation elders in handling problems today. First, let the problem and related facts be plainly stated. Next, let reliable witnesses give clear,

---

5-7. (a) In what sense was there "much disputing"? (b) What testimony was presented? (c) How were the Scriptures brought to bear on the matter? (d) What mature determination did James make, leading to what final decision? (e) What kind of action followed?

8. (a) How is the modern-day Governing Body guided in making decisions? (b) What are some matters that have been clarified recently? 9. What procedure must elders follow in handling problems today?

factual evidence bearing on the matter. Search the Scriptures to get Jehovah's viewpoint, making use also of help that may be available in the Watch Tower Society's publications. Prayerfully work toward reaching a unanimous solution, in harmony with the teaching of Jehovah's Word, that will benefit the congregation. —Isaiah 48:17; 1 Corinthians 14:33.

Rejoicing—Then and Now

[10] When they heard of the governing body's decision, members of the congregation in Antioch "rejoiced over the encouragement." Similarly today, Jehovah's Witnesses rejoice to learn of organizational decisions and clarifications of doctrine that promote the spiritual health of God's people and the advancement of Jehovah's work. (Compare Titus 2:1.) But it is no longer necessary for the Governing Body to write letters of instruction by hand and to circulate these by messengers traveling on foot. Modern means of communication and printing facilities in more than 30 Watch Tower branches around the earth have made it possible to convey "the good news of the word of Jehovah" to the millions of God's people in a minimum of time. This is done principally through the *Watchtower* magazine. Thus, the congregations worldwide continue "to be made firm in the faith and to increase in number from day to day."—Acts 15:30–16:5.

[11] Those who have read *The Watchtower* over the years have rejoiced also to see its increasing circulation. In 105 years of publication, this expanded from 6,000 copies in English once a month to 11,150,000 copies in 102 languages, all major editions being semimonthly. Unquestionably, *The Watchtower* has been used mightily by our Grand Instructor, Jehovah God, in fulfilling the promise: "Happy are all those keeping in expectation of him. . . . Your own ears will hear a word behind you saying: 'This is the way. Walk in it, you people,' in case you people should go to the right or in case you should go to the left." —Isaiah 30:18-21.

[12] *Now there is further reason to rejoice.* Starting into the year 1985, *The Watchtower* is being published *simultaneously,* as to contents, in 23 languages!* All these editions have the same cover design. They contain the same series of opening articles and the same articles for study. This provides for a simultaneous "feeding" program that will unite Jehovah's people in growing spiritually "until we all attain to the oneness in the faith." It should stimulate us the more, that 'with one accord we may with one mouth glorify the God and Father of our Lord Jesus Christ.' —Ephesians 4:13; Romans 15:6.

[13] When you hold this magazine in your hand at the weekly congregation study of *The Watchtower,* does it not thrill you to know that most of your brothers worldwide will be unified in partaking of this same spiritual food on the same day? Yes, this will be happening in all of North and South America, in most of Europe, in Japan and in many places in southern Afri-

---

* These languages are: Afrikaans, Danish, Dutch, English, Finnish, French, German, Italian, Japanese, Norwegian, Portuguese, Spanish, Swedish, and Thai; the African dialects: Sepedi, Sesotho, Tsonga, Tswana, Venda, Xhosa, and Zulu; and two languages in lands where the work of Jehovah's Witnesses is restricted.

---

10. (a) As in the first-century congregation, how should theocratic decisions affect us today? (b) How have modern developments led to strengthening and increasing God's people?
11. How has Jehovah used *The Watchtower* in fulfilling Isaiah 30:18-21?

12. (a) Why do we now have further cause for rejoicing? (b) How should this new arrangement benefit us?
13. (a) How extensive is this program? (b) What application of 1 Corinthians 1:10 may therefore be made?

ca! It is estimated that already more than 90 percent of those attending the *Watchtower* study around the earth—some 2,500,000 persons each week—are now sharing in this simultaneous "feeding" arrangement. Together, these are being "fitly united in the same mind and in the same line of thought." (1 Corinthians 1:10) As circumstances permit, other languages will be added.

14 Hitherto, because of language differences, members of one family may have been months apart in studying particular *Watchtower* articles. But now they can be united in this respect. For example, immigrant parents better acquainted with another language may sit down with their English-speaking children to prepare together the same week's *Watchtower* lesson in both languages. In bilingual families, parents will be better equipped to carry out the instruction of Ephesians 6:4 and 2 Timothy 3:14, 15.

15 Consider, too, our public ministry with the magazines. In this additional way, Kingdom publishers around the globe can now "cry out joyfully in unison" as they present identical information to the world public at the same time. (Isaiah 52: 8, 9) In doing magazine street witnessing in multilanguage territories, publishers can display magazines with the same cover theme in two or more languages. Think of it! During the early part of 1985, Kingdom publishers all over the earth will be giving a rousing, united testimony concerning Armageddon! In due time, Jehovah may direct his people to make other powerful, unified declarations worldwide as they serve "side by side for the faith of the good news." (Philippians 1:27) The simultaneous publication of *The Watch-*

tower in many languages will make possible such pronouncements.—Compare Daniel 11:44.

Looking Ahead

16 During the year 1984, Jehovah's Witnesses have given wide distribution to the companion magazines *The Watchtower* and *Awake!* This activity has been richly blessed by Jehovah, as can be seen from the statistics published on pages 8, 9, and 25 in this magazine. Worldwide, the field distribution of our magazines during 1984 increased by 11.1 percent to a grand total of 287,358,064, while placements of magazine subscriptions increased by 3.2 percent to 1,812,221. There is no question that more and more people are wanting to know why the nations are in anguish, "not knowing the way out." (Luke 21:25, 26) Parents want a happy future for their children—something better than an earth roasted in a nuclear war. Our magazines hold out a living hope!—Matthew 12: 18, 21; Romans 15:4.

17 What, then, of 1985? The message in *The Watchtower* and *Awake!* is becoming ever more pointed. This is to be expected as the last days for Satan's world wind down. (Revelation 12:12) Make no mistake! The Devil would like to discourage us from sharing regularly in Jehovah's service. Yes, Satan would like to separate us from the body of God's people and its activity, and so devour us. (1 Peter 5:8) But we can resist him by regularly meeting to take in accurate knowledge, and by using this increased knowledge in serving Jehovah.—Ephesians 6:11, 14-16; Colossians 1:9-11.

---

14. How will families be benefited?
15. (a) In our public ministry, what can we now do in line with Isaiah 52:8, 9? (b) What is made possible for early 1985, and for the future?

16. (a) What does this *Watchtower* tell us about magazine activity on pages 8, 9, and 25? (b) Why do people need our magazines today?
17. How will our magazines help us to resist the Devil?

¹⁸ Are you a Kingdom publisher? If so, you hold the key position in the modern-day theocratic society. As a dedicated Christian, you may have other responsibilities in the congregation. Yet, in living up to Jehovah's name, you must be a zealous minister in the field. United in brotherly love and in having tender affection for one another, let all of us continue to be aglow with the spirit as we "slave for Jehovah." (Romans 12:10, 11) No matter what pressures we experience from Satan and his world, we must continue as one body, yes, 'with one accord and with one mouth,' to glorify Jehovah by making known his Kingdom purposes.

¹⁹ Many of us have to contend with persecution or with territories that are unresponsive to our preaching. However, let us continue to show the same mental attitude that Christ Jesus had. (John 16:33; 1 Peter 4:1, 2) As a united body let us manifest true courage—the internal spiritual strength that endures and does not crumble under pressure. (Psalm 27:14; Philippians 1:14) Let us never slack the hand in searching for sheeplike ones. Let us keep ourselves "in expectation" of Jehovah and his day of reckoning, serving him shoulder to shoulder as we call upon his name and speak the "pure language" of truth. —Zephaniah 3:8, 9.

²⁰ Unitedly, may all who glorify God "put on the new personality which was created according to God's will in true righteousness and loyalty." (Ephesians 4:24) This results in true happiness. It is illustrated at Isaiah 11:6-9, which tells of the spiritual paradise now existing among Jehovah's restored people. What peace and harmony! What absence of greedy, harmful personality traits! As the finale of this paradisaic description, we note these words: "They will not do any harm or cause any ruin in all my holy mountain; because the earth will certainly be filled with the knowledge of Jehovah as the waters are covering the very sea." Jehovah's "holy mountain" of united worship is firmly established today in all the earth. Why? It is because Jehovah has moved his witnesses to glorify his name 'with one accord and with one mouth.' Thus "the earth," the spiritual estate of His people, has been filled with "the knowledge of Jehovah."

²¹ May we, in the strength that Jehovah provides, give *The Watchtower* and its companion magazine *Awake!* the widest possible distribution. And may we do so in the hope that all the ends of the earth and all the families of the nations, representatively, "will remember and turn back to Jehovah."—Psalm 22:27; Revelation 15:4.

21. Why should we give our magazines the widest possible distribution?

18. (a) How great is your responsibility as a Kingdom publisher? (b) How can we apply the counsel of Romans 12:10, 11 and 15:5, 6?
19. (a) How can we successfully contend with persecutions and other problems? (b) What counsel does Zephaniah 3:8, 9 provide for us?
20. (a) How can we find true happiness? (b) Isaiah 11:6-9 has had what remarkable fulfillment?

Reviewing This Article—

☐ How did the first-century congregation function?

☐ What benefits should result from simultaneous publication of *The Watchtower?*

☐ What fine magazine effort was put forth in 1984?

☐ How may we prosper spiritually, even in times of trial?

Christians Must Witness

In recent years church leaders have been quite vocal about the need for a Christian witness. And so they should be, for the word "witness," and its derivatives, as based on the Greek word *martýs,* occurs 47 times in the Christian Greek Scriptures ("New Testament"), *King James Version.* Let us examine some of the statements coming out of Christendom.

POPE JOHN PAUL II is quoted in *L'Osservatore Romano* (weekly edition in English) of April 30, 1984, as saying: "Witness, as my predecessor Paul VI stressed, 'is an essential element of evangelization, and generally the first' (*Evangelii Nuntiandi,* n. 21). It is particularly urgent in our era, in the disorientation of minds and in the eclipse of values that are shaping a crisis which is revealed ever more clearly as a total crisis of civilization." A year earlier, another issue of the same journal reported on a papal audience under the headline "World of work needs Christian witnesses."

Thus the need for witnessing is emphasized by the Roman Catholic Church. But what do Protestant spokesmen say about the importance of witnessing?

The sixth General Assembly of the World Council of Churches, which now has 301 members, met in Vancouver from July 24 to August 10, 1983, and later published its *International Review of Mission* (October 1983) including a 36-page article entitled "Witnessing in a Divided World." Under a subheading, "All Christians Are Called to Witness," this article stated forthrightly: "For a Christian, the task and act of witnessing is a response to and an expression of loyalty to God. . . . Witnessing is by divine mandate. We witness to the supremacy and love of God the creator and giver of life."

The Baptist theological journal *Review and Expositor* gives similar emphasis, saying: "A study of the book of Acts reveals that new believers were added to the church because Christians were witnessing. If new converts are not being brought in, then, most likely, Christians are not witnessing."

Though the sects of Christendom are hopelessly divided as to ideology and doctrine, they appear to agree on the need for witnessing. But are their members living up to the obligation of witnessing?

On this point, Michael Green, rector of St. Aldgate's Church, Oxford, England, writes: "Our forefathers in the faith were accused of 'turning the world upside down' with the good news they told people about Jesus (Acts 17:6). . . . That is where we differ so enormously from the early church, where every man and woman saw it as his task to bear witness to Jesus Christ by every means at his or her disposal."

A Baptist booklet, *Witnessing in Today's World,* states: "A dedicated Christian may say, 'Why, I wouldn't know where to start in trying to witness to someone else.'" It adds: "The immediate reaction of many Baptist church members when witnessing is mentioned is, 'We pay the pastor to do that.'"

Further, a Westminster publication, *The Christian as Communicator,* confesses: "It is quite possible that the responsibility for communicating the gospel is being bypassed simply because Christians do not have very much to say."

True, members of Christendom's sects "do not have very much to say." And therein lies the crux of their problem. They have failed to recognize the modern-day fulfillment of "the sign" that Jesus gave concerning his "presence" in Kingdom glory and "the conclusion of the system of things." Those who see that "sign" are impelled to witness about it. How happy we can be that true Christians today have *a great deal to say,* as they witness zealously concerning Jehovah's incoming Kingdom by Christ Jesus.—Matthew 24: 3-14; Isaiah 43:12.

A Centennial to Remember

GOD'S people have been privileged to observe many modern-day miracles. Outstanding among these has been the growth of the global organization that Jehovah is now using to declare his name throughout the earth. It all started in Pittsburgh during the early 1870's with a small group of earnest Bible students. These multiplied rapidly, so that it soon became necessary to form a legal corporation to care for the expanding organization. Thus, Zion's Watch Tower Tract Society was duly incorporated on December 13, 1884, under the laws of the Commonwealth of Pennsylvania.

Recently, on Saturday, October 6, 1984, the 100th annual meeting of the members of the corporation—known now as the Watch Tower Bible and Tract Society of Pennsylvania—was held in Pittsburgh. A special occasion indeed! Just as important events in ancient times were memorialized, so it was appropriate that Jehovah's Witnesses should mark this centennial of the Watch Tower Society by a special gathering. Thus they could render thanks and praise to the Sovereign Lord Jehovah, who has protected and shepherded this expanding organization through the troublesome years of the past century.—Joshua 4:4-8, 20-24; Esther 9:20-22; Psalm 23:1-6.

Corporate Meeting

Promptly at ten o'clock on the morning of October 6, the annual corporate meeting of the Society was opened at the Coraopolis Assembly Hall of Jehovah's Witnesses, Pittsburgh. Among worldly organizations, corporate meetings are usually cut-and-dried, busi-

ness-only affairs. But this meeting was different.

Of the 429 members of the corporation, 259 were present in person, together with their guests —an assembly totaling 1,615 persons. These had traveled to the meeting from 53 different countries—from such widely scattered places as Alaska, Antigua, Argentina, Australia, Austria, and through the alphabet to Zimbabwe. The formal election of four directors of the Society was followed by a spiritually strengthening program of talks. One of these, based on the yeartext chosen by Jehovah's Witnesses for 1985, 2 Timothy 4:5, exhorted everyone: "Fully accomplish your ministry."

There followed a stirring address by the Society's 91-year-old president, F. W. Franz. He stated that he had never been so thrilled as when, some 65 years ago, along with J. F. Rutherford, he first heard the phrase "God's organization." After tracing the development of the organization in the earth, he expressed thankfulness that this is the 100th year that Jehovah's organization has used the incorporated Society to bring us life-saving Scriptural information. Brother Franz' voice rose to a triumphant crescendo as he quoted the last verse of the Psalms, saying, 'Every breathing thing—let it praise Jah—HALLELUJAH!'

'Jehovah Is With His People'

Outstanding brotherly love and hospitality were displayed by the Pittsburgh congregations of Jehovah's Witnesses. (Hebrews 13: 1, 2) Self-sacrificing attention was given to provide fine meals, accommodations and transportation, and every organizational detail was cared for in readying Pittsburgh's famous Three Rivers Stadium for the three-hour evening meeting that followed.

It was like a smile of approval from Jehovah that weather conditions for this autumn day were ideal. Thus, the crowd of 37,733 at the stadium could listen in comfort and with appreciation. Telephone tie lines carried the program to 34 Assembly Halls of Jehovah's Witnesses in the United States and in Canada, where another 59,715 listened—making a grand total of 97,448 in attendance. All of these were provided with copies of a colorful 32-page brochure-style program as a memento of the happy event.

The evening session commenced with joyful song and prayer. Then ten members of the Governing Body of Jehovah's Witnesses shared with many other long-time servants of Jehovah in developing the theme: "Jehovah Has Always Proved to Be With His People." As the program brochure stated: "There is, indeed, much evidence that Jehovah has proved to be with his people and that he has blessed and established the work of their hands—accomplished by the instrumentality of the Watch Tower Society. Therefore, in accord with the thoughts of Psalm 78:2-7, it is appropriate that we use this occasion to relate to the newer generation 'the praises of Jehovah . . . and his wonderful things that he has done.'"

That is just what the program accomplished! Hitler and apostate religionists had tried to exterminate Jehovah's Witnesses "like vermin," but such opposers have gone, as always, "like snow in the sun." Bible translator Goodspeed described the first century Christians as "a translating and publishing people." And how true this is also of 20th-century Witnesses! During the 105 years ending in 1984, these Christians published, in 200 and more languages, 8.8 billion Bibles, books, booklets, magazines, and tracts. The *New*

World Translation of the entire Bible, or at least the Greek Scriptures, was printed in 14 languages to a total of 51,034,000 copies. Very soon a pocket edition of this Bible, and also a large-print edition in four volumes, will become available. Thus the Watch Tower Society will continue to be a leader in Bible publication.

The brochure said: "A testimony to the caliber of faithful men who have served with the Watch Tower Society can be seen in the fact that during a period of 100 years only four different men have served in the responsible position of president of the Society." Jehovah's organization moves on grandly toward final victory. As Martin Poetzinger, who kept integrity through nine years in Nazi concentration camps, commented: "Stick to Jehovah and Christ Jesus and God's organization, and you will see his triumphant victory over all opposers."

The final speaker of the evening, president F. W. Franz, described this centennial day as "an occasion that will never be duplicated." How true! Reviewing the thrilling history of the Society, Brother Franz recalled the words of J. F. Rutherford, the second president, who died in 1942. Shortly before his death, he said, "Well, Fred, it looks to me the great [crowd] is not going to be so great after all." Brother Franz commented, "He died too soon." At that time Jehovah's Witnesses numbered fewer than 100,000 worldwide. Today, literally 'millions of those who will never die' have been added to the ranks of these loyal servants.

Brother Franz concluded with these words: "We are stirred to say in unison: 'All hail to Jehovah God the Universal Sovereign.'" By thunderous applause all present expressed their wholehearted agreement. After final song and prayer they left for their home countries and congregations with joyful determination to go on in Jehovah's work to the finish.

WITNESSING
Brings Kingdom Increase

"May Jehovah . . . increase you a thousand times as many as you are, and may he bless you just as he has promised you."
—DEUTERONOMY 1:11.

A THOUSANDFOLD INCREASE! That is what Moses petitioned for Jehovah's "holy nation," Israel. Jehovah had promised great things for that nation. (Exodus 19:5, 6; see also Genesis 12:2, 3.) Did he fulfill those promises?

2 Well, some 500 years after Moses spoke the above words, it was reported: "Judah and Israel were many, like the grains of sand that are by the sea for multitude, eating and drinking and rejoicing." The queen of Sheba, coming from afar to behold the splendor of that kingdom, exclaimed to Solomon: "Look! I had not been told the half. You have surpassed in wisdom and prosperity the things heard to which I listened. . . . May Jehovah your God come to be blessed . . . because Jehovah loves Israel to time indefinite." (1 Kings 4:20; 10:7-9) As long as that people served faithfully as Jehovah's witnesses, he did indeed prosper and increase them.

3 More than a millennium after Solomon's day, the apostle Peter, while testifying before the Christian governing body in Jerusalem, "related thoroughly how God for the first time turned his attention to the nations to take out of them a people for his name." (Acts 15:14) The Israelites had been a people for God's name. But now, again, God was gathering out "a people for his name"—the Christian congregation, spiritual Israel—who also would witness for Jehovah, making known his Kingdom purposes. (Galatians 6:16) Appropriately, this people is recognized today earth wide by the name that Jehovah himself makes prominent at Isaiah 43:10-12, 'Jehovah's Witnesses.' What is involved in their being a people for Jehovah's name?

"Witnesses of Me"

4 Jesus himself commissioned this people, saying: "You will be witnesses of me . . . to the most distant part of the earth." (Acts 1:8) "Witnesses of me"—do these words of Jesus mean that it is concerning Jesus only, and not Jehovah, that the witness must be given? Far from it! At that crucial time, when Jehovah's favor was being transferred from fleshly to spiritual Israel, it was necessary to give a thorough witness concerning the Christ upon whom this new arrangement is built. However, Jesus remains always subject to his Father. He set the example for us in witnessing concerning Jehovah's name and Kingdom.—John 5:30; 6:38; 17:6, 26; 18:37.

1, 2. (a) What did Jehovah promise Israel? (b) How did he fulfill his promises, but depending on what?

3. (a) What did Peter testify as to God's "people for his name"? (b) Why is the name Jehovah's Witnesses appropriate for that people?

4. (a) Why must Jehovah's Witnesses also be 'witnesses of Jesus'? (b) According to the Scriptures, Jesus left us what example in witnessing for Jehovah?

⁵ Jesus Christ is the Mediator of the new covenant and anointed Christians in it are called to inherit the Kingdom. He is "the Chief Agent of life" whom Jehovah uses in redeeming mankind from death. Jesus "must rule as king" until all enemies of God and man are subdued and a glorious paradise is restored to this earth. He is "the Son of God" who calls the dead from their tombs in the resurrection. (Hebrews 9:15; Acts 3:15; Psalm 110:1, 2, 5; 1 Corinthians 15:25-28; Luke 23:42, 43; John 5:25-29) Hence, as Jehovah's Witnesses, we witness also concerning the Son's outstanding part in vindicating Jehovah's name. In this, we follow in the steps of our Master, who was himself the preeminent witness for Jehovah—"the Faithful Witness."—Revelation 1:5; 3:14; John 18:37; 1 Peter 2:21.

Who Is Witnessing?

⁶ Today, a united people is witnessing "to the most distant part of the earth." It is the people spoken of by the apostle Peter —the 'people for God's name'—that is bearing witness to Jehovah and his Kingdom by Christ Jesus. Concerning this, Jesus himself told his disciples: "He that exercises faith in me, that one also will do the works that I do; and he will do works greater than these, because I am going my way to the Father." (John 14:12) From his Father's right hand in the heavens, the King Jesus Christ now directs the most extensive witness ever conducted here upon earth. As Jesus prophesied, when "this good news of the kingdom" has been "preached in all the inhabited earth for a witness to all the nations . . . then the end will come."—Matthew 24:14.

⁷ "This good news of the kingdom" is the most thrilling news that has ever been proclaimed to humans. It is the glorious good news concerning which the religious sects of Christendom are completely silent. They have no Kingdom hope for the future. No wonder that they fail to witness! They have failed to take note of the most exciting event in all history—the arrival in Kingdom glory of the Son of man to sit down on his glorious throne and judge the nations and peoples of earth. That *is* something about which to witness! Hence, under angelic direction, witnesses for Jehovah and his Christ are now declaring "everlasting good news . . . as glad tidings to those who dwell on the earth, and to every nation and tribe and tongue and people." Are you sharing zealously in this witness?—Revelation 14:6, 7; Matthew 25:31-33.

Grand Witness in 1984

⁸ The 1984 Service Year Report of Jehovah's Witnesses Worldwide, appearing on pages 20-23 of this magazine, shows how abundantly our God, Jehovah, is blessing the efforts of his humble witnesses. In all, 203 lands are represented. Of these, 172 lands report a publisher increase. And happily, these Kingdom proclaimers also speak of how 'the Lord has caused them to increase, yes, made them abound, in love to one another and to all.' (1 Thessalonians 3:12) The loving unity among Jehovah's people, together with the Kingdom witness, is attracting multitudes of new disciples. To these Jesus is saying: "You will know the truth, and the truth will set you free."—John 8:31, 32.

5. (a) Concerning what features related to Jesus must we witness? (b) In this, how do we follow in Jesus' steps?
6. (a) Who alone today are giving the Kingdom witness? (b) Why can it be said that these are doing 'greater works'?

7. (a) Why do Christendom's sects fail to witness? (b) In contrast, why are Jehovah's Witnesses so zealous in their service?
8. (a) Why should we be happy about the 1984 Service Year Report? (b) What attracts new disciples?

1984 SERVICE YEAR REPORT OF JEHOVAH'S WITNESSES WORLDWIDE

Country	Population	1984 Peak Pubs.	Ratio, One Publisher to:	1984 Av. Pubs.	% Inc. Over 1983	1983 Av. Pubs.	1984 No. Bptzd.	Av. Pio. Pubs.	No. of Congs.	Total Hours	Av. Bible Studies	Memorial Attendance
Alaska	484,287	1,748	277	1,654	10	1,501	74	156	24	285,136	1,005	4,397
Algeria	19,800,000	41	482,927	29	45	20	1		3	1,715	26	71
American Samoa	32,297	90	359	80	8	80	4	11	1	21,913	123	260
Andorra	41,627	98	425	84		78		4	1	10,396	46	248
Anguilla	6,524	16	408	14		14	3	1	1	2,882	6	35
Antigua	70,794	208	340	196	4	188	11	23	4	42,302	168	558
Argentina	29,627,000	50,151	591	48,282	10	43,815	4,646	4,709	715	9,287,554	51,070	109,140
Aruba	68,008	298	228	287	3	280	12	14	5	40,366	178	962
Australia	15,451,900	40,486	382	39,052	9	35,982	2,264	3,295	591	7,198,583	18,539	78,701
Austria	7,555,338	15,618	484	15,317	4	14,771	790	916	228	2,498,014	7,388	26,500
Azores	250,700	276	908	257	-5 *	271	12	30	12	57,317	260	887
Bahamas	209,505	635	330	607	10	554	63	86	11	149,231	890	2,244
Bangladesh	100,000,000	19	5,263,158	15		15		6	1	6,765	36	54
Barbados	265,000	1,431	185	1,356	4	1,310	63	109	16	224,155	1,168	4,225
Belau	13,000	35	371	31	15	27	1	11	1	15,808	87	186
Belgium	9,793,017	20,499	478	20,043	4	19,342	1,009	1,239	294	3,290,261	8,144	40,387
Belize	145,000	696	208	666	12	594	62	66	17	142,429	715	3,136
Benin	3,700,000	1,462	2,531	1,248	18	1,062		46	66	181,633	937	7,029
Bermuda	55,000	323	170	302	7	281	24	33	4	63,485	274	710
Bolivia	5,500,000	3,899	1,411	3,639	13	3,228	423	617	83	1,129,983	5,779	17,671
Bonaire	9,927	47	211	40	11	36		4	4	8,994	41	170
Botswana	936,600	419	2,235	390	14	342	29	40	17	80,302	411	1,635
Brazil	132,580,000	160,927	824	150,732	13	133,765	15,702	11,853	2,661	24,311,347	126,870	474,450
Britain	54,932,383	97,495	563	92,616	5	87,732	5,166	7,924	1,167	16,613,530	46,166	187,709
Brunei	190,300	10	19,030	5	-44 *	9		1	1	796	11	47
Burkina Faso	7,318,695	223	32,819	209	12	186	28	45	8	76,088	365	778
Burma	35,400,000	1,284	27,570	1,197	9	1,103	53	194	68	329,601	914	3,308
Burundi	4,600,000	348	13,218	298	16	256	20	45	10	89,305	604	959
Canada	24,994,200	80,939	309	76,866	5	73,139	4,407	6,398	1,153	12,983,116	37,198	154,213
Cape Verde Rep.	301,500	184	1,639	166	14	145	13	19	7	45,083	292	700
Cayman Islands	16,821	61	276	54	17	46	4	8	1	12,745	63	150
Central Afr. Rep.	2,400,000	1,236	1,942	1,144	2	1,118	95	125	41	254,809	1,095	6,069
Chad	4,200,000	155	27,097	132	16	114	18	30	10	53,749	197	981
Chile	11,878,419	23,985	495	21,983	14	19,323	2,095	2,107	293	4,365,250	28,052	75,029
Colombia	29,730,300	23,117	1,286	21,442	14	18,827	2,330	1,780	306	4,078,143	24,964	96,422
Congo	1,600,000	1,102	1,452	936	11	845	6	35	39	138,671	965	2,942
Cook Islands	17,975	61	261	61	13	54		8	4	14,443	66	256
Costa Rica	2,460,226	8,316	296	7,811	12	6,946	700	578	156	1,439,950	8,253	24,427
Curaçao	167,563	1,050	160	1,021	10	930	79	104	11	215,849	1,285	2,988
Cyprus	500,000	1,061	471	1,047	1	1,033	62	75	13	167,080	477	1,949
Denmark	5,112,130	14,337	357	13,903	2	13,580	391	790	234	1,861,389	4,602	23,359
Djibouti	335,000	8	41,875	7	-30 *	10	1	2	1	1,116	9	30

Country												
Dominica	70,302	222	317	207	5	198	9	23	7	42,721	134	863
Dominican Rep.	5,647,977	8,192	689	7,904	6	7,432	503	860	129	1,694,517	11,935	31,282
Ecuador	8,830,000	8,362	1,056	7,814	13	6,892	1,016	871	124	1,803,637	11,462	40,728
El Salvador	5,229,096	13,427	389	12,583	14	11,085	1,610	1,553	217	3,127,225	18,823	49,344
Equatorial Guinea	300,000	111	2,703	84	40	60	27	17	3	36,917	250	441
Falkland Islands	1,830	3	610	3		3		1	1	427	5	8
Faroe Islands	44,805	89	503	84	22	69	5	20	4	20,456	45	147
Fiji	685,440	950	722	849	12	761	71	148	24	215,304	805	3,682
Finland	4,868,268	15,263	319	14,600	4	14,000	629	1,337	256	2,441,895	6,844	24,414
France	54,334,871	82,458	659	79,568	6	75,209	4,708	4,617	1,230	13,751,717	42,404	166,109
French Guiana	73,022	341	214	297	11	268	21	28	4	73,171	521	1,140
Gabon	900,000	477	1,887	435	15	378	21	21	13	73,729	603	1,640
Gambia	695,886	16	43,493	15	25	12	48	4	1	6,811	31	71
Germany, F. R.	59,397,300	109,102	544	107,479	2	104,931	4,288	5,391	1,508	16,310,070	42,520	182,857
Ghana	12,205,574	27,730	440	24,112	9	22,082	2,514	2,873	493	5,345,456	31,199	104,151
Gibraltar	29,073	109	267	104	8	96	7	4	1	13,011	31	194
Greece	9,740,417	22,037	442	21,715	6	20,533	825	1,733	434	3,769,326	8,008	38,382
Greenland	52,347	82	638	75	10	68	2	7	7	13,982	49	170
Grenada	112,000	349	321	334	6	314	17	39	7	72,245	375	1,175
Guadeloupe	328,000	3,514	93	3,352	6	3,064	273	128	43	551,011	3,828	9,921
Guam	105,979	229	463	211	5	211	11	44	1	64,788	327	690
Guatemala	7,250,000	7,558	959	7,047	11	6,325	613	507	112	1,283,710	7,145	25,233
Guinea	5,143,284	186	27,652	155		152	2	37	11	59,995	260	943
Guinea-Bissau	530,000	5	106,000	4	-33 *	6			1	313	4	11
Guyana	842,000	1,283	656	1,219	6	1,147	76	226	29	320,194	1,340	4,451
Haiti	6,000,000	3,595	1,669	3,537	9	3,248	244	294	77	722,696	4,825	25,801
Hawaii	1,023,200	5,082	201	5,013	4	4,812	220	734	60	1,186,695	4,639	14,143
Honduras	4,093,545	3,663	1,118	3,450	9	3,162	349	362	68	781,895	4,698	17,005
Hong Kong	5,300,000	1,206	4,395	1,169	9	1,077	81	258	14	413,110	1,699	2,805
Iceland	238,175	153	1,557	141	6	133	5	17	2	31,374	102	325
India	720,000,000	6,552	109,890	6,132	10	5,574	465	624	270	1,221,922	3,557	17,461
Ireland	4,989,959	2,350	2,123	2,278	7	2,124	111	362	78	623,689	1,059	4,651
Israel	5,484,600	306	17,924	295	5	281	21	24	5	57,463	216	635
Italy	56,556,911	116,555	485	111,951	9	102,714	9,060	12,984	1,580	25,856,432	72,831	250,868
Ivory Coast	9,273,167	1,948	4,760	1,828	11	1,640	250	217	49	452,899	2,632	7,018
Jamaica	2,300,000	7,517	306	7,110	7	6,842	392	483	166	1,133,195	5,934	23,684
Japan	119,316,468	92,022	1,297	87,460	13	77,577	9,276	32,458	1,603	39,382,375	127,527	224,696
Jordan	3,500,000	50	70,000	43	-20 *	54	5	1	2	5,279	26	155
Kenya	19,000,000	3,248	5,850	3,101	9	2,840	375	642	102	1,094,017	4,700	11,129
Kiribati	60,000	14	4,286	12	9	11		2	1	3,637	21	55
Korea	40,682,603	35,560	1,144	33,794	9	31,044	2,857	7,919	594	10,491,233	31,643	77,428
Kosrae	6,005	27	222	24	-11 *	27		4		5,736	37	104
Lebanon	3,000,000	2,054	1,461	1,930	3	1,865	73	83	48	283,042	1,097	4,127
Lesotho	1,518,635	747	2,033	681	4	657	57	79	40	147,194	603	3,413
Liberia	1,800,000	1,189	1,514	1,151	6	1,082	68	139	31	290,832	1,603	6,440
Libya	3,096,000	15	206,400	8	14	7		1		1,549	12	17
Liechtenstein	26,512	43	617	41	11	37		3	1	6,192	28	71
Luxembourg	435,500	1,129	386	1,103	5	1,048	54	89	21	207,725	762	2,537

Country	Population	1984 Peak Pubs.	Ratio, One Publisher to:	1984 Av. Pubs.	% Inc. Over 1983	1983 Av. Pubs.	1984 No. Bptzd.	Av. Pio. Pubs.	No. of Congs.	Total Hours	Av. Bible Studies	Memorial Attendance
Macao	375,000	15	25,000	13	18	11		5	1	8,529	31	62
Madagascar	9,672,660	1,800	5,374	1,672	19	1,408	151	171	31	374,882	2,913	8,977
Madeira	258,240	451	573	429	8	396	78	24	10	68,657	352	1,248
Malaysia	13,745,241	704	19,524	654	6	618	41	92	17	185,875	1,015	1,730
Mali	7,000,000	50	140,000	48	20	40	2	23	1	36,488	160	198
Malta	320,000	271	1,181	243	21	201	49	27	3	56,847	171	497
Marshall Islands	31,042	203	153	155	14	136	1	37	2	48,918	288	876
Martinique	328,566	1,635	201	1,545	13	1,370	169	125	24	309,881	1,652	4,548
Mauritius	965,201	679	1,422	642	17	549	68	67	9	136,610	631	1,478
Mayotte	55,000	14	3,929	9	50	6	3	2	1	2,961	25	35
Mexico	76,791,819	151,807	506	141,876	16	122,327	14,267	14,278	4,905	28,954,633	179,956	695,369
Montserrat	12,335	24	514	20	-9*	22		2	1	3,177	18	103
Morocco	21,663,105	87	249,001	78	-5	82	1	8	2	17,519	53	207
Nauru	6,000	6	1,000	4	100	2				167	1	22
Nepal	15,000,000	30	500,000	29	12	26		4	1	6,890	24	101
Netherlands	14,420,042	27,812	518	27,263	1	26,995	841	1,693	302	4,025,856	8,062	46,703
Nevis	11,230	32	351	29		29	1	6	1	10,345	33	120
New Caledonia	149,500	649	230	593	20	495	82	64	8	136,381	689	1,886
New Zealand	3,232,700	8,805	367	8,203	8*	7,580	523	709	132	1,458,589	4,809	18,066
Niger	5,800,000	73	79,452	60	-10*	67	9	18	5	31,804	99	238
Nigeria	94,000,000	113,537	828	108,425	6	102,356	4,085	7,720	2,254	18,503,248	93,285	319,959
Niue	2,800	19	147	14	75	8		3	1	4,125	31	89
Norway	4,140,634	7,670	540	7,420	4	7,140	328	303	176	874,902	2,322	14,228
Pakistan	94,000,000	231	406,926	215	4	207	13	50	6	76,943	330	656
Panama	2,134,236	4,131	517	3,804	10	3,462	257	332	87	731,165	4,607	14,022
Papua New Guinea	3,006,799	1,682	1,788	1,601	3	1,557	143	152	83	317,470	1,660	7,704
Paraguay	3,191,784	2,041	1,564	1,923	11	1,734	60	231	32	413,123	1,962	5,139
Peru	19,400,000	19,021	1,020	17,944	14	15,788	1,812	2,843	356	4,892,988	24,897	75,080
Philippines	52,000,000	75,257	691	69,869	8	64,601	5,521	9,378	2,301	14,207,610	36,884	236,999
Ponape	23,140	78	297	69	3	67		22	1	28,835	108	523
Portugal	9,345,000	27,220	343	25,705	10	23,341	1,859	1,632	400	3,879,613	17,917	72,140
Puerto Rico	3,350,000	19,371	173	18,917	5	17,991	1,099	1,290	249	3,171,674	14,543	53,266
Réunion	530,900	849	624	806	8*	744	44	51	12	146,171	566	2,288
Rodrigues	35,919	18	1,996	16	-6	17	2	11		2,002	12	53
Rota	1,274	10	127	7	17	6	1	2		3,189	11	30
Rwanda	5,775,000	374	15,441	367	13*	324	69	52	14	121,702	689	1,133
St. Eustatius	1,335	3	445	2	-33*	3		1		314	4	21
St. Helena	6,000	94	64	85	8	79	4	12	2	8,458	34	230
St. Kitts	35,135	137	256	124	19	104	10	12	2	26,358	127	361
St. Lucia	120,000	328	366	279	1	275	9	41	5	65,666	341	1,216
St. Martin	15,926	89	179	80	4	77	8	6	1	13,612	64	331
St. Pierre & Miquelon	6,000	17	353	11	10	10			1	1,521	5	19
St. Vincent	110,000	134	821	128	2	125		16	4	29,690	113	415
Saipan	15,519	26	597	20	-5*	21	3	8	1	13,631	57	72
San Marino	21,622	84	257	79	8	73	6	4	1	14,499	33	160

São Tomé	80,000	20	4,000	14		14	2	1	1	3,760	53	9
Senegal	6,000,000	422	14,218	400	7	375	44	68	10	131,688	629	1,166
Seychelles	70,000	54	1,296	51	2	50	6	4	1	9,096	56	156
Sierra Leone	3,354,000	679	4,940	624	2	614	32	120	31	197,012	884	3,197
Solomon Islands	258,193	640	403	591	4	567	40	66	32	125,184	578	3,210
South Africa	32,281,729	34,363	939	32,882	8	30,345	1,927	2,994	939	6,377,172	24,320	103,751
South-West Africa	1,032,000	340	3,035	323	7	302	12	28	12	68,026	298	1,106
Spain	38,496,000	56,717	679	55,251	7	51,485	3,671	4,988	852	10,902,831	36,476	125,040
Sri Lanka	15,605,000	803	19,433	762	7	715	44	118	26	222,819	848	2,416
Sudan	22,000,000	180	122,222	162	22	133	15	31	3	54,043	390	463
Suriname	350,000	1,010	347	957	8	887	63	111	15	209,018	1,005	3,362
Swaziland	638,419	749	852	659	1	652	55	48	40	140,735	541	2,644
Sweden	8,340,014	19,526	427	19,029	3	18,439	845	1,773	318	3,187,863	9,248	33,753
Switzerland	6,423,100	12,378	519	12,119	5	11,582	713	493	240	1,834,771	6,948	23,144
Syria	9,100,000	209	43,541	134	113	63	10	15	5	19,058	63	169
Tahiti	166,753	578	289	561	14	492	52	47	11	106,343	591	1,626
Taiwan	18,886,737	994	19,001	975	5	932	51	198	23	296,669	1,069	3,059
Tanzania	20,400,000	2,150	9,488	2,056	12	1,837	97	251	80	496,729	1,760	6,239
Thailand	50,731,000	831	61,048	814	3	793	64	127	28	215,098	716	1,816
Togo	2,801,197	2,420	1,158	2,169	14	1,907		166	70	345,222	2,942	7,568
Tonga	100,230	47	2,133	40	14	35	4	9	2	14,928	60	269
Trinidad	1,128,600	3,845	294	3,663	9	3,367	283	459	45	764,664	3,874	11,130
Truk	38,650	39	991	38	9	35		14	2	21,023	121	411
Tunisia	6,650,000	45	147,778	39	-7 *	42		1	1	3,913	19	65
Turkey	45,000,000	819	54,945	790	2	771	29	49	10	143,500	469	1,442
Turks & Caicos Isls.	8,000	33	242	31		31		7	1	13,019	72	163
Tuvalu Islands	8,000	25	320	23	28	18		4	1	4,231	30	176
Uganda	14,500,000	282	51,418	262	9	240	27	47	11	87,984	562	1,228
U.S. of America	235,925,000	690,830	342	648,704	5	616,058	35,618	62,563	7,980	115,047,299	416,987	1,611,310
Uruguay	2,990,000	5,150	581	4,789	7	4,458	217	520	90	984,841	5,717	14,801
Vanuatu	131,000	67	1,955	59	23	48	5	6	2	13,736	117	354
Venezuela	17,500,000	25,305	692	23,699	16	20,392	2,804	2,656	238	5,525,163	33,436	93,263
Virgin Isls. (Brit.)	12,000	83	145	80		80	4	4	3	13,465	88	339
Virgin Isls. (U.S.)	96,000	492	195	449		448	24	35	8	76,628	435	1,667
West Berlin	1,852,000	4,929	376	4,907		4,893	177	250	61	744,630	2,024	7,590
Western Samoa	156,349	166	942	141	4	136	21	17	2	38,128	124	616
Yap	9,320	48	194	44	-4 *	46	2	13	1	18,127	82	148
Zaïre	30,100,000	32,208	935	29,435	12	26,234	4,598	5,239	941	8,903,678	48,652	139,856
Zambia	6,440,000	58,925	109	54,605	3	52,994	3,087	4,204	1,462	9,629,840	63,858	393,431
Zimbabwe	7,768,500	13,621	570	12,640	9	11,552	631	976	488	2,257,409	9,202	38,979
175 Countries		2,581,112		2,444,167	7.5	2,272,626	168,795	252,031	43,284	479,956,954	1,915,866	6,968,317
# 28 Other Countries		261,419		236,107	3.1	229,096	10,626	6,905	4,585	25,631,083	131,247	448,657
GRAND TOTAL (203 countries)		2,842,531		2,680,274	7.1	2,501,722	179,421	258,936	47,869	505,588,037	2,047,113	7,416,974

* Percentage of decrease
\# Work banned and reports are incomplete

MEMORIAL PARTAKERS WORLDWIDE: 9,081

⁹ How has this marvelous service report been compiled? It has been made up from the field service reports that you—the individual Kingdom publisher—have faithfully turned in each month. Do you not rejoice that you have had your own small part in this grand report? These figures show how wonderfully Jehovah has 'emptied out a flood of blessings' upon his Witnesses—this "people for his name"—whom he has united in a global bond of loving service.—Malachi 3:10; Psalm 56:10, 11; Colossians 3:14.

¹⁰ Much of this witnessing has been accomplished under persecution or hardship and at great self-sacrifice. This is to be expected, for the word "witness" as here used is a translation of the Greek *martýs* or *martyr,* from which is also derived the word "martyr," meaning one who bears witness by his death. This emphasizes that we, as Jehovah's Witnesses, should be self-sacrificing, determined always to expend ourselves and to keep integrity under all circumstances, even to the death if necessary.—Luke 9:23; compare Job 2:3; 27:5; 31:6; Acts 22:20; Revelation 2:10.

Integrity-Keepers Blessed

¹¹ In times of persecution, Jehovah's 'name people' have needed "power beyond what is normal" in order to overcome the vehement attacks of Satan and his demonic hordes. Jehovah supplies that power and delivers and prospers his faithful witnesses. (2 Corinthians 4:7-9; Isaiah 54:17; Jeremiah 1:19) Take for example the situation in the Axis powers of World War II, headed by Germany, Italy, and Japan. Using cruel dictatorial governments, the Devil 'disgorged from his mouth a river' of persecution, to drown out the witness work directed by God's heavenly womanlike organization. But did Satan succeed in this? Not at all! Jehovah maneuvered events so that the democratic nations of earth swallowed up that flood. 'The wicked ones were cut off' and Jehovah's loyal witnesses now prosper wonderfully in those lands.—Revelation 12:15, 16; Psalm 37:28, 29.

¹² Recently, in those three countries, the Watch Tower Society has needed to build and equip large factories in order to send forth a different kind of flood—millions upon millions of Bibles and related Kingdom publications for the edification of Jehovah's Witnesses and other truth-hungry people. In Germany, Italy, and Japan, today more than 300,000 publishers of the Kingdom are carrying the witness to the homes of people. And throughout the world field Jehovah is blessing his integrity-keeping people with increase!—Compare Psalm 115:12-15.

¹³ However, the Devil, knowing that his time is short, continues to wage war with those "who observe the commandments of God and have the work of bearing witness to Jesus." (Revelation 12:12, 17) Satan's opposition is particularly vicious in the lands listed in the accompanying report as "28 Other Countries." Witnesses in these territories have faithfully lived up to our yeartext for 1984, "showing all the more courage to speak the word of God fearlessly." (Philippians 1:14) Their publisher increase of 3.1 percent is most commendable. Stimulated by their example, may all of us zealously continue offering "to God a sacrifice of praise, that is, the fruit of lips which make public declaration

---

9. (a) How might you have been privileged to share in making this report? (b) What do the figures indicate as to Jehovah and his people?
10. (a) What emphasizes that witnesses must be self-sacrificing? (b) What do the Scriptures say about integrity keepers and their reward?
11, 12. (a) Jehovah gives us what strengthening assurances? (b) How have his people triumphed over totalitarian oppressions?

---

13. (a) What in the Year Report shows that faithful witnesses have lived up to the 1984 yeartext? (b) How should this stimulate us?

to his name."—Hebrews 13:15.

¹⁴ As world conditions worsen, others of us, no doubt, will be persecuted, haled into court and imprisoned. Jesus spoke of such experiences among the things "destined to occur" before the end, and added: "It will turn out to you for a witness." In all situations, then, Jehovah's Witnesses must continue to witness concerning God and Christ. Many continue to do this despite bitter family opposition, mockings by fellow employees or schoolmates, and reproaches heaped upon them in their preaching territory. Are you witnessing courageously despite trying circumstances? Then you are one of those to whom Jesus says: "By endurance on your part you will acquire your souls."—Luke 21:7, 9-19.

Kingdom Increase!

¹⁵ "Kingdom Increase"—what an appropriate theme for our district conventions of the summer of 1984! For this indeed has been our finest year of increase. Just look at the chart on this page! This has been compiled from the reports of the 95 Watch Tower Society branches that supervise the witness work in 203 lands.

¹⁶ Space does not permit us to publish all the written expressions of joy that have been received from those branch offices together with their annual reports, but

World Report Comparison

	1984	1983	Increase
Watch Tower Branches	95	94	
Lands Reporting	203	205	
Peak of Publishers	2,842,531	2,652,323	7.2%
Average Publishers	2,680,274	2,501,722	7.1%
Average Pioneers	258,936	206,098	25.6%
Auxiliary Pioneers (April)	323,644	217,860	48.6%
Total Field Hours	505,588,037	436,720,991	15.8%
Literature Placed	36,639,925	36,039,400	1.7%
Subscriptions Placed	1,812,221	1,756,153	3.2%
Magazines Placed	287,358,064	258,698,636	11.1%
Return Visits	195,819,093	174,687,309	12.1%
Av. Bible Studies	2,047,113	1,797,112	13.9%
Memorial Attendance	7,416,974	6,767,707	9.6%
Memorial Partakers	9,081	9,292	

here are some samplings from around the globe:

Alaska: The whole village of Metlakatla came to see 230 Jehovah's Witnesses construct a beautiful Kingdom Hall in 32 hours; it was dedicated on Sunday of that same weekend.

Honduras: 3,663 publishers was our highest peak ever; with a Memorial attendance of 17,005 much more remains to be done.

Brazil: New peaks culminated in 160,927 publishers, with 474,450 persons attending the Memorial.

Thailand: The pioneer spirit is alive, with 22 percent of all publishers in this service in April.

Papua New Guinea: Peak auxiliary pioneers increased by 91 percent; Memorial attendance rose by more than 1,000—to 7,704.

Austria: The pioneer spirit is catching on, and we had five consecutive peaks in that field; we had seven peaks of publishers, the latest being 15,618.

Zambia: We reached an all-time peak of 58,925 publishers: Memorial attendance was 393,431—110,447 more than last year.

¹⁷ Reports show that faithful missionaries and pioneers continue to take the lead

---

14. (a) What may turn out to us "for a witness"? (b) In spite of what situations should we continue to witness courageously, and why?
15. What are some outstanding points in the chart on this page?
16. Cite some typical, joyful expressions from around the globe.

17. (a) How is the pioneer field expanding? (b) What practical goals are recommended, and for whom? (c) What is the new publisher peak, and what may have contributed toward this?

'Joyful, Happy, Thankful'

From a land where the work of Jehovah's Witnesses has been restricted for more than 40 years comes this report: "The greatest joy [we] have been experiencing is the increased preaching and teaching activity in the field. Many have been serving as auxiliary pioneers. One of them expressed his feelings in these words: 'I am filled with joy, rejoicing and happiness, and with deep satisfaction.' Another auxiliary pioneer said: 'I am so happy that I do something that is pleasing to Jehovah. I was able to start five new home Bible studies.' Another one added: 'I am thankful to Jehovah who helped me to cultivate the love needed to help other people.' In one congregation of 61 publishers 38 served as auxiliary pioneers in one month. As a result, 66 new Bible studies were started."

in carrying the witness to territories new and old. It is encouraging indeed to see the increase in pioneers. The total of auxiliary pioneers reporting in April mushroomed to an all-time peak of 323,644 for a 49-percent increase. Not a few of these have seen their privilege of advancing into the regular pioneer ranks. Further, many of our young Kingdom publishers are setting pioneer service as their goal and are making practical preparation to that end during their final years in high school. The overall result is shown in the splendid increase of pioneers. This has helped also to build a spirit of zeal in our congregations, contributing, no doubt, to the new worldwide peak of 2,842,531 publishers, a 7.2-percent increase over the 1983 peak. Do you not rejoice that you have shared in this forward surge?

[18] The joyful witness given during 1984 is reflected also in the increased place-

---

18. (a) What other grand increases were there in 1984? (b) The Memorial report indicates what potential for expansion, and how can our readers respond?

ments of magazines and other literature, the record number of field-service hours reported, the outstanding increase in return visits to interested persons and in home Bible studies conducted with these. How we look forward to further fruits from this zealous service! And there is great potential for a still larger ingathering! This is shown by the remarkable attendance at the Lord's Evening Meal last April 15. In the congregations of Jehovah's Witnesses around the earth, a total of 7,416,974 attended, of whom 9,081 indicated that they were of the Lord's "little flock" by partaking of the bread and the wine. May all our readers continue to grow spiritually, in order to make room for sharing in the grand witness and ingathering that yet lies ahead.—Compare Ephesians 4:15; Philippians 1:9-11.

[19] Truly, we may repeat Moses' words in saying of Jehovah's Witnesses, the modern day "people for his name": "Jehovah your God has multiplied you, and here you are today like the stars of the heavens for multitude." (Deuteronomy 1:10) It is our prayer that our Sovereign Lord, Jehovah, will continue to prosper the Kingdom witness and add to the increase!

---

19. For what can we thank Jehovah, and what is our prayer regarding the future?

What Would You Say?

□ Why must Jehovah's Witnesses be 'witnesses of Jesus' also?

□ What grand witness was given during 1984?

□ What shows that Jehovah blesses faithful witnesses?

□ In what ways should the 1984 report stimulate us?

Kingdom Proclaimers Report

Kingdom Increase Worldwide

ISAIAH the prophet aptly foretold the expansion of Kingdom interests in our day when he said: "Of the increase of [Christ's] government and peace there shall be no end." (Isaiah 9:7, *King James Version*) Reports from over 200 countries where Jehovah's Witnesses are preaching the good news show Jehovah's blessing on the work done. Here are a few expressions from different parts of the earth.

□ Africa: The Senegal branch says that "this service year has once again seen Jehovah's rich blessing." In the island of Mauritius, where the work started in 1951, the number of Witnesses reached 100 in 1964 and 679 in 1984. Ghana reports that Witnesses in that country have increased from 30 in 1938 to 25,755 today! The pioneer ministry is going very well in Africa too. A pioneer in Sierra Leone gives the reason why she is in full-time work: "I chose to pioneer because going to college or university would be a waste of precious time that could be used to aid honest-hearted ones to gain accurate knowledge about Jehovah and his Son, Jesus Christ, before the end comes." Recent conventions held in South Africa manifested unity. The Watch Tower branch there states: "This year we had the first full-scale interracial conventions in this country . . . The multiracial baptism of 343 was an outstanding example of the unity of Jehovah's sheep in this multiracial country." In Zimbabwe a local politician accepted the truth and turned in his resignation to the party. "This caused a great disturbance and the matter was taken up with a visiting official at a public meeting. When asked what to do with this brother the official said, 'You will do nothing. That is their policy everywhere in the world. If he continues as a party member he is not a real Jehovah's Witness.'"

□ Asia and the Pacific: The spirit of full-time pioneer service has been outstanding in Japan where 40 percent of all publishers were in full-time service during May. The Philippine branch states that it has enrolled close to 200 new pioneers each month. Australia says that "the pioneer spirit has been really outstanding this year." India has new branch facilities and a new peak of 6,506 publishers. They held 14 conventions with 7 more being held for the first time in the local languages. Over 9,000 attended, and 246 were baptized. We are happy to see increase in this vast country. Expansion is very evident in Korea also. Their new branch was dedicated in 1982 but is now too small. They are building again to double their floor space. Regular pioneers have increased 56 percent in that country. Western Samoa is a branch newly formed to care better for the needs of the Samoan islanders. So Jehovah's "field" in Asia and the Pacific is being harvested.

□ Europe: Kingdom increase is evident in Europe. Portugal writes: "There has been an 'explosion' of interest on every front. No sooner is a peak reached than it is surpassed the following month." Belgium echoes this sentiment, stating: "Everywhere expansion is taking place." Selters, Germany, dedicated the second-largest branch complex in the world, with all but one member of the Governing Body of Jehovah's Witnesses participating. One brother was moved to write: "Can you imagine how we felt after 60 years of service—20 years of which we spent in prison due to two waves of persecution—to be able to share in this wonderful spiritual banquet in a spiritual paradise?"

□ Americas: Canada had an outstanding year of increase with 80,939 reporting service. The branch there makes this comment: "It is most encouraging that despite growing pressures and enticements from a decaying world . . . we continue to grow marvelously. This parallels the outstanding expansion of early Christianity during the decadent last days of the Roman world. (2 Timothy 3:1-5)" Belize, Central America, says that one of the highlights of the year was a "field trip to visit the Mayan Indian villages in the south of the country. To reach these remote villages (12 in number), one must walk 113 miles (180 km) along jungle paths." Twelve brothers made the trip equipped with backpacks and briefcases, a six-volt slide projector, and motorcycle batteries. They showed slides of Jehovah's Kingdom work worldwide. One person who had never before seen a slide showing described it as "big picture on wall with bright light." Mexico has grown from 81 publishers in 1931 to a peak of 151,807 in 1984 (a 16-percent increase for the year), and 695,769 attended the Memorial last April. The United States had a grand new peak of 690,830 publishers.

The Kingdom increase continues worldwide.

Beginnings of Royalty in Israel

The Two Books of Samuel

"SO YOU have not read what David did when he and his men were hungry? He went into the House of God and took the sacred bread to eat and gave it to his men, though priests alone are allowed to eat it, and no one else." (Luke 6:3, 4, *The New English Bible*) With these words, Jesus silenced some Pharisees who had accused his disciples of Sabbath breaking because they had plucked a few grains to eat during the Sabbath day.

He also demonstrated something else. The historical account about David and "the sacred bread" is recorded in the first book of Samuel. (1 Samuel 21:1-6, *NE*) Jesus' reference to it to refute an objection shows his familiarity with the book and suggests that we, too, would do well to become familiar with it. Along with its companion, Second Samuel, it contains information that was valuable to Jesus and is valuable to us today.—Romans 15:4.

What are the two books of Samuel? They are historical books found in the Hebrew Scriptures that describe a turning point in the history of God's people. Previously, the Israelites had been ruled by a succession of judges. These two books describe the end of that era and the beginning of rule by Israelite royalty. They are filled with exciting events and fascinating people. We meet Samuel himself, the last of the judges, and the first two kings, Saul and David. We also meet a host of other unforgettable characters: the sad figure of Eli, the wise and tactful Abigail, the valiant but kindly Jonathan, as well as the brothers Abishai and Joab, mighty for Jehovah but cruel in their personal vendettas. (Hebrews 11:32) The two books teach principles that are still important and describe events that had long-lasting effects on God's people, in fact on all mankind.

A King Who Failed

The first one anointed by Jehovah to be king over Israel was Saul. He started well but later failed to show proper reliance on Jehovah in the face of an impending attack by the Philistines. Hence, Samuel told him that his sons would not inherit the kingship. Rather, said Samuel, "Jehovah will certainly find for himself a man agreeable to his heart; and Jehovah will commission him as a leader over his people." (1 Samuel 13:13, 14) However, Saul continued as king for the rest of his life.

Later, this first king was commanded to wage punitive war against the Amalekites. Saul did not completely fulfill Jehovah's orders and thus incurred further displeasure. Samuel is moved to say: "Does Jehovah have as much delight in burnt offerings and sacrifices as in obeying the voice of Jehovah? Look! To obey is better than a sacrifice, to pay attention than the fat of rams." (1 Samuel 15:22) Here is a principle that is still vital for

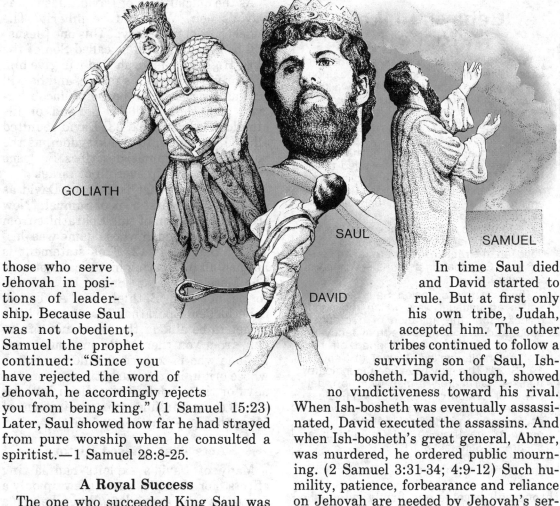

GOLIATH

SAUL

SAMUEL

DAVID

those who serve Jehovah in positions of leadership. Because Saul was not obedient, Samuel the prophet continued: "Since you have rejected the word of Jehovah, he accordingly rejects you from being king." (1 Samuel 15:23) Later, Saul showed how far he had strayed from pure worship when he consulted a spiritist.—1 Samuel 28:8-25.

A Royal Success

The one who succeeded King Saul was David, son of Jesse. David was different from Saul. In his youth, he had shown reliance on Jehovah when he slew the Philistine giant, Goliath. Then, when he had to flee for his life because of Saul's jealousy, he nevertheless kept obeying Jehovah in all things. More than once, David could have killed Saul. But he refrained, waiting on Jehovah's time for him to become king. It was during this difficult time that Ahimelech the priest gave him the showbread to eat in the incident mentioned by Jesus to the Pharisees.

In time Saul died and David started to rule. But at first only his own tribe, Judah, accepted him. The other tribes continued to follow a surviving son of Saul, Ishbosheth. David, though, showed no vindictiveness toward his rival. When Ish-bosheth was eventually assassinated, David executed the assassins. And when Ish-bosheth's great general, Abner, was murdered, he ordered public mourning. (2 Samuel 3:31-34; 4:9-12) Such humility, patience, forbearance and reliance on Jehovah are needed by Jehovah's servants in any age.

The "Son of David"

When David finally became king over a reunited nation, one of his first thoughts was to build a permanent home for the ark of the covenant, the symbol of Jehovah's presence in Israel. Jehovah did not consent to this, but in recognition of David's outstanding faithfulness he made a remarkable covenant with him: "Your house and your kingdom will certainly be steadfast to time indefinite before you; your very

"Behaving Like a Prophet"

What does the Bible mean when it says: "The spirit of God came to be upon [Saul], yes, him, and he went on walking and continued *behaving like a prophet*"? —1 Samuel 19:23.

When the prophets of Jehovah were delivering God's messages, they spoke under the influence of holy spirit that 'filled them with power' and doubtless led them to speak with an intensity and feeling that were truly extraordinary. (Micah 3:8; Jeremiah 20:9) Probably their behavior appeared strange—perhaps even irrational—to others. Nevertheless, once it was established that they were speaking from Jehovah, their messages were taken seriously by God-fearing persons.—Compare 2 Kings 9:1-13.

Thus, on this occasion Saul began to act in an unusual way, which reminded onlookers of the agitation of a prophet about to deliver a message from Jehovah. While acting thus, he stripped off his clothes and lay naked all night. (1 Samuel 19:23, 24) This may have been to indicate that he was merely a man with no regal power or authority when he stood against Jehovah God's purposes. On a previous occasion when King Saul "behaved like a prophet," he tried to kill David with a spear.—1 Samuel 18:10, 11.

throne will become one firmly established to time indefinite."—2 Samuel 7:16.

David thus became a link in the long, unbroken chain of descent that led from Adam, through Abraham, Isaac, Jacob and Judah down to the promised Messiah. (Genesis 3:15; 22:18; 26:4; 49:10) When the Messiah would finally arrive, he would be a descendant of David. This Jesus was, on both his foster father's side and his mother's side. (Matthew 1:1-16; Luke 3: 23-38) In the Gospel accounts, he is frequently called the "Son of David."—Mark 10:47, 48.

As the official "Son of David," Jesus was David's heir. What did he inherit? The angel Gabriel told Mary: "This one [Jesus] will be great and will be called Son of the Most High; and Jehovah God will give him the throne of David his father, and he will rule as king over the house of Jacob forever, and there will be no end of his kingdom." (Luke 1:32, 33) David reunited all God's people into one kingdom, as the book of Second Samuel describes. So Jesus inherited rulership over all of Israel.

Note, too, another fact about David as reported by the first book of Samuel: "Now David was the son of this Ephrathite from Bethlehem of Judah whose name was Jesse." (1 Samuel 17:12) This statement is not just an interesting historical footnote. The Messiah, too, as "Son of David," was to be born in Bethlehem: "And you, O Bethlehem Ephrathah, the one too little to get to be among the thousands of Judah, from you there will come out to me the one who is to become ruler in Israel, whose origin is from early times, from the days of time indefinite." (Micah 5:2) Jesus, of course, fulfilled this requirement of Messiahship.—Matthew 2:1, 5, 6.

Acts That Altered History

Many of David's exploits had lasting effects. For example, David grew up only a few miles from Jerusalem. When he was a boy the city was in the hands of the Jebusites, and David must often have admired its almost impregnable position on a steep rocky outcrop known as Mount Zion. Now, as king, he was in a position to do more than admire it. The second book of Samuel tells graphically how, despite the taunting of the Jebusite inhabitants, "David proceeded to capture the stronghold of Zion, that is, the City of David." (2 Samuel 5:7) Thus Jerusalem moved to center stage in world history where it has been—on and off—ever since.

The city became David's royal capital and remained the capital of God's earthly kings for hundreds of years. In the first century, the "Son of David," Jesus, preached there. It was into Jerusalem that Jesus rode on an ass to present himself as King to the Jews. (Matthew 21: 1-11, 42–22:13; John 7:14) And it was outside the gates of Jerusalem that he offered his life for mankind, after which he was resurrected and ascended into heaven, patiently waiting—as David had before him—for Jehovah to say when he should begin reigning as King.—Psalm 110:1; Acts 2:23, 24, 32, 33; Hebrews 13:12.

David's ruling in Jerusalem also reminds us that his descendant, Jesus, now also rules in a Jerusalem, the "heavenly Jerusalem." (Hebrews 12:22) And the location of that heavenly Jerusalem in heaven is called "Mount Zion," reminding us of the rocky outcrop that was the site of the original city.—Revelation 14:1.

Toward the end of his reign David conducted an illegal census of the nation. In punishment Jehovah plagued the nation, and the plague-carrying angel finally stopped at a threshing floor belonging to a Jebusite landowner named Araunah. David bought the land from Araunah and built an altar to Jehovah there. (2 Samuel 24:17-25) This act, too, had lasting results. That stretch of land became the site of Solomon's temple and, later, of the rebuilt temple. Thus, for centuries it was the world center of true worship. Jesus himself preached in Herod's temple, which was also built around what was once the threshing floor of Araunah the Jebusite.—John 7:14.

Yes, the two books of Samuel introduce us to real people and explain important principles. They show why Israel's first king was a failure and why her second king, despite some tragic mistakes, was an outstanding success. They carry us through an important juncture in history, the beginnings of human royal rule among God's people. We watch Jerusalem become the capital city of that royalty and note the purchase of the site of what would become, for some centuries, the world center of true worship. And we learn an important clue to help identify the coming Messiah. He would have to be a "Son of David."

Truly, these are remarkable books. Every Christian should read them for himself.

In Our Next Issue

- The Middle East
  —Site of Armageddon?

- How Much Can Humans Accomplish?

- A Government That Accomplishes What Man Cannot

'You Have Brought Me Much Courage'

In a letter requesting subscriptions to the *Watchtower* and *Awake!* magazines, a woman from Quebec, Canada, wrote:

"I have been reading your literature for some years now and I find it simply tremendous. How often you have comforted me or very often corrected me or brought joy to my heart. You have also brought me much courage. . . . My four daughters and myself say 'thank you.'"

January 15, 1985

The Watchtower

Announcing Jehovah's Kingdom

ARMAGEDDON
and the Middle East

January 15, 1985
Vol. 106, No. 2

The Watchtower®
Announcing Jehovah's Kingdom

In This Issue

Cover picture courtesy of British Aerospace

THE PURPOSE OF "THE WATCHTOWER" is to exalt Jehovah God as the Sovereign of the universe. It keeps watch on world events as they fulfill Bible prophecy. It comforts all peoples with the good news that God's Kingdom will soon destroy those who oppress their fellowmen and that it will turn the earth into a Paradise. It encourages faith in the now-reigning King, Jesus Christ, whose shed blood opens the way for mankind to gain eternal life. "The Watchtower," published by Jehovah's Witnesses continuously since 1879, is nonpolitical. It adheres to the Bible as its authority.

"WATCHTOWER" STUDIES FOR THE WEEKS

February 17: Can Human Accomplishments Ward Off Catastrophe? Page 10. Songs to Be Used: 23, 21.

February 24: A Government That Accomplishes What Man Cannot. Page 15. Songs to Be Used: 16, 187.

Average Printing Each Issue: 11,150,000

Now Published in 102 Languages

SEMIMONTHLY EDITIONS AVAILABLE BY MAIL
Afrikaans, Arabic, Cebuano, Chichewa, Chinese, Cibemba, Danish, Dutch, Efik, English*, Finnish, French, German, Greek, Hiligaynon, Igbo, Iloko, Italian, Japanese, Korean, Lingala, Malagasy, Maltese, Norwegian, Portuguese, Sepedi, Sesotho, Shona, Spanish, Swahili, Swedish, Tagalog, Thai, Tswana, Xhosa, Yoruba, Zulu

MONTHLY EDITIONS AVAILABLE BY MAIL
Armenian, Bengali, Bicol, Bulgarian, Croatian, Czech, Ewe, Fijian, Ga, Greenlandic, Gujarati, Gun, Hausa, Hebrew, Hindi, Hiri Motu, Hungarian, Icelandic, Kannada, Kikuyu, Kiluba, Malayalam, Marathi, New Guinea Pidgin, Pangasinan, Papiamento, Polish, Rarotongan, Romanian, Russian, Samar-Leyte, Samoan, Sango, Serbian, Silozi, Sinhalese, Slovenian, Solomon Islands-Pidgin, Tahitian, Tamil, Telugu, Tshiluba, Tsonga, Turkish, Twi, Ukrainian, Urdu, Venda, Vietnamese
*Study articles also available in large-print edition at same cost.

The Bible translation used is the "New World Translation of the Holy Scriptures," unless otherwise indicated.

Twenty cents (U.S.) a copy

Watch Tower Society offices	Yearly subscription rates Semimonthly
America, U.S., Watchtower, Wallkill, N.Y. 12589	$4.00
Australia, Box 280, Ingleburn, N.S.W. 2565	A$6.00
Canada, Box 4100, Halton Hills (Georgetown), Ontario L7G 4Y4	$4.50
England, The Ridgeway, London NW7 1RN	£5.00
Ireland, 29A Jamestown Road, Finglas, Dublin 11	£5.00
New Zealand, 6-A Western Springs Rd., Auckland 3	$7.00
Nigeria, P.O. Box 194, Yaba, Lagos State	₦3.50
Philippines, P.O. Box 2044, Manila 2800	₱50.00
South Africa, Private Bag 2, Elandsfontein, 1406	R5.60

Remittances should be sent to the office in your country or to Watchtower, Wallkill, N.Y. 12589, U.S.A.

Changes of address should reach us 30 days before your moving date. Give us your old and new address (if possible, your old address label).

The Watchtower (ISSN 0043-1087) is published semimonthly for $4.00 (U.S.) per year by Watch Tower Bible and Tract Society of Pennsylvania, 25 Columbia Heights, Brooklyn, N.Y. 11201. Second-class postage paid at Brooklyn, N.Y., and at additional mailing offices.

Postmaster: Send address changes to Watchtower, *Wallkill, N.Y. 12589.*

Published by
Watch Tower Bible and Tract Society of Pennsylvania
25 Columbia Heights, Brooklyn, N.Y. 11201, U.S.A.
Frederick W. Franz, President

The Middle East—Site of
ARMAGEDDON?

"AS THE world races toward its final hour of struggle, the important city to watch is not New York, Moscow, Paris, Peking, or Cairo. The city to watch is Jerusalem!" So declared theologians John F. and John E. Walvoord in their book *Armageddon, Oil and the Middle East Crisis.*

Many are indeed casting a nervous eye at both Jerusalem and the troubled region in which it is situated. Says the *Times* of London,

"The Middle East is becoming more frightening." Some fear that a future U.S.-Soviet confrontation there is almost inevitable. By January 1984, relations between the rival superpowers had so deteriorated that the *Bulletin of the Atomic Scientists* moved its famous "doomsday clock" (a symbol of how near the world is to nuclear annihilation) to *three minutes before midnight.* Declared the *Bulletin*: "We thus stand at a fateful juncture, at the threshold of a period of confrontation, a time when the blunt simplicities of force threaten to displace any other form of discourse between the superpowers. This is an appalling prospect."

A growing number of fundamentalist preachers, theologians, and TV evangelists, though, applaud these developments. Escalating Middle East tensions have worked to give seeming credence to their startling predictions that Armageddon is soon to take place in that vicinity! And by sounding the alarm in books, lectures, and television productions, they have gathered a considerable following.

These commentators quarrel over the exact sequence of events. But a typical 'Armageddon scenario' goes like this: The starting of the 'doomsday countdown,' they say, was the establishment of the State of Israel. They therefore feel that the so-called rapture is imminent. According to them, soon true Christians will suddenly disappear from the earth—being snatched up to heaven. During the ensu-ing seven years of "tribulation," many evangelists even predict that the nation of Israel will be converted to Christianity. Most of the human race, though, will supposedly be brought under the spell of a charismatic dictator (the "Antichrist") who will lead a ten-nation coalition. Even Israel, they believe, will align itself with him. But a confederacy of Arab nations and others, led by Russia, will make a surprise invasion of Israel. God will miraculously halt this invasion, say these fundamentalists. Soon to follow, however, will be another attack from the "Antichrist," triggering all-out war in the Middle East—Armageddon.

Perhaps this sounds quite plausible to some. After all, the Bible *does* predict a gathering of nations for war at "Armageddon." (Revelation 16:14-16, *King James Version*) But does the Bible really indicate that this event will take place in the Middle East? And what significance does the location of this battle have?

ARMAGEDDON,
the Middle East, and the Bible

"**T**HE center of the entire prophetic forecast," claims author Hal Lindsey, "is the State of Israel." (*The 1980's: Countdown to Armageddon*) Critical to the fundamentalists' 'Armageddon scenario,' therefore, is their belief that God has special dealings with Israel. God, they believe, will intervene when her enemies seek to destroy her.

The Bible, however, indicates that the Jewish nation lost God's favor and protec-tion when they rejected his Son, Jesus Christ. (Acts 3:13, 14, 19) Jesus himself plainly told them: "The kingdom of God will be taken from you and be given to a nation producing its fruits."—Matthew 21:43.

Rejected Entirely?

Theologians John F. and John E. Walvoord (previously quoted) nevertheless counter by saying: "The Apostle Paul clearly indicated that the Old Testament promises for Israel were still to be fulfilled. Paul wrote, 'I ask then, Did God reject his people? By no means!' (Rom. 11:1; NIV.)" They fail, though, to quote the rest of that verse: "For I also am an Israelite, of the seed of Abraham, of the tribe of Benjamin." What did Paul mean by this?

Paul could not have believed that the Israelites as a nation still had a special place with God, for the apostle expressed "great grief and unceasing pain in [his] heart" over their unresponsiveness to God's goodness. (Romans 9:2-5) At Romans 9:6 Paul adds: "However, it is not as though the word of God [to Abraham] had failed. For not all who spring from [natural] Israel *are really 'Israel.'*" Note what Paul is saying: that because the Jews rejected Christ, God *no longer considered them to be Israel!* The anointed congregation of Jesus Christ's followers was now

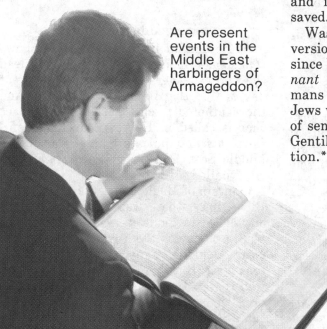

Are present events in the Middle East harbingers of Armageddon?

the *real* "Israel," the instrument through which God would bless all mankind.—1 Peter 2:9; Galatians 3:29; 6:16; Genesis 22:18.

God, though, did not reject the Jewish people as *individuals,* for Paul pointed out: "For I also am an Israelite." Yes, individuals within the Jewish nation, like Paul, could become part of spiritual Israel if they accepted Christ. Only "a remnant," a minority, chose to do so.—Romans 11:1, 5.

A Future Conversion?

Some, however, anticipate a dramatic change of heart on the part of all natural Jews. "The great tribulation, which will follow the rapture of the Church," claims one fundamentalist writer, "will be the means of Israel's conversion [to Christianity]." Interestingly, Paul does say at Romans 11:25, 26: "A dulling of sensibilities has happened in part to Israel *until the full number of people of the nations has come in,* and in this manner *all Israel* will be saved."

Was Paul predicting a future mass conversion of the Jews? How could that be so, since he himself indicated that only a *remnant* of Jews would accept Christ? (Romans 11:5) True, Paul did say that the Jews would experience a spiritual "dulling of sensibilities" *until* "the full number" of Gentiles came into the Christian congregation.* However, Greek scholar Richard

---

* Christendom's religions fail to recognize that a definite number, revealed in the Bible to be 144,000, makes up spiritual Israel. (Revelation 7:4) As a result, some draw the erroneous conclusion that Paul predicted a mass conversion of both the Jews and "the whole pagan world." (*The Jerusalem Bible*) Paul's illustration of the olive tree in Romans, chapter 11, however, makes little sense without a definite number being involved.

Lenski shows that here the word "until" does *not necessarily* imply some later conversion. (Compare the use of "until" at Acts 7:17, 18 and Revelation 2:25.) Paul is actually saying that the natural Jews' sensibilities would *remain* 'dull' right down to the end. God, however, wisely completes "the full number" of spiritual Israel (144,000) by bringing believing Gentiles into the Christian congregation. "And in *this manner* [not by the Jewish nation's change of heart] all [spiritual] Israel will be saved."

Possessing the Promised Land —"For Ever"?

What, though, about the land on which the State of Israel is situated? Does God have some sort of special interest in it? Many, such as Protestant theologian William Hurst, think so. Said Hurst: "No parcel of land on the face of the earth has been more sought after or more constantly in the attention of the society of nations than has the land of the Jew." Quoting Genesis 13:14, 15, he reminds us that God promised that he would give this land to Abraham's seed *"for ever."—King James Version.*

Is Jehovah God thus obliged to protect the land of Israel from invasion? If so, a Middle Eastern "Armageddon" could be imminent. Nevertheless, God merely told Abraham that his offspring would occupy this land, not *forever,* but for an "indefinite" period of time.* (Genesis 13: 14, 15) By rejecting Jesus Christ, they

---

* Although the Hebrew word 'oh·lam is rendered by some as "forever," according to Hebrew authority William Gesenius, it means *"hidden time, i. e. obscure and long, of which the beginning or end is uncertain or indefinite." Nelson's Expository Dictionary of the Old Testament* adds: "With the preposition *'ad,* the word can mean 'into the indefinite future.'"—Compare Deuteronomy 23:3; 1 Samuel 1:22.

Is Jerusalem the key to the events leading to Armageddon?

lost all claim to this land—and God's protection.

Armageddon—Where?

At Revelation 16:14, 16 the Bible shows that demon-inspired propaganda will lead the world's leaders "to the war of the great day of God the Almighty." It adds: "And they gathered them together to the place that is called in Hebrew Har-Magedon." Does *this* not indicate a final war in the Middle East? No, for no geographic location called "Har-Magedon" (literally, "Mountain of Megiddo") actually exists. In Bible times, there was a Middle Eastern city called Megiddo. It was located in the plain shown on the cover of this issue. Near Megiddo many significant battles took place. But there was, and is, no mountain there. "Har-Magedon," or "Armageddon," must therefore be a *symbolic* location. Symbolic of what?

Ezekiel's prophecy shows that Armageddon is precipitated by the attack of a multinational army upon "Israel." The attackers are led by 'Gog of Magog,' whose forces swoop down from "the remotest parts of the north." Who is this "Gog"? Fundamentalist theologian Hal Lindsey confidently declares (as do others): "There is only one nation to the 'uttermost north' of Israel —the U.S.S.R." He likewise theorizes that those making up Gog's "military force" (called Meshech, Tubal, Persia, Ethiopia, Put, Gomer, and Togarmah in the Bible) will be Soviet allies, primarily Arab nations.—Ezekiel 38:1-9, 15.

The nations listed as Gog's confederates, though, were not especially prominent on the world scene in Ezekiel's day. The prophecy's fulfillment was thus to take place in "the final part of the years," when ancient Israel's traditional enemies had passed off the earthly scene. (Ezekiel 38:8) Therefore, Gog's *obscure* and *remote* "land of Magog" would not picture the *prominent* and far from *remote* Soviet Union.

Who, then, is it that dwells in a 'remote' land and harbors fierce animosity toward God's people? At Revelation 12:7-9, 17, the Bible answers: "War broke out in heaven: Michael and his angels battled with the dragon . . . So down the great dragon was hurled, the original serpent, the one called *Devil and Satan.*" How did Satan react to being cast out of heaven into the debased spirit realm? Says the Bible: "And the dragon grew wrathful at the woman [God's heavenly organization], and went off to *wage war* with the remaining ones of her seed, who observe the commandments of God and have the work of bearing witness to Jesus."

Satan, therefore, is "Gog." For decades, Satan and his demon hordes have carried out this warfare against the remnant of spiritual Israel—the anointed Christian congregation. (Galatians 6:16) These Christians are spread throughout the earth; they are not in some central location that could be invaded by a Middle Eastern confederacy of troops. But as Ezekiel prophesied, they are "dwelling in security" under God's protection. (Ezekiel 38:11) Present-day natural Israel, surrounded by hostile neighbors and suffering internal difficulties politically and socially, is hardly "dwelling in security."

The Bible, however, indicates that the world scene will undergo a drastic change. "Babylon the Great," the world empire of false religion, will suffer sudden destruction. (Revelation, chapter 18) With this debacle of false religion, the remaining true Christians will seem vulnerable, and Satan, or "Gog," will not be able to resist attempting to destroy them. He will see to it that under demonic influence "the kings of the entire inhabited earth" are gathered together "to the war of the great day of God the Almighty" at Har–Magedon. —Ezekiel 38:12-16; Revelation 16:14, 16.

"Har–Magedon" is, therefore, not some tiny location in the Middle East. Rather, it is a *world situation.* The entire world will be united in its opposition to Jehovah God and his witnesses. (Isaiah 43:10-12) It is Satan's vicious attack upon true Christians—not a battle between nations in an area of the Middle East—that arouses God to warfare in defense of His people!—Ezekiel 38:18-23; Zechariah 2:8.

True Christians today are therefore doing more than keeping a passive watch on the Middle East. Their prime concern is to direct people to what God's Word really says about this coming war. Jehovah's Witnesses have gained a worldwide reputation for fearlessly taking this message to the homes of people. Nevertheless, you may wonder why a God of love would bring about such a war. Is it possible to survive it? Our next two issues of *The Watchtower* will address themselves to these very questions.

She Had Faith and Courage —Do You?

THIS little Israelite girl is being taken captive by a marauding band of Syrians. Eventually she is brought to the wife of Naaman, the commander of the Syrian army. In this enemy territory, far from her home in Israel, she becomes a servant of Naaman's wife.

Naaman is a valiant, mighty man who is held in high esteem. However, this great military commander is afflicted with the terrible disease leprosy, which eats away parts of a person's body. Back in Israel, before she was captured, the little Israelite girl heard about the miracles Jehovah God performed through his prophet Elisha, including even the restoring of life to a woman's dead son. (2 Kings 4:8-37) Unlike so many others, the little girl has complete faith in God's miracles, and she has the courage to speak up about them.

So one day, as you can see, the little girl tells Naaman's wife: 'If my master would go to Samaria, Jehovah's prophet there would cure him of leprosy.' Well, eventually, someone goes to Naaman and reports what the little Israelite girl said. How this must have impressed Naaman!

As here pictured, we can imagine Naaman approaching the little girl and saying something like this: 'I am the chief of the army of Syria. Yet you dare to urge me to go to your country, to the prophet of your God, that I might be cured of my leprosy. Little one, you have great faith and unselfish courage, risking my displeasure to render me this kindness. I will ask permission of the Syrian king to go to Israel.'—2 Kings 5:1-5.

Can you see yourself in a position similar to that of the little Israelite girl? Do *you* know about Jehovah's goodness and how he purposes to create a new system of things in which all people will be healthy and can live forever? (2 Peter 3:13; Revelation 21:3, 4) Why, most people today know little if anything about these things!

So, as a youngster, you might find yourself in a situation like that of the young girl pictured here. The teacher and the other students in this class do not know about Jehovah. In such a case, if you had the opportunity, would you have the faith and courage to speak up and help others to go where they can receive spiritual healing?

But what happened to Naaman? Was he healed? That is another story, and we will consider it later.

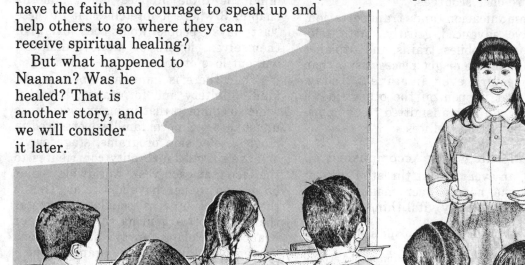

Can Human Accomplishments Ward Off Catastrophe?

"It does not belong to man who is walking even to direct his step."—JEREMIAH 10:23.

IN OUR 20th century, mankind has accomplished amazing things. Great strides have been made in education, in science, and in technical fields. Today many reap the benefits of this in their daily lives. In various lands there are modern conveniences such as indoor electric lighting, plumbing, and helpful appliances. Also, medical science is helping to control certain diseases, such as smallpox, that were once scourges.

[2] Communication and transportation, too, have advanced greatly. With telephones, automobiles, trains, and airplanes we communicate or get places faster than our ancestors ever imagined. Today, events that happen on the other side of the earth can be transmitted to us immediately by space satellites.

Vital Things Not Accomplished

[3] Yet, an ever-present threat of nuclear catastrophe hovers over mankind, and there are absolutely vital things that humans have not been able to accomplish. For example, has the advance in education seen a similar advance in the educating of people to be more honest, truthful, and moral? In the United States, tax losses from cheating come to over 100 billion dollars annually. In another country, in one large city alone, 17,000 police officers reportedly were dismissed for corruption in seven years. Such dishonesty brings to mind the Bible prophecy at 2 Timothy chapter 3 where it foretells that in these "last days" people would be 'lovers of themselves, lovers of money, disloyal, without love of goodness.'

[4] Then there is immorality of a sexual kind. Adultery and fornication have become so common that in many places it is unusual to see moral families portrayed in movies, television programs, stage plays, or novels. And immorality contributes to the fact that each year, worldwide, about 55 million women have abortions! This is the destruction of a population greater than that of Argentina, or Canada, or France, or Poland, or 145 other nations —every year! So while one branch of medical science hails advances that save the

---

1, 2. What are some of mankind's accomplishments in this 20th century?

3, 4. What vital things have humans not accomplished, as accurately foretold in Bible prophecy?

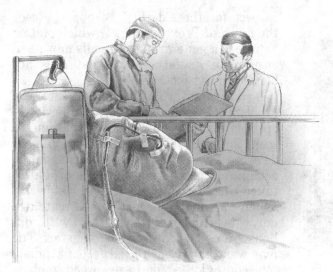

Medical science has not stemmed the tide of disease and death

lives of some children, another branch murders millions of the unborn. Just as the Bible foretold, in these "last days" many people are "without self-control" and have "no natural affection."—2 Timothy 3:3.

[5] Sexual immorality is causing an epidemic of sexually transmitted diseases. Many types are now resistant to drugs. The widespread disease known as genital herpes has seen no cure so far. And there is a sharp rise in the number of babies who have it, born from infected mothers. About half of these babies die, and of the rest, half are physically or mentally damaged. Nor has any cure been found so far for AIDS (Acquired Immune Deficiency Syndrome), the deadly disease that has baffled doctors. AIDS has appeared in at least 33 nations "and now poses a global health threat" says the Associated Press. It has especially affected homosexuals, calling to mind Romans 1:27.

[6] Medical science cannot stem the tide of many other diseases. In Africa alone, millions have malaria, sleeping sickness, leprosy, and other illnesses. In developed nations cancer, heart trouble, diabetes, cirrhosis, and emotional disorders are on the rise. Some of these are brought on, or worsened, by the anxieties or by-products of modern industrial society. Others result from permissive life-styles.

[7] If more diseases were controlled, could medical science keep us in good health indefinitely? No, say many scientists. They show that while the life span might be lengthened by a few years, other illnesses would become bigger killers. A scientist concluded: "There is little chance that we will greatly increase life expectance or postpone aging in the near future." Accurately, the Bible stated long ago at Psalm 90:10: "The days of our years are seventy years; and if because of special mightiness they are eighty years, yet their insistence is on trouble and hurtful things; for it must quickly pass by."

Problem of Poverty Unsolved

[8] Technology has made living more convenient for some people, true. But many others do not have enough money to buy the products of technology. The publication *World Military and Social Expenditures 1983* reported: "2,000,000,000 people live on incomes below $500 [U.S.] per year." It continued: "At least one person in five is trapped in absolute poverty, a

5. What are some health consequences of rampant immorality today?

6. Has medical science stemmed the advance of disease throughout the world?
7. Is it likely that advances in medicine could keep us in good health indefinitely?
8. How did the Bible accurately foretell that technology would not solve the poverty problem?

Human governments cannot
eliminate global poverty

state of destitution so complete that it is silent genocide." It then noted that each year "11,000,000 babies die before their first birthday" from malnutrition or disease.—Revelation 6:5-8.

⁹ In some countries, states *The Detroit News,* "many women find themselves with too many children and no means to care for them. . . . All too often, such mothers simply deposit an unwanted child . . . on the street." There are millions of such children. In other places, parents are abandoned. An Asian journalist writes: "Thousands of old people are being turned out of their homes because their families cannot feed them anymore. There are no welfare agencies to provide help. Many times the children of these elderly ones take them on a train and drop them off someplace or abandon them at train stations." The writer adds: "What a shocking change in a culture that had so much

respect for the elderly." So our age sees the truth of Proverbs 30:11, which states: "There is a generation that calls down evil even upon its father and that does not bless even its mother."

¹⁰ Human governments cannot solve the problem of global poverty. Underdeveloped lands have a crushing burden of mounting debt that they cannot pay. Even developed countries have excessive debts. Symptomatic of this, dozens of banks failed in the United States last year. When one of the largest was threatened, only government intervention with billions of dollars prevented disaster. The fear was that if such a large bank failed, "the contagion would have spread to other banks as well, threatening the entire financial system," reported *The New York Times.* Thus, it is becoming increasingly difficult to ward off catastrophe. In fact, with each passing year the observation of England's *Guardian* takes on added force: "The world is on the verge of a human catastrophe and a political disaster . . . Whole continents have seen their hopes for the future disappear."—Luke 21: 25, 26.

Technology's Effect on War

¹¹ Technology has made much worse something else that governments are unable to stop: war. It was technology that made World War I such a slaughter with the mass use of machine guns, submarines, warplanes, tanks, and flamethrowers. British author Richard Rees said: "The 1914-18 war brought two facts to light: first, that technological development had reached a point where it could continue without disaster only in a unified

---

9. What sad situation prevails in many lands?

10. How secure is the world's financial situation, bringing to mind what prophecy of Jesus?
11. What additional problem that governments cannot solve has been made much worse by technology?

world and, second, that the existing political and social organizations in the world made its unification impossible." World War II proved his point, as newer weapons killed about 55 million people.

¹² Today war weapons are far more hideous, and governments are far from united. Regarding nuclear weapons, author Herman Wouk said: "The ingenuity, labor, and treasure poured out on this . . . insanity truly stun the mind. If nations did not learn war any more, there would be nothing mankind could not do." Astronomer Carl Sagan said of nuclear war: "There is little question that our global civilization would be destroyed." And while this threat of earth-wide catastrophe hangs over the human family, numerous other conflicts take countless lives. The Center for Defense Information in the United States reported that in 1984 there were 42 different wars and rebellions in progress *at the same time!* Governments cannot even stop the tidal wave of crime and violence in their own lands, much less bring global peace.

¹³ All of this fits the prophecy at Revelation 6:4 about the ride of one of the 'four horsemen of the Apocalypse' since 1914: "And another came forth, a fiery-colored horse; and to the one seated upon it there was granted to take peace away from the earth so that they should slaughter one another; and a great sword was given him."

Why Human Efforts Fail

¹⁴ Why is there reason to fear that human accomplishments will not ward off catastrophe? Indeed, why are humans un-

able to accomplish their aims? The Bible shows one major reason: "Through one man sin entered into the world and death through sin, and thus death spread to all men because they had all sinned." (Romans 5:12) Our first parents, Adam and Eve, were created perfect in body and mind. But that perfection depended on their staying inside the boundaries of God's beneficial laws. Within those laws they were given much freedom of choice. But Genesis chapter 3 shows that our first parents took free choice too far. They desired independence from God and his laws, wanting to decide for themselves what was right or wrong, an authority that belongs only to God. After they made that choice, they were on their own. The Bible states: "Jehovah is with you as long as you prove to be with him; . . . but if you leave him he will leave you." (2 Chronicles 15:2) Separated from God, Adam and Eve began to degenerate. Sickness, sorrow, and eventually death overtook them. —Genesis 2:16, 17.

¹⁵ After our first parents became imperfect, the law of genetics saw to it that all their offspring inherited imperfection. The psalmist acknowledged: "With error I was brought forth with birth pains, and in sin my mother conceived me." (Psalm 51:5) There is no way whatsoever that medical science can overcome the consequences of inherited imperfection. Looking for some medical breakthrough to eliminate sickness and death is looking for something that humans cannot accomplish—ever.

¹⁶ Inherited imperfection also affects our mental condition. We are all born with the tendency to do the wrong thing. Now, this does not mean that humans cannot control their actions. They can if they take

---

12. What threats confront the human family today?
13. Does global violence in our time fit Bible prophecy?
14, 15. What is a major reason why humans cannot accomplish their aims now?

---

16. How has imperfection affected mankind's mental condition?

corrective measures. Proverbs 3:6 shows this, saying: "In all your ways take notice of him [Jehovah], and he himself will make your paths straight." However, when humans ignore the proper correction, then they get into deep trouble. And the farther away individuals and nations get from God's laws, the more ruinously they act, feeding the inborn tendency to be selfish. In this regard a *New York Times* editorial commented: "You can hardly take a casual look at today's headlines without wondering where the world is going. . . . See what happens when men, institutions and nations put their selfish interests ahead of everything else. . . . The plain fact in all countries is that playing the selfish game is not working."

Satanic Influence

17 Another major factor that helps to explain why humans cannot achieve their aims and ward off catastrophe is the influence noted at 2 Corinthians 4:4, which speaks of "the god of this system of things." Some who are not familiar with the Bible may think that the god referred to here is Almighty God. But the same verse adds that this god "has blinded the minds of the unbelievers." Surely, the loving Creator would not do that. The god referred to is the same one mentioned at 1 John 5:19, which says: "The whole world is lying in the power of the wicked one."

18 The god who controls this present world is identified at Revelation 12:9 as "the one called Devil and Satan, who is misleading the entire inhabited earth." The name Satan means "Resister" or "Adversary." The name Devil means "False Accuser," or "Slanderer." These are appropriate terms, for the rebellion of Adam

17, 18. What other major factor helps to explain why humans cannot accomplish their aims?

Questions in Review

☐ What vital things have humans been unable to accomplish?

☐ How has technology worsened the effects of war?

☐ Why do human efforts so often fail?

☐ In view of man's record, what is the wise course?

and Eve was instigated by this rebel in the spirit realm. It was he who told Eve, in effect: 'You do not need God's laws. You can decide for yourself what is right and what is wrong.' However, by pulling away from God, Satan became mentally debased. This can be seen by his works, for just look at the world under his control! The ugly, evil history of mankind verifies that it has an ugly, evil influence behind it.

What Hope?

19 Some observers of this chaotic world have made interesting observations about the remedy for mankind's ills. *The Gazette* of Montreal said: "About 150 groups of national politicians pull in different directions, steering planet earth toward chaos. Yet most of the world's major problems are global in scope because transportation and communications technology have shrunk the world into a global community or village." It then recommended: "*Some form of world government will be necessary.*" Sociologist Erich Fromm said that this world's ills can be done away with "only if the whole [social and political] system as it has existed during the last 6000 years of history can be *replaced by a*

19. What have some observers suggested as remedies for this world's ills?

fundamentally different one."—Italics ours.

20 Such observers do not realize it, but the whole social and political system *is* going to be "replaced by a fundamentally different one"! There *will* soon be just one world government for all mankind. But it will not come about by human efforts. Humans alone are unable to ward off catastrophe. They surely cannot replace this present system of things with a better one, as history has proved. They cannot get rid of inherited imperfection, sickness,

---

20. (a) Why will desired goals never come about by human efforts? (b) In whom should we put our trust for the future?

and death. And they cannot get rid of Satan and his demons. Instead, the past course of human events has proved true the inspired words: "It does not belong to man who is walking even to direct his step." (Jeremiah 10:23) Thus God's Word counsels: "Do not put your trust in nobles, nor in the son of earthling man, to whom no salvation belongs." (Psalm 146:3) In whom, then, should you place confidence? Proverbs 3:5 urges: "Trust in Jehovah with all your heart and do not lean upon your own understanding." Why should we have such confidence in Jehovah? Because he can do what man cannot, as the following article will prove.

A Government That Accomplishes What Man Cannot

"Come, you people, and see the activities of God. His dealing with the sons of men is fear-inspiring."
—PSALM 66:5.

JEHOVAH has the power to do what man cannot. To illustrate: Men are in awe of the power of the nuclear bomb; but its power is dwarfed by the tremendous power that exists in our sun. Yet the sun is just one of about 200 billion stars in our

---

1, 2. (a) How does the visible universe display the awesome power of the Creator? (b) Why should we believe what Jehovah's prophetic Word says about our time?

Milky Way galaxy alone. Astronomers estimate that throughout the universe there may be about 100 billion galaxies, each with billions of stars. What stupendous power it took to create all of that! (Isaiah 40:26) This awesome power of the Creator makes the power of humans pale into insignificance.—Isaiah 40:15.

2 Thus no one should doubt that Jehovah can accomplish what he says he will do.

(Isaiah 46:9, 10; 55:11) We should believe it when his prophetic Word tells us that we are nearing the end of the time limit he has allowed for humans to go their independent way. History shows that what people have done to human life and to animal life, as well as to the earth itself, is a disgrace, a blot on God's universe. Thus, Jehovah is fully justified in erasing this blot once and for all.—Hosea 4:1-3; Jude 14, 15.

³ What is taking place on the world scene today is clear evidence that this system of things is indeed in the final part of "the last days" foretold at 2 Timothy chapter 3. Soon Jehovah will crush this system out of existence and immobilize its head, Satan the Devil. That will be followed by an entirely new system of things on earth, controlled by the heavenly government for which Jesus taught his followers to pray when he said: "Let your kingdom come. Let your will take place, as in heaven, also upon earth."—Matthew 6:10; Daniel 2:44; Romans 16:20.

The Principle of Repurchase

⁴ Human governments cannot eliminate sin, sickness, and death. Yet, God's government will do what humans cannot. We get some insight as to how this will work by examining Jehovah's dealings with his people of ancient Israel. Back then, God used the principle of repurchase, or ransom. For instance, if an Israelite became poor, he might have to sell himself as a slave to a non-Israelite. But a close relative could ransom him if he had the adequate purchase price.—Leviticus 25:47-49.

⁵ In a similar way, God has provided for the repurchasing of mankind out of slavery to sin. The price had to be the equivalent of what was lost. (Deuteronomy 19:21) Adam lost perfect, eternal human life. Since nothing that sinful humans possess equals that in value, they cannot "redeem even a brother." (Psalm 49:7) However, the Bible foretold the coming of the one who could. That one proved to be Jesus Christ. It was revealed that Jesus had a prehuman existence in heaven. But his life was transferred to the womb of Mary by Jehovah's power. In this way he was born as a human. But with God as his Father, he did not inherit the sinfulness that had crippled all the rest of mankind.—Matthew 1:18-21; John 1:1, 14; 1 Peter 2:22.

⁶ Thus, Jesus possessed the only thing equal in value to a perfect human life —another perfect human life. But unlike disobedient Adam, Jesus remained obedient to God. And when he offered up his life for the human family, Jehovah accepted it as the suitable repurchase price. (Galatians 1:4) But does this mean that everyone is automatically freed from sin and will gain perfection under Kingdom rule? No, for John 3:16 states: "God loved the world so much that he gave his only-begotten Son, in order that *everyone exercising faith in him* might not be destroyed but have everlasting life." Only if we accept the repurchase provision *and do something about it* will we experience the regeneration of our bodies and minds to perfection in Paradise.—Revelation 21:4.

Education in the New Order

⁷ The mind has a huge potential for learning, even in man's present imperfect condition. But this is only a fraction of what it will be able to learn in the New Order, where sin will not block its functioning. In *The Brain Book* the

3. What does Bible prophecy say about the near future?
4. How did Jehovah use the principle of repurchase in ancient Israel?
5, 6. (a) How does the repurchase principle work in relieving mankind of inherited sin? (b) Is everyone automatically freed from sin?

7, 8. What potential for future learning lies within the human brain?

Under Kingdom rule, truth-loving people "will all be taught by Jehovah"

author states: "Within our own heads lies one of the most complex systems in the known universe. Its power and versatility far surpass that of any man-made computer." He adds: "It is frequently stated that we use only 10 percent of our full mental potential. This, it now appears, is rather an overestimate. We probably do not use even 1 percent—more likely 0.1 percent or less."

8 Imagine what the brain will enable humans to accomplish when it reaches its full potential in the New Order. Think of all the fascinating things that Jehovah has put on this earth about which we can learn, such as its animal, marine, and plant life. Think, too, of learning about the amazing universe with its billions of galaxies. Consider all the skills we will be able to master in art, music, crafts, and a host of other things.

9 There is another type of education in the New Order that will bring the greatest benefit of all. Jesus said: "They will all be taught by Jehovah." (John 6:45) This is the highest level of education. And it will be made available to all the subjects of God's Kingdom, including those who survive the end of this system of things. (Revelation 7:9, 14) Other Kingdom subjects are noted at John 5:28 and 29, where Jesus said: "The hour is coming in which all those in the memorial tombs will hear his voice and come out." This resurrection of billions of dead persons—utterly impossible for humans to accomplish—means that a vast educational work will have to be done in their behalf.

10 Today there are many conflicting systems of education. But in the New Order, God's heavenly government will provide one worldwide system of education to teach people the truth about Jehovah in a unified way. Part of this will be to teach people about proper human relationships. There will be no teaching of pride of race, nationality, or social standing. Instead, earth's inhabitants will learn to love one another, respecting one another's dignity. Such education will also result in a whole-

9. What type of education will bring the greatest benefits in the New Order?

10. How will education proceed in the New Order?

some remaking of personalities to mirror the superior qualities of Jehovah.—Acts 10:34, 35; Colossians 3:9-12.

[11] Can such education really work? We are certain that it can and will. One reason is that Jehovah, who cannot lie, says that it will. (Titus 1:2) Furthermore, this kind of education *is working right now!* Jehovah already has a worldwide teaching organization that is instructing millions of people about his Kingdom government and its requirements. This is happening because Kingdom rule has been in operation since "the last days" began in 1914.

[12] Since that time, the prophecy of Matthew chapter 25 has been undergoing fulfillment. It shows that Jesus comes to Kingdom power while God's enemies are still on earth. Verse 32 says: "All the nations will be gathered before him, and he will separate people one from another, just as a shepherd separates the sheep from the goats." These sheeplike ones are now being taught by Jehovah through his growing, visible organization. Appreciating what they learn, they work to remake their personalities in God's image. And the fact that this education is affecting millions of persons for the good right now is a sure

11, 12. How can we be certain that such education in the New Order will succeed in its purpose?

In Our Next Issue

■ Armageddon
    —From a God of Love?

■ Who Can Read the "Sign" Aright?

■ Can a Blind Man "See"?

token that it will do so on a much grander scale in God's New Order.

Building a Paradise

[13] Another kind of work under Kingdom rule will be that of turning this earth into a paradise. And Paradise could not include slums or poverty. People want decent homes and some land with trees, flowers, and gardens. Those who are willing to be taught by God will have just that. Isaiah 65:21 and 22 foretells: "And they will *certainly* build houses and have occupancy; and they will *certainly* plant vineyards and eat their fruitage. They will not build and someone else have occupancy; they will not plant and someone else do the eating. . . . The work of their own hands my chosen ones will use to the full."

[14] Do not doubt what Jehovah will accomplish with the willing hearts and hands of his people in the New Order. Even today the construction world is amazed at what Jehovah's Witnesses accomplish in putting up buildings, such as quickly built Kingdom Halls. After one of these was built in the United States, a newspaper editorial said: 'Something more valuable than a building was created by those 2,000 volunteers. Civic leaders should look closer at what was accomplished last weekend. Enthusiasm, dedication and desire to meet a goal were harnessed with astounding results. If only local groups could bridle those same resources, any goal—be it recycling, crime prevention, or community development—could be within reach. An army of workers proved what potential lies within the soul when a community is unified. We hope the Kingdom Hall is the site for a fountain of inspiration to the congregation of Witnesses. Its existence is al-

13. What grand construction work will take place under Kingdom rule?
14, 15. Why can we be confident that Jehovah's servants will be able to construct a paradise?

Peace and unity are already a reality among those who submit to the Kingdom government

ready an inspiration to us all.'

¹⁵ This willingness and growing skill of Jehovah's servants will be employed with even greater benefits in God's New Order. And how enjoyable it will be to replace all undesirable areas with beautiful homes and surroundings! How satisfying it will be to know that every day your efforts will bring the earth one day closer to being a global paradise!

A United Global Family

¹⁶ Nor will the inhabitants of the New Order ever have to feel threatened by crime, rioting, or war. Psalm 46:9 says: "[God] is making wars to cease to the extremity of the earth." The "Prince of Peace," Jesus Christ, will enforce enduring global peace, for "to the abundance of the princely rule and to peace there will be no end." (Isaiah 9:6, 7) With true peace, and with the entire human family educated in the same high standards, all will be united in an unbreakable bond of love. Thus, there will no longer be any divisive national boundaries.

¹⁷ Are such promises too good to be true?

16. Why will inhabitants of the New Order never feel threatened by violence?
17. How far reaching are the peace and unity God's servants have even now?

No, because peace and unity are already a reality among those who loyally submit to Kingdom rule! Consider this: Over two and a half million witnesses of Jehovah are spread around the earth. Yet, they already are fulfilling Isaiah 2:4, which says: "And they will have to beat their swords into plowshares and their spears into pruning shears. Nation will not lift up sword against nation, neither will they learn war anymore." Under no circumstances will Jehovah's Witnesses intentionally take the lives of their brothers, or anyone else, in any land. As the Italian publication *Il Corriere di Trieste* observed: "They are ready to face death rather than violate the basic precept . . . THOU SHALT NOT KILL!" Because of adhering to God's standards, Jehovah's Witnesses have true peace and unity, which it is impossible for this world to attain. And the fact that millions of them enjoy this condition in the midst of this strife-torn world testifies to what will take place when God's Kingdom controls all earth's affairs.—John 13: 34, 35; 1 John 3:10-12.

[18] In addition to this international peace and unity, adherence to God's superior standards produces people who care for their neighbor and their neighbor's property. Thus they 'conduct themselves honestly in all things.' (Hebrews 13:18) Regarding this, a French-Canadian columnist, writing in *Le Journal de Montreal,* said of Jehovah's Witnesses: "If they were the only people in the world, we would not at night have to bolt our doors shut and put on the burglar alarm."

[19] These loyal subjects of God's government have no crime problem among themselves, while it is out of hand in the world. Too, since they adhere to the Bible's high moral standards, they are not plagued by the sexually transmitted diseases or abortions that are epidemic in every nation. And Jehovah's servants hold marriage in deep respect, in contrast with the world's permissive view of the marital arrangement. Why can Jehovah's Witnesses maintain such standards? Because Jehovah is guiding his loyal worshipers, and "with God all things are possible."—Matthew 19:26.

Gather to True Worship

[20] Whether people realize it or not, the global gathering of sheeplike persons into Jehovah's organization is the most significant movement of modern times. This is fulfilling the remarkable prophecy of Isaiah 2:2, 3: "And it must occur in the final part of the days that the mountain of the house of Jehovah [his exalted true worship] will become firmly established above the top of the mountains, and it will certainly be lifted up above the hills; and to it *all the nations must stream*. And many peoples will certainly go and say: 'Come,

18, 19. What are some other benefits that come to those who adhere to God's high standards?
20. What is the most significant movement of modern times?

you people, and let us go up to the mountain of Jehovah, . . . and he will instruct us about his ways, and we will walk in his paths.'"

[21] We encourage all honest-hearted people to be part of this thrilling world movement toward true worship and righteous government. Enjoy blessings that right now come from associating with a people being educated in God's laws and principles. Loyally submit to the Kingdom government that will soon begin to turn this earth into a paradise. Put your trust in that Kingdom and not in the schemes of this world, for as Psalm 127:1 says: "Unless Jehovah himself builds the house, it is to no avail that its builders have worked hard on it." Respond to the invitation of Psalm 66:5: "Come, you people, and see the activities of God. His dealing with the sons of men is fear-inspiring." So come to the God who guarantees the best government for mankind, the government that will accomplish what man cannot, the government that very soon will be the *only one* this earth will have.

21. What are honest-hearted people encouraged to do?

How Would You Answer?

□ Why can we be certain that Jehovah will accomplish his purposes?

□ How does the principle of repurchase work for relieving one of sin?

□ What great education and construction works will there be in the New Order?

□ What evidence is there now that peace, unity, and love will exist earth wide in the New Order?

Insight on the News

Threat of "Apocalypse"

According to the nuclear-winter theory, if bombs equivalent to 5,000 million tons of TNT were detonated in a nuclear war, the resulting smoke and soot—particularly from large cities—would plunge the northern hemisphere into months of darkness and freezing, life-threatening weather. "If the analysis is correct," states Nobel laureate Herbert A. Simon in the magazine *Science,* "then no nation can make a major nuclear attack even against an unarmed opponent without committing suicide."

Many experts feel that if this theory is verified, it will be a great incentive for nuclear disarmament. "Recognition of the nuclear-winter problem, awful as it is, seems a piece of immense good fortune at the eleventh hour," writes Thomas Powers in *The Atlantic.* But would this end the arms race? Hardly. Powers maintains that the superpowers would be compelled to construct "a whole new generation of weaponry" with "a much larger number of much smaller, extremely accurate weapons that would allow targets in cities to be destroyed without burning down the cities around them." He concludes that the nuclear-winter problem "does not end the possibility of a big war . . . , but it does push planners in a new direction, away from apocalypse."

Rather than offering hope, the threat of nuclear winter simply raises new fears. Would the superpowers not be *more* likely to deploy "suicide-proof" weapons to settle their confrontations? In desperation, might not warring nations still use nuclear weapons at the risk of suicide to avoid defeat? The selfish military strategies that nations employ provide yet another reason for Almighty God to bring about *his* war of Har–Magedon. This he will do soon, and his Word assures us that "there is no king saved by the abundance of military forces." —Psalm 33:16; Revelation 16: 14, 16.

Armageddon —What Is It?

In a televised debate, U.S. President Ronald Reagan said that no one knows whether Bible prophecies mean "that Armageddon is a thousand years away or day after tomorrow." But summing up some of Reagan's statements, Andrew Lang, research director of the Christic Institute, an ecumenical public-policy center, says: "What we have are a series of repetitions that Armageddon may happen in our generation, that Armageddon may happen in the Middle East and that Armageddon may involve Soviet forces."

The Bible indicates that "the kings of the entire inhabited earth" will be gathered to Armageddon for destruction, though a "great crowd" in God's favor will survive. (Revelation 7:14, 15; 16: 14, 16; 19:19-21) Armageddon (Hebrew, "Har–Magedon," meaning, "Mountain of Megiddo") is not an actual site in the Middle East. Nor could the armies of the nations squeeze into the area surrounding Megiddo, an ancient Biblical city. Armageddon is, therefore, a situation, that is, the world's assembling or lining up in opposition to Jehovah God. This situation will follow the "sign," which we are presently witnessing. Armageddon *will* occur in our generation.—Matthew 24:3-15, 21, 34.

Teenage Childbearing

"There is a strong tendency among those of us who are alarmed at the rise in pregnancy and child-bearing among black teen-agers to try to solve the problem by focusing on the pragmatic side of it," writes black columnist William Raspberry. What does he mean? Teenage girls are told not to have babies "because it interrupts their education, preempts their career prospects and damages their life chances. Their babies are likely to be of low birth weights and subject to learning disabilities." But, says Raspberry, "what fascinates and dismays me is how seldom the question of morality enters any of these discussions."

Indeed, teenagers need to be taught that promiscuity, which often results in pregnancy, violates the Bible's moral laws. (Galatians 5:19-23) They should also be taught principles in God's Word that deal with marriage and child rearing. The apostle Paul indicates that Christians should cultivate self-control and wait until they are "past the bloom of youth," when sexual desires first bloom, or become strong, before they get married. (1 Corinthians 7:8, 9, 36) Modern-day studies, which indicate that mature people make the best parents, confirm these moral laws and principles.

"Kingdom Increase" Conventions
—What Rich Spiritual Feasts!

JEHOVAH promised that 'the little one would become a thousand and the small one a mighty nation.' He himself would "speed it up in its own time." (Isaiah 60:22) And in some lands since World War II, Kingdom proclaimers have increased a thousandfold. To this very day, Jehovah's Witnesses are experiencing splendid increases in Brazil, Italy, Japan, Mexico—indeed around the earth. How appropriate, then, that their recent assemblies should be called "Kingdom Increase" District Conventions!

More important than numerical increases, of course, are the rich spiritual blessings we enjoy as witnesses of Jehovah. And how many we enjoyed at this convention! A review of program highlights should refresh our minds, gladden our hearts, and strengthen our determination to apply the fine counsel.

The Overall Effect

In the contiguous United States alone, 117 conventions were held. A total of 1,159,898 were present (35,828 more than last year), and 10,625 were baptized. The four days were filled with spiritual feasting and rejoicing, and the program was like a trumpet sounding distinct notes —Scriptural counsel to strengthen the heart and conscience.

"The talks zeroed in on every facet of life," said one conventioner. Heard, too, were comments like these: 'On getting home, I will have more to think about than I have had after any other convention.' "It always seems that this year's convention is better than last year's, but this year's *was* the best ever!" Yes, the program truly was outstanding.

These conventions also served to advertise Jehovah's name and Kingdom. For instance, this was done when many Kingdom proclaimers shared in the field ministry on Friday afternoon. Then, too, there was much good coverage by the media. Newspaper, radio, and television reports focused on convention activities and the beliefs of Jehovah's Witnesses.

"The Little One Becomes a Thousand"

Based on Isaiah 60:22, this was the theme of the opening day. The talk "Listen and Become Wise in Your Future" urged conventioners to listen to counsel especially applicable to them and work on those points when they returned home. (Proverbs 19:20) Then came the chairman's talk "Together Let Us Exalt God's Name," a most encouraging discussion of Psalm 34. Exalting Jehovah's name means praising it under all circumstances and showing respect for all the Creator's spiritual provisions. And how grateful we should be for the superb spiritual provisions he makes through his organization!

Heartwarming, indeed, was the feature "Declaring Jehovah's Works to the Next Generation." For years, the older ones among us have experienced God's goodness and therefore have much to tell those who are younger. And elderly Witnesses do not retire. Why, all members of the Governing Body keep very active although their ages range from 59 to 91 years! Moreover, Scriptural and modern-day examples show how fitting it is for the younger generation to respect and cooperate with older servants of Jehovah.

The importance of holiness was emphasized in the talk "Keeping Spotless, Unblemished and in Peace." (2 Peter 3:14) To keep spotless, we must avoid the world's immorality and greed. Maintaining peaceful relations with others requires that we be yielding as regards our preferences and that we conduct ourselves as lesser ones.

Next, conventioners were urged to be "Talking About the Glory of His Kingship." For instance, we can witness informally if we carry tracts and other literature, make good use of our opportunities and cultivate a positive frame of mind. The feature entitled "The Increase Is On" showed that large numbers are responding to the good news. Why, in 40 years Jehovah's Witnesses have increased from about 126,000 to more than 2,842,500, with over 7,416,900 attending the Memorial! Encouraging expressions were heard from some who shared in this grand increase.

The first day's program ended with the stirring talk "Survivors Into a New Earth" and the release of a new book entitled *Survival Into a New Earth.* It focuses attention on 47 prophetic patterns and descriptions of people who will survive the end of this system and inherit the earthly realm of God's Kingdom. This publication certainly was received with great enthusiasm.

"Declaring Abroad the Kingdom"

The second day of the convention had this as its theme, and the program emphasized our privilege of declaring the Kingdom message. Pioneers interviewed during the talk "Will You Enter the Large Open Door?" told about the sacrifices they made to become full-time ministers but testified that entering this large door had resulted in deep satisfaction and the blessing that makes one truly rich. (Proverbs 10:22) Those not in the full-time ministry had reason for serious reflection when the speaker asked: "Do our circumstances permit us to enter the pioneer service?"

As aptly shown in the next talk, the apostle Paul was "Intensely Occupied With the Kingdom Good News." (Acts 18:5) Since preaching the good news is one of the main reasons for the existence of the Christian congregation, each present-day witness of Jehovah may wisely ask: "Am I a zealous proclaimer of the Kingdom? Is there any reason why I cannot share regularly each week in some feature of Kingdom preaching?"

The talk "In Your Training Aim for Godly Devotion" showed that such devotion means being personally attached to

Modern-day applications
of Bible principles give
convention dramas
added impact

in 1931 and the proper identification of the "great crowd" in 1935. (Isaiah 43: 10-12; Revelation 7:9) Attention was drawn to the increases we enjoyed during World War II and since then, fulfilling Isaiah 60:22.

All of this was an apt prelude to the talk "A Joyful People—Why?" What reasons we have for joy! Ours is a happy God, and joy is a fruit of his spirit. We enjoy the light of truth, the protection of Bible-based morality, the finest association, and the privilege of making Jehovah's heart glad by maintaining our integrity and preaching the good news. In fact, many conventioners joyfully shared in the Kingdom-preaching work that afternoon, following a talk that heightened appreciation for the great variety of printed material so helpful in our ministry.

Jehovah. And while some secular education is necessary, we may well ask: What is my goal, a secular career or trying to please Jehovah?

Secular education also was considered in the modern-day drama *Divine Education Increases Kingdom Fruitage.* This highlight contrasted the dangers common to attending college with the rewards of full-time service. Youths appreciated the straightforward counsel, and one young man remarked: "That drama was not an exaggeration."

A delightful surprise that morning was the release of *Kingdom Melodies* No. 5. And ever so many expressed appreciation for the new songs used on the program.

The afternoon program began with the keynote address "Kingdom Fruitage Increasing in All the World." It interwove a verse-by-verse discussion of Isaiah chapter 60 with a review of Kingdom increase since 1919, noting such high points as the adoption of the name Jehovah's Witnesses

"Practicing the Things We Learn"

The third day began with two elders discussing the daily text and focusing attention on the foregoing theme. Then came a symposium entitled "Measuring Up as a Christian Family." First considered was the responsibility of the Christian husband, who needs to answer such questions as these: Are you careful never to use your headship for selfish ends? Do you set a fine example by keeping material interests in their proper place as you teach your children to put the Kingdom first in life? Are weekends viewed merely as times for recreation or primarily as opportunities to share in sacred service?

The next talk, "A Wife Who Shows Deep Respect," pointed out that the wife's Scriptural role originates with a wise, just, and loving God who knows what is best for all. Of course, a wife should also be accorded respect. It may not always be easy for a woman to show deep respect for her husband, because he is not perfect. But showing such respect gains Jehovah's approval, results in family harmony, and will bring a woman happiness.

Especially did young people benefit from the talk "Children Who Honor Their Parents." Honoring parents requires obeying them from the heart and guarding against wrong inclinations. So a Christian youth may wisely ask: Is what I am doing bringing honor to God, my parents, and me?

Further counsel for young people was presented in the feature "Youths, Do Not Be Deceived." It included several fine interviews and emphasized the need to resist the Devil's attempts to deceive us. This was fol-

lowed by the talk "Sons Who Make Jehovah's Heart Glad," which showed that Jesus, David, and others gladdened Jehovah's heart in their youth. Similarly, by fine conduct and zealous service, many youths among us are making Jehovah's heart glad today. (Proverbs 27:11) What a privilege!

The baptism talk, "Subjecting Ourselves Under Jehovah's Mighty Hand," emphasized the fact that a person is loyal either to God's organization or to Satan's. Dedication and baptism require changes in the way we think, speak, and act and call for regular presence at meetings and a full share in the Christian ministry.

Three main responsibilities of overseers were driven home in the afternoon discourse "Elders, Imitate the Great Shepherd." (1) Elders must take seriously the obligation to feed God's flock, avoiding last-minute preparation. (2) By example and precept they must protect the flock

The thousands baptized have subjected themselves under Jehovah's mighty hand

from such dangers as permissiveness, excessive pleasures, illicit sex, and apostasy. (3) Elders need to share regularly in the shepherding work.

A discussion between an elder and a ministerial servant next clarified "What It Means to Submit to Kingdom Authority." The root of disregard for rightful authority is selfishness, which got its start with the Devil. Submitting to Kingdom authority means following Bible principles and being submissive to those appointed to take the lead among us.

Yet what if a close friend tells us that he has committed a gross sin but wants us to keep it secret? The soul-searching talk "Do Not Share in the Sins of Others" stressed the need to be loyal to Jehovah and his organization. If we are unable to persuade our conscience-stricken friend to confess to the elders, we should go to them about the matter. Actually, this is for the wrongdoer's own spiritual well-being, and reports indicate that a number of individuals have acted in harmony with this counsel.

A talk that elicited much favorable comment was the one entitled "At Which Table Are You Feeding?" By extending the principle of the apostle Paul's counsel at 1 Corinthians 10:

14-22, we realize that to feed at Jehovah's table means to give God the worship due him and to feed on his truths. We must therefore avoid "the table of demons" by being on guard against such things as illicit sex, materialism, improper entertainment, and philosophies critical of God's Word. Limiting ourselves to Jehovah's table results in joy, contentment, and a sure hope.

The third day's closing talk was entitled "The Sacred Scriptures Increase Our Accurate Knowledge of God." After tracing the Watch Tower Society's record in printing various Bibles, the speaker thrilled his listeners by announcing the release of the *New World Translation of the Holy Scriptures—With References*. It contains over 125,000 cross-references, very helpful footnotes, and a valuable appendix. What a boon to Bible students!

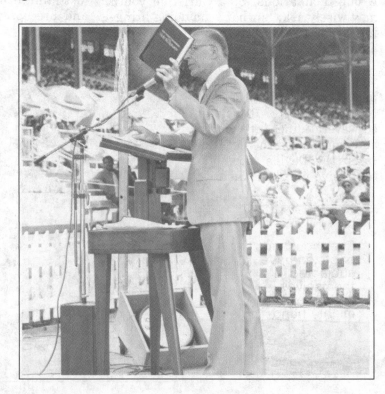

Conventioners were thrilled to receive the superb reference edition of the *New World Translation*

A stirring Bible drama underscored the need to guard against disgraceful folly

portrayed were the bad consequences of Achan's greed. (Joshua, chapter 7) The drama also showed how a similar incident of disgraceful folly could impede the flow of God's holy spirit in a congregation. How this underscored the need to do our part to keep the organization clean while guarding our own hearts against temptation!

"No End to the Abundance of Kingdom Rule"

This was the theme of the convention's fourth and final day. The first major talk centered attention on the question "Do You Abhor What Is Bad?" We need wisdom to determine what is bad and must actually hate, or loathe, badness, for following a wrong course brings Jehovah's disfavor and can harm us and others. (Romans 12:9) Moreover, we need to realize that when Jehovah says something is bad, *it really is bad* and should be avoided.

Next, it was stressed that "Kingdom Increase Adds Responsibility." Yes, great increase places an obligation on all those who have been in the truth longer. They have to care for the spiritual interests of newer ones. Among other things, this can be done by showing hospitality and by setting a fine example in all forms of sacred service.

Guard Against Disgraceful Folly was the title of the second drama. Effectively

The afternoon began with the public talk "A Government That Accomplishes What Man Cannot." You can read information from this heartening message on pages 10 through 20 of this issue of *The Watchtower.*

Next came the talk "The Honor of Bearing Jehovah's Name." It was based on the brochure *The Divine Name That Will Endure Forever,* released that forenoon. The speaker noted that the Bible's most important truth is not the ransom or the hope of life in Paradise but the fact that Jehovah is the one true God. As bearers of Jehovah's name, we must acknowledge that he is the Great Purposer, love his qualities, and do our best to imitate them, making his name known at every opportunity.

In the final talk, "Kingdom Organization Geared for More Increase," the speaker stressed our great privilege to be living in this time of increase. However, we must

Works of Faith
Promote Kingdom Increase

KINGDOM INCREASE is a reality today because Jehovah is blessing his faithful witnesses. Some idea of the works of faith that are promoting this theocratic growth can be gleaned from experiences related at the recent "Kingdom Increase" conventions. Among them were the following:

Outstanding works of faith are being shown in the field ministry. For instance, a recently baptized brother in Korea wanted to share fully in the subscription campaign. So he contacted his business associates and obtained 76 subscriptions to *The Watchtower* and *Awake!* in just one month. He was so encouraged that in nine months he placed 656 subscriptions—as many as 164 in a single month!

How fine it is when our young ones take Kingdom preaching very seriously! In Japan a young Kingdom publisher in the third grade heard that his class was going to a Shinto shrine for an art lesson. With his mother's help, he prepared a letter to his teacher and then telephoned her to explain why he would not be going. Greatly impressed, the teacher told his mother that she had been a publisher while in school but had given up because of family opposition. What resulted from the young boy's stand? Why, the teacher has become an active Witness once again!

One five-year-old in Kenya told his mother, who is a pioneer, that he wanted to become a special pioneer. She felt that he could not even be a regular pioneer since he was not conducting a Bible study. Her suggestion was that he take *My Book of Bible Stories* and try to teach other children. So he invited some youngsters to study the Bible with him, and before long ten were doing so regularly. If the young students could not answer the review questions he asked at the end of the study, he would go over the material again. Soon eight of the children were attending congregation meetings. But what about the other two? Well, they were just too small.

Places to meet are essential as Kingdom increase continues. However, when certain Witnesses in Chad decided to build a Kingdom Hall, it so upset the church people who met across the street that several times they broke down what the brothers had put up. Finally, the opposers became so ashamed of their unchristian conduct that they stopped hindering the Witnesses, and the hall was completed. How thrilled that small congregation was when 73 people came to the Memorial!

Other evidence of faith in action also contributes to Kingdom increase. For instance, in Papua New Guinea a group of interested people, including 15 husbands, wives, and children, were determined to attend a district convention to be held 70 miles (110 km) from their homes. To get there they had to go by dugout canoe with an outboard motor to power it. But when the weather turned bad, they faced powerful river currents and rough seas. They had to bail out water furiously, but they finally made it to their destination after ten hours. And just think—the one who organized this expedition is blind! But how their faith was rewarded at that rich spiritual feast!

maintain the quality of our worship, and individually we should keep moving forward. As one speaker said in closing: "With Jehovah and his Son giving us divine support, let us go forward as a Kingdom organization geared for more increase. We have every reason to exalt God's name together, now and forevermore."

So it was that the "Kingdom Increase" District Conventions struck a positive and spiritually stimulating note. From beginning to end, they truly were rich spiritual feasts.

How Do You View Jehovah's Name?

THIS challenging question was raised for delegates at the "Kingdom Increase" District Conventions of Jehovah's Witnesses. It was occasioned by the release of a new brochure, *The Divine Name That Will Endure Forever.* Why was the question important?

Right from the earthly history of creation, the name Jehovah was used to refer to the only true God. (Genesis 2:4; 4:1) "Jehovah's friend" Abraham used it freely. (James 2:23; Genesis 18:30-33) Moses learned that Jehovah is the Creator's name "to time indefinite." (Exodus 3:15) Jesus made God's name manifest to his followers. (John 17:6) And his disciples traveled far and wide to help people 'call on the name of Jehovah and be saved.' —Acts 2:21.

Others, though, dishonored the name. Israelites who failed to keep Jehovah's law profaned his name. (Leviticus 18:21; 19:12) Those Israelites at the foot of Mount Sinai who used God's name in connection with their worship of the golden calf brought reproach upon his name. (Exodus 32:4, 6) Similarly, the Jews who later superstitiously refused to pronounce God's name dishonored it, as did the Jewish mystics who viewed it as a magic symbol.

Uninformed professing Christians, too, covered over the name when, like the Jews, they ceased to use it and even removed it from the Greek translation of the Hebrew Scriptures. And this, in turn, has led to a modern abuse. People today ignore God's name, viewing it as unimportant or nonessential for worship.

Keep Honoring the Name

In fact, only Jehovah's Witnesses today follow the example of Jesus' early disciples and help people worldwide to 'call on the name of Jehovah and be saved.' They alone can truly be called "a people for his name." (Acts 15:14) Is it possible, though, that we, too, may brush aside Jehovah's name?

Well, if we break Jehovah's laws and practice unrighteousness, we are in fact dishonoring his name. (2 Timothy 2:19) And if we use Jehovah's name in our worship, but our actions show that our real hope for the future is based on material things or something similar, we are not very different from those ancient Israelites who used Jehovah's name but actually were worshiping a golden calf. Moreover, Jehovah's name is not a charm. If we were to display it as the Tetragrammaton or in modern spelling in our house or on our vehicle in the hope that it would protect us or bring us "good luck," how would we differ from those superstitious Jews who viewed it as a magic symbol?—Exodus 20:7.

Thus, how we view God's name is important. The name Jehovah is God's eternal memorial. (Exodus 3:15) It represents his changeless qualities and purposes. (Deuteronomy 32:3-43) Jehovah richly blesses those who fear him and honor his name. (Malachi 3:16) The new brochure, *The Divine Name That Will Endure Forever,* with its in-depth discussion of the divine name, its meaning and correct use, will surely help thousands more to honor the name of their Creator, Jehovah.—Revelation 4:11.

The Bible —A Book to Be Read

THE Bible is by far the most widely circulated book in all history. It is the most translated, the most quoted, and the oldest book. Yes, and it is also the book that has survived the most violent opposition. Unhappily, though, it is unlikely that the Bible is the most *widely read* book in the world.

Yet the Bible *should* be read. Consider some facts about it.

Why Read It Regularly?

Our English word "Bible" comes from the Greek term *bi·bli'a,* meaning "little books." This reminds us that the Bible is made up of a number of books—though some are not so "little"! These were written over a period of more than a thousand years. Although written by men, they were inspired by a higher Source. Even today, millions agree that "all Scripture is inspired of God and beneficial." (2 Timothy 3:16) Yes, these "little books" are filled with the thoughts of Jehovah God himself. (Isaiah 55:9) No wonder they have endured so long!

The practice of reading the Scriptures regularly has certainly been beneficial in times past. Kings of Israel were to make personal handwritten copies of the Law, now an important part of the Bible. They were to read in it daily, as a constant reminder to serve humbly and adhere to God's commandments. (Deuteronomy 17: 18-20) Surely, we can derive similar benefits from regular Bible reading.

And how important to pay attention to Bible prophecy! Because of the prophet Daniel's personal study of the Scriptures, he was able to discern that an important prophecy in the book of Jeremiah was about to be fulfilled.—Daniel 9:1, 2; Jeremiah 29:10.

When John the Baptizer was preaching, "the people were in expectation" of the Messiah. (Luke 3:15) This suggests that many among them were familiar with the prophecies about the Christ that had been recorded in the Scriptures. This is very interesting, since books were not readily available in those days. Copies of Bible books had to be made painstakingly by hand. So how did people become familiar with them?

In many cases by public reading. The disciple James remarked: "From ancient times Moses has had in city after city those who preach him, because he is read aloud in the synagogues on every sabbath."—Acts 15:21.

Today it is easy for individuals to own a personal copy of the Bible, and at least some of the "little books" are available in the languages of 97 percent of the world's population. Thus it is sad that many are not very interested in finding out what the Bible has to say to them.

Encouraged to Read It

Jehovah's Witnesses have made it a prominent part of their work to encourage regular reading of the Bible. In bold letters

For years, a sign on the Watchtower Society's printing plant at 117 Adams Street, Brooklyn, New York, has urged passersby to read the Holy Scriptures

READ GOD'S WORD THE HOLY BIBLE DAILY

on one of their printing plants at their world headquarters in Brooklyn, New York, appears the statement "READ GOD'S WORD THE HOLY BIBLE DAILY."

In the more than 46,000 congregations of Jehovah's Witnesses throughout the world, there is the weekly Theocratic Ministry School. Public reading of a selected portion of the Bible each week is a part of the course. All in attendance have a weekly assignment to read a few Bible chapters in the privacy of their own home, and those who keep up with this schedule eventually read the whole Bible.

This is in harmony with the *Theocratic Ministry School Guidebook,* one of the textbooks used in this course. It states: "Your personal schedule should include time for reading the Bible itself. There is great value in reading it right through from cover to cover. . . . However, your goal in reading should never be just to cover material, but to get the overall viewpoint of it with the intention of remembering. Take time to ponder on what it says."—Page 21.

Jehovah's Witnesses feel that modern-day Christians should be knowledgeable about the Bible. With this in mind, they have promoted a 20th-century version of public Bible reading. They have recorded readings of many of the "little books" of the Bible on cassette tapes. Thus those who feel that they cannot take the time to sit down and read for long periods can now listen to recordings of Bible books while working around the house, while driving, or doing a number of other things. Of course, the tapes are also a fine help when we *do* sit down to read the Bible. It is a delightsome experience to listen to a reading of the Scriptures while following along in your own copy of the Bible.

By all means, avail yourself fully of the spiritual guidance provided in true Christian publications provided by God through "the faithful and discreet slave." (Matthew 24:45-47) But why not also make it *your* habit to read the Bible daily. The benefits will be great, as was noted in the command given long ago to the Israelite leader Joshua: "This book of the law should not depart from your mouth, and you must in an undertone read in it day and night, in order that you may take care to do according to all that is written in it; for then you will make your way successful and then you will act wisely."—Joshua 1:8.

'Children Just Love Them'

Millions of families have enjoyed *My Book of Bible Stories.* Its 116 Bible accounts give the reader an idea of what the Bible is all about. Now this 256-page *Bible Stories* book has been recorded on four cassette tapes with a heartwarming appeal for children. A mother from Vancouver, British Columbia, writes:

"I cannot tell you how much joy we've received from having these tapes in our home. We have 2 girls, ages 10 and 6, and they just love following the stories with their books in their hands. I also find it a great aid in helping my younger one to read, as she can follow most of the words in the book. She can follow about 30 stories and still can't get enough."

February 1, 1985

The Watchtower

Announcing Jehovah's Kingdom

ARMAGEDDON —FROM A GOD OF LOVE?

February 1, 1985
Vol. 106, No. 3

The Watchtower®

Announcing Jehovah's Kingdom

In This Issue

THE PURPOSE OF "THE WATCHTOWER" is to exalt Jehovah God as the Sovereign of the universe. It keeps watch on world events as they fulfill Bible prophecy. It comforts all peoples with the good news that God's Kingdom will soon destroy those who oppress their fellowmen and that it will turn the earth into a paradise. It encourages faith in the now-reigning King, Jesus Christ, whose shed blood opens the way for mankind to gain eternal life. "The Watchtower," published by Jehovah's Witnesses continuously since 1879, is nonpolitical. It adheres to the Bible as its authority.

"WATCHTOWER" STUDIES FOR THE WEEKS

March 3: Who Can Read the "Sign" Aright? Page 8. Songs to Be Used: 210, 61.

March 10: Seeing the "Sign" With Understanding. Page 13. Songs to Be Used: 33, 14.

March 17: Act Promptly Upon the "Sign"! Page 19. Songs to Be Used: 6, 181.

Average Printing Each Issue: 11,150,000

Now Published in 102 Languages

SEMIMONTHLY EDITIONS AVAILABLE BY MAIL
Afrikaans, Arabic, Cebuano, Chichewa, Chinese, Cibemba, Danish, Dutch, Efik, English*, Finnish, French, German, Greek, Hiligaynon, Igbo, Iloko, Italian, Japanese, Korean, Lingala, Malagasy, Maltese, Norwegian, Portuguese, Sepedi, Sesotho, Shona, Spanish, Swahili, Swedish, Tagalog, Thai, Tswana, Xhosa, Yoruba, Zulu

MONTHLY EDITIONS AVAILABLE BY MAIL
Armenian, Bengali, Bicol, Bulgarian, Croatian, Czech, Ewe, Fijian, Ga, Greenlandic, Gujarati, Gun, Hausa, Hebrew, Hindi, Hiri Motu, Hungarian, Icelandic, Kannada, Kikuyu, Kiluba, Malayalam, Marathi, New Guinea Pidgin, Pangasinan, Papiamento, Polish, Rarotongan, Romanian, Russian, Samar-Leyte, Samoan, Sango, Serbian, Silozi, Sinhalese, Slovenian, Solomon Islands-Pidgin, Tahitian, Tamil, Telugu, Tshiluba, Tsonga, Turkish, Twi, Ukrainian, Urdu, Venda, Vietnamese
*Study articles also available in large-print edition at same cost.

The Bible translation used is the "New World Translation of the Holy Scriptures," unless otherwise indicated.

Twenty cents (U.S.) a copy

Watch Tower Society offices	Yearly subscription rates Semimonthly
America, U.S., Watchtower, Wallkill, N.Y. 12589	$4.00
Australia, Box 280, Ingleburn, N.S.W. 2565	A$6.00
Canada, Box 4100, Halton Hills (Georgetown), Ontario L7G 4Y4	$4.50
England, The Ridgeway, London NW7 1RN	£5.00
Ireland, 29A Jamestown Road, Finglas, Dublin 11	£5.00
New Zealand, 6-A Western Springs Rd., Auckland 3	$7.00
Nigeria, P.O. Box 194, Yaba, Lagos State	₦3.50
Philippines, P.O. Box 2044, Manila 2800	₱50.00
South Africa, Private Bag 2, Elandsfontein, 1406	R5,60

Remittances should be sent to the office in your country or to Watchtower, Wallkill, N.Y. 12589, U.S.A.

Changes of address should reach us 30 days before your moving date. Give us your old and new address (if possible, your old address label).

The Watchtower (ISSN 0043-1087) is published semimonthly for $4.00 (U.S.) per year by Watch Tower Bible and Tract Society of Pennsylvania, 25 Columbia Heights, Brooklyn, N.Y. 11201. Second-class postage paid at Brooklyn, N.Y., and at additional mailing offices.

Postmaster: Send address changes to Watchtower, *Wallkill, N.Y. 12589.*

Published by
**Watch Tower Bible and Tract Society
of Pennsylvania**
25 Columbia Heights, Brooklyn, N.Y. 11201, U.S.A.
Frederick W. Franz, President

ARMAGEDDON
—From a God of Love?

Chicago Tribune, Oct. 11, 1984 — Is Reagan arming for real Armageddon?

New York Post, Aug. 13, 1984 — **Prez plays with Armageddon – no sweat, just a test**

Guardian Weekly, May 16, 1982 — Timetable for Armageddon

The Auckland Star, May 14, 1984 — Superpowers 'gear for Armageddon'
Belief in the biblical prophesies of Armageddon figure in American defence thinking, says the Campaign for Nuclear Disarmament.

India Today, Nov. 30, 1981 — Racing Toward Armageddon

The New York Times, Oct. 24, 1984 — ARMAGEDDON VIEW PROMPTS A DEBATE

WHAT do you think of when you see the word "Armageddon?" For many it means a violent confrontation between the world's superpowers. Most envision the ultimate disaster—a nuclear holocaust that reduces our earth to a devastated, radioactive cinder with few, if any, survivors. Yet, contrary to such popular opinions, that is *not* what Armageddon is at all.

The word "Armageddon" finds its source in the Bible. And there it occurs only once —in the 16th chapter of the book of Revelation. After telling how "all the kings of the world" will be gathered together "for the war of the Great Day of God the Almighty," the prophecy states: "They called the kings together at the place called, in Hebrew, Armageddon."—Verses 13 to 16, *The Jerusalem Bible.*

"The war of the Great Day of God the Almighty"! Clearly, Armageddon is *God's* war. True, it involves the kings, or nations, of the world. But they come, not to battle with one another, but to fight against God and the heavenly armies led by his appointed King Jesus Christ—who is depicted as mounted on a white horse. With what outcome? The Bible account reads: "The kings of the earth and their armies gathered together to wage the war with the one seated on the horse and with his army. . . . [They] were killed off with the long sword of the one seated on the horse . . . And all the birds were filled from the fleshy parts of them."—Revelation 19:19-21.

A Sanguinary War

So devastating will Armageddon be that the carnage is referred to as a reaping of "the harvest of the earth" by means of a sharp sickle. "And the angel thrust his sickle into the earth and gathered the vine of the earth, and he hurled it into the great winepress of the anger of God. And the winepress was trodden outside the city, and blood came out of the winepress as high up as the bridles of the horses, for a distance of a thousand six hundred furlongs."—Revelation 14:15-20.

Yes, blood will run deep under the hand of God's executional forces. The 69 million deaths of two world wars will pale in comparison to those slain in God's war of Armageddon. Concerning them the prophet Jeremiah wrote: "Those slain by Jehovah will certainly come to be in that day from one end of the earth clear to the other end of the earth. They will not be bewailed, neither will they be gathered up or be buried. As manure on the surface of the ground they will become."—Jeremiah 25: 30-33.

The burning missiles, fiery showers, and other cataclysmic forces that accompany God's judgment will strike terror into the hearts of mankind earth wide. In confusion they will turn, each one against his neighbor, as God's executional forces strike without regard to age or sex. For God instructs them to show no mercy: "Strike. Let not your eye feel sorry, and do not feel any compassion. Old man, young man and virgin and little child and women you should kill off—to a ruination."—Ezekiel 9:5, 6; Zechariah 14:12, 13.

But how can this be? How can a God of love issue such an order? Or is he just a cold, uncaring, and vengeful God with little regard for his human creation? Would a God of love really bring about such a war as Armageddon?

Why
ARMAGEDDON
Must Be Fought

"**G**OD IS LOVE." Not only does God show love, says the apostle John, but he *is* love—the very embodiment of love.—1 John 4:8.

Yet, this same God of love is often portrayed by some as a vindictive god who brings cruel punishment upon those who have fallen from his favor. Consequently, many have either lost faith in God or ridiculed the Bible, claiming it could not have originated with such a God. Particularly do portions of the book of Revelation come in for censure where God's judgments

upon the wicked are described, culminating in the battle of Armageddon.

For example, Joseph Wheless writes in his book *Is It God's Word?:* "Surely the gentle reader would not endure the apocalyptic vision revealing the genial repentant soul among poor sinners (either of original or of mortal sin), who are there 'tormented with fire and brimstone in the presence of the holy angels, and in the presence of the Lamb,' who all look on complacent while 'the smoke of their torment ascendeth up for ever and ever: and they have no rest day nor night' from the fierceness of the wrath of Almighty God (Rev. xiv, 10, 11). This is the inspired revelation of the God of all love."

Also taking issue with the Revelation account, Professor Gerald A. Larue of the University of Southern California recently wrote in the magazine *Free Inquiry:* "Nonbelievers are plunged into an abyss of suffering that staggers the imagination. The punishment is not the *lex talionis,* the an eye-for-an-eye justice; nor is it like vendetta justice, where a total group may be wiped out (cf. Gen. 4:23, [24]; Josh. 6; etc). Here punishment is for eternity. There is no mercy, punishment is never-ending. There is no forgiveness, only punishment that denies the peace of annihilation. This is no Jesus-meek-and-mild imagery." Then, quoting Revelation 14:9-11, he continues: "No turning of the other cheek here—only vicious, furious reprisal in savagery that makes the Nazi tortures look tame by comparison."

Understandably, thoughts of cruel suffering while sinners are tortured eternally can raise questions about a 'God of love.' But such ideas are based on a misunderstanding of the Bible and the symbolisms used therein. Nowhere does the Bible teach that the soul is immortal. Rather, the Scriptures point out that "the wages sin pays is death"—not eternal torment—and that at death one's senses, including the ability to feel pain, cease.—Romans 6:23; Ecclesiastes 9:5, 10.

It is the *punishment,* not the *punishing,* that lasts eternally—as the wicked are totally annihilated in "the lake of fire," a symbol of complete destruction. (Revelation 20:14, 15; 21:8) Still, the battle of Armageddon will bring untold suffering and hardship to humankind and will be the most sanguinary war ever fought. (Matthew 24:21, 22; Revelation 14:20; 19:17, 18) Does it emanate from 'the God of love?' Will God really bring about such a war?

An Expression of God's Love

Actually, it is *because* of God's love that the battle of Armageddon must be fought. Jehovah God's purpose for the earth is to restore it to its original Paradise state and to have mankind live on it in peace and perfection "with no one to make them tremble." (Ezekiel 34:28; Micah 4:3, 4; Revelation 21:4) What, then, is to be done with those who, by their crime and violence, would mar the security of the restored Paradise? No system devised by man has yet successfully dealt with such a problem. The only way to ensure perfect peace is to eliminate even the threat of wickedness. Yes, God must destroy the incorrigibly wicked for the sake of those who want to do what is right. Out of love, he acts to clear the earth of those who would ruin it.—Revelation 11:18.

But no one *needs* to die. "[God's] will is that all sorts of men should be saved," writes the apostle Paul. (1 Timothy 2:4) And Peter, also writing under inspiration, states: "He does not desire any to be destroyed but desires all to attain to repentance." (2 Peter 3:9) God has arranged for the "good news of the kingdom" to be proclaimed so that each individual will have opportunity to work out his own salvation. (Matthew 24:14; Philippians 2:12; Galatians 6:5) You *can* live forever in perfection on a paradise earth. The choice is yours. (Romans 2:5-9; Ezekiel 18:23, 32) Is this not what you would expect from a God of love?

The Issue of Sovereignty

In order to ensure perfect peace and tranquillity, there will be only one government ruling over all the earth—God's Kingdom. Is it not the many human governments, all striving for their own selfish

ARMAGEDDON. . .

nationalistic gains, that have caused much of the strife and bloodshed earth wide? These governments must be removed to make way for the righteous rule of God's Kingdom under Christ. (Daniel 2:44) You have prayed for that heavenly government when you repeated the model prayer that Jesus gave his disciples: "Let your kingdom come. Let your will take place, as in heaven, also upon earth."—Matthew 6:10.

But which government do you know that is willing to renounce its sovereignty and subject itself fully to God's Kingdom? Do governments not rather cling tenaciously to their own sovereignties, continually seeking to expand their sphere of influence in defiance of God's established Kingdom? (Psalm 2:1-9) Has there ever been any indication that the nations will relinquish their rulerships to God and Christ? The ineffectiveness of the United Nations organization as an instrument for world peace shows the unwillingness of nations to budge where selfish national interests are concerned and to submit to a single authority. The nations are determined to run earth's affairs their way. (Revelation 17:13, 14; 19:19) So the battle of Armaged-

don must be fought to break this stalemate and forever settle the issue of who has the right to rule the earth.

To Satisfy Man's Needs

Jehovah's actions at Armageddon will be with mankind's best interests in mind. Think. How do *you* feel about the present world conditions? Do you like them as they are? Do you feel secure under the threat of nuclear annihilation? Do you tremble at seeing violence increasing, your own neighborhood becoming less safe? Do you fear for your children and their future? What relief do you see? Has any government ever shown that it could bring peace and prosperity to all mankind? Has any ever been able to eliminate sickness or death from the earth? Instead, have not conditions worldwide worsened despite man's technological achievements, and often because of such developments? It is only God's righteous Kingdom that will fully satisfy the needs of mankind. It is only by means of it that true peace will prevail over all the earth. The battle of Armageddon must be fought!

But how about the human suffering and

. . . paves the way for peace

hardship that will result as God goes into action to cleanse the earth? These have always been products of war. They will occur at Armageddon only because the nations entrench themselves in opposition to theocratic rule. They are determined to fight and resist. (Psalm 2:2, 3) That is not God's fault. He gives them due warning: "And now, O kings, give heed; take warning, you rulers of the earth. Serve the Lord with fear, and rejoice before him; with trembling pay homage to him, lest he be angry and you perish from the way, when his anger blazes suddenly. Happy are all who take refuge in him!"—Psalm 2:10, 11, *The New American Bible.*

Now think. What would world conditions be like if God refrained from stepping in to straighten out world affairs? Would not wars, violence, and hatreds continue unabated as they have down through the centuries of human rulership? Do they not even now intensify to the point where all mankind is threatened with the horrors of nuclear warfare and its radiation poisoning? Armageddon is actually the best thing that could happen to our globe! It will put an end to the nations' selfish suicidal course. It will clear out the systems that bring misery to humankind and make way for a truly righteous new system of things where all man-made sorrow, pain, and death will be forever removed. Then 'the former things will have passed away,' according to God's promise.—Revelation 21:4; 2 Peter 3:13.

We must remember that God in his wisdom knows what is best for mankind and what is needed to achieve it. Even human governments have proposed and engaged in war to rectify seeming injustices or to fight for what was thought to be a noble cause. But only God has the wisdom to fight a truly just war. Only he can fight a truly selective war where right-hearted individuals, wherever they may be on earth, will be preserved. (Matthew 24: 40, 41; Revelation 7:9, 10, 13-17) And only God has the right to impose his sovereignty over all the earth, for it is his creation. Yes, in order to remove all traces of wickedness forever, end injustice, oppressive false worship, even the cause of sin, and fully sanctify God's holy name—Armageddon must be fought. And it will be, because "God is love!"

Who Can Read the "SIGN" Aright?

"Hypocrites, you know how to examine the outward appearance of earth and sky, but how is it you do not know how to examine this particular time?"—LUKE 12:56.

WISE mariners know how to interpret the appearance of the sky, and they heed its indications. As a well-known rhyme puts matters: "Red sky at night, sailors' delight,/Red sky at morning, sailors take warning."

[2] The Lord Jesus Christ made a similar point even more dramatically when confronted by his enemies. Concerning that encounter the Gospel writer Luke reported: "Then he went on to say also to the crowds: 'When you see a cloud rising in western parts, at once you say, "A storm is coming," and it turns out so. And when you see that a south wind is blowing, you say, "There will be a heat wave," and it occurs. Hypocrites, you know how to examine the outward appearance of earth and sky, but how is it you do not know how to examine this particular time?'"—Luke 12:54-56.

[3] Those proud foes could forecast the weather, but they were too hypocritical and

spiritually ignorant to understand matters of much greater significance. Jesus performed various signs that helped honest-hearted ones to believe in him. (John 2:23) However, especially was his death on Passover Day of 33 C.E. and his resurrection on the third day a "sign" proving that he was the Messiah, or Christ. (Matthew 12:38-41; Luke 11:30) Naturally, Jesus' enemies tried to obscure that "sign." (Matthew 27:62–28:20; Acts 4:1-4) But before he ascended to heaven upwards of 500 Jews became witnesses of his resurrection. (1 Corinthians 15:3-6) Similarly, today there is a "sign" that cannot be obscured. Reading it aright is a matter of life and

---

1, 2. What could Jesus' enemies determine from the sky's appearance, but what could they not understand?
3. What "sign" proving that Jesus was the Messiah were his foes unable to obscure?

death. But what is that "sign"? And who can accurately read it?

The "Sign" for Our Day

4 Jesus' disciples had asked him: "What will be the sign of your presence and of the conclusion of the system of things?" In response, Christ foretold unparalleled wars, food shortages, earthquakes, and other features of the "sign" of his invisible "presence" in Kingdom power. A principal feature is the globe-encircling work of Kingdom preaching now being done in 203 lands by over 2,840,000 witnesses of Jehovah. Watch Tower publications have often pointed to this and other evidence now fulfilling the "sign" of Jesus' "presence." —Matthew, chapters 24, 25; Mark, chapter 13; Luke, chapter 21.

5 There is no denying the fact that since the outbreak of World War I in 1914 the evidence in fulfillment of the "sign" has been multiplying. What significance should this have for us? Well, we do not want to be like the Jews of 19 centuries ago who were good weather-forecasters, but who ignored the plain evidence before their eyes and did not want to draw the conclusion to which it logically led. Long before that, God had empowered Moses to perform three signs to prove his divine authorization to the suffering Israelites. (Exodus 4: 1-31) But in the face of many more than three signs, the Jews of that first-century generation were unwilling to accept as the Messiah the One greater than Moses. (John 4:54; Hebrews 2:2-4) So Jesus was not overstating the case when he called them "a wicked and adulterous generation."—Matthew 12:39.

6 People of this 20th-century generation who do not desire or believe in the second coming of Jesus Christ do not read aright the "sign" of this system's end. But present conditions are by no means heartening, as shown by the following samples:

"United Nations Secretary General Javier-Perez de Cuellar has observed that the world has come to a most critical stage in the evolution of international affairs and the drive towards a just, peaceful and stable international order seems to have been weakened. . . . 'The . . . decline of mutual trust among nations provides a fertile breeding ground for tension and conflict,' the UN Secretary General said."—*Indian Express*, October 22, 1983.

"Many of us have been saying for years that nuclear war would kill many millions of innocent people and would make large portions of the world uninhabitable . . . A group of respected scientists has reached an even more dismal conclusion—that a nuclear war, or even one general nuclear exchange by the superpowers, could touch off a worldwide climatic disaster that in turn could kill billions rather than millions and possibly could end human life on earth. The two-year study was made for the Conference on the Long-term Worldwide Biological Consequences of Nuclear War. Its conclusions were endorsed by more than 100 scientists . . . Carl Sagan . . . put the consequences of nuclear war in stark terms: 'The extinction of the human species would be a real possibility.' "—*The Express* (Easton, Pa.), November 3, 1983.

7 Such is the gloomy outlook of certain responsible, authoritative commentators. It is especially dark because they cannot point to any way out of the disaster they envision. Surely, lovers of life in a better world want hope-inspiring information. Happily, there is a way out of impending

---

4. Today, what "sign" is in evidence, and what are some of its features? (Matthew 24:3)
5. Why was Jesus not overstating the case when he called the first-century Jews "a wicked and adulterous generation"?

6. Informed people are now saying what about world conditions?
7. Where must lovers of life in a better world look for reassurance?

world calamity, for there were survivors of an equally threatening global peril. Why, if there had been no survivors of the Deluge in Noah's day, the earth would not now teem with over 4,000,000,000 human inhabitants! Only one book —the Holy Bible—gives us an accurate account of how only eight humans, along with specimens of animal life, survived that global catastrophe.

[8] Since the same reliable Book gives us Jesus' description of the conditions that would obtain on the earth when the present collapsing system of things would be removed, should we not try to read that "sign" aright? Thirty-seven years before Jerusalem was destroyed by Roman legions in 70 C.E., Jesus gave that long list of features of the composite "sign" that would precede the global catastrophe prefigured by the Flood. And among other things, he said: "There will be signs in sun and moon and stars, and on the earth anguish of nations, not knowing the way out because of the roaring of the sea and its agitation, while men become faint out of fear and expectation of the things coming upon the inhabited earth; for the powers of the heavens will be shaken. And then they will see the Son of man coming in a cloud with power and great glory. But as these things start to occur, raise yourselves erect and lift your heads up, because your deliverance is getting near."—Luke 21:25-28.

[9] Part of that prophecy appeared on the front cover of the *Watch Tower* issues of

Those who read the "sign" aright can survive the end of this system, as eight persons survived the Flood

January 1, 1895, through October 1, 1931. Above that Bible quotation was a watchtower sending out rays of light, while a raging sea beat against the rock foundation upon which the tower stood. Thus this journal indicated its mission to a generation, members of which are yet alive and are reading this very issue.

[10] Today, men of affairs, whose hearts are growing faint out of fear, place their own interpretation upon features of the composite "sign." But our best interpreter is Jesus Christ, and if we attach to the "sign" the significance he gave it, we shall not suffer the fears common to the human leaders who do not know the way out of the present world mess. Rather, we shall rejoice because our deliverance from this wicked system is getting near.

8. In contrast with others, what were Jesus' disciples to do when the present system of things was about to be removed?
9. From 1895 to 1931, how was this journal's mission indicated on its front cover?

10. How can we avoid suffering the fears experienced by human leaders today?

October, 607 B.C.E. — October, 1 B.C.E. =	606 years
October, 1 B.C.E. — October, 1914 C.E. =	1,914 years
SEVEN GENTILE TIMES	= 2,520 years

The Marked Time for the "Sign" to Appear

[11] World events are happening right on time. How so? Well, before Jesus gave the prophecy recorded at Luke 21:25-28, he foretold the second destruction of Jerusalem. True to his word, it occurred in 70 C.E. As for the surviving Jews, Jesus said: "They will fall by the edge of the sword and be led captive into all the nations; and Jerusalem will be trampled on by the nations, until the appointed times of the nations are fulfilled." Those nations were non-Jewish, or Gentile. Hence, the period of trampling is often called "the times of the Gentiles." (Luke 21:24, *NW; King James Version*) When did they end? Well, more is involved than what happened to earthly Jerusalem. So the date when the Israelis took over control of the old walled city of Jerusalem, or the fact that it is the capital of the modern independent nation of Israel, is not the determining factor. God's timetable is what matters!

[12] The Gentile Romans began trampling down Jerusalem in 63 B.C.E. But before them the Gentile Greeks, Persians, and Babylonians had trodden down that "city of the great King" Jehovah. (Matthew 5: 34, 35) The Babylonians destroyed it and its temple in 607 B.C.E. From that time onward, the Gentile trampling upon what represented God's Kingdom began, and the Gentile Times really started. Those Gentile Times were to be seven in number, each corresponding with a prophetic year of 360

days. On the basis of "a day for a year," all "seven times" would total 2,520 years. (Numbers 14:34; Ezekiel 4:6; Daniel, chapter 4) Beginning with Jerusalem's desolation in 607 B.C.E., they would end in 1914 C.E.

[13] As early as 1880, the *Watch Tower* magazine said that the Gentile Times would extend to the year 1914. Then with the publication of the book *The Time Is at Hand* in 1889, Bible students earth wide were further alerted to the fact that the Gentile Times would end in the autumn of 1914.

[14] Well, then, in that year, did old Jerusalem cease to be trampled on by non-Jewish, or Gentile, nations? No, for in 1914 the historic city was still in the hands of the Turkish Empire, the ally of imperial Germany. On December 9, 1917, it was taken from the Turks by British troops under General Allenby. Jerusalem continued under British rule by mandate of the League of Nations until 1948. Then the Jews rose up and captured the western part of modern Jerusalem outside the old walled city. The walled city was taken over by the Muhammadans. How, then, can we say that the Gentile Times ended in 1914? Because in that year the government of the great King Jehovah was born in heaven.

[15] When Jesus was on earth, the temple

---

11. How did Jesus indicate that world events betokening the end would occur right on time?
12. When did the Gentile Times start, how long were they, and when did they end?

---

13. Since when have Bible students known the date for the Gentile Times to end?
14. Despite what happened to Jerusalem in 1948, why can we say that the Gentile Times ended in 1914?
15, 16. (a) When did old Jerusalem cease to be "the city of the great King" Jehovah, but what more exalted Jerusalem exists? (b) Where, then, would Jehovah have installed Jesus Christ as King?

of God stood in Jerusalem, and Jesus worshiped there. So Jerusalem could then be called "the city of the great King" Jehovah. (Matthew 5:34, 35) But certainly at the miraculous ripping of the inner temple curtain at the death of Jesus on Passover Day of 33 C.E., it ceased to be Jehovah's royal city. The destruction of Jerusalem and its temple by the Gentile Romans in 70 C.E. confirmed that fact. Happily for the Jewish Christians then, and for all Christians since, there is another Jerusalem, a more exalted one, "heavenly Jerusalem."—Hebrews 12:22.

¹⁶ In line with this fact, Jesus' prophecy recorded at Luke 21:24 began with an application to earthly Jerusalem but must end with reference to "heavenly Jerusalem." Yes, for "heavenly Jerusalem" has replaced earthly Jerusalem as "the city of the great King" Jehovah God. There, in that celestial "city," was the place for "the great King" Jehovah to install his glorified Son Jesus Christ at the end of the Gentile Times in 1914.

¹⁷ That was the divinely appointed time for Jehovah to issue to his enthroned Son Jesus Christ the command embodied in the words of Psalm 110:2, 3: "The rod of your strength Jehovah will send out of Zion, saying: 'Go subduing in the midst of your enemies.' Your people will offer themselves willingly on the day of your military force. In the splendors of holiness, from the womb of the dawn, you have your company of young men just like dewdrops." True to this prophecy, the dedicated "people" who followed in Jesus' footsteps and recognized the end of the Gentile Times in 1914 offered themselves willingly to serve as announcers of the newly begun rule of

---

17. At the end of the Gentile Times, what divine command was given to the enthroned King Jesus Christ, and who offered themselves willingly for his service?

What Is Your Answer?

□ What "sign" is in evidence today, and what are some of its features?

□ How can we avoid the fears now experienced by human leaders?

□ When did the Gentile Times begin and end?

□ In what "Jerusalem" has Jehovah installed Jesus Christ as King?

□ How did Jehovah's people view the League of Nations?

Jehovah God in heavenly Zion by means of the Lord Jesus Christ. But the so-called Christian nations did not submit willingly to Jehovah's newly enthroned King. Actually, they proved to be his "enemies," for they engaged in the first world war of human history over the issue of world domination. Worldwide they also interfered with the proclamation of God's Kingdom.

¹⁸ Enmity against God's Kingdom became particularly evident in 1918. On May 8, 1918, the editor of the *Watch Tower* magazine and a number of his fellow workers were arrested amid war hysteria. Later, on June 21, they were sentenced to many years of imprisonment in the federal penitentiary in Atlanta, Georgia, U.S.A. Only after the war had ended and they had spent nine months in prison were these ministers of God's Kingdom admitted to bail. In due course, they were exonerated of all the false charges lodged against them.

¹⁹ World War I ended on November 11, 1918, and in the following month the Fed-

---

18. In 1918, what proof was there of enmity against God's Kingdom?
19. After World War I, what position did the Federal Council of American churches take toward the League of Nations?

eral Council of the Churches of Christ in America publicly declared itself to be in favor of the then-proposed League of Nations. That religious body declared the League to be "the political expression of the Kingdom of God on earth." Ignoring that religious recommendation, for political reasons the United States of America refused to join the League, joining only the World Court. Yet the League went into operation at the start of 1920, and the members of the Federal Council of Churches gave it their blessing and support.

[20] On the other hand, the *Watch Tower*

20. What position did Jehovah's people take toward the League, and what did they start to advertise?

magazine and Jehovah's people circulating it refused to recognize the League of Nations as the political substitute for God's Kingdom. They never recognized it as the fulfillment of the model prayer as taught by Jesus Christ: "Let your kingdom come. Let your will take place, as in heaven, also upon earth." (Matthew 6:9, 10) They did not offer themselves for the service of that man-made substitute, that fake! Rather, they gave their allegiance to the real Kingdom of God in the hands of Jesus Christ in "heavenly Jerusalem." With God's help, they had read aright the "sign" of Jesus' "presence and of the conclusion of the system of things." So they set out to advertise the Kingdom worldwide.

Seeing the "SIGN" With Understanding

"While he was sitting upon the Mount of Olives, the disciples approached him privately, saying: 'Tell us, When will these things be, and what will be the sign of your presence and of the conclusion of the system of things?'"
—MATTHEW 24:3.

THE world-shaking events since World War I of 1914-18 have not been accidental. They were foretold 19 centuries ago by Jesus Christ. He had told his disciples about many startling things to come, and for that reason they asked him: "Tell us, When will these things be, and what will be the sign of your presence and of the conclusion of the system of things?" —Matthew 24:3.

1. Why have the world-shaking events since 1914 not been accidental, and what did Jesus' disciples ask him?

[2] Those apostles wanted to know more than what would occur between that time and the destruction of Jerusalem. Jesus did not return either visibly or invisibly on that calamitous occasion. Nor did the system of things that had existed since the Deluge conclude at Jerusalem's destruction in 70 C.E. In reality, "the sign of [Jesus' unseen] presence and of the conclusion of the system of things" was

2. Why did the apostles want to know more than what would happen before Jerusalem's destruction in 70 C.E.?

due to appear long after the earthly lifetime of his apostles.

³ By means of prophetic parables regarding God's Kingdom, Jesus had told his apostles about the religious rebellion that was to take place after his return to heaven and their death. During all the time of that apostasy, would there be any worldwide preaching of "this good news of the kingdom"? (Matthew 24:14) Certainly not by Christendom's religions, when as late as December 1918 the Federal Council of the Churches of Christ in America hailed the then proposed League of Nations as "the political expression of the Kingdom of God on earth." In spite of that religious endorsement, however, the League failed at the outbreak of World War II in 1939. But with that failure, did the true Kingdom of God fail? No! Nor will it fail when the League's successor, the United Nations, fails shortly. Rather, that divine Kingdom will destroy the United Nations, no matter how many heavenly angels may be needed to do this!

3. (a) What shows that "this good news of the kingdom" was not preached by Christendom's religions during the post-apostolic apostasy? (b) Will God's Kingdom fail when the United Nations fails?

⁴ All the foregoing helps to make possible a sharper understanding of this important fact: It was in response to the request for a "sign" that Jesus told his followers: "This good news of the kingdom will be preached in all the inhabited earth for a witness to all the nations; and then the end will come." (Matthew 24:14) This signifies that such earth-wide preaching of the Kingdom would be part of the composite "sign" that would mark "the conclusion of the system of things." It would also be visible evidence of Jesus Christ's invisible "presence." The manner in which Jesus lined up the succession of events prior to his prophecy about the Kingdom-preaching work is noteworthy. In part he said:

⁵ "You are going to hear of wars and reports of wars; see that you are not terrified. For these things must take place, but the end is not yet. For nation will rise against nation and kingdom against kingdom, and there will be food shortages and earthquakes in one place after another. . . . And because of the increasing of lawlessness the love of the greater number will cool off. But he that has endured to the end is the one that will be saved." —Matthew 24:6-13.

4. Why was the Kingdom-preaching work to be part of the "sign"?
5. What are some features of the "sign" that Jesus mentioned before foretelling worldwide Kingdom preaching?

'Tell us, what will be the sign of your presence?'

⁶ True, there had been wars, food shortages, earthquakes, and pestilences down through the centuries of our Common Era until 1914. (Luke 21:11) Nevertheless, there had been nothing to compare with what has taken place since the Gentile Times ended in that momentous year. The international strife that was surprisingly stirred up in the summer of 1914 grew into a military engagement in which 28 nations eventually took part. Along with that human upheaval came natural earthquakes. There were food shortages, or famines, and in the final year of that world war there came the thieflike pestilence called the Spanish influenza that took the lives of more than 20,000,000 humans. All of this was not just a continuation of the previously occurring pattern of things. It was the start of a series of events making up a "sign" that this system of things is in its foretold "time of the end." (Daniel 12:4) The Bible's last book —The Apocalypse, or Revelation—makes this certain.

⁷ The apostle John, who received the Revelation, was commanded to write it down for a special purpose. What purpose? This: "To show [God's] slaves the things that must shortly take place." And at the close of the Revelation the Lord Jesus Christ says: "Yes; I am coming quickly." At that, John responds: "Amen! Come, Lord Jesus." Many things thus "presented . . . in signs" would, at their appearing in history, signify that we are living in "the time of the end" of this system of things. (Revelation 1:1; 22:20) Yes, they would be helpful to us in seeing the composite "sign" with understanding.

⁸ In Revelation chapter 6 appears the account of what has been called the ride of "the four horsemen of the Apocalypse." Appearing first is the rider of "a white horse," the glorified Jesus Christ, going forth to make war against his foes. This he was authorized by God to do at the end of the Gentile Times, when Jesus' foes in heaven and on earth should have submitted to his rule.—Psalm 2:1-12.

⁹ The rider on the "fiery-colored" second horse pictured international war, for a military weapon, "a great sword," was given to him. On the third mount, "a black horse," was a rider picturing food shortage. How do we know this? Because he carried a pair of scales with which to measure out basic food supplies at inflated prices. The fourth rider, on a sickly-looking "pale horse," pictured pestilence, for the account says: "The one seated upon it had the name Death. And Hades [the grave] was closely following him." True, this fourth rider was given authority "to kill with a long sword" of war "and with food shortage . . . and by the wild beasts of the earth." Notably, though, he was also authorized to make victims for the grave (Hades) by means of "deadly plague." —Revelation 6:1-8.

¹⁰ After the apostle John saw those visions of features that were to mark "the conclusion of the system of things," he saw the opening of the prophetic scroll's fifth and sixth seals. At that point, he saw a vision of terrifying natural phenomena, starting with "a great earthquake." Finally, earth's inhabitants were obliged to ad-

6. Why are the features of the "sign" not just a continuation of a previous pattern of things?
7. Why was the book of Revelation recorded, and what would many things therein "presented . . . in signs" signify?

8. Who is the rider on the "white horse," and when did God authorize him to go forth against his foes?
9. What is pictured by the rider on (a) the "fiery-colored" horse? (b) the "black horse"? (c) the "pale horse"?
10. What was to occur after the fifth and sixth seals were opened, and what would earth's inhabitants have to admit?

mit: "The great day of their wrath [that of Jehovah God and Jesus Christ] has come." The closing of that symbolic day of wrath would signify that the end had at last come for supporters of this world.—Revelation 6: 9-17.

Gathering Those Approved for Salvation

¹¹ In giving the "sign" of his "presence and of the conclusion of the system of things," Jesus said: "Now learn from the fig tree as an illustration this point: Just as soon as its young branch grows tender and it puts forth leaves, you know that summer is near. Likewise also you, when you see all these things, know that he is near at the doors. Truly I say to you that this generation will by no means pass away until all these things occur. Heaven and earth will pass away, but my words will by no means pass away."—Matthew 24:32-35.

¹² When the Romans destroyed Jerusalem and its temple in 70 C.E. just as Jesus had predicted, this terrible tribulation upon the Jews did not signify that he had come the second time and that his invisible presence had begun. (Matthew 24: 15-21) Since the Bible uses ancient Jerusalem as a type, that shocking catastrophe of 70 C.E. was really a prophetic type. It portrayed in miniature what was to occur on a world scale after the Gentile Times ended in 1914 and therefore after Jesus Christ actually had begun his invisible presence. That is why Jesus had also said:

¹³ "Immediately after the tribulation of those days the sun will be darkened, and the moon will not give its light, and the stars will fall from heaven, and the powers of the heavens will be shaken. And then the sign of the Son of man will appear in heaven, and then all the tribes of the earth will beat themselves in lamentation, and they will see the Son of man coming on the clouds of heaven with power and great glory. And he will send forth his angels with a great trumpet sound, and they will gather his chosen ones together from the four winds, from one extremity of the heavens to their other extremity."—Matthew 24:29-31.

¹⁴ The foretold gathering of those "cho-

---

11. What illustration did Jesus use to show the certainty of what he foretold regarding his "presence" and "the conclusion of the system of things"?

12, 13. (a) What did the Jewish national calamity of 70 C.E. not signify? (b) Of what was that catastrophe a prophetic type? (c) So, what did Jesus go on to prophesy concerning his coming?

---

14. What covenant and sacrifice are referred to at Psalm 50:5?

sen ones" during the conclusion of this system of things is in fulfillment of God's command: "Gather to me my loyal ones, those concluding my covenant over sacrifice." (Psalm 50:5) Since Jehovah calls it "my covenant," it could not be a dedication that an individual makes to God upon becoming a Christian and that he could make binding by sacrificing himself. No, this covenant concluded between Jehovah and the "loyal ones" is God's promised "new covenant" with the house of spiritual Israel. The sacrifice upon which that new covenant is based is the ransom sacrifice of "the Son of man," Jesus Christ.—Jeremiah 31:31-34; Matthew 24:30.

¹⁵ The "loyal ones" taken into the new covenant are made spiritual Israelites. (Luke 22:19, 20) God calls for the gathering to take place so that he can examine those gathered, approve the *loyal* and reject those not living up to their claims about being in his covenant, the new covenant. (Psalm 50:16) Since World War I, the evidence is that Christendom, which claims to be in the new covenant, has not proved acceptable to Jehovah God. In sharp contrast stands a small remnant of truly dedicated, baptized disciples of the new covenant's Mediator, Jesus Christ. They have proved to be spiritual Israelites. These loyal adherents to the new covenant are the "chosen ones" whom the Son of man gathers to himself by means of his angels. They carry out the obligations of the new covenant, "my covenant," as God calls it. Because of their activity in support of God's Kingdom by Jesus Christ, they have become a 'sign' to the whole world.—Isaiah 8:18; Hebrews 2:13, 14.

---

15. Who are the "loyal ones," and they now serve as what to the world?

¹⁶ For that remnant of "loyal ones," there had to be a spiritual awakening during the early part of "the conclusion of the system of things." This was an outstanding feature of the "sign" that Jesus foretold in his great prophecy. For the remnant, the time of that awakening was one of great joy, a joy like that of the five discreet, or wise, virgins awakened by the midnight cry: "Here is the bridegroom! Be on your way out to meet him." (Matthew 25:1-6) That joyous awakening occurred in the spring of 1919, when the anointed remnant began to recover from the effects of the worldwide persecution and interference they had experienced during the dark period of World War I. The Bridegroom of the parable of the ten virgins is, of course, Jesus Christ, and his symbolic bride is his loyal congregation of 144,000 members who are to be associated with him in the heavenly Kingdom. (Revelation 14:1-4) Bible chronology and modern correspondencies indicate that the Bridegroom King came to the spiritual temple in the spring of 1918. Then he began to resurrect from the dead the faithful members of the spiritual bride and to unite them to himself in the heavenly Kingdom. As the expression of the remnant of the bride, pictured by the discreet virgins, Revelation 19:7 states: "Let us rejoice and be overjoyed, and let us give him the glory, because the marriage of the Lamb has arrived and his wife has prepared herself."

¹⁷ Yes, the time of the spiritual awakening of the 'discreet virgin' class and their coming to understand the meaning of the

---

16. (a) When was there a spiritual awakening for the remnant of the "loyal ones"? (b) In the parable of the ten virgins, who is the Bridegroom, and who make up his symbolic bride?
17. (a) Why could the 'discreet virgin' class rejoice? (b) The discreet virgins brought what along, and therefore could do what?

"sign" that began to appear in 1914 was the occasion for great rejoicing. Then applicable to them were the words: "Happy are those invited to the evening meal of the Lamb's marriage." (Revelation 19:9) In Jesus' parable, the five discreet virgins brought along a reserve supply of illuminating oil so as to be able to relight their lamps and thus join the happy marriage procession with lighted lamps. When the Bridegroom arrived, "the virgins that were ready went in with him to the marriage feast; and the door was shut." —Matthew 25:1-10.

[18] True to the picture of the five discreet virgins, the anointed remnant proceeded to give a bright and gladsome welcome to the heavenly Bridegroom, the time for whose marriage to his bridal congregation had arrived. After their spiritually disconcerting experiences during World War I, they still had enough of God's enlightening Word and his holy spirit within themselves as "earthen vessels" to rekindle their work of enlightening mankind concerning God's Kingdom by means of his Bridegroom-King. (2 Corinthians 4:7) Accordingly, on September 1-8, 1919, the 'discreet virgin' class held their first international convention at Cedar Point, Ohio. There the proposed publishing of a new magazine in addition to *The Watch Tower* was announced. This new journal was to be called *The Golden Age,* a name descriptive of the kind of age restored mankind will enjoy during the Thousand Year Reign of the Bridegroom-King Jesus Christ. That magazine is still being published, now under the name *Awake!*

[19] Shortly after that convention, the first issue of *The Golden Age*—that of October 1, 1919—was published. With that journal and other publications of the Watch Tower Bible and Tract Society, the loyal 'virgin class' went forth on their mission of world illumination. They launched out on the postwar work of 'preaching this good news of the kingdom for a witness to all the nations' before the end of this system of things would come. (Matthew 24:14) In this way the anointed remnant, the 'discreet virgin' class, became an outstanding feature of the composite "sign" marking Jesus' invisible "presence" as empowered King and "the conclusion of the system of things." That enlightening work is further weighty proof that "the time of the end" began at the close of the Gentile Times in 1914. Happy are all those who with understanding see this foretold feature of the "sign" in all its significance!

---

18. (a) After World War I, the anointed remnant still had enough of God's enlightening Word and his holy spirit within themselves to do what? (b) What was announced at their first postwar convention?

19. (a) How did the 'discreet virgin' class become an outstanding feature of the "sign" of Jesus' "presence"? (b) Who are now the happy ones on earth?

How Would You Reply?

□ Of what is the Kingdom-preaching work a feature?

□ Who or what is pictured by the rider on the white horse; the fiery-colored horse; the black horse; the pale horse?

□ The Jewish national calamity of 70 C.E. was a prophetic type of what?

□ Who constitute the 'discreet virgin' class, and why can they rejoice?

Act Promptly Upon the "SIGN"!

"Keep awake, because you do not know the day nor the hour."
—MATTHEW 25:13, *Byington.*

IN THE light of the incoming golden age for the world of redeemed mankind, how unwise it is to be like the five foolish virgins of Jesus' parable! They acted too late and did not make it into "the kingdom of the heavens." Those foolish ones did not act as illuminators at the needed time. (Matthew 25:1-12) When "this good news of the kingdom" shall have been preached "in all the inhabited earth for a witness" and "the end" is due, they will have lost their opportunity to share in that never-to-be-repeated privilege of service.—Matthew 24:14.

2 That is why Jesus Christ closed his parable with this admonition: "Keep on the watch, therefore, because you know neither the day nor the hour."—Matthew 25:1-13.

3 Those words of the Bridegroom Jesus Christ are very timely, especially now, 71 years into this "conclusion of the system of things." Even at this late date the remnant of the 'discreet virgin' class does not know the day or hour when "the door" will be shut to further opportunity for admittance into the heavenly Kingdom to be with the Bridegroom to whom they are espoused. Constantly it behooves those seeking to prove themselves discreet virgins to keep supplied with spiritual oil. In doing so they let the light shine by spreading "this good news of the kingdom" for an earth-wide, international witness until "the end" comes.—Matthew 24:14; Mark 13:10; Revelation 14:6, 7.

"Sheep" and "Goats" Now Being Separated

4 Before "the end" comes to "the conclusion of the system of things," another work of separating people must take place and serve as part of the "sign" indicating that we are in "the time of the end." (Daniel 12:4) This is the fulfillment of Jesus' parable of the sheep and the goats, with which Matthew closes his account of Christ's great prophecy concerning the "sign" of His invisible "presence" and of "the conclusion of the system of things."

5 Note now what Jesus foretold about this, as recorded at Matthew 25:31-46. He began the parable by saying: "When the Son of man arrives in his glory, and all the angels with him, then he will sit down on his glorious throne. And all the nations will be gathered before him, and he will separate people one from another, just as

---

1. Why would it be unwise to be like the foolish virgins of Jesus' parable?
2, 3. (a) With what admonition did Jesus conclude the parable of the ten virgins? (b) Why is that admonition still timely, and with what does the 'discreet virgin' class therefore need to keep supplied?

4. According to Matthew's account, what final parable of Jesus must be fulfilled as part of the "sign" of His "presence"?
5. When was the separating of people like sheep and goats to take place?

As a shepherd separates sheep from goats, so Jesus Christ is separating people today. Are you a sheeplike person?

a shepherd separates the sheep from the goats. And he will put the sheep on his right hand, but the goats on his left." What follows next? Jesus continued:

6 "Then the king will say to those on his right, 'Come, you who have been blessed by my Father, inherit the kingdom prepared for you from the founding of the world. For I became hungry and you gave me something to eat; I got thirsty and you gave me something to drink. I was a stranger and you received me hospitably; naked, and you clothed me. I fell sick and you looked after me. I was in prison and you came to me.'

7 "Then the righteous ones will answer him with the words, 'Lord, when did we see you hungry and feed you, or thirsty, and give you something to drink? When did we see you a stranger and receive you hospitably, or naked, and clothe you?

When did we see you sick or in prison and go to you?' And in reply the king will say to them, 'Truly I say to you, To the extent that you did it to one of the least of these my brothers, you did it to me.'"

8 "The goats" do not act promptly on the "sign." They do not do the things done by "the sheep" class. Thus we read: "Then he will say, in turn, to those on his left, 'Be on your way from me, you who have been cursed, into the everlasting fire prepared for the Devil and his angels. For I became hungry, but you gave me nothing to eat, and I got thirsty, but you gave me nothing to drink. I was a stranger, but you did not receive me hospitably; naked, but you did not clothe me; sick and in prison, but you did not look after me.' Then they also will answer with the words, 'Lord, when did we see you hungry or thirsty or a stranger or naked or sick or in prison and did not minister to you?' Then he will answer

---

6. What does the Shepherd-King say to the people on his right?
7. What inquiry will the righteous, sheeplike people make, and how will the King reply?

---

8. (a) The goatlike people did not act promptly to do what? (b) So where will the King send them in contrast with the righteous, sheeplike ones?

them with the words, 'Truly I say to you, To the extent that you did not do it to one of these least ones, you did not do it to me.' And these will depart into everlasting cutting-off, but the righteous ones into everlasting life."

9 Likely you are taking part in the fulfillment of this prophetic illustration. Did you note the good things Jesus mentioned? Have you done such things to his "brothers"? Happy you can be if you have acted as a "sheep" toward them!

10 Jesus drew a distinction between his spiritual "brothers" and those proving to be like sheep or goats. At the time of this parable's fulfillment, his "brothers" are those who have imitated him by unreservedly giving themselves to God. Like Jesus, they have offered public evidence of this by getting baptized in water. Moreover, Jehovah, the Father of the King Jesus Christ, has become their heavenly Father by begetting them with His holy spirit and thus making them spiritual "brothers" of his Son. This puts them in line for a place in the heavenly Kingdom with their Elder Brother, Jesus Christ, the "King of kings and Lord of lords." (Revelation 19:16) In this connection it was written concerning him: "For both he who is sanctifying and those who are being sanctified all stem from one, and for this cause he is not ashamed to call them 'brothers,' as he says: 'I will declare your name to my brothers; in the middle of the congregation I will praise you with song.'" (Hebrews 2:11, 12) Here Psalm 22:22 is applied to the glorified Son of God, Jesus Christ.

11 There is yet on earth a remnant of those spiritual "brothers" of the reigning King Jesus Christ. As a class, or "congregation," they make up "the faithful and discreet slave" that Jesus foretold in his prophecy on "the conclusion of the system of things." He said: "Who really is the faithful and discreet slave whom his master appointed over his domestics, to give them their food at the proper time? Happy is that slave if his master on arriving finds him doing so. Truly I say to you, He will appoint him over all his belongings."—Matthew 24:45-47.

12 Historical facts answer Jesus' question about the identity of this "slave." "The congregation" that serves as the "slave" is made up of his God-given "brothers" still on earth. It is the same as the 'discreet virgin' class. Since 1919 this "slave" has been outstanding in serving fresh spiritual food from the Bible to the "domestics" of the Master's household, doing so at a time most "proper" for it. Hence, the invisible Master has appointed this dependable "slave" class "over all his belongings" of a spiritual kind. Particularly is this so in connection with the preaching of "this good news of the kingdom" throughout all the earth, over which he rules. Until now this Kingdom witness has increased! "The faithful and discreet slave" in action is a prominent part of the "sign" showing us what time it is.

13 It is to the members of the "slave" class that the righteous "sheep" have done good things. The symbolic sheep and goats

9. For having done what during the present-day fulfillment of Jesus' parable of "the sheep" and "the goats" can you be happy?
10. How did Jesus draw a distinction between his "brothers" and those pictured by "the sheep" and "the goats," and what basis is there in the Bible for this?

11. Are there many of Jesus' spiritual "brothers" now on earth, and what class, or "congregation," do they make up?
12. (a) Since 1919 the "slave" class has been outstanding in doing what? (b) Over what "belongings" has the "slave" been appointed? (c) The "slave" now in action is part of what?
13. Since when have "all the nations" been gathered before the King, and when did the "slave" begin gathering "the sheep" to His right side?

are people of all the nations to which the Kingdom witness now is being given. So, as represented by such sheep and goats, "all the nations" have been gathered before the King seated on his heavenly throne since the end of the Gentile Times in 1914. In line with that foretold gathering, noteworthy is the year 1935. The Watch Tower Bible and Tract Society, which is used by the "slave" class, then had some 49 branch offices earth wide. In that same year the attention of the "slave" was specifically directed to the earthly sheeplike ones, with a view to gathering them to the right side of the reigning King Jesus Christ. Thus, these out of all nations came into closer association with the "slave" class.

¹⁴ Those righteous, sheeplike ones no longer were to be given a broad general classification as "men of good will." (Luke 2:14, *Douay Version*) No more were they to be viewed as an indefinite, unorganized class of God-fearing people in all nations —lost sheep, as it were. Jesus said he would gather "other sheep" and make them "one flock" with the remnant of the "slave" class. (John 10:16) The gathering

---

14. In the light of John 10:16, what new view was taken of the righteous sheeplike ones, and how many branch offices of the Watch Tower Society now serve them?

In Our Next Issue

■ **Armageddon—A War That Leads to True Peace**

■ **Nisan 14 —A Day for Remembering**

■ **Does Greed Sometimes Grip You?**

of such "other sheep" from then on is an outstanding part of the "sign" marking "the conclusion of the system of things." And to serve them the Watch Tower Society now has 95 branch offices.

Timely Action on the "Sign" Rewarded

¹⁵ According to Jesus' parable, the righteous "sheep" must meet certain requirements during "the conclusion of the system of things." They have to recognize and acknowledge Christ's spiritual "brothers" who make up "the faithful and discreet slave" class. "The sheep" must also do good things to the "slave" class, even visit them when they are unjustly confined in prison. This "the sheep" must do so as to enjoy the blessing of the heavenly Father and have the King Jesus Christ invite them to "inherit the kingdom prepared for [them] from the founding of the world."—Matthew 25:34.

¹⁶ Since these "sheep" are not the King's spiritual "brothers," he does not invite them to sit on heavenly thrones and rule with him for the special thousand years of his reign. By his words "inherit the kingdom," he is inviting them to enter the Kingdom era after he has destroyed all the ungodly kingdoms of this world during "the war of the great day of God the Almighty" at Har–Magedon. (Revelation 16:13-16) Many of the sheeplike ones now living will survive that war of all wars and enter into Christ's Thousand Year Reign without dying.

¹⁷ So the King Jesus Christ speaks to these "sheep" as to his children whose

---

15. To "inherit the kingdom," what requirements must "the sheep" meet?
16. By the words "inherit the kingdom," the King invites "the sheep" to enter what, surviving what "war"?
17. How does the King speak to "the sheep," and how did he acquire something to bequeath to them?

time has come to enter into an inheritance from him. By his death as a perfect human to provide a ransom sacrifice for all mankind, he gave up all prospects of personally enjoying the earthly Paradise. (Luke 23: 39-43) In this respect Jesus, "the last Adam," is unlike "the first man Adam" who sinned and forfeited the earthly Paradise for all his offspring. Thus the resurrected Jesus Christ, who becomes the "Eternal Father" of all the redeemed world of mankind, had something to bequeath to these sheeplike ones on earth. (1 Corinthians 15:45; Isaiah 9:6, 7) The human family was founded in "the first man Adam," with all his Paradise prospects and opportunities. But that lost Paradise is to be restored by means of God's Kingdom in the hands of "the last Adam," Jesus Christ.

[18] Not until after they had been driven out of the first Paradise did Adam and Eve begin to have children. Their second son, righteous Abel, was murdered by their first son, Cain. So their son Seth was viewed as taking Abel's place. With the birth of such offspring, the world of mankind was founded. But before this, when the parents of the world of mankind were driven out of Paradise, Jehovah God made his merciful promise concerning a "seed" that would bruise, or crush, the head of the symbolic Serpent, Satan the Devil. That "seed" was to be a royal Seed, and this involved a Kingdom, according to God's purpose and forevision. (Genesis

3:15) When Satan the Serpent and his seed are put out of action, therefore, the redeemed ones of mankind would enter into a Kingdom realm on earth, under the heavenly government of the victorious Seed that crushes the Serpent and his seed. In this way "the kingdom" that the sheeplike ones "inherit" from their Eternal Father, Jesus Christ, is the Kingdom realm that was "prepared for [them] from the founding of the world."

[19] Since the symbolic goats will be cut off in destruction at Armageddon, the surviving "sheep" will give a righteous start to the post-Armageddon system of things on a Paradise earth. Regarding this, Jesus said: "These [goatlike ones] will depart into everlasting cutting-off, but the righteous ones into everlasting life."—Matthew 25:46.

[20] During this "conclusion of the system of things" since the end of the Gentile Times in 1914, "the sheep" and "the goats" differ in the way they interpret the "sign" of Jesus' "presence." Since we unquestionably are in a time of judgment, this question is of vital concern: What does the "sign" signify to us? If left to our own judgment, we might misinterpret the features of that "sign." So we do well to ask: What does Jesus Christ say that this composite "sign" should indicate to us? According to him, it should signify that the present system of things is to end shortly in a "great tribulation" more de-

---

18. In what sense was the Kingdom realm "prepared for [the sheep] from the founding of the world"?

19. What kind of start will the post-Armageddon system of things have on earth?

20. How can we avoid misinterpreting the features of the "sign"?

structive than the global Flood of Noah's day.—Matthew 24:21.

21 Yet, rejoice, for this "sign" also signifies that the Millennial Reign of Jesus Christ is at hand, is ready to begin after the destruction of Satan's system of things on earth. (Luke 21:28) Therefore, under divine protection you have the priceless opportunity of surviving that "great tribulation" right on into the new system of things, in which righteousness is to dwell forever. Indeed, there is set before you the possibility of never dying but of living endlessly and blessedly in a paradise earth under the universal sovereignty of Jehovah God!

22 Whether we are Christ's spiritual "brothers" or the righteous "sheep," then, let us act on the "sign" promptly and aright. Let us have a further part in the outworking of its prominent feature: "This good news of the kingdom will be

---

21. (a) Although the "great tribulation" is ahead, why should we rejoice? (b) What opportunity and possibility exist for "the sheep" class of today?
22. (a) If we act on the "sign" promptly and aright, what will we do? (b) In connection with the "sign," how will Jesus Christ be vindicated?

Can You Answer?

□ When were people to be separated like sheep and goats?

□ You can be happy for doing what during the fulfillment of Jesus' parable of the sheep and the goats?

□ Who constitute the King's "brothers" and "the faithful and discreet slave"?

□ In order to "inherit the kingdom," what requirements must sheeplike ones meet?

□ What will we do if we act promptly and aright on the "sign" of Jesus' "presence"?

preached in all the inhabited earth for a witness to all the nations." Then we shall have nothing to fear when "the end" comes. Instead, our joy will overflow! Then, too, Jesus Christ will be vindicated as the reliable forecaster of the many-featured "sign . . . of the conclusion of the system of things."—Matthew 24:3–25:46.

Barren Environment for Children

LITTLE BY LITTLE modern society has changed the environment for healthy child growth from a fertile one into a sterile one, says Professor Edward A. Wynne, University of Illinois. He blames extreme individualism, affluence, and the failure of religion. "It's understandable why some parents feel embattled," states Professor Wynne in *The Wall Street Journal.* "Some throw up their hands and capable married couples plan to postpone or even avoid child-rearing." He advises counter measures, such as married couples making a serious commitment to proper child rearing, which may include associating with a religion that encourages family unity and expects involvement from its members, mixing love with discipline, and sacrificing prestigious goals.

The Bible emphasized this need centuries ago. It advises parents: "Bring them [children] up with Christian teaching in Christian discipline." (Ephesians 6:4, *Phillips*) God's Word further exhorts: "Congregate the people, the men and the women *and the little ones* . . . in order that they may listen and in order that they may learn." (Deuteronomy 31:12) The consistent application of these principles will surely help families to counteract the downward pull of modern society.

Putting On the New Personality

THE Bible commands: "Strip off the old personality with its practices, and clothe yourselves with the new personality, which through accurate knowledge is being made new according to the image of the One who created it." (Colossians 3: 9, 10) Many of those who are Jehovah's Witnesses today were once a part of Satan's dishonest world. On getting an accurate knowledge of what God requires of Christians, they changed, clothing themselves with the new personality. The following experiences illustrate how such changes can be made.

☐ A confirmed thief in Spain with kleptomaniac tendencies started studying the Bible with Jehovah's Witnesses. His home was full of stolen goods. As he continued to progress in accurate knowledge of Bible principles, his conscience began to bother him and he made the decision to return the things he had stolen to the owners.

He approached his former employer and confessed that he had stolen a new washing machine from him. This man, impressed with the reasons for his changed attitude, permitted him to pay the price of the washing machine, which was $292 (U.S.), and said he would not inform the police.

Next he visited the town's mayor and confessed that he had broken two expensive light bulbs in the city, and he offered to pay for them. Seeing that this man had put on "the new personality" due to a study of the Bible, the mayor forgave him and would not accept any payment.

The man also visited others in his neighborhood, returning stolen items, and they all expressed surprise at his great change of attitude due to applying Bible principles.

But the owners of many of the items still in his possession were unknown to him. So after praying to Jehovah, he went to police headquarters and turned in six stereo radio cassette players, which he had removed from parked cars. The police were surprised because he had a clean record with them. They

> "Let the stealer steal no more, but rather let him do hard work, doing with his hands what is good work, that he may have something to distribute to someone in need."
> —Ephesians 4:28

had him pay a fine and serve a short time in jail.

Now he has a clean conscience before Jehovah. In harmony with Ephesians 4:28, "Let the stealer steal no more," and appreciating that thieves will not "inherit God's kingdom," he has stopped stealing and has put on "the new personality." —1 Corinthians 6:9, 10.

☐ The honesty of those with Christlike personalities is often recognized by outsiders, as illustrated by an experience in Italy. A terrible car accident was witnessed by one of Jehovah's Witnesses. She approached one of the cars involved to see if she could help, and noticing a man badly injured and bleeding, she spoke to him mentioning Jehovah's name. The man raised his head and asked if she was one of Jehovah's Witnesses, to which she answered yes. He said: "Miss, I feel quite bad. I have a bag in the car that contains many millions [of lira] in cash. Please take it to your home. I know it will be in good hands. Otherwise all this money will disappear. When I am well you can return the money to me!" The Witness took the money and returned it to him when he recovered. He was very thankful.

Jehovah blesses those who "put away the old personality" and "put on the new personality."—Ephesians 4:22-24.

Can a Blind Man "See"?

As told by Bernardo de Santana

"IT IS just too bad, Bernardo," Germiro said. "You used to work right along with us; you were able to see then, but now . . . that's the way it goes. God willed it that way, didn't he?"

"That's right, Germiro," I answered. "It's God's will, so there's nothing we can do about it."

I really felt that it was God's will that I had lost my sight, but in my heart there were unanswered questions. Here I was—32 years old, single, a devout Catholic, and in a shaky financial condition. I asked myself: 'Why did God "will" that I lose my sight? How will I ever care for my parents?' When I had first noticed my sight failing, I prayed fervently for help to Santa Luzia, the "saint" for sight, kneeling before her image in the hospital that bears her name. 'Why did she fail me?' I wondered.

At one time I made my living selling vegetables in the Market of the Seven Doors in Salvador, Brazil. It was not lucrative, but it was steady work. Ever since I was ten years old I had worked on a farm in Sergipe State. So when we moved to Salvador it was natural for me to take up selling vegetables.

One day I noticed that my vision was failing. A specialist confirmed that I had cataracts, but he was hopeful that surgery would restore my sight. An operation on my right eye in 1960 did improve my vision some, but a second operation on the left eye, four years later, proved unsuccessful. From then on it was just a matter of time until I was completely blind. Although I had known for years that I was losing my sight, it is hard to express my feelings once the darkness became complete.

I continued to work in the market but with certain adjustments. Before I left for work, my family divided the money, putting bills of different denominations in separate pockets. This enabled me to make change. But I had to be constantly alert so as not to make mistakes. My fellow workers were sympathetic, and their kind words prevented me from getting discouraged. But some of their expressions, such as those of Germiro mentioned at the outset, only served to raise questions in my mind.

Beginning to "See"

It was at this point in my life that one of my acquaintances, a Jehovah's Witness named Clovis, spoke to me about the promises in the Bible. He told me that God would make a New Order where the blind would see and the deaf would hear again. (Isaiah 35:5) His words struck a responsive chord in my heart. Eager to learn more, I sought him out constantly to ask questions. Observing my interest, he asked me: "Bernardo, how about my coming to your home one afternoon so we can talk more about the Bible?" I accepted eagerly. This was the beginning of our weekly Bible discussions.

Although handicapped, I was anxious to learn. With Clovis' patient help, not only did I discover God's name—Jehovah—but I also learned of His wonderful acts in the past. They were a guarantee that His promises for a righteous Paradise earth would be fulfilled. Then even physical disabilities, such as mine, would be no more. It was not long before I was talking to others about my new hope, even preaching from house to house. Finally, on November 18, 1973, I was baptized. Especially from then on my life began to take on a real purpose, making it easier to cope with my handicap.

From my study of the Bible I knew that God had not willed that I become blind. Rather it was just as the Bible states at Ecclesiastes 9:11: "Time and unforeseen occurrence befall them all." Like all of mankind, I was born of imperfect parents who had inherited sin and imperfection from our first human parents, Adam and Eve. (Romans 5:12) Rather than being God's will that I lose my sight, I learned that his will is that I *see again*. Under the Kingdom rule of God's Son and on the basis of his ransom sacrifice, all imperfections and defects will be removed from believing mankind, and this in the near future. I began to "see" so many things that I could not see before when I had my good eyesight.

My prayers now were directed to Jehovah rather than to Santa Luzia and other "saints." Rather than praying for a miraculous healing to occur now, I prayed sincerely that 'His will take place, as in heaven, also upon earth.' Included in my prayers was a petition that I might someday find a "helper" and "complement," a wife with whom I could share my joys and troubles.

One day while offering Bible literature to people in the business section of Salvador, I heard a female voice say, "I'm one of Jehovah's Witnesses too." I stopped to talk with her. She was the owner of a small street stand. I asked: "Is your husband one of Jehovah's Witnesses too?" She answered: "I have no husband. I'm single." That chance encounter began a friendship that blossomed into courtship, and on June 14, 1975, Ambrosina and I were married. To this day she continues to be my fine helper and complement.—Genesis 2:18.

Working With the Handicap

Ever since my baptism, my desire has been to tell others of what I had learned from the Bible. I was happy that my handicap did not prevent me from doing this. How amazing it was to find that my faculties of hearing and touch tended to make up for my loss of sight. What a sense of accomplishment I felt the first time I went preaching from door to door alone! I wondered if I could not devote more time to this work. A talk by a traveling overseer of Jehovah's Witnesses helped to answer my question. He quoted a number of examples of persons with handicaps, some worse than mine, who actually served as full-time preachers of the good news, called pioneers. Encouraged, I filled out my application to serve as an auxiliary pioneer.

Due to my blindness, I had some problems pioneering, but with the help of loving brothers in the congregation, these were all solved. For example, on rainy days I needed three hands. In one hand I carried my briefcase and in the other my cane. But the umbrella? How much I appreciated the "third hand" offered by my Christian brothers who accompanied me in the ministry! Difficulties arose, too, in working territories where the streets were unknown to me, but again understanding brothers helped me.

How did I find my way around the preaching territory? Usually, I had no problem, since I had taken a special course to help the blind get around. I learned how best to use my cane, to train my hearing and sense of touch, to get on and off buses, and to climb up and down stairs. The course helped me to learn many little things that I had taken for granted before. I would memorize names of streets and then keep count of them as we crossed them. I learned also to keep a mental record of each house on the street, and in this way I was able to make return visits on

---

"He told me that God would make a New Order where the blind would see and the deaf would hear again"

For my door-to-door ministry I memorize the Bible texts I will use, as well as the page in the Bible where they are found

persons interested in Bible study. Also, although we live about two and a half kilometers (1.5 mi) from the Kingdom Hall, I have no problem in going there by myself.

In this regard a visiting traveling overseer was heard commenting: "When I visited the congregation I was really impressed when I worked with Bernardo. He knows the streets and even the houses, can climb stairs and go up and down hills. I was amazed to see how he locates the homes of the persons with whom he conducts Bible studies. We went to one study on the fourth floor of an apartment building, and he took us there without difficulty."

Preparation and Efforts Rewarded

My door-to-door ministry requires special preparation. I memorize ahead of time the Bible texts I will use, as well as the page in the Bible where they are found. At the doors I ask the householder to read the texts, citing the page number, but if the house-holder prefers not to read, then I will quote the texts from memory.

When I conduct Bible studies, I encourage the student to prepare well. Next, I have him read the question first for my benefit, then the paragraph, and finally the question again. This helps me to determine if he answers the question correctly. Using this method I aided two persons to dedication and baptism. Also, I conduct studies with three other families.

For years I have shared in the Theocratic Ministry School of our congregation. In preparation for my talks I have someone read the material aloud to me, recording it on tape at the same time. Then I listen to the recording and form a mental outline of my talk, memorizing also the Bible texts to be included. I am then ready to give my talk. At least I am never counseled about depending too much on written notes! Following the same procedure enables me to comment regularly at the study of *The Watchtower* in the congregation.

The year 1977 was a milepost in my life as a dedicated Christian. I was appointed as a regular pioneer, a ministerial servant, and Congregation Book Study conductor, which privileges I continue to enjoy. I follow the same procedure in the Congregation Book Study as with my Bible students.

In conclusion: Can a blind man "see"? I can see the fulfillment of so many Bible prophecies in our day and hence I realize the need to help others to learn the truth that leads to eternal life. (John 17:3) In a spiritual way I have experienced the fulfillment of Isaiah 35:5: "At that time the eyes of the blind ones will be opened." I have full confidence that in Jehovah's due time this prophecy will also have a literal fulfillment on thousands of persons who, like me, have lost their sight. In the meantime, my desire is to continue doing his will to the best of my ability so as to be found worthy to live in his New Order of righteousness.

Determined to Assemble Together

"**H**EAVIEST rainfall in 80 years kills 28," the next day's headlines read. In just six hours, from 2 a.m. to 8 a.m., a total of about 10 inches (25 cm) had fallen on northern Taiwan. Especially hard hit was Taipei City. In those few hours, what was normally a month's precipitation fell, causing flooding as high as 13 feet (4 m) in some places. But northern Taiwan was the area from which Jehovah's Witnesses were to congregate that day, and Taipei the city where their assembly was being held! Would they still be able to assemble on this second day of their semiannual circuit assembly?

When we awoke that day, June 3, 1984, my wife and I did not realize just how bad the storm was. Strong downpours are quite common in the monsoon season, and we thought little of it. Gradually, an unusual quietness became apparent. The city buses, which normally stop every few minutes in front of the apartment house where we were staying, were not running. And when, at 7:30 a.m., the electricity went off, we began to appreciate that this was no normal monsoon shower. Concerned over the assembly that was scheduled to start at 9:55 a.m., I called the one in charge of sound at the assembly to make sure there would be battery-operated amplifying equipment and flashlights there in case of power failure during the program.

At about that time, we started to hear from our neighbors and friends about widespread flooding in our part of the city. Determined to be at the assembly on time for the morning session, we left shortly after 8 a.m. on our motorbike for what would normally be a 20-minute ride to the Assembly Hall. As soon as we left our street, we realized there would be problems in getting through. The four different routes we tried proved to be impassable when we approached lower ground. Many times in the past we had ridden through water 12-16 inches (30-40 cm) deep while visiting congregations during the rainy season. But now, even buses and trucks were getting stuck in the waist-deep water. So we took the motorbike back home and decided to try to walk out of the area. We were still determined to assemble with our spiritual brothers that day.

Walking also proved to be difficult. Although the rain had now stopped, the water continued to rise. Brown water spouted out like fountains from the gutters and manholes as we approached the Ching Mei River, for the swollen waters behind the levees were already much higher than the surrounding land. We hooked arms tightly and slowly waded through the swift current—cautiously checking each step so that we would not fall into any holes. It was only when we got to the top of the river bridge that we fully realized the seriousness of the situation. What was normally a little stream amid a wide riverbed used for growing vegetables and raising hogs, some 49 feet (15 m) below the bridge, was now a wild torrent filling the bed almost to the top of the levees—and just about 3 feet (1 m) below the bridge!

Flooding on the other side of the bridge looked even more serious. But some men coming through mentioned that conditions down the road were not as bad and that buses and taxis were traveling the streets there. So we struck out for that area. But the farther we went, the stronger the current seemed to become. My wife, shorter than I, had to hang on tightly to me just to keep her balance. Then we came to a spot that seemed impassable. From a side street, a strong, deep, riverlike flood of water was shooting out. Happily, two ropes had been strung across this section, and by hanging on to them we were able to make our way through. As we progressed to higher ground the water decreased and finally we were able to stop, empty our boots of water and thus lighten the load on our feet.

Arriving at the first unflooded road, we faced another problem that stood in the way of our reaching the Assembly Hall: The few buses running were hopelessly crowded and most of the taxis refused to take passengers. But finally one, already with a passenger, stopped for us. After many detours to get around flooded areas we arrived at the Assembly Hall at a little after 10 a.m.

To our delight, most of the Witnesses were already there and waiting for the assembly to start. All had made great efforts to get there, wading through varying depths of water, as buses and motorcycles—usually used by most—could not get through. How wonderful it was to see their appreciation for the assembly program! There are only 417 Witnesses in this section, but many interested persons also braved the floods in their determination to assemble with them and be refreshed with the Bible's spiritual truths. The attendance of 629 at the morning session swelled to 764 for the main talk in the afternoon! Over 30 persons had died by drowning or in mud slides in our area of northern Taiwan, yet none of those who were determined to assemble had suffered any harm. Thankful for Jehovah God's protection, they enjoyed the fine program.

Yes, we were confident that Jehovah would protect all of us in our determination to get to the assembly—without our worrying overly much about our homes and the things there. And really, none attending suffered any serious loss or damage. But we all gained much by the sweet association with our fellow Christians and the outstanding program presented. This proved to us that, although it is easy to put off going to Christian meetings or assemblies when there are some inconveniences, those who make the effort will be richly rewarded.—*Contributed.*

1985 District Conventions

YEAR after year Jehovah's Witnesses have had basic aspects of their beliefs and activities serve as themes for their annual district convention. Among these were "Victorious Faith," "Joyful Workers," "Divine Love," "Kingdom Loyalty," and "Kingdom Unity." The theme chosen for the 1985 district convention is likewise most basic to their activities, namely "Integrity Keepers" Convention.

How important the keeping of integrity is! It is so important that Jehovah accepted the Devil's challenge over this issue, Jehovah being fully confident that among earth's intelligent creatures, there would be those that would keep integrity, prove Jehovah God true and the Devil a base, gross liar.

Keeping integrity is by no means an easy, simple thing to do. It is anything but following the lines of least resistance or doing what comes natural. Knowing what is involved Satan the Devil does all within his power to cause Jehovah's servants to break their integrity. And not only do we have Satan and his demons opposing us in our efforts to keep integrity but we also have to contend with his wicked world that brings all kinds of temptations and pressures to bear upon us. Furthermore, we have our inherited downward tendencies to resist.

To keep integrity by successfully resisting these three foes, we need all the help we can possibly get. The "Integrity Keepers" Convention is designed to give the greatest possible help to all concerned with keeping their integrity toward Jehovah God and proving the Devil a liar. As in other years the convention will, in most lands, begin on Thursday afternoon and last for four days. Make plans now to attend all four days, and come prepared to benefit fully from the program as well as to share in other convention activities.

1985 "Integrity Keepers" Convention Locations

United States

June 13-16, 1985: **AMARILLO, TX**, Civic Center Coliseum, 3rd & Buchanan Sts. **BATON ROUGE, LA** (Sign language also), Assembly Center, Louisiana State University. **CICERO, IL**, Hawthorne Race Course, 35th & Cicero Ave. **GREENVILLE, SC**, Greenville Memorial Auditorium, 300 E. North St. **JACKSONVILLE, FL**, Memorial Coliseum, Gator Bowl Sports Complex. **MONROE, LA**, Civic Center Arena, Civic Center Expwy. **NEW HAVEN, CT**, Veterans Memorial Coliseum, 275 S. Orange St. **OGDEN, UT**, Dee Events Center, 4600 South 1400 East. **PONTIAC, MI**, Silverdome, 1200 Featherstone. **SAN DIEGO, CA**, Jack Murphy Stadium, 9449 Friars Rd. **TUCSON, AZ**, Community Center, 260 S. Church. **WHEELING, WV**, Civic Center, Two 14th St.

June 20-23, 1985: **BIRMINGHAM, AL**, Civic Center Coliseum, One Civic Center Plaza. **CICERO, IL**, Hawthorne Race Course, 35th & Cicero Ave. **DENVER, CO**, McNichols Sports Arena, 1635 Clay St. **FRESNO, CA**, Convention Center, 700 "M" St. **GREENVILLE, SC**, Greenville Memorial Auditorium, 300 E. North St. **LANDOVER, MD**, Capital Centre, Beltway Exit 15 E. or 17. **MIDLAND, TX**, Chaparral Center, Midland College, 3600 N. Garfield. **MONROE, LA**, Civic Center Arena, Civic Center Expwy. **NEW HAVEN, CT**, Veterans Memorial Coliseum, 275 S. Orange St. **OGDEN, UT**, Dee Events Center, 4600 South 1400 East. **RICHFIELD, OH**, The Coliseum, 2923 Streetsboro Rd. **ST. LOUIS, MO**, The Arena, 5700 Oakland Ave. **SOUTH BEND, IN**, N.D.U. Athletic Center, Juniper Rd. **TACOMA, WA**, Tacoma Dome, 2727 E. "D" St. **TUCSON, AZ** (Sign language also), Community Center, 260 S. Church. **WEST PALM BEACH, FL**, West Palm Beach Auditorium, 1610 Palm Beach Lakes Blvd. **WHEELING, WV**, Civic Center, Two 14th St. **WICHITA, KS**, Kansas Coliseum, I-135 at 85th St. N.

June 27-30, 1985: **CICERO, IL** (Sign language also), Hawthorne Race Course, 35th & Cicero Ave. **DENVER, CO** (Sign language also), McNichols Sports Arena, 1635 Clay St. **ERIE, PA**, Convention Center Arena, 809 French St. **FRESNO, CA**, Convention Center, 700 "M" St. **GREENSBORO, NC**, Greensboro Coliseum, 1921 W. Lee St. **GREENVILLE, SC**, Greenville Memorial Auditorium, 300 E. North St. **LANDOVER, MD**, Capital Centre, Beltway Exit 15 E. or 17. **MADISON, WI**, Dane County Memorial Coliseum, John Nolen Dr. **RICHFIELD, OH** (Sign language also), The Coliseum, 2923 Streetsboro Rd. **ROCHESTER, NY**, Memorial Auditorium, 100 Exchange St. **ST. LOUIS, MO**, The Arena, 5700 Oakland Ave. **ST. PETERSBURG, FL**, Bayfront Center, 400 1st St. S. **SAN FRANCISCO, CA**, Cow Palace, Geneva Ave. **SAVANNAH, GA**, Civic Center Arena, Orleans Square. **SOUTH BEND, IN**, N.D.U. Athletic Center, Juniper Rd. **TACOMA, WA** (Spanish and sign language also), Tacoma Dome, 2727 E. "D" St. **WEST PALM BEACH, FL**, West Palm Beach Auditorium, 1610 Palm Beach Lakes Blvd. **WHEELING, WV**, Civic Center, Two 14th St.

July 4-7, 1985: **ALBANY, GA**, Albany Civic Center, 100 West Oglethorpe Ave. **BEAUMONT, TX**, Civic Center Assembly Hall, 701 Main St. **BILLINGS, MT**, Yellowstone Metra, Hwy. #10. **CHATTANOOGA, TN**, U.T.C. Arena, Douglas & E. 5th St. **CICERO, IL** (Spanish only), Hawthorne Race Course, 35th & Cicero Ave. **DULUTH, MN**, Duluth Arena-Auditorium, 350 South 5th Ave. W. **FRESNO, CA** (Spanish only), Convention Center, 700 "M" St. **GREENSBORO, NC**, Greensboro Coliseum, 1921 W. Lee St. **HAMPTON, VA**, Hampton Coliseum, 1000 Coliseum Dr. **LANDOVER, MD** (Sign language also), Capital Centre, Beltway Exit 15 E. or 17. **LOS ANGELES, CA** (Sign language also), Dodger Stadium, 1000 Elysian Park Ave. **LOUISVILLE, KY**, Coliseum, Kentucky Fair & Exposition Center. **MADISON, WI**, Dane County Memorial Coliseum, John Nolen Dr. **MONROE, LA**, Civic Center Arena, Civic Center Expwy. **OKLAHOMA CITY, OK**, Myriad, One Myriad Gardens. **RICHFIELD, OH**, The Coliseum, 2923 Streetsboro Rd. **ROCHESTER, NY**, Memorial Auditorium, 100 Exchange St. **ST. PETERSBURG, FL**, Bayfront Center, 400 1st St. S. **SAN FRANCISCO, CA**, Cow Palace, Geneva Ave. **SAVANNAH, GA**, Civic Center Arena, Orleans Square. **WEST PALM BEACH, FL**, West Palm Beach Auditorium, 1610 Palm Beach Lakes Blvd.

July 11-14, 1985: **ALBANY, GA** (Sign language also), Albany Civic Center, 100 West Oglethorpe Ave. **BISMARCK, ND**, Bismarck Civic Center Arena, 6th & Sweet Sts. **CHATTANOOGA, TN**, U.T.C. Arena, Douglas & E. 5th St. **DULUTH, MN**, Duluth Arena-Auditorium, 350 South 5th Ave. W. **EL PASO, TX** (Spanish only), Special Events Center, Baltimore at Mesa. **FT. WORTH, TX**, Will Rogers Memorial Coliseum, One Amon Carter Sq. **FRESNO, CA** (Spanish only), Convention Center, 700 "M" St. **HAMPTON, VA**, Hampton Coliseum, 1000 Coliseum Dr. **LONG ISLAND CITY, NY** (French only), Jehovah's Witnesses Assembly Hall, 44-17 Greenpoint Ave. **LOS ANGELES, CA** (Spanish only), Dodger Stadium, 1000 Elysian Park Ave. **LOUISVILLE, KY** (Sign language also), Coliseum, Kentucky Fair & Exposition Center. **MOBILE, AL**, Municipal Auditorium, 401 Auditorium Dr. **PHILADELPHIA, PA**, Veterans Stadium, S. Broad & Pattison Ave. **PROVIDENCE, RI**, Providence Civic Center, One LaSalle Sq. **RENO, NV**, Centennial Coliseum, 4590 S. Virginia St. **ST. PETERSBURG, FL** (Sign language also), Bayfront Center, 400 1st St. S. **SAN FRANCISCO, CA** (Sign language also), Cow Palace, Geneva Ave. **SPRINGFIELD, IL**, Convention Center Arena, One Convention Center Plaza.

July 18-21, 1985: **BILOXI, MS**, Mississippi Coast Coliseum, 3800 W. Beach Blvd. **CHARLESTON, WV**, Charleston Civic Center Coliseum, 200 Civic Center Dr. **DES MOINES, IA**, Veterans Memorial Auditorium, 833 5th Ave. **FT. LAUDERDALE, FL** (French only), Jehovah's Witnesses Assembly Hall, 20850 Griffin Rd. **FT. WORTH, TX** (Sign language also), Will Rogers Memorial Coliseum, One Amon Carter Sq. **GREEN BAY, WI**, Memorial Arena, 1901 S. Oneida St. **HIALEAH, FL** (Spanish only), Hialeah Park Race Track, E. 32nd St. at E. 2nd Ave. **LONG ISLAND CITY, NY** (French only), Jehovah's Witnesses Assembly Hall, 44-17 Greenpoint Ave. **PROVIDENCE, RI**, Providence Civic Center, One LaSalle Sq. **RENO, NV**, Centennial Coliseum, 4590 S. Virginia St. **ST. PETERSBURG, FL**, Bayfront Center, 400 1st St. S. **SAN ANTONIO, TX** (Spanish only), Convention Center Arena, S. Alamo & Market Sts. **SAN FRANCISCO, CA** (Chinese, Japanese, and Korean also), Cow Palace, Geneva Ave.

July 25-28, 1985: **FT. WORTH, TX**, Will Rogers Memorial Arena, One Amon Carter Sq. **HIALEAH, FL** (Spanish only), Hialeah Park Race Track, E. 32nd St. at E. 2nd Ave. **HOUSTON, TX**, Astrodome, Loop 610 at Kirby Dr. **KNOXVILLE, TN**, Civic Auditorium, 500 Church Ave. **S.E. LINCOLN, NE** (Sign language also), Devaney Sports Center, 16th & Military. **RENO, NV**, Centennial Coliseum, 4590 S. Virginia St. **SAN ANTONIO, TX** (Spanish only), Convention Center Arena, S. Alamo & Market Sts. **SPRINGFIELD, MA** (Sign language also), Civic Center, 1277 Main St.

August 1-4, 1985: **ELMONT, NY** (Spanish only), Belmont Park Race Track, Hempstead Tpk. at Cross Island Pkwy. **RENO, NV**, Centennial Coliseum, 4590 S. Virginia St.

August 8-11, 1985: **ELMONT, NY**, Belmont Park Race Track, Hempstead Tpk. at Cross Island Pkwy.

August 15-18, 1985: **ELMONT, NY** (Sign language also), Belmont Park Race Track, Hempstead Tpk. at Cross Island Pkwy.

August 22-25, 1985: **ELMONT, NY**, Belmont Park Race Track, Hempstead Tpk. at Cross Island Pkwy.

Britain

June 27-30, 1985: **DERBY**, Derby County Football Club, The Baseball Ground. **SOUTHAMPTON**, Southampton Football Club, The Dell, Milton Road.

July 4-7, 1985: **EDINBURGH**, Rugby Union Ground, Murrayfield. **MANCHESTER**, Manchester City Football Club, Maine Road, Moss Side. **PLYMOUTH**, Plymouth Argyle Football Club, Home Park.

July 11-14, 1985: **LEEDS**, Leeds United Football Club, Elland Road. **NORWICH**, Norwich City Football Club, Carrow Road. **WOLVERHAMPTON**, Wolverhampton Wanderers Football Club, Molineux.

July 18-21, 1985: **CARDIFF**, Welsh National Rugby Ground, Cardiff Arms Park.

July 25-28, 1985: **LONDON**, Rugby Union Ground, Whitton Road, Twickenham.

Ireland

July 11-14, 1985: **NAVAN**, Navan Exhibition Centre.

August 1-4, 1985: **BELFAST**, Grenville Nugent Hall, The Kings Hall, Balmoral.

Canada

July 4-7, 1985: **EDMONTON, ALTA.** (Ukrainian sessions also), Edmonton Northlands Coliseum, 75 St. & 118 Ave. **KAMLOOPS, B.C.**, Kamloops Exhibition Association. **PRINCE GEORGE, B.C.**, Kin Centre, Arenas I & II. **SASKATOON, SASK.**, Saskatoon Arena, 19 Street East. **VANCOUVER, B.C.** (Portuguese also), Pacific Coliseum, Exhibition Park. **WINNIPEG, MAN.** (Ukrainian sessions also), Winnipeg Convention Centre, 375 York Ave.

July 11-14, 1985: **MONTREAL, QUE.** (French, Chinese, and Korean also; Hungarian and Ukrainian sessions also), Olympic Stadium, Pie IX Blvd. & Sherbrooke St.; Arabic and Italian: Velodrome, Olympic Park; Greek and Portuguese: Centre Pierre Charbonneau, 300 Viau St.; Spanish: Arena Maurice-Richard, 2800 Viau St. **REGINA, SASK.** (Ukrainian sessions also), The Agridome, Exhibition Grounds. **VICTORIA, B.C.**, Victoria Memorial Arena, 1925 Blanshard St.

July 18-21, 1985: **LETHBRIDGE, ALTA.**, The Sportsplex, 2510 Scenic Dr. **PENTICTON, B.C.**, Peach Bowl Convention Centre, Power St. & Westminster Ave. W. **ST. JOHN'S, NFLD.**, Feildian Gardens, Pennywell Rd.

July 25-28, 1985: **CASTLEGAR, B.C.**, Castlegar & District Community Complex, 2101 6th Ave. **LONDON, ONT.**, Grandstand Western Fairgrounds, Queen's Park.

"I have just finished reading *You Can Live Forever in Paradise on Earth,*" a woman from Chicago, Illinois, recently wrote. "Next to the Bible itself I have found this book to be the most accurate, inspiring, and motivating piece of literature I have ever read." She went on to explain:

"My first encounter with the Jehovah's Witnesses was a rather negative one. At first I found it embarrassing when they would persistently come to visit my home to inform me of the Scriptures. Certain members of my family thought I was crazy for ever listening to them. . . . Now that I have had the chance to witness what the truth is all about by reading this book . . . I would really appreciate it if I could receive regular Bible studies with someone in the organization."

You Can Live Forever in Paradise on Earth

A Most Inspiring Book!

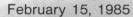
February 15, 1985

The Watchtower

Announcing Jehovah's Kingdom

ARMAGEDDON
A War That Brings
TRUE PEACE

February 15, 1985
Vol. 106, No. 4

The Watchtower®

Announcing Jehovah's Kingdom

THE PURPOSE OF "THE WATCHTOWER" is to exalt Jehovah God as the Sovereign of the universe. It keeps watch on world events as they fulfill Bible prophecy. It comforts all peoples with the good news that God's Kingdom will soon destroy those who oppress their fellowmen and that it will turn the earth into a paradise. It encourages faith in the now-reigning King, Jesus Christ, whose shed blood opens the way for mankind to gain eternal life. "The Watchtower," published by Jehovah's Witnesses continuously since 1879, is nonpolitical. It adheres to the Bible as its authority.

"WATCHTOWER" STUDIES FOR THE WEEKS

March 24: Nisan 14—A Day for Remembering. Page 10. Songs to Be Used: 114, 205.

March 31: The "Other Sheep" and the Lord's Evening Meal. Page 15. Songs to Be Used: 150, 105.

Average Printing Each Issue: 11,150,000

Now Published in 102 Languages

SEMIMONTHLY EDITIONS AVAILABLE BY MAIL
Afrikaans, Arabic, Cebuano, Chichewa, Chinese, Cibemba, Danish, Dutch, Efik, English*, Finnish, French, German, Greek, Hiligaynon, Igbo, Iloko, Italian, Japanese, Korean, Lingala, Malagasy, Maltese, Norwegian, Portuguese, Russian, Sepedi, Sesotho, Shona, Spanish, Swahili, Swedish, Tagalog, Thai, Tswana, Xhosa, Yoruba, Zulu

MONTHLY EDITIONS AVAILABLE BY MAIL
Armenian, Bengali, Bicol, Bulgarian, Croatian, Czech, Ewe, Fijian, Ga, Greenlandic, Gujarati, Gun, Hausa, Hebrew, Hindi, Hiri Motu, Hungarian, Icelandic, Kannada, Kikuyu, Kiluba, Malayalam, Marathi, New Guinea Pidgin, Pangasinan, Papiamento, Polish, Rarotongan, Romanian, Samar-Leyte, Samoan, Sango, Serbian, Silozi, Sinhalese, Slovenian, Solomon Islands-Pidgin, Tahitian, Tamil, Telugu, Tshiluba, Tsonga, Turkish, Twi, Ukrainian, Urdu, Venda, Vietnamese
*Study articles also available in large-print edition at same cost.

The Bible translation used is the "New World Translation of the Holy Scriptures," unless otherwise indicated.

Twenty cents (U.S.) a copy

Watch Tower Society offices	Yearly subscription rates Semimonthly
America, U.S., Watchtower, Wallkill, N.Y. 12589	$4.00
Australia, Box 280, Ingleburn, N.S.W. 2565	A$6.00
Canada, Box 4100, Halton Hills (Georgetown), Ontario L7G 4Y4	$4.50
England, The Ridgeway, London NW7 1RN	£5.00
Ireland, 29A Jamestown Road, Finglas, Dublin 11	£5.00
New Zealand, 6-A Western Springs Rd., Auckland 3	$7.00
Nigeria, P.O. Box 194, Yaba, Lagos State	₦3.50
Philippines, P.O. Box 2044, Manila 2800	₱50.00
South Africa, Private Bag 2, Elandsfontein, 1406	R5,60

Remittances should be sent to the office in your country or to Watchtower, Wallkill, N.Y. 12589, U.S.A.

Changes of address should reach us 30 days before your moving date. Give us your old and new address (if possible, your old address label).

The Watchtower (ISSN 0043-1087) is published semimonthly for $4.00 (U.S.) per year by Watch Tower Bible and Tract Society of Pennsylvania, 25 Columbia Heights, Brooklyn, N.Y. 11201. Second-class postage paid at Brooklyn, N.Y., and at additional mailing offices.

Postmaster: Send address changes to Watchtower, **Wallkill, N.Y. 12589.**

Published by
**Watch Tower Bible and Tract Society
of Pennsylvania**
25 Columbia Heights, Brooklyn, N.Y. 11201, U.S.A.
Frederick W. Franz, President

"ARMAGEDDON"—what does this Bible name signify? Introduced each time by a meaningful cover, a series of informative articles on this topic has been featured in the four issues of *The Watchtower* for January and February 1985. It is hoped that these Scriptural discussions are comforting you with knowledge as to what is the real ARMAGEDDON.

The End of All War —Can It Be Achieved?

"COME, you people, behold the activities of Jehovah, how he has set astonishing events on the earth. *He is making wars to cease to the extremity of the earth.* The bow he breaks apart and does cut the spear in pieces; the wagons he burns in the fire."—Psalm 46:8, 9.

The above words of the inspired psalmist agree with the heartfelt desire of people throughout the ages. Really, who has not longed for the day when war will be no more? As much as we would like to see it, however, the end of war has, so far, eluded all human efforts. Not only is war still very much with us but it also has become so destructive and deadly that for the first time in human history the continuation of civilization, and even life itself, is threatened.

In view of the grave danger looming ahead, we cannot help but ask: Why have human efforts to prevent war been such miserable failures? Is war really inevitable? Indeed, why are wars fought in the first place?

Why Human Efforts Fail

"If you live in a neighborhood where there are no police and everybody has guns and lives in constant fear of being attacked, then there is going to be a lot of shooting," writes journalist and military historian Gwynne Dyer. "That is the sort of neighborhood that all the countries of the world live in," he continues. "There are no international police, so each country keeps itself armed and ready for violence; but the kind of violence that countries get involved in has a special name. We call it war."

Though that is a rather simplified explanation, it does point out several of the basic factors that make for war. There must be the *means* to wage war as well as the *inclination* to do so. Along with these, we note also the *lack of law and order* in the "neighborhood," which in this case is the world.

The famous historians Will and Ariel Durant pointed to these same basic factors when they wrote in their book *The Lessons of History:* "In the present inadequacy of international law and sentiment a nation must be ready at any moment to defend itself; and when its essential interests are involved it must be allowed to use any means it considers necessary to its survival. The Ten Commandments must be silent when self-preservation is at stake."

Consequently, the success or failure of any effort to bring war to an end would depend largely on how it deals with these basic factors. Has any human scheme, no matter how noble in concept, been successful in doing so? Let us examine the facts.

Lack of International Order

Many attempts have been made in the past to create some sort of world agency with the power to police the nations and to maintain international law and order. The League of Nations, for example, was formed at the end of World War I to ensure that the world would not again be plunged into war. In effect it sank into oblivion with the outbreak of World War II. Then, in 1945, the United Nations organization emerged, to be praised and adored by the clergy of Christendom as mankind's hope for peace. What has been its record? Once again history gives the reply. "Over four million people are engaged now in 42 different wars, rebellions and civil uprisings. . . . Between one million and five million people have been killed in these struggles," reported *The New York Times* in 1984. Today few people believe that the UN has the ability to prevent wars and conflicts from erupting. Its existence does little to allay the fear of a third world war or a nuclear holocaust.

Mounting Threat and Tension

One reason that agencies such as the UN are powerless to prevent war is that the nations around the world are fully dedicated to national sovereignty and rights. They care little about international responsibility or rules of conduct. To reach their ends, some nations feel fully justified in using any means that they consider necessary—massacres, assassinations, hijackings, bombings, and so on—often with the innocent being the victims. Even the major powers of the world often push one another to the limit in the name of self-preservation and national interest. How long will the nations put up with one another in such senseless and irresponsible conduct? How many Falklands, Afghanistans, Grenadas, Korean 007's, and so on can the world survive without a major confrontation? It is not difficult to see why nationalism and self-determination have become major obstacles to bringing an end to war.

Armed and Ready

By now it is common knowledge that the arsenals of the superpowers are stocked with enough nuclear devices to destroy all human life on earth many times over. But what about the other nations? According to a U.S. government report, developing nations around the world, though hard pressed economically, have spent well over $230 billion in the last decade acquiring some of the most advanced aircraft, missiles, and tanks available. The result? "It has reached the point now where many of the buyers are having problems absorbing all their new hardware." These nations are literally armed to the teeth, as the saying goes. The fact that they have only so-called conventional weapons makes them that much more willing and ready to put them to use.

Any Reason for Hope?

The repeated failure of human efforts to bring an end to war merely emphasizes the Bible truth that "it does not belong to man who is walking even to direct his step." (Jeremiah 10:23) As much as humans may want to see the end to war, they of themselves simply do not know how to achieve it. What, then, about the promise that 'wars will be made to cease to the extremity of the earth'? Is it given just to arouse hope or to mock us? Certainly not. For Jehovah assures us regarding any word or promise from his mouth: "It will not return to me without results." (Isaiah 55:11) How, then, will this promise be realized? What sound basis is there for us to believe that God will succeed where man has failed repeatedly?

Armageddon
A War That Leads to True Peace

IN THE language of those who deal with international relations, the word used to describe the world situation today is MAD—Mutual Assured Destruction. That term is most appropriate. In the 40 years since the first atomic bomb exploded in warfare over Hiroshima, Japan, the world's nuclear arsenals have grown unbelievably. Some reports claim that they amount to the equivalent of 12 thousand million tons of TNT, or about 3 tons for each person on earth!

As the One "who did not create [the earth] simply for nothing, who formed it even to be inhabited," Jehovah God will not, in fact, cannot, allow the nations to continue in their suicidal course. (Isaiah 45:18; see also Psalm 104:5.) Before they have occasion to unleash all their deadly weapons on one another, and in the process destroy themselves and the environment, the Maker and Owner of the earth and everything upon it will rise up to action. He has promised that this will be "the war of the great day of God the Almighty," the Biblical Armageddon!—Revelation 16:14, 16.

Armageddon, therefore, will be much more than just another war to resolve the present-day political deadlock. It will accomplish what man throughout the ages could only hope for. It will do away with all causes of human war. It will establish true peace on the earth. Above all, it will restore the rightful rulership of earth's Owner, Jehovah God, over all his creation. How will all of this be accomplished? Let us see.

Peace—By Eliminating the Means to Wage War

One of the reasons that the nations have not been able to do away with war is that they have not been able to do away with the means to wage war. Even though they know that the spiraling arms buildup is suicidal, they are not willing to give it up or to slow it down. It will be "astonishing," indeed, when Jehovah takes action and accomplishes what the nations cannot do: "The bow he breaks apart and does cut the spear in pieces; the wagons he burns in the fire."—Psalm 46:8, 9.

Jehovah has in the past demonstrated his ability to neutralize the most advanced or formidable weapons that the nations could brandish. For example, he delivered his seemingly defenseless people, the Israelites, from the military might of the first world power, Egypt, by wielding the elemental forces of the waters of the Red Sea. (Exodus 15:3-5) Similarly, Canaanite King Jabin's sophisticated tactical weapons, "nine hundred war chariots with iron scythes," in the command of his army chief Sisera, were rendered totally inoper-

ative when Jehovah unleashed the powers of a flash flood. The enemy ranks were thrown into total confusion, leading to their liquidation down to the last man. The outcome was that "the land had no further disturbance for forty years."—See Judges, chapter 4 and 5:21, 31.

Significantly, that decisive battle against King Jabin's forces took place in the torrent valley of Kishon, "by the waters of Megiddo." (Judges 5:19-21) It therefore provides us with a dramatic preview of Jehovah's total victory in the forthcoming battle of Armageddon.

What "mysterious" forces, if any, Jehovah will use against his enemies we do not know. What we do know is that he does have at his disposal forces that can completely devastate the military establishments of the nations. Scientists are aware, for example, that a powerful electromagnetic pulse—something even they can generate by a high-altitude nuclear explosion—is capable of knocking out the communication and military control systems of a nation, thus throwing everything into chaos. Reasonably, Jehovah will

At the Red Sea Jehovah displayed his ability to neutralize formidable weapons of war

nullify all the nations' arsenals in order to lay the foundation for total peace.

Peace—Only for Those Who Want It

It has been said often that wars are fought by people, not by weapons. Therefore, even though it is essential that the means to wage war be eliminated, that in itself will not guarantee lasting peace. Logically, if we want to see true peace, the political, racial, and nationalistic hatreds that divide the world into ever so many blocs and camps must also be done away with. This, Jehovah God will do by bringing to pass what millions throughout the world have been praying for: "Let your kingdom come."—Matthew 6:9, 10.

Even though fulfilled Bible prophecies clearly show that the Messianic Kingdom in the hands of Jesus Christ was established in the heavens in the World War I year of 1914, it was not welcomed by the nations. Not one of them would give thought to laying down their arms and surrendering their sovereignty. Instead, in their frantic struggle for world domination, they were embroiled in the greatest war ever to take place up to that time.

Prophetically, the second Psalm describes the situation: "Why have the nations been in tumult and the national groups themselves kept muttering an empty thing? The kings of earth take their stand and high officials themselves have massed together as one against Jehovah and against his anointed one." That is why Jehovah's command to his designated King, Jesus Christ, is: "You will break them with an iron scepter, as though a potter's vessel you will dash them to pieces."—Psalm 2:1, 2, 9; 110:2.

This conquest by God's anointed King is described in figurative detail at Revelation 19:11–20:3. The Word of God, Jesus Christ, supported by angelic armies, is seen astride a white horse, "and he judges and carries on war in righteousness. . . . Out of his mouth there protrudes a sharp long sword, that he may strike the nations with it." The resulting slaughter of the wicked is very great. In his sweeping victory, the triumphant King will then deal with the real culprit behind all the woes and suffering on earth. The vision in Revelation describes this as though it has already been accomplished, saying: "He seized the dragon, the original serpent, who is the Devil and Satan, and bound him for a thousand years."

Peace—A Thousand Years and Beyond

Can you imagine what a thousand years of peace will mean for mankind? Authorities today recognize that hunger, diseases, and poverty among the nations could be eliminated if only a fraction of the hundreds of billions of dollars spent on armaments each year was used to deal with them. Think of what will be accomplished when all earth's resources are put to constructive use. It was no wishful dream of a visionary when Isaiah was inspired to prophesy about the rule of the "Prince of Peace," Jesus Christ: "To the abundance of the princely rule and to peace there will be no end."—Isaiah 9:6, 7.

The pressing question is: Will you survive the destruction at Armageddon to enjoy the endless peace? You may ask, 'What must I do to survive?' Here is the Bible's admonition: "Seek Jehovah, all you meek ones of the earth, who have practiced His own judicial decision. Seek righteousness, seek meekness. Probably you may be concealed in the day of Jehovah's anger." (Zephaniah 2:2, 3) Jehovah's Witnesses will be glad to help you to do so. In that case, Armageddon will turn out to be for you, not a war that brings total destruction, but a war that leads to true peace.

God's Word Is Alive

A Proud Man Humbles Himself

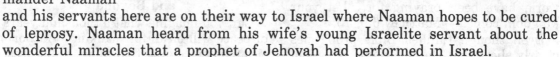

THE proud Syrian military commander Naaman and his servants here are on their way to Israel where Naaman hopes to be cured of leprosy. Naaman heard from his wife's young Israelite servant about the wonderful miracles that a prophet of Jehovah had performed in Israel.

Naaman carries a letter from the Syrian king that introduces him to the king of Israel. The letter requests that Naaman be cured of his leprosy. Arriving in Israel, Naaman presents the letter to King Jehoram, who becomes extremely upset because he cannot cure this man. Jehoram exclaims, 'The king of Syria is only seeking a quarrel with me.' When Jehovah's prophet Elisha learns of this, he asks that Naaman be sent to him.

So Naaman, with his horses and war chariots, goes to Elisha's house. But Elisha does not even come out to meet him. He simply sends out a messenger who directs Naaman: 'To be cured you must go and bathe seven times in the Jordan River.'

God's Word Is Alive

Proud Naaman is offended and leaves in a rage. 'I thought that he would at least come out to me,' he says, 'and pray to Jehovah and wave his hand over the diseased spot. I could just as well have bathed in the rivers of Syria.' Yet one of Naaman's servants calms him by reasoning: 'Sir, if the prophet had told you to do something difficult, you would have done it. Now why can't you just bathe, as he directed, and be cured?'

Naaman listens to his servant. He goes to the Jordan and plunges into its waters. And, miraculously, after the seventh time, his leprosy vanishes! Naaman is moved with appreciation and travels all the way back to Elisha to thank him, a trip of perhaps 30 miles (48 km).

Naaman offers Elisha expensive gifts and he then requests: 'Let me have two muleloads of earth to take home.' For what purpose? So that he there might offer sacrifices to Jehovah on Israel's soil. In fact, Naaman vows that henceforth he will not offer sacrifices or burnt offerings to any god except Jehovah.—2 Kings 5:5-17.

What a remarkable change Naaman made! It is indeed a fine example for us to consider. But we can learn another lesson from this incident, which we will consider in a future issue of this magazine.

Nisan 14
—A Day for Remembering

"Keep doing this in
remembrance of me."
—1 CORINTHIANS 11:24.

"**T**AKE courage! I have conquered the world." With such words of comfort and encouragement, Jesus strengthened his 11 faithful apostles the night before he died. Jesus had proved himself to be a world conqueror! He had successfully resisted every attempt of his Adversary, Satan the Devil, to break his loyalty to Jehovah. And now, with death on a torture stake facing him in a few hours, he was confident of maintaining his course of faithful integrity right to the very last.—John 16:33; Hebrews 12:2.

² This event of universal importance took place nineteen hundred and fifty-two years ago on the 14th day of Nisan, the first lunar month of the Jewish sacred calendar. This day would be one that was never to be forgotten by his devoted footstep followers. To ensure that his loyal followers would never overlook the significance of what was then to take place, Jesus instituted a special commemorative evening meal, described by the apostle

Paul as "the Lord's evening meal." Under divine inspiration Paul relates that on this occasion Jesus commanded his disciples then present: "Keep doing this in remembrance of me." (1 Corinthians 11:20, 24) If you are concerned with being one of Jesus' followers, do you appreciate why he commanded that, what it calls on you to do, and what it can mean for your future?

A Memorable Day

³ This was not the first time in man's history that Nisan 14 had been set aside as a day for remembering. In 1513 B.C.E., Jehovah, through his servant Moses, commanded the Israelites: "This day [Nisan 14] must serve as a memorial for you, and you must celebrate it as a festival to Jehovah throughout your generations." What prompted the celebration back then? Jehovah himself answered: "It is the sacrifice of the passover to Jehovah, who

---

1. How did Jesus conquer the world?
2. Why did Jesus institute "the Lord's evening meal"?

---

3. Why, and under what circumstances, was Nisan 14 first made a day for remembering?

passed over the houses of the sons of Israel in Egypt when he plagued the Egyptians."—Exodus 12:14, 27.

4 That awesome deliverance in Egypt of every Israelite firstborn, involving both man and beast, took place on that night of Nisan 14. It was the culmination of nine preceding blows against the demon gods worshiped by the Egyptians, underscoring Jehovah's previously stated purpose given to haughty Pharaoh: "In fact, for this cause I have kept you in existence, for the sake of showing you my power and in order to have my name declared in all the earth." A few days later Jehovah's name and power were further manifested when he delivered millions of Israelites and a great mixed company at the Red Sea, while drowning the flower of Pharaoh's armies. Little wonder that Moses and the sons of Israel sang: "Let me sing to Jehovah, for he has become highly exalted"! —Exodus 9:16; 15:1.

---

4. What important issues were involved in Israel's deliverance from Egypt?

5 After the Israelites became settled in the land promised to their forefather Abraham, the Passover was to be celebrated nationally once each year in Jerusalem, in obedience to the command at Deuteronomy 16:1-8. Jehovah thus arranged that Nisan 14 should always stand out in the minds of his typical people. What purpose would this serve? It was to be a day for exalting Jehovah's name, for remembering his great acts of deliverance. So centuries later the significance of the Passover would be uppermost in the hearts and thoughts of Jesus' parents who, we are told, "were accustomed to go from year to year to Jerusalem for the festival of the passover." According to Jewish custom, their son Jesus would be with them. —Luke 2:41, 42.

6 Following Jesus' baptism in the Jordan and the start of his ministry, he likely would continue to celebrate the Passover with Mary, his earthly mother, and her sons, his half brothers. However, for Nisan 14, 33 C.E., Jesus arranged to celebrate the feast with his 12 apostles. Luke's account tells us how Jesus felt about this occasion: "I have wanted so much to eat this Passover meal with you before I suffer!" (Luke 22:15, Today's English Version) Why such a great desire on Jesus' part? Because he knew the significance of the events shortly to take place on that memorable day that had started at sundown. Jesus also knew that such events would far eclipse those that happened back in 1513 B.C.E. They would exalt Jehovah's name more than ever before and would lay the basis for the ultimate blessing of all the families of the earth. Also, he had much to tell his disci-

---

5. What purpose was served by the Passover celebration?

6. For what reasons was Jesus anxious to keep the Passover of 33 C.E. with his faithful apostles?

ples before he died, instilling courage in them to remain his loyal followers. The detailed Gospel accounts allow us to listen in, as it were, on what Jesus said and did. —John 12:31; 17:26.

What Occurred? What Did It Mean?

⁷ While the meal was in progress, Jesus got up and washed the feet of his disciples, thus setting a perfect example in humility. Then Jesus said, "One of you will betray me." Shortly afterward, he turned to Judas and said, "What you are doing get done more quickly." John's account relates: "He went out immediately. And it was night." (John 13:21, 27, 30) It was after this that Jesus instituted the Memorial of his death. Let us hear how eyewitness Matthew describes what happened: "As they continued eating, Jesus took a loaf and, after saying a blessing, he broke it and, giving it to the disciples, he said: 'Take, eat. This means my body.' Also, he took a cup and, having given thanks, he gave it to them, saying: 'Drink out of it, all of you; for this means my "blood of the

---

7. (a) What events during Jesus' last Passover meal led up to his instituting the Memorial of his death? (John 13:1-30) (b) Describe Jesus' procedure in setting up the Lord's Evening Meal.

covenant," which is to be poured out in behalf of many for forgiveness of sins. But I tell you, I will by no means drink henceforth any of this product of the vine until that day when I drink it new with you in the kingdom of my Father.' Finally, after singing praises, they went out to the Mount of Olives."—Matthew 26:26-30; see also Mark 14:22-26, Luke 22:19, 20, and 1 Corinthians 11:23-26.

⁸ What was the full meaning of what Jesus said and did on that occasion? Paul emphasized how important it is for all of Christ's anointed followers to appreciate this, saying: "Consequently whoever eats the loaf or drinks the cup of the Lord unworthily will be guilty respecting the body and the blood of the Lord." Surely none of the anointed would want to be 'unworthy' in Jehovah's eyes, resulting in his adverse judgment. Further, the "great crowd" should want to be counted worthy as companions of the anointed remnant. So, with the approach of another Memorial on Thursday, April 4, 1985, it is timely that all of us reexamine this matter together in detail.—1 Corinthians 11:27.

⁹ Jesus said, "This means my body."* In saying these words, Jesus put a special meaning on the loaf—it was a symbol of

---

* Some Bible versions read, "This is my body." (See *King James Version,* Catholic *Douay Version, The New English Bible,* and some modern versions.) However, the Greek word used for "is" is *e·stin,* in the sense of signifying, importing, representing. (See footnote on Matthew 26:26, *NW Ref. Bi.*) The same Greek word appears in Matthew 9:13 and 12:7 and in both cases is translated "meaneth" (*KJ*) and "means" (*NE* and other modern translations).

8. Why is it so important to understand the meaning of Jesus' words and actions in instituting the Memorial?
9. (a) Why is the rendering of Jesus' words, "This means my body" more correct than, "This is my body"? (See footnote.) (b) What special meaning did Jesus put on the loaf? (c) On the wine?

his own sinless fleshly body that he gave "in behalf of the life of the world." (John 6:51) Similarly, when he said respecting the cup of wine, "This means my 'blood of the covenant,' . . . poured out . . . for forgiveness of sins," he was using the fermented wine in the cup as a symbol of his own blood. This blood was to be the basis for putting into operation "a new covenant." His shed blood was also going to be a means of providing "forgiveness of sins."—Matthew 26:28; Jeremiah 31: 31-33; Hebrews 9:22.

¹⁰ What, then, is implied on the part of those who partake of the bread and the wine during the Memorial celebration? The act itself demonstrates to the partakers, and to onlookers, that they have *already* benefited from the ransom sacrifice of Christ Jesus, but in a special way and for a special purpose. How does this work out? On the basis of their faith in Christ's sacrifice and their dedication to Jehovah, God credits them with the merit of Jesus' human sacrifice. For what purpose? So that they can have imputed to them human perfection and thus have a righteous standing before God. Jehovah then begets these by his holy spirit and they become his spiritual sons. They are now in a position to sacrifice their right to live on earth in return for a heavenly inheritance. All of this has taken place before they share in the Lord's Supper.—Romans 5:1, 2, 8; 8: 15-17; James 1:18.

¹¹ Consider now what else is implied by drinking the wine. Although Jehovah has imputed righteousness to his spiritual sons and has adopted them as sons, they are still in the imperfect flesh. They are yet prone to sin and they recognize this. In drinking the wine, they thereby acknowledge their daily dependence on the blood of Christ Jesus, which has been "poured out in behalf of many for forgiveness of sins."—1 John 1:9, 10; 2:1.

¹² There is still something else, however, that is implied by drinking the wine. The partakers testify that they have been brought into the "new covenant" that Jehovah long ago foretold through the prophet Jeremiah. This covenant was made operational by the blood of Jesus. The parties to that covenant are Jehovah God and his spiritual sons, who collectively make up spiritual Israel. Each member is chosen by God. Jesus is the Mediator of the covenant, by which he assists those 144,000 covenant members to become part of the seed of Abraham. (Jeremiah 31: 31-34; 2 Thessalonians 2:13; Hebrews 8: 10, 12; 12:22-24; Galatians 3:29) These are also the ones that Jesus takes into a 'covenant for a kingdom.' As a result, they will eventually be used along with their King Jesus Christ to channel Jehovah's blessings of life to all the families of the earth.—Luke 22:28-30; John 6:53; Revelation 5:9, 10; Genesis 22:15-18.

10. What does partaking of the bread and wine imply?
11, 12. (a) What two additional things are indicated by drinking the wine? (b) Explain the covenant that Jesus makes with those who partake.

13 Truly, as we examine the full meaning of Jesus' words spoken on this day for remembering, we are forcibly reminded of Jehovah's love in making the provision of his dear Son. We are also reminded of Jesus' love in providing his life as a ransom for all believing mankind. (John 3:16; Romans 5:8; 1 Timothy 2:5, 6) However, there are other precious truths that Jesus discussed with his followers that evening. Of the Bible writers, only the apostle John records this very intimate conversation.

Glory, Love, and Unity

14 Jesus said: "Now the Son of man is glorified, and God is glorified in connection with him." (John 13:31) Ever since Israel's deliverance from Egypt, Nisan 14 had been associated with the vindication of God's name, his sovereignty, and his power. Now, with Jesus' faithfulness to death and his subsequent glorious resurrection by God's power, still greater honor and glory were being brought to God's name. (Compare Proverbs 27:11.) Jesus told his disciples that they would give proof of discipleship by keeping "a new commandment," to 'love one another just as he had loved them.' (John 13:34, 35) The depth of *our* brotherly love is a reflection of our appreciation for the love that Jesus expressed for us at that time. —1 John 4:19.

15 The hope of one day living in a heavenly home is part of the joy set before those chosen to be corulers with Christ. (Revelation 20:6) Jesus introduces this

hope, saying: "I am going my way to prepare a place for you. . . . I am coming again and will receive you home to myself." (John 14:2-4) What a homecoming awaits all who remain faithful to the end! Hence, Jesus admonishes, "If you love me, you will observe my commandments." This means *all* of his commandments, including the command to teach and to make disciples.—John 14:15, 21; Matthew 28:19, 20.

16 How important it is for Jesus' followers to be in unity with him and one another! Jesus uses the illustration of a vine and its branches to stress this fact. Unity results in bearing fruit and this, in turn, glorifies the Father. (1 Corinthians 1:10; John 15:1, 5, 8) Persecution and opposition face all of Jesus' followers. But how faith-strengthening to know that Jesus maintained his integrity as a world conqueror despite all of Satan's attacks! —John 15:18-20; 16:2, 33.

17 Jesus brings the evening to a close with a heartfelt prayer to his Father. The glorification of his Father takes first place in his petition. He prays that his followers

---

13. What are the things that should now be remembered on Nisan 14?
14. (a) How is Jehovah glorified by each Memorial celebration? (b) What part does love play in remembering Jesus, and what self-examination should this prompt in the minds of all participants?
15. (a) What hope of life is set before all who partake worthily? (b) How is love for Jesus proved?

16. (a) How did Jesus stress the need for unity among his followers, and why is this unity so important? (b) To what must all of Jesus' followers face up, but what helps them to do this?
17. Discuss some of Jesus' requests in his prayer recorded in John chapter 17.

Can You Recall—

□ Who partake of the Memorial emblems?

□ What important matters should the Memorial bring to mind?

□ How is daily remembrance of Jesus proved?

□ What important issue is always associated with Nisan 14?

will be protected from the wicked one, Satan, as they remain separate from the world. And he also prays that the same loving unity that exists between him and the Father may continue to grow among his ever-increasing number of footstep followers.—John chapter 17.

¹⁸ We have considered only a few of the precious truths and thoughts that Jesus shared with his disciples on that night about 1,952 years ago, but surely these help us to understand why Nisan 14 is indeed a day for remembering. Little wonder it is, then, that last year 7,416,974 of Jehovah's Witnesses and their friends saw the importance of assembling together to observe the Lord's Evening Meal. And yet, of that vast multitude, there were only 9,081 who partook of the em-

---

18. Considering the total number attending the Memorial in 1984, why did so few partake of the emblems?

blems. Why? Because the vast majority of Jehovah's Witnesses today see themselves as part of the "great crowd" that stands *before the throne and before the Lamb.*" These look forward to living on planet Earth as their everlasting home, not to living in the heavens where the 144,000 will "rule as kings with [Christ] for the thousand years."—Revelation 7:9; 20:6; Psalm 37:11.

¹⁹ Some questions, however, have arisen regarding the relationship between the Lord's Evening Meal and the "great crowd" of "other sheep." (John 10:16) It seems appropriate, then, that these matters be discussed in the following article, so that there will be no misunderstanding on the part of anyone as another Memorial celebration draws near.—1 Thessalonians 5:21.

---

19. What forms the basis for next week's study, and why is it important that all should attend?

The "Other Sheep" and the Lord's Evening Meal

"[Jesus] is a propitiatory sacrifice for our sins, yet not for ours only but also for the whole world's."—1 JOHN 2:2.

JESUS said: "This good news of the kingdom will be preached in all the inhabited earth for a witness to all the nations; and then the end will come."

---

1. What positive results have come from the 'preaching of the good news of the kingdom'?

(Matthew 24:14) Some of the generation of 1914 still survive to testify that Jehovah's Witnesses have faithfully carried out this command. As a result, hundreds of thousands of honest-hearted people, disillusioned by this world's failures, have responded positively to the good news. They have dedicated themselves to Jehovah God and given their allegiance to his Kingdom, making known this dedication by water baptism. There were 179,421 that took such a course of wisdom during 1984. In effect, they said to God's name people: "We will go with you people, for we have heard that God is with you people." —Zechariah 8:23.

2 This ever-increasing "great crowd" of worshipers is part of those described by Jesus as his "other sheep." (Revelation 7: 9, 15; John 10:16) They have the grand hope of living forever in an earthly paradise. (Psalm 37:29) Jesus foretold that he would bring together these faithful followers of his *after first* giving his undivided shepherding attention to the gathering of a "little flock" of sheeplike ones toward whom he mediates the new covenant. (Luke 12:32; Hebrews 9:15) Having in mind this gathering of two sheeplike classes of people into "one flock," we can understand why the apostle John stated that Jesus Christ "is a propitiatory sacrifice for our sins, yet not for ours only but also for the whole world's."—1 John 2: 1, 2.

Changes in Viewpoint

3 Many newly gathered ones of the "other sheep" used to celebrate Mass or Communion, the frequency and manner of celebration being governed by the beliefs of the particular religious organization to which they belonged. Now, however, these have come to realize that the Lord's Evening Meal should be celebrated only *once* each year. Why is this so? Well, the Jewish Passover was celebrated just *once* each

2. What factor has governed the timing for Jesus' gathering his "other sheep"?
3, 4. (a) What changed viewpoint have many had regarding celebrating the Lord's Evening Meal? (b) What did Paul mean by saying, "For as often as you eat . . . and drink"?

year, and Jesus started the Memorial on that same Passover night, Nisan 14. He then told his disciples: "Keep doing this in remembrance of me." Paul adds: "For as often as you eat this loaf and drink this cup, you keep proclaiming the death of the Lord, until he arrives." (1 Corinthians 11: 24-26) Jesus clearly meant that his disciples should keep the celebration of his death on the Passover Day, which came once a year. Therefore, it has been celebrated "often" during the lifetime of the Christian congregation. In fact, the Memorial has already been celebrated 1,952 times.

4 There is another important difference in viewpoint that the "other sheep" class have come to appreciate. Instead of partaking of the bread and the wine as many of them formerly did in some church, they now find their situation "readjusted" to that of onlookers. Why is this so, and do we have Scriptural support for a procedure that allows for onlookers as well as partakers?—2 Corinthians 13:11; 2 Timothy 3:16, 17.

5 For anyone to benefit from the "propitiatory sacrifice" of Christ Jesus, there are certain steps that need to be taken, regardless of whether that one entertains the hope of life in heaven or he entertains the hope of life in the earthly Paradise. These fundamental steps are as follows: (1) taking in accurate knowledge of God's Word (Romans 10:13-15); (2) exercising faith (Hebrews 11:6); (3) repentance (Matthew 4:17); (4) conversion (Acts 3:19); (5) dedication (Luke 9:23); and (6) baptism (Matthew 28:19). It is after these steps have been taken that God acts in a special way toward a person he chooses to be one of the 144,000, or "little

5. (a) Describe the fundamental steps a person must take to benefit from Jesus' sacrifice. (b) Why has God specially acted on behalf of 144,000 of Christ Jesus' followers?

The Memorial deepens love for Jehovah and his Son

flock." For what purpose? In order for the person to become God's spiritual son with the prospect of being a priest and a king with Christ Jesus. (Revelation 20:4, 6) There is only a remnant of such spiritual sons now living, and these are the ones who properly partake of the emblems. This, then, accounts for the vast majority of Jehovah's Witnesses being observers and not partakers.

The Passover and the Memorial

6 Some have suggested that the increasing great number of "other sheep" should partake of the emblems. Their reasoning is: Since "the Law has a shadow of the good things to come," and since one of the

requirements of the Law was the keeping of the Passover by both Israelites and circumcised alien residents, this would imply that both classes of sheeplike ones in the "one flock" under the "one shepherd" ought to partake of the Memorial emblems. (Hebrews 10:1; John 10:16; Numbers 9:14) This raises an important question: Was the Passover a type of the Memorial?

7 It is true that *certain features* of the Passover observance in Egypt were undoubtedly fulfilled in Jesus. Paul likens Jesus to the Passover lamb, saying, "Christ our passover has been sacrificed." (1 Corinthians 5:7) The sprinkling of the Passover lamb's blood on the doorposts

___
6. Why have some contended that the "other sheep" should partake of the emblems, and what question does this raise?

___
7. In what respects was the Passover "a shadow of the good things to come"?

and lintels assured deliverance for the firstborn within each Israelite home. Similarly, it is through the sprinkling of Christ's blood that "the congregation of the firstborn who have been enrolled in the heavens" receive their deliverance, or "release by ransom." (Hebrews 12:23, 24; Ephesians 1:3, 7) Furthermore, not a bone of the Passover lamb was to be broken, and this also found fulfillment in Christ Jesus. (Exodus 12:46; Psalm 34:20; John 19:36) Hence, it is true to say that the Passover, in certain respects, was *one* of the many features in the Law that provided "a shadow of the good things to come." All these features pointed forward to Christ Jesus, "the Lamb of God."—John 1:29.

8 Nevertheless, the Passover was *not strictly* a type of the Lord's Evening Meal. Why not? When the Passover was instituted in Egypt, the flesh of the roasted lamb was eaten, but none of the blood of the Passover lamb was eaten. In contrast, however, when Jesus instituted the Memorial of his death he specifically instructed those then present to eat his flesh and

---

8-10. (a) In what important respect concerning the blood did the Passover differ from the Memorial? (b) How do the covenants associated with the Memorial highlight another difference? (c) To what conclusion does this lead us?

In Our Next Issue

■ **Unraveling the Mystery of Kimbilikiti**

■ **Shedding Forth Light Amidst Earth's Gloom**

■ **'Preaching in Favourable Season and in Troublesome Season'**

drink his blood, symbolized by the bread and the wine. (Exodus 12:7, 8; Matthew 26:27, 28) In this very important aspect —the blood—the Passover was not a type of the Lord's Evening Meal.

9 There is something else that should not be overlooked. Jesus discussed two related covenants with his disciples, "the new covenant" and 'a covenant for a kingdom.' (Luke 22:20, 28-30) Both covenants had to do with the partakers' being in line to share as priests and kings with Christ Jesus. But in Israel no circumcised alien resident could ever become a priest or a king. In this respect, also, we find a distinction between the Passover feast in Israel and the Lord's Evening Meal.

10 So to what conclusion does this lead us? The fact that the circumcised alien resident ate of the unleavened bread, bitter herbs, and lamb of the Passover does not establish that those today of the Lord's "other sheep" who are present at the Memorial should partake of the bread and the wine.

3-27-96

Importance of Attending the Memorial

11 Does this, however, indicate that it is not important for those of the "other sheep" class to be present at the celebration of the Memorial? Certainly not! This is an occasion for all of Jesus' sheeplike followers to remember Jesus in a very special sense. The "other sheep" on that occasion recall that they have already benefited because of their faith in Christ's shed blood to the extent that they are now viewed by Jehovah as having "washed their robes and made them white in the blood of the Lamb." This is why they are able to render "sacred service day and night in [God's] temple." (Revelation 7:

---

11. For what important reasons should the "other sheep" attend the Memorial?

14, 15) They can also remember that they have to keep on 'seeking Jehovah, righteousness, and meekness' with the hope of being spared during "the day of Jehovah's anger," and thereafter having the joy of attaining to human perfection. Finally they can be declared actually righteous by Jehovah, which will be after Jesus hands over the Kingdom to his Father.—Zephaniah 2:2, 3; 1 Corinthians 15:24; Revelation 20:5.

[12] Another important reason to be in attendance is the fact that the truths discussed during the Memorial talk are among "the deep things of God," 'solid food belonging to mature people,' not just the milk of "primary doctrine." (1 Corinthians 2:10; Hebrews 5:13–6:1) The Scriptural discourse will deepen appreciation for the love Jehovah displayed in setting

12. What benefits result from listening to the Memorial talk?

3-27-96

Showing Respect for the Lord's Evening Meal

Emblems to Be Used

Unleavened bread: Bread, such as unseasoned Jewish matzoth, made only with wheat flour and water may be used. Do not use matzoth that are made with added ingredients such as salt, sugar, malt, eggs or onions. You can make your own unleavened bread using the following recipe: Mix one and a half cups of wheat flour (if unobtainable, use rice, corn or another grain flour) with one cup of water, making a moist dough. Then roll dough to wafer thickness. Place it in a baking pan and liberally fork it with small holes. Bake it in a hot oven until it is dry and crisp.

Wine: Use an unadulterated red grape wine such as Chianti, Burgundy, or a claret. Avoid dessert wines that have been fortified or altered with brandy, such as sherry, port or muscatel. Do not use wines with spices or herbs added to them, like Dubonnet and other aperitif wines. A homemade red wine may also be used if it has not been sweetened, spiced or fortified.

Kingdom Hall Preparation

Table for emblems: Cover table with a clean tablecloth and sufficient plates and wine glasses for efficient serving. The bread may be broken and the wine poured prior to the meeting. Jesus did not establish any ritualistic precedent regarding this matter. If conditions demand, cover the emblems with a clean cloth to protect from insects.

Servers: Instruct beforehand regarding procedure to be followed so as to avoid any delay or confusion in serving emblems to all in attendance, including the speaker and the servers.

Attendants: Sufficient attendants should be on hand well before the start of the meeting so that all can be welcomed on arrival and provided with a seat.

Flower decoration: This may be provided, but it should be simple and tasteful.

Meeting Procedure

Time of celebration: Although the talk may start earlier, the emblems should not be passed until after sundown. It should be determined locally when sundown occurs on April 4 in your locality.

Memorial talk: The speaker should prepare well so that he can present his material within the allotted time. It should be clearly presented and encouraging to all present.

up such a wonderful Kingdom arrangement for the blessing of the human family. It is also an opportunity for 'looking more intently at the Chief Agent and Perfecter of our faith, Jesus.' Never should the love Jesus displayed on our behalf, nor the sufferings he went through, be taken for granted. (Hebrews 12:2, 3) Furthermore, we all can agree that many of the precious thoughts Jesus discussed with his apostles when instituting the Memorial—thoughts regarding unity, love, and glorification of Jehovah's name—can be shared by the "other sheep" as well as the "little flock."

Showing Loving Concern for All

[13] It is important that everyone present at the Lord's Evening Meal be reminded of the procedure instituted by Jesus. The actual passing of the bread and the wine from one to the other helps to deepen appreciation for the sacred things that have just been discussed that evening. It also enables each one to go on record as indicating what his hope of life is—heavenly or earthly.* Following the proper procedure brings the congregation into line with what is being done earth wide that evening.—1 Corinthians 14:40.

[14] Suppose one of the anointed in a congregation is sick and unable to attend the Memorial. What then? Every effort should be made to have one of the elders take the emblems to that ill Christian and, if convenient, the elder can make a few appro-

---

* In one large congregation the practice has been for those serving the emblems to stand at the end of each row of seats and gesture to those in the row. Anyone wishing to partake had to indicate this to the server. However, as indicated above, this would not be appropriate.

---

13. Why is it important to have the emblems passed to all in attendance?
14. How can the elders show loving concern for one of the anointed who is sick on the night of the Memorial?

priate comments before offering the emblems and closing with a fitting prayer. How encouraged the sick person will feel! Such acts of loving concern promote a spirit of love within the congregation. (See also page 31.)—Psalm 133:1.

[15] Other interesting questions have been raised regarding procedure and the type of emblems to be used at the Memorial. The answers to these questions will be found on page 19 under "Showing Respect for the Lord's Evening Meal." The responsible elders would do well to follow carefully what is outlined therein.

The Need for Self-Examination

[16] There are some who are distressed by doubts as to whether they are entitled to partake of the emblems. This question sometimes arises in the weeks before another celebration of the Lord's Evening Meal. Frequently such inquiries are made by some who have recently become associated with Jehovah's Witnesses. Are you one who has had doubts of this kind pass through your mind? How can you determine the right course to take?

[17] Paul recommended regarding the Lord's Evening Meal: "First let a man approve himself after scrutiny, and thus let him eat of the loaf and drink of the cup." (1 Corinthians 11:28, 29) Did you notice that Paul says you are the one who is to do the 'approving after scrutiny'? Of course, it is not wrong to talk over such a serious matter with a mature Christian, but you alone must determine your personal relationship with Jehovah and his Son. God leaves none of the 144,000 in

---

15. Describe some other ways by which respect can be shown for the Lord's Evening Meal.
16, 17. (a) What question have some asked regarding participation in the Memorial, and who alone can give the answer? (b) How does God provide convincing evidence for those begotten by his spirit?

doubt. We are assured: "The spirit itself bears witness with our spirit that we are God's children." It is God's spirit that awakens in the heart of any member of Christ's body the conviction that he is one of God's spiritual sons. The chosen one knows this and does not have to ask another in the congregation for confirmation.—Romans 8:15, 16.

[18] The modern history of Jehovah's Witnesses shows that since 1931 more attention started to be given to the "other sheep" through the Kingdom message. Then on May 31, 1935, with the delivering of the talk "The Great Multitude,"* the "great crowd" that the apostle John saw in vision was clearly identified with the "other sheep." What did this new emphasis indicate? Surely that the gathering of the "little flock" was drawing to a close and the time had come for Jesus, through the administration of "the faithful and discreet slave," to turn his attention to gathering the "other sheep."—Matthew 24: 45-47.

[19] With the foregoing in mind, we say to all those who have recently become associated with Jehovah's people and who may have made some claim to being one of the anointed class: Examine carefully your relationship with Jehovah. Ask yourself, Is the heavenly hope that I profess to have somehow a holdover from a previously held church teaching that all church members go to heaven? Is my hope in any way connected with some selfish desire or emotional feelings? Paul said: "It is impossible for God to lie." (Hebrews 6:18) Nor can the

holy spirit of adoption lie. Therefore, anyone genuinely begotten by God's spirit is not continually disturbed with doubts but is able to testify in all good conscience that he is one of God's sons.

Celebrating in 1985

[20] The Lord's Evening Meal is, without question, the year's greatest celebration for all true Christians. There is no other occasion like it in regard to importance, purpose or procedure. Hence, as the earth turns on its axis, causing the sun progressively to sink below the horizon around the earth, every congregation of Jehovah's Witnesses, large and small alike, and every isolated group will meet together in obedience to the Master's command.

[21] All sheeplike disciples are therefore overjoyed at the prospect of sharing together in another Memorial celebration. May this year's occasion prove to be a time of upbuilding encouragement to all of Jehovah's servants. May it instill in them the same spirit of confidence as that of their Exemplar, Jesus Christ, who said: "Take courage! I have conquered the world."—John 16:33.

---

20. Of what importance is the Memorial to Jehovah's Witnesses?
21. What attitude and expectations should the Memorial in 1985 raise in the hearts of God's people?

---

* This talk was given at Washington, D.C., by J. F. Rutherford, then president of the Watch Tower Bible and Tract Society.

---

18. What historical facts regarding the "other sheep" are of interest to us?
19. What personal examination may be advisable for those newer ones who have laid claim to being of the anointed?

Can You Recall—

☐ Why was the Passover not a type of the Memorial?

☐ What six steps must be taken before benefiting from Jesus' sacrifice?

☐ Why is your attendance at the Memorial so vital?

☐ Why is self-examination beneficial before the Memorial?

Does Greed Sometimes Grip You?

HAVE you been at a party where delicious food and alcoholic drinks were plentiful and you were tempted to overindulge? Many will admit that, at times, a form of greed does grip them. Can you always resist it? Or has it sometimes overtaken you, resulting in a headache or a hangover or worse? What are some other consequences of greed? How can we overcome its subtle grip? This is a vital matter, for the Bible says that no 'greedy person will inherit God's kingdom.' —1 Corinthians 6:10.

Greed has been defined as excessive desire, or avarice, a rapacious desire for more than one needs or deserves. It can take different forms, including: love of money, desire for power or fame, voraciousness for food, drink, sex, and material possessions. It is the basic cause of many evils that bedevil us today. Why are illicit sex and crime of all kinds increasing? Why are millions of people overfed and other millions starving? Why is so much money squandered in gambling and lotteries? What lies behind the embezzlement of private and public funds, commercial exploitation, and corruption of public officials? And what is behind wars with their ghastly aftermath of ruin and suffering? The depraving grip of greed.

Sexual Greed and Its Consequences

Greed can take very ugly forms and seriously degrade one's life. For example, a married man with a fine family had an inordinate greed for sex. One day, under the influence of alcohol, he followed two girls to their home, hoping to seduce them. But their father and a relative came out and beat him up. He was taken to the hospital with a cracked skull, broken jaw, and badly damaged eye. His young daughter was so upset that she tried to commit suicide. His whole family felt shocked and degraded. What a price for his giving in to sexual greed!

An experience of King David of Israel confirms this point. David already had a number of wives. But one day he saw from his rooftop the beautiful woman Bath-sheba bathing herself. Instead of immediately turning away and dismissing the thought, he allowed illicit sexual desire to take root in his heart. He then committed adultery with her while her husband, Uriah, was away fighting in David's army.

When Bath-sheba became pregnant, David first tried to have his adultery covered up by having Uriah come home and lie with his wife. However, when that ruse failed, and he was faced with the terrible alternative of having Bath-sheba stoned as an adulteress, he opted for having Uriah exposed to sure death in battle. But nothing goes unobserved by Jehovah. He sent his prophet Nathan to rebuke David for his heinous crimes—adultery and bringing about the death of the woman's husband. David was cut to the heart and humbly accepted the rebuke. Still, he paid a heavy price. His first son by Bath-sheba died as a babe, and his family from then

Judas Iscariot came to be gripped by greed

on was plagued with calamities.—2 Samuel 11: 1–12:23; chapter 13.

This warning example of yielding to temptation well illustrates the chain reaction of sin as set forth in the Bible: "Each one is tried by being drawn out and enticed by his own desire. Then the desire, when it has become fertile, gives birth to sin; in turn, sin, when it has been accomplished, brings forth death." (James 1: 14, 15) The mistake David made was to allow the seed of greedy sexual desire to take root and grow in his heart. Once the sinful desire was triggered, he let sexual greed motivate him into misconduct.

What a contrast was Joseph in Egypt when he was enticed by Potiphar's wife to lie down with her! How did Joseph react to this temptation? The account tells us: "So it turned out that as she spoke to Joseph day after day he never listened to her to lie alongside her, to continue with her." Even without the moral guidance of the Ten Commandments, which had not yet been given, he had answered her insistence by saying: "How could I commit this great badness and actually sin against God?" Then finally one day she grabbed hold of him, saying, "Lie down with me!" Did Joseph stay around and try to reason

or rationalize? He "took to flight and went on outside." He did not even give sexual greed a chance to germinate in his heart. He fled.—Genesis 39:7-16.

No sincere Christian would actually lay plans to pursue a course that manifests sexual greed. But, then, David had not planned to sin as he did. So his example should move all of us to strengthen our personal resolve to resist any stirring toward greed in illicit sexual matters. We —whether single or married, youthful or older—need to be absolutely determined to reject any such temptations as soon as they arise.—Romans 13:13, 14.

Greed for Money and Its Consequences

A gross example of a greedy person was the most infamous traitor in human history—Judas Iscariot. When chosen by Jesus as an apostle, he must have been faithful up to that point and not greedy. In fact, Jesus made him the trustee of their

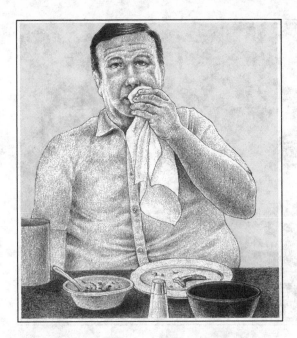

etary excess and overweight in the adult are not good for life expectancy."

Far more serious to a Christian is the spiritual danger inherent in greed. Materialism has caused some Christian wives, whose husbands earn reasonable pay, to seek employment even if the result is neglect of their children and fewer blessings in the preaching work. It has caused young Christians to succumb to the glitter of well-paying jobs without even seriously considering entering the full-time ministry. Catering to the flesh, whether illicit sex or greed for money (and pleasures and possessions it can buy) can lead to serious sins and even loss of everlasting life. "For the minding of the flesh means death, . . . for if you live in accord with the flesh you are sure to die."—Romans 8:6, 13.

How Can We Prevent or Overcome the Grip of Greed?

Once greed has gripped a person, it is hard to break loose. Therefore prevention is better than cure. Parents need to curb greedy trends in themselves first and then in their children. Most children tend to be selfish. A story is told that one day Abraham Lincoln was taking his two small sons for a walk, but they were crying. A neighbor inquired: "What's the matter with the boys?" Replied Lincoln: "Just what's the matter with the whole world. I've got three walnuts, and each wants two."

Parents should "train up" boys and girls in the way of unselfishness and consider-

funds. But in time Judas began to steal some of the money. "He was a thief and had the money box and used to carry off the monies put in it."—John 12:6.

Obviously, Judas had become a practicing thief, a greedy person. When the climactic Passover drew near in 33 C.E., Judas, after having been rebuked by Jesus, made a deal with the murderous chief priests to betray the Lord for 30 pieces of silver. Later, Judas felt the enormity of his deed and committed suicide. Greed's deadly grip claimed another victim. —Luke 22:3; Matthew 26:14-16.

The evil consequences of greed are legion. Many who greedily pursue a lot of money spend much of it on a luxurious life-style. They may turn their back on simple food and concentrate on highly refined luxury foods. Yet overindulging in rich foods that wealth can purchase often boomerangs on them in indigestion or worse problems that can hasten death. Says a medical expert: "It is a hard business fact of the insurance world that diation for others, consistently and lovingly. (Proverbs 22:6) This will help them very much during the teenage stage when sexual appetites and other selfish desires may become strong. Young people are constantly besieged these days by sexual provocation. However, the Bible says: "Let fornication and uncleanness of every sort or greediness *not even be mentioned among you,* just as it befits holy people; neither shameful conduct nor foolish talking nor obscene jesting, things which are not becoming . . . No fornicator or unclean person *or greedy person—which means being an idolater—*has any inheritance in the kingdom of the Christ and of God." —Ephesians 5:3-5.

Note that a "greedy person" is also "an idolater." How so? Those who become obsessed with desire for sex, love for money (such as expressed by thieving, embezzling, and gambling), voraciousness for food and drink, or ambition for power and fame, become slaves to such desires and make them their idols, as it were. Their chief aim in life is to satisfy their greedy desire. Christians who practice such things in an idolatrous way are unquestionably "greedy persons," in Biblical terminology, and could be excluded from the congregation. They have put worship of their "gods" above worship of Jehovah, who is "a God exacting exclusive devotion."—Exodus 20:3-6, 17.

Giving attention to radio and TV programs or books and magazines that stir up greed for harmful things is very dangerous for Christians—young and old. Remember that David failed to avert his gaze from Bath-sheba bathing and, in a weak moment, got caught in sensual greed. Do you turn off the TV or walk out of the cinema when immorality is featured?

David, in spite of his lapse, had a deep love for Jehovah. This helped him to recover from his transgression. Similarly, a long-time Christian in Africa was able to recover from a bad case of greed for money. Due to certain difficulties he had got into debt. Being responsible for the financial affairs of the firm he worked for, he was tempted to "borrow" money without permission. He allowed that "seed" of greed to germinate, and he embezzled a large amount. When his employers began to inquire into the matter, he panicked and fled the country, leaving his wife and children behind. But his conscience soon smote him, and he realized he had made a terrible mistake. He returned home and eventually restored the whole amount. He was reproved by Christian elders and is now making commendable progress.

What helped him to recover? Prayer and Bible reading. He found that many expressions in David's psalms struck a sympathetic chord in his own heart, helping him to pray more fervently and meaningfully. Here are a few examples of those psalms: "Show me favor, O God, according to your loving-kindness. According to the abundance of your mercies wipe out my transgressions. Create in me even a pure heart, O God, and put within me a new spirit, a steadfast one." "Also from presumptuous acts hold your servant back; do not let them dominate me."—Psalm 51:1, 10; 19:13.

If you want to avoid or overcome the grip of greed, "draw close to God, and he will draw close to you." (James 4:8) When a Christian's heart is filled with love for Jehovah, for the Christian brothers, and for the many who need help in these distressing times, then the ugly "seed" of greed finds it more difficult to germinate. Moreover, the holy spirit is an excellent greed killer! So let that powerful force pour into your heart, cleansing it of unclean desires, and filling it with a deep longing to serve Jehovah. Then the loathsome force of greed will not grip you.

Insight on the News

Churches Under Pressure

"The issue of homosexuality is troubling religious groups throughout America," states *The New York Times.* "They are under pressure from the outside to ease their traditional hostility and from within to revise their theology." Underlying factors behind the pressures are the changing attitudes toward sex and the contention that Bible passages have been "misinterpreted or even mistranslated by opponents of homosexuality." For example, critics of the traditional interpretation say that the city of Sodom was destroyed for lack of hospitality, so vital to ancient travelers, and for intention to rape the visitors—not for homosexual practices. They also maintain that, at Romans 1:26, 27, the apostle Paul's reference to changing "the natural use of themselves into one contrary to nature," simply means "departures from cultural norms, not homosexuality as an aberration from nature." Consequently, a number of churches have been modifying their attitude toward homosexuals, and some have even accepted homosexuals as ministers.

But is such "modernization" in harmony with *God's* will? "No; I, Yahweh, do not change," the Creator emphatically states at Malachi 3:6. (*The Jerusalem Bible*) The Bible also states explicitly that neither "men kept for unnatural purposes, nor men who lie with men . . . will inherit God's kingdom." (1 Corinthians 6:9, 10; compare Leviticus 20:13.) Rather than calling on Christians to adopt a more liberal view toward those who sin against God, the Bible advises: "Put away all filthiness and that superfluous thing, badness, and accept with mildness the implanting of the word which is able to save your souls." —James 1:21.

Religious Revival?

"Gallup surveys show that more Americans think religion is important to them than similar polls showed five years ago," reports *The New York Times.* It adds: "On every scale measured by Gallup, Americans profess conventional theological beliefs." Total church membership has also increased. But is this truly a religious revival? "While we are clearly a religious country," says George Gallup, Jr., "religion doesn't appear to be the center of many lives. The commitment is low in terms of religion having primacy." Moreover, a comparison of church members and nonmembers revealed little difference as to personal morality. "Both samples," says the *Times,* "showed considerable deviation from traditional Christian moral standards."

While some analysts concede that there is a religious awakening, they find serious omissions. "It hasn't sparked a revival of ethical rigor or study of the Bible for ethical principles," says Professor Timothy Smith, church history specialist at Johns Hopkins University. "Without that, many people can feel spiritual and still indulge their secular yearnings for wealth, power and achievement. They can claim to be religious but not apply it to the ethical part of their lives." As Jesus pointed out, such persons 'honor God with their lips, yet their heart is far removed from him.' Mere lip service, however, does not please the Creator. Such worship, he says, is "in vain." (Matthew 15:8, 9) Rather, what is required is for a person to dedicate his life to God and to love Him with his whole heart, soul, mind, and strength. (Mark 12:30) Yes, God looks for those who will worship him "with spirit and truth."—John 4:23, 24.

Discipline Needed

Impatient, self-centered, and contrary children are a growing trend, says child psychologist Thomas Millar. He holds that such children are linked to the increase in juvenile delinquency, broken marriages, and mental disease. The problem, says Millar in the *Toronto Star,* is discipline. Modern child-rearing theories have caused parents to feel guilty and afraid to discipline their children. "You can't have a society without rules," says Millar. "The parent has to train the kid to belong to society . . . this leaves the door open for a much richer life." This advice, however, is not new. Centuries ago the Bible noted that "foolishness is tied up with the heart of a boy; the rod of discipline is what will remove it far from him." It advised: "Train up a boy according to the way for him; even when he grows old he will not turn aside from it."—Proverbs 22:15, 6.

Ugandans Express Appreciation for "the Real Life"

SUDAN
KENYA
ZAIRE
UGANDA
Kampala●
Lake Victoria

THE sunrise over Kampala, Uganda's capital, is often strikingly beautiful. From any one of its seven hills, you can breathe the invigorating morning air. Fresh carpets of green shaded by trees of many forms are offset by the multicolored blossoms of hibiscus, poinciana and bougainvillea. Sunbirds, hornbills and shrikes move about in the branches, and the cry of the ibis resounds from above. How wonderful life can be!

Contemplating such scenes in this beautiful country, it is difficult not to feel thankful for life and the wonderful opportunity offered by the Giver of life to live in an earthly paradise forever.

Yet many people do not easily think of that. To them Uganda is not "the Pearl of Africa." In their minds Uganda evokes memories of trouble. Many people in Uganda itself are preoccupied with the fear of crime, and they worry about inflation. In less than ten years bread prices have soared from 1/20 shilling to 200 shillings. Most families have lost relatives and friends in violent death, which has led to the general conclusion that "life is cheap these days." But the Originator of life, Jehovah God, attaches great value to life, as his written Word reveals. About half of Uganda's 15 million people claim to accept the Bible as God's Word, and many respond when their attention is turned to the Bible's explanation of the root causes of suffering and God's purpose to have happy humans taste "the real life" on a paradise earth.—1 Timothy 6:19.

Forty Years of Early Efforts

The good news of God's Kingdom and of "the real life" first came to Uganda in 1931. Full-time pioneer preachers of Jehovah's Witnesses from Southern Africa sailed to Mombasa, traveled through what today is Kenya, and reached fertile Uganda. It was a country of perpetual summer with even rainfall—a land full of cotton, coffee, plantains, cassava, and other crops. The visitors found a mixture of over 30 tribes, some of which were very proud of a history that included past kingdoms. Since many people knew English as a second language, much initial interest concerning God's Kingdom was easily located. A similar journey was made in 1935, but the pioneers had to move on, and years went by without much preaching work in the Ugandan field.

> **By close association at meetings and a regular diet of spiritual food, they remained cheerful**

By 1952 Kampala had a small congregation of four publishers. Three years later, N. H. Knorr, then the president of the Watch Tower Society, and M. G. Henschel, still a member of the Governing Body of Jehovah's Witnesses, visited Kampala, and the first Ugandan baptism took place in Lake Victoria. Later some of the publishers moved, and other setbacks occurred. So in 1958 just one publisher of the life-giving good news was left.

In 1962 Uganda ceased being a colony. During this time period the first group of foreign Witnesses moved in, mainly from Britain and Canada, to help where a greater need existed for making Jehovah God's purposes known. Soon the first graduates of the Watchtower Bible School of Gilead arrived, and other towns were reached with the Kingdom message. Steady increase ensued, leading up to 110 publishers in 1971.

Times of Turbulence and Trial

Dramatic political changes then occurred, and these have become well known all over the world. Instability and fear provoked an exodus of foreigners and Ugandans alike. The missionaries of Jehovah's Witnesses had to leave in 1973. Religious freedom was restricted by bans. A climate of fear persisted. Daily necessities vanished from the shops. Many people disappeared without court trials. Daily, people lived in the shadow of death. Finally, in 1979, war broke out, leading to subsequent changes in government.

While some Ugandans became despondent during these times, others hungered for comfort all the more. Jehovah's Witnesses knew that all of this was temporary and that God provides not only practical guidance in such difficult times but also the solution to all man's problems. By close association at meetings and a regular diet of spiritual food, they remained cheerful. Observers could see that they had something special that other religions did not have. Interesting experiences can be told from these turbulent times.

A family man experienced Jehovah's protection often. He belonged to a tribe whose members were denounced and hunted down for extermination. On one occasion his house was assaulted with grenades and bullets for an hour. While this was happening he reminded his wife and children to remember Jehovah's words to Joshua, "Be courageous and strong," and they prayed together. (Joshua 1:6) Surprisingly, no bullet pierced the house, and the grenades rebounded from the exterior walls, exploding at a distance. Then the brother went outside and reasoned with the attackers. Some neighbors spoke in his favor too. During a search of the house the attackers found his Bible study aids, so they left him alone as a religious man. During the next two days he was denounced again and had two more encounters with death, but with Jehovah's help he survived.

A former high official who had taken his stand for true Christianity was arrested several times. Two of his sons disappeared, never to be seen again. This did not shatter his trust in the Giver of life, nor dim his wonderful hope of the resurrection and "the real life" ahead. He zealously preached to his fellow prisoners, starting several Bible studies. A former soldier especially showed great appreciation and made rapid progress. After a few months, that man began to share in the preaching work in prison. Hence, when the Witness was released, six Bible studies were turned over to the care of the former soldier. What a fine surprise it was for the former high official and the former soldier when, some years later, they met at a class of the Pioneer Service School arranged by Jehovah's Witnesses for full-time preachers. Yes, the former soldier had also become a pioneer! The brother who taught him the truth could say, "I have lost my fleshly sons, but now I have gained a spiritual son."

A mother of seven children who has been a Witness for over 13 years had her endurance tested many times. At first her husband opposed her new faith. Then turbulent events made him flee to Kenya, leaving her alone with all the children for two years. Upon his return he was arrested, and during his imprisonment thieves broke into the house, stealing practically all the family's possessions. This sister's keeping active in the truth and shunning worldly associations helped her to find comfort and to endure. Her steadfastness and joy impressed her husband, who upon his release showed interest in the Bible before death overtook him at an early age. But the congregation strengthened this faithful woman. A fellow Witness helped her to start a small business so she could care for her children. She teaches her children and others the wonderful hope of everlasting life on earth without problems, and she conducts six Bible studies.

Elderly people are generally respected in Uganda, and Anna, well into her 60's, used her opportunities by becoming a pioneer preacher. Instead of joining her neighbors in talking about miseries, she talked to them about good news during these turbulent times. Then she had the joy of attending a special school for pioneer ministers conducted in the neighboring land of Kenya. While there, she received mail from relatives urging her

The hills of southwest Uganda

not to return to Uganda, as life was too dangerous and too difficult. One relative living in Kenya offered to house her and to look after her, but she told all that she had a message of comfort and hope of a better life, which people in Uganda needed. So she returned to Uganda.

Appreciation for Assemblies

With the changes in government after the war of 1979, freedom of worship was restored, which made all of Jehovah's Witnesses very happy. Assemblies could once again be held, and the enormous demand for Bible literature indicated that many people yearn for good news of a better life. District conventions were arranged, and in December 1983 a Bible drama was presented for the first time. It made a deep impression on the audience, for it dealt with family life. The next day 572, about twice the number of all of Uganda's active Witnesses, came to the Sports Hall at Kampala's Lugogo Stadium and enjoyed Kingdom unity with people who truly appreciate life.

A group of newly baptized Witnesses

Many had made sacrifices to be there. In some instances the train fare for a married couple was higher than a schoolteacher's monthly salary. For several families the convention trip cost up to four months' salary! Many who were present showed such appreciation for the spiritual things.

Missionary Experiences

Late in 1982 four foreign missionaries were able to take up service in Kampala. They were like a new generation of missionaries after an interruption of many years. The very first person with whom one of them shared the good news was a young man who must have been waiting for the message of hope. A Bible study was started immediately and held twice a week. On the first day that the young man joined another Witness in the field ministry, the two were held up by armed criminals. Though inexperienced, he trusted in Jehovah and started to preach to them. For several tense minutes the thieves debated whether or not to kill them. Then one of the gun-toting men told his associates to let the two go. What did the young man do following this nerve-shaking experience? Without hesitation he and his partner went on to the next house to continue preaching! He is now baptized and has his eyes set on the treasure of the pioneer ministry.

One of the missionaries met a man who had worked in Mozambique. He immediately said he had high regard for Jehovah's Witnesses, for he had seen their clean and orderly camps in Mozambique.* This man was particularly touched when one day he saw a destitute family of Witnesses arriving at a camp. They were warmly welcomed by spiritual brothers from different tribes. Immediately their material needs were cared for, including a house, a field, utensils, and clothes. Now this man has tasted the same love and brotherhood himself as he enjoys a Bible study and regularly shares in Christian meetings with Jehovah's Witnesses.

It is easy to see from such experiences that the missionaries, along with their Ugandan brothers and sisters, have reason for joy. They have often experienced shortages of food, water, and electricity, and they have often heard the sound of gunshots and explosions, yet they are grateful for gradual improvements. They are content to help people see the value of "the real life." The 250 proclaimers of God's Kingdom here spent an average of over 14 hours per month in the preaching activity. There is much interest, and many are taking up the full-time preach-

* Jehovah's Witnesses from Mozambique and Malawi have been put in camps by the authorities.

ing work. At present over 500 Bible studies are being conducted in this beautiful part of the earth that, in spots, provides a foregleam of an earthly paradise. Many Ugandans are learning to turn their vision to "the real life" of eternity purposed for the very near future by the loving Provider of life, Jehovah.

Questions From Readers

■ If a Christian cannot be at the celebration of the Lord's Evening Meal, what should he do?

It is important that Christians attend the annual celebration of the Lord's Evening Meal, for Jesus said when instituting it: "Keep doing this in remembrance of me." (Luke 22:19) The early Christians did so. The apostle Paul thus could write about the Corinthian brothers who each year 'met as a congregation,' or 'came together,' for the Memorial of Jesus' sacrificial death. (1 Corinthians 11:20, *The New English Bible; NW*) But what would they have done about the Memorial in difficult circumstances? For example, what did Paul himself do during the years that he was imprisoned (under guard and perhaps even chained) in Caesarea? —Acts 23:35; 24:26, 27.

In view of Jesus' plain command, even if Paul was in isolation on the occasion of the Lord's Evening Meal, he certainly would have reviewed the Scriptural aspects of the event. Being a spirit-anointed Christian, he would have made every effort to partake of the most appropriate things he could use for emblems. Wine was then a common beverage, so despite being a prisoner Paul might have had some wine and a type of bread to use. That was even more likely when he was later confined in Rome, where he was permitted to have visitors. Probably some brothers

from Rome tried to "come together" with him in a small group to celebrate the Lord's Evening Meal.—Acts 28:30.

Around the earth today, congregations of Jehovah's Witnesses gather on the date corresponding to Nisan 14 for the Memorial of Christ's death. But sometimes unusual obstacles arise. On occasion, raging storms or floods have prevented a congregation, or some of its members, from meeting together as planned. In rare cases, martial law has been in effect with armed soldiers barring citizens from being out-of-doors after sunset. Other Christians have not been able to be at the congregation's celebration because of being hospitalized or seriously ill. What can be done in such instances?

While it is fitting for the whole congregation to unite for this important event, circumstances such as noted above may make that impossible. When extreme weather, a natural disaster, or the like, absolutely prevents a family or a portion of a congregation from meeting with the congregation, the isolated ones can meet and discuss Scriptural accounts such as found in Luke 22: 7-23, 28-30 and 1 Corinthians 11:20-31, as well as discussing the meaning of the occasion. Similarly, if an enforced curfew

makes it impossible for a congregation to gather on the appropriate night, meeting in Congregation Book Study groups or neighborhood groups might be the best alternative, the sum of those in attendance serving as the congregation's attendance report. A brief talk may even be given if a capable, dedicated brother is in the group. There need not be concern that no suitable emblems are available as long as no one in this emergency situation previously partook of the bread and the wine as an anointed Christian.

God's Law to Israel had a special arrangement for someone who was not in a position to partake of the regular Passover meal; the individual could do so a month (30 days) later. (Numbers 9:10, 11; 2 Chronicles 30: 1-3, 15) Comparably, in an extreme situation with a spiritual Israelite who absolutely cannot attend or be served the emblems on Nisan 14, he or she could partake 30 days later. This would apply only in the case of an anointed Christian who is under command to partake of the bread and the wine.—Galatians 6:16.

On April 4, 1985, after sundown, congregations of true Christians around the earth will gather in obedience to Jesus' command: "Do this as a memorial of me." We invite you to assemble with them.—1 Corinthians 11:25, *NE*.

March 1, 1985

The Watchtower

Announcing Jehovah's Kingdom

Their Loved Ones Were Massacred —Why?

March 1, 1985
Vol. 106, No. 5

The Watchtower®
Announcing Jehovah's Kingdom

In This Issue

THE PURPOSE OF "THE WATCHTOWER" is to exalt Jehovah God as the Sovereign of the universe. It keeps watch on world events as they fulfill Bible prophecy. It comforts all peoples with the good news that God's Kingdom will soon destroy those who oppress their fellowmen and that it will turn the earth into a paradise. It encourages faith in the now-reigning King, Jesus Christ, whose shed blood opens the way for mankind to gain eternal life. "The Watchtower," published by Jehovah's Witnesses continuously since 1879, is nonpolitical. It adheres to the Bible as its authority.

"WATCHTOWER" STUDIES FOR THE WEEKS

Average Printing Each Issue: 11,150,000

Now Published in 102 Languages

SEMIMONTHLY EDITIONS AVAILABLE BY MAIL
Afrikaans, Arabic, Cebuano, Chichewa, Chinese, Cibemba, Danish, Dutch, Efik, English*, Finnish, French, German, Greek, Hiligaynon, Igbo, Iloko, Italian, Japanese, Korean, Lingala, Malagasy, Maltese, Norwegian, Portuguese, Russian, Sepedi, Sesotho, Shona, Spanish, Swahili, Swedish, Tagalog, Thai, Tswana, Xhosa, Yoruba, Zulu

MONTHLY EDITIONS AVAILABLE BY MAIL
Armenian, Bengali, Bicol, Bulgarian, Croatian, Czech, Ewe, Fijian, Ga, Greenlandic, Gujarati, Gun, Hausa, Hebrew, Hindi, Hiri Motu, Hungarian, Icelandic, Kannada, Kikuyu, Kiluba, Malayalam, Marathi, New Guinea Pidgin, Pangasinan, Papiamento, Polish, Rarotongan, Romanian, Samar-Leyte, Samoan, Sango, Serbian, Silozi, Sinhalese, Slovenian, Solomon Islands-Pidgin, Tahitian, Tamil, Telugu, Tshiluba, Tsonga, Turkish, Twi, Ukrainian, Urdu, Venda, Vietnamese
*Study articles also available in large-print edition at same cost.

The Bible translation used is the "New World Translation of the Holy Scriptures," unless otherwise indicated.

Twenty cents (U.S.) a copy

Watch Tower Society offices	Yearly subscription rates Semimonthly
America, U.S., Watchtower, Wallkill, N.Y. 12589	$4.00
Australia, Box 280, Ingleburn, N.S.W. 2565	A$6.00
Canada, Box 4100, Halton Hills (Georgetown), Ontario L7G 4Y4	$4.50
England, The Ridgeway, London NW7 1RN	£5.00
Ireland, 29A Jamestown Road, Finglas, Dublin 11	£5.00
New Zealand, 6-A Western Springs Rd., Auckland 3	$7.00
Nigeria, P.O. Box 194, Yaba, Lagos State	₦3.50
Philippines, P.O. Box 2044, Manila 2800	₱50.00
South Africa, Private Bag 2, Elandsfontein, 1406	R5,60

Remittances should be sent to the office in your country or to Watchtower, Wallkill, N.Y. 12589, U.S.A.

Changes of address should reach us 30 days before your moving date. Give us your old and new address (if possible, your old address label).

The Watchtower (ISSN 0043-1087) is published semimonthly for $4.00 (U.S.) per year by Watch Tower Bible and Tract Society of Pennsylvania, 25 Columbia Heights, Brooklyn, N.Y. 11201. Second-class postage paid at Brooklyn, N.Y., and at additional mailing offices.

Postmaster: Send address changes to Watchtower, *Wallkill, N.Y. 12589.*

Published by
**Watch Tower Bible and Tract Society
of Pennsylvania**
25 Columbia Heights, Brooklyn, N.Y. 11201, U.S.A.
Frederick W. Franz, President

Martyred for Their Faith!

IT WAS very early on a Sunday morning. A mob of some 500 people surrounded a house in the village of Pangi, in Kivu province, Zaire. Christians sleeping peacefully in the home were rudely awakened by the noisy crowd and loud banging on the door. The outcome? Seven Christian men were dragged outside, mercilessly beaten and forced to march seven kilometers (4 mi) to the village of Kilungulungu in the heart of the forest.

There these peace-loving Christian men had their throats cut and one was mutilated. Their bodies were buried under a riverbed after the water had been dammed up for the occasion. Later the dam was unstopped, and the river flowed over their common grave, leaving no trace of the horrible event!

Why This Massacre of Innocents?

This massacre of faithful witnesses of Jehovah was the climax of a wave of persecution that began in 1978 throughout the part of Kivu region dominated by the Rega tribe. Why did the massacre take place? Because Jehovah's Witnesses refuse to comply with "Kimbilikiti." Leaders of this ancestral religion of the Waregas believe that the Witnesses represent the greatest threat to their whole tribal structure and must therefore be eliminated.

From 1978 to 1983 several Kingdom Halls of Jehovah's Witnesses were burned down by fanatical members of this cult. They threatened many Witnesses, chased them away from their homes, and confiscated their belongings. Often efforts were made to liquidate the Witnesses by means of sorcery and spells. Since none of these measures proved successful, the persecutors resorted to brutal mass murder.—Compare Numbers 23:23.

The Horrifying Incident

Let us, however, take a closer look at those tragic events of Sunday, August 14, 1983. Looking at the *1983 Yearbook of Jehovah's Witnesses,* how appropriate are the text and comment for that day! The day before the murder of the seven faithful

Village of Pangi

Christian men, most members of the little congregation of Jehovah's Witnesses at Pangi had walked from surrounding villages to attend their usual Saturday meeting. They all stayed overnight so as to be on hand for their Sunday morning meeting for worship. Seven people stayed in the house of Kalumba Malumalu, a full-time minister and the presiding overseer of the congregation. That made a total of 11, including Brother Malumalu, his wife, and their 2 small children. Five others found lodging in the home of Brother Kikuni Mutege.

After the Saturday meeting, the Witnesses spent a pleasant evening around a fire, singing Kingdom songs and telling experiences. They noticed that small groups of people kept drifting by with unusual regularity, all of them heading in the direction of a village two kilometers (1.2 mi) from Pangi. How could the Witnesses know what that gathering of their enemies would mean?

At about five o'clock the next morning the house of the presiding overseer was surrounded by a crowd headed by Group Chief Mulamba Musembe. It was demanded that Brothers Kampema Amuri and Waseka Tabu accompany them to the Chief of the Collectivity (Katunda Banangozi) in order to perform "Salongo" (obligatory community work for the maintenance of roads, bridges, and the like). Brother Kampema politely explained that an arrangement already had been made with Chief Katunda to do the work on the following day. But the Group Chief chose to view this reply as disrespectful and ordered that Brother Kampema be beaten. This was followed by an order to beat the other brothers.

At that point the mob realized that "pastor" Kalumba Malumalu (the presiding overseer) had gone back into his house. So they all pushed against the house until they broke through one wall. At that, several of them rushed inside to find Brother Malu-

malu. In the ensuing scuffle the sisters were manhandled, but they and their children managed to flee to the local police chief for protection.

Meanwhile, two brothers staying at the other house were able to escape. One of them (Hemedi Mwingilu) hid in an unfinished house and witnessed the incident. The other brother (Lulima Kazalwa) fled into the forest.

Finally, seven brothers were seized, beaten, and taken away with their hands bound. During the entire five-kilometer (3-mi) march to the forest near Kilungulungu, they were bullied and struck by their captors. Although the brothers were barely conscious upon arrival there, they were determined not to compromise their faith —and that even though their death was evidently imminent. They met death bravely and with dignity, as have so many other faithful Christians of ancient and modern times.—Matthew 24:9; Revelation 2:10.

Path to execution site

One other brother, Amisi Milende, was murdered shortly thereafter. He was away on a trip to Kama, but men sent there arrested him and brought him bound to Binyangi (15 kilometers [9 mi] from Pangi) to appear before Kibonge Kimpili, another Group Chief. While awaiting the Chief's arrival, this zealous Witness encouraged one of his cousins spiritually and told his persecutors that although he was about to die, he would only be waiting for Jehovah God to resurrect him on this earth that was to become a paradise. This faithful young man was put to death by several men. His own uncle was an accomplice in this; he was especially bitter because two of his sons had become Jehovah's Witnesses through Brother Milende's assistance. In fact, these two sons, Malala Ramazani and Akilimali Walugaba, were among the seven other Witnesses slaughtered!

What of the Survivors?

These terrible events resulted in the murder of eight men who left behind widows and orphans. The survivors and the other local Witnesses and interested people became objects of increased hatred. So they eventually fled to Kindu, the nearest large town, and were well cared for by members of the three congregations of Jehovah's Witnesses there. The Watch Tower Society's branch office in Kinshasa also helped these bereaved ones by sending them clothing, blankets, and money. This loving aid was greatly appreciated and resulted in a fine witness to unbelieving family members and other observers. (John 13:34, 35; James 1:27) Governmental authorities also intervened. The perpetrators were arrested and judicial measures were taken against them.

These shocking incidents raise many questions. What kind of religion is Kimbilikiti? Of what nature are beliefs and practices that could prompt this kind of persecution? And why should only Jehovah's Witnesses and no other religion be the object of such hatred?

Unraveling the Mystery of Kimbilikiti

KIMBILIKITI is the ancestral religion of the Rega tribe in Kivu province, situated in east-central Zaire. Rega men hunt in the dense forests, the women fish in the rivers, and families cultivate the land. But the lives of all are completely dominated by Kimbilikiti, the great tribal spirit to whom they must show implicit obedience. And they must jealously guard all secrets associated with devotion to him, for divulging any of these is punishable by immediate death. In fact, any protest over the death of a family member at the hands of Kimbilikiti likewise results in immediate execution.

How did this powerful religion get its start? For an answer, we must look to the past.

A Mystery in the Making

According to legend, very far back in tribal history a certain man had three

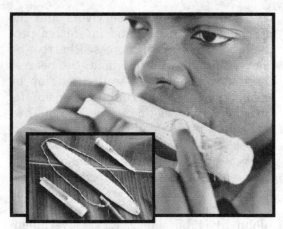
Kimbilikiti "flutes"

sons. Katima Rega, the firstborn, was an ugly dwarf, so handicapped that he was unable to get married. Mentally, however, he was extremely bright and possessed a very fertile imagination. He enjoyed eating to the point of gluttony. To help him get food without working, he invented some simple flutelike bamboo instruments that produced weird sounds. He also fashioned a flat, boat-shaped piece of wood with a cord attached to one end. When this device was twirled rapidly above one's head, it produced a loud, eerie, whirring sound.

This legendary inventor first tried his devices on his two nephews, convincing them that the sounds came from a spirit and thus frightening them into stealing food and tobacco for him from his two brothers. Deciding to enlarge his field of activity, he hid in the bush and waited for the women to catch fish and put them in baskets. Then he manipulated his instruments, causing the women to return to the village in terror, leaving behind their catch.

At first, the reports of the panic-stricken women were doubted. But when the same situation kept recurring and the villagers no longer had fish to eat, the men cautiously closed in on the "demon-animal," only to find that it was Katima Rega. Some wanted to kill him on the spot, but others concluded that what he had devised was very clever and voted to adopt "the voice" as their tribal spirit. It would be guarded as a secret and would be a mystery to all the uninitiated. Every member of the tribe would have to obey all orders, instructions, and decrees coming from "the voice," the spirit of the forest. But what should it be called? All agreed when a wise elder suggested "Kimbilikiti."

Thus the Rega tribal religion was born. An entire framework of rules, practices, and superstitions was built up around that simple beginning. In time, three other invisible "spirits" were added as associates of Kimbilikiti. Kabile, sometimes considered his sister and at other times his wife, was a very beautiful and extraordinary woman. All adolescent males are supposed to be miraculously circumcised through sex relations with her! Twamba, a younger brother of Kimbilikiti, is said to have such strength that he can produce storms, cause houses to collapse, and so forth. His "voice" is heard through the whirring of the boat-shaped piece of wood! The third spirit is Sabikangwa, or Mukungambulu. He is another younger brother of Kimbilikiti and appears to play the role of his messenger.

Secret Initiation Rites

In the visible realm, Kimbilikiti is represented by a hierarchy of high priests (the wise Bami). One of them, called Mukuli, presides over circumcision rites. Kitumpu, another high priest, acts as doctor and actually does the circumcising of adolescents. A third, Kilezi, takes care of the newly circumcised boys. The role of mediator between the initiation camp and the ordinary villagers is played by the Bikundi, a group of those already initiated.

The initiation rites (called Lutende) are held deep in the forest, the supposed dwelling of Kimbilikiti. Strict secrecy shrouds these rites, and any female (animal or human) venturing near the spot is strangled immediately! On initiation day, great festivities are held in the various villages, with nonstop games and dancing from early morning. This is designed to test the resistance of the young boys who will be initiated. Afterward, they listen to the history of Kimbilikiti, complete with all the myths built up over the years. The boys are made to believe that Kimbilikiti and his sister-wife Kabile are real persons. These youngsters are told to prepare themselves to struggle with Kabile, after which they will have sexual relations with her and be miraculously circumcised. If any of them fails these two tests, Kabile will angrily complain to Kimbilikiti, who will liquidate the offender!

Once in the forest, however, the boys see none of the things they were told. Instead, the three high priests (Mukuli, Kitumpu, and Kilezi) seize each one in turn and perform the circumcision. That, they say, is the struggle with Kabile! If a boy should not heal properly before the appointed time for him to return to the village, he is strangled and disposed of, for such a condition would destroy the myth of miraculous circumcision following relations with beautiful, supernatural Kabile.

Despite such high esteem for Kabile, during the initiation ceremonies the boys are taught vile sex expressions to be pronounced against women, including their own mothers and sisters. When the initiates return to their villages, women are forced to appear almost naked and walk on their knees and dance before them and to be objects of their newly learned insults.

During the initiation periods, the Bikundi (those already initiated) go from village to village extorting food or possessions. Families are forced to give whatever is asked for Kimbilikiti and those away at the initiation camp. Roads are even blocked and passersby are obliged to pay what the devotees of Kimbilikiti demand. Perpetuated in this way is the original objective of "the voice"—getting food without working for it.

In reality, then, what is Kimbilikiti? A hoax built around some pieces of bamboo! To uphold it, however, a system of terror has been devised with fear of death as the basic instrument. (Hebrews 2:14, 15) The other tools are superstition, greed, and obscenity. And all of this is maintained by a hierarchy of high priests. But how could this have any bearing on persecution experienced by Jehovah's Witnesses?

Integrity-keeping Witnesses in the Pangi area

Persecuted for Telling the Truth

JEHOVAH'S WITNESSES do not support the beliefs and practices of Kimbilikiti, for these run counter to Scriptural principles. The Witnesses have been set free by the truth found in God's Word the Bible. (John 8:31, 32) Hence, they refuse to allow their sons to be circumcised according to the initiation rites of Kimbilikiti. The Witnesses also refuse to give food, money, or goods demanded during initiation periods, and their women do not participate in compulsory fishing sessions organized for the same purpose.

Interestingly, in connection with the slaughter of the Witnesses mentioned earlier, the state prosecuting attorney said this in his recommendation to the court: 'Certain Warenga who in the past participated in the rites of Kimbilikiti and know the secrets are now associated with Jehovah's Witnesses. They have revealed the secrets, particularly those that concern the nonexistence of the spirit called Kimbilikiti. Consequently, they have exposed the falsity of the offerings demanded by the said spirit who, according to Jehovah's Witnesses, is a vast deception organized by the old men that direct the ceremonies.'

As individuals of the Rega tribe accept genuine Bible teachings, superstition and fear of death are replaced by truth and the resurrection hope. (John 5:28, 29) Insults to mothers, wives, and sisters yield to respect for women.—Ephesians 5:21–6:4; 1 Timothy 5:1, 2.

In striking contrast, the many churches and missions of Christendom allow their members to practice tribal religion under a thin veneer of so-called Christianity. In fact, many priests and high priests of Kimbilikiti are considered loyal, respected members of the various churches. How unlike the attitude of the apostle Paul! He wrote: "Do not become unevenly yoked with unbelievers. For what fellowship do righteousness and lawlessness have? Or what sharing does light have with darkness? . . . And what agreement does God's temple have with idols?"—2 Corinthians 6:14-16.

Very often, those with strong ties to both Kimbilikiti and the orthodox churches have stirred up trouble for Jehovah's Witnesses. These opposers have been much like the idol makers of ancient Ephesus. They saw their trade jeopardized by Paul, who proved that 'the ones made by hands are not gods.' (Acts 19:23-28) The same principle applies to the truth that the spirit Kimbilikiti does not exist.

Jehovah's Witnesses feel an obligation to make known such truths as these. Of course, because of speaking the truth, they have sometimes suffered persecution. But what can be learned from their faithful endurance?

Truth and Faith Prevail

JEHOVAH'S WITNESSES are determined to worship God "with spirit and truth." (John 4:23, 24) Yes, the Bible message they declare does expose error, but like the apostle Paul they ask: 'Have we become your enemies because we tell you the truth?' (Galatians 4:16) Of course not! These Christians love their neighbors and want them to enjoy the spiritual freedom that only the truth makes possible.—John 8:32.

The Witnesses are also determined to maintain strong faith, even if they are persecuted for speaking the truth. Indeed, the faith of the humble Christians in Pangi provides evidence that with Jehovah's help his servants can maintain integrity to him down to the end. That may be the final end of this wicked system of things or one's own death in faithfulness, perhaps in the face of cruel, religiously inspired persecution.—Matthew 24:13.

Faith in Action

Those lovers of truth massacred in Kivu province were not the only ones manifesting strong faith. For example, consider Bingimeza Bunene, an elderly sister. Two of her sons, Malala Ramazani and Akilimali Walugaba, were among those murdered at Pangi. Moreover, tribal elders persuaded her husband to join the killers of his nephew, Amisi Melende. When her two sons and her nephew were murdered, she was abandoned by her entire family, including her husband. However, she took comfort in the psalmist's words: "In case my own father and my own mother did leave me, even Jehovah himself would take me up." (Psalm 27:10) Her brothers and sisters in the faith welcomed and consoled her, with loving reminders of the wonderful resurrection hope.

This sister's husband, Ramazani Musombwa, was imprisoned for involvement in the death of his nephew, but eventually was released. Afterward, he admitted being impressed by his wife's courageous stand and the love that fellow Witnesses showed her and the bereaved daughters-in-law. Now he expresses great regret and is accompanying his wife to meetings of Jehovah's Witnesses. Because of his complete change, he has become the object of much criticism and mockery but is determined to serve Jehovah from now on.

All the other bereaved young widows were rejected by their families due to fear of death at the hands of Kimbilikiti. These young women all stood firm and refused to renounce their faith in Jehovah. They were taken in by their fellow believers and have experienced what Jesus foretold in saying: "No one has left house or brothers or sisters or mother or father or children or fields for my sake and for the sake of the good news who will not get a hundredfold now in this period of time, houses and brothers and sisters and mothers and children and fields, with persecutions, and in the coming system of things everlasting life."—Mark 10: 29, 30.

Faith and Truth Have Prevailed

Today, the circumstances of Jehovah's Witnesses in the Pangi area are back to normal. All the bereaved ones and interested people obliged to flee to other villages and towns have returned to their homes. Once again the Witnesses are preaching the Kingdom message there, with renewed zeal and determination. Despite everything they have undergone, they are like 'the brothers who felt confidence by reason of Paul's prison bonds and were showing all the more courage to speak the word of God fearlessly.'—Philippians 1:14.

Of course, there is sadness over the massacre of all eight faithful Christian men of the Pangi Congregation. But another pioneer minister now serves as presiding overseer, and Jehovah's people there in the heart of Africa have confidence in God's love for them through Christ, as expressed in Paul's words: "Who will separate us from the love of the Christ? Will tribulation or distress or persecution or hunger or nakedness or danger or sword? . . . To the contrary, in all these things we are coming off completely victorious through him that loved us."—Romans 8:35-39.

However, why would Jehovah permit the murder of these faithful witnesses? In today's violent world, there have been many cases where Jehovah obviously protected his people. In doing so, he demonstrates how he can bring them safely through the "great tribulation." (Matthew 24:21; Isaiah 26:20) But, just as Jesus stated at John 16:1-3, there may be occasions when he permits opposers to go to the extent of actually killing individuals among Jehovah's Witnesses. Their keeping integrity in such situations, as our faithful brothers did in Kivu province, serves as a witness and as proof that God's servants are determined to keep integrity even to the death.—Job 27:5; Proverbs 27:11.

We are reminded of the great witness that resulted after the death of the first-century martyr Stephen. (Acts 8:1-8) So it may be that the dreadful massacre will cause many of the Rega tribe and others in Zaire and elsewhere to give Bible truth serious thought. How happy Jehovah's Witnesses will be to help such honest-hearted people to break free from the fear and superstition attached to the religion of Kimbilikiti! And what freedom will be enjoyed by all who embrace God's wonderful truth!

Perpetrators Pay the Penalty

WHEN reports of the massacre reached Kinshasa, government authorities took steps to ensure that justice would be done. For this, the authorities are to be commended.

Trucks and military personnel were dispatched to the region. Eventually, the perpetrators were rounded up and brought to trial in the district court of Kindu, Kivu.

Judging the case was not easy, for the judges experienced constant threats and pressure to pervert justice. Huge bribes were offered to them. When the guilty verdict was handed down, they even received an anonymous letter saying that Kimbilikiti would avenge himself upon them.

Interestingly, even during the trial the defendants insisted that Kimbilikiti was a spirit and that this spirit pushed them to act. During the hearing, Judge Tumba wisely arranged for the Kimbilikiti instruments to be sounded within earshot of the courtroom. He reasoned that if Kimbilikiti was a spirit, the sound of the instruments would have no effect on the Rega people in the courtroom. The result? When the weird sounds were produced, there was an uproar in the courtroom. The women fled in terror, fearing that they might see Kimbilikiti and be put to death. The men hung their heads in shame and left the courtroom, leaving behind only the defendants, the court personnel, and some spectators not of the Rega tribe. So once again Kimbilikiti was exposed as a superstitious hoax holding the Rega people in captivity.

The Kindu court sentenced to death six of those directly responsible for the murders. A number of others received prison sentences and fines. Additionally, some compensation was ordered for the bereaved widows. (The sentences were appealed to a higher court at Bukavu, Kivu.)

The responsible action of the authorities calls to mind the apostle Paul's words: "Those ruling are an object of fear, not to the good deed, but to the bad. . . . [The authority] is God's minister, an avenger to express wrath upon the one practicing what is bad." (Romans 13:1-4) Thus Jehovah's Witnesses continue to make "supplications, prayers, intercessions, offerings of thanks . . . concerning all sorts of men, concerning kings and all those who are in high station; in order that we may go on leading a calm and quiet life with full godly devotion and seriousness." Paul added: "This is fine and acceptable in the sight of our Savior, God, whose will is that all sorts of men should be saved and come to an accurate knowledge of truth."—1 Timothy 2: 1-4.

As a result of these events in Pangi, we are convinced that many sincere Rega people will "come to an accurate knowledge of truth" and will thus be freed from the bondage of superstitious deception. For these and other honest-hearted people around the earth, Jehovah's Witnesses will continue to search. We are delighted, indeed, to act in faith and share Kingdom truth with all lovers of righteousness, even to the remotest parts of Africa.

Kingdom Proclaimers Report

The Many Islands Rejoice

JESUS' declaration to his disciples was: "You will be witnesses of me . . . to the most distant part of the earth." (Acts 1:8) That commission would eventually take in the vast expanse of the Western Pacific, where the Kingdom work in all Micronesia is now under the supervision of the Guam branch of the Watch Tower Bible and Tract Society. Many of the inhabitants of these beautiful islands rejoice today. Why? Psalm 97:1 gives the reason: "Jehovah himself has become king! Let the earth be joyful. Let the many islands rejoice."

Many languages are spoken on the different islands in this part of the world, and this is a major problem in spreading the good news that "Jehovah himself has become king." Hence, one highlight of this service year was receiving the monthly edition of *The Watchtower* in five of the major languages, as well as *My Book of Bible Stories* and the brochure *Enjoy Life on Earth Forever* in a number of Micronesian languages. Having literature in the local languages for these isolated people is a real blessing and fulfills a great need. The local populace responds well, especially since the religions of Christendom as a rule do not bother to translate literature into their languages.

□ For example, on the lovely island of Moen in Truk the missionaries reported that *My Book of Bible Stories* in Trukese caused quite a stir as householders received it and showed it to their friends and relatives.

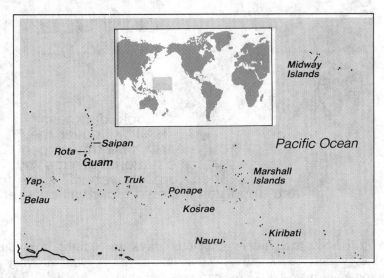

People stopped missionaries on the streets asking for the book, and some even went to the missionary home before 6:30 a.m. asking for it. Still others went to the Department of Education to get copies from one of Jehovah's Witnesses who works there.

One educator asked how it is that Jehovah's Witnesses can produce such a book in Trukese when the Catholics and the Protestants have been there for ages and produced nothing like it. Even some former opposers wanted the book.

□ One experience from the Marshall Islands shows how Bible truth can bring unity and happiness to a home. The husband was a drunkard and a heavy smoker, as well as a zealous, practicing Catholic. Two young Witnesses called on him

at his home and, over the objection of his wife, he accepted a Bible study. The wife opposed him for the next three years. But on observing how the truth changed him as he stopped smoking, no longer got drunk, and began doing things with his family, she finally listened to the good news and shared what she learned with others. The couple legalized their marriage and symbolized their dedication to Jehovah by baptism. The man now serves as an elder in the congregation, while his wife is looking forward to the pioneer service.

Happiness and peace have come to this home as they have to many such homes in the islands that the psalmist said would rejoice because Jehovah has become King.—Psalm 144:15.

Shedding Forth Light Amidst Earth's Gloom

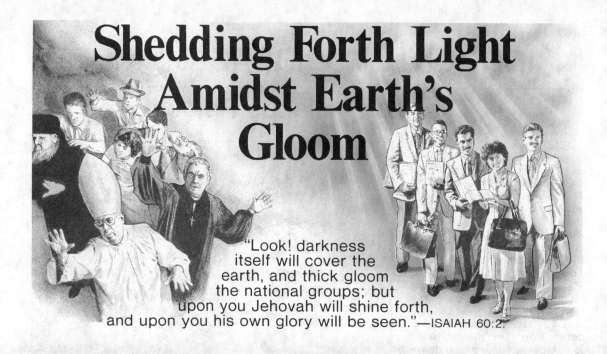

"Look! darkness itself will cover the earth, and thick gloom the national groups; but upon you Jehovah will shine forth, and upon you his own glory will be seen."—ISAIAH 60:2.

THESE are indeed glorious days in which to be alive! 'Glorious days?' someone may ask. 'How can you say that, when the entire world flounders in political, economic, and religious disunity, amidst the nuclear-age gloom that envelops the nations?' But glorious days these are—because of the good news that is now being proclaimed in all the earth, enlightening truth-hungry humans concerning the meaning of our times and the happy prospect of even more glorious days that they may live to see!

² The Source of our marvelous hope is none other than the Sovereign Lord Jehovah, the grand Creator of heaven and earth. (Isaiah 45:12, 18) He it is who gives the command recorded at Isaiah chapter 60, verse 1: "Arise, O woman, shed forth

light, for your light has come and upon you the very glory of Jehovah has shone forth." Who is this "woman"? She is no lifeless Statue of Liberty; nor is she any fleshly female campaigning for women's liberation. Rather, she is the dynamic, forward-moving, heavenly organization of Jehovah God, his devoted helpmate made up of myriads of loyal angels and now including resurrected "holy ones"—those who have proved themselves faithful even to death as anointed Christians here upon earth.—Revelation 11:18; 2:10.

³ "Arise, O woman," commands Jehovah. Obediently, God's heavenly organization has arisen from a centuries-long barren, desolate condition to a state of fruitful productivity. In 1914 she gave birth to the Messianic Kingdom. (Revelation 12:1-5) Since 1919 she has brought the remaining ones of her anointed sons

1. What positive answer can be given to the questions here raised?
2. (a) What words of encouragement does Jehovah give in Isaiah chapters 45 and 60? (b) Who is God's "woman"?

3. How has God's woman (a) 'arisen,' and (b) "shed forth light"?

on earth into a "land," or condition, of glorious spiritual prosperity. (Isaiah 66:8) Furthermore, God's heavenly organization has "shed forth light" on marvelous Kingdom prophecies. Her numerous sons are being "taught by Jehovah."—Isaiah 54: 1, 13.

Light Amidst Thick Gloom

4 "Your light has come," declares Jehovah. Indeed, "the very glory of Jehovah has shone forth" upon his heavenly organization, and this has been reflected in a wonderful way by Jehovah's restored people on earth. However, Jehovah next draws a contrast, saying: "Look! darkness itself will cover the earth, and thick gloom the national groups." (Isaiah 60:2) Does that not well describe global conditions since 1914?

5 Christendom in particular has rejected the prophetic 'sign of Jesus' presence and of the conclusion of the system of things.' Therefore, she stumbles around in thickening spiritual darkness. Christendom's religions have shown themselves to be part and parcel of the world empire of false religion, Babylon the Great—far, far removed from the light of truth. (Matthew 24:3-14; Revelation 17:3-6) Worldly religion has supplied no solution for the problems of this nuclear age, nor can it dispel the heavy gloom, the sickening hopelessness, that has engulfed mankind. False religion's involvement in the affairs of the political nations will lead ultimately to her own devastation.—Revelation 17:16, 17.

6 In contrast, Jehovah goes on to say of his heavenly organization: "Upon you Jehovah will shine forth, and upon you his

---

4. Jehovah tells of what contrast between God's people and the nations of earth?
5. Why can false religion find no solution to nuclear-age problems?
6, 7. (a) How did Jehovah's glory "shine forth" during the years 1919-31? (b) What climax did this reach in 1931?

"Weapons of terrifying destructiveness are piled up at an increasing tempo. . . . The arms race today extends into the oceans of the world and into outer space. In fact it is ironic that the accumulation of arms is one of the few expanding industries in a period of economic depression and gloom."—UN Secretary-General, Mr. Javier Perez de Cuellar

"There, under the door at home the other day, was another familiar message in the form of a religious leaflet. 'Are we nearing Armageddon?' read the words superimposed over a lowering sky and a bolt of jagged lightning bearing down on us. There was a time when that sort of message would bring indulgent smiles. Suddenly, it no longer seems funny."—Haynes Johnson, *The Washington Post*

own glory will be seen." (Isaiah 60:2) This glory is reflected to anointed Christians here on earth, so that they in turn may 'let their light shine before men.' (Matthew 5:16) The years 1919 through 1931 were glorious years for the shining forth of Kingdom light, with God's people casting off completely the remaining shackles of Babylonish doctrine, thinking, and customs. During those years, the small remnant of true Christians began to give a positive answer to the question "WHO WILL HONOR JEHOVAH?"—this being the title of the study article in the January 1, 1926, issue of *The Watch Tower*.

7 Then, in 1931, Jehovah's glory came more fully to be seen upon his "servant," as they accepted the name that he himself had given them—JEHOVAH'S WITNESSES. (Isaiah 43:10, 12) During 12 fruitful, action-packed years up until 1931, Kingdom proclaimers increased from a handful to tens of thousands of zealous witnesses.

Further 'Shining Forth'

[8] However, would Jehovah "shine forth" only in behalf of the anointed ones of the 'little flock of Kingdom heirs'? (Luke 12:32) No, for the years 1931 through 1938 proved to be a grand period of further enlightenment, as *The Watch Tower* began to focus clearly on another group. The study article in its issue of September 1, 1931, was entitled "MAN WITH THE WRITER'S INKHORN," this being based on Ezekiel 9:1-11. After identifying the 'writer' as the anointed remnant, *The Watch Tower* made this comment:

[9] "The commandment is given to put a 'mark upon the foreheads of the men that sigh, and that cry, for all the abominations that be done in the midst' of Christendom. . . . The Lord tells of a class of persons whom he will 'deliver in a time of trouble and keep alive and bless upon the earth.' (Ps. 41:1, 2) This must be the class of persons that are often described as 'the millions now living that will never die'." Today, it is thrilling actually to see millions of these being marked for preservation, as they put on the true Christian personality, in a dedicated relationship to Jehovah through Christ Jesus.—Genesis 22:15-18; Zephaniah 2:1-3; Ephesians 4:24.

[10] Especially noteworthy were study articles in the *Watchtower* issues of July 1 through August 1, 1932. Referring to Second Kings chapters 9 and 10, these showed how King Jehu foreshadowed Jehovah's Executioner, the King Jesus Christ, represented on earth by the anointed remnant, who warn others about Jehovah's coming execution of judgment.

But who was pictured by Jehu's companion, Jehonadab? *The Watchtower* answered:

[11] "Jehonadab represented or foreshadowed that class of people now on the earth during the time that the Jehu work is in progress who . . . are out of harmony with Satan's organization, who take their stand on the side of righteousness, and are the ones whom the Lord will preserve during the time of Armageddon, take them through that trouble, and give them everlasting life on the earth." *The Watchtower* next showed these to be the ones 'blessed by the Father' in Jesus' parable of 'the sheep and the goats.' (Matthew 25:31-46) It said: "These constitute the 'sheep' class that favor God's anointed people, because they know that the anointed of the Lord are doing the Lord's work."

[12] These flashes of prophetic light prepared the ground for the historic discourse on "The Great Multitude," given May 31, 1935, by the president of the Watch Tower Society, J. F. Rutherford, at the Washington, D.C., convention of Jehovah's Witnesses. What a revelation of divine truth that was! Presented at that time was conclusive proof identifying the "great crowd" of Revelation 7:9 with the Lord's "other sheep" of John 10:16, with the Jehonadab class, with those marked in the forehead for survival, with the millions now living who will never die, and with "the sheep" that are separated from "the goats" and will inherit everlasting life in the earthly realm of God's Kingdom. All of this was covered in *The Watchtower,* August 1 and 15, 1935.

[13] In the years that followed, God's or-

8, 9. (a) In 1931, what other group did *The Watch Tower* bring into focus? (b) According to the Scriptures, how are these 'marked'?
10, 11. (a) How did Jehu foreshadow Jesus? (b) Identify the modern-day "Jehonadab."

12. What thrilling revelation of divine truth was made in 1935?
13. What further suggestion was made in 1938?

ganization proceeded to give much attention to the "great crowd" and their grand hope of surviving into the restored Paradise on earth. During September 9-11, 1938, Jehovah's Witnesses met in convention in London, England, two principal talks being conveyed by direct telephone tie-ins to other conventions around the world. On the basis of previous mandates given to humans, one of these discourses, entitled "Fill the Earth," suggested that the "Jonadabs" surviving the great tribulation may, at least for a time, marry and bring forth children in the New Order after Armageddon.—Genesis 1:28; 9:1, 7; see *The Watchtower,* October 15 and November 1, 1938.

14 During those years, the Master Jesus Christ proceeded to gather and send out more workers. Thus publishers in the field grew to about 50,000 in 1938.—Matthew 9:37, 38.

"Kings" and "Nations"

15 This gathering work is beautifully described in Isaiah chapter 60, verses 3 through 10. There Jehovah speaks of "kings" who appear in connection with Zion's "shining forth" and who minister to that wifely organization. When God's people of ancient times returned from Babylonian captivity, King Darius the Mede and King Cyrus of Persia took the lead in making provision for the restoration of Jehovah's worship at Jerusalem. (Daniel 5:30, 31; 9:1; Ezra 1:1-3) In this, they aptly pictured the Almighty King, Jehovah, and his associate King, Jesus,

14. How did Jehovah prosper his people during those years?
15, 16. How did "kings" share in the fulfillment of Isaiah 60:3-10 (a) in ancient times, and (b) in modern times? (c) How do "foreigners" now serve with the "kings"?

who have directed the restoration of true worship among Jehovah's people of modern times. (Revelation 11:15, 17) Moreover, an anointed remnant of true worshipers—prospective "kings," "joint heirs with Christ"—have been taking the lead in the modern-day witness work. Serving with them are "foreigners"—those not of spiritual Israel, but who will become earthly subjects of the Kingdom and who share even now in building up theocratic activity earth wide.—Romans 8:17; compare Isaiah 61:5, 6.

16 Jehovah himself invites us: "Raise your eyes all around and see!" The gathered Kingdom heirs are now being joined by that "great crowd . . . out of all nations"! (Revelation 7:9; Zechariah 8:23; Isaiah 2:2, 3) 'The praises of Jehovah they announce,' in zealous ministry. They also expend themselves on such projects as building Kingdom Halls for worship —some of these erected in only two days. They "minister," in wholehearted support of the global expansion of Kingdom interests.—Isaiah 60:4-7.

17 Jehovah next asks this pertinent question: "Who are these that come flying just like a cloud, and like doves to their birdhouse holes?" First to come to God's organization are her "sons from far away," separating completely from all Babylonish religion. These anointed ones bring precious things, dedicating their all "to the name of Jehovah," their God. As "the Holy One of Israel," he has put his name upon them and beautified them with the privilege of serving him as his witnesses. They take the lead in exalting the name of their Sovereign Lord, Jehovah, as the grandest, the most illustrious, the

17, 18. (a) Happily, what thrilling 'flight' is now taking place? (b) How does a seasonal event in Palestine appropriately illustrate this 'flight'?

most glorious name in all the universe.
—Isaiah 60:8, 9.

¹⁸ Happily, the anointed remnant have not been alone in this. It could be quite difficult if they were! This aging group grows smaller, as one by one they finish their earthly course in integrity. About 9,000 now remain. But others, numbering into the millions, are flocking like doves to their "birdhouse holes," or "dovecotes," finding refuge in God's organization. (*NW; The New English Bible*) They are like the flocks of doves seen in Palestine at certain seasons—flying just like a cloud, so numerous that they actually darken the sky.

'Wide-Open Gates'

¹⁹ Mercifully, Jehovah has opened wide the gates of his organization, which he now addresses in these words: "Your gates will actually be kept open constantly; they will not be closed even by day or by night, in order to bring to you the resources of the nations." It is that way now as the peace-loving "great crowd" ever increases in number. Joyfully, these "foreigners" contribute their resources of time, energy, and means in "sacred service day and night." They avail themselves of the "large door that leads to activity" and share with the prospective kings in bringing beauteous praise to Jehovah's name.—Isaiah 60: 10, 11; Revelation 7:4, 9, 15; 1 Corinthians 16:9.

²⁰ Next, Jehovah addresses his organization, saying: "Any nation and any kingdom that will not serve you will perish; and the nations themselves will without fail come to devastation." All prideful worldly nations and other opposers will be humbled at Armageddon. In contrast, Jehovah beautifies his own sanctuary of worship. He 'glorifies the very place of his feet,' the earthly courtyards of his great spiritual temple of worship, as he gathers there the ever-increasing numbers of the great crowd. By means of another prophet, Jehovah declares: "I will rock all the nations, and the desirable things of all the nations must come in; and I will fill this house with glory." (Haggai 2:7) But persecutors, apostates, and other disrespectful opposers will be compelled to 'bow down'—acknowledging in chagrin that Jehovah's Witnesses do indeed represent God's organization—"the city of Jehovah, Zion of the Holy One of Israel."—Isaiah 60:12-14.

19. Why do the "gates" of Jehovah's organization remain open, and what response do "kings" and "foreigners" make?
20. (a) Who will "come to devastation"? (b) What happy contrast do we here note?

²¹ Jehovah will never abandon his wifely helper however much the opposers revile her 'sons and daughters' here on earth. Rather, he tells his loyal organization: "I will even set you as a thing of pride to time indefinite, an exultation for generation after generation. And you will actually suck the milk of nations." In a figurative way the earthly representatives of God's organization thus use all available resources in advancing true worship. They make practical use of modern facilities of communication, transport, and printing to get the good news preached. Jehovah's watchcare and guidance have been with Jehovah's Witnesses in this work. These, too, in serving on behalf of Jehovah's heavenly organization, rejoice at the ful-

21, 22. (a) What reassurance does Jehovah here give? (b) How, representatively, do his people "suck the milk of nations"? (c) What further thrilling study awaits us?

Questions in Summary

☐ What contrast between light and gloom is apparent today?

☐ What progressive 'shining forth' was there during 1919-38?

☐ How is Isaiah 60:8 being fulfilled in modern times?

☐ How do "kings" and "foreigners" enter 'wide-open gates'?

fillment of his promise: "You will be certain to know that I, Jehovah, am your Savior, and the Powerful One of Jacob is your Repurchaser."—Isaiah 60:15, 16.

²² What further encouragement does Jehovah give us at Isaiah 60:17-22? That will be the thrilling subject of our next study.

Jehovah 'Speeds It Up'

"I myself, Jehovah, shall speed it up in its own time."—ISAIAH 60:22.

TODAY, rejoicing and exultation are to be found not only in Jehovah's heavenly organization but also throughout the organization of Jehovah's Witnesses here on earth. Our happiness stands out in sharp contrast to the gloom that has engulfed Satan's world. (Psalm 144:15) We have spiritual food and drink in abundance, so that we "cry out joyfully because of the good condition of the heart." (Isaiah 65:13-19) We are not ignorant as to the reason for the present world crisis. Our

hope for early deliverance by God's Kingdom is fortified as we see Bible prophecies being fulfilled in the relentless countdown to Armageddon. We know that this "war of the great day of God the Almighty" will come exactly at "the appointed time," for the vision "keeps panting on to the end, and it will not tell a lie."—Revelation 16: 14, 16; Habakkuk 2:3.

² As in heaven, so on earth there is permanency to Jehovah's theocratic organization. Further, since Jehovah is the

1. How does the outlook of Jehovah's people contrast with that of Satan's world, and why?

2. What conditions abound in Jehovah's organization, leading to what question?

Watchtower covers of the 1930's depicted Ezekiel's vision of Jehovah's dynamic organization

Source of dynamic energy, he makes 'full might abound in those who are hoping in him.' (Isaiah 40:29-31) His organization is alive with activity and is constantly on the move. (Compare Ezekiel 1:15-21.) The 47,-869 congregations of Jehovah's Witnesses in 203 lands throughout the earth are well organized to press forward zealously in the Kingdom work. (Matthew 24:14) How was this dynamic global organization brought forth?

3 "Organization" was the title of the study articles in *The Watchtower* of June 1 and 15, 1938. These discussed at length Isaiah 60:17, where Jehovah addresses his heavenly organization, saying: "Instead of the copper I shall bring in gold, and instead of the iron I shall bring in silver, and instead of the wood, copper,

---

3. (a) How has Isaiah 60:17 been fulfilled in modern times? (b) What similar arrangements brought prosperity in Bible times?

and instead of the stones, iron; and I will appoint peace as your overseers and righteousness as your task assigners." In reflecting this better condition, Jehovah's organization on earth was revitalized. Just as gold is more valuable than copper (and it is similar with the other materials here mentioned), so the theocratic arrangement that the Watch Tower Society explained to the congregations of God's people back in 1938—and which they wholeheartedly accepted—is much to be preferred over former democratic procedures. It is Scriptural. It makes for good organization in getting God's work done, just as similar arrangements brought prosperity in Moses' time and in the early days of the Christian congregation.—Exodus 18:25; Acts 6:3-7; Titus 1:5; 1 Peter 5:1-3.

4 Thus, in 1938, a year before the outbreak of World War II, the "overseers" and "task assigners" in all congregations became "peace" and "righteousness." A strong, unified organizational arrangement moved forward with fruitful increase. Jehovah blessed his united witnesses. Their numbers almost doubled, from 71,509 to 141,606 between 1939 and 1945, despite the pressures and persecutions of those war years.

'No More Violence'

5 However, what of the post-World War II period? There has been no peace among the nations of the earth. In fact, it has been reported that more than 30,-000,000 persons have perished in the "minor" wars that have been fought since 1945. As many as 40 "pocket-size wars" have been

---

4. (a) How were Jehovah's Witnesses fortified for the trials of 1939-45? (b) What proved that Jehovah's blessing was upon that theocratic arrangement?
5. As to "peace," how do Jehovah's people differ from the world?

raging around the globe at one time. How happy we are, therefore, to serve with an organization that has rejected violence! (Isaiah 2:4; Proverbs 20:22) Moreover, as a global organization, we enjoy peace within our ranks. By walking with "the God of peace," we have come to experience "the peace of God that excels all thought." —Philippians 4:7-9.

⁶ Since "peace" and "righteousness" prevail among Jehovah's people, we stand out as distinct from Satan's world. Taking note of this, some of our neighbors have said, 'We admire you people, but we don't like your religion.' However, is it not our religion that has made us the people that we are? We have no interest in the opposing ideologies and hatreds that divide the nations. Rather, our twofold interest is (1) to instruct meek persons in the way of salvation through Christ's Kingdom and (2) to praise Jehovah, keeping his name before all peoples as a witness. We are "no part of the world."—John 17:14, 16.

⁷ Thus, we have shared in the fulfillment of Jehovah's promise: "No more will violence be heard in your land, despoiling or breakdown within your boundaries. And you will certainly call your own walls Salvation and your gates Praise." (Isaiah 60:18) All praise to our God Jehovah! The religious leaders of Christendom (and all of their apostate bedfellows) dishonor that name—even to the point of hypocritically trying to purge it from translations of the Bible. "But we, for our part, shall walk in the name of Jehovah our God to time indefinite, even forever."—Micah 4:5.

⁸ Jehovah encourages us to walk in his name. At Isaiah 60:19-21, he assures his heavenly organization that he will be to her "an indefinitely lasting light," even eclipsing the brightness of sun and moon. Spiritually, he becomes her beauty, fulfilling also his promise toward her people: "All of them will be righteous; to time indefinite they will hold possession of the land, the sprout of my planting, the work of my hands, for me to be beautified." Truly, Jehovah has prospered "the land," or domain of activity, of his witnesses. Increasingly, it 'sprouts' with fruitfulness as multitudes of new ones are gathered to the side of the Kingdom and helped to put on the Christian personality. (Colossians 3:10, 12-14) This 'beautifies' Jehovah, bringing honor to his precious name.

⁹ A recent example is Mexico. In the past two years, the peak of publishers in that land has increased from 113,823 to 151,807—a commendable 33 percent! (Their 1984 celebration of the Memorial of Jesus' death was attended by 695,369.) Our Mexican brothers are most zealous in their field activity. A Monterrey newspaper recently took note, also, of their integrity in meeting the neutrality issue, saying among other things: "What a profound respect their steadfastness and courage of conviction inspire in us. Even though their children are expelled from school they prefer to remain loyal to their faith, their belief. How would it be if all of us Christians were that way, without distinction of group and denomination? Mexico would be the branch office of heaven."

¹⁰ Jehovah's Witnesses continue to bring forth this fruitage of praise, even in lands where there is no letup in persecu-

6, 7. (a) What makes God's people stand out as distinct? (b) How has Isaiah 60:18 been fulfilled toward us? (c) In what outstanding way do we differ from false religionists?
8. (a) What encouragement does Jehovah give his people at Isaiah 60:19-21? (b) What 'sprouting' beautifies Jehovah, and how?

9. (a) How is Jehovah blessing his witnesses in Mexico, and why? (b) What did one newspaper say on noting their integrity?
10. (a) What shows Jehovah's Witnesses to be fruitful even under ban? (b) What question is here posed?

tion. How thrilling it was to note in the 1984 Service Year Report that in 28 countries where there are governmental bans or other restrictions the total number of publishers increased 3.1 percent, to well over a quarter of a million, and pioneers increased 23 percent! Can you imagine pioneering under those circumstances? An average of 6,905 of our brothers and sisters in these lands have been doing so each month! If you have comparative freedom where you live, could you reach out for regular pioneering, or at least part-time auxiliary pioneering?—Compare Luke 17:5, 6.

'Becoming a Thousand'

¹¹ Over his own precious name, Jehovah now makes a threefold promise. (Isaiah 60:22) First he tells us: "The little one himself will become a thousand." As you read each *Yearbook of Jehovah's Witnesses,* have you noticed how a start was made by just one Kingdom publisher, or a few, in some lands where there now are thousands? For example, the pioneer brother who was the first to witness in Chile rented an apartment and invited people to a Sunday meeting. At last one interested person came. This man asked the question, 'And the others, when will they come?' The pioneer assured him: "They will come." And come they did. After some 50 years, that little one has become 23,985.

¹² In Italy, Jehovah's Witnesses were bitterly persecuted by Mussolini's fascist regime. In the postwar year of 1946, only 120 of them were reporting service. But remember that only about 120 were present at Pentecost in the year 33 C.E. And just think of what got started at that time! (Acts 1:15; 2:1-4, 41) Now, in another respect, Jehovah's spirit has been poured out in Italy. In 38 years publishers have grown to a peak of 119,408, at last report, very close to a thousandfold increase. As in so many Catholic countries around the earth, Jehovah's Witnesses in Italy are experiencing a phenomenal growth. —Compare Psalm 69:9; Isaiah 63:14.

"A Mighty Nation"

¹³ The second part of Jehovah's three-fold promise is this: "The small one [will become] a mighty nation." It was indeed a "small one," a dispersed remnant of anointed ones, that was restored to Jehovah's "land" of favor in 1919. But it multiplied, until all spiritual Israel had come in—the full number of 144,000 Kingdom heirs. (Romans 11:25, 26) Truly, as part of God's "holy nation," the anointed remnant on earth has been called out of darkness into his wonderful light. They have rejoiced to declare abroad the excellencies of their God, Jehovah. (1 Peter 2:9) Though comparatively few in number, they have been mighty by God's spirit. "'As for me, this is my covenant with them,' Jehovah has said. 'My spirit that is upon you and my words that I have put in your mouth —they will not be removed from your mouth or from the mouth of your offspring or from the mouth of the offspring of your offspring,' Jehovah has said, 'from now on even to time indefinite.'"—Isaiah 59:21.

¹⁴ By this statement Jehovah assures us that our proclaiming "good news of good things" must meet with sure success, and for this we pray fervently in this 'day of Jehovah.' Our preaching has gained mo-

---

11, 12. (a) What is the first part of the promise that Jehovah himself now makes? (b) What are some examples of 'a little one becoming a thousand'? (c) Why has there been such rapid growth?

13, 14. (a) How has the second part of Jehovah's promise been fulfilled? (b) In this connection, how do 1 Peter 2:9 and Isaiah 59:21 apply? (c) What has given our preaching greater momentum?

A healthy pioneer spirit has helped toward
'speeding up' the harvest work

mentum as the figurative "offspring" of the anointed remnant, the "great crowd," and also *their* "offspring" (new ones whom *they* have directed to God's organization) have taken this message of salvation into their mouths, making public declaration thereof. As a result, all congregations continue to grow in spirituality, as well as in numbers.—Romans 10:10, 15; Psalm 118: 24, 25; 1 Thessalonians 3:12.

15 In recent times, how marvelously the Kingdom fruitage has increased! With the addition of large numbers of the "great crowd," God's figurative nation now totals 2,842,531 active Witnesses as a peak. This "nation" is more populous than some 92 nations and geopolitical divisions of the world. With joy we repeat the words of the sweet singer: "To time indefinite the very counsel of Jehovah will stand; the thoughts of his heart are to one genera-

tion after another generation. *Happy is the nation whose God is Jehovah,* the people whom he has chosen as his inheritance."—Psalm 33:11, 12.

'Speeding It Up'

16 Jehovah adds a third part to his promise: "I myself, Jehovah, shall *speed it up* in its own time." As we stand at the brink of the "great tribulation," the time for this is NOW! (Mark 13:10, 18, 19) The rapid acceleration of the Kingdom work during the past two years bears this out. This 'speeding up' is to be observed earth wide, even in lands where Jehovah's Witnesses must demonstrate their love for Jehovah God and Jesus Christ by preaching in the

---

15. How populous has God's figurative "nation" become, and why is it happy?

16, 17. (a) What indicates that the third part of Jehovah's promise is now being fulfilled? (b) How has love for God and Christ been demonstrated? (c) What joyful activity and spirit has helped to "speed it up"? (d) How does Matthew 9:35-38 apply today?

face of persecutions or other circumstances that endanger their very lives. With the ranks of the full-time publishers ever increasing, the pioneers are to the forefront. And what joy they find in Jehovah's service!—Proverbs 10:22.

¹⁷ This happy pioneer spirit has encouraged congregations everywhere to 'speed up' their share in the final ingathering. Even with the grand increase, we can say that "the harvest is great, but the workers are few." In this hopeless world of today, we can feel pity for the people, as Jesus did when on earth, for indeed they are "skinned and thrown about like sheep without a shepherd." So we "beg the Master of the harvest to send out workers into his harvest," and we rejoice to see our prayers so wonderfully answered.—Matthew 9:35-38.

¹⁸ To take just one of many stimulating examples: In April of 1984, Ecuador reported 1,048 auxiliary pioneers in the field, 106 percent more than the previous April. By June this land was reporting 12,238 home Bible studies, a 24-percent increase for the year, and 8,044 publishers, a 17-percent increase. Memorial attendance mushroomed to 40,728, a ratio of more than 5 for each publisher. From around our globe come similar reports, and the worldwide attendance of 7,416,974 at the Memorial celebration of April 15, 1984, shows that the fields are "white for harvesting" those who are being gathered "for everlasting life."—John 4:35, 36.

¹⁹ Often Jehovah 'speeds it up' in striking ways. A traveling overseer writes this from the jungles of northern Papua New Guinea: "A person who was contacted by a special pioneer returned to his isolated home in a mountain village. Several years

later, he reappeared at a circuit assembly —with a request. This as-yet-unbaptized man had witnessed to his village and the surrounding 'wilds' so effectively that the village elders now wanted Jehovah's Witnesses to come and care for the spiritual interests of the whole area." Once the seed is planted, it is God who 'keeps making it grow.'—1 Corinthians 3:6.

²⁰ In many ways, Jehovah has been preparing his people for the grand increase that is now coming forth. We rejoice that, in recent years, Jehovah has so wonderfully cared for the expanding of the Watch Tower branch facilities. Today, these branches are equipped to help massive flocks of "doves."

²¹ Therefore, let all of us share in beaming forth the light of the Kingdom good news to millions more! Let us point all homing "doves" to the way of "salvation" behind the protective walls of Jehovah's organization and increase "praise" to him at its gates. Let it be our prayer that the Sovereign Lord Jehovah and the head of the Christian congregation, our beloved King Jesus Christ, will continue to "speed it up" as the Kingdom proclamation moves on toward its climax!

---

20. How have Watch Tower branches been expanded to handle the increase?
21. How can we continue to share in 'speeding it up'?

18, 19. What are some reports showing the world field to be "white for harvesting"?

Reviewing This Study:

□ What notable fulfillment of Isaiah 60:17 took place in 1938?

□ In line with Isaiah 60:18, what interests do we have?

□ How are reports from the field 'beautifying' Jehovah?

□ How is the threefold promise of Isaiah 60:22 moving to a climax?

You Can Survive!

THE matter of survival is prominently on the minds of people worldwide. Although the Bible reveals that what faces mankind is far more awesome than the prospects that are envisioned by certain scientists, it also shows that there are dependable prospects for survival. It was most appropriate, therefore, that on the opening day of a recent international series of conventions held by Jehovah's Witnesses, the Watch Tower Society released for widespread distribution a book entitled *Survival Into a New Earth.* What does it contain?

The book offers a realistic consideration of the problems that face us in the 1980's. There are vital factors that people in general leave out of consideration, and as a result many see no way out of the escalating world crisis. These vital factors are brought into clear focus in the opening chapter, "What Will Become of Planet Earth?" Some people earnestly hope that election of new officials or resorting to mass protests or even violent revolution will bring them relief. But the facts show that they simply exchange one set of problems for another. The book analyzes the underlying reason for this and identifies the truly vital issues that will determine our future.

With God's Word as the authority, this new book answers the question "How Long Will the Present System Last?" And, after showing that people now living have the prospect of surviving this world's end, the book paints a vivid and well-founded picture of "The Kind of Life That Awaits Survivors." It is the kind of prospect that makes any lover of righteousness want to be among the survivors. What is presented in this publication will doubtless be a source of great encouragement to millions of honest-hearted people.

Thrilling Prophetic Bible Dramas

At the time of releasing the book *Survival Into a New Earth,* the speakers at the various conventions explained that it gives special attention to many of the thrilling prophetic Bible dramas and other prophecies that relate particularly to those who will survive the coming "great tribulation" and live forever on a paradise earth. (Matthew 24:21; Revelation 7:14) Those Bible dramas provide real-life examples that demonstrated how Jehovah will deal with people now living. They show what is required in order to have his favor. However, instead of simply telling us what we must do in order to gain God's approval, these accounts make those divine requirements come to life for us. They stir our emotions and strengthen our desire to do what is right.

"In Jonah chapter 3, for example," the convention speakers explained, "is a drama that emphasizes the need for urgent action to avoid calamity. Jehovah had commissioned Jonah to go to Nineveh, to a people who made no profession of worshiping the God of Abraham, to proclaim that their great city would be overthrown in just 40 days. How did they react? Instead of scoffing, 'the men of Nineveh began to put faith in God.' They proclaimed a fast and put on sackcloth. In response to the urging of their king, they called out earnestly to God and turned back from their bad ways. Because of their genuine repentance, Jehovah spared them. Jesus later showed that the events recorded by Jonah are not mere dead history. (Matthew 12:39-41) Does their prophetic significance reach down even to our day?

"Are there people today who are like those ancient Ninevites?" the speakers asked. "Yes. When Jehovah's Witnesses deliver the divine warning that the wicked world will soon be destroyed, many who pay heed are persons who never professed to worship the God of the Bible, people who did not at all know the difference between their right hand and their left, religiously speaking. [Jonah 4:11] But now they put faith in Jehovah, repent of their former ways, and become part of the 'great crowd,' with the prospect of surviving the 'great tribulation.'"—Revelation 7:9, 14.

Altogether, the book considers 21 different groups or individuals who are mentioned in the Bible and who foreshadowed people now living who will inherit the earthly realm of God's Kingdom without dying. It also treats 26 other prophetic descriptions of this favored group who

In Our Next Issue

- **Jehovah—A Cruel or a Loving God?**

- **Working With the Organizer of All the Universe**

- **Parents, Protect Your Children**

have the delightful prospect of perfect human life.

Foundation of the New Earth

Those who are spared by Jehovah God through the coming "great tribulation" will become the foundation of the foretold new earth, being the first members of a new society, one that will spread worship of the true God around the globe. (2 Peter 3:13) They will have the joy of sharing in the education of the billions who will later be raised from the dead. So, as the convention speakers pointed out, it is important that the foundation for the new earth be sound.

Right now the prospective members of that new earth are being instructed in Jehovah's ways. They are being helped to gain heartfelt appreciation of how the issue of universal sovereignty affects our daily lives. They are learning how vital it is to 'trust in Jehovah with all their heart and not to lean on their own understanding.' (Proverbs 3:5, 6) They are being afforded opportunities to prove that they are zealous and loyal supporters of God's Kingdom. They are gaining experience as part of a global society in which people out of all nations, languages, and races work together in loving brotherhood. Are you an active part of that group?

Rather than merely discussing the subject of survival, the new book released at the recent series of conventions held by Jehovah's Witnesses is directed to the reader, helping him to examine his own life in the light of the requirements of God's Word. Whether you are a new student of the Bible or one who has read it for many years, you will benefit by allowing the book *Survival Into a New Earth* to stimulate your thinking. If you have not yet read it, we urge you to do so now. Then share it with others so they, too, can embrace the marvelous prospect it presents.

'Preaching in Favourable Season and in Troublesome Season'

THE Australian outback beckoned me when I was a lad of 19. The first world war had left England economically depressed. Millions, including me, could find no work. One morning my father showed me a newspaper notice of a government plan to help youths emigrate to Queensland, Australia. So 25 of us sailed from London in 1922.

As told by Harold E. Gill

My first job was in a vineyard. But after a few months I moved to a large property that was being cleared to grow wheat. There I learned many things: how to milk cows, to use an axe and a crosscut saw, to tell time by the sun to within ten minutes, to kill a poisonous snake safely, to plow with a team of horses, to build fences, to make a tree fall where you want it, and to do many other jobs that are part of life in outback Australia.

There I experienced a plague of grasshoppers too. They were so dense that truck drivers had to fix chains to the wheels to get up the hills. Another time there were thousands of mice doing enormous damage in the barn. Yet a week later they moved on just as suddenly as they came. And I lived through the heartrending horror of a drought, with sheep—thousands of them—lying dead everywhere.

In 1927 I leased virgin land near Gympie, southern Queensland, cleared it, and planted bananas. My neighbours, Tom and Alec Dobson, were Bible Students, as Jehovah's Witnesses were called in those days. One day I mentioned that I was going to Brisbane, the state capital, for a short visit. They invited me to call on their parents. That I did, spending the whole day discussing the Bible with their father. What struck me was the simplicity of the Bible's great recurring theme—the Kingdom of God. I also liked the name "International Bible Students." It painted a picture of an international family, all students of the Bible, all worshipping God harmoniously. When I returned to the bananas, I had with me J. F. Rutherford's book *Creation*. Upon reading it, I at last found answers to many of my questions and therefore sent for more literature.

The more I read, the more I wanted to tell others about the Kingdom. As secretary of the social and cricket clubs for the area, I had many friends and felt sure that they, too, would be enthusiastic about the truths I was learning. So I bought an old motorbike to get around. To my great surprise, however, I found that what was thrilling to me left them cold. They thought I was crazy. I suppose I was a bit

Pioneering the outback, Queensland, Australia

too insistent, but I was just so full of what I was learning!

It was obvious that I needed training and instruction from the Bible Students. So I sold the banana plantation and joined a congregation in Brisbane. Six months later, on April 2, 1928, I was baptized. Then I took another farming job. But as the months rolled by I became increasingly restless. The outback life I had so much enjoyed no longer satisfied me. A desire to spend my time and energy in another kind of harvest was growing strongly within me. The apostle Paul's counsel to Timothy impressed me: "Preach the word, be at it urgently in favorable season, in troublesome season . . . Do the work of an evangelizer."—2 Timothy 4:2, 5.

Keen to get going, I wrote to the Watch Tower Society in Sydney requesting appointment to the spiritual harvest as a full-time minister, a pioneer. They accepted my application and in 1929 assigned me to Toowoomba, southern Queensland.

Preaching in the Outback

A few months later, I received a letter from the Society telling me of a motorized caravan (van) for sale and suggesting that if I bought it, George Schuett could join me. And that is what happened. George was in his 60's and had been a lifelong student of the Bible. I was still in my 20's and very inexperienced. His help, counsel, and Bible knowledge were of inestimable value to me, though I am sure I sorely tried his patience many times.

Our territory was 100,000 square miles (260,000 sq km) of far western Queensland. We covered it three times. The towns were small and far apart. Even sheep and cattle stations (ranches) were 60 to 70 miles (95 to 115 km) from one another. These isolated people eagerly took the sets of ten hardbound books that we offered for a contribution of only 10 shillings (about $2, U.S.). As they were most hospitable, we were never without a meal and a bunk for the night.

In the outback, roads were just tracks. All year round we carried wheel chains to cope with mud, wire netting for sand, and a winch to haul us out of trouble. On one occasion a flood marooned us for a week. Food and water ran very low, but we survived. Another time we were driving along a rough bush track in the vicinity of a bushfire. Suddenly we realized that the wind had changed and the fire was veering toward us. The track was so narrow we could not turn. All we could do was offer a prayer and step on the gas. We escaped by a whisker. I still shudder when I think of how close we came to disaster.

At the Australian Headquarters

In 1931 Alex MacGillivray, the branch overseer, invited me to join the Bethel family in Sydney. I was delighted, though a bit overawed. At that time the Society's Australian branch office was responsible for the preaching of the good news in

China, most lands of the Far East, and the isles of the South Pacific—a region spreading over a quarter of the globe. Brother J. F. Rutherford, then the Society's president, was eager that those areas be penetrated by the "good news." (Matthew 24:14) Brother Mac, as we all called the branch overseer, was equally keen about this. When I entered Bethel, I never dreamed that I would soon be going to some of those very places myself.

Missionary work always involves putting up with hardships. But in those pre-World War II days there was no Gilead School for training missionaries, and there were no missionary homes. Communications were slow, emphasizing the isolation. Nor was there any financial support other than the meagre contributions for literature, which, through the generosity of the brothers, the Society provided at well below cost. Those who responded to the call for evangelizers had to be trailblazers, pioneers in the fullest sense. The work meant going, usually in pairs, to the teeming cities of the East or the isolated islands of the Pacific, there to plant seeds of Bible truth in virgin soil. We had to cope with totally different beliefs, languages, and ways of life, and this called for complete trust in and loyalty to Jehovah.

To New Zealand

My first overseas assignment was to New Zealand in 1932. I was to pay particular attention to the organizing of the preaching work, especially the pioneer service. So, in addition to visiting congregations, I worked in the field with the pioneers. Some of them had formed travelling groups, equipped with camping gear and vehicles, including the trusty old bike. I served for some time with such a group in the South Island.

On one occasion we hired the Civic Theatre in Christchurch to present a recorded lecture by Brother Rutherford. A young man, Jim Tait, came and manifested keen interest. I met him again the following evening and was so impressed with his enthusiasm that I suggested he consider joining us in the pioneer group. How premature such an invitation would be today, for he had not yet been baptized! But home he went, packed his few things on his bike, took leave of his parents, and joined our happy band. To this day he remains a stalwart Witness. Those were 'favourable seasons' indeed.

The Far East

In 1936 I returned to Australia to be briefed for a trip to Batavia (now Djakarta) and Singapore. I was to recommend which city was more suitable for an office to provide closer contact with our missionaries in the Far East. I chose Singapore as a better hub and stayed there to run the office and preach in the city. Jehovah blessed the work, and within 18 months the Singapore congregation was established.

Later the Society's 52-foot (16-m) ketch *Lightbearer* was based in Singapore. Its crew of ministers visited and preached in many ports of what are now Indonesia and Malaysia. One of my jobs was to keep them supplied with literature. I recall that in 1936 alone, they distributed 10,500 publications in ten languages.

Islands of the Pacific

In July 1937 I was recalled to Sydney and sent to Fiji. Since our literature was banned there, we concentrated on preaching by sound car, using a Fijian translation of Brother Rutherford's lectures made by Ted Heatley, a Fijian. He accompanied me in order to do the talking over the loudspeaker. We went to every village on Viti Levu (Big Fiji), the main island, and were well received. Additionally, we helped

With crew of *Lightbearer*—Singapore

to establish the Suva congregation and to expand the house-to-house preaching work.

In 1938 Brother Rutherford visited Australia and New Zealand on a tremendous wave of publicity. Although much of it was hostile, it served only to arouse curiosity. I went to New Zealand to arrange his visit there. As I drove him to the Auckland Town Hall for the meeting, I drew his attention to a newspaper placard bearing a distortion of the title of a lecture he had given years earlier. The placard read, "Millions now living would rather die than listen to Judge Rutherford." He laughed heartily. It was all good publicity. The Town Hall was packed out.

Back to Fiji

One day in 1940 I was working in the Sydney office when Brother Mac asked me, "Is your passport all right?" I told him it was. "There is a boat sailing for Fiji in three days. I want you to go there and challenge the government in the courts over the banning of our literature." At that, I packed a carton of the offending literature and returned to Fiji. The recommended solicitor was fearful, so I dropped him and found another not quite so afraid.

He said he would prepare the case but would not present it in court. As a result, I found myself conducting the case with the Attorney General as my opponent. As it turned out, we lost on a timing technicality due to the dithering of the first solicitor.

After that setback, I requested an appointment with the Governor, Sir Harry Charles Luke, which he granted. Present with the Governor were the Prime Minister and the Chief of Police. I entreated Jehovah to be with me. In presenting our case, I provided evidence showing that the Roman Catholic Church was chiefly responsible for the ban. At the end of the discussion, the Governor came over to me, handed back the banned books I had produced in evidence, and quietly said: "You know, Mr. Gill, I am not quite so ignorant of the machinations of the Roman Catholic hierarchy as you think I am. My advice to you is to carry on your evangelical work." I thanked him and went off to cable Sydney for a shipment of literature.

American Samoa

Next I was sent to American Samoa. During my three months there, I stayed with High Chief Taliu Taffa, chief government interpreter and a highly respected man. His niece, a Witness in Fiji, had sent word ahead. So his smiling face greeted me as the boat docked. Throughout my stay, he was most hospitable. Of course, his household lived on the native diet, mostly raw fish and yams. The Samoans thrived on it, but after a while it became too much for me. I broke out in a rash of boils and became ravenous for European food, but I just did not have the money to buy any.

Well, by then I was used to surviving 'troublesome seasons.'

My task in American Samoa was to distribute 3,500 copies of the newly translated booklet *Where Are the Dead?* On arrival, I paid a courtesy call on the Governor to acquaint him with the booklet and to give him a copy. He thought there was already enough religious representation on the island—the navy's padre, the London Missionary Society, the Seventh-Day Adventists, and the Roman Catholics. However, he suggested that I presented a booklet to each of them and have them advise the Attorney General whether they thought it suitable for distribution. The padre was sarcastic but not hostile. The Adventists cared not what I did as long as I took none of their flock. The Missionary Society parson was affable once we got onto common ground—the papacy. I never did get to see the Catholic priest because a curious thing happened.

I had given a copy of the booklet to the Samoan policeman who had escorted me to the Governor. When I saw the policeman a few days later, I asked if he enjoyed it. He said: "My boss [the Attorney General] said to me, 'You go see your priest and ask him if this good book.' I get under tree and read book. I say, 'This very good book, but if I show priest, he say, "No good book."' I say to my boss, 'Boss, my priest say, "Very good book."'"

Later, while I was witnessing along the harbour front, the Attorney General came over and invited me to his office. There I

My Samoan host,
High Chief Taliu Taffa

outlined the booklet's message as he looked through it. Then he picked up the phone and ordered its release. The season had become very 'favourable' indeed! I bought a bike and set about distributing the booklets. In three months I had distributed all but one carton of 350 booklets.

Western Samoa

These remaining booklets I took to Western Samoa, a few hours away by boat. Word must have gone ahead though, for on my arrival a policeman told me that I was not allowed ashore. I produced my passport and read to him the rather glorious preamble that requests all concerned to allow His Britannic Majesty's subject "to pass freely without let or hindrance and to afford him every assistance and protection." That gained me an interview with the Governor, who allowed me to stay until the next boat sailed in five days. I hired a bike and toured the island, leaving the booklets far and wide.

Then it was back to American Samoa. The war was raging in the Pacific, with patriotic feelings running high. Since the authorities could not understand our strictly neutral stand, they banned us in many places. (John 15:19) However, they politely asked me to leave Samoa, and I returned to Australia.

Back to New Zealand

By that time a "troublesome season" had come the way of my brothers in New Zealand. That was my next assignment. But in October 1940, not long after I arrived, our work was banned there too. Many letters and telegrams to the government brought no response. Included was this telegram that we sent to the Attorney General: "DOES YOUR GOVERNMENT DENY US THE RIGHT AS CHRISTIANS TO ASSEMBLE AND WORSHIP GOD WITH SONG, PRAYER, SCRIPTURE STUDY? PLEASE ANSWER YES OR NO."

The following day the Prime Minister's secretary phoned to offer us an interview, which Brother Robert Lazenby and I accepted. With the Prime Minister, Peter Fraser, were the Attorney General and a high police official. They were pleasant and courteous but gave us the impression that their hands were tied. However, on May 8, 1941, the government amended the ban so as to permit our meetings, although we had been holding them all along in small groups in private homes. We could also preach unhindered as long as we did not distribute our literature. Later, in March 1945, while the war in the Pacific was still hot, the ban was completely withdrawn.

Return to England

I returned to Sydney in 1941. By that time we were banned in Australia too. After some discussion, Brother Mac agreed that I should go to London to see if anything could be done there about the bans. I sailed on October 2, 1941. But due to the hazards of war, I did not reach Liverpool until December 22, nearly three months later.

In London I tried to get an interview with Lord Alexander, first Lord of the Admiralty and a friend of my father. But in the heat of war that was not possible. In fact, London viewed our problems as the sole business of the governments concerned.

After a trip to the Society's headquarters in New York, I returned to England and obtained passage for Australia. My baggage was searched and sealed in London and I went to the ship. Brothers with whom I stayed gave me a few presents for the journey, which I put in my overnight bag. When I was going aboard, a customs officer asked, "Why are these not sealed?" My simple explanation did not satisfy them; so they arrested me, stripped me, and, though they found nothing incriminating, charged me with attempt to evade inspection. I spent a month in Walton prison. To this day I am quite sure I was framed to prevent my return to Australia.

After that it was impossible to get passage. So I settled in England. First I enjoyed a fruitful ministry in Alfreton, Derbyshire. Later I visited congregations as a circuit overseer. Then I went to Malta to serve where the need was very great. Now I am back in Sheffield, the city I left as a lad 62 years ago. It is my privilege to serve as secretary of the Ecclesall Congregation, one of 15 in the city. And during these later years, I have enjoyed the fine support of my wife, Joan, one of a family with whom I studied 35 years ago.

I can now look back over a half century of service as an evangelizer, both 'in favourable season and in troublesome season.' How I have prized the twin qualities of trust and loyalty! Yes, trust in Jehovah, whatever the circumstances. Trust that he and his vast army of angels are with us. Never do we stand alone.

And remain loyal. Maintain loyalty not only to Jehovah and Jesus Christ but also to God's earthly organization that nurtures and cherishes us. To be sure, our loyalty does get put to the test through adjustments within the organization, through trouble brought upon us, or through that which comes from our own foolishness. But the precious qualities of loyalty and trust will see us through —through 'favourable season and troublesome season' too.

Questions From Readers

■ When Abraham (and later Isaac) represented his wife as his sister, was this an example of the wife-sister relationship that once existed in the Middle East?

Modern scholarship has advanced that theory, but there seems to be more underlying Abraham's and Isaac's conduct.

Professor E. A. Speiser presented the wife-sister idea in *The Anchor Bible*. He noted discoveries about the ancient Hurrians who appear to have lived in northern Mesopotamia, including Haran where Abraham resided for a time and where Rebekah may have lived. Speiser wrote:

"In Hurrian society the bonds of marriage were strongest and most solemn when the wife had simultaneously the juridical status of a sister, regardless of actual blood ties. This is why a man would sometimes marry a girl and adopt her at the same time as his sister, in two separate steps recorded in independent legal documents. Violations of such sistership arrangements were punished more severely than breaches of marriage contracts . . . The wife-sister relationship is attested primarily among the upper strata of Hurrian society . . . Not only was Rebekah a native of Hurrian-dominated Har(r)an, but she was actually given as wife to Isaac, through an intermediary, by her brother Laban . . . There are thus sufficient grounds for placing the two marriages, those of Abraham and Sarah and of Isaac and Rebekah, in the wife-sister category."

The Genesis history tells us that Abraham twice represented his wife Sarah (who actually was his half sister) as his sister, not as his wife. This happened when they were in Egypt and again in Philistia. (Genesis 12:10-20; 20: 1-7) Isaac followed a similar course with Rebekah. Since Isaac and Rebekah were related, he could call her his sister.—Genesis 26:6-11.

In these cases Abraham and Isaac wanted their wives thought of as a sister because of an apparent danger to the husbands if it became known that the beautiful women were married. (Genesis 12:12; 26:9) So it does not seem that the men were appealing to a supposed wife-sister status as a means of protection; the object was to hide the marital status of Sarah and Rebekah.

Abraham married his half sister prior to God's giving Israel laws against such close unions. Still, many have been critical of his (and Isaac's) representing his wife as his sister. Of course, we must not forget that the Bible sometimes relates events without approving of the conduct involved. (Genesis 9:20, 21; 19:30-38) Yet there are ways of viewing what Abraham/Sarah and Isaac/Rebekah did that are consistent with their exemplary standing with God.

Before these events took place, God told Abraham: "I shall make a great nation out of you and I shall bless you and I will make your name great; and prove yourself a blessing. And I will bless those who bless you, and him that calls down evil upon you I shall curse, *and all the families of the ground will certainly bless themselves by means of you.*"(Genesis 12:2, 3) Jehovah also indicated that the blessing depended on Abraham's seed. (Genesis 12:7; compare Genesis 15:4, 5; 17: 4-8; 22:15-18.) Hence, Abraham (and later Isaac) needed to stay alive to produce offspring.

This may well have moved Abraham and Isaac to represent their faithful wives as their sisters. If public knowledge that Abraham was the legal husband of desirable Sarah, and Isaac of lovely Rebekah, would endanger the line of the seed, these men of faith might have determined that it was prudent not to let such relationship be known while they were in dangerous territory.

Sarah is singled out as an example of faith and a woman who 'hoped in God.' (1 Peter 3:5, 6; Hebrews 11:11) She chose to accept the position taken by her family head and for a time did not publicize her married state. It would be kind to view this as being done out of selflessness, a subordinating of personal feelings and interests so that all mankind would have a blessing available. And, seeing that Jehovah protected her from Pharaoh and later from Abimelech, king of Gerar, it is not surprising that Rebekah confidently followed a similar course in cooperation with Isaac, who was also a man of noteworthy faith.—Hebrews 11:20.

Consequently, whether people in Canaan and Egypt knew about the wife-sister status that seems to have existed in Haran or not, the course followed by Abraham/ Sarah and Isaac/Rebekah was, according to the things involved, motivated by high principles and objectives.

"No Empty Pep Talk"

That is what one reader writes regarding the new book *Survival Into a New Earth.* "This is one publication that won't stay on the shelf. Once you've opened it you're obliged to continue reading how your future will unfold," he explains. "The faith-strengthening, confident choice of words can only move one to say, 'Amen!' I already feel butterflies and am only on chapter eight!"

SURVIVAL INTO A NEW EARTH

March 15, 1985

The Watchtower

Announcing Jehovah's Kingdom

JEHOVAH
AWE-INSPIRING BUT LOVING

March 15, 1985
Vol. 106, No. 6

The Watchtower.
Announcing Jehovah's Kingdom

In This Issue

Photo on cover and on page 7 courtesy of NASA.

THE PURPOSE OF "THE WATCHTOWER" is to exalt Jehovah God as the Sovereign of the universe. It keeps watch on world events as they fulfill Bible prophecy. It comforts all peoples with the good news that God's Kingdom will soon destroy those who oppress their fellowmen and that it will turn the earth into a paradise. It encourages faith in the now-reigning King, Jesus Christ, whose shed blood opens the way for mankind to gain eternal life. "The Watchtower," published by Jehovah's Witnesses continuously since 1879, is nonpolitical. It adheres to the Bible as its authority.

"WATCHTOWER" STUDIES FOR THE WEEKS

April 21: Working With the Organizer of All the Universe. Page 10. Songs to Be Used: 52, 93.

April 28: At Unity With the Creator of the Universal Organization. Page 15. Songs to Be Used: 213, 100.

Average Printing Each Issue: 11,150,000

Now Published in 102 Languages

SEMIMONTHLY EDITIONS AVAILABLE BY MAIL
Afrikaans, Arabic, Cebuano, Chichewa, Chinese, Cibemba, Danish, Dutch, Efik, English*, Finnish, French, German, Greek, Hiligaynon, Igbo, Iloko, Italian, Japanese, Korean, Lingala, Malagasy, Maltese, Norwegian, Portuguese, Russian, Sepedi, Sesotho, Shona, Spanish, Swahili, Swedish, Tagalog, Thai, Tswana, Xhosa, Yoruba, Zulu

MONTHLY EDITIONS AVAILABLE BY MAIL
Armenian, Bengali, Bicol, Bulgarian, Croatian, Czech, Ewe, Fijian, Ga, Greenlandic, Gujarati, Gun, Hausa, Hebrew, Hindi, Hiri Motu, Hungarian, Icelandic, Kannada, Kikuyu, Kiluba, Malayalam, Marathi, New Guinea Pidgin, Pangasinan, Papiamento, Polish, Rarotongan, Romanian, Samar-Leyte, Samoan, Sango, Serbian, Silozi, Sinhalese, Slovenian, Solomon Islands-Pidgin, Tahitian, Tamil, Telugu, Tshiluba, Tsonga, Turkish, Twi, Ukrainian, Urdu, Venda, Vietnamese
*Study articles also available in large-print edition at same cost.

The Bible translation used is the "New World Translation of the Holy Scriptures," unless otherwise indicated.

Twenty cents (U.S.) a copy

Watch Tower Society offices	*Yearly subscription rates* *Semimonthly*
America, U.S., Watchtower, Wallkill, N.Y. 12589	$4.00
Australia, Box 280, Ingleburn, N.S.W. 2565	A$6.00
Canada, Box 4100, Halton Hills (Georgetown), Ontario L7G 4Y4	$5.20
England, The Ridgeway, London NW7 1RN	£5.00
Ireland, 29A Jamestown Road, Finglas, Dublin 11	£5.00
New Zealand, 6-A Western Springs Rd., Auckland 3	$7.00
Nigeria, P.O. Box 194, Yaba, Lagos State	₦3.50
Philippines, P.O. Box 2044, Manila 2800	₱50.00
South Africa, Private Bag 2, Elandsfontein, 1406	R5,60

Remittances should be sent to the office in your country or to Watchtower, Wallkill, N.Y. 12589, U.S.A.

Changes of address should reach us 30 days before your moving date. Give us your old and new address (if possible, your old address label).

The Watchtower (ISSN 0043-1087) is published semimonthly for $4.00 (U.S.) per year by Watch Tower Bible and Tract Society of Pennsylvania, 25 Columbia Heights, Brooklyn, N.Y. 11201. Second-class postage paid at Brooklyn, N.Y., and at additional mailing offices.

Postmaster: Send address changes to Watchtower, *Wallkill, N.Y. 12589.*

Published by
**Watch Tower Bible and Tract Society
of Pennsylvania**

25 Columbia Heights, Brooklyn, N.Y. 11201, U.S.A.
Frederick W. Franz, President

JEHOVAH
A Cruel or a Loving God?

"**B**UT the God of the Bible is a *cruel* God," the Japanese man insisted. The missionary standing in his doorway found himself before a person familiar with God's Word, the Bible.

"What about God's drowning people in the Flood?" the man continued. "And what about his incinerating Sodom and Gomorrah, not to mention his having the Israelites exterminate the Canaanites? How can you say that God is anything other than cruel? Besides, the God of the 'New Testament' is entirely different. Jesus taught about a God of peace and love."

This perception of the "Old Testament" God as cruel and warlike permeates the thinking of many. Consequently, some people view even the "New Testament" God of love as suspect. How could anyone be moved to serve a God who appears to have a split personality?

"All His Ways Are Justice"

Humans, though, are hardly in a position to criticize God's actions. Does a child at once comprehend why his father makes him endure the pain of a dentist's chair? Likewise, we might not at first understand all of God's actions. "Know that Jehovah is God," said the psalmist. "It is he that has made us, and not we ourselves."—Psalm 100:3.

Is it not unwise, then, hastily to conclude that God's actions are cruel? "'The thoughts of you people are not my thoughts, nor are my ways your ways,' is the utterance of Jehovah. 'For as the heavens are higher than the earth, so my ways

Was Jehovah just in sending the Flood, in destroying Sodom and Gomorrah, and in executing the Canaanites?

are higher than your ways, and my thoughts than your thoughts.'" (Isaiah 55:8, 9) Moreover, the Bible assures us that "all his ways are justice." Jehovah is identified as "a God of faithfulness, with whom there is no injustice." (Deuteronomy 32:4) Let us therefore look at some cases in which God has seen fit to execute judgment.

The Flood

"Jehovah saw that the badness of man was abundant in the earth and every inclination of the thoughts of his heart was only bad all the time." (Genesis 6:5) Such was the pre-Flood world. Yes, Jehovah God "saw the earth and, look! it was ruined, because all flesh had ruined its way on the earth." (Genesis 6:12) Some might argue that God should have left people alone, letting them do what they wanted. But there were still honest, morally upright people left on the earth. Would it not have been cruel for God to allow the wicked to exterminate the last vestige of morality left on earth? God therefore arranged for a global deluge to rid the earth of its ruiners.

A cruel God would have made no provision for the survival of man or beast. Yet Jehovah did so. A cruel God would never have warned of the coming cataclysm. Yet he assigned Noah to be "a preacher of righteousness" for at least some 40 or 50 years! (2 Peter 2:5) People could choose either survival or death.

Sodom and Gomorrah

When two angels visited Sodom, the inhabitants soon revealed their perverted nature. The men of Sodom surrounded Lot's house, "from boy to old man, all the people in one mob. And they kept calling out to Lot and saying to him: 'Where are the men who came in to you tonight? Bring them out to us that we may have intercourse with them.'" (Genesis 19:4, 5) This was 'going after flesh for unnatural use.'—Jude 7; see also Romans 1:26, 27.

God, "who searches the hearts," saw that the cities were unsalvageable. Their annihilation was deserved. (Romans 8:27) Why, not even ten righteous men could be found in Sodom! (Genesis 18:32) The conduct of the Sodomites posed a real threat to righteous Lot and his family. Therefore, God's rescue of Lot and his daughters was an act of love!—Genesis 19:12-26.

Executing the Canaanites

Jehovah promised Abraham that his seed would eventually occupy the land of Canaan. Note, though, that no execution was to take place in Abraham's day. Why not? "Because the error of the Amorites [the dominant Canaanite tribe] has *not yet come to completion*," said Jehovah. (Genesis 15:16) Some 430 years would pass before the wickedness of that nation had reached such proportions that Moses could say: "It is for the wickedness of these nations [of Canaan] that Jehovah your God is driving them away from before you."—Deuteronomy 9:5.

Says the book *Archaeology and the Old Testament:* "The brutality, lust and abandon of Canaanite mythology . . . must have brought out the worst traits in their devotees and entailed many of the most demoralizing practices of the time, such as sacred prostitution, child sacrifice and snake worship . . . utter moral and religious degeneracy." Nevertheless, the Gibeonites and residents of three other cities were spared. (Joshua 9:17, 18) Would a cruel God have allowed this?

A Split Personality?

However, some insist that the "Old Testament" God underwent a personality change in the "New Testament." 'Jesus' teachings focused on *love,*' they say. —Matthew 5:39, 44, 45.

Yet, the destruction of Jerusalem in 70 C.E. came as a judgment from Jehovah, even as Jesus foretold. (Matthew 23: 37, 38; 24:2) Further, unrighteous *individuals* such as Ananias, Sapphira, and Herod were put to death. God had not changed. (Acts 5:1-11; 12:21-23; Malachi 3:6) Nor were Jesus' teachings about love a new development. Much earlier, the Mosaic Law had commanded: "You must love your fellow as yourself." (Leviticus 19:18)

Jesus' teachings about *self-sacrificing love,* though, went further than this command. (John 13:34) Remember, too, that he also pronounced strong denunciations on hypocritical religious leaders. Read all of Matthew chapter 23 for yourself and see how powerfully Jesus denounced such ones.

The Bible record thus stands, not as a proof of God's being cruel, but as evidence of his deep and abiding love for mankind. Thus we are moved to learn more about Jehovah and his loving ways. Our next article can help you to do just that.

JEHOVAH
Awe-Inspiring but Loving

"TO WHOM can you people liken me"? asked Jehovah God. Even the loftiest of language could never fully convey God's incomparable power and glory. He himself invites us to consider the expanse of the heavens, saying: "Raise your eyes high up and see. Who has created these things? It is the One who is bringing forth the army of them even by number, all of whom he calls even by name. Due to the abundance of dynamic energy, he also being vigorous in power, not one of them is missing."—Isaiah 40:25, 26.

The thousands of stars visible to the naked eye are just a fraction of the some 100 *billion* stars that make up our galaxy alone! Yet Jehovah has numbered and named all the stars in the entire universe! Consider, too, the massive volume of energy locked up in all of this matter. Our sun has a central temperature of 27 million degrees Fahrenheit (15 million degrees Celsius). What "dynamic energy" Jehovah must have to have created *billions* of these nuclear furnaces!

Understanding Jehovah fully is therefore beyond our limited capabilities. Said Elihu: "As for the Almighty, we have not found him out; he is exalted in power . . . Therefore let men fear him." (Job 37:23, 24) Jehovah, however, wants more than just our awe or fear. "You must *love* Jehovah your God with all your heart and all your soul and all your vital force," the Bible commands. (Deuteronomy 6:5) But can we love someone we cannot fully understand? Yes, for though Jehovah's dwelling is high in the heavens, he deals lovingly with imperfect humans and allows them to gain at least a partial understanding of him.—Compare Psalm 113: 5-9.

His "Eyes," "Ears," and "Face"

One way in which Jehovah helps us understand him is by allowing himself to be described in human terms. The apostle Peter said: "The *eyes* of Jehovah are upon the righteous ones, and his *ears* are toward their supplication; but the *face* of Jehovah is against those doing bad things."—1 Peter 3:12; compare Exodus 15:6; Ezekiel 20:33; Luke 11:20.

Of course, these are metaphors, not to be taken literally, any more than when the Scriptures call God "a sun," "a shield," or "the Rock." (Psalm 84:11; Deuteronomy 32:4, 31) 'But does not the Bible say that we are made in his "image"?' reason some. (Genesis 1:26, 27) Yes, but claiming that God has a literal mouth, nose, and ears creates serious problems. Would an almighty God's hearing, for example, really be limited by what sound waves would carry to literal ears? No, for the Bible indicates that God can "hear" even voiceless expressions made in the human heart. (Genesis 24:42-45) Nor does his ability to "see" depend upon light waves.—Psalm 139:1, 7-12; Hebrews 4:13.

Perfect man thus mirrored, not physical features, but God's qualities such as love and justice. Especially do Christians manifest such qualities as they heed the counsel of the apostle Paul, who urged: "Clothe yourselves with the new personality, which through accurate knowledge is being made new according to the *image* of the One who created it."—Colossians 3:10.

Visions of Glory

In ancient times, certain servants of Jehovah had the privilege of receiving inspired visions of Jehovah's heavenly glory. Ezekiel was one of these individuals. (Eze-

Men such as Ezekiel and John had visions that give us only an idea of Jehovah's awe-inspiring glory

kiel 1:1) What he saw in vision defied description! Ezekiel resorted to metaphors and similes, often stating that what he saw was "something like" familiar material things. For instance, the prophet said:

"There was something in appearance like sapphire stone, the likeness of a throne. And upon the likeness of the throne there was a likeness of someone in appearance like an earthling man upon it, up above. And I got to see something like the glow of electrum, like the appearance of fire all around inside thereof, from the appearance of his hips and upward; and from the appearance of his hips and downward I saw something like the appearance of fire, and he had a brightness all around. There was something like the appearance of the bow that occurs in a cloud mass on the day of a pouring rain. That is how the appearance was of the brightness round about. It was the appearance of the likeness of the glory of Jehovah."—Ezekiel 1: 26-28.

What glory Ezekiel described! The apostle John had a similar vision of Jehovah, and he wrote: "Look! a throne was in its position in heaven, and there is one seated upon the throne. And the one seated is, in appearance, like a jasper stone and a precious red-colored stone, and round about the throne there is a rainbow like an emerald in appearance." (Revelation 4:1-3) Although Jehovah is represented in such grandeur, he is not depicted as a cruel God. Rather, the setting is calm, peaceful like the rainbow.—Compare Genesis 9: 12-16.

The fact that God allowed even such limited views of his heavenly majesty

shows that his intentions toward mankind are peaceful. Surely, then, those who love God can confidently approach him as the benevolent "Hearer of prayer."—Psalm 65:2.

The man Job said of God: "Look! These are the fringes of his ways, and what a whisper of a matter has been heard of him!" (Job 26:14) There is, indeed, much to learn about Jehovah God, who has blessed his servants with the prospect of living eternally. (John 17:3) But even "time indefinite" will not be enough for us to "find out the work that the true God has made from the start to the finish."—Ecclesiastes 3:11.

What honest-hearted ones *do* know or learn, however, can motivate them to love and obey Jehovah. (1 John 5:3) Are you one of such individuals? Obeying God is not always easy. But when you have truly come to know Jehovah God and his loving ways, no effort seems too great. Are you determined, therefore, to know more fully this awe-inspiring yet loving God?

A Man Ruined by Greed

NAAMAN is grateful for being healed of his leprosy. He shows his gratitude by trying to give Elisha a gift of thousands of pieces of gold and silver, as well as ten changes of fine clothes. But Elisha refuses the gift. Jehovah actually performed the miraculous healing, and Elisha refuses to take any credit by accepting a gift.

But what of Elisha's servant Gehazi? He greedily looks at those beautiful clothes and all that money. What will happen if Gehazi keeps wishing he could have some of these things? The improper desire could lead to his being drawn out and enticed so that he does what is bad.—James 1:13-15.

Well, eventually Naaman and his servants say good-bye and start off for their homes in Syria. But Gehazi does not stop thinking about those beautiful clothes and all that money. Look there! Gehazi is running off. Where is he going?

Gehazi chases after Naaman and catches up with

him. Naaman greets Gehazi, asking: 'Is everything all right?' 'Yes,' Gehazi replies. 'But Elisha sent me to tell you that two visitors just came. And Elisha would like you to give them two changes of clothes and some silver.' But this is a lie. Gehazi wants these things for himself. Naaman, however, does not know this, and so he is delighted to provide this gift. He even insists that Gehazi take more money than he asks for.

When Gehazi arrives back home, Elisha inquires: 'Where have you been?'

'Oh, nowhere,' he replies. However, Jehovah has revealed to Elisha the bad thing Gehazi has done. So Elisha says: 'This is no time to accept money and clothes! Now Naaman's disease will come upon you and your offspring.' Immediately Gehazi is struck with leprosy, and this terrible disease sticks to him for the rest of his life. What happened to Gehazi shows how greed can lead to ruin. —2 Kings 5:5, 15-27.

Working With the Organizer of All the Universe

"For we are God's fellow workers. You people are God's field under cultivation, God's building."—1 CORINTHIANS 3:9.

"**G**OD'S ORGANIZATION." That expression was used by a member of the Watch Tower Society's editorial staff during the daily Bible discussion at the Bethel dining tables over 60 years ago. How it thrilled the headquarters family in Brooklyn, New York! That unique phrase, "God's organization," served to guide the future thinking, speech, and writing of those Bible Students. It broadened their spiritual vision with regard to all creation and greatly influenced their attitude toward the marvelous Organizer of the universe, Jehovah God.

2 Today, that may seem strange, since the word "organization" is used regularly among Jehovah's Witnesses, who cherish their privilege of working with the Organizer of the universe. (1 Corinthians 3: 5-9) The word "organization" is drawn from the Greek term *or'ga·non.* Among other things, it signifies an instrument or implement with which work is accomplished. It appears in the *Septuagint Version* a number of times and is used to refer to a musical instrument, such as David's harp. The root of this word is *er'gon,* a noun meaning "work." So an organization is an arrangement of things put in force to get something done or worked out in the best way possible and with the least expenditure of time and energy.

Early Views of Organization

3 Years ago, however, the Bible Students had some difficulty in applying the word "organization." For instance, in the *Watch Tower* issue of March 1883, it was stated:

"But, though it is impossible for the natural man to see our organization, because he cannot understand the things of the Spirit of God, we trust that you can see that the true Church is most effectually organized, and is in the best possible working order. . . . We have unbounded faith in our Captain; and this perfect organization, invisible to the world, marches on to certain and glorious victory."

4 However, the *Watch Tower* issue of December 1, 1894, said:

"But as that work of organizing the church of the new Gospel dispensation was no part of the harvest work of the old Jewish dispensation, so the present harvest work or reaping of the Gospel dispensation is also separate and distinct from the work of the new Millennial dispensation now drawing on. . . . It is plain that the forming of a visible organization of such gathered out ones would be out of

---

1. What expression voiced over 60 years ago thrilled its hearers, and what effect did it have on earnest Bible Students of that time?
2. As indicated by its Greek origin, how may the word "organization" be defined?

3. What did the March 1883 issue of this journal say about "our organization"?
4. What view of organizing was presented in the December 1, 1894, issue of this magazine?

harmony with the spirit of the divine plan; and if done would seem to indicate on the part of the church a desire to conform to the now popular idea of organization or confederacy. (See Isa. 8:12) The work now is not organization, but division, just as it was in the Jewish harvest proper. (Matt. 10:34-36) . . .

"While, therefore, we do not esteem a visible organization of the gathered ones to be a part of the Lord's plan in the harvest work, as though we expected as an organization to abide here for another age, we do esteem it to be his will that those that love the Lord should speak often one to another of their common hopes and joys, or trials and perplexities, communing together concerning the precious things of his Word."

⁵ So the Christian congregation was not then considered to be an organization. But it was thought well to set in order the congregation, or ecclesia. For example, Study V of the book *The New Creation,* published in 1904, was entitled "The Organization of the New Creation" and opens by saying: "As the New Creation will not reach its perfection or completion until the First Resurrection, so its organization will be completed only then. The temple figure illustrates this: as living stones we are now called, or invited to places in the glorious temple."

⁶ Interestingly, the book *Thy Kingdom Come,* published in 1891, said regarding those anointed ones of the "new creation": "As for Isaiah 54:1-8, the Apostle Paul has thrown the light of superhuman wisdom upon it, and has applied it to spiritual Zion, our mother or covenant, symbolized by Sarah. The fleshly seed of Abraham had been cast out from being heir of the promise, and the true seed, Christ (typified by Isaac and Rebecca), had been received as the only seed of promise.—Gal. 4:22, 24, 26-31."

⁷ This statement had nothing to do with the Zionist World Organization, founded by Theodor Herzl in 1897. That organization dealt with Jerusalem below, here on earth, not "the Jerusalem above," the "mother" of the Christian congregation. (Galatians 4:26) The book *Thy Kingdom Come* did not go on to develop the fact that the husbandly owner of the "mother" of the Christian congregation is God, who was pictured by Abraham. Jehovah is married, not to the Abrahamic covenant or the new covenant, but to "Jerusalem above," pictured by Isaac's mother Sarah. Like her, as a "mother," "the Jerusalem above" must be something alive and having personality.

⁸ Who, then, is "Jerusalem above"? To find out, let us first consider Isaiah 54:1-8, which reads in part:

"'Cry out joyfully, you barren woman that did not give birth! Become cheerful with a joyful outcry and cry shrilly, you that had no childbirth pains, for the sons of the desolated one are more numerous than the sons of the woman with a husbandly owner,' Jehovah has said. . . . 'For your Grand Maker is your husbandly owner, Jehovah of armies being his name; and the Holy One of Israel is your Repurchaser. The God of the whole earth he will be called. For Jehovah called you as if you were a wife left entirely and hurt in spirit, and as a wife of the time of youth who was then rejected,' your God has said. 'For a little moment I left you entirely, but with great mercies I shall collect you together. With a flood of indignation I concealed my face from you for but a moment, but with loving-kindness to time indefinite I will have mercy upon you,' your Repurchaser, Jehovah, has said."

---

5. Regarding organization, what was said in the book *The New Creation?*
6. How did the book *Thy Kingdom Come* identify the "mother" of members of the "new creation"?

7, 8. Who is the husband of the "mother" of the Christian congregation, and what does Isaiah 54:1-8 say in this regard?

⁹ There, in the first instance, Jehovah was not talking to a covenant. He was addressing a nation, his chosen people in the Mosaic Law covenant with him. From God's standpoint, that nation made up a composite "woman" that was like a wife to him. According to the apostle Paul's letter to the Galatians, that figurative "woman" was typical, but he does not say that she is a covenant, or compact. A covenant could not be comforted, consoled. Rather, Paul shows that the antitypical "woman" is something alive, like a "mother," just as the "husbandly owner," Jehovah, is alive as a Person having intelligence and ability to give comfort. Speaking of women of ancient history, the apostle wrote: "Now this Hagar [the maidservant who substituted for her mistress Sarah in bearing Ishmael to Abraham] means Sinai, a mountain in Arabia, and she [Hagar] corresponds with the Jerusalem today [when Paul was on earth], for she is in slavery [to the Mosaic Law covenant] with her children. But the Jerusalem above is free, and she is our mother."—Galatians 4: 25, 26.

The Jerusalem in Slavery

¹⁰ Hagar does not typify, or represent, the Mosaic Law covenant. Nor is that covenant with its Ten Commandments pictured by Mount Sinai, with which Hagar corresponds. Of course, God did not make any covenant with Mount Sinai. But it was there that he brought the Israelites, whom he had freed from Egyptian bondage, into a covenant relationship with himself, and he dealt with them as a free

How was earthly Jerusalem in slavery?

nation. This took place centuries after God made a unilateral covenant with Abraham, promising him a male seed.

¹¹ When Moses, the mediator of the Law covenant, came down from Mount Sinai, his face had a superhuman effulgence of such intensity that he had to veil it so that the Israelites could look at him. (2 Corinthians 3:12-16) But up on Mount Sinai, Moses was not in direct touch with Jehovah, for it was by means of an angel that God entered into the covenant with the Israelites. (Acts 7:37, 38; Hebrews 2:2) In that way the nation of Israel became subject to the Law covenant. Centuries later, however, that covenant was removed, being nailed to Jesus' torture stake in 33 C.E.—Colossians 2:13, 14.

¹² Paul wrote that Mount Sinai corresponded with the Jerusalem below of his day. Of course, Jerusalem was not a covenant; it was a prized city occupied by Jewish residents. As the capital city, it stood for the nation and was the symbolic "mother" of "children," that is, of all members of the Jewish, or Israelite, nation. (Matthew 23:37) In Jerusalem stood the temple of Jehovah, the God with whom the

9. (a) At Isaiah 54:1-8, to whom or to what was Jehovah speaking comfortingly? (b) According to Galatians 4:25, 26, who is the figurative "woman" addressed in the antitype?
10, 11. (a) What significant development involving the Israelites took place at Mount Sinai? (b) With regard to the Law covenant, what happened in 33 C.E.?

12. (a) Of whom was earthly Jerusalem a "mother"? (b) Jerusalem on earth was under what servitude 19 centuries ago, and why did she never get free?

Israelites were in covenant relationship. But the Jewish people did not then have an independent kingdom of their own ruled by a descendant of King David. Hence, they were not free but were in servitude under Gentile political authorities. More importantly, they were in religious slavery. Only the promised Messiah, Jesus Christ, could free them from that, as well as from slavery to sin. But that Jerusalem did not accept Jesus as Messiah and King and never did get free. Instead, she perished at Roman hands in 70 C.E., with disaster for her "children."

The Free Jerusalem

13 Paul contrasted enslaved earthly Jerusalem with "Jerusalem above," which is "free." Quoting from Isaiah 54:1-8, he wrote:

"But the Jerusalem above is free, and she is our mother. For it is written: 'Be glad, you barren woman who does not give birth; break out and cry aloud, you woman who does not have childbirth pains; for the children of the desolate woman are more numerous than those of her who has the husband.' Now we, brothers, are children belonging to the promise the same as Isaac was. But just as then the one born in the manner of flesh began persecuting the one born in the manner of spirit, so also now. Nevertheless, what does the Scripture say? 'Drive out the servant girl and her son, for by no means shall the son of the servant girl be an heir with the son of the free woman.' Wherefore, brothers, we are children, not of a servant girl, but of the free woman. For such freedom Christ set us free. Therefore stand fast, and do not let yourselves be confined again in a yoke of slavery." —Galatians 4:26–5:1.

14 The Galatian Christians thus addressed were "God's children as a result of

his promise." (Galatians 4:28, *Today's English Version*) Foreshadowing this, Isaac was born to the centenarian Abraham and his 90-year-old wife Sarah in fulfillment of Jehovah's promise to that faithful patriarch. Yes, Isaac's birth to Abraham was miraculous, absolutely not "in the manner of flesh." (Genesis 18:11-15) So it had to be "in the manner of spirit." Yes, the spirit of the Greater Abraham, Jehovah God, surely was needed to revive the reproductive powers of the free woman Sarah, as well as those of Abraham. (Romans 4:19) It is noteworthy that the "promise" itself was not old when Isaac was born in 1918 B.C.E., for that was only 25 years after Abraham's entry into the promised land of Canaan in 1943 B.C.E., when the "promise" went into effect.

15 "Jerusalem above" was "desolate," childless as it were, much longer than Sarah had been. Actually, "Jerusalem above" was in that state from 1943 B.C.E., when the promise to Abraham went into effect, until Jesus was baptized in 29 C.E. It was then that Jesus was begotten by the spirit of the Greater Abraham, Jehovah, and was anointed with His spirit to be the Christ or Anointed One, the Messiah. But "Jerusalem above" was to have more than one spiritual child. So at Pentecost of 33 C.E., after Jesus' resurrection and ascension to heaven, about 120 of his faithful disciples were begotten by the spirit of the Greater Abraham. They were then anointed with that spirit to become the spiritual brothers of the Greater Isaac, Jesus Christ. Later that day about 3,000 more Jews got baptized as Jesus' disciples and were anointed with the holy spirit. (Acts 2:1-42) Thus on that day "Jerusalem above" became "mother" to many children.

13. What did Paul say about the free Jerusalem, and in freedom from what should her "children" stand fast?
14. Why was Isaac's birth "in the manner of spirit"?

15. For how long was "Jerusalem above" childless, and when did her offspring begin to become numerous?

The queen of Sheba was amazed when she visited Solomon. He worked with the Organizer of the universe. Are you also working with Jehovah God?

ral Jews who rejected Jesus Christ as the promised "seed" not only of the patriarch Abraham but also of the Greater Abraham, Jehovah God.—Matthew 23:37-39.

Work With the Great Organizer

[18] Jesus Christ, who had God's heavenly organization as his "mother," was greater and wiser than King Solomon, the renowned son of David and ruler in ancient earthly Jerusalem. Solomon's glory and wisdom surely attracted the attention of the non-Israelite nations, even as Jesus indicated in saying: "The queen of the south will be raised up in the judgment with this generation and will condemn it; because she came from the ends of the earth to hear the wisdom of Solomon, but, look! something more than Solomon is here." (Matthew 12:42; Luke 11:31) In part, Solomon displayed that outstanding wisdom in the way he arranged the affairs of his administration. How he had everything wisely organized was a cause of wonderment.

[19] Accordingly, at 1 Kings 10:4, 5 we read: "When the queen of Sheba got to see all the wisdom of Solomon and the house that he had built, and the food of his table and the sitting of his servants and the table service of his waiters and their attire and his drinks and his burnt sacrifices that he regularly offered up at the house of Jehovah, then there proved to be no more spirit in her." (NW; Rotherham;

[16] The apostle Paul reveals that the woman addressed at Isaiah 54:1-8 is "the Jerusalem above." Jehovah God is her "husbandly owner," as well as her Grand Maker. Figuratively speaking, she is his "woman," his "wife," or wifelike organization in heaven above. Like a husband, he is the One who makes her fruitful so as to produce the true "seed" promised in Abraham's day.—Galatians 3:16, 26-29.

[17] To become the primary "seed" of the Greater Abraham, the only-begotten Son of God had emerged from Jehovah's wifelike celestial organization. Thus she became like a "mother" to God's Son. Jesus Christ was not the figurative son of the earthly Jerusalem of his days on earth, for that city then was in bondage, or slavery, with her "children," and Jesus never was enslaved. (Galatians 4:25) Earthly Jerusalem was the "mother" of those natu-

16. What is the identity of "Jerusalem above"?
17. How did "Jerusalem above" become the "mother" of the primary "seed" of the Greater Abraham?

18. Why was earthly Jerusalem a center of attention in the days of King Solomon?
19. What was there about King Solomon's reign that amazed the queen of Sheba?

Young; Revised Standard; Septuagint. See also 2 Chronicles 9:4.) The queen of Sheba had reason to be impressed with the arrangement of Solomon's staff. And in having things well arranged and in good order, he was in harmony with the God of Order.—1 Corinthians 14:33.

[20] In keeping with Solomon's humble prayer, Jehovah gave him "a wise and understanding heart." (1 Kings 3:5-14) The Great Organizer of all the universe gave Solomon the ability to organize things in behalf of good order and efficiency. Hence, it became the obligation of the king of Jehovah's covenant people to work with the divine Organizer of all created things in heaven and on earth. Compa-

20. (a) In response to Solomon's prayer, what did Jehovah give him? (b) As "something more than Solomon," what does Jesus Christ do, and what is the course of his followers?

rably, the glorified Jesus Christ, who is "something more than Solomon," wisely does so. Therefore, his faithful followers on earth also need to do this, and they do.

What Do You Say?

□ How would you define the word "organization"?

□ Earthly Jerusalem was the "mother" of whom, and she never was freed from what servitude?

□ What is the identity of "Jerusalem above," and who are her "children"?

□ How did Solomon use his God-given wisdom, and what is being done by the Greater Solomon and His followers?

At Unity With the Creator of the Universal Organization

"Look! How good and how pleasant it is for brothers to dwell together in unity!"—PSALM 133:1.

THE Creator of the universal organization desires to keep it pure, righteous, and unified. But shortly after the beginning of mankind's existence some 6,000 years ago, a disturbing factor appeared on

1, 2. (a) What disturbing factor appeared some 6,000 years ago? (b) What does the Bible call this renegade, and how did he try to make himself like the Most High?

the universal scene. This occurred when a superhuman resister broke away from the Creator's organization and set out to form his own independent organization.

[2] Because this renegade opposed his Creator, the Bible calls him Satan, meaning "Resister." He is the archresister of Jehovah, the rightful Sovereign of the universe. (Job 1:6, 7) Ambitious to make

himself like the Most High in having his own organization, the Resister would not stop short of trying to act as a rival organizer and god. Satan thus made himself attractive-looking. Satan's attitude was reflected in the dynasty and brilliant worldly position taken by "the king of Babylon," to whom the terms "shining one" and "Lucifer" were aptly given. (Isaiah 14:4, 12-14; *King James Version; An American Translation*) To this day, but only by Jehovah's permission, Satan is "the god of this system of things."—2 Corinthians 4:4.

³ Likely in order to undermine Jehovah's organization, Satan first struck at its lowest part, Adam, the appointed head of the human family. (Genesis 3:1-24; Psalm 8:3-5; Romans 5:12) Later, many angels disobediently forsook their "original position," or proper dwelling place in heaven, and materialized in flesh so as to marry and cohabit with good-looking, though imperfect, women. (Jude 6) Their hybrid offspring, abnormal in size and strength, were called Nephilim. This term, believed to mean "fellers," was apropos since they apparently caused mere humans to fall by violence. At the time of the Flood, the disobedient angels dematerialized and returned to the spirit realm. (Genesis 6:1–7:23) By disuniting themselves from Jehovah's organization, they made themselves demons, and Satan the Devil became their ruler.—Deuteronomy 32:17; Psalm 106:37; Matthew 12:24; Luke 11:15-19.

⁴ In that way, Satan set up the invisible, superhuman spirit part of his organization. The Flood survivors, Noah and his family, remained at unity with Jehovah's invisible heavenly organization. (Genesis 6:9; 8:18-21) But Satan set out to break up the unity of faithful Noah's descendants. What was the Devil's objective? Why, to bring forth a visible part to his wicked organization!

⁵ It took some time for the International Bible Students to discern that Satan has an organization. But *The Watch Tower* of May 1, 1921, said: "Not content with what he had already done, Satan seduced these of the heavenly host and caused them to debauch mankind and to fill the earth with

---

3. (a) At what part of Jehovah's organization did this resister first strike? (b) What developments resulted in the Devil's becoming the ruler of the demons?

4. What did the human Flood survivors do, but what did Satan set out to do, and with what objective?

5. How did *The Watch Tower* of May 1, 1921, suggest that Satan has an organization?

Jehovah's people have always been at unity with one another and with the Creator of the universal organization

violence. He organized a system invisible to human eyes, as well as a system on earth that is visible to human eyes, and has sought to counterfeit every part of the revealed plan of God."

⁶ "Satan's Purpose" was a subheading under which *The Watch Tower* of December 1, 1922, plainly said: "We are now in the evil day. The fight is on between Satan's organization and God's organization. It is a desperate fight. Satan is attempting to destroy the morale of the Lord's organization and, if possible, to destroy the members of the house of sons. To this end he resorts to every possible scheme."

───────

6. What did *The Watch Tower* of December 1, 1922, say about Satan's purpose?

⁷ Discerning the two antagonistic organizations helped to clarify many Bible teachings and prophecies. For example, Revelation chapter 12 was not correctly understood until the article "Birth of the Nation" appeared in *The Watch Tower* of March 1, 1925. Its theme text (Revelation 12:5, *KJ*) reads: "And she brought forth a man child, who was to rule all nations with a rod of iron: and her child was caught up unto God, and to his throne."

⁸ On pages 67 and 68 this article stated:

"What has been the outstanding feature of the divine plan during the ages? . . . The establishment of the kingdom for which Jesus taught us to pray. That means the birth of the new nation, which shall rule and bless all the families of the earth. . . . What has been the opposing power that has kept the people in ignorance of this glorious new nation and the blessings it will bring to them? . . . Satan the devil, and his organization. . . . The real fight is God against the devil, the kingdom of righteousness putting out of possession the kingdom of wickedness and darkness, and establishing the kingdom of truth instead. . . . Following 1918 the devil's organization, financial, political and ecclesiastical, particularly the latter, openly repudiated the Lord and his kingdom; and then and there the wrath of God against the nations began to be expressed. From that time forward the battle has gone on in the earth. Prior to that the battle was fought in heaven."

⁹ It was then mistakenly thought that both Isaiah 66:7 and Revelation 12:5 foretold the birth of the same "man child." (*KJ*) So the above-quoted *Watch Tower* also said:

"The 'woman' seems clearly to symbolize that part of Zion, God's organization, which gives birth to the new government or nation

───────

7, 8. (a) How was it helpful to discern the two antagonistic organizations? (b) In *The Watch Tower* of March 1, 1925, what was shown to be against the figurative "man child"?
9. In 1925, what was the "woman" of Revelation chapter 12 explained to be?

which shall rule the nations and peoples of the earth with a rod of iron and with righteousness. . . . (Galatians 4:26) In other words Zion or Jerusalem, God's organization, is the mother which gives birth to the new nation, or governing factors. The anointed ones on earth are a part of 'the woman', and surely represent her. The woman 'clothed with the sun' means Zion in heaven and the approved ones on earth of God's organization at the time the Lord comes to his temple. . . . Now in his temple encompassing the temple class or investing them with his robe of righteousness, his organization producing the new nation, otherwise designated Zion, shines as the sun."

10 The "dragon," now understood to be Satan the Devil himself, failed to devour the "man child," the Messianic Kingdom born in heaven at the end of the Gentile Times in 1914. (Luke 21:24, *KJ*) During the war that followed in heaven, the spirit part of Satan's organization was cast down to the vicinity of the earth, never again to enter heaven and exercise a disunifying influence there. That demoted organization now goes after the visible part of Jehovah's universal organization, relentlessly waging war "with the remaining ones of her seed, who observe the commandments of God and have the work of bearing witness to Jesus."—Revelation 12:17.

United Service

11 God's figurative "woman" is likened to the chosen city Jerusalem, poetically called Zion. Hence, Paul's words about the free "Jerusalem above" can now be applied to "the remaining ones of her seed" against whom the "dragon," Satan the Devil, continues to "wage war." (Galatians 4:26) Earthly Jerusalem was strongly built and closely knit together in the days of David, who said: "I rejoiced when they were saying to me: 'To the house of Jehovah let us go.' Our feet proved to be standing within your gates, O Jerusalem. Jerusalem is one that is built like a city that has been joined together in oneness, to which the tribes have gone up, the tribes of Jah, as a reminder to Israel to give thanks to the name of Jehovah."—Psalm 122:1-4.

12 What a lovely picture of the unity of Jehovah's universal organization! Especially was unity evident at national festivals, when the 12 tribes of Israel joined in united worship of Jehovah at the sacred tabernacle in Jerusalem. And during the reign of their shepherd-king David, the tribes remained united not just due to fleshly ties but primarily because of the organized worship of their God. Yes, Jerusalem was the divinely approved center of united, organized worship under the one priesthood taken from the tribe of Levi and the family of Israel's first high priest, Aaron, the older brother of the prophet Moses. Moreover, all 12 tribes were in the one Law covenant that divided them off from all the demon-worshiping nations.

13 What unifying factors all these things were! They kept God's people united as one national organization for their safety and blessing. David put it this way: "Look! How good and how pleasant it is for brothers to dwell together in unity! It is like the good oil upon the head, that is running down upon the beard, Aaron's beard, that is running down to the collar of his gar-

---

10. What has happened to the spirit part of Satan's organization, and what war is it now waging?
11. (a) To whom can Paul's words about "Jerusalem above" be applied today? (b) What did David say about earthly Jerusalem, where Jehovah's house of worship was situated?

12. (a) To what unity do the words of Psalm 122: 1-4 apply today? (b) Jerusalem and the sacred tabernacle there had what bearing on the unity of Israel's tribes?
13. What did David say about the unity enjoyed by the ancient Israelites?

ments. It is like the dew of Hermon that is descending upon the mountains of Zion. For there Jehovah commanded the blessing to be, even life to time indefinite." —Psalm 133:1-3.

¹⁴ The national unity that inspired such heartfelt expressions is being duplicated today. By whom? By "the Israel of God," the spiritual Israelites whose one motherhood Paul called to mind in saying: "But the Jerusalem above is free, and she is our mother." (Galatians 6:16; 4:26) She does not put her spirit-begotten children under bondage to the Law covenant. Although "the Israel of God" is pictured as consisting of 12 tribes, all 144,000 members thereof are sealed with the same "seal of the living God," and all are depicted as standing on the one heavenly "Mount Zion." (Revelation 7:1-8; 14:1-4) What a choral group they make up as they unitedly sing "the song of Moses the slave of God and the song of the Lamb," Jesus Christ! (Revelation 15:3, 4; John 1:29, 36) That "song" delights God and bespeaks victory!

¹⁵ The 144,000 and their Choirmaster, "the Lamb," are organized for more than making the heavens ring with their singing. Theirs is a royal organization that is to reign a thousand years for the vindication of Jehovah's universal sovereignty and the blessing of all responsive mankind. (Revelation 20:4-6) The word "organization," an antonym of "disorganization," pertains to an arrangement of things with each part being put in its proper place and given its assignment of work so that they all operate together to bring about a common result. Thus, organization makes for unity, cooperation, good order, and harmony—not friction.

¹⁶ The goal of Christian unity was set more than 19 centuries ago, when "gifts in men" were given in the form of apostles, prophets, evangelizers, shepherds, and teachers. When the *Watch Tower* magazine began to be published in 1879, God also gave spiritual "shepherds and teachers." This provision has brought Jehovah's Witnesses to their present "oneness in the faith and in the accurate knowledge of the Son of God." (Ephesians 4:8, 11-16) How grateful we are that Jehovah has done this after all the centuries of worldwide religious confusion and disorganization!

¹⁷ Clearly, God had more than the unity of anointed Christians in mind, for "he purposed in himself for an administration at the full limit of the appointed times, namely, to gather all things together again in the Christ, the things in the heavens and the things on the earth." (Ephesians 1:9, 10) In this regard, Jesus foretold: "I have other sheep, which are not of this fold; those also I must bring, and they will listen to my voice, and they will become one flock, one shepherd." —John 10:16.

¹⁸ These "other sheep" are among "the things on the earth" that must be gathered together. So, under the influence of God's spirit, about 21 years after Jesus Christ started reigning in 1914, special attention began to be given to the "other sheep." During a convention of Jehovah's Witnesses in Washington, D.C., in 1935,

---

14. (a) By whom is Israel's national unity being duplicated today? (b) Where are the spiritual Israelites depicted as standing, and what "song" do they sing in unison?
15. (a) The 144,000 are organized for what besides for singing? (b) How does the very word "organization" denote unity?

16. According to Ephesians 4:8, 11-16, what goal was set more than 19 centuries ago, and what has been achieved among Jehovah's Witnesses?
17. How do we know that God had more than the unity of anointed Christians in mind, and in this regard what did Jesus foretell?
18. (a) Who are among "the things on the earth" that must be gathered together? (b) In 1935, how was special attention given to the "other sheep"?

the president of the Watch Tower Society explained that the "great multitude" were "other sheep" eventually to be gathered by the Fine Shepherd, Jesus Christ. (Revelation 7:9-17, *KJ*) Did Jesus gather any "other sheep" at that epoch-making convention? Yes, for 840 conventioners then recognized themselves as being gathered by the Fine Shepherd and got baptized in symbol of their dedication to Jehovah God.

¹⁹ That only began the gathering of the "great multitude" of "other sheep," who already number over 2,800,000. By uniting with the visible part of Jehovah's organization—that is, with the remnant of the "little flock" in "this fold" of the Fine Shepherd—they have come into unity with the Grand Creator of the universal organization. And they are determined to maintain that unity throughout their eternal life on the Paradise earth that the Supreme Shepherd, Jehovah, will provide for them.—Luke 12:32; 23:43.

²⁰ As the anointed remnant and the increasing "great multitude" contemplate all that the Supreme Shepherd has done universally since the Gentile Times ended in 1914, heartfelt gratitude moves them to sing together the grand Hallelujah psalm: "Praise Jah, you people! Praise God in his holy place. Praise him in the expanse of his strength. Praise him for his works of mightiness. Praise him according to the abundance of his greatness. Praise him with the blowing of the horn. Praise him with the stringed instrument and the harp. Praise him with the tambourine and the circle dance. Praise him with strings

and the pipe. Praise him with the cymbals of melodious sound. Praise him with the clashing cymbals. Every breathing thing —let it praise Jah. Praise Jah, you people!"—Psalm 150:1-6.

²¹ Soon the present "heavens" and "earth" will be dissolved amid "the war of the great day of God the Almighty," and the long-awaited "new heavens and a new earth" will be immovably established. (2 Peter 3:7-13; Revelation 16:14, 16) Then, indeed, "every breathing thing" that survives on this cleansed earth will praise Jah, the Grand Creator of the universal organization of righteousness. All members of that organization in heaven and on the earth will exultantly praise Jehovah and will loyally and lovingly work with him for the eternal vindication of his universal sovereignty and the sanctification of his most worthy name. O what magnificent unity all of this bespeaks!

---

21. (a) When will "every breathing thing" praise Jehovah? (b) With whom and with what purpose will all members of the universal organization then work?

How Would You Answer?

□ What developments led to Satan's becoming the ruler of the demons?

□ How was it helpful to discern between the two great organizations?

□ Psalm 122:1-4 applies to what unity today?

□ Why can it be said that Jehovah had more than the unity of Jesus' anointed followers in mind?

□ When will "every breathing thing" praise Jehovah God?

---

19. (a) So far, how large has the "great multitude" become? (b) By uniting with Jehovah's visible organization, the "great multitude" have come into unity with whom, and what determination is theirs?

20. As the anointed remnant and the "great multitude" contemplate what the Supreme Shepherd has done since 1914, what expressions are they moved to make?

How Expansive Is Your Love?

THE acorn barnacle is a small, shelled creature that lives in water. Few people give it much thought. However, the barnacle has one remarkable ability: It knows how to stick to things. Its secret? It makes a glue so strong that a film a mere 3/10,000 of an inch (0.0762 mm) thick has a "shear strength" of 7,000 pounds per square inch (493 kg/sq cm)! Anyone who has tried to pry a barnacle from its chosen mooring will testify to the strength of its powerful bonding agent.

Christians are familiar with something similar. Jehovah's organization on earth is made up of people from all nations, languages, races, and social groups. Yet it is firmly united. Its secret? It, too, has a powerful bonding agent, one much stronger than the glue of the lowly barnacle. The apostle Paul told us what that bonding agent is when he wrote: "Clothe yourselves with *love,* for it is a perfect bond of union." —Colossians 3:14.

Of course, not everything called love serves to unite. Many wars have been fought in the name of "love of country." Selfish love may lead to jealousy. "Love of money is a root of all sorts of injurious things." (1 Timothy 6:10) And today's critical times are due, in part, to the fact that many men are "lovers of themselves." —2 Timothy 3:1, 2.

What kind of love, then, serves to unite Christians? An unselfish, expansive love.

Where Is the Source of This Love?

This question is answered in three short words penned by the apostle John: "God is love." (1 John 4:8) Jehovah's love is shown by his kindness to us. Everything good that we have comes ultimately from him. "Every good gift and every perfect present is from above." (James 1:17) This is true of the physical world that we enjoy, and more especially of the spiritual blessings given so abundantly to appreciative Christians.

Jesus Christ drew our attention to a further remarkable manifestation of Jehovah's love, saying: "He [Jehovah] makes his sun rise upon wicked people and good and makes it rain upon righteous people and unrighteous." (Matthew 5:45) And Jehovah's love for mankind as a whole goes beyond providing material blessings, for Jesus explained: "God loved the world so much that he gave his only-begotten Son, in order that everyone exercising faith in him might not be destroyed but have everlasting life." (John 3:16) What more expansive love could there be?

By showing such love for mankind, Jehovah is expressing a love that is firmly rooted in principle. In the Greek language, that love is called *a·ga'pe.* Jehovah shows this love toward Christians too. However, his love toward them takes on an additional flavor. When a person responds to God's love, Jehovah expresses *phi·li'a,* a Greek word meaning "friendship" or "affection." Jesus assures us: "The Father himself has affection for you, because you have had affection for me."—John 16:27.

Imitate God's Love

The love that serves as a uniting bond for Christians follows Jehovah's own magnificent example. As the apostle John said:

"We love, because he first loved us." (1 John 4:19) Such love is the mark of a true Christian and is, indeed, a fruit of God's holy spirit.—John 13:34, 35; Galatians 5:22.

A Christian's love must be directed first and foremost toward his heavenly Father. Then, he should show love to fellow humans. (Matthew 22:37-39) Since God's love is widely embracing, our love for fellow believers, too, must be expansive, 'widened out.' Accordingly, the apostle Paul told the Corinthian Christians: "Our mouth has been opened to you, Corinthians, our heart has widened out. . . . You, too, widen out."—2 Corinthians 6:11-13.

How can we imitate Jehovah's expansive love? Let us consider a few examples.

"Widen Out" Love in the Family

Paul warned that in "the last days" there would be a lack of "natural affection." (2 Timothy 3:1-3) Nevertheless, in the Christian family, love should abound, both the love rooted in principle (a·ga′pe) and the friendly, affectionate type of love (phi·li′a).—Matthew 10:37; Ephesians 5:28; Titus 2:4.

Showing love is not always easy. Money problems often cause hurt feelings in the family. One marriage mate may sometimes resent the demands made on the time of the other mate. A wife may come to feel that she is being neglected or taken for granted. Many teenagers feel that their parents do not understand them. How can these and similar problems be solved?

Basically, the solution is for everyone concerned to imitate God's example and "widen out" his love. "You wives, be in subjection to your husbands, as it is becoming in the Lord," urged Paul. "You husbands, keep on loving your wives and do not be bitterly angry with them. You children, be obedient to your parents in everything, for this is well-pleasing in the Lord. You fathers, do not be exasperating your children, so that they do not become downhearted."—Colossians 3:18-21.

Prayer for help in manifesting love surely is effective when problems arise. So are good family communication and regular Bible discussion. (Deuteronomy 6:4-9) As a basis for such loving communication, many families have found it helpful to use the feature "God's Word Is Alive" in The Watchtower and the one entitled "Young People Ask" in the Awake! magazine.

Expansive Love in the Congregation

It is sad when parents and children fail to love one another. It is also sad when fellow Christians fail to show love for one another. The apostle John affirms: "He who does not love his brother, whom he has seen, cannot be loving God, whom he has not seen."—1 John 4:20.

Love helps us to hope for the best for our spiritual brothers. (1 Corinthians 13:4, 7) We may see our brother struggling with problems—perhaps even 'reaping what he has sown' by previous unwise actions. (Galatians 6:7) Nevertheless, love will help us to maintain a positive attitude toward him. We will avoid such thoughts as, 'I always had my doubts about him.' Even though our brother may be weak in faith, we can reflect on Jehovah's patience with weak ones and can try to imitate His loving mercy.—2 Peter 3:9.

The love existing among Jehovah's servants helps to stabilize young Christians through the difficult teenage years. When a young African girl was asked what had helped her stick to true worship, she commented: "I think it has been not just what I have learned from the Bible but the love I have seen when I attended Christian meetings and how I was accepted that impressed me the most."

Yes, an expansive love can serve to bond together the congregation. But remember,

Jehovah's love reaches out to all mankind. How can we imitate him in this?

Loving Those We Do Not Know

Jesus highlighted one outstanding way to express love even for people we do not know. He said: "This good news of the kingdom will be preached in all the inhabited earth for a witness to all the nations; and then the end will come." (Matthew 24:14) Yes, Jehovah's Witnesses show their love for others when they preach the good news to people who are complete strangers.

Love for mankind in general moves Christians to help strangers in other ways too. Like the Samaritan of Jesus' parable, they try to be good neighbors, 'working good toward all,' often with unexpectedly pleasant results. (Galatians 6:10; Luke 10: 29-37) For example, a young girl in Alaska who was sharing in the evangelizing work some 160 miles (260 km) from her home met a financially destitute family whose car had broken down. Upon hearing of their plight, the girl's father drove 320 miles (520 km) to render aid. This afforded an opportunity to tell the family about Jehovah's purposes and Kingdom. After studying the Bible, the husband and wife symbolized their dedication to Jehovah. Now they, too, are experiencing the joy of sharing the good news with others.—Acts 20:35.

Can You Love Those Who Hate You?

Christian love goes further than loving strangers, however. Jesus urged his disciples: "Continue to love your enemies and to pray for those persecuting you; that you may prove yourselves sons of your Father who is in the heavens, since he makes his sun rise upon wicked people and good and makes it rain upon righteous people and unrighteous."—Matthew 5:44, 45.

Is it really possible to love those who persecute us? During World War II, Jehovah's Witnesses in Nazi Germany were brutally beaten and forced to do hard work on meager rations. Obviously, they could not feel much affection and friendliness (*phi·li'a*) for their persecutors. Nevertheless, they *did* show them the same principled love (*a·ga'pe*) that Jehovah has shown to all mankind. Thus, when possible, the Witnesses shared with the persecutors the life-giving message of truth. And some of these enemies eventually became Christians.

Many of those who persecute God's servants do so in ignorance, as did Saul, who later became the apostle Paul. (Galatians 1:13, 14) When we realize that such persecutors are, in a way, victims of Satan's lying propaganda, we are helped to have a more loving attitude toward them.—2 Corinthians 4:4.

Jehovah, the God of warmth and feeling, takes delight in rewarding those who show expansive love in the family, in the congregation, to strangers, and even to enemies. Such love binds family and congregation members together tightly, even as the glue of a barnacle enables it to cling so firmly to a rock. Moreover, love encourages outsiders to come and share in Christian unity. Do we not have reason, then, to respond appreciatively to God's love by expanding our love even more? Indeed we do! So let us "go on doing it in fuller measure."—1 Thessalonians 4:9, 10.

In Our Next Issue

■ **What Is Most Important in Your Life?**

■ **Messages From Heaven**

■ **Keep Avoiding the Snare of Greed**

Insight on the News

"All in Good Fun"?

"Suddenly, I spotted movement, an enemy soldier. I crouched behind a tree and sighted through my Uzi machine gun, awaiting a clear shot. The adrenaline coursed through my veins. My temples throbbed." Such were the intense emotions that gripped this soldier. Then, unexpectedly, a stinging pain ripped into his side. "I looked down and saw red oozing from my camouflage fatigues. I had been hit. It was all over for me."

Yet 20 minutes later he was fighting again. How is this possible? Simply because this soldier had not been hit with a real bullet. He was participating in a war game at a mock battlefield—one of many throughout North America—where customers pay to fight, reports *The Express* of Easton, Pennsylvania. Using rented air guns, modeled after Israeli Uzi machine guns, two opposing teams try to "kill" each other with pellets that splatter water-soluble dye on their targets, eliminating their enemies from the game. The object is to capture the enemy team's flag. "It's all in good fun," says an advertising brochure.

But Thomas Radecki, chairman of the National Coalition on Television Violence, says that a dozen research experts on the effects of aggression agreed unanimously that "this game would be likely to increase people's tendency toward anger and aggression in general." Whether that is true or not, could genuine Christians participate? The Scriptures admonish them to be "gentle toward all," not "stirring up competition with one another." (2 Timothy 2:24; Galatians 5:26) Additionally, the prophetic words of Isaiah 2:4, "neither will they learn war anymore," apply to God's people today. They avoid amusements that promote warlike thinking, and "pursue the things making for peace."—Romans 14:19.

"Beyond Science"

"We need to discredit the belief held by many scientists that science will ultimately deliver the final truth about everything," says Nobel laureate Sir John Eccles, a pioneer in brain research. Citing some examples, he says that by learning more about the brain, "many scientists and interpreters of science . . . argue that someday science will explain values, beauty, love, friendship, aesthetics and literary quality." But, concludes Eccles, "that view is nothing more than a superstition." The basic questions of life (Who am I? Why am I here? and so forth) "are all mysteries that are beyond science," adds Eccles. He thus reminds us that much of what is called science today is really based on shaky human thinking.

Wrote the psalmist: "It is better to take refuge in Jehovah than to trust in earthling man." (Psalm 118:8) Why is this true? In part because science cannot go beyond the material world. But Jehovah has infinite knowledge and gives us satisfying explanations of our origin, our makeup, and our purpose for living. (Genesis 1: 26-28; 2:4; Ecclesiastes 12:13) Nevertheless, the Bible says that some things are beyond human understanding. (Psalm 139:1-6; Romans 11:33) Wisely, then, let us not overestimate what science will do.

'Whistle-Blowing' Hazards

The term "whistle-blower" has come to describe a venturesome government or corporate employee who exposes high-level illegalities or abuses. But, says psychiatrist Donald R. Soeken, who runs a counseling service for such people, "whistle blowers end up with a variety of emotional and physical problems." He cites conditions like depression, paranoia, and stress-related disorders. Many of his clients, most of whom are federal employees, "act out of a sense of moral outrage," says *The New York Times* in reporting Soeken's views, "believing somewhat naïvely that the system will ultimately support their cause and even reward them." When "the system" does not do so, or even punishes them, "the psychological effect can be devastating," says the report.

Today many people wish to see justice meted out to those in power who commit illegal acts. But "the system," or any worldly organization, rarely rights the wrong. Why is this too much to expect? Because, says the Bible, "that which is made crooked cannot be made straight." (Ecclesiastes 1:15; 1 John 5:19) Yet, if righteously inclined people cannot bring about improvements, who can? Only God can, and he will do so soon. Under his Kingdom government, all corruption will be eliminated. The effect on all earth's inhabitants will be delightful.—Daniel 2:44; Psalm 37: 37-40.

Parents,
Protect Your Children

IF YOUR son told you he was being pressured by schoolmates to take drugs, what would you do? Or, if your daughter told you the boys at school were bothering her, how would you react?

Surely you would waste no time in doing something about it, would you? You would try to learn the facts and see what you could do to protect your child. That, you feel, is how you as a parent would respond. But in reality things do not always happen that way. Usually, by the time parents find out about such things it is already too late. Far too often, the only reaction is: "How could this happen to my boy (or my girl)?"

Youth Under Pressure

If you are a parent, do you know the kind of pressure under which your children are? Are you aware of what they are facing each day? The apostle Peter warned: "Keep your senses, be watchful. Your adversary, the Devil, walks about like a roaring lion, seeking to devour someone." (1 Peter 5:8) Although Satan aims at conquering and enslaving all mankind, young and old, he is clearly a greater threat to inexperienced youths, thus putting them under severe pressure.

Consider just a few examples. Under the headline "Crime By Minors Now 52% Of Total," Japan's *Mainichi Daily News* reports that among juvenile delinquents "crimes committed by 14-year-olds top the list." In the United States, 3.3 million among those aged 14 to 17 are problem drinkers, one in every six teenagers uses drugs regularly, and nearly half a million children are born to unwed teenage mothers each year. The fact is that no matter where you live, your children are not immune to the wave of juvenile crime, violence, and immorality that is sweeping the earth.

You Can Help Them

All of this emphasizes that the youths of today are involved in a difficult fight. Whether they realize it or not, to come off victorious they need help from mature, experienced people. If you are a parent, are you in position to provide such help for your children? And are you willing to make the necessary effort to help them?

Much has been said and written about helping children; there is no lack of advice on the subject. In fact, if anything, the problem is in deciding which among the many conflicting opinions one should follow. For example, one expert may say that spanking is good. Another says it should never be done. Or one specialist may tell you not to reward your child for accomplishments if you do not want a spoiled child. But another says that commendation and rewards are essential if you do not want an insecure child. It is no wonder that, in the words of a staff member of the Hospital for Sick Children in Toronto, Canada, what we have is "a generation of parents who are almost afraid to be parents."

Seeing the grave situation, and the many cases of failure, you may wonder if it is really possible to bring up children to be mature, balanced, and, above all, godly individuals in this day and age. Before you resign yourself to the view that this cannot be done, remember that the apostle Paul wrote: "You, fathers, do not be irritating your children, but go on bringing them up in the discipline and mental-regulating of Jehovah." (Ephesians 6:4) Surely, God would not have given this responsibility to parents if it was something that could not be carried out.

Consistent guidance, good communication, and loving correction are essential in training your children

An Exemplary Family

Noah and his family lived at a time very similar to ours. According to the Bible record, at that time "Jehovah saw that the badness of man was abundant in the earth and every inclination of the thoughts of his heart was only bad all the time. . . . God saw the earth and, look! it was ruined, because all flesh had ruined its way on the earth."—Genesis 6:5, 12.

How would you feel if you had to bring up your children under those circumstances? Comparing Genesis 5:32 with Genesis 7:6, we note that Noah's sons were all born within a hundred-year period before the Flood. And yet, 120 years before the Flood, conditions already were so bad that Jehovah God said: "My spirit shall not act toward man indefinitely in that he is also flesh. Accordingly his days shall amount to a hundred and twenty years."—Genesis 6:3.

In spite of such adverse conditions, Noah and his wife successfully reared their three sons to be God-fearing young men. Through obedient cooperation with their parents, they survived the Deluge that destroyed that ungodly generation.

What was the key to Noah's success? The apostle Paul was inspired to say, at Hebrews 11:7: "By faith Noah, after being given divine warning of things not yet beheld, showed godly fear and constructed an ark for the saving of his household." In fact, Genesis 6:22 tells us: "Noah proceeded to do according to all that God had commanded him. He did just so."

Undoubtedly, Noah's faithfulness and diligence before Jehovah had firmly impressed on the minds of his sons how important it was for them to show the same qualities in their lives. During the ark-building project, he must have spent a lot of time working and talking with them, sharing and doing things with them. And, being "a preacher of righteousness," Noah must have taught his own family Jehovah's laws and requirements. As a result, Noah's family survived the end of that ancient "world of ungodly people."—2 Peter 2:5.

What You Can Do

It should be quite apparent, then, that parental example plays an important role in successfully teaching and training children. When a newspaper columnist was asked to name the biggest obstacle parents face in training children, he simply answered: "Themselves." Parents who do not practice what they preach are working against their own interests and those of their children. (Compare Romans 2: 21-23.) *Consistency* in this regard is essential. Thus, parents need to ask themselves: What do I believe are the most important things in life? What are my personal goals?

At Deuteronomy 6:7, parents are commanded: "You must inculcate them [words from Jehovah] in your son and speak of them when you sit in your house and when you walk on the road and when you lie down and when you get up." That means *communication*. But not all speaking is necessarily communicating. A 17-year-old boy related that twice he tried to talk to his mother about the drug problem he was experiencing at school. "My mother told me to stay away from [the pushers]," he said. Did that help? Evidently not, because the boy still felt trapped by the pressure and did not know how to break away from it.

When youths are confronted with problems they cannot handle, their first recourse usually is to turn to their parents for answers, and this is a good thing. But such trust can easily be destroyed if parents fail to show understanding of their situation. Even if no immediate solution is available, where understanding is shown the lines of communication are kept open.

Correction is another essential in training children. A Bible proverb says: "The rod and reproof are what give wisdom; but a boy let on the loose will be causing his mother shame."—Proverbs 29:15.

Some time ago, the Houston, Texas, Police Department distributed a pamphlet entitled "12 rules for raising delinquent children." Its tongue-in-cheek style may merit a chuckle, but nearly every one of the sobering "rules" has to do with correction or the lack of it. Here are a few examples:

☐ "Begin with infancy to give the child everything he wants. In this way he will grow to believe the world owes him a living."

☐ "When he picks up bad words, laugh at him. This will make him think he's cute. . . ."

☐ "Never give him any spiritual training. Wait until he is 21 and then let him 'decide for himself.'"

☐ "Avoid use of the word 'wrong.' It may develop a guilt complex. . . ."

Christian parents naturally are concerned about bringing up their children "in the discipline and mental-regulating of Jehovah." (Ephesians 6:4) This does not happen without effort—a great deal of it. But no investment of time and effort is too great when the end result is life for you and for your children.—Deuteronomy 6:2.

A Rewarding Assignment

"Look! Sons are an inheritance from Jehovah; the fruitage of the belly is a reward," says the psalmist. (Psalm 127:3) In spite of the passing of time and the change in social customs, that statement is still true. The proof can be seen in the many, many youths in the Christian organization of Jehovah's Witnesses who have grown up to be responsible, respectable, and resourceful young people. They are a credit to themselves, to their parents, and above all, to their Creator, Jehovah God.

You can reap the reward of bringing up your children with such satisfying results if you now take steps to train, teach, and protect them.

Responding to the 'Macedonian Call' in Japan

SUMMER generally means vacation trips and the great outdoors for most people. Many of Jehovah's Witnesses, however, have had the incomparable joy of spending the summer months in a unique activity—calling on people living in remote and isolated areas to bring them the good news of God's Kingdom.

For several years now, the Watch Tower Society's branch office in Japan has made a concentrated effort to reach the four million people living in such areas in that country. Early last year, a call was sent out to all the congregations of Jehovah's Witnesses: "Step over into Macedonia and help us!" (Acts 16:9) Let us go along with some of those who accepted the invitation and experience their challenges and joys.

Why They Responded

Obviously, love for God and for neighbor was their prime motivation. But it is interesting to observe the reasons that different ones gave for their decision.

A couple who applied to serve for a month in a small village in the mountains said this: "Here we are at middle age. We have no major problems, no health problems. Our two children have grown up strong in faith, both serving as full-time workers—in the pioneer field and at the branch office of the Society. We want to show our appreciation to Jehovah for the many blessings we have. And, too, we want to go out, just the two of us, and taste Jehovah's help and blessing away from all our comforts."

The father of a family of four from Saitama Prefecture related: "I could see the children growing into teenagers and facing many problems at school. They had to spend more and more time away from us, and I, being busy with my business, am limited in the time I can spend with them. I wanted to take the time with them and do something to encourage them in the truth and create the pioneer spirit." He had his work for August transferred to September so that he and his family could spend a month in unassigned territory.

A single woman said of her efforts: "I felt it was a way I could really get close to Jehovah and show complete reliance on him to provide for my necessities." Some young Witnesses felt the same way. Two girls just out of school applied to serve in an isolated area for three months. They felt that by fending for themselves, with only Jehovah's help, they could prepare themselves for full-time service anywhere.

Did only families or single ones respond? By no means. Many congregations also applied. An overseer in one of these groups stated: "We felt it would be a fine way to strengthen the bonds of love and fellowship in the congregation, as well as to give the young and newer ones an opportunity to see the importance of the preaching work." Of the 114 publishers, more than 80 were able to participate sometime during the six weeks the congregation served in unassigned territory.

Meeting the Challenges

Right from the start, 'stepping over into Macedonia' to preach has had its challenges. Invariably, the first one is: "Where shall we stay?" The way this problem has been met fully demonstrates the truthfulness of Jesus' admonition: "Keep on, then, seeking first the kingdom and his righteousness, and all these other things will be added to you."—Matthew 6:33.

Two women from Tokyo had an assignment to work an out-of-the-way village in the mountains. Ahead of time, they went to look for suitable lodging but with no success. Deciding to leave the matter in Jehovah's hands, they went to their assignment anyway. At the end of their first day of preaching activity, they still had not found any permanent accommodations. What would they do?

"On the second day in service," one of them related, "I came across a vacant drive-in restaurant. The owner was an elderly man who displayed a very favorable attitude. When we asked if we could rent the place, he offered to let us have it for just 10,000 yen [$45, U.S.] for the three months we had arranged to serve. This gave us a place to stay and to hold meetings. The man's daughter and her husband accepted a set of books. Later on in the day, we met the man's son and his wife. They, too, accepted literature and agreed to study the Bible with us. However, when they learned that we were staying at his father's restaurant, they were amazed. Up to that time, the father had shown a very hostile attitude toward all religions. We certainly felt Jehovah's hand in the matter."

Prejudice, suspicion, and deeply ingrained traditions often pose special challenges, but Jehovah opens the way. Such was the experience of the middle-aged couple mentioned earlier. When they first arrived, they were greeted with suspicion by their landlady, who scrutinized their every move. This gave them an idea of the reaction they might expect in the territory and what they had to do to break down the barrier and reach the people.

"We decided we would first spend a full day cleaning and setting up housekeeping," the husband related. "We opened all the sliding doors on the sides of the house so the neighbors could have a full view of what was going on. They could see our Bibles and Bible literature sitting on the table. They could see how we arranged everything. They could see how we lived. In effect, we were telling them, 'Come on in if you want. Visit us. We have nothing to hide. We trust you.'

"As we went about preaching, we would introduce ourselves as people from the big city and would ask if they could teach us something about the country and their customs. We made it a point to greet everyone, even the farmers working in the fields. We shopped in the local farmers' cooperative. All of this helped the people to see that we were sincerely interested in them and not just in 'selling books.' They saw that we were just ordinary people like them and they became friendly. After a while, we did not even have to introduce ourselves. It was not unusual to be greeted at the doors with remarks such as: 'It's hot outside. Why not come in for a cool drink?' or, 'We have just prepared lunch. Please eat with us.' Our efforts succeeded in opening their minds and hearts to the message."

Where the entire congregation participated, the challenges were multiplied. In line with Jesus' implied advice to 'count the cost,' much advance planning had to be done in connection with rooming, cleaning, trucking, field service, and so on. (Luke 14:28) One congregation reported: "Although we planned to serve from the end of July to the first week of September, we went to look for housing in May. We went

Kingdom proclaimers joyfully share good news with others in Japan

to the city office and told them our needs. We explained that we were family groups and young people interested in teaching the Bible in the area. They were very cooperative and suggested several possibilities.

"When we finally found a suitable place, we sent the cleaning crew one week in advance to get it ready. Maps for the territory were prepared, posters advertising our meetings were made, and handbills were printed. Since we received permission to use a new recreation center for our meetings, we had good publicity and left a fine impression.

"We knew that all work and no play would not be good when there were so many young ones with us. So each day after the preaching work was done, or on the rest day of the week when all had finished their assigned chores, we would go hiking, boating, or fishing and would be refreshed by the beautiful scenery and healthful mountain air."

Was It Worth It?

The family of four from Saitama Prefecture gave this answer: "During our month in the territory, we placed 920 magazines, 240 books, had 13 interested persons at the public meetings we arranged, and started 4 Bible studies that continued after we left. These results alone made it worth the effort, but there is much more. Our children learned the joy of the ministry and have developed a real pioneer spirit. As a family, our unity increased as we shared chores and field experiences. We are making definite plans to go again next year."

The middle-aged couple who tried hard to befriend the people submitted this report: "After we had covered the territory once, we spent our afternoons making return visits. We made friends with the local people and some even shed tears when we left the area. They accepted us and the good news and left us with glowing memories. Unless you experience it yourself, you just cannot know how wonderful it is. We realized that we could do anything with Jehovah's help."

One Witness who has been active for over 20 years stated in her report: "My 82-year-old partner and I have never felt closer to Jehovah than we do now after serving just two weeks in isolated territory. Our hearts are full to overflowing."

A Unique Privilege

Those who have responded to the 'Macedonian call' in Japan fully appreciate Jesus' words: "The harvest is great, but the workers are few. Therefore, beg the Master of the harvest to send out workers into his harvest."—Matthew 9:37, 38.

The joyful experiences of those responding to the call show that "the Master," Jehovah God, is answering that prayer. Young and old alike count it a unique privilege to share in the ingathering. (Exodus 23:16) Are you doing all you can in this grand work?

Questions From Readers

■ Was it predetermined that Adam and Eve would have to die, since Hebrews 9:27 says that "it is reserved for men to die once for all time, but after this a judgment"?

No, this statement is not dealing with Adam and Eve, who were created with the prospect of endless life on earth. Had they obeyed God, they could have lived forever. Rather than their death being predetermined, it resulted from their willful sin. (Genesis 2:15-17) The context shows that the primary application of Hebrews 9:27 is to the high priest in ancient Israel, who on Atonement Day foreshadowed Jesus Christ.—Hebrews 4:14, 15.

In 1915 Charles T. Russell, then president of the Watch Tower Society, was asked about Hebrews 9:27. He referred to what had earlier been published, such as in *Studies in the Scriptures* and *Tabernacle Shadows of the Better Sacrifices* (1899). Hebrews 9:27 was explained contextually.

In Hebrews chapters 8 and 9, Paul showed that many details of the Mosaic Law were "a typical representation and a shadow of the heavenly things." (Hebrews 8:5) This was particularly so regarding sacrificial procedures on the annual Day of Atonement. Only on that special day could the high priest enter the innermost compartment of the tabernacle. This room, the Most Holy, was screened off by a curtain, and the high priest had to prepare the way in by introducing special incense. Then he could enter with the sacrificial blood of a bull and a goat. Even when the priest carefully followed all the exacting requirements, the resulting covering of the Israelites' sins was limited in time; the sacrifices had to be offered each year.

Continuing his argument, Paul said that "Christ came as a high priest," but after his death and resurrection, he "entered, not into a holy place made with hands, ... but into heaven itself, now to appear before the person of God for us." (Hebrews 9:11, 12, 24) Would *that* sacrifice have to be repeated? No. Christ "manifested himself once for all time." (Hebrews 9:25, 26; Romans 6:9) Paul then said: "And as it is reserved for men to die once for all time, but after this a judgment, so also the Christ was offered once for all time to bear the sins of many." —Hebrews 9:27, 28.

With this review of the context we can appreciate the comments on Hebrews 9:27 in *Tabernacle Shadows*: "Each time a Priest went into the Most Holy on the Atonement Day he risked his life; for if his sacrifice had been imperfect he would have died as he passed the second veil [the curtain]. He would not have been accepted into the Most Holy himself, nor would his imperfect sacrifices have been acceptable as an atonement for the sins of the people. Hence any failure meant his death, and the condemnation of all for whose sins he attempted to make reconciliation. This was the *judgment* mentioned in this text, which was passed every year by the typical priests."

Tabernacle Shadows then drew a contrast with Christ Jesus, who died a sacrificial death: "Had his sacrifice been in any manner or degree *imperfect* he would never have been raised out of death, the 'judgment' of justice would have

gone against him. But his resurrection, on the third day, proved that his work was perfectly performed, that it stood the test of the divine judgment."

So, viewed contextually, Hebrews 9:27 is an observation on the superiority of Christ's priestly service.

It is also possible, however, to refer to Hebrews 9:27 in making a general expression on mankind's experience. Though Adam and Eve had the possibility of endless life, that has not been true of their descendants. Adam and Eve had children only after they had sinned. Hence, all their imperfect descendants were born dying. (Romans 5:12; 6:23) Inherited death, therefore, comes to mankind only once. That will be true even in the future. If, after the application of the benefits of Christ's sacrifice for mankind, and if during God's judgment day of a thousand years, a resurrected person proves deserving of everlasting destruction, his death will result from his own wickedness, not from Adamic sin.—Revelation 20:13-15.

Contrariwise, those who previously had died from inherited sin, but who after resurrection prove faithful, will receive the favorable judgment of everlasting life. —Revelation 21:3-6.

Consequently, Hebrews 9:27 refers in context to Jesus' service as high priest in contrast with the high priests in Israel. It also has been used to describe the general experience of humans having inherited Adamic death. But it does not support the unscriptural predestinarian view that even before they were created it was predetermined that Adam and Eve would die.

A Night to Remember

The date Nisan 14 is the anniversary of Israel's deliverance from Egypt. It is an anniversary the Jews were instructed to remember each year with a special meal. During it they were to explain to younger ones how the blood of the Passover lamb placed on the doorposts and above the doorway protected the firstborn of the Israelite households from God's executional angel.—Exodus 12: 21-27.

Just 1,545 years later, also on Nisan 14, Jesus Christ instituted for his disciples in line for the heavenly Kingdom a new celebration that was to replace the Passover. During a simple ceremony, Jesus used unleavened

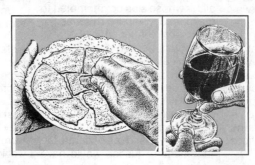

bread and wine as symbols of his human life, which he was to sacrifice for mankind. His sacrifice has saving power superior to that of the Passover lamb. (John 1:29) When instituting the memorial of his sacrifice, Jesus said: "Keep doing this in remembrance of me."—Luke 22:19.

Jehovah's Witnesses invite you to be present for the observation of this very important Memorial celebration. This year the date in our calendar that corresponds to Nisan 14 is Thursday, April 4, after sunset. You can attend on that day at the Kingdom Hall nearest to your home. Check with Jehovah's Witnesses locally for the exact time.

April 1, 1985

The Watchtower

Announcing Jehovah's Kingdom

What Is
MOST
IMPORTANT
in Your Life?

The Watchtower.
Announcing Jehovah's Kingdom

April 1, 1985
Vol. 106, No. 7

In This Issue

THE PURPOSE OF "THE WATCHTOWER" is to exalt Jehovah God as the Sovereign of the universe. It keeps watch on world events as they fulfill Bible prophecy. It comforts all peoples with the good news that God's Kingdom will soon destroy those who oppress their fellowmen and that it will turn the earth into a paradise. It encourages faith in the now-reigning King, Jesus Christ, whose shed blood opens the way for mankind to gain eternal life. "The Watchtower," published by Jehovah's Witnesses continuously since 1879, is nonpolitical. It adheres to the Bible as its authority.

"WATCHTOWER" STUDIES FOR THE WEEKS

May 5:   How Different Are You From the World? Page 10. Songs to Be Used: 2, 160.

May 12: Keep Avoiding the Snare of Greed. Page 16. Songs to Be Used: 217, 62.

Average Printing Each Issue: 11,150,000

Now Published in 102 Languages

SEMIMONTHLY EDITIONS AVAILABLE BY MAIL
Afrikaans, Arabic, Cebuano, Chichewa, Chinese, Cibemba, Danish, Dutch, Efik, English*, Finnish, French, German, Greek, Hiligaynon, Igbo, Iloko, Italian, Japanese, Korean, Lingala, Malagasy, Maltese, Norwegian, Portuguese, Russian, Sepedi, Sesotho, Shona, Spanish, Swahili, Swedish, Tagalog, Thai, Tswana, Xhosa, Yoruba, Zulu

MONTHLY EDITIONS AVAILABLE BY MAIL
Armenian, Bengali, Bicol, Bulgarian, Croatian, Czech, Ewe, Fijian, Ga, Greenlandic, Gujarati, Gun, Hausa, Hebrew, Hindi, Hiri Motu, Hungarian, Icelandic, Kannada, Kikuyu, Kiluba, Malayalam, Marathi, New Guinea Pidgin, Pangasinan, Papiamento, Polish, Rarotongan, Romanian, Samar-Leyte, Samoan, Sango, Serbian, Silozi, Sinhalese, Slovenian, Solomon Islands-Pidgin, Tahitian, Tamil, Telugu, Tshiluba, Tsonga, Turkish, Twi, Ukrainian, Urdu, Venda, Vietnamese
*Study articles also available in large-print edition at same cost.

The Bible translation used is the "New World Translation of the Holy Scriptures," unless otherwise indicated.

Twenty cents (U.S.) a copy

Watch Tower Society offices	Yearly subscription rates Semimonthly
America, U.S., Watchtower, Wallkill, N.Y. 12589	$4.00
Australia, Box 280, Ingleburn, N.S.W. 2565	A$6.00
Canada, Box 4100, Halton Hills (Georgetown), Ontario L7G 4Y4	$5.20
England, The Ridgeway, London NW7 1RN	£5.00
Ireland, 29A Jamestown Road, Finglas, Dublin 11	£5.00
New Zealand, 6-A Western Springs Rd., Auckland 3	$7.00
Nigeria, P.O. Box 194, Yaba, Lagos State	₦3.50
Philippines, P.O. Box 2044, Manila 2800	₱50.00
South Africa, Private Bag 2, Elandsfontein, 1406	R5,60

Remittances should be sent to the office in your country or to Watchtower, Wallkill, N.Y. 12589, U.S.A.

Changes of address should reach us 30 days before your moving date. Give us your old and new address (if possible, your old address label).

The Watchtower (ISSN 0043-1087) is published semimonthly for $4.00 (U.S.) per year by Watch Tower Bible and Tract Society of Pennsylvania, 25 Columbia Heights, Brooklyn, N.Y. 11201. Second-class postage paid at Brooklyn, N.Y., and at additional mailing offices.

Postmaster: Send address changes to Watchtower, **Wallkill, N.Y. 12589.**

Published by
**Watch Tower Bible and Tract Society
of Pennsylvania**
25 Columbia Heights, Brooklyn, N.Y. 11201, U.S.A.
Frederick W. Franz, President

What Is MOST IMPORTANT in Your Life?

HE WAS reputed to be the richest man in the world. His personal fortune ran into billions of dollars. He was admired by many as having reached the pinnacle of success. Yet two years before he died, J. Paul Getty said: "Money doesn't necessarily have any connection with happiness. Maybe with unhappiness."

In the pursuit of what many consider important in life, the famous oil magnate certainly had succeeded to an outstanding degree. But did he sound like a man who had found happiness through what he had worked so hard to acquire? Or did he sound more like one who had come to realize finally that what he had worked so hard for was not that important after all?

Ideal and Reality

What do you consider most important in your life? Some people may say that *freedom* is what they treasure the most. Others may say that *success* means the most in their lives. Still others put *personal fulfillment* ahead of everything else.

Though they do not want to admit it, many people's life pattern and actions betray that *money* and *pleasure* are really the most important things in their lives. They are so determined to get rich or are so bent on 'having a good time,' that they do not mind neglecting their family, their health, and their spiritual well-being in doing so. And interestingly, the Bible foretold that in "the last days" people would become "lovers of themselves, lovers of money" and "lovers of pleasures rather than lovers of God."—2 Timothy 3: 1, 2, 4.

Something More Important

Jesus Christ, the founder of Christianity, posed a thought-provoking question. "Does a person gain anything if he wins the whole world but loses his life?" he asked. (Mark 8:36, *Today's English Version*) Think about that. What would a person be able to do without life? Nothing! —Ecclesiastes 9:5, 10.

You may still be young and so feel that you have plenty of time to do all the things you want to do. But do you really? Wars, crime, diseases, and accidents have struck down countless able-bodied men and women—suddenly and unexpectedly. What happened to all their plans and goals?

You may have a family or may be along in years. So you may feel that you must put all your time and effort into building a secure future for yourself and your loved ones before you can think about anything else. But what would you consider to be secure? As you know, inflation, recession, and unemployment have eaten up the life savings of many, leaving them destitute and homeless. Besides, with conditions around the world so unstable, what guarantee is there that the things you worked hard for will not be eliminated by some unexpected turn of events?

Doubtless you see, therefore, the importance of examining your personal goals. So, what do you really consider most important in your life?

HAPPINESS
Through a
PRECIOUS RELATIONSHIP

"A LIVE dog is better off than a dead lion." (Ecclesiastes 9:4) In those few words, King Solomon of old stated the fundamental truth that life is more important than any material possessions or any ambitious goals we may hope to achieve. Without life, we cannot benefit from any of these things. Yes, life is essential in our pursuit of happiness.

Something "Better Than Life"

As precious as life is, however, there is something that is even better. 'Is that possible?' you might wonder. 'What could be more precious than life itself?'

King David of ancient Israel supplied us with the answer. Addressing the Creator, Jehovah God, he said with deep appreciation: "Because your loving-kindness is better than life, my own lips will commend you." (Psalm 63:3) David's heartfelt words show that to be the recipient of God's loving-kindness, which is based on having a fine relationship with him, is even more precious than life itself. Why is this so?

What Makes Life Possible

Suppose you were given a gift, something that you really liked. Of course you would be very happy to receive the gift and perhaps get a great deal of enjoyment from using it. But you would be ungrateful, indeed, if your thoughts did not go beyond the gift to the giver. Was it not the personal relationship between you and the giver that prompted the gift? If that relationship did not exist, there would have been no gift and no enjoyment of it.

The same is true with life. Precious as it is, we must bear in mind where our life came from and how it has been sustained. Certainly we did not create it ourselves, nor can we sustain it independent of all the marvelous provisions Jehovah has made on earth. (Psalm 100:3; Acts 14:17) The very fact that we have life, and undoubtedly we are enjoying it in some measure, is an expression of loving-kindness on the part of the Grand Creator, Jehovah God. Can we not see why King David wholeheartedly felt that God's "loving-kindness is better than life"?

There is another reason why having an approved relationship with the Creator is more important than having life itself —our future depends on it. Let us see how this is so.

If you are grateful to the giver . . .

In spite of this, it is the purpose of our loving Creator that all those who love and obey him will be liberated from the frustration and futility that is our lot today. Jehovah assures us with this wonderful promise: "They will not build and someone else have occupancy; they will not plant and someone else do the eating. For like the days of a tree will the days of my people be; and the work of their own hands my chosen ones will use to the full." —Isaiah 65:22.

Is this expression of God's loving-kindness not better than our present limited and uncertain life? To be the recipient of his loving-kindness, yes, to live in that

Do you not agree that life is transitory and full of uncertainties? A person may work very hard for many years in order to achieve some materialistic goal he considers worth while. Yet, death soon robs him of everything he has attained. It is just as wise King Solomon said: "What does a man come to have for all his hard work and for the striving of his heart with which he is working hard under the sun? For all his days his occupation means pains and vexation, also during the night his heart just does not lie down. This too is mere vanity."—Ecclesiastes 2: 22, 23; compare 2:3-11.

. . . what about the greatest giver, Jehovah God?

New Order and to enjoy life filled with purpose and meaning would certainly be a most worthwhile goal. To realize that happy prospect, one must gain Jehovah's approval now and maintain a close relationship with him and his people.

Short-Term Interest Versus Long-Term Benefit

In view of the foregoing points, it certainly would be shortsighted and unwise for us to occupy ourselves solely with the pursuit of self-interest, be it fame, fortune, career, academic achievement, personal fulfillment, or anything else considered worth while in this system of things. While these goals may not be wrong in themselves, pursuing any one of them as the most important thing may very well cause us to neglect our responsibilities before our Creator. Ultimately, we may lose his approval and fail to gain "the real life."—1 Timothy 6:19; Luke 9:24.

To take such a course can be likened to a youngster who drops out of school and goes to work as an unskilled laborer just to get some spending money. He may feel that he is finally freed from the restrictions of school and is having a good time. But is he not sacrificing his long-term welfare for the sake of some doubtful short-term interest? Similarly, then, is a person not short-sighted when he neglects his relationship with the Creator because he is too busy pursuing some personal goal?

Busy as all of us are, we usually manage to find the time and energy to do the things we really consider important, do we not? Thus, with an unerring understanding of human nature, Jesus succinctly points out: "For where your treasure is, there your heart will be also."—Matthew 6:21.

So on what sort of "treasure" have you set your heart? The glitter and tinsel of the world may seem very attractive. But ask yourself: How lasting are the supposed benefits gained from such things? Do they bring true happiness or just temporary pleasures, like a drug, leaving an undesirable or even painful aftermath?

Make a Wise Choice

There is a valuable lesson to be learned from the people of Lot's day. "They were eating, they were drinking, they were buying, they were selling, they were planting, they were building," said Jesus. In other words, they were busy pursuing what they considered important, without paying any attention to God's will. The result? "On the day that Lot came out of Sodom it rained fire and sulphur from heaven and destroyed them all." Then, for our benefit, Jesus added: "The same way it will be on that day when the Son of man is to be revealed."—Luke 17:28-30.

All indications are that "that day" is upon us. Out of concern for our eternal welfare, Jehovah God has been issuing repeated calls through his Word and his organized people in all the nations. The invitation is to turn back from selfish pursuits and become reconciled to him. It would be truly unwise for us to let our personal interests occupy *all* our time and energy, so that we fail to respond to this loving call. Rather, as the apostle Paul put it, we should recognize the urgency of the times: "Look! Now is the especially acceptable time. Look! Now is the day of salvation."—2 Corinthians 5:20; 6:2.

Will you be among those who are blessed with the happy prospect of surviving the end of the present wicked system of things into the righteous New Order of God's promise? That depends on what you consider most important in your life now and what you do about gaining an approved relationship with God. The choice is yours!

Jesus' Life and Ministry

**Beginning with this magazine issue, a new feature
on the above theme will appear in *The Watchtower*.**

FOR the past five years, since March of 1980, *The Watchtower* has once a month carried the two-page, illustrated feature "God's Word Is Alive." By means of pictures combined with an easy-to-read text, many Bible doctrines and historical accounts were discussed in a vivid, easy-to-understand manner. Now a new feature, highlighting the life and ministry of Jesus Christ, will replace "God's Word Is Alive."

On the following two pages you will see the first segment of this new feature. For the next several months, you can look forward to receiving a new installment in each issue of *The Watchtower*. This new series of articles will have the same generously illustrated, two-page format of "God's Word Is Alive."

It is appropriate that Jesus Christ be featured in this way in *The Watchtower,* for Jesus has had a greater influence on the history of mankind than any other human. Yet, much more importantly, the lives of millions of people of all races and nationalities have been beneficially changed when they have come to appreciate his life and teachings.

You probably already know much about Jesus and his ministry. But do you have fixed in mind the time and place of events so as to relate them to one another and so as to remember them better? For example, when did Jesus choose his 12 apostles —early in his ministry or considerably later? Was it before or after the Samaritan woman identified him as the Christ? And where was he when he chose the 12, or miraculously fed the 5,000, or gave the Sermon on the Mount? Since this new feature will chronologically tell the story of Jesus' life and ministry and provide both visual settings and descriptive commentary, it will help you fix more indelibly in your mind these momentous events.

This feature will be helpful to long-time Bible readers as well as to newer Bible students, and to parents when they study with their children. Questions are provided for this purpose. What a fine way to acquaint them with the founder of Christianity and his teachings! You may foresee ways you can use these articles in ministering to your family and others. Remember, practically everyone likes stories, and many enjoy them in serial form where they receive segments at regular intervals.

So, right from its first installment, encourage others to keep up with this continuing story. You will observe that Bible quotations are paraphrased for easier understanding, with the Bible source being provided at the end of each story. Encourage the reading of these Bible accounts. Yes, put this new feature in *The Watchtower* to good use in your disciple-making work!

Messages From Heaven

THE entire Bible is, in effect, a message from heaven, having been provided by our heavenly Father for our instruction. However, two special messages were delivered nearly 2,000 years ago by an angel who "stands near before God." His name is Gabriel. Let us examine the circumstances of these two important visits to earth.

The year is 3 B.C.E. In the Judean hills, probably not too far from Jerusalem, lives a priest of Jehovah by the name of Zechariah. He has grown old, and so has his wife Elizabeth. And they have no children. Zechariah is taking his turn at priestly service in God's temple in Jerusalem. Suddenly Gabriel appears at the right side of the incense altar.

Zechariah is very much afraid. But Gabriel quiets his fears and says: 'God has heard your prayers. Elizabeth will have a son, and you must name him John. He will get ready for Jehovah a prepared people.' But Zechariah cannot believe it. It seems so impossible that, at their age, he and Elizabeth could have a child. So Gabriel says, 'Because you have not believed me, you will not be able to speak until these things happen.'

Well, in the meantime, the people outside are wondering why Zechariah is taking so long in the temple. When he finally comes out, he cannot speak but can only make signs with his hands, and they realize he has seen something supernatural.

After Zechariah finishes his period of temple service, he returns home. And

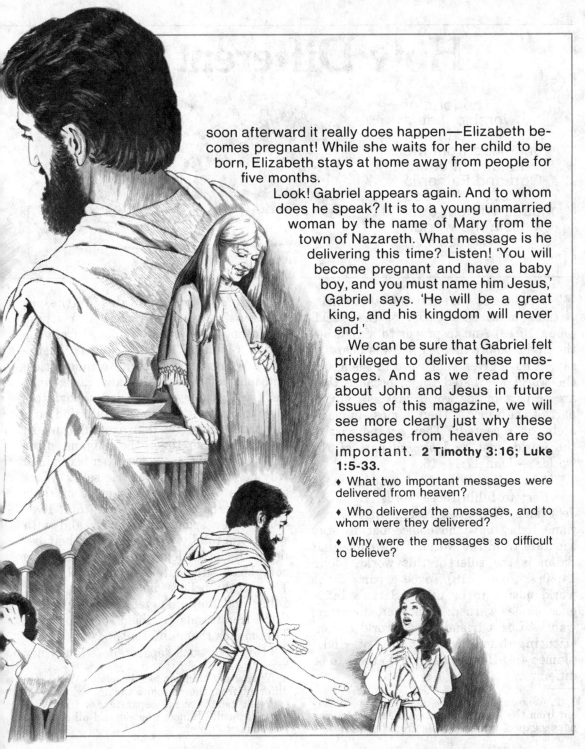

soon afterward it really does happen—Elizabeth becomes pregnant! While she waits for her child to be born, Elizabeth stays at home away from people for five months.

Look! Gabriel appears again. And to whom does he speak? It is to a young unmarried woman by the name of Mary from the town of Nazareth. What message is he delivering this time? Listen! 'You will become pregnant and have a baby boy, and you must name him Jesus,' Gabriel says. 'He will be a great king, and his kingdom will never end.'

We can be sure that Gabriel felt privileged to deliver these messages. And as we read more about John and Jesus in future issues of this magazine, we will see more clearly just why these messages from heaven are so important. **2 Timothy 3:16; Luke 1:5-33.**

♦ What two important messages were delivered from heaven?

♦ Who delivered the messages, and to whom were they delivered?

♦ Why were the messages so difficult to believe?

How Different Are You

"The form of worship that is clean and undefiled from the standpoint of our God and Father is this: . . . to keep oneself without spot from the world."
—JAMES 1:27.

IT WAS Jesus who first said that Christians must be no part of the world. (John 15:19) And in prayer to his Father the night before he died, he was heard to say: "I have given your word to them, but the world has hated them, because they are no part of the world, just as I am no part of the world." Then, almost immediately, he repeated: "They are no part of the world, just as I am no part of the world."—John 17:14, 16.

² Most religions of Christendom make no effort to fulfill those words. However, Jehovah's Witnesses realize that Christians today have no choice but to stay separate from the world. They know that Satan is the ruler of this world. (John 14:30; 1 John 5:19) To be a part of the world means to be under Satan's influence. James warned: "Whoever, therefore, wants to be a friend of the world is constituting himself an enemy of God." (James 4:4) Hence, we should *expect* to be different.

³ But *how* are Jehovah's Witnesses different? Jesus said that Christians would not be physically removed from the world. (John 17:15) And, indeed, Jehovah's Witnesses live in its communities, and most of them marry and raise families, just like everyone else. They, too, have to find work, cope with inflation, and pay their taxes. Yet they are different. In an article about them, the religion editor of a United States newspaper explained why he thought this was. He said: "What separates Witnesses from most of their critics, perhaps, is that their total lives —how they spend their hours and with whom—is totally wrapped up in their beliefs." Exactly! Jehovah's Witnesses are completely dedicated to Jehovah God. They truly believe his promises in the Bible, and they take very seriously all of God's commands to them. (1 John 5:3) This makes them different.

⁴ However, such separateness is neither

1, 2. Who said that Christians would be different from the world? Why should Jehovah's Witnesses expect to be different from the world?

---

3. What basic things make Jehovah's Witnesses different from those around them?
4. What factors make separateness from this world difficult? Hence, what should all of us do from time to time?

From the World?

popular nor easy. In our day-to-day lives, the pressure toward conformity is strong. Most of us have an instinctive desire to be not too different from everyone else. When issues arise involving neutrality, it takes strong conviction to be different and obey Jehovah's commands. (Acts 5:29; 15: 28, 29) Hence, it is wise for each individual to examine himself from time to time to see how he stands in the matter of being separate from the world.—2 Corinthians 13:5.

Zealous in Field Service

5 For example, Jehovah's Witnesses are well known for their zeal in preaching. This truly makes them different. Some admire them for it, while others are annoyed by it. Missionaries from one evangelical organization report that wherever they go in the world they meet up with local people who are active, zealous witnesses for Jehovah! "Talk for very long to almost any . . . missionary anywhere in

the world about local situations, and you'll hear Jehovah's Witnesses mentioned," said one of their publications. Why are the Witnesses so zealous in this work? The reason is that preaching the good news is God's will and an identifying mark of a true Christian. (Matthew 28:19, 20; Ephesians 6:14, 15; Revelation 22:17) Today, this preaching by Jehovah's Witnesses is a public demonstration of their loyalty to God's Kingdom and their desire to help others to worship Jehovah.—Isaiah 2:2-4; Matthew 24:14.

6 How important is the preaching work to you? In the world, most feel that making a living, or even recreation, is more important than religious practices. (2 Timothy 3:4; 1 John 2:16) However, Paul wrote to Timothy: "Pay constant attention to yourself and to your teaching. Stay by these things, for by doing this you will save both yourself and those who listen to you." (1 Timothy 4:16) Do you have this view? Do you also remember the warning of the apostle Peter that you

5. (a) What do some non-Witnesses say about Jehovah's Witnesses' zeal in the preaching work? (b) What are some Bible principles that move the Witnesses to be zealous in this work?

6. What are some questions we should ask ourselves to examine our feelings toward the work of preaching the good news of the Kingdom?

should 'keep close in mind the presence of the day of Jehovah'? (2 Peter 3:12) If so, then you know that preaching the good news of the Kingdom is a matter of urgency. This may move you to act in ways that seem strange to non-Witnesses.

7 For example, John, a schoolteacher in Ghana, took the Scriptures seriously. So he resigned from his job in order to spend more time telling neighbors about the Kingdom. Brian, an English boy, sacrificed his opportunity to go to a university so that he could be a full-time preacher; and Eve, an American girl, left college after a few semesters for the same reason. Were these young people impractical or foolish? Really, to anyone who takes the Bible seriously, what they did was reasonable and logical. Far from endangering their future, they were helping to *ensure* it. As Paul said, the work they chose means salvation, 'both to them and to those who listen to them.' —1 Timothy 4:16.

A Different Kind of Conduct

8 Here is another principle that makes Christians different from the world: "You loved righteousness, and you hated lawlessness." (Hebrews 1:9) In the context, these words are addressed to Jesus Christ, but Jehovah's Witnesses recognize that they provide a standard for Christians too. (1 Peter 2:21) We have to love what God says is right and hate what God says is lawless.

9 The apostle Paul identified some kinds of lawlessness in these words: "Neither fornicators, nor idolaters, nor adulterers, nor men kept for unnatural purposes, nor men who lie with men, nor thieves, nor greedy persons, nor drunkards, nor revilers, nor extortioners will inherit God's kingdom." (1 Corinthians 6:9, 10) Today, the world is grossly permissive, particularly in matters of morality. But Bible standards are not negotiable. The Bible says that any Christian getting involved in immoral practices should be lovingly helped to change his way. (Galatians 6:1; James 5:19, 20) If he refuses to make a change, then he should be shunned by Christians.—1 Corinthians 5:9-13.

10 Some have charged that this way of handling matters is unloving or fanatical. They prefer the world's more liberal approach. Do you feel that way? Or do you realize that such actions show not so much a lack of love for the sinner as a hatred of his lawless acts. And do you understand that the Christian congregation *must* act in this way if it is to remain Christian? James said: "Religion that God our Father accepts as pure and faultless is this: . . . to keep oneself from being polluted by the world." (James 1:27, *New International Version*) How could a group claim to have the true religion if it allowed itself to be polluted by serious sin?

11 A Christian's 'hatred of what is bad' goes further. The Bible says: "Let fornication and uncleanness of every sort or greediness not even be mentioned among you, just as it befits holy people; neither shameful conduct nor foolish talking nor obscene jesting." (Ephesians 5:3, 4) So *real* Christians are known among their associates for not using filthy language, telling dirty jokes, or getting prurient enjoyment out of discussing unclean things. Clean minds and clean speech are increasingly rare today.

7. What step have many taken with regard to the preaching work? Why?
8. What Biblical principle in Hebrews 1:9 also helps to make Jehovah's Witnesses different?
9. (a) What are some forms of lawlessness? (b) How does a Christian congregation's attitude toward lawlessness differ from that of the world?

10. Why do Jehovah's Witnesses *have* to protect themselves from lawless acts?
11. How do Christian standards affect a Christian's speech?

Jehovah's Witnesses have learned to be cautious about the entertainment offered by the world

¹² Jehovah's Witnesses even differ when it comes to entertainment. Since "the whole world is lying in the power of the wicked one," they have learned to be cautious about entertainment offered by the world. (1 John 5:19) They avoid completely the many party games, magazines, videos, films, music, and television shows that have demonic or pornographic content, or that highlight sick, sadistic violence. They are wary, too, of so-called family entertainment that promotes promiscuous or permissive ideas that Christians cannot approve. (1 Corinthians 15:33) Anyone who takes the Bible seriously would not look for entertainment in things that should not even be *mentioned* among Christians.

---

12. How are Jehovah's Witnesses different from the world when it comes to entertainment?

¹³ Is this your opinion? Or do you feel that such views make Jehovah's Witnesses narrow-minded or restrictive? If so, consider: When a food product is discovered to be polluted and is immediately removed from the store shelves, consumers do not complain that their freedom is restricted because they can no longer purchase it. Rather, they are grateful to be protected from food poisoning. Jehovah's Witnesses, similarly, do not complain that their freedom is somehow restricted when the pollution of much worldly entertainment is pointed out to them. Rather, they are relieved to be protected from the danger such pollution poses.

They Love One Another

¹⁴ Here is another measure of a Christian's separateness from the world. The night before he died, Jesus said to his followers: "By this all will know that you are my disciples, if you have love among yourselves." (John 13:35) Why would love be a sign to outsiders? Because, as a whole, the situation in the world today is just as Paul said it would be: "Men will be lovers of themselves, lovers of money, . . . having no natural affection." (2 Timothy 3:2, 3) In such an environment, a worldwide *community* of people who have love among themselves would be a phenomenon. Such a brotherhood exists among Jehovah's Witnesses.—1 Peter 2:17.

¹⁵ This love is very noticeable and often draws comments from outsiders when the Witnesses get together at their conventions. When there are large-scale disasters, the Witnesses are quickly on the

---

13. Is it narrow-minded to restrict ourselves so much in the matter of entertainment? Explain.
14. What quality did Jesus say would make the Christian community stand out from the world around it?
15. What are some situations in which Jehovah's Witnesses have the opportunity to show love for one another?

scene, bringing aid to their brothers. And within the congregation, genuine Christians show love and consideration for one another. Even when there are personality problems, they try hard to 'put up with one another and forgive one another freely.'—Colossians 3:12-14.

They Do Not Stumble One Another

16 Such love makes the Witnesses different in another way. Today, many are concerned with and jealously protect their

16. (a) What situation did Paul discuss that gave first-century Christians a fine opportunity to show the depth of their love for one another? (b) What principle did he explain that has many modern applications?

rights. The apostle Paul, however, set a different standard: "Let us pursue the things making for peace and the things that are upbuilding to one another." (Romans 14:19) In the context, Paul was speaking about a problem that existed then regarding food. Christians, unlike the Jews under the Mosaic Law, were free to eat whatever they wanted as long as they were not gluttons. Some, though, who from childhood had viewed certain foods as repugnant, were disturbed when they saw fellow Christians eat them. Did those other Christians insist on their right to eat anything they wanted anyway? Not if they followed Paul's counsel.

Honesty Makes Them Different Too

HIS heart sank when he saw the parking ticket under the automobile's windshield wiper. The fine was $25 (U.S.), and he was pained because it was unjust. There were no signs prohibiting parking. Worse yet was the fact that he was from a distant place and could not afford to return to the city to appeal his case. So he took photographs of the area to prove that there were no warning regulations posted anywhere. And being one of Jehovah's Witnesses, he asked a fellow Witness to appear in traffic court for him.

Here is his friend's report of what took place in court that morning:

"When you are called before the judge, you must give your name and address. Then they administer the oath of truthfulness. Before they gave me the oath, the court clerk, an older gentleman, asked me to repeat my street address. When I said, '124 Columbia Heights,' he evidently recognized it as the address of the world headquarters of the Watch Tower Society and Jehovah's Witnesses. Turning to the judge, he said: 'You have nothing to worry about here, Judge. These are good people. They do not lie! They never lie! They cannot lie! Their religion does not allow it, and they hold strictly to it. I have never known any of their men or even their women to tell a lie. They are as honest as you can get. I have seen plenty of times when they could have escaped a parking ticket just by telling a little fib, but they would not do it.'

"Then, turning to me, he declared, 'I know you would not tell a lie because you know who would roll over in his grave if you did?' 'Who is that?' I asked. 'The Judge, Judge Rutherford [onetime president of the Watch Tower Society],' he answered. 'I used to deliver mail to him 47 years ago. I knew Jehovah's Witnesses before they grew big. The Judge was some man!'

"After all of this, the court judge did not even bother to swear me in with the oath. He asked me to present my case, which I did. His verdict? 'Not guilty.'"

Jehovah's Witnesses 'wish to conduct themselves honestly in all things.' (Hebrews 13:18) And their adherence to honesty is one of the many ways that they differ from the world.

He said: "It is well not to eat flesh or to drink wine or do anything over which your brother stumbles." (Romans 14:21) What loving counsel! Can you see how it could guide us in some other areas?

¹⁷ For example, the Bible permits Christians to drink alcoholic beverages in moderation. (1 Timothy 3:8; 5:23) But some are sensitive about strong drink. Others are not used to it or cannot handle it. If you were at a gathering with someone like that, would you try to pressure or shame him to join you in drinking alcohol? Or would you yourself not rather abstain so as not to cause him problems?

¹⁸ Consider another example: the matter of clothing. The Bible does not describe what kind of clothing a Christian should wear, although it does say that it should be modest and neat. (1 Timothy 2:9) Today, most countries have certain dress codes that are considered acceptable in formal society. Usually, this code allows for reasonable variety, but any wide deviation from it seems egocentric, sensuous, or eccentric. Christians, both men and women, have to bear this in mind. Are you willing to limit your freedom in the matter of clothing for the sake of the good news and so as not to stumble your brothers?

¹⁹ Yes, Jesus was right when he said that Christians would be "no part of the world." (John 17:16) In preaching the good news, in shunning what is bad, and in love and consideration for one another, Jehovah's Witnesses really are different. This separateness brings blessings to the

Witnesses, not least because it protects them from many of the problems that plague the world today.

²⁰ Do you treasure and cultivate this separateness in your own life? Remember, if Jehovah's Witnesses were any less separate, they would be more similar to the world, of which Satan the Devil is the god. (2 Corinthians 4:4) They would lose their clear identification as a 'holy people,' and would fail to keep themselves "uncontaminated by the world." Thus, they would no longer have "pure, unspoilt religion, in the eyes of God." (James 1:27, *The Jerusalem Bible;* 1 Peter 1:14-16) If you find yourself wishing you could be more like the world, remember the warning at James 4:4.

²¹ The apostle Paul prophesied that another trait would dominate in the world today. He said that men would be "lovers of money." (2 Timothy 3:1, 2) True to his words, pursuit of money is now such a powerful force that for many it is *the* strongest influence on their lives. Are Christians different in this too? Is it possible to survive in today's world without being a 'lover of money'? We will discuss this in the succeeding article.

17, 18. (a) How can the principle at Romans 14:21 be applied in the matter of strong drink? (b) How can it be applied in the matter of clothing? (c) What other areas can you think of in which applying this same principle will help us to show love for one another?
19-21. (a) Why do Jehovah's Witnesses work to maintain their separateness from the world? (b) In what other field do we have to strive to be separate from the world?

Can You Recall?

□ Why should a Christian expect to be different from the world?

□ What scriptures help Jehovah's Witnesses to have a right view of the preaching work?

□ In what different ways does the application of Hebrews 1:9 make Jehovah's Witnesses different from the world?

□ What effect does applying the principle explained in Romans 14:21 have on their conduct?

Keep Avoiding

"Be on your guard against greed of every kind, for even when a man has more than enough, his wealth does not give him life."
—LUKE 12:15, *The New English Bible.*

WE ARE living in a world that worships material prosperity. Commercial interests constantly appeal to people's greed to enrich themselves. Success is usually measured by the size of a paycheck. Hence, the Bible's many warnings against greed and the related vice of covetousness are timely. (Colossians 3:5; 1 Timothy 6:10) According to the dictionary, greed and covetousness share the element of "having or showing a strong desire for possessions and especially material possessions." Greed can be as serious as fornication or idolatry, for Paul warned: "Quit mixing in company with anyone called a brother that is a fornicator or a *greedy person* or an idolater or a reviler or a drunkard or an extortioner, not even eating with such a man."—1 Corinthians 5:11; Ephesians 5:3, 5.

² Jesus warned his followers: "Guard against every sort of covetousness." (Luke 12:15) And Jehovah himself included a commandment against this vice among the Ten Commandments: "You must not desire your fellowman's house. You must not desire your fellowman's wife, nor his slave man nor his slave girl nor his bull nor his ass nor anything that belongs to your fellowman."—Exodus 20:17; Romans 13:9.

No One Can Relax

³ The fact is, no one can lower his guard against greed and covetousness. When Eve sinned in the garden of Eden, it was because of greed: "The woman saw that the tree was good for food and that it was something to be longed for to the eyes, yes, the tree was desirable to look upon." (Genesis 3:6) On one occasion in the wilderness, the Israelites showed disgusting greediness. When, in response to their complaints about having only manna to eat, Jehovah provided an abundant supply of quail, they acted like gluttons and were severely punished.—Numbers 11: 4-6, 31-33.

⁴ Later, at the battle of Jericho, it was

1. Why is Paul's warning against greed timely?
2. What warnings did Jesus and Jehovah give us against covetousness?

3. How did greed overtake Eve and later the Israelites?
4. What other historical examples show the dangers of greed?

the Snare of Greed

greed that prompted Achan to steal some silver and gold and an expensive garment from the spoils of the city. (Joshua 7: 20, 21) Greed caused Gehazi, Elisha's attendant, to try to gain financial advantage out of the miraculous cure of Naaman's leprosy. (2 Kings 5:20-27) King Ahab was another greedy man. He allowed Jezebel, his pagan wife, to plot the death of Naboth, his neighbor, so that he could get his hands on Naboth's vineyard. (1 Kings 21: 1-19) Finally, Judas Iscariot, a member of Jesus' intimate circle, greedily used his position to steal from the common fund. And greed led him to betray Jesus for 30 pieces of silver.—Matthew 26:14-16; John 12:6.

⁵ All these greedy ones were punished. But did you notice the different *types* of people that fell into the snare of greed? Eve was a perfect woman living in Paradise. Achan and the Israelites had personally witnessed Jehovah's miracles. Ahab was a king, perhaps the richest man in the land. Gehazi and Judas were blessed with

rich spiritual association and high privileges of service. Yet they all became greedy. Thus anyone—however rich, however high his privilege of service, or whatever his experience—can fall into this trap. No wonder Jesus warned: "Guard against every sort of covetousness"! —Luke 12:15.

⁶ But how can we do that? Only by self-control and constant self-scrutiny. Greed starts in the heart. To avoid the snare of greed, we have to examine our hearts constantly to see if some manifestation of greed is taking root there. The Bible helps us to do that. How? For one thing, it records what Jesus and his disciples said about greed. When we examine those comments, they suggest some searching questions that we should ask ourselves to see where we stand in the matter of greed.

Examining Our Motives

⁷ Jesus' warning against covetousness

---

5. What do we learn from the experiences of different *types* of people who fell into the trap of greed?

6. What is needed if we are to avoid the trap of greed?
7. How does Jesus' answer to the man involved in an inheritance dispute help us to examine ourselves?

was prompted by a request from one of his listeners: "Teacher, tell my brother to divide the inheritance with me." Jesus answered: "Man, who appointed me judge or apportioner over you persons?" (Luke 12: 13, 14) Then he went on to warn against covetousness. Jesus did not want to get involved in a quarrel over material things, in view of the important spiritual task he was here to fulfill. (John 18:37) But this conversation suggests searching questions that we could ask ourselves. Suppose we were not in any particular need, but we felt we had a claim to some disputed property or wealth, or to a disputed inheritance. To what extent would we fight to succeed in our case? How much would we sacrifice of our service to Jehovah or of our relationship with our brothers to win what we viewed as our rights?—Proverbs 20:21; 1 Corinthians 6:7.

8 Consider another comment by Jesus. He warned his followers: "Look out for the scribes who . . . devour the houses of the widows." (Luke 20:46, 47) What a cruel manifestation of greed! Christians, of course, are obligated to care for widows, not prey on them. (James 1:27) However, suppose you knew a widow who had received a sizable insurance settlement, and you needed money in a hurry for an emergency. Would your first thought be to approach the widow, feeling that she would be the easiest to persuade, or that she *ought* to help because 'she's got plenty of money'? Or suppose you have already borrowed money, and now you are having problems paying it back. Would you feel justified in holding off repaying the widow, because she 'won't cause too much trouble,' or perhaps because you think 'she doesn't really need the money'? We have to be careful not to let our thinking

on principles become warped when we face financial problems.

9 Jude also described a way that greed may ensnare us. He spoke about persons who had infiltrated the Christian congregation and were corrupting it with their greed and loose conduct, "proving false to our only Owner and Lord, Jesus Christ." (Jude 4) Also, they were "admiring personalities for the sake of their own benefit." (Jude 16) We would not want to be like that. But consider: Do we find ourselves preferring to spend time with wealthier Christians and not giving so much attention to the poorer ones in the congregation? If so, could it be that we hope to benefit in some way? (Compare Acts 20:33; 1 Thessalonians 2:5.) When we show hospitality to responsible ones in the organization, do we do so out of love or because we hope for some privileges in return? If the latter, perhaps we, too, are 'admiring personalities for the sake of our own benefit.'

10 One manifestation of greed that irritated Jesus very much was when he "found in the temple those selling cattle and sheep and doves and the money brokers in their seats." Zeal for Jehovah's house made him drive these out of the temple and exclaim: "Stop making the house of my Father a house of merchandise!" (John 2:13-17) Do we have a similar zeal? Then it would be good to ask ourselves: Would I discuss business matters at the Kingdom Hall? Do I promote business ventures among fellow Christians because their being spiritual brothers makes it harder for them to say no? Do I use the many friends I have in the organization to widen my business contacts? Certainly,

8. How can we avoid being like the scribes mentioned by Jesus in Luke 20:46, 47?

9. How may we fall into the trap of 'admiring personalities for our own benefit'?
10. In what ways is it possible to make financial profit out of our worship of Jehovah? If we do this, whose example are we following?

we should not greedily make financial gain out of exploiting our relationship with our brothers.

¹¹ Does that mean that Christians can never do business together? No. It is just that there is a time and place for business, and another time and place for worship. (Ecclesiastes 3:1) However, when Christians do have business relationships, they should not forget Bible principles. When a Christian makes a business agreement, he should not seek legal loopholes to get out of his moral obligations. (Matthew 5:37) Neither will he become relentless or vindictive if a business goes sour and he loses money. The apostle Paul wrote to the Corinthians: "Really, then, it means altogether a defeat for you that you are having lawsuits with one another. Why do you not rather let yourselves be wronged? Why do you not rather let yourselves be defrauded?" (1 Corinthians 6:7) Could you, for the sake of the congregation, choose to be defrauded rather than go to court?

¹² Any Christian engaged in business needs to be very careful. Today many business practices are cutthroat, yet a Christian cannot act like that. He must never forget that he is a disciple of Christ. He does not want the reputation of being dishonest or of resorting to sharp practices. (Compare Proverbs 20:14; Isaiah 33:15.) And he should never forget Jesus' warning against making wealth a god, or John's warning against "the desire of the flesh and the desire of the eyes and the showy display of one's means of life." (1 John 2:16; Matthew 6:24) As a Christian businessman or businesswoman, can you resist the temptation to appeal to other people's greed in order to increase

| When doing business together, Christians should never forget Bible principles |

sales? Or would you play on their vanity or pride to further your business? Do you conduct your secular work in such a way that you are not ashamed to talk to Jehovah about it in your prayers?—Matthew 6:11; Philippians 4:6, 7.

¹³ Finally, Paul wrote to Timothy: "Those who are determined to be rich fall into temptation and a snare and many senseless and hurtful desires, which plunge men into destruction and ruin." (1 Timothy 6:9) Being rich is not a sin, although wealth brings its own problems and temptations. (Matthew 19:24-26) The danger is 'being determined to be rich.' For example, one elder said: "The problem often arises when a man looks at his wealthy Christian brother and says: 'Why can't I be like that?'"

¹⁴ The Bible urges: "Let your manner of life be free of the love of money, while you are content with the present things. For he has said: 'I will by no means leave you nor by any means forsake you.'" (Hebrews 13:5) If you are wealthy, do you view that as a gift, something you can use in Jehovah's service? On one occasion, Jesus told a rich young man that if he wanted to follow him, he would have to give away all his wealth. If Jesus had said that to you, would you have chosen to keep your wealth or to follow Jesus? (Matthew 19: 20-23) If you are not wealthy, can you be

11. What Christian principles help us to maintain a right attitude when we conduct business with one another?
12. What Bible principles will help those engaged in business to avoid the trap of greed?

13, 14. (a) What balance do wealthy Christians have to maintain? And those who are not wealthy? (b) How does the prayer at Proverbs 30:8 help us to learn reasonableness in the matter of wealth?

content with that? Can you avoid the trap of covetousness? Are you willing to trust Jehovah's promise: "I will by no means leave you nor by any means forsake you"? —See also Proverbs 30:8.

Be Rich Toward God

[15] When Jesus warned his listeners to "guard against every sort of covetousness," he went on to tell of a farmer whose fields produced exceptionally well. The man "began reasoning within himself, saying, 'What shall I do, now that I have nowhere to gather my crops?' So he said, 'I will do this: I will tear down my storehouses and build bigger ones, and there I will gather all my grain and all my good things; and I will say to my soul: "Soul, you have many good things laid up for many years; take your ease, eat, drink, enjoy yourself."'" However, that very night, the man died. All that accumulated wealth helped him not one little bit. Jesus concluded: "So it goes with the man that lays up treasure for himself but is not rich toward God."—Luke 12:16-21.

[16] Did the man commit any overt sin, such as extortion or theft? The parable does not say so. Still, he had a problem. He relied on his wealth for a secure future and forgot something more important: being "rich toward God." It is precisely because true Christians make their relationship toward God the most important thing in their lives that they can avoid the trap of greed and thus are no part of the world. —John 17:16.

[17] Jesus once counseled: "Never be anxious and say, 'What are we to eat?' or, 'What are we to drink?' or, 'What are we to put on?' For all these are the things the nations are eagerly pursuing." (Matthew 6:31, 32) True, all of us face the same problems that "the nations" face. Most of us have to work hard for a living to buy the necessary things to eat, drink, and wear. (2 Thessalonians 3:10-12) But we refuse to let such concerns overshadow our being "rich toward God."

[18] Jehovah is the source of all wealth. (Acts 14:15, 17) He has promised to take special care of his servants. Jesus said: "Your heavenly Father knows you need all these things. Keep on, then, seeking first the kingdom and his righteousness, and all these other things will be added to you." (Matthew 6:32, 33; Psalm 37:25) Do you believe that promise? Are you confident that Jehovah will keep it? Will you be satisfied with the provisions Jehovah makes? If so, you will be able to avoid the snare of greed. (Colossians 3:5) Your service to Jehovah and your relationship with him will always have first place, and your whole way of life will be a demonstration of your faith in him.

---

18. How will trust in Jehovah enable us to avoid the snare of greed?

15, 16. (a) What illustration did Jesus use to strengthen his counsel about covetousness? (b) What was the basic problem of the man in Jesus' parable?
17. How does a balanced Christian view the problem of earning a living?

Do You Remember?

□ What kinds of people are affected by greed?

□ How can we guard against greed?

□ How does greed sometimes manifest itself?

□ What questions help us to see whether we are avoiding the snare of greed or not?

□ What is a great protection against greed?

Kingdom Proclaimers Report

Angelic Direction of Our Ministry

EXPERIENCES often show that the Christian ministry has angelic direction. (Revelation 14:6, 7) Did not an angel direct Philip to the sincere Ethiopian eunuch who wanted to understand the Bible? (Acts 8:26, 27) And when the right-hearted Gentile Cornelius earnestly prayed to God for help, was not an angel sent to help him? (Acts 10:3-33) The following experience from Denver, Colorado, U.S.A., helps us appreciate that our ministry today has angelic direction as we search for those sincere of heart.

□ In their house-to-house ministry, two of Jehovah's Witnesses were told by the lady of the house that she was very busy. One Witness asked her if she ever wondered if one could speak to the dead? The Witnesses were invited in and scriptures were read about the cause of death, the condition of the dead, and the hope of the resurrection. (Ecclesiastes 9: 5, 10; John 5:28, 29) The woman was interested and a Bible study was arranged. After three months of study she asked if the Witnesses in the future could come at 4:30 p.m. for the study. This they agreed to.

The next week the woman *and* her husband were waiting for the Witnesses, as the husband wanted to know what his wife was learning. He asked many questions, one of which was: "Who is the antichrist and the man of lawlessness?" This question was answered satis-

factorily from the Bible by the Witnesses, and he then asked for six copies of the book *The Truth That Leads to Eternal Life*, published by Jehovah's Witnesses.

The following week the man and his wife, with their six children, were present for the study. The children were well mannered and obedient. Soon all of them began to attend the meetings of Jehovah's Witnesses at the Kingdom Hall.

The man asked the Witnesses to call on his married daughter and her husband and also on his aunt and her daughter. This was done and Bible studies were arranged with both families.

After a year of Bible study, this man, his wife, and two teenage daughters asked to get baptized in symbol of their ded-

ication to Jehovah. It was then learned that this man had been a Methodist minister. But after two months of Bible study with the Witnesses, he and his family had left the church. It was also learned that at the time of the initial call, the wife had planned to take her life and had prayed to God to take care of her family thereafter.

From that initial call, ten persons have accepted the truth. The man is now an elder, one of his daughters is a pioneer, and his son-in-law is a ministerial servant.

It is evident that angelic direction was on the ministry of those two Witnesses. Now these ten persons who were helped to a knowledge of the truth are all happily serving Jehovah, free from the bonds of false religion.

Serving God as a Family

As told by Otto Rittenbach

CAROL and I were married in November of 1951. The following year our first child, Brenda, was born. In the next six years we had five more children—Rick in July 1954, Rhonda in June 1955, JoDene in May 1956, Wayne in June 1957, and Kenan in July 1958. By then I was still only 27 and Carol just 23. Indeed, heavy family responsibilities for a young couple!

Today, we are thankful that all of us are united in God's service. Rick serves at Bethel, the world headquarters of Jehovah's Witnesses in Brooklyn, New York. Carol and I, along with our younger sons Wayne and Kenan, are at Watchtower Farms about 95 miles (150 km) north of Brooklyn. And Brenda, Rhonda, and JoDene each graduated from the Watchtower Bible School of Gilead and are now missionaries—Brenda in the Middle East and Rhonda and JoDene in Colombia, South America.

Never in our fondest hopes did we envision that our entire family would have these grand privileges of service. We were just a young couple with a bunch of kids who tried our best to keep up with the directions that we received from God through his Word and visible organization. It wasn't always easy. There were difficult times. But we all agree that keeping God's service our first priority has resulted in our living rich and rewarding lives. Let me tell briefly about our background and the rearing of our family.

Learning Bible Truth

I was born in 1930 on a farm in the prairie area of North Dakota, the 13th of 14 children. The Nylens, another farm family, lived about four miles (6 km) away. They were known in the community as Jehovah's Witnesses, even though they were not baptized and did not regularly attend congregation meetings.

In the course of taking care of farming business, I made frequent visits to their farm and became acquainted with Carol Nylen. Our relationship grew, and soon after Carol graduated from high school we were married. Two months later, early in 1952, I was drafted and spent two years in the army, including 14 months in Germany.

After I returned from Germany, we

rented a farm about a quarter mile (.4 km) from the Nylens. We had practically no money so we had to get FHA (Farmers Home Administration) loans to buy a herd of milk cows and some farm machinery. Farming was very time consuming in those days. Yet, with encouragement from Carol and my in-laws who by then were active Witnesses, I accepted a home Bible study. It was faithfully conducted with me by Carol's brother Roland. With additional spiritual help from visits of circuit overseers and other Witnesses, I eventually made a dedication to Jehovah and was baptized in August of 1956.

7-16-97

A Hardworking Companion

Life on the farm in those days lacked many modern conveniences. Our rented farm house, for example, had no running water or indoor plumbing, so all the water had to be carried from the well, and we had to go outside to use the toilet facilities. We had few home furnishings, but we made do with what we had and what was given to us. Carol became so adept at home decorating that even the owners said the place was like a doll's house. She also made all the kids' clothes, mainly out of old garments given to her. And she often gave me a hand outside with the chores, including milking the cows, which we did by hand.

During those years Carol, whose mother had been a schoolteacher, did a marvelous job training the children. In addition, reading the Bible and Watchtower publications had impressed upon us the value of training our children from infancy. (2 Timothy 3:15) So, regularly, each morning from about 9:30 to 11, one end of our small kitchen became a school. Among the earliest memories of all the children is sitting in little red chairs in a semicircle around a blackboard. Today, these instruction sessions are recalled by the children with fondness. The ones that were yet infants would learn to sit quietly and fold their hands for up to an hour. Afterward they were ready for their regular forenoon nap.

By the time the children were about a year and a half old, they were active participants. Carol taught them the alphabet and how to read and write by use of homemade flash cards. She also helped them to memorize key Bible texts, as well as the names of the apostles, and related to them Bible stories along with the practical lessons that these taught. It was intriguing to watch how easily and how much our children were able to learn at an early age. Some may find it hard to believe, yet they were able to recite the names of all 66 books of the Bible by the time they were a year and a half old, and by the age of two or three each of them could read.

In addition, we had a regular family study during which we would prepare with the children the lessons to be studied at our regular congregation meetings. Of course, this meant breaking the material down so that they could understand it, especially when we were studying the book *Your Will Be Done on Earth,* and later *Let Your Name Be Sanctified,* as well as lessons in the *Watchtower* magazine. This training helped the children not only to progress spiritually but also to excel in school.

Dealing With Problems

Yet, despite all our efforts, not everything went as smoothly as we would have liked. For example, when Brenda came home from her first day at school, we excitedly asked her about her day. One of our questions was about the flag salute. She answered, "Oh, no, I didn't salute the flag; I just pledged allegiance." Something, obviously, had been missing in our instruction!

JoDene, Brenda, and Rhonda
learned Bible stories
at an early age

Then there was the occasion when a turkey dinner was served in the school cafeteria just before Thanksgiving vacation. Rick, who was in the first grade at the time, refused to eat it. Only after persistent explaining by the teacher that it was not Thanksgiving Day nor a real Thanksgiving dinner, and after a phone call to Carol, did Rick's conscience allow him to eat that meal.

There were also problems of another kind, ones we could hardly believe would arise, but which illustrate the wayward inclinations of youth. (Genesis 8:21; Proverbs 22:15) Rhonda seemed intent in the third grade to have a ready-made, store-bought coat. So she fabricated the story that the teacher said she had to have one by May 1! She almost had us convinced.

Then there was the matter of stealing. When Wayne and Kenan were in the second and first grades, they took candy from the teacher's desk. When we learned of this, we reasoned with them, trying to draw out of their hearts what motivated them to do this bad thing. We had them make retribution by buying candy and presenting it to the teacher and telling her what they had done. We tried to root out bad motives from our children's hearts once these were discerned and tried to replace them with good and pure motives by reasoning with them.

Full Attention Required

Very early on we realized that rearing a family in Jehovah's service is a career that requires full attention. We found that children need to be kept busy, to be given a sense of order and scheduling. They need to know when to get up in the morning, when nap time is, when it is time to eat, and so forth. All of this needs to be inculcated while they are yet infants and carried through and expanded as they grow older.

We began teaching our young ones obedience in infancy. When we asked them to do something, even if it was as simple as, "Fold your hands," or, "Sit down," we expected and received immediate compliance. We made sure that *each* command was carried out. Wholesome control and guidance from infancy to adulthood drastically reduces problems at a later date. One practice that we exercised in their infancy was to wrap our children in a swaddling manner when it was time for them to sleep, even as Jesus was wrapped as an infant. (Luke 2:7) This helped them to feel secure and to go to sleep almost instantly.

From a very early age we also taught the children to work. Under the watchful eye of my wife, they learned to pick up things, to wash dishes, and to fold clothes. Later they learned to darn socks, to sew on buttons, to make bread, to plant and weed the garden, and to help with the canning and freezing of its produce. Both the boys and the girls learned all these things. They also learned to make minor repairs around the house, to do painting, and to keep the yard looking attractive. We taught them to be thorough at whatever they did, to do a good job, and we saw to it that they did. It took time, but it really paid off in later years.

We also recognized the need of recreational activities. These, however, seldom included watching television. In fact, our family made a combined decision NOT to have one. Our recreation mostly consisted of doing things together—playing games, having picnics, enjoying congregational activities, and going to assemblies. Often, in connection with travel to the assemblies, we scheduled vacation trips to interesting places.

We always placed priority on spiritual activities. At first we had to travel 55 miles (90 km) each way to the Kingdom Hall, and North Dakota winters can be severe. But by taking reasonable precautions and being blessed with relatively good health, we seldom missed a meeting. Circuit assemblies were real highlights in our lives, sometimes involving a trip of 250 miles (400 km) to share in a three-day program back in those days.

The field ministry was a regular feature of every weekend, regardless of -20° F. (-29° C.) weather. Some people may think it extreme to have young ones out in such weather, but it helped to impress upon the children that nothing should stand in the way of our service to Jehovah.

Keeping Kingdom Interests First

In 1961 we were faced with a big decision when the farm that we were renting came up for sale. Should I buy the farm, or should I seek different employment? Farm life was good for the children, and as the boys grew up it could become their means of livelihood. However, to do it

Wayne, Rick, and Kenan
—now all in Bethel service

justice, farming would take most of our time, and we reasoned that it could become a snare to us. Earlier my dad had given me some land, which was really not large enough to farm. I sold this and bought a backhoe and related equipment and went into excavation work.

We moved to the nearby town of Butte, North Dakota, population about 200. I excavated basements and installed farm sewers, and I learned to lay cement blocks and to do plumbing. To supplement what was a rather meager income, I also drove the school bus. Yet we always could feel Jehovah's concern and help for us as our family put spiritual things first. Despite our being a large, relatively poor family and our having to contend with severe weather at times, we always managed to attend congregation meetings and assemblies, and also to share regularly in the field ministry.

In time we were able to buy an old house and, with the generous help of Carol's father, remodel it into a very attractive but modest home. A congregation was formed in our area, and we had the privilege of helping to build a small Kingdom Hall. As a result, we now had to travel only 15 miles (25 km) instead of 55 miles (90 km) to get to the meetings. Since the congregation was small, we had parts on the meetings every week, which kept us busy preparing for them.

In so many ways we felt Jehovah's watchcare. To illustrate: In March of 1965 I was invited to attend the Kingdom Ministry School in South Lansing, New York, which at the time provided a month-long course of instruction for Christian elders. But the car we had was old and not dependable enough for my family to get to the meetings and a circuit assembly while I would be away. So we went to the biggest nearby town to look for a car. We had looked unsuccessfully most of the day when, about 45 minutes before I had to return home to drive the school bus, I stopped at one more dealer.

The salesman took me to a dark underground garage and showed me a car that I thought would serve our purposes. A test drive revealed that it ran well, but the salesman said the price was $300, much more than I could pay. As I was about to leave, the salesman said to wait while he asked the manager what was the least he could take. The manager stalled, pondered, and reluctantly said, $150. We made the deal and drove the car home.

Later that spring, money was tight. I had just returned from the Kingdom Ministry School. It was too early to start outside work as the frost was still in the ground. I had a job coming up right across the street to dig a waterline and sewer and put in a bathroom and plumbing. It would be a month or more before I could do it, but one day, to my surprise, our neighbor called up. He said he would like to advance me $500 on the job!

In 1967 I received a job offer in a town about 100 miles (160 km) away. I decided to accept it. One reason was that my excavating business was taking me farther and farther away from home, and it was at the point where I would need to expand and become more involved with the business at the expense of spiritual activities. So we sold our house and moved to New Rockford, North Dakota, where I became a bulk fertilizer salesman for a farm store. Although this new job did not allow me the freedom that being self-employed did, I decided to take it since the children were now older and well established in the Christian way.

A Happy Family in the Full-Time Ministry

Because the children turned down scholarships upon their graduation, their teachers and others in the community thought their scholastic abilities were being wasted. Yet, despite pressures to continue their secular education, on completing high school each of them started in the full-time ministry as a pioneer.

Brenda started pioneering in 1970, followed by Rick in 1972. He then went to Bethel that December. The following year both Rhonda and my wife began pioneering. In 1974 JoDene and I joined them in the pioneer work, and the following spring Wayne brought the number of pioneers in the family to six. In 1976 Wayne went to serve at Watchtower Farms, but Kenan graduated and kept the number in the family pioneering at six.

When I decided to pioneer, my employer refused my request for part-time work, so I quit the farm store. I was subsequently hired as a fuel-truck driver, but when my employer insisted that I become involved in dishonest business practices, I quit there also. However, I was by this time

Part of the
Rittenbach family today
—all in full-time service

pioneering with Carol and the children, the desire of a lifetime, so nothing could now deter me.

Within a week of quitting my job, I was called by another employer who asked me if I could work two days a week during the winter servicing furnaces. Amazing? Not really, for hadn't we been promised that if we put Kingdom interests first, we would be cared for? (Matthew 6:33) The children by this time each had part-time jobs, and their contributing to household expenses made possible our pioneering together as a family.

Then, in June 1977, Carol and I along with Kenan were invited to Watchtower Farms. Being a mother and leaving behind our home and three darling daughters tugged at my wife's heart. But she reasoned that it was Jehovah's leading and truly an inestimable privilege. The girls viewed it that way, too, and urged us to go. The following summer we returned on vacation, sold our house and other material possessions, and helped our daughters move to their first special-pioneer assignment about 100 miles (160 km) away.

While the girls were serving as special pioneers in Grand Island, New York, they were called to Watchtower Farms in August 1981 to work along with us until they entered the 72nd class of Gilead School

commencing that October. The following March they graduated, and soon all three were on their way to a missionary assignment in Colombia, South America.

Rhonda and JoDene are still in Colombia, but Brenda married a Gilead classmate in March of 1983 and joined him in the Middle East. Then, in March of 1984, Rhonda married a Gilead graduate who joined her in Colombia. Also, each of the boys married lovely pioneer girls who are now serving with them either at Brooklyn Bethel or at Watchtower Farms. So our pioneer family has grown to 13, including my wife and me.

All of us are truly happy to be in the full-time service of our God, Jehovah, and as a family we know that to continue enjoying these privileges of service, we must behave in a manner worthy of the good news. (Philippians 1:27) We are grateful for the fine counsel that Jehovah has provided through his visible organization, since it has been the application of it in our lives that has resulted in our now enjoying as a family our present glorious treasure of service.

Turkish Court Sends Jehovah's Witnesses to Prison

ON DECEMBER 12, 1984, a shocking decision was rendered by the State Security Court in Ankara, Turkey. It sentenced five of Jehovah's Witnesses to prison, each for six years and eight months, with an additional two years and two months in exile! Eighteen other Witnesses were sentenced to four years and two months in prison, with another year and four months in exile. Other Witnesses are to have a separate trial before a criminal court.

What was their "crime"? They were found guilty of violating article 163 of the Turkish Penal Code. According to this, it is a crime 'to make religious propaganda with the aim of changing the social, economic, political, or legal order of the state.' So it was claimed that a very small number—a mere handful—of Jehovah's Witnesses were trying to change the existing governmental order in Turkey. But how could this tiny group of people who are peaceful, unarmed, and totally untrained in political subversion be a threat to overthrow the entire established system of the nation?

Law-Abiding People

Jehovah's Witnesses are well known throughout the world as a law-abiding people. For example, a governor-general of Nigeria said of them: "They have added greatly to the spiritual upbuilding of our people in Nigeria." He also said: "If all the religious denominations were like Jehovah's Witnesses, we would have no murders, burglaries, delinquencies, prisoners and atomic bombs. Doors would not be locked day in and day out."

Also, Jehovah's Witnesses never have mixed in politics. Their neutrality in such affairs is well known. The Italian publication *Il Corriere di Trieste* said that "Jehovah's Witnesses should be admired." Why, among other reasons? Because, it said, their religion teaches them 'not to mix politics with religion and not to serve the interests of political parties.'

Thus, during their more than a hundred years of history, they never have tried to change any political order of any state. Rather, they do what the Bible tells them to do—accept the existing governments as "superior authorities" to which they must give respect. (Romans 13:1) Therefore it is against their religious convictions to engage in any subversive activity. That is why nations that are not dictatorial recognize that Jehovah's Witnesses are certainly a religion and have given them the freedoms of other citizens, including the freedom of worship.

The sentences are also completely unwarranted for another reason. On March 24, 1980, the Supreme Court of Appeals in Turkey ruled that Jehovah's Witnesses cannot be punished, as their religion does not violate the law. The court had acquitted them of charges of subversion.

Events Leading to Trial

So the question arises: What information did the court use to reach its decision? Have Jehovah's Witnesses changed their activity or beliefs since 1980? Let us briefly consider the circumstances that led up to the trial, as well as the court records.

On November 20, 1974, a district court in Istanbul gave legal approval to Jehovah's Witnesses as a religion. Accordingly, the Witnesses could legally register their religion on their identification cards, which they did. And from December 1974, Jehovah's Witnesses began to meet freely for worship in various cities of the country. The military government that came to power in September of 1980 also permitted their public meetings in their "Halls of Worship."

However, in March of 1984, three families in Eskişehir applied to the court to have their religion registered as Jehovah's Witnesses. That event made headlines in the local newspaper. Being former Muslims, their application aroused the animosity of fanatical Muslims, who began to attack and defame Jehovah's Witnesses in various newspapers.

Among the opposers was the "High Council of Religion in the Directorate of Religious Affairs," a Muslim governmental office. This council stated: "This movement [Jehovah's Witnesses], which in no country is being accepted as a religion . . . is a Christian order under Jewish influence." It further stated that "if this movement will be permitted [in Turkey] it will be a danger for the State as well as for Islam."

After the malicious newspaper campaign, suddenly two Witnesses were arrested in Ankara for offering their publications to another person. Yet, those publications were being printed legally in Turkey.

During the following days, the police in Ankara arrested the five elders of a congregation, as well as others who were known as Jehovah's Witnesses. Altogether 31 were arrested. Some were arrested at their homes, others at their place of work, and some after their meeting at their "Hall of Worship." Of the 31 originally arrested, 23 were held and the others released.

False Charges

As the court hearing proceeded, it became more and more evident that it was not actually a case of violating the law. Rather, it was a religious issue that the court was deciding.

For example, as supposed evidence of guilt, the prosecution used a statement from the Directorate of Religious Affairs. In this statement, Jehovah's Witnesses are labeled as "a crazy Christian movement" that has "no prophets and no special holy book." On the contrary, Jehovah's Witnesses are known as a very sane, law-abiding, peaceful society of people. And they most assuredly have a prophet —Jesus Christ—who, incidentally, even Muslims acknowledge as a prophet. And

In Our Next Issue

■ **A Cure for All Diseases**
——**It Can Be Found!**

■ **Accept God's Help**
to Overcome Secret Faults

■ **Mourning Customs**
——**How Do You View Them?**

Jehovah's Witnesses do not subvert any government

they need no other "special holy book," for they already have one—the Holy Bible, which is "inspired of God."—2 Timothy 3:16.

It was also claimed that Jehovah's Witnesses do not accept "the existent nations and states and their national boundaries." This, too, is totally false. Their religion specifically requires them to "be in subjection to the superior [governmental] authorities" and all the laws that do not conflict with God's laws. That is what the Bible says to do.—Romans 13:1; Acts 5:29.

In addition, the Directorate of Religious Affairs claimed that Jehovah's Witnesses engage in an activity "to establish a Bible-based religious order over the entire world," and that God's Kingdom would be established between the "Euphrates and Nile" rivers. This statement tries to prove that Jehovah's Witnesses would change the established political order in Turkey, since the Euphrates River passes through Eastern Turkey.

That is another totally false charge. Jehovah's Witnesses have never believed that the Kingdom of God will be on earth. Instead, they have always taught that it will be a heavenly rule. So it could not possibly be located in any part of Turkey. —Matthew 4:17; 6:9, 10.

False Religious Testimony

The court also appointed three "experts" to examine the publications and beliefs of Jehovah's Witnesses. One was a member of the Directorate of Religious Affairs. The second was an assistant professor of an Islamic faculty. The third was an assistant professor of the legal faculty of the University of Ankara.

The defense counsel objected to the appointment of two of the religious "experts." These had already expressed their opinion against Jehovah's Witnesses in a book. Therefore, it could not be expected that they would give an unbiased opinion to the court. However, the court refused the request of the defense and allowed these prejudiced religious persons to participate.

When these three handed in their report, it was as expected. The religious examiners found Jehovah's Witnesses guilty. However, the law expert did not find any guilt. He stated: "They are expecting the coming change in the world by God after the war of Armageddon," and not by any human intervention.

The religionists claimed that Jehovah's Witnesses are not a religion. That is obviously another false charge. They also claimed that the belief of Jehovah's Witnesses in God and in Jesus Christ "serves only as a religious cover in order to hide the real purpose." And what would that "real purpose" supposedly be? The religious advisers said: "Under the appearance of the Kingdom of God they lay a foundation for some political developments in an unknown future." Quoting unrelated passages from the publications of Jehovah's Witnesses, they concluded that they were 'a secret organization under Zionistic influence that is using religious meetings as a cover.'

However, these two religious persons did not produce a single piece of evidence that Jehovah's Witnesses have ever tried to subvert the Turkish state. They could not produce such evidence because the Witnesses do not subvert existing governments. It is God himself who holds governments accountable. He is the Judge, not any human. And anyone who is familiar with the Witnesses knows that they have no connection whatsoever with Zionism.

Defense Provides Evidence

On the other hand, the defense provided much evidence that Jehovah's Witnesses were not guilty of violating any law. In addition to the decision of the Supreme Court of Appeals on March 24, 1980, the defense presented three other decisions of the Supreme Court. These also had previously acquitted Jehovah's Witnesses from the same charges.

The defense also presented a second opinion from another professor of law who had examined the publications of Jehovah's Witnesses. He did not find any violation of law in them.

The court was also referred to about 20 other court decisions rendered during the past 30 years in Turkey. All those courts had acquitted the Witnesses from the same charges.

Last, but not least, even the police officer who had been appointed to control the meetings of the Witnesses testified before the court. He declared that he had "not observed any violation of the law during the entire year" that he had controlled the meetings.

Court Rejects the Evidence

Nevertheless, the court rejected all the evidence of the defense! It accepted only the slanderous and totally unfounded writings that the prosecutor presented.

These were the statements from the Directorate of Religious Affairs and also the report from the two prejudiced religious commentators.

The sentences raise serious questions. Were the judges of the court also prejudiced by their Muslim beliefs? Was the court put under religious pressure to sentence Jehovah's Witnesses?

Of course, the decision is being appealed. So the Supreme Court will have the opportunity to review the matter. It is hoped that this court will render a judgment in full harmony with the facts. Unfortunately, until that time the 23 Witnesses—15 men and 8 women—remain in prison.

Certainly, fair-minded and freedom-loving people throughout the world ask: How could such a thing happen in a country that claims to be a democratic state? How could Turkish courts do such a thing when the Turkish government also has signed the Declaration of Human Rights, which guarantees freedom of religion?

If you feel indignant at peaceful, innocent persons being so unjustly sentenced to prison, you have the opportunity to express your opinion. You can write to any or all of the officials below and let them know how you feel about this matter:

President of the Republic:
    His Excellency Kenan EVREN, Bakanliklar, Ankara, Turkey

Prime Minister:
    Mr. Turgut ÖZAL, Bakanliklar, Ankara, Turkey

Minister of Interior:
    Mr. Yildirim AKBULUT, Bakanliklar, Ankara, Turkey

Minister of Justice:
    Mr. M. Necat ELDEM, Bakanliklar, Ankara, Turkey

Also, you may write to the Turkish Ambassador in your area.

"My Guide, My Counselor"

The book *Your Youth—Getting the Best out of It* has served as such for a youth from Senegal, West Africa. "As a Muslim," he explains, "I was greatly impressed by the way you examine problems of youth. You wisely deal with adolescence. Your book is for me more than a book—it is my guide, my counselor, and will be so for always.

"Being a fatherless child since the age of eleven, I lived with my grandmother until I was nineteen. Now I am twenty. If my way of life has a good influence on people around me, it is thanks to the *Youth* book. I cannot count how many times I have read and reread it. Every subject you deal with gives me the feeling it is especially for me. I have also shared your book with all my friends. They, too, say it is a treasure house of knowledge."

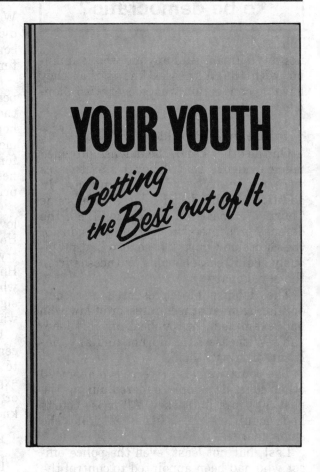

YOUR YOUTH

Getting the Best out of It

April 15, 1985

The Watchtower

Announcing Jehovah's Kingdom

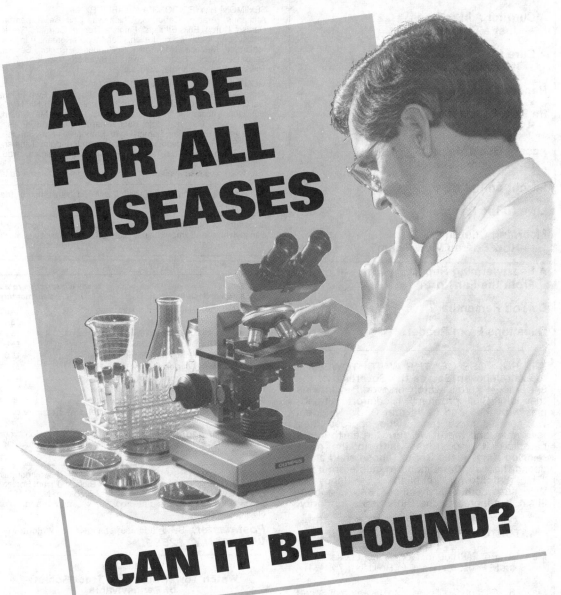

A CURE FOR ALL DISEASES

CAN IT BE FOUND?

April 15, 1985
Vol. 106, No. 8

The Watchtower
Announcing Jehovah's Kingdom

THE PURPOSE OF "THE WATCHTOWER" is to exalt Jehovah God as the Sovereign of the universe. It keeps watch on world events as they fulfill Bible prophecy. It comforts all peoples with the good news that God's Kingdom will soon destroy those who oppress their fellowmen and that it will turn the earth into a paradise. It encourages faith in the now-reigning King, Jesus Christ, whose shed blood opens the way for mankind to gain eternal life. "The Watchtower," published by Jehovah's Witnesses continuously since 1879, is nonpolitical. It adheres to the Bible as its authority.

"WATCHTOWER" STUDIES FOR THE WEEKS

May 19: Be Faithful to God "Who Looks On in Secret." Page 10. Songs to Be Used: 79, 111.

May 26: Accept God's Help to Overcome Secret Faults. Page 15. Songs to Be Used: 9, 163.

Average Printing Each Issue: 11,150,000

Now Published in 102 Languages

SEMIMONTHLY EDITIONS AVAILABLE BY MAIL
Afrikaans, Arabic, Cebuano, Chichewa, Chinese, Cibemba, Danish, Dutch, Efik, English*, Finnish, French, German, Greek, Hiligaynon, Igbo, Iloko, Italian, Japanese, Korean, Lingala, Malagasy, Maltese, Norwegian, Portuguese, Russian, Sepedi, Sesotho, Shona, Spanish, Swahili, Swedish, Tagalog, Thai, Tswana, Xhosa, Yoruba, Zulu

MONTHLY EDITIONS AVAILABLE BY MAIL
Armenian, Bengali, Bicol, Bulgarian, Croatian, Czech, Ewe, Fijian, Ga, Greenlandic, Gujarati, Gun, Hausa, Hebrew, Hindi, Hiri Motu, Hungarian, Icelandic, Kannada, Kikuyu, Kiluba, Malayalam, Marathi, New Guinea Pidgin, Pangasinan, Papiamento, Polish, Rarotongan, Romanian, Samar-Leyte, Samoan, Sango, Serbian, Silozi, Sinhalese, Slovenian, Solomon Islands-Pidgin, Tahitian, Tamil, Telugu, Tshiluba, Tsonga, Turkish, Twi, Ukrainian, Urdu, Venda, Vietnamese
*Study articles also available in large-print edition at same cost.

The Bible translation used is the "New World Translation of the Holy Scriptures," unless otherwise indicated.

Twenty cents (U.S.) a copy

Watch Tower Society offices	Yearly subscription rates Semimonthly
America, U.S., Watchtower, Wallkill, N.Y. 12589	$4.00
Australia, Box 280, Ingleburn, N.S.W. 2565	A$6.00
Canada, Box 4100, Halton Hills (Georgetown), Ontario L7G 4Y4	$5.20
England, The Ridgeway, London NW7 1RN	£5.00
Ireland, 29A Jamestown Road, Finglas, Dublin 11	£5.00
New Zealand, 6-A Western Springs Rd., Auckland 3	$7.00
Nigeria, P.O. Box 194, Yaba, Lagos State	₦3.50
Philippines, P.O. Box 2044, Manila 2800	₱50.00
South Africa, Private Bag 2, Elandsfontein, 1406	R5,60

Remittances should be sent to the office in your country or to Watchtower, Wallkill, N.Y. 12589, U.S.A.

Changes of address should reach us 30 days before your moving date. Give us your old and new address (if possible, your old address label).

The Watchtower (ISSN 0043-1087) is published semimonthly for $4.00 (U.S.) per year by Watch Tower Bible and Tract Society of Pennsylvania, 25 Columbia Heights, Brooklyn, N.Y. 11201. Second-class postage paid at Brooklyn, N.Y., and at additional mailing offices.

Postmaster: Send address changes to Watchtower, **Wallkill, N.Y. 12589.**

Published by
**Watch Tower Bible and Tract Society
of Pennsylvania**
25 Columbia Heights, Brooklyn, N.Y. 11201, U.S.A.
Frederick W. Franz, President

A Cure for All Diseases
Just a Dream?

JOHN was a very old man. He had been in exile on a small island for some time. It might appear he was to live out his life in isolation. But in that situation he received a message full of encouragement for him—and for us.

In a dramatic vision John heard a loud voice from heaven saying: "Look! The tent of God is with mankind . . . He will wipe out every tear from their eyes, and death will be no more, neither will mourning nor outcry nor pain be anymore. The former things have passed away."

Then, he saw a river with sparkling, crystal-clear waters. Along its banks he saw luxuriant fruit trees. The leaves of the trees were for the curing of the nations. What an exhilarating experience!

If you heard and saw what John did, would you not be excited to learn that some day all pain and suffering will cease and that all ills will be cured? Indeed, it seems too good to believe!

Why So Hard to Believe

What happened there was a historical event that took place in the year 96 C.E. on the island of Patmos, off the coast of modern-day Turkey. The elderly John was the beloved apostle of Jesus Christ, and what he saw he recorded in the Holy Bible.—Revelation 1:9; 21:3, 4; 22:1, 2.

Even so, most people today find it difficult to believe that there is to be a time when diseases will be no more. Why? Human nature being what it is, we tend to reject anything that seems to go contrary to our common experience.

Regarding man's long struggle against disease, Richard Fiennes, pathologist to the Zoological Society of London, wrote in his book *Man, Nature and Disease:*

"Is the end of the battle then in sight? Man fights a hydra. When one head is removed, another appears in its place. Premature illness, incapacity, and death are still the most pressing of human problems; where in days gone by tuberculosis, pneumonia, and death in childbirth were the problems, today, coronary heart disease, stroke, cancer, and other ailments have taken their place."

The killers of "days gone by" are not

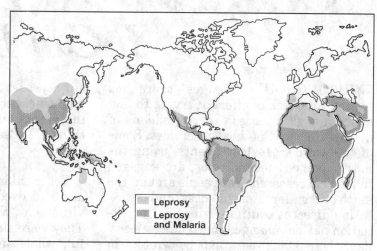

Leprosy

Leprosy and Malaria

Killers of the past still infect wide areas

totally banished either. *The Economist* of London reports that "in Asia, Africa and South America, one person in 10 is in some way disabled. Most of the poor will suffer diseases such as acute diarrhoea and pneumonia during their lifetimes. . . . Millions more will succumb to parasitic diseases such as malaria or schistosomiasis (ie, bilharzia [caused by a blood parasite]); others will be crippled by leprosy."

Even in the developed countries other heads of the "hydra" have baffled experts. "Doctors today are encountering exotic diseases that can be even more deadly than the classic killers such as smallpox and diphtheria," writes Edward Edelson in New York's *Daily News.*

A few years ago, the acronym AIDS would have meant hardly anything to most people. Today, this deadly disease has become known virtually to everyone, as have also Legionnaires' disease and toxic shock syndrome. Waiting in the wings are other potential killers: Ebola fever, Lassa fever, Korean hemorrhagic fever, Reye's syndrome, Kawasaki disease, hemolytic uremic syndrome, and so on. "One thread that runs through the story of these exotic diseases is that they often present medicine with unsolved puzzles," says Edelson.

Despite medical advances, most people have resigned themselves to believing that sickness and death are ultimately unavoidable. It is difficult for them to imagine that there could ever be a time when death, pain, and disease will be no more.

What, then, about the stirring vision that John received? Will it finally turn out to be just an unfulfilled dream? We have good reasons to believe that this will not be so. Immediately after hearing the marvelous promises, John received this assurance: "Write, because these words are faithful and true." (Revelation 21:5; 22:6) How will these words come true? And will we see the fulfillment of them in our lifetime?

A Cure for All Diseases
It Can Be Found!

THROUGHOUT the ages, there has been no lack of effort at trying to find a cure for all diseases. Yearly, billions of dollars are spent on health services. Some of the world's greatest talents, using the most advanced technologies, are engaged in medical research. Yet people around the earth still suffer from sickness, and devastating diseases continue with us. Our situation has not changed much since Moses' day. Over 3,000 years ago he wrote: "In themselves the days of our years are seventy years; and if because of special mightiness they are eighty years, yet their insistence is on trouble and hurtful things."—Psalm 90:10.

A Healthy Start
Yet mankind had a perfect start. Adam and Eve lived in a clean, disease-free environment, the beautiful garden of Eden. They were supplied with plenty of healthful, wholesome food. They had stimulating, rewarding work to do. And they were

sound in body and mind.—See Genesis 1: 26-30.

God also told them how to maintain their perfect state. First he told them what they should do: "Be fruitful and become many and fill the earth and subdue it." Then he told them what they should not do: "As for the tree of the knowledge of good and bad you must not eat from it, for in the day you eat from it you will positively die." (Genesis 1:28; 2:17) If they, and eventually their offspring, would obey these two basic directives, they would be able to maintain their healthy, happy, and perfect state forever.

Many people today feel that the account of Adam and Eve is unscientific, merely a myth. But rather than dismissing these matters lightly, let us take a closer look.

In terms that we are familiar with today, the first command told them that they must take care of their *environment*. The second told them that they must keep their *life-style* within certain bounds set by God. Is this unscientific myth or does it underline a basis for healthful living? Note what the book *Health and Disease* by René Dubos and Maya Pines says on the matter: "One of the least appreciated influences on disease is environment. Where a man lives and how he lives may have a greater effect on his health—often in unsuspected ways—than the microbes he encounters or the genes he inherits."

What Is Disease?

In this context, disease is very much related to how we live and how we deal with our environment. Today we feel that our civilized way of life has done much to improve the general condition of health. But note what Dubos and Pines say: "The Australian aborigines, living in relative isolation in a Stone Age culture, are remarkably free of disease. In fact, it is only in the most advanced societies that civilized man, through the science of modern medicine, begins to approximate the good health the world's least civilized people enjoy as a birthright."

Another of these "least civilized people" cited by the authors are the Mabaans of the Sudan. "The Mabaans enjoy longevity that would be remarkable in the most medically pampered society. Furthermore, their declining years are almost free of the usual degenerative diseases of old age. Scientists are still puzzled by the Mabaans' extraordinary health, but their stable, tranquil environment is almost certainly an important factor." To emphasize the influence of environment, the authors added: "When a Mabaan moves from home to the city of Khartoum, 650 miles [1,050 km] away, he is beset by a host of ills he has never known before."

In contrast, our "civilized" way of life has brought pollution of air and water, deforestation, overpopulation, and malnutrition for large segments of the population. Man's careless treatment of the environment has not only posed serious hazards to his health but also threatened the prospect of his continued existence on earth.—See Revelation 11:18.

It is not surprising, therefore, that disease has sometimes been defined as "a by-product of a civilized way of life." We consider ourselves civilized because we no longer live in the wild. Rather, we may live in cities in close contact with, if not literally on top of, one another. In fact, the word "civilized" comes from a Latin root meaning citizen or city dweller. But from where did the idea of city dwelling come?

The first record of it is given at Genesis 11:4: "They now said: 'Come on! Let us build ourselves a city and also a tower with its top in the heavens, and let us make a celebrated name for ourselves, for fear we may be scattered over all the surface of the earth.'" That proposal during the days of Nimrod was in contradiction to God's purpose stated to Adam, namely, for humans to "fill the earth and subdue it." To do so, they were to spread out as their numbers increased. For refusing to do this, as well as for other reasons, Nimrod came to be known as being "in opposition to Jehovah." (Genesis 10:9) That defiant course, added to the rebellion in the garden of Eden, accelerated mankind down the road of decadence, disease, and death.

Even today, most of the diseases plaguing those in the affluent nations are the result of their life-style.

The Search for Health

Authorities have come to realize that mankind's health problems are not solved simply by having more medicine, more doctors, or more hospitals, even though these undoubtedly would provide short-term improvement. Rather, radical changes in the way people live and the way people deal with the environment are called for. For example, Dr. Halfdan Mahler, director-general of WHO (World Health Organization), in an essay on World Health Day, April 7, 1983, wrote:

"What *can* people do about their health? To give a few examples, they can take individual and community action to ensure that they have sufficient food of the right kind. They can get together to make the most of whatever safe water is available, or can be made available, making sure that it is protected from pollution. They can insist on acceptable standards of hygiene in and around their homes, in market places and shops, in schools, in factories, in canteens and restaurants. They can learn how to space the children they desire in such a way as to give each and everyone of them a good chance of survival, a reasonable education, and a decent quality of life."

Clearly, these are steps toward good health. But the obvious questions are: How are the poor people in the underdeveloped countries to get sufficient food, safe water, and acceptable hygiene? Where will they get the finances and the skills needed to provide these essential things?

Interestingly, an article in *World Health,* the official magazine of WHO, declares: "Imagine an ideal world in which all the ingenuity, expense and human and material resources which are at present poured into military weaponry were instead devoted to improving the health of the world!" What would that do? Well, that article estimated that the arms race costs the world about $600 thousand million a year, or one million dollars a minute, to maintain. Yet "the 14-year campaign to wipe out the killer disease of smallpox between 1967 and 1980 cost the world just $300 million." Thus it concludes: "Clearly, if even a part of the resources at present allocated to military expenditure could be shifted instead to prevention, cure and research in the field of health, the world would be given a prodigious boost towards the goal of Health for all by the year 2000."

What about people in the developed countries? They may be better off in some respects, but, according to Dr. Mahler, they, too, "must rise to their health responsibilities, eating wisely, drinking moderately, smoking not at all, driving carefully, taking enough exercise, learning to live under the stress of city life, and helping one another to do so."

Thus we must ask: Will the nations be willing to change their policies and give the pursuit of health high priority? Will they be willing to put aside their political differences and pool their resources and efforts toward conquering disease? And will the people change their life-style to one that is more healthful? Realistically, you will have to admit that this is very unlikely. A cure of all diseases will never be realized if we have to look to the nations for it.

The Cure Is at Hand!

To whom, then, shall we look? Well, recall the vision that the aged apostle John saw. He described it this way:

"He showed me a river of water of life, clear as crystal, flowing out from the throne of God and of the Lamb down the middle of its broad way. And on this side of the river and on that side there were trees of life producing twelve crops of fruit, yielding their fruits each month. And the leaves of the trees were for the curing of the nations."—Revelation 22: 1, 2.

The symbolic "river of water of life" is seen flowing out from "the throne of God and of the Lamb." Clearly, then, it is to Jehovah God and the Messianic Kingdom of his Son that we must look for "the curing of the nations." Is that not logical? God is the Creator of the human body and of the entire earth. He—more than any doctor or scientist—knows how matters can best be handled so that diseases can be overcome. Under God's Kingdom rulership, mankind will be freed from the disease-causing and death-dealing contamination plaguing us now. Sustained and nourished by the pure, crystal-clear "water of life" and the fruits and leaves of the "trees of life"—Jehovah's entire provision for gaining everlasting life—mankind will be cured permanently of all its diseases, spiritual and physical.* Humans will be brought back to the happy, healthy, perfect state enjoyed by their ancestors, Adam and Eve, at the beginning.

---

* For a detailed explanation of these verses, please see *"Babylon the Great Has Fallen!" God's Kingdom Rules!*, published by the Watchtower Bible and Tract Society of New York, Inc.

The time for God's Kingdom to take action "to bring to ruin those ruining the earth" is at hand. (Revelation 11:18) Then many features of Bible prophecy will become a reality in a restored paradise. (Isaiah 33:24; 35:5, 6) This is good news for all those who desire good health God's way. Soon the "new earth" that John saw will be here, in which "death will be no more, neither will mourning nor outcry nor pain be anymore."—Revelation 21: 1, 4.

Will you be among those who survive the end of this polluted and decaying system of things into that clean "new earth"? By making wise use of the time still available for learning more about God's Kingdom and doing what he requires, you will live to see the day when a cure of all diseases will be realized.

Honored Before He Was Born

THE angel Gabriel has just finished telling the young woman Mary that she will give birth to a baby boy who will become an everlasting king. But Mary asks, 'How is this possible, since I have had no relations with a man?'

'God's holy spirit will come upon you,' Gabriel explains, 'and for this reason the boy will be called God's Son.' To help Mary, Gabriel continues: 'Your aged relative Elizabeth, who people said could not have children, is now six months pregnant.' Mary believes Gabriel and says: 'Let it happen to me just as you have said.'

Soon after Gabriel leaves, Mary gets ready and goes to visit Elizabeth who lives with her husband Zechariah in the mountainous country of Judea. From Mary's home in Nazareth, this is a long trip of perhaps three or four days.

When Mary finally arrives at Zechariah's house, she enters and offers a greeting. At that Elizabeth is filled with holy spirit, and she says to Mary: 'Blessed are you among women, and blessed is the child you will have. What a privilege it is to have the mother of my Lord come to me! For, look! as soon as I heard your greeting, the infant in my womb leaped with great gladness.'

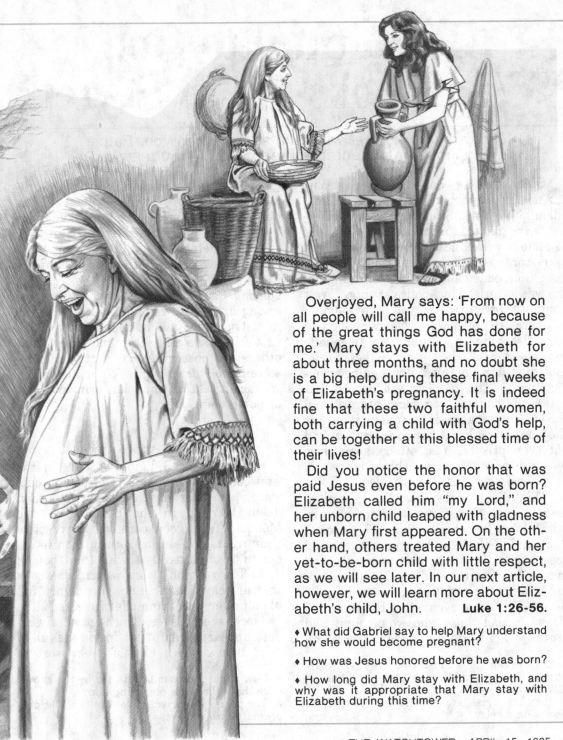

Overjoyed, Mary says: 'From now on all people will call me happy, because of the great things God has done for me.' Mary stays with Elizabeth for about three months, and no doubt she is a big help during these final weeks of Elizabeth's pregnancy. It is indeed fine that these two faithful women, both carrying a child with God's help, can be together at this blessed time of their lives!

Did you notice the honor that was paid Jesus even before he was born? Elizabeth called him "my Lord," and her unborn child leaped with gladness when Mary first appeared. On the other hand, others treated Mary and her yet-to-be-born child with little respect, as we will see later. In our next article, however, we will learn more about Elizabeth's child, John.　**Luke 1:26-56.**

♦ What did Gabriel say to help Mary understand how she would become pregnant?

♦ How was Jesus honored before he was born?

♦ How long did Mary stay with Elizabeth, and why was it appropriate that Mary stay with Elizabeth during this time?

Be Faithful to God "Who Looks On in Secret"

"Pray to your Father who is in secret; then your Father who looks on in secret will repay you."—MATTHEW 6:6.

SOME years ago one of Jehovah's Witnesses telephoned her brother in Long Island, New York. Since he was of a different faith, she told him about God's promise to remove wickedness from the earth and to restore paradisaic conditions. As the discussion ended and her brother hung up, she was surprised by a voice saying, "Wait a minute, I want to ask you a question."

2 It was the telephone operator. She had been listening in, which the telephone equipment back then enabled her to do, though it was unethical and against company policy. The Witness was pleased that her words had sparked such interest, and she made arrangements to follow it up, yet she was startled that her conversation had not been private. Yes, others sometimes see and hear what we think is secret. —Ecclesiastes 10:20.

3 This should not present major problems for true Christians, who strive to be faithful to God at all times. The apostle Paul said: "We have become a theatrical spectacle to the world, and to angels, and to men." (1 Corinthians 4:9) He was alluding to a practice at the gladiatorial arena. Before the final event the Romans displayed unclad those who would fight and probably die. Christians today are also on display before unbelieving relatives, workmates, neighbors, and schoolmates. The observers may form a good or a bad opinion of Christianity based on what they see in us.—1 Peter 2:12.

4 When we know that others are observing, we might tend to rise to the occasion, sharing Paul's desire: "In no way are we giving any cause for stumbling, that our ministry might not be found fault with." (2 Corinthians 6:3) Our knowledge that others are observing may fortify our resolve to do what is right. What, though, if we face a test of Christian principles out of public view?

He Looks Beyond Outward Appearances

5 Many Jewish religious leaders in the first century were one sort of person outwardly, another sort of person inwardly. Jesus warned in the Sermon on the Mount: "Take good care not to practice your righteousness in front of men in order to be observed by them." (Matthew 6: 1, 2) The religious leaders were like cups that are clean outside but 'inside are full of plunder and immoderateness,' like "whitewashed graves, which outwardly indeed appear beautiful but inside are full of dead men's bones and of every sort of

---

1, 2. How can it be illustrated that seemingly private matters can become public? (1 Samuel 21:7; 22:9)
3. In what sense are the lives of Christians always on display?

4. How might a person be affected by the knowledge that others are observing him?
5. The public and private lives of Jewish leaders presented what contrast?

uncleanness."—Matthew 23:25-28; compare Psalm 26:4.

6 Those words should help us to appreciate that Jehovah is interested in more than what might be seen by other humans. Jesus counseled: "When you pray, go into your private room and, after shutting your door, pray to your Father who is in secret; then your Father *who looks on in secret* will repay you." (Matthew 6:6) Yes, God can hear our prayers offered when we are isolated from other humans. Nothing is beyond God's notice. He is able to observe the embryonic formation of a person, perhaps reading the genetic material that later will shape the individual's characteristics. (Psalm 139:15, 16; Genesis 25:23) He even can read the secret leanings of our hearts. (1 Samuel 16:7; 1 Kings 8:39; Jeremiah 17:10; Acts 1:24) Consider how these facts should affect us.

7 To become true Christians we had to work at overcoming serious faults and sins, even as did the early Christians. (1 Corinthians 6:9-11; Acts 26:20; 1 Peter 4:1-4) Yet what about faults that may not be known to other humans? That these failings are not publicly known does not make them any less significant. This is indicated by David's words: "Anyone slandering his companion in secrecy, him I silence. Anyone of haughty eyes and of arrogant heart, him I cannot endure." (Psalm 101:5) Even if it was done secretly, to just one listener, slander was wrong. So David would not condone this 'secret' sin.

8 Nor should the wrongdoer fool himself by thinking that the error would escape the notice of God "who looks on in secret." Actually, God has proved that he is interested in humans' being faithful even when their actions are not publicly known. Recall the case of Achan. The Israelites were to destroy Jericho and its inhabitants, wicked Canaanites. Only the silver, gold, and copper were excepted, these being for the treasure of God's sanctuary. (Joshua 6: 17-19) Achan, however, gave in to temptation and took a costly garment, some silver and gold. He hid this under his tent, perhaps feeling that no one would know. But did he deceive the One "who looks on in secret"? No. God saw to it that Achan's sin was publicly exposed, bringing death to him and to his household.—Joshua 7:1, 16-26.

9 Elihu wisely explained about Jehovah: "For his eyes are upon the ways of man, and all his steps he sees. There is no darkness nor any deep shadow for those practicing what is hurtful to conceal themselves there." (Job 34:21, 22) If, then, we desire to gain and retain Jehovah God's approval, we must seek to live according to his principles both when we know that others are observing us and when it appears that our conduct is hidden. At all times "his eyes are upon the ways of man."

10 A Christian may undergo some test that is hidden to fellow worshipers. That happened to Paul while he was in prison. The Jews had charged him with "stirring up seditions" and 'trying to profane the temple.' (Acts 24:1-6) Paul testified to his innocence before Roman procúrator Felix, who historians say was cruel and immoral. Felix detained Paul in prison "hoping for money to be given him by Paul." (Acts 24: 10-21, 26) While the apostle knew the Bible's counsel about not giving or accepting gifts to affect judgment, he could have reasoned that giving a bribe would be an

---

6. What is Jehovah able to observe about us?
7. Wherein might a Christian have room for improvement?
8. How do we know that hidden wrongdoing does not escape Jehovah's notice?

9. What must we do to gain and retain God's approval?
10. (a) Paul set what fine example as to hidden conduct? (b) The possibility of secret faults in what areas deserves our attention?

expedient way to get free. Since the bribe could be hidden from others, Paul would not need to worry about stumbling them. (Exodus 23:8; Psalm 15:1, 5; Proverbs 17:23) Yet Paul did not reason that way. Many of Jehovah's people in modern times have faced other tests, such as those involving God's law on blood, self-abuse, and misuse of alcohol. Let us consider how such tests could confront you or your loved ones.

Obedience Tested Over Blood

[11] God's law on blood certainly is not new or unclear. Through our common forefather Noah, Jehovah commanded all mankind: "Flesh with its soul—its blood—you must not eat." (Genesis 9:4) The sacredness of blood, representing life from God, was stressed in the Mosaic Law. Blood could be used on the altar, but otherwise it was to be 'poured out on the ground as water.' (Leviticus 17:11-14; Deuteronomy 12:23-25) Did the prohibition against sustaining life with blood continue after the Mosaic Law ended? Absolutely. At what some might call the first Christian council, the apostles and older men (who comprised the governing body) concluded that Christians must 'abstain from idolatry, from fornication, from what is strangled [having blood left in] and from blood.' Misuse of blood was as serious a moral wrong as illicit sex relations.—Acts 15:20, 21, 28, 29.

[12] The early Christians obeyed God's law about blood. Though some people back then drank the blood of gladiators as a "cure" for epilepsy, true Christians would not. Nor would they eat food containing blood, even when their refusal meant death for them and their children. Since that time, various theologians and others have acknowledged that Christians are under God's law against sustaining life by taking in blood.

[13] In recent times blood transfusion has become a popular medical tool. The Christian may thus face a test involving it. Doctors, nurses, and even relatives may strongly urge him to accept blood. Informed persons, of course, know that transfusions themselves pose grave risks. *Time* magazine (November 5, 1984) said that "some 100,000 Americans contract hepatitis each year from blood transfusions," mainly from "a mystery virus that can be identified only by a process of elimination." *Time* also reported on over 6,500 cases of AIDS (acquired immune deficiency syndrome), some being "transfusion-linked cases." The report said: "Nearly half the victims have died, although the ultimate mortality rate may be 90% or higher." Of course, Jehovah's Witnesses do not base their refusal on the argument that blood is bad medicine. Even if doctors could give assurance that a transfusion would be totally safe, God's Word commands us to 'keep ourselves from blood.' —Acts 21:25.

[14] Imagine if *you* were told that you badly needed a transfusion. God's law on blood would come to your mind, would it not? And your resolve to obey God, no matter what the immediate results of this, likely would be strengthened if fellow Christians were present. (Compare Daniel 3:13-18.) However, what if in private a doctor or a judge pressured you to accept blood, even telling you to let him bear the responsibility before God?

---

11. What is the basis for the Christian position on use of blood?
12. The early Christians took what stand on blood?
13. (a) Why might you sometime be confronted with a test regarding blood? (b) What major reason for Christians' not accepting blood should we keep in mind?
14. What "secret" test involving blood might you face?

¹⁵ Reports from various lands indicate that sometimes doctors, hospital officials, and judges mistakenly think that Jehovah's Witnesses publicly object to blood transfusion but privately or inwardly feel differently. In one case a judge arbitrarily concluded "that the crux of the problem lay, not in [the patient's] religious convictions, but in her refusal to sign a prior written authorization for the transfusion of blood. She did not object to receiving the treatment involved—she would not, however, direct its use." On the contrary, rather than weakly refusing to 'sign authorization for blood,' Jehovah's Witnesses are on record as being strongly desirous of signing legal documents relieving medical personnel of any liability connected with refusing blood.*

15. Some doctors and officials have what incorrect view as to our stand on blood?

* Many hospitals use Form P-47 REFUSAL TO PERMIT BLOOD TRANSFUSION as printed in the American Medical Association's *Medicolegal Forms with Legal Analysis.*

God's Law on Blood Recognized as Still Valid

JOSEPH PRIESTLEY (1733-1804) is most noted as the scientist who discovered oxygen, but he was also a theologian. He wrote: "The prohibition to eat blood, given to Noah, seems to be obligatory on all his posterity." As to the claim that the Christian prohibition on blood was only temporary, Priestley added: "There is no intimation, or hint, of its being temporary, or any mention made of a time when the prohibition was to cease. . . . If we interpret this prohibition of the apostles by the practice of the primitive Christians, who can hardly be supposed not to have rightly understood the nature and extent of it, we cannot but conclude, that it was intended to be absolute and perpetual."

In 1646 *A Bloody Tenet Confuted, or, Blood Forbidden* (modern spelling) was published. On page 8 it concluded: "Let us lay aside this cruel custom of eating the lives of beasts, as it is used throughout all England, in unhallowed black [blood] puddings, as we will show our selves therefore to be merciful men, not inhumane; as we will not be found to be disobeyers of God in such express precepts, but obeyers of his will, and doers of those things that are right in his eyes, as we would have the favor of God, . . . and not to be cut off from our people, and have the face of God continually set against us for evil."

Gaspard Bartholin was a 17th-century professor of anatomy at the University of Copenhagen. Writing on 'The Misuse of Blood,' he observed: 'Those who drag in the use of human blood for internal remedies of diseases appear to misuse it and to sin gravely. Cannibals are condemned. Why do we not abhor those who stain their gullet with human blood? Similar is the receiving of alien blood from a cut vein, either through the mouth or by instruments of transfusion. The authors of this operation are held in terror by the divine law, by which eating of blood is prohibited.'

Revelation Examined with Candour (1745) dealt with God's commands about blood. It reasoned: "A command given by God himself to *Noah,* repeated to *Moses,* and ratified by the apostles of *Jesus Christ;* given immediately after the flood, when the world, as it were, began anew; and the only one given on that great occasion; repeated with awful solemnity, to that people whom God separated from the rest of mankind, to be holy to himself; repeated with dreadful denunciations of divine vengeance, both against the *Jew* and the *stranger* that should dare to transgress it; and ratified by the most solemn and sacred council, that ever was assembled upon earth; acting under the immediate influence of the Spirit of God! transmitted from the sacred assembly to the several churches of the neighbouring nations, by the hands of no meaner messengers, than two bishops, and two apostles . . . Will any man, after this, dare to vilify this command? Will any man in his senses pronounce a precept, so given, so repeated, and so ratified by God himself, unmeaning and unimportant?"

The conduct of one Witness may make it easier for the next one to be faithful to God

¹⁶ Doctors and judges may try to persuade you to accept blood because they have seen people of other religions object to some medical step but then accept it 'behind closed doors.' Some officials have even claimed to know of a Witness who agreed to a secret transfusion. *If* that did occur, it might have involved someone who was just acquainted with Jehovah's Witnesses. Devoted servants of God know well that no such compromise would escape his notice. Recall when David sinned concerning Bath-sheba and Uriah. Jehovah saw it all and sent Nathan with the message: "Whereas you [David] acted in secret, I, for my part, shall do this thing in front of all Israel and in front of the sun." As God stated, David later felt the sad consequences of his "secret" sin.—2 Samuel 11: 27–12:12; 16:21.

¹⁷ Love for your Christian brothers should also help you to resist pressure to agree secretly to violate God's law on

16. If someone in private urged you to accept blood, what should you not forget?
17. (a) How could accepting a blood transfusion in secret make trouble for others? (b) Explain how one sister stood firm on the blood issue even in private, and what was the outcome of this?

blood. How so? Well, if a doctor or a judge tried to coerce you into accepting blood, even in secret, you should think of the added trouble that would bring on the next Witness. Note this experience:

Sister Rodriguez was being treated for an infection. Then she got very ill; her doctor diagnosed internal bleeding and advised her to rush to a major hospital. Sister Rodriguez told the emergency-room personnel: "No matter what, I cannot take a blood transfusion." She held to this later when nurses pressured her by their claiming that some Witnesses had taken blood. For days this sister continued to lose blood and weaken, finally being moved to the Intensive Care Unit. Then the hospital called in a judge of the state Supreme Court.

Some months later in the hospital's amphitheater, this judge spoke to over 150 doctors on the subject "Whose Life Is It, Anyway?" He, too, said he had encountered persons who at first refused blood but who acquiesced once a judge was involved. What though about Sister Rodriguez? He related that in privacy he had tried to convince her to let him 'bear the responsibility' by having the transfusion given under court order. What did she do? The judge told the assembled doctors that with all the strength she could muster,

---

How Would You Answer?

☐ God has what ability that should affect our actions?

☐ Achan's experience should teach us what vital lesson?

☐ What harm can result if a Christian secretly breaks God's law on blood?

☐ You should resolve what regarding Jehovah's view on blood?

Mrs. Rodriguez told him that she was not going to accept blood and that he should leave her alone and get out of the room. Consequently, the judge explained, he had no basis for ordering blood against her wishes.

[18] This underscores the importance of making it absolutely clear that our position on blood is *nonnegotiable.* The apostles took such a resolute stand, declaring: "We must obey God as ruler rather than men." (Acts 5:29) Sister Rodriguez' case also shows the effect a Witness' compromise could have on others. While sick and physically weakened, she had to face extra pressure just because someone earlier may secretly have broken God's law. Of course,

such a violation would be no secret to "the Judge of all the earth." (Genesis 18:25) Happily, Sister Rodriguez was as uncompromising in private as she had been in public. And later, in good health, she explained to the same medical assembly her continued determination to be faithful to God.

[19] We, too, must be faithful whether our actions are public or not. Jehovah delights in such faithfulness and will reward it; he will justly respond to the works—public or private—of those unfaithful to his standards. (Psalm 51:6; Job 34:24) Lovingly he provides perfect counsel that will help us to overcome any hidden faults we have, as we will next consider.

---

18. What determination should we make clear regarding the blood issue, and with what likely results?

19. At all times, we should be conscious of what fact?

Accept God's Help to Overcome Secret Faults

"For all things I have the strength by virtue of him who imparts power to me."—PHILIPPIANS 4:13.

THE lad was an epileptic.* He foamed at the mouth, had convulsions, and at times fell into the water or the fire. His worried father sought out a man noted for curing the sick. When it seemed that there was a lack of confidence in that man's ability, the father cried: "I have faith! Help me out where I need faith!"

---

* Matthew 17:14-18, Mark 9:17-24, and Luke 9:38-43 show that demon possession caused his condition. The Bible distinguishes between this epilepsy and that from natural causes.—Matthew 4:24.

---

1. What request did one concerned father make?

[2] We can learn something from this father who sought Jesus' aid. The man admitted that his faith might be faulty; he also was sure that Jesus wanted to help. It can be that way with us, as we face our own faults—even secret ones—and work to overcome them. We can trust that Jehovah God *wants* to help us, as he has helped others in the past. (Compare Mark 1: 40-42.) He, for example, helped the apostle Paul to cope with faults that can result

---

2. How can we be sure that God wants to help us overcome faults?

from having an abundance or being in want. A poor person might crave riches; a wealthy person's failing might be his smugly trusting in success and looking down on those having less. (Job 31:24, 25, 28) How did Paul overcome or avoid such faults? He says: "For all things I have the strength by virtue of him who imparts power to me." —Philippians 4:11-13.

3 Drawing on God's power, we are wise to work at conquering our faults, not ignoring them just because they presently may be secret. The psalmist said of Jehovah: "He is aware of the secrets of the heart." (Psalm 44:21) If we do not overcome our faults, they may surface to our greater detriment. The principle applies: "The sins of some men are publicly manifest, leading directly to judgment, but as for other men their sins also become manifest later." (1 Timothy 5:24) Let us examine two common faults meriting attention by Christians who want to please Jehovah.

A Secret Fault Involving Sexual Desire

4 One of God's finest gifts is marriage, along with the ability and desire to reproduce. (Genesis 1:28) Sexual desire expressed in marital relations is natural and clean. The Bible commends finding sexual enjoyment with one's own mate. (Proverbs 5:15-19) However, sexual appetite cannot go unrestrained. As a comparison, consider our desire for food. That we have a returning appetite does not mean that we ought to develop an inordinate craving for food, or that we need no control as to when, where, and how we eat.—Proverbs 25:16, 27.

5 Paul may once have been married, and

he knew that normal sexual expressions between mates were fitting. (1 Corinthians 7:1-5) So he had to be referring to something else when he wrote: "Deaden, therefore, your body members that are upon the earth as respects fornication, uncleanness, *sexual appetite, hurtful desire, and covetousness.*" (Colossians 3:5) He must have meant sexual expressions beyond the proper marital setting and means. The apostle also said: "Each one of you should know how to get possession of his own vessel in sanctification and honor, not in *covetous sexual appetite.*" (1 Thessalonians 4:4, 5) This frank, inspired counsel is beneficial both for married and for single Christians.

6 One way in which such "lust of carnal desire" (1 Thessalonians 4:5, *The New Testament for English Readers,* by Henry Alford) often is expressed is by a person's stimulation of his or her own sexual organs for the pleasure involved. This is called masturbation, or self-abuse. It is very common among single males and females. But it is engaged in also by many a married person. Its commonness leads many doctors to claim that it is normal and even beneficial. However, this practice runs contrary to God's counsel against "covetous sexual appetite." We can better appreciate why, and why Christians should overcome the habit, by considering some counsel that Jesus gave.

7 Jesus said: "Everyone that keeps on looking at a woman *so as to have a passion for her has already committed adultery with her in his heart.*" (Matthew 5:28) He knew that passionate thoughts of adultery are often the precursors of immoral acts. Yet, even those who excuse masturbation admit that it usually involves sexual fantasies. After speaking of youths' "con-

---

3. Why is it wise for us to try to conquer our weaknesses?
4, 5. (a) The Bible presents what balanced view of sexual desire? (b) What warnings do we find in the Scriptures regarding sexual desire?

---

6. Why do Christians rightly avoid self-abuse?
7. How does Matthew 5:28 provide added reason to abstain from masturbation?

scious attention to the pleasure masturbation can bring," the book *Talking With Your Teenager* adds: "They may imagine themselves in wild sexual situations or with partners of the same sex or with older people like teachers, relatives, even [parents]. They might have fantasies about sexual violence. All of this is absolutely normal." But is it? How could Christians consider such fantasies and masturbation "normal" in the light of Jesus' warning about 'adultery in the heart' or

He Overcame Self-Abuse

AS A YOUNG MAN, C—— had normal sexual feelings, but he also had a problem. From the age of 13 he had the habit of self-abuse, usually in the secrecy of his bedroom. He was a bit ashamed of it, but he felt that it was not hurting anyone else.

By the time he was 19, the practice was ingrained. On occasion C—— confessed it to his priest, but he was told that though wrong, it was not too serious. When C—— joined the military, he did not have much privacy. Hence, he seldom resorted to self-abuse, which, incidentally, shows that his past habit was not the result of uncontrollable passion.

Upon getting out of the military, C—— returned home. He began purchasing pornographic magazines and, aroused by these, he was soon back to his former ways. When he began living alone, it was easy to get sexually stimulating material. Often he masturbated several times a day.

Then he began to study the Bible with a minister of Jehovah's Witnesses. As he learned God's view of immorality, C—— felt ashamed of purchasing pornographic materials, and he wanted to break the habit of self-abuse. He tried. But after a week or two he would feel sexual tension, would stop by some newspaper stand, and would become aroused by the immoral material. Back home, he would feel that since he had already failed, he might as well go one step farther. Afterward, remorse would come. Would he never be able to break this bad habit?

Finally C—— spoke to a spiritual elder at the congregation. This minister was understanding and helped him to look up Bible-based material that would help him to improve his self-control. The minister also explained:

'Imagine the desire to be like a chain. The first link is small and weak. But each successive link gets larger and harder. That is the way it is with urges leading to masturbation. So you need to stop the impulse as soon as possible. The longer it goes on, the more intense your desire becomes. Finally it will be almost unstoppable. Yes, try to break the chain at the first link. As soon as you sense the urge coming, DO SOMETHING! Get up and change your position, polish your shoes, empty the garbage can—anything to break the link. You might begin reading something out loud, such as the Bible or a Christian publication that will channel your thoughts along clean lines.'

This minister would inquire of C—— at the meetings as to how things were going, regularly commending and encouraging him in his resolve. For seven weeks C—— succeeded. Then, when he was frustrated and discouraged over another problem, he succumbed again, buying some erotic literature. That led to a relapse. Such episodes were setbacks, but the minister urged him to continue the struggle. Gradually the intervals lengthened to 9 weeks, then 17 weeks, then even longer. Slowly his confidence grew that he would be able to master the secret problem.

Finally C—— faced up to the fact that Jehovah knew all that he was doing. Thus, if he wanted to serve God with a completely clear conscience, he would have to get this practice out of his life totally. He did it! Now he is not even able to recall how long it has been. As an exemplary Christian, C—— has been given responsibility in the congregation, and he is making plans to increase his service to God's praise. He is a different person.

Paul's counsel against "covetous sexual appetite"? No, such fantasies and self-abuse—whether by a youth or by an adult, by a single person or by a married person—need to be overcome.

Overcoming This Private Fault

8 If a Christian had this secret fault, what could he do to conquer it, "to get possession of his own vessel in sanctification and honor"? (1 Thessalonians 4:4) Through his Word, God provides valuable help.

9 First it is important to recognize that Jehovah does have standards. He makes plain the wrongness of extramarital sex, both fornication and adultery. (Hebrews 13:4) Hence, if we believe that his ways are the best, we will seek satisfying rewards of sexual expression only within marriage. (Psalm 25:4, 5) The book *Adolescence,* by E. Atwater, points out that regarding masturbation, youths commonly express 'reticence, embarrassment and misgivings.' One reason given is that 'the closeness of a love relationship that accompanies sexual intercourse is missing in masturbation.' Yes, there is benefit in controlling sexual desire until this can be expressed in loving marital relations.

10 God's Word provides additional help by counseling: 'Whatever things are true, whatever things are of serious concern, whatever things are righteous, whatever things are chaste, whatever things are well spoken of and whatever virtue there is, continue considering these things.' (Philippians 4:8) Clearly, erotic pictures and immoral novels are not 'chaste and well spoken of or virtuous.' Yet these things are often the fare of masturbators. Anyone determined to overcome this fault

must, then, absolutely avoid such erotic material. Experience has proved that if a person's desires begin to be drawn toward the erotic in a way that previously resulted in masturbation, determined concentration on what is righteous and chaste can cool the desires. This is especially important if a person is alone or in the dark, when the secret fault of self-abuse is most common.*—Romans 13:12-14.

11 A related aid is keeping active, in line with the admonition: "Keep strict watch that how you walk is not as unwise but as wise persons, buying out the opportune time for yourselves, because the days are wicked." (Ephesians 5:15, 16) Ask a mature Christian confidant for suggestions about positive things to do. (Isaiah 32:2) Many who have overcome this fault admit that their knowing that a concerned Christian would be checking with them on their progress helped them to develop self-control. Of course, the One who should be our closest confidant is Jehovah. So it is vital to turn to him in prayer, seeking his help. (Philippians 4:6, 7) If someone who has battled this fault for a time should "stumble," he can ask God for power, then he can renew his efforts and likely succeed again, for an even longer period.—Hebrews 12:12, 13; Psalm 103:13, 14.

Battling Misuse of Alcohol

12 'Wine makes God and men rejoice,' says one Bible verse. (Judges 9:13) You may agree, for alcoholic beverages have been an aid to relaxation and a source of pleasure for many. (Psalm 104:15) Few

---

* Sometimes during sleep the body experiences an *involuntary* sexual release, which natural occurrence is not the same as *conscious* self-abuse.

8, 9. Appreciation of what facts can help a person to break the masturbation habit?
10. What are some steps that a person can take to help himself overcome the practice?

11. Describe additional things that have proved beneficial in coping with this fault.
12. What is the Christian view of alcoholic beverages?

would deny, however, that using alcohol can pose both physical and moral dangers. A major problem is outright drunkenness. This fault is so serious that God warns that drunkards can be expelled from the congregation and barred from the Kingdom. (1 Corinthians 5:11-13; Galatians 5: 19-21) Christians are aware of this and would agree that they must avoid getting drunk. But, aside from drunkenness, how might use of alcohol become a secret fault?

[13] A Christian could drink only moderately, yet still have a serious fault. Consider the experience of a man whom we will call Heinz.

He, his wife, and children became true Christians and were very active in the local congregation. In time Heinz was appointed as an elder and came to be viewed as a 'pillar' among the congregations in the city. (Galatians 2:9) Understandably, he faced pressures in rearing his family and some anxiety in caring for the flock. (2 Corinthians 11:28) His job, though, brought on him a lot of stress because the company he worked for was growing, and his boss wanted him to handle numerous problems and decisions.

Many evenings Heinz was quite tense. He found that a drink or two would help him to relax. Of course, being a mature Christian he carefully avoided overdrinking or drunkenness. Though he did have some drinks to unwind in the evening, he did not *need* alcohol during the day, nor did he even drink with most meals. He was not known to be 'given to a lot of wine.'—1 Timothy 3:8.

Unexpectedly Heinz was hospitalized for a common operation. Some unusual symptoms appeared. What was their cause? It did not take the medical staff long to determine that Heinz was experiencing withdrawal symptoms. Yes, his body had become dependent on alcohol. This came as a surprise to the family, but they rallied around him and supported his resolve to avoid alcohol completely.

13. Illustrate how dependence on alcohol could develop.

[14] Some sense that alcohol has taken on an unusual role in their lives, so they try to conceal their drinking, not wanting family and friends to realize how much they drink or how often. Others may not feel that they are dependent on alcohol, still, drinking has become a focal point of their day. Those in either category are at great risk of overdrinking on some occasion or of being hidden alcoholics. Consider this proverb: "Wine is a ridiculer, intoxicating liquor is boisterous, and everyone going astray by it is not wise." (Proverbs 20:1) The point is that drinking too much can cause a person to act boisterously and be ridiculous. However, wine might ridicule someone in another sense. A person merits ridicule if he thinks that his drinking is hidden from God.

[15] One of the fruits of God's spirit is self-control, and we need that in all aspects of life. (Galatians 5:22, 23) Paul likened the Christian to a runner. In a normal race the runner "exercises self-control in all things" just to "get a corruptible crown." Similarly, the Christian needs to display "self-control in *all* things" in order to gain a prize of much higher value—LIFE. Paul stressed that

14. What could lead to being ridiculed by alcoholic beverages?
15. How do Paul's words at 1 Corinthians 9: 24-27 bear on a Christian's use of alcohol?

we must 'lead our body as a slave' to be sure 'that after we have preached to others we might not become disapproved somehow,' such as over a secret fault involving alcohol.—1 Corinthians 9:24-27.

[16] What can help a Christian to deal with this fault? It is helpful to appreciate that though a drinker may conceal his pattern from other humans, he is not hiding it from God. (1 Corinthians 4:5) Thus, honestly—in the sight of God—a person should think about his drinking habits. (We mean drinking for pleasure or effect, not just a small amount as a common beverage with meals.) Some, however, may say, 'But I don't *have* to drink. I just enjoy it; it relaxes me. I could abstain if I wanted to.' Well, in view of the potential dangers of overdrinking or alcohol dependency, why not do just that for a month or two? Or, since there is a strong tendency to deny that there is a problem, resolve for a month to abstain at all times when having a drink is normal. For example, the person who usually has a drink after work, before going to bed, or at a social gathering could avoid doing so. He can thus monitor how he feels. If it is difficult, or he 'just can't relax,' he has a serious fault.

[17] Once a sincere Christian realizes before God that he has a fault involving alcohol, it will be easier to overcome it. He may already know that the Bible says that it is 'a person of stupidity' who reasons 'that stolen waters are sweet, and bread [or alcohol] taken in secrecy—it is pleasant.' However, such ones, says Proverbs, will wind up impotent in death. In contrast, the wise person loves reproof, and he happily 'leaves the inexperienced ones and *keeps living* by walking straight in the way of understanding.' (Proverbs 9:1, 6, 8, 13-18) Yes, God provides additional help to overcome secret faults by letting us know what lies ahead, what the end results will be.

God Rewards Private Actions

[18] Some people live in fear that their bad ways will be found out, by men or by God. Let that not be so with us. Instead, let us live with an awareness that we cannot hide things from Him, "for the true God himself will bring every sort of work into the judgment in relation to every hidden thing, as to whether it is good or bad." (Ecclesiastes 12:14) Let us accept Jehovah's help to overcome our faults, even hidden ones. We then can look forward to the time when "the secret things of darkness" are brought to light and "the counsels of the hearts" are made manifest. "Then each one will have his praise come to him from God."—1 Corinthians 4:5; Romans 2:6, 7, 16.

18. As we overcome our secret faults, of what can we be confident? (Proverbs 24:12; 2 Samuel 22:25-27)

16. How can a person determine whether alcohol has become a fault in his case?
17. Why must a Christian having a hidden fault involving alcohol work to conquer it?

Do You Recall?

☐ How does God feel about secret faults on which we may be working?

☐ What Scriptural counsel indicates that self-abuse is to be avoided?

☐ How can a Christian overcome the habit of self-abuse?

☐ Since the Bible does not condemn it, how could the use of alcohol become a secret fault?

☐ What wise steps can be taken in dealing with a private fault involving alcoholic beverages?

Insight on the News

Blood-Substitute Research

● Fluosol-DA, an oxygen-carrying blood substitute made from chemicals, failed to pass medical tests in the United States, and experimentation with the fluid on humans has been stopped by its manufacturer. For almost five years, Alpha Therapeutic Corporation, the U.S. producer of the "synthetic blood," Fluosol-DA 20%, had been working with selected hospitals in the United States and Canada on clinical trials of its use. More than 120 patients were studied. Reports indicate that Fluosol was not as valuable a stand-in for blood as had been hoped for and that other readily available solutions were just as effective as Fluosol. The *Chicago Tribune* reported that one hospital used for the research gave two reasons for Fluosol's failure. "It didn't carry enough oxygen to vital organs," said the article, "and it didn't stay in a person's system long enough to keep him alive until natural production replenished red blood cells."

The Fluosol study did highlight, though, that surgeons use blood too freely and, according to the *Tribune,* "that it is possible to operate on someone who is quite anemic without blood transfusions." Dr. Bruce Friedman, a director at the University of Michigan hospitals, said: "My guesstimate is that 25 percent to 33 percent of the blood used in this country isn't needed." Although testing on humans has ceased, it appears that research to improve fluorocarbon "artificial blood" will continue.

● A similar blood substitute is being developed by Dr. Henry A. Sloviter at the University of Pennsylvania's School of Medicine. This "artificial blood" is a chemical compound treated with ultrahigh-frequency sound waves and then coated with egg-derived lecithin. It has been tested only on animals so far, but no harmful effects were seen even when large amounts of the milky-white fluid were infused. The *Almanac,* published by the university, notes that it has these advantages over natural blood: "Appears to be safe without regard to blood type; does not require refrigeration; and eliminates the risk of transmitting infectious diseases such as AIDS, hepatitis and malaria in transfusions." It will not be ready for general use for at least three years.

● Research continues on another continent. "Australian scientists have developed a blood substitute which they say is better for most uses than human whole blood and plasma," claims *The Bulletin,* an Australian financial magazine. Named CH (casein hydrolysate), it is a protein and can be made from milk or soybeans. Dr. Louis Hissink, one of the developers of CH, "believes that it is dangerous to introduce blood from another person into a patient," continues the article, "not only for the chance of bringing disease but also because of immune reactions set up." Hissink says: "At last, it is becoming clear to people that blood (from donors) is not such a great thing after all." CH has yet to gain Australia's state health department approval.

Jehovah's Witnesses have always been interested in this type of research. While the Witnesses may allow nonblood fluids to be used for transfusion purposes, they will not compromise their religious beliefs —even when faced with danger—to allow for a blood transfusion. At all times these Christians hold firm to the Biblical injunction: "Keep abstaining from . . . blood."—Acts 15:29.

Alcohol Abuse

● Alcohol abuse has affected even the young and the elderly. A survey conducted for the Division of Alcoholism and Alcohol Abuse of 27,414 New York State students aged 12 to 18 found that 10 percent got drunk at least once a week. On the other end of the age scale, the journal *Medical Aspects of Human Sexuality* states that alcohol abuse "is a significant problem among older people with an expected incidence of 10% to 15%—the prevalence being higher among those who are institutionalized." Interestingly, one evidence of mankind's being "in the last days" is that people are "without self-control." (2 Timothy 3:1-3) And the abuse of alcohol is but one indication of lack of self-control.

Love to the Rescue

EARLY last September two storm systems collided over Korea. In a matter of hours, some areas were drenched with more than 20 inches (50 cm) of rain. The result was the worst flood to hit the country in 40 years. Over 200,000 people were left homeless, and 181 were reported dead or missing. Property loss ran into millions of dollars, and crop damage was beyond reckoning.

The downpour started Friday evening and continued all day Saturday. Six dams on the upper Han River overflowed, swelling the river to more than a foot and a half (0.5 m) over its safety level. Early Sunday morning, without any warning, a drainage sluice gave way, and the surging river spilled into the surrounding countryside. By the time the waters began to subside that evening, some 60,000 people in this area were rendered homeless.

Every section of the country was hit by flooding. But the capital city of Seoul, where there are 174 congregations of Jehovah's Witnesses, was hit the hardest, especially the two areas served by the Mangwondong and Sungnaedong Congregations. Between them a total of 130 Witness families lost their homes. Immediately and spontaneously, Jehovah's Witnesses in Korea responded to the needs of their fellow Christians.

Although phone lines were down in many areas, reports started to come in to the branch office of the Watch Tower Society. Two committees were quickly formed to organize relief for Witnesses in the two badly devastated areas. The traveling circuit overseers in Seoul were instructed to get in touch with the brothers to see what the needs were or what could be done to aid those in the two worst-hit areas.

Witnesses in other areas learned about the extent of the damage through TV news reports. They started calling the branch asking where to send donations for their brothers in distress. (The Watch Tower branch in Japan also phoned, offering to help.) Donations of money started to come in from all over the country. Rice, noodles, and other foodstuffs, along with clothing and blankets, were also made available. These were distributed quickly by the committees on the scene. The brothers contributed so generously that soon the Seoul office had to make it known that no more money donations were needed.

Next came the enormous task of cleaning up. Three hundred Witnesses volunteered for this service. They were sent out in twos to each home to assist with the cleanup and to help get things back to normal as quickly as possible. One volunteer observed: "Through the training in our assembly and convention organizations, we know how to cooperate and get things done." Many in the community were upset when they saw some people taking advantage of the victims. On the other hand, they were surprised to see the calm, joyful, and generously helpful attitude of the Witnesses, even in such dire circumstances.

"Once more it has been demonstrated," said one Witness at the scene, "that disaster can take away our material goods quickly, but it cannot take away our faith." With tears of joy, a Witness woman said: "Even though we lost everything, we are not helpless. The warm love of our brothers has given us strength."

Truly, it was wonderful to see love in action. The initiative by the Witnesses on the scene and the immediate response of those 'related in the faith' were outstanding. (Galatians 6:10) The brothers in Korea were greatly encouraged by this experience. They were convinced by the well-organized assistance so lovingly given that there can be only one explanation —love came to the rescue!

Mourning Customs
How Do You View Them?

THROUGHOUT history, death has been the common experience of mankind. But long-time acquaintance has not lessened the devastating effect that death has on the survivors. The knowledge that someone who was a part of your life has gone seldom fails to cause deep and lasting grief, and an aching sense of loss.

Religion should soften the pain that death causes, but often it does the opposite. In some lands the pain death brings to bereaved ones is turned into terror when they are told that their parents and relatives who have died are now vengeful spirits who have to be placated with proper mourning ceremonies. Otherwise they will haunt the living. In addition, when a Christian family is bereaved, there may be decisions to face regarding local customs, such as wearing special garments and engaging in rituals that others may expect.

Jehovah God has promised one day to remove the painful experience of death from the human family. (Revelation 21:4) And meantime he has given us his Word, the Bible, as a 'light to our roadway.' (Psalm 119:105) Whenever we are in doubt as to the proper thing to do, the Bible shows us the way God wants us to act. (Isaiah 30:21) Let us consider the guidance it gives for that saddest of times, when someone close to us dies.

Mourning Is Proper

As already noted, it is natural to feel deep sadness when someone we love dies. But Christians know that there will be a resurrection. Hence, they do not have the hopeless, frantic sorrow that those without hope often manifest. (1 Thessalonians 4:13) Death does not necessarily mean good-bye forever, though it does mean that for a time.

Thus, Abraham 'bewailed Sarah and wept over her' when she died. (Genesis 23:2) Isaac, his son, needed "comfort after the loss of his mother." (Genesis 24:67) The sadness of the friends and relatives of the dead Lazarus was so great that Jesus himself "gave way to tears." (John 11:35) It is an act of love for friends of the bereaved family to visit and offer comfort during such a stressful time.—John 11:31.

However, you will notice that in the Scriptural accounts of mourning, and of comforting the bereaved, appeasement of the dead is never mentioned. God's servants knew that the dead were asleep, unconscious. (John 11:11-14; Ecclesiastes 9:5, 10) The dead do not suffer in an afterlife, nor do they turn into vengeful, dangerous spirits. (Psalm 146:3, 4) Hence, Jehovah's people were not to copy the surrounding nations in actions that reflected a wrong attitude toward the dead.—Deuteronomy 14:1; 18:10-12.

Today, too, when considering things that are commonly practiced out of 'respect for the dead,' we must determine what that practice means *at present*. Is it now linked with a wrong teaching or some superstition? If it is, should a Christian follow it?—Romans 13:12-14.

What Mourning Customs?

Among some peoples of the world, widows and widowers are supposed to wear special garments and stay in a state of mourning, with many restrictions on their freedom, for a year. Is this custom compatible with Christian beliefs?

Understandably, a Christian who has lost a loved one might dress and act more subdued for a time. (Compare 2 Samuel 13:19; 2 Kings 6:30.) But this is quite different from wearing, for a lengthy period, clothing that in the minds of the community is connected with non-Biblical beliefs about the dead. When Christian widows have refused to follow such customs, they have sometimes been threatened by relatives and neighbors who claim that "bad luck" will come to them or that the "spirit" of the dead husband will be upset and bring calamity upon them. These superstitious ones may also fear that the rain will be held back, or that there will be a crop failure.

One widow did not follow the customs, whereupon her son said: "My father's spirit will not rest in peace." In another place, the chief of the tribe threatened to dismiss all servants of Jehovah from that area! Some local people were so upset that they vandalized the local Christian meeting place with crowbars and axes. In still another area, a Christian widow was stripped naked and brutally lashed with a *sjambok* (whip) by tribal police.

Why did these Christian widows refuse to do what their neighbors expected of them? Perhaps you personally see little harm in going along with local customs for the sake of "decency." And with some customs, that may indeed be true. But how would a Christian be viewed if he or she shared in rituals designed to appease the "spirits of the ancestors"? Remember, those who engaged in such practices in earlier times were not allowed to remain part of the Israelite community or the early Christian congregation.—Deuteronomy 13:12-15; 18:9-13; 2 Corinthians 6: 14-18; 2 John 9, 10.

Consider some of the reasons for this. For one thing, by having any part in such rituals, a person would be supporting and, in effect, promoting a non-Christian religion. He would be showing that in his heart he is still a part of false religion. —Revelation 18:4.

All around the world, Jehovah's Witnesses are well known for teaching the Bible. One Biblical truth that they highlight is that the dead are unconscious, neither suffering in hell nor wandering the earth and able to harm their descendants. The Bible says: "As for the dead, they are conscious of nothing at all." (Ecclesiastes 9:5) This teaching has comforted hundreds of thousands. Thus, people in most communities do not generally expect these Christians to take part in rituals designed to appease the dead.

What would happen, then, if true Christians, because of pressure from their relatives or neighbors, consented to follow non-Christian mourning customs? Would the neighbors not conclude that perhaps the Christians do not really believe what they preach? That perhaps they can be made to compromise in other areas? Undoubtedly. Thus, a lot of good work would be destroyed, and people might be stumbled.—Matthew 18:6; 2 Corinthians 6:3.

Hence, the elders and others in the congregations of Jehovah's Witnesses give as much support as possible to those who have recently been bereaved. They give whatever support is needed to help them stand firm for truth in the face of any pressure to follow unchristian practices. —Compare 2 Corinthians 1:3, 4.

What if, despite such help, a Christian begins to follow non-Christian mourning customs? Elders would act with kindness. The apostle Paul counseled: "Brothers, even though a man takes some false step before he is aware of it, you who have spiritual qualifications try to readjust such a man in a spirit of mildness." (Galatians 6:1) The disciple James adds: "My brothers, if anyone among you is misled from the truth and another turns him back, know that he who turns a sinner back from the error of his way will save his soul from death and will cover a multitude of sins."—James 5:19, 20.

It is good to remember that God himself "does not desire any to be destroyed but desires all to attain to repentance." (2 Peter 3:9) The elders would first try hard to restore the erring one. In most cases it will doubtless be found that intense grief combined with fear of neighbor has pressured the mourning one to take the wrong step. Hopefully, with kind, empathetic help, he will henceforth 'make straight paths for his feet, that what is lame may not be put out of joint, but rather that it may be healed.'—Hebrews 12:13.

However, if a Christian follows non-Christian mourning customs and, refusing the help of fellow Christians, insists on continuing with the non-Christian course, then eventually the elders may have to act to make sure that such practices do not confuse onlookers or introduce wrong practices into the Christian congregation. Anyone who worships his ancestors is no longer a true Christian, and steps should be taken to make sure that everyone recognizes this fact.—1 Corinthians 5:13.

Blessings From Faithfulness

Many Christians have found that faithfulness in this important matter brings good results. Edwina Apason, a Christian woman in Suriname, relates her experience: "Once, when conducting a Bible study, I received a shocking message. While participating in a protest demonstration, my oldest son, who was not a Witness, had been shot to death. This painful loss triggered more strain, for my relatives said: 'If you don't follow the mourning customs, you have no motherly feelings for your son.' Custom required that I cut my hair, wrap my head in a white scarf, wear mourning clothes for months, deliberately walk slowly, and talk softly in a muffled voice—all of this to show the people and the supposed 'spirit of the dead' that I really was sad. Yet, if I did these things, surely my preaching would be in vain and I would lose my clean conscience before God." Hence, Edwina did not compromise.

Another man claimed that his dead aunt regularly visited him at night. What did he think she wanted? He replied: "That a sacrifice be made for her down at the edge of the river." What if the sacrifice was not made? There was the threat of death. While living, this aunt had been a very loving person. But, after dying, she supposedly acted like a menacing, threatening tyrant. Could this really be the same person? With reasoning and the use of the Scriptures, this man and others like him have been freed from fear of the dead. These people have learned that the visions, voices, and apparitions are the work of fallen angels, demons.—Compare 2 Corinthians 11:3, 14; Ephesians 6:12.

Jehovah's servants are aware that if they stay in the way that he sets out for them, this will eventually lead to the blessing of everlasting life. (Isaiah 30:21) Satan is constantly using cunning and devious means to try to trip them and make them stray from that way. (1 Peter 5:8, 9) He recognizes that they may be especially vulnerable when mourning the death of a loved one. Nevertheless, Christians are determined to be faithful to Jehovah in all things, despite any pressure. In this, as in other matters, they "must obey God as ruler rather than men." (Acts 5:29) Thus they prove the depth of their devotion to Jehovah God, and they can look forward to his rewarding them with life in his new system where death and mourning "will be no more."—Revelation 21:4.

A Heartwarming Report From the Far North

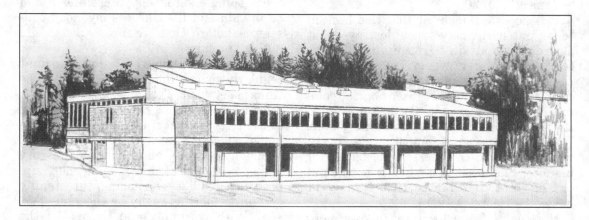

FINLAND is situated in the far north of Europe, its northern reaches stretching well into the Arctic Circle. It is famous for the scenic beauty of its forests, lakes, coastline, and offshore islands. It is noted also for seasonal contrasts, for long winter nights, and for the summer midnight sun.

Over 90 percent of the five million Finns are nominally members of the Evangelical Lutheran Church, the state religion of Finland. But, with the standard of living steadily rising, interest in spiritual things has generally lost its place in their lives. There is, however, a different kind of spiritual growth taking place in this country. The result is that there are now more than 15,000 Jehovah's Witnesses in Finland, one of every 320 inhabitants of the land. Using the words of the prophet Isaiah, the time came for Jehovah's Witnesses in Finland to "stretch out the tent cloths" and to "make the place of [their] tent more spacious"—once again.—Isaiah 54:2.

"Are they really going to build again?"

That was the reaction of some of the older members of the Finnish Bethel, or headquarters, family when they learned of the plans to expand the branch facilities once again. But, in spite of the inconveniences during the construction period, they were happy to be on hand at the dedication of the new extension on May 5, 1984, when M. G. Henschel, a member of the Governing Body of Jehovah's Witnesses, was a special guest.

Early Flashes of Truth

"In the past the King of Sweden ordered the Finns to be converted by force," said Erkki Kankaanpää, the coordinator of the Finnish Branch Committee, in his opening speech on the dedication program. He was referring to the clergy's strong grip on the people when Finland was under Swedish domination. "But that was not the flash of truth in Finland."

That "flash" came in 1909 when some colporteurs, or full-time preachers, came to Finland, distributing C. T. Russell's books. As a result, Österman, a businessman, and Harteva, an engineer, became interested. They obtained more books from the Swedish branch office and started to translate and publish them in Finnish. In 1912 the *Watchtower* magazine was published in Finnish.

The two brothers were most courageous and resourceful in preaching the good news. Once Brother Harteva was relating the newfound truth to a former schoolmate.

"And how many are there of you people in Finland?" the schoolmate asked.

"There are two of us," he replied unhesitatingly. "But, if you join us, that will make three."

At another time, Brother Österman was offering the passersby at a marketplace a booklet entitled *What Say the Scriptures About Hell?* on a contribution of two Finnish marks. He surely had their attention when he shouted: "A ticket to hell—one mark in, and another one out!"

Brother Russell visited Finland in 1912. The October 1, 1912, issue of *The Watch Tower* reported: "The public meeting was crowded to the capacity of the hall—1000—many standing; some almost in tears because they could not gain admission." Although the work was still new, said the report, "it seems to make excellent progress. The number of Colporteurs engaged, and the fact that it is self-sustaining, speak well for the depth of interest."

Subsequent visits by other members from the Brooklyn headquarters, including J. F. Rutherford, the second president of the Society, proved to be most strengthening to the brothers. In fact, in December 1945, when Brother N. H. Knorr and Brother M. G. Henschel visited Finland for the first time, there were some 1,800 Witnesses.

Today, Jehovah's Witnesses enjoy complete freedom of worship in Finland, and

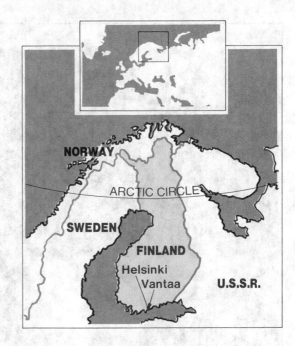

they are making full use of it. Last April an all-time peak of 15,263 persons shared in preaching the Kingdom good news throughout the country. More than 900 have taken up full-time preaching work as pioneers, special pioneers, or serving as members of the Bethel family at the branch headquarters.

Developments at the Branch

The first branch building in Finland was constructed in 1933 in Helsinki, the capital. It consisted of a factory and a Bethel Home, and it was well situated for its purpose. But after many years of service, it became too small. Thus in 1957, a site for a new branch was obtained in the city of Vantaa, about 17 kilometers (10 mi) from Helsinki.

In January 1962 the branch was transferred to the new facility. Everyone thought at that time that this new home would be all that would ever be needed to support the preaching work in Finland.

In 1913 J. F. Rutherford (with hat at his feet) met with a large group of Finnish brothers

That was not to be the case. Since then, the dining room, dormitory, office, bindery, in fact, nearly all the facilities have been expanded to care for the increase in the number of publishers and the resulting growth of the Bethel family.

The Finnish Bethel is ideally located in that it is convenient to transportation and enjoys the peace and quiet of the countryside. It is situated on a small hill and has a beautiful garden for a yard. That it is an asset to the community is recognized even by the authorities, who have been most accommodating. For example, some time ago, when the original plans for a highway would have put it right through our property, they agreed to alter the plans upon our request. And, even though the area had been designated as a park, we were granted permission to expand our facility. Naturally, we are grateful for such special consideration.

The expansion this time consists of a new wing with 3,400 square meters (36,-500 sq ft) of floor space. It includes an underground level for parking and storage. On the ground level are the machine shop, carpenter shop, and garage. On the upper floor is the bindery, along with adequate space for the locker rooms and some recreational facilities. The structure matches the existing building in design —red bricks with exposed wood beams in an attractive blond color.

Volunteers to Meet the Challenge

When the building project was announced, many Witnesses volunteered their services. Forty-five of them were invited to come and work for about a year. Who would supervise this challenging project? A brother who is an architect and a pioneer who used to own a construction business were among the volunteers. The job of excavating for the basement was done by a brother who owns an earth-moving company. Another brother who is an expert in explosives took care of the boulders. Still another brother took a two-month course for operating the large crane so that there was no need to hire an outsider to do the job.

Due to the willing spirit of the brothers, the project was completed at only about a third of the cost that a commercial contractor would charge. But what about the quality? "You could not get such quality work even if you spent the big money with commercial contractors," remarked one of the inspectors when he saw the completed building. What a testimony to the whole-hearted service rendered by the brothers!

The Task Ahead

"However, it is not the architecture or the building materials that are significant to Jehovah," said Brother Henschel in his dedication talk. "It is the way the building is used that matters." He referred to the temple in Jerusalem built by King Solomon. It was undoubtedly the most glorious building in existence then, or perhaps ever. Yet Jehovah rejected it when the Israelites failed to render pure worship in his house.

So the new building is dedicated to advancing the Kingdom interests in Finland. Jehovah has indeed blessed the work in this part of the field. In the 1984 service year, 127,625 books and 128,083 booklets were produced in Finland. Over 562,531 copies of the book *The Truth That Leads to Eternal Life* have been published. That is enough to provide one of every two Finnish households with a copy! Also, every month more than 350,000 copies of the *Awake!* and *Watchtower* magazines are produced.

All of this presents a tremendous challenge to the Finnish Bethel family, which now consists of 73 members. But that is nothing new. Two years ago, the Bethel family took on the challenge of converting from letterpress to offset printing. Brothers throughout the country provided the finances, and those at Bethel worked hard to acquire the new skills. The result has been gratifying. The factory in the Finland branch is capable of producing multicolored magazines and books.

For the task ahead, more expansion is planned. Already, work is underway for a new, spacious Kingdom Hall to be added to the Bethel Home. Thereafter, 28 new rooms, together with a new kitchen and a dining room, will be built to accommodate additional members of the family. Jehovah has provided the means and the strength for tackling similar tasks in the past, and the Witnesses in Finland are confidently looking ahead to future blessings. They echo the sentiments of one Witness at the dedication program: "It is wonderful to be one of Jehovah's Witnesses in these times!"

In Our Next Issue

■ **Why God Has Not Yet Executed His Judgment**

■ **Accepting the Challenge of Christian Maturity**

■ **Single and Happy as a Pioneer**

Do You Remember?

Have you found the recent issues of *The Watchtower* to be of practical value? Then why not test your memory with the following:

□ **What is Armageddon?**

Armageddon is the worldwide situation where all earthly nations will battle against God's Son, Christ Jesus, and his angelic army in "the war of the great day of God the Almighty." (Revelation 16:13, 14, 16)—1/1, page 6.

□ **Who today holds the key position in Jehovah's earthly organization?**

The Kingdom publisher holds the key position because, in living up to Jehovah's name, the publisher must be a zealous minister.—1/1, page 14.

□ **Why is it that agencies such as the UN are powerless to prevent wars?**

The nations around the earth are dedicated to national sovereignty and rights, so they care little about international sovereignty or rules of conduct. Their repeated failure emphasizes the Bible truth that "it does not belong to man who is walking even to direct his step." (Jeremiah 10:23)—2/15, page 4.

□ **Why is a "greedy person" also called "an idolater" in Ephesians 5:3-5?**

Those who are obsessed with a desire for sex, love for money, voraciousness for food and drink, or an ambition for power and fame, become slaves to such desires and make them, as it were, their idols. Hence, their chief aim in life now becomes a satisfying of their greedy desires.—2/15, page 25.

□ **What was it, in all probability, that moved Abraham and Isaac to represent their wives as their sisters?**

Jehovah had already indicated to Abraham that the blessing of "all the families of the ground" depended on Abraham's seed: (Genesis 12:2, 3) Hence, Abraham (and later Isaac) needed to stay alive to produce offspring and thus fulfill Jehovah's promise. For this reason, when they were in dangerous territory with their wives, these men probably determined that it was prudent not to let their marriage relationship be known. In so doing, the line of the seed would not be endangered.—3/1, page 31.

□ **How did Noah set a fine example for family heads today?**

Of Noah it is recorded: "Noah proceeded to do according to all that God had commanded him. He did just so." (Genesis 6:22) Noah's faithfulness and diligence impressed on the minds of his sons the importance of showing the same qualities in their lives. He spent a lot of time talking to and working with his sons. They were sharing and doing things together as a family. Being "a preacher of righteousness," Noah also taught his own family Jehovah's laws and requirements. (2 Peter 2:5) In all these aspects Noah set a fine example for family heads today. —3/15, page 26.

□ **In what ways are Jehovah's Witnesses different from the world?**

They are different in being zealous preachers of the good news of God's Kingdom, in their shunning what is bad in God's eyes, in maintaining neutrality toward worldly affairs, and in their demonstrating their love and consideration for the whole association of their Christian brothers. (Matthew 24:14; Hebrews 1:9; John 15:19; 13:35) —4/1, pages 10-14.

Questions From Readers

■ If a Christian feels that someone in the congregation is not the best of association because of that person's conduct or attitude, should he personally 'mark' that individual in accord with 2 Thessalonians 3:14, 15?

Those who become part of the Christian congregation do so because they love Jehovah and sincerely want to live by his principles. It is better to fellowship with these than with worldly people.

We may be more comfortable with certain Christians, as Jesus 'especially loved' the apostle John and was particularly close to 3 of the 12. Still, he chose, was interested in, and loved all of them. (John 13:1, 23; 19:26; Mark 5:37; 9:2; 14:33) Though all brothers have failings of which we must be understanding and forgiving, we know that for the most part fellow believers are wholesome companions. (1 Peter 4:8; Matthew 7:1-5) Love for one another is an identifying mark of the Christian congregation.

—John 13:34, 35; Colossians 3:14.

On occasion, however, someone may have an attitude or way of life of which we personally do not approve. The apostle Paul wrote about some in Corinth whose personal views about the resurrection were not right and who may have had an 'eat, drink, and be merry' attitude. Mature Christians in the congregation needed to be cautious about such ones, for Paul advised: "Do not be misled. Bad associations spoil useful habits."—1 Corinthians 15:12, 32, 33.

This general counsel is also valid today. For example, a Christian couple may find that their children are adversely affected when they spend time with certain other youngsters, who may not yet take the truth seriously or may be worldly minded. These other children may yet benefit from godly training. But until there is evidence of that, the couple might restrict their children as to playing with and visiting those youngsters. This would not be a 'marking' such as spoken of in 2 Thessalonians chapter 3. The parents simply are applying Paul's advice to avoid "bad associations."

Situations that call for 'marking' are more serious than the above example involving children. Occasionally a person in a congregation pursues an unscriptural course that is very disturbing, though it does not yet justify the disfellowshipping action mentioned at 1 Corinthians 5:11-13. Such conduct occurred in the congregation of ancient Thessalonica, so Paul wrote: "We hear certain ones are walking disorderly among you, not working at all but meddling with what does not concern them."—2 Thessalonians 3:11.

What were other Christians in Thessalonica to do? Paul wrote: "We are giving you orders, broth-

ers, in the name of the Lord Jesus Christ, to withdraw from every brother walking disorderly and not according to the tradition you received from us. For your part, brothers, do not give up in doing right. But if anyone is not obedient to our word through this letter, keep this one marked, stop associating with him, that he may become ashamed. And yet do not be considering him as an enemy, but continue admonishing him as a brother."—2 Thessalonians 3:6, 13-15.

Thus, without naming the lazy meddlers, Paul exposed to the congregation their serious course. All Christians who were aware of the identity of the disorderly ones would then treat them as "marked." The counsel, "keep this one *marked*," used a Greek word meaning "be you putting sign on," that is, 'taking special notice of someone.' (*New World Translation Reference Bible,* footnote) Paul said, "Stop associating with" the marked one "that he may become ashamed." Brothers would not completely shun him, for Paul advised them to "continue admonishing him as a brother." Yet by their limiting social fellowship with him, they might lead him to become ashamed and perhaps awaken him to the need to conform to Bible principles. Meanwhile the brothers and sisters would be protected from his unwholesome influence.—2 Timothy 2:20, 21.

The Christian congregation today also applies this counsel.* *The Watchtower* of February 1, 1982, page 31, stressed that marking is not to be done over mere private opinions or when a Christian personally chooses to avoid close association with someone. As shown by the case in Thessalonica, marking involves serious violations of Bible princi-

* See *The Watchtower,* May 15, 1973, pages 318-20.

ples. First the elders try repeatedly to help the violator by admonishing him. If the problem persists, they may, without naming the person, give a warning talk to the congregation concerning the disorderly conduct involved, even as Paul warned the Thessalonians. After that, individual Christians would keep the erring person "marked."

Good judgment is needed rather than predetermined rules about every aspect of marking. Paul did not give detailed rules regarding that problem in Thessalonica, such as stipulating how long someone had to have been refusing to work before he could be marked. Similarly, the elders are in touch with the flock and can use reasonableness and discernment in determining whether a particular situation is sufficiently serious and disturbing so as to require a warning talk to the congregation.*

One purpose of marking is to move a disorderly Christian to feel ashamed and stop his unscriptural course. Individuals who had marked him, particularly the elders, will continue to encourage him and note his attitude as they have contact with him at meetings and in field service. When they see that the problem and attitude necessitating the marking have changed for the better, they can end their limitation as to socializing with him.

Consequently, marking should not be confused with a personal or family application of God's advice to avoid bad association. While marking is not something that is needed often, it should be plain that marking is a Scriptural step that is taken when it is warranted, which step our Thessalonian brothers took.

_____

* For example, elders should exercise discernment in dealing with a Christian who is dating a person not "in the Lord."—See *The Watchtower* of March 15, 1982, page 31.

THAT is what people say about the book *"Let Your Kingdom Come."* A letter of appreciation explains: "It gives a clear picture of what the Kingdom is, how it is established and maintained, and what it will do for us and for the earth. It certainly helps to keep alive in our hearts that Kingdom hope and sharpens our desire to strive diligently to be among those who will be granted life at that time."

'It Makes the Kingdom Real'

"Let your Kingdom come"

May 1, 1985

The Watchtower

Announcing Jehovah's Kingdom

Is God Delaying His Judgment?

May 1, 1985
Vol. 106, No. 9

The Watchtower®
Announcing Jehovah's Kingdom

In This Issue

THE PURPOSE OF "THE WATCHTOWER" is to exalt Jehovah God as the Sovereign of the universe. It keeps watch on world events as they fulfill Bible prophecy. It comforts all peoples with the good news that God's Kingdom will soon destroy those who oppress their fellowmen and that it will turn the earth into a paradise. It encourages faith in the now-reigning King, Jesus Christ, whose shed blood opens the way for mankind to gain eternal life. "The Watchtower," published by Jehovah's Witnesses continuously since 1879, is nonpolitical. It adheres to the Bible as its authority.

"WATCHTOWER" STUDIES FOR THE WEEKS

June 2: Accepting the Challenge of Christian Maturity. Page 8. Songs to Be Used: 128, 43.

June 9: "Go On Walking Orderly in This Same Routine." Page 13. Songs to Be Used: 202, 42.

Average Printing Each Issue: 11,150,000

Now Published in 102 Languages

SEMIMONTHLY EDITIONS AVAILABLE BY MAIL
Afrikaans, Arabic, Cebuano, Chichewa, Chinese, Cibemba, Danish, Dutch, Efik, English*, Finnish, French, German, Greek, Hiligaynon, Igbo, Iloko, Italian, Japanese, Korean, Lingala, Malagasy, Maltese, Norwegian, Portuguese, Russian, Sepedi, Sesotho, Shona, Spanish, Swahili, Swedish, Tagalog, Thai, Tswana, Xhosa, Yoruba, Zulu

MONTHLY EDITIONS AVAILABLE BY MAIL
Armenian, Bengali, Bicol, Bulgarian, Croatian, Czech, Ewe, Fijian, Ga, Greenlandic, Gujarati, Gun, Hausa, Hebrew, Hindi, Hiri Motu, Hungarian, Icelandic, Kannada, Kikuyu, Kiluba, Malayalam, Marathi, New Guinea Pidgin, Pangasinan, Papiamento, Polish, Rarotongan, Romanian, Samar-Leyte, Samoan, Sango, Serbian, Silozi, Sinhalese, Slovenian, Solomon Islands-Pidgin, Tahitian, Tamil, Telugu, Tshiluba, Tsonga, Turkish, Twi, Ukrainian, Urdu, Venda, Vietnamese
*Study articles also available in large-print edition at same cost.

The Bible translation used is the "New World Translation of the Holy Scriptures," unless otherwise indicated.

Twenty cents (U.S.) a copy

Watch Tower Society offices	Yearly subscription rates Semimonthly
America, U.S., Watchtower, Wallkill, N.Y. 12589	$4.00
Australia, Box 280, Ingleburn, N.S.W. 2565	A$6.00
Canada, Box 4100, Halton Hills (Georgetown), Ontario L7G 4Y4	$5.20
England, The Ridgeway, London NW7 1RN	£5.00
Ireland, 29A Jamestown Road, Finglas, Dublin 11	£5.00
New Zealand, 6-A Western Springs Rd., Auckland 3	$10.00
Nigeria, P.O. Box 194, Yaba, Lagos State	₦6.00
Philippines, P.O. Box 2044, Manila 2800	₱50.00
South Africa, Private Bag 2, Elandsfontein, 1406	R5.60

Remittances should be sent to the office in your country or to Watchtower, Wallkill, N.Y. 12589, U.S.A.

Changes of address should reach us 30 days before your moving date. Give us your old and new address (if possible, your old address label).

The Watchtower (ISSN 0043-1087) is published semimonthly for $4.00 (U.S.) per year by Watch Tower Bible and Tract Society of Pennsylvania, 25 Columbia Heights, Brooklyn, N.Y. 11201. Second-class postage paid at Brooklyn, N.Y., and at additional mailing offices.

Postmaster: Send address changes to Watchtower, **Wallkill, N.Y. 12589.**

Published by
**Watch Tower Bible and Tract Society
of Pennsylvania**
25 Columbia Heights, Brooklyn, N.Y. 11201, U.S.A.
Frederick W. Franz, President

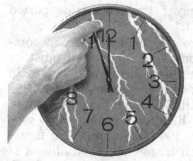

Is God Delaying His Judgment?

IMAGINE you are awaiting an out-of-town visitor who has told you the day of his arrival but not the hour. As time passes, and he still has not come, you begin to wonder if he has been delayed. Was this really the day he said he would come? Could there have been a misunderstanding? Slowly, what was at first only impatience gives way to something more disconcerting, something called doubt.

This may well describe how some people feel about the promised arrival of God's time to execute judgment against wickedness. After all, his worshipers have been waiting so long for it. Take, for example, faithful King David. Over 3,000 years ago he said: "Jehovah himself at your right hand will certainly break kings to pieces on the day of his anger. He will *execute judgment among the nations.*" So can anyone today be blamed for wondering, When?—Psalm 110:5, 6.

By comparing world conditions with Bible prophecy and by taking into account Bible chronology, serious Bible students have become convinced that God's day of judgment is finally near. But have not many people in the past felt the same way, only to find out later that they were mistaken? Is there any *sure* way of determining exactly when God's judgment will be executed?

At God's "Appointed Time"

Jesus indicated that judgment would take place at a definite time. But in warning to his followers, he said: "Keep awake, for you do not know when *the appointed time* is."—Mark 13:33.

Habakkuk, commissioned by God six centuries earlier to write about the execution of divine judgment, also said it would be "for *the appointed time.*" And as a warning against becoming impatient, or perhaps even doubtful, he promised at God's direction: "It will not tell a lie. Even if it should delay, keep in expectation of it; for it will without fail come true. It will not be late."—Habakkuk 2:2, 3.

But if God's judgment is "for the appointed time" and if it "will not be late," why does Habakkuk say "even if it should delay"? Evidently to show that some of God's people would expect it to come sooner than it actually would. Why? Because the *exact* time of its coming would remain unknown to them.

While on earth, even Jesus did not know the exact time, for he said: "Concerning that day or the hour nobody knows, neither the angels in heaven nor the Son, but the Father." (Mark 13:32) What he did know, however, was the *time period* during which judgment would occur. Thus, at his disciples' request, he gave a sign that would enable them to recognize this time period once it had begun. Its first evidence, Jesus said, would be "like the first pains of childbirth." Now, of course, a pregnant woman going into labor does not know the exact time her child will be born.

Many of the generation of 1914
hope to see
"all these things occur"

She does know, however, that its birth is imminent.—Matthew 24:3-8, *Today's English Version.*

"This Generation Will by No Means Pass Away"

Besides knowing when the time period for divine judgment would come, Jesus was able to put a limit on its length. Using the illustration of a fig tree, he said: "Just as soon as its young branch grows tender and it puts forth leaves, you know that summer is near. Likewise also you, when you see all these things, know that he is near at the doors. Truly I say to you that this generation will by no means pass away until all these things occur."—Matthew 24:32-34.

Thus judgment would be executed sometime during the life span of people seeing the first evidence of the time period foretold by Jesus. The start of this time period would mark the beginning of the end for Satan's world, against which God's newly established Kingdom in heaven would execute divine judgment. Bible chronology and the fulfillment of Bible prophecy pro-

vide ample proof that this time period began in 1914.*

Thus before the 1914 generation completely dies out, God's judgment must be executed. This generation still exists in goodly numbers. For example, in 1980 there were still 1,597,700 persons alive in the Federal Republic of Germany who were born in 1900 or before. The figure would be even larger had not millions of its citizens experienced premature death during the two world wars.

In promising that "this generation will *by no means* pass away," Jesus used the two Greek negatives *ou* and *me. The Companion Bible* explains this usage as follows: "The two negatives when combined lose their distinctive meanings, and form the strongest and most emphatic asseveration [affirmation]." Only now, at a time when it appears that the generation *could* pass away before all is fulfilled, do Jesus' words "by no means" take on real significance.

A Test of Faith

Habakkuk's warning words indicate that there would be an apparent delay in Jehovah's judgment, serving as a test of faith. Logically this test could not arise until late in the generation of which Jesus spoke. In reference to the example at the beginning of this article, consider this: When would you begin seriously doubting that your visitor was coming? Certainly not at nine o'clock in the morning, nor at noon, possibly not even in the late afternoon. But likely your faith *would* be tested once evening had set in. However, remember that even at 11:30 p.m. your visitor still would have sufficient time to come in fulfillment of his promise!

---

* A detailed explanation can be found in chapters 16 and 18 of the book *You Can Live Forever in Paradise on Earth,* published in 1982 by the Watchtower Bible and Tract Society of New York, Inc.

There is no reason to worry that God's Word will go unfulfilled. It has never failed. Joshua's words to the Israelites over 3,000 years ago are as true now as they were then: "Not one word out of all the good words that Jehovah your God has spoken to you has failed. They have all come true for you. Not one word of them has failed."—Joshua 23:14.

"Respecting the fulfilment of prophecy it seems to be natural for us, and for all humanity, to be impatient and to expect things to be done more rapidly than they usually come to pass." So said *The Watch Tower* in its May 1, 1910, issue, adding: "This is a delay as respects our expectations, but we may be sure that there is no delay in the matter as respects the divine intention . . . We have no doubt that the results will be attained in the fulness of time—God's time."

In retrospect, faithful Christians living today can see good reasons why God's judgment has not yet been executed. In fact, they rejoice that it has not. Our next article explains why.

Why God Has Not Yet Executed His Judgment

ABOUT two decades after Jesus' death, some Christians were already expecting Jehovah to "arrive" in judgment. This prompted the apostle Paul to write them, saying: "The day of Jehovah . . . will not come unless the apostasy comes first and the man of lawlessness gets revealed, the son of destruction." Although Paul admitted that "the mystery of this lawlessness" was "already at work" in his day, it obviously was not to the extent necessary, so that divine judgment could come. —2 Thessalonians 2:2, 3, 7, 8.

A Twofold Ingathering

The apostasy, although sure to come, would not hinder God's purpose to choose 144,000 faithful Christians to be joint rulers with his Son, Jesus, in heaven. (See Revelation 14:1-5.) Only after their number had been completed and they had finally been sealed by God could the execution of Jehovah's judgment take place. Revelation 7:2, 3 explains: "To the four angels [it was said]: 'Do not harm the earth or the sea or the trees [by bringing the destructive winds of God's judgment against the nations], until *after* we have sealed the slaves of our God in their foreheads.'" As we now know, this work had not been finished when the Kingdom was established in 1914.

Thus, even though some were hopeful that it might, God's execution of judgment could not come at that time. The January 1, 1914, issue of *The Watch Tower* left room for this development, stating that although "the Year 1914 is the last one of what the Bible terms 'Gentile Times' . . . we are by no means confident that this year, 1914, will witness as radical and swift changes of dispensation as we have expected." Still, as the article went on to explain, Christians were grateful that Bible chronology had awakened them to the imminence of divine judgment. It said: "We believe that the chronology is a blessing. If it should wake us a few minutes earlier or a few hours earlier in the morning than we would otherwise have waked, well and good! It is those who are awake who get the blessing."

Also among those getting a blessing would be what the Bible describes as "a great crowd, which no man was able to number, out of all nations and tribes and peoples and tongues." Not until 1935 was it fully understood that this "great crowd" would be composed of persons "that come out of the great tribulation," that is to say, those who abandon Satan's organization and take their stand on God's side, so as to survive the execution of God's judgment. For some five decades now, the work of gathering this "great crowd" has been proceeding in accordance with Jehovah's purpose. We can rejoice that divine judgment will not be executed until this lifesaving work has been completed.—Revelation 7:9, 14.

Political Developments

Certain political developments were also foretold to occur before the execution of God's judgment. A fulfillment of Daniel's prophecy about "two kings" (chapter 11) is now clearly seen as edging toward completion.* At the culmination of this fulfillment, God will execute judgment.—Compare Daniel 2:44.

---

* This prophecy is explained in detail in the book *"Your Will Be Done on Earth,"* published in 1958 by the Watchtower Bible and Tract Society of New York, Inc.

Although opposed to each other, the superpowers and their blocs—"the king of the south" and "the king of the north"—are both represented in the global political organization that today causes people to "wonder admiringly." What an apt description of the post-World War I League of Nations and its post-World War II successor, the United Nations organization. —Daniel 11:40; Revelation 17:8.

Ideologically and politically divided, and yet at the same time "united," these "two kings" have much to say about preserving world "peace and security." This, too, is significant, for Bible prophecy says that "whenever it is that they are saying: 'Peace and security!' then sudden destruction is to be instantly upon them." To what extent these "two kings," separately and in conjunction with the United Nations organization, will be able to solve the world's political, economic, environmental, and social problems so as to feel justified in making this cry, we at present do not know.—1 Thessalonians 5:2, 3.

What we do know, however, is that sometime during its rule, the United Nations organization, together with all its

---

WHAT MUST PRECEDE EXECUTION OF JUDGMENT

The apostasy—2 THESSALONIANS 2:2, 3

The sealing of the 144,000 —REVELATION 7:2, 3

The gathering of the "great crowd" for survival—REVELATION 7:14

The appearing of the League of Nations and then the United Nations—REVELATION 17:8

The final confrontation between the two great blocs of nations—DANIEL 11:40, 44, 45

The global cry of "Peace and security"—1 THESSALONIANS 5:2, 3

Peter regarded God's patience as salvation, whereas Jonah complained. Whose example will you follow?

member nations—including most prominently these "two kings"—will experience God's judgment and 'go off into destruction.' We also know that the 1914 generation is well into the evening of its existence, thus allowing only little time for this prophecy yet to be fulfilled. But we also know—for this we have Jesus' own promise—that "this generation will *by no means* pass away until all these things happen."—Revelation 17:11; Mark 13:30.

Jehovah Will Not Delay—Will You?

If you are studying the Bible and learning about Jehovah's purposes, do not delay in fleeing to God's symbolic place of protection. "Seek righteousness, seek meekness," so that "you may be concealed in the day of Jehovah's anger."—Zephaniah 2:1-3.

Keep in mind the first-century Christians who fled from Jerusalem in 66 C.E. upon recognizing the sign that Jesus had given of its impending judgment. Any who delayed their flight—for whatever reason—were probably lulled into a false sense of security when the Romans, who had encircled the city and then unexpectedly withdrawn, failed to return. Weeks passed. Weeks turned into months. Months turned into years. Some may have thought that Jehovah was delaying the execution of his judgment. But suddenly the Romans returned in 70 C.E. For those inside the city, there was no escape. —Luke 21:20-22.

People today, on the other hand, who have already dedicated their lives to doing God's will and have fled to his place of safety, should not delay in fulfilling their Christian obligations. They should not beg off preaching Jehovah's message of judgment as Jonah tried to do when he was instructed to warn the Ninevites of divine judgment. Neither should they withdraw into inactivity to sulk, as he did, because things have not developed as they expected or as rapidly as they hoped.—Jonah 1:1, 2; 4:2, 5, 10, 11; 2 Peter 3:15.

Appropriately *The Watch Tower* of June 1, 1906, stated concerning God's execution of judgment: "Time will fully manifest the divine wisdom in what seems to short-sighted humanity like pitiless delay . . . God has kindly brought us to his standpoint of view and bidden us look into the glorious future . . . and in proportion as we are able to comprehend and believe it, we may rest and rejoice in it. But in the meantime, being thus graciously refreshed by the cheering prospect, we must patiently wait for the end, however painful the waiting season may be."

And wait we will, with this full conviction: "It will without fail come true. It will not be late."—Habakkuk 2:3.

"Speaking the truth, let us by love grow up in all things into him who is the head, Christ."
—EPHESIANS 4:15.

Accepting the Challenge of Christian Maturity

A HEALTHY, bouncing baby is truly a bundle of joy. Few people can resist its amusing antics. It is a source of endless excitement and delight, the center of attention wherever it goes. Understandably, parents love it as their 'pride and joy' in spite of all the toil and turmoil it brings. Indeed, "the fruitage of the belly is a reward."—Psalm 127:3.

² Lovable as a baby may be, however, what happens if it fails to give any sign of growth? If it remains in that state after months or perhaps even years of loving care from the parents, then clearly something is seriously wrong. Indeed, growth has come to be synonymous with life; we expect it of all living things. It is a testimony to Jehovah's creative power and wisdom.—Luke 2:52.

Spiritual Growth Essential

³ True to Jesus' prophecy, growth of another kind is taking place. Around the world, a spiritual "harvest" is in progress. (Matthew 9:37) During the 1984 service year, for example, six countries reported averages of over a hundred thousand Kingdom publishers. Just three years earlier, in 1981, only two countries did. In the last six years, 827,144 new witnesses of

Jehovah got baptized and over 5,000 new congregations were formed. Jehovah has speeded up his work.—Isaiah 60:22.

⁴ These figures show that about one in every three persons who regularly associate with Jehovah's people and share in the preaching work today got baptized within the last six years. Are you one of them? If so, you have been a source of great joy to those who assisted you in learning the truth, to all your Christian associates, and to your heavenly Father, Jehovah God. (Proverbs 27:11) Like the first step taken by an infant, the step you have taken to dedicate yourself to Jehovah was an exciting event. It signified a forward, progressive move on your part. It was a sign of growth.

⁵ What about since then? With the loving attention of your fellow Christians, are you showing evidence of steady spiritual growth? 'How can I tell?' you may ask. Well, recall what the apostle Paul said about growth: "When I was a babe, I used to speak as a babe, to think as a babe, to reason as a babe; but now that I have become a man, I have done away with the traits of a babe." (1 Corinthians 13:11) So, it was not just the passing of time but the doing away with "the traits of a babe" that

1, 2. (a) In what ways is 'the fruitage of the belly' a reward? (b) What is expected of newborn infants?
3. What growth was foretold by Jesus, and what fulfillment is seen?

4. What has been the result of the worldwide growth among Jehovah's people?
5. What questions should each individual ask himself? What can help in finding the answers?

made him a mature man. What are these traits?

⁶ One thing about infants is that they have a very short attention span. Though they are curious about everything around them, they are also unpredictable, changeable, and unsettled. Obviously, anyone remaining in such a state is in grave spiritual danger. He is likely to be "tossed about as by waves and carried hither and thither by every wind of teaching by means of the trickery of men, by means of cunning in contriving error," as the apostle Paul described it at Ephesians 4:14.

⁷ Waves and wind can break forth as quickly as they dissipate. Today, when it is planned for things to go obsolete, trends, fads, and fashions come and go. Things that were considered essential just a short while ago are completely outdated and forgotten. Whether it is in the field of entertainment, dress and grooming, or anything else, how unwise—and childish—it is to be caught up in always wanting or getting the latest in everything, only to be outclassed and disappointed quickly. In spiritual matters, the consequence of such unsteadiness can be disastrous.—Compare James 1:6-8.

6, 7. (a) Describe one 'trait of a babe' and the danger it poses. (b) How is this trait manifest? What can be the outcome?

⁸ Another 'trait of babes' is that they have very little conception of what is good or bad, right or wrong. Similarly, spiritual babes have not yet had their "perceptive powers trained to distinguish both right and wrong," and that is why the apostle Paul urged his fellow Christians to "press on to maturity, not laying a foundation again." (Hebrews 5:14; 6:1) Those who are spiritual babes need constant reassurance that what they have accepted as truth is indeed truth, and what they have been taught to do is indeed what they ought to do. They need help in even the most fundamental things. Otherwise they are easily confused, frustrated, and overtaken by doubts that can damage their faith.

⁹ Have you ever noticed that children are always eager to do what they see adults do? To them, of course, it is only a game. Part of the fun, no doubt, is in being able to do what they want to do without having to accept the responsibility that goes with it. That, after all, is what a child's life is all about. (See Matthew 11:16, 17.) But with growth and

development come duty and responsibility. It is a challenge that a child must be helped to accept. How well he responds to it will determine, to a large extent, his success or failure in later life. Spiritually, it is even more important that each one of us seriously consider the challenge of

8. What is another 'trait' of spiritual babes, and what danger does it present?
9. Why must we accept the challenge of Christian maturity?

Christian maturity. Are you willing, even eager, to accept the responsibility that comes with being a full-grown, mature, spiritual person? Or do you merely coast along, letting others shoulder your responsibility for you?—Galatians 6:4, 5.

Christian Maturity—What Is It?

¹⁰ When the apostle Paul urged Christians to "press on to maturity," what did he have in mind? (Hebrews 6:1) The context shows that Paul originally had much to say to the Hebrew Christians concerning the "high priest according to the manner of Melchizedek," Jesus Christ. But he felt that they were not ready for it because what he had in mind was "hard to be explained." (Hebrews 5:10, 11) Instead, he reminded them: "You have become such as need milk, not solid food. For everyone that partakes of milk is unacquainted with the word of righteousness, for he is a babe. But solid food belongs to mature people, to those who through use have their perceptive powers trained to distinguish both right and wrong."—Hebrews 5:12-14; compare Jude 3.

¹¹ Does this mean, then, that maturity is just a matter of having knowledge of the deeper things of the Bible? While Christian maturity includes knowledge and understanding of the Bible, there is much more to it. An understanding of the words used by the apostle Paul will help us see the matter more clearly. The Greek word translated "maturity" is *te·lei·o'tes,* and the adjective "mature" is translated from *te'lei·os.* These words are related to *te'los,* which means "end." W. E. Vine's *Expository Dictionary of New Testament Words,* therefore, explains that being mature (*te'lei·os*) "signifies having reached its end (*te'los*), finished, complete, perfect." Thus,

a mature Christian is one who has reached a certain end, or goal. What is this goal?

¹² The apostle Paul, in Ephesians 4:11-13, explained that Christ Jesus, as the head of the Christian congregation, has made many provisions to help the "holy ones" to reach that goal, namely, that "we all attain to the oneness in the faith and in the accurate knowledge of the Son of God, to a full-grown man, to the measure of stature that belongs to the fullness of the Christ." Here, being mature, or full-grown (Greek, *te'lei·os*), is related not only to having "accurate knowledge" but also to "oneness in the faith" and to measuring ourselves according to the stature attained by Christ.

¹³ "Oneness in the faith" signifies unity. Before a person comes to learn of the "one faith," he may have his own ideas and opinions about how things should be done, about what is right and what is wrong, and so on. (Ephesians 4:4, 5.) If he allows such ideas to persist, he will find it very difficult to grow spiritually. Paul once called the Christians in the ancient Corinthian congregation "babes in Christ" and "fleshly" because they were torn by "jealousy and strife," some claiming to follow Paul, others Apollos. (1 Corinthians 3:1-4) It can easily be seen, therefore, that unity, or "oneness in the faith," goes hand in hand with Christian maturity. There cannot be one without the other. So we must ask ourselves: Have we abandoned our former worldly ways of thinking? Do we see the importance of unity in thought and action with Jehovah's people? "Oneness in the faith" is an indispensable ingredient of Christian maturity.—Ephesians 4:2, 3.

---

10. Why did Paul urge the Hebrew Christians to "press on to maturity"?
11. What does being mature signify?

12. According to Ephesians 4:11-13, what does maturity involve?
13. Why can there be no Christian maturity without "oneness in the faith"?

Many today choose the ministry above materialistic pursuits

[14] Christian maturity is also related to having "the measure of stature that belongs to the fullness of the Christ." What does this mean? Paul goes on to say that those who reach this stature are no longer babes, "tossed about as by waves and carried hither and thither by every wind of teaching by means of the trickery of men" who cunningly contrive error. Rather, they have an accurate knowledge of the truth. They have grown up in the love of the Christ, and they show forth other godly qualities, such as wisdom, righteousness, and power. (Ephesians 4:13, 14; John 15: 12, 13; 1 Corinthians 1:24, 30; 2:7, 8; Proverbs 8:1, 22-31) While we, as imperfect humans, may not be able to attain completely to the 'stature of the Christ,' we can certainly make him our Exemplar, setting for ourselves the end, or goal, of developing the same kind of godly personality. (Colossians 3:9) To the extent that we reach out for this goal we become mature.

14. To what else is maturity related?

Grow Up by Love

[15] Having considered the meaning embodied in the term "Christian maturity," we need to know how we can attain it. As we have seen, Hebrews 6:1 shows that in the quest for Christian maturity there is a certain foundation on which we must build. Once this is done, further efforts can be directed toward pressing on to maturity. First among the various elements making up that foundation is "repentance from dead works."

[16] Obviously, "dead works" would include works of the fallen flesh, which, if unchecked, will lead to death. We readily come to recognize outright transgressions such as fornication, uncleanness, loose conduct, idolatry, and spiritism as sinful, and we shun them. But the works of the flesh, "dead works," also include what some might call personality traits such as enmities, strife, jealousy, fits of anger, contentions, divisions, sects, and envies. (Galatians 5:19-21) Unless such personality traits are stripped off and replaced by "the new personality which was created according to God's will in true righteousness and loyalty," it is very unlikely that one will make any headway toward attaining Christian maturity.—Ephesians 4: 22-24.

[17] Besides the works of the flesh, the "dead works" of which we must divest ourselves also include works and pursuits that are *spiritually* dead, vain, and fruitless. They may be money-making, get-rich-quick schemes. They may be ambitious and time-consuming plans for advanced education, or they may be worldly movements for social reform, peace, and so on. All these things may appear to have

15. What is the first step in the quest for maturity?
16. From what "dead works" must we repent?
17. What else can be considered "dead works"? Why?

some merit in themselves, but they are "dead works" because they may spell spiritual death for those who become entangled in them. All those who are interested in attaining Christian maturity must 'repent from' or desist from pursuing, such "dead works" and follow Jesus' admonition to "keep on, then, seeking first the kingdom and [God's] righteousness."
—Matthew 6:33.

18 Once the foundation is built upon, what then? Paul advises: "But speaking the truth, let us by love grow up in all things into him who is the head, Christ." (Ephesians 4:15) First of all, we note that Paul mentions the need for "speaking the truth." This expression evidently involves much more than just speech; it actually means "maintaining truth." (*Kingdom Interlinear*) Other translations render it as "live by the truth"; "lovingly follow the truth at all times—speaking truly, dealing truly, living truly".—Ephesians 4:15, *The Jerusalem Bible; The Living Bible.*

19 Thus, the pursuit of Christian maturity requires that we maintain, or uphold, the truth by the way we live, speak, act, and deal with others. This means putting to use in our everyday affairs the Bible knowledge we have gained and thus come to be among "those who through use have their perceptive powers trained to distinguish both right and wrong." (Hebrews 5:14) Are you doing this? Do you reason along the lines of Bible principles each time you are faced with a decision? Do you accept the challenge of becoming a mature Christian, upholding the truth by word and deed, or would you rather remain a spiritual babe, free from responsibilities and free to pursue your own desires and wishes?

18, 19. (a) In Ephesians 4:15, what is meant by "speaking the truth"? (b) How is it related to Christian maturity?

20 Paul says: "Let us by love grow up in all things into him who is the head, Christ." (Ephesians 4:15) Here, Paul points to the heart of the matter—the motivation. At 1 Corinthians 13:1-3 he shows that works that might otherwise be of value become totally profitless if they are done without the proper motivation. Thus we must examine our motive for everything that we do. Is it done to be viewed by others, to impress them so that they will think we are mature? Or, rather, is it done out of love for God and love for our neighbor? When love is our motive, we will "grow up in all things," becoming balanced, dependable, mature Christians, in full recognition of "him who is the head, Christ."

21 While striving to reach Christian maturity is a worthwhile goal, it is not the end. Once a person has reached this goal, is there something more for him to do? What about those who have been in the truth for a number of years and have attained the goal of Christian maturity? This we will consider in the next article.

20, 21. (a) How is love involved in growing to maturity? (b) What questions await further discussion?

Can You Explain?

□ What are some "traits of a babe," and what dangers do they pose?

□ How are "oneness in the faith" and "fullness of the Christ" related to maturity?

□ To reach Christian maturity, what "dead works" must we abandon?

□ How does one "by love grow up"?

"Go On Walking Orderly in This Same Routine"

WHEN Alisa was little more than two years old, she delighted everyone by being able to sing through the names of all the 66 books of the Bible, recite the names of the 12 apostles, and describe by gestures the nine fruits of God's spirit. (Matthew 10:2-4; Galatians 5:22, 23) By the time she was in the fifth grade at school, she was conducting a weekly Bible study with a girl in the third grade, who, in turn, was able to get her older brother interested in the Bible. Alisa and her little companion have set a goal for themselves. They look forward to being partners in full-time preaching work as special pioneers in due time.

2 Surely, it would be a delight for any one of us to know children such as these, and very likely you do. At the same time, however, we cannot help but wonder: What will they turn out to be when they grow up? Will they continue their spiritual development until they reach their goal? Or will they be distracted by other things and fall by the wayside?

Continued Advancement

3 Obviously such youngsters need a great deal of spiritual development before they reach their goal. But is it only the young or the new ones that need to make advancement? In fact, is advancement necessary only until one reaches spiritual maturity or becomes qualified for a certain privilege? Not so. Consider the apostle Paul. Rather than being satisfied with what he had achieved, he said in his letter to the Philippians: "Not that I have already received it or am already made perfect, but I am pursuing to see if I may also lay hold on that for which I have also been laid hold on by Christ Jesus."—Philippians 3:12.

4 Clearly, Paul was not talking about attaining maturity, for there was no question but that he already was a mature Christian. Yet he said he was "pursuing" something that he had not yet "received." What was it? Paul went on to explain: "I am pursuing down toward the goal for the prize of the upward call of God by means of Christ Jesus." (Philippians 3:14) The goal he was pursuing was not just Christian maturity or qualification for a certain position, but it was something greater. For him and his fellow anointed Christians, it was "the upward call," the hope of heavenly life through a resurrection.

1, 2. (a) How are exemplary youths a source of encouragement? (b) Yet, what questions about them come to mind?
3. Who need to make advancement?

4. What "goal" was the apostle Paul pursuing?

⁵ This helps us to see the reason for continuing to grow and develop spiritually no matter how long we have been in the truth. If a person made advancement only to the point of being considered mature, or only to the point of qualifying for some special privilege, what lasting benefit would there be for him? Maturity and special privileges are no guarantee that we will reach our final goal—everlasting life. Instead, we must do as the apostle Paul did: 'Forget the things behind and stretch forward to the things ahead.' (Philippians 3:13) Not only should we leave behind the unprofitable things we may have done before coming to a knowledge of the truth but we should also be careful not to become self-satisfied with what we have done since that time. In other words, the advice is not to rest on one's laurels but to press forward without letup. Are you doing this, or are you, for one reason or another, slowing down?—See 1 Corinthians 9:26.

⁶ With this possibility in mind, Paul continued: "Let us, then, as many of us as are mature, be of this mental attitude; and if you are mentally inclined otherwise in any respect, God will reveal the above attitude to you." (Philippians 3:15) Earlier, in verse 12, Paul indicated that he did not consider himself as "already made perfect." Yet here he said "as many of us as are mature," or, "perfect ones." (*Kingdom Interlinear*) This is not a contradiction. Rather, it only makes the point that even mature Christians such as Paul must bear in mind that they have not yet reached the ultimate goal, and they must continue to make advancement in order to reach it. That is why he summed it up this way: "At

Alisa and her Bible student have the full-time ministry as their goal

any rate, to what extent we have made progress, let us go on walking orderly in this same routine."—Philippians 3:16.

Orderly Routine

⁷ When Paul encouraged Christians to "go on walking orderly in this same routine," was he telling them to work out a comfortable pattern of activity and stay put until the time came for them to receive their reward? To do so would be doing like the slave in Jesus' illustration who buried the one talent his master had given him and simply waited for the master's return. (Matthew 25:14-30) Even

5. (a) Why is continuous growth essential? (b) What may "forgetting the things behind" include?
6. Comparing Philippians 3:12 with 3:15, what can be said about making advancement?

7. What "routine" was Paul urging Christians to follow?

though the slave did not lose the talent or quit his service, he was called "good-for-nothing" and rejected by the master. Surely Paul was not telling us just to hold on to what we have for fear that we might lose it. He was speaking about making progress. By "routine" Paul evidently had in mind a set course of forward movement, something like that of a soldier who is not standing at attention but is marching forward.

⁸ Paul's advice should help us to recognize the importance of putting forth continuous and strenuous effort to advance, improve, and better ourselves in Jehovah's service. "To what extent we have made progress," whether elders, ministerial servants, pioneers, or publishers, our chief concern should be to improve the quality and, if possible, the quantity of our service. We must be careful not to fall into the same frame of mind as the delinquent Israelites of Malachi's day who thought they were getting away with offering inferior sacrifices to Jehovah. But how did Jehovah feel about it? "Yes, you have brought it [the lame and sick offering] as a gift," he said. Then he added: "Can I take pleasure in it at your hand?"—Malachi 1:13.

⁹ To the contrary, we should take our service to God seriously. As Paul reminded the Romans, whatever privilege of service we may be given, we should be 'at it,' "in real earnest" and not 'loiter at our business.' (Romans 12:6-8, 11) To loiter is to hang around aimlessly, with no forward movement toward any specific goal. Interestingly, the Greek word used here literally means "slothful," a most fitting description. A report shows that, though capable of rapid movement, over a period of

168 hours, one sloth slept or remained completely motionless for 139 hours —83 percent of the time. No wonder we are admonished not to be "slothful" but to "be aglow with the spirit" and "slave for Jehovah"! What can help us to do this?

¹⁰ At 1 Timothy 4:12-16 the apostle Paul spelled out in detail the things Timothy should do so that his advancement might "be manifest to all persons." At the time, the disciple Timothy was neither a youngster nor a novice. In fact, by then he had worked closely with Paul for more than ten years and had considerable responsibility and authority entrusted to him in the Christian congregation, no doubt because of the advancement he already had made up to that point. Yet, Paul still gave Timothy such counsel. Clearly, it behooves all of us to pay close attention to what Paul had to say.

Become an example in speech and conduct

¹¹ First, in verse 12, Paul said: "Let no man ever look down on your youth. On the contrary, become an example to the faithful ones in speaking, in conduct, in love, in faith, in chasteness." This list reminds us of "the fruitage of the spirit," which Paul detailed at Galatians 5:22, 23. Who can deny that every one of us needs to produce this fruitage to a greater extent in our lives? Most of us put forth a great deal of effort to *learn* and *memorize* the nine fruits of the spirit, and to teach the

---

8. With what should we concern ourselves regarding our service to God?
9. How is Paul's counsel at Romans 12:6-8, 11 related to making advancement?

10. Why should we be keenly interested in Paul's counsel to Timothy at 1 Timothy 4:12-16?
11, 12. (a) What is the first area we should give attention to in making advancement? (b) Why is it more important than advancement in knowledge or skill?

young and the new ones to do the same. But do we put forth at least that much effort to *cultivate* them? Paul made the point that those who are mature should be exemplary in these matters. Surely, this is one area in our lives where all of us can easily make advancement.

12 In one sense, perhaps, these qualities are even more of an indicator of our spiritual progress than knowledge and skills are, because the former are products of God's spirit, whereas the latter are often related to one's natural abilities and education. The scribes and the Pharisees of Jesus' day were well versed in the Scriptures, and they were scrupulous in observing the intricate details of the Law. Yet, Jesus condemned them, saying: "Woe to you, scribes and Pharisees, hypocrites! because you give the tenth of the mint and the dill and the cumin, but you have disregarded the weightier matters of the Law, namely, justice and mercy and faithfulness." (Matthew 23:23) How important it is for us to continue to make advancement in cultivating these "weightier matters" in our lives!

Application to reading, exhortation, and teaching

13 Next, Paul admonished Timothy to "continue applying [himself] to public reading, to exhortation, to teaching." (1 Timothy 4:13) Elsewhere in his letters, Paul spoke highly of Timothy as an able and faithful minister. (Philippians 2:20-22; 2 Timothy 1:4, 5) Yet he advised Timothy to continue giving attention to

these essential responsibilities of an overseer. If you are an appointed overseer in the congregation, do you "continue applying yourself" to these matters? For example, do you take seriously the suggestions offered in the *Theocratic Ministry School Guidebook* and work on your deficiencies, or do you feel that this counsel is only for the beginners? Do you study the Bible and the Society's publications carefully so that you can "exhort, with all long-suffering and art of teaching"?—2 Timothy 4:2; Titus 1:9.

Do not neglect the gift of service

14 While only a few are appointed to teach in the congregation, all Christians are commissioned by Jesus Christ to share in the Kingdom witnessing and the disciple-making work. (Matthew 24:14; 28:19, 20) This involves teaching honesthearted ones the Bible truth, exhorting them to make changes in their lives and to take their stand on Jehovah's side. Do you "continue applying yourself" to improve your ministerial skills? Do you conscientiously make use of the suggestions offered in *Our Kingdom Ministry* and the weekly Service Meeting so as to 'do the work of an evangelizer, fully accomplishing your ministry'?—2 Timothy 4:5.

15 Previously, Paul had given Timothy this reminder: "Do not be neglecting the gift in you that was given you through a prediction and when the body of older men laid their hands upon you." (1 Timothy

---

13. How can appointed overseers benefit from Paul's counsel at 1 Timothy 4:13?

14. How can we show advancement in our field ministry?
15. What was Timothy's "gift," and what about today?

4:14) Apparently, through the operation of the holy spirit, Timothy had been designated for and subsequently appointed to some special service in the Christian congregation. (1 Timothy 1:18; 2 Timothy 1:6) Similarly, today there are many in the organization who have cultivated God-given abilities, resulting in their being appointed as traveling overseers, missionaries, regular or special pioneers, elders, and so on. Even though no special prediction or laying on of hands is involved, the counsel "do not be neglecting the gift in you" applies with similar force.

[16] To neglect something, according to the dictionary, means to give little attention to it or to leave it undone through carelessness. When something becomes commonplace, it is easy to neglect it. This could happen if we stop making progress, or advancement, but take our assignments for granted. Therefore, we can profit from what Paul said at Colossians 3:23, 24: "Whatever you are doing, work at it whole-souled as to Jehovah, and not to men, for you know that it is from Jehovah you will receive the due reward of the inheritance. Slave for the Master, Christ."

Continuous Effort Brings Blessings

[17] When we give close attention to the matters discussed above, we can be assured that we will not fall into the trap of complacency or self-satisfaction. "Ponder over these things; be absorbed in them, that your advancement may be manifest to all persons," said Paul. (1 Timothy 4:15) The "advancement," of course, is not for the purpose of showing off or impressing others. When we, young and old, grow and develop spiritually, we bring joy and

encouragement to all who associate with us, as did young Alisa and her companion, mentioned earlier in this article.

[18] A double blessing awaits us if we apply Paul's counsel diligently. "Pay constant attention to yourself and to your teaching," said Paul. "Stay by these things, for by doing this you will save both yourself and those who listen to you." (1 Timothy 4:16) Yes, by constantly examining ourselves as to whether we are doing what we teach others to do, that is, to advance, grow, and develop spiritually, we will avoid the tragedy of 'becoming disapproved somehow.' (1 Corinthians 9:27) Rather, the happy prospect of life in God's promised New Order is assured for us and for those whom we have the joyful privilege to help. Thus, for our blessing and for the blessing of others, and for the praise of Jehovah God: "Go on walking orderly in this same routine"!—Philippians 3:16.

18. What double blessing awaits us if we apply Paul's counsel diligently?

Do You Remember?

□ What is the ultimate "goal" we should have in mind? How do we pursue it? (Philippians 3:12, 13)

□ What is the "routine" in which we should walk? (Philippians 3:16)

□ Why must we continue to improve in Christian conduct and speech? (1 Timothy 4:12)

□ How can elders, ministerial servants, and others make advancement in their teaching skill? (1 Timothy 4:13)

□ What must we do not to neglect "the gift" entrusted to us? (1 Timothy 4:14)

16. What can prevent us from neglecting our "gift"?
17. How only will we see the result of our efforts?

Welcome to the 1985 "Integrity Keepers" Convention!

JEHOVAH'S WITNESSES are well known not only for their zealous house-to-house ministry but also for their large Christian conventions. These have been featured for more than a hundred years now, going back all the way to 1879. There is good Scriptural precedent for these conventions.

Three times each year the Israelites were required to come together for their festivals. Jehovah considered these so important that he repeatedly had Moses stress them in the Pentateuch. See Exodus 23:14-17; 34:22-24; Leviticus 23:4-22; Numbers 28:16–29:12; Deuteronomy 16:1-16. We also read that Jesus' parents regularly went up to Jerusalem for the Passover festival.—Luke 2:41, 42.

For 38 years now, assemblies of Jehovah's Witnesses have been following a pattern similar to that in ancient Israel. Twice each year we rejoice to come together for our circuit assemblies, involving anywhere from 8 to 20 congregations. Then we look forward eagerly to assembling once each year for our district, national, or international conventions. Do we appreciate these gatherings as much as we should? Not all our brothers throughout the earth have this blessing. Thus a recent report from a Balkan country where the work has long been under restrictions tells that "for the first time we could hold a district convention in a public hall . . . The brothers were very happy about it."

They had reason to be happy, for it does seem that the greater the number of Witnesses that come together, the greater the happiness. One country reported in 1983 that "the 'Kingdom Unity' convention in December was indeed the highlight of the year," and another described it as "the high point of the year." It is no wonder that most of Jehovah's Witnesses make plans, often at great self-sacrifice, to attend district conventions all three and a half days.

Last year we were privileged to attend "Kingdom Increase" conventions. The program told how fitting that theme was in view of the great increases in Kingdom publishers worldwide. Further, it stressed the obligations of each individual Witness in connection with that increase. And what fine instruments we received for our ministry —the Reference Edition of the *New World Translation of the Holy Scriptures,* the Bible study aid *Survival Into a New Earth,* and the brochure *The Divine Name That Will Endure Forever!* This year another treat is in store! We rejoice to assemble in the "Integrity Keepers" convention. This theme calls attention to the importance of our sharing in the vindication of Jehovah's name by keeping integrity through to the end of Satan's system.

How important that theme is! It is bound up with the most important issue facing all intelligent creatures, namely, the rightfulness of Jehovah's sovereignty, as upheld by creatures keeping their integrity in spite of all that Satan the Devil can do. It is not easy to be an integrity keeper in these "critical times hard to deal with." (2 Timothy 3:1-5) It is the very opposite of following the line of least resistance. It means 'going through the narrow gate and walking on the cramped road that leads to life.'—Matthew 7:13, 14.

Keeping integrity as ministers of Jehovah God involves two basic requirements. On the one hand there is the need to bring forth the fruitage of the spirit so that we may "adorn the teaching of our Savior, God, in all things." (Titus 2:10) On the other hand we have the commission to preach and to make disciples, as we share in fulfilling Bible prophecy.—Matthew 24:14; 28:19, 20.

To meet these two requirements, we need to keep on seeking first the Kingdom and God's righteousness. We must fight against all the machinations of Satan the Devil, all the temptations that this old world puts in our way in the form of materialism and pleasure seeking, and we must do as Paul did, 'pummel our bodies and lead them about like slaves.' (1 Corinthians 9:27; 1 Peter 5:8; 1 John 2:15-17) Successfully overcoming threats to our integrity is no easy matter.

If we appreciate fully the challenge of keeping our integrity, we will come to the convention 'conscious of our spiritual need.' (Matthew 5:3) We will pay close attention to what is said from the platform, take notes, join heartily in the singing, and enter into the spirit of the prayers offered. Also, we will listen carefully to the counsel given on keeping our integrity toward Jehovah God, toward our marriage mates, and toward our fellow Christians. By talks, interviews, demonstrations, and dramas we will be encouraged and equipped to be more determined than ever to keep integrity down to the end of this old, wicked system of things.

Nor would we want to overlook the fact that our large gatherings serve as a witness to the world. This past January the "King-dom Increase" convention was held at the River Plate Stadium, Buenos Aires, Argentina, for four days. It made big news! The local news publication *Ahora* presented a fine color-illustrated report on the convention, with the banner headline, "Faith Fills Stadiums."

Under a large heading, "A Kingdom That Is Growing—That of Jehovah's Witnesses," a two-page article said in part: "Certainly incredible. Seeing is believing. Faith moves mountains. It has to be faith that motivated an average of 42,000 persons silently and with admirable order to fill the football stands of the River Plate Stadium during four days of this torrid summer. It has to be faith, also, that was able to assemble no fewer than 46,000 faithful without distinction of sex, age, culture, race, or nationality for the last day of the district convention of Jehovah's Witnesses. . . . Whether or not we share their ideas and doctrines, this entire multitude deserves our greatest respect. They show themselves to be humble, far removed from the trivial things of daily life and the modern world it is our lot to share; they make a dogma of peace and love among the brothers."

The article went on to say: "What about their organization? All was perfect. The police detailed there were bored as they had nothing to do . . . Not so much as a minor incident, provocation, or disorder occurred in the four days. . . . We are left with an immeasurable peace that the Witnesses appear to have . . . Wrong or not, they won our respect. What moves them? That faith. That faith that moves mountains."

There is no question that, by our conducting ourselves as Christian ministers of Jehovah God, we can provide a fine witness to outsiders. True it is, being a Christian never was easy. Jesus said it meant taking up a torture stake. Doing justice to our "Integrity Keepers" convention will help us to be fine followers of Jesus Christ.—Matthew 16:24.

The Preparer of the Way Is Born

ELIZABETH is almost ready to have her baby. For these past three months Mary has been staying with her. But now it is time for Mary to say good-bye and to make the long trip back home to Nazareth. In about six months she, too, will have a baby.

Soon after Mary leaves, Elizabeth gives birth. What joy there is when the birth is successful and Elizabeth and the baby are all right! When Elizabeth shows the little one to her neighbors and relatives, they all rejoice with her.

The eighth day after his birth, according to God's law, a baby boy in Israel must be circumcised. For this occasion friends and relatives come to visit. They say that the boy should be named after his father, Zechariah. But Elizabeth speaks up. 'No!' she says. 'He is to be called John.' Remember, that is the name the angel Gabriel said should be given to the child.

However, their friends protest: 'There is no one among your relatives with that name.' Then, using sign language, they ask what his father wants to name the boy. Asking for a writing tablet, Zechariah, to the astonishment of all, writes: 'His name is John.'

With that Zechariah's speech is miraculously restored. You will recall that he lost his ability to speak when he did not believe the angel's announcement that Elizabeth would have a child. Well, when Zechariah speaks, all those living in the neighborhood are amazed and say to themselves: 'What really will this child become?'

Zechariah is now filled with holy spirit, and he foretells regarding his son: 'He will be called a prophet of the Most High, and he will go ahead of Jehovah and prepare the way for him. He will tell the people that they must be saved by having their sins forgiven.'

By this time Mary, who evidently is still an unmarried woman, has arrived home in Nazareth. What will happen to her when it becomes obvious that she is pregnant? **Luke 1:56-80; Leviticus 12:2, 3.**

♦ How much older was John than Jesus?

♦ What things happened when John was eight days old?

♦ What work was John foretold to do?

Kingdom Proclaimers Report

Witnessing at School

"DO YOUR utmost to present yourself approved to God, a workman with nothing to be ashamed of, handling the word of the truth aright," wrote the apostle Paul to the young man Timothy. (2 Timothy 2:15) Many children of Jehovah's Witnesses have opportunity to give a witness about the good news of God's Kingdom at school. They are not ashamed to do so and are appreciated for it by many of the other students.

□ An example of this comes from Martinique. A young girl who is known in school as one of Jehovah's Witnesses was often asked her opinion on religious subjects by her teacher.

She had had several conversations with this teacher, and the teacher accepted some of the Watch Tower literature.

One day a discussion came up in class about the overpopulation of the earth. In discussing how to stop overcrowding the earth, contraception and abortion were mentioned. Some students were for abortion and some against it. The teacher asked the young sister for her opinion. She said that she would be pleased to give a complete explanation the next day. That night she prepared, and the next day brought to school some *Awake!* magazines that dealt Scripturally with the subject of abortion. After reading the material, she asked the class questions, and at the end of the discussion "all in the class expressed themselves against abortion," she said. Some students subscribed to the *Awake!* magazine.

□ Another experience comes from Sweden where the brothers have often been invited to give lectures in schools. One special-pioneer minister of Jehovah's Witnesses had been invited to give several lectures in a class. The teacher said: "We have had other pastors here, but they just play the guitar and tell the students to be good. That is all right," said the teacher, "but I want my students to learn something too." Then he made arrangements to have the Witness come and conduct a regular Bible study with the class.

Students in the classroom, as well as people everywhere in the world today, have many questions about world conditions or family and social problems that they want answered. What a privilege for Jehovah's Witnesses who are still in school to apply themselves diligently in personal study and at congregation meetings, so as to get an understanding of the Bible and help such ones to learn the Bible's answers! The Biblical proverb counsels: "Do not hold back good from those to whom it is owing, when it happens to be in the power of your hand to do it."—Proverbs 3:27.

Single and Happy as a Pioneer

As told by Margaret Stephenson

MOMBASA, East Africa, 1958. The tropical heat bore down, covering everything with a shimmering haze. Flies buzzed irritatingly around me. Under the tin roof of the customs shed at the harbour, the temperature was nearing 40 degrees Celsius (104° F.). As I waited patiently, the perspiration rolled down my cheeks. The humidity hung over us like a steamy blanket, and the air—dank and stuffy—was almost too thick to breathe. Was all of Kenya going to be like this?

I began to wonder whether this was a good place for a single woman. I had seen pictures of vast rolling plains filled with game, lush forests, even snowcapped mountains, but here . . . "Oh, what have I done?" I asked myself. "What have I let myself into?"

It was all so very different from Ottawa, Canada, where I had been living. The trip by sea had taken five weeks. Ten thousand miles just to get here! Would there be anyone to meet me? I did not know whether there were any Jehovah's Witnesses in Mombasa, so you can imagine my surprise and relief to see a group of smiling faces. It was so heartening! And what a warm welcome!

The first meeting that very night also did much to allay my fears about this land so new and strange to me. Just two families—how appreciative and encouraged they were to hear experiences and to have some company. There is such a great work to be done here, I thought. How could I possibly leave these few brave people to do

it all by themselves? That first night helped me greatly to be determined to stay and help as long as I could.

Answering the Call

"Step over into Macedonia!" was the invitation extended by the speaker almost 18 months earlier at the 1957 assembly of Jehovah's Witnesses in Seattle, Washington, U.S.A. We had all been asked to consider seriously whether our personal circumstances would permit us to answer the call for more workers in the field, helping as preachers of the good news of the Kingdom even in foreign lands. I thought to myself: 'Is there really anything holding me back? Is there any reason why I cannot make myself available?

I am single with no one to support. I have always been a person who likes to do things with a whole heart, and here is a direct request from Jehovah that I should respond to.' Hurriedly, I started to write down all the places the speaker designated as modern "Macedonias," in memory of the place of great need to which the holy spirit invited the apostle Paul in the first century.—Acts 16:9, 10.

You may wonder what makes a somewhat fragile woman over 50 years of age take courage and strike out on her own to a distant part of the globe. Adventure? No, not at all; I am definitely not the adventurous type. Perhaps it was the influence of elderly Sister Bartlett, who so patiently and lovingly taught me the truth up to my baptism in 1954. She was always encouraging the full-time service, stressing its joys and blessings. But what changes that would mean for me! My father had already shown deep respect for the Bible and *The Watchtower,* but he had never come to the point of taking a clear stand for Bible truths. I, too, hesitated for a while. For two and a half years Sister Bartlett had tried to encourage me to take part in the house-to-house preaching work. I understood why this work was necessary, but I was terrified. Finally, after covering four large study books and

---

In Our Next Issue

- **True Friends
  —How to Find Them**

- **"You Are the
  Salt of the Earth"**

- **Bible Truth Triumphs
  Amid Tradition**

---

while I was still offering lame excuses, she urged me into magazine street work. "If you've any pride left," she said, "that will get rid of it." How marvelously Jehovah supplies to all of us the power we need to accomplish his will!—Philippians 4:13.

As I look back now, I am so grateful that the pioneer work and its rewards were always set before me as a goal. Having tasted and seen that the ministry was indeed a truly satisfying work, in 1956 I decided to do it full time as a pioneer. Since I was due to retire from my work the following year, I decided: 'Why not do it now, straight away?' So I did—and loved it. "Should I apply for Gilead missionary school?" I asked a mature couple. "No," came their reply, "you are too old!" "Well, then, should I apply to work at the Society's headquarters?" Again came the reply, "You're too old, Margaret!" 'Oh, well,' I thought, 'I'll just have to serve where the need is greater.' Wisely they encouraged a move within Canada first to see how I could adapt and get along with changes before trying another country.

After receiving an assignment, I packed up and travelled the 2,500 miles (4,000 km) from Vancouver right across Canada to Ottawa. There I met Aubrey and Eunice Clarke, just assigned from Gilead School and going to Kenya. They were positive and kindly offered to write and provide all the information they thought would be helpful to me. After a number of letters filled with practical advice, encouragement, suggestions, and warnings, and many other things that would help me in deciding whether I could make it, I was off.

Was I scared? Oh, no! . . . not until the moment I arrived in Mombasa. But the warmth that the local brothers showed, and the efforts they all put forth to make me feel welcome and wanted, soon helped me to settle in. After only two days at the coast, I travelled up to the capital, Nairobi, 300 miles (480 km) inland.

An Enlarged Field

At first, our witnessing was mostly informal and only among Europeans, as our work had not yet been legally recognized in Kenya. Under these circumstances, the challenge was great indeed. We had so many people to reach with the good news and few people to do it! Still, a foundation was being laid for greater expansion. What a happy day it was in 1962 when total recognition and acceptance as a Bible association was granted! With this new freedom, we could go from house to house and witness to the local African people.

So we started, armed with great excitement and rather limited, memorized Swahili sermons. The reaction really gave us a thrill. Many new Bible studies were started, and the people were so pleased to learn! But the conditions were very different from what I had been used to, and I remember thinking, 'Oh, how people need the life-giving message of the truth!'

The hospitality of the people especially was an endearing quality. How many cups of tea we drank I cannot remember. And now and then in the midst of it all a spark of interest would be kindled, and the appreciation the new ones showed for the truth was a great stimulus to all of us to stick with our work.

Lonely?

Was I lonely as a single person so far from home? Not really. There were so many friends and such a lot of work! We did things together, visited one another, and kept busy. There have been opportunities for marriage in my life, but I just never got around to it. Instead, I was able to use the extra freedom and mobility that singleness affords to keep busy in the ministry, and this has brought me great

'The reaction to our Swahili sermons gave us a thrill'

happiness. Admittedly, when making return visits on interested families, I used to think, 'Well, I suppose a husband would have his uses!' Since certain families kindly included me in things they would do, I was rarely on my own. Here in Kenya I have a spiritual family made up of about 15 different ones I have been privileged to help along to dedication and baptism. Even now, as I look at the congregation, I see that one of these individuals and her five children are publishing the good news too. Surely, this is what makes all the sacrifice and effort worth while. These new ones, along with my dear spiritual brothers and sisters, have so filled my life that there is always something to do and not too much time for loneliness.

Work Banned! Stay or Leave?

What a shock! Like a bolt out of the blue, one morning we awoke to a total ban on our work. No preaching, no large gatherings, missionaries soon to be expelled, and literature proscribed. The future looked quite uncertain. What was I to do? I went to see a brother in the Watch Tower Society's branch office. He himself was packing to leave. "Should I go or should I stay?" I asked. He replied: "If you can, you had better stay. You might still be able to help." 'Well,' I thought, 'I have come to serve the people and to preach the good news as best I can, and for me this is still possible.' So I stayed. But what a loss I felt as I waved good-bye to the missionaries at the airport! So many fine friends and associates gone, and all at once! I missed them greatly and still do.

When I look back, how thankful I am that I had taken the initiative to make friends and build up relationships with the local brothers and others who remained! Had I not done this, I would have been totally on my own. Together, we weathered the storm. And how thrilled and relieved we were when, just a few months later, matters were cleared up, the ban was cancelled, and our work was legally recognized again!

Slowly, more help arrived. How that gave all of us and the work a boost! What a joy to see how the work has progressed! When I first arrived in Kenya, there were only about 30 brothers and interested ones struggling to bring the light of truth to the people. Now we have some 3,000 Kingdom publishers and well over 4,000 Bible studies in the country. I used to know everyone at our small assemblies. But as I look at large, colourful, and packed grandstands these days, that is impossible. I remember, too, the first little branch office. Now, instead of a small two-room office, we have a fine new branch office and printing facilities.

Jehovah's Sustaining Power Always Evident

Not too long ago my eyes began troubling me, requiring some rather costly operations. This would have put quite a strain on my already dwindling resources. Here again, I had to decide whether to return to Canada or to try to stay in my pioneer assignment. I made this problem a matter of prayer. So you can imagine my excitement when I heard the news that the Canadian government was just changing the laws to allow pensions to be paid to citizens even though they were not residing in Canada. Jehovah had shown me the way out, and I was thrilled, for I had made Kenya my home and really wanted to stay.

Over the years my relationship with Jehovah has deepened. As a single woman in an African country, I have seen him as a Protector. He sustains us, too, for at 77 I am still pioneering and have now been doing so for the past 27 years. I have also learned to stick with what is right when problems arise. Eventually, things always change; they do not remain the same forever. And then how glad you are that you remained faithful! As for me, well, just as long as I can, I hope to continue serving Jehovah as a happy pioneer.

"**Happy is the one who has the God of Jacob for his help,**
Whose hope is in Jehovah his God,
The Maker of heaven and earth,
Of the sea, and of all that is in them,
The One keeping trueness to time indefinite."
—PSALM 146:5, 6.

Insight From the Two Books of Kings

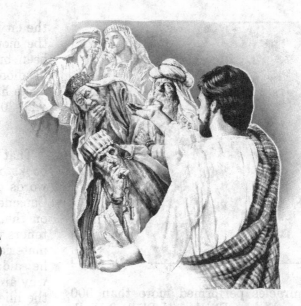

ON ONE occasion when Jesus was speaking in his hometown of Nazareth, he said something that provoked a surprisingly strong reaction. The inhabitants of Nazareth seemingly were wondering why he had not performed as many miracles there as he had in other towns. In telling them why, Jesus used two Scriptural examples. Here is what he said:

"Truly I tell you that no prophet is accepted in his home territory. For instance, I tell you in truth, There were many widows in Israel in the days of Elijah, when the heaven was shut up three years and six months, so that a great famine fell upon all the land, yet Elijah was sent to none of those women, but only to Zarephath in the land of Sidon to a widow. Also, there were many lepers in Israel in the time of Elisha the prophet, yet not one of them was cleansed, but Naaman the man of Syria." (Luke 4: 24-27) At these words, those listening became filled with anger and tried to kill Jesus. Why did they respond so violently?

To find the answer, we have to look back into the Hebrew Scriptures and read the histories of Elijah and Elisha. The first-century Christians were thoroughly familiar with these books, and so were their Jewish listeners. On numerous occasions Christian Bible writers referred to events and personalities in these earlier books to illustrate a point, as Jesus did here. These references were instantly recognized and understood by the listeners. If we are to get the full point of Jesus' teachings, we need to recognize those references too.

The truth is, it is impossible to understand the Christian Greek Scriptures fully unless we are familiar with the Hebrew Scriptures. The histories of the prophets Jesus referred to, Elijah and Elisha, are recorded in the two books of Kings. Let us consider these two books to illustrate this point and see how a knowledge of them gives us a deeper and more vivid understanding of the Christian Greek Scriptures.

An Unfavorable Comparison

First of all, why were the inhabitants of Nazareth so upset when Jesus referred to

two miracles performed more than 900 years earlier by Elijah and Elisha? Well, Jesus was clearly comparing the Nazarenes with the Israelites of the northern kingdom of Israel during the days of Elijah and Elisha, and according to the two books of Kings, Israel was not in a good spiritual condition at that time. The Israelites had gone right over to Baal worship and were persecuting the prophets of Jehovah. Elijah was actually fleeing from his own countrymen when a widow in Zarephath, in a foreign country, took him in and fed him. That was when he performed the miracle Jesus referred to. (1 Kings 17:17-24) Israel was still riddled with Baal worship when Elisha healed the Syrian army chief Naaman of his leprosy. —2 Kings 5:8-14.

The inhabitants of Nazareth did not appreciate being compared with the paganized Jews of those days. Was Jesus' comparison justified? Evidently so. Just as Elijah's life was in danger in Israel, so Jesus' life was now in danger. The record tells us: "All those hearing these things in the synagogue became filled with anger; and they rose up and hurried him outside the city, and they led him to the brow of the mountain upon which their city had been built, in order to throw him down headlong." But Jehovah protected Jesus, as he had earlier protected Elijah.—Luke 4:28-30.

King Solomon's Glory

That is one example of how the two books of Kings flesh out, as it were, the words of Jesus and the early Christians. Consider another example. In his Sermon on the Mount, Jesus encouraged his listeners to rely on Jehovah in the matter of material necessities. Among other things, he said: "Also, on the matter of clothing, why are you anxious? Take a lesson from the lilies of the field, how they are growing; they do not toil, nor do they spin; but I say to you that not even Solomon in all his glory was arrayed as one of these." (Matthew 6:28, 29) Why did Jesus refer to Solomon here?

His Jewish listeners would have known because they were familiar with the glory of Solomon. It is described at some length in the book of First Kings (as well as in Second Chronicles). They would likely have remembered, for example, that the food for Solomon's household each day "proved to be thirty cor measures of fine flour and sixty cor measures of flour, ten fat cattle and twenty pastured cattle and a hundred sheep, besides some stags and gazelles and roebucks and fattened cuckoos." (1 Kings 4:22, 23) That was a lot of food.

Besides that, the weight of gold that came to Solomon in one year amounted up to "six hundred and sixty-six talents of gold," well over 250 million dollars (U.S.) at current values. And all the ornaments of Solomon's house were of gold. "There was nothing of silver; it was considered in the days of Solomon as nothing at all."

(1 Kings 10:14, 21) As Jesus triggered their recollections of these things, his listeners quickly got the point of what he was saying.

Jesus referred to Solomon in another context. Some scribes and Pharisees had demanded that he perform a sign, and Jesus answered: "The queen of the south will be raised up in the judgment with this generation and will condemn it; because she came from the ends of the earth to hear the wisdom of Solomon, but, look! something more than Solomon is here." (Matthew 12:42) Why was this reference a strong rebuke to the listening religious leaders?

If we are familiar with the first book of Kings, we know that "the queen of the south" was the queen of Sheba. She was clearly a great lady, queen of a wealthy realm. When she visited Solomon, she brought with her "a very impressive train," expensive oil and "very much gold and precious stones." (1 Kings 10:1, 2) Peaceful communications between national rulers are usually undertaken by means of ambassadors. Hence, for the queen of Sheba, a reigning monarch, to travel personally all the way to Jerusalem to see King Solomon was unusual. Why did she do it?

King Solomon was very wealthy, but so was the queen of Sheba. She would not undertake such a journey just to see a rich monarch. However, Solomon was not only rich but he "was greater in riches and *wisdom* than all the other kings of the earth." (1 Kings 10:23) Under his wise rule "Judah and Israel continued to dwell in security, everyone under his own vine and under his own fig tree, from Dan to Beer-sheba, all the days of Solomon." —1 Kings 4:25.

It was Solomon's wisdom that attracted the queen of Sheba. She was "hearing the

report about Solomon in connection with the name of Jehovah. So she came to test him with perplexing questions." When she arrived in Jerusalem, "she came on in to Solomon and began to speak to him all that happened to be close to her heart. Solomon, in turn, went on to tell her all her matters. There proved to be no matter hidden from the king that he did not tell her."—1 Kings 10:1-3.

Jesus, too, possessed outstanding wisdom "in connection with the name of Jehovah." In fact, he was "more than Solomon." (Luke 11:31) The queen of Sheba, who was not a Jewess, made a long, inconvenient journey just to see Solomon for herself and to benefit from his wisdom. Thus, surely the scribes and Pharisees should have listened appreciatively to the one 'greater than Solomon' when he was right there in front of them. But they did not. "The queen of the south" appreciated God-given wisdom far more than they did.

Allusions to the Prophets

During the period of history covered in the books of First and Second Kings, the rulers in the 12-tribe kingdom—and later in the divided kingdoms of Israel and Judah—were kings. At that time Jehovah's prophets were very active among His people. Outstanding among these were Elijah and Elisha, to whom we have already referred. Jesus' reference to them in Nazareth was not the only time they were mentioned in the Christian Greek Scriptures.

The apostle Paul in his letter to the Hebrew Christians wrote about the faith of God's servants of earlier times and, as one example of this, said: "Women received their dead by resurrection." (Hebrews 11:35) Doubtless he had in mind Elijah and Elisha, both of whom were used to perform resurrections. (1 Kings 17:17-24; 2 Kings 4:32-37) When three of Jesus' apostles became 'eyewitnesses of Jesus' magnificence' during the transfiguration vision, they saw Jesus talking with Moses and Elijah. (2 Peter 1:16-18; Matthew 17:1-9) Why was Elijah chosen to represent the line of pre-Christian prophets who bore witness to Jesus? If you read the account of First Kings and see his great faith and the mighty way he was used by Jehovah, you will understand the answer.

Nevertheless, Elijah was really just an ordinary person like us. James referred to another event in First Kings when he wrote: "A righteous man's supplication, when it is at work, has much force: Elijah was a man with feelings like ours, and yet in prayer he prayed for it not to rain; and it did not rain upon the land for three years and six months. And he prayed again, and the heaven gave rain and the land put forth its fruit."—James 5:16-18; 1 Kings 17:1; 18:41-46.

Further Echoes From Kings

Many other references in the Christian Greek Scriptures contain echoes from the two books of Kings. Stephen reminded the Jewish Sanhedrin that Solomon built a house for Jehovah in Jerusalem. (Acts 7:47) Many of the details of that building work are in the first book of Kings. (1 Kings 6:1-38) When Jesus spoke to a woman in Samaria, the woman said to him in surprise: "'How is it that you, despite being a Jew, ask me for a drink, when I am a Samaritan woman?' (For Jews have no dealings with Samaritans.)" (John 4:9) Why did the Jews have no dealings with the Samaritans? The account in Second Kings describing the origin of this people sheds light on the matter.—2 Kings 17:24-34.

A letter found in the book of Revelation to the congregation of Thyatira contains this strong counsel: "Nevertheless, I do hold this against you, that you tolerate that woman Jezebel, who calls herself a prophetess, and she teaches and misleads my slaves to commit fornication and to eat things sacrificed to idols." (Revelation 2:20) Who was Jezebel? The daughter of a Baal priest in Tyre. As the first book of Kings tells us, she married King Ahab of Israel and became queen of Israel. Dominating her husband, she introduced Baal worship into an already apostate Israel, brought a host of Baal priests into the land and persecuted Jehovah's prophets. Ultimately, she died a violent death. —1 Kings 16:30-33; 18:13; 2 Kings 9: 30-34.

The woman showing the spirit of Jezebel in the congregation of Thyatira was evidently trying to teach the congregation to practice immorality and to violate God's laws. Such a spirit had to be exterminated in the congregation, just as the family of Jezebel had to be exterminated from the Israelite nation.

Yes, we need the Hebrew Scriptures in

order to understand the Christian Greek Scriptures. Many details would be meaningless without the background that the Hebrew Scriptures provide. Jesus and the early Christians, as well as the Jews that they spoke to, were thoroughly familiar with them. Why not take the time to make yourself equally familiar with them? Thus you will take the fullest advantage of *"all Scripture,"* which is "inspired of God and beneficial for teaching."—2 Timothy 3:16.

Questions From Readers

■ In view of reports that doctors may be able to reverse a voluntary sterilization, might not some Christians choose it as a form of birth control?

The Bible shows that God has high regard for reproductive powers. He purposed that humans fill the earth by reproducing their kind. (Genesis 1:28; 9:6, 7) Later, Israelites regarded large families as a blessing from Jehovah, and tampering with reproductive powers brought divine disfavor. (Psalm 127:3-5; Deuteronomy 1:11; 23:1; 25:11, 12) Such points in the Hebrew Scriptures have influenced the thinking of many of God's servants with regard to the practice of voluntary sterilization.*

What, though, do we find in the Christian Greek Scriptures bearing on the matter? For one thing, we learn that Christians are not under the Mosaic Law. (Galatians 3:24, 25) Further, Jesus urged the expansion of Christianity by preaching the good news, not by procreation. Since a great harvest of disciples would result, Jesus advised disciples who could make room for it to become eunuchs in a spiritual sense, expressing self-control as single persons. Of similar import,

* See, for example, "Questions From Readers," *The Watchtower* of March 1, 1975.

the apostle Paul encouraged Christians not to marry and thus to have greater freedom to preach and teach. That way they would gather in spiritual children. Even married couples were to remember that "the time left is reduced"; their goal should be 'freedom from the anxieties' of family life.—1 Corinthians 7:29-32, 35; Matthew 9:37, 38; 19:12.

When we last discussed voluntary sterilization in this column* most physicians considered the procedure irreversible and thus permanent. However, medical developments in the last decade have changed the situation somewhat. For example, *Population Reports* (November-December 1983, Johns Hopkins University) says about vasectomies: "In recent reports reversals have restored patency —that is, sperm have been found in the ejaculate—in 67 to 100 percent of men. Functional success—that is, pregnancies among the wives of men who have had reversals—has ranged from 16 to 85 percent." New surgical procedures and methods of implanting temporary

blocks are also pointed to as indicating that reversal success will yet increase.

Since the Christian Greek Scriptures give no direct guidance on such matters, Christians must make personal decisions about limiting the size of their family and about birth control. As to sterilization, they should bear in mind that even though a reversal is theoretically more possible now than it was a decade ago, physicians *cannot guarantee* that reproductive ability can be restored.

Above all, a couple should keep a clear conscience before Jehovah and toward their fellow Christians. If a couple is thinking of sterilization as a form of birth control, they still should consider any effect their actions may have on others. Though married couples do not usually publicize their decision about birth control, if it became widely known that a couple had resorted to voluntary sterilization, would the congregation be greatly upset and lose respect for them? (1 Timothy 3:2, 12, 13) These are factors to consider very seriously, even in this private and personal matter. In the final analysis, Paul's statement is appropriate: "To his own master [Jehovah] he stands or falls."—Romans 14:4, 10-12.

My Book of Bible Stories
Stories 1-16

csmy-1

1
SIDE
A

A Fabulous Memory Aid

The cassette recordings of *My Book of Bible Stories* are just that. A mother from Alberta, Canada, explains:

"One day I was reading a story from *My Book of Bible Stories* to my four-and-a-half-year-old son, Shaun. As I paused at one point I found that to my amazement he began to continue the story, word for word, as it appears in the *Bible Stories* book. At first I thought it was just one story that he knew. So I tried another and then another and he had memorized every one. . . .

"As he listens to the tape he studies the picture in the book that is associated with each story. It seems that in this way he has actually memorized, word for word, the first 33 stories, including difficult names of places and people. If he has a memory lapse, it often takes just a word and no more than three or four words to prompt him and he is able to continue again."

May 15, 1985

The Watchtower

Announcing Jehovah's Kingdom

You Can Find
True Friends

May 15, 1985
Vol. 106, No. 10

The Watchtower
Announcing Jehovah's Kingdom

In This Issue

THE PURPOSE OF "THE WATCHTOWER" is to exalt Jehovah God as the Sovereign of the universe. It keeps watch on world events as they fulfill Bible prophecy. It comforts all peoples with the good news that God's Kingdom will soon destroy those who oppress their fellowmen and that it will turn the earth into a paradise. It encourages faith in the now-reigning King, Jesus Christ, whose shed blood opens the way for mankind to gain eternal life. "The Watchtower," published by Jehovah's Witnesses continuously since 1879, is nonpolitical. It adheres to the Bible as its authority.

"WATCHTOWER" STUDIES FOR THE WEEKS

June 16: Cultivating the Finest Friendship in All the Universe. Page 8. Songs to Be Used: 217, 165.

June 23: The Finest Friendship Endures in an Unfriendly World. Page 13. Songs to Be Used: 58, 212.

June 30: "You Are the Salt of the Earth." Page 22. Songs to Be Used: 191, 38.

Average Printing Each Issue: 11,150,000

Now Published in 102 Languages

SEMIMONTHLY EDITIONS AVAILABLE BY MAIL
Afrikaans, Arabic, Cebuano, Chichewa, Chinese, Cibemba, Danish, Dutch, Efik, English*, Finnish, French, German, Greek, Hiligaynon, Igbo, Iloko, Italian, Japanese, Korean, Lingala, Malagasy, Maltese, Norwegian, Portuguese, Russian, Sepedi, Sesotho, Shona, Spanish, Swahili, Swedish, Tagalog, Thai, Tswana, Xhosa, Yoruba, Zulu

MONTHLY EDITIONS AVAILABLE BY MAIL
Armenian, Bengali, Bicol, Bulgarian, Croatian, Czech, Ewe, Fijian, Ga, Greenlandic, Gujarati, Gun, Hausa, Hebrew, Hindi, Hiri Motu, Hungarian, Icelandic, Kannada, Kikuyu, Kiluba, Malayalam, Marathi, New Guinea Pidgin, Pangasinan, Papiamento, Polish, Rarotongan, Romanian, Samar-Leyte, Samoan, Sango, Serbian, Silozi, Sinhalese, Slovenian, Solomon Islands-Pidgin, Tahitian, Tamil, Telugu, Tshiluba, Tsonga, Turkish, Twi, Ukrainian, Urdu, Venda, Vietnamese
*Study articles also available in large-print edition at same cost.

The Bible translation used is the "New World Translation of the Holy Scriptures," unless otherwise indicated.

Twenty cents (U.S.) a copy

Watch Tower Society offices	Yearly subscription rates Semimonthly
America, U.S., Watchtower, Wallkill, N.Y. 12589	$4.00
Australia, Box 280, Ingleburn, N.S.W. 2565	A$6.00
Canada, Box 4100, Halton Hills (Georgetown), Ontario L7G 4Y4	$5.20
England, The Ridgeway, London NW7 1RN	£5.00
Ireland, 29A Jamestown Road, Finglas, Dublin 11	£5.00
New Zealand, 6-A Western Springs Rd., Auckland 3	$10.00
Nigeria, P.O. Box 194, Yaba, Lagos State	₦6.00
Philippines, P.O. Box 2044, Manila 2800	₱50.00
South Africa, Private Bag 2, Elandsfontein, 1406	R5,60

Remittances should be sent to the office in your country or to Watchtower, Wallkill, N.Y. 12589, U.S.A.

Changes of address should reach us 30 days before your moving date. Give us your old and new address (if possible, your old address label).

The Watchtower (ISSN 0043-1087) is published semimonthly for $4.00 (U.S.) per year by Watch Tower Bible and Tract Society of Pennsylvania, 25 Columbia Heights, Brooklyn, N.Y. 11201. Second-class postage paid at Brooklyn, N.Y., and at additional mailing offices.

Postmaster: Send address changes to Watchtower, **Wallkill, N.Y. 12589.**

Published by
**Watch Tower Bible and Tract Society
of Pennsylvania**
25 Columbia Heights, Brooklyn, N.Y. 11201, U.S.A.
Frederick W. Franz, President

TRUE FRIENDS
Why So Hard to Find?

"**I** WANT to have a million friends." So goes a popular Brazilian song. But just what *is* a friend? At times the word "friend" is used so loosely that it is applied to practically every acquaintance who is not hostile. A true friend, however, is more than a mere acquaintance. Concerning friendship, Francis Bacon wrote: "It redoubleth joys and cutteth griefs in half."

To be sure, a true friend is one who adds to your happiness and who, when needed, helps you cope with sorrow. A person without friends, therefore, cannot be completely happy. Millions, though, complain that finding true friends is difficult.

Why True Friends Are Hard to Find

The Bible foretold that today men and women would be "lovers of themselves, . . . self-assuming, haughty, . . . unthankful, disloyal, having no natural affection, not open to any agreement, slanderers, without self-control, fierce, without love of goodness, betrayers, headstrong, puffed up with pride." (2 Timothy 3:1-4) No wonder, then, that loyal friends are hard to find! The environment in which people are raised works against their developing the qualities needed in a friend.

But there are other factors. Some people are superficial, concerned only with the surface aspects of life. Others are not willing to make the sacrifices necessary for friendship. "Don't get involved!" is the advice one hears so often these days. The world's emphasis on materialism has also taken its toll on friendship. People often prefer possessions—even dogs and cats—to people. Any love they might show to fellow humans tends to be superficial. As one elderly woman observed: "They love, but from a distance." Even in cultures where profuse hugging and kissing are common courtesies, there may be a lack of real support when dire need strikes.

A lack of time, too, is a common hindrance to friendship. In their daily rush, often people are too busy or too exhausted to cultivate friendships. Or some may feel that friends must be treated to lavish entertainment and thus conclude they cannot afford friends!

Shallow Friendships

Many people, nevertheless, claim that they *do* have friends. But how much depth is there to such relationships? Often a person takes an interest in someone because of what that one has to *offer,* not because of what he *is.* Such friendships are therefore likely to be short-lived, for as soon as the "friend" ceases to be useful, he or she is promptly discarded.

Even having things in common is not always a sufficient basis for a lasting friendship. The *Brazil Herald* once told of two close "friends" who enjoyed making the rounds of taverns and drinking heavily on weekends. Once, though, they got into a dispute over which one of them was the better he-man. To prove his claim, one of them emptied his gun into the other. The killer later said that he had murdered his "best friend."

In spite of all the difficulties and obstacles in the way of friendship, however, the fact remains that we all have an innate *need* for friends. Where and how, then, can they be found?

TRUE FRIENDS
How to Find Them

"THE only way to have a friend is to be one," said Ralph Waldo Emerson. Many, though, have chosen the route of solitude. Rather than reaching out and *being* a friend, they cut others off. The result? "People who spend a lot of time by themselves tend to feel 'very passive, unhappy, left out of the world,'" a Brazilian newspaper quoted a researcher as saying. He continued: "When there's nothing else to do, when there's no one to talk to, you turn inwards. It's much easier to get caught up in your problems."

You need not reach such a stage, however. Almost anyone can learn to be a friend and thus gain friends. But how does a person start? A big factor in the ability to make friends is our own person-

ality. An ancient proverb truthfully says: "A man's attraction lies in his kindness." (Proverbs 19:22, *The Jerusalem Bible*) True friendship, therefore, comes to those who express kindness. For example, when we let others know we appreciate them, they are more likely to take an interest in us.

A kind person also *listens* to others. Someone who dominates the conversation or talks excessively about himself will have a hard time finding anyone who is interested in his feelings and aspirations. Kindness also means watching what we say to others. "There exists the one speaking thoughtlessly as with the stabs of a sword, but the tongue of the wise ones is a healing." (Proverbs 12:18) To illustrate:

You may notice that someone is depressed or consumed with worry. Says a proverb: "Worry can rob you of happiness, but kind words will cheer you up." (Proverbs 12:25, *Today's English Version*) On such an occasion, your healing tongue could win a loyal friend for you.

The Value of Loyalty

The writer of Proverbs 18:24 showed deep insight into human relationships when he wrote: "Some friends bring ruin on us, but a true friend is more loyal than a brother." (*The New American Bible*) Yes, who wants a fair-weather friend? But consider the example of David and Jonathan. Jonathan could have had ill will toward David, since Jonathan was the heir to the throne of Israel but knew that David would actually become king. Yet Jonathan showed loyalty, not jealousy, toward David, even risking his life on David's behalf.—1 Samuel 18:1-3; 20:17, 31, 32; 2 Samuel 1:26.

Ruth was another loyal friend. Rather than abandoning her mother-in-law Naomi, she stuck with her. In fact, observers rightly declared that Ruth was 'better than seven sons' to Naomi.—Ruth 1: 16, 17; 4:15.

Do you show such loyalty? For example, when you observe flaws in your associates, do you thoughtlessly reveal them to others?

But what if someone dear to you has a serious fault that needs immediate attention? The loyal friend does not hold back from telling the truth out of fear of the other person's reaction. "The wounds inflicted by a lover are faithful," says the Bible. (Proverbs 27:6) This, of course,

True friendship knows no age limit

does not mean that you should be harsh or tactless. Christians in ancient Galatia once needed some outspoken correction. But note how skillfully the apostle Paul handled the situation and then asked: "Well, then, have I become your enemy because I tell you the truth?" (Galatians 4:16) A true friend will love you for 'telling the truth,' even if it is corrective counsel.—Proverbs 9:8.

Happiness in Giving

Genuine, lasting friendship does cost something. People who are always striving to get something without giving anything in return will never come to know the happiness Jesus spoke of when he said, "There is more happiness in giving than there is in receiving." (Acts 20:35; Luke 6:31, 38) Therefore, learn to look at people from the standpoint of what you

We can win true friends by being
liberal, ready to share

can *do* for them, instead of what you can *get out* of them.

The Bible encourages Christians to be "generous," "liberal, ready to share." (Proverbs 11:25; 1 Timothy 6:18) Your material resources may be quite limited, but what about your *time?* Do you have the habit of always being in a hurry? Friendship takes *time,* and unless a person is willing to make time for others, relationships will not thrive. For example, you may use the well-worn greeting "How are you?" But are you generous enough with your time to stop and be prepared to listen to the answer to this question? Remember that although Jesus Christ was very busy, he always found the time to attend to those who sought him out.—Mark 6: 31-34.

Keeping Our Friendships Alive

Once a friendship has been established, every effort should be made to keep it alive. True, as you get to know each other, certain weaknesses and flaws will become apparent. Yet you will do well to recognize and accept minor weaknesses. And when in doubt, the noble thing to do is to give your friend the benefit of the doubt, avoiding undue suspicion. 'Put up with one another in love,' counsels Paul. And Peter adds: "Above all things, have intense love for one another, because love covers a multitude of sins." —Ephesians 4:2; 1 Peter 4:8.

Then, too, how wise it is never to take friends for granted! Even the closest friends need some privacy. Lengthy, frequent, or untimely visits may eventually become wearisome and unwanted. Discernment and respect would suggest making arrangements beforehand when at all possible. Proverbs 25:17 counsels: "Make your foot rare at the house of your fellowman, that he may not have his sufficiency of you and certainly hate you."

It is also the course of wisdom to avoid being overly inquisitive, personal, or possessive. Modesty will move us to avoid being dogmatic. Surely, friendship does not give us the right to force our opinions or personal tastes on one another. Indeed, if we are governed by "the wisdom from above," we will be reasonable.—James 3:17.

Be supportive of your friends, following Paul's advice at Romans 12:15: "Rejoice with people who rejoice; weep with people who weep." Yes, be willing to share your friends' sorrows, disappointments, joys, and successes. Display a sense of humor, too, being willing to laugh at your own mistakes, not just those of others. Good-

A Friendship That Unites

Jehovah's Witnesses are not only spiritual brothers and sisters but also friends. And since their friendship is based on mutual obedience to the commands of Jesus Christ, it is not limited by national boundaries. (John 15:14) This type of friendship receives God's blessing, which keeps them just as united and secure as a flock of sheep are in their pen.—Micah 2:12.

Often friendship and unity are absent at a construction site. Yet, when Jehovah's Witnesses gather to construct their "quick-build" Kingdom Halls, a healthy spirit of cooperation and camaraderie is seen. For example, Witnesses from the United States, England, and Wales cooperated and shared their methods in building halls. The result?

"I've never seen anything like it in my life," said Roger, a bricklayer from England. "I just couldn't see carpenters working with bricklayers because it never happens in the world. But on a Kingdom Hall site you see brothers working on the roof, while carpenters and bricklayers work underneath with the painters and the carpet layers. All work together. It is wonderful!"

Mike, a father of two, from Wales noted that "everyone can share in that camaraderie." And his friend Malcolm observed why, commenting: "When all the brothers work in unity as one, in God's name, then he blesses that project with his spirit."

natured remarks can even serve to ease tension at awkward moments. Yes, friendship is *work*. But is it not worth the effort?

Finding True Friends

Where, though, can one find true friends? A good place to start would be the local congregation of Jehovah's Witnesses. These genuine Christians enjoy such good relations that they frequently refer to one another as "the friends," as did their fellow believers of the first century. (3 John 14) Such ones have put away nationalism and racial pride, factors that alienate people. They are endeavoring to clothe themselves with what the Bible calls "the new personality." This means cultivating such attractive qualities as "the tender affections of compassion, kindness, lowliness of mind, mildness, and long-suffering." (Colossians 3:10-12) You will certainly be able to find desirable friends among people who do this!

By associating with Jehovah's Witnesses, you will also learn how to make friends with Jehovah God and his Son Jesus Christ. Said Jesus: "You are my friends if you do what I am commanding you." (John 15:14) And Abraham of old was called "Jehovah's friend." Abraham attained that very desirable relationship because of his faith and righteous works, and you can do the same.—James 2:23.

So while it is good to make the effort to cultivate earthly friends, be even more determined to establish friendly relations with our heavenly Friend Jehovah God. He will soon restore Paradise to this earth, allowing all his earthly servants to live in peace and security. Yes, earth's inhabitants will then be surrounded by millions who will eternally prove to be true friends.—Luke 23:43; Revelation 21:3, 4; Psalm 37:10, 11.

In Our Next Issue

- **Adam and Eve**
  —Myth or Reality?

- **Jesus' Birth**
  —Where and When?

- **Subjecting Ourselves to Jehovah by Dedication**

Cultivating the
Finest Friendship
in All the Universe

"But you, O Israel, are my servant, you, O Jacob, whom I have chosen, the seed of Abraham my friend."—ISAIAH 41:8.

HOW precious a true friend! But what is the basis for having a genuine friend? What is at the rock bottom of an enduring friendship? It is something that never fails, so that a true friend never fails. What is it? Why, it is the quality that the apostle Paul cited when saying, "Love never fails"!—1 Corinthians 13:8.

2 In the Hebrew Scriptures, the noun translated "love" is drawn from a verb meaning "to love." (Deuteronomy 6:4, 5; compare Matthew 22:37.) And in the Greek *Septuagint Version,* the verb translating "you must love" from the Hebrew text is *a·ga·pan'.* However, in that ancient version and in the Christian Greek Scriptures the noun translated "friend" is not based upon that verb but is the Greek noun *phi'los,* derived from a verb meaning "to have affection for." So, according to the original Greek, loving affection is expressed toward a friend or between friends. Even in the English language the word "friend" is drawn from an Anglo-Saxon verb meaning "to love."

3 The Greek verb from which "friend" is drawn therefore expresses an emotion warmer and more intimate than the love expressed by the verb *a·ga·pan',* appearing in the Greek text of John 3:16, where Jesus is quoted as saying: "God loved the world so much that he gave his only-begotten Son, in order that everyone exercising faith in him might not be destroyed but have everlasting life." Thus the love (Greek, *a·ga'pe*) on the part of Jehovah God is broad enough to embrace the whole world of mankind in spite of the sinfulness of the human race. But the only-begotten Son of God told his 11 faithful apostles that they were bound to him by a warmer, more intimate kind of love.

A Precious Kind of Friendship

4 Jesus told those apostles that they would continue to be his "friends" if they kept on doing the things that he commanded them to do. Showing that this would include the privileged intimacy resulting from mutual confidence, he said: "I no longer call you slaves, because a slave

---

1. What is it that causes a genuine friendship never to fail?
2. The verb from which the Greek word for "friend" is derived has what special meaning?

3. Compared with God's love for the world of mankind, with what kind of love were Jesus' disciples bound to him?
4. By doing what could Jesus' disciples continue as his "friends," and to what intimacy would this status admit them?

does not know what his master does. But I have called you friends, because all the things I have heard from my Father I have made known to you." (John 15:14, 15) In saying that, Jesus applied the term *phi'los* to each one of those apostles.

⁵ According to Proverbs 18:24, the inspired wise man declared: "There exist companions disposed to break one another to pieces, but there exists a friend sticking closer than a brother." Such a friendship is not based upon fleshly relationships; it rests upon an appreciation of the true worth of the one befriended. Yes, fleshly relatives may part company with one another for various selfish reasons, but a solid friend will be unwavering and will adhere to his friendship regardless of the trialsome or difficult conditions, or the heart-searching circumstances that may develop.

⁶ Here we may think of Jonathan, son of

rejected King Saul, and of David, whom Jehovah God had chosen and anointed to be Israel's king. Their friendship persisted down to the death of Jonathan on the field of battle. On hearing the sad news, David gave way to the lament recorded in 2 Samuel 1:17-27. Showing how tender his relationship with Jonathan was, David said: "I am distressed over you, my brother Jonathan, very pleasant you were to me. More wonderful was your love to me than the love from women." A friendship like that was not to be forgotten or to go unrequited. It accounted for King David's display of mercy toward Mephibosheth, the surviving son of Jonathan.—2 Samuel 9:1-10.

⁷ That precious kind of friendship has not died off the face of the earth. Today, in this "conclusion of the system of things" when 'the love of the greater number has cooled off,' the warmth of such a loving friendship is strongly felt among

---

5. The friendship referred to at Proverbs 18:24 rests upon what, and how solid is such a relationship?
6. Of whose strong friendship are we reminded, and how did David later requite that friendship?

7. (a) Has friendship like that of David and Jonathan died off, especially in this "conclusion of the system of things"? (b) To what expression of intimacy does such friendship admit a person, as Jesus explained to his faithful apostles?

David and Jonathan enjoyed heartfelt, precious friendship. So can you

the dedicated, baptized witnesses of Jehovah God who are giving the worldwide Kingdom witness that Jesus foretold. (Matthew 24:3-14) Friends are inclined to reveal things to one another because of having confidence in one another. Remember that while conversing late at night with the 11 apostles that had stuck with him, Jesus said: "I have called you friends, because all the things I have heard from my Father I have made known to you." (John 15:14, 15) Yes, the spiritual things of God's Word that are due to be fulfilled or to be applied would be disclosed first to the true spirit-begotten "friends" of the Master, Jesus Christ. Then these "friends" would have the privilege and responsibility to disclose such hitherto secret things to those wanting to enter into friendly relations with Jehovah God, with whom such secret things originate.

8 That is the way Jehovah has proceeded with his spirit-begotten worshipers taken into his new covenant through the Mediator, Jesus Christ. When instituting the Lord's Evening Meal, Jesus said: "This cup means the new covenant by virtue of my blood, which is to be poured out in your behalf." (Luke 22:20) This was in harmony with Psalm 25:14, which says: "The intimacy with Jehovah belongs to those fearful of him, also his covenant, to cause them to know it." What extraordinary knowledge is imparted to those who come into a friendly relationship with Jehovah God and his Mediator, Jesus Christ!

Those Whom Jehovah Befriends

9 Oh, but can we really have the Most High and Almighty God as our personal Friend? Has he really humbled himself to such an extent as to become our Friend? It is not presumptuous to think so. In a letter written to spiritual Israelites before the destruction of Jerusalem in 70 C.E., James wrote: "The scripture was fulfilled which says: 'Abraham put faith in Jehovah, and it was counted to him as righteousness,' and he came to be called 'Jehovah's friend.'" (James 1:1; 2:23; Genesis 15:6; Galatians 6:16) In one Hebrew "scripture" to which James there referred we read this appeal made to God by King Jehoshaphat when the security of Jerusalem was threatened by a large-scale invasion: "Did not you yourself, O God of ours, drive away the inhabitants of this land from before your people Israel and then give it to the seed of Abraham your lover ["thy friend," *King James Version*], to time indefinite?" (2 Chronicles 20:7) Here we can note that the basic Hebrew word translated "friend" (*KJ*) means "a lover." Indisputably, Abraham was a lover of Jehovah, the God who called him out of Ur of the Chaldeans and brought him into the Promised Land. As such a lover, Abraham was a man whom Jehovah could befriend, or take into His friendship.

10 However, at Isaiah 41:8 Jehovah spoke for himself and said these encouraging words to the descendants of Abraham as a nation: "But you, O Israel, are my servant, you, O Jacob, whom I have chosen, the seed of Abraham my friend." The Most High God honored this friendship with Abraham by assigning him to be the illustrious forefather of Jesus Christ, the Savior of all mankind, including Abraham himself. This descendant of Abraham was

---

8. To whom does Jehovah accord intimacy with him, and how did Jesus refer to the covenant involved with such intimacy?
9. Is it presumptuous for us to think that Jehovah would take mere human creatures into his friendship, and what Bible texts can we furnish to verify our answer?

---

10. At Isaiah 41:8, who spoke for himself on the matter of friendship, and on the basis of what attitude toward Jehovah was Abraham given a special rating with God?

more than a friend of Jehovah God, for he is God's beloved Son.—John 3:16.

¹¹ From all the foregoing, what conclusion can we draw? That it is possible for human creatures down here on Jehovah's "footstool" to be his friends. (Isaiah 66:1) Of course, our precious friendship with him in this old world will be put to the test, for Satan the Devil, "the god of this system of things," will try to break it up. —2 Corinthians 4:4.

¹² Consider the case of that outstanding man of ancient times named Job, of whom the Christian disciple James said: "Look! We pronounce happy those who have endured. You have heard of the endurance of Job and have seen the outcome Jehovah gave, that Jehovah is very tender in affection and merciful." (James 5:11) Job was no mythical person but actually lived in the land of Uz. The Devil doubted the enduring quality of Job's friendship with God, and Jehovah let Satan put Job to a very severe test. By means of heartbreaking calamities that he brought upon Job, Satan endeavored to make him renounce Jehovah. But Job refused to support the Devil by renouncing God, which would have resulted in Job's dying on Satan's side of the issue of universal sovereignty. To the contrary, Job proved Satan the Devil to be a base liar. On earth, Jesus Christ proved the same thing. But what about us today? Those who treasure Jehovah's friendship are determined to uphold his side of this controversy of universal interest. And they will do so until Satan and his demons are finally abyssed and put to silence before the Millennial Reign of Jesus Christ.—Revelation 20:1-4.

Abraham was "Jehovah's friend." Are you?

¹³ No friendship in existence outranks that with the Most High God, Jehovah. Friendship with the only-begotten Son of God ranks next. Such an amicable relationship with them means everlasting life in boundless happiness for us. They rightly demand exclusive allegiance from us. We cannot be hobnobbing with this doomed old world and at the same time be cultivating their friendship. Spiritually speaking, we do not want to be classified as adulteresses, according to James 4:4, which puts the matter point-blank and says: "Adulteresses, do you not know that the friendship with the world is enmity with God? Whoever, therefore, wants to be a friend of the world is constituting himself an enemy of God." Those words were directed to the spiritual Israelites of the first century C.E., but they also apply to Jehovah's Witnesses living in this 20th-century world, or system of things.

---

11. Why is friendship with Jehovah bound to be put to the test?
12. Like Job of the land of Uz, what should we be determined to do about our own friendship with the Most High?

13. How does friendship with Jehovah God and his only-begotten Son rank, and what course must we pursue in order not to be classified figuratively as "adulteresses"?

Shun Friendship That Will Fail

14 Because of not constituting themselves friends of this corrupt, violent old world, Jehovah's Witnesses are misrepresented, maltreated, and persecuted. So was the greatest witness of Jehovah ever on earth, Jesus Christ, and they are not better than he was. (Revelation 1:5; 3:14) Because they honestly keep adjusting their thinking according to the Word of their finest Friend, Jehovah God, they have been spared the experience described prophetically at Zechariah 13:4-6, where it is written: "It must occur in that day that the prophets will become ashamed, each one of his vision when he prophesies; and they will not wear an official garment of hair for the purpose of deceiving. And he will certainly say, 'I am no prophet. I am a man cultivating the soil, because an earthling man himself acquired me from my youth on.' And one must say to him, 'What are these wounds on your person between your hands?' And he will have to say, 'Those with which I was struck in the house of my intense lovers ["friends," *KJ*].'"

15 For centuries now, the clergymen of Christendom have worn 'official garments' for the purpose of calling attention to their religious profession and for the self-honoring purpose of distinguishing themselves from the members of their congregations whom they style "the laity." This these clerics do, although there is not a shred of evidence to prove that Jesus Christ and his apostles and the evangelizers he sent out ever wore official religious garments to call attention to their status and to magnify it. Now we are deep into "the conclusion of the system of things"

What Are Your Thoughts?
□ Only by doing what can Jesus' disciples continue to be his friends?
□ How do we know that humans can enjoy Jehovah's friendship, and to whom does he grant intimacy with him?
□ Why is friendship with God bound to be put to the test?
□ With regard to friendship, how do Jehovah's Witnesses avoid experiencing what was foretold at Zechariah 13:4-6?

that began with the end of "the appointed times of the nations," or "the times of the Gentiles," in the year 1914. (Matthew 24:3; Luke 21:24; *KJ*) Long have the clergy tried to be the best of friends with the commercial, military, and political elements of this world. This they have done for their own selfish benefit and without any qualms of conscience. But their selfish friendships of this kind will be short-lived!

16 The clergy and the laity alike find themselves in a highly scientific age. Worldly relationships are being strained to the limit under the pressure of these times. The clergy, despite their claimed standing with the God of heaven, have gained no favor from him for the commercial, military, and political arrangement of things and are providing no relief for the worsening world situation. Shortly, their worldly "friends" will be brought to the realization that the clergy are worthless, yes, burdensome to them, false in their prophecies of materially better times apart from Jehovah's Kingdom by Christ.

---

14. As regards friendship, how do Jehovah's Witnesses avoid having the experience foretold at Zechariah 13:4-6?
15. Why have the clergymen of Christendom worn special garments publicly, and with whom have they made self-seeking friendships?

---

16. (a) According to Bible prophecy, what will worldly "friends" shortly do to the clergy class? (b) Even though in a new status, what final experience will the clergy not escape?

Indeed, those worldly "friends" will finally be moved to give full vent to their loss of confidence, their contempt, yes, their hatred. They will violently destroy the clergy or at least defrock them of their professional official garment and reduce them to an unprofessional, laical position, as explained at Zechariah 13:4-6. But this change of status will not spare them from annihilation with Babylon the Great, the world empire of false religion, as foretold in Revelation chapters 17 and 18. The clergy's worldly "friends" will fail them utterly.

¹⁷ In the face of this, how important it is to shun selfish friendships of the wrong kind! But how precious the finest friendship in all the universe should be to us! It is worthy of our cultivating it forever.

---

17. What friendship is worthy of cultivation, and for how long?

The Finest Friendship
Endures in an Unfriendly World

"Make friends for yourselves by means of the unrighteous riches, so that, when such fail, they may receive you into the everlasting dwelling places."—LUKE 16:9.

"EVEN to his fellowman one who is of little means is an object of hatred, but many are the friends of the rich person." (Proverbs 14:20) This proverb of King Solomon of Israel did not apply to the greatest man ever on earth, Jesus Christ, the one greater than Solomon. Jesus did not draw Israelites into intimate association with himself by means of material riches; neither did he recognize earthly wealth as the basis for true, enduring friendship.

² It is true that on one occasion Jesus said: "Make friends for yourselves by means of the unrighteous riches, so that, when such fail, they may receive you into the everlasting dwelling places." (Luke 16:9) But the "friends" Jesus had in mind were Jehovah God, the Source of all worthwhile possessions, and himself as the Son of his boundlessly rich Father. If we today follow that same counsel, we are brought into the finest friendship that can be enjoyed on earth, that of Jehovah God by means of his self-sacrificing Son, Jesus Christ.

³ Because of their immortal life, these heavenly Ones can remain our firm Friends and can usher us into "everlasting dwelling places." That is so whether these "everlasting dwelling places" are to be in heaven above with all the holy angels or down here on this earth in Paradise restored.—Luke 23:43.

---

1. Why did Proverbs 14:20 not apply to Jesus Christ on earth?
2. What friendships did Jesus tell his disciples to make, and for what reason?

3. Into what "dwelling places" can these heavenly Friends usher us?

Admittance Into
the Finest Friendship

4 The friendship of the Most High God and of his only-begotten Son, Jesus Christ, cannot be bought with money. This fact was emphasized in the case of Ananias and Sapphira in the first-century Christian congregation. Without seeking fame and reputation as they did, we can use our earthly possessions in a way approved by Jehovah God and Jesus Christ. (Acts 5:1-11) This is what was meant when Jesus Christ said: "Use worldly wealth to gain friends for yourselves, so that when it is gone, you will be welcomed into eternal dwellings."—Luke 16:9, *New International Version.*

5 When Jesus spoke those words, he was not seeking to gain the favor of the tax collectors of the Roman Empire and other sinners. He was not interested in gaining any material wealth for himself on earth, for he had told his disciples to lay up treasures for themselves in the heavens above. Zacchaeus, a Jewish tax collector for the Roman government, decided to act upon this counsel of the Messiah Jesus and openly declared his purpose to do so. In view of this action in support of Kingdom interests, the most notable guest of Zacchaeus declared: "This day salvation has come to this house, because he also is a son of Abraham. For the Son of man came to seek and to save what was lost." (Luke 19:1-10) "What was lost" included the tax collector Zacchaeus himself.

6 Zacchaeus was admitted into the finest friendship in all the universe, that of the God and Father of the special guest he was then entertaining. Whether Zacchaeus saw Jesus after His resurrection from the dead and was one of about 120 disciples gathered together in an upper room in Jerusalem on the momentous day of Pentecost of 33 C.E. is not stated in the Bible record. Doubtless, though, Zacchaeus was to be found among the 5,000 spirit-begotten, anointed disciples that were reported on shortly thereafter. (Acts, chapters 2 and 4; 1 Corinthians 15:1-6) But what a contrast we have in Ananias and Sapphira, mentioned earlier! Those two individuals associated with the Jerusalem congregation tried to enhance their reputation among the disciples by falsifying the amount of the contribution that they had made. The punishment that befell them for their dishonesty cost them the finest friendship and serves as a warning to all Christians today.—Acts 4:34–5:11.

7 In spite of the unfriendliness of this 20th-century world, Jehovah's Witnesses continue to enjoy the finest friendship in all existence. But why should they be enjoying this rarity whereas the more than a thousand diverse religious systems are not doing so? The evidence shows that it is because the witnesses of Jehovah have done something vital that the religionists of Christendom have not done. For one thing, the Witnesses have come out of false religious systems, for they recognize that these make up the world empire of false religion, designated in the Bible as Babylon the Great. Of course, getting out of some false religion does not automatically put one into Jehovah's organization, for a person could join some other religious system of the world empire of false religion.

---

4. (a) What Bible example shows whether God's friendship can be bought? (b) In what proper way can we use our possessions?
5. What course did Zacchaeus pursue, and with what result?
6. Into what was Zacchaeus admitted, but whose wrong course serves as a warning?

7. Despite the unfriendliness of this world, what rarity do Jehovah's Witnesses enjoy?

Zacchaeus was taken into the finest friendship in all the universe. Has that been your experience?

8 We should note that the divine command to get out of Babylon the Great is addressed to "my people." (Revelation 18:4) According to the Hebrew Scriptures, this divine call is similar to a command given by God to the exiles of Israel in the land of Babylon. (Isaiah 52:11) Hence, the specification "my people" applies directly to the remnant of the spirit-begotten, anointed disciples of Jesus Christ yet on earth. During World War I of 1914-18, Babylon the Great had taken these anointed ones captive by means of the political, military, and judicial elements of this world in order to put this spiritual remnant out of action. Figuratively speaking, the remnant came into a captive condition, losing freedom of movement in Jehovah's service.

9 In Revelation chapter 17, Babylon the Great is pictured as a harlot riding a wild beast with seven heads and ten horns. That symbolic wild beast that goes down into the abyss and comes up again pictures the present-day organization for world peace, namely, the United Nations, the successor to the League of Nations that went into the abyss at the outbreak of World War II. So when Jehovah's people, whom he designates as "my people,"

obeyed his call to get out of Babylon the Great, what did they do? They got out not only from under the domination and power of that world empire of false religion but also from under the domination of her political associates, the political elements now embodied in the UN.

10 The anointed remnant have adopted and maintained strict neutrality with regard to the political and military matters of this system of things. (John 15:19) They undividedly stand for the Kingdom of God by Jesus Christ, established in the heavens at the close of the Gentile Times in 1914. In defiance of the Kingdom, the League of Nations was set up and endorsed by Babylon the Great after the end of World War I in 1918. Hence, this international man-made organization is abominable, disgusting to Jehovah God and also to the faithful remnant of spiritual Israelites on earth. They trust in Jehovah's Kingdom itself and not in any supposed earthly substitute for it. (Matthew 24: 15, 16) And so does the modern-day "great

8. To whom is the command to get out of Babylon the Great directly addressed today?
9. To what extent did Jehovah's Witnesses have to go in getting out of Babylon the Great?

10. With what international organization today do Jehovah's Witnesses have nothing to do, and why so?

crowd," symbolized by the Nethinim and "the sons of the servants of Solomon." —Revelation 7:9-17; Ezra 2:43-58.

11 When Jesus stood on trial for his life before the Roman governor Pontius Pilate, he said: "My kingdom is no part of this world. If my kingdom were part of this world, my attendants would have fought that I should not be delivered up to the Jews. But, as it is, my kingdom is not from this source." (John 18:36) So it would be totally wrong for Jesus' "attendants," or disciples, to be friends of this world. Earlier, Jesus had told the first ones of his "attendants," the 11 faithful apostles, that they were "no part of the world" of which Satan the Devil is "the ruler." (John 14:30; 15:19; compare 2 Corinthians 4:4.) This was why the world hated them or was unfriendly toward them. No less so, Jesus' disciples of this 20th century find themselves in an unfriendly world. Despite this, they continue to enjoy the finest friendship in all the universe, that of the God of the righteous world to come, with its "new heavens and a new earth."—2 Peter 3:13.

12 When a person gets out of Babylon the Great and away from her worldly partners, Big Business and Politics and Militarism, there can be only one other place to go. That is onto the side of the universal organization of the one living and true God, Jehovah. There is no middle ground. This requires that an individual endure the unfriendliness of this world, a factor that makes it so hard for a person to decide to forsake Babylon the Great and the world of which it is a vital part.

---

11. (a) Why is it wrong for Jesus' disciples to be friends of this world? (b) What attitude does this world take toward Jehovah's Witnesses, but they continue to enjoy what?
12. When a person gets out of Babylon the Great and away from her worldly paramours, on what side only must he take his stand, and what does this entail?

A "New Name" From the Finest Friend

13 Our cherished friendship with God makes us happy to be called Jehovah's Witnesses. True, Christ's disciples of the first century had not adopted the name "Jehovah's Witnesses." But please consider their relationship with the finest Friend of all. Acts 11:26 reports: "It was first in Antioch [Syria] that the disciples were by divine providence called Christians." You will note that the *New World Translation of the Holy Scriptures* says that they were "by divine providence called Christians." The Greek word here rendered "by divine providence called" implies something more than mere random calling. The finest Friend in the universe approved of that name "Christians."

14 From the term "Christian" has developed the name Christendom, which is applied to the whole realm of professed Christians with its multiplicity of religious sects and denominations. So the title "Christendom" has not been conferred "by divine providence," either through the apostles or 'providentially' according to God's will. Thus the situation today is far different from that in the first century. Only genuine Christians can enjoy the finest friendship in this unfriendly world. So the big question today is, Who are the genuine, real Christians conforming to the inspired Scriptures? Another significant question is, Are Jehovah's Witnesses true Christians having Jehovah God and Jesus Christ as their Friends? In this regard the self-chosen name of God, Jehovah, is at stake.

---

13. In the first century C.E., what were Jesus' disciples providentially called?
14. What can be said regarding the term "Christendom," and what questions require consideration?

¹⁵ How could Christendom, with its many religions, enjoy friendship with Jehovah? Christendom has pushed the name of Jesus Christ to the fore, almost to the exclusion of his heavenly Father's name, Jehovah. However, in keeping with Bible prophecies, the time has come for Jehovah to make a name for himself. Therefore, his name has to come to the fore. In this behalf, he would use his true witnesses, his chosen people, those enjoying his friendship. At a special first-century meeting held by the apostles and other foremost followers of Jesus Christ, the disciple James said: "Symeon has related thoroughly how God for the first time turned his attention to the nations to take out of them a people for his name."—Acts 15:14.

¹⁶ It would be expected that 'a people for God's name' would be his friends and would uphold the divine name. But what has happened in Christendom? In its popular Bible translations, Jehovah's name has been overshadowed by a title. Why, his name is to be found only four times in the most popular English version of today! (Exodus 6:3; Psalm 83:18; Isaiah 12:2; 26:4, *King James Version*) Moreover, even in Jewish translations of the Hebrew Scriptures, God's name has been rendered as "the Lord." Such attempted suppression of Jehovah's name is *not* the work of his friends.

¹⁷ In the year 1950, however, the *New World Translation of the Holy Scriptures* began to come on the religious scene, and it has reproduced the divine name every time it occurs in the original Hebrew Bible text. The *New World Translation* has also restored the divine name to its rightful place in the main text of the Christian Greek Scriptures, the so-called New Testament—yes, 237 times. This *is* the work of Jehovah's friends.

¹⁸ Of interest to Jehovah's friends are the words of Isaiah 62:2. This verse, addressed to the visible organization of God's dedicated, baptized, spirit-begotten disciples of the Messiah, reads: "And the nations will certainly see your righteousness, O woman, and all kings your glory. And you will actually be called by a new name, which the very mouth of Jehovah will designate." That "name" refers to the blessed condition into which these modern-day anointed disciples have been gathered. Further, in order to be 'a people for God's name,' the remnant of the members of his visible organization should rightly have his name called upon them, should bear that name. This fact was realized in due time. So, in the spirit of Isaiah 62:2, God's spirit-begotten organization, gathered in convention at Columbus, Ohio, in 1931, joyfully adopted the name "Jehovah's witnesses." Following that example, all the congregations of Jehovah's dedicated people adopted that name. And that name has stuck despite worldly predictions to the contrary. At Revelation 3:14 the glorified Jesus Christ called himself "the faithful and true witness." Fittingly, then, from that memorable year of 1931 onward, the congregations of his disciples on earth have providentially espoused that name. Since then, they have endeavored to fulfill their responsibility to live up to that name and make it known. Consequently, Jehovah's name—the peerless name of their finest

---

15. In view of what circumstances has the time come for Jehovah to make a name for himself, and what part are the "people for his name" now having in this connection?
16, 17. What has been done about God's name in Christendom's Bible translations, but what is true of the *New World Translation* in this regard?

18. In the spirit of Isaiah 62:2, what step did God's people take in 1931, and what responsibility have they been fulfilling?

Delighted to have God as their finest Friend, in 1931 Jehovah's Witnesses resolved to be known by his matchless name

Friend—has been brought to the fore throughout the whole earth. And Jehovah has given outstanding evidence that his friendship toward his witnesses has been enduring down to this late date.

¹⁹ Since Jehovah God is for us as his dedicated witnesses, who can really be against us with any success? (Romans 8: 31-34) So we do not fear the unfriendliness of this enemy world. Hence, we carry on as ambassadors or as envoys of the Messianic Kingdom, calling upon sheeplike people to become reconciled to Jehovah God through his royal High Priest, Jesus Christ. (2 Corinthians 5:20) Although for this reason the animosity of this world continues to mount against the anointed remnant and their companions, the "great crowd," the finest friendship in all the universe, that of Jehovah God,

loyally continues to endure. (Revelation 7:9) It will never be broken off toward us as keepers of integrity toward him. In fact, soon, as at no earlier time, that friendship will be demonstrated during that war of all wars, "the war of the great day of God the Almighty," at Har-Magedon. (Revelation 16: 14, 16) There, face to face with Satan the Devil and his horde of demons and all his visible earthly organization, Jehovah will vindicate His universal sovereignty by His most tremendous victory of all the ages. We, toward whom Jehovah's fine friendship has endured till now, will then be favored with preservation and with the honor of being eyewitnesses of his superlative triumph by means of the conquering King, Jesus Christ. (Psalm 110:1, 2; Isaiah 66:23, 24) All our heartfelt thanks and praise go to Jehovah God for his enduring friendship! —Psalm 136:1-26.

---

19. (a) Why do Jehovah's dedicated witnesses not fear the unfriendliness of this world, and with what privilege will integrity keepers be rewarded at Har-Magedon? (b) For what should all our thanks and praise go to Jehovah?

How Would You Answer?

□ Jesus urged his disciples to make what friendships, and into what "dwelling places" can they thus be ushered?

□ What attitude does the world have toward Jehovah's Witnesses, but what friendship do they continue to enjoy?

□ The 'people for God's name' have been fulfilling what responsibility regarding his name?

□ Why do Jehovah's dedicated witnesses not fear this world's unfriendliness?

Insight on the News

'Hitting a Raw Nerve'

On December 22, 1984, a dramatic incident on a subway car in New York City made headlines. Thirty-seven-year-old commuter Bernhard Hugo Goetz was approached by four youths who, he said, threatened to rob him. Goetz, previously a victim of muggers, pulled out a handgun and shot all four, paralyzing one of them for life.

The shooting touched off a nationwide debate on crime and public safety. "This case hit a real raw nerve," said the co-host of a cable news show. "There is a broad sense of frustration and anger over the state of the criminal justice system." An editorial in *The New York Times* elaborated: "Government has failed [the public] in its most basic responsibility: public safety. To take the law into your own hands implies taking it out of official hands. But the law, on that subway car on Dec. 22, was in no one's hands."

The public's overwhelming interest in the Goetz case revealed feelings shared by many: terror over the threat of being robbed or mugged, and frustration and anger over the fact that more is not being done to ensure public safety. Of course, problems from thieves are not new. (Compare 2 Corinthians 11:26.) What is new is the extent to which crime and other worrisome conditions have made people "faint out of fear and expectation." (Luke 21:26) However, under God's Kingdom government such fear will soon end. In that promised new system, all earth's inhabitants will live in peace and harmony, and "there will be no one making them tremble."—Micah 4:4.

"Higher" Education

"Most colleges promise to make you better culturally and morally, but it is not evident that they do," says William J. Bennett, the new secretary of education in the United States. "They are not delivering on their promises." There is another reason why he is negative about the state of college education today. "There's a kind of assumption that college graduates are a priestly class and that wonderful things must come to pass when you get a degree," says Bennett. "If my own son . . . came to me and said 'You promised to pay for my tuition at Harvard; how about giving me $50,000 instead to start a little business?' I might think that was a good idea."

While college may promise a bright future, does it guarantee success? Obviously not. Yet for many people, there is something that does. True Christians today can testify to the cultural, moral, and even financial benefits that they have received from study of God's Word and application of it in their lives. They know, as Paul said, that "all Scripture is . . . beneficial for teaching, for reproving, for setting things straight, . . . that the man of God may be fully competent, completely equipped for every good work." (2 Timothy 3:16, 17) A Bible education carries no risk. Tapping wisdom from the God 'whose thoughts are higher than our thoughts' leads to genuine success.—Isaiah 55:9.

Abortion Divides

"Nearly 10 years ago," says William V. Shannon of *The Boston Globe,* "a Roman Catholic bishop said to me privately, 'I am concerned that we as a church are driving the wrong way down a one-way street on this abortion issue. . . . Look at Poland. It is probably the most Catholic country in Europe. . . . And yet last year, Polish women had 400,000 abortions. If the Polish bishops cannot stamp out abortion in Poland, which is about 90-per-cent Catholic, how can we hope to do so in this country where we are a minority?'" Continues Shannon: "It was a relevant question then. It is even more relevant today when . . . the number of abortions in [Poland] . . . has climbed to 800,000 a year."

The abortion issue remains a touchy subject for the Vatican, both in politics and within the church itself. In October 1984 a full-page ad in *The New York Times,* endorsed by 24 nuns and 73 other Catholics, stated that the church's condemnation of abortion in all instances was not "the only legitimate Catholic position"—a statement with which the Vatican has taken issue. The ad cited data from a recent survey that indicated that only 11 percent of Catholics disapproved of abortion in all cases. Clearly, the abortion issue divides the church. But God's Word exhorts true Christians to "speak in agreement" and to "think in agreement."—1 Corinthians 1:10; 2 Corinthians 13:11.

Pregnant
but Not Married

MARY is in the third month of pregnancy. You will remember that she spent the early part of her pregnancy visiting Elizabeth, but now she has returned home to Nazareth. Soon her condition will become public knowledge in her hometown. She, indeed, is in a distressing situation!

What makes the situation worse is that Mary is engaged to become the wife of the carpenter Joseph. And she knows that, under God's law to Israel, a woman engaged to one man, but who willingly has sexual relations with another man, is to be stoned to death. How can she explain her pregnancy to Joseph?

Since Mary has been gone three months, we can be sure Joseph is eager to see her. When they meet, likely Mary breaks the news to him. She may do her best to explain that it is by means of God's holy spirit that she is pregnant. But, as you can imagine, this is a very difficult thing for Joseph.

Joseph knows the fine reputation Mary has. And apparently he loves her dearly. Yet, despite what she may claim, it really seems she is pregnant by some man. Even so, Joseph does not want her to be stoned to death or to be disgraced publicly. So he makes up his mind to divorce her secretly. In those days, engaged persons were viewed as married, and a divorce was required to end an engagement.

Later, as Joseph is still considering these matters, he goes to sleep. Jehovah's

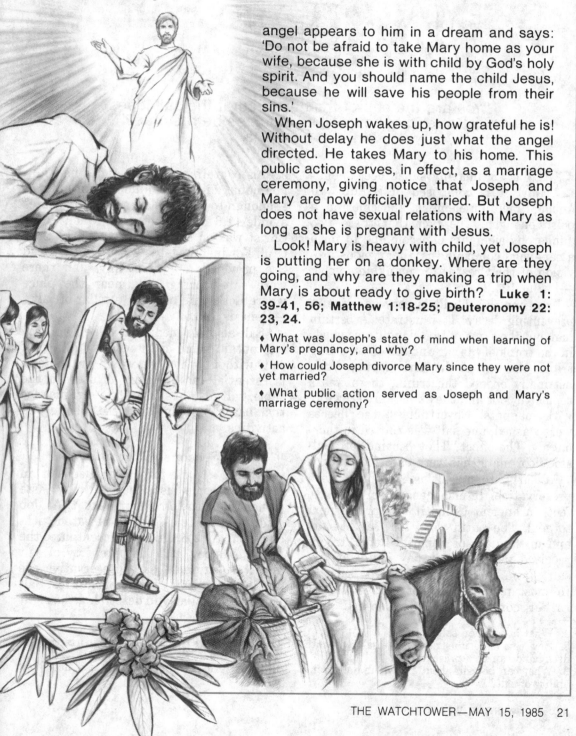

angel appears to him in a dream and says: 'Do not be afraid to take Mary home as your wife, because she is with child by God's holy spirit. And you should name the child Jesus, because he will save his people from their sins.'

When Joseph wakes up, how grateful he is! Without delay he does just what the angel directed. He takes Mary to his home. This public action serves, in effect, as a marriage ceremony, giving notice that Joseph and Mary are now officially married. But Joseph does not have sexual relations with Mary as long as she is pregnant with Jesus.

Look! Mary is heavy with child, yet Joseph is putting her on a donkey. Where are they going, and why are they making a trip when Mary is about ready to give birth? **Luke 1: 39-41, 56; Matthew 1:18-25; Deuteronomy 22: 23, 24.**

♦ What was Joseph's state of mind when learning of Mary's pregnancy, and why?

♦ How could Joseph divorce Mary since they were not yet married?

♦ What public action served as Joseph and Mary's marriage ceremony?

"You Are the Salt of the Earth"

"You are the salt of the earth; but if the salt loses its strength, how will its saltness be restored?"
—MATTHEW 5:13.

SALT is an amazing substance. Chemically, it is composed of sodium, an unusual metallic element, and chlorine, a poisonous gas. The fact that these two dangerous elements can combine to form a beneficial compound is a marvelous provision of the Creator for mankind's good. —Psalm 104:24.

2 For one thing, salt is very effective in preventing decay. To illustrate: A certain man put the skins of two slaughtered sheep in the trunk of his car and set off on a long trip in the heat of the African sun. When he finally opened the trunk, there was a repulsive odor and the skins were crawling with maggots! Nevertheless, the fleeces were washed, and salt was rubbed in thoroughly. The effect? They became soft bedside floor mats that were used for years.

3 Clearly, then, salt is invaluable as a preservative. It also has other value. In fact, in ancient China it was prized next to gold. The Latin word for "salt" is sal, and in the days of imperial Rome, troops received part of their pay (salarium) in salt. From this comes the word "salary." In most places today, of course, salt is rather common and inexpensive. The oceans contain some four and a half million cubic miles (19 million cu km) of salt —enough to bury the entire United States a mile (1.6 km) deep! Even when Jesus Christ was on earth, salt was fairly plentiful. For instance, the waters of the Dead Sea provided a good supply, and there were salt-bearing hills near the place where Lot's wife became "a pillar of salt." —Genesis 19:26.

4 Salt also has medicinal value. Our bodies contain some eight ounces (230 g) of salt, without which we would die. So salt is essential for life. But as used in the Bible, salt also has figurative significance that has a bearing on Christian life and activities.

"Seasoned With Salt"

5 When a cook forgets to use salt in preparing some dish, the food may taste so flat that people refuse to eat it. As Job said: "Will tasteless things be eaten without salt?" (Job 6:1, 6) Salt accentuates the flavor of food. Both this property of salt and its usefulness as a preservative are applied figuratively in the Scriptures. Salt is used particularly in describing the right kind of speech.

1. What is common salt?
2. How can it be illustrated that salt prevents decay and can be a preservative?
3. What can be said about the value and availability of salt?

4. Why can we say that salt has importance with regard to life?
5. As regards food, what purpose does salt serve?

⁶ The apostle Paul wrote: "Let your utterance be always with graciousness, seasoned with salt, so as to know how you ought to give an answer to each one." Another translation reads: "Let your conversation be always gracious, and never insipid." (Colossians 4:6; *The New English Bible*) True Christians spend many hours talking to people about God's Kingdom. Of course, not all of Jehovah's Witnesses are naturally fluent speakers. Yet, if they appreciate the message deeply and speak with conviction and warmth, they can turn the hearts of many people to the truth of God's Word. How vital it is, then, for the speech of Jehovah's servants to be gracious and appealing!

⁷ A Christian's "seasoned" words not only enable the hearer to get the fine flavor of the Bible's message but also tend to preserve the lives of those listening to it. So, just as salt is essential for life, the speech of Jehovah's servants can mean life to those who listen appreciatively to what they say about God's purpose and Kingdom.—Compare John 6:63, 68.

⁸ Accordingly, graciousness should characterize the speech of Christians as they speak to unbelievers. Sometimes hearers of the Kingdom message reply in a harsh or rude manner. But Jehovah's servants must never answer back in that way. Rather, they must always be gracious. What does it mean to be gracious? It means to be kind, pleasing, courteous, and merciful. A Christian's kind, patient way of handling questions, objections, criticism, or bad manners often make a vital difference. As a proverb says, "An answer, when mild, turns away rage." (Proverbs

15:1) Graciousness, courtesy, and tactful replies in the Christian ministry can soften people who, although hard and bitter in manner, really have good hearts.—Proverbs 25:15.

⁹ How, then, should Christians communicate with fellow believers? Ungraciously? Never! Why? Because these dedicated servants of Jehovah are also part of "the flock of God," which is to be treated with tenderness.—Compare 1 Peter 5:2-4; Acts 20:29.

¹⁰ Should a servant of Jehovah use bad language when speaking to workmates who may have irritated him? Would it be proper for a Christian foreman to use unclean speech when workers disappoint him? When Christian husbands and wives are somewhat annoyed, should they scream abuses at each other or at their children? Never! Paul wrote: "Let a rotten saying not proceed out of your mouth . . . Let all malicious bitterness and anger and wrath and screaming and abusive speech be taken away from you along with all badness. But become kind to one another, tenderly compassionate, freely forgiving one another just as God also by Christ freely forgave you."—Ephesians 4:29-32.

"Have Salt in Yourselves"

¹¹ Since we are imperfect, we all have times when we speak in a manner that is unsuitable for a Christian. As the disciple James candidly admitted: "We all stumble many times. If anyone does not stumble in word, this one is a perfect man, able to

---

6. How does Colossians 4:6 apply to the ministry of Jehovah's Witnesses?
7. A Christian's "seasoned" words can have what good effect?
8. Why should graciousness characterize the speech of Christian ministers?

9. How should Christians communicate with fellow believers, and why?
10. What bearing should Ephesians 4:29-32 have on the language used by Jehovah's servants?
11, 12. To "salt" of what kind was Jesus referring at Mark 9:50, and those words would call for what kind of speech and action?

bridle also his whole body." (James 3:2, 8-10) Jesus' early disciples were no exception to this, and they had to be reproved for failing to speak graciously to one another. For instance, on a certain occasion the disciples argued hotly about who was the greatest among them. Jesus gave the entire group some fine counsel against stumbling others and thus being "salted with fire," or being destroyed in Gehenna. He then concluded with the words: "Have salt in yourselves, and keep peace between one another."—Mark 9:33-50.

[12] Obviously, Jesus was not there referring to the small amount of literal salt found in the physical bodies of his disciples. Rather, he was referring to their being considerate, tactful, wholesome, and peaceable in word and conduct—acting in good taste toward others. This is vital so that true Christians can remain at peace with one another.

"The Salt of the Earth"

[13] Concerning his followers, Jesus also said: "You are the salt of the earth." (Matthew 5:13) By saying this, Jesus did not mean that his disciples literally were salt. Rather, salt is a preservative, and the message that Jesus' followers carried to the people would preserve the lives of many. Indeed, his disciples had a preserving influence upon those who listened to their message, preventing spiritual and moral decay among such individuals. There was no question about the fact that the good news declared by Jesus' followers would preserve life.—Acts 5:20; 13:46-48.

Salt Preserves From Corruption

[14] From Jehovah God's elevated and pure standpoint, this entire wicked sys-tem of things must appear much like the sheepskins mentioned earlier. Before the cleansing process and use of salt, they created a bad stench and were crawling with vermin. Well, to some extent, everyone is affected by the conditions in this world, and to resist corruption that reaches into every aspect of life, a person needs courage and must maintain his integrity to God. Only in this way can an individual preserve himself from moral decay. He needs not only graciousness of speech but also the preservative quality that enables him to say no to corruption in all its forms. In his case, there is an urgent need for "salt."—1 Peter 4:1-3.

[15] A faithful servant of Jehovah must know how to say no to bad practices and temptations. Remember that Jesus said no three times when he was tempted by Satan in the wilderness. (Matthew 4:1-10) And consider the example provided by the prophet Daniel. He learned to say no at a comparatively tender age. When Daniel was a young man in the royal court of Babylon, he and his companions were offered "a daily allowance from the delicacies of the king." But Daniel and his friends refused. This was not a case of refusing a hospitable offer. Rather, the four young Hebrews insisted on a diet consisting solely of vegetables and water because they were anxious to avoid food prohibited by Jehovah's Law or defiled by pagan rituals. Real courage was required to take that course. The outcome was rewarding, for at the end of the set period of testing, their physical appearance was better than that of those who had accepted the royal diet. And spiritually those Hebrews enjoyed Jehovah's blessing and favor.—Daniel 1:5-17.

---

13. What did Jesus mean when he told his followers, "You are the salt of the earth"?
14. To resist worldly corruption, what is needed?

15. What fine examples were set by Jesus and Daniel?

¹⁶ Jehovah God saw to it that Daniel and his associates were preserved because of 'having salt in themselves.' But we can learn more from Daniel. He was appointed to a high office in the Babylonian government. Under those circumstances he must have had to say no many times, for he was surrounded by pagan people, and the royal court no doubt was full of immorality, lying, bribery, political intrigue, and other corrupt practices. Daniel was under heavy pressure many times. But although he was in the midst of the "world" of that day, he was "no part of the world." (John 17:16) Daniel was a faithful, "well-salted" servant of Jehovah. Why, Daniel's enemies, perhaps irritated because his integrity and honesty reflected badly on them, even tried to destroy him! Nevertheless, they had to admit that "he was trustworthy and no negligence or corrupt thing at all was found in him." (Daniel 6:4, 5) What a fine example!

¹⁷ Like young Daniel and his friends, Christian youngsters today face difficult tests. Especially at school, they have to contend with drugs, tobacco, alcoholic beverages, unclean talk, immorality, cheating, a spirit of rebelliousness, false worship, nationalism, bad associations, false teachings such as evolution, and other powerful influences. It takes a "well-salted" Christian youngster to remain a clean integrity keeper in the face of all that temptation.

¹⁸ Therefore, Christian parents, consider carefully the condition of your family.

At an early age, Daniel learned to say no

Are all members of it making spiritual progress? Have you prevented worldly corruption from contaminating your own youngsters? Do you know what they do and what they really think and feel about true worship? Do they have a loathing for the unclean things of this world or are they in danger of succumbing to them? (Amos 5:14, 15) If, as parents, you are not close enough to your children to help them, or you find this difficult, why not make it a matter of earnest prayer to Jehovah? Surely, he can help you to overcome this barrier.—1 John 5:14.

¹⁹ As Christian parents, what sort of example are you setting? Do you firmly say no to harmful overeating and heavy drinking and the many forms of immorality and uncleanness practiced around you? Do you say no to bribery, to petty pilfer-

---

16. Why can it be said that Daniel was a "well-salted" servant of Jehovah?
17. What difficult tests confront Christian youngsters today?
18. (a) Christian parents would do well to consider what questions? (b) What is recommended for parents who find it difficult to help their children?

---

19. What are some things to which Christian parents should say no?

ing, and to the obscene jokes and speech of worldly people? At work or in your neighborhood, are you known as clean, honest, upright individuals? Saying no at the right time is vital to being "the salt of the earth."

Permanence and Loyalty

[20] Doubtless because salt represented freedom from corruption, it was used in Israel's worship of Jehovah. For instance, all offerings on the altar had to be salted. In the Law given through Moses, it was stated: "You must not allow the salt of the covenant of your God to be missing upon your grain offering. Along with every offering of yours you will present salt." And "a covenant of salt" was considered to be binding.—Leviticus 2:13; Numbers 18:19; 2 Chronicles 13:4, 5.

[21] As witnesses of Jehovah, his servants today are "the salt of the earth." This requires that they be incorruptible, faithful, and loyal. They must be diligent in cultivating the fruitage of God's holy spirit—love, joy, peace, long-suffering, kindness, goodness, faith, mildness, and self-control. (Galatians 5:22, 23) The spirit's fruitage is the source of spiritual, saltlike qualities. But the fact that some have served Jehovah for years is, in itself, no guarantee that they will not fall away. (1 Corinthians 10:12) Jesus himself warned us about this.

[22] Remember that just after Jesus said, "You are the salt of the earth," he added: "But if the salt loses its strength, how will its saltness be restored? It is no longer usable for anything but to be thrown out-
side to be trampled on by men." (Matthew 5:13) Some of the salt used when Jesus was on earth was mixed with foreign matter. Thus if the pure salt was washed away by rain or in some other way, what was left was fit only to be thrown outside, perhaps cast on paths and trampled upon by passersby. Unless the salt was kept in the right condition, it could easily become useless.

[23] As loyal servants of Jehovah and his Son Jesus Christ, then, let us be careful never to 'lose our strength,' or pure salt-like qualities. Rather, let us make every effort to cultivate the fruitage of God's spirit. May we always be gracious in speech, zealously declaring the Kingdom message and thus helping to preserve the lives of others. May we never be overreached by this corrupt world, but may we always keep in mind the depth of meaning and the great privilege associated with Jesus' words: "You are the salt of the earth."

___

23. As Jehovah's Witnesses, what should be our view of Jesus' words, "You are the salt of the earth"?

___

20. How was salt used in connection with worship of Jehovah in ancient Israel?
21. As "the salt of the earth," what is required of Jehovah's servants today?
22. What is the significance of the latter part of Matthew 5:13?

Check Your Memory

☐ How can we 'let our utterances be seasoned with salt'?

☐ Why is it vital for Christians to 'have salt in themselves'?

☐ How are Jesus' followers "the salt of the earth"?

☐ What are some things avoided by "well-salted" Christians?

☐ In view of Matthew 5:13, what should be the viewpoint of Jehovah's servants today?

Bible Truth Triumphs Amid Tradition

BRITAIN

ONE hundred years ago, the Bible had a prime place in most British households. The *King James Version* of 1611, an established part of the nation's Protestant tradition, was greatly loved and respected. Thus, when Charles T. Russell, the first president of the Watch Tower Society, visited the British Isles for the first time in 1891, he was impressed by the "religious fervor" of the people. He described the country as "fields ready and waiting to be harvested," and saw the urgent need to bring this interest together and to distribute more Bible literature in the country.

To meet this need, Russell opened a book depot in London, and by 1898 there were nine congregations of Bible Students (as Jehovah's Witnesses were then known) meeting in Britain. Two years later, in 1900, the first branch office of the Watch Tower Society was organized in London, and in 1911 it became located at 34 Craven Terrace. The nearby London Tabernacle became the center for many historic assemblies. The evangelizing work prospered throughout the country.

With the outbreak of World War I in 1914, however, the scene was set for change. Support for traditional religion began to wane, the erosion continuing to our day. Who would then have thought it possible that 70 years later the Anglican Church, steeped in tradition with its ancient churches and cathedrals, customs and celebrations, would be losing 75 percent of its congregation before they reach the age of 20? Or that the Church of Scotland's membership would tumble to less than a million, or about 18 percent of the population? Or that many Welsh chapels would end up as garages, supermarkets, or recreational centers? But such is the picture today.

On the other hand, who would ever have dreamed that Jehovah's Witnesses in Britain would, in 1984, number over 95,000 active preachers? Or that their 1,170 congregations would be engaged in an unprecedented program of Kingdom Hall construction? Yet, the facts are there for all to see. How are we to account for this seemingly paradoxical development? Why are Jehovah's Witnesses prospering in Britain? And what challenges are they facing today?

Power of Bible Truth

Traditions die hard, as the saying goes. Even so, love of Bible truth has enabled many who had long been staunch church supporters to break free from the grip of such traditions. Others, too, have allowed the power of Bible truth to transform their life. Indeed, in the following experiences, we can clearly see how Bible truth triumphs amid tradition in Britain.

One elderly lady who had been a stalwart member of the Church of England all her life was well known for her love of the Bible. Although she knew and admired a number of Witnesses in her community, she never allowed herself to get involved too deeply when it came to discussing religion with them. But when the book *You Can Live Forever in Paradise on Earth* was scheduled to be considered at a nearby Bible study group, she accepted the invitation to attend and was deeply impressed by what was being discussed. From that first meeting, she became a regular attender there and at the congregation's Kingdom Hall. When the vicar called to inquire about her absence from church, she told him frankly that she would never be going back as she had learned more about the Bible during the past few weeks than she had learned during her 86 years as a member of his church.

"Confession followed talk with Witnesses" was the headline given to the following story by *The West Wales Guardian*. A 30-year-old man was arrested for stealing. He instructed his lawyer to enter a plea of "Not Guilty." Before the court hearing, however, he started to study the Bible with Jehovah's Witnesses. The outcome? A statement to the court and a last-minute change of plea to "Guilty"! In summarizing the case, the chairman of the magistrates declared: "We are delighted that you have decided to live by the law of the land." The man's wife, appreciating the profound changes her husband had already made in his life,

exclaimed: "This really is the best way of life!"

Bible Truth Benefits Children

For years, a bone of contention in households where only one of the parents is a Witness has been that the children are deprived, particularly when it comes to traditional religious celebrations. A recent High Court judgment, however, puts this emotional topic in a different perspective by saying, in part:

"There is nothing immoral or socially obnoxious in the beliefs and practice of [Jehovah's Witnesses]. There is a great risk, because we are dealing with an unpopular sect, in overplaying the dangers to the welfare of these children inherent in the possibility that they may follow their mother and become Jehovah's Witnesses."

Rather than being deprived, children of Jehovah's Witnesses often receive commendation because of their Christian training and upbringing. For example, one teacher in Glasgow, Scotland, noted that they "do well in school, not because they are more intelligent, but because, from an early age, they are taught how to sit and listen and how to apply what they learn." He also observed that Witness teenagers tend to be more balanced and therefore, in his opinion, better able to cope with the problems peculiar to the adolescent years.

'Seek First the Kingdom'

What happens when the children grow up? Does the training they receive when young result in any advantage in later life? With three and a half million unemployed people in Britain now, putting spiritual things first in life can be a real test. Yet, as Jesus promised, "seeking first the kingdom" does lead to rich dividends, as borne out by the following experience. —Matthew 6:33.

Quickly built Kingdom Hall at Northampton, England

While trying to decide between the full-time ministry and a secular profession, a young Witness was offered a promising job with an engineering firm with the stipulation that he enroll for special study courses on Tuesday and Thursday evenings. The young man, however, decided to make it clear that as one of Jehovah's Witnesses he attended congregation meetings on those two evenings. "Which will you put first?" the manager wanted to know. Unwilling to compromise, the young man turned down the offer but took part-time employment to support himself and started in the full-time ministry.

Looking back over four years of happy, fruitful activity, the young man, now with foreign missionary service as his goal, has seen many of his contemporaries who went to universities still without employment. Others have become dropouts from society. What of the company that made the offer? Soon thereafter it went into liquidation and is no more.

The full-time ministry, or pioneering, is not just for the young. One Witness, a family man in the north of England, sold his prosperous business and took part-time work in order to pioneer regularly. With his fine lead, three of his four children pioneered straight from school, leaving the remaining daughter keen to join them when her turn comes. The mother

also sets a fine example by serving as an auxiliary pioneer, spending 60 hours or more a month in the preaching work whenever she can.

The auxiliary pioneer work has caught on well in Britain. In May 1984, a peak of 12,108 Witnesses volunteered for this privilege of service. Imagine the enthusiasm in one Scottish congregation when a 23-year-old brother who had been a thalidomide baby born with no arms and only one leg, took the lead and enrolled. With the kind help of the congregation, he is able to witness from door to door.

The Challenge of a Mixed Community

Although Britain is a small country, it is not without its challenges as far as varying traditions, languages, and dialects are concerned. In Wales, for example, most people, though English speaking, are still conversant with their native tongue, Welsh. A few, in more remote areas of the Principality, are solely Welsh speaking. To help them, the Society has recently printed some Bible study aids in the Welsh language, and initial reports indicate that they are being very well received.

Since World War II, there has been a steady influx of British citizens from former colonies. Besides large numbers of

West Indians, reports show that over one million Asians from India, Pakistan, and Bangladesh now live in Britain. Their languages have presented a most interesting challenge to Jehovah's Witnesses. Though Bible literature is available in both Gujarati and Punjabi—the two main tongues involved—initial breakthrough is not easy. Witnesses who set their minds to learn the languages and to understand the social and religious traditions of these people are warmly welcomed by the communities.

As a result, the London newspaper *Garavi Gujarat* reports: "Many Gujaratis have broken away from the traditional Hindu Caste System and have now become Jehovah's Witnesses." A similar headline in the *Wembley Midweek* proclaims: "Bible breaking caste barriers." Those who break away, however, are faced with considerable family pressure, especially regarding the tradition of arranged marriage. Confronted with this situation, one young Indian girl witnessed at length to the men who were introduced to her as prospective husbands. Each in turn decided that he did not want to marry her in view of her strong religious faith. Eventually, with her parents' consent, she married an Indian Witness. They are now a united family in Jehovah's service. Today, over 500 Witnesses of Asian background are active across the country, among them 35 full-time preachers!

Building for the Future

In the months just prior to the second world war, the first Kingdom Halls were built in London, in the suburbs of Harrow and Ilford. Now, there are 140 congregations in London alone, including 4 Greek, 2 Italian, and one Spanish, along with Chinese, Gujarati, Japanese, Portuguese, and Punjabi groups. The challenge to acquire new Kingdom Halls, in the face of the wildly escalating cost of property, is greater than ever.

Speeding things up, however, is the new two-day Kingdom Hall building program. The first such hall in Europe was erected in 1983 in the Midlands town of Northampton. Witnesses experienced in this unique field of construction came from the United States and Canada to oversee the project. At a nearby school, the headmaster gave permission for the pupils to visit the building site at regular intervals to see firsthand what he called "a challenging view of a great community undertaking." But it was more than that. It was an *international* project, with about 500 volunteers from as far afield as Japan, India, France, and Germany.

This spirit of unity is now a source of much comment in Britain. No longer are Jehovah's Witnesses looked upon as an insignificant minority. They are seen as a people with a purpose, building for the future with, as one Church of England clergyman put it, "an efficient organisation as well as burning enthusiasm." He further observed: "They show a detailed knowledge of the Bible. They can quote it and find their way easily about it. Their ordinary members seem to be extraordinarily well trained." Herein lies the reason for their unity and strength: Jehovah's Witnesses use the Bible as sole authority for all that they believe and preach, a fact readily acknowledged today.

In Britain in the 1980's, the Bible is still a best-seller, and respect for it remains. True, there may no longer be the "religious fervor" so readily apparent one hundred years ago. But by holding high the truth of the Bible, Jehovah's Witnesses there are gathering a bountiful harvest. A total of 187,709 persons gathered with them for the 1984 annual commemoration of the death of the Lord Jesus Christ—a peak attendance! With good reason, therefore, they remain confident that in this land of tradition thousands more will yet embrace Bible truth to become worshipers of Jehovah, the God of truth, as this system of things draws to its close.—Matthew 24:3, 14.

Questions From Readers

■ Since it was the two-tribe kingdom of Judah that was taken captive to Babylon in 607 B.C.E., how was it that members of all 12 tribes of Israel returned from Babylon 70 years later?

It appears that there are two primary reasons for this. First, at the time of the splitting of the kingdom of Israel and the subsequent withdrawal of 10 tribes, representatives of all 12 tribes evidently remained in Judah's territory. And second, prior to 740 B.C.E., it is likely that some from all the ten tribes fled to Judah's territory to escape Israel's idolatry.

The division of the united kingdom of Israel took place when Jehovah became displeased with Solomon "because his heart had inclined away from Jehovah." God informed him: "I shall without fail rip the kingdom away from off you, and I shall certainly give it to your servant. . . . Out of the hand of your son I shall rip it away. . . . One tribe I shall give to your son." (1 Kings 11:9-13) Solomon's son Rehoboam, who was of the tribe of Judah, was given the tribe of Benjamin, thus forming the two-tribe southern kingdom.

Although Rehoboam ruled over only two tribes, he continued to reign over some of "the sons of Israel [that is, members of the northern ten tribes] that were dwelling in the cities of Judah." (1 Kings 12:17; see also 2 Chronicles 10:17.) Additionally, when King Jeroboam of the northern kingdom established calf worship and put in office his own priests, the priests of Jehovah and the Levites who lived in the territory of that kingdom sided with Rehoboam. We read: "The Levites left their pasture grounds and their possession and then came to Judah and Jerusalem, because Jeroboam and his sons had discharged them from acting as priests to Jehovah." At that time, representatives from "all the tribes of Israel" joined the priests and Levites and went to Jerusalem. (2 Chronicles 11:13-17) Further desertions by members of various ones of the ten tribes are reported in the reign of King Asa. —2 Chronicles 15:9, 10.

In 740 B.C.E., when the Assyrians overthrew the northern capital city of Samaria, they applied their policy of transplanting populations of conquered areas to reduce the possibility of uprisings. (1 Chronicles 5:6, 26) Thus the northern kingdom of Israel ceased to exist. However, this did not affect those members of the ten tribes who were by then living in the southern kingdom of Judah. These individuals were among those taken captive to Babylon when Judah fell in 607 B.C.E. And some of their descendants would have returned at the time of the restoration in 537 B.C.E. Perhaps even some descendants of those exiled by the Assyrians in 740 B.C.E. also returned at that time.

Interestingly, Ezekiel, in the book bearing his name, mentioned "the house of Israel" far more often than he referred to "the house of Judah," despite his being a prophet to Judah while in captivity in Babylon. Moreover, his prophecy indicated that the two 'houses' would be reunited as one. (Ezekiel 37:19-28; see also Jeremiah 3:18; Hosea 1:11.) With good reason, then, no distinction is made between the two after the Babylonian captivity.

Hence, the ripping away of the ten tribes in 740 B.C.E. did not result in the loss of their identity. They were accounted for in the return from captivity in 537 B.C.E. And regarding the inauguration of the rebuilt temple in Jerusalem, the priest Ezra stated: "The sons of Israel, the priests and the Levites and the rest of the former exiles held the inauguration of this house of God with joy. And they presented . . . as a sin offering for all Israel twelve male goats, according to the number of the tribes of Israel." (Ezra 6:16, 17) Also indicating that the returning remnant included representatives of all tribes of Israel, not merely Judah and Benjamin, Isaiah wrote: "For although your people, O Israel, would prove to be like the grains of sand of the sea, a mere remnant among them will return." (Isaiah 10:22) Hence, among the returnees were representatives of *all* the tribes of Israel.

"I Couldn't Put It Down"

That is what an appreciative reader said after finishing the book *Making Your Family Life Happy*. She wrote:

"Yesterday I finished reading *Making Your Family Life Happy*. I couldn't put it down until it was finished. It was just excellent. I pray that we can make proper application of all the fine points in this book."

June 1, 1985

The Watchtower

Announcing Jehovah's Kingdom

Adam and Eve

Myth or Reality?

The Watchtower

Announcing Jehovah's Kingdom

June 1, 1985
Vol. 106, No. 11

THE PURPOSE OF "THE WATCHTOWER" is to exalt Jehovah God as the Sovereign of the universe. It keeps watch on world events as they fulfill Bible prophecy. It comforts all peoples with the good news that God's Kingdom will soon destroy those who oppress their fellowmen and that it will turn the earth into a paradise. It encourages faith in the now-reigning King, Jesus Christ, whose shed blood opens the way for mankind to gain eternal life. "The Watchtower," published by Jehovah's Witnesses continuously since 1879, is nonpolitical. It adheres to the Bible as its authority.

"WATCHTOWER" STUDIES FOR THE WEEKS

July 7: Walk by Faith! Page 10. Songs to Be Used: 144, 124.

July 14: Walk With Confidence in Jehovah's Leadership. Page 15. Songs to Be Used: 8, 1.

Average Printing Each Issue: 11,150,000

Now Published in 102 Languages

SEMIMONTHLY EDITIONS AVAILABLE BY MAIL
Afrikaans, Arabic, Cebuano, Chichewa, Chinese, Cibemba, Danish, Dutch, Efik, English*, Finnish, French, German, Greek, Hiligaynon, Igbo, Iloko, Italian, Japanese, Korean, Lingala, Malagasy, Maltese, Norwegian, Portuguese, Russian, Sepedi, Sesotho, Shona, Spanish, Swahili, Swedish, Tagalog, Thai, Tswana, Xhosa, Yoruba, Zulu

MONTHLY EDITIONS AVAILABLE BY MAIL
Armenian, Bengali, Bicol, Bulgarian, Croatian, Czech, Ewe, Fijian, Ga, Greenlandic, Gujarati, Gun, Hausa, Hebrew, Hindi, Hiri Motu, Hungarian, Icelandic, Kannada, Kikuyu, Kiluba, Malayalam, Marathi, New Guinea Pidgin, Pangasinan, Papiamento, Polish, Rarotongan, Romanian, Samar-Leyte, Samoan, Sango, Serbian, Silozi, Sinhalese, Slovenian, Solomon Islands-Pidgin, Tahitian, Tamil, Telugu, Tshiluba, Tsonga, Turkish, Twi, Ukrainian, Urdu, Venda, Vietnamese
*Study articles also available in large-print edition at same cost.

The Bible translation used is the "New World Translation of the Holy Scriptures," unless otherwise indicated.

Twenty cents (U.S.) a copy

Watch Tower Society offices	Yearly subscription rates Semimonthly
America, U.S., Watchtower, Wallkill, N.Y. 12589	$4.00
Australia, Box 280, Ingleburn, N.S.W. 2565	A$6.00
Canada, Box 4100, Halton Hills (Georgetown), Ontario L7G 4Y4	$5.20
England, The Ridgeway, London NW7 1RN	£5.00
Ireland, 29A Jamestown Road, Finglas, Dublin 11	£5.00
New Zealand, 6-A Western Springs Rd., Auckland 3	$10.00
Nigeria, P.O. Box 194, Yaba, Lagos State	₦6.00
Philippines, P.O. Box 2044, Manila 2800	₱50.00
South Africa, Private Bag 2, Elandsfontein, 1406	R5,60

Remittances should be sent to the office in your country or to Watchtower, Wallkill, N.Y. 12589, U.S.A.

Changes of address should reach us 30 days before your moving date. Give us your old and new address (if possible, your old address label).

The Watchtower (ISSN 0043-1087) is published semimonthly for $4.00 (U.S.) per year by Watch Tower Bible and Tract Society of Pennsylvania, 25 Columbia Heights, Brooklyn, N.Y. 11201. Second-class postage paid at Brooklyn, N.Y., and at additional mailing offices.

Postmaster: Send address changes to Watchtower, *Wallkill, N.Y. 12589.*

Published by
Watch Tower Bible and Tract Society of Pennsylvania
25 Columbia Heights, Brooklyn, N.Y. 11201, U.S.A.
Frederick W. Franz, President

Did Adam and Eve Really Exist?

"THE first man was Adam and the first woman was Eve; they were our first parents." Such was the viewpoint expressed in 1947 in *The Catechism for Use by French Dioceses,* the basic textbook for teaching French children the Catholic faith.

But a year later, in 1948, the church-authorized French encyclopedia *Catholicisme* said: "Any evolutionary doctrine that allows for the soul's being created by God is not in disagreement with the Bible." That very same year, the Papal Biblical Commission described the Genesis account of creation as being "a popular description of the origins of the human race" explained in "simple figurative language suited to the intelligence of less-developed humans."

In 1981 Pope John Paul II made the following statement before the Papal Academy of Sciences:

"The Bible itself speaks of the origin and constitution of the Universe not as a scientific treatise but to clarify man's proper relationship with the Universe." And *La Bible de la Liturgie* (Liturgical Bible), officially approved in 1976, sums up the opinions of many Catholic theologians on the subject of the Genesis creation account, stating: "Actually, it is neither historical nor scientific truth."

Other churches claiming to be Christian are not to be outdone as far as upholding the evolution theory is concerned. Alexandre Westphal, who was emeritus professor of religious history and Biblical theology at the Protestant Theology School in Montauban, France, stated in his *Dictionnaire Encyclopédique de la Bible* that the account in Genesis concerning Adam and Eve and their first two children "should not be considered a description of events that actually took place in four people's lives, but a narration, using figurative style and basic imagery, of the beginnings of mankind's relations with God." (Genesis 2:7–4:16) In 1949 the Archbishop of Canterbury, considered to be the senior bishop of the Church of England, went so far as to say: "The Christian Church as a whole has accepted the theory of evolution as scientifically established."

Thus, in a peremptory tone the French-language weekly *L'Express* claims that man's belonging to the animal kingdom is undisputed today by anyone "except ignoramuses and a few cranks."

Creation Account and Science

But does the creation account, which was accepted for many centuries, now deserve to be scornfully rejected? Admittedly, the book of Genesis does not supply technical details about how plant and animal life was created, but its general outline is in perfect harmony with scientific facts.

For instance, the Bible shows that all men have a common origin, springing from the first human couple, Adam and Eve. Confirming mankind's common stock, André Langaney, assistant department head at the *Musée de l'Homme* (Museum of Man) in Paris, explained in a special issue of the French monthly *Science et Vie:* "Biological and historical facts show that Man's unity goes deep, prevailing over differences in skin color or frequency of genes in the Gm system [blood globulins characteristic of certain population groups]."

The book of Genesis also supplies information on questions that go beyond the understanding of scientists. When answering a question concerning the "incredible paradox of the aging process," put to him by Paris weekly *L'Express,* Nobel-prize-winning biologist François Jacob admitted: "The mechanism is not understood. Indeed, it is utterly paradoxical that an organism that managed to produce itself by an extraordinarily complicated process should then be incapable of maintaining itself in good condition. The fact that a human being can be produced from a fertilized egg cell is probably the most stupendous event that could happen on earth."

The Bible, too, indicates that it is, in a way, paradoxical that man should die. According to the creation account in the book of Genesis, man was created to live, to 'maintain himself in good condition,' forever. However, this was dependent on his maintaining good relations with the One who created him. When the first humans deliberately rebelled against His requirements, they sinned. It was sin that introduced for mankind the "paradox" of dying. Sin 'worked out death' in humans, as God had warned that it would.—Romans 7:13; Genesis 3:16-19.

Hence, it is not unreasonable to believe the account of man's origin found in the

Bible. In fact, the following article will present evidence to show that a Christian cannot reject this account of man's creation without dire consequences to his belief in the very basis of Christianity —Christ's sacrificial death. Please read on.

Adam and Eve
Myth or Reality?

"IS IT not a flagrant contradiction of the Bible to say that Adam and Eve issued from the animal kingdom?" This question, raised by the Roman Catholic daily *La Croix,* puts in a nutshell the problem many Christians are up against. They are wondering what Christianity is all about if creation is called into question.

For a better understanding of the problems involved, we will need to investigate what the Bible has to say on the subject of sin and death. First of all, we must go back to the account of what happened in the garden of Eden.

Sin and the Ransom

Genesis chapter 2 relates that God gave the first man a command. He was not to eat of a certain tree called "the tree of the knowledge of good and bad." (Genesis 2:17) As *The Jerusalem Bible* explains in a footnote, when he transgressed God's commandment, man assumed a right that did not belong to him, "the power of deciding for himself what is good and what is evil and of acting accordingly, a claim to complete moral independence by which

man refuses to recognise his status as a created being."

By disobeying God's law, Adam sinned and introduced imperfection into the human race, resulting in death as God had foretold. Having lost their perfection, the first human couple could pass on only imperfection to their offspring. All future descendants of Adam and Eve—in other words, the entire human race—would be destined to death.—Genesis 3:6; Psalm 51:5; Romans 5:14, 18, 19.

How could mankind ever again have the hope of everlasting life that was forfeited by Adam? The "life for life" principle expressed in God's Law given through Moses made clear what was required: a *perfect life* had to be offered up for the *perfect life* that Adam lost. (Deuteronomy 19:21, *The New English Bible*) Jesus, the foundation stone of Christianity, was fully qualified for this. Free from sin and imperfection, he alone was able to offer up a perfect human life as "a corresponding ransom for all." (1 Timothy 2:5, 6) Christ showed that this was one of the main purposes of his coming to earth, when he stated: "The Son of man came, not to be

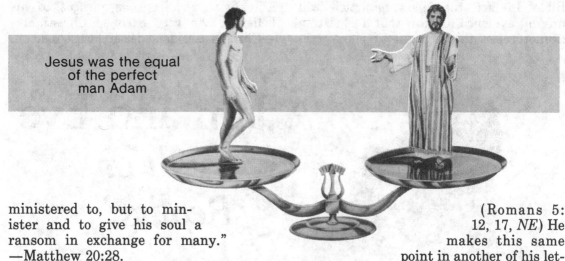

Jesus was the equal
of the perfect
man Adam

ministered to, but to minister and to give his soul a ransom in exchange for many." —Matthew 20:28.

This same requirement—namely, that the ransom must be offered by someone superior to imperfect man—is also made clear in Psalm 49:7, where we read concerning man's lot: "None of them can by any means redeem his brother, nor give to God a ransom for him." (*King James Version*) Why is it that no one can "redeem his brother"? Simply because no imperfect life could ever compensate for the perfect life lost by Adam.

Two Pieces of Weighty Evidence

By an investigation of what the apostle Paul and Christ himself said on the subject, we can judge for ourselves whether the Adam and Eve account was symbolic and whether they really existed or not.

The apostle Paul draws a parallel between the part Adam played and that played by Jesus, explaining: "It was through one man [Adam] that sin entered the world, and through sin death . . . For if by the wrongdoing of that one man death established its reign, through a single sinner, much more shall those who receive in far greater measure God's grace, and his gift of righteousness, live and reign through the one man, Jesus Christ."

(Romans 5: 12, 17, *NE*) He makes this same point in another of his letters, where he calls Jesus "the last Adam," thereby showing that only Jesus could redeem what Adam had lost. Then, after his resurrection to spirit life in the heavens, Jesus could become "a *life-giving* spirit" in behalf of all those being saved. (1 Corinthians 15:45) Now, if Adam were just a symbol of humanity, or a "collective being," as a footnote in the French *Traduction Œcuménique de la Bible* (Ecumenical Translation of the Bible) expresses it, what basis would the apostle Paul's argument have?

However, the most important testimony concerning the authenticity of the Genesis account about Adam and Eve was provided by Christ himself, who referred to it when questioned by the religious leaders of his day. He declared: "'Have you never read [in Genesis] that the Creator made them from the beginning male and female?'; and he added, 'For this reason a man shall leave his father and mother, and be made one with his wife; and the two shall become one flesh. . . . What God has joined together, man must not separate.'" (Matthew 19:4-6, *NE*) Can we imagine Jesus basing his teaching about the sacredness of marriage on something that was imaginary or mythological?

Wisdom of the World or Wisdom of God?

The French Jesuit priest Teilhard de Chardin brought about one of the biggest changes in Catholic thought. He considered evolution to be a gradual climb to a spirit existence. According to his theory, life forms evolve, passing through the animal and human stages, being finally destined to become united at a focal omega point—Christ. Although initially condemned by the church, the theory gained the approval of many Catholic ecclesiastics. However, it was clearly contrary to Scriptural evidence and heaped reproach on God himself, denying the necessity of the ransom for humans to recover perfect human life.

This pseudoscientific theory has had very serious consequences for the church. As was explained in the book *L'épopée des adamites* (The Epic of the Adamites) by Jean Rondot: "All seditious or revolutionary trends in the Church, among both clergy and laity, literally surged into the breach opened up by Teilhard. Now that a certain liberty in Scripture interpretation was permitted (even if it meant changing the spirit of the text), why not make the most of it and build a new religion according to individual taste?"

The fruitage of this trend is particularly visible today. In 1980 a poll organized by an important French institute showed that only 40 percent of French Catholics believed in Adam and Eve and original sin. Doubt had also contaminated other equally important areas, since only 59 percent of Catholics in France now believed in the fundamental Christian doctrine of the resurrection of Jesus Christ.

Far from sticking close to Scriptural teaching, the different churches that have adopted the evolution theory reveal that they are seeking above all to embrace popular, fashionable philosophies. Paul warned the early Christians against such thinking. He reminded the Corinthians that Christianity had nothing in common with the ideas or philosophies in vogue in his day. He wrote: "Where is the wise man? Where the scribe? Where the debater of this system of things? Did not God make the wisdom of the world foolish? . . . For both the Jews ask for signs and the Greeks look for wisdom; but we preach Christ impaled, . . . to the nations foolishness."—1 Corinthians 1:20-23.

Similarly today, the pursuit of such "wisdom of the world" cannot lead man to a knowledge of God nor to obtaining His approval. (Compare John 17:3.) Salvation leading to everlasting life is available to all who fully accept Christ's sacrifice, the ransom he paid to buy back the perfect life that Adam lost. Only on the basis of this sacrifice can men approach God and have their sins forgiven. The apostle Peter was totally convinced of this when he declared before religious leaders gathered at Jerusalem: "There is no salvation in anyone else [apart from Jesus], for there is not another name under heaven that has been given among men by which we must get saved."—Acts 4:12.

Hundreds of thousands of people have already placed their confidence in this "life-giving spirit." They are eagerly awaiting the near future when Paradise will be restored to earth and they will be able to realize the hope Adam lost, that of living forever on earth. If you have not already done so, you can acquire this vital Bible knowledge by studying with Jehovah's Witnesses, free of charge, and by attending their Christian meetings. Thus you will learn what is required in order to become one of Jesus' disciples. By means of him, "the last Adam," you may inherit marvelous blessings from God.—1 Corinthians 15:45; Revelation 21:3, 4.

Jesus' Birth— Where and When?

WITH the time getting near for Mary to give birth, why is Joseph taking a long trip? Well, the emperor of the Roman Empire, Caesar Augustus, has made the law that everyone must return to the city of his birth to be registered. So Joseph is going to his birthplace, the city of Bethlehem.

A lot of people are in Bethlehem to register, and the only place that Joseph and Mary can find to stay is in a stable. Here, where donkeys and other animals are kept, Jesus is born. Mary wraps him in strips of cloth and lays him in a manger, the place that holds the food for the animals.

Surely it was at God's direction that Caesar Augustus made his registration law. It made it possible for Jesus to be born in Bethlehem, the city the Scriptures had long before foretold would be the birthplace of the promised ruler.

What an important night this is! Out in the fields a bright light gleams around a group of shepherds. It is Jehovah's glory! And Jehovah's angel tells them: 'There has just been born to you today in Bethlehem a Savior, who is Christ the Lord. You will find him lying in a manger.' Suddenly many more angels appear and sing: "Glory in the heights above to God, and upon earth peace among men of goodwill."

When the angels leave, the shepherds say to one another: 'Let us go all the way to Bethlehem to see this thing that Jehovah has made known to us.' They go in a hurry and find Jesus just where the angel said they would. When the shepherds relate what the angel told them, all who hear about it marvel. Mary safeguards all these sayings and cherishes them in her heart.

Many people today believe that Jesus was born on December 25. But December is a rainy, cold season in Bethlehem. Shepherds would not be out in the fields overnight with their flocks at that time of the year. Also, the Roman Caesar would not likely have required a people who were already inclined to revolt against him to make that trip in the dead of winter to register. Evidently Jesus was born sometime in the early autumn of the year. **Luke 2:1-20; Micah 5:2.**

♦ Why did Joseph and Mary travel to Bethlehem?
♦ What marvelous thing happened the night Jesus was born?
♦ How do we know that Jesus was not born on December 25?

Walk by Faith!

"We are . . . always of good courage and know that, while we have our home in the body, we are absent from the Lord, for we are walking by faith, not by sight."
—2 CORINTHIANS 5:6, 7.

ONE of the marvels of the human body is the eye. By means of this astounding photographic mechanism, we not only avoid obstacles but also take in a vast number of impressions, many of which affect our relations with others. It is evident that the Designer of the eye did not intend that we should grope about our planetary home in darkness. Moreover, it was his purpose that we behold and enjoy his wondrous creations—humans and animals, mountains and rivers, lakes and seas, flowers and other plants, the sky and the glorious hues of a sunset. Appreciative beholders can exclaim with the psalmist: "How many your works are, O Jehovah! All of them in wisdom you have made. The earth is full of your productions."—Psalm 104:24.

² Marvelous though physical sight is, however, walking by it alone is fraught with great danger. If we are to enjoy divine favor, we must walk by faith in the Designer of the human eye. We must seek his guidance so as to practice what is good. Writing to fellow anointed Christians, the apostle Paul fittingly declared: "We are . . . always of good courage and know that, while we have our home in the body, we are absent from the Lord, for we are walking by faith, not by sight. But we are of good courage and are well pleased

rather to become absent from the body and to make our home with the Lord [by dying and being resurrected to heavenly life]. Therefore we are also making it our aim that, whether having our home with him or being absent from him, we may be acceptable to him. For we must all be made manifest before the judgment seat of the Christ, that each one may get his award for the things done through the body, according to the things he has practiced, whether it is good or vile."—2 Corinthians 5:6-10.

³ *All* dedicated servants of Jehovah —whether of the anointed remnant or of the increasing "great crowd" with earthly hopes—want to practice what is good. (Revelation 7:9) But why can it be said that there is such great danger in 'walking by sight'? And what does it mean to 'walk by faith'?

Dangers of 'Walking by Sight'

⁴ If we take everything at face value and depend only upon outward appearances, there is the danger of being deceived to our own harm. For example, a person may be walking along a sandy stretch when he suddenly finds himself engulfed in quicksand. Or an individual may be thrown off guard by the friendly appearance of some-

1. What are some of the blessings we enjoy because of the human eye?
2. Why is it not sufficient to walk by sight, and what did Paul say in this regard?

3. What should be the desire of all dedicated servants of Jehovah, and what questions merit our consideration?
4. (a) Why not take everything at face value? (b) How does the Maker of the eye view things?

one who turns out to be 'a wolf in sheep's covering.' (Matthew 7:15) So we must be vigilant. The Maker of the eye is not guided by mere external appearance. He told the prophet Samuel: "Not the way man sees is the way God sees, because mere man sees what appears to the eyes; but as for Jehovah, he sees what the heart is." (1 Samuel 16:7) Indeed, the One who formed the eye discerns the inmost thoughts and intentions, and his appraisal of anyone or anything is always accurate. (Compare Hebrews 4:12.) In view of his perfect sight and insight, he truly is the all-seeing One.

5 As mere humans, however, we cannot discern clearly what is in the heart of another person. Even with our God-given faculties, we are imperfect and can often be deceived. In fact, our own heart may mislead us, for it "is more treacherous than anything else and is desperate." (Jeremiah 17:9) So it is vitally important that we be forewarned about the perils of 'walking by sight.' Has Jehovah provided for this urgent need? Indeed he has! For our instruction, he has caused a record to be made of some outstanding happenings that show the dangers of walking merely by sight.—Romans 15:4.

6 The experiences of God's ancient people, the Israelites, are very much to the point. Even though the unerring guidance of Jehovah was available to that highly favored nation, its faithless multitudes stubbornly walked "in their own counsels." (Psalm 81:12) 'Walking by sight,' they turned to the worship of idols or gods visible to the natural eye. Being guided by outward appearances, they trembled in fear of their enemies' overwhelming numbers. Moreover, because of 'walking by sight, not by faith,' the Israelites also challenged Moses' God-given leadership and complained about their lot in life. (Compare Jude 16.) Yes, and many of them apparently looked with envy upon what seemed like freedom and prosperity in surrounding nations, ignoring the fact that those people were steeped in degradation and subject to demonic influence. —Leviticus 18:1-3, 30.

7 What happened to the Israelites who insisted on going their own way, rejecting divine guidance? Why, they incurred Jehovah's displeasure, and he withdrew his protective care so that they were defeated by their enemies! Even in the Promised Land, the Israelites often became slaves to their merciless foes. (Judges 2:17-23) Unlike Moses, who refused to enjoy the worldly comforts of Egypt's ruling class, the people of Israel sought "the temporary enjoyment of sin" and did not continue to walk "as seeing the One who is invisible." They lacked faith. And remember, "without faith it is impossible to please [God] well."—Hebrews 3:16-19; 11:6, 24-27.

8 Jehovah's modern-day servants can take warning from those events of the past. We, too, are in danger of becoming weak in faith or even losing our faith. Is it not a fact that we can be unduly influenced by the outward appearance of things and thus again start 'walking by sight'? Yes, and that is why Jehovah kindly provided guidance for those who would serve him in faith. He used the Israelites and his dealings with them as object lessons for later generations, including our own. (1 Corinthians 10:11) Thereby we are fortified by accurate knowledge, by strong hope, and by endurance.

5. Why is it vital that we be forewarned about the perils of 'walking by sight'?
6. 'Walking by sight' had what effects upon the Israelites?

7. What happened to the Israelites who rejected divine guidance?
8. Why should Jehovah's modern-day servants take warning from the experiences of the ancient Israelites?

While fellow witnesses of Jehovah are engaging in theocratic pursuits, are you and your family often heading for some recreation spot?

⁹ Without this sure direction from our loving Creator, we would be in danger of challenging the Greater Moses, Jesus Christ, forgetting that God and Christ are directing true Christians today. (Compare 1 Corinthians 11:3; Ephesians 5:24.) We might view the organization of Jehovah's Witnesses as being of mere human origin and might thus feel free to do what seems right in our own eyes. (Compare Judges 21:25.) Additionally, we could fall into the error of some who appear to think that as long as some course of action does not trouble their conscience, it is all right. Others might start thinking that the theocratic organization is for their comfort and convenience and that all its requirements should be made easy, with no self-sacrifice required of them. Another danger could be entertaining the idea that the arrangements of the organization should be made to conform to our will instead of

God's will. Yet, our Exemplar, Jesus Christ, always did his heavenly Father's will joyfully.—Psalm 40:8; Hebrews 10: 5-10.

¹⁰ Because of overlooking divine direction or treating it lightly, some might think our meetings should be shortened, assembly locations should not be so far away, and study material should always be simple, never including "solid food." (Hebrews 5:12) In lands where Christians enjoy peace and quiet, some may take Kingdom blessings for granted, feeling that there should be no exertion in sacred service. If we develop such attitudes, we could even become "lovers of pleasures rather than lovers of God," possibly reserving nearly every weekend for recreation instead of using such time in the field ministry and other theocratic activities that show wholehearted devotion to

9. If we were to 'walk by sight,' how might we feel about certain actions and about theocratic arrangements?

10. How might our attitude toward the field ministry and other theocratic activities be affected if we overlook divine direction or treat it lightly?

Jehovah. (2 Timothy 3:1, 4) If that happened, could we honestly say that we were really "walking by faith, not by sight"?

¹¹ There is also the danger of pampering ourselves. It is easy to talk ourselves into thinking that a slight headache or some similar problem is worse than it really is. Our imperfect flesh may prompt us to use this as an excuse not to fulfill a responsibility, such as giving a talk in the Theocratic Ministry School. But is it possible that we would never think of letting the same indisposition stop us from participating in some form of recreation? Of course, we should use a sound mind and not treat serious symptoms lightly. However, we do need to exert ourselves vigorously. (Luke 13:24) And surely faith should figure largely in our decisions so that we do not 'walk by sight' alone, in accord with our own unaided counsel. —Romans 12:1-3.

¹² Never forget that we are in a fight against wicked spirit forces. (Ephesians 6: 11-18) Our chief enemy, Satan the Devil, can bring tremendous influences to bear upon us by wielding his weapons designed to destroy our faith in Jehovah. Satan will appeal to every selfish propensity in humans and will overlook no type of persuasion that might sway us in our thinking. If we are associated with "the remaining ones" of the "seed" of God's "woman," or heavenly organization, we are in a war. It is one from which there can be no furlough until Jehovah, who strengthens us to withstand satanic attack, brings the Devil's entire organization to its end. (Revelation 12:16, 17; 1 Peter 5:6-11) So, should we now be courageous and have a sense of urgency? Assuredly we should!—Psalm 31:24.

What It Means to 'Walk by Faith'

¹³ "Walking by faith" means moving along through difficult conditions with faith in God, in his ability to guide our steps, and in his willingness to see us to safety. (Psalm 22:3-5; Hebrews 11:6) It means refusing to be guided by mere outward appearances of things or by unaided human reasoning. Faith will move us to walk in the direction in which Jehovah points, regardless of how difficult the path may be. If we 'walk by faith,' we will be like David, who said of God: "You will cause me to know the path of life. Rejoicing to satisfaction is with your face; there is pleasantness at your right hand forever." (Psalm 16:11) Moreover, if we allow Jehovah to direct our steps, he will grant us peace of mind and will help us to gain the victory, no matter how great the odds against us. (John 16:33; Philippians 4: 6, 7) Among other things, "walking by faith" will regularly take us into association with our spiritual brothers and sisters for united Bible study and prayer. —Hebrews 10:24, 25.

¹⁴ In effect, "walking by faith" also makes us the companions of Jehovah's faithful servants of the past. The principal one among them was Jesus Christ, "the Chief Agent and Perfecter of our faith." As we strive to "follow his steps closely," what do we find?—Hebrews 12:1-3; 1 Peter 2:21.

¹⁵ Jesus shunned involvement in worldly politics and never sought the riches and prestige many were pursuing. Instead, he pointed out that his Kingdom is "no part of this world," and far from being a materialist, he had 'nowhere to lay his head.' (John 6:14, 15; 18:36; Luke 9:57, 58) Al-

---

11. Pampering ourselves might have what effect, but there is a need for us to do what?
12. In what kind of fight do we find ourselves, calling for what attitude on our part?

13. What does it mean to 'walk by faith'?
14, 15. (a) What was Jesus' attitude toward riches, prestige, and involvement in politics? (b) As revealed in the Scriptures, how did Jesus view God's guidance?

Jesus Christ set us a superb example. Like him, are you "walking by faith"?

though Jesus had a perfect mind, he did not act independently but looked to his heavenly Father for guidance.—John 8: 28, 29.

¹⁶ In view of Jesus' example, what can be said about Jehovah's Witnesses today? Well, as advocates of God's heavenly Kingdom, we respect governmental "superior authorities" but maintain neutrality in political affairs. (Romans 13:1-7; Matthew 6:9, 10; John 17:16) Rather than seeking riches and prestige in this world, we 'seek first the Kingdom,' confident that Jehovah will provide the necessities of life. (Matthew 6:24-34; Psalm 37:25) And like Jesus, we 'do not lean on our own under-

standing' but gratefully accept the guidance of our loving God. (Proverbs 3:5, 6) Certainly, all of this helps us to 'walk by faith.'

Tests and Blessings

¹⁷ In many lands our fellow witnesses of Jehovah must endure unusual inconveniences and tribulations, even brutal persecution, as they 'walk by faith.' Of course, trials of faith appear in a variety of forms. For example, consider the hardships and faithful service of one elderly Ecuadorian brother. He came in contact with the truth at the age of 80, then learned to read and write. He was baptized two years later. Since he lived in the jungle, he had to walk for three hours to reach the Kingdom Hall. His opposed wife would hide his clothes and money to discourage him from attending Christian meetings. But these problems did not overwhelm this faithful brother. He served as a temporary, or auxiliary, pioneer every month for ten years and preached in many villages, often being mistreated by the villagers. However, when pioneers and missionaries later witnessed in those areas, many people approached them and asked for Bible studies. So, good things resulted from the hard work of this zealous brother. He died of cancer at the age of 92 but spent 40 hours in the ministry the very month that he died.

¹⁸ We, too, must persevere despite problems and hardships. (Matthew 24:13) If we are to enjoy divine favor, it is vital that we apply the counsel of God, rely on him, and remain separate from the world, its attitudes, and its ways. (Psalm 37:5; 1 Corinthians 2:12; James 1:27) So let us

16. In the light of Jesus' example, what can be said about the attitude of Jehovah's Witnesses?

17. Jehovah's people must endure what as they 'walk by faith'? Please illustrate this.
18. (a) What must we do if we are to enjoy divine favor? (b) What rewards will be ours if we keep "walking by faith, not by sight"?

strive to imitate our Exemplar, Jesus Christ. Let us be self-sacrificing and willing to exert ourselves in Jehovah's glorious service. As we do this, we can confidently look to the fulfillment of our heavenly Father's grand promises to his loyal worshipers. And to what wonderful blessings this will lead in his promised New Order! Above all, "walking by faith, not by sight" will bring us the reward of sharing in the vindication of Jehovah's universal sovereignty.

Do You Recall?

☐ What are the dangers of 'walking by sight'?

☐ The experiences of the Israelites furnish what warning for Jehovah's people today?

☐ Instead of pampering ourselves, what do we need to do?

☐ "Walking by faith" means doing what?

Walk With Confidence in Jehovah's Leadership

"Be courageous and strong. Do not be afraid or suffer a shock before them, because Jehovah your God is the one marching with you. He will neither desert you nor leave you entirely."
—DEUTERONOMY 31:6.

JEHOVAH proved to be a matchless leader when he brought the Israelites out of slavery in Egypt. Not only did he guide them through the wilderness but he also provided their food and drink and gave them flawless instruction. Thus the Levites of Nehemiah's day could say: "You, even you [Jehovah God], in your abundant mercy did not leave them in the wilderness. The pillar of cloud itself did not depart from over them by day to lead them in the way, nor the pillar of fire by night to light up for them the way in which they should go. And your good spirit you gave to make them prudent, and your manna you did not hold back from their mouth, and water you gave them for their thirst. And for forty years you provided them with food in the wilderness. They lacked nothing. Their very garments did not wear out, and their feet themselves did not become swollen."—Nehemiah 9:19-21.

² By discipline administered with fatherly kindness, the Divine Teacher taught the Israelites what it meant to be just and righteous. Everything he did was in their best interests. Even when they murmured and rebelled, he was long-

1. How did Jehovah prove to be a matchless leader of the Israelites?

2. Why could Moses urge the Israelites to "be courageous and strong"?

suffering and did not abandon them. Particularly when overwhelming enemy armies confronted them did Jehovah give evidence of skillful leadership and wreak havoc upon the ranks of the attackers. Moses spoke the truth when he encouraged the Israelites with these words: "Be courageous and strong. Do not be afraid or suffer a shock before them, because Jehovah your God is the one marching with you. He will neither desert you nor leave you entirely." (Deuteronomy 31: 1, 6) God would be "marching" with them if they exercised faith. What an incentive for us to walk with confidence in Jehovah's leadership!

Warnings From the Past

³ Yet, the experiences of the Israelites provide warnings for us. Although they had been free of Egyptian bondage only a short time, they repeatedly sinned against their invisible Leader. While Moses was on Mount Sinai receiving the Law, they showed ingratitude for all that God had done for them. They prevailed upon Aaron to make a golden calf and worshiped it in what Aaron called "a festival to Jehovah." (Exodus 32:1-6) Ten of the 12 spies sent to search out Canaan proved faithless, only Joshua and Caleb urging the people to go on into the land and take it. But Israel did not act with faith in God, who therefore decreed that all males "from twenty years old upward," excluding the tribe of Levi and faithful Caleb and Joshua, would die during a 40-year period in the wilderness. (Numbers 13:1–14:38; Deuteronomy 1:19-40) Surely, all of this should warn us against similar ingratitude and lack of confidence in Jehovah's leadership!

---

3. Soon after being released from Egyptian bondage, how did the people of Israel show ingratitude and lack of confidence in Jehovah?

⁴ Though the Israelites wandered in the wilderness for 40 years, Jehovah did not forsake them. He continued to fight their battles. After the death of Moses and Joshua, God raised up judges to deliver his people from oppressive enemies. But at that time the people of Israel did what was right in their own eyes, and lawless violence, immorality, and idolatry began to abound. (Judges 17:6–19:30) Later, when they wanted a human king so as to be like surrounding nations, Jehovah granted their request but warned them of the consequences. (1 Samuel 8:10-18) However, even the kingship of David's house did not satisfy the people, and ten tribes rebelled in the days of Rehoboam. (1 Kings 11: 26–12:19) More and more, the very idea of having God lead them faded in the minds of the majority. The destruction of Jerusalem and the temple as well as the overthrow of the kingdom of Judah at Babylonian hands in 607 B.C.E. were well-deserved judgments upon a people who had failed to walk with confidence in Jehovah's leadership. What a warning for us!

Jehovah's Leadership of a New Nation

⁵ Like the Israelites of old, Jehovah's later servants walked through changing circumstances, but he unfailingly directed them. When Jesus of Nazareth submitted to water baptism in 29 C.E., God provided a Prophet and Leader greater than Moses. As the Messiah, he would lead people out of this wicked world lying in Satan's power. (Matthew 3:13-17; Daniel 9:25; Deuteronomy 18:18, 19; Acts 3:19-23; 1 John 5:19) But what people? Why, those Jews and others who would exercise faith in the

---

4. How did Israel's history justify the calamity that befell Judah, Jerusalem, and the temple in 607 B.C.E.?
5. What did Jehovah provide in the person of Jesus, and what would Jesus do?

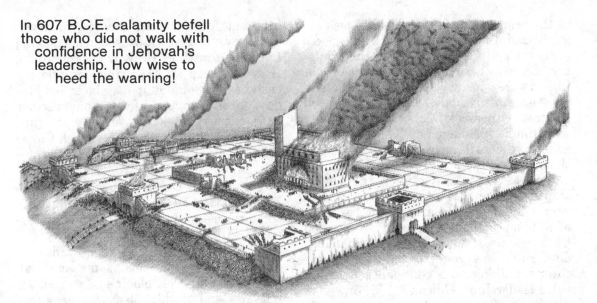

In 607 B.C.E. calamity befell those who did not walk with confidence in Jehovah's leadership. How wise to heed the warning!

Messiah provided by the great heavenly Leader, Jehovah God!

⁶ Jesus taught his followers the marvelous truth of God and gave them needed instruction for the ministry. (Luke 10: 1-16) Thus when Christ completed his ministry and presented himself as a sacrifice on behalf of sinful mankind, he left behind followers trained to carry on the preaching work and to administer the affairs of the growing organization of those believing in him. During the apostolic period, there was fierce persecution. But Jehovah's hand was with his people, and their hardships were balanced by marvelous increases in the number of believers. (Acts 5:41, 42; 8:4-8; 11:19-21) After Jesus' apostles and their immediate co-workers died, the professed followers of Christ came under the rulership of cruel and arrogant clergymen and kings. (Acts 20:28-30) Since this condition continued for some 15 centuries, it appeared

that the light of Bible truth had been extinguished.

⁷ Then, however, like 'a voice crying in the wilderness,' came the announcement: 'The Kingdom is at hand!' (Compare Isaiah 40:3-5; Luke 3:3-6; Matthew 10:7.) In the latter part of the 19th century, Jehovah again asserted his leadership and began calling his genuine worshipers out of this wicked world and its Babylonish religious systems. (Revelation 18:1-5) By means of his written Word and the holy spirit, God revealed to his modern-day servants that the year 1914 marked the end of uninterrupted rule by Gentile nations and also the heavenly enthronement of the glorified Jesus Christ, God's choice as King over all mankind.—Luke 21:24; see *1975 Yearbook of Jehovah's Witnesses*, pages 34-37.

⁸ Subsequently, a new nation comprised

---

6. (a) Why were Jesus' followers able to preach and to care for a growing organization? (b) Why did it later appear that the light of Bible truth had been extinguished?

---

7. When and how did Jehovah again assert his leadership, and what did he reveal to his modern-day servants?
8. (a) Subsequently, what was organized? (b) Jesus' anointed followers have been joined by whom, and how has the leadership of God and Christ become evident?

of the remnant of spiritual Israel was organized, further enlightened as to God's purposes and fully trained for the ministry. Later, these anointed followers of Christ were joined by a multitude of believers with earthly hopes. Now, together, all of these witnesses of Jehovah are joyfully proclaiming his name and Kingdom to the ends of the earth. (Isaiah 66:7, 8; Galatians 6:16; Revelation 7:4, 9, 10) In the Witnesses' organized activity, the leadership of Jehovah and his royal Son has been very evident, particularly in the response of millions of honest-hearted people who have become staunch advocates of Kingdom rule. Are you part of this happy throng walking with confidence in Jehovah's leadership?—Micah 4:1, 2, 5.

9 Eventually, Jesus' followers were to be witnesses of him "to the most distant part of the earth." (Acts 1:6-8; Mark 13:10) Accordingly, Jehovah's Witnesses are now proclaiming the good news of the Kingdom around the earth, and those "rightly disposed for everlasting life" are embracing the truth with joyful hearts. They are becoming part of a worldwide association of spiritual brothers and sisters who have gladly accepted God's leadership and have subjected themselves to theocratic rule. (Acts 13:48; 1 Peter 2:17) Like them, do you have complete confidence that Jehovah God and his King-Son, Jesus Christ, are directing this organization of Kingdom proclaimers?

Guard Against Loss of Confidence

10 Can recipients of all the blessings resulting from Jehovah's leadership fall into the snare of lack of faith and confidence in him? Yes, for we are warned: "Beware,

brothers, for fear there should ever develop in any one of you a wicked heart lacking faith by drawing away from the living God; but keep on exhorting one another each day, as long as it may be called 'Today,' for fear any one of you should become hardened by the deceptive power of sin." (Hebrews 3:12, 13) Therefore, each Christian should examine himself very carefully.

11 A person's conscience can become so hardened that he sees nothing wrong with some course of action that is out of harmony with the spirit of Christianity and that betrays a lack of faith and confidence in Jehovah. For instance, some could fall into the snare of placing materialistic pursuits and fleshly pleasures on a par with or even ahead of their service to God. Others may become immoral or may speak disparagingly of responsible men in the congregation. In the first century C.E., "ungodly men" who had slipped into the congregation were "defiling the flesh and disregarding lordship and speaking abusively of glorious ones" shouldering congregational responsibility. (Jude 4-8, 16) Those false Christians had lost true faith in Jehovah and in his leadership. May that never happen to us!

12 Often coupled with 'disregard for lordship' is an independent and rebellious spirit that ignores the fact that Jehovah is directing his organization. This spirit had dire consequences for Korah and others who challenged the God-given authority of Moses and Aaron. (Numbers 16: 1-35) But what a contrast we find in David! Content to wait on God to rectify

9. What worldwide association has come into existence, and with what attitude toward God's leadership and theocratic rule?
10. What warning should move each Christian to examine himself very carefully?

11. (a) In what ways may a person's conscience become hardened? (b) What happened to some in the first century C.E.?
12. (a) An independent and rebellious spirit ignores what? (b) What contrast was there between Korah and David?

Abraham,
Sarah, David,
Jesus, and others
walked with confidence
in Jehovah's leadership. Is that how you are walking?

wrongs, David would not slay his wicked enemy King Saul because he was "the anointed of Jehovah." (1 Samuel 24:2-7) Yes, Jehovah appointed Moses, Aaron, Saul, David, Jesus Christ, and others. Similarly, in God's organization today service appointments are made in harmony with Scriptural requirements and under the direction of Jehovah's holy spirit.—1 Timothy 3:1-13; Titus 1:5-9; Acts 20:28.

¹³ Since 'it does not belong to man to direct his step,' we should be grateful for Jehovah's leadership. (Jeremiah 10:23) Abraham and his devoted wife Sarah obeyed God and acted with faith. Boaz and Ruth complied with divine arrangements. Yes, and many other faithful men and women gladly accepted Jehovah's guidance. (Hebrews 11:4-38; Ruth 3:1–4:17) Like earlier servants of God, then, we should shun an independent spirit, joyfully cooperate with God's theocratic organization, and walk with complete confidence in Jehovah's leadership.

---

13. (a) Why should we be grateful for Jehovah's leadership? (b) Like whom should we be walking, and with what attitude?

Confidently "Throw Your Burden Upon Jehovah"

¹⁴ What can help us, as Jehovah's loyal witnesses, to guard against a rebellious spirit? Well, first we need to acknowledge that it is wrong to be rebellious and presumptuously ignore God's direction. (Nehemiah 9:16, 28-31; Proverbs 11:2) We can pray to our heavenly Father as did David, who pleaded: "From presumptuous acts hold your servant back; do not let them dominate me. In that case I shall be complete, and I shall have remained innocent from much transgression." (Psalm 19:13) It will also be helpful to remember how much love Jehovah has shown for us. This ought to increase our love for him and should motivate us to accept his leadership at all times.—John 3:16; Luke 10:27.

¹⁵ We must not lose sight of the fact that God is directing his organization,

---

14. What can help us to guard against a rebellious spirit?
15. What course is recommended if a brother thinks he has not been appointed as a ministerial servant or an overseer because the elders have something against him?

although walking with confidence in Jehovah's leadership may not be easy at times. To illustrate: Suppose a brother thinks that he has not been appointed as a ministerial servant or an overseer because the elders have something against him. Instead of reacting in a way that could disturb the congregation's peace, he should remember that Jehovah is directing the theocratic organization. Hence, the brother may seek some explanation in a humble, peaceful manner. (Hebrews 12:14) Then how wise it would be for him to acknowledge any weaknesses called to his attention and prayerfully strive to make improvement! Thereafter, he can leave matters in God's hands, in keeping with the words: "Throw your burden upon Jehovah himself." (Psalm 55:22) In time and as we qualify spiritually, Jehovah is sure to give us plenty to do in his service. —Compare 1 Corinthians 15:58.

16 Even if we have suffered some real wrong at the hands of a brother or a sister, would that give us just cause to stop associating with the congregation? Would we thus be justified in ceasing to render sacred service to Jehovah? No, for such a course would be one of unfaithfulness to God and ingratitude for his leadership. It would also indicate that we did not love our loyal fellow believers earth wide. (Matthew 22:36-40; 1 John 4:7, 8) Moreover, if we were to break our integrity to Jehovah, that would give Satan a basis for taunting God—something we surely do not desire! —Proverbs 27:11.

17 So, then, let us 'bless Jehovah and

never forget all the doings of the One who crowns our life with loving-kindness and mercies.' (Psalm 103:2-4) If we always remember our loving God and act in harmony with his Word, we will maintain strong confidence in his unfailing leadership. (Proverbs 22:19) To turn away from Jehovah and his organization, to spurn the direction of "the faithful and discreet slave," and to rely simply on personal Bible reading and interpretation is to become like a solitary tree in a parched land. But in contrast, a person whose confidence is in our Great Leader, Jehovah, "will certainly become like a tree planted by the waters, that sends out its roots right by the watercourse; and he will not see when heat comes, but his foliage will actually prove to be luxuriant." Moreover, "in the year of drought he will not become anxious, nor will he leave off from producing fruit" to God's glory. (Matthew 24:45-47; Jeremiah 17:8) That can be your blessed experience if you resolutely continue to walk with confidence in Jehovah's leadership.

---

16. Even if we have suffered some real wrong inside the congregation, what course should we not take, and why?
17. (a) What should help us to maintain our confidence in Jehovah's leadership of his organization? (b) What will be the experience of those who continue to walk with confidence in Jehovah's leadership?

Can You Answer?

☐ In what ways did Jehovah prove to be a matchless leader of the Israelites?

☐ As to God's leadership, ancient Israel provides what warnings?

☐ Over whom is Jehovah exercising leadership today?

☐ What can help us to guard against loss of confidence in Jehovah's leadership?

☐ Even if we suffer some wrong inside the congregation, what attitude should we have toward Jehovah's leadership?

Kingdom Proclaimers Report

Search for the Truth Rewarded

THE Bible tells us to "search for Jehovah, . . . call to him." (Isaiah 55:6) Solomon was informed by Jehovah: "If you search for [Jehovah], he will let himself be found by you." (1 Chronicles 28:9) A young girl in Finland searched for the truth about Jehovah and was richly rewarded.

She belonged to the State Church of Finland and attended Confirmation School, hoping that she would find the truth about God. She was disappointed, however. They did not read the Bible very much in school. In fact, the priest warned her *not* to read it, as it would upset her mental balance.

Nevertheless, she started to read the Bible after finishing the school. She also went to church, but she found no contentment there. Then she went to the Pentecostal Church where she "entered the faith." They prayed for her and told her that she had now gained faith. But she did not feel any closer to God than she had previously felt.

She wrote to the "Gang and Street Service Center" for help, but they gave her only a phone number. When she called, the phone was answered by a Methodist who said a prayer for her and told her that it did not matter which church she attended as long as she did not join Jehovah's Witnesses or the Mormons!

She attended the People's Mission and was given tracts to distribute entitled *Jehovah's Witnesses, the Deception of the Time of the End*. This still did not satisfy her search for the truth or give her a purpose in life.

Then she visited her aunt who shocked her by telling her that she believed that Jehovah's Witnesses were teaching the truth. The aunt calmly read scriptures from the Bible that proved it was God's purpose to make this earth a paradise, and she gave her the book *The Truth That Leads to Eternal Life*. The girl read the book with the purpose of finding fault with it—to disprove it—but instead she soon realized that it contained the truth, showing her the purpose in life for which she had been searching. She wrote to the publishers for other books and asked for someone to visit her. Only two days later, two pioneer sisters arrived at her doorstep. A Bible study was arranged and the girl started attending meetings at the Kingdom Hall, where she was deeply impressed and touched by the loving atmosphere that existed there. She continued her Bible study, was baptized a year later, started to pioneer, and attended the Pioneer Service School. "At last I can be happy," she said. Her search for the truth was rewarded.

Similar experiences have been repeated thousands of times during 'the conclusion of this system of things,' when Jesus, the Fine Shepherd, is gathering his "other sheep" as foretold in John 10:16. (Matthew 24:3) Happy, then, are those who search for the truth of the Bible and whom God rewards. —Matthew 7:7.

How Priceless Your Friendship, O God!

As told by Daniel Sydlik

L IFE for me began on a farm near Belleville, Michigan, in February 1919. A midwife assisted at my birth, since my immigrant mother considered a doctor unnecessary. "Why go to hospital? I not sick," she would say in her broken English to anyone asking where the child would be born.

Times on the farm were hard. In search of a better life our family moved to Detroit. Not long after that, Dad became ill and died when I was about three. He had been actively associated with the International Bible Students, known today as Jehovah's Witnesses.

Mother was now left with six children and debts to pay. She had opposed Dad's religion bitterly, but after his death she turned to the Bible to find out why it had so fascinated him. A number of years later she also became one of Jehovah's Witnesses.

After Dad died, Mother worked as a waitress at night and cared for the family during the day. This continued until she remarried several years later. My stepfather argued successfully that the best place to rear children was in the open countryside and not in some overcrowded concrete jungle.

A farm of 55 acres (22 ha) was purchased near Caro, Michigan. When we arrived in the spring of 1927, the orchards were ablaze with blossoms. The air was sweet with the fragrance of wild flowers, and trees were in bloom. There were swimming holes, trees to climb, and animals to play with. Life here was wonderful! Nothing like the city. However, country life was difficult for Mother. It was pioneering at its roughest—no running water, no inside plumbing, no electricity.

Winters were long and severe. We children slept in the attic, where snow would often sift through the shingled roof and literally cover the beds. In the morning it would be sheer torture to put on ice-cold pants that at times were frozen stiff. The barn chores had to be done before breakfast. Then came the hike through the woods to the school, which had but one classroom where eight grades were taught by one teacher.

Spiritual Beginnings

Mother had genuine love for God and that greatly influenced us children. She would say in Polish: "God has given us a beautiful day." We kids would go outside to find out what she was talking about —only to find it raining. To Mother everything that happened was in some way because of God. When a new calf was born or when the chickens laid their eggs or when the snow fell, it had something to do with God as far as she was concerned. God was responsible for these good things in some way.

Mother was a believer in prayer. Prayer was a must for us at mealtimes. "Dogs wag their tails when you feed them. Are we less appreciative than dogs?" she would say. She also wanted us to say our prayers before we went to bed. Since none of us knew the Lord's Prayer in English, she would have us kneel and recite the words in Polish after her.—Matthew 6: 9-13.

Those were the days long before television. After sunset, there was little to do but go to bed. Mother encouraged us to read. She read her Bible by a kerosene lamp. And we youngsters would read publications obtained from traveling ministers of the International Bible Students, such as *The Harp of God, Creation,* and *Reconciliation.* Thus a friendship with God began to be cultivated.

In the early 1930's some Bible Students from Saginaw, Michigan, visited and encouraged us to preach to others. But since there was no organized Bible study group or congregation nearby, our preaching efforts were negligible. Our spiritual growth for the most part lay dormant.

Because of the depression of the 1930's, it was necessary for me to leave home and find work in Detroit. The farm was heavily mortgaged, and it was my desire to bring us out from under that burden. Detroit, however, was then a city of breadlines. Thousands of men stood in lines, sometimes all night, huddled over wood and charcoal fires, trying their best to keep warm until the employment offices opened their doors. I was fortunate to get a job in an auto factory.

Olive Perkins was an inspiration to me

Spiritual Development

It was not until the latter part of that decade, when I was in Long Beach, California, that my spiritual interest was rekindled in a productive way. An invitation to a public talk was handed to me. That Sunday I attended my first meeting at a Kingdom Hall. There I met Olive and William (Bill) Perkins, wholesome people with a priceless relationship with Jehovah God.

Sister Perkins was a remarkable teacher of God's Word, using her Bible as skillfully as a surgeon uses his knife. She would lay her big King James Version Bible on her left arm, lick the thumb of her right hand, and flip the pages from verse to verse. The people were fascinated by her skill and by what they were learning from the Bible. She was instrumental in bringing many people to an understanding of God's purpose. Working with her in the ministry was an inspiration. It encouraged me to take up the full-time pioneer ministry in September 1941.

Sister Wilcox was another one who helped me. She was a tall, dignified, white-haired woman in her 70's who wore her hair swept up neatly on her head, climax-

The Boyd family helped work the territory in San Pedro, California

ing in a bun. Her costume was always topped with a lovely wide-brimmed hat. In her neatly tailored, ankle-length dress she looked special, like someone who had just stepped out of the 1880's. Together we preached in the business districts of Long Beach.

Managers were instantly impressed at the sight of Sister Wilcox. And with a certain anxious enthusiasm they would invite her into their offices. I would tag along. "What is it?" they would ask with a sense of respect. "May I help you?"

Without hesitation Sister Wilcox, with the perfect English of a professor at her command, would reply: "I am here to tell you about the old whore of Revelation who is riding the beast." (Revelation 17:1-5) Managers would wince and adjust themselves in their seats, wondering what was coming next. She would paint them a vivid picture of the end of this system of things. The reaction was almost always decisive. They wanted whatever she had. Daily we would place literally cartons of literature. My job was to play the phonograph whenever she asked for it to be played,

and to be as fearless and as courageous as possible when she was speaking.

New Assignments

An envelope from the Watchtower Society always charged me with excitement. It was such an envelope, received in 1942, that contained an assignment to serve as a special pioneer in San Pedro, California. There Bill and Mildred Taylor opened their home to me. It took great self-discipline to work alone in the field ministry day after day. But it drew me close to Jehovah, so that I really felt his friendship. Then the Society sent Georgia and Archie Boyd, along with their son and daughter, Donald and Susan, to help work the territory. The Boyds lived in an 18-foot (5.5-m) trailer with all their supplies and belongings.

Another envelope from the Society arrived for us! Chills ran up and down our spines as we read of our new assignment —Richmond, California, just to the north of San Francisco. Despite the improbability that our old car and trailer would ever make it, we packed and started out. We looked like gypsies on the move, repairing the engine and patching tires on the way. When we finally arrived in Richmond, the rain was falling in sheets.

World War II was by now in full swing. The Kaiser shipyards were in mass production building "Liberty Ships," as they were called. Our job was to preach to the people who had flocked here to work. From early in the morning to late at night, we talked about the Kingdom, often returning home hoarse from speaking so much. Many Bible studies were started. These shipyard workers were generous and hos-

At the 1946 "Glad Nations" convention with fellow Witnesses recently released from McNeil Island prison

pitable people who supplied our every need. The territory actually supported us without our having to take up secular part-time jobs.

Prison Experiences

Young men were being drafted into the armed forces. My fleshly brothers, who were not Witnesses, had volunteered and were serving in the paratroops and the engineering corps. I applied for exemption as a minister conscientiously opposed to war. The Draft Board refused to recognize my ministerial status. I was arrested, tried, and on July 17, 1944, sentenced to three years of hard labor at the McNeil Island Federal Penitentiary in Washington State. In prison I learned that Jehovah's friendship lasts forever.—Psalm 138:8, *The Bible in Living English.*

For a month I was kept in the county jail in Los Angeles, awaiting transfer to McNeil Island. First impressions of prison life are hard to forget, how inmates shouted obscenities at the guards and at us as we were brought in. Or how the guards ordered: "Watch the gates!" The rumbling sound of the electric gates rolling shut resembled sounds of thunder in the distance. As the gates closed one by one, the sound would draw ever closer until one's own gate would quiver and roll

shut with a clashing clang! There was that trapped feeling and a wave of fear. I quickly prayed to God to help me, and almost instantly a warm peaceful glow swept over me, an experience I will never forget.

On August 16, along with a group of other prisoners, I was handcuffed and chained. Then, under the watchful eye of an armed police force, we were escorted through the noon crowd of Los Angeles onto a bus and then transferred to a prison train for McNeil Island. Those prison chains filled me with joy, for they linked me to the company of Christ's apostles who were also chained for keeping their integrity.—Acts 12:6, 7; 21:33; Ephesians 6:20.

While I was being booked into McNeil prison, an official behind a desk asked me: "Are you a J.W.?" That caught me by surprise, for it was the first time I had heard the term "J.W." But it soon dawned on me what he was talking about, so I said, "Yes!"

"Step over there," he said. I was surprised to hear him ask the man directly behind me the same question: "Are you a J.W.?" The man quickly replied, "Yes!"

"You big liar!" the officer said, laughing. "You don't even know what a J.W. is." I learned later that the man was a hardened criminal with a prison record as long as his arm. "J.W." stood, of course, for "Jehovah's Witness," and that he was not.

It was late, and a guard ushered me through the dark to my bunk. It was hard to believe that I was in a federal prison hundreds of miles away from home or from anyone I knew. Just then I saw someone coming toward me in the dark. "*Shhh!*" he said as he sat next to me on the bunk. "I'm a brother. The grapevine had it that a Witness would be coming." He introduced himself and offered words of encouragement, telling me about the group *Watchtower* study that was permitted within the prison on Sunday afternoons. It was against the rules to be out of one's bunk once the lights were out, so he stayed only briefly. But in those few moments, I felt the precious friendship of Jehovah manifesting itself through his dedicated servant.

Highlights of my prison stay were the periodic visits of A. H. Macmillan from the Society's headquarters in Brooklyn. He was a "Barnabas," an encourager, if ever there was one. When he came we were allowed to have the mess hall, and all of us Witnesses and many other prisoners would crowd in to hear him. He was a fantastic speaker,

and even prison officials enjoyed listening to him.

We organized the cellblocks and dormitories into preaching territory. Systematically we preached the Kingdom good news in these areas as we had in a city block before we were imprisoned. The reception was mixed and difficult to predict. But there were hearing ears. Bank robbers and others, including prison guards, turned to Jehovah and were baptized. I still rejoice when I recall such experiences.

Moves That Shaped My Life

Early in 1946, with the war ended, I was released from prison. Awaiting me was another envelope from the Society! My next special-pioneer assignment would be Hollywood, California! The city of make-believe. Talk about challenges! There were times when it would have been easier to sell refrigerators to Eskimos than to get these people to study the Bible. Yet, slowly but surely, "sheep" of the Lord were found.

While attending the "Glad Nations" international convention in Cleveland, Ohio, in August 1946, Milton Henschel, secre-

A Sunday morning broadcast over WBBR

tary to Nathan Knorr, the then president of the Watchtower Society, stopped me and asked: "When are you coming to Bethel, Dan?" I told him I was happy pioneering. "But we need you at Bethel," he said. After a few more words, I ran out of excuses. I loved California and dreaded the thought of living in New York. But I remember saying to myself, 'Dan, if Jehovah wants you in Brooklyn, then Brooklyn it is.' So on August 20, 1946, I began my service at Bethel, the Brooklyn headquarters of Jehovah's Witnesses.

For years I worked in the Brooklyn factory bindery doing a variety of physically demanding jobs. Eventually I was sent to the Subscription Department, which offered a new direction. Then came mental challenges, such as writing radio scripts and broadcasting for the Society's radio station WBBR. I also worked in the Writing Department for 20 years, trying to meet its high standards. In the meantime, there were appointments to the Pennsylvania and New York corporations of the Watchtower Society, recording sessions for dramas, speaking assignments at district and international conventions, and a host of other privileges of service too numerous to mention.

Then in November 1974, another envelope arrived. This one contained an unbelievable, unthinkable assignment. I was invited to serve as a member of the Governing Body of Jehovah's Witnesses. I felt totally inadequate and humbly grateful. Some ten years have gone by since that appointment, and the feelings are still the same.

The passing years have been enriched by human relationships with dedicated and devout men who loved Jehovah more than life itself—men such as Judge Rutherford, whom I had the privilege to meet in his home in San Diego, California. It was also my privilege to work side by side with other such men, including Hugo Riemer, Nathan Knorr, Klaus Jensen, John Perry, Bert Cumming, and a host of others who were spiritual giants, "big trees of righteousness."—Isaiah 61:3.

And to be privileged to see Jehovah's organization grow from a mere handful of 50,000 Kingdom publishers earth wide to nearly three million is no small honor. It is thrilling to have witnessed the growth of the publishing from just a few printing facilities to dozens of factories supported by 95 branches declaring the good news in 203 lands of the earth. The changes and adaptations in technology and computerization have been nothing short of awesome. Witnessing all of this, one cannot help but repeat the words of Matthew 21:42: "From Jehovah this has come to be, and it is marvelous in our eyes."

It has been a rich and rewarding life, to say the very least. Somewhere along the way time was found to get married to a lovely girl from Hebburn, England. Marina, my wife, is a God-sent support. How true the words of Proverbs 19:14: "The inheritance from fathers is a house and wealth, but a discreet wife is from Jehovah."

Throughout life's experiences, like an encircling shelter, there has been the ever-sustaining power of God's friendship. Meditating on Jehovah's Word, reflecting on its meaning, and searching for insight and understanding have filled my waking hours with spiritual riches and contentment. Even at this very moment, sheer joy overwhelms me when I read the psalmist's words: "Happy the nation that has Jehovah for its God, the people that he chose as his estate! Our souls are waiting for Jehovah; he is our help and our shield; for our hearts are glad in him because we have confidence in his hallowed name. Let your friendship be over us, Jehovah, as we rest our expectations on you."—Psalm 33: 12, 20-22, *By*.

A Doubly Joyous Occasion

MARCH 3, 1985, was a doubly joyous occasion, especially for the 42 students of the 78th class of the Watchtower Bible School of Gilead. It was not only graduation day —reason enough to be joyous—but also the first time that a Gilead graduation was held at the new Brooklyn Assembly Hall, dedicated only the day before.

By 10:00 a.m., the 2,400-seat hall was filled by a capacity crowd consisting of the graduating students, their families and friends, and, for the first time in many years at a Gilead graduation, the entire Brooklyn Bethel family. The air was charged with excitement. And the conversation was dominated by comments on how beautifully the brothers had remodeled the hall. It was very evident that no one was holding back the joy and gratitude with which his heart was overflowing.

Promptly at 10:00 a.m., Theodore Jaracz, chairman for the day, called the audience to order. He drew a thunderous round of applause when he simply remarked: "It's fine to be here, isn't it?" Clearly, he struck a responsive chord with those words.

The topic of happiness appeared to be much on the minds of the speakers for the day. George Gangas of the Governing Body spoke on the subject "Enjoy Happiness in the Missionary Field—How?" He told the graduating students that as Jehovah used the angels in the past, "Jehovah will use you to deliver people from bondage in Satan's prison." Imagine the happiness that will bring them! Then Daniel Sydlik advised the students to "take along a close friend" as they go to their foreign assignments. The Bible is that friend. They can depend on it in their hour of need, he told them. It is so powerful that only a sentence, or even a word, from it is at times enough to help someone. Read it and listen to it daily, he exhorted the students, and help others to do the same.

Elaborating on the theme of happiness, Robert Wallen of the Bethel Home Committee urged the students to maintain the "Here I am! Send me" attitude, and Joel Adams of the Service Department Committee told the class: "To enjoy happiness in its fullest measure, we must be completely devoted to doing God's will. The two are inseparable."

The students also received some parting counsel from their two instructors. Ulysses Glass reminded them that "missionary life is not all going to be sunshine and light." Recounting the prophetic drama of Elijah and Elisha, he urged them to imitate the modern-day Elisha class and stick to their work to the finish. Jack Redford surprised everyone by saying: "Last year I met a man who had not made a mistake in 4,000 years." He was referring to an Egyptian mummy in a museum. The point, of course, was that only dead men do not make mistakes. But when we are confronted with our mistakes, do we act like Saul, who tried to justify his errors, or like David, who readily admitted his? Thought-provoking questions indeed!

The final speaker of the morning was the president of the Watchtower Bible School of Gilead, F. W. Franz. Calling the establishment of Gilead School "a magnificent exemplification of faith," he recounted how the school has spearheaded the work of proclaiming the Kingdom good news worldwide. Now the 42 students of the 78th class have the privilege of going forth to 14 lands to assist in this grand work.

After receiving their diplomas, one of the students, Gordon Grant, came forward and read a letter of appreciation from the class. "We came as needy men and women, although we didn't realize it at the time," he said. "Today, at the end of just five months, we are leaving rich and full." They are resolved to put their training and spiritual riches to good use in their new assignments.

The afternoon program began with the students participating in an abbreviated *Watchtower* Study conducted by Calvin Chyke of the Factory Committee. Then the students put on a spirited revue of experiences and musical numbers, highlighting what they had learned simply through observation and association with the Bethel family and others. Finally, they enacted a touching Bible drama, based on the eventful account of Joseph and his brothers. There were many moist eyes in the audience.

As the chairman brought the day's proceedings to a close, everyone in attendance wholeheartedly agreed that it had been fine for them to be there. Yes, it had been a day filled with spiritual good things—a doubly joyous occasion!

Subjecting Ourselves to Jehovah by Dedication

"WE KNOW we originate with God, but the whole world is lying in the power of the wicked one." With that statement the apostle John establishes an unwelcome truth for most people, namely, that the whole world lies in the power of "the evil one," Satan. However, Satan "does not fasten his hold" on those who originate with the true God, Jehovah. Thus the whole human family must find itself either under Satan's rule or under Jehovah's rule. It is a matter of personal choice. To whom will you submit yourself? To Satan or to Jehovah?—1 John 5:18-20; *New International Version; Today's English Version.*

Now more than ever is the time for each one to choose. (Luke 21:31, 32) Jesus showed that there can be no in-between position, or sitting on the fence. He stated, "He that is not on my side is against me, and he that does not gather with me scatters." (Matthew 12:30) How can we be sure that we are gathering with Christ? So many divided and diverse religions claim to be Christian, to be "saved" and "born again," that these very terms have been cheapened. (Matthew 19:16-26; John 3:3; 10:9) The guideline is: Do we believe and proclaim what Jesus believed and proclaimed? As a Jew, he certainly did not try to glorify himself by teaching a mystifying Trinity doctrine. (John 14:28; 17:1-5) But he did proclaim a clear message, that of God's Kingdom. Conscious of his commission, Jesus said: "Also to other cities I must declare the good news of the kingdom of God, because for this I was sent forth."—Luke 4:43.

"Let It Be, This Time"

Before Jesus started his public ministry of announcing God's Kingdom, he took a vital step that serves as an example for all those who, like him, would subject themselves to his Father. Matthew's account tells us: "Then Jesus came from Galilee to the Jordan to John, in order to be baptized by him." When John protested that he was the one who should be baptized, Jesus' reply was: "Let it be, this time, for in that way it is suitable for us to carry out all that is righteous." —Matthew 3:13-15.

Having set the example in "all that is righteous" by immersion in the Jordan, Jesus could later give the command to his disciples: "Go therefore and make disciples of people of all the nations, baptizing them in the name of the Father and of the Son and of the holy spirit, teaching them to observe all the things I have commanded you." (Matthew 28:19, 20) Among other things, this step of baptism would serve to identify those who have opted for submission to the true God, Jehovah, in place of submission to Satan. During the past service year (September 1983–August 1984) nearly 180,000 people worldwide indicated their choice by water baptism. They showed that they prefer Jehovah's sovereignty to that of Satan.—Proverbs 27:11.

Decision Based on Knowledge

Likewise this year many thousands are contemplating the step of baptism during the "Integrity Keepers" Convention that will be held in many locations worldwide. Before reaching this point of baptism, all candidates have carefully reviewed with congregation elders the Bible's principal doctrines and guidelines for Christian conduct to make sure they really qualify for baptism. Thus the decision to be baptized is by no means a sudden emotional reaction. Rather, each one has 'proved for himself the good and acceptable and perfect will of God' and wishes to submit to that will. —Romans 12:2.

At the close of the convention baptism

In Our Next Issue

■ **Popular Misconceptions About the Bible**

■ **How to Make Your Bible Reading Fruitful**

■ **Finding Joy in a Trouble-Filled World**

> Since June 1984, a total of 808 "Kingdom Increase" Conventions of Jehovah's Witnesses have been held around the earth. The overall attendance reported was 5,002,684. Of these 63,556 were baptized.

talk, the baptism candidates will be in position to answer with depth of understanding and heartfelt appreciation two simple questions that serve to confirm that they recognize the implications of following Christ's example. The first question is:

On the basis of the sacrifice of Jesus Christ, have you repented of your sins and dedicated yourself to Jehovah to do his will?

The second is:

Do you understand that your dedication and baptism identify you as one of Jehovah's Witnesses in association with God's spirit-directed organization?

Having answered *yes* to these questions, candidates are in a right heart condition to undergo Christian baptism.

Proper Decorum

Sometimes questions are raised about proper dress for those being baptized. Certainly modesty should prevail in the type of bathing suit used. This is important today when fashion designers seem to want to flaunt sexuality and achieve almost total nudity. Another factor to take into account is that some suits that appear modest when dry are less than that when wet. No one getting baptized would want to be a cause for distraction or stumbling at an event as serious as baptism.—Philippians 1:10.

In the past, some have gone to extremes in giving costly gifts and holding large parties for newly baptized persons. Baptism is an occasion for great joy that can be shared, but perhaps a word of caution is appropriate here. The Bible states: "Better is the end afterward of a matter than its beginning." (Ecclesiastes 7:8) Baptism is a beginning—the beginning of the Christian race for salvation to life. Certainly no lengthy record of faithful service has yet been established. So why cause the newly converted ones to feel unduly self-important?—Compare 1 Timothy 3:6.

What does the Bible record say took place after three thousand were baptized at Pentecost 33 C.E.? "They continued devoting themselves to the teaching of the apostles and to sharing with one another, to taking of meals and to prayers." They concentrated on spiritual things and shared hospitality with one another. (Acts 2:41, 42) Baptism is a time for meditation and sober thought. We are joyful to see our Bible students take this essential step. And our decorum at the baptism site should indicate to onlookers that a vital decision has been made—to submit to God as the Sovereign Lord and, as a witness for Jehovah, to be no part of the world that lies "in the power of the wicked one."—1 John 5:19; Matthew 4:10.

Questions From Readers

■ Are there things that we should avoid saying when we pray to Jehovah?

Yes, there are. We should avoid saying things in our prayers that sound overly familiar and suggest to others (in public prayers) that we are being disrespectful. Such expressions as "Good afternoon, Jehovah" and "Give our love to Jesus" are not fitting, nor are humorous comments or even jokes in our prayers. Why?

For one reason, when such expressions are used in public prayer, they are likely to shock or offend those listening. (Romans 14:21) But there is a deeper reason why like expressions should be avoided, even in our private prayers. These are expressions that we use in conversation between equals. When used in prayer, they suggest a lack of reverence and respect, and they give the impression that the one thus praying has forgotten his total insignificance in comparison with Jehovah.—Genesis 18:27; compare Luke 18:9-14.

It is true that Christians are encouraged to develop a close relationship with Jehovah. We love him and he is our heavenly Father. (Matthew 6:9; 22:37) In fact, some humans may be called his friends. (James 2:23) Additionally, we are invited to speak to Jehovah with freeness of speech and to express our deepest thoughts and most intimate problems to him.—Psalm 55: 1, 2; Philippians 4:6; Hebrews 4:16; 1 John 3:21, 22.

Nevertheless, Jehovah demands a proper attitude from those who approach him. He said: "To this one, then, I shall look, to the one afflicted and contrite in spirit and trembling at my word." (Isaiah 66:2) Earnestness of heart is also a requirement. "Come back to me with all your hearts," Jehovah said to his people. (Joel 2:12, 13) Before him we have no claim of merit, no reason to presume, no right to demand.

The Bible gives this further counsel to those who pray to Jehovah: "Let men fear him. He does not regard any who are wise in their own heart." "The desire of those fearing him he will perform, and their cry for help he will hear, and he will save them." (Job 37:24; Psalm 145:19; see also Psalm 39:5, 12.) Hence, while Jehovah is always ready to listen to our prayers, the way we address him should show our sense of our own unworthiness, as well as our great respect for him. Any other approach would suggest presumptuousness, lack of humility, or lack of seriousness.

Sometimes children in their prayers use very familiar expressions that cause even their parents to smile. Such expressions are an appealing demonstration of childish innocence and show how real Jehovah is to them. Nevertheless, adults, with their greater realization of what is involved, should avoid levity. They ought to approach Jehovah earnestly, reverently, humbly, with dignity and seriousness.—1 Corinthians 13:11.

The "Integrity Keepers" Convention Is at Hand

A rewarding four days of Bible instruction awaits you at the "Integrity Keepers" Convention of Jehovah's Witnesses beginning this month. By means of instructive discourses, interviews with experienced ministers, and practical demonstrations, vital Christian guidance will be provided.

Be there for the opening session at 1:30 Thursday afternoon. The chairman's address, "Let Integrity Safeguard Us," highlights the convention theme and will whet anticipation for the whole four-day program. Also, in the opening session you will receive what will prove to be long-lasting assistance to reason with others from the Scriptures.

On Friday morning, there will be the dramatic presentation *Your Future—A Challenge*. This will be a real encouragement to young ones. No doubt you will appreciate so much what you receive on Friday that you will be eager to share it with others in the community.

Saturday's program is filled with practical instruction for Christian living. What it means to keep your eye simple and how a checkup can be made of your figurative heart will be explained. The day's concluding presentation, "Integrity to Truth in a Godless World," will provide you with something beautiful that not only will be a treasure to you but also should make a tremendous impact on our activity in the field ministry.

The program on Sunday, the final day, will highlight the full-costume dramatic presentation *Fear God, Turn Away From Bad*, as well as the public talk, "God's Times and Seasons—To What Do They Point?" Truly an instructive, thrilling four-day program! BE THERE!

Since over a hundred conventions are scheduled in the United States alone, there will be a convention not far from your home. Check with Jehovah's Witnesses locally for the time and place of the one nearest you.

June 15, 1985

The Watchtower

Announcing Jehovah's Kingdom

How to Read the Bible

The Watchtower
Announcing Jehovah's Kingdom

June 15, 1985
Vol. 106, No. 12

THE PURPOSE OF "THE WATCHTOWER" is to exalt Jehovah God as the Sovereign of the universe. It keeps watch on world events as they fulfill Bible prophecy. It comforts all peoples with the good news that God's Kingdom will soon destroy those who oppress their fellowmen and that it will turn the earth into a paradise. It encourages faith in the now-reigning King, Jesus Christ, whose shed blood opens the way for mankind to gain eternal life. "The Watchtower," published by Jehovah's Witnesses continuously since 1879, is nonpolitical. It adheres to the Bible as its authority.

"WATCHTOWER" STUDIES FOR THE WEEKS

July 21: Digging Deeper Into God's Word. Page 8. Songs to Be Used: 203, 123.

July 28: Sustaining Ourselves on the Fulfillment of Jehovah's Utterances. Page 13. Songs to Be Used: 135, 177.

Average Printing Each Issue: 11,150,000

Now Published in 102 Languages

SEMIMONTHLY EDITIONS AVAILABLE BY MAIL
Afrikaans, Arabic, Cebuano, Chichewa, Chinese, Cibemba, Danish, Dutch, Efik, English*, Finnish, French, German, Greek, Hiligaynon, Igbo, Iloko, Italian, Japanese, Korean, Lingala, Malagasy, Maltese, Norwegian, Portuguese, Russian, Sepedi, Sesotho, Shona, Spanish, Swahili, Swedish, Tagalog, Thai, Tswana, Xhosa, Yoruba, Zulu

MONTHLY EDITIONS AVAILABLE BY MAIL
Armenian, Bengali, Bicol, Bulgarian, Croatian, Czech, Ewe, Fijian, Ga, Greenlandic, Gujarati, Gun, Hausa, Hebrew, Hindi, Hiri Motu, Hungarian, Icelandic, Kannada, Kikuyu, Kiluba, Malayalam, Marathi, New Guinea Pidgin, Pangasinan, Papiamento, Polish, Rarotongan, Romanian, Samar-Leyte, Samoan, Sango, Serbian, Silozi, Sinhalese, Slovenian, Solomon Islands-Pidgin, Tahitian, Tamil, Telugu, Tshiluba, Tsonga, Turkish, Twi, Ukrainian, Urdu, Venda, Vietnamese
*Study articles also available in large-print edition at same cost.

The Bible translation used is the "New World Translation of the Holy Scriptures," unless otherwise indicated.

Twenty cents (U.S.) a copy

Watch Tower Society offices	Yearly subscription Semimonthly
America, U.S., Watchtower, Wallkill, N.Y. 12589	$4.00
Australia, Box 280, Ingleburn, N.S.W. 2565	A$6.00
Canada, Box 4100, Halton Hills (Georgetown), Ontario L7G 4Y4	$5.20
England, The Ridgeway, London NW7 1RN	£5.00
Ireland, 29A Jamestown Road, Finglas, Dublin 11	£5.00
New Zealand, 6-A Western Springs Rd., Auckland 3	$10.00
Nigeria, P.O. Box 194, Yaba, Lagos State	₦6.00
Philippines, P.O. Box 2044, Manila 2800	₱50.00
South Africa, Private Bag 2, Elandsfontein, 1406	R5,60

Remittances should be sent to the office in your country or to Watchtower, Wallkill, N.Y. 12589, U.S.A.

Changes of address should reach us 30 days before your moving date. Give us your old and new address (if possible, your old address label).

The Watchtower (ISSN 0043-1087) is published semimonthly for $4.00 (U.S.) per year by Watch Tower Bible and Tract Society of Pennsylvania, 25 Columbia Heights, Brooklyn, N.Y. 11201. Second-class postage paid at Brooklyn, N.Y., and at additional mailing offices.

Postmaster: Send address changes to Watchtower, **Wallkill, N.Y. 12589.**

Published by
Watch Tower Bible and Tract Society of Pennsylvania
25 Columbia Heights, Brooklyn, N.Y. 11201, U.S.A.
Frederick W. Franz, President

Popular Misconceptions About the Bible

OVER 8,000,000 pounds sterling! What a fabulous price to pay for one book! Yet, when the auctioneer's gavel came down at the sale held in London during December 1983, that was the price paid by the buyer, representing the Federal Republic of Germany. What book could possibly be worth that much? It was a part of the Bible, actually a 12th-century illuminated book of the Gospels.

Whatever the reasons for paying this enormous sum for this manuscript book, it is of interest that such a price for a work of art should be for a portion of the Bible. It reflects the view of many people that the Bible is priceless. Others, however, consider the Bible with suspicion or even hostility. Why?

Popular Misconceptions

Many people, particularly in Protestant lands, claim that the Bible is like an old fiddle that can be used to play many tunes. They feel that the Bible can be used to prove many conflicting doctrines. They say: 'It all depends upon the way you interpret it.' Is this correct?

Admittedly, the Bible *can* be quoted in attempted support of differing viewpoints. But if statements are taken out of context, cannot the work of any author be made to appear to contradict itself? Would this be honest, though? Jehovah's Witnesses maintain that an honest reading of the Bible does not allow for conflicting interpretations of key doctrines.

The Bible itself states, "For you know this first, that no prophecy of Scripture springs from any private interpretation." (2 Peter 1:20) In other words, the force instigating the writing of the prophetic Scriptures was no mere native human force, but it was the holy spirit, or active force, of God. He is the first of all prophets and Inspirer of all true Bible prophecy by means of his invisible active force.

Another popular misconception is that, whereas the God of the inspired Christian Greek Scriptures is kind and loving, the God of the inspired Hebrew Scriptures is cruel and vengeful. French essayist Stendhal wrote that God "is a despot, and, as such, is full of ideas of revenge; his Bible speaks only of dreadful punishment." This opinion is not surprising, coming from a man known as an atheistic libertine. Unfortunately, that same opinion is shared by many who call themselves Christians, including some clergymen.

The fact is that both in the portion originally written in Hebrew and in the portion written in Greek, the Scriptures state categorically that there is only "one God." (1 Corinthians 8:6; Deuteronomy 6:4) Both parts show God to be merciful, just, loving, and firm. (Exodus 34:6, 7; Psalm 103:6-8; 1 John 4:8; Hebrews 12:28, 29) Some of the most tender passages of Scripture are found in the Hebrew part of the Bible, such as in the Psalms. Conversely, the "New Testament" contains striking descriptions of severe judgment meted out to the wicked. (2 Thessalonians 1:6-9; Revelation, chapters 18 and 19) The Bible from beginning to end holds out a wonderful hope to the righteous. (Genesis 22:17, 18; Psalm 37:10, 11, 29; Revelation 21:3, 4) Thus, the Bible is in agreement with itself from start to finish.

A "Protestant Book"?

A misconception common among the world's hundreds of millions of Catholics is that the Bible is a "Protestant book." Sincere Catholics are not to be blamed for this view. For centuries the Roman Catholic Church forbade the reading of the Bible in any language other than Latin. This put the Scriptures beyond the reach of most lay Catholics. True, since 1897 and more particularly since the second Vatican Council (1962-1965), Catholics have had the right to read common-language Bibles approved by Rome. But traditions die hard. So in predominantly Catholic countries, Bible reading is still associated with Protestantism.

Many of the practicing Catholics who in recent years have obtained a Bible cannot yet pick it up without some apprehension. Why is that? Because their church still teaches that reading the Bible can be dangerous. Why? Because the Roman Catholic Church says that the Bible does not contain the complete revelation of Christian truth; it needs to be completed by "tradition." In his book La Parole de Dieu (The Word of God), Georges Auzou, Catholic professor of Sacred Scripture, wrote: "Tradition precedes, envelops, accompanies and goes beyond the Scriptures. . . . [This] helps us to understand why the Church has never made Bible reading or Bible study a strict obligation or an absolute necessity."

Why Read the Bible?

Nevertheless, many sincere Catholics the world over are procuring a Bible and are seeking help to understand it. The same is true of many disappointed Protestants and even of some who had placed their hopes in communism, socialism, or science.

Analyzing the reasons for the renewed interest in spiritual matters, religious correspondent Alain Woodrow wrote in the Paris daily Le Monde: "This is firstly a natural reaction to the disillusionment brought about by the failure of the great systems of thought, ideologies, politics, and science." He gave as further reasons "disappointment in the institutional churches because of their compromising with the political and financial powers of this world," and, lastly, what he called "apocalyptic fear."

You may be one of those who has begun reading the Bible. If so, you will need to know how to make your Bible reading fruitful.

How to Make Your Bible Reading Fruitful

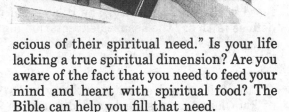

"BLESSED are the poor in spirit." Such are the opening words of Jesus' celebrated Sermon on the Mount, according to several English-language Bibles. (Matthew 5:3, *Revised Standard Version,* Protestant and Catholic editions) Can you understand what Jesus really meant by "poor in spirit"? Was he referring to those who are discouraged? Or could he have meant the feeble-minded? The latter may seem unlikely, but surely it is important to know.

Jehovah's Witnesses, who are recognized even by their critics as excellent Bible students, have found that the *New World Translation of the Holy Scriptures* admirably meets the requirements of clarity and accuracy. It renders that passage from the Sermon on the Mount: "Happy are those *conscious of their spiritual need.*"

Some Bible commentaries admit that this is what "poor in spirit" means. Why, then, do many current versions, such as the Catholic *Jerusalem Bible* and the *New International Version,* persist in using the expression "poor in spirit"?

This example shows that in order to make one's Bible reading fruitful, it is necessary to choose a translation that is faithful, clear, and understandable.

Proper Attitude

Fruitful Bible reading also requires a proper attitude on the part of the reader. Those same words of the Sermon on the Mount nicely sum up what our attitude should be, namely: "Happy are those conscious of their spiritual need." Is your life lacking a true spiritual dimension? Are you aware of the fact that you need to feed your mind and heart with spiritual food? The Bible can help you fill that need.

However, you will not find food for mind and heart in the Bible if you read it as you would any other piece of literature. You must approach it, "not as the word of men, but, just as it truthfully is, as the word of God." (1 Thessalonians 2:13) You will be reading, not human philosophy or nationalistic history, but God's thoughts and the history of his dealings with his servants on earth. It also contains amazing prophecies, some of these having already been fulfilled, while others are being fulfilled before our eyes or are yet due to come to pass for mankind's greatest good.

Since the Bible is the Word of God, to read it fruitfully a person should seek His help. Prayer to God is, therefore, an appropriate prelude to Bible reading. In simple words, expressed from your heart, ask him to help you to understand what you read and how to apply it in your personal life. Sometimes we lack the ability to use the knowledge we have acquired, which ability is wisdom. The Bible itself counsels: "If any one of you is lacking in wisdom, let him keep on asking God, for he gives generously to all and without reproaching; and it will be given him. But let him *keep on asking in faith,* not doubting at all." —James 1:5, 6.

Reading With Faith

You may say: 'How can I pray in faith and read with faith if I lack faith?' Well, if you approach Bible reading 'conscious of your spiritual need,' your faith will increase as you gain knowledge of Jehovah God and his marvelous purposes centered upon Christ. True faith is not to be confused with blind credulity. The Bible itself defines faith as "the assured expectation of things hoped for, the evident demonstration of realities though not beheld."—Hebrews 11:1.

True faith requires an underlying basis of knowledge, and such knowledge makes the things promised by God become as real as though they were beheld. Faith is, therefore, something that can be acquired. It follows the reading and hearing of things pertaining to God and his wonderful purposes for mankind. As the apostle Paul puts it, "Faith follows the thing heard. In turn the thing heard is through the word about Christ."—Romans 10:17.*

As your faith increases, your Bible reading will become more fruitful. Why? Because your "expectation of things hoped for" will become more "assured." This might be illustrated by a new friendship between you and another person. As time passes and you get to know the person better, your confidence in that one grows. Finally, after living through many situations in which your friend has never let you down, you come to put implicit trust in

* See footnote, Reference Edition of the *New World Translation of the Holy Scriptures,* 1984.

that person. If he or she writes to you, you know how to get the spirit of what is meant. Even if a sentence is not too clear, you know the person so well that you have no difficulty in grasping the thought. You read that friend's letter in a trusting way, not with suspicion.

Similarly, the more you get to know the Bible and its Author, Jehovah God, the more trust you will have in both God and his Word. Even some episodes in Bible history that may seem difficult to understand will not shake that trust. For instance, even if the reason for drastic action by God against some person or nation is not immediately apparent, you will have confidence that it was necessary. It is much the way you might say of a trusted friend: 'Well, if he did that, there must have been a good reason.'

Of course, your faith in God will be strengthened if you *can* find the reason why he acted in such a way or why he sometimes appears to delay in acting against the wicked. But you may need help. That brings us to another important aspect of fruitful Bible reading.

The Need for Help

It is an excellent thing to read the entire Bible. At the rate of one chapter a day, it would take you over three years to get through both the Hebrew and the Greek Scriptures. If you read three or four chapters a day, it will take you about a year. However, to get a general idea of what the Bible contains, you might start with Psalms and Proverbs. Then go back to Genesis, Exodus, and First Samuel before moving on to the Christian era, with Matthew, Acts, and a few of the letters written to the early Christians, such as Philippians, James, and First or Second Peter.

While doing this, you will come to realize that in order to get practical and spiritual benefit from the Bible, it is good to find out

The Ethiopian recognized what is needed to understand the Bible

what it says on a given subject. Passages bearing on one subject may be widely separated. You will likely feel the need for Bible study aids that will help you to learn what the Scriptures say, topic by topic. Also, since the books of the Bible are not arranged in strictly chronological order, such aids can help you to grasp the time sequence. Geographic and historical background material can also be very useful in understanding the Scriptures.

Where can such Bible study help be found? In recent years Catholic authors have published many books ostensibly meant to help Catholics in their Bible reading. But such authors find themselves on the horns of a dilemma. If such authors truly help Catholics to understand the Bible, the latter quickly discover that much Catholic dogma cannot be found in it. On the other hand, if the authors justify Catholic doctrine, they undermine the readers' confidence in the Bible because they subordinate Scripture to church tradition. —Compare Mark 7:13.

More and more sincere Catholics are accepting help from Jehovah's Witnesses. In many lands, thousands of Catholic people are struggling to read the Bible with understanding but are receiving little or no help from their local priests. They resemble the Ethiopian official who was reading the book of Isaiah. When the evangelizer Philip asked if he really understood what he was reading, the Ethiopian humbly replied: "How can I, unless some one guides me?" (Acts 8:31, *RS*, Catholic edition) Philip helped him, and a little later this sincere man became a baptized Christian. Similarly, as they go from door to door Jehovah's Witnesses meet Catholics, and when these say that they have a Bible in their home, the Witnesses ask if they would like help to make their Bible reading really fruitful.

Reading That Produces Fruitage

In their Bible educational work, Jehovah's Witnesses use a wide range of Bible study aids, such as *My Book of Bible Stories* (116 Bible accounts presented in simple language and in chronological order), *Is the Bible Really the Word of God?* (for scientific and historical evidence of the Bible's authenticity), *"All Scripture Is Inspired of God and Beneficial"* (a book-by-book summary of the Bible's contents, with geographic and historical background information), and *You Can Live Forever in Paradise on Earth* (which gathers scriptures on 30 vital topics, including the wonderful hope God's Word sets before sincere Bible readers today).

These Bible study aids, together with the personal help that Jehovah's Witnesses will be happy to offer you free of charge, will make your Bible reading pleasurable and fruitful. You will find guidance for everyday living and a wonderful hope for life in God's promised New Order, where, at long last, the will of God will "be done, on earth as in heaven."—Matthew 6: 10, *JB*.

Digging Deeper Into God's Word

"HAPPY is the man that has found wisdom, and the man that gets discernment, for having it as gain is better than having silver as gain and having it as produce than gold itself. It is more precious than corals, and all other delights of yours cannot be made equal to it. Length of days is in its right hand . . . It is a tree of life to those taking hold of it, and those keeping fast hold of it are to be called happy."—Proverbs 3:13-18.

> 'If as for hid treasures you keep searching for it, you will find the very knowledge of God.'
> —PROVERBS 2:4, 5.

² True Christians are happy, indeed, to have found wisdom. That means the ability to use their knowledge of God's Word in their active worship, in solving their day-to-day problems, and in making decisions concerning their goals in life. Before being accepted for baptism by Jehovah's Witnesses, each candidate's basic Bible knowledge is tested by a comprehensive series of pointed questions. One of the concluding questions asks: "Following your baptism in water, why will it be vital for you to maintain a good schedule for personal study and to share regularly in the ministry?" This impresses on the mind of that baptismal candidate the need to continue to study beyond the elementary things and "press on to maturity." (Hebrews 6:1) But do all heed this advice?

---

1. What is a true source of happiness, and why?
2. Why are Jehovah's Witnesses happy, but what advice are they given from the time of their baptism?

³ In his first letter to the Corinthian Christians, the apostle Paul complained that he was unable to speak to them "as to spiritual men," but that he needed to speak to them "as to babes in Christ." (1 Corinthians 3:1) Similarly, he wrote, likely to Christians living in Judea: "Concerning him we have much to say and hard to be explained, since you have become dull in your hearing. For, indeed, although you ought to be teachers in view of the time, you again need someone to teach you from the beginning the elementary things of the sacred pronouncements of God; and you have become such as need milk, not solid food. For everyone that partakes of milk is unacquainted with the word of righteousness, for he is a babe."—Hebrews 5:11-13.

⁴ Today, likewise, it would appear that some, when once they have acquired sufficient knowledge to dedicate themselves to Jehovah, with the hope of living forever in Paradise on earth, do not develop serious, long-term study habits. They may feel that they know enough to "get along," spiritually speaking. They do not go beyond the "milk" stage. Paul states frankly that such ones remain "unacquainted with the word of righteousness," that is, they

---

3, 4. (a) What did Paul state about some Christians in Corinth and in Judea? (b) What appears to be the case with some Christians today?

are unaccustomed to using "the word of righteousness" to test things out. Paul adds: "But solid food belongs to mature people, to those who through use have their perceptive powers trained to distinguish both right and wrong."—Hebrews 5:14.

"Solid Food" Needed for Growth

⁵ How many years have you been a dedicated servant of Jehovah? Reflect on your spiritual growth over those years. Are you able to explain from the Bible only the basic truths, "the elementary things of the sacred pronouncements of God"? A few who have been in the Christian way for 10 or 20 years are still at the "milk" stage. What would people think of a child 10 years old, or of a young man or woman aged 20, who was still being bottle-fed on milk? Would this not be an anomaly? Would not such a milk diet stunt the person's growth? The individual might survive, but he or she would not grow into a strong and healthy adult. The same is true spiritually.

⁶ Why are some who have been Christians for years not spiritually strong enough to take an active part in helping the normal "babes," those who have just taken their stand for Jehovah? These who have not advanced have for years received of the time and attention of Christian elders and other mature ones. Still, as Paul says, they themselves "ought to be teachers in view of the time." To become teachers, they must progress beyond the "milk" diet and get used to eating "solid

food." How can they do this?—Hebrews 5:12.

⁷ Paul says that "solid food belongs to mature people," and he defines such as "those who through use have their perceptive powers trained to distinguish both right and wrong." In other words, those who make a habit of using whatever knowledge of God's Word they have to distinguish both right and wrong will gradually train their perceptive powers and will attain Christian maturity. They will become accustomed to using "the word of righteousness" to test things out and thus distinguish between what is wholesome and what is hurtful morally, spiritually, and even physically. By applying what they learn, they will no longer be "unacquainted with the word of righteousness." They will become "mature people," those to whom "solid food belongs."—Hebrews 5:13, 14.

Develop Good "Eating" Habits

⁸ Sick people who have been put on a milk diet over a long period of time have

---

5, 6. (a) What is true of some who have been in the truth for years, and why is this abnormal? (b) What did Paul say to such ones, and so what should they do?

7. According to Hebrews 5:14, for whom is "solid food" appropriate, and how does a Christian become one of such?
8. How could a Christian limit himself to a "milk" diet, but how can he change his spiritual "eating" habits?

to accustom their body to taking in solid food once more. Similarly, those who have developed the habit of "pecking" at the spiritual food served by "the faithful and discreet slave," leaving on the side of their plate, as it were, those choice morsels that require a little more "chewing" (thought and research), will need to put forth an effort to develop good spiritual "eating" habits. They will need to 'arouse their clear thinking faculties' and 'exert themselves vigorously.'—Matthew 24:45; 2 Peter 3:1, 2; Luke 13:24.

9 Three things can help a person who has been sick to recover his appetite for solid, nourishing food: (1) proper motivation, that is, the desire to get well and strong again, (2) appetizing food served at regular intervals, and (3) sufficient fresh air and exercise. How could these points help someone who has lost his appetite for the deeper things of God's Word?

10 Any person who has dedicated his life to Jehovah should have strong motivation for increasing his knowledge of God's Word. Our love for Jehovah moves us to become better acquainted with his wonderful qualities, his will, and his purposes. This requires deep study and meditation. (Psalm 1:1, 2; 119:97) Moreover, our hope to live forever in God's Paradise earth depends upon our continually 'taking in knowledge of the only true God and of his Son, Jesus Christ.' (John 17:3) But our desire for everlasting life should not be our primary motive for studying the Scriptures. That was the mistake some faithless Jews made. Our "searching the Scriptures" must be done primarily out of love for God and with the desire to do his will.—John 5:39-42; Psalm 143:10.

11 The abundance of appetizing spiritual food served regularly and "at the proper time" by "the faithful and discreet slave" should move all of us to show our appreciation by taking full advantage of the good things provided. (Matthew 24:45) We should develop good spiritual "eating" habits by setting aside sufficient time to read and study all the fine material published in the Watch Tower Society's books and magazines. Spiritual food is served at regular times at the five weekly meetings organized in the congregations of Jehovah's Witnesses throughout the world. Are you present at all these meetings and well prepared to assimilate the food served?

12 Love for God as well as love for neighbor should move us to study His Word. (Luke 10:27) A person who has lost his physical appetite can benefit from fresh air and exercise. So, too, the Christian who wants to build up an appetite for "solid food" can be helped by getting out in the preaching work and using his knowledge to spread "this good news of the kingdom" and to "make disciples of people of all the nations." (Matthew 24:14; 28:19, 20) Remember, Paul said to those who had "become such as need milk," or spiritual babes, that they "ought to be teachers in view of the time." (Hebrews 5:12) Where do *you* stand, in view of the time you have been a true Christian? If you are a brother, have you advanced to the stage where you can be useful as a "teacher" in the field, and perhaps also as an elder in the congregation? If you are a Christian sister, are you able to conduct upbuilding Bible studies in the homes of people who show interest in God's truth or

9. What can help someone who has lost his appetite?
10. What proper motivation should move us to increase our knowledge of God's Word?

11. How are we served appetizing food at regular times?
12. (a) What is another way in which a Christian can build up his spiritual appetite? (b) So, what questions may we ask ourselves?

Factors that can help a person have spiritual health

1. **Proper motivation:** Develop a strong desire to become better acquainted with Jehovah

2. **Regular diet:** Take advantage of the spiritual food served regularly by "the faithful and discreet slave"

3. **Exercise:** Use knowledge to help others, such as by getting out in the preaching work

perhaps to help your Christian sisters in the witnessing work?

Make Study a Pleasure

13 It has been said that reading is a pleasure whereas studying is work. There is some truth in that. Much upbuilding reading can be done for pleasurable relaxation. What could be more enjoyable than an hour or two spent in a comfortable position reading a report from the *Yearbook of Jehovah's Witnesses* or an issue of the *Awake!* magazine? Study, however, means work. A dictionary states: "Study implies sustained purposeful concentration with such careful attention to details as is likely to reveal the possibilities, applications, variations, or relations of the thing studied." Yes, study requires effort. But just as any work well done can be satisfying and remunerative, study can be pleasurable and spiritually rewarding. It is in our interest to make it so. How?

14 For study to be enjoyable and really beneficial, it is necessary to devote sufficient time to it. Since "study implies sus-

tained purposeful concentration" and "careful attention to details," how often can you honestly say that you have *studied* your *Watchtower* or the publication used for your Congregation Book Study? Would it not be more accurate to say that oftentimes you skim through the study material and quickly underline the answers to the questions, without really getting down to the details and the *reasons* for the explanations given? If this is the case with you, probably the first step you should take to improve your spiritual "eating" habits is to 'buy out the opportune time' for study. (Ephesians 5:15-17) This may mean making drastic transfers of time from other less essential activities. But you may be surprised how enjoyable study can become when you have the time to do the material justice rather than having to rush through it.

15 Not unrelated to the time factor is the matter of prayer. Jehovah's blessing is essential for study to be spiritually beneficial. We need to pray to him, in the name of Jesus, asking him to open up our minds and hearts and to make them really receptive to the truths to be studied. How often have you had to sit down hurriedly to prepare for a meeting, only to realize later that you forgot to ask Jehovah for his blessing and for wisdom to apply in your daily life the things learned? Why deprive yourself of Jehovah's help when it is there for the asking?—James 1:5-7.

Digging Deeper

16 Proverbs 2:4, 5 states: 'If as for hid treasures you keep searching for it, you will find the very knowledge of God.' The context of that passage speaks of the need

13. What is the difference between reading and studying?
14. What may you need to do to make your personal study more pleasurable and beneficial?

15. What else is indispensable for study to be both enjoyable and spiritually beneficial?
16. In line with the theme text for this study, what must we do to find knowledge, discernment, and understanding?

to seek out Jehovah's "sayings," "commandments," "wisdom," "discernment," and "understanding." Searching for treasures requires effort and perseverance. It calls for much digging. It is not different when searching for "the very knowledge of God," for "discernment," and for "understanding." This also requires much digging, or penetrating below the surface. Do not feel that it is sufficient to skim over the surface of God's Word.

¹⁷ A psalmist exclaimed: "How great your works are, O Jehovah! Very deep your thoughts are." (Psalm 92:5) The apostle Paul wrote admiringly: "O the depth of God's riches and wisdom and knowledge!" (Romans 11:33) In another letter, he spoke of "the deep things of God." (1 Corinthians 2:10) True, as Paul explains, God reveals such deep things "through his spirit," which active force acts powerfully upon the anointed Christians appointed by Christ Jesus to provide spiritual food. We should be truly thankful for the spiritual digging that the "slave" class does to make clearer and clearer for us "the hidden depths of God's purposes."—1 Corinthians 2:10, *Today's English Version.*

¹⁸ But that does not relieve each individual Christian of the responsibility to dig deeper into God's Word, for the purpose of getting the full depth of the thoughts explained. This involves looking up the scriptures cited. It means reading the footnotes in *Watchtower* articles, some of which refer the reader to an older publication that provides a fuller explanation of a certain passage or prophecy. It requires digging deeper, putting forth effort to lo-

---

17. What do the Scriptures say about Jehovah's thoughts, and so for what should we be thankful?
18. How can each Christian dig deeper into God's Word, and what special digging tools have been provided?

By Way of a Reminder

☐ Why do some remain spiritual "babes"?

☐ What can help a person to become mature?

☐ How can we develop good spiritual "eating" habits?

☐ What can make our personal study more pleasurable?

☐ Why is it necessary to dig deep into God's Word?

---

cate that older publication and then studying the pages referred to. It consists of making full use of specialized Bible study aids that the "slave" class has made available over the years, such as indexes, concordances, *Aid to Bible Understanding,* and *"All Scripture Is Inspired of God and Beneficial."* Yes, Christians have been provided with excellent digging tools, the latest of which is the new English-language Reference Bible, which, in time, will be available in a number of other languages. Let us use these digging tools to good advantage.

Study With a Purpose

¹⁹ The purpose of our digging deeper into God's Word is not to make us feel superior to our brothers or to make a show of our knowledge. This is often the case with worldly people. In principle, what Paul wrote is true here: "Knowledge puffs up, but love builds up." (1 Corinthians 8:1) Love will move us humbly to use our knowledge in the preaching and disciple-making work and in contributing discreetly to the spiritual value of Christian meetings.

---

19. What word of caution is vital about knowledge?

²⁰ Let us "no longer be babes," but "grow up in all things into him who is the head, Christ." (Ephesians 4:13-15) "Let us press on to maturity." (Hebrews 6:1) Let us be mature people, able to assimilate "solid food" that will make us spiritually strong and useful within the Christian congregation. However, this involves more than taking in knowledge by study. It requires feeding upon Jehovah's utterances or published expressions with appreciation, which we will consider in the following article.—Psalm 110:1; Isaiah 56:8; 66:2.

20. What exhortations does Paul give in this connection?

Sustaining Ourselves on the Fulfillment of Jehovah's Utterances

JEHOVAH is the Great Food Provider. He presented himself as such to man in the very first chapter of the Bible. (Genesis 1:29, 30) Much later, the psalmist David gratefully said to Jehovah: "To you the eyes of all look hopefully, and you are giving them their food in its season. You are opening your hand and satisfying the desire of every living thing." (Psalm 145:15, 16) Yes, Jehovah has provided an abundance of food for both man and animal. There is a difference though. Whereas animals require only physical food, Jesus showed that man needs more than physical bread, or food. He 'must live also on every utterance coming forth through Jehovah's mouth.'—Matthew 4:4.

> **"Man must live, not on bread alone, but on every utterance coming forth through Jehovah's mouth."**
> **—MATTHEW 4:4.**

² Jesus made this statement in reply to Satan, who had tried to tempt Him into miraculously converting stones to bread. The Devil did not press the point but quickly moved on to another temptation. Judging by the erroneous way he then applied Psalm 91:11, 12, maybe Satan did not even understand what Jesus meant in His reply to the first temptation. (Matthew 4:3-7) But we servants of Jehovah are very interested in what Jesus said. We who enjoy digging deeper into the Bible so as to get the maximum spiritual benefit can ask: Did Jesus mean that in order to lead a full life, man must study

1. How is Jehovah the Great Food Provider, but what statement did Jesus make about man's needs?

2. What should we know concerning the meaning of Jesus' words at Matthew 4:4?

and perhaps memorize "every utterance coming forth through Jehovah's mouth"? Or what did he mean?

Jehovah's Utterances

[3] In rebutting Satan, Jesus quoted Deuteronomy 8:3 according to the Greek *Septuagint* version of this Hebrew scripture. The Greek word translated "utterance" (*rhe′ma*) has a twofold meaning. It is sometimes translated "word," "expression," or "utterance." But, like its Hebrew equivalent (*da·var′*), it can also mean "thing."

[4] In Luke 1:37 we read: "With God no declaration [*rhe′ma*] will be an impossibility." Luke 2:15 reads: "The shepherds began saying to one another: 'Let us by all means go clear to Bethlehem and see this thing [*rhe′ma*] that has taken place, which Jehovah has made known to us.'" So, particularly as used in connection with Jehovah, this Greek word can imply a "word," a "declaration," or an "utterance" of God. Or it can imply a "thing," whether that refers to an "event," or "action" described, the *result* of what is said, the *word fulfilled.*

[5] Thus understood, Luke 1:37 does not mean that God can say just anything. That could be true of a man, even if what he said was unlikely to occur or was meaningless. But regarding God's statements, the import of Luke 1:37 is that no word or declaration of Jehovah can go unfulfilled. The declaration that the angel had made to Mary was thus bound to come to pass. The thought behind the Hebrew and the

What does Jesus' response to Satan's temptation mean to you?

Greek words used for Jehovah's "word," "utterance," "expression," or "declaration" is beautifully expressed in the book of Isaiah. Jehovah states: "For just as the pouring rain descends, and the snow, from the heavens and does not return to that place, unless it actually saturates the earth and makes it produce and sprout, and seed is actually given to the sower and bread to the eater, so my word [Hebrew, *da·var′*; Greek, *rhe′ma*] that goes forth from my mouth will prove to be. It will not return to me without results, but it will certainly do that in which I have delighted, and it will have certain success in that for which I have sent it."—Isaiah 55: 10, 11.

"Not on Bread Alone"

[6] Now, coming back to the point, what did Jesus mean when, quoting Deuteronomy 8:3, he said that "man must live, not

---

3, 4. What twofold meaning do the Greek and Hebrew words for "utterance" have? Illustrate.
5. What is the meaning of Luke 1:37?

6, 7. What was the historical and geographic context of Deuteronomy 8:2, 3?

on bread alone, but on every *utterance* coming forth through Jehovah's mouth"? (Matthew 4:4) Was he saying that the godly man is sustained just by utterances, words, or declarations? Would head knowledge of such divine expressions be sufficient? Let us examine the historical context of the words Jesus quoted from Deuteronomy.

7 The Bible study aid *"All Scripture Is Inspired of God and Beneficial"* informs us, on page 36: "The book of Deuteronomy contains a dynamic message for Jehovah's people. After wandering in the wilderness for forty years, the sons of Israel now stood on the threshold of the Land of Promise." The year was 1473 B.C.E. The place? The plains of Moab. In his second discourse to the assembled Israelites, Moses declared: "You must remember all the way that Jehovah your God made you walk these forty years in the wilderness, in order to humble you, to put you to the test so as to know what was in your heart, as to whether you would keep his commandments or not. So he humbled you and let you go hungry and fed you with the manna, which neither you had known nor your fathers had known; in order to make you know that not by bread alone does man live but by every expression of Jehovah's mouth does man live."—Deuteronomy 8:2, 3.

8 Just imagine! Several million Israelites—old and young, men, women, and children—had been walking for 40 long years in "the great and fear-inspiring wilderness, with poisonous serpents and scorpions and with thirsty ground that [had] no water." (Deuteronomy 8:15) They had needed water to drink and food to eat. Jehovah had, at times, allowed them to be thirsty and hungry. Why? So as to im-

press upon their minds that "not by bread alone does man live but by every expression of Jehovah's mouth."

9 What was the connection between the Israelites' needs and the expressions, or utterances, coming forth from Jehovah's mouth? Well, what tangible things had come to pass among the Israelites as a *result* of Jehovah's utterances? Moses wrote: "Your mantle did not wear out upon you, nor did your foot become swollen these forty years. . . . [Jehovah] brought forth water for you out of the flinty rock; [and he] fed you with manna in the wilderness." (Deuteronomy 8:4, 15, 16) The connection is this: The Israelites would have received none of these things if Jehovah had not commanded them to take place. Thus, the Israelites had literally lived "by every expression [or, command] of Jehovah's mouth."

Sustained by Jehovah's Utterances

10 Besides depending on Jehovah for such material benefits as food, water, and clothing, how else were the Israelites able to be sustained by Jehovah's utterances? There were spiritual benefits too. Moses told the Israelites that Jehovah had caused them to go through these experiences in the desert 'in order to humble them, to put them to the test so as to know what was in their heart, as to whether they would keep his commandments or not.' He added: "You well know with your own heart that just as a man corrects his son, Jehovah your God was correcting you . . . so as to do you good in your afterdays."—Deuteronomy 8:2, 5, 16.

11 Yes, if the Israelites had taken full advantage of their experiences in the wilderness, they would have learned to 'live

8. What had been the situation of the Israelites, and why had Jehovah allowed this?

9. How had the Israelites' needs been filled by Jehovah's utterances?

10, 11. In what other ways were the Israelites able to be sustained by Jehovah's utterances?

The Israelites' living "by every expression of Jehovah's mouth" had direct physical benefits

by every expression of Jehovah's mouth,' not only by learning to obey his written commandments but actually by experiencing the results of Jehovah's utterances in their life as a nation and in their individual lives. They had been given ample opportunity to "taste and see that Jehovah is good." (Psalm 34:8) These enriching experiences in connection with Jehovah's words—both uttered and fulfilled—should have sustained them spiritually.

¹² Joshua, who succeeded Moses as leader of Israel, informed himself of Jehovah's utterances by filling his mind with them. His faith was strengthened by observing their fulfillment. After Moses' death, Jehovah made this utterance to Joshua: "This book of the law should not depart from your mouth, and you must in an undertone read in it day and night, in

order that you may take care to do according to all that is written in it; for then you will make your way successful and then you will act wisely."—Joshua 1:8.

¹³ Toward the end of his life, after having faithfully obeyed Jehovah's word and observed its fulfillment upon Jehovah's people, Joshua was able to testify: "So Jehovah gave Israel all the land that he had sworn to give to their forefathers, and they proceeded to take possession of it and to dwell in it. Furthermore, Jehovah gave them rest all around, according to everything that he had sworn to their forefathers, and not one of all their enemies stood before them. All their enemies Jehovah gave into their hand. Not a promise [Hebrew, da·var'; Greek, rhe'ma] failed out of all the good promise that Jehovah had made to the house of Israel; it all came true." (Joshua 21:43-45) Joshua truly lived and was sustained, not on literal bread alone, "but on every utterance com-

---

12, 13. How did Joshua familiarize himself with Jehovah's utterances, and to what did he testify?

ing forth through Jehovah's mouth."
—Matthew 4:4.

Living Today by Jehovah's Utterances

14 Having dug a little deeper into the above words quoted by Jesus in reply to the Devil's temptation, we are better able to understand what Jesus meant. The historical and geographic context of Moses' account, quoted from by Jesus, shows that the utterances of Jehovah by which godly men and women must live are not just words learned by rote. For those Israelites, "every expression of Jehovah's mouth" was linked with the manna, the water, and the clothing that did not wear out. Yes, the utterances included their fulfillment, the wonderful things Jehovah did for his people. It was their experiencing these things, in fulfillment of Jehovah's utterances, that strengthened the appreciative Israelites.

15 Similarly today, what nourishes Jehovah's people is not simply reading and studying Jehovah's utterances, as necessary as this is. It is *experiencing,* collectively and individually, the wonderful way in which Jehovah deals with us and acts on our behalf. The more we are conscious of Jehovah's dealings with us, the more such fulfilled utterances will nourish us, strengthening our faith, our spirituality.

16 A psalmist wrote: "I shall remember the *practices* of Jah; for I will remember your marvelous *doing* of long ago. And I shall certainly meditate on all your *activity,* and with your *dealings* I will concern myself." (Psalm 77:11, 12) If we concern ourselves with Jehovah's practices, doings, activities, and dealings on behalf of his people, realizing that they are a tangible expression of his utterances, these divine providences will be like spiritual bread for us. They will draw us into a closer personal relationship with Jehovah. We will be like Jesus. He refused to turn stones into loaves of bread at the Devil's bidding. Likewise we will take care not to allow material things or undue concern about material needs to cause us to fall into the Devil's trap and abandon Jehovah's worship.

17 Jesus stated: "My food is for me to do the will of him that sent me and to finish his work." (John 4:34) He was a wonderful example, showing us in a practical way that "man must live, not on bread alone, but on every utterance coming forth through Jehovah's mouth."—Matthew 4:4.

Awaiting Further Instructions

18 Jehovah, through his Son, has stated that "this good news of the kingdom will be preached in all the inhabited earth" before the end comes. (Matthew 24:14)

---

14. (a) By digging deeper into Matthew 4:4, how can we better understand what Jesus meant? (b) What strengthened appreciative Israelites?
15. How can Jehovah's utterances nourish us?
16. (a) With what did a psalmist concern himself? (b) How should we do likewise, and how will this help us?

17. In what way was Jesus a wonderful example?
18. What divine utterance is now being fulfilled?

In Our Next Issue

- **Captives of Superstition Find Freedom**

- **Triumphing in "the Final Part of the Days"**

- **Peaceable People Are Truly Needed!**

That divine utterance is in course of fulfillment as a result of the worldwide preaching work of Jehovah's Witnesses. Are you 'living' on that utterance from Jehovah's mouth by having a full share in the preaching work and thus receiving spiritual sustenance because you are doing his will?

19 Other utterances of Jehovah are due to cause exciting events in the near future. "The ten horns" and "the wild beast" will turn against "the harlot," Babylon the Great. Yes, the destruction of that world empire of false religion by antireligious elements within the United Nations will be an outstanding action resulting from the carrying out of one of Jehovah's utterances.—Revelation 17:16, 17.

20 Another remarkable divine utterance will come to pass when Jehovah symbolically puts "hooks" in the jaws of Gog, or Satan, challenging him and his "military force" to attack His people on earth. (Ezekiel 38:2-4, 8-12) Yet another divine utterance will bring the destruction of Gog's hordes. (Ezekiel 39:1-6)* This will mean "the war of the great day of God the Almighty" at Har–Magedon. (Revelation 16:14, 16; 19:11-21) How thrilling it will be for Jehovah's faithful people to observe the fulfillment of these divine utterances and, in the midst of the fray, to hear figuratively this further utterance: "Stand still and see the salvation of Jehovah in your behalf."—2 Chronicles 20:17.

21 Then, carrying out another divine utterance, Christ will bind Satan and his

demons and hurl them into the abyss for "a thousand years." (Revelation 20:1-3) That thousand years will allow for the fulfillment of other utterances of Jehovah, including the resurrection of the dead and "the curing of the nations," obedient mankind. (Revelation 20:11-15; 22:1, 2) During this thousand-year judgment period, Jehovah evidently will give additional instructions, unknown to us at present, as new "scrolls" are opened. (Revelation 20:12) How marvelous it will be for the survivors of the "great tribulation" and for the resurrected dead to gain instruction and guidance from these further instructions as set forth on these unrolled "scrolls" of Jehovah and to carry them out delightfully!

22 With such a wonderful prospect before us, let us take full advantage of the opportunity we now have to acquaint ourselves with Jehovah's utterances and do deep personal study of his Word and participate in the preaching work with an ever-increasing consciousness of Jehovah's actions on our behalf.

---

22. What are we encouraged to do now?

---

* See chapters 19, 20 in "The Nations Shall Know That I Am Jehovah"—How? published by the Watchtower Bible and Tract Society of New York, Inc.

19, 20. What other divine utterances will shortly cause exciting events?
21. The carrying out of Jehovah's utterances will bring about what developments?

Can You Recall?

□ How did the Israelites learn to live "by every expression of Jehovah's mouth"?

□ How could the Israelites feed spiritually on Jehovah's utterances?

□ How can we live today by Jehovah's utterances?

□ What utterances of Jehovah are to be fulfilled?

Insight on the News

Hospitals Seek Witnesses

The press reports that a few California hospitals are now actively seeking Jehovah's Witnesses as patients. Some hospitals have been reluctant to operate on the Witnesses because they refuse blood transfusions on religious grounds. Why the change in attitude? Since the economy of the medical industry is in trouble, administrators are looking for additional sources of revenue. But another reason is given. "Recent medical advances making bloodless surgery—the term used to describe operations in which transfusions of blood or blood parts are withheld—less risky also have made the hospitals and doctors involved more willing to operate on Witnesses," reports the *Daily News* of Van Nuys, California. "Most forms of surgery can be performed without giving blood if you are very cautious and patient with the patient," admits general surgeon Dr. Sheldon N. Lipshutz.

Although Jehovah's Witnesses accept nonblood alternatives, such as saline solutions, they refuse to 'thrust aside their faith and good conscience' for a medical practice that is unscriptural. (1 Timothy 1:19; Acts 15:20) They have found that obeying God's laws is also medically sound. "Fifteen or 20 years ago, I didn't want (Witnesses) in my hospital," one administrator told the *Daily News.* "Today there are too many cases of AIDS and hepatitis spreading through transfusions not to question the desirability of routine blood transfusions. The Jehovah's Witness point of view makes increasing sense."

Learning to Do Good

Why did some in Nazi Germany risk their lives in order to save or help people in danger of persecution or death while others who could have helped turned the other way? Dr. Samuel Oliner, a sociologist at Humboldt State University in Arcata, California, along with his associates, is endeavoring to find out. Already, reports *The New York Times,* their findings "converge on the formative experiences people have in childhood, which seem to make them, many years later, more predisposed than others to come to the aid of the distressed."

Concurring is Ervin Staub, a psychologist at the University of Massachusetts. "The parents who transmit altruism most effectively," said Dr. Staub, "exert a firm control over their children. Although they are nurturant, they are not permissive. They use a combination of firmness, warmth and reasoning. They point out to children the consequences to others of misbehavior—and good behavior. And they actively guide the child to do good, to share, to be helpful."

It is no wonder, then, that parents are instructed to bring their children up "in the discipline and mental-regulating of Jehovah" because "he that does good originates with God."—Ephesians 6:4; 3 John 11.

No "Truth"?

"You will know the truth, and the truth will set you free," Jesus stated at John 8:32. Yet a growing trend is to think that the goal of knowing the truth is unattainable. Note the remarks of Bishop John S. Spong, as quoted in *The Sunday Star-Ledger* of Newark, New Jersey: "We must . . . move from thinking we have the truth and others must come to our point of view to the realization that ultimate truth is beyond the grasp of all of us." He added: "Every religious tradition . . . revolves around a center none of us finally can claim or capture." Speaking to a convention of some 600 Episcopal clergymen and lay delegates, the bishop questioned "the traditional, imperialistic claims of Christianity."

But if "ultimate truth" is not to be found, why did Jesus insist that God must be worshiped "with spirit and truth"? Or why did he state that his followers would be guided "into all the truth"? (John 4:23, 24; 16:13) And why would the apostle Paul state that it is God's will that individuals should "come to an accurate knowledge of truth"? (1 Timothy 2:3, 4) Or why did he speak of some doctrines as being a 'deviation from the truth'? (2 Timothy 2:18; 4:3, 4) Certainly, as with the early Christian congregation, a group of worshipers having the truth can be expected to be present today.

The Child of Promise

INSTEAD of returning to Nazareth, Joseph and Mary remain in Bethlehem. And when Jesus is eight days old they have him circumcised, as God's Law to Moses commands. It is apparently the custom also to give a baby boy his name on the eighth day. So they name their child Jesus, as the angel Gabriel had directed earlier.

More than a month passes, and Jesus is 40 days old. Where do his parents now take him? To the temple in Jerusalem, which is only a few miles from where they are staying. According to God's Law to Moses, 40 days after giving birth to a son, a mother is required to present a purification offering at the temple.

That is what Mary does. But she brings two small birds as her offering. This reveals something about the economic situation of Joseph and

Mary. The Law of Moses indicates that a young ram, which is much more valuable than birds, should be offered. But if the mother could not afford this, two turtledoves or pigeons would suffice.

In the temple an old man takes Jesus into his arms. His name is Simeon. God has revealed to him that he will not die before he has seen Jehovah's promised Christ, or Messiah. When Simeon comes to the temple on this day, he is directed by holy spirit to the child carried by Joseph and Mary.

As Simeon holds Jesus he thanks God, saying: 'You have kept your promise, for I

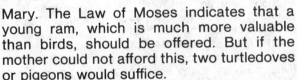

have seen with my own eyes the means of salvation that you have prepared.' Joseph and Mary are amazed when they hear this. Then Simeon blesses them and says to Mary that her son "is laid for the fall and the rising again of many in Israel" and that sorrow, like a sharp sword, will pierce her soul.

Present on this occasion is the 84-year-old prophetess named Anna. In fact, she is never missing from the temple. In that very hour she comes near and begins giving thanks to God and speaking about Jesus to all those who will listen.

How happy these events at the temple have made Joseph and Mary! Surely, it only confirms to them that the child is the Promised One of God.   Luke 2:21-38; Leviticus 12:1-8.

♦ When was it apparently the custom to give a baby Israelite boy his name?

♦ What was required of an Israelite mother when her son was 40 days old, and how did the fulfilling of this requirement reveal Mary's economic situation?

♦ Who recognized the identity of Jesus on this occasion, and how?

'Lengthening the Tent Cords' in Japan

"**M**AKE the place of your tent more spacious. And let them stretch out the tent cloths of your grand tabernacle. Do not hold back. Lengthen out your tent cords, and make those tent pins of yours strong."—Isaiah 54:2.

By those words, the prophet Isaiah pointed to the time when true worship of Jehovah God would undergo rapid expansion. Today, in one country after another around the world, we are witnessing just such marvelous theocratic expansion. This is, perhaps, nowhere more evident than in Japan, where there are some 96,000 worshipers of the true God.

Growth Through the Years

It was early in the second decade of this century that the good news of God's Kingdom first reached Japan. Charles T. Russell, the first president of the Watch Tower Society, made a 700-mile (1,100-km) tour through the Japanese islands and saw the need for preaching true Christianity. In 1926 an American-Japanese was assigned to Japan as the Watch Tower Society's first missionary.

For some 20 years, many seeds of truth were sown and scores of persons learned about Jehovah's Kingdom. Many of them underwent severe trials for their faith at the hands of the military government during the period of 1933-45.*

In 1949 the preaching work in Japan got a fresh start. Gilead-trained missionaries

---

* For a detailed account, see *1973 Yearbook of Jehovah's Witnesses,* pages 214-22.

began arriving. By August, there were seven missionaries working in Tokyo, and, on an average, nine persons shared in the evangelizing work each month. Six more missionaries arrived in October, five of these starting the preaching work in Kobe. How would this preaching be received in this country of Buddhist and Shinto believers, recovering from the shock of World War II?

In less than ten years the number of Kingdom preachers grew to 1,000. But the 'place of the tent was yet to be made more spacious.' By November 1970 the number of Witnesses had multiplied tenfold, and three years later it reached 20,000. In another three and a half years that number was to double again—for a new peak of 40,000-and-more Kingdom preachers! However, there were many sheeplike ones yet to be found, and Jehovah continued to pour out his blessing on the zealous activities of his people in Japan. In a little over six years, by June 1983, the 40,000 had doubled once again to over 80,000, and, as of this report, the number of Kingdom publishers in Japan has reached 97,305!

Those Who Preached Full Time

Clearly, Jehovah God has been the One behind the expansion. However, the zealous missionaries and other full-time preachers have played an important role.

By 1952 the missionary group had grown to about 50, and several new native Witnesses were entering the pioneer work. The example of the zealous missionaries en-

Growth in Kingdom publishers in Japan in the past 37 years

9	1,000	10,000	20,000	40,000	80,000	97,305
1949	1958	1970	1973	1976	1983	1985 (Feb.)

couraged more and more of their newly baptized companions to devote themselves full time to Jehovah's service. Today, 37 years after the first missionaries entered the country, nearly 40 percent of all Witnesses in Japan are in the full-time (pioneer) work each month, with 36,118 reporting even in the short midwinter month of February 1985. Many of the missionaries who shared in this expansion from the start are still serving there, but the present group of 76 missionaries is now like a small 'drop in the ocean' of tens of thousands of local pioneers.

Would you like to meet some of these zealous ones? Let us get acquainted with at least a few, representing the spectrum of these pioneers.

First, meet some of the old-timers. Iwako Kono is our oldest special pioneer. At age 70 she has enjoyed this privilege of service for about 28 years and has helped almost 50 persons to dedication and baptism. Then there is Sadakichi Shimada. At 87 years of age he is the oldest regular pioneer in Japan. Toyoko Umemoto was 26 years old when she started to special pioneer. Now,

with more than 29 years of faithful service, she has served the longest of any native Japanese special pioneer.

At the other end of the scale, there are many young ones who are using their youth to serve Jehovah. Meri Aida was 14 years old when she received her appointment to serve as a regular pioneer. Before that she had shared in auxiliary pioneer service for 41 months since her baptism at age 11. She did so while going to school.

Akiko Goto was seven years old when her mother started to do regular pioneer work, in spite of caring for two babies. Akiko followed her mother's fine example and became a regular pioneer when she was 18, and then two years later she became the youngest special pioneer in Japan. Hisako Wakui was 21 when she started as a special pioneer. Now, after some 28 years, she has had the privilege of helping at least 37 persons to become worshipers of Jehovah.

Many have gone out from the big cities to the small towns and villages to bring the "good news of the kingdom" to all the deserving ones. Interestingly, about 60 percent of all regular pioneers are housewives, and the majority of them do not have believing husbands. This marvelous pioneer spirit has spearheaded the growth of Kingdom interests in Japan.

The Urgent Need for Meeting Places

The Japanese Witnesses fully appreciate the Bible command not to 'forsake the gathering of ourselves together, and all the more so as we behold the day drawing near.' (Hebrews 10:25) In the early years, most congregations held their meetings in small rooms in labor halls or civic auditoriums. Many of these were rented on a weekly basis. Often the brothers would arrive for their meetings only to be told that the room would not be available that day. This meant scurrying around to find another

Toyoko Umemoto has the longest record of special pioneering

location and then, in less than an hour, setting it up for the meetings!

Happily, most of that is in the past. The majority of the congregations now have their own meeting places. Some rent on a yearly basis while others have renovated vacant buildings or warehouses. But the price of land in Japan is so high—ranging anywhere from $35 to $50 (U.S.) per square foot—that few congregations can afford to own the land where their Kingdom Halls stand. Some brothers who own property have torn down their houses and rebuilt with a Kingdom Hall on the first floor and their residence above. In several unusual cases, persons who are not Jehovah's Witnesses or not even interested in Christianity have offered to build Kingdom Halls on their property and rent them to Jehovah's Witnesses, even asking the Witnesses to submit plans for their hall. This has resulted in some truly unusual Kingdom Halls.

For example, in Yokohama, a parking-lot owner agreed to build a Kingdom Hall on stilts over his lot and to rent the hall to the Witnesses. One in Tokyo is on the second floor of a building anchored between the supports of an elevated railway. At last report, the brothers there have got used to the noisy trains overhead.

As the congregations have grown larger, so have the circuit assemblies. Whereas 20 years ago a circuit assembly might have only 300 to 400 in attendance, now there may be 1,500 to 2,000, or more. Facilities for assemblies this large are difficult to find. Thus, in 1975, a bankrupt bowling establishment outside of Tokyo was leased and remodeled to become Japan's first Assembly Hall, with a seating capacity of 1,200. The second one, a fine ferroconcrete building, followed in 1982. It is in the central (Kansai) area of Japan and was built entirely by the volunteer labor of Witness men, women, and children. It seats 1,800. The third Assembly Hall has been built by volunteer workers on the property of the Watch Tower Society's branch headquarters in Ebina. It will seat 3,000.

The last time all the publishers in Japan came together for one assembly was at the international convention at Ōsaka in 1973, with 31,263 in attendance. Since then, due to lack of suitable facilities, smaller conventions have proved to be more practical, and a Kingdom witness can be given in more places. Twenty-four such conventions were held in 1984, with 179,439 attending and 3,236 being baptized.

Expansion at the Branch

To keep pace with the rapid growth in the field, the Society's branch office has undergone tremendous expansion through the years. From 1949 to 1962 the office was located in a two-story Japanese-style house in Minato Ward, Tokyo. It was finally replaced by a seven-story building that served as the headquarters until 1972. By then the Society saw the need to do its own printing. So a new factory and a Bethel home were built on an acre (0.4 ha) of land in Numazu City, 75 miles (120 km) southwest of Tokyo.

Within five years, however, the facilities at Numazu were taxed to the limit. Thus, 18 acres (7 ha) were purchased in Ebina, and a fine factory and a Bethel home, three times the size of the facilities in Numazu, were built. This complex, constructed entirely by the Witnesses themselves, was dedicated on May 15, 1982.

Magazine production was started with a new rotary offset printing press while construction was still in progress. After construction was completed, another four-color rotary offset press was added. The brothers were especially excited when tens of thousands of copies of the Japanese *New World Translation of the Holy Scriptures* rolled off the Society's press in 1982. To keep up with the increasing demand for magazines and other literature, a five-unit rotary offset press was installed in January 1984. It can produce a thousand magazines a minute and can print *The Watchtower* and *Awake!* simultaneously.

To do all this printing and shipping and to look after the needs of the workers, the Bethel family has grown to 345 members. In addition, 165 have been working on the new construction project. Interestingly, there are 19 sets of fleshly brothers in this family.

Even though it was just three years ago that the Ebina facilities were dedicated, work is already under way for further expansion. Under construction on the same property are a new eight-story Bethel home, which will house 250 persons, and a six-story factory addition. Indeed, the "tent cords" are being extended beyond all anticipation.

Sadakichi Shimada is the oldest regular pioneer in Japan

Future Prospects

In this land of Buddhist and Shinto beliefs, there are many people who are looking for something in which they can put faith. How many will yet come to Jehovah's "tent" remains to be seen. An indication of further progress is the fact that 224,696 persons met together on April 15, 1984, to commemorate Jesus' death. And a concerted effort is being put forth to help the interested ones. Each month, some 142,000 home Bible studies are being conducted.

When the first missionaries arrived in 1949, who could have imagined that after 37 years there would be over 97,000 active praisers of Jehovah in this land? Yet, Jehovah has brought it about. True to his promise, he has indeed 'stretched out the tent cloths' and 'lengthened the tent cords' for his people. His Witnesses will continue to work hard and look to him to bring in the harvest before the end of this system of things.

Finding Joy
in a
Trouble-Filled World

"ALWAYS rejoice in the Lord," commanded the apostle Paul. "Once more I will say, Rejoice!" (Philippians 4:4) But for many, such joy seems elusive. 'How can you be joyful when you have to put up with poverty, unemployment, unruly workmates, immoral enticements, or pressures at school?' wonder some.

It would hardly be reasonable for God to expect his people to be in a perpetual state of jubilance. God himself inspired Paul to predict that these would be "critical times hard to deal with." (2 Timothy 3:1-5) Nevertheless, the Bible does clearly show that even in the worst of circumstances, one can have at least a *measure* of joy. Jesus, for example, "endured a torture stake" and "contrary talk by sinners." Certainly there was little joy in being painfully nailed to a stake or in being jeered at by crowds. Paul even speaks of Christ's agonies as being so intense that he had to petition God "with strong outcries and tears." Yet Jesus was able to endure all of this "for the *joy* that was set before him." —Hebrews 12:2, 3; 5:7.

Early Christians likewise "endured a great contest under sufferings, sometimes while [they] were being exposed as in a theater both to reproaches and tribulations." Yet, Paul says, they "*joyfully* took the plundering of [their] belongings." (He-brews 10:32-34) But how was this possible?

Joy—From Without or Within?

Joy is not something external. It is a quality of the heart. (Compare Proverbs 17:22.) True, external things such as family, friends—even a favorite food—can to a limited extent bring a feeling of joy. (Acts 14:16, 17) Why, just *anticipating* something good can bring joy! (Compare Proverbs 10:28.) However, the joy a person derives from external circumstances or material things can be short-lived.

On the other hand, external circumstances at times seem to rob us of joy. For example, a young man named Jim expresses how his secular job affected him: "I hated my job . . . I couldn't see spending my life just to advance some company that didn't seem to really care about me as a person. Plus, many of the people I worked with were backstabbing, insincere people." Trying to induce joy artificially likewise proved a dead end. Recalls Jim: "I've been involved with drugs of all kinds since I was ten years old. But I became a very mixed-up person. I was sick of the life I was leading: drinking, taking drugs, and partying. Life had no meaning or purpose. I asked myself, 'Where can I find something better?'"

Jim's experience in this regard reminds us of that of King Solomon. He, too, learned the futility of trying to find joy through self-indulgence:

"I said, even I, in my heart: 'Do come now, let me try you out with rejoicing. Also, see good.' And, look! that too was vanity. I said to laughter: 'Insanity!' and to rejoicing: 'What is this doing?' I explored with my heart by cheering my flesh even with wine, while I was leading my heart with wisdom, even to lay hold on folly until I could see what good there was to the sons of mankind in what they did under the heavens for the number of the days of their life. I engaged in greater works. I built houses for myself; I planted vineyards for myself. I made gardens and parks for myself . . . And anything that my eyes asked for I did not keep away from them. . . . And I, even I, turned toward all the works of mine that my hands had done and toward the hard work that I had worked hard to accomplish, and, look! everything was vanity and a striving after wind."—Ecclesiastes 2:1-5, 10, 11.

Is there a way of life that is not vain, one that brings joy even under the direst of circumstances?

The Source of Real Joy

"The joy of Jehovah is your stronghold," said Nehemiah. (Nehemiah 8:10) Yes, joy emanates from Almighty God because, for one thing, he is the Creator of all good things that can bring true joy. "Strength and joy are at his place," says the Bible. (1 Chronicles 16:27) The real way to attain joy, therefore, is to have a friendship, a relationship, with the Creator himself such as Abraham enjoyed! (James 2:23) Can such a friendship bring joy? Consider what the psalmist said: "Your [God's] friendship is better than life." (Psalm 63:3, *The Bible in Living English*) In passing let it be noted that Jim in time came to appreciate these facts. Today he is a joyful Christian.

How could friendship with God bring joy? For one thing, God is "the rewarder of those earnestly seeking him." (Hebrews 11:6) In serving God, one need not fear that one's efforts are in vain or go unnoticed. The smallest acts of devotion are deeply appreciated by him. (Compare Mark 12:41-44.) And when Jehovah blesses his faithful friends, his blessing "makes rich, and he adds no pain with it." (Proverbs 10:22) In fact, lovers of God look forward to enjoying the reward of eternal life in his New Order where "righteousness is to dwell." (2 Peter 3:13) Such a hope is a real cause of joy for Christians!

Another thing to consider is that "joy" is a fruit of God's spirit. Yet God generously gives his spirit to his friends upon request. (Galatians 5:22; Luke 11:13) What is the result? The psalmist proclaimed, "Happy is the people whose God is Jehovah!"—Psalm 144:15.

Keeping Our Joy

Nevertheless, even anointed Christians in Paul's day felt low at times. (1 Thessalonians 5:14) And today the stresses and strains of life exact an even greater toll. But since joy is a quality that dwells deep in one's heart, these pressures need not cause you to lose your joy. Consider, for example, Jesus Christ. We earlier observed that "for the joy that was set before him he endured a torture stake." (Hebrews 12:2) Though being impaled was obviously a wretched experience, Jesus' relationship with his Father was far too strong to allow him to focus his thoughts on self-pity. The dominant thought in Jesus' mind was clearly "the joy that was set before him": the privilege of vindicating Jehovah's name, the prospect of rescuing the entire human race from sin, the honor of serving as the King of God's Kingdom! Even in his darkest moments, Christ could reflect upon these things and have feelings of intense joy!

Early Christians likewise could endure persecution, even 'joyfully taking the plundering of their belongings,' not because they derived some masochistic pleasure from misery, but because their minds were focused on *why* they had to endure these things. They could rejoice "because they had been counted worthy to be dishonored in behalf of [God's] name." They could rejoice because of the 'hope of everlasting' life set before them.—Acts 5:41; Titus 1:2.

Today we also can maintain our joy, even when confronted with serious problems. Rather than withdrawing into ourselves and dwelling on our problems, we can try to remind ourselves of the blessings of having a friendship with Jehovah and the support of loving brothers and sisters. Often this is enough to make our suffering seem insignificant. Jesus illustrated the matter this way: "A woman, when she is giving birth, has grief, because her hour has arrived; but when she has brought forth the young child, she remembers the tribulation no more because of the joy that a man has been born into the world."—John 16:21.

In the Christian congregation today are many fine examples of individuals who allow joy to overshadow their problems. A Christian woman named Evelyn, for example, has suffered a variety of illnesses, including cancer. She walks with difficulty and is often visibly in pain. Yet she is regular in attendance at meetings and usually has a radiant smile on her face. The secret of her joy? "I lean on Jehovah," she is fond of saying. Yes, rather than dwelling on her misery, she makes an effort to focus her mind on the reasons she has to be joyful. This gives her the strength to cope with her illnesses.

Of course, we can easily lose our joy. Some become consumed with a desire for material things or recreation. They neglect Christian meetings, personal study, and field service. Rather than bringing joy into his life, the one who lusts for material riches 'stabs himself all over with many pains.'—1 Timothy 6:10.

Pursuing the selfish "works of the flesh" is another way of destroying one's joy. Fornication, uncleanness, or loose conduct may bring momentary pleasure, but they are diametrically opposed to God's spirit, which produces joy. (Galatians 5:19-23) The one who indulges in wrongdoing risks cutting himself off from the Source of joy —Jehovah!

How much better it is, therefore, for a Christian jealously to safeguard his joy. If, for some reason, you find yourself lacking joy, see what you can do to regain it. Perhaps there is a need on your part for further study and meditation on the Bible. It is only by constantly reminding ourselves of our hope that we can "rejoice in the hope" ahead, even when suffering difficulties. (Romans 12:12) Or perhaps there is a need to have a greater share in preaching the "good news of the kingdom." (Matthew 24:14) "Giving" in this way almost inevitably brings a greater measure of joy!—Acts 13:48, 52; 20:35.

Our problem-filled world will continue to cause us trouble. But by drawing close to our heavenly Friend, we can hold on to our joy and gain entrance into God's New Order where all the obstacles to joy will be forever removed!—Revelation 21:3, 4.

EXACTLY two years ago, *The Watchtower* published the article "Jehovah's Standards Help Us." (Psalm 20:4) It gave as one example of the help available from God's safe and sure guidelines, the protection coming to Christians who obey his law against taking in blood. At that time in the United States attention was just beginning to be focused on a new health threat—AIDS. There were suspicions that this fatal syndrome might be spread through blood transfusions. However, readers in Europe and elsewhere might then have felt that this threat from violating God's law was limited to some distant location. As an update two years later, consider this recent information from Great Britain.

Britain, Blood, and AIDS

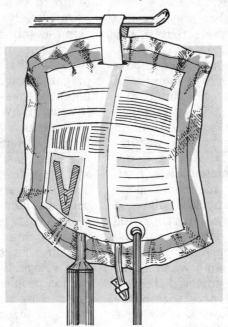

"**M**Y SISTER needs to have an operation but is terrified of contracting AIDS. We are not Jehovah's Witnesses, but can you please help by recommending a surgeon who would operate without the use of blood?" That was just one of the heartfelt requests received recently by Jehovah's Witnesses at their London, England, headquarters. What lies behind these appeals?

Since its inception, the British Blood Transfusion Service has prided itself on its blood supply from voluntary donors. "A rest after the donation [of a unit of blood], a drink and biscuits, and back to work. Why not give it a try?" encourages their advertising leaflet. As a result, two million *voluntary* donations are made each year by 3 percent of the population.

"Blood collected from unpaid volunteers, as it is in Britain, is qualitatively superior to that collected from people who are paid for it," claims *The Guardian*. In other words, the view has long been that Britain has avoided the risk of infection from blood *purchased* from alcoholics or others who have little else to sell. But recent events have revealed serious flaws in this picture, resulting in an unprecedented loss of public confidence. Following the death of two haemophiliacs, a spokesman for the Haemophiliac Society said that National Health Service 'blood supplies can no longer be regarded as safe.' What happened?

Although it has been well known for years that it is impossible to screen blood for every disease and that serious infections, such as hepatitis or malaria, can be passed by transfusion, such dangers were

What Is AIDS?

AIDS is an acronym derived from Acquired Immune Deficiency Syndrome. AIDS itself does not kill. But, as its name implies, the victim is left with a crippled immune system. Lacking this protection, a person with the disease will usually die from an infection, such as a unique type of pneumonia or a rare form of skin cancer, Kaposi's sarcoma. Research into detection and diagnosis is in its early stages, and there is, as yet, no known cure for AIDS.

not widely publicized in Britain. The inference always was that donated blood gives no cause for alarm. But two shocking factors have combined, causing *The Daily Telegraph* to conclude: "Britain has lost the battle to prevent the Aids virus infiltrating blood supplies."

The first shock came when press reports revealed that for many years Britain has in fact been buying blood from abroad. "Blood is being bought from people in poor countries where there is a high increase of blood-transmitted diseases," confided a union representative at a blood-products laboratory. Furthermore, some 70 million units of concentrated Factor VIII are imported from the United States and are used to treat British haemophiliacs. Each batch of Factor VIII is made from plasma that is pooled from as many as 2,500 blood donors. It seems that by importing this blood product the AIDS virus was transferred to the British supply.

An additional shock came when AIDS was confirmed as having infected the system from homosexual donors within the British Isles. Although homosexuals have been among those asked not to donate blood because of their higher risk of having AIDS, the warning was not as strongly worded as it should have been, admitted the Department of Health. The warning in their pamphlet on AIDS referred only to "Homosexual men who have many different partners." A current overprinting of the leaflet *A.I.D.S. and how it concerns blood donors* specifies that "Practising male homosexuals and bisexuals" are "par-

ticularly susceptible" to AIDS. But the warning came too late. By the beginning of 1985 more than 40 individuals, including a newborn baby, were infected. Furthermore, there is the troubling fact that the AIDS virus has an incubation period of up to two years. So how many more have already been infected? There is a "time-bomb element," as *The Sunday Times* put it. Accordingly, the National Blood Transfusion Service has recently prepared an additional pamphlet for all potential blood donors in Britain, *Some Reasons Why You Should Not Give Blood.*

There have already been some 50 deaths from AIDS in Britain, out of over 100 reported cases. The number of people suffering from the disease is presently doubling every eight months. A medical correspondent for *The Sunday Times* estimated that there could be over 12,000 cases within five years. An even more startling estimate out of the United Kingdom's Royal College of Nursing is that one million people in the British Isles could be affected by the year 1991 if no action is taken to check the spread of AIDS.

The inquirer mentioned above said: "It seems to me that you Jehovah's Witnesses are being proved right on this matter of blood transfusion." More accurately, of course, it is Jehovah God, through his Word, the Bible, who is being vindicated. Centuries ago he commanded Christians to 'abstain from blood.' (Acts 15:29; 21:25) His counsel and standards have certainly proved to be a protection for his people and will continue to be.

Questions From Readers

■ Was Dinah, the daughter of Jacob, raped by Shechem, and was it solely an act of violence, or did he want to marry her?

Evidently Shechem had sex relations with Dinah against her will. He raped her. However, her frequent, friendly visits with the Canaanites put her in a compromising situation and evidently had led to his strong attachment to her and his desire to have her as his wife.

The account at Genesis 34:1-3 reads: "Now Dinah . . . used to go out to see the daughters of the land. And Shechem the son of Hamor the Hivite, a chieftain of the land, got to see her and then took her and lay down with her and violated her. And his soul began clinging to Dinah the daughter of Jacob, and he fell in love with the young woman." Despite the efforts of her father to discourage association with the immoral people of Canaan by pitching his camp *outside* the city of Shechem and establishing a separate water supply, Dinah still "used to go out to see the daughters of the land." (Genesis 33:18; John 4:12) The Hebrew verb translated "used to go out" is in the imperfect tense, which indicates continuous action. This verb in the same tense is also rendered, according to the setting, "regularly went out" and "customarily came up." (1 Samuel 18:13; 1 Kings 10:29) So Dinah's venture was not her first outing. She apparently wanted to "see," become better acquainted with, her neighbors in the city.

On one occasion during her regular visits, Shechem "took [Dinah] and lay down with her and violated her." Regarding the Hebrew word rendered "violated,"

A Hebrew and English Lexicon by William Gesenius states: "to deflower a woman, usually by force." This same word at Judges 19:24 and 20:5 is rendered "raped." However, a measure of consent on the part of the woman is indicated at Deuteronomy 22:24 where this same Hebrew word is used. Perhaps at the outset neither Shechem nor Dinah had in mind sex relations, but as his passion became aroused by the charms of this young, inquisitive virgin, he, without any godly moral restraints, did what most Canaanite men would have considered natural. After all, she had come into *his* environment! When Dinah evidently objected to "going that far," he simply overpowered her.

Even if there was no measure of consent by Dinah, she still bore some responsibility for losing her virginity. Though she only visited "the *daughters* of the land," just imagine the morals of these. The fact that Esau's Hittite (or, Canaanite) wives were "a source of bitterness of spirit" to godly Isaac and Rebekah is certainly an indication of the badness already manifest among "the daughters of the land." (Genesis 26:34, 35; 27:46) Sexual immorality, including incest, homosexuality, sodomy, and bestiality eventually became a part of "the way the land of Canaan" did. (Leviticus 18: 2-25) So what did Dinah talk about during such visits? Did she really believe she could avoid fellowship with the girls' brothers and boyfriends? For a woman to mingle, apparently unattended,

among such immoral people was inviting trouble. Dinah knew what happened to her ancestors Sarah and Rebekah while in Canaan. In the eyes of the depraved men of Canaan, Dinah became legitimate prey. She put herself in a compromising situation and paid for such with the loss of her virginity, despite any last-minute resistance.—Genesis 20:2, 3; 26:7.

After the affair Shechem detained Dinah in his home and "kept speaking persuasively" to her, as it were 'to her heart.' His father said: "His soul is attached to [Dinah]." It is unlikely that such ardent attachment would have developed simply from one encounter. He apparently had noticed her good qualities previously, perhaps during her frequent visits. Now he wanted to marry her. He and his father also may have felt that the marriage proposals would somehow atone for the son's deed and correct the situation, keeping peaceful relations with the prosperous household of Jacob. —Genesis 34:3, 8.

This whole episode led to the massacre of Shechem, his father, and all the males of the city. This brought ostracism on Jacob's household and led to his stern denunciation of his sons' anger many years later. (Genesis 34:30; 49:5-7) What a horrendous chain of events, and all because Dinah failed to guard her associations. This episode in the inspired record is a warning to young Christian women today who may, out of curiosity, be tempted to mingle socially with those who are not servants of God.—Proverbs 13:20.

'I've Listened to Them Dozens of Times'

TO WHAT? To dramatized Bible accounts on cassette tapes. An appreciative listener from Albuquerque, New Mexico, writes:

"I've listened to the tape 'Beware of Losing Faith by Drawing Away From Jehovah' in my car at least 25 times. It gives me so many things to ponder over. It's helped me to see issues much more clearly in my life by hearing the Israelites' discussions—they are such real people, and it becomes so obvious what they should or should not do.

"Different phrases, such as 'it's such a little thing' or 'you take the Law so literally . . . your view is narrow and restricted,' ring in my mind over and over. It makes me joyful because it's helped me take a firm stand (like Moses, Aaron, and Joshua) for what's right—not even desiring to compromise, thus beginning to draw away from Jehovah."

July 1, 1985

The Watchtower

Announcing Jehovah's Kingdom

TRUE WORSHIP
Man-Made or Revealed by God?

July 1, 1985
Vol. 106, No. 13

The Watchtower®

Announcing Jehovah's Kingdom

THE PURPOSE OF "THE WATCHTOWER" is to exalt Jehovah God as the Sovereign of the universe. It keeps watch on world events as they fulfill Bible prophecy. It comforts all peoples with the good news that God's Kingdom will soon destroy those who oppress their fellowmen and that it will turn the earth into a paradise. It encourages faith in the now-reigning King, Jesus Christ, whose shed blood opens the way for mankind to gain eternal life. "The Watchtower," published by Jehovah's Witnesses continuously since 1879, is nonpolitical. It adheres to the Bible as its authority.

"WATCHTOWER" STUDIES FOR THE WEEKS

August 4: Jehovah's Goodness in "the Final Part of the Days." Page 18. Songs to Be Used: 77, 90.

August 11: Triumphing in "the Final Part of the Days." Page 23. Songs to Be Used: 195, 113.

Average Printing Each Issue: 11,150,000

Now Published in 103 Languages

SEMIMONTHLY EDITIONS AVAILABLE BY MAIL
Afrikaans, Arabic, Cebuano, Chichewa, Chinese, Cibemba, Danish, Dutch, Efik, English*, Finnish, French, German, Greek, Hiligaynon, Igbo, Iloko, Italian, Japanese, Korean, Lingala, Malagasy, Maltese, Norwegian, Portuguese, Russian, Sepedi, Sesotho, Shona, Spanish, Swahili, Swedish, Tagalog, Thai, Tswana, Xhosa, Yoruba, Zulu

MONTHLY EDITIONS AVAILABLE BY MAIL
Armenian, Bengali, Bicol, Bulgarian, Croatian, Czech, Ewe, Fijian, Ga, Greenlandic, Gujarati, Gun, Hausa, Hebrew, Hindi, Hiri Motu, Hungarian, Icelandic, Kannada, Kikuyu, Kiluba, Malayalam, Marathi, New Guinea Pidgin, Pangasinan, Papiamento, Polish, Rarotongan, Romanian, Samar-Leyte, Samoan, Sango, Serbian, Silozi, Sinhalese, Slovenian, Solomon Islands-Pidgin, Tahitian, Tamil, Telugu, Tshiluba, Tsonga, Turkish, Twi, Ukrainian, Urdu, Venda, Vietnamese
*Study articles also available in large-print edition at same cost.

The Bible translation used is the "New World Translation of the Holy Scriptures," unless otherwise indicated.

Twenty cents (U.S.) a copy

Watch Tower Society offices	Yearly subscription Semimonthly
America, U.S., Watchtower, Wallkill, N.Y. 12589	$4.00
Australia, Box 280, Ingleburn, N.S.W. 2565	A$6.00
Canada, Box 4100, Halton Hills (Georgetown), Ontario L7G 4Y4	$5.20
England, The Ridgeway, London NW7 1RN	£5.00
Ireland, 29A Jamestown Road, Finglas, Dublin 11	£5.00
New Zealand, 6-A Western Springs Rd., Auckland 3	$10.00
Nigeria, P.O. Box 194, Yaba, Lagos State	₦6.00
Philippines, P.O. Box 2044, Manila 2800	₱50.00
South Africa, Private Bag 2, Elandsfontein, 1406	R5,60

Remittances should be sent to the office in your country or to Watchtower, Wallkill, N.Y. 12589, U.S.A.

Changes of address should reach us 30 days before your moving date. Give us your old and new address (if possible, your old address label).

The Watchtower (ISSN 0043-1087) is published semimonthly for $4.00 (U.S.) per year by Watch Tower Bible and Tract Society of Pennsylvania, 25 Columbia Heights, Brooklyn, N.Y. 11201. Second-class postage paid at Brooklyn, N.Y., and at additional mailing offices.

Postmaster: Send address changes to Watchtower, **Wallkill, N.Y. 12589.**

Published by
**Watch Tower Bible and Tract Society
of Pennsylvania**
25 Columbia Heights, Brooklyn, N.Y. 11201, U.S.A.
Frederick W. Franz, President

True Worship
—Man-Made or Revealed by God?

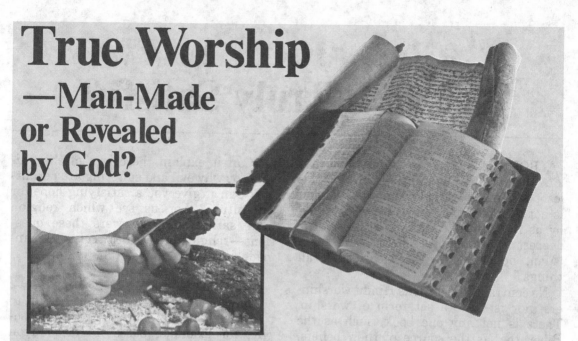

ALMOST everything man knows, he has had to discover for himself.

The most basic of shreds of knowledge —how to grow food and cook it, how to build a roof over his head—have come only by painful trial and error. But the last century has seen man rapidly expand his horizons beyond mere domestic needs. Now he splits the atom, flies faster than the speed of sound—even routinely sends men into outer space. Does this mean, however, that man is equally capable of figuring out for himself how best to serve God?

Not according to the writer of Psalm 143:10, who said: "Teach me to do your will, for you are my God. Your spirit is good; may it lead me in the land of uprightness." The psalmist thus recognized that man, for all his know-how and ingenuity, needs divine assistance in order to learn God's will. (Compare Jeremiah 10:23.) This would mean, however, that God must somehow reveal himself to man.

Has such a thing occurred? For millions, the Bible is evidence that such a divine revelation has already taken place. Others, however, disagree. They are so bedazzled by man's ingenuity that they see no need for such a revelation. These ones may claim that religious knowledge is "inborn in every person" or that such knowledge "can be acquired by the use of reason" rather than "through either revelation or the teaching of any church."

However, if this is true, it would, in effect, be up to man to invent his religion, to develop his own doctrines and moral standards. Does this seem reasonable to you? What purpose would a man-made religion serve? Would it really be able to satisfy man's spiritual needs? (Matthew 5:3) Could it really answer the questions that truth-seeking individuals ask about God?

Let us explore these questions by taking a brief look at a religion that has tried to find God through human reasoning and philosophies—the Hindu faith.

Man-Made Religion
—Can It Truly Satisfy?

ABOUT 450,000,000 people embrace the Hindu religion. Says Hindu philosopher Dr. S. Radhakrishnan: "Religion is not so much a revelation to be attained by us in faith as an effort to unveil the deepest layers of man's being." He adds: "Man, no doubt, is the measure of all things."

No central body governs Hindu worshipers, nor is there a set form of worship. There is not any one book, such as the Bible, that is the source of their beliefs. Over the centuries a vast array of Hindu writings have appeared, and six different schools of Hindu philosophy have developed: *Nyāya* (analytical reasoning), *Vaiśeshika* (knowledge of physics), *Sānkhya* (synthesis of elements), *Yoga* (union with deity), *Mīmāmsā* (inquiry), and *Vedānta* (fulfillment of Veda).

These philosophies have been developed by various Hindu teachers at different times and stages in history, and each uses a different approach to worship. *Nyāya,* for its part, uses complicated systems of logic to prove God's existence by inference (for example, inferring the reality of wind from the rustle of trees).

This approach obviously has some validity, inasmuch as the Bible similarly says: "For his invisible qualities are clearly seen from the world's creation onward, because they are perceived by the things made, even his eternal power and Godship." (Romans 1:20) Nevertheless, can a system of logic really acquaint you with the Creator? Can such a system reveal what his name

is? Can it explain the origin of the universe or why evil and suffering are permitted? Can it give you a satisfying hope for the future? Let us see which religion more satisfactorily answers these questions—religion of revealed truths or man-made religion.

Human Teachings Versus the Bible

The Hindus have given much thought to the nature of God. The *Vedānta* philosophy, for example, bases its ideas upon the religious writings called *Upanishads.* These writings inquire into the nature of God and his relationship to humans.

However, the Bible excels in giving insight about God, and it does so clearly and consistently. He is identified as the Creator of all things. (Revelation 4:11) He is portrayed as a Person, not as some nameless force. "Let them praise the name of Jehovah, for his name alone is unreachably high. His dignity is above earth and heaven," says the Bible at Psalm 148:13. He is described as "a God merciful and gracious, slow to anger and abundant in loving-kindness and truth." (Exodus 34:6) He even invites imperfect humans to come to know him and have a relationship with him! (Psalm 34:8) Is not what the Bible says about God far more satisfying than philosophical inquiries?

The *Upanishads* also search into the makeup of the human soul. The Bible, however, clearly explains that "Jehovah God proceeded to form the man out of dust from the ground and to blow into his

Millions embrace
man-made religions,
but have they provided
satisfactory answers to
questions about God?

nostrils the breath of life, and the man came to be a living soul." (Genesis 2:7) So man *is* a soul —not the possessor of some shadowy spirit that experiences repeated reincarnations. Nor is this soul immortal. The Bible says, "The soul that is sinning—it itself will die."—Ezekiel 18:4.

The *Upanishads* probe into the nature of *Self* and *Ego*. Only the Bible, however, gives the key to the understanding of man by exposing his sinful nature. "For all have sinned and fall short of the glory of God." (Romans 3:23) As a result, man must constantly battle wrong impulses.—Romans 7:20, 25.

The *Upanishads* delve into questions regarding the reality of evil and recompense. The Bible, however, clearly says that wickedness on this earth is a result of man's choosing an independent course. "See! This only I have found, that the true God made mankind upright, but they themselves have sought out many plans." (Ecclesiastes 7:29) As to the ultimate recompense for evil, the Scriptures say: "And he will render to each one according to his works: everlasting life to those who are seeking glory and honor . . . ; for those who are contentious and who disobey the truth but obey unrighteousness there will be wrath and anger, tribulation and distress . . . For there is no partiality with God."—Romans 2:6-9, 11.

And while the *Upanishads* struggle to

explain the path to salvation, the Bible simply says, "Salvation belongs to Jehovah." (Psalm 3:8) Those following Jehovah's way are promised: "The righteous themselves will possess the earth, and they will reside forever upon it."—Psalm 37:29.

The Bible supplies simple, straightforward, understandable answers to questions that perplex human speculators. No philosopher could have developed these answers on his own.

The Bible —A Revelation From God?

Does this necessarily mean, though, that you can trust the Bible as a revelation from God? There are many reasons why you can.

First of all, it is only reasonable to assume that God would reveal himself to man in some way. What do you think of a man who fathers children but then runs away and abandons them? What if such a man left his children in complete ignorance about himself, not even leaving them his name? Would you not be outraged with him? Is it not, therefore, only reasonable to conclude that a loving Creator would in some way reveal himself to his earthly children?

'But why would he do so through a book?' you might ask. 'Would not an Almighty God use something more dramatic—perhaps a voice from the sky?' God did speak from heaven on several occasions, as when he gave the Ten Commandments. At that time the people were so terrified by the display of natural phenomena that they pleaded with Moses, "Let not God speak with us for fear we may die." So they stood at a distance while Jehovah spoke to Moses. (Exodus 20:18-22)* But even Moses could have forgotten those words spoken by God. Jehovah therefore wisely chose to have Moses and, later, other faithful men preserve His words in writing. (Exodus 34:28) Thus, people can read God's thoughts at their leisure. They can ponder, meditate on, and study what God has to say.—See Joshua 1:8; also 1 Timothy 4:15.

True, the Bible was written by men, just as surely as men wrote the Hindu writings. But the men writing the Bible were under the influence of Jehovah God's holy spirit. (2 Peter 1:21) Their writings were not mere philosophical musings. And the Bible has the earmarks of God's direction. Can anything other than God's direction account for the Bible's accurately telling the order in which life appeared on the earth? (Genesis, chapter 1) Can anything other than God's direction account for the Bible's accurately stating, more than 2,700 years ago, that the earth not only is round but hangs "upon nothing"? (Job 26:7; Isaiah 40:22) Can anything other than divine direction account for the Bible's unerring accuracy when it comes to prophecies, such as the one at Isaiah 44:28, wherein the Persian conqueror Cyrus the Great was mentioned by name some 130 years before he was born? Could any human have foretold 2,500 years ago the development of the two rival superpower blocs that hold the center of the world stage today?—Daniel 11:27, 36-40.

The Bible not only stated that the earth is round but also said that it hangs "upon nothing." Does this not argue for divine inspiration?

So there are solid reasons to believe in the Bible as a revelation of God's will. We invite you to examine open-mindedly what it has to say. Jehovah's Witnesses are pleased to help individuals do this. In this way your worship will not be a vain pursuit of human wisdom. (Matthew 15:9) Nor will you, like the ancient Samaritans, be worshiping "what you do not know." (John 4:22) With the help of God's spirit, you can actually come to know even "the deep things of God." (1 Corinthians 2:10) For "if you search for him, he will let himself be found by you." —2 Chronicles 15:2.

* See also Exodus 33:11; Matthew 3:17; 17:5; John 12:28.

Three Captives of Superstition Find Freedom

Edmond Kouadio

Adama Traore

Athanase Kouassi

THEY called him M. Tout-Blanc, which means "Mr. All-White." A resident of the Ivory Coast town of Dimbokro, Edmond had worn white clothes exclusively for the last 16 years! And if you asked Edmond why he wore only white, he would simply tell you that it was because he was obedient. But to whom—or to what—he did not say.

Adama's prized possession was his woven "guinea-fowl" shirt. It was called that because its black and white colors were a reminder of the guinea fowl. The design was characteristic of the work of the Tagbana tribe in north-central Ivory Coast. Adama had received the shirt as a child, but even in adulthood he carefully secured it in a safe place. He somehow felt he *had* to.

Athanase similarly had something that he treasured—a perfume bottle filled with, of all things, a mixture of kaolin (white clay) powder, sand, and water. Yet he was actually afraid to throw it away!

All three men were captives of superstitious, religious fears—fears that actually took over their lives! Millions more suffer similar captivity. In Africa many believe that items such as amulets, rings, statues, and necklaces have supernatural power to ward off wicked spirits. Promoters of su-perstition, such as fetish priests, make a living off such fears. And Africa is not unique in this regard. Many followers of Western culture have similar beliefs when it comes to "lucky" objects, such as the rabbit-foot and the horseshoe. Nevertheless, as Edmond, Adama, and Athanase learned, there is a way out of this captivity.

Edmond and the "Spirit of the Stream"

Some of Edmond's earliest memories are those of accompanying his parents to a "sacred" mountain outside their village. Nearby was a stream where sacrifices of cattle and sheep were offered to please the spirit of the stream. People would come and consult this spirit for solutions to their problems. Everyone had heard emanating from the stream a voice that often gave them counsel.

Certain children in each family were said to have a special relationship with this spirit. Edmond was one of these, according to the fetish priest. He could, therefore, depend on the spirit to guide him. When Edmond became old enough to work, he would consult the spirit if it appeared that other workers were in line to get a promotion that he wanted. The spirit would tell him to offer a chicken or a sheep as a sacrifice. By thus appeasing the spirit, he was sure that "bad luck" would befall his colleagues. Edmond made fast progress and came to have a responsible position where he worked. Even his parents, recognizing his "special relationship," would come to Edmond if they needed to contact the spirit.

Oddly enough, Edmond saw no conflict between practicing spiritism and Catholicism. At the Catholic Church that he regularly attended, pagan rites, such as the playing of sacred tam-tams (drums), were carried on side by side with "Christian" ritual.

Eventually, Edmond's job brought him to the capital city, Abidjan. There he became interested in yet another spirit —one his brother-in-law consulted regularly. This spirit, however, was associated with the lagoons and the ocean. They called it Mami-Wata. Near one of the lagoons was a secluded spot that Edmond would frequently visit in order to consult this spirit for advice.

One day, however, the spirit appeared to be perturbed. "What is the trouble?" Edmond asked. The spirit complained that Edmond's brother-in-law was no longer coming to consult him. "Why?" asked Edmond. He was told that it was because of his brother-in-law's new religion. Edmond was intrigued, for he was a Catholic, and the spirit had never complained about that. There had to be something different about this new religion. Soon Edmond was to be visited by a member of this religion, and his days of consulting Mami-Wata would also come to an end.

Adama's
Search for Success

Adama's ambition was to succeed in life. His parents were animists, believing that each material object has a soul. So they gave him a fetish object—the "guinea-fowl" shirt—for good luck so that he would do well in school. When he failed his school exams, however, he concluded that other students must have had fetishes that were more effective than his.

He spoke to his parents about this, and they now gave him a goat's horn. By means of a very thin thread, he was to attach this to a nail in the ceiling of his room. In the morning he could consult the fetish object, telling it all that he wanted. Then the thin thread would break! Now, depending on the way the goat's horn fell, he could decide whether to go ahead with his plans for the day or not. This new fetish, too, proved ineffective.

After Adama finished school, he went to the town of Agboville. There, one of his friends directed him to a fetish priest, who said he could guarantee Adama success in finding a job. Obeying the instructions of the priest, Adama bought a small padlock. He was told to speak into the opening of the padlock and say all the things he wanted in life. "I want to find a job," he said into the padlock, closed it, and waited for success. But it did not come.

Nevertheless, Adama did not despair. He was sure that he was still protected by the magical charm of his precious "guinea-fowl" shirt.

Adama did eventually find work in the town of San Pedro. It was not the kind of work he wanted, but it was work. In the evening Adama would visit a friend's home. One evening he found that his friend had a visitor—a teacher of the Bible. A fervent Catholic, Adama disputed what this visitor had to say. Yet he was intrigued by the idea of studying the Bible to learn about the Creator. One evening when the topic of discussion was "Are There Wicked Spirits?" Adama could not resist participating in the discussion fully.

His days as a fetish worshiper were also coming to an end.

Athanase and His Talisman

Athanase was brought up a "Harrist" —a nominal Christian sect founded by William Wade Harris. He was a Liberian who claimed to have been appointed as a prophet by the angel Gabriel. About the year 1913, Harris left Liberia for the Ivory Coast and began preaching. One book says: "At his voice, the fetishes fell in powder, those ministering to idols renounced their false gods, whole villages accepted his religion. . . . He advanced, supporting himself on a cane surmounted by a wooden cross, followed by six women all dressed in white as he was and whom he called his 'disciples.'"

Athanase's father told him that he was to become a Harrist priest when he grew up. While the Harrists supposedly condemned fetishes, they claimed that the Bible had miraculous powers! Like their founder, Harrist priests would use the Bible to bless and to heal people. Athanase observed, however, that few actually read, much less followed, the Bible.

When he finished school, he decided to spend two weeks with a high official of the Harrist religion, hoping that this would result in his obtaining a job. To his great surprise, the religious leader gave him a talisman—a perfume bottle filled with kaolin powder, sand, and water—and told him that this would guarantee his success in finding work. "But," said the official, "if you throw it away, you will go mad and eventually die!"

Athanase was confused. He could see no difference between this perfume bottle and the fetishes used by members of other faiths. However, out of fear of his parents and the religious leader, he kept the talis-man. It did not bring the good luck he had been promised. A whole year was spent looking for work but without success. Nevertheless, Athanase, too, came in contact with someone who freed him from the fear of the talisman.

The Truth About Fetishes

All three men had come in contact with Jehovah's Witnesses. Through a Bible study with the Witnesses, they learned the origin of the spirits. The Bible showed that before the Noachian Flood, angels rebelled against God and materialized so as to enjoy sexual relations with women. The Flood forced the spirits to dematerialize, and they have been trapped in the spirit realm ever since. No wonder these demons place so much emphasis on material objects, such as fetishes!—Genesis 6: 1-5; 2 Peter 2:4.

In time each of these three men built up a love for Jehovah God and a hatred for spiritistic practices. The Bible quite explicitly condemns seeking contact with wicked spirits, saying at Deuteronomy 18: 10-12: "There should not be found in you anyone who makes his son or his daughter pass through the fire, anyone who employs divination, a practicer of magic or anyone who looks for omens or a sorcerer, or one who binds others with a spell or anyone who consults a spirit medium or a professional foreteller of events or anyone who inquires of the dead. For everybody doing these things is something detestable to Jehovah, and on account of these detestable things Jehovah your God is driving them away from before you." Not wanting Jehovah's disfavor, the three of them now followed the advice of the Christian disciple James: "Subject yourselves, therefore, to God; but oppose the Devil, and he will flee from you."—James 4:7.

Breaking free from religious captivity was not easy, however. Edmond, for example, had to burn amulets that apparently linked him to Mami-Wata. But he made fine progress thereafter, even dedicating his life to God and being baptized in symbol of this. Then, just one week after his baptism, the spirits began to bother him. Voices told him to quit this newfound faith. But Edmond prayed and called on the name of Jehovah. Eventually the wicked spirits ceased harassing him.—Proverbs 18:10.

Adama, too, had his problems. Desiring to help others break from Satanic influence, he became a full-time preacher. However, for a while he was plagued with feelings of discouragement. He felt that he was not making good progress and that in spite of much Christian activity, his spirituality was low. What could be the reason for such negative thoughts? Suddenly Adama realized that he still had that "guinea-fowl" shirt his parents had given him. He searched his house, finding that last link with the spirit world and destroy-ing it. "I felt greatly relieved in my mind," he said.

Athanase, too, had to throw out something—that talisman he had been given. After doing this, he became very sick. 'Could it be because of disobeying the order not to throw it out?' he wondered. But he, too, turned to Jehovah in prayer. Rather than succumbing to pressure from his relatives to resort to spiritism again, he sought medical help. In time his health, both physical and spiritual, improved. Athanase now spends his weekends helping neighbors learn Bible truths.—John 8:44.

The experiences of these three former captives of superstition confirm that the Word of God is able to work mightily on those who come to believe. (1 Thessalonians 2:13; Acts 19:18-20) More than 2,000 others in the Ivory Coast are working with these young men in helping people to gain freedom from religious captivity. Jehovah's Witnesses in your area, too, will gladly help you find such freedom.

Adjust the Bible to Polygamy?

IN *Bijeen* (Together), a Roman Catholic magazine from the Netherlands, columnist Sjef Donders discussed the conflict that exists in some African countries between the Biblical command on monogamy and the accepted custom of polygamy. That conflict is resolved, he said, by "simply declaring the church doctrine [on monogamy] invalid."

Demonstrating the ambiguous views of the church, Donders quoted American priest Eugene Hillman, a member of the Holy Ghost Fathers, a Roman Catholic order that has spearheaded Catholic missionary work in Africa. In a book dealing with polygamy, Hillman wrote: "If, due to one or other natural disaster or man-caused calamity, there ever would be all of a sudden almost no more men, but almost only women, then there certainly would be found reasons in the Bible to permit these men to have relations with several women."

Would there? Regardless of the priest's liberal views, polygamy is not to be condoned for any Christian regardless of nationality or circumstance. Monogamy was God's arrangement for mankind in Eden, and Jesus Christ indicated that there should be a return to this in the Christian congregation. (Matthew 19:4-6) Under inspiration the apostle Paul wrote: "The overseer should . . . be irreprehensible, a husband of one wife." (1 Timothy 3:2) And with regard to all Christians, he counseled: "Because of the prevalence of fornication, let each man have his own wife and each woman have her own husband." (1 Corinthians 7:2) This leaves no room for polygamy among true Christians.

Kingdom Proclaimers Report

Jehovah Blesses Godly Zeal

JESUS had godly zeal. On seeing his godly zeal, his disciples recalled the prophecy concerning him: "The zeal for your house will eat me up." (John 2:17) This zeal was manifest in his ministry: "And he journeyed through from city to city and from village to village, teaching," and he told his disciples to 'exert themselves vigorously.' (Luke 13:22-24) Jehovah blessed the godly zeal of Jesus' disciples then and he does so today, as the following experiences from Uruguay show.

□ Two women who were Jehovah's Witnesses lived about 45 miles (70 km) from the nearest congregation. Since they were so isolated, they decided to hold weekly meetings in their own home, to which they would invite interested persons. They were very zealous despite their isolation. One conducted six Bible studies, and the other seven. When the circuit overseer visited them, 36 adults attended his talk. One of the sisters raised five children in the truth, and today all of them are zealously working in Jehovah's organization. Surely, Jehovah blessed the godly zeal of these two sisters.

□ Another sister showed godly zeal by regularly walking with her children 7 miles (11 km) to attend congregation meetings, usually arriving an hour early. She never felt that since the book study was for just one hour, it would not be worth while walking that long distance when she could simply read the book at home. Today she counts her blessings. Her fine example of self-sacrifice, perseverance, and determination as a wife and mother has had a powerful effect on her children. All six of them are in the truth. One son who is a pioneer shows the same zeal by riding his bicycle 36 miles (58 km) to care for an isolated group. To do this he has to ford a river with his bicycle. Jehovah blesses his godly zeal too.

□ In 1982 one group of brothers worked a certain isolated territory and placed many books. The next year they returned to work the same territory. At one home they encountered a very unusual objection. After hearing their Bible presentation, the householder stated that he did not want to change his religion as he felt he already had the truth. He said: "You see, I am one of Jehovah's Witnesses." He was overjoyed when he learned that his callers, too, were Jehovah's Witnesses.

He explained that he was away from home when the brothers worked the territory, but his family had accepted literature. He read it, discerned that it taught the truth from the Bible, and began telling his neighbors what he had learned. The brothers made arrangements to help this new "sheep" progress to maturity and really become one of Jehovah's people.

Yes, Jehovah blesses godly zeal for true worship. We are happy to be a part of Jehovah's organization of brothers worldwide, and we want to manifest this godly zeal for the ministry. Being delivered from Satan's wicked system and cleansed by Bible truth should encourage us to be "zealous for fine works." —Titus 2:14.

Peaceable People Are Truly Needed!

THE theme was promising: "International Literature Congress—Writers for Peace." The location was picturesque: the old German city of Cologne, overlooking the Rhine River. The atmosphere of the convention was tranquil until it was shattered by a brawl between delegates. According to news reports of the 1982 convention, some attenders shouted, pushed, and shoved—even grappled for control of the stage. The ruckus was over whose government is the aggressor in world conflicts.

Whether the battlefield be some distant land, a convention floor, or your next-door neighbor's living room, why cannot more people get along in peace? The answer is simple: Genuine peace cannot exist if the God of peace, Jehovah, is excluded from people's lives.—1 Thessalonians 5:23.

At Galatians 5:22, 23, the Bible lists peace as one of the fruits of God's holy spirit. True and lasting peace can be in our lives only if God's spirit causes its growth in our hearts. How is this done? We must first come to know Jehovah God and his Son Jesus Christ, and then exercise faith in them. (John 17:3) Thus, there will be fulfilled toward us the fervent petition of the apostle Paul: "May the God who gives hope fill you with all joy and *peace* by your believing, that you may abound in hope with power of *holy spirit*." And note that Paul concludes his admonition in this same letter with this further petition: "May the God who gives peace be with all of you."—Romans 15:13, 33.

The peace that God's holy spirit produces is different from the peace that the world seeks. In what way?

A Different Peace

Internationally, a peacemaker is someone who is good with words and protocol; someone who by compromise can appease two opposing parties without necessarily changing their attitudes and motives. Thus a communist can come to be at peace with a capitalist without either one of them changing his philosophy. Being at peace with God, though, is different. God sets the terms for peace. He defines these and shows how they are applied. With Jehovah God it is not compromise but a *total* surrendering of our motives, attitudes, manner of life—our whole self.—Matthew 22:37.

Therefore, what is needed today is peace rooted in divine wisdom, not human wisdom. On reading James 3:13-18, we note the benefits that heavenly wisdom gives:

"Who is wise and understanding among you? Let him show out of his fine conduct his works with a mildness that belongs to wisdom. But if you have bitter jealousy and contentiousness in your hearts, do not be bragging and lying against the truth. This is not the wisdom that comes down from above, but is the earthly, animal, demonic. . . . The wisdom from above is first of all chaste, then peaceable, reasonable, ready to obey, full of mercy and good fruits, not making partial distinctions, not hypocritical. Moreover, the fruit of righteousness has its seed sown under peaceful conditions for those who are making peace."

The peace that comes from God's wisdom

does more than prevent conflict; it earnestly and actively pursues a good relationship with others.

In addition, being peaceable in a godly way helps prevent harmful inclinations, seeded in mankind's heart since the time of the rebellion in Eden, from growing into deadly, sinful acts. (Genesis 8:21; Matthew 15:19; Romans 5:12) Referring to the effectiveness of this protective shield, the apostle Paul wrote that "the peace of God that excels all thought will guard your hearts [motives] and your mental powers by means of Christ Jesus." —Philippians 4:7.

This indicates that "the peace of God" is conveyed by him through the Son. Jesus said: "I give you my peace. I do not give it to you the way that the world gives it." (John 14:27) True peace is not a result of social, economic, political, or environmental reform but, rather, a result of worshiping Jehovah in imitation of his Son Jesus Christ. It is appropriate, therefore, that the apostle Paul starts so many of his letters with expressions such as: "May you have undeserved kindness and peace from God our Father and the Lord Jesus Christ." —Romans 1:7; 1 Corinthians 1:3; 2 Corinthians 1:2.

Are You a Peaceable Person?

Peaceable Christians realize that apart from Jehovah they have no lasting peacemaking ability. The human flesh is weak. It needs to be bolstered by God's spirit. Paul reminded Christians: "You must love your neighbor as yourself." Then he added: "If, though, you keep on biting and devouring one another, look out that you do not get annihilated by one another. But I say, Keep walking by spirit and you will carry out no fleshly desire at all. For the flesh is against the spirit in its desire, and the spirit against the flesh; for these are opposed to each other, so that the very things that you would like to do you do not do."—Galatians 5:14-17.

The peace that God's holy spirit produces is different
from the peace that the world seeks

When opposed by someone, a person's 'fleshly desires' may deceive him into believing that he is right when, in fact, he is wrong. The ugly traits of egotism, envy, and uncontrolled competitiveness are glossed over. In the person's mind, these take on the appearance of aggressiveness and zealousness, which to him are the keys to becoming a winner, or a success. That is what happened to some first-century Christians living in the province of Galatia. They allowed their 'fleshly desires' to mar the beauty of peace not only in their own lives but also in the congregation. "Enmities, strife, jealousy, fits of anger, contentions" spotted up their congregation's spiritual appearance, and they had to remove those spots in order to restore peace.—Galatians 5:20, 22.   •

Today, unchristian traits can similarly rob our spiritual paradise of its peace. Business, work, school, social, and congregational activities provide circumstances that test whether we have a tight grip on the fruit of peace or not. To ensure that you are a peacemaker rather than a peace robber, ask yourself these questions:

□ Do I crave self-importance and recognition, or am I humble and modest?—Proverbs 11:2; Matthew 18:1-4.

□ Do I have a strong desire for material acquisitions, or am I content with sustenance and covering?—1 Timothy 6:4-10; Hebrews 13:5.

□ Do I show favoritism to prominent ones or to the materially wealthy in the congregation, or do I welcome all in the faith?—Romans 15:7; James 2:1-4.

Replace Human Wisdom With Divine Wisdom

The sinister spirit that impels habitual peace robbers stems from selfish desires. Notice how the disciple James pinpoints the origin of bad fruitage at James 4:1, where he writes: "From what source are there wars and from what source are there fights among you? Are they not from this source, namely, from your cravings for sensual pleasure that carry on a conflict in your members?" Disturbers of congregational harmony resist becoming peaceable because they allow selfish desires to 'carry on a conflict within them.' They permit a warring spirit to camp inside their bodies. Hence, their selfish desires, like an invading army, go on the warpath, campaigning for importance, greater influence, possessions, and the like, while snatching peace from their relationship with God and with fellow believers.

Likely every day we are faced with some situation, or with someone, that we find disagreeable. How do we handle the matter? Some may protest loudly and angrily, hoping that this will cause the problem to back off and change. Others, desiring to protect their position and status in life, may campaign actively against any improved methods. Such actions destroy peace. They slow down progress and accomplishment at home, at work, or in the congregation. On the other hand, "the wisdom from above is . . . peaceable." (James 3:17) And peace in action unites people with people, and people with God. (Ephesians 4:3) That is why divine wisdom further instructs:

In Our Next Issue

- Does Your Religion
  Really Please God?

- "Let No Man Deprive You
  of the Prize"

- Are You Resisting
  the Spirit of Discontent?

> **The peace that comes from God's wisdom does more than prevent conflict; it earnestly and actively pursues a good relationship with others**

☐ "If, then, you are bringing your gift to the altar and you there remember that your brother has something against you, leave your gift there in front of the altar, and go away; first make your peace with your brother, and then, when you have come back, offer up your gift."—Matthew 5:23, 24.

☐ "If possible, as far as it depends upon *you,* be peaceable with all men."—Romans 12:18.

☐ "So, then, let us pursue the things making for peace and the things that are upbuilding to one another."—Romans 14:19.

Peacemakers Are Evangelizers

The apostle Peter, recognizing that Jehovah God is the Sponsor of a worldwide message of peace, said, "He sent out the word to the sons of Israel to declare to them the good news of peace through Jesus Christ: this One is Lord of all others." (Acts 10:36) Jesus not only "came and declared the good news of peace" himself but also trained his followers to do so. (Ephesians 2:17) He explained that this would be through a house-to-house 'search for deserving ones,' and he instructed them, "Wherever you enter into a house say first, 'May this house have peace.'"—Matthew 10:11; Luke 10:5.

However, as in the first century, so too now, not all appreciate "the good news of peace." To them it awakens, not a peaceful reaction, but rather a fighting spirit. Jesus anticipated this type of response to the evangelizing work, for he said: "When you are entering into the house, greet the household; and if the house is deserving, let the peace you wish it come upon it; but if it is not deserving, let the peace from you return upon you." (Matthew 10: 12, 13) Some would eagerly accept this peace from God; others would not. But, in either case, the Christian would not lose his peace with God or with man.

People who spurn God's peace are really at war with him. Included in Jesus' prophecy that lists events marking the sign of his presence in Messianic Kingdom power is this warning illustration: "When the Son of man arrives in his glory, and all the angels with him, . . . he will separate people one from another, just as a shepherd separates the sheep from the goats." (Matthew 25:31-33) The issue causing separation centers on God's Kingdom by Christ. How individuals respond to the "good news of the kingdom" that is brought to them by the 'least of Christ's brothers' is what weighs heavily in their judgment. (Matthew 24:14; 25:34-46) In his dividing work, Christ uses only peaceable people to deliver the message of good news. In this way no opposer would have grounds for saying: 'They made me so angry I couldn't understand "the message of peace."'

Therefore, in a world peppered by day-to-day conflicts of both a personal and an international nature, peaceable people are truly needed. You will find such people in the true Christian congregation. Let the "God of peace" give you his holy spirit. Calmness, serenity, and tranquillity, as well as freedom from friction, strife, doubt, and fear, will then be your happy lot. (Isaiah 32:17, 18) In addition, by spreading "the good news of peace," you will enjoy the grand privilege of helping others to become peaceable.—Ephesians 2:17; Matthew 28: 19, 20.

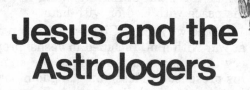

Jesus and the Astrologers

A NUMBER of men come from the East. They are astrologers —people who claim to interpret the position of stars. While they were at home in the East, they saw a new star, and they have followed it hundreds of miles to Jerusalem.

When the astrologers get to Jerusalem, they ask: 'Where is the child born to be king of the Jews? We saw his star and have come to bow down to him.'

When King Herod at Jerusalem hears about this, he is very upset. So he calls the chief priests and asks: 'Where is the Christ to be born?' Basing their reply on the Scriptures, they answer: 'In Bethlehem.' At that Herod has the astrologers brought to him and tells them: 'Go search for the child, and when you find him, come back and tell me so that I can go and bow down to him too.' But, at heart, Herod wants to find the child to kill him!

After they leave, an amazing thing happens. The star they had seen when they were in the East travels ahead of them. Clearly, this is no ordinary star, but it has been specially

provided to direct them. The astrologers keep following it until it stops right above the house where Joseph and Mary are staying.

When the astrologers enter the house, they find Mary with her young child, Jesus. At that they all bow down to him. And they take out of their bags gifts of gold, frankincense, and myrrh. Afterward, when they are about to return and tell Herod where the child is, they are warned by God in a dream not to do that. So they leave for their own country by another way.

Who do you think provided the star that moved in the sky to guide the astrologers? Remember, the star did not guide them directly to Jesus in Bethlehem. Rather, they were led to Jerusalem where they came in touch with King Herod, who wanted to kill Jesus. And he would have done so if God had not stepped in and warned the astrologers not to tell Herod. It was God's enemy, Satan the Devil, who wanted Jesus killed, and he used that star to try to accomplish his purpose. **Matthew 2:1-12; Micah 5:2.**

♦ What shows that the star the astrologers saw was no ordinary star?

♦ Where was Jesus when the astrologers found him?

♦ Why do we know that Satan provided the star to guide the astrologers?

Jehovah's Goodness in "the Final Part of the Days"

"Come, you people, and let us go up to the mountain of Jehovah."—ISAIAH 2:3.

"THE FINAL PART OF THE DAYS." Why does Bible prophecy repeatedly use this expression? Does it mean that the days of mankind are numbered and that finally our earth and all life upon it will perish in some global catastrophe? World leaders often talk apprehensively of such a possibility. For example, in a television interview on January 13, 1985, Moscow's foreign minister Andrei Gromyko warned the people of the Soviet Union that "a grave danger, a grave threat is looming over the whole of mankind." He added: "Everything possible should be done to remove that threat, so that the Armageddon with which people have been scared for centuries should not happen."

² On a number of occasions, President Ronald Reagan of the United States has also referred to Armageddon. The New York *Daily News* of October 30, 1983, quoted him as saying: "I turn back

---

1, 2. (a) What grave danger now threatens mankind? (b) What are world leaders saying about Armageddon?

to your ancient prophets in the Old Testament and the signs foretelling Armageddon, and I find myself wondering if—if we're the generation that is going to see that come about." More recently, on February 8, 1985, *The Wall Street Journal* reported: "President Reagan says he thinks and talks about Armageddon, . . . but he isn't planning for it."

³ Yes, world leaders are talking about Armageddon. But do they realize what that Bible word means? Apparently not, for Armageddon is no man-made holocaust. It is God's universal war by which he and his associate King, Jesus Christ, execute judgment upon wicked nations and wicked men. It comes as a climax to "the final part of the days." (Daniel 10:14; Revelation 16:14, 16) And what are we to understand by "the final part of the days"? Other translations render this expression as "the afterpart of the days," "the latter end of the days." (*Rotherham, Young*) The Hebrew words so translated are *'a·charith' hay·ya·mim'.* According to the *Theological Dictionary of the Old Testament,* they often mean "The End Time," indicating not merely the future but "how history will culminate, thus its outcome."

⁴ For some 70 years, mankind has been living through "the conclusion of the system of things," foretold by Jesus at Matthew 24:3–25:46. This period, beginning in 1914, is the "End Time" during which events progressively move forward to their culmination. That will be in the "great tribulation" when all of Satan's wicked organization will be destroyed. (Matthew 24:21, 22) The grand outcome will be the vindication of Jehovah's holy name.—Ezekiel 38:16, 23.

3. (a) What really is Armageddon? (b) What is meant by "the final part of the days"?
4. How will the "End Time" move to its culmination, and with what outcome?

Jehovah's Goodness

⁵ Jehovah is a God of encouragement. What marvelously stimulating expressions he has scattered throughout his Word, the Holy Bible! One such expression is to be found at Hosea 3:5, which reads: "Afterwards the sons of Israel will come back and certainly look for Jehovah their God, and for David their king; and they will certainly come quivering to Jehovah and to his goodness *in the final part of the days.*"

⁶ A remnant of Israel returned from captivity in Babylon in 537 B.C.E. to resume worshiping Jehovah in Jerusalem. Similarly in modern times, in 1919 the anointed remnant of spiritual Israel 'came back' from captivity to Satan's organization, earnestly 'looking for Jehovah their God.' How different from the apostate sects of Christendom! None of these want to recognize Jehovah as "their God." Rather than "look for Jehovah," they avoid any use of his name.

⁷ Early in "the final part of the days," the January 1, 1926, issue of *The Watch Tower* published the challenging article "Who Will Honor Jehovah?" The regathered remnant of spiritual Israel loyally answered that call, and in 1931 they rejoiced to accept the name Jehovah's Witnesses. (Isaiah 43:10, 12) To this day they continue to hold the name of Jehovah prominently before earth's inhabitants. Why, in 1984 they published, by the millions of copies in many languages, the attractive color brochure entitled *The Divine Name That Will Endure Forever.*

5. What encouraging words are found at Hosea 3:5?
6. How has spiritual Israel differed from Christendom's sects?
7. How have Jehovah's people honored his name?

Hosea encourages us to imitate Jehovah's goodness

⁸ However, Hosea also foretold that these spiritual sons would "come back and certainly look for . . . David their king." Fleshly Israel has had no king since the overthrow of the Davidic dynasty in 607 B.C.E. That began 2,520 years of godless rule—"the appointed times of the nations," or Gentile Times. (Luke 21:24; Daniel 4:16) But in 1914, as "the final part of the days" began, God installed the One whom David typified—Jesus Christ—as King in Zion, the "heavenly Jerusalem." —Hebrews 12:22; Psalm 2:6.

⁹ Jehovah's people on earth did not immediately understand all of this. However, their search for 'David our king' was climaxed when *The Watch Tower* of March 1, 1925, published the article "Birth of the Nation." This set forth conclusive proof, based on Revelation chapter 12, that Jehovah's Messianic Kingdom had been born in the heavens in 1914 and that Christ is now 'ruling in the midst of his enemies.'—Psalm 110:1, 2, *King James Version;* 2:1-6.

¹⁰ The anointed remnant, and indeed all who make a dedication to Jehovah, are deeply conscious of their sins of former times. Humbly, they have "come quivering to Jehovah," asking forgiveness for past sins. And now as "the final part of the days" moves on toward its climax, lovers of Jehovah watch all the more carefully that they do not transgress against God and his righteous laws. We must continue to "come quivering to Jehovah," pummeling our bodies, in order to find salvation into God's New Order. (1 Corinthians 9:27) We must always remember that "the fear of Jehovah is the beginning of wisdom."—Psalm 111:10.

¹¹ How, though, may we "come quivering . . . to his goodness"? Jehovah is altogether good. He is the epitome of moral excellence. He is complete in providing for our every need. Thus, we can confidently say as did David: "Jehovah is my Shepherd. I shall lack nothing. . . . Surely goodness and loving-kindness themselves will pursue me all the days of my life." (Psalm 23:1-6) Now, and through to the end of "the final part of the days," we must 'come quivering to Jehovah's goodness,' confident that our sins will be covered by the precious sacrifice of his Son, Jesus. (1 John 2:1, 2) Thankfully, we declare: "O Jehovah, . . . how abundant your goodness is, which you have treasured up for those fearing you!"—Psalm 31:17, 19.

¹² As Satan's world sinks ever deeper into the morass of badness, may we imitate Jehovah's goodness by making known to our neighbors the Kingdom good news and by displaying godly qualities in our own lives. May we really *cultivate* the fruits of the spirit, including goodness, in all our relationships—in our families, in our congregations, and in our contacts with people of the world. (Galatians 5:

8, 9. (a) What is meant by 'looking for David their king'? (b) When and where was the King installed? (c) How did Jehovah's people come to understand this matter?
10. (a) Who "come quivering to Jehovah," and how? (b) Why is "the fear of Jehovah" so important today?

---

11. (a) In what respects is Jehovah good? (b) Why must we 'come quivering to Jehovah's goodness'?
12. (a) How may we imitate Jehovah's goodness? (b) Why is it essential that we do so?

22, 23; Psalm 119:65-68) Doing this is essential if we are to survive "the final part of the days."

Patriarchal Advice

¹³ Some 3,700 years ago, the patriarch Jacob (also named Israel) gave a deathbed prophecy. Addressing his 12 sons, the heads of Israel's tribes, he said: "Gather yourselves together that I may tell you what will happen to you *in the final part of the days.*" His words apply today to the remaining ones of spiritual Israel and by extension to their companions, the "other sheep." None of these may with impunity disregard Jehovah's moral standards, as did Reuben, nor can they allow room for violent dispositions like those of Simeon and Levi. Rather, they must cultivate qualities such as courage, reliance on Jehovah, and fruitfulness, as displayed by other sons of Israel.—Genesis 49:1, 3-7, 9, 18, 22; John 10:16; compare 2 Peter 1: 8-11.*

¹⁴ However, particular counsel is provided for the "other sheep" who have the prospect of surviving the "End Time." We find this stated, as if for emphasis, in two related Bible prophecies, at Isaiah 2:2-5 and Micah 4:1-5.

Streaming to God's House

¹⁵ Isaiah 2:2 reads: "And it must occur *in the final part of the days* that the mountain of the house of Jehovah will become

_____
* See the *Watchtower* issues of June 15 and July 1, 1962, for a detailed discussion of Jacob's prophecy.

13. (a) Who today may benefit by considering Jacob's deathbed prophecy? (b) What counsel does that prophecy contain?
14. What two related prophecies on the "End Time" provide counsel particularly for the "other sheep"?
15. (a) How has Isaiah 2:2 been fulfilled? (b) What contrast do meek persons now see, and how do they respond?

Jacob describes desirable and undesirable qualities

firmly established above the top of the mountains, and it will certainly be lifted up above the hills; and to it all the nations must stream." For more than 50 years, since 1935, these "desirable things of all the nations" have been gathering to Jehovah's house of worship, 'filling that house with glory.' This 'streaming' appears to intensify as "the final part of the days" moves ever closer to its culmination. The symbolic mountain of Jehovah's pure worship is becoming more prominent, so that meek persons can see how it contrasts with the sectarian "hills" and "mountains" of Satan's permissive world. They "get out" of false religion and flee in growing numbers to Jehovah's mountain of worship.—Haggai 2:7; Revelation 18:2, 4, 5; Psalm 37:10, 11.

¹⁶ These meek ones answer the call of Isaiah 2:3: " 'Come, you people, and let us go up to the mountain of Jehovah, to the house of the God of Jacob; and he will instruct us about his ways, and we will walk in his paths.' For out of Zion law will go forth, and the word of Jehovah out of Jerusalem." Already, Jehovah is fulfilling his promise to "speed it up in its own time." (Isaiah 60:22) An increasing "great crowd . . . out of all nations" are flocking to Jehovah's worship. Of these, 138,540 were baptized in

_____
16. (a) What call do meek ones now answer? (b) How is Jehovah fulfilling his promise to "speed it up"?

Isaiah invites us to "walk in the light of Jehovah"

1982; 161,896 in 1983; and 179,421 in 1984. They want to be saved through "the final part of the days."—Revelation 7:9, 14.

¹⁷ These new Witnesses appreciate Jehovah's goodness in bringing them to the light of truth, and they are earnestly desirous of showing goodness to others. They welcome the instruction that Jehovah provides through his Word and his organization. The Law of Moses contained many 'must nots,' and Israel properly had to observe these. (See Exodus 20:3-17.) But the two great commandments for Christians, as stated by Jesus, are positive commands to 'love Jehovah our God with our whole heart, soul, mind, and strength, and our neighbor as ourself.' (Mark 12:29-31) Unitedly, Jehovah's Witnesses now obey the "law" that God sends forth from the "heavenly Jerusalem," applying its righteous principles.

¹⁸ This does not mean, however, that Jehovah's people do not need to observe any rules. The apostle Paul reminds us: "Let all things take place decently and according to order." (1 Corinthians 14:40, *NW Ref. Bi.*, footnote) A few rules may be needed at our Kingdom Halls, for example, to economize on the use of electricity or to prevent young children from using God's house of worship as a playground after meetings. Family heads may need to make some orderly arrangements, such as providing for regular consideration of the daily Bible text in the home. In Bethel families there are rules, such as requiring that family members adorn the good news by modest dress and grooming. (1 Timothy 2:9) The "scrolls" to be opened during Jesus' Thousand Year Reign will no doubt contain rules that will benefit mankind. It is good now to become accustomed to obeying healthful rules that are made for orderliness and out of consideration for others.—Revelation 20:12; 1 Corinthians 10:24; Philippians 2:3, 4.

In This World of Violence

¹⁹ We are moving rapidly toward the time when every man's hand will "come up against the hand of his companion." (Zechariah 14:13) As the world becomes ever more lawless and violent, how do Jehovah's people react? They act in harmony with Micah 4:3, which says: "They will have to beat their swords into plowshares and their spears into pruning

───────

19, 20. (a) How have Jehovah's people reacted to the principle at Micah 4:3? (b) How is this benefiting them during "the final part of the days"?

───────

17. (a) How may new Witnesses show appreciation for Jehovah's goodness? (b) What positive commands do all of us need to obey?
18. (a) What kinds of rules do we need to observe? (b) Of what advantage is it to obey healthful rules?

───────

Questions in Summary

□ What do you understand by "the final part of the days"?

□ How may we 'come quivering to Jehovah and his goodness'?

□ What guidance does Jacob's deathbed prophecy provide?

□ What positive steps may we take in harmony with Isaiah 2:2-5 and Micah 4:1-5?

Micah encourages us to 'walk in Jehovah's name forever'

shears." Jehovah's Witnesses renounce every kind of violence. "Neither will they learn war anymore." Doubtless, this will continue to work to their advantage throughout "the final part of the days." It has done so already.

20 For example, when the July 15, 1983, *Watchtower* magazine pointed out that guns were not for Christians, Jehovah's Witnesses in New Caledonia got rid of their firearms. Shortly thereafter, a local political group searched through a town, burning down every house where they found firearms. But no Witness houses were destroyed. Known neutrality is often the best defense, as has proved true in Northern Ireland, Lebanon, Zimbabwe, and other lands.

21 Happy we are if we answer the call of Isaiah 2:5: "Come and let us walk in the light of Jehovah"! Happy, too, are all of us who join in the firm resolve expressed by the prophet Micah who, after describing the paradisaic security and peace that exist among God's own people, goes on to say: "All the peoples, for their part, will walk each one in the name of its god; but we, for our part, shall walk in the name of Jehovah our God to time indefinite, even forever." Surely Jehovah's goodness will be expressed toward all of us who continue to unite peacefully in true worship, for survival through "the final part of the days."

---

21. (a) What call should we answer, and what resolve should we make if we want to be truly happy? (b) How may we be assured of sharing in Jehovah's goodness?

> "There exists a God in the heavens who is a Revealer of secrets, and he has made known . . . what is to occur in the final part of the days."—DANIEL 2:28.

Triumphing in "the Final Part of the Days"

JEREMIAH, EZEKIEL, DANIEL —what thrilling prophecies those names bring to mind! Almost 2,600 years ago, those three courageous servants of

---

1. (a) How are the prophecies of Jeremiah, Ezekiel, and Daniel of vital interest to us today? (b) Why were those inspired writings preserved?

---

the Sovereign Lord Jehovah lived through the final days of an apostate Jerusalem, though serving in different locations and under far different circumstances. But each from his own vantage point prophesied concerning events that would culminate in a later "final part of the days."

Those inspired writings have been preserved for the encouragement of all who love God and righteousness, and who desire to survive the "great tribulation" that impends in our time.—Matthew 24:3-22; Romans 15:4.

² Jeremiah prophesied at Jerusalem. As calamity approached, both rulers and people had fallen into lawlessness and corruption. Hence, Jehovah strengthened his prophet like "a fortified copper wall" to stand firm amid their badness.—Jeremiah 15:11, 20; 23:13, 14.

Prophets of Peace

³ Concerning Jerusalem's delinquent religious leaders, Jehovah declared through Jeremiah: "Do not listen to the words of the prophets who are prophesying to you people. They are making you become vain. The vision of their own heart is what they speak—not from the mouth of Jehovah. They are saying again and again to those who are disrespectful of me, 'Jehovah has spoken: "Peace is what you people will come to have."'" Those false prophets were saying, "There is peace! There is peace!" when there was no peace.—Jeremiah 23:16, 17; 6:14.

---

2. Why did Jeremiah need strength from Jehovah?
3. What false words were the prophets speaking?

Jeremiah points to the true hope for peace

THE LOGO approved by the UN for its International Year of Peace (1986) shows an olive wreath, a dove, and human hands. These are explained as follows: "The dove is the symbol of peace in association with the olive wreath emblem of the United Nations. Human hands supporting the dove ready for flight underline the role of human beings in the maintenance of peace."

In this nuclear age, there is indeed a crying need to establish and maintain peace. But can human hands accomplish that? Jeremiah reminds us: "I well know, O Jehovah, that to earthling man his way does not belong. It does not belong to man who is walking even to direct his step." And the prophet adds this petition: "O Jehovah, . . . pour out your rage upon the nations who have ignored you." —Jeremiah 10:23-25.

The dove and the olive leaf are borrowed from the Bible record about Noah's day. (Genesis 8:11) How was peace restored at that time? It was by an act of God, the global deluge that wiped out a corrupt generation of mankind. Jesus said that "the days of Noah," with their violence and badness, were prophetic of the time of his "presence," which is now.—Matthew 24:37-39; Genesis 6:5-12.

Once again, "the God who gives peace" must wipe out a satanic system of things, after which the "Prince of Peace," Jesus Christ, will usher in eternal peace.—Romans 16:20; Isaiah 9:6, 7; 33:7.

⁴ Likewise, in apostate Christendom today, there are prophets of peace. Many of these cling to what Pope Paul VI described as "the last hope of concord and peace," the United Nations. Shortly, that body is to proclaim 1986 as the International Year of Peace. In announcing its intention to participate in the Year, the Holy See declared that it "nourishes the hope that this Year will produce the desired results and will mark a significant stage in bringing about peaceful relations among peoples and nations." But is it realistic to expect the nations to establish true peace?

---

4. To what hope do many in Christendom cling?

⁵ God himself describes what will happen: "Look! The windstorm of Jehovah, rage itself, will certainly go forth, even a whirling tempest. Upon the head of the wicked ones it will whirl itself. The anger of Jehovah will not turn back until he will have carried out and until he will have made the ideas of his heart come true. *In the final part of the days* you people will give your consideration to it with understanding [or, "you will fully understand," *The New English Bible*]." (Jeremiah 23: 19, 20; see also 30:23, 24.) Yes, the leaders of false religion will come to understand what "the final part of the days" means for them. But any consideration they give to it will be too late!—Compare Revelation 18:10, 16; 19:11-16; Matthew 24:30.

⁶ Happily, though, many individuals who were once captives to false religion are 'giving consideration to it.' They answer the call: "Get out of her [false religion], my people," since they do not want to share in her sins or receive part of God's judgment against her. If you are one of these, may you continue to heed what God's Word says about "the final part of the days" and the glorious era of peace to follow.—Revelation 18:2, 4, 5; 21:3, 4.

Attack by Gog

⁷ How do God's own people fare during "the final part of the days"? Let the prophet Ezekiel tell us. As a young man, he doubtless knew Jeremiah, but then Ezekiel was carried away to Babylonia. There, by the river Chebar, he was commissioned in 613 B.C.E. to act as Jehovah's prophet and watchman on behalf of the Jews in exile, a service that he faithfully carried out for at least 22 years. However, his prophecies look

Ezekiel warns us to prepare now for the attack by Gog

far beyond his own time. In chapters 37 and 38, he tells about 'Gog of Magog.'

⁸ Who is this 'Gog of Magog'? Well, who is Jehovah's arch enemy with whom he must settle the major issue of "the final part of the days," that of universal sovereignty? He is Satan the Devil, whom the Shepherd-King, Jesus Christ, hurled down from heaven following His own enthronement in 1914. The debased and angry Gog is now confined to a limited spirit realm, "the land of Magog," close to this earth. This means "woe for the earth" because Gog knows that time is short for carrying out his nefarious policy of 'rule or ruin.' —Ezekiel 37:24-28; 38:1, 2; Revelation 11: 18; 12:9-17.

⁹ Ezekiel quotes the Sovereign Lord Jehovah as saying: "Here I am against you, O Gog, you head chieftain [world ruler] . . . And I shall certainly turn you around and put hooks in your jaws and bring you forth with all your military force, . . . many peoples with you." (Ezekiel 38:3-6; John 12:31) Yes, Gog has many peoples with him, for "the whole world is lying in the power of the wicked one." (1 John 5:19) Yet, Jehovah can put figurative hooks in Gog's jaws to maneuver him. But why, and how?

---

5. What does Jehovah foretell, and how will it be fulfilled in "the final part of the days"?
6. What happy outcome will there be for many?
7. Under what circumstances did Ezekiel prophesy?

8, 9. (a) What major issue must be settled, and when? (b) Who is Gog, who follow him, and what policy does he pursue? (c) What will Jehovah do to Gog?

[10] Under Gog's prompting, the superpowers today argue that world peace depends on their stockpiling ever more horrendous nuclear armaments. And other nations lend their support. However, God's people "gathered together out of the nations" have renounced weapons of violence. Jehovah's Witnesses are the only "nation" on earth that can truthfully state, "In God we trust." (Isaiah 2:4; 31:1; Proverbs 3:5) These peaceable witnesses of Jehovah are "dwelling in security, all of them dwelling without wall, and they do not have even bar and doors." They are "dwelling in the center of the earth," for in all nations, they hold the center stage as the one people that Gog has not overreached. (Ezekiel 38:11, 12) Hence, the infuriated Gog of Magog brings his entire demonic organization to the war zone. Like a roaring lion, the debased Satan gets ready for an all-out assault. For survival, we must all 'take our stand against him, solid in the faith.'—1 Peter 5:8, 9.

[11] Jehovah instructs Ezekiel: "Therefore prophesy, O son of man, and you must say to Gog, 'This is what the Sovereign Lord Jehovah has said: "Will it not be in that day when my people [spiritual] Israel are dwelling in security that you will know it?"'" Gog and his mob envy the security and prosperity that they see among Jehovah's Witnesses today. They are enraged that these should make themselves "no part of [Satan's] world." Thus Jehovah taunts Gog, arousing him to attack the defenseless Witnesses. Jehovah tells Gog: "You will be bound to come up against my people Israel, like clouds to cover the land. *In the final part of the days* it will occur, and I shall certainly bring you against my land, for the purpose that the nations may know me when I sanctify myself in you before their eyes, O Gog."—Ezekiel 38: 14, 16; John 17:14, 16.

[12] The enraged Gog moves to invade the prosperous "land" of Jehovah's people. However, is Gog the only one to be enraged? What of the Sovereign Lord Jehovah's rage against Gog and his dupes? At Ezekiel 38:18-23 Jehovah describes how he 'sanctifies himself in the eyes of the nations' by bringing Gog to ruin and rescuing his loyal servants. Closing out the report of his triumph over Gog and his mob, the Sovereign Lord himself declares: "They will have to know that I am Jehovah." His glorious name is vindicated!

'Secrets Revealed'

[13] While Ezekiel was prophesying among the exiled Jews near Babylon, youthful Daniel, who was of princely Jewish descent, was being educated in the royal court of Nebuchadnezzar. There, as an integrity keeper, he set a fine example for all young servants of Jehovah today. —Daniel 1:8, 9.

[14] In the second year after Jerusalem's fall, Nebuchadnezzar was agitated by a dream. On awakening, he could not even remember the dream. But God-fearing Daniel made known to the king both the dream and its interpretation. In doing so, he gave God all the credit, saying to the king: "There exists a God in the heavens who is a Revealer of secrets, and he has made known to King Nebuchadnezzar what is to occur *in the final part of the days.*" (Daniel 2:28). What do we learn

10. (a) In contrast to the nations, where do Jehovah's Witnesses place their trust? (b) Why do Gog and his mob become enraged? (c) We must do what in order to survive?
11. How does Jehovah 'bring Gog against His land,' and for what purpose?

12. According to Ezekiel 38:18-23, what is the outcome of Gog's attack?
13. How did Daniel set a fine example for youthful Witnesses?
14. In what matter did young Daniel give all credit to God?

Daniel discloses the outcome of "the final part of the days"

from the dream and its application to "the final part of the days"?

¹⁵ Here we see a colossus, an immense image, made up for the most part of different metals in succession. Daniel explains that these represent a series of kingdoms and tells Nebuchadnezzar, "You yourself are the head of gold," referring apparently to the Babylonian dynasty. There follow other world powers, the silver breasts and arms standing for Medo-Persia, the copper belly and thighs for Greece, and the iron legs for Rome and, later, the world power of Britain and America. (Daniel 2:31-40) Down through "the appointed times of the nations," from 607 B.C.E. to 1914 C.E., these powers have held sway in the kingdom of 'the god of this world.'—Luke 21:24; 4:5, 6; 2 Corinthians 4:4.

¹⁶ However, it is "in the final part of the days" that "the offspring of mankind," the common man, comes to the fore. In many lands kings, kaisers, and czars are replaced by revolutionary and democratic rulers. Human misrule of the earth becomes a hodgepodge of harsh dictatorships and more pliable democratic forms of government. Like iron and clay, these do not mix. Even in the United Nations they do not cleave together but engage, rather, in angry debates and threats. Truly, 'the

kingdom proves to be divided.'—Daniel 2:41-43.

¹⁷ Thus, in "the final part of the days," the issue of world domination comes to its culmination. And what is the solution? Look! Already set in motion since 1914 is God's Messianic Kingdom. It is the "stone" cut out of the "mountain" of Jehovah's universal sovereignty. No human politician shares in that! Here it comes, right on course, with pinpoint accuracy. At God's due time, it smashes the feet of the image and grinds the entire colossus to powder. Like chaff before the wind, man-rule is carried away, with no trace being left. But the "stone"—the Kingdom of the grand God and his Christ—becomes a large mountain that fills the whole earth. That kingdom 'will never be brought to ruin and will never be passed on to any other people.' It will stand forever. How we thank Jehovah for his advance 'revealing' of such secrets!—Daniel 2:29, 44, 45.

A Modern-Day "Pushing"

¹⁸ However, Daniel had something more to say about human government and "the final part of the days." Some 70 years after making known Nebuchadnezzar's dream, the aged Daniel was still in Babylon but serving under Cyrus, king of Persia. While he was on the bank of the river Hiddekel, an angel appeared to him, saying: "I have come to cause you to discern what will befall your people *in the final part of the days,* because it is a vision yet for the days to come." (Daniel 10:14) The angel went on to describe in great detail rulers and events that would appear in the history of Persian, Greek, Egyptian, Roman, Germanic, Anglo-American, and

---

15, 16. What is the interpretation of Nebuchadnezzar's dream?

17. How is the prophecy fulfilled at "the final part of the days"?
18. (a) What later vision was given to Daniel? (b) What is remarkable about this vision?

socialistic forms of rulership. How remarkable that all this history, covering more than 2,500 years, could be written in advance! It gives us great confidence in the inspired prophetic Word of Jehovah God!*

¹⁹ This prophecy tells that, in the course of time, two superpowers would appear, "the king of the south" and "the king of the north." At last, the angel says, the northern king will "magnify himself above every god; and against the God of gods he will speak marvelous things"—not favorable things, for it is 'to the god of fortresses that he gives glory.' Against this boastful "king," there is pitted "the king of the south," who is also powerful in military might. As foretold, these two kings "engage . . . in a pushing." The modern-day cold war between the superpowers is well illustrated by this. At times they 'push' rather rudely as they argue for some parity of nuclear armaments, while escalating their war preparations to the limit.—Daniel 11:36-45.

²⁰ Though the prophecy predicts that "the king of the north" will storm like a flood into many lands, that will not determine the outcome. The determining factor is stated at Daniel 12:1: "And during that time Michael will stand up, the great prince who is standing in behalf of the sons of your people." This Michael is Jesus Christ, who 'stood up' in his Kingdom in 1914, promptly to eject Satan from the heavens. And it is this "King of kings" who goes into action at Armageddon to consign all "the kings of the earth," including those of the "north" and the

"south," to destruction.—Revelation 12:7-10; 19:11-19.

²¹ There, at the culmination of "the final part of the days," the outcome will become apparent, with the triumph of God's Kingdom. The angel describes it in these further words: "And there will certainly occur a time of distress such as has not been made to occur since there came to be a nation until that time."—Daniel 12:1; compare Jeremiah 25:31-33; Mark 13:19.

²² Should we fear that time of tribulation and distress? Not if we are on Jehovah's side, for the angel goes on to say: "During that time your people will escape, every one who is found written down in the book." (Daniel 12:1) Let all of us, therefore, apply ourselves in diligent Bible study and exert ourselves in serving Jehovah. Thus, at "the final part of the days," may we find our names written in God's "book of remembrance" that is "written up before him for those in fear of Jehovah and for those thinking upon his name." (Malachi 3:16) So doing, we shall be privileged to share in his triumph "in the final part of the days."

21. What, then, is the outcome at "the final part of the days"?
22. As God's people, how should we react to these prophecies and with what prospect?

---

* For details, see the book "Your Will Be Done on Earth," published in 1958 by the Watchtower Bible and Tract Society of New York, Inc., pages 220-323.

19. What modern events does the prophecy foretell?
20. What determines the outcome, and how is "Michael" involved in this?

With regard to "the final part of the days"—

☐ What outcome did Jeremiah prophesy as to world peace?

☐ Gog's attack results in settling what issue, and how?

☐ Nebuchadnezzar's dream points to what grand climax?

☐ How will the power struggle between the two "kings" end?

Bishops
—Lords or Slaves?

THOMAS WOLSEY was born in Ipswich, England, in 1475. He became a priest in 1498 and was favored by King Henry VIII. His rise was swift. He was appointed bishop of Lincoln in 1514, archbishop of York a few months later, cardinal in 1515, and papal legate just three years later. In addition, the king made him lord chancellor. Thus he virtually ruled England from 1515 until 1529. Cardinal Wolsey was typical of many clerics who have exercised power as both secular and spiritual "lords."

In the first century C.E., a "bishop" of another sort served. Called Timothy, he was the son of a Greek man, though his mother Eunice and grandmother Lois were Jewesses. They lovingly raised him in the way of Christianity. About the year 50 C.E., while still a young man, Timothy seized the opportunity to join the apostle Paul as a missionary. After years of training, he became a Christian overseer, or e·pi′sko·pos (from which the word "bishop" is derived), and was much loved for his selfless devotion. Wrote Paul: "Like a child with a father he *slaved* with me in furtherance of the good news."—Philippians 2:22.

Thomas the lord, Timothy the slave —which one set the right example for true Christian "bishops," or overseers?

The Pattern of a Christian Overseer

The Founder and only Head of true Christianity, Jesus Christ, established a basic pattern for overseers, when he said: "You know that *among the pagans the rulers lord it over them,* and their great men make their authority felt. This is not to happen among you. . . . Anyone who wants to be first among you must be your *slave,* just as the Son of Man came not to be served but to serve, and to give his life as a ransom for many."—Matthew 20:25-28, Catholic *Jerusalem Bible;* italics ours.

Peter, one of the first Christian overseers, confirmed the above pattern by commanding Christian elders: "Shepherd the flock of God in your care, not under compulsion, but willingly; neither for love of dishonest gain, but eagerly; *neither as lording it* over those who are God's inheritance, but becoming examples to the flock." (1 Peter 5:2, 3) Peter practiced what he preached. When visiting Cornelius, the first Gentile to become a Christian, the latter "fell down at his feet and did obeisance to him. But Peter lifted him up, saying: 'Rise; I myself am also a man.'" —Acts 10:25, 26.

Interestingly, Peter wrote his words at 1 Peter 5:1 to the "older men." The Greek word Peter used for "older men" was *pre·sby·te′rous,* from which the word "priest" is derived. In Christendom "bishops" are now considered superior to "priests." But when the apostle Paul "sent to Ephesus and called for the older men [*pre·sby·te′rous*] of the congregation," he said to them, among other things: "Pay attention to yourselves and to all the flock, among which the holy spirit has appointed you *overseers* [*e·pi·sko′pous*]." (Acts 20:17, 28) Hence, elders (*pre·sby·te′rous*) and overseers (*e·pi·sko′pous*) had the same rank in Bible times. The term "elder" highlights the experience and spiritual maturity needed by those accepting this responsibility, whereas the term "overseer" describes the kind of work such ones do in supervising and caring for members of the congregation.

But did one man reign as "overseer," or "elder," over a congregation in Bible times? Not according to what the Bible says at Titus 1:5, 7. There Titus was told to "make appointments of older men [*pre·sby·te′rous*] in city after city." *The Jerusalem Bible* renders this verse, "and appoint elders in every town" with a footnote saying: "In the earliest days each Christian community was *governed by a body of elders.*"—Italics ours.

Timothy was also commissioned to appoint overseers in many congregations. To him Paul wrote, according to the *King James Version:* "If a man desire the office of a bishop [*e·pi·sko′pos*], he desireth a good work." (1 Timothy 3:1) *The Jerusalem Bible* renders this: "To want to be a presiding elder is to want to do a noble work." It adds in a footnote: "The word '*episcopos,*'" used here by Paul, "has *not yet acquired the same meaning as 'bishop'.*" (Italics ours.) Hence, Catholic scholars admit that the lordly bishops of Christendom are not the same as the humble overseers of the early Christians. As *The New Bible Dictionary* states: "There is no trace in the New Testament of government by a single bishop." Elmer T. Merrill, M.A., LL.D., similarly states in his book *Essays in Early Christian History:* "For the first hundred years . . . the bishop was at most only the unassuming chairman of a college [organized body] of fellow presbyters [older men.]"

Christendom's Bishops —Scripturally Qualified?

When writing to Titus, the apostle Paul said that an overseer must be "free from accusation." (Titus 1:6) Was Cardinal Wolsey "free from accusation"? The *Encyclopædia Britannica* says that he was "unchaste —he had an illegitimate son and daughter." He is not alone in this. Through the centu-

ries, countless priests and bishops have been similarly guilty. As the book *Age of Faith* says: "By the ninth century, clerical chastity and even celibacy had become a mockery." One of the 11th-century popes, Gregory VII, admitted: "I find but few bishops whose appointments and whose lives are in accordance with the laws of the Church, or who govern God's people through love and not through worldly ambition."

Paul further wrote that a Christian elder should not be "a lover of money." (1 Timothy 3:3) Concerning Wolsey, however, the *Encyclopædia Britannica* says: "He was worldly, greedy for wealth" and "used his vast secular and ecclesiastical power to amass wealth that was second in value only to that of the King." He had two palaces, one of which, York Place, was so sumptuous that Henry VIII, after inspecting it, became "incensed by the wealth which he found" and took it over.

Similarly today, church clerics have used the payment of church dues, collections, tithing, and revenue from lands and property to enrich themselves. (Revelation 18:7) For example, a bishop in South Africa, head of one of the thousands of African sects, not long ago bought a new Buick automobile costing R37,000.* This was despite his already having four luxury automobiles at his disposal. Asked what was wrong with one of the present cars, a church official explained: "It's a nice car, but the bishop needs the extra bit of space in the big Buick."

How fleeting such material gain can be! Thomas Wolsey failed to arrange the marriage annulment that Henry VIII wanted and thus fell from favor in 1529. According to history, he then "retired in disgrace to his diocese of York, *which he had never visited*"—in 15 years! (Italics ours.) Wolsey, however, had not merely lost in the game of politics. His real failure was ne-

---

* 1 Rand = 87 cents.

glecting to follow "the fine shepherd [Jesus, who] surrenders his soul in behalf of the sheep."—John 10:11.

In contrast, Timothy did not meddle in politics. He was therefore "no part of the world." (John 15:19) Rather than lording it over others, he became such a devoted slave of fellow Christians that Paul could write: "I have no one else of a disposition like his who will genuinely care for . . . you."—Philippians 2:20.

How grateful we can be that today Jehovah has likewise raised up thousands of faithful overseers who "genuinely care" for the flock of God. Almost all overseers in congregations of Jehovah's Witnesses are men of modest means. Most support their families by secular employment and carry out their spiritual duties in their time after work. Most of that time is taken up with preparing for and attending five meetings a week; taking the lead in preaching from house to house; conducting Bible studies with interested people; visiting the sick, elderly, and spiritually weak; and caring for their own families. These are very busy men, dedicated "slaves," who receive no payment for these services. To the contrary, out of their personal funds they share in contributing to the upkeep of the local Kingdom Hall. They wear no peculiar garb, have no special titles, and are distinguished only by their Bible knowledge, their Christian maturity, and their zeal in Jehovah's service. Such men merit deep respect and wholehearted cooperation as they shepherd the flock and prove by their humble, devoted service that they are slaves—not lords!

Questions From Readers

■ What is symbolized by "the feet and the toes" of the "immense image" described at Daniel 2:31-45?

This prophecy was inspired by the One "who is a Revealer of secrets," the Sovereign Lord Jehovah God himself, and reaches its culmination in "the final part of the days," when the issue of world domination is to be settled once and for all time. (Daniel 2:28) Up until our day, from the start of "the times of the Gentiles" in 607 B.C.E., there has been a succession of world powers, commencing with imperial Babylon and proceeding with Medo-Persia, Greece, Rome, and the Anglo-American empire. These are represented by the metallic parts of the image.—Luke 21:24, King James Version.

However, with the ending of the Gentile Times in 1914, a conglomeration of different kinds of man-rule has appeared here on the earth. (Matthew 24:3-12) The common man ("the offspring of mankind" made from the dust of the ground) wields greater influence in affairs of government. Socialistic and democratic rulerships have come to the fore, along with other ironlike oppressive forms of government. They are like the "iron mixed with moist clay" that make up the feet and toes of the image.

Various views have been expressed about the ten "toes." But since "ten" is often used in the Bible to signify completeness as to things on earth, the ten "toes" appear logically to represent the entire global system of rulership at the culmination of the days. It is against the feet and toes of the image that 'God's Kingdom comes,' grinding to powder the final manifestations of man-rule. How happy we can be that the peaceful, prosperous rule of Christ's Kingdom will then fill the entire earth!*—Matthew 6:9, 10; compare Isaiah 11:1, 9.

The further dream of Nebuchadnezzar described in Daniel chapter 4 points also to events following the end of the Gentile Times. At last people must come to "know that the Most High is Ruler in the kingdom of mankind, and that to the one whom he wants to he gives it," that is, to the King, Jesus Christ.—Daniel 4:25; 7:13, 14.

---

* See "Your Will Be Done on Earth," published in 1958 by the Watchtower Bible and Tract Society of New York, Inc., pages 108-27, for a more detailed discussion of the "immense image."

United in Worship
of the Only True God

"This Wonderful Jewel"

That is what a reader from Quebec, Canada, called the publication *United in Worship of the Only True God.* She writes: "I have never felt I learned so much as with this book, which contains counsel that is really motivating. This book has really given me a thirst for spiritual knowledge."

July 15, 1985

The Watchtower

Announcing Jehovah's Kingdom

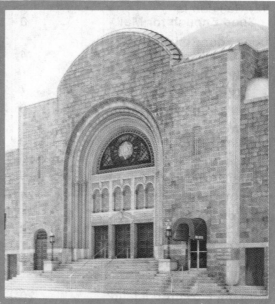

Does Your Religion Really Please God?

July 15, 1985
Vol. 106, No. 14

The Watchtower®
Announcing Jehovah's Kingdom

THE PURPOSE OF "THE WATCHTOWER" is to exalt Jehovah God as the Sovereign of the universe. It keeps watch on world events as they fulfill Bible prophecy. It comforts all peoples with the good news that God's Kingdom will soon destroy those who oppress their fellowmen and that it will turn the earth into a paradise. It encourages faith in the now-reigning King, Jesus Christ, whose shed blood opens the way for mankind to gain eternal life. "The Watchtower," published by Jehovah's Witnesses continuously since 1879, is nonpolitical. It adheres to the Bible as its authority.

"WATCHTOWER" STUDIES FOR THE WEEKS

August 18: "Let No Man Deprive You of the Prize." Page 10. Songs to Be Used: 222, 109.

August 25: 'Run in Such a Way That You May Attain the Prize.' Page 15. Songs to Be Used: 25, 27.

Average Printing Each Issue: 11,150,000

Now Published in 103 Languages

SEMIMONTHLY EDITIONS AVAILABLE BY MAIL
Afrikaans, Arabic, Cebuano, Chichewa, Chinese, Cibemba, Danish, Dutch, Efik, English*, Finnish, French, German, Greek, Hiligaynon, Igbo, Iloko, Italian, Japanese, Korean, Lingala, Malagasy, Maltese, Norwegian, Portuguese, Russian, Sepedi, Sesotho, Shona, Spanish, Swahili, Swedish, Tagalog, Thai, Tswana, Xhosa, Yoruba, Zulu

MONTHLY EDITIONS AVAILABLE BY MAIL
Armenian, Bengali, Bicol, Bulgarian, Croatian, Czech, Ewe, Fijian, Ga, Greenlandic, Gujarati, Gun, Hausa, Hebrew, Hindi, Hiri Motu, Hungarian, Icelandic, Kannada, Kikuyu, Kiluba, Malayalam, Marathi, New Guinea Pidgin, Pangasinan, Papiamento, Polish, Rarotongan, Romanian, Samar-Leyte, Samoan, Sango, Serbian, Silozi, Sinhalese, Slovenian, Solomon Islands-Pidgin, Tahitian, Tamil, Telugu, Tshiluba, Tsonga, Turkish, Twi, Ukrainian, Urdu, Venda, Vietnamese
*Study articles also available in large-print edition at same cost.

The Bible translation used is the "New World Translation of the Holy Scriptures," unless otherwise indicated.

Twenty cents (U.S.) a copy

Watch Tower Society offices	Yearly subscription Semimonthly
America, U.S., Watchtower, Wallkill, N.Y. 12589	$4.00
Australia, Box 280, Ingleburn, N.S.W. 2565	A$6.00
Canada, Box 4100, Halton Hills (Georgetown), Ontario L7G 4Y4	$5.20
England, The Ridgeway, London NW7 1RN	£5.00
Ireland, 29A Jamestown Road, Finglas, Dublin 11	£5.00
New Zealand, 6-A Western Springs Rd., Auckland 3	$10.00
Nigeria, P.O. Box 194, Yaba, Lagos State	₦6.00
Philippines, P.O. Box 2044, Manila 2800	₱50.00
South Africa, Private Bag 2, Elandsfontein, 1406	R5,60

Remittances should be sent to the office in your country or to Watchtower, Wallkill, N.Y. 12589, U.S.A.

Changes of address should reach us 30 days before your moving date. Give us your old and new address (if possible, your old address label).

The Watchtower (ISSN 0043-1087) is published semimonthly for $4.00 (U.S.) per year by Watch Tower Bible and Tract Society of Pennsylvania, 25 Columbia Heights, Brooklyn, N.Y. 11201. Second-class postage paid at Brooklyn, N.Y., and at additional mailing offices.

Postmaster: Send address changes to Watchtower, **Wallkill, N.Y. 12589.**

Published by
Watch Tower Bible and Tract Society of Pennsylvania
25 Columbia Heights, Brooklyn, N.Y. 11201, U.S.A.
Frederick W. Franz, President

'My Religion Is Good Enough for Me!'

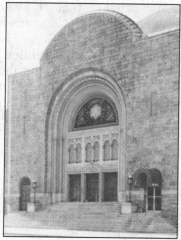

HAVE you ever reacted with such words when one of Jehovah's Witnesses called at your home? Perhaps you added: 'It was good enough for my parents and my grandparents. So why bother with any other religion?'

Of course, we benefit greatly from the wisdom and experience of our parents. But is that necessarily a wise basis for following a religion? Certainly we do not imitate our parents and grandparents in everything we do. Why not? Because there has been progress in knowledge and understanding.

To illustrate: Over 40 years ago when people got sick, they may have died simply because available treatment was inadequate. Since 1943, antibiotics have been available and have saved many lives. Do we refuse to consider using antibiotics just because our grandparents did not know of them? No, we keep an open mind

and weigh the merits of new developments. That same attitude is wise with regard to religion.

The apostle Paul's case further illustrates that the religion of our forebears is not necessarily true worship that pleases God. Prior to Paul's conversion to Christianity, his reaction to the Christian "Way" was violent in the extreme, for he "kept on persecuting the congregation of God and devastating it." But why? Because he was 'zealous for the traditions of his fathers.' His sincere adherence to his former religion prevented him from recognizing the truth about Jesus Christ—and that could not have pleased God.—Acts 9: 1, 2; Galatians 1:13, 14.

Your Religion —By Choice or by Chance?

In most cases, a person's religion is really a matter of coincidence. In what sense? In that you may have been born a Catholic, a Protestant, a Hindu, a Taoist, or a Buddhist because that was the religion of your parents. But suppose you had been born in another country or family. Perhaps you would now be fervently professing a different religion. Therefore, is it logical to assume that the religion of your birth is automatically the true one?

Whether you were born into your religion or not, you may still feel that it is good enough for you. But is right religion just a matter of personal opinion or taste? Is that a reliable guideline?

Perhaps we can illustrate this with food. Ask a child to tell you which he prefers—a slice of cake or a dish of spinach. Most likely he will choose the cake. But will that choice be the most nutritious? Similarly, the fact that a religion appeals to your personal taste does not necessarily mean that it is the best for you spiritually. —Compare Romans 10:2, 3.

Religion is not just a matter of subjective opinion. It involves the worship of God, so it must please him. Therefore, the vital question is not, Is my religion good enough for me? Rather, it is, Does my religion really please God?

Does Your Religion Really Please God?

'GOD is not a God of disorder but of peace.' (1 Corinthians 14:33) Surely, then, the many religions with their conflicting doctrines could not all have God's approval. Hence, there can be only one religion that meets his requirements for true worship. How can we find that one religion that really pleases God?

Doubtless, many feel that such a search would be like looking for a needle in a haystack. Sifting through it would be quite a task! Yet there is a simpler method —using a powerful magnet. It would attract the steel needle and separate it from the straw. Likewise, the Bible can be used as a magnet to separate truth from error. But how does the Bible do that? By defining acceptable worship from God's viewpoint.

The apostle Paul wrote: "All Scripture is inspired of God and beneficial for teaching, for reproving, for setting things straight, for disciplining in righteousness, that the man of God may be fully competent, completely equipped for every good work." (2 Timothy 3:16, 17) Accurate knowledge of the Bible is essential if we are to avoid the pitfall of reducing religious devotion only to what is convenient or pleasing to us.

Additionally, Jesus Christ, the Son of God, stated: "God is a Spirit, and those worshiping him must worship with spirit and truth." (John 4:24) How can we "worship with spirit and truth"? By following the truthful guidelines that God has provided, through inspiration, in his Word, the Holy Bible.

How would you find the true religion?

How would you find a needle in a haystack?

True Worshipers Exhibit Love

What does God's Word lead us to expect of true worship? We have an immediate clue in three words: "God is love." (1 John 4:16) Therefore, worship that pleases God must be based on genuine love.

In practical terms, what does that mean? Religion that pleases God cannot inculcate or allow for hatred of fellow humans. The Bible's simple command is, "You must love your neighbor as yourself." (Matthew 22:39) That means separating from this world's hatreds, prejudices, and conflicts. It means learning war no more and pursuing peace.—Isaiah 2:2-4.

To illustrate the point: Could we imagine a "French" apostle Paul going out to kill a "German" apostle Peter just because their respective nations had declared war? Yet, during the second world war most religions were so deeply involved in the war efforts of their nations that they even supplied chaplains for the armies! At the same time, "Christian" clergymen on both sides prayed to the same God for victory. But does God stand divided? Can he be dragged into what Professor Albert Einstein described as the "infantile sickness" of nationalism, "the measles of humanity"? Of course not! That is why worshipers who really please God must remain neutral and practice genuine love. (John 13:34, 35; 17:16) They 'do not wage war according to what they are in the flesh.' —Compare 2 Corinthians 10:3, 4.

True Worship Exalts God's Name

The apostle Paul pointed to another mark of religion that is pleasing to God when he said that although many are called gods and lords, among true worshipers there is only "one God the Father." (1 Corinthians 8:5, 6) Surely, then, those pleasing God would know and use his name.

The Bible, in its original languages, specifically mentions the name of God over 7,000 times. For instance, Psalm 83:18

BELIEFS OF JEHOVAH'S WITNESSES

BELIEF	BIBLICAL BASIS
Jehovah is God's name	Exodus 6:3; Psalm 83:18
The Bible is God's Word	John 17:17; 2 Timothy 3:16, 17
Jesus Christ is God's Son	Matthew 3:16, 17; John 14:28
Man did not evolve but was created	Genesis 1:27; 2:7
Human death is due to Adam's sin	Romans 5:12
Soul ceases to exist at death	Ecclesiastes 9:5, 10; Ezekiel 18:4
Hell is mankind's common grave	Job 14:13; Revelation 20:13, *King James Version*
Resurrection is the hope of the dead	John 5:28, 29; 11:25; Acts 24:15
Christ's earthly life was the ransom for obedient humans	Matthew 20:28; 1 Peter 2:24; 1 John 2:1, 2
Prayers must be directed only to Jehovah through Christ	Matthew 6:9; John 14:6, 13, 14
Bible's laws on morals must be obeyed	1 Corinthians 6:9, 10
Images must not be used in worship	Exodus 20:4-6; 1 Corinthians 10:14
Spiritism must be avoided	Deuteronomy 18:10-12; Galatians 5:19-21
Blood must not be taken into one's body	Genesis 9:3, 4; Acts 15:28, 29
A Christian must keep separate from the world	John 15:19; 17:16; James 1:27; 4:4
Christians must witness, declaring the "good news"	Isaiah 43:10-12; Matthew 24:14; 28:19, 20
Baptism by complete immersion symbolizes dedication to God	Mark 1:9, 10; John 3:23; Acts 19:4, 5
Religious titles are improper	Job 32:21, 22; Matthew 23:8-12
We are now in "the time of the end"	Daniel 12:4; Matthew 24:3-14; 2 Timothy 3:1-5
Christ's presence is in spirit	Matthew 24:3; John 14:19; 1 Peter 3:18
Satan is the invisible ruler of the world	John 12:31; 1 John 5:19
God will destroy present wicked system of things	Daniel 2:44; Revelation 16:14, 16; 18:1-8
Kingdom under Christ will rule the earth in righteousness	Isaiah 9:6, 7; Daniel 7:13, 14; Matthew 6:10
"Little flock" to rule with Christ in heaven	Luke 12:32; Revelation 14:1-4; 20:4
Other people God approves will receive eternal life on a paradise earth	Luke 23:43; John 3:16

reads: "That people may know that you, whose name is Jehovah, you alone are the Most High over all the earth." Then why do adherents of so many religions worship a nameless God? And why do they omit his name from their Bible translations? That certainly is not the way to please God, for Jesus prayed: "Let your *name* be sanctified."—Matthew 6:9.

The Religion That Pleases God

Is there any worldwide religious group that fulfills the two basic requirements of true worship that we have just discussed? Is there any religion that really practices the love that Christ taught? And do those same worshipers truly glorify God and honor his name in this 20th century?

It is a well-attested fact that Jehovah's Witnesses maintain neutrality toward the wars of the nations. For this reason, they have suffered in concentration camps and prisons. Rather than compromising their Bible-based principles, they have preferred the pathway of martyrdom trodden by the early Christians. This stand has been motivated by their love for God and fellow humans. Such love is one mark of true worship that pleases God.

Many have noted the fine record of Jehovah's Witnesses in this respect. For example, a few years ago a South American newspaper publisher noted that the Witnesses "refuse for conscientious reasons to serve in the armed forces." He continued: 'Even as children, Jehovah's Witnesses are aware that on reaching the age of eighteen they will have to serve an extended period in prison because of their neutrality. They accept the punishment as part of their religious faith. They are gentle and peaceful.'

What about another requirement of religion that pleases God? Indeed, who honor the divine name, Jehovah? It is self-evident that only Jehovah's Witnesses are doing this worldwide by both their preaching and their conduct.—Romans 10:13-15.

Why not get better acquainted with Jehovah's Witnesses? The accompanying chart lists some of their beliefs, along with Scriptural reasons for them. Submit the Witnesses' form of worship to this simple test: Does it meet God's standards of truth as laid down in the Bible? Is it producing the peaceable fruit of love that must form a part of true worship? Does it honor God's name? If you find that it does all of this, you will have discovered the religion that *really* pleases God.

The Watchtower
—Aid in Crime Prevention

NAOMI, a seven-year-old girl living in Manchester, England, excitedly wrote to the London office of the Watch Tower Society: "When I went into our Post Office, I saw a big poster of one of our magazines, the one of the lady having her handbag stolen by a man with a knife. The Greater Manchester police have copied it to warn people about muggings!" What is the story behind this unusual crime-prevention poster?

While witnessing on a Manchester street, one of Jehovah's Witnesses placed with a man a copy of the November 1, 1984, issue of *The Watchtower* with the theme "Our Critical Times—Why So Violent?" The gentleman put the magazine in his pocket, but he was mugged on his way home. As he sat recovering from the shock of the event, he remembered the magazine and began to read it. When visited by an officer of the Police Crime Prevention Department, he showed him the magazine, commenting that he never thought he would be a mugging victim himself.

The police officer was greatly impressed by the cover photograph, saying that it contained in graphic detail all that was necessary to alert the public to the dangers of mugging. Permission to reproduce the picture as a crime-prevention poster was readily granted, resulting in the distribution of 3,000 of them in the Greater Manchester area.

Escape From a Tyrant

WHY does Joseph wake Mary up in the middle of the night? 'Jehovah's angel just appeared to me,' Joseph tells her. 'And he said to take you and the child and to flee into Egypt, for Herod is about to hunt for Jesus to kill him.'

The three of them make their escape. And it is just in time because Herod has learned that the astrologers have tricked him and have left the country. Remember, they were supposed to report back to him when they found Jesus. Herod is furious. So in an attempt to kill Jesus, he gives orders to put to death all the boys in Bethlehem and its districts who are two years of age and younger. He bases this age calculation on the information that he obtained earlier from the astrologers.

The slaughter of all the baby boys is something horrible to see! Herod's

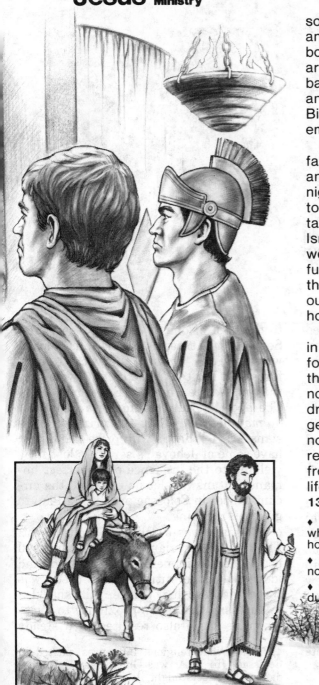

soldiers break into one home after another. And when they find a baby boy, they grab him from his mother's arms. We have no idea how many babies they kill, but the great weeping and wailing of the mothers fulfills a Bible prophecy of God's prophet Jeremiah.

In the meantime, Joseph and his family have safely made it to Egypt, and they are now living there. But one night Jehovah's angel again appears to Joseph in a dream. 'Get up and take Jesus and his mother back to Israel,' the angel says, 'for those who were trying to kill him are dead.' So, in fulfillment of another Bible prophecy that says God's Son would be called out of Egypt, the family return to their homeland.

Apparently Joseph intends to settle in Judea, where they were living before they fled to Egypt. But he learns that Herod's wicked son Archelaus is now the king of Judea, and in another dream Jehovah warns him of the danger. So Joseph and his family travel north and settle in the town of Nazareth. Here in this community, away from the center of Jewish religious life, Jesus grows up. **Matthew 2: 13-23; Jeremiah 31:15; Hosea 11:1.**

♦ When the astrologers did not return, what terrible thing did King Herod do, but how was Jesus protected?
♦ On returning from Egypt, why did Joseph not again stay in Bethlehem?
♦ What Bible prophecies were fulfilled during this period of time?

"Let No Man Deprive You of the Prize"

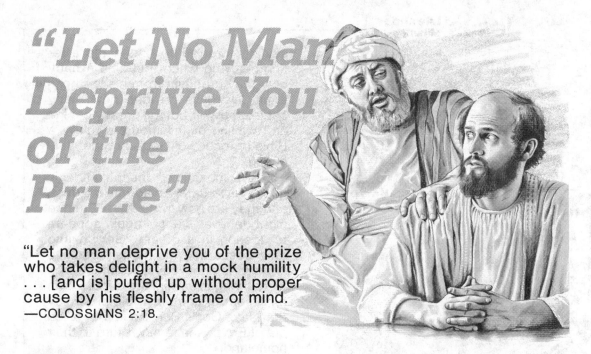

"Let no man deprive you of the prize who takes delight in a mock humility . . . [and is] puffed up without proper cause by his fleshly frame of mind. —COLOSSIANS 2:18.

THE first human sinner, Eve, was led to her death by a crafty, superhuman spirit creature. The second sinner, Adam, was seduced by his wife—a mere human. —1 Timothy 2:14; Genesis 3:17.

2 Eve was the first of a procession of individuals whose urgings, if heeded, would have worked against the eternal interests of fellow humans. Listen as their words echo throughout the Bible! Potiphar's wife to Joseph: "Lie down with me." (Genesis 39:7) Job's wife: "Curse God and die!" (Job 2:9) The Israelites to Aaron: "Get up, make for us a god who will go ahead of us." (Exodus 32:1) Peter to Jesus Christ: "Be kind to yourself, Lord; you will not have this destiny at all."—Matthew 16:22.

3 All too often such urgings have worked

to the ruin of one of Jehovah's servants. So while it is true that Christians "have a wrestling . . . against the wicked spirit forces," it is often *fellow humans* who pose the immediate threat. (Ephesians 6:12) The apostle Paul therefore warned: "Let *no man* deprive you of the prize." (Colossians 2:18) What is this prize? And why have some of Jehovah's servants lost it by yielding to the influence of imperfect humans? In answer, let us examine the circumstances in Colossae prompting Paul to give this warning.

4 Colossae was a religious melting pot. The native Phrygians were an emotional people deeply immersed in spiritism and idolatrous superstition. Then there was the city's Jewish populace, still shackled to Judaism. Colossae's proximity to a major trade route also resulted in a steady

1, 2. How have many worked against the eternal interests of fellow humans, and can you cite further examples of this from the Bible?
3. What warning did Paul give at Colossians 2: 18, and what questions arise as a result?

4, 5. (a) What religious influences existed in Colossae? (b) What was Gnosticism, and what dangerous effects might its influence have produced?

stream of visitors. Likely, these foreigners loved to spend their leisure time telling or listening to something new. (Compare Acts 17:21.) This led to the spread of new philosophies, among them slowly emerging Gnosticism. Says scholar R. E. O. White: "Gnosticism was a climate of thought as widespread as evolutionary theory is today. It probably came into prominence in the first century or earlier and reached its zenith in the second. It combined philosophic speculation, superstition, semi-magical rites, and sometimes a fanatical and even obscene cultus."

5 In such a climate, religion in Colossae seems to have become a kind of ongoing experiment—a hybrid mixture of Judaism, Greek philosophy, and pagan mysticism. Would Christianity, too, be cast into the same melting pot?

'Deprived of the Prize'—How?

6 Paul's powerful letter to the Colossians would have counteracted the influence of any who might have wished to fuse Judaism and pagan philosophy with Christianity. Repeatedly, he called attention to *Christ.* Paul wrote: "Carefully concealed in *him* [Christ, not any Judaizer or pagan philosopher] are all the treasures of wisdom and of knowledge." The Colossians were urged to "go on walking in union with *him* [Christ], rooted and being built up in him and being stabilized in the faith." Otherwise, they might be led astray. So Paul warned: "Look out: perhaps there may be someone who will carry you off as his prey through the philosophy and *empty deception* according to the tradition of men, according to the *elementary things* of the world and not according to Christ."—Colossians 2:3, 6-8.

---

6. (a) How would Paul's words have counteracted the influence of pagan philosophies and Judaism? (b) Why was there a need for Christians to "look out"?

7 Perhaps some new followers of Jesus Christ missed the awe of mysticism or the stimulation of philosophy. Certain Jewish Christians may have had a lingering fondness for the obsolete traditions of Judaism. The teachings of pagan philosophers and Judaizers would therefore have had a certain appeal to such individuals. Yet, however convincing or eloquent these false teachers may have seemed, they offered nothing more than "empty deception." Instead of expounding the pure word of God, they were merely parroting "the elementary things of the world" —useless philosophies, precepts, and beliefs. Embracing those erroneous ideas would spell disaster for a Christian. Hence, Paul said: "Let no man deprive you of the prize."—Colossians 2:18.

8 "The prize" was immortal life in the heavens. It was likened to the reward given the victorious runner after an exhausting footrace. (1 Corinthians 9: 24-27; Philippians 3:14; 2 Timothy 4:7, 8; Revelation 2:7) Ultimately, only Jehovah God through Jesus Christ could disqualify someone from the race for life. (John 5: 22, 23) Nevertheless, if a false teacher brought a Christian under his tutelage, this could have the *effect* of depriving him of the prize. The deceived one could veer so far from the truth that he could *fail to finish the race!*

Personality of the False Teachers

9 Was there any way, then, of identifying a person who was intent on 'depriving a Christian of the prize'? Yes, for Paul

---

7. (a) Why might the teachings of pagan philosophers and Judaizers have appealed to some Christians? (b) Why were their teachings really "empty deception"?
8. (a) What was "the prize," and what scriptures support your answer? (b) How could anointed Christians be deprived of "the prize"?
9. What four things characterized the false teachers among the Colossians?

The 'worship of angels' threatened the Christian congregation in Colossae. Similar idolatry persists among professed Christians today

gave the personality profile of the false teachers at Colossae. Such a man (1) "takes delight in a mock humility and a form of worship of the angels"; (2) is "'taking his stand on' the things he has seen"; (3) is "puffed up without proper cause by his fleshly frame of mind"; whereas (4) "he is not holding fast to the head," Jesus Christ.—Colossians 2:18, 19.

¹⁰ What a clever ruse! Ignoring Jesus' condemnation of ostentatious fasting, the false teacher presented an appealing facade of humility. (Matthew 6:16) Indeed, the false teacher 'took delight' in making a show of fasting and other forms of religious self-denial. (Colossians 2:20-23) His sad-faced appearance was carefully de-

signed to emit a false piety. Indeed, the false teacher was 'practicing his righteousness in front of men in order to be observed by them.' (Matthew 6:1) But all of this was a sham, "a mock humility." As The Expositor's Bible puts it: "A man who knows that he is humble, and is self-complacent about it, glancing out of the corners of his downcast eyes at any mirror where he can see himself, is not humble at all."—Italics ours.

¹¹ Nevertheless, this sham humility added seeming credibility to an otherwise absurd practice—the "worship of the angels." Paul does not explain exactly how this worship was performed. The evidence is, however, that it was a form of false worship that persisted in the area of Colossae for centuries. A fourth-century council at nearby Laodicea found it necessary to declare: "Christians ought not to forsake the Church of God, and . . . call upon the names of angels. . . . If any one, therefore, be found to exercise himself in this private idolatry, let him be accursed." However, fifth-century theologian and scholar Theodoret indicates that "this vice" of angel worship still existed there in his day. To this day, the Catholic Church "encourages the faithful to love, respect, and invoke the angels," promoting "Masses and Divine Offices in honor of guardian angels."—New Catholic Encyclopedia, volume I, page 515.

¹² Using a basic line of reasoning similar to that of Catholic theologians, the false teacher may have said: 'What a marvelous privilege the angels have! Was not the Mosaic Law transmitted through them? Are they not close to God in heaven? Surely we should give these mighty ones their

10. How did the false teachers 'take delight in a mock humility'?

11. (a) What was the worship of angels? (b) What evidence is there that the worship of angels persisted in Colossae?
12. How might the false teachers have reckoned that the worship of angels was acceptable?

due honor! Would this not show true *humility* on our part? After all, God is so high, and we humans are so low! The angels can, therefore, serve as our *mediators* in approaching God.'

¹³ Worship of angels in whatever form, though, is wrong. (1 Timothy 2:5; Revelation 19:10; 22:8, 9) But the false teacher would try to waive this objection aside by '"taking his stand on" the things he had seen.' According to *The Vocabulary of the Greek Testament,* this expression was used "in the mystery religions to denote the climax of initiation, when the mystês [initiate] 'sets foot on' the entrance to the new life which he is now to share with the god." By using pagan phraseology, Paul mocked the way the false teacher prided himself on having special insight—perhaps even claiming to have had supernatural visions.

¹⁴ Though claiming to be spiritual, however, the false teacher was really puffed up without proper cause by his *fleshly frame of mind.* The sinful flesh tainted his outlook and motives. "Puffed up" with pride and arrogance, his mind was "on the works that were wicked." (Colossians 1:21) Worst of all, he was not holding fast to the head, Christ, for he was giving more weight to the speculations of worldlings than to the teachings of Jesus.

Still a Danger?

¹⁵ The prize of everlasting life—be it in heaven or on a paradise earth—is still held out to Jehovah's servants. True, the Gnostics and the Judaizers have long

---

13. (a) Is the worship of angels acceptable? (b) How did the false teacher '"take his stand on" the things he had seen'?
14. How were the false teachers 'puffed up by a fleshly frame of mind'?
15. (a) What attitudes are noted among some Christians today? (b) Where do such attitudes originate, and how do they compare with the counsel of the Bible?

since been gone. Yet there are individuals who might now hinder a Christian from gaining this prize. They may not do so deliberately. However, because they have allowed themselves to be unduly affected by this system's "philosophy and empty deception," they may remark:

'I try to be honest, but it's hard when you're running a business. This is a dog-eat-dog world, and sometimes you just have to compromise.' (Compare this view with Proverbs 11:1; Hebrews 13:18.)

'You mean you're still just a housewife? Times have changed! Why not get a job and *do* something with your life!' (Compare Proverbs 31:10-31.)

'I know my job cuts into meetings and the field ministry quite a bit. But it takes a lot of money to support our life-style. And what's wrong with having a few nice things?' (Contrast this reasoning with Luke 21:34, 35; 1 Timothy 6:6-8.)

'I get so tired of hearing the elders always talking about field service! I work all week and deserve to *relax* on the weekends.' (Compare Luke 13:24; Mark 12:30.)

'Pioneering is not for everybody. Besides, in today's economy you need a university education if you're going to make it.' (Contrast this with Matthew 6:33; 1 Corinthians 1:19, 20; 1 Timothy 6:9-11.)

Materialistic and fleshly reasoning is part and parcel of "the elementary things of the world"—the fundamental precepts and beliefs of *worldlings!* Yielding to it can cause irreparable spiritual damage.

¹⁶ Self-appointed judges and teachers pose yet another danger. Like those in Colossae, they may make issues of purely personal matters. They are often characterized by "mock humility." (Colossians 2: 16-18) Their holier-than-thou attitude betrays a wrong motive—a desire to elevate themselves above others. They are often

---

16. How might some today become hypocritical judges?

"righteous overmuch," quick to go beyond what the 'faithful slave' has said or published. Thus they may ignite controversies over such matters as recreation, health care, styles of dress and grooming, or the use of alcoholic beverages. (Ecclesiastes 7:16; Matthew 24:45-47) Attention is thereby diverted from spiritual matters and focused on fleshly desires.—Compare 1 Timothy 6:3-5.

¹⁷ Today, some even go so far as to 'take their stand on' personal views of Scripture, or they claim to have special insight. One woman, who had been baptized only a year, claimed to be of the anointed and thought that this gave her opinions added weight. Thus she expressed a strong desire to "teach and encourage others" in some official capacity. (But see 1 Timothy 2:12.) Since Jehovah hates "self-exaltation and pride," Christians should have a modest view of their own opinions. (Proverbs 8:13) They avoid the snare of being "puffed up without proper cause by [their] fleshly frame of mind." (Colossians 2:18) Any who advance their personal ideas and put the counsel of Christ's appointed 'faithful slave' in a poor light are not holding fast to the head. Surely, then, Jehovah's loyal witnesses should guard against ungodly influence that could rob them of the prize of life.

¹⁸ Satan still uses man to hinder fellow humans from gaining life. What are some other ways in which the Devil employs this stratagem? And how can a witness of Jehovah tenaciously hold on to the prize?

17, 18. (a) How have some 'taken their stand on' personal views, and why is this dangerous? (b) What will our next lesson discuss?

Do You Recall?

☐ What religious influences threatened Christians in ancient Colossae?

☐ What were the identifying traits of those who would deprive Christians of "the prize"?

☐ How do some Christians today show that they have been influenced by "the elementary things of the world"?

☐ How might false teachers steer Christians into a wrong course?

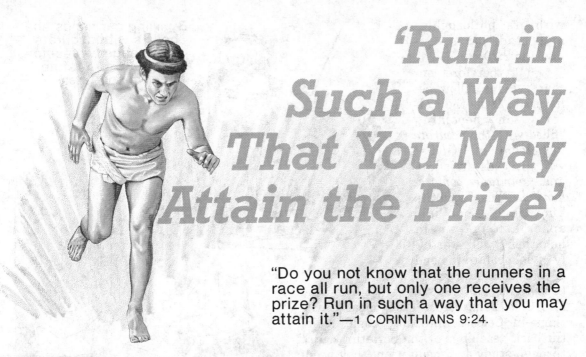

'Run in Such a Way That You May Attain the Prize'

"Do you not know that the runners in a race all run, but only one receives the prize? Run in such a way that you may attain it."—1 CORINTHIANS 9:24.

IT WAS to have been the grand climax to 12 years of grueling preparation. But just over half way into the race, the young athlete fell in a heap, abruptly ending her dreams of an Olympic gold medal. The news media called her fall a "tragedy."

2 Far more tragic, however, would be the failure of a witness of Jehovah to finish the race for life, especially with the promised New Order so near! (2 Peter 3:13) Appropriately, then, the apostle Paul said: "Do you not know that the runners in a race all run, but only one receives the prize? Run in such a way that you may attain it." (1 Corinthians 9:24) Some in ancient Corinth were in danger of losing out because they selfishly did as they pleased, even at the cost of 'wounding the consciences' of others. (1 Corinthians 8:

1-4, 10-12) Winning the race, though, entailed sacrifice, for Paul said: "Every man taking part in a contest exercises self-control . . . I pummel my body and lead it as a slave, that, after I have preached to others, I myself should not become disapproved somehow."—1 Corinthians 9: 25-27.

3 Later, when writing to the Colossians, Paul warned of yet another potential danger—men who would 'deprive them of the prize' of life. (Colossians 2:18) So how could Christians 'run in such a way as to attain it'? Did the apostle suggest that they study philosophy and mysticism in order to debate successfully with false teachers? No, for Christians had 'died toward the elementary things of the world' and should have wanted nothing to do

---

1, 2. (a) What would be a great tragedy for a Christian today? (b) What counsel did Paul give at 1 Corinthians 9:24, and how did it apply to Christians at Corinth?

---

3. (a) What situation existed at Colossae that could have prevented Christians there from finishing the race? (b) Was it advisable for Christians at Colossae to study philosophy and mysticism?

with its philosophies and traditions.—Colossians 2:20.

⁴ Paul, therefore, encouraged his fellow believers to focus their efforts on becoming "filled with the *accurate knowledge* of [God's] will in all wisdom and *spiritual comprehension.*" Yes, "accurate knowledge"—not idle speculations—would help them "walk worthily of Jehovah to the end of fully pleasing him." (Colossians 1:9, 10; see also Colossians 3:10.) True, most Christians in Colossae probably could recite the basic teachings of the Scriptures. But through study and meditation, they needed to go beyond the basics and become firmly "established on the foundation" of Christ. (Colossians 1:23; 1 Corinthians 3:11) After gaining such depth, 'no man could delude them with persuasive arguments.' (Colossians 2:4) Through skillful use of God's Word, they could effectively refute the claims of any angel worshipers or Judaizers.—Deuteronomy 6:13; Jeremiah 31:31-34.

⁵ Have *you,* though, gone beyond "the primary doctrine" and peered into "the deep things of God"? (Hebrews 6:1; 1 Corinthians 2:10) For example, can you identify the beasts of Revelation or explain what the spiritual temple is? (Revelation, chapter 13; Hebrews 9:11) Can you explain the *Scriptural* basis for the modern-

By filling our minds and hearts with accurate knowledge, we equip ourselves to refute erroneous ideas

day organization of Jehovah's Witnesses? Are you well grounded in Bible doctrine? One Christian sister found it difficult to defend her beliefs when discussing the Trinity with a certain woman. Later, the woman gave our sister literature that slandered Jehovah's organization. "I got very depressed spiritually," this Witness recalls. Happily, an elder was able to expose the false claims of the opposers and restore our sister's faith. (Jude 22, 23) "Now I understand," she says, "why the Society always says pray, study, and meditate."

"Trembling at Men"

⁶ "Trembling at men is what lays a

---

4. How would gaining "accurate knowledge" help Christians in Colossae?
5. (a) Give some examples of "deep things" that a mature Christian should know and understand. (b) How does one sister's experience show the danger of not taking in "accurate knowledge"?

6. (a) What has proved to be a stumbling block to some servants of God? Give some Biblical examples. (b) What often causes the fear of man?

snare," warned the wise man. (Proverbs 29:25) And at times a morbid "fear of death" or an inordinate desire for acceptance by others pushes a person into this snare. (Hebrews 2:14, 15) Elijah, for one, fearlessly stood up against practicers of Baal worship. But when Queen Jezebel ordered his execution, "he became afraid . . . and began to go for his soul and came to Beer-sheba." (1 Kings 19:1-3) The night Jesus was arrested, the apostle Peter likewise gave in to fear of man. Although Peter had boasted, "Lord, I am ready to go with you both into prison and into death," when charged with being one of Christ's disciples, "he started to curse and swear: 'I do not know the man!'"—Luke 22:33; Matthew 26:74.

7 Fearful desire for acceptance may have been the real reason why some sought to blend Christianity with Judaism. When Judaizers arose in Galatia, Paul exposed their hypocrisy, saying: "All those who want to *make a pleasing appearance* in the flesh are the ones that try to compel you to get circumcised, *only that they may not be persecuted.*" (Galatians 6:12) Could it be that a similar desire for popular acceptance has also been the force motivating some who have recently left Jehovah's organization?

8 Christians must work to overcome such fears. If you are reluctant to preach in territories close to your home, or you hold back from witnessing to relatives, fellow workers, or schoolmates, remember the question that Jehovah asks at Isaiah 51:12: "Who are you that you should be afraid of a mortal man that will die, and of a son of mankind that will be rendered as mere green grass?" (Compare Matthew 10:28.) Remind yourself that anyone "trusting in Jehovah will be protected." (Proverbs 29:25) Peter overcame his fear of man, eventually dying a martyr's death. (John 21:18, 19) And many brothers today show similar courage.

9 A missionary serving in a country where the preaching work was under ban said: "It takes faith to go to a meeting or in the service, knowing that it is possible that you will be picked up by the police." But like the psalmist the brothers there said: "Jehovah is on my side; I shall not fear. What can earthling man do to me?" (Psalm 118:6) And the work in that country flourished, recently attaining legal recognition. Regular participation in the field ministry is sure to help *you* develop the same confidence in Jehovah.

Family Ties

10 A book entitled *The Individual, Marriage, and the Family* states: "A universal need of the individual in all societies and in all segments of society is the need to 'belong' and to have a significant other who 'belongs' to him." This need is usually fulfilled through the family arrangement, an institution of Jehovah. (Ephesians 3: 14, 15) Satan, though, often exploits the attachment we feel to family members. Adam's strong feelings for his wife evidently prodded him to ignore the consequences and join her in rebellion. (1 Timothy 2:14) And what about Solomon? In spite of his renowned wisdom, "it came about in the time of Solomon's growing old that his wives themselves had inclined his heart to follow other gods; and his heart did not prove to be complete with

---

7. (a) Likely, what was the real reason why some in Colossae sought to blend Christianity with Judaism? (b) Who today appear to be similarly motivated?
8, 9. (a) How might a Christian today manifest the fear of man? (b) How can this fear be overcome?

10. (a) What emotional need is universal, and how is it usually fulfilled? (b) Give Bible examples of men whose attachment to their wives was stronger than their relationship with Jehovah.

Peter denied Jesus because of fear of man. Later, the apostle conquered such fear. So must all true Christians

Jehovah his God . . . And Solomon began to do what was bad in the eyes of Jehovah."—1 Kings 11:4-6.

¹¹ Do you remember aged Eli, a high priest of Israel? His sons Hophni and Phinehas were "good-for-nothing men" who "did not acknowledge Jehovah." They showed brazen disregard for sacrifices to Jehovah and committed sexual immorality "with the women that were serving at the entrance of the tent of meeting." Yet Eli offered only the meekest of protests ("Why do you keep doing things like these?"), while making no effort to remove them from their privileged office. In effect, he was 'honoring his sons more than Jehovah,' this resulting in his—and their—death!—1 Samuel 2:12-17, 22, 23, 29-34; 4:18.

¹² Misdirected loyalties could, therefore, hinder you in your race for life. Jesus told his disciples: "He that has greater affection for father or mother than for me is not worthy of me; and he that has greater affection for son or daughter than for me is not worthy of me." (Matthew 10:37; Luke 14:26) But what if a loved one left the truth or was disfellowshipped? Would you go along with the worldly notion that "blood is thicker than water" and follow that relative into destruction? Or would you put faith in the words of Psalm 27:10: "In case my own father and my own mother did leave me, even Jehovah himself would take me up"?

11. How did Eli 'honor his sons more than Jehovah'?

12. (a) What warning did Jesus give regarding family ties? (b) What worldly line of reasoning might some pursue when it comes to relatives, but is this Scripturally proper?

¹³ The sons of Korah had such faith. Their father led a rebellion against the authority of Moses and Aaron. Jehovah, however, dramatically proved that he backed Moses and Aaron by executing Korah and his coconspirators. Yet "the sons of Korah did not die." (Numbers 16:1-3, 28-32; 26:9-11) Apparently they refused to join their father in rebellion, and Jehovah blessed their loyalty by preserving them alive. Their descendants later had the privilege of writing portions of the Bible! —See the superscriptions of Psalms 42, 44-49, 84, 85, 87, 88.

¹⁴ Loyalty today likewise results in blessings. One young Witness remembers the stand he and his brothers took when their mother, long inactive as a Christian, entered an adulterous marriage. "We reported matters to the elders," he recalls, "and since she did not live at home, we decided to limit association with her until the elders could handle matters. It was the hardest thing we ever had to do." The mother protested, "Does your everlasting life mean more to you than *I* do?" To this they replied, "Our relationship with Jehovah means more than *anything.*" The woman was jolted into manifesting sincere repentance, was restored spiritually, and serves again as an active publisher of the good news.

¹⁵ Some have allowed their own children to be stumbling blocks. Failing to recognize that "foolishness is tied up with the heart of" youngsters, some parents have allowed their children to associate closely with worldlings, attend unsavory social affairs, and even date when far too young for marriage. (Proverbs 22:15) What are often the tragic consequences of such permissiveness? Spiritual shipwreck. (1 Timothy 1:19) Some even compound the wrong by deviously covering up the wrongdoing of their children! (Proverbs 3:32; 28:13) However, by loyally sticking to Bible principles, a parent helps both himself and his children to gain the prize of life.—1 Timothy 4:16.

Your Friends—"Wise" or "Stupid"?

¹⁶ The book *Sociology: Human Society* observes: "Desire for the esteem of one's close friends exerts a strong pressure for conformity to their standards." The book *Adolescence* shows that young people are particularly vulnerable to such pressure. It states: "[This is because] of the changes they are experiencing in their bodies, self-concepts, and relationships with their families. As a result, adolescents begin spending more time with their friends and less with their families."

¹⁷ Not to be overlooked are the words of Proverbs 13:20: "He that is walking with wise persons will become wise, but he that is having dealings with the stupid ones will fare badly." One Christian girl confesses: "All the bad association at my school is really starting to affect me. I caught myself saying a curse word in school today . . . I almost said it, but I didn't." Sad to say, some Christian youths have been led into very serious acts of misconduct by so-called friends. But if you are a young person desirous of gaining the

---

13. How did the sons of Korah prove their loyalty to Jehovah, and how were they blessed for this?
14. What experience illustrates the blessing that results from placing loyalty to Jehovah above loyalty to relatives?
15. (a) How have some parents allowed their own children to be stumbling blocks? (b) How can a parent help both himself and his offspring to gain life?

16. (a) How can our friends be a powerful influence? (b) Who are particularly vulnerable to the influence of friends, and why?
17. (a) Illustrate the truthfulness of the words of Proverbs 13:20. (b) What kind of friends could be considered "wise"? (c) How can young people today follow the example of young Samuel?

prize, search out wise friends—those who are spiritually minded, upright in their conduct, upbuilding in their speech. Remember, young Samuel did not associate with the bad sons of Eli. He stayed busy "ministering to Jehovah," thus remaining untouched by their corruption.—1 Samuel 3:1.

Attain the Prize!

[18] Beware, then, of anyone who would deprive you of the prize of life. This, of course, does not mean that you should view your brothers with suspicion. At times, though, perhaps unwittingly, some brothers may say things that discourage you. ('Why do you keep *pushing* yourself? Do you think you're the only one who will gain life?') They may even harshly judge your sincere efforts. ('I just don't see *how* you can pioneer with a family. It just isn't fair to your children.') However, recall that Jesus rejected Peter's admonition to 'take it easy.' (Matthew 16:22, 23) Use your Bible-trained ears to "test out words," and do not be influenced by those that do not ring true. (Job 12:11) Remember that Paul said: "If anyone contends even in the games, he is not crowned unless he has contended *according to the rules.*" (2 Timothy 2:5) Yes, God's "rules" —not unscriptural opinions—must guide your thinking.—Compare 1 Corinthians 4: 3, 4.

[19] True, at times a fellow Christian may 'stab' you with some thoughtless word. (Proverbs 12:18) *Do not let this make you quit the race for life!* Remember Joseph.

---

18. (a) How may some brothers, perhaps unwittingly, hinder us in our race for life? (b) What can protect us from such unwholesome influences?
19, 20. (a) How did Joseph's brothers seek to do him harm, and how did Joseph respond to their unkindness? (b) How can we avoid stumbling over imperfect humans? (c) What should be our resolve with regard to the prize, and why?

His own brothers considered murdering him, and though restrained from doing so, they finally sold him into cruel slavery. Joseph, however, did not allow this to embitter him or 'enrage him against Jehovah.' (Proverbs 19:3) Rather than taking revenge, he later gave them opportunity to demonstrate a changed attitude. And upon observing their repentance, he "proceeded to kiss all his brothers and to weep over them." As Jacob later said, "the archers [Joseph's jealous brothers] kept harassing him and shot at him and kept harboring animosity against him." Yet Joseph repaid their hatred with kindness. Rather than being weakened by the experience, "the strength of his hands was supple."—Genesis 37:18-28; 44:15–45:15; 49:23, 24.

[20] So rather than stumbling over imperfect humans, keep on 'running in such a way as to attain' the prize! Like Joseph, let trialsome encounters *strengthen* rather than weaken you. (Compare James 1:2, 3.) Let your love for God prove to be so strong that no human will become a stumbling block to you. (Psalm 119:165) Always remember that Jehovah holds out the prize of everlasting life—a prize beyond description, beyond comprehension. Let no man deprive you of it!

Do You Recall?

□ Why is accurate knowledge of such value to Christians?

□ How can one overcome the fear of man that has prevented some from gaining life?

□ How could one's own family prove to be a stumbling block?

□ How should a Christian respond to discouraging or even hurtful words from fellow Christians?

Insight on the News

Economic Pastoral

"The U.S. bishops have stirred the waters, even kicked up a storm, with the release of their pastoral on the economy," proclaimed the *National Catholic Reporter*. The pastoral, a letter entitled "Catholic Social Teaching and the U.S. Economy," was released in preliminary form last November. Although it is not expected to be in final form until 1986, the letter has already elicited widespread criticism from many American businessmen and economists, including Catholics. Why? In part, because it advocates strong political reforms.

For example, the bishops propose that the government reduce unemployment to 3 or 4 percent, create more job-training programs, reduce or eliminate taxes for the poor, and increase the level of public assistance. But should followers of Christ take a stand on such highly controversial political issues?

Jesus Christ was very concerned with the condition of the poor and underprivileged. Furthermore, the early Christian congregation, out of concern, made provision for the care of its members who had limited resources. (Luke 14:13, 14; 18: 22; Galatians 2:10; 1 Timothy 5:16) Yet Jesus and his followers avoided involvement in worldly affairs of their day. (John 6:15) Why? Because they centered their attention on the real solution to mankind's problems—God's Kingdom.—Matthew 6:33; John 17:16; 18:36.

Likewise, true Christians today maintain neutrality and do not seek to promote human political solutions for social ills. Doing so would divert attention from God's Kingdom, which will soon replace the governments of our day and bring an end to all poverty and want. (Daniel 2:44) While the bishops' pastoral makes scant reference to such a blessed prospect, true Christians proclaim this as welcome news.

Life—From Clay?

"Scientists in California . . . reported a major discovery that supports the emerging theory that life on earth began in clay rather than the sea," said *The New York Times*. Working at the Ames Research Center in Mountainview, California, the scientists discovered that ordinary ceramic clay has the capacity to store and transfer energy. This, they speculate, could have enabled clay to convert inorganic raw materials into chemicals that led to the first life forms. "The theory is also evocative of the biblical account of the Creation," says the report. "In Genesis, it is written, 'And the Lord God formed man of dust of the ground,' and in common usage this primordial dust is called clay." Still, according to this theory, life arose spontaneously. Does the Bible support this view?

No, it does not. The Bible says that *God* 'created all things, and because of *his* will they existed and were created.' (Revelation 4:11) In harmony with this, the amazingly complex and diverse life forms on earth bespeak the work of an intelligent Creator —a fact that precludes life's arising by chance.—Compare Hebrews 3:4.

True, Jehovah God used "clay" or "dust from the ground" to create man. (Genesis 2:7; Job 33:6) But nowhere does the Bible suggest that life of any kind began as a random chemical reaction. To the contrary, the psalmist says of God: "With you is the source of life." —Psalm 36:9.

Help for Marriages

Premarital counseling apparently is on the increase. "The attitude seems to be that if you can get help before the problems begin, you have a better chance," says Suzanne Prescod, editor in chief of the newsletter *Marriage and Divorce Today*. Indeed, of 90 married couples monitored between 1968 and 1978 by Dr. Claude Guldner of the University of Guelph in Ontario, Canada, the 30 who received counseling both before and just after their weddings were getting along the best.

Interestingly, a Biblical proverb urges: "Listen to counsel and accept discipline, in order that you may become wise in your future." (Proverbs 19:20) The best counsel one can receive is that given in the Bible by Jehovah God, the Originator of marriage.—Compare Ephesians 5:21-33; 1 Corinthians 7: 3, 4; 2 Corinthians 6:14, 15.

Are You Resisting the Spirit of Discontent?

MURMURING in the spirit of complaint is early brought to our attention in the Holy Scriptures. (Exodus 15:24) Today murmuring of this type is all around us and is swelling to a veritable roar. It threatens to engulf everyone, for it exerts a strong influence. The spirit behind it often finds expression in complaint, perhaps in a low murmuring tone, a muttering in discontent or dissatisfaction. Such murmuring must be resisted by true Christians. But how can we resist the spirit of discontent?

How It Began

There are legitimate reasons not to be contented with some circumstances. Understandably, "the cry of complaint about Sodom and Gomorrah" became loud because of the wickedness of their inhabitants. (Genesis 18:20, 21) But unwarranted complaint and murmuring are rooted in discontent. And the original promoter of the spirit of discontent was Satan the Devil, "who is misleading the entire inhabited earth." (Revelation 12:9) In the garden of Eden he brought about a situation designed to produce discontent, first in Eve and then in Adam. (Genesis 3:1-7) Ever since that time, Satan has been successful in producing situations that promote discontent.

Centuries after the revolt in Eden, Jehovah made a name for himself by delivering the Israelites from Egypt and organizing them into a nation. (Exodus 9:16) Were they grateful to their Deliverer? Why, during their 40 years in the wilderness, they repeatedly murmured against Jehovah, either directly or indirectly by finding fault with Moses and Aaron! In one case, Jehovah asked: "How long will this evil assembly have this murmuring that they are carrying on against me?" (Numbers 14:26, 27; Exodus 16:2, 7) The spirit of discontent persisted in ancient Israel all through its history.—Ezekiel 18:25.

Complaining About One's Lot in Life

Of course, because of being imperfect, a person could improperly let his circumstances become a cause of complaint. The righteous man Job was so unhappy about his terrible experiences that he called down evil on the day of his birth. (Job 3:1-3) Can professing Christians become discontented with their lot in life? Yes, they can, and some have.

Referring to "ungodly men" who had slipped into the first-century Christian congregation, the disciple Jude wrote: "These men are murmurers, complainers about their lot in life, proceeding according to their own [degraded, immoral] desires, and their mouths speak swelling things, while they are admiring personalities for the sake of their own benefit." (Jude 3, 4, 16) To remain faithful as Christians, we must shun such complainers. And how much better it is to count our many blessings as Jehovah's servants, thus maintaining a spirit that has divine approval!—Galatians 6:18.

Against Brothers or Associates

Servants of Jehovah should desire to maintain a loving, cooperative attitude toward one another. Yet, murmuring can be detrimental to good relations with others. The Levite Korah and his company murmured against Moses and Aaron and manifested a spirit of envy. Because Jehovah was greatly displeased with this, the murmurers met death.—Numbers, chapter 16.

Centuries later, the apostle John mentioned position-hungry Diotrephes, who was 'chattering about him with wicked words.' If John was able to come to that congregation, he intended to give that murmurer suitable attention.—3 John 9, 10.

We therefore need to guard against be-ing discontented, murmuring about our privileges within the congregation. For instance, we will do well to curb feelings of discontent over someone else's appointment to care for certain responsibilities for which we consider ourselves better suited. We may be wrong, and surely we do not want to have a spirit like that of Korah or Diotrephes.

Seek Bible Remedies

All of us, being imperfect and living in stressful times, no doubt occasionally have feelings of discontent. But we do have needed aid, for the Scriptures show us how to overcome the spirit of discontent and the tendency to complain.

A basic point to acknowledge is that murmuring is not approved by Jehovah, as it betrays lack of faith and lack of love of God. Thus the apostle Paul warned: "Neither be murmurers, just as some of them [the Israelites in the wilderness] murmured, only to perish by the destroyer." (1 Corinthians 10:10; Numbers 14:35-38) Paul also wrote: "Keep doing all things free from murmurings and arguments." (Philippians 2:14) Actually, how can a person be whole-souled in serving "the *happy* God" and yet be a chronic complainer? (1 Timothy 1:11) So we need to adopt Jehovah's view of matters and exercise implicit confidence in his ability to make us contented and happy. Remember that the fruitage of his spirit includes *joy*.—Galatians 5:22, 23.

In resisting the spirit of discontent, it is helpful to realize that in this life there is constant change. Hence, any cause for complaint is strictly temporary. (Compare 2 Corinthians 4:17.) An awareness of this should help us to find joy in serving Jehovah at all times. Rather than yielding to anxiety or discontent, "having sustenance and covering," let us "be content with these things." (1 Timothy 6:8) It is heartwarming to note that Jehovah assures us: "I will by no means leave you nor by any means forsake you." Safe and secure in our heavenly Father's care, therefore, let us not complain about our lot in life, but may we be "content with the present things."—Hebrews 13:5.

Remember Our Blessed Position

Do you sometimes feel discontented about what you have accomplished in your life? If so, reflect on your former status and your present favored position in the spiritual paradise enjoyed by true Christians. (Compare 2 Corinthians 12:1-4.) Anointed followers of Christ have been 'called out of darkness into God's wonderful light.' Their associates, the "great crowd," are also enjoying the marvelous light of truth and have grand prospects before them. (1 Peter 2:9; Revelation 7: 9-14) Should we not be contented—in fact, supremely happy—that we enjoy spiritual light and are privileged to know and serve Jehovah God and our King, Jesus Christ?

We are part of an international association of brothers and sisters, a great publicity organization that Jesus Christ is directing through "the faithful and discreet slave." This worldwide brotherhood is accomplishing Jehovah's will in preaching the good news of the Kingdom and in making disciples. (Matthew 24:14, 45-47; 28:19, 20; 1 Peter 2:17) What grand reasons for contentment!

If we personally are not contented with some aspect of congregational function, however, it may well be that we have misunderstood certain developments or are somewhat wrong in our viewpoint —something that surely is not impossible among imperfect humans and even dedicated Christians. (Compare Proverbs 16:2; Galatians 2:11-14; Philippians 4:2.) On the other hand, if we are right, should we not have confidence that Jehovah can bring about any needed adjustments, doing so through his Son, the Head of the congregation? (Ephesians 5:22, 23) How much better to be patient rather than discontented!

When we meditate on Jehovah's dealings with his people as an organization, we have sound reasons to be content. For instance, Bible doctrines have been made very clear, and this has upbuilt Jehovah's people spiritually. God's viewpoint on clean conduct has been clarified, so that Jehovah's Witnesses, although not perfect, are of outstanding morality. Our understanding of how the true Christian organization should function has improved to the extent that we are serving Jehovah in harmony with Scriptural directions for congregational organization. (Philippians 1:1) Should this not add to our contentment as dedicated Christians?

Faithful Christians also have a glorious hope for the future, one that should enable us to overcome any temporary lack of complete contentment. Now so near is the time when every living thing will be praising Jehovah! (Psalm 150) Meanwhile, let us not give place to murmuring. Rather, may we serve our loving heavenly Father with godly contentment.

In Our Next Issue

■ Religion and Politics
　—On a Collision Course?

■ True Christians Are
　Kingdom Preachers

■ Missionary Service
　—Come What May!

Despite My Infirmity, Let Jehovah Be Praised!

Bill and Janice Adams "listening" to a Bible discourse

THOSE who serve Jehovah God faithfully despite serious infirmities have constant evidence that he supports them. "Never will he allow the righteous one to totter."—Psalm 55:22.

Such comforting words have real meaning for Bill and Janice, both in their late 20's. Married for about three years, they are associated with a congregation of Jehovah's Witnesses in Washington, D.C. Bill serves as a pioneer, a full-time Kingdom proclaimer, and conducts a number of home Bible studies. Four of these are held with deaf individuals.

Janice was born deaf, and complications associated with her form of deafness caused her to become blind as well. During the "Kingdom Increase" District Convention last year, Janice sat in a section reserved for the deaf, to whom the spoken word was communicated by means of sign language. Of course, since Janice is also blind, she could not get the message in that way. Therefore, an interpreter was assigned to sit next to her. By placing her hand on the dominant hand of the interpreter, Janice could "hear" the program.

During the singing of one of the Kingdom songs, an interpreter failed to appear on the platform because of a misunderstanding regarding the schedule. So Bill, who was interpreting for Janice at the time, got up on the platform with her and signed the song. She, in turn, put her hand on his and sang with the others—something that brought tears to many eyes.

Bill and Janice have been "walking in the truth" for about two years. (3 John 4) And although Janice is physically blind and deaf, she is helping others to see and hear God's truth. She has been blessed with three home Bible studies, all conducted in sign language because the students are also deaf. So where there is an earnest desire to praise Jehovah and help others spiritually, his servants find a way.

Kingdom Truth Blossoms in 'the Flowered Island'

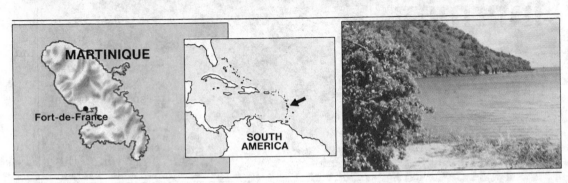

THE island of Martinique, basking in the blue waters of the Caribbean Sea and cooled by the gentle trade winds, is as paradisaic as any place can now be. Appropriately, the native Caribs called this 425-square-mile (1,100-sq-km) island in the West Indies Madinina, 'the flowered island.' Here, the brilliant purples and reds of the bougainvillea mingle with the scarlet of the flame trees and the iridescent hues of the crotons. There is a veritable symphony of colors, dazzling and spectacular, all over the island.

Blossoming of Kingdom Truth

Like the colorful flowers, blooming throughout the island today are 24 congregations of Jehovah's Witnesses. Fort-de-France, the capital city with its 100,000 inhabitants, has eight of them. All of this, however, is the result of divine blessing upon the seeds of Kingdom truth planted over the past 35 years.

In 1949 four graduates of the Watchtower Bible School of Gilead sowed the first seeds of Kingdom truth. Though the local authorities allowed the missionaries to remain for only two years, they kept busy sowing and watering, all the while trusting in Jehovah's promise: "In me the islands themselves will hope, and for my arm they will wait."—Isaiah 51:5.

Such trust in God was rewarded, for Jehovah's arm is never too short. In 1954 a couple from France came to Martinique. They were Xavier and Sarah Noll, full-time ministers. With hard work and Jehovah's blessing, by 1963 the number of Kingdom proclaimers had grown to 138. By 1976 there were 1,055 individuals busily preaching the good news in this 'flowered island.'

The year 1984 saw seven successive peaks of Kingdom proclaimers. The number of regular pioneers increased from 19 to 44, and 491 took up the auxiliary pioneer work in April. During the year, a peak of 1,635 individuals, about one out of every 200 inhabitants of the island, shared in proclaiming the good news. Truly, as the prophet Isaiah foretold, 'Jehovah must be glorified in the islands of the sea.'—Isaiah 24:15.

Branch Dedication

The blossoming of Kingdom truth in Martinique reached a high point on August 22, 1984. Some 2,000 guests from France, Canada, French Guiana, Guadeloupe, and the United States assembled for the dedication of a beautiful four-story building, the new Watch Tower branch office and Bethel home for Martinique.

A rich spiritual program was arranged for the morning. It started with Brother Noll's recounting the small beginning of the preaching work on the island. The audience was thrilled to learn that the first missionaries were present among them that morning.

Next on the program was a report on the construction, given by Brother Faustini, a missionary. For two and a half years, 40 brothers worked full time on the project. But on weekends, 100 to 200 volunteers from the local congregations would come to help. Among the full-time workers were brothers from Canada, French Guiana, Guadeloupe, and France, who for a while left jobs, homes, friends, and relatives to come and help with the work. Several of them took the opportunity to express their appreciation for the privilege of having a share in Kingdom expansion in this part of the field.

The climax of the morning was a vigorous speech on the theme "Moving Ahead With Jehovah's Organization." It was given by J. E. Barr, a member of the Governing Body of Jehovah's Witnesses. He emphasized the need to work harmoniously in order to accomplish God's will and to press forward to the things ahead. Clearly, the Witnesses in Martinique have done this, as attested to by the expansion and the blossoming of Kingdom truth on the island.

The news media responded enthusiastically. Coverage by television brought the event before the public. The newspaper *France-Antilles* observed that the high quality of workmanship seen in the structure reflected a "great love for work well done" and called the building "an architectural masterpiece" worthy of close inspection by experts in the field.

A Hospitable People

The appeal of Martinique is not limited to its reputation as 'the flowered island.' Among its friendly and hospitable people, it is a matter of custom to invite a visitor in and listen to him and not let him leave without offering him something. Even though people are more in a hurry nowadays, they still take time to talk and listen. All of this makes the preaching work a real pleasure. That was the experience of the Nolls on their first day of preaching in Martinique.

"Of course we were anxious to find out how the people would receive us, but what happened exceeded all our expectations," recalled Brother Noll. "That morning my wife and I had to return home twice to refill our bags with Bible literature. Some accepted the literature as soon as they saw that it talked about God; others took it simply because we called. How stimulating to see such hospitality! Whereas in other places we have to see that we do not stay

Young ones, too, are joyfully responding
to Kingdom truth

too long because people are busy, here we must avoid being detained too long in order to visit as many people as possible."

The experience of a traveling overseer showed how hospitable and generous the islanders are. "Our brothers have never hesitated to share what they have," he said. "One day a couple invited us to an evening meal. When we arrived in their tiny one-room home that had no running water or electricity, we were surprised by what we saw. There, set out on a tiny table, were only two plates. 'Why only two?' we asked. With their small income, they only had two plates, two forks, and two spoons. They told us they would eat as soon as we finished. Every time we thought about this couple, tears would come to our eyes."

Love for God's Word

Most people in Martinique have a deep reverence for the Holy Scriptures. Often the Bible, opened to the book of Psalms, is prominently displayed on a table. They believe that the Bible protects the house when they are out. Of course, when individuals learn the truth, they no longer look upon the Bible as a charm but as God's message to mankind.

This was the case with the headmistress of a local school. When she learned what the Bible says about image worship, she destroyed all her religious idols. (Psalm 115:4-8; 1 Corinthians 10:14) When the neighbors learned what she did with her "saints," the news got around the small town quickly. An uproar followed, fanned by the angry remarks of the local priest from the pulpit. But that did not deter her from embracing the truth. Today, this 75-year-old Witness is zealously making true worship blossom out in her part of the island.

A young man living in an isolated area started studying the Bible with Jehovah's Witnesses by correspondence. Shortly thereafter, he attended a circuit assembly and was so impressed by what he heard that he told all his friends about it upon returning to his town, where he was the bell ringer at the local church. Astonished at the Bible knowledge he had acquired in such a short time, one of his friends went to see the priest to ask his opinion of the Witnesses. "Just between you and me," the priest told him, "Jehovah's Witnesses teach the truth." Soon, the Witness conducting the study received this message from the young man: "I have decided to stop smoking and stop ringing the bells." Today, he is busy helping people hear the sound of the truth and serves as an elder in one of the congregations in Fort-de-France.

Even the children show remarkable interest in God's Word. To illustrate: A Witness schoolteacher showed her class the book *Your Youth—Getting the Best out of It,* and four pupils wanted a copy. When the Witness brought four copies of the book to school the next day, she was flooded with so many requests from the other students that she had to arrange for them to come to her house for the book. "A few days later, a woman approached me and asked me for two copies of the book," the sister related. The woman so appreciated the book her daughter had obtained that she wanted to study it with her children. "With her I placed the 105th copy of this book meant for the youths," said the sister.

Bible Truth Changes Lives

As in many parts of the world, drug abuse is taking its toll in Martinique. However, one young man, who was once bearded, long-haired, and heavily involved with drugs, was so impressed by the love and warmth of the Witnesses and the clear Bible message they offered that he gave up his drug habit, changed his life-style, and dedicated his life to Jehovah God.

One day a car pulled up when he was offering the *Watchtower* and *Awake!* magazines to passersby on the street. The driver, a police officer, called out: "But it's G——! What did you do to change so much?" He recognized the young man because in the past he had arrested him at the same spot for possession of illegal drugs. The young Witness, taking the Bible and the magazines out of his book bag, answered: "Here is what changed me!" Pleasantly surprised, the police officer encouraged him to continue. But he was not able to leave without the young man placing two magazines with him.

Marital problems have been an obstacle for some in making spiritual progress. However, God's Word can help those who truly love their Creator to break free from even the most difficult situations. One woman with six children by three different men and cohabiting with the third man started to study the Bible with the Witnesses. Soon she realized that her life was out of harmony with God's requirements. Her love for God and her desire to serve him gave her courage to tell the man she was living with to leave, in spite of the heavy responsibility of supporting six children by herself. Other women in similar situations have acted in faith and have been richly blessed for doing so.

Assemblies Give a Witness

The circuit assemblies and district conventions have contributed much toward the blossoming of Kingdom truth in Martinique. The first circuit assembly was held in 1955 at the home of Brother and Sister Noll. The five local Witnesses were supported by 27 others from Guadeloupe, the neighboring island. Though the total attendance was under 40, that assembly was a most upbuilding experience for the brothers.

Today, the Witnesses can no longer find facilities large enough for them to come together for a large assembly. Instead, they have built several sectional metal structures that can be assembled on football fields. This has made it possible to hold assemblies in the smaller towns on the island. The local people are always impressed by the orderly throng of Witnesses coming to the assembly and by the efficient way in which they put up and take down the assembly facilities. More than 4,000 people attended the two district conventions in 1984, and a fine witness was given.

What About the Future?

The building of the branch and Bethel home has strengthened the love, that "perfect bond of union," among all the brothers in Martinique. (Colossians 3:14) It was also an opportunity for all to cultivate the spirit of generosity. Many brought meals or gifts of fruits, vegetables, timber, machines, furniture, and so on. Others donated money and expensive jewelry. What a demonstration of unselfish love!

No doubt, the new branch facility will play an important role in the further blossoming of Kingdom truth in this 'flowered island.' Much work of cultivation remains to be done, because on April 4, 1985, there were 4,848 individuals in attendance at the Memorial of the death of Jesus Christ. All the Witnesses in Martinique are looking forward to the time when the entire earth will become a flowered garden—a paradise—under the righteous rule of God's Messianic Kingdom. —Luke 23:43.

Questions From Readers

■ Did 2 John 10, which says not to receive into one's home or to greet certain ones, refer only to those who had promoted false doctrine?

In context this counsel concerned the "many deceivers" who had gone forth, "persons not confessing Jesus Christ as coming in the flesh." (2 John 7) The apostle John offered directions on how Christians back there should treat one who denied that Jesus had existed or that he was the Christ and Ransomer. John directed: "If anyone comes to you and does not bring this teaching, never receive him into your homes or say a greeting to him. For he that says a greeting to him is a sharer in his wicked works." (2 John 10, 11) But the Bible elsewhere shows that this had a wider application.

At one time among the Christians in Corinth, a man was practicing immorality, and the apostle Paul wrote them to "quit mixing in company with anyone called a brother that is a fornicator or a greedy person or an idolater or a reviler or a drunkard or an extortioner, not even eating with such a man." (1 Corinthians 5:11) Now, did that apply to former brothers who had been expelled only for the gross wrongs there listed?

No. Revelation 21:8 shows also that such individuals as unrepentant murderers, spiritists, and liars are included among those who merit the second death. Surely the counsel in 1 Corinthians 5:11 would also have been applied with equal force to former Christians guilty of these wrongs. Further, John wrote that some "went out from us, but they were not of our sort; for if they had been of our sort, they would have remained with us. But they went out that it might be shown up that not all are of our sort." (1 John 2: 18, 19) John did not say that they had been expelled for gross sin. Perhaps some of them just quit, deciding that they no longer wanted to be in the congregation because they disagreed over a doctrine. Others may have grown tired and given out.—1 Corinthians 15:12; 2 Thessalonians 2: 1-3; Hebrews 12:3, 5.

Of course, if a brother had begun to stray into sin, mature Christians would have tried to help him. (Galatians 6:1; 1 John 5:16) If he had doubts, they would have attempted to 'snatch him out of the fire.' (Jude 23) Even if he had become inactive, not going to meetings or in the public ministry, spiritually strong ones would have striven to restore him. He might have told them that he did not want to be bothered with being in the congregation, reflecting his weakened faith and low spirituality. They would not have badgered him, but they might occasionally have made a friendly visit on him. Such loving, patient, merciful efforts would have reflected God's interest that none be lost.—Luke 15:4-7.

In contrast, John's words indicate that some went further than spiritual weakness and inactivity; they actually repudiated God's congregation. Someone may have come out openly in opposition to God's people, declaring that he no longer wanted to be in the congregation. He may even have renounced his former faith formally, such as by a letter. Of course, the congregation would have accepted his decision to disassociate himself. But how would they then have treated him?

John says: "Everyone that pushes ahead and does not remain in the teaching of the Christ does not have God. He that does remain in this teaching is the one that has both the Father and the Son. If anyone comes to you and does not bring this teaching, never receive him into your homes or say a greeting to him." (2 John 9, 10) Those words certainly would have applied to a person who became an apostate by joining a false religion or by spreading false doctrine. (2 Timothy 2: 17-19) But what about those who John said "went out from us"? While Christians in the first century would know that they should not associate with an expelled wrongdoer or with an active apostate, did they act similarly toward someone who was not expelled but who willfully renounced the Christian way?

Aid to Bible Understanding shows that the word "apostasy" comes from a Greek word that literally means "'a standing away from' but has the sense of 'desertion, abandonment or rebellion.'"* The *Aid* book adds: "Among the varied causes of apostasy set forth in apostolic warnings were: lack of faith (Heb. 3:12), lack of endurance in the face of persecution (Heb. 10:32-39), abandonment of right moral standards (2 Pet. 2:15-22), the heeding of the 'counterfeit words' of false teachers and 'misleading inspired utterances' (. . . 1 Tim. 4:1-3) . . . Such ones willfully abandoning the Christian congregation thereby become part of the 'antichrist.' (1 John 2:18, 19)"

A person who had willfully and formally disassociated himself

from the congregation would have matched that description. By deliberately repudiating God's congregation and by renouncing the Christian way, he would have made himself an apostate. A loyal Christian would not have wanted to fellowship with an apostate. Even if they had been friends, when someone repudiated the congregation, apostatizing, he rejected the basis for closeness to the brothers. John made it clear that he himself would not have in his home someone who 'did not have God' and who was "not of our sort."

Scripturally, a person who repudiated God's congregation became more reprehensible than those in the world. Why? Well, Paul showed that Christians in the Roman world daily contacted fornicators, extortioners, and idolaters. Yet he said that Christians must "quit mixing in company with anyone called a brother" who resumed ungodly ways. (1 Corinthians 5:9-11) Similarly, Peter stated that one who had "escaped from the defilements of the world" but then reverted to his former life was like a sow returning to the mire. (2 Peter 2:20-22) Hence, John was providing harmonious counsel in directing that Christians were not to 'receive into their homes' one who willfully 'went out from among them.' —2 John 10.

John added: "For he that says a greeting to him is a sharer in his wicked works." (2 John 11) Here John used the Greek word of greeting *khai'ro* rather than the word *a·spa'zo·mai*, found in verse 13.

Khai'ro meant to rejoice. (Luke 10:20; Philippians 3:1; 4:4) It was also used as a greeting, spoken or written. (Matthew 28:9; Acts 15:23; 23:26) *A·spa'zo·mai* meant *"to enfold* in the arms, thus *to greet, to welcome."* (Luke 11: 43; Acts 20:1, 37; 21:7, 19) Ei-

ther could be a salutation, but *a·spa'zo·mai* may have implied more than a polite "hello" or "good-day." Jesus told the 70 disciples not to *a·spa'se·sthe* anyone. He thus showed that their urgent work allowed no time for the Eastern way of greeting with kisses, embraces, and long conversation. (Luke 10:4) Peter and Paul urged: 'Greet [*a·spa'sa·sthe*] one another with a kiss of love, or a holy kiss.'—1 Peter 5:14; 2 Corinthians 13:12, 13; 1 Thessalonians 5:26.

So John may deliberately have used *khai'ro* in 2 John 10, 11 rather than *a·spa'zo·mai* (verse 13). If so, John was not urging Christians then to avoid merely *warmly greeting* (with an embrace, kiss, and conversation) a person who taught falsehood or who renounced the congregation (apostatized). Rather, John was saying that they ought not even greet such an individual with *khai'ro,* a common "good-day."*

The seriousness of this counsel is evident from John's words: "He that says a greeting to him *is a sharer in his wicked works."* No true Christian would have wanted God to view him as sharing in wicked works by associating with an expelled wrongdoer or with one who rejected His congregation. How much finer to be a sharer in the loving Christian brotherhood, as John wrote: "That which we have seen and heard we are reporting also to you, that you too may be having a sharing with us. Furthermore, this sharing of ours is with the Father and with his Son Jesus Christ."—1 John 1:3.

---

* *Webster's New Collegiate Dictionary* says "apostasy" is "1: renunciation of a religious faith 2: abandonment of a previous loyalty."

---

* Regarding the use of *khai'ro* in 2 John 11, R. C. H. Lenski comments: "[It] was the common greeting on meeting or on parting. . . . Here the sense is: Do not even give the proselyter this greeting! Already this makes you a participant in the wicked works for which he has come. John [refers] . . . to a greeting of any nature."

"Solution to All Our Problems"

That is what a young person from Puerto Rico says is found in the book *Your Youth—Getting the Best out of It.* He writes:

"Not too long ago I wrote to you concerning a problem I had, masturbation, and asked that you favor me with some advice by means of presenting some information in your magazine. Well, a friend of mine, one of Jehovah's Witnesses, gave me the book *Your Youth—Getting the Best out of It* to read. This happened about a month ago. I would like to let you know that since I read chapter 5 of this book, I have not practiced this habit again. I have come to realize that masturbation isn't really something one needs. . . .

"I would like it if every young person would read this book, regardless of his religious affiliation. All young people have the same problems, and this book is like a treasure, for it has the solution to all our problems. . . . You should continue publishing books for youths because in a world filled with drugs and immorality, this book is like a glass of very cool, refreshing water."

August 1, 1985

The Watchtower

Announcing Jehovah's Kingdom

Religion and Politics
A Lasting Partnership?

August 1, 1985
Vol. 106, No. 15

The Watchtower

Announcing Jehovah's Kingdom

THE PURPOSE OF "THE WATCHTOWER" is to exalt Jehovah God as the Sovereign of the universe. It keeps watch on world events as they fulfill Bible prophecy. It comforts all peoples with the good news that God's Kingdom will soon destroy those who oppress their fellowmen and that it will turn the earth into a paradise. It encourages faith in the now-reigning King, Jesus Christ, whose shed blood opens the way for mankind to gain eternal life. "The Watchtower," published by Jehovah's Witnesses continuously since 1879, is nonpolitical. It adheres to the Bible as its authority.

Average Printing Each Issue: 11,150,000

Now Published in 103 Languages

SEMIMONTHLY EDITIONS AVAILABLE BY MAIL
Afrikaans, Arabic, Cebuano, Chichewa, Chinese, Cibemba, Danish, Dutch, Efik, English*, Finnish, French, German, Greek, Hiligaynon, Igbo, Iloko, Italian, Japanese, Korean, Lingala, Malagasy, Maltese, Norwegian, Portuguese, Russian, Sepedi, Sesotho, Shona, Spanish, Swahili, Swedish, Tagalog, Thai, Tswana, Xhosa, Yoruba, Zulu

MONTHLY EDITIONS AVAILABLE BY MAIL
Armenian, Bengali, Bicol, Bulgarian, Croatian, Czech, Ewe, Fijian, Ga, Greenlandic, Gujarati, Gun, Hausa, Hebrew, Hindi, Hiri Motu, Hungarian, Icelandic, Kannada, Kikuyu, Kiluba, Malayalam, Marathi, New Guinea Pidgin, Pangasinan, Papiamento, Polish, Rarotongan, Romanian, Samar-Leyte, Samoan, Sango, Serbian, Silozi, Sinhalese, Slovenian, Solomon Islands-Pidgin, Tahitian, Tamil, Telugu, Tshiluba, Tsonga, Turkish, Twi, Ukrainian, Urdu, Venda, Vietnamese
*Study articles also available in large-print edition at same cost.

The Bible translation used is the "New World Translation of the Holy Scriptures," unless otherwise indicated.

Twenty cents (U.S.) a copy

	Yearly subscription
Watch Tower Society offices	Semimonthly
America, U.S., Watchtower, Wallkill, N.Y. 12589	$4.00
Australia, Box 280, Ingleburn, N.S.W. 2565	A$6.00
Canada, Box 4100, Halton Hills (Georgetown), Ontario L7G 4Y4	$5.20
England, The Ridgeway, London NW7 1RN	£5.00
Ireland, 29A Jamestown Road, Finglas, Dublin 11	£5.00
New Zealand, 6-A Western Springs Rd., Auckland 3	$10.00
Nigeria, P.O. Box 194, Yaba, Lagos State	₦6.00
Philippines, P.O. Box 2044, Manila 2800	₱50.00
South Africa, Private Bag 2, Elandsfontein, 1406	R5,60

Remittances should be sent to the office in your country or to Watchtower, Wallkill, N.Y. 12589, U.S.A.

Changes of address should reach us 30 days before your moving date. Give us your old and new address (if possible, your old address label).

The Watchtower (ISSN 0043-1087) is published semimonthly for $4.00 (U.S.) per year by Watch Tower Bible and Tract Society of Pennsylvania, 25 Columbia Heights, Brooklyn, N.Y. 11201. Second-class postage paid at Brooklyn, N.Y., and at additional mailing offices.

Postmaster: Send address changes to Watchtower, **Wallkill, N.Y. 12589.**

Published by
Watch Tower Bible and Tract Society of Pennsylvania
25 Columbia Heights, Brooklyn, N.Y. 11201, U.S.A.
Frederick W. Franz, President

Religion and Politics
A Lasting Partnership?

THE Russian ruler Vladimir I decided one day that his pagan people should become "Christians." He himself had been converted in 987 C.E., after marrying a Greek Orthodox princess, and he now decreed mass baptism of his subjects—at sword point if necessary. Gradually the Russian Church gained independence from its "mother," the Greek Church, eventually even becoming a department of the State. And though the Soviet rulers today officially deny the existence of God, Church and State in Russia still maintain an uneasy partnership.

Centuries later, King Henry VIII of England also succeeded in forming a close partnership between Church and State, though by different methods. In 1532 he was worried because his wife, Catherine of Aragon, had failed to produce a male heir to the throne. To solve the problem, Henry secretly married his ladylove, Anne Boleyn. This was with the connivance of the Archbishop of Canterbury, who pronounced Henry's first marriage annulled. In 1534 this adulterer and tyrant declared himself the head of the Church of England, a title enjoyed by England's monarch to this very day. Church Synod decisions are subject to

The first head of the Church of England

parliamentary approval, and bishops, as members of the House of Lords, take part in governing Britain. Church and State have thus been married in England for over 450 years.

Modern Church-State Marriages

In 1936 a revolt in Spain against the Republican government led to civil war and General Franco's rise to power. To the dismay of left-wingers, Franco gave the clergy considerable power in return for their exuberant support.

In 1983 the WCC (World Council of Churches) assembled in Vancouver, Canada. Its general secretary, Philip Potter, told them to "stay political." Grants of money from the WCC to militant political groups in a number of countries have been a source of grave concern to many churchgoers.

There is, therefore, little question that religion meddles in politics. The crucial question, though, is, *Should* it do so? Is it good or bad? Does religion's political involvement raise the moral standards of politics, or does it pervert religion? And what of the future? Will religion and politics continue to enjoy their 'love affair,' or will it sour and place them on a collision course?

Religion and Politics

On a Collision Course?

THE policy of combining political and religious power in one man did not originate with Henry VIII. In his day it was already a well-tried political ploy designed to promote national unity.

For example, the ancient empire of Egypt had many gods. "Pharaoh himself was one of the gods, and a central figure in his subjects' lives," says *The New Bible Dictionary*. The Roman Empire likewise had a pantheon of gods, including the emperors. One historian describes emperor worship as "the most vital force in the religion of the Roman world."

But in spite of the fact that Church-State unions are centuries old, Christendom's modern-day excursions into politics have placed her on a collision course with the very ones whose favor she woos. Why so? To answer this question, let us now take a look at how Christendom became involved in politics in the first place.

True Christianity—A Contrast

Jesus Christ, the founder of Christianity, rejected all political power. On at least one occasion, the people, enthused by his miracles, tried forcibly to make him king, but he "withdrew again into the mountain all alone." (John 6:15) Asked by the Roman governor if he was a king, Jesus replied: "*My kingdom is no part of this world.* If my kingdom were part of this world, my attendants would have fought that I should not be delivered up to the Jews."—John 18:36.

Christ further told his disciples: "*Because you are no part of the world,* but I have chosen you out of the world, on this account the world hates you." (John 15:19) So, early Christians did not become sidetracked by social or political problems. Slavery, for example, was then a major problem, but Christians did not campaign so as to abolish it. Instead, Christian slaves were commanded to be obedient to their masters.—Colossians 3:22.

Rather than dabbling in politics, these early Christians set about to accomplish the work of preaching "concerning the kingdom of God." (Acts 28:23) In just a few decades their message reached the limits of the then-known world. (Colossians 1:23) And with what effects? Thousands responded and became spiritual 'brothers and sisters.' (Matthew 23:8, 9) Jews and Gentiles who became Christians ceased their hostilities. Between the Jews and the Samaritans even major differences disappeared because of the "intense love" Christians had for one another.—1 Peter 4:8.

Christian love, however, extended even to their enemies. (Matthew 5:44) They therefore refused to join Caesar's armies. 'But,' some may object, 'did not Jesus say, "Pay back . . . Caesar's things to Caesar?"' True. However, was Jesus talking about military service? No, he was merely discussing the issue of whether to 'pay taxes to Caesar or not.' (Matthew 22:15-21) So Christians paid their taxes. But they viewed their lives as being dedicated to God and refused to do harm to their fellowman.

Becoming a Friend of the World

'But look at Christendom today,' some may say. 'It is hopelessly divided, its members often slaughter one another, its clergy are embroiled in politics. What *happened* to Christianity?' Well, Jesus warned that false Christians would be 'sown' in among true Christians. (Matthew 13:24-30) Paul likewise prophesied: "I know that . . . oppressive wolves will enter in among you and . . . men will rise and speak twisted things to draw away the disciples after themselves."—Acts 20: 29, 30.

Even in the first century this trend had begun. The disciple James found it necessary to write these graphic words: "You are as unfaithful as adulterous wives; don't you realise that *making the world your friend is making God your enemy?*" (James 4:4, *The Jerusalem Bible*; italics ours.) Many chose to disregard this divine counsel—so much so that in the fourth century a wolf in sheep's clothing, the Emperor Constantine, was able to compromise corrupt "Christianity" further by making it the official religion of the Roman Empire. But in becoming a 'friend of the world,' Christendom became God's enemy. An eventual collision became inevitable.

By the 13th century the Church, ruled by its "pope," or "father," had reached "the summit of its power," setting the stage for an even closer marriage of Church and State. Pope Innocent III became convinced that "the Lord gave Peter the rule not only of the Universal Church *but also the rule of the whole world.*" (Italics ours.) Continues professor of history T. F. Tout in *The Empire and the Papacy*: "Innocent's work was that of an ecclesiastical statesman, . . . making and unmaking kings and emperors at his will." But adds the same writer: "The more political the papal authority became, the more difficult it was to uphold its prestige as the source of law, of morality, of religion."

Religion and War

War is politics on a more violent scale. Pope Innocent III, however, personally organized a military campaign against the Albigenses of southern France. This led to the ghastly massacre of thousands at Béziers in 1209 and the mass burning of victims by the Holy Inquisition. A crusade, originally intended for Palestine, was diverted by political intrigue to include Constantinople. There, "Christian" knights engaged in a "hideous three days of plunder, murder, lust, and sacrilege." On whom? On fellow "Christians"! Says one historian: "The very churches were ruthlessly pillaged."

The un-Christlike methods of the Church eventually led to Martin Luther's nailing of his challenging theses to the

In 1914, at a drum altar on the steps of St. Paul's, the Bishop of London stirred up patriotism in British troops

castle church door at Wittenberg in 1517 —and the Reformation was on. But, says H. A. L. Fisher, in *History of Europe:* "The new confession was . . . closely dependent upon princely and governmental favour." Germany became divided along politico-religious lines. In France, Calvinists likewise mixed with political leaders. The ensuing wars of religion were therefore fought not only for religious liberty but also because of "rivalry between Protestants and Roman Catholic nobles for control of the Crown." Thus, the history of religion in Europe is written in blood!

The 20th century dawned with Briton and Boer locked in combat in South Africa. Clergymen on both sides fanned the flames with "exhortations from the pulpit." Says historian R. Kruger: "The volume of supplication addressed heavenward by either side in the course of the war was only matched by its variety of denominational inspiration." White "Christians" slaughtered one another while asking God to help them do it!

This pattern was repeated on a colossal scale in 1914 when German troops marched into Belgium wearing belts inscribed with the words *"Gott mit uns"* (God with us). On both sides the Church was prolific in prayers for victory and vitriolic in abuse of the enemy.

Multitudes were disillusioned by religion's role in World War I. Calling religion "the opium of the people," atheists and communists multiplied. Nevertheless, the clergy continued their involvement in politics, supporting Fascist dictators such as Mussolini and Franco. In 1933 the Roman Catholic Church even concluded a concordat with the Nazis. Cardinal Faulhaber wrote to Hitler: "This handshake with the Papacy . . . is a feat of immeasurable blessing . . . May God preserve the Reich Chancellor [Hitler]."

Even the possibility of another world war has not swayed the clergy from politics. One recent trend has been for some churches to swerve toward a left-wing political stance. Says one writer: "The latest generation of theologians from Latin America . . . insists that Marxism is the unavoidable political expression of Christianity." But the Bible warns: "They sow the wind, they will reap the whirlwind." —Hosea 8:7, *JB*.

Reaping the Whirlwind

Yes, the Bible sounds a solemn warning: A terrible clash between religion and politics is coming. In Revelation chapter 17, the Bible depicts the world empire of false religion stained with blood as a "great harlot who sits on many waters." These "waters" represent 'peoples and nations.' (Verses 1, 15) The harlot is named "Babylon the Great, the mother of the harlots and of the disgusting things of the earth," and she is "drunk with the blood of the holy ones." (Verses 5, 6) "Babylon" is a fitting name for organized false religion, inasmuch as many of her doctrines stem from the ancient city of Babylon.* She has earned her murderous reputation by her persecution of true Christians throughout the centuries.

The world empire of false religion is further pictured as riding a beast with "seven heads and ten horns . . . [which] mean ten kings." (Verses 3, 12) Previous articles in this journal have identified this "beast" as the instrument entrusted with maintaining world peace, the United Nations. The churches have gone on record

---

* For details, see the book *"Babylon the Great Has Fallen!" God's Kingdom Rules!*, published by the Watchtower Bible and Tract Society of New York, Inc.

as supporting this organization. In October 1965, Pope Paul VI described the UN as "the last hope of concord and peace." In 1979, Pope John Paul II addressed the UN General Assembly. Without ever mentioning Christ or his Kingdom, he spoke of the UN as "the supreme forum of peace and justice."

But why is this union of religion and the UN so dangerous? Because "the ten horns . . . and the wild beast, these will hate the harlot and will make her devastated and naked . . . and will completely burn her with fire." (Verse 16) False religion is therefore headed straight for a catastrophic collision with politics. Being denuded and her rank uncleanness revealed, she will be destroyed utterly.

That will spark the "great tribulation" that Jesus spoke of, culminating in the battle of Armageddon. Christ, backed by invincible heavenly hosts, will "crush and put an end to" Satan's worldwide system, leaving only the 'meek that will inherit the earth.' These will be true Christians who have, among other things, steered clear of divisive politics.—Matthew 24:21; Daniel 2:44; Psalm 37:10, 11; Matthew 5:5; Revelation 6:2; 16:14-16.

If you are one who is distressed over the suffering and reproach that false religion has brought on God's name, what should you now do? The Bible commands: "Get out of her [false religion], my people, if you do not want to share with her in her sins." (Revelation 18:4) Only Jehovah's Witnesses are urging people to heed this command. They, like the early Christians, keep out of war and politics and hence will not be in line for destruction when religion collides with politics. So contact them. They will gladly show you how to find the "narrow gate" that leads not to destruction but to everlasting life.—Matthew 7:13, 14; John 17:3.

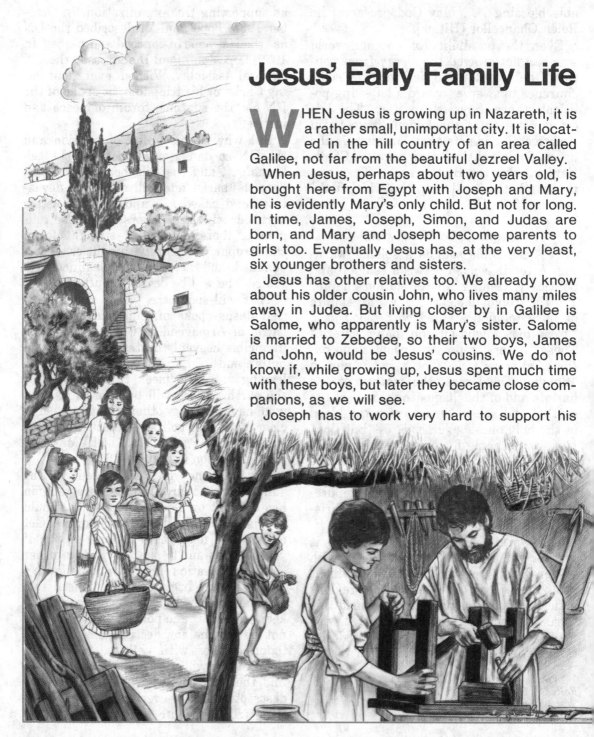

Jesus' Early Family Life

WHEN Jesus is growing up in Nazareth, it is a rather small, unimportant city. It is located in the hill country of an area called Galilee, not far from the beautiful Jezreel Valley.

When Jesus, perhaps about two years old, is brought here from Egypt with Joseph and Mary, he is evidently Mary's only child. But not for long. In time, James, Joseph, Simon, and Judas are born, and Mary and Joseph become parents to girls too. Eventually Jesus has, at the very least, six younger brothers and sisters.

Jesus has other relatives too. We already know about his older cousin John, who lives many miles away in Judea. But living closer by in Galilee is Salome, who apparently is Mary's sister. Salome is married to Zebedee, so their two boys, James and John, would be Jesus' cousins. We do not know if, while growing up, Jesus spent much time with these boys, but later they became close companions, as we will see.

Joseph has to work very hard to support his

Jesus' Life and Ministry

growing family. He is a carpenter. Joseph raises Jesus as his own son, so Jesus is called 'the carpenter's son.' Joseph teaches Jesus to be a carpenter too, and he learns well. That is why people later say of Jesus, 'This is the carpenter.'

The life of Joseph's family is built around the worship of Jehovah God. In keeping with God's law, Joseph and Mary give their children spiritual instruction 'when they sit in their house, when they walk on the road, when they lie down, and when they get up.' There is a synagogue in Nazareth, and we can be sure that Joseph also regularly takes his family along to worship there. But no doubt they find their greatest enjoyment in regular trips to Jehovah's temple in Jerusalem, as we will consider in our next article. **Matthew 13:55, 56; 27:56; Mark 15:40; 6:3; Deuteronomy 6:6-9.**

♦ How many younger brothers and sisters did Jesus have, and what were the names of some of them?

♦ Who were three well-known cousins of Jesus?

♦ What was Jesus' secular occupation?

True Christians Are Kingdom Preachers

"This good news of the kingdom will be preached in all the inhabited earth for a witness to all the nations; and then the end will come."—MATTHEW 24:14.

ANNOUNCING JEHOVAH'S KINGDOM. For decades, that has been the main objective of this journal. In fact, it is part of its copyrighted title. And it is vital that the Kingdom message *now* be declared worldwide. Why? Because of what Jesus Christ said after citing other features comprising "the sign" of his invisible "presence" and the end of this system. Jesus said: "This Good News of the kingdom will be proclaimed to the whole world as a witness to all the nations. And then the end will come."—Matthew 24:3, 14, *The Jerusalem Bible.*

² Today, "the end" is near indeed. Hence, each dedicated witness of Jehovah might well ask: How do I feel about the Kingdom-preaching work? Am I participating in it regularly? And is my ministry being carried out with skill and zeal?

The Commission to Preach

³ No genuine Christian can rightly shun the privileged work of proclaiming the "good news" to others. Jesus told his disciples: "You are the light of the world. A city cannot be hid when situated upon a mountain. People light a lamp and set it, not under the measuring basket, but upon the lampstand, and it shines upon all those in the house. Likewise let your light shine before men, that they may see your fine works and give glory to your Father who is in the heavens." (Matthew 5:14-16) That indicated that Jesus' disciples would be Kingdom preachers.

⁴ Concerning the foremost Kingdom preacher, it has been said: "As our Lord preached the kingdom He proceeded . . . to prepare and organize its Ministry . . . He began the *prophetic ministry* . . . and made both the Twelve and the Seventy partakers of the same. As He preached the coming kingdom and wrought 'signs,' He sent them before His face with a like message and like powers. By a wonderful course of minute teaching, . . . He trained them the meanwhile for positions of higher trust afterwards to be given."—*A Church History,* by Milo Mahan.

⁵ Jesus provided fine instruction for his apostles and the 70 disciples he sent out. (Luke 6:12-16; 10:1-22) Moreover, our Exemplar himself "went journeying from city to city and from village to village, preaching and declaring the good news of the kingdom of God." With him

---

1, 2. (a) Why must the Kingdom message now be declared worldwide? (b) What questions might each witness of Jehovah ask?
3. Jesus' words recorded at Matthew 5:14-16 indicate what about his followers?

4. What has been said about the foremost Kingdom proclaimer?
5. As regards Kingdom preaching, what did Jesus do?

were the apostles and certain women "who were ministering to them from their belongings." (Luke 8:1-3) Yes, Jesus was a zealous proclaimer of the good news and took steps to initiate a Kingdom-preaching organization.

6 After a three-and-a-half-year ministry, Jesus finished his earthly course. But before he ascended to heaven, he gave his followers this commission: "Go . . . and make disciples of people of all the nations, baptizing them in the name of the Father and of the Son and of the holy spirit, teaching them to observe all the things I have commanded you. And, look! I am with you all the days until the conclusion of the system of things." (Matthew 28:19, 20) They would, indeed, be Kingdom preachers.

7 When Jesus was about to leave the earth, his disciples asked: "Lord, are you restoring the kingdom to Israel at this time?" In reply, he told them: "It does not belong to you to get knowledge of the times or seasons which the Father has placed in his own jurisdiction." Even though the disciples then lacked accurate knowledge about the Kingdom, Jesus could assign them to be its proclaimers, for they would have the needed help to carry out their commission. "But you will receive power when the holy spirit arrives upon you," Jesus added, "and you will be witnesses of me both in Jerusalem and in all Judea and Samaria and to the most distant part of the earth." (Acts 1:6-8) Under the guidance of the holy spirit, Jesus' followers eventually would realize that the Kingdom would be a *heavenly government*. (John 16:12, 13) And in time the facts about that Kingdom would be

---

6. Before ascending to heaven, what commission did Jesus give his followers?
7. Although Jesus' disciples originally lacked accurate knowledge about the Kingdom, why would they succeed in being his witnesses?

proclaimed "to the most distant part of the earth."

8 Those witnesses did their work very well. Of course, Jehovah was with them, and they had the support of the glorified Jesus Christ. (Acts 8:1-8; 11:19-21) No wonder that as early as 60 to 61 C.E. the apostle Paul could say that the "good news" had already been 'preached in all creation under heaven'!—Colossians 1:23.

9 Regarding the work of witnessing, it has been written: "The proclamation of the gospel is . . . not one activity among many in which the Church of the N[ew]

---

8. How successful was the first-century preaching work?
9. As here noted, what is the chief work of the Christian congregation?

Jesus told his followers: 'Go, make disciples.' Are you zealously doing this chief work of all true Christians?

T[estament] engages, but it is her basic, her essential activity. . . . Note well, Jesus did not say [at Acts 1:8], You shall witness to me, or, You shall bear witness to me, but, You shall *be* my witnesses. The use of the verb 'to be' here has a value which must be taken with full and literal seriousness. The expression [in Greek] does not merely state what the Church would *do,* but what the Church would *be.* . . . The Church of Jesus Christ is . . . a witnessing body." (*Pentecost and the Missionary Witness of the Church,* by Harry R. Boer, pages 110-14) Yes, witnessing is the chief work of the true Christian congregation.

By Divine Providence

[10] First-century Kingdom proclaimers received direction from a governing body. Traveling elders served within the organization, and congregational duties were shouldered by overseers and ministerial servants. (Acts 15:1, 2, 22-36; Philippians 1:1) But what happened when new circumstances developed?

[11] Well, consider what took place shortly after Pentecost of 33 C.E. Greek-speaking Jews began murmuring against Hebrew-speaking Jews "because their widows were being overlooked in the daily distribution." To solve the problem, the apostles appointed "seven certified men" to care for this food distribution. (Acts 6:1-8) Concerning this we read: "At first, the care that the daily public meals were impartially distributed was all, so far as we are told, for which the 'seven' were set apart, but, of course, other duties would be added as they rose, for while the principles of the new faith were unchangeable, the machinery and modes of presentment, by which these might be most effectually es-

tablished and extended, were left to the wisdom and practical experience of successive generations . . . Adaptation and modification of non-essential details . . . is imperative in any great organisation." —*Hours With the Bible,* New Testament Series, volume II, by Cunningham Geikie.

[12] Prayerful reliance upon God, along with "the wisdom and practical experience" of the governing body, contributed to the progress of early Christianity. And things certainly were happening by divine providence. For instance, Jesus' early followers were said to belong to "The Way." (Acts 9:1, 2) But perhaps as early as 44 C.E. at Antioch, Syria, "the disciples were *by divine providence* called Christians." (Acts 11:26) This was a God-given name that they readily accepted.—1 Peter 4:16.*

[13] Among those early Christians, other developments also were within the divine providence. For instance, as Jehovah's Witnesses now use modern publishing methods, so the early Christians pioneered the use of the codex—a real boon to their zealous Kingdom-preaching work. In this regard, C. C. McCown wrote: "The Christians' religious books, both the Old Testament and the new writings . . . were not for the leisurely reading of the well-to-do. Hard-working business people wanted as much as they could get into a book. They and the earnest Christian missionaries wished to be able to refer to this or that proof text quickly, without having to un-

---

* See page 316 of *Aid to Bible Understanding,* published by the Watchtower Bible and Tract Society of New York, Inc.

10, 11. (a) Basically, how were first-century Kingdom proclaimers organized? (b) What happened when new circumstances developed?

12. (a) What contributed to the progress of early Christianity? (b) Where and how did Jesus' followers come to be called Christians?

13. As Jehovah's Witnesses now use modern publishing methods, what did the early Christians put to use in their Kingdom-preaching work?

Are you regularly witnessing from house to house? Jesus' early apostles did it. So did the zealous Kingdom proclaimer Paul

roll many feet of papyrus." —*The Biblical Archaeologist Reader,* page 261.

¹⁴ Being "able to refer to this or that proof text quickly" was very important because of the Kingdom-preaching methods employed by the early Christians. At times, of course, they witnessed to people informally, as Jehovah's Witnesses often do today. Of this it has been said: "One of the peculiar features of the apostolic preaching was its incidental character. There was no waiting of an apostle for a great opportunity. His only state occasion was when, like Paul before Felix, he was led as a prisoner before a ruler in purple to give an account of himself and answer the charge of infraction of the laws. He was not without his opportunities, but they were furnished him in the prison, by the wayside, and in the humble home where he might be sheltered for the night. . . . He felt that his message was largely to human units, though equally ready to present it to the multitude. He was equally at home with any audience. He had not forgotten the example of Christ, . . . [whose] stoa was the dusty highway, or the crowded street, or the pebbly shore of Jewish Galilee . . . [The apostles] had not forgotten that he had given them early in their companion-

ship with him special instructions as to the best methods of preaching his doctrines, had reinforced these first lessons by others, and, just before his ascension, pointed them to the world as their field and every creature as their auditor." —*History of the Christian Church,* by John F. Hurst, volume I, page 96.

"From House to House"

¹⁵ In the days following Pentecost of 33 C.E., Jesus' disciples were already using a superb method of preaching the "good news." After the persecuted apostles had been dishonored because of Jesus Christ's name, what did they do? Why, "every day in the temple and *from house to house* they continued without letup teaching and declaring the good news about the Christ, Jesus"! (Acts 5: 41, 42) Yes, the apostles witnessed from house to house.

---

14. Jesus' apostles were eager to preach under what circumstances?

---

15. How were the apostles carrying out the preaching work in the days following Pentecost of 33 C.E.?

[16] Later, the apostle Paul could remind appointed elders from Ephesus: "I did not hold back from telling you any of the things that were profitable nor from teaching you *publicly and from house to house*. But I thoroughly bore witness both to Jews and to Greeks about repentance toward God and faith in our Lord Jesus." (Acts 20:20, 21) Paul did not mean that he was teaching appointed elders in their homes. Rather, he was witnessing to unbelieving Jews and Greeks about repentance toward Jehovah God and faith in Jesus Christ. Without question, Paul also taught those elders how to witness from house to house.

[17] Concerning the apostle's ministry in Ephesus, it has been said: "Paul's general practice was to work at his trade from sunrise till 11 a.m. (Acts 20:34-35) at which hour Tyrannus had finished his teaching; then from 11 a.m. to 4 p.m. to preach in the hall, hold conferences with helpers and private talks with candidates, plan extensions into the interior; then lastly to make a house-to-house evangelistic canvass that lasted from 4 p.m. till far into the night (Acts 20: 20-21, 31)." (A. E. Bailey) Other scholars have stated: "He was not content merely to deliver discourses in the public assembly, and dispense with other instrumentalities, but zealously pursued his great work in private, from house to house, and literally carried *home* the truth of heaven to the hearths and hearts of the Ephesians." (A. A. Livermore) "Publicly and from house to house, in the city and throughout the province, he had preached the gospel." (E. M. Blaiklock) "It is worth noting that this greatest of preachers

What Is Your Understanding?

□ Why should the Kingdom message now be declared earth wide?

□ What is the chief work of all true Christians?

□ Why can it be said that among Jehovah's servants things do happen by divine providence?

□ The house-to-house preaching work of Jehovah's Witnesses has what sound basis?

preached from house to house and did not make his visits merely social calls." —A. T. Robertson.

[18] House-to-house witnessing was done by Jesus' apostles in 33 C.E. It was part of Paul's ministry in Ephesus and undoubtedly elsewhere. So there is a solid Scriptural basis for the house-to-house ministry of Jehovah's Witnesses. And this is true of various other methods they use to spread the Kingdom message. Interestingly, McClintock and Strong's *Cyclopedia* states: "Our Lord and his apostles found places for preaching wherever people could be assembled. The mountain-side, the shores of seas and rivers, the public street, private houses, the porch of the Temple, the Jewish synagogue, and various other places were found available for the proclamation of the Gospel." (Volume VIII, page 483) Like Jesus and his early disciples, Jehovah's Witnesses preach the Kingdom message in "the public street, private houses, . . . and various other

---

16. In what kind of preaching activity did Paul give training to the elders in Ephesus?
17. What have various scholars said about Paul's house-to-house ministry in Ephesus?

---

18. (a) Why would you say that there is a solid Scriptural basis for the house-to-house ministry of Jehovah's Witnesses? (b) Like Jesus and his early disciples, where and how do Jehovah's Witnesses preach the Kingdom message?

places." For instance, they engage in magazine street work (with this journal and its companion *Awake!*) and are especially known for their house-to-house witnessing.

19 The basic forms of the ministry now used by Jehovah's Witnesses were well established in the first century, and, besides this, it is proper for the present-day Governing Body of anointed Christians to decide what preaching methods are suitable at this time. Such decisions can partly be based on "the wisdom and practical experience" of these men. Especially, however, do they make decisions as did the first-century Christian governing body. God's direction and the guidance of his holy spirit are sought in prayer, and Scriptural precedents are followed when determining what preaching methods

are most suitable in these "last days." —2 Timothy 3:1; Acts 15:23, 28.

20 It is evident that the preaching methods used by Jehovah's Witnesses are within the divine providence, for God has crowned these efforts with abundant success and blessing. (Proverbs 10:22) Throngs are embracing true worship and joining the remnant of Jesus' anointed followers as part of the only organization that honors Jehovah's holy name and fearlessly declares the good news of the established heavenly Kingdom. May all of Jehovah's servants therefore continue exerting themselves in the disciple-making work as this system nears its end. This we must do faithfully, for true Christians unquestionably are Kingdom preachers.

19. How are decisions made regarding the preaching methods now used by Jehovah's Witnesses?

20. (a) Why can we be sure that there is divine approval of the preaching methods used by Jehovah's Witnesses? (b) What attitude should all of Jehovah's servants have toward the Kingdom-preaching work?

Teach With Skill and Zeal

"Go therefore and make disciples of people of all the nations, . . . teaching them to observe all the things I have commanded you."—MATTHEW 28:19, 20.

JEHOVAH'S WORD encourages skill and industriousness. For instance, it states: "Have you beheld a man skillful in his work? Before kings is where he will station himself; he will not station himself before commonplace men." (Proverbs 22: 29) Of course, there is nothing demeaning

about working for "commonplace men." But the skillful artisan's fine work will not remain a secret. Why, news of his skill may reach the ears of a king, who may well seek his services!

2 Knowledge and skill are needed in any

1. What is encouraged by Proverbs 22:29, and how so?

2. (a) To develop skill in any profession, what is necessary? (b) Why is a Christian minister's effectiveness as a teacher so important?

profession. A man may study carpentry and may also learn much by observing those skilled in that trade. But to develop skill himself, he must put acquired knowledge to work on the job. A surgeon needs to be educated. But to become competent, he must put his knowledge to use in the operating room. And in that profession skill is vital, for competence can often make the difference between life and death for the patient. Yet, of far greater importance is proficiency as a minister. Why? Because the minister's effectiveness as a teacher can well affect the way that people respond to the good news. In turn, their response can make the difference between everlasting life and eternal death for them. —Deuteronomy 30:19, 20; John 17:3.

3 The commission that Jesus Christ gave his followers involves teaching. He said: "Go therefore and make disciples of people of all the nations, baptizing them in the name of the Father and of the Son and of the holy spirit, *teaching* them to observe all the things I have commanded you. And, look! I am with you all the days until the conclusion of the system of things." (Matthew 28:19, 20) Of course, skill is required to teach the honest-hearted all the things Jesus commanded.

4 Such skillful teaching should be done with zeal. Yes, Christians should be "zealous for fine works," and these certainly include the imparting of spiritual instruction in the ministry and in the congregation. (Titus 2:14) As skillful teachers, Aquila and Priscilla "took [Apollos] into their company [at Ephesus] and expounded the way of God more correctly to him." This benefited Apollos greatly, for later in Achaia "with intensity he thoroughly proved the Jews to be wrong publicly,

while he demonstrated by the Scriptures that Jesus was the Christ." (Acts 18: 24-28) Clearly, Apollos taught with both skill and zeal.

'Pay Attention to Your Teaching'

5 The apostle Paul told his Christian associate Timothy: "Pay constant attention to yourself and to your teaching. Stay by these things, for by doing this you will save both yourself and those who listen to you." (1 Timothy 4:16) Since the very salvation of both teacher and student is at stake, surely such instruction should be imparted skillfully and zealously.

6 Carpenters and surgeons surely must pay attention to themselves. They must be able to use their tools or instruments competently. So must the Christian minister, whose chief implement is 'the sword of the spirit, God's word.' (Ephesians 6:17) How can you become adept in handling the Scriptures? Through regular study and use, of course. So, have you read the Bible from cover to cover, taking time to meditate on its superb counsel? Do you read it daily? Are you using it regularly in the field ministry? And are you taking full advantage of the rich spiritual food being provided by Jehovah through "the faithful and discreet slave"?—Matthew 24:45-47.

7 Be sure to set aside time for study of God's Word and true Christian publications. This will fill your mind with wholesome information that will benefit you and that can be used to answer sincere inquirers. (1 Peter 3:15; Colossians 4:6) Times for study and meditation vary with families and with individuals. Some may find it

---

3. The making of disciples requires what?
4. (a) Skillful teaching should be done with what attitude? (b) How did Apollos benefit from being in the company of Aquila and Priscilla?

5. According to 1 Timothy 4:16, why should we teach skillfully and zealously?
6. How can you become adept in handling the Scriptures, and what appropriate questions can be considered?
7. What suggestions are offered regarding time for study, and how can the need for study be shown Scripturally?

Visualizing Bible events can help you to become a better teacher

those you already know. This will help you to outline information in your mind so that you can explain matters clearly when teaching others. Doubtless, you have used association when studying in the past. For instance, at one time you may not have realized that Christians are to be in *relative* subjection to governmental "superior authorities." But you now know that obedience to God must come first. (Romans 13:1-8; Mark 12:17; Acts 5:29) You understand this because you have associated new points with those already known.

9 Another way to enhance your teaching ability is by visualizing incidents recorded in the Bible. Why not do this now with Judges 7:19-22? Under the cover of darkness, Gideon and 300 men surround a Midianite camp where sentries have just been posted. Suddenly, you hear Gideon's band of 100 blow their horns, and you see them smash the large water jars they have been carrying. The 200 other Israelites do the same thing. And as they all raise flaming torches aloft, you hear them shout: "Jehovah's sword and Gideon's!" As the terrorized Midianites begin to flee, Gideon's three companies continue blowing their horns, and you find that Jehovah has set the swords of the fleeing enemies against one another. Because you have visualized this event, doubtless you will remember it well and will be able to use it when teaching others. Surely, one lesson it teaches is that Jehovah can deliver his people without a powerful human military force. —Psalm 94:14.

10 Fine illustrations, including those in the Scriptures, can also enhance your skill as a teacher. As an example, consider

beneficial to study at day's end. Others may be more alert upon arising. Still others may find a midday hour to be most suitable for them. In any case, regularity and diligence are of utmost importance. Joshua and kings of Israel were to read God's Word daily.—Joshua 1:7, 8; Deuteronomy 17:18-20.

Work to Become a Better Teacher

8 Improvement of teaching skill calls for hard work. One way to enhance your ability as a teacher is to use mental association when studying the Bible or Christian publications. Associate new ideas with

___

8. How can the use of mental association improve your teaching skill?

9. Illustrate how you can visualize an incident recorded in the Bible.
10. In teaching, how might you use the illustration found at Judges 9:8-15?

Judges 9:8-15. Gideon's son Jotham told of a time when the trees went to anoint a ruler over them. Whereas the olive tree, the fig tree, and the vine refused a position of rulership, the lowly bramble eagerly accepted it. The valuable plants represented worthy persons who did not seek kingship over their fellow Israelites. However, the bramble, useful only as fuel, represented the kingship of arrogant, murderous Abimelech, who wanted to dominate others but met a bad end in fulfillment of Jotham's prophecy. (Judges 9:50-57) This illustration might be used to emphasize the need to do what is right and to be humble, not arrogant.—Psalm 18:26, 27; 1 Peter 5:5.

[11] The Great Teacher, Jesus Christ, is well known for his excellent illustrations. For example, consider his words: "The kingdom of the heavens is like a traveling merchant seeking fine pearls. Upon finding one pearl of high value, away he went and promptly sold all the things he had and bought it." (Matthew 13:45, 46) Jesus thus illustrated the preciousness of the Kingdom and showed that a person appreciating the true value of gaining it would be willing to part with anything in order to do so. There was nothing complicated about that illustration, and Christian teachers do well to keep that standard in mind when using illustrations as a teaching aid.

Meetings Can Make Us More Skillful

[12] Christian meetings play a significant role in making Jehovah's servants skillful and zealous teachers. As Jesus' Sermon on the Mount shows, public talks are a fine means of providing spiritual instruction. (Matthew 5:1–7:29) Hence, public talks are among the meetings of Jehovah's Witnesses today. Do you attend regularly? Are you an attentive listener? Do you consult your Bible when texts are read by the speaker? Is it your practice to take notes? These are ways to improve your ability as a teacher, and the fine Scriptural instruction should increase both your skill and your zeal as a disciple maker.

[13] The disciple-making work took on particular significance among Jehovah's servants with the call to 'Advertise the King and Kingdom,' first sounded during their convention at Cedar Point, Ohio, in 1922. Also in that year, group studies of *The Watch Tower* were first organized. This journal certainly has kept Bible teaching and Kingdom preaching to the fore, its very name being *The Watchtower Announcing Jehovah's Kingdom*. Are you an avid reader of God's Word with *The Watchtower* as an aid? Do you actively participate in the weekly *Watchtower* Study?

[14] The weekly Congregation Book Study also provides opportunities to improve your ability as a teacher of the good news. When answering questions at these smaller gatherings, as well as at the *Watchtower* Study, do you express matters in your own words? Do your comments reflect what you believe in your heart?

[15] Prior to 1922, Jehovah's servants customarily gathered for a midweek Prayer, Praise, and Testimony Meeting. It was an occasion for singing, giving testimonies,

---

11. (a) What points are emphasized by Jesus' illustration recorded at Matthew 13:45, 46? (b) The nature of that illustration suggests what about the illustrations used by Christian teachers?
12. How can attending public talks help you to improve your teaching ability?

13, 14. (a) When did the disciple-making work take on particular significance among Jehovah's servants? (b) What questions can well be asked regarding the *Watchtower* Study and the Congregation Book Study?
15. What is the purpose of the Service Meeting, and how is guidance provided for it?

The Theocratic Ministry School instructor helps students to be skillful in Kingdom service

and engaging in prayer. But with the increased emphasis on house-to-house Kingdom proclamation, this gathering developed into the Service Meeting, which stresses the preaching work. Of particular help was the *Bulletin,* which contained field service instructions and "canvasses," or testimonies, that could be used in the ministry. Today, *Our Kingdom Ministry* provides similar assistance, as well as guidance for weekly "Meetings to Help Us Make Disciples." Do you regularly participate in such meetings? Are you applying the counsel designed to help you teach with skill and zeal?

16 To promote skillful teaching, the Theocratic Ministry School was instituted in the congregations of Jehovah's Witnesses in 1943. Regarding the school's chief purpose, its first guidebook stated: "This course is not provided to take away from your time spent in field service, but is arranged to make you more proficient therein. Stated in more specific terms, the purpose of this 'Course in Theocratic Min-

istry' is to prepare all 'faithful men', those who have heard God's Word and proved their faith therein, to 'be able to teach others' by going from door to door, by making back-calls [return visits], by conducting model studies and book studies, and, in short, by engaging in every phase of the Kingdom service. It is to the one end of making each one a more efficient Theocratic minister to the honor of the Lord's name; that he may be better equipped to publicly present the hope that is within him; that he may be 'apt to teach, patient, in meekness instructing'. (2 Tim. 2:24, 25) Let no one lose sight of this primary purpose of the course." (*Course in Theocratic Ministry,* page 4) This remains the principal purpose of the Theocratic Ministry School. Have you been applying the fine information on teaching, reading, public speaking, and the like, that appears in this school's textbooks?* Are you an enrollee? Do you gratefully accept and fulfill your assignments on the school program? This

---

16. As stated at its inception, what is the purpose of the Theocratic Ministry School?

---

* For instance, please see *Theocratic Ministry School Guidebook* and *Qualified to Be Ministers* (Revised Edition), published by the Watchtower Bible and Tract Society of New York, Inc.

provision of Jehovah through his organization can help to make you a skillful and zealous minister.

Training for Zealous Teaching

¹⁷ Jehovah is making abundant spiritual provisions for those privileged to teach others his sacred truth. Among other things, he provides Bible literature, weekly meetings, and larger assemblies. Such fine provisions enable his dedicated Witnesses to become skillful and zealous teachers.

¹⁸ But what if we are appointed as elders or are more experienced witnesses of Jehovah? Then love for others should move us to help new and less experienced Christians to become more skillful and zealous teachers. Surely this is proper, for Jesus sent out the 70 disciples only after giving them instructions for their ministry. (Luke 10:1-24) Paul taught the overseers of Ephesus "publicly and from house to house," and this would involve training them to witness to unbelievers while going from door to door in the field ministry. (Acts 20: 20, 21) Similarly, elders, pioneers, and others may gladly train fellow Witnesses in the field ministry today. Do you sense a need for such training? Then by all means seek it and accept it. Are you an elder? Then make arrangements for training others in the ministry while you yourself take a zealous lead in the field service.

Continue Developing Skill

¹⁹ Surgeons, carpenters, and others can become more skillful through continued study and application of acquired knowledge. The same is true of Christian ministers. Therefore, how vital it is that each dedicated witness of Jehovah work hard to increase his skill as a teacher of the good news! And since this is Jehovah's work, it should be the subject of our earnest prayers. If we seek God's help and guidance, we can be confident that he will bless our zealous ministry. As the apostle John said: "Whatever we ask we receive from [Jehovah God], because we are observing his commandments and are doing the things that are pleasing in his eyes." —1 John 3:22.

²⁰ As the present wicked system of things nears its end, therefore, may we exert ourselves vigorously in the ministry. May we 'pay attention to ourselves and our teaching,' to our own salvation and to that of those who heed the Kingdom message. Yes, let us make every effort to teach with skill and zeal.

---

20. As Jehovah's Witnesses, what should be our determination as this system nears its end?

---

17. What spiritual provisions has Jehovah made for those who teach others his sacred truth?
18. Following the examples of Jesus and Paul, what arrangements may elders make to advance field ministry today?
19. Why should we pray about our ministry?

What Would You Say?

□ Besides preaching, the disciple-making work calls for what?

□ Why is it so important to 'pay attention to your teaching'?

□ What are some ways to enhance teaching skill?

□ How can Christian meetings help us to be skillful and zealous teachers of God's Word?

□ What may elders and other experienced Witnesses do as regards the field ministry?

Kingdom Proclaimers Report

'They Adorn the Teaching of Our God'

THE simplicity and clarity of Kingdom truth can be 'adorned' by those who proclaim it to others. How? By their good conduct. Notice how the apostle Paul showed this. Christian slaves were counseled to exhibit "good fidelity to the full, so that they may adorn the teaching of our Savior, God, in all things." (Titus 2:10) The following experiences from Argentina demonstrate the practicalness of this counsel.

□ Six of Jehovah's Witnesses were employed in a supermarket where the owner was considered to be very strict. When they asked for time off to attend the Memorial of Christ's death, they were told, "Choose between your work and your meetings." Although work was scarce, they chose to attend the Memorial. The next day, they went to work thinking that they would be fired. What a surprise they had when not only were they kept on but four of them who were temporary workers were given permanent jobs. And all six received an increase in pay! Later, two of them decided to become regular pioneers, so the supermarket owner gave them a shift arrangement for their convenience. His reason for being so considerate of them? He did not want his honest, diligent workers to quit.

So the honesty and good work habits of these six Witnesses 'adorned' their teaching to Jehovah's honor.

□ A sister was working in a pharmacy, but because of the long hours, she was not attending all the Christian meetings, nor could she be a pioneer, which was her desire. The owner of the pharmacy would not give her the work schedule she wanted, so she left her job. She then worked as a maid, and this permitted her to auxiliary pioneer. A few months later, the pharmacy owner came to her house and offered her a job "with whatever working schedule she wanted." Why? "Because of her excellent conduct," says the report.

□ The good conduct of one Witness 'adorned' her teaching in a different way. The report from Argentina explains that when two Witnesses approached the door of a beautiful, luxurious house with a big, modern car outside, they felt a little afraid because of the evident show of wealth. How surprised they were to receive a cordial welcome. A two-hour discussion followed, answering questions. The Witnesses stated: "We agreed to return the following week. We left very happy but puzzled because we did not know the real reason for such a welcome. The following week we found out what that reason was."

The lady of the house explained: "I used to live in Mar del Plata and knew a young woman who led a very wild life. In time she began to study the Bible with Jehovah's Witnesses, and immediately a change in her personality became evident.

The neighbors and I could not believe the change in her because not a trace of her former wild personality was noticeable. She is now a respectable woman, the wife of an elder, as you call them, and now has a family that is an example to all."

The changed conduct of this young person when she became one of Jehovah's Witnesses now moved the lady to consider seriously the teachings of Jehovah's Witnesses. A Bible study was arranged then and there with this couple, and they began to attend the meetings at the Kingdom Hall. The Witnesses concluded this experience by stating: "This shows that our conduct can also give a witness, all to the glory and honor of Jehovah's name."

Missionary Service
—Come What May!

As told by Eric Britten

THE place: Coventry, England. The time: seven o'clock in the evening, November 14, 1940. Suddenly, air-raid sirens began to wail as a prelude to what was to be one of the longest raids in the history of modern warfare. When the bombs started falling, ten other pioneers (full-time preachers) and I huddled together under the stairway of our "pioneer home." My thoughts turned to my wife, who was away visiting her mother. Was she safe?

We poured out our hearts to Jehovah for protection. How happy we were to come through this ordeal unscathed and to learn later that my wife and all members of our little congregation were also safe! We felt as did the psalmist who declared, "Your own loving-kindness, O Jehovah, kept sustaining me."—Psalm 94:18.

Early Tragedy

From the time of my birth in January 1910, I was reared in a strict religious home, and that early Bible training helped me considerably in later years. This was especially true after my mother's death in January 1922, when I was just 12 years old.

About that time my father, although a Christadelphian, obtained from the Bible Students (as Jehovah's Witnesses were then known) a set of C. T. Russell's *Studies in the Scriptures*. One thing that impressed my father was the reasonable explanation of the ransom doctrine. (Matthew 20:28) Father felt strongly that if a Christian accepts the ransom doctrine, he is responsible to tell others about it. He realized, too, that the Bible Students were doing just that, so he sought them out.

In the early 1920's he began attending meetings of the Bible Students in Coventry and took me along with him. Soon we both began to share in the preaching work. Dad reached the point of consecration (now called dedication), and in 1924 he was baptized. In 1926, at the age of 16, I, too, was baptized. The following year, in October 1927, tragedy struck again—my father died, leaving me and my younger sister to be cared for. She went to live with our grandparents, whereas I continued to live alone.

I was just 17, and I had to identify Father's body and make the necessary arrangements for his burial. To me this was a formidable task, but the Christian brothers came to my aid. They invited me to their homes for meals, studied the Bible with me, and accompanied me in the preaching work until I felt stronger again. How I appreciated their kindness during this difficult period!

Although living in Coventry, I found employment in the nearby city of Birmingham. During the week, I was able to attend meetings there. It was at these midweek meetings that I later met Christina, who was to become my wife.

Although raised a Methodist, Chris visited other churches, searching for something more satisfying. One Sunday morning two Bible Students visited her home and left three booklets with her. Shortly thereafter, Chris' mother attended a meeting of the Bible Students and acquired three books for Chris. Little did her mother realize how these books were to influence her daughter's life, even to the point of Chris' going from house to house with the Kingdom message—something Chris had said she would never do!

War Declared

In 1934 Chris and I were married. We both entered married life with the purpose of 'seeking first God's Kingdom,' and we can truthfully say that Jehovah has blessed us for pursuing this course. (Matthew 6:33) As our goal, we kept in mind entering the full-time pioneer ministry. So we made arrangements for others to share our home and to work as pioneers along with us. But by this time, 1939, war clouds were looming up, and it seemed as though everyone in Coventry was making arrangements for a long period of austerity and for protection against possible bombings.

World War II was a very difficult period for everyone but especially for our brothers. For nearly six years, Coventry, as an industrial centre, was the special target of the German bombers. This meant many sleepless nights. We took turns staying up one night a week to protect our "pioneer home" and also the homes of our neighbours, while they in turn protected our home on other nights. There were some pretty close calls too. Why, on one occasion Chris was visiting a home to share a Bible message when a raid started. Bombs fell, and the houses on both sides of the home she was visiting were completely destroyed.

In and Out of Prison

Adding to our discomfort was the harassment by the authorities because of our neutrality. As a result, Chris and I were imprisoned for a short term. As soon as I had served my sentence, I was charged again, and I ended up going back to prison. This we called cat and mouse, since a cat will often release a mouse only to pounce on it again.

Even though we had little contact with the prison officers, at times we were able to preach to some of them. I recall one officer, named Beveridge, who during my first sentence ridiculed our neutral stand. When I was imprisoned the second time, his attitude had improved some. During my third sentence, he was quite favourable, although opportunities to talk with him were limited. When I finally left prison, I lost contact with him.

Years later, when we were in Portugal, a letter came from the Society's office in Brooklyn advising us that Eric Beveridge, a graduate of Gilead (the Watchtower school for training missionaries) was being assigned to Portugal. How happy we were to learn that his father had been that favourable prison officer! He later retired from prison service and became a baptized Witness.

Missionary Service and Unusual Challenges

With the end of the war in 1945, the Kingdom work in England, as in other parts of the earth, entered a period of prosperity and expansion. Brother Knorr, then the president of the Watch Tower

In Brazil, we had to learn how to "knock" at a door—by clapping our hands loudly at the front gate

Society, and Brother Henschel visited England and held a special meeting with all pioneers interested in attending the Watchtower Bible School of Gilead, which had been opened in February 1943. Christina and I attended the meeting, filled out our preliminary applications, and wondered if we would ever be called.

In 1946 the Society invited me to do circuit work in England, visiting a number of congregations. I enjoyed this privilege for three years, and then, when least expected, the final applications for missionary school arrived! These we filled out immediately, and shortly thereafter we were invited to attend the 15th class, beginning in February 1950. The next five months in Gilead School in upper New York State were an unforgettable experience of intensive Bible study and mature Christian association. Before we realized it, we were attending graduation at Yankee Stadium on July 30, 1950. Our assignment? Brazil.

A missionary home was opened in the coffee-exporting port of Santos, Brazil, and we were part of a group of eight missionaries assigned to start our work there. There was the initial period of adapting to new customs and the Portuguese language. For a child, learning a new language may be relatively simple. But for us, at 40 years of age, it was far from easy. On one occasion I went with another missionary to buy bread. The Portuguese word for bread (*pão*) sounds similar to the word for stick (*pau*), the former having a slight nasal sound. Not yet having mastered the nasal sound, we asked for sticks (*paus*), and the astonished baker said that he did not have any!

Another custom that it took a while to get used to was how to accept hospitality when a householder offered it. We would say: *"Muito obrigado"* (Thank you very much), expecting to receive some refreshments. This, however, to the householder meant no! Finally, we learned the right expression: *"Aceito"* (I accept), which brought pleasure to the householder—and to us.

We found that we even had to learn how to "knock" at a door. You see, the Brazilian custom is to clap the hands loudly at the front gate. At first it was always a surprise for us to have the householder answer our "knock," but we soon got used to it.

Unhappily, within six months of our arrival in Brazil, I contracted an intestinal disorder with amoebas. The prolonged treatment for the illness left me very weak, and finally, in March 1954, acting upon the doctor's advice, we sadly returned to England. There, in the temperate climate, I gradually recovered, but during my recuperation we received an unexpected letter.

A Very Different Missionary Assignment

The Society invited us to go to Portugal! There the work had been banned, and the two previous branch overseers had been expelled from the country. I was able to gain entrance into Portugal as a business representative of an English firm, and we arrived there in November 1954.

Having worked in Brazil where our preaching work was carried on openly, we soon realized that here in Portugal we would have to exercise care and much tact. Since our work was banned, we could not openly identify ourselves as Jehovah's Witnesses. Door-to-door preaching was a challenge since we never knew whom we would meet. If anyone seemed overly curious or antagonistic, we simply left the territory, to return another day. It was not easy to get invited into the homes since people were understandably suspicious of strangers. However, Chris did start a study with a lady who later told her that she really had been afraid to let anyone into her home. Why did she do so?

It seems that this lady had been praying to God to show her the right way. But Chris' knock came so soon after her prayer that she felt wary about letting her in! A Bible study was started, and the lady and her teenage daughter both progressed to dedication and baptism. They are still firm in the truth.

At that time Chris and I were the only missionaries in Portugal, but gradually the Society was able to have more sent into the country. The work progressed rapidly, especially in the capital, Lisbon. This increase aroused opposition. Several brothers were imprisoned, and much literature was confiscated.

Finally, for us the worst blow came in 1962 when we, along with four other missionaries, were ordered to leave the country. We requested an interview with the

> **We have always tried to 'seek first God's Kingdom' in our lives, with resultant blessings**

chief of the secret police to ask for a reconsideration of our case, since we were merely teaching people the Bible. His reply: "You have abused Portuguese hospitality for seven years and will never set foot in Portugal again!" We were shattered.

It is extremely difficult to describe our feelings at having to leave after seven happy years in that missionary field. Actually, leaving Portugal was much harder for us than leaving England back in 1950 to go to Gilead. We had worked intimately with the brothers; we had shared their joys and their problems. We felt we were leaving when our help and support were most needed. But we had no choice. 'Our missionary days are over,' we sadly thought as we set sail for England.

From England to the Amazon!

In England we continued in the full-time ministry as special pioneers, but we felt incomplete. We always remembered the happy times in missionary service, and we wanted to get back to it—so much so that we finally wrote to the Society about the possibility of another assignment, even though by now I was over 50 years of age and Chris was 49. How great our joy when we received an invitation to return to Brazil and work from a missionary home in Belém, a city at the mouth of the Amazon River!

We did appreciate the Society's letter giving us an idea of the climate in Belém —"hot and humid," it said—and giving us the option of turning down the assignment. However, we were overjoyed at the prospect of returning to Brazil, even though it was to a different part of the country. We gladly accepted, and early in 1964 we arrived in our new assignment.

After serving one year in Belém, I was invited to do circuit work, visiting congregations in that region. This was a real challenge. The circuit was some 800 miles* long and 300 miles wide, taking in both sides of the Amazon River. The heat? Well, we just had to get accustomed to it! Conditions were often primitive. Even dirt highways were few in those days. Clouds of dust arose from them in the dry season. With the rainy season, they became impassable.

Besides trusting in Jehovah for his protection, having a good sense of humor helped. On one visit with an isolated Witness family, we had to sleep in a stable. In the morning Chris awoke to find herself covered with blood. We called out to the brother, thinking that something serious had happened. Imagine our surprise when he calmly informed us that she had apparently been bitten by a vampire bat! One reference work explains that among bats in the Amazon region are 'bloodsucking vampires (*Dysopes*), although these are by no means as dangerous as travelers' tales would lead one to believe.' Had we known that before, we would have been less fearful of the outcome!

After serving a year in that circuit, we were transferred to Rio de Janeiro and later to São Paulo, where we have been serving now for several years. The Brazilian people are very open and friendly, and it has been a joy to experience the love and hospitality of the brothers in this part of the country as well. At the same time, we have enjoyed many fine experiences in the field.

At one house a youngster came in answer to Chris' handclapping. He said that

_____
* One mile equals 1.6 kilometers.

his mother could not come to the door because she was crying. Sensing something wrong, Chris said, "Tell her that senhora Christina would like to speak to her." The mother came to the door, asking, "Do you know anything about the Bible?"

"That is just why I am here!" Chris answered. She invited Chris inside. On the table was a large Bible, open where the lady had been reading, seeking comfort. She was very upset because her husband had been away for a week, after a quarrel between them.

"He's a good husband and father," she said, "and I'm sure he hasn't gone away with someone else." Chris shared some Bible principles on family life and started a Bible study in the book *The Truth That Leads to Eternal Life.* That very night the lady went to the Kingdom Hall. Since we had to leave that week for the next congregation, the study was turned over to a local publisher. How happy we were when we visited the congregation again six months later and met not only the lady but her husband and three children! Some time later, both husband and wife were baptized as Jehovah's Witnesses.

Now, though both of us are over 70 years of age, we are still able, by Jehovah's loving-kindness, to continue serving in our missionary assignment, although not travelling as much as in the past. It has been a marvelous privilege to meet and work with so many mature missionaries and local brothers and sisters. We are glad that from the very beginning we have tried to 'seek first God's Kingdom' in our lives. For over 30 years missionary service has been our joy. We are ever mindful of the words of the psalmist, when he said: "For Jehovah is good; his loving-kindness is to time indefinite." (Psalm 100:5) And how we have appreciated that!

"Walk Worthily . . . With Long-Suffering"

SHE was repeatedly arrested and subjected to intense interrogation. Once she was even paraded through the streets in front of a jeering crowd in company with nine male prisoners whose crimes varied from murder to rape and theft. Altogether she was imprisoned and separated from her family for more than 20 years.

This Christian woman's experience is perhaps not unique, for many have similarly endured long prison terms. But her "crime" was certainly unusual: She was one of Jehovah's Witnesses. Renouncing her faith could have brought immediate relief. What therefore enabled this woman not only to submit to such treatment but also to retain a measure of happiness?

To answer this question, let us make reference to another faithful Christian who was also arrested because of the religious stand that he took. This was the apostle Paul. Writing to the congregation at Ephesus, he said: "I, therefore, the prisoner in the Lord, entreat you to walk worthily of the calling with which you were called, with complete lowliness of mind and mildness, with long-suffering [longness of spirit], putting up with one another in love, earnestly endeavoring to observe the oneness of the spirit in the uniting bond of peace." —Ephesians 4:1-3.

Christians in Ephesus had a marvelous "calling" to heavenly life with Christ Jesus. (1 Peter 1:3, 4) But in order to attain to it, they had to "walk," or conduct themselves, in a way that proved they were worthy of it. Paul indicated that "long-suffering" was vital to their doing this. "Long-suffering," however, meant more than merely suffering pain or inconvenience for a prolonged period of time. A man with a broken leg 'suffers long,' but does he have any other choice? The long-suffering person, however, endures ill-treatment without retaliation or irritation for a *purpose*. His slowness to express anger is an exercise of *deliberate restraint*.

Paul showed such restraint in enduring house arrest. He knew it served "for the advancement of the good news." (Philippians 1:12) Also, it allowed Paul to demonstrate his loyalty and devotion to Jehovah God, to prove he was 'walking worthily' of his calling to heavenly life. Paul thus happily endured imprisonment. And many Christians since then have similarly demonstrated long-suffering. Not all have had the heavenly "calling." But they have been moved to "walk worthily" of the prize of everlasting life, whether that be in the heavens or in the earthly realm of the Kingdom.

Nevertheless, comparatively few have had to suffer the rigors of prison life. Is long-suffering valuable under other circumstances? Yes, indeed, for Paul encouraged the entire Ephesian congregation to "walk worthily . . . with long-suffering." Ephesus was the most important city in the Roman province of Asia. Its wealth was a potential snare for Christians. It was also a city noted for loose conduct, demonism, sorcery, and magic, a city filled with worshipers of the goddess Artemis, or Diana. Said ancient historian Lucius Seneca concerning such ones: "Men seek pleasure from every source. No vice remains within its limits . . . We are overwhelmed with forgetfulness of that which is honourable." 'Walking worthily' was therefore a trying experience for Christians there.

No wonder, then, that Paul further wrote the Ephesians: "This, therefore, I say and bear witness to in the Lord, that you no longer go on walking just as the nations also walk in the unprofitableness of their minds, while they are in darkness mentally, and alienated from the life that belongs to God." (Ephesians 4:17, 18) How difficult it must have been to live among such depraved people! But by being long-suffering, a Christian could at least lead a tolerable life.

Needed Today

We today similarly find ourselves surrounded by wickedness, materialism, and demonic influence. In fact, there is even greater pressure on Christians today because Satan has been cast down to the vicinity of the earth and is set on destroying our faith. (Revelation 12:12, 17) We must therefore pay more than the usual attention to how we walk if we are to prove worthy. And like Christians of old, we must be long-suffering. True, it is unusual for a person to show such restraint. Nevertheless, long-suffering is an evidence of God's spirit upon a Christian. "The fruitage of the spirit is . . . long-suffering," says Galatians 5:22. How, though, does it benefit us?

In Our Next Issue

■ All Men Are Equal—How?

■ Youth's Greatest Opportunity

■ Train Your Child to Develop Godly Devotion

Long-suffering helps us tolerate economic difficulties, health problems, and other pressures of 20th-century living. We know *why* such problems exist and we also know that relief is in sight! (2 Timothy 3:1-5; Luke 21:28) Even when we encounter strong opposition to the work of spreading the good news of the Kingdom, long-suffering acts like a restraining wall that not only helps us endure but also keeps our hope alive.

Following Paul's advice to "be long-suffering with joy" has also helped improve touchy domestic situations. (Colossians 1:11) At times Christians are yoked in marriage to unbelievers. Said one man: "Not only was our family life very much disturbed but I also had to endure all kinds of hardships . . . No meals were prepared . . . No clothing was cleaned and ready . . . Sometimes it was filthy language on her part toward me." But this Christian man was long-suffering. "I turned each time to Jehovah in prayer," he said, "and I trusted Him to help me develop the good quality of long-suffering in order not to lose my Christian balance . . . This has helped me to endure." The outcome? After 20 years of opposition, his wife became a Christian too! "How grateful I am to Jehovah," says this man, "that he helped me cultivate the fruit of the spirit, long-suffering."

Long-Suffering Toward One Another

Since long-suffering is a product of God's holy spirit, it is incompatible with "the works of the flesh," such as enmities, strife, jealousy, fits of anger, contentions, and envies. (Galatians 5:19-21) What results when we allow these "works" to surface and dominate in our dealings with one another?

A situation involving Moses illustrates what can happen. He was said to be "by far the meekest of all the men who were upon the surface of the ground." (Numbers 12:3) On one occasion, however, he ceased being long-suffering. When the nation's water supply ran out, the faithless people cried out: "Why have you men brought Jehovah's congregation into this wilderness for us and our beasts of burden to die there?" (Numbers 20:4) This situation required on Moses' part both restraint and sober reflection on the fact that their rebellious talk was really directed against Jehovah himself! Moses, however, allowed fleshly impulses to dominate him. Said the psalmist: "Further, they caused provocation at the waters of Meribah, so that it went badly with Moses by reason of them. For they embittered his spirit and he began to speak rashly with his lips."—Psalm 106:32, 33.

As if *he* were the miraculous provider of water, Moses bitterly said: "Hear, now, you rebels! Is it from this crag that we shall bring out water for you?" (Numbers 20:10) Yes, Moses allowed the quarrelsome and complaining spirit of others to get the better of him. And because of his loss of restraint and also his failing to glorify Jehovah, he was denied entry into the Promised Land.

Christians today must beware of falling into this snare. At times our own Christian brothers can be a source of provocation, as the Israelites were to Moses. "But a slave of the Lord does not need to fight, but needs to be gentle toward all, qualified to teach, keeping himself restrained under evil." (2 Timothy 2:24) The exhortation at 1 Thessalonians 5:14 is thus appropriate: "Be long-suffering toward all."

Worthy Examples to Imitate

Christ set a perfect example of long-suffering. He had to endure not only "contrary talk by sinners" but also problems that arose among his own disciples. (Hebrews 12:3) At times they were slow either to comprehend or to apply his teachings. Yet, never did he deal harshly with them. When on the night of his betrayal his disci-

ples fell asleep, Christ kindly exhorted them by saying: "Why are you sleeping? Rise and carry on prayer, that you do not enter into temptation."—Luke 22:46.

Since his resurrection, Jesus has continued to manifest patience and long-suffering. Saul, for example, was a persecutor of Christians, a blasphemer, and an insolent man. Yet Christ showed him mercy in a way that led to Saul's becoming a prominent follower of Christ. Paul (formerly Saul) explains: "The reason why I was shown mercy was that by means of me as the foremost case Christ Jesus might demonstrate all his long-suffering for a sample of those who are going to rest their faith on him for everlasting life."—1 Timothy 1: 15, 16.

The Scriptures tell us to "follow his [Christ's] steps closely." (1 Peter 2:21) Do you show the same patience toward fellow believers when they are slow to apply some Bible principle? Do you grant a similar long-suffering spirit toward people of the world who are ignorant of the truth? Are you moved to help such ones find the truth?

The incomparable example of long-suffering, however, is Jehovah. "Jehovah is merciful and gracious, slow to anger and abundant in loving-kindness." (Psalm 103:8; Exodus 34:5-7) Though men such as Moses became frustrated with the stubborn Israelites, Jehovah said: "All day long I have spread out my hands toward a people that is disobedient and talks back." (Romans 10:21) But there was purpose behind such long-suffering. Like a father with a wayward son, Jehovah refused to give up hope for improvement in his strained relationship with Israel. And his forbearance produced results—a remnant of that nation was saved!

Limits to Long-Suffering

God's patience is not limitless, however. Israel's persistent resistance to Jehovah's warnings resulted in their being alienated from God as a nation. Said Isaiah: "But they themselves rebelled and made his holy spirit feel hurt. He now was changed into an enemy of theirs; he himself warred against them." (Isaiah 63:10) Yes, in time "the rage of Jehovah came up against his people." (2 Chronicles 36:15, 16) His long-suffering came to its end.

This has serious implications for us today. It would be unreasonable to conclude that God will forever tolerate wrongdoing. True, as Paul says: "God, although having the will to demonstrate his wrath and to make his power known, tolerated with much long-suffering vessels of wrath made fit for destruction." Yet there has been a purpose in such toleration: to "make known the riches of his glory." (Romans 9:22, 23) Yes, as a result of God's restraint, his name has been declared throughout the earth. Also, God has announced his "day of vengeance" by means of his people. (Isaiah 61:2) It is true that many mock and ridicule this warning message, like the Epicureans and Stoics in Paul's day who said, "What is it this chatterer would like to tell?" (Acts 17:18) But remember, God will bring "vengeance upon those who do not know God and those who do not obey the good news about our Lord Jesus."—2 Thessalonians 1:8.

In the meantime, however, we must continue with the work of preaching God's judgments until God reveals that it is time to stop. We must 'exercise patience until the presence of the Lord.' (James 5:7) But patiently enduring the various evils that life in this system brings upon us will produce tangible results. It will increase our dependence upon Jehovah. It will smooth out our relationships with others and prevent needless problems from developing. Long-suffering may mean hardship, but regardless of who we are or where we may be living, whether free or imprisoned, experiencing opposition either at home or in the Christian ministry, the peace and unity that long-suffering promotes will add joy and contentment to our lives. (Ephesians 4:2) By all means, then, walk worthily with long-suffering.

Annual Meeting
October 5, 1985

THE ANNUAL MEETING of the members of the Watch Tower Bible and Tract Society of Pennsylvania on October 5, 1985, will be held at the Assembly Hall of Jehovah's Witnesses, 973 Flatbush Avenue in the Borough of Brooklyn, New York City. A preliminary meeting of the members only will be held at 9:30 a.m., followed by the general annual meeting at 10:00 a.m., Saturday, October 5, 1985.

It will be appreciated if the members of the Corporation will inform the Secretary's Office of any change in their mailing addresses during the past year so that the regular letters of notice and proxies can reach them shortly after August 15.

The proxies, which will be sent to the members along with the notice of the annual meeting, are to be returned so as to reach the Office of the Secretary of the Society not later than September 1. As each member knows, he should complete and return his proxy promptly, stating whether he is going to be at the meeting personally or not. The information given on each proxy should be definite on this point, as it will be relied upon in determining in advance those who will actually be personally present.

It is expected that the entire session, including the formal business meeting and reports, will be concluded by 1:00 p.m. or shortly thereafter. There will be no afternoon session. Due to limited space, admission will be by ticket only. No arrangements will be made for tying in the annual meeting by telephone lines to other locations.

Questions From Readers

■ How does the holy spirit work along with the modern-day Governing Body in the appointment of elders?

The apostle Paul told Christian elders from Ephesus: "Pay attention to yourselves and to all the flock, among which *the holy spirit has appointed you overseers,* to shepherd the congregation of God, which he purchased with the blood of his own Son."—Acts 20:28.

Paul did not explain in detail how God's spirit functioned in such appointments. However, we can gain insight from what occurred when the first-century governing body considered a question concerning circumcision. In summarizing their conclusion, they wrote: "For *the holy spirit* and we ourselves have favored adding no further burden to you, except these necessary things." (Acts 15:28) How did God's spirit, his impersonal active force, contribute to the binding decision reached at that time?

Acts chapter 15 shows that first Paul and Barnabas outlined the question. Then a discussion took place. The apostle Peter related what had led up to baptism of the uncircumcised Gentile Cornelius and his household. Peter explained that 'God bore witness by giving them the holy spirit, just as he did to us also.' (Acts 15:7, 8; 10:9-48) Next Paul and Barnabas 'related the many signs and portents that God did through them among the nations.' (Acts 15:12) Thus, by its operation on Peter, Cornelius, Paul, and Barnabas, the holy spirit indicated that Gentiles did not need to be circumcised.

Yet there were additional operations of the spirit involved in that decision reached by the governing body. We can assume that they had asked for the help of the spirit on their deliberations. Such help may have moved the disciple James to recall the prophecy at Amos 9: 11, 12, and to see its application. That prophecy had, of course, been written under the inspiration of the holy spirit. (Acts 15:13-20) Furthermore, "the apostles and older men in Jerusalem" who made up the governing body were Christians who were anointed with holy spirit and who manifested its operation in their lives, such as by producing its fruits.—Acts 15:2; Romans 8:14-17; 1 Corinthians 7:40; Galatians 5: 22, 23.

So without there being some audible directive from heaven on the circumcision question, those of the governing body could accurately say that "the holy spirit" had led to their decision.

It is similar with the appointment of Christian men to be elders, or overseers, in the congregations today. Periodically a group of elders (likely including a traveling overseer of the Society) meet to consider recommending brothers for appointment as overseers. Those in the group have themselves been appointed as elders and they manifest in their lives that they have the spirit. Their discussion is opened with prayer for the spirit's guidance. Then, during the meeting, they analyze whether each brother being considered measures up to the qualifications for elders set out in the Bible, which have been recorded under the direction of holy spirit. (1 Timothy 3:2-7; Titus 1:5-9) They also consider whether the brother evidences in his manner of life that he is "full of spirit and wisdom." (Acts 6:3) If they agree that he is of that sort and meets the qualifications to a reasonable degree, their recommendation is forwarded to the spirit-designated Governing Body or its chosen representatives. Later the congregation may be informed that the brother has been appointed.

Understandably, the appointed elder is still imperfect and may have limitations. But the apostles were imperfect, both before Jesus chose them and later when they served on the governing body. (Luke 9:46, 54; 22:54-62; Galatians 2:11-14) They certainly did, though, have God's spirit and were appointed under its guidance. Comparably, brothers and sisters can be confident that 'the holy spirit has appointed the overseers, to shepherd the congregation.' (Acts 20:28) It is regarding such men that the counsel is given: "Remember those who are taking the lead among you, who have spoken the word of God to you, and as you contemplate how their conduct turns out imitate their faith."—Hebrews 13:7.

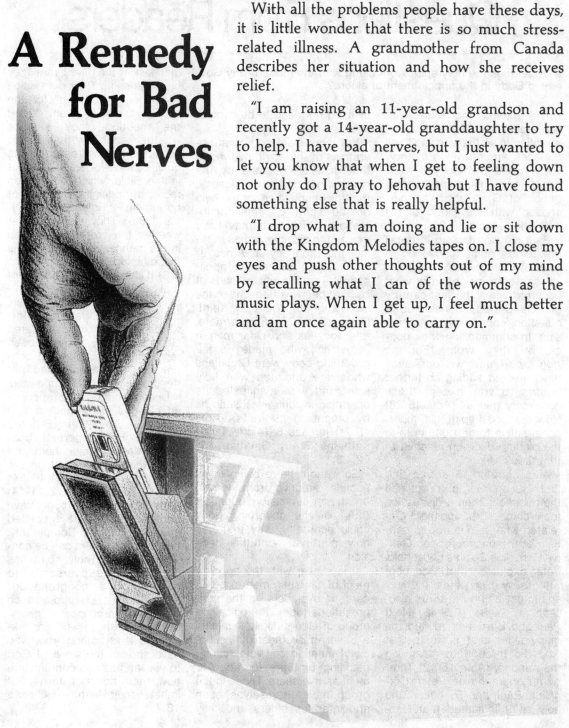

A Remedy for Bad Nerves

With all the problems people have these days, it is little wonder that there is so much stress-related illness. A grandmother from Canada describes her situation and how she receives relief.

"I am raising an 11-year-old grandson and recently got a 14-year-old granddaughter to try to help. I have bad nerves, but I just wanted to let you know that when I get to feeling down not only do I pray to Jehovah but I have found something else that is really helpful.

"I drop what I am doing and lie or sit down with the Kingdom Melodies tapes on. I close my eyes and push other thoughts out of my mind by recalling what I can of the words as the music plays. When I get up, I feel much better and am once again able to carry on."

August 15, 1985

The Watchtower

Announcing Jehovah's Kingdom

All
Men
Are
EQUAL—
How?

August 15, 1985
Vol. 106, No. 16

The Watchtower®
Announcing Jehovah's Kingdom

In This Issue

THE PURPOSE OF "THE WATCHTOWER" is to exalt Jehovah God as the Sovereign of the universe. It keeps watch on world events as they fulfill Bible prophecy. It comforts all peoples with the good news that God's Kingdom will soon destroy those who oppress their fellowmen and that it will turn the earth into a paradise. It encourages faith in the now-reigning King, Jesus Christ, whose shed blood opens the way for mankind to gain eternal life. "The Watchtower," published by Jehovah's Witnesses continuously since 1879, is nonpolitical. It adheres to the Bible as its authority.

"WATCHTOWER" STUDIES FOR THE WEEKS

September 15: Youth's Greatest Opportunity. Page 11. Songs to Be Used: 183, 157.

September 22: Train With Godly Devotion as Your Aim. Page 16. Songs to Be Used: 221, 211.

September 29: Train Your Child to Develop Godly Devotion. Page 22. Songs to Be Used: 164, 66.

Average Printing Each Issue: 11,150,000

Now Published in 103 Languages

SEMIMONTHLY EDITIONS AVAILABLE BY MAIL
Afrikaans, Arabic, Cebuano, Chichewa, Chinese, Cibemba, Danish, Dutch, Efik, English*, Finnish, French, German, Greek, Hiligaynon, Igbo, Iloko, Italian, Japanese, Korean, Lingala, Malagasy, Maltese, Norwegian, Portuguese, Russian, Sepedi, Sesotho, Shona, Spanish, Swahili, Swedish, Tagalog, Thai, Tswana, Xhosa, Yoruba, Zulu

MONTHLY EDITIONS AVAILABLE BY MAIL
Armenian, Bengali, Bicol, Bulgarian, Croatian, Czech, Ewe, Fijian, Ga, Greenlandic, Gujarati, Gun, Hausa, Hebrew, Hindi, Hiri Motu, Hungarian, Icelandic, Kannada, Kikuyu, Kiluba, Malayalam, Marathi, New Guinea Pidgin, Pangasinan, Papiamento, Polish, Rarotongan, Romanian, Samar-Leyte, Samoan, Sango, Serbian, Silozi, Sinhalese, Slovenian, Solomon Islands-Pidgin, Tahitian, Tamil, Telugu, Tshiluba, Tsonga, Turkish, Twi, Ukrainian, Urdu, Venda, Vietnamese
*Study articles also available in large-print edition at same cost.

The Bible translation used is the "New World Translation of the Holy Scriptures," unless otherwise indicated.

Watch Tower Society offices	Yearly subscription Semimonthly
America, U.S., Watchtower, Wallkill, N.Y. 12589	$4.00
Australia, Box 280, Ingleburn, N.S.W. 2565	A$6.00
Canada, Box 4100, Halton Hills (Georgetown), Ontario L7G 4Y4	$5.20
England, The Ridgeway, London NW7 1RN	£5.00
Ireland, 29A Jamestown Road, Finglas, Dublin 11	£5.00
New Zealand, 6-A Western Springs Rd., Auckland 3	$10.00
Nigeria, P.O. Box 194, Yaba, Lagos State	₦6.00
Philippines, P.O. Box 2044, Manila 2800	₱50.00
South Africa, Private Bag 2, Elandsfontein, 1406	R5,60

Remittances should be sent to the office in your country or to Watchtower, Wallkill, N.Y. 12589, U.S.A.

Changes of address should reach us 30 days before your moving date. Give us your old and new address (if possible, your old address label).

The Watchtower (ISSN 0043-1087) is published semimonthly for $4.00 (U.S.) per year by Watch Tower Bible and Tract Society of Pennsylvania, 25 Columbia Heights, Brooklyn, N.Y. 11201. Second-class postage paid at Brooklyn, N.Y., and at additional mailing offices.

Postmaster: Send address changes to Watchtower, **Wallkill, N.Y. 12589.**

Published by
Watch Tower Bible and Tract Society of Pennsylvania
25 Columbia Heights, Brooklyn, N.Y. 11201, U.S.A.
Frederick W. Franz, President

The Pursuit of Equality

NO ONE likes to feel inferior. "I am as good as the next man" is a common saying. Do we not find an air of superiority distasteful? Basically, it is reassuring to feel equal to others. However, it is easier to think and talk about equality than to attain it, as many have experienced. Consider this example.

In 1776 the English colonies in North America asserted their claim to self-government. Their famed Declaration of Independence proclaimed among "truths to be self-evident" that "all men are created equal." They further declared that it was the right of all citizens to enjoy "life, liberty, and the pursuit of happiness."

At the time that the 13 colonies broke from Britain, their population was about three million. Of these, more than half a million were slaves. It took almost a hundred years to abolish slavery in the United States of America. Thomas Jefferson, a prime mover behind the Declaration, remained a slave owner throughout his life. The aims of that Declaration were noble, yet time was needed for even *part* of such fundamental equality to be realized.

Around the earth many still lack much freedom, or they suffer discrimination. Realizing this, various individuals devote their lives to trying to remove all sorts of injustices and inequalities. One recent United Nations publication on the subject of freedom refers more than a dozen times to being equal and to the need of equality. Evidently it is still an elusive goal. Why?

The problem is that equality has many facets and is not an easy thing to define. People look for equality in different ways, depending on their circumstances. To what extent, then, can it be said that men are equal? What may we reasonably expect, both now and in the future, as to equality with our fellowman?

Equality—How Real Today?

A prince and a pauper may be born in the same city on the same day, but the silver spoon of wealth and privilege will likely favor the one just as poverty will affect the other. This is just one aspect that shows why it cannot be said that all people today are *born* equal.

Much depends upon the community in which we live and the degrees of equality it has developed over the years. The *Encyclopædia Britannica* sums it up nicely: "All societies necessarily make arrangements for the sharing of wealth, power, and other values. Among individuals and groups these arrangements exhibit all degrees of equality and inequality."

In any community, every individual has something to give that is unique to him. Some have thus sought to draw on the individual talents and abilities of all and equitably to distribute wealth and the means of production. Hence the communistic dictum: "From each according to his ability, to each according to his needs." Also: "From each according to his ability, to each according to his work." Despite the seeming appeal of such philosophies, though, inequalities persist under all human governmental systems.

The fact is that, rather than advancing the cause of equality, some political systems have sought to capitalize on supposed racial inequalities. Recall the Nazi emphasis on a "master race." Yet the existence of any master race has long since been discredited. Aside from evident differences in physical characteristics, "the possible existence of true racial differences in behaviour and intelligence becomes difficult to establish," to quote again from the *Encyclopædia Britannica*. Such racial equality is basic.

Education and Ability

Education can be a great equalizer when its facilities are readily available, but it does not always work out that way. In many countries, hard-earned money still must be paid for even the most rudimentary aspects of learning.

For example, in one country of the southern hemisphere, only 20 percent of the people are literate. It is not uncommon there to find a family in which the two oldest children are reasonably well educated but the rest receive no education at all, simply because the family budget will not allow for it. Other developing countries face similar problems.

This situation tends to sustain inequality because, in our modern society, possible advancement is economically weighted in favor of the educated. Still, degrees from some universities are more sought after than those from others because the former carry greater prestige. So education is by no means the final answer to today's problem of inequality.

Fundamental Rights

Genetic factors may determine that humans can never be identical in every respect, yet do you not agree that in certain fundamentals equality should exist? Would not mankind be much better off if progress could be made in these areas:

RACIAL EQUALITY: How can we ever overcome the stigma so often attached by one race or class to another? Resentments go deep and cause many problems. What can be done to ensure the treatment of individuals as equals, according them the dignity they deserve?

FOOD: When you see pictures of starving children and read of the millions who die each year of malnutrition or its related illnesses, how do you react? It is well established that there could be enough food for the world's population. Why, then, should there not be a more equitable distribution of it to alleviate such suffering?

WORK: Unemployment can bring heartache and frustration—even suicide. Is it not possible for all to be gainfully employed? Can there not be equal opportunity of work for all?

EDUCATION: Should not all individuals have access at least to basic education, so that illiteracy could be eliminated? Rather than tending to increase the differences between classes ('the rich getting richer and the poor, poorer'), could not education help to improve the condition of *all?* That would especially prove to be so if education covered more than technical matters, if it included morality and principles for quality human relations.

Certainly, you will agree that the pursuit of equality has a long way to go!

All Men Are Equal —How?

IS IT possible for men and women of all nations to view one another as equals —and act accordingly? Not if the present world order is anything to go by. Yet we can take heart that it *is* possible. Why? Because there are millions of Christians who have proved it to be so.

It is well known that true Christianity has been linked with equality. For example, the apostle Paul wrote: "We are no longer Jews or Greeks or slaves or free men or even merely men or women, but we are all the same—we are Christians." (Galatians 3:28, *The Living Bible*) But was this just idealistic talk? How did it work out in practice for the early Christians living in a world rife with inequalities?

Much has been written of the tremendous impact that the early Christians made upon the world of their time as they developed the brotherhood taught by Jesus Christ. Eberhard Arnold says in his book *The Early Christians After the Death of the Apostles*:

"The equal esteem in which the Christians held all their fellow-men as brothers, sharing the same judgment and the same call as themselves, resulted in equality and fellowship in all things. This equal esteem resulted in the equal title of all, the equal obligation to work, and equal opportunity in life for all. . . . The mutual esteem in which the Christians of that time held each other resulted in a social solidarity, which was founded on love, on a basis of complete equality of birth."

What a splendid testimony to a God-given unity!

Equals in a United Body

Individuals in the early Christian congregation had various natural abilities and capacities. Some may have excelled in music, while others had better memories or stronger muscles. Aside from such variety, the holy spirit imparted differing gifts and abilities, though these complemented one another. Paul could thus write: "For just as the body is one but has many members, and all the members of that body, although being many, are one body, so also is the Christ. For truly by one spirit we were all baptized into one body, whether Jews or Greeks, whether slaves or free." (1 Corinthians 12:11-13) All were preachers, even though there was rich variety in the "gifts in men," as those who shepherded the congregation were prophetically described.—Ephesians 4:8; Psalm 68:18.

The overseers were spiritually mature and called e·pi′sko·poi in Greek. Writing of the related verb e·pi·sko·pe′o (to take oversight), W. E. Vine states: "The word does not imply the entrance upon such responsibility, but the fulfilment of it. It is not a matter of assuming a position, but of the discharge of the duties." Working along with these appointed overseers were di·a′ko·noi, a Greek word translated "ministers," "ministerial servants," or "deacons." W. E. Vine says that this word "primarily denotes a servant, whether as doing servile work, or as an attendant rendering free service, without particular reference to its character." For either office, the privileges of service were the main thing. The position was not emphasized, for as worshipers of God they had equality and were all his servants.

Although Jesus chose 12 men to be his apostles, women also enjoyed association with him. They were very active, Mary Magdalene, Joanna, and Susanna being specifically spoken of as ministering to Jesus. Women, too, received the gifts of the holy spirit at Pentecost 33 C. E. They were thus able publicly to talk in foreign tongues and witness about the truths of their Christian faith. Christian sisters, however, did not take the lead in teaching in the congregations, but they shared along with the brothers in publicly preaching God's Word.—Luke 8:1-3; Acts 1:14; 2:17, 18; 18:26.

On a more personal level, too, the Christians set a precedent in helping one another. For example, when visitors to Jerusalem came in contact with the miraculous work of the apostles at the time of Pentecost 33 C.E., they stayed longer than they had intended and ran short of both food and money. Yet the Scripture record states: "There was not one in need among them; for all those who were possessors of fields or houses would sell them and bring the values of the things sold" for free distribution under the apostles' direction. What a fine spirit, revealing the love and equality of those first Christians to be a practical reality! It could be said that "they had all things in common."—Acts 4: 32, 34, 35.

Practical Equality Today

Amid the divisions and social structures of the world today, attempting to imitate those early Christians is not easy. But to do so has always been a goal of Jehovah's Witnesses. That they have had considerable success is apparent. The *Encyclopedia Canadiana* observes:

"The work of Jehovah's Witnesses is the revival and re-establishment of the primitive Christianity practised by Jesus and his disciples during the first and second centuries of our era. . . . All are brothers."

Just as it did 1,900 years ago, this Christian brotherhood today gives practical aid in times of trouble. When, in November 1980, parts of Italy were rocked by a severe earthquake, the first truckload of supplies prepared by the Witnesses arrived in the stricken area the same evening. An official report reads:

"The brothers were amazed at how quickly the necessary help arrived. We immediately set up our own kitchen from which food cooked by sisters was distributed to the brothers every day. The other inhabitants of the town had yet to receive assistance and were doing the best they could for themselves. Of course, the brothers were not selfish, and food was shared with many non-Witnesses."

Following the death of Swaziland's King Sobhuza II in August 1982, Jehovah's Witnesses, because they would not share in traditional religious mourning customs, were subjected to persecutions. In Britain two Witnesses, one white and the other black, made joint representation to the local Swaziland High Commission in seeking to alleviate the situation. After listening for a while, the Swazi official turned to the black Witness, a well-educated executive, and asked: "But why are you here?" Came the reply: "Because I am concerned about the well-being of my Christian brothers in your country." The official found it difficult to understand how such an affluent man could equate himself with Africans living in a country he had never even visited.

Why not attend a meeting at your local Kingdom Hall or a larger convention and see for yourself? You will find a society in which you are welcome whether young or old, rich or poor, whether you have had a

At meetings of Jehovah's Witnesses, you will observe equality

college education or you have had no schooling at all. Each one is called brother or sister, and the individual is not measured by race, background, or secular position. Each is appreciated for his Christian personality and qualities.

With appointed elders and ministerial servants, the pattern of teaching is based on the structure of the first Christian congregation. And the meetings reflect equality, or harmony, earth wide. Commented one Church of England clergyman:

"Every meeting, whether formal or informal, is a meeting for intensive instruction. Members are expected to prepare for their Sunday meetings by reading through the *Watchtower* article, checking Bible references and working out answers to the questions of which they have advance knowledge. At the meetings themselves, there is good congregational participation. They are supported by the knowledge that the same teaching is being promulgated everywhere in the world at the same time."

If you take this issue of *The Watchtower* with you to the local congregation on the dates listed on page 2, you will be able to follow such a discussion.

These discussions often embrace the hope of those in the congregation: life on a paradise earth where wars will cease and people will put their talents to constructive activity, truly enjoying "the work of their own hands." All obedient humans will live under the rule of the Kingdom of God. Starvation will be gone as food in abundance is provided for all from a bountiful earth. The scourges of disease will also be things of the past, all of earth's inhabitants enjoying equally the vitality of perfect health.—Isaiah 2:4; 33:24; 65: 22, 23; Zechariah 8:11, 12.

Yes, this Christian hope is real, as is the knowledge that the present structure of the Christian congregation will be carried through into the earthly Paradise. The solid foundation already laid for the complete removal of all class and national barriers will be enlarged. How can we be sure? Because the Bible foretells that Christians "out of all nations and tribes and peoples and tongues" will then continue their true worship of Jehovah God. They will have an equal standing before him. You and your family can be among them.—Revelation 7:9, 10.

Trips to Jerusalem

SPRING has arrived. And it is time for Joseph's family, along with friends and relatives, to make their yearly trip to Jerusalem to celebrate the Passover. As they leave on what is about a 65-mile (105-km) journey, there is the usual excitement. Jesus is now 12 years old, and he looks forward with special interest to the festival.

To Jesus and his family, the Passover is not just a one-day affair. They also stay for the following seven-day Festival of Unfermented Cakes, which they consider part of the Passover season. So the entire trip from their home in Nazareth, including the stay in Jerusalem, takes about two weeks. But this year, due to something that involves Jesus, it takes longer.

The problem comes to light on the return trip from Jerusalem. Joseph and Mary assume that Jesus is in the group of relatives or friends traveling together. Yet he does not show up when they stop for the night, and they go hunting for him among their traveling companions. He is nowhere to be found. So Joseph and Mary go all the way back to Jerusalem to look for him.

For a whole day they hunt but without success. The second day they cannot find him either. Finally, on the third day, they go to the temple. There, in one of its halls,

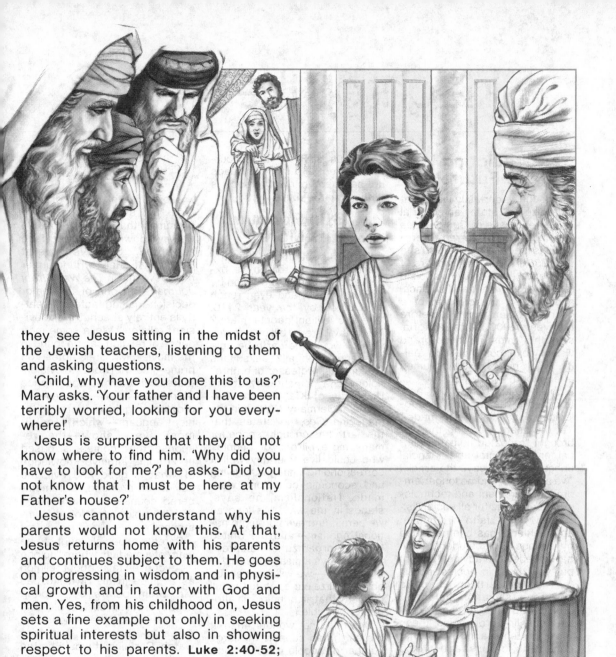

they see Jesus sitting in the midst of the Jewish teachers, listening to them and asking questions.

'Child, why have you done this to us?' Mary asks. 'Your father and I have been terribly worried, looking for you everywhere!'

Jesus is surprised that they did not know where to find him. 'Why did you have to look for me?' he asks. 'Did you not know that I must be here at my Father's house?'

Jesus cannot understand why his parents would not know this. At that, Jesus returns home with his parents and continues subject to them. He goes on progressing in wisdom and in physical growth and in favor with God and men. Yes, from his childhood on, Jesus sets a fine example not only in seeking spiritual interests but also in showing respect to his parents. **Luke 2:40-52; 22:7.**

♦ What springtime trip did Jesus regularly make with his family, and how long did it take?

♦ What happened during the trip when Jesus was 12 years old?

♦ What example did Jesus set for youths today?

Insight on the News

Predicting the Future

"The future certainly isn't what it used to be!" states an editorial in a recent issue of *Compressed Air Magazine*. It referred to predictions made from the 1930's to the 1950's, when "the thinkers of the period had virtually a blind faith in government and science, and foresaw the creation of a nearly Utopian lifestyle before the year 2000." The editorial says that "most of these grand visions never come close to reality." Why not? It was assumed after World War II that "all . . . problems were behind us," and, admittedly, "astounding technological advances were made." Yet the years following the war brought "repeated human, political, environmental and financial upheaval." Now, says the article, "we are wiser, and no longer embrace government and technology as panaceas for all social ills."

Such "blind faith" in human achievements has been avoided by serious Bible students who have heeded the advice: "Do not put your trust in nobles, nor in the son of earthling man, to whom no salvation belongs." (Psalm 146:3) Based on the Bible's unfailing prophecies, these Bible students announced that conditions of this age would worsen, until God stepped in and replaced all human rulerships with his Kingdom.—Daniel 2:44; Matthew 24:6-8, 14.

Although faced with the same social upheavals around them, servants of God do not have the "uncertain resignation" that the writer mentions. Rather, they follow Jesus' advice: "Raise yourselves erect and lift your heads up, because your deliverance is getting near."—Luke 21:28.

Still Room for More

Earth's population, recently estimated at 4.5 billion, is expected to increase to 6 billion by the year 2000, and even reach 10.5 billion by the year 2110. "Are 4.5 billion people many? Too many? Are 10 billion unbearable or would the earth be able to support them all?" asks Hans W. Jürgens, professor of anthropology and demography at the University of Kiel, Federal Republic of Germany. Writing in the magazine *Geo,* he states that the earth has enough "space for many more billions of people," who could live tolerably well if corresponding changes in living and economic conditions were made. Nationalism, he says, stands in the way. "As long as we permit and even promote national egotism—and the United Nations organization unintentionally plays a disastrous role in this matter—we will scarcely be able to utilize our earth to the full capacity that, in principle, is altogether possible."

One need not wonder, then, if the earth can support the large number of people who, in God's due time, will be released from mankind's common grave. (John 5:28, 29; Revelation 20:12, 13) They will be brought back, not to an earth divided by selfish, nationalistic interests, but to one that is righteous, peaceful, and capable of providing abundant food for all.—Psalm 72:7, 8, 16.

"Religious Wasteland"

People in television dramas face "the same problems and dilemmas that ordinary people walking down the street face each day." So says novelist Benjamin J. Stein, writing under the above title in *The Wall Street Journal.* "But one of the major decision-making factors in reality is entirely absent from television: religion." While some incidence of religion can be found in the movies, Mr. Stein notes, "on prime-time network television, there is virtually no appearance of religion at all. Whenever a problem requiring moral judgment appears—which is on almost every show—the response that comes is based upon some intuitive knowledge of what is good and evil, the advice of a friend, a remembered counsel, or, more likely, the invisible hand of circumstance."

Parents especially ought to be wary of a medium where "no one . . . ever even talks about religion as a guide in his own life," as Mr. Stein points out. Young minds are impressionable and tend to imitate the actions and views of celebrities that they watch. Certainly it would be the prudent course to monitor carefully what is watched on TV. Even more important, parents do well to train their children to use the Bible as their guide. Children need to be brought up "in the discipline and mental-regulating of Jehovah."—Ephesians 6:4; Philippians 4:8.

Youth's Greatest Opportunity

"Godly devotion is beneficial for all things, as it holds promise of the life now and that which is to come. Faithful and deserving of full acceptance is that statement."—1 TIMOTHY 4:8, 9.

WHAT is the greatest opportunity that life holds out to you? Recent surveys of a cross section of young people reveal that the majority consider "getting a job that I enjoy" and "being very well-off financially" to be their most important goals. Increasing numbers of youths are career-minded, and in some places they are entering universities in record numbers in a quest for well-paying jobs. Many look to such material opportunities to find security, strength, and fulfillment in life. If you are a youth, is that how you feel? And how do you who are adults, especially parents, *really* consider such opportunities? Are these the key to the "good life"?

2 If ever young people needed strength and fulfillment, it is now during these "last days" when times are "hard to deal with." (2 Timothy 3:1-5) Today's young folks have grown up under stresses that would have been unimaginable a generation ago. The rapid changes in society, such as the breakdown of family life and morals, have caused great emotional turmoil.

1, 2. (a) What do many youths consider important opportunities, and what questions are raised? (b) Why are there special pressures on today's youth?

The Need for Strength and Fulfillment

3 More and more young people find that they lack the inner strength to cope with the pressures of life. (Compare Ephesians 3:16.) A recent National Institute of Mental Health report concludes that one out of five youths is seriously depressed.* From 1961 to 1975, the rate of juvenile suicide in the United States more than doubled! In that one land nearly 8,000 youths die by their own hands annually, yet 50 times that number attempt suicide. Some authorities call the problem a pandemic. Reports also show that a surprising number of youths are being admitted to mental hospitals.#

------
* "A number of experts in adolescent development and behavior see such depression as a major contributing factor to serious teen problems such as truancy and trouble at school, drug and alcohol abuse, sexual acting out, pregnancy, running away from home and suicide," reports author Kathleen McCoy in *Coping with Teenage Depression*.

While in the United States the number of admissions of all age groups has declined during a 13-year period, the 15-24 age group increased 19 percent, and the under-15 group increased 158 percent!

3, 4. What evidence shows that many youths lack inner strength, and why do material advantages not provide such?

THE WATCHTOWER—AUGUST 15, 1985   11

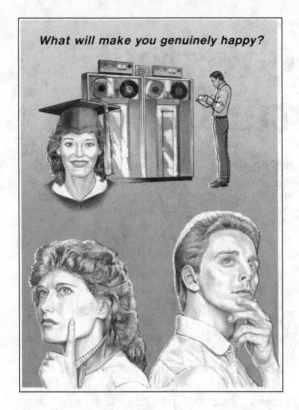

What will make you genuinely happy?

things eventually bring satisfaction, the "good life"? Wealthy King Solomon admitted: "I, even I, turned toward all the works of mine that my hands had done and toward the hard work that I had worked hard to accomplish, and, look! everything was vanity and a striving after wind." (Ecclesiastes 2:3-11) Though his attainments brought him some pleasure, he still sensed a feeling of emptiness, of vanity.

⁶ Many today herald higher education as one of the keys to the future "good life." One former U.S. state governor even called such schooling "a necessity for strength, fulfillment and survival." Is it really? Well, 846 graduates from a prestigious university compiled a "class report" about how they were faring ten years after being graduated. "While jolly good cheer spreads through the report," observed one class member, "there is an underlay of pessimism, bitterness and even despair." After 25 years, one graduate had achieved "certain financial goals," but he admitted: "The failures in my own personal life so outnumber the successes that both will mercifully go unreported." Is this the best that life offers?

The Greatest Opportunity

⁷ In his inspired letters to the Christian disciple Timothy, the apostle Paul pointed to something much better. This young man had been assigned to serve in Ephesus, one of the greatest commercial centers in ancient times. What careers he must have seen! He himself could have striven to become a prosperous merchant or sought fame either at the school of Tyrannus or in the local theater. (1 Timothy 1:3; Acts 19:1, 9, 29) Timothy could

⁴ Of course, not all young people live in circumstances that offer material opportunities. However, when you consider that the reports mentioned earlier involve a major country where material opportunities abound, it is clear that such alone do not help young people to 'remove vexation from their heart and calamity from their flesh.' (Ecclesiastes 11: 9, 10) Material advantages supply little strength to a person whose heart is plagued with discouraging self-doubts, insecurities, or guilts. The Bible observes: "Have you shown yourself discouraged in the day of distress? Your power will be scanty."—Proverbs 24:10.

⁵ But will laying hold on material

5, 6. Will gaining material things bring the "good life" in the future? Illustrate.

7. For what careers could Timothy have trained, but what did Paul recommend?

no doubt have trained for a lucrative secular career, but Paul wrote: "Be training yourself with godly devotion as your aim. For bodily training is beneficial for a little; but godly devotion is beneficial for all things, as it holds promise of the life now and that which is to come." Yes, godly devotion is "beneficial for *all* things." This was not mere speculation, for Paul added: "Faithful and deserving of full acceptance is that statement." From personal experience, Paul knew what would open up the best way of life.—1 Timothy 4:7-9; 2 Corinthians 6:10.

8 What is this godly devotion? It is personal attachment to God springing from a heart stirred by deep appreciation of his appealing qualities. While "godly fear" (Hebrews 12:28) means primarily reverential dread of doing anything displeasing to God, "godly devotion" is a response of the heart that will move you to live in a way that pleases God because you love him.* Such a quality of the heart leads to an "intimacy with God," a personal relationship wherein you sense his approval and help. (Job 29:4) The opportunity to have this personal friendship with God is more valuable than anything else that may be offered to you.—Compare Jeremiah 9:23, 24.

9 Does having godly parents or getting baptized as a Christian automatically bring about this relationship with God? No, because sincerity of heart must be

---

* "The spontaneous feeling of the heart [toward God]" is how the *Lexicon* by Edward Robinson defines the original Greek word *eu·se′bei·a.* J. A. H. Tittmann, in his *Remarks on the Synonyms of the New Testament,* adds: "[Godly devotion] expresses that reverence for the Deity which shows itself in actions, . . . but [godly fear] indicates that disposition, which dreads and avoids the doing of any thing contrary to right, . . . [godly devotion] is the energy of piety in the life."

8, 9. (a) What is godly devotion? (b) What is your greatest opportunity, and why is effort needed to take advantage of it?

cultivated, along with other Christian virtues. (2 Peter 1:5-8) You must become a person 'whose heart impels' him to render "deeds of godly devotion." (Compare Exodus 36:2; 2 Peter 3:11; Colossians 3:22.) Though reared from infancy in the way of the truth, Timothy had to develop godly devotion. Today, too, rigorous effort is necessary, yet this godly devotion will prove to be "a means of great gain." (1 Timothy 6:6) How so?

An Elevated Way of Life

10 In Ephesus, Timothy pursued godly devotion among people who were 'walking in the unprofitableness of their minds.' (Ephesians 4:17) What filled their minds was of no real profit but was vanity. "What a picture!" states Bible scholar R. C. H. Lenski about Ephesians 4:17. "Men with thinking, willing minds, rational creatures, walking and walking on and on throughout life, following the dictates of a mind that leads them at every step and at the end to nothing, to monumental, tragic failure!"

11 Timothy could see that the Ephesians' course of life was vain and debasing. Many worshiped the goddess Artemis, but their fanatical worship was directed to a lifeless image. It included wild orgies and ceremonial prostitution. (Acts 19:23-34) Timothy's way of life, though, was elevated above that of the nations, who were "alienated from the life that belongs to God . . . [and] past all moral sense." (Ephesians 2:6; 4:18, 19) His godly course in living "the life that belongs to God" had given him the greatest Friend in the universe! The opportunity to develop this relationship with the *living* God through godly devotion is most precious indeed! Can you lay hold on it?

10, 11. How did godly devotion elevate Timothy's life?

Timothy trained with godly devotion as his aim. This elevated his life above that of the immoral Ephesians

¹² Many today worship sex, pleasure, riches, and higher education with the same intensity that the ancient Ephesians did Artemis. (Matthew 6:24; Ephesians 5:3-5; Philippians 3:19) However, those pursuing godly devotion enjoy a superior quality of life. "I look at the kids I used to run around with before I began to study the Bible," reports one 24-year-old Christian. "Half of them are in jail. Most are on drugs, and many of the girls have illegitimate babies. Their lives are a mess. Several are even dead. I am so thankful to be able to look at my life and be proud of what I see." Other Christian youths heartily agree!

¹³ Those who live with godly devotion have the treasure of the ministry. (2 Corinthians 4:1, 7; 2 Timothy 4:5) This provides real purpose and challenge. Rather than the pseudo excitement of some fic-

tional TV or movie drama, Christians involved in the ministry visit the homes of *real* people to help them. They deal also with *real* problems. What indescribable joy as they see people who have lived immoral, violent, or hopeless lives respond to Bible instruction and put away former bad habits, develop self-respect, and serve Jehovah. No other career is as meaningful or produces such lasting good!

Contentment and a Clean Conscience

¹⁴ "To be sure, it is a means of great gain, this godly devotion along with self-sufficiency. . . . So, having sustenance and covering, we shall be content with these things. However, those who are determined to be rich . . . have stabbed themselves all over with many pains." (1 Timothy 6:6-10) In 1981 a survey by *Psychology Today* revealed that young people think "much more" about money than any other age group. However, *half*

---

12. What did one Christian youth say about the "great gain" of godly devotion? How do you feel about that?
13. Why does following the command at 2 Timothy 4:5 add meaning to life?

14, 15. How does godly contentment as to money make for a better life?

the group of respondents who were most concerned about money (including wealthy and poor) complained of "constant worry and anxiety."

15 A young man in Japan succeeded in going from 'rags to riches,' but in doing so he damaged his health. Later, with the help of a Bible study, he developed godly devotion. "When I think back to when my chief goal in life was to become wealthy, there is no comparison as to how much happier I've been since I changed my goal," he concludes. "Truly there is nothing that can match the contentment and satisfaction that come with using one's life in the service of the Grand Creator."* —Proverbs 10:22; Ecclesiastes 5:10-12.

16 Paul urged Timothy to 'hold a good conscience.' How? One way was for him to treat women "with all chasteness." (1 Timothy 1:19; 5:2) However, chastity has all but vanished from among many youths as their consciences have become seared. (1 Timothy 4:2) But immorality does not bring inner peace and satisfaction. One study considered the sexual attitudes and conduct of several hundred adolescents. Concerning those who were the most sexually promiscuous, the report stated: "They believe they are functioning with little purpose and self-contentment." Nearly half of these felt: "The way I'm living right now, most of my abilities are going to waste."

17 If, in time, a couple pursue honorable marriage, they will be benefited by showing "love out of a clean heart and out of a good conscience." (1 Timothy 1:5) In 1984 the *Journal of Marriage and the Family*

---

* Read the life story of Shozo Mima, "Finding Something Better Than Wealth," in *The Watchtower* of March 1, 1978.

16. What is the result to those who fail to 'hold a good conscience'?
17. Why does 'love out of a good conscience' help us to get the best out of life?

reported that a study of 309 recently married couples showed that premarital sex was associated with "significantly lower marital satisfaction for both spouses." But what a contrast with those who are chaste! "It is such a beautiful feeling looking back and knowing I am clean," states one young Christian wife who has now been happily married for seven years. Yes, a clean conscience is a rich reward to youths who "become an example . . . in chasteness."—1 Timothy 4:12.

Inner Strength

18 No doubt Timothy met with many pressures in Ephesus. The temptations of the prosperous and immoral city with its emphasis on 'fun and games' could bring external stress. Timothy's apparent diffidence as well as his "frequent cases of sickness" certainly created pressures within him. (1 Timothy 5:23) But Paul reminded him: "God gave us not a spirit of cowardice, but that of power and of love and of soundness of mind."—2 Timothy 1:7.

19 Indeed, how many of your peers yearn for such strength! One young woman fully overcame a life of prostitution and drug addiction. "It was only by Jehovah's help," she said. "There are certain times I will get those old feelings back, but I just

---

18, 19. (a) Timothy had to deal with what pressures? (b) How did God help him?

start praying—immediately. The ability to overcome these problems is more exciting than anything I have ever accomplished in my life!" No question about it, God can 'infuse power' into you and give you the inner strength to cope with any pressure and to make sound decisions. —2 Timothy 4:17.

20 So godly devotion brings you a host of benefits. Your "course of life" takes on a purpose that towers over the goals of those who reach only for material opportunities. (2 Timothy 3:10) As one Christian youth who gave up a college scholarship and became a full-time evangelizer exclaimed: "I have the best career anyone could want, being a teacher of the good news and helping others to learn of our loving Father! And the 'fringe benefit' —my own improved personality—is better than anyone could offer. Add to that the reward of living in a paradise forever with no more sorrows. Now ask: What better life could anyone ever want?"

21 You may say, 'How can I develop godly devotion?' For an answer, read the following article.

20, 21. (a) Relate some of the benefits of godly devotion. (b) What will be considered in the following article?

Train With Godly Devotion as Your Aim

"Be training yourself with godly devotion as your aim."—1 TIMOTHY 4:7.

SHE was the best runner on the team in her event. Previous victories had given her a national rating. So it was expected that she would win at this distinguished track meet. However, to the disappointment of her coach, teammates, and herself, she ran the worst race of her career. Why? "I slouched off in practice and stopped training hard," admitted the young woman, deeply embarrassed. "My coach tried to push me to do harder workouts and warned me, but I did not listen." Her failure to train properly cost her the victory for which she was aiming.

2 As a Christian, particularly if you are young, you also have a vital training. "Be training yourself with godly devotion as your aim." (1 Timothy 4:7) The Greek word for "be training" (gy·mna′zo) described the strenuous and often painful exercises that athletes performed in the gymnasium. Therefore, regarding godly devotion and its rewards, the apostle Paul added: "To this end we are working hard and exerting ourselves." (1 Timothy 4:10) This essential quality is not something that just comes naturally or that rubs off

---

1. Why did one good runner fail to win?

2. In what way must Christians train, and why should all want to know how?

from godly parents. But what steps must you take? Christians of all ages should want to know.

Good Communication With God

³ Since godly devotion involves heartfelt appreciation for Jehovah's qualities, you need to know what he is really like. Jehovah communicates this in the Bible. But you must carefully study his Word and Bible-based publications, thereby being "nourished with the words of the faith and of the fine teaching." (1 Timothy 4:6) Such study will help you to see "the pleasantness of Jehovah."—Psalm 27:4.

⁴ "It makes you feel closer to Jehovah the more you learn about him," states a 22-year-old, full-time evangelizer (pioneer). "When I read prophecies and see how they are fulfilled, it makes me stand in awe of him. Personal study is what really helps me." A 16-year-old, who had been severely depressed, wrote about one of the articles in the series "Young People Ask" that appears regularly in the *Awake!* magazine: "Just when I had given up all hope, this article came out. I was so excited I could not put it down! It made me feel so much closer to Jehovah, and I realized that he understands and cares very much. I feel now I can cope."* Do you make it a point to read each issue of our journals? Though it requires exertion, do you make time to nourish your mind and heart by personal Bible study? By doing your own research, you can really prove for yourself that you have the truth. When such knowledge reaches the heart, it almost

---

* "Why Do I Get So Depressed?" in the August 22, 1982, issue of *Awake!,* companion magazine of *The Watchtower.*

3. (a) Why is personal study so important? (b) What qualities of God draw you to him?
4. What experiences show the value of personal study, and what questions should you seriously consider?

Some Qualities of Our Warmhearted God

■ He has feelings. Therefore, our actions can cause him either to "feel hurt" or to rejoice.—Psalm 78:40; Proverbs 27:11.

■ While humans often look just at another's appearance, he "sees what the heart is."—1 Samuel 16:7.

■ He cares for us and invites us to throw our anxieties upon him, and he is "a stronghold in the day of distress."—Nahum 1:7; 1 Peter 5:7.

■ He is called "the happy God," and he "takes delight" in his servants.—1 Timothy 1:11; Psalm 35:27.

■ He will never act unjustly or show partiality.—Job 34:10; Acts 10:34, 35.

■ While not condoning wrongdoing, when we repent over a mistake or a weakness, he is "ready to forgive," not doing "to us even according to our sins" nor bringing "upon us what we deserve."—Psalm 86:5; 103:8-14.

■ He is approachable, and he encourages his loyal creatures to use their abilities. Despite his infinite wisdom, he listens to suggestions. "Your own humility will make me great," wrote King David.—Psalm 18:35; 1 Kings 22:19-22.

---

certainly will motivate you, for it is "the teaching that accords with godly devotion."—1 Timothy 6:3; Romans 12:2.

⁵ Good communication with God also involves heartfelt and specific prayers. These help toward building a personal friendship with Jehovah. When you make mistakes, be willing to plead as did David: "The sins of my youth and my revolts O do not remember." (Psalm 25:7, 11) And know that he will forgive you if you are repentant. Learn to linger in prayer, pouring out your heart. One youth, though reared in a godly home, had allowed a

---

5, 6. What kind of prayers draw you closer to God? Illustrate.

speech impediment to hinder her involvement in the true religion. "Then one night," revealed this 22-year-old, "I begged Jehovah, 'Help me to want to serve you, and not just because the elders or my parents want me to.'" How her life began to change! Despite her stuttering, she became fully involved in the ministry. Joyfully she declares, "I trust in Jehovah a whole lot more now because I know he always comes through."—Psalm 62:8.

6 One young Christian prayed specifically regarding her plans to pioneer. When her prayers were answered, she exclaimed: "I knew Jehovah was real and that he cares for us! Before this I thought I had a relationship with him, but now he is more like a friend—my best one." Jehovah will not always answer in some spectacular way, but if you are earnest and work in harmony with your prayers, you will come to appreciate his loving guidance.—Psalm 145:18.

Hold a Good Conscience

7 When Paul urged Timothy to continue "holding . . . a good conscience," the apostle knew that it would require determined effort. (1 Timothy 1:19) Why so? Our conscience is our God-given capacity to examine ourselves and pass judgment on what we have done or contemplate doing. It can either 'accuse' us, painfully condemning our course, or 'excuse' us, approving what we do as right. (Romans 2:15) But if it becomes warped, it can send out defective messages. Some with defective consciences can act like ruthless animals, yet the 'inner voice' does not 'accuse' them. They can even "publicly declare they know God" but "disown him by their works." How can you guard against developing a defective conscience?—Titus 1:10-16.

---

7. What is the conscience, and why must you hold a good one?

8 Paul had told Timothy that some Christians had "thrust aside" their good conscience by 'paying attention to false stories' and "empty speeches that violate what is holy." (1 Timothy 1:4, 19, 20; 6:20; 2 Timothy 2:16-18) Because they listened to these things, their faith was subverted, and this resulted in spiritual shipwreck. Paul, however, showed that other things besides apostate teachings were "in opposition to the healthful teaching." At 1 Timothy 1:9, 10 he lists such things as murder, fornication, and homosexuality.

9 Today violence and sexual immorality pervade movie and TV presentations as well as the printed page. If we feed our mind on such, our conscience can gradually become seared. This happened to a young Christian couple who committed fornication shortly before their wedding day. "I think it had to do with what we had been watching on TV," admitted the young woman. "You see persons all the time necking and petting, so it does not seem to be serious. You get used to it. So we started doing it. If I had only thought more about how serious it was!" Before she realized it, she lost her good conscience. The young man added: "I also had a problem with masturbation, and this sears your conscience so it is not so hard to engage in necking and petting and then finally in fornication." Though they seemed to be setting a good example before others, what they watched for entertainment, together with a secret unclean practice, had worked toward deadening the conscience just as flesh is cauterized by repeated touches from a red-hot branding iron.—1 Timothy 4:2.

---

8. How did some in the first century "thrust aside" a good conscience?
9, 10. (a) What can be learned from the example of a Christian couple who failed to hold a good conscience? (b) How can we prevent our conscience from becoming seared?

¹⁰ Could your conscience be similarly deadened by what you watch or read for entertainment? Are you really working hard to overcome any bad habit that could defile your conscience? For your protection, you could take positive action by reading—and rereading—Bible-based literature that specially deals with your problem or by discussing the problem with an elder. A good, clean conscience is a precious gift from God that will help you to develop godly devotion. Do not let anything cause you to lose it!

Choose Proper Associates

¹¹ The apostle Paul writes: "In a large house [the congregation] there are vessels not only of gold and silver but also of wood and earthenware, and some for an honorable purpose but others for a purpose lacking honor. If, therefore, anyone keeps clear of the latter ones, he will be a vessel for an honorable purpose, sanctified, useful to his owner, prepared for every good work." (2 Timothy 2:20, 21) Our emotions and conduct are greatly affected by those whom we choose as friends. Obviously, unbelievers are not the best associates. But Paul here shows frankly that even within the congregation there could be

11, 12. (a) What warning is given at 2 Timothy 2:20, 21? (b) How can you heed that warning?

In Our Next Issue

■ **Belief in God—Is It Enough?**

■ **My Family's Love for God Despite Prison and Death**

■ **Kingdom Ministers Meet the Challenge**

persons who are undesirable associates. True, you may find such ones fun to be around, but their influence will never help you to "flee from the desires incidental to youth" or to develop godly devotion. Reach out for upbuilding associates within the congregation. Paul continues in verse 22: "Pursue righteousness, faith, love, peace, along with those who call upon the Lord out of a clean heart."—Compare Philippians 4:8, 9.

¹² Take the case of one Christian youth who, despite godly training, was always getting into trouble. "It was largely because of the people I was associating with," she said. When she saw her life becoming a failure, she changed her friends. She concludes: "If you have friends around you who love Jehovah, it helps you to keep a sensitive conscience and stay out of trouble. When they express disgust for wrongdoing, it makes you feel the same way." By keeping clear of questionable associates, she has become a vessel "useful to [her] owner, prepared for every good work." Having served for ten years as a pioneer, she adds: "I find that now Jehovah has used me to help others."—2 Timothy 2:21; Proverbs 15:31.

¹³ Hence, realistically consider your associates. Do they pursue righteousness, faith, principled love, and peace? Are they full of Christian zeal? By making such ones your close companions, you yourself may become an example in speaking, in conduct, in love, in faith, in chasteness, just as did Timothy, the close associate of Paul. This does not mean that you should become cold or unfriendly toward less exemplary ones. Your joyful example may stir these, also, to make straight paths for their feet.—1 Timothy 4:12; Hebrews 12:12-15.

13. How can you determine who are good associates, and how may they influence you?

Many Christians find deeper joy in the ministry than in high-paying jobs

Make Sacrifices for God

¹⁴ During Timothy's day, while athletes were in training they exercised "self-control in all things," denying themselves many legitimate pleasures. (1 Corinthians 9:25) They followed a strict diet. According to Horace, poet of the first century B.C.E., they "abstained from women and wine" to "reach the longed-for goal." Similarly, to train with godly devotion as your aim requires sacrifice. Paul said of Timothy: "I have no one else of a disposition like his . . . for all the others are seeking their own interests, not those of Christ Jesus. But . . . he slaved with me in furtherance of the good news."—Philippians 2:19-22.

¹⁵ Timothy was commanded: "Do the work of an evangelizer, fully accomplish your ministry." (2 Timothy 4:5) Regardless of how appealing any of his personal interests might have been, he sacrificed these to complete God's work. Are you willing to do the same? Today some young Christians who are free of heavy Scriptural responsibilities have pursued higher education or high-paying full-time jobs rather than making the Christian ministry their career. One of these was eagerly awaiting such a job. However, before he started work, he accepted the invitation to work with a pioneer couple in the field service all summer. He loved it. As a result, he sacrificed that coveted full-time job and took less interesting part-time work in order to pioneer. With this same Timothy-like spirit, he now serves at the world headquarters of Jehovah's Witnesses. The willingness to sacrifice is evidence of genuine love, and the sacrifices deepen that love, as he found out.

¹⁶ As "a preacher and an apostle," Paul emphasized the desirability of modesty in

---

14, 15. (a) What was required of ancient athletes while training? (b) What work requires sacrifice, and what good examples do we have?

16. What are some sacrifices that young people may have to make?

dress. Would you be willing to sacrifice a certain style of dress or grooming that could upset others or hinder your effectiveness as a preacher? (1 Timothy 2:7-10) Continuing, Paul wrote: "All those desiring to live with godly devotion . . . will also be persecuted." (2 Timothy 3:12) Are you willing to stand up for the truth when it may mean ridicule, sacrificing a favored position with your classmates? All such sacrifices done with the right motive will help you to develop godly devotion and at the same time teach you to rely on Jehovah and consider his feelings above all else.

Keep Advancing

¹⁷ Developing godly devotion is an ongoing process. Paul told Timothy: "Ponder over these things; be absorbed in them, that your advancement may be manifest to all persons." (1 Timothy 4:15) Some, because of being too young to be a ministerial servant or an elder, may feel unable to advance, thinking that progress is measured solely by congregational responsibilities and privileges. True, Timothy had qualified not only in spiritual development but also in years to serve as an elder. But Timothy was to continue applying himself, and in this he set an outstanding example for all young ministers to follow in whatever field may be open to them. —1 Timothy 4:12, 13.

¹⁸ So, like Timothy, you maturing servant of Jehovah can be "an example to the faithful ones" by letting the truth deeply influence the way you live and by improving in your ministry. Right now you can strive to advance by learning to cultivate such qualities as being moderate in habits, orderly, hospitable, and serious. By mak-

---

17. In making advancement, how was Timothy an example for young ministers today?
18. In what ways can young Christians make advancement?

ing yourself available to the elders and by taking seriously any task they ask you to perform, you can work toward proving your 'fitness under test.' (1 Timothy 3:1, 2, 8-10) Even if your progress is not quickly recognized by others, be assured that Jehovah sees. In time, others will also. —1 Timothy 5:25.

¹⁹ Never forget that it is by developing godly devotion that you may attain to an approved personal relationship with Jehovah. Lack of spiritual training results in a loss far greater than that of the embarrassed runner mentioned at the outset of this article. Developing godly devotion is hard work. But all over the world, multitudes of joyful young voices thunder: IT IS WORTH ALL THE EFFORT! Gaining this quality leads to a satisfying way of life now, with no regrets, and it opens up the hope of eternal happiness. So keep training. Continue to do your best, even when it is difficult. Take comfort that "the God of all undeserved kindness . . . will himself finish your training, he will make you firm, he will make you strong. To him be the might forever. Amen."—1 Peter 5: 10, 11.

---

19. Despite the effort, why should you train with godly devotion as your aim?

Can You Answer?

□ What effort is needed to maintain good communication with God?

□ What is involved in holding a good conscience?

□ How may 2 Timothy 2:20-22 be applied in developing godly devotion?

□ How can young Christians make advancement?

Train Your Child to Develop Godly Devotion

"Train up a boy according to the way for him; even when he grows old he will not turn aside from it."—PROVERBS 22:6.

A CIRCUS performer trying to teach her son the art of the trapeze noticed he had trouble getting over the bars. "If you will just throw your heart over the bars," she suggested, "your body will follow." Similarly, those who are 'training up' their child to develop godly devotion must motivate the heart. This is especially difficult during the teenage years.—Proverbs 4:23.

² "For years it was not hard to find out what was going on deep inside my boys," stated a Christian father in Germany. "But that changed like a bolt of lightning as soon as they entered puberty." During this time of transition to adulthood, many new and exciting desires, fueled by body and hormonal changes, affect a young person's heart. Yet all too often such years are marred by painful mistakes. Even faithful Job bemoaned facing "the consequences of the errors of [his] youth." (Job 13:26) Emotional pressures can create "anxious care in the heart" of a young person. Proverbs 12:25 says that this will cause the heart "to bow down, but the good word is what makes it rejoice." How can you help your child with good communication during these critical years?

---

1. What must be reached to train a child successfully, and why?
2. Why are the teenage years difficult, and how can parents help?

Heart Communication

³ Consider the contrast in the counseling approaches of Elihu and of the three "friends" of Job. This will make clear what will, or will not, promote communication. Elihu was a good listener. While the others remained aloof, never acknowledging their own human frailties, he said: "Look! I am to the true God just what you are; from the clay I was shaped, I too." He urged Job to 'reply,' speak his heart, and not to be terrified. (Job 33:5-7) On the other hand, the three "friends" put on an appearance of sympathizing with and comforting Job, but they listened with minds already made up. "Hear, please, my counterarguments, and to the pleadings of my lips pay attention," implored Job without effect. (Job 13:6) Yes, their approach had raised a barrier.

⁴ If not careful, a parent can raise similar barriers without realizing it. So hear your child out. (Proverbs 18:13) Think over carefully how your reply will come across. "There exists the one speaking thoughtlessly as with the stabs of a sword, but the tongue of the wise ones is a healing." (Proverbs 12:18) True, at times the attitude and/or words of a youngster can irritate. But remember, behind such "wild

---

3, 4. (a) How did the counseling approaches of Elihu and of Job's three "friends" differ? (b) What will hinder heart communication?

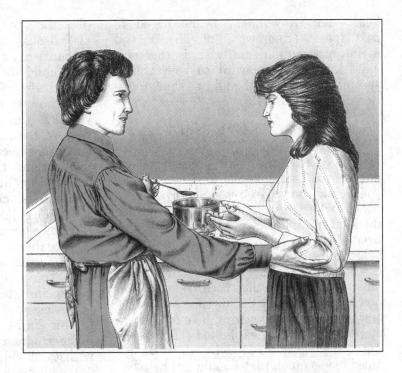

Attentive listening, even when inconvenient, will encourage heartfelt communication

talk" may be a heart laden with turmoil. Thoughtfully use your tongue to heal. —Job 6:2, 3.

⁵ Attentive listening, which includes tactful questions, will help draw out the child and make it easier for him to talk about what is bothering him. (Proverbs 20:5) "A lot of times my son would start a conversation at a seemingly inappropriate time and just say one or two sentences, perhaps about an incident in school," observed the mother of an 18-year-old. "But it was up to me to kindly 'draw up' what was in his heart with questions such as, 'Then what happened?' Or, 'How did you feel about it?' Or, 'What did you do or say?' This is what he was looking for, and he opened up with his problem. But this took a lot of time!" Take such time with your child! Perhaps during long walks or while relaxing together, get to know what is on his mind. Many parents have found that, by referring back to information provided over the years in the Watch Tower Society's publications, they are helped to understand their youngsters better and to have meaningful discussions with them. As a result, heartfelt dialogue has increased among family members. However, more than good communication is needed to develop godly devotion.

5. (a) What will help a parent to draw out the intentions of the child's heart? (b) How can referring back to the Society's publications help?

Promote Spiritual Nourishment

⁶ Timothy's mother was not passive regarding the spiritual matters that meant life for her son. Of him it was written: "From infancy you have known the holy writings, which are able to make you wise for salvation." (2 Timothy 3:15) Similarly today, those parents whose children develop godly devotion are intensely concerned about their children's spiritual nourishment. They teach them to do personal study at an early age.

⁷ Have you seen to it that your child has his own Bible literature and prepares for the congregation meetings? Do you strongly encourage him to schedule time to dig into the treasures of the Word of God? (Proverbs 2:1-5; 1 John 2:14) While at the meetings, do you sit with him to provide encouragement for his mind—and

6, 7. What did Timothy's mother accomplish, and how can parents imitate her?

heart—not to wander? Is he urged to participate? (Hebrews 10:23-25) Do you maintain a regular family study that provides knowledge relevant to your child's specific needs? Give thought to these questions.—Proverbs 24:5.

"Make Jehovah Real"

8 However, simply filling a head with facts may leave the heart and conscience untouched. To develop a good conscience, your child must see that Jehovah is a person who is dynamic and intensely interested in him and in what he does. But first a love for Jehovah must fill your own heart and move you to speak regularly of his loving care and his greatness. You must love and live the truth. When asked how her children, both full-time evangelizers, developed such strong love for God, a mother in England explained: "By speaking to them of how real Jehovah is. He has aided me so much that I could not help but make Jehovah real to them. Everything centers around him." Train your child, also, to talk to Jehovah "with every form of prayer and supplication . . . [carrying] on prayer on every occasion in spirit." (Ephesians 6:18) Let the child hear your earnest, heartfelt prayers and discuss with him the contents of his own.—Deuteronomy 11:1, 2, 18, 19; Proverbs 20:7.

9 The youthful conscience can be powerfully influenced by real-life examples. (Compare 1 Corinthians 8:10.) From time to time you may hear of individuals who suffer because of breaking God's laws. In a nonaccusing manner, discuss such examples with your child, thereby helping him to appreciate Paul's words: "You can't fool God. Whatever you sow you'll reap."

(Galatians 6:7, *Beck*) For a positive example, discuss together the moving Gospel accounts of Jesus' life. You will be helping your child to gain "the mind of Christ." (1 Corinthians 2:16) But you have to make the accounts live! Encourage the child to visualize the dramatic scenes and to reflect on the masterful way Jesus handled matters. Select material from Bible-based publications that detail Jesus' life and personal qualities, and to add variety, use these occasionally on your family study.*

10 Your child must also strive to imitate Christ's example. Only then will the youth by actual experience get "to know the love of the Christ which surpasses knowledge." (Ephesians 3:19) Therefore, encourage him to imitate more closely Jesus' hatred of lawlessness, his love of people, his zeal for his Father's worship, his mercy and bigheartedness, and his willingness to withstand ridicule. (Hebrews 1:9; Mark 6:34; John 4:34; Luke 23:34; 1 Peter 2:23) Warmly commend your child when he responds. He must see that, though we are imperfect, the closer we follow the Master's pattern the happier we are and the better tuned our conscience becomes. We also draw closer to God, since Jesus reflects his Father's personality. (John 14: 6-10) Always remind your child to value this relationship. As one successful Christian mother of four said: "My husband never lets a day go by without putting his arm around each one and telling them how much he loves them and how proud he

---

* For an epitome of Jesus' earthly life, see the article "Get a Firm Hold on the Real Life," in the January 1, 1973, *Watchtower.* The article "Prove Yourselves to Be True Disciples of Christ," in the July 1, 1977, *Watchtower,* considers many of his personal qualities, as does *Aid to Bible Understanding* (published by the Watchtower Bible and Tract Society of New York, Inc.), pages 927-32.

---

8. Where does Deuteronomy 11:18, 19 show that godly devotion must start, and how can parents apply this with a child today?
9. How can parents use real-life examples to train a child's conscience?

10. How can you help your child "to know the love of the Christ"?

knows Jehovah must be of their conduct. 'Jehovah loves you,' he says. 'Don't let him down.'"—Proverbs 27:11.

The Need for Loving Discipline

11 Despite being taught by God "from [his] youth on," David still pleaded, "The sins of my youth and my revolts O do not remember." (Psalm 71:5, 17; 25:7) Yes, every child has 'foolishness tied up with his heart.' But "the rod of discipline is what will remove it far from him." (Proverbs 22:15) This "rod" of parental authority often may be a word of correction or a firm restriction. So when the treacherous heart of your child craves to do something harmful, there is need for firmness to say no!—Jeremiah 17:9; Proverbs 29:17, 19, 21.

12 In disciplining, especially when punishing, follow the pattern of Jehovah who 'corrects according to what is right.' Isaiah 28:26-29 shows that he is like the farmer who uses discernment in determining which instrument to use for effective threshing of different kinds of grains and how long to thresh, not 'incessantly treading it out.' So ask yourself: Is the restriction reasonable in the light of my child's age and progress toward maturity? Is the punishment in propor-

11. Why does every child need discipline?
12, 13. How can you make discipline effective?

tion to the seriousness of the wrong deed as well as consistent and not simply due to my mood? And does the child really know why he is being punished?—Job 6:24.

13 Unreasonable restrictions or inconsistent discipline will irritate or exasperate the child.* (Ephesians 6:4; Colossians 3:21) Yet loving firmness will protect your child from circumstances that can destroy all the good teachings that you have stored in his heart. Especially is this important regarding his associations. (Proverbs 13:20; 28:7) But what if after all your effort your child gets into real trouble?

---

* A research study involving 417 young people that was published in the journal *Adolescence* concluded: "A very restrictive home leads to frustration and then to aggression, while a very permissive home leads to frustration, in not knowing what the parental expectations are, which then leads to aggression, in search of norms."

When Trouble Strikes

14 Painful disappointment has caused some parents to give up quickly on an erring child. While Jehovah gave fitting punishment and reproof, he was not quick to give up on the ancient nation of Israel that once was like a "son" to him. (Hosea 11:1; 2 Chronicles 36:15, 16; Psalm 78: 37, 38; Nehemiah 9:16, 17) Just as ancient trainers were able to dress wounds and set fractures when an athlete got injured, parents must now strive to "straighten up the hands that hang down . . . that what is lame may not be put out of joint, but rather that it may be healed."—Hebrews 12:12, 13.

15 To straighten out a child who is spiritually "lame" and to prevent his condition from worsening requires readjusting the child's thinking. "Even though a man [or a child] takes some false step before he is aware of it," counseled Paul, "you who have spiritual qualifications try to readjust such a man in a spirit of mildness." (Galatians 6:1) The Greek word rendered "readjust" was a medical term used during Paul's time for 'setting bones.' Certainly this painful procedure required the utmost skill to prevent a broken bone from becoming a lifelong handicap. The same basic word is translated "mending" (nets) and "to make good." (Mark 1:19; 1 Thessalonians 3:10) To "mend" a youngster's heart, endeavor with the "art of teaching" to reach him. Rather than verbally fighting, follow the vital Bible suggestion: "Be gentle . . . keeping [yourself] restrained under evil, instructing with mildness those not favorably disposed; as perhaps God may give them repentance."—2 Timothy 2:24-26; 3:16; 4:2.

16 To readjust a child's erroneous thinking requires that a parent intensify his training efforts. The parent may need to make adjustments in his life-style to give the necessary attention. In a parable that shows the appropriate effort to regain "one sinner," Jesus describes a woman who virtually dropped everything to recover her lost drachma coin. (Luke 15:7-10) A child trained in godliness can become overwhelmed with feelings of worthlessness and guilt when his sin comes to light, so a parent may need to confirm his love for the child. Help the child to see that it is his conduct that is disliked, not himself, and that this conduct can be corrected. —Jude 23.

17 One father, whose son was disciplined by the congregation for immorality, began to take long walks with his son several times a week, engaging in long, relaxed conversations. He also selected Bible-based publications that dealt with his son's specific needs. The father studied these with him, in addition to having the lad share in the study that the father had with the whole family. The parent adjusted his work load as a congregation elder to

14. Why should a parent not give up quickly when a child becomes involved in serious trouble?
15. How can a parent apply Galatians 6:1 in restoring an erring child?

16. (a) What adjustments may have to be made to regain an erring child? (b) What should be made clear to the child?
17, 18. (a) How did one father restore his son? (b) What usually brings success?

What Do You Say?

□ How can a parent improve heart communication with a child?

□ What will help a child to develop a good conscience?

□ What will make discipline effective?

□ How can an erring child be restored?

---

give his son the full emotional and mental attention he needed. The boy was restored.

[18] However, at times a son or a daughter may become totally rebellious, even 'despising obedience.'* (Proverbs 30:17) Happily, such extreme situations are rare among God's people. How encouraging to know that, in the vast majority of situations, when the parents—while not condoning the wrong conduct—do not quickly give up on the child but patiently try to reach him, the results are good!

Hard Work—But Worth It!

[19] Rearing children, especially in these "last days," is a formidable task. Parents who take such responsibility seriously are to be commended! Continually evaluate your priorities. Never let the anxiety to provide "many things" of a material nature for your loved ones prevent you from grasping spiritual opportunities with them. Remember, Jesus told Martha that only "a few things, though, are needed, or just one." Yes, a simple meal was sufficient. Be like Mary, who enjoyed a spiritually good time with Jesus. Choose "the good portion" for your family by engaging in spiritual activities as a family.—Luke 10:38-42.

[20] Some years after successfully helping her six children to love Jehovah, a parent received a card from one of them. In part it read: "Mom, I love you very much, much more than you will ever know. Thanks for giving me direction and guidance . . . You gave me the best hope in the world and that is the truth. Thanks for saving my

* See "Questions From Readers" in the May 1, 1960, *Watchtower,* pages 287-8.

19. How can you imitate the example of Mary in caring for your family?
20. What rewards await successful Christian parents?

life." How this mother rejoiced! As Proverbs 23:24, 25 states: "You can take pride in a wise son [or daughter]. Let your father and mother be proud of you; give your mother that happiness." (*Today's English Version*) With Jehovah's help, may such happiness be yours!

Annual Meeting
October 5, 1985

THE ANNUAL MEETING of the members of the Watch Tower Bible and Tract Society of Pennsylvania on October 5, 1985, will be held at the Assembly Hall of Jehovah's Witnesses, 973 Flatbush Avenue in the Borough of Brooklyn, New York City. A preliminary meeting of the members only will be held at 9:30 a.m., followed by the general annual meeting at 10:00 a.m., Saturday, October 5, 1985.

It will be appreciated if the members of the Corporation will inform the Secretary's Office of any change in their mailing addresses during the past year so that the regular letters of notice and proxies can reach them shortly after August 15.

The proxies, which will be sent to the members along with the notice of the annual meeting, are to be returned so as to reach the Office of the Secretary of the Society not later than September 1. As each member knows, he should complete and return his proxy promptly, stating whether he is going to be at the meeting personally or not. The information given on each proxy should be definite on this point, as it will be relied upon in determining in advance those who will actually be personally present.

It is expected that the entire session, including the formal business meeting and reports, will be concluded by 1:00 p.m. or shortly thereafter. There will be no afternoon session. Due to limited space, admission will be by ticket only. No arrangements will be made for tying in the annual meeting by telephone lines to other locations.

Bermuda Rejoices in Kingdom Increase

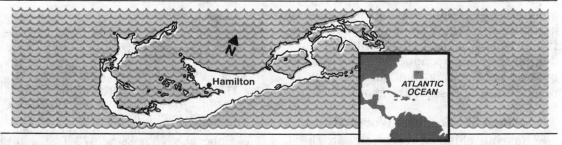

"JEHOVAH himself has become king! Let the earth be joyful. Let the many islands rejoice." So sang the Biblical psalmist. (Psalm 97:1) Among these "many islands" is Bermuda, a self-governing British colony in the West Atlantic, some 700 miles (1,100 km) southeast of New York City.

With its famous pink beaches and clear blue waters, Bermuda certainly is one of the beauties among the islands of the Atlantic. Visitors are delighted by its charming way of life. "In place of automobile horns, factory whistles, traffic lights, skyscrapers, subways, and hurrying throngs," a longtime admirer once observed, "there was the clippety-clop of horses' hoofs, the jingle of bicycle bells, carriage drivers wearing pith helmets, 'bobbies' directing traffic that keeps to the left, business men in shorts, veranda cafés, the dazzling cleanliness of pastel-colored buildings and low, white-roofed houses."

That observation was made in 1939. What about today? Modern travel and communication have made this small group of islands very much a part of Western society. This has brought many ad-

vantages and material prosperity. But has this resulted in a totally joyful way of life for the islanders? Not really.

To illustrate, one newspaper recently said: "Premier gives Bermudians a stern warning . . . the Island's economy was facing serious challenges." A later article reported: "Minister says changes must be made, tourism sinking."

Compared with many other places, Bermuda may still seem rather paradisaic. Nevertheless, crime is reported to be rising at about 4 percent a year. Other newspaper articles speak of "the existence of a hard drug culture in Bermuda" and the "Saturday night specials or deadly automatics" that "are back on streets." No wonder that a recent survey revealed that "about one Bermudian in four thinks that conditions are not as good now as they were in the past and will get worse in the next five years."

Yet, is there hope for a brighter future? Can Bermudians find a sound basis for happiness and true joy?

Joyful Message Comes to Bermuda

The hope of a joyful future through God's Kingdom first reached Bermuda in 1913. At that time a Bible Student named Nelson distributed some Watch Tower publications in the islands. Later, however, local authorities asked him to leave.

Religious prejudice against Jehovah's Witnesses persisted for many years. Thus, in 1933, the Roberts family from the West Indies was forced to leave Bermuda. Many others experienced similar treatment —simply for trying to spread the Bible's joyful message. Among them was Fredricia "Freddy" Johnson, who in the 1930's often visited these islands as a full-time minister of the good news. In 1940, however, she was haled into court and told: "You are not the kind of person we want in Bermuda, and the sooner you leave the better."

Despite continuing pressure, Kingdom proclaimers did not cease to spread the Bible's joyous message. In 1945 two graduates of the Watchtower Bible School of Gilead arrived. Although they were deported in 1947, for some 19 months they had carried out a fruitful ministry, helping the islanders to learn what the hope of Jehovah's Witnesses is and what type of people they are. The Witnesses let their conduct speak for them, and Jehovah rewarded their persistent efforts.

Two specially trained graduates of Gilead School arrived in 1951. By this time, the authorities had developed a more tolerant attitude toward the Witnesses.

Kingdom Increase Brings Joy

In 1950 there were only five Kingdom publishers associated with the one congregation in Bermuda. Ten years later, the number of publishers had risen to 43, and by 1970, 118 Witnesses of Jehovah were serving joyously in that congregation. Another decade gave evidence of Kingdom increase as the number of congregations

had risen to four, with a total of 214 publishers. By January of 1985, more than 310 individuals associated with these congregations were actively sharing their joyous hope with others.

However, it is not just the numerical growth that brings joy. It is seeing the changes in the lives of those who embrace the good news that brings delight. While more and more people, young and old, turn to drugs and alcohol, others are taking up the truly happy way of life.

For example, Randy became involved in the use of drugs at the age of 12. "Due to my bad associations, I started off with marijuana. This led to such hard drugs as speed and LSD. My first 15 trips were beautiful—or so I thought at the time. Then the bad trips started. On one occasion, I spent four to five hours drinking milk and water because I thought my insides were on fire. Another frightening experience was sitting in a corner thinking my body was shrinking and at the same time my feet were getting larger and larger. If I had had a gun at that time, I would have shot myself. . . .

"Hardly a day went by that I did not smoke marijuana. . . . I also lived a very immoral life, which at the time seemed to me to be quite normal."

After living in this way for 11 years, Randy came in touch with the truth. His brother and sister had begun studying the Bible with Jehovah's Witnesses, and his sister would leave Bible literature in his room. He never read it. Then one day he was attracted by the cover of an *Awake!* magazine on the subject of world peace. He read the magazine with interest and admitted this to his sister, who immediately gave him the book *The Truth That Leads to Eternal Life.* "I took it to work with me every day," said Randy, "and in one week I read it through. This was the

**Kingdom Halls
—centers of true
worship in Bermuda**

first book I had read from cover to cover."

Randy's brother invited him to attend a meeting at the Kingdom Hall, but he was somewhat reluctant because he "hated to dress up." However, he did attend and now says: "Since then I have never stopped enjoying these wonderful arrangements that Jehovah is providing." Shortly thereafter, he was baptized in symbol of his dedication to Jehovah God. "From then on I spent 75 to 90 hours a month telling others of my hope for the future," continued Randy. "I especially made sure I told all my former friends about this good news." In time Randy married a zealous preacher of the good news. In January 1983 she became a regular pioneer. One year later he was able to join her in this purposeful and joyous way of service to Jehovah. Also, for over six years now he has served as an appointed elder in one of the local congregations. Says Randy: "I thank Jehovah every day for opening my heart to the truth!"

Many other individuals in Bermuda have been able to change their lives and become better and happier husbands, wives, mothers, fathers, brothers, and sisters. Especially among the youth and young adult population do we see keen interest in a reliable hope for the future. Consider one family that provides a fine example of this.

Gretchen first started studying the Bible with Jehovah's Witnesses in 1961. She could see the error in the doctrines taught by other religions, so she expected to find something wrong in the things she was taught by the Witnesses. But she could not do so. Gretchen was baptized in 1963. Today, over 20 years later, two of her sons and three of her daughters also serve as baptized and joyful witnesses of Jehovah.

Joyful Service Ahead

All these young people, along with their spiritual brothers and sisters older in years, are reaping the joys of sacred service to Jehovah.

During 1984, there was a ratio of one Witness to every 170 inhabitants. But is there hope of greater Kingdom increase? Indeed there is, for about 300 home Bible studies are now being conducted with interested persons. Clearly, then, there are grand prospects of further Kingdom increase that will surely bring greater joy to Bermuda.

Do You Remember?

Have you enjoyed the last several issues of *The Watchtower?* See if you can remember the following points:

□ **What can help Christians to overcome secret faults?**

Christians who want to please Jehovah should live with an awareness that they cannot hide their faults from God. Also, they should accept Jehovah's help to overcome such weaknesses. (Ecclesiastes 12:14; Philippians 4:13)—4/15, page 20.

□ **What challenge involving Christian maturity should each servant of Jehovah seriously consider?**

Is Jehovah's servant willing and eager to accept the responsibility that comes with being a full-grown, mature spiritual person? Or is he content merely to coast along, letting others shoulder that responsibility for him? (Galatians 6:4, 5)—5/1, pages 9, 10.

□ **How can we show kindness by cultivating true friendship?**

Kindness on our part is shown when we let the others know that we appreciate them. This we can do by listening to others and not dominating the conversation by talking exclusively about ourselves. Kindness is further shown by watching what we say to others. (Proverbs 12:18) —5/15, page 4.

□ **What did Jesus mean when he said at Mark 9:50: "Have salt in yourselves"?**

Jesus was referring to his disciples' being considerate, tactful, wholesome, and peaceable in word and conduct—acting in good taste toward one another. —5/15, page 24.

□ **What are some facts that argue against Jesus' having been born on December 25?**

December is a rainy, cold season in Bethlehem, so shepherds would not be out at night with their flocks. The people would not likely have been asked by the Roman Caesar to travel in winter for registration because the Jews were already at the point of revolting against the Romans.—6/1, page 8.

□ **Why should baptism be a time for meditation and sober thought by candidates?**

Baptism is the time when an individual shows that he has made a vital decision—to submit to God as the Sovereign Lord and, as a Witness for Jehovah, to be no part of the world. (Luke 3:21; Matthew 4:10; 1 John 5:19) —6/1, page 31.

□ **What did Jesus mean when he said at Luke 1:37: "With God no declaration will be an impossibility"?**

Jesus' words do not mean that God can say just anything but, rather, that no word or declaration given by Jehovah can go unfulfilled. (Isaiah 55:10, 11) —6/15, page 14.

□ **How do Jehovah's people today feed on "every utterance coming forth through Jehovah's mouth" (Matthew 4:4)?**

This feeding is not done simply by personally reading and studying God's Word the Bible, but it is by Jehovah's people experiencing, collectively and individually, the wonderful way in which Jehovah fulfills his utterances toward his people, acting on their behalf.—6/15, page 17.

□ **What are some chief characteristics of the Hindu religion?**

Hindu worshipers are not governed by any central body; there is no set form of worship; their source of beliefs is not any one book like the Bible; but, instead, over the centuries a vast array of Hindu writings have appeared, and six different schools of philosophy have been developed. —7/1, page 4.

□ **How did Christians in the first century act toward someone who was not an expelled wrongdoer, but who willfully renounced the Christian way?**

The apostle John gave counsel about persons who had 'gone out from among us' and about those who brought false teaching. (1 John 2:19) At 2 John 10 he advised that Christians were not to 'receive such persons into their home' or greet them. The word "apostasy" is from a Greek word that has the sense of 'desertion, abandonment, or rebellion,' and a person who had willfully and formally disassociated himself from the Christian congregation would have matched such a description. Loyal Christians would not have wanted to fellowship with such an apostate.—7/15, page 31.

□ **How can the true religion be determined?**

True religion should meet God's standards of truth as laid down in the Bible; it ought to produce the peaceable fruit of love; and it must also honor God's name, Jehovah.—7/15, page 7.

The Pastor Forgot to Go to Church

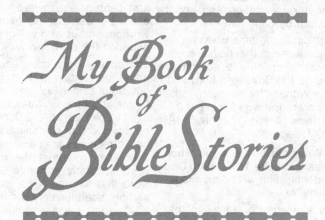

September 1, 1985

The Watchtower

Announcing Jehovah's Kingdom

BELIEF IN GOD
Is It Enough?

September 1, 1985
Vol. 106, No. 17

The Watchtower®
Announcing Jehovah's Kingdom

THE PURPOSE OF "THE WATCHTOWER" is to exalt Jehovah God as the Sovereign of the universe. It keeps watch on world events as they fulfill Bible prophecy. It comforts all peoples with the good news that God's Kingdom will soon destroy those who oppress their fellowmen and that it will turn the earth into a paradise. It encourages faith in the now-reigning King, Jesus Christ, whose shed blood opens the way for mankind to gain eternal life. "The Watchtower," published by Jehovah's Witnesses continuously since 1879, is nonpolitical. It adheres to the Bible as its authority.

"WATCHTOWER" STUDIES FOR THE WEEKS

October 6: Kingdom Ministers Meet the Challenge. Page 16. Songs to Be Used: 72, 204.

October 13: God's Ministers Prove Their Qualification. Page 21. Songs to Be Used: 82, 10.

Average Printing Each Issue: 11,150,000

Now Published in 103 Languages

SEMIMONTHLY EDITIONS AVAILABLE BY MAIL
Afrikaans, Arabic, Cebuano, Chichewa, Chinese, Cibemba, Danish, Dutch, Efik, English*, Finnish, French, German, Greek, Hiligaynon, Igbo, Iloko, Italian, Japanese, Korean, Lingala, Malagasy, Maltese, Norwegian, Portuguese, Russian, Sepedi, Sesotho, Shona, Spanish, Swahili, Swedish, Tagalog, Thai, Tswana, Xhosa, Yoruba, Zulu

MONTHLY EDITIONS AVAILABLE BY MAIL
Armenian, Bengali, Bicol, Bulgarian, Croatian, Czech, Ewe, Fijian, Ga, Greenlandic, Gujarati, Gun, Hausa, Hebrew, Hindi, Hiri Motu, Hungarian, Icelandic, Kannada, Kikuyu, Kiluba, Malayalam, Marathi, New Guinea Pidgin, Pangasinan, Papiamento, Polish, Rarotongan, Romanian, Samar-Leyte, Samoan, Sango, Serbian, Silozi, Sinhalese, Slovenian, Solomon Islands-Pidgin, Tahitian, Tamil, Telugu, Tshiluba, Tsonga, Turkish, Twi, Ukrainian, Urdu, Venda, Vietnamese
*Study articles also available in large-print edition.

The Bible translation used is the "New World Translation of the Holy Scriptures," unless otherwise indicated.

Twenty cents (U.S.) a copy

	Yearly subscription
Watch Tower Society offices	*Semimonthly*
America, U.S., Watchtower, Wallkill, N.Y. 12589	$4.00
Australia, Box 280, Ingleburn, N.S.W. 2565	A$6.00
Canada, Box 4100, Halton Hills (Georgetown), Ontario L7G 4Y4	$5.20
England, The Ridgeway, London NW7 1RN	£5.00
Ireland, 29A Jamestown Road, Finglas, Dublin 11	£5.00
New Zealand, 6-A Western Springs Rd., Auckland 3	$10.00
Nigeria, P.O. Box 194, Yaba, Lagos State	₦6.00
Philippines, P.O. Box 2044, Manila 2800	₱50.00
South Africa, Private Bag 2, Elandsfontein, 1406	R5,60

Remittances should be sent to the office in your country or to Watchtower, Wallkill, N.Y. 12589, U.S.A.

Changes of address should reach us 30 days before your moving date. Give us your old and new address (if possible, your old address label).

The Watchtower (ISSN 0043-1087) is published semimonthly for $4.00 (U.S.) per year by Watch Tower Bible and Tract Society of Pennsylvania, 25 Columbia Heights, Brooklyn, N.Y. 11201. Second-class postage paid at Brooklyn, N.Y., and at additional mailing offices.

Postmaster: Send address changes to Watchtower, *Wallkill, N.Y. 12589.*

Published by
**Watch Tower Bible and Tract Society
of Pennsylvania**
25 Columbia Heights, Brooklyn, N.Y. 11201, U.S.A.
Frederick W. Franz, President

Belief in God —Is It Enough?

"DO YOU believe in God or a universal spirit?" asked famous pollster George Gallup, Jr. Perhaps to the surprise of some, *95 percent* of both the adults (over 30 years of age) and the teenagers polled said yes! But to what extent does belief translate into action? Apparently very little. For Mr. Gallup reported that when some young adults were asked, "To what degree do your religious beliefs affect your daily thinking or acting," a mere 26 percent said, "a great deal."*—*The Search for America's Faith,* by George Gallup, Jr., and David Poling.

Obviously, then, mere belief in God is not enough. Wrote the disciple James: "You believe there is one God, do you? You are doing quite well. And yet the demons believe and shudder. . . . Faith apart from works is inactive." (James 2:19, 20) On the other hand, the Bible tells of individuals who went beyond mere belief. Enoch, for example, "kept walking with the true God." (Genesis 5:24) The relationship between Enoch and his God thus became so close that it was as if they walked together! But why was Enoch favored with this

---

* Thirty-nine percent said "some," 14 percent said "hardly any," and 12 percent said "not at all."

unique relationship? For one thing, though he lived in the midst of a degenerate religious atmosphere where shocking "ungodly deeds" were commonplace, Enoch followed a righteous way of life. With courage and frankness he exposed the evil ways of his contemporaries, prophesying: "Look! Jehovah came with his holy myriads, to execute judgment against all, and to convict all the ungodly concerning all their ungodly deeds that they did in an ungodly way, and concerning all the shocking things that ungodly sinners spoke against him."—Jude 14, 15.

Walking with God put Enoch in grave danger. His enemies apparently schemed to assassinate him and end his irritating prophesying. The God with whom he walked, however, intervened. Says the Bible: "By faith Enoch was transferred so as not to see death, and he was nowhere to be found because God had transferred him." Yes, "God took him" in death, apparently sparing him a violent death at the hands of his enemies.—Hebrews 11:5, 13; Genesis 5:24; compare John 3:13.

Noah was another man who "walked with the true God." Like Enoch, "Noah was a righteous man. He proved himself faultless among his contemporaries." (Genesis 6:9) And this in spite of the fact that in his day loose conduct was prevalent and violence ran rampant. Noah, though, displayed godly fear and stood out as "a preacher of righteousness." God therefore preserved him and his family when he brought a deluge upon that ancient world! —2 Peter 2:5; Hebrews 11:7; Genesis 6: 5, 11.

Does God still extend the invitation to walk with him? Yes indeed! The apostle Paul said that God "is not far off from each one of us," if we but "grope for him and really find him." (Acts 17:27) But how can we do this? And what does walking with God really entail?

You Can Walk With God

"**W**ILL two walk together unless they have met by appointment?" asked the prophet Amos. (Amos 3:3) But can you make an "appointment" to walk with God?

Yes! For, in fact, God takes the initiative by extending to us the invitation to be his friends. He does not coerce us into such friendship. Rather he draws us to him by his magnificent qualities. Why, creation alone provides abundant testimony to God's goodness! "His invisible qualities are clearly seen from the world's creation onward, because they are perceived by the things made, even his eternal power and Godship." (Romans 1:20) Or as the apostle Paul said at Acts 14:17: "He [God] did not leave himself without witness in that he did good, giving you rains from heaven and fruitful seasons, filling your hearts to the full with food and good cheer."

Men such as Enoch and Noah were therefore eager to accept God's offer of friendship. They perceived that God was "worthy . . . to receive the glory and the honor." (Revelation 4:11) So they responded to God's invitation and approached him in faith. "Without faith it is impossible to please him well," said Paul, "for he that approaches God must believe that he is and that he becomes the rewarder of those earnestly seeking him." (Hebrews 11:6) So by seeking out a relationship with God, you, too, can make an "appointment" with Him. And, said the psalmist, "Happy is the one you [God] choose and cause to approach."—Psalm 65:4.

Since a friendship with God is made on his terms, one must study his Word, the Bible, in order to find out what is "the good and acceptable and perfect will of God." (Romans 12:2) "Really, how could I ever [understand Isaiah's prophecy] unless someone guided me?" asked a sincere seeker of God back in Bible times. And perhaps you feel the same way. However, God saw to it that a disciple named Philip approached this man and explained the prophecy. (Acts 8:30-35) Does God show any less interest in sincere seekers of him today? Why, the mere fact that you are reading this Bible-based journal demonstrates God's interest in you! Would it not be wise to allow those from whom you obtained this journal to help you to learn even more about God?

Seeing the Invisible One

As you grow in your knowledge of God, he will become more and more real to you. You will soon appreciate that he is not some nameless bundle of energy but rather a Person with a name! Says the Bible at Psalm 83:18: "That people may know that you, whose name is Jehovah, you alone are the Most High over all the earth." As a Person, Jehovah has qualities, likes and dislikes—even feelings! —Compare Exodus 34:6, 7; Psalm 78:40.

God also has righteous standards. For example, Proverbs 3:32 says: "The devious person is a detestable thing to Jehovah, but His intimacy is with the upright ones." Joseph was one of the "upright ones." The Bible tells of how the wife of his Egyptian master, Potiphar, repeatedly pleaded with Joseph to have immoral relations with her. Yet he refused, saying, "How could I commit this great badness and actually sin against God?"—Genesis 39:9.

Jehovah was real to Joseph. He had a healthy fear of Him and acted as though he was in His literal presence. Joseph was like the psalmist who said: "I have placed Jehovah in front of me constantly. Because he is at my right hand, I shall not be made to totter." (Psalm 16:8; compare Proverbs 3:5, 6) Moses had similar faith. He "continued steadfast as seeing the One who is invisible."—Hebrews 11:27.

Walking with God, therefore, means more than taking in knowledge. It means adopting a way of life that harmonizes with God's revealed will and purpose! As the apostle Paul put it: "Therefore, whether you are eating or drinking or doing anything else, do all things for God's glory."—1 Corinthians 10:31.

Walking With God—Its Benefits

"For all its economy of muscle and energy," wrote Sussman and Goode in their book *The Magic of Walking,* "walking is endorsed by medical and health authorities for an astonishing variety of benefits." Among the claimed benefits are weight control, better sleep, release of tension, and prevention of heart disorders. If such is true of physical walking, we can expect that walking with God is even more advantageous.

Do not expect, however, some profound emotional experience. But as you "draw close to God" by praying and acting in faith, you will enjoy "the peace of God that excels all thought." (James 4:8; Philippians 4:6, 7) One woman, for example, used to engage in heavy drinking and drug use because of constant depression. She also experimented with a number of sects of Christendom. But then she began studying the Bible with Jehovah's Witnesses. Said she: "While nothing else I tried could relieve my depression, understanding Jehovah's purposes gave me a real purpose in living." Yes, as a person begins walking with God, he is led in a path that is sure to bring him spiritual and emotional benefits.—Compare Isaiah 30:21.

Another benefit was pointed out by a discerning woman named Abigail. She told King David: "When man rises up to pursue you and look for your soul, the soul of my lord will certainly prove to be wrapped up in the bag of life with Jehovah your God." Imagine that! When threatened by his enemies, David's life would be under Jehovah's protective custody as if it were a precious object carefully wrapped

God's Word, spirit, and organization can help us to continue faithfully 'walking with God'

up for safekeeping. Although this does not necessarily imply that physical protection will always be given God's servants, He is sure to protect the eternal interests of those who walk with him today!—1 Samuel 25:29; compare Psalm 116:15.

This, though, does not mean that you will be exempt from problems common to mankind, as if Christians lead some sort of charmed life. Solomon observed that "time and unforeseen occurrence befall" all mankind. (Ecclesiastes 9:11) The apostle Paul, for example, suffered from "a thorn in the flesh," possibly some sort of physical infirmity. (2 Corinthians 12:7; Galatians 4:13-15) His companion Timothy likewise suffered from "frequent cases of sickness." (1 Timothy 5:23) Similarly, Christians today have their share of illnesses and even occasional feelings of discouragement or depression.

Further, Jehovah God at times permits momentary trials so as to refine us, as he did when allowing Joseph to be impris-

oned. (Psalm 105:17-19) Some may suffer a premature death at the hands of violent persecutors as did Stephen. (Acts 7:57-60) But never should God's friends feel abandoned. (Compare 2 Corinthians 4:8, 9.) "For God is not unrighteous so as to forget your work and the love you showed for his name." (Hebrews 6:10) Said one Christian woman who was sustained through years of unjust imprisonment: "I am deeply convinced that none of those who zealously endure in Jehovah's service will experience disappointment. With my whole heart I have trusted Jehovah and his assuring words, 'I will by no means leave you nor by any means forsake you.'"—Hebrews 13:5.

Help in Keeping Up Our Fight

Keeping such a faithful course is not easy. Satan and his wicked spirit forces are intent on entrapping us. (Ephesians 6:12) Then there is the present wicked system of things with its attractive lures.

A Christian in the first century named Demas was sidetracked because "he loved the present system of things." (2 Timothy 4:10) Finally, there is our own sinful flesh with its inclination toward evil. (Romans 7:21-23) A constant fight against these influences is needed if we are to continue walking with God.

God, though, has made three powerful instruments available to help us: (1) His Word, the Bible, which provides needed guidance. (Psalm 119:105) (2) His visible organization, the Christian congregation, which is carrying out God's spiritual feeding program. (Matthew 24:45-47; Ephesians 4:11-16) The Watch Tower Society, the publisher of this magazine, is closely associated with that organization. (3) His holy spirit, which we receive through prayer, study of the Scriptures, and association with his people. It would be a serious mistake to neglect any one of these provisions. The prophet Micah exhorts us, "Be modest in walking with your God." (Micah 6:8) That means recognizing our limitations and being totally dependent upon God.

Indeed, our walking with God can be compared to a little girl who is walking with her father during a powerful storm. If she were to let go of his hand or decide to go her own way, she would soon get lost. But if she holds on tightly, she can walk safely and confidently with her father. We, too, must take care to submit to God's direction as given through his Word and organization. Independence can only get us hopelessly lost. By modestly walking with God, however, we can be led safely through the oncoming storm of Armageddon and survive into a promised new order. There, death and pain will be things of the past. (Revelation 16:16; 21:3, 4; 2 Peter 3:13) Will you, therefore, accept God's gracious invitation to walk with him?

Religion—A Uniting Force?

HAS religion as a whole been a uniting force in the world? Or, rather, has it been a force for death and destruction? In answer we must say, the world has witnessed a century of conflict—ignited by nationalism but fueled by religion. Since 1909, at least 14 major world conflicts have had religious roots. "From ancient times to the present," says Ernest Lefever, president of the Ethics and Public Policy Center in Washington, D.C., "very few wars have been fought in which religion has not played at least some part."

Yet, theoretically, religion should be able to keep the world at peace. Writes syndicated columnist Mike Royko: "If soldiers refused to kill somebody simply because they practice the same religion, it would be [very] hard to get a war going." Then after noting that people of the same non-Christian faith have "been eagerly slaughtering each other by the tens of thousands," he says: "Nor have Christians ever been squeamish about waging wars on other Christians. If they had been, most of the liveliest wars in Europe would never have occurred."

Is it any wonder, then, that many people want nothing to do with anything that smacks of religion? The pages of history have repeatedly been bloodied by warring religionists who have either ignored God's Word the Holy Bible or twisted its meaning to suit their own selfish interests.

However, the way of life outlined in the Bible, when correctly followed, does not lead to conflict but only to peace and unity. (Proverbs 3:1-6) Jesus urged his followers, "Continue to love your enemies, to do good to those hating you." (Luke 6:27) Jesus also pointed to this identifying mark of his genuine followers when he said: "By this all will know that you are my disciples, if you have love among yourselves."—John 13:35.

John

Prepares the Way

SEVENTEEN years have passed since Jesus was a child of 12 questioning the teachers in the temple. It is the spring of the year 29 C.E., and everybody, it seems, is talking about Jesus' cousin John, who is preaching in all the country around the Jordan River.

John is indeed an impressive man, both in appearance and in speech. His clothing is of camel's hair, and he wears a leather girdle around his loins. His food is insect locusts and wild honey. And his message? "Repent, for the kingdom of the heavens has drawn near."

This message excites his listeners. Many realize their need to repent, that is, to change their attitude and to reject their past course of life as undesirable. So from all the territory around the Jordan, and even from Jerusalem, the people come out to John in great numbers, and he baptizes them, dipping them beneath the waters of the Jordan. Why?

John baptizes people in symbol, or acknowledgment, of their heartfelt repentance for sins against God's Law covenant. Thus when some religious Pharisees and Sadducees come out to the Jordan, John condemns them. "You offspring of vipers," he says. "Produce fruit that befits repentance."

Due to all the attention John is receiving, the Pharisees send out priests and Levites to him. They ask: "Who are you? that we may give an answer to those who sent us. What do you say about yourself?"

John explains: "I am a voice of someone crying out in the wilderness, 'Make the way of Jehovah straight,' just as Isaiah the prophet said." John is preparing the way by getting people in a proper heart condition to accept the Messiah, who will become King. Of this One, John says: "The one coming after me is stronger than I am, whose sandals I am not fit to take off."

Thus John's message, "the kingdom of the heavens has drawn near," serves as a public notification that the ministry of Jehovah's appointed King, Jesus Christ, is about to begin. **John 1:6-8, 15-28; Matthew 3:1-12; Luke 3: 1-18; Acts 19:4.**

♦ What kind of man is John?
♦ Why does John baptize people?
♦ Why could John say the Kingdom has drawn near?

My Family's Love for God Despite Prison and Death

(Circuit overseeer) 12-8-94

As told by Magdalena Kusserow Reuter

MY BROTHER Wilhelm was to be executed by the Nazis the following morning. His crime? Conscientious objection to service in the German army. He was 25 years old and well aware of his impending execution by firing squad. During that evening of April 26, 1940, he wrote us the following farewell letter, after which he peacefully went to bed and slept soundly.

"Dear parents, brothers, and sisters:

All of you know how much you mean to me, and I am repeatedly reminded of this every time I look at our family photo. How harmonious things always were at home. Nevertheless, above all we must love God, as our Leader [Führer] Jesus Christ commanded. If we stand up for him, he will reward us."

In his final night our dear Wilhelm was thinking of us—his Christian parents and his five brothers and five sisters, an unusually large and harmonious family. Through the turmoils of time, as a family we have seen to it that our love for God has always come first.

Our "Golden Age" Home

My parents, Franz and Hilda Kusserow, had been zealous Bible Students, or *Bibelforscher* (Jehovah's Witnesses), from the time of their baptism in 1924, the year I was born as their seventh child. The years of youth that we 11 children spent with our parents were a marvelous time.

Since my father retired from secular work early in life, he was able to devote much time to us. This he did in harmony with Bible principles. Not a day passed without our receiving Biblical counsel and instruction. Our parents recognized that children will not automatically become praisers of Jehovah just because their parents are.

In 1931 Father followed the Watchtower Society's invitation to move his large family to a territory where no local congregation existed at that time. In Paderborn and surroundings—about 200 towns and villages were included—we had a lot of work to do in preaching the Kingdom message. My oldest sister, Annemarie, served as a special pioneer, and Dad and my 15-year-old brother, Siegfried, as regular pioneers.

Even from a distance, people could see two big signs painted on both sides of our house in Bad Lippspringe. There, in German, Father had written: LESEN SIE 'DAS GOLDENE ZEITALTER' (READ 'THE GOLDEN AGE,' the former name of the *Awake!* magazine). The house was situated alongside a tramway line connecting Paderborn and Detmold. Whenever the tram stopped in front of the house, the driver would call out: "Streetcar stop, GOLDEN AGE!" And of a truth, our house, located on three acres (1.2 ha) of land and surrounded by a beautiful garden with bushes and trees, became for us a center of education and activity, all revolving around the golden age of God's Kingdom to come.—Matthew 6:9, 10.

All in Harmony

A family blessed with so many children required management. There were often vegetables and fruits to harvest. The chickens and the ducks had to be cared for, and the family lamb needed its feeding bottle. Dachshund "Fiffi" and the cat "Pussi," also beloved family "members," needed attention. So Father scheduled the work of housekeeping, gardening, and caring for the domestic animals. Each child shared in the various chores, which were rotated weekly between the boys and the girls.

Dad also included time for recreation, which included music, painting, and a number of other things, all supervised by Mother, a professional teacher. We had five violins, a piano, a reed organ, two accordions, a guitar, and several flutes. Yes, not only did our parents supervise our school homework but they also made music and singing a part of our educational program.

What I consider of most importance today is that there was not a single day that passed without our receiving some spiritual instruction, whether at the table receiving answers to our questions or by means of learning by heart different Bible texts. Father also insisted that we learn to express ourselves correctly. In other words, we had an ideal family life, better than any story could tell. Of course, we also had our weaknesses, and Father would often discipline us with words that hurt more than any physical punishment. He always taught us to apologize for our errors and to be forgiving to others. We did not realize then how important all this training was going to be.

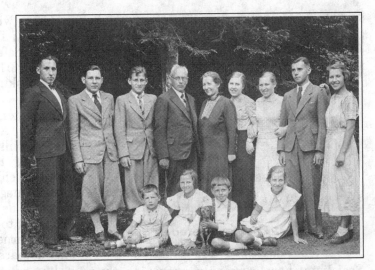

The last photo ever taken of the entire family. Left to right, rear: Siegfried, Karl-Heinz, Wolfgang, Father, Mother, Annemarie, Waltraud, Wilhelm, Hildegard. Below: Paul-Gerhard, Magdalena, Hans-Werner, and Elisabeth

The youngest member of the family, little Paul-Gerhard, was born in 1931. He was welcomed by his brothers, Wilhelm, Karl-Heinz, Wolfgang, Siegfried, and Hans-Werner, as well as by me and my sisters, Annemarie, Waltraud, Hildegard, and Elisabeth.

Tribulation Begins

About this time Adolf Hitler was coming to power in Germany. It seemed that Father knew that problems were on the way, and more and more he prepared us for the difficult years to come. He showed us from the Bible that some faithful Witnesses would be persecuted, thrown into prison, and even killed. (Matthew 16:25; 2 Timothy 3:12; Revelation 2:10) I remember thinking that this would not necessarily happen to our family. Little did I know what the future held for us.

The first blow was the death of my brother Siegfried by accidental drowning at the age of 20. Then in the spring of 1933 we came under scrutiny by the National

The family house located at the streetcar stop "GOLDEN AGE"

Socialists, now commonly known as the Nazis. The secret police ordered that the signs on our house be painted out. But the paint in those days was so poor that you could still see "GOLDEN AGE" shining through! And the tram driver continued to call out: "Streetcar stop, GOLDEN AGE!"

Gradually the pressures became stronger. Fellow Witnesses, severely mistreated by the Gestapo, sought refuge in our home. Father's pension was cut because he refused to say "Heil Hitler." Between 1933 and 1945, the Gestapo searched our house some 18 times. But did all of this intimidate us children? My sister Waltraud remembers: "Even with persecution running high, we drew strength from our parents, who regularly studied the Bible with us. We still followed Father's schedule."

The Youngest Under Pressure

With butterflies in our stomach, the youngest of us went to school each day. The teachers demanded that we salute the flag, sing Nazi songs, and raise our arms while saying "Heil Hitler." Because we refused, we were made objects of derision. But what helped us remain steadfast? We all agree that the secret was that Father and Mother daily discussed our individual

problems with us as they occurred. (Ephesians 6:4) They showed us how to act and how to defend ourselves with the Bible. (1 Peter 3:15) Often we held practice sessions, asking questions and giving answers.

My sister Elisabeth recalls a severe test she had: "A most difficult moment for us that we will never forget was when, in the spring of 1939, the school principal accused us children of being spiritually and morally neglected and arranged by court to have us hauled off from school and abducted to an unknown place. I was 13, Hans-Werner 9, and little Paul-Gerhard only 7 years old."

Just recently, over 40 years later, Paul-Gerhard received a letter from an official whose conscience was still bothering him. He wrote: "I was the policeman who took you and your brother and sister to the reform school. I handed you over that same evening." Imagine, those three defenseless children abducted from school without a word to our parents!

Mother tried to find out where they had been taken. At last, after some weeks, she located them in a reform school in Dorsten. The director soon realized that the children were well mannered and that they did not belong there, so after several months they were released. But they failed to arrive home. What had happened?

My brothers and sister had been intercepted by the Gestapo and taken from Dorsten to Nettelstadt near Minden and placed in a Nazi training school. Visits by relatives, of course, were forbidden, but mother tried in every possible way to strengthen her children, including sending hidden letters. Once she was even able to meet and speak with them secretly. Later the children were separated and taken to different places. They maintained integrity, however, and refused to salute the flag or to say "Heil Hitler." They pointed to

Acts 4:12, where of Jesus Christ it is said: "There is no salvation [*Heil,* in German] in anyone else."

Entire Family Put to the Test

In the meantime, Father served two prison sentences. On August 16, 1940, he was released from prison, only to be sent eight months later for his third sentence to the penitentiary at Kassel-Wehlheiden. But during this short period of freedom, what a joy it was for him to be able to baptize three of us—19-year-old Hildegard, 18-year-old Wolfgang, and me, then 16.

Father was reimprisoned at the same time that Mother and Hildegard were incarcerated. I was also taken to court, and at 17 years of age was sentenced to solitary confinement in the juvenile prison at Vechta. There I had hardly anything to do. Arising early and just sitting around the whole day looking at whitewashed walls was not easy. I tried to remember as much as possible of what I had learned and was amazed at the spiritual riches I found. I recalled entire Kingdom songs and worked out Bible themes. How thankful I was for all the careful training that my parents had given me!

When my first six months in prison were about to end, the prison director called me to her office and explained that I would be released if I signed a paper renouncing my beliefs as false teaching. Again I had the privilege of defending my faith. Her reply was silence. Then she said with a sad voice that she would have to return me to the Gestapo. Four months later I was transported to the Ravensbrück concentration camp.

My mother and Hildegard were still in another prison. I met them later when they were assigned to Ravensbrück. Then Mother and I were able to stay together until the end of the war. Annemarie and Waltraud were also serving time in prison. Every member of the family had now been either put behind bars or abducted. The large house in Bad Lippspringe, once filled with the laughter and singing of carefree children, was now empty. The signs on both sides of the house had been painted over again and again. The GOLDEN AGE had faded from sight.

Ravensbrück—Friends and Foes

When I arrived at Ravensbrück, in spite of my apprehension I was looking forward to meeting other Witnesses. But how would I find them among all those thousands of prisoners? Part of the reception procedure was delousing. The prisoner who examined my head asked in a low voice "Why are you here?" "I am a *Bibelforscher,*" I answered. Joyfully she replied, "A heartfelt welcome, my dear sister!" I was next taken to the *Bibelforscher* block where Sister Gertrud Poetzinger took me under her wing.

The next day I was called to the camp commander's office. On his desk was a big Bible opened to Romans chapter 13. He ordered me to read the first verse, which says: "Let every soul be in subjection to the superior authorities." After I had finished he said: "And now you will explain to me why you do not want to obey the superior authorities." I answered: "In order to explain this, I would have to read the whole chapter." With that he closed the Bible abruptly and then dismissed me. Thus I started my three and a half years in Ravensbrück.

Apart from the brutality of the SS guards, the winters, perhaps, were the worst part of that experience. We used to stand out on parade in the freezing cold for the official head count every morning. That started at 4 a.m. and could last anywhere from two to five hours! We were not allowed to put our hands in our pockets, and I got chilblains on my hands and feet and needed medical attention.

But we also used those wasted hours on parade to build one another up spiritually. When the SS guards were out of earshot, we would all repeat a text from mouth to mouth and thus center our minds on God's Word. On one occasion we all learned Psalm 83, repeating it one after the other, being careful that no guard caught us. This spiritual aid helped us to endure. But let us return to the spring of 1940.

The First Martyr

My older brother Wilhelm was sentenced to death and executed publicly in the hospital garden in Münster. He was the family's first martyr. Mother and I visited him shortly before his death. We were impressed by his resolute composure. He wanted Mother to take his overcoat, saying, "I don't need it now."

Hitler turned down Wilhelm's third appeal against the death sentence and personally signed his execution warrant. But even as Wilhelm's eyes were being bound, he was offered a last chance to renounce his faith. He refused. His last wish? That they should shoot straight. His court-appointed counsel later wrote the family: "He died immediately, meeting death standing erect. His attitude impressed the court and all of us deeply. He died in accordance with his convictions."

Mother immediately went to Münster to claim the body. She was determined to bury him in Bad Lippspringe. As she said, "We will give a great witness to the people who knew him." She added, "I will make Satan pay for killing my Wilhelm." She applied for Father to have four days leave from the prison to attend the funeral, and to our surprise it was granted!

Father gave the prayer at the funeral, and Karl-Heinz, the next eldest son, spoke Biblical words of comfort to a large crowd of mourners gathered at Wilhelm's grave. Some weeks later, without a trial, Karl-Heinz was also sent to a concentration camp, first to Sachsenhausen and later to Dachau.

A Second Martyr

My other older brother, Wolfgang, had taken a stand for the true God when he got baptized, even though he knew it could also lead to his death. But he could not forget the outstanding examples of steadfastness on the part of his father and brothers, indeed those of the entire family. On March 27, 1942, a year and a half after his baptism, he himself was sitting in a cell in Berlin writing the following farewell letter:

"Now, as your third son and brother, I must leave you tomorrow morning. Do not be sad, for the time will come when we will be together again. . . . How great our joy will then be, when we are reunited! . . . Now we have been torn apart, and each of us must stand the test; then we will be rewarded."

Hitler had decided that death by shooting was too good for conscientious objectors. He ordered beheading by guillotine. As our family's second martyr, Wolfgang was beheaded in Brandenburg penitentiary. He was only 20 years of age.

Love for God Still Comes Foremost

What has become of the family members who survived the Nazi era? Waltraud and Hans-Werner were the first to arrive back in Bad Lippspringe at the end of World War II. Hildegard, Elisabeth, and Paul-Gerhard followed. Father, with a broken leg, set out for home nestled between sheep riding on a livestock wagon.

"We were so happy to have Father free and back with us again," Waltraud recalls. "But he was very sick. In June 1945, a nurse brought our seriously ill brother

Karl-Heinz back from Dachau concentration camp. In July 1945, Annemarie, in a roundabout way, arrived back from Hamburg-Fuhlsbüttel penitentiary. The last members of the family, Mother and Magdalena, after many difficulties returned from Ravensbrück in September 1945. How much we had to talk about!"

Did this period of persecution and family loss deaden our love for God? By no means! Father, although sick, did not have a quiet moment until he had reorganized the work, including house-to-house preaching activity, and had arranged for holding meetings. While setting up a family schedule, which provided care for the sick and also saw to the need of making a living, we did not forget that our love for God should come foremost. We considered the possibilities of full-time service. So it was that Elisabeth and I became special pioneers in 1946, while Annemarie and Paul-Gerhard served as regular pioneers.

The Aftereffects

But the aftereffects of persecution on our health soon became apparent. In October of 1946, at the age of 28, Karl-Heinz died of tuberculosis. In July of 1950 my beloved father finished his earthly course in the conviction that his works would go along with him. My mother, who likewise had a heavenly hope, died in 1979. (See Revelation 14:13.) Elisabeth had to quit her full-time service but continued faithful until her death in 1980. In 1951 Mother had taken up pioneer service and, although over 60 years old, was able to continue for three and a half years. And what a great joy for her to see, before her death, most of her grandchildren take up the full-time ministry.

My youngest brother, Paul-Gerhard, worked in the printery at the German Bethel until he was invited to attend the missionary school of Gilead. He graduated with the 19th class in 1952. After several further years of full-time service, he was forced to quit when his wife became seriously ill. Even though she is still bedridden, he serves as an elder, and their daughter Brigitte is now serving as a special pioneer. Their son Detlef has been pioneering for 14 years. Elisabeth's two children, Jethro and Wolfgang, have also been in the full-time service for many years.

In 1948 I, too, went to serve in the Wiesbaden Bethel. Within the Bethel family I felt secure, just like at home. We worked hard, often working well into the night, unloading huge shipments of books from Brooklyn headquarters. In 1950 I married George Reuter, a fellow Bethel worker. With that, a new period began for me, with wonderful experiences at the side of my husband in circuit, district, and missionary service in Togo, Africa, in Luxembourg, and now in southern Spain.

And the rest of the family? In 1960, Annemarie, Waltraud, and Hildegard, together with Mother, moved to a large German city where they could work with English- and Italian-speaking congregations. Hildegard, who had survived nearly five years of prisons and concentration camp, finally succumbed to death in 1979. Annemarie and Waltraud have carried on with their self-sacrificing spirit and devoted work.

Truly, our family, whose love for God came first, has experienced the words of Jesus that "the Devil will keep on throwing some . . . into prison," testing the faithfulness of God's servants "even to death." But we have never forgotten what Jesus also said: "He that conquers will by no means be harmed by the second death." —Revelation 2:10, 11.

Therefore, we have every reason to look forward to being united in the coming "GOLDEN AGE"—no longer just painted on a wall. Under God's Kingdom it will be reality!—Revelation 20:11–21:7.

Kingdom Ministers Meet the Challenge

"What, then, is Apollos? Yes, what is Paul? Ministers through whom you became believers."—1 CORINTHIANS 3:5.

THE authority of ministers of religion is being challenged today. More and more, this is the case as the political element of this world turns against religion, including the "Christian" religion, regarding it as a profit-seeking racket. Even graduates of religious seminaries are discounted as duly authorized ministers and are put under ban in nations that are turning antireligious. Yes, the world empire of false religion is under assault and is threatened with an earth-wide attack that will spell its annihilation. The divine Author of true worship foretold this and fixed his own due time for the fulfillment of his prophecy. Creature life in the whole universe will benefit from this stupendous event!

2 Yet, irreligion will not long remain to dominate the earth, but the vindicated Creator of the universe will remain! Yes, and the true religion of this deathless and Most High God will remain! For that matter, although earth's billions deny the facts, right now practicers of God's pure worship are alive and active on earth. And the following centuries-old statement is true today: "His invisible qualities are clearly seen from the world's creation onward, because they are perceived by the things made, even his eternal power and Godship, so that they are inexcusable." —Romans 1:20.

3 When those words were written during the first century of our Common Era, Jehovah God had his ministers on the earth. Thus the apostle Paul could write: "What, then, is Apollos? Yes, what is Paul? Ministers through whom you became believers, even as the Lord granted each one. I planted, Apollos watered, but God kept making it grow."—1 Corinthians 3:5-9.

4 Jehovah must also have ministers on earth today. But he is not using the religious ministers of Babylon the Great, the world empire of false religion. In fact, they will soon be out of a job. That will be when Babylon the Great itself is put out of existence. Foretelling this, Revelation 16:19 says: "The great city split into three parts, and the cities of the nations fell; and Babylon the Great was remembered in the sight of God, to give her the cup of the wine of the anger of his wrath."

5 What, then, about people who remain the loyal adherents of the religious systems served by the professional ministers

_____
1. (a) Religiously, what is being questioned today, and why? (b) What empire is being threatened, and what will happen to it?
2. As to religion, what will remain and what will not?

_____
3, 4. (a) How can it be proved that Jehovah has ministers on earth? (b) How do we know that the religious ministers of Babylon the Great will soon be out of a job?
5. What happened in ancient Babylon in 539 B.C.E., and what about ministers and other supporters of the religions of Babylon the Great?

of Babylon the Great? Well, consider what happened on that night of 539 B.C.E. when King Belshazzar and his invited lords were praising Babylonian gods at an outstanding feast in defiance of the besieging Medes and Persians. First, notice was served on the revelers when they saw miraculous handwriting on the wall of the banquet hall and heard the interpretation given by Jehovah's prophet Daniel. Then, with Babylon's fall that very night, the king and apparently the other banqueters extolling false gods were slain by the invading conquerers. (Daniel, chapter 5) A similar disaster awaits ministers and those remaining loyal to the religious systems of Babylon the Great.

God's Ministers Urgently Needed

⁶ No one can reasonably question the fact that we are now living in the most critical period of human history since the global Flood of Noah's day. (2 Timothy 3:1-5) So it is vital that there now be genuine ministers of the God of Noah. Surely, as Jehovah gave warnings to the people of Noah's time and to the revelers at Belshazzar's feast, He must have had an urgent message for the

6. (a) In this critical period, what must God have for the human family? (b) When did the Gentile Times end, and what did Jesus say about this?

As Jehovah used Daniel to serve notice on revelers at Belshazzar's feast, so He has ministers to deliver an urgent message today

human family since 1914, when the first world war broke out. Actually, on a wide public scale, for some four decades God's servants had pointed to that year as marking the end of the Gentile Times, regarding which Jesus said: "Jerusalem shall be trodden down of the Gentiles, until the times of the Gentiles be fulfilled."—Luke 21:24, *King James Version.*

⁷ For some 53 years after 1914, or until the Six-Day War of 1967, earthly Jerusalem continued to be trodden down by non-Jewish nations. Evidently, however, Jesus was not referring finally to the Jewish Jerusalem of today but to what that city represented up until 607 B.C.E. And what did it represent? Why, the Kingdom of

7. (a) Until when was earthly Jerusalem trodden down by non-Jewish nations? (b) To what was Jesus referring finally when he spoke of Jerusalem's being "trodden down of the Gentiles"?

Jehovah God by means of his anointed King of the royal house of David!—Luke 1:32; 1 Chronicles 29:11.

⁸ Jesus Christ was the one to whom Jehovah God would give the kingdom of his forefather David of old. Before Pilate as judge, Jesus said that His Kingdom was not of this world, meaning that it would be heavenly. (John 18:36) Logically, then, Jesus' future installation in the Kingdom at the end of the Gentile Times would take place in the invisible heavens. Thus his enthronement would be invisible to human eyes, and that is why neither we nor the Gentile nations literally saw him enthroned in his rightful, God-given Kingdom in 1914. Those nations certainly did not believe that this event took place, despite the fact that it had been proclaimed by Jehovah's people since the 1870's.

⁹ Without regard for the Kingdom message, in the autumn of 1914 the nations became engulfed in war. As foretold at Psalm 2:1-12, they proved themselves to be Jesus' enemies, refusing to "kiss" the newly installed King as a sign of their submission and allegiance. Hence, it became necessary to carry out Psalm 110: 1, 2, where we read: "The utterance of Jehovah to my Lord is: 'Sit at my right hand until I place your enemies as a stool for your feet.' The rod of your strength Jehovah will send out of Zion, saying: 'Go subduing in the midst of your enemies.'"

¹⁰ Jewish opposers displayed their enmity toward Jesus' apostles when Jesus sat down at God's right hand to await the time to start ruling amid his enemies. (Acts 4:24-26) Correspondingly, it was among enemies that the glorified Jesus Christ began his rule at the close of the Gentile Times in 1914. Thus in this 20th century, as in the past, it has been among enemies that Jehovah has had bearers of his message, his genuine ministers of the Kingdom. They are his witnesses.—Isaiah 43:10-12.

Defending Our Qualification as Ministers

¹¹ All along, it has been necessary for genuine God-ordained Kingdom ministers to defend their authorization for the ministry. That certainly has been true of Jehovah's Witnesses in this 20th century. Their qualification as duly ordained ministers of God has been challenged and discounted. By whom? Particularly by Christendom's theological-seminary graduates who receive a certificate of ordination and become paid clergymen. They consider themselves duly schooled and adequately qualified to be the exclusive professional ministers of the God of the Bible.

¹² The situation was similar in the first century C.E. In the Roman province of Galatia, even the inspired writer of about half the books of the Christian Greek Scriptures met with a development that challenged his qualification as an apostle of Jesus Christ, for it put in question the correctness of what he was teaching as Christianity. So he was obliged to tell the Galatians: "I marvel that you are being so quickly removed from the One who called you with Christ's undeserved kindness

---

8. To whom would Jehovah give the kingdom of David, and why would humans not be able to see the foretold enthronement?
9. (a) What did the nations do without regard for the Kingdom message? (b) In view of what the nations did in 1914, what became necessary?
10. (a) Under what circumstances did Jesus begin ruling in 1914? (b) Who have been representing Jehovah in the 20th century?

---

11. By whom has the authorization of Jehovah's Witnesses as God-ordained Kingdom ministers been challenged?
12. The authorization of what prominent first-century Christian was challenged, and how was anyone bringing a different sort of good news to be viewed?

over to another sort of good news. But it is not another; only there are certain ones who are causing you trouble and wanting to pervert the good news about the Christ. However, even if we or an angel out of heaven were to declare to you as good news something beyond what we declared to you as good news, let him be accursed. As we have said above, I also now say again, Whoever it is that is declaring to you as good news something beyond what you accepted, let him be accursed."—Galatians 1:6-9.

¹³ True, that writer, the apostle Paul, did not first learn Christian teachings by personal contact with Jesus Christ or His 12 apostles. Later, Paul did spend some time with the apostle Peter, or Cephas. (John 1:42; Galatians 1:18, 19) But in defense of his being a qualified minister of the good news from God by Christ, Paul could tell the unstable Galatian Christians: "Yes, when they came to know the undeserved kindness that was given me, James and Cephas and John, the ones who seemed to be pillars, gave me and Barnabas the right hand of sharing together, that we should go to the nations, but they to those who are circumcised." (Galatians 2:9) So those Galatians should have asked themselves: If Jesus' apostles Peter, James, and John recognized Paul as a bearer of the true good news, what basis do we have for challenging his message and moving away from it?

¹⁴ But what about Jehovah's people today? Well, since a person like Paul was obliged to defend his qualifications as a minister of God and Christ, why should we be surprised if we, as dedicated, baptized witnesses of Jehovah, are challenged and have to defend our standing as Kingdom

Religious leaders were too proud to accept even Jesus Christ as a minister of God

ministers? Of course, as in Paul's case, such baseless challenging of us proves nothing.

Even Jesus Was Challenged

¹⁵ The Lord Jesus Christ himself was challenged and confronted with the unwillingness of his own people to accept him as an authorized minister of God. For instance, we read: "When by now the festival [of tabernacles] was half over, Jesus went up into the temple and began teaching. Therefore the Jews fell to wondering, saying: 'How does this man have a knowledge of letters, when he has not studied at the schools?'" Jesus met that challenge head-on, declaring: "What I teach is not mïne, but belongs to him that sent me. If anyone desires to do His will, he will know concerning the teaching whether it is from God or I speak of my own originality. He that speaks of his own originality

13. Why should the Galatians not have questioned Paul's authority?
14. Why is it not strange that the ministerial status of Jehovah's Witnesses is challenged?

15. Who, ranking higher than the apostles, was also challenged as to his teaching authority, and to whom did he ascribe his authority?

is seeking his own glory; but he that seeks the glory of him that sent him, this one is true, and there is no unrighteousness in him."—John 7:14-18.

¹⁶ The religious leaders of Judaism looked upon Jesus Christ as a mere Galilean. Of course, they did not think that he could not read because of not having attended school, especially something like a theological seminary. After all, Jesus already had shown that he could read the text of the Hebrew Scriptures. (Luke 4:16-21) What proved unacceptable to such Jews of Judea and Jerusalem was that this former carpenter was not a theologian and could not be ranked with the scribes, Pharisees, and Sadducees of their nation. Why, then, should he publicly presume to know what the Hebrew Scriptures meant and how they applied, speaking with such authority as he did? This is what made those Jews too deaf spiritually to hear the ring of the divine truth. They were too proud to accept what

---

16. Why did the religious leaders of Judaism feel they had grounds for questioning Jesus' teaching ability?

came from a man who had not graduated from a theological school.

"Taught by Jehovah"

¹⁷ Those worldly-wise Jews overlooked the One who really had been teaching Jesus Christ. Why, Jesus' own skill as a teacher had come from "the greatest teacher of all," Jehovah God! (Job 36:22, *Today's English Version*) Referring to God in this capacity, Jesus said: "When once you have lifted up the Son of man, then you will know that I am he, and that I do nothing of my own initiative; but just as the Father taught me I speak these things." (John 8:28) So Jesus proved himself to be the finest pupil in the universal school of the highest Teacher in existence. This was a credit to the One who taught him. No wonder the Nazarenes said of their former townsman: "Where did this man get this wisdom and these powerful works?"—Matthew 13:54.

¹⁸ To understand the Bible, we want and need the best teacher possible. And that teacher is the Inspirer of that unsurpassable Book. Speaking to those who were members of that Teacher's visible, earthly organization during his earthly lifetime, Jesus said: "No man can come to me unless the Father, who sent me, draws him; and I will resurrect him in the last day. It is written in the Prophets, 'And they will all be taught by Jehovah.' Everyone that has heard from the Father and has learned comes to me." (John 6:44, 45) Jesus was there quoting Isaiah 54:13, which reads: "And all your sons will be persons taught by Jehovah, and the peace of your sons will be abundant."

---

17. In connection with Jesus Christ, the Jewish religious leaders overlooked what Teacher, and what kind of scholar was Jesus?
18. (a) What sort of teacher should we want? (b) What did Jesus say about the greatest Teacher and those taught by Him?

¹⁹ However, we ask: The "sons" of whom were to be "persons taught by Jehovah"? That prophetic promise was made to a figurative "woman," a prospective mother of certain "sons," or children. This "woman" is the one addressed at Isaiah 54:1, where it is said: "'Cry out joyfully, you barren woman that did not give birth! Become cheerful with a joyful outcry and cry shrilly, you that had no childbirth pains, for the sons of the desolated one are more numerous than the sons of the woman with a husbandly owner,' Jehovah has said."

²⁰ Since Jehovah is the One who ad-

dresses this "woman" and is to be the Teacher of her "sons," he must be her figurative Husband, and she must be his womanlike heavenly organization. Her "sons," or children, are students of "the greatest teacher of all." Of course, it is vital that those "sons," Jesus' anointed followers, and their companions, the "great crowd," continually apply the instruction provided by Jehovah. (Revelation 7:9) That surely is one way to heed Paul's admonition: "Keep testing whether you are in the faith, keep proving what you yourselves are." (2 Corinthians 13:5) If dedicated, baptized Christians continue to do this and remain diligent students of the greatest Teacher, they should have the needed qualification as Kingdom ministers authorized by Jehovah. We shall next see how God's ministers prove their qualification.

---

19. The "sons" of whom were to be taught by Jehovah?
20. In view of 2 Corinthians 13:5, what must dedicated Christians continue to do, and what bearing does this have on their qualification as Kingdom ministers?

God's Ministers Prove Their Qualification

"And who is adequately qualified?"—2 CORINTHIANS 2:16.

IN TODAY'S religiously divided world, this question may be asked in all sincerity: Who actually is an authorized minister of God? Similarly, the apostle Paul asked: "Who is adequately qualified for these things?" When challenged, Paul and his colaborers could say, "We are"! (2 Corinthians 2:16, 17) But today, who have a

solid basis, the right, and the courage to reply, "We are"?

² Before answering that question, let us consider these words of Paul to Christians in Corinth: "But thanks be to God! For . . . wherever we go he uses us to tell others about the Lord and to spread the Gospel like a sweet perfume. As far as God is

---

1. In today's religiously divided world, what question may be raised in all sincerity?

2. What is the essence of Paul's words at 2 Corinthians 2:14-17?

concerned there is a sweet, wholesome fragrance in our lives. It is the fragrance of Christ within us, an aroma to both the saved and the unsaved all around us. To those who are not being saved, we seem a fearful smell of death and doom, while to those who know Christ we are a life-giving perfume. But who is adequate for such a task as this? Only those who, like ourselves, are men of integrity, sent by God, speaking with Christ's power, with God's eye upon us. We are not like those hucksters—and there are many of them—whose idea in getting out the Gospel is to make a good living out of it."—2 Corinthians 2:14-17, *The Living Bible; see The Watchtower,* May 1, 1944, pages 133-4.

³ Peddling God's Word for selfish profit —how repulsive such a thought! Paul did not seek financial gain by preaching that Word so as to live a life of ease, eventually to retire from the ministry and take it easy the rest of his days. He was willing to make tents as sideline work to provide funds for himself and help his associates in Jehovah's service. (Acts 18:1-4) Paul did not become a financial burden to those to whom he preached the good news. So he could ask the Corinthian Christians: "Did I commit a sin by humbling myself that you might be exalted, because without cost I gladly declared the good news of God to you?" (2 Corinthians 11:7) That question had to be answered with a positive no!

⁴ Today Jehovah's Witnesses imitate the apostle's fine example in not peddling the priceless Word of God but in making it available to all. They do not commercialize such a holy thing. Thus they have no paid clergy, their public speakers do not charge for lectures, and a collection plate is never passed at their meetings. If anyone desires to contribute money for the work, he can drop any amount, even one like the widow's "two small coins of very little value," into a contribution box at the Kingdom Hall or elsewhere. (Luke 21:1-4) Such freewill contributions are used to defray expenses and not to enrich any individual. Even private homes are freely opened for meetings of Jehovah's Witnesses.—Philemon 1, 2.

"Adequately Qualified"

⁵ But who today has qualified Jehovah's Witnesses to carry on after such a Scriptural pattern despite all the persecution and opposition they constantly experience? No one can account for this but the Individual that adequately qualified Paul and his companions for sacred service. Please note the purity of Paul's motive, in contrast with a religious peddler's motivation, as he explained: "As out of sincerity, yes, as sent from God, under God's view, in company with Christ, we are speaking." (2 Corinthians 2:17) This is the way Jehovah's Witnesses are speaking today. But are we recommending ourselves as ministers? Do we need to publish letters of recommendation from others?

⁶ Paul disavowed qualification for his ministry as something he developed. He said: "Our being adequately qualified issues from God, who has indeed adequately qualified us to be ministers of a new covenant." (2 Corinthians 3:4-6) Unlike Paul, the clergy of Christendom claim to be "adequately qualified" because of having

---

3. (a) How should we react to the thought of peddling God's Word for selfish profit? (b) What did Paul do to avoid becoming a financial burden to those to whom he preached?
4. How do Jehovah's Witnesses imitate Paul's example in connection with God's Word?

5. Who has qualified Jehovah's Witnesses for sacred service?
6. (a) Why do Christendom's clergy think they are "adequately qualified"? (b) But what is the basis for a person's having adequate qualification for the true Christian ministry?

graduated from theological seminaries. So they deny that those who are not seminary graduates are qualified ministers having authority to teach. But Paul's special schooling in Judaism did not qualify him for the Christian ministry pertaining to the new covenant. Nor did Jesus establish any theological seminary for his 12 apostles or anyone else to attend. No less so today, a person's being adequately qualified for the true Christian ministry must issue from Jehovah, the greatest Teacher. Of course, such a minister would have to furnish proof beyond all denial.

Jesus taught his disciples to be ministers, but he did not establish any theological seminary

"Who Gave You This Authority?"

7 Religious leaders challenged the right of even God's Son to preach the good news and perform miracles. In the temple, "the chief priests and the older men of the people came up to him while he was teaching and said: 'By what authority do you do these things? And who gave you this authority?'" (Matthew 21:23) They refused to draw the conclusion the Jewish ruler Nicodemus reached when he told Jesus: "Rabbi, we know that you as a teacher have come from God; for no one can perform these signs that you perform unless God is with him."—John 3:1, 2.

8 Jesus could have told his challengers, 'Let my works speak for themselves!' After more than three years of his public career, the chief priests and older men had many signs on which to base a correct conclusion as to Jesus' identity and right to perform miracles and teach the truth about God's Kingdom. They simply were too stiff-necked to accept all the evidence Jehovah was furnishing to prove that Jesus was the promised Messiah.

9 In view of what happened in Jesus' case, it does not surprise Jehovah's Witnesses that their qualification as authorized ministers of his Father is called into question by religious leaders today. Since those who challenged Jesus' authority ignored his many miraculous works, he raised a question that put them on the spot. And his present-day disciples can do the same thing in the case of those who willfully overlook the works of those disciples.

7. In what way did the religious leaders differ from Nicodemus in the way they viewed Jesus' authority?
8. After more than three years of Jesus' ministry, how did Jewish leaders react to proof of his identity and authority?

9, 10. (a) Why should it not surprise Jehovah's Witnesses that their qualification as ministers is questioned today? (b) How did Jesus deal with religious leaders who challenged his authority, and what effect did this have?

[10] When the chief priests and older men asked Jesus, "Who gave you this authority?" he did not pose an abstract question but said: "I, also, will ask you one thing. If you tell it to me, I also will tell you by what authority I do these things: The baptism by John, from what source was it? From heaven or from men?" The account adds: "But they began to reason among themselves, saying: 'If we say, "From heaven," he will say to us, "Why, then, did you not believe him?" If, though, we say, "From men," we have the crowd to fear, for they all hold John as a prophet.' So in answer to Jesus they said: 'We do not know.' He, in turn, said to them: 'Neither am I telling you by what authority I do these things.'" (Matthew 21: 23-27) Today, Jehovah's Witnesses can question the clergy Scripturally in a way that has a similar effect.*

[11] From 1876 onward, Jehovah's people served notice upon the world, and particularly upon Christendom, that the Gentile Times would end in the fall of 1914. (Luke 21:24, *King James Version*) The clergy could not ignore this preliminary work of almost 40 years—a work corresponding to that of John the Baptizer. Those clergymen waited eagerly to pounce upon this journal's editor should 1914 pass without any outstanding events to correspond with those about which he warned. But, oh, how they were silenced when on July 28, 1914, peace was shattered by the outbreak of World War I!

[12] The war's devastation and the withdrawal of many men from agricultural pursuits brought food shortages. Earthquakes shook various parts of the earth,

causing much damage and suffering. In 1915 an earthquake at Avezzano, Italy, killed 29,970, and a tremendous quake in 1920 brought death to 200,000 in Kansu Province, China. In 1923, more than 140,-000 died in the Great Kanto earthquake in Japan. On the heels of the war came the Spanish flu that in one year killed more victims than had four years of war. Not to be passed over was the persecution of Jehovah's servants during that first world conflict, climaxed by the unjust nine-month imprisonment of the president and the secretary-treasurer of the Watch Tower Society and six of their co-workers.

[13] Since the end of World War I, Jehovah's Witnesses have asked Christendom's clergy: 'Are the catastrophic events that have afflicted our earth from 1914 onward a fulfillment of Jesus' prophecy at Matthew 24:3-13?' If those clerics honestly said yes, they would have to admit that Jesus Christ came into his heavenly Kingdom in 1914. Naturally, since Jesus said that 'the world would behold him no more' and he now is an immortal spirit person, his "coming," or "presence," is invisible. (John 14:19; Matthew 24:3, *KJ;* 1 Peter 3:18) But admitting all of this would debar the clergy from arguing that the world-shaking events of 1914-18 were merely a routine flare-up of nations in the course of history.

[14] Moreover, if the clergy of Christendom admitted that the events of 1914-18 marked the start of the end for the old

---

* See, for example, paragraphs 13 and 14 below.

---

11. What work did Jehovah's people do prior to 1914, and how were their critics silenced?
12. What hardships accompanied and followed World War I?

13. What have Jehovah's Witnesses asked Christendom's clergy, and what would these critics have to admit if they answered honestly?
14. (a) If religious leaders made the right admission, in what work would this oblige them to share? (b) What makeshift for the Kingdom would they have to renounce, but what course have they pursued?

system of things, they would be obliged to acknowledge the other features of "the sign" of Jesus' "presence" and would have to take part in the fulfillment of his words: "This good news of the kingdom will be preached in all the inhabited earth for a witness to all the nations." (Matthew 24:14) That would mean preaching, not the Gospel they have preached for centuries, but the good news of the Kingdom established in heaven at the close of the Gentile Times in 1914. They would have to renounce the League of Nations as "the political expression of the Kingdom of God on earth" and view it and its successor, the United Nations, as 'the abomination of desolation standing in the holy place.' (Matthew 24:15, *KJ*) But down to the year 1985, the clergy of Christendom refuse to brand the League of Nations and the United Nations as that "abomination," or "disgusting thing."

¹⁵ So Christendom's clergy refuse to take a stand for Jehovah's Kingdom by Jesus Christ. For failing to support it, they will be destroyed in the "great tribulation" just ahead. But unlike them, Jehovah's Witnesses have abandoned Babylon the Great, the world empire of false religion, and are preaching the Kingdom message in 203 lands. This unparalleled work is an outstanding feature of "the sign" proving that in 1914 Jesus was installed as heavenly King, to rule amid his enemies.—Matthew 24:3, 14, 21; Psalm 110:1, 2; Revelation 18:1-5.

15. What future awaits the clergy, but what have Jehovah's Witnesses been doing?

Any Need for a Recommendation?

¹⁶ Are we baselessly recommending ourselves as Jehovah's anointed witnesses? Or are we adroitly maneuvering matters so as to establish such a recommendation for Jesus' "other sheep"? (John 10:16) Paul did not do such a thing but could say to those Corinthians who became Christians due to his tireless efforts: "Are we starting again to recommend ourselves? Or do we, perhaps, like some men, need letters of recommendation to you or from you? You yourselves are our letter, inscribed on our hearts and known and being read by all mankind. For you are shown to be a letter of Christ written by us as ministers, inscribed not with ink but

16. What questions arise as to recommendation, and what did Paul have to say about this?

with spirit of a living God, not on stone tablets, but on fleshly tablets, on hearts." —2 Corinthians 3:1-3.

[17] With the help of Jehovah's spirit, Paul wrote a number of Bible books and made many converts to Christianity. So he certainly proved to be adequately qualified for the Christian ministry. In a modern parallel, especially since this journal was first published in 1879, the anointed remnant of Christ's disciples, though not inspired as was Paul, have produced much Bible literature. Since 1920, they have published thousands of millions of books, booklets, magazines, and tracts in many languages. This literature has been distributed at reduced cost, much of it being given free to the poor. The Watch Tower Society has also arranged for free Bible lectures and has sent missionaries to unserved territories around the globe. Tens of thousands have responded to the printed and vocal message and have symbolized their dedication to Jehovah God by being baptized, particularly since 1935 when it was first made clear that an unlimited "great crowd" of Jesus' "other sheep" can look forward to eternal life in a restored paradise on earth.—Revelation 7:9-17; Luke 23:43.

[18] Consequently, what if the clergy challenge the anointed remnant to produce certificates as Doctors of Divinity? Why, these servants of Jehovah can provide far more significant evidence! They can now point to over two and a half million "other sheep" earth wide and can say: 'There is our letter of support!' They can take up Paul's words and declare to members of the "great crowd": "You yourselves are our letter, inscribed on our hearts and known and being read by all mankind." (2 Corinthians 3:2)

17. Why can it be said that Paul was adequately qualified for the ministry, and in this regard, what may be said of Jehovah's Witnesses?
18. If challenged to prove their qualification as ministers, to what can the anointed remnant point?

Let Christendom's clergy read that living letter made up of dedicated, baptized Christians who are serving Jehovah God day and night at his temple and who are helping to 'preach this good news of the kingdom in all the earth for a witness to all the nations.' (Matthew 24:14) Like the anointed remnant, they are proving themselves to be adequately qualified for the Christian ministry.

[19] This unique letter of recommendation will not be wiped out in the impending "war of the great day of God the Almighty" at the symbolic place called Har-Magedon. (Revelation 16:14-16) Rather, it will be guarded and preserved by the Omnipotent God for display in the post-Har-Magedon system of things under Christ the King. What a powerful letter that "great crowd" will be to the billions of human dead whom Jehovah God, by Jesus Christ, will then resurrect from the memorial tombs all around the earth! So keep on writing, you anointed remnant! And keep on assisting them, you "great crowd" of the Fine Shepherd's "other sheep"!

19. What unique letter of recommendation will be preserved through Har-Magedon?

What Are Your Comments?

☐ How do Jehovah's Witnesses imitate Paul in not peddling God's Word?

☐ What is the basis for a person's being adequately qualified for the true Christian ministry?

☐ If religious leaders made the right admission, in what work would they be obliged to share?

☐ The anointed remnant can point to what unique letter proving that they are adequately qualified ministers?

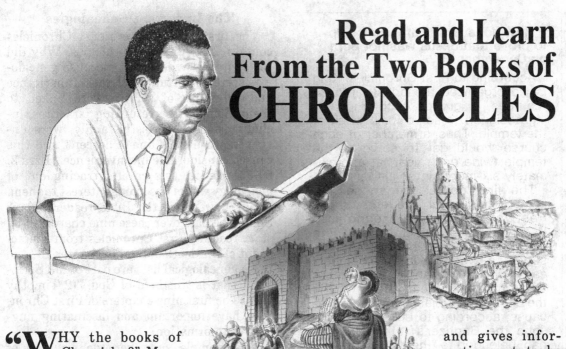

Read and Learn
From the Two Books of
CHRONICLES

"WHY the books of Chronicles?" Many students have asked this question when reading the Bible through for the first time. They read the books of Samuel and Kings and see the history of God's people under the kings presented in a vivid, masterly fashion. Now they face the two books of Chronicles: nine long chapters of genealogies followed by a repetition of much of what they have read before. *Eerdmans' Bible Handbook* comments: "On the face of it, Chronicles seems to repeat in duller and more moralistic fashion what we already have in 2 Samuel and Kings."

But that is only on the surface. Just as the four Gospels in the Christian Greek Scriptures all cover the same general material, but each gives a different perspective and adds information unique to itself, so the writer of the books of Chronicles, while covering the same general material as previous books, has his own perspective and gives information not to be found elsewhere. He was writing for a special period of time and he had certain, well-defined goals. When we understand this, we can enjoy reading the books and learn lessons that will help us today.

They Filled a Need

The books of Chronicles were written, probably by Ezra, for the benefit of the Jews who returned to the Promised Land at the end of the 70 years' captivity in Babylon. After telling about the rule of David and Solomon and the subsequent division of God's people into two nations, the writer concentrated on the southern kingdom of Judah and presented its history in a way that would provide lessons for the returned exiles. He traced the development of the important royal line of David, and in so doing he answered vital questions: Why did Jehovah allow his chosen nation to be exiled

According to First Chronicles, King David organized the priests into 24 "courses," or groups, each group being assigned to serve for a week at the temple. Thus, a member of each course would get to serve at the temple twice each year, at approximately six-month intervals.

The first course began serving immediately after the end of the Festival of Booths, around late September/early October. The eighth group, named after Abijah, served a week in late November/early December, and then another week in late June/early July. Why is the division of Abijah significant? Because, according to Luke's account, John the Baptizer's father, Zechariah, belonged to "the division of Abijah," and he was actually serving in the temple when the angel appeared to him and announced the coming birth of John.—Luke 1:5, 8, 9.

As Luke's record shows, John was conceived very soon after this. Hence, he was born nine months later, either early September or early April. Luke's record also shows that Jesus was six months younger than John. (Luke 1:26) Thus this detail from the book of Chronicles shows that, rather than being born at the end of December, Jesus was born either early March, or early October. Other scriptures show that the latter is the correct time.—For more details, see *The Watchtower*, June 15, 1954, page 382.

The Important Genealogies

The first nine chapters of 1 Chronicles contain long lists of genealogies. Why did the writer include these? Because genealogies were important in Israel. Inheritance and privileges of service were linked to them. Some of the returning Israelites, including some of priestly family, were unable to prove their line of descent, and this caused considerable inconvenience. (Ezra 2:59-63) Hence, this careful tracing out of genealogy was of absorbing interest to them.

But how about the Bible reader today? Should he pass over these nine chapters and start reading First Chronicles from the account of the death of Saul in chapter 10? No, these genealogical lists are part of "all Scripture" that is "inspired of God." (2 Timothy 3:16) The first nine chapters of First Chronicles have important and fascinating nuggets of information.

For example, only here do we read of Jabez, a descendant of Judah who proved himself exceptionally honorable. (1 Chronicles 4:9, 10) Here, too, we find a useful list of the royal line of David, which reveals the important fact that Zerubbabel, the governor of the Jews after their return from Babylon, was of that line.—1 Chronicles 3:10-19.

Telling Us More About David

The remaining chapters of First Chronicles flesh out the historical narratives of previous books, particularly rounding out our knowledge of King David. In previous books the Bible reader got to know David as a devoted servant of Jehovah, an effective warrior, a poet, and a fine leader of men. In First Chronicles we learn that he was also a master organizer. He organized the nation and the army, and he organized worship at the temple, making 24 divisions of priests, Levites, and singers.—1 Chronicles 23:1-27:22.

Second Samuel describes David's intense

in a pagan land? And how could the returned Jews (as well as true Christians today) avoid making the mistakes that led to this punishment?

desire to build a "house," or a temple, for the ark of the covenant. (2 Samuel 7:2-5) Jehovah would not allow David to go ahead with his plans, and First Chronicles explains why. David was a man of blood. The temple would be built by David's successor, a peaceful man. (1 Chronicles 22:8-10) Second Samuel also tells us how David came to buy the threshing floor where the temple was eventually built. (2 Samuel 24:18-25) First Chronicles adds to that by describing the huge contribution that David amassed and all the arrangements he made, so that when Solomon was in a position to start constructing the temple, everything would be ready for him. (1 Chronicles 22:6-19) Why, Jehovah even gave David the temple layout, which was faithfully passed on to Solomon.—1 Chronicles 28:9-21.

Jehovah's Blessing . . .

As you continue reading the second book of Chronicles, you will notice that a theme begins to stand out: When the kings of Judah showed complete confidence in Jehovah, they were blessed. When they did not, the people suffered. For example, King Rehoboam's son Abijam, fighting a war against Israel, was badly outmaneuvered by Jeroboam, the warrior king of the northern kingdom. Abijam's army found itself completely surrounded, so "they began to cry out to Jehovah, while the priests were loudly sounding the trumpets." The result? "God himself defeated Jeroboam and all Israel before Abijah [Abijam] and Judah." —2 Chronicles 13:14, 15.

Similarly Asa, Abijah's son, defeated a huge army of one million Ethiopians because he relied on Jehovah. (2 Chronicles 14:9-12) Asa's son Jehoshaphat was saved from the combined attack of Ammon, Moab, and the Edomites, while many years later his descendant, King Hezekiah, was saved from the might of Assyria, because of that same confidence.—2 Chronicles 20:1-26; 32:9-23.

> **Why did Joseph become father of *two* tribes of Israel, while his brothers fathered only one tribe each?**
>
> First Chronicles helps us to answer this question. Joseph was given the double portion that belonged to the firstborn. True, Joseph was almost the youngest of the 12 sons of Jacob, but he was the older son of Jacob's favorite wife, Rachel. By birth, the right of firstborn should have gone to Jacob's eldest son, Reuben, his firstborn by Leah. But, as First Chronicles tells us, Reuben forfeited this because of a serious sin. The record says: "Reuben . . . he was the firstborn; but for his profaning the lounge of his father his right as firstborn was given to the sons of Joseph the son of Israel, so that he was not to be enrolled genealogically for the right of the firstborn." The account goes on: "For Judah himself proved to be superior among his brothers, and the one for leader was from him; but the right as firstborn was Joseph's."—1 Chronicles 5:1, 2.

. . . and Displeasure

Nevertheless, many of the kings did not show this confidence, usually for one of three reasons. The first was that many fell into the snare of idolatry. Jehoash, Jehoshaphat's great-grandson, started out well, but then turned to idolatry. Jehovah withdrew his protection, and Jehoash was defeated in battle by the Syrians and was finally assassinated. (2 Chronicles 24:23-25) Jehoash's son, Amaziah, showed how seductive idolatry can be. Amaziah started by showing exemplary faith in Jehovah. Then, after a successful war in which he defeated the Edomites, incredibly he took the gods of the Edomites and began to worship them! (2 Chronicles 25:14) So, again, Jehovah withdrew his protection from the king.

Perhaps the worst example of idolatry is Manasseh. Not only did this king worship false gods but he actively persecuted those who stuck to Jehovah's worship. It was because "he filled Jerusalem with innocent blood" that Jehovah determined to destroy Judah. "Jehovah did not consent to grant forgiveness." (2 Kings 21:11; 23:26; 24:3, 4) Yet, surprisingly, Manasseh was the son of Hezekiah, one of the most faithful of Jewish kings. In fact, his birth was the result of a miracle. He was born after Jehovah miraculously extended his father Hezekiah's life. (Isaiah 38:1-8; 2 Chronicles 33:1) And there is a final surprise. After many years of persecuting worshipers of Jehovah, Manasseh repented and at the end of his life was a servant of Jehovah!—2 Chronicles 33:1-6, 12-17.

A second thing that trapped the kings of Judah was foreign alliances. These got the good king Asa into trouble, as well as the not-so-good king Ahaz. (2 Chronicles 16:1-5, 7; 28:16, 20) A tragic result of a foreign alliance was seen in the case of Jehoshaphat. This fine servant of Jehovah unwisely cultivated an alliance with Baal-worshiping King Ahab of Israel. He followed Ahab on unwise military expeditions and allowed Jehoram, his son, to marry Ahab's daughter, Athaliah. Athaliah was a bad influence on her husband, Jehoram, and on Ahaziah, her son, when they became kings in their turn. Then, when Ahaziah died, she usurped the throne and killed most potential rivals. Happily, Jehovah maneuvered things so that the royal line of King David was preserved, but what a tragic result from unnecessary foreign entanglements!

A third snare that some of the kings fell into was haughtiness. It blemished the last years of good King Asa, and because of it, King Uzziah, the military genius, spent the final part of his life as an isolated leper. Even faithful King Hezekiah fell into this snare when he was visited by emissaries from Babylon and proudly showed them the temple treasury.—2 Chronicles 32:25, 26; Isaiah 39:1-7.

Read and Learn From Them

Yes, the two books of Chronicles are a rich mine of information. They show the kind of conduct that pleases Jehovah, and they demonstrate that even kings can fall into sin. What a warning that is today, especially to those in positions of authority in the Christian congregation! Modern idolatry is just as subtle as was idolatry in the days of the Israelite kings, and we must be determined to avoid it. (Ephesians 3:19; Colossians 3:5; Revelation 13:4) We, too, must avoid unnecessary entanglements with the world. (John 17:14, 16; James 4:4) And certainly, the weakness of pride, or haughtiness, is still a problem that we have to fight against.—Proverbs 16:5, 18; James 4: 6, 16.

Reading and learning from the two books of Chronicles will fortify our determination to serve Jehovah by following the good examples and avoiding the bad examples that are presented to us from Jewish history. It will encourage us to imitate the good and avoid the bad, that "through our endurance and through the comfort from the Scriptures we might have hope."—Romans 15:4.

In Our Next Issue

- Adversity
  —How Can We Face It?

- Ministerial Servants—A
  Blessing to Jehovah's People

- Do You Show
  Godlike Kindness?

Kingdom Proclaimers Report

Expansion at the "Hub"

IN INDUSTRIAL circles, the city of Kitwe, Zambia, is often called the "hub" of the Copperbelt. This is because Kitwe lies right at the center of the mining district. Kitwe, however, is also a hub of another sort—the center of theocratic activities in Zambia. Since 1962 the branch office has been located there, and during these two decades the number of publishers in Zambia has virtually doubled, from 30,129 in 1962 to a peak of 58,925 in 1984. The Memorial attendance for 1984 was 393,431, which is one person for every 16 of Zambia's total population.

With such rapid growth, the old branch facilities soon became inadequate. At first, the present structure was simply expanded, adding another dining room for the headquarters staff and space for storage and shipping. However, soon the Zambian branch ventured into the field of printing Bible literature. And in no time at all the small printing room became so cramped that there was little space for movement or storage.

Too, since the branch office was in a residential area, it was difficult to carry on a factory operation without disturbing the neighbors.

So the brothers in Zambia put in an application for a site on which to build a new factory. Obtaining such a site, however, was not easy. The first site offered was rejected by the city council as being 'zoned for government use.' However, a brother came forward and offered some land that he owned. As soon as the brothers got the clearance, they hired an international architectural firm to make plans and present them to the city council for approval. News of this electrified the brothers in Zambia! Many came to help with the construction, which was done under the supervision of a brother who is a professional contractor. In just two years, in 1984, the building was finished.

It was a joyous occasion, indeed, when the dedication program for the buildings took place. Although the brothers were told that seats at the program were extremely limited, over 4,000 from all parts of Zambia attended the meeting! They were thrilled to hear the branch coordinator speak on the history of the work in Zambia and show how Jehovah has backed the work there. Following this, some experiences from old-timers were heard. Some had in times past served as special pioneers in such countries as Tanzania, Kenya, and Uganda when the work there was supervised by the Zambian branch. Now these countries are cared for by the branch that was established in Kenya.

Brother John McBrine, who was visiting from Zimbabwe as zone overseer, concluded the program by encouraging the Zambian brothers to put these new facilities to good use. The literature produced at this factory will further the cause of pure worship and help good-hearted persons to come to a knowledge of the truth! And what will doubtless result from this? Further expansion at the "hub" of theocratic activities in Zambia!

New Watch Tower branch facilities at Kitwe, Zambia

COURAGE
to Face Death

"My husband recently died of cancer," wrote a woman from California. "It is a disease that can destroy both hope and life. Yet the information in the book *You Can Live Forever in Paradise on Earth* helped my husband die with courage. It can most certainly help others to live with hope. Everyone should read it."

You Can Live Forever in Paradise on Earth

September 15, 1985

The Watchtower

Announcing Jehovah's Kingdom

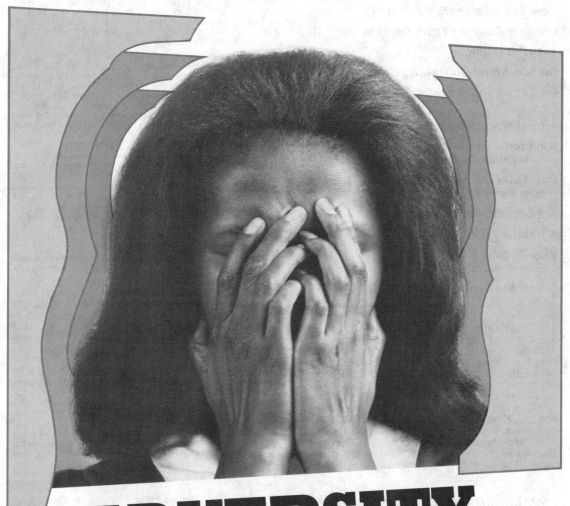

ADVERSITY
—How Can We Face It?

The Watchtower®

Announcing Jehovah's Kingdom

September 15, 1985
Vol. 106, No. 18

In This Issue

THE PURPOSE OF "THE WATCHTOWER" is to exalt Jehovah God as the Sovereign of the universe. It keeps watch on world events as they fulfill Bible prophecy. It comforts all peoples with the good news that God's Kingdom will soon destroy those who oppress their fellowmen and that it will turn the earth into a paradise. It encourages faith in the now-reigning King, Jesus Christ, whose shed blood opens the way for mankind to gain eternal life. "The Watchtower," published by Jehovah's Witnesses continuously since 1879, is nonpolitical. It adheres to the Bible as its authority.

"WATCHTOWER" STUDIES FOR THE WEEKS

October 20: Ministerial Servants—A Blessing to Jehovah's People. Page 14. Songs to Be Used: 10, 34.

October 27: Ministerial Servants—Maintain a Fine Standing! Page 19. Songs to Be Used: 37, 155.

Average Printing Each Issue: 11,150,000

Now Published in 103 Languages

SEMIMONTHLY EDITIONS AVAILABLE BY MAIL
Afrikaans, Arabic, Cebuano, Chichewa, Chinese, Cibemba, Danish, Dutch, Efik, English,* Finnish, French, German, Greek, Hiligaynon, Igbo, Iloko, Italian, Japanese, Korean, Lingala, Malagasy, Maltese, Norwegian, Portuguese, Russian, Sepedi, Sesotho, Shona, Spanish,* Swahili, Swedish, Tagalog, Thai, Tswana, Xhosa, Yoruba, Zulu

MONTHLY EDITIONS AVAILABLE BY MAIL
Armenian, Bengali, Bicol, Bulgarian, Croatian, Czech, Ewe, Fijian, Ga, Greenlandic, Gujarati, Gun, Hausa, Hebrew, Hindi, Hiri Motu, Hungarian, Icelandic, Kannada, Kikuyu, Kiluba, Maiayalam, Marathi, New Guinea Pidgin, Pangasinan, Papiamento, Polish, Rarotongan, Romanian, Samar-Leyte, Samoan, Sango, Serbian, Silozi, Sinhalese, Slovenian, Solomon Islands-Pidgin, Tahitian, Tamil, Telugu, Tshiluba, Tsonga, Turkish, Twi, Ukrainian, Urdu, Venda, Vietnamese
* Study articles also available in large-print edition.

The Bible translation used is the "New World Translation of the Holy Scriptures," unless otherwise indicated.

Twenty cents (U.S.) a copy

Watch Tower Society offices	Yearly subscription Semimonthly
America, U.S., Watchtower, Wallkill, N.Y. 12589	$4.00
Australia, Box 280, Ingleburn, N.S.W. 2565	A$7.00
Canada, Box 4100, Halton Hills (Georgetown), Ontario L7G 4Y4	$5.20
England, The Ridgeway, London NW7 1RN	£5.00
Ireland, 29A Jamestown Road, Finglas, Dublin 11	£5.00
New Zealand, 6-A Western Springs Rd., Auckland 3	$10.00
Nigeria, P.O. Box 194, Yaba, Lagos State	₦6.00
Philippines, P.O. Box 2044, Manila 2800	₱50.00
South Africa, Private Bag 2, Elandsfontein, 1406	R5,60

Remittances should be sent to the office in your country or to Watchtower, Wallkill, N.Y. 12589, U.S.A.

Changes of address should reach us 30 days before your moving date. Give us your old and new address (if possible, your old address label).

The Watchtower (ISSN 0043-1087) is published semimonthly for $4.00 (U.S.) per year by Watch Tower Bible and Tract Society of Pennsylvania, 25 Columbia Heights, Brooklyn, N.Y. 11201. Second-class postage paid at Brooklyn, N.Y., and at additional mailing offices.

Postmaster: Send address changes to Watchtower, **Wallkill, N.Y. 12589.**

Published by
Watch Tower Bible and Tract Society of Pennsylvania
25 Columbia Heights, Brooklyn, N.Y. 11201, U.S.A.
Frederick W. Franz, President

A World Full of
Adversity

NEVER before in history has mankind undergone so much affliction, oppression, and suffering. Disasters have become almost as common as the air we breathe. Describing the period since the year 1914, one journal commented: "This has been a time of extraordinary disorder and violence, both across national frontiers and within them."

Especially agonizing is the tendency toward uncontrolled brutality in present-day warfare. In one small African country, a seven-year struggle took more than 20,000 lives. There were abductions, rapings, and similar acts. Elderly people and young children became victims of land mines, rocket fire, and just plain brutality.

When we view adversity from the standpoint of individuals, the sadness of the situation stands out very clearly. For instance, try to put yourself in the place of a woman who, with her children present, was forced at gunpoint to sing and clap her hands while a gang of men slowly hacked her husband to death. What would your reaction be? Yes, there is truly "anguish of nations," and the *individual* suffers the adversity.—Luke 21:25.

Christians often avoid calamities because of maintaining strict neutrality and keeping away from places where violence is most likely to occur. (John 17:16) However, they cannot avoid all calamity, and at times they suffer, as do those who are part of the world. Through violence and deceit, Satan the Devil can cause untimely deaths. Since part of the message declared worldwide by Jehovah's Witnesses includes exposing the Devil's works, should we not expect Satan to use his "means to cause death" in an effort to do away with these message bearers? The Scriptures so indicate.—Hebrews 2:14, 15; Revelation 2:10; 12:12, 17.

Christians Face Further Sufferings

In addition to the adversities confronting people in general, faithful followers of Jesus Christ must endure the persecution that comes upon them because of their firm stand for the Universal Sovereign, Jehovah God, and his Kingdom. After describing distressing events that would portend the conclusion of the system of man-rule under Satan, Jesus said: "Then people will deliver you [Jesus' disciples] up to tribulation and will kill you, and you will be objects of hatred by all the nations on account of my name." Mark quotes Jesus as adding, "And you will be beaten." —Matthew 24:3, 7-9; Mark 13:9.

Yes, because of their determination to preach "this good news of the kingdom" earth wide under all circumstances, Jehovah's people have had to endure the additional trial of persecution—beatings, bans, imprisonments, and other forms of mistreatment. (Matthew 24:14) Why, persecutors have even killed some Christians whose only "offense" was teaching that the Kingdom of God is the sole hope for mankind!

Jesus did say: "He that has endured to the end is the one that will be saved." (Mark 13:13) However, can we endure and not give out? Is there any source of comfort in even the greatest of adversity? Do we have examples of those who have endured?

How You Can Endure
Adversity

"**B**Y ENDURANCE on your part you will acquire your souls." Jesus Christ spoke those words when giving his prophecy concerning "the time of the end." (Luke 21:19; Daniel 12:4) In his statement, these two points stand out: (1) Endurance is essential to the saving of our life, and (2) it is possible to endure.

But how can you endure? To answer this question, we first need to know why Jehovah permits suffering and persecution to come upon his servants.

Suffering and Persecution—Why?

The prime reason is that Satan challenged the rightfulness and righteousness of Jehovah's sovereignty. (Genesis 3:1-19) Jehovah has arranged to meet this challenge for his own name's sake and for the sake of others.

God has also allowed his people to suffer for purposes that can prove to be very beneficial to us if we view such affliction in the right way. For example, if we endure when under trial without resentment toward our adversities, we are proving that our faith is genuine, the kind of faith that pleases God. (1 Peter 1:6, 7; Hebrews 11:6) But affliction can also show up such personality flaws as pride, impatience, and love of ease. With the help of God's spirit, we can work to overcome such traits and more fully 'clothe ourselves with the new personality.'—Colossians 3:9-14.

The psalmist expressed this point for us very well, saying: "It is good for me that I have been afflicted, in order that I may learn your regulations." (Psalm 119:71) What a fine way to view affliction! No complaining or murmuring. No selfish concern for any personal loss that the affliction might have caused. Rather, here is wise realization that what Jehovah permitted to come upon the psalmist could help him to appreciate the regulations of Jehovah more fully. Do we allow suffering to have the same effect on us?

The apostle Paul benefited from the tribulation he experienced in the district of Asia. For one thing, this adversity made him depend more fully upon Jehovah. It also underlined the apostle's belief in the resurrection, for he endured his hardships with complete trust in "the God who raises up the dead." (2 Corinthians 1: 8-10) Yes, Paul enjoyed benefits because of his endurance under suffering.

The same is true of those Christians who have the right view of affliction today. In Zimbabwe, a country once plagued with guerrilla warfare, a congregation of Jehovah's people was moved into a protected village. Due to the wartime conditions, each of the three appointed elders in the congregation had lost a child in death. Moreover, the local people were putting great pressure on these Christian parents to compromise their faith by appeasing the spirits that were said to have been angered. How did the elders feel about this? Speaking for all three, one of them said: "While the nation is at war, we are also at war with the wicked spirits. We have an advantage over the enemy [wicked spirit forces] in that we have a hope, a living one. So, even if we die in the fight, as long as we die faithful to Jehovah, we shall be resurrected. We shall have conquered the enemy." These three faithful men never lost sight of Jehovah's power to deliver. Noting their firm stand, we, too, should be convinced that we can endure!

When Persecution Is Brutal

'But what if the persecution is brutal, with cruel methods of torture being used?' you may ask. 'Can we even then endure and not give out in our faith?' Well, early Christians were able to endure horrible treatment without compromising their faith.

Similarly, full faith in Jehovah was demonstrated by a present-day Christian living in an isolated rural area of Zimbabwe. He was alone on one occasion because his wife had gone to visit their married daughter. Suddenly, he was accosted by some armed men who made false accusations because of his Christian stand. After beating him severely, these men tied red-hot bricks between his legs and also made him walk on such bricks. Then he was left alone to die. Because the sudden change of conditions in the area had made travel impossible, the man's wife was not aware of her husband's plight. Neighbors were ordered on pain of death not to help him. So he remained alone in this condition for three whole months, daily expecting to die.

This suffering Christian man was able to sustain himself on supplies of water and maize meal at his home. But because of the mistreatment he had received, he could not walk. Therefore, when nearby firewood ran out, he had to break up his furniture and use this to make cooking fires. The water became rusty and full of worms. His burns continued to fester.

This was the brother's condition when his wife was finally able to return home three months later. Imagine how she felt upon seeing him! Immediately, she made preparations to get him to a hospital. To do this, she had to take him in a wheelbarrow to the nearest bus stop and from there get him to town where there was a hospital. Three weeks later, he was discharged from the hospital and went to the home of his daughter, where he received spiritual aid and encouragement from members of the congregation of Jehovah's Witnesses in that area.

What helped this loyal supporter of God's Kingdom to endure brutal treatment? For three months he was entirely on his own. He fully expected to die. And yet, when asked how he felt during this ordeal, his answer was, "I felt that Jehovah was with me all the time." There were no complaints against his persecutors or lamenting over what had happened to him —just firm conviction that Jehovah never forsakes his loyal servants.—Psalm 37:28.

Yes, Christians can endure. They know that if Jehovah allows tribulation, it is for a good purpose, and endurance is possible. God's Word and the experiences of others assure us of this fact. (Matthew 24:13) However, while enduring trials, we often need to be comforted, do we not? But where should we turn for such comfort?

Drawing Comfort
From God's Word

JEHOVAH is "the Father of tender mercies and the God of all comfort, who comforts us in all our tribulation." (2 Corinthians 1:3, 4) Therefore, it is to him and his Word that we must turn to receive true comfort and solace in times of distress.—Romans 15:4.

If we are faithful to God, then he 'will by no means leave or forsake us.' Confidently, we can say: "Jehovah is my helper; I will not be afraid. What can man do to me?" (Hebrews 13:5, 6; Psalm 37:39, 40; 145:20) Surely, therefore, we need not be depressed or discouraged, even when suffering great affliction.

As part of his great prophecy being fulfilled in our time, Jesus said: "You will be delivered up even by parents and brothers and relatives and friends, and they will put some of you to death; and you will be objects of hatred by all people because of my name." But just after that Jesus added: "And yet not a hair of your heads will by any means perish." (Luke 21: 16-18) How could that be? Because of the resurrection, the very same hope that sustained Paul. (John 5:28, 29; 2 Corinthians 1:9, 10) Is it not comforting to know that even death itself cannot take away our wonderful hope for the future?

Think of the comfort that this hope and the assurances of God's help can bring to persecuted Christians enduring physical torture, to those crippled and maimed because of cruelties, to godly women who have been raped, to parents forcibly separated from their children. Yes, in Jehovah's Word we find many expressions of comfort and assurance that can even cause us to rejoice when under tribulation. —Matthew 5:10-12.

Keep in Mind the Reward

When experiencing adversity and affliction, remember that nothing is happening to us that has not happened to other faithful servants of Jehovah. We can resist the Devil's attempts to cause us to stop serving Jehovah if we do what the apostle Peter urged: "Take your stand against [the Devil], solid in the faith, knowing that the same things in the way of sufferings are being accomplished in the *entire association* of your brothers in the world." (1 Peter 5:9) Yes, other Christians endure similar trials for the sake of the good news and do so without compromising. We can do the same.

We should take note not only of those who stood firm but also of the rewards they received. To illustrate: Satan, bent on proving that Job served Jehovah only for selfish reasons, brought one calamity after another upon this man of God. First his animals were destroyed, then his servants, and finally even his ten children. Not satisfied with that, Satan struck Job with "a malignant boil from the sole of his foot to the crown of his head." (Job, chapters 1 and 2) Did Job break his integrity to God because of these calamities?

No, he did not. But what about the reward? Well, Jehovah restored Job's health, gave him "in double amount" all that had been his, and granted him an extended, satisfying life. (Job 42:10-17) In addition to these rewards, there is the far greater one of a resurrection with the prospect of everlasting life on a paradise earth. (Job 14:13-15) Surely, Job's experience gives comfort and strength to suffering Christians today.

"Jehovah Helps"

Now, consider the case of a Christian woman who endured many years of suffering in concentration camps in Germany during World War II. In addition to dreadful conditions, brutal persecution, and privations was a forced separation from her husband and child for five years, not knowing what was happening to them. Finally, after years of faithful endurance, she was reunited with her husband and child, and the three of them have been serving Jehovah faithfully ever since. Note her comments concerning her experience:

Job's experience gives strength to suffering Christians today

"My years in German concentration camps taught me an outstanding lesson. It is how greatly Jehovah's spirit can strengthen you when you are under extreme trial! Before I was arrested, I had read a sister's letter that said that under severe trial Jehovah's spirit causes a calmness to come over you. I thought that she must have been exaggerating a bit. But when I went through trials myself, I knew that what she had said was true. It really happens that way. It's hard to imagine it, if you have not experienced it. Yet it really happened to me. Jehovah helps."

Are you not comforted and strengthened by these expressions? Because of holding fast her integrity under trial, this Christian woman, along with her family, looks ahead to realizing her hope of everlasting life. (Hebrews 10:39) What a grand reward for faithfulness!

After experiencing trials for years, how did our beloved brother Paul feel? Discouraged? Downhearted? Depressed? Not at all! He was confident, hopeful, glad that he had endured. "I have fought the fine fight, I have run the course to the finish, I have observed the faith," said Paul. "From this time on there is reserved for me the crown of righteousness, which the Lord, the righteous judge, will give me as a reward in that day." (2 Timothy 4:7, 8) Paul held his course without wavering and has received his heavenly reward. (Philippians 3:4-14) Who is not comforted by such a fine example? May we similarly endure adversity, draw comfort from the Scriptures, and remain loyal to our loving God, Jehovah.

Jesus' Baptism

ABOUT six months after John begins preaching, Jesus, who is now 30 years old, comes to him at the Jordan. For what reason? To pay a social visit? Is Jesus simply interested in how John's work is progressing? No, Jesus asks John to baptize him.

Right away John objects. "I am the one needing to be baptized by you, and are you coming to me?" he asks. John knows that his cousin Jesus is God's special Son. Why, John had jumped with gladness in his mother's belly when Mary, pregnant with Jesus, visited them! John's mother Elizabeth no doubt later told him about this. And she would also have told him about the angel's announcement of Jesus' birth and about the appearance of angels to shepherds the night he was born.

So Jesus is no stranger to John. And John knows that his baptism is not for Jesus. It is for those repenting of their sins, but Jesus is without sin. Yet, despite John's objection, Jesus insists: "Let it be, this time, for in that way it is suitable for us to carry out all that is righteous."

Why is it right for Jesus to be baptized? Because Jesus' baptism is a symbol, not of repentance for sins, but of his presenting himself to do the will of his Father. Jesus was a carpenter, but now the time has come for him to begin the ministry that God sent him to earth to perform. Do you think John expected anything unusual to happen when he baptized Jesus?

Well, John later reported: "The very One who sent me to baptize in water said to me, 'Whoever it is upon whom you see the spirit coming down and remaining, this is the one that baptizes in holy spirit.'" So John was expecting God's spirit to come upon someone he baptized. Perhaps, therefore, he was not really surprised when, as Jesus came up from the water, 'God's spirit came upon him like a dove.'

Jesus' Life and Ministry

But more than that happened at Jesus' baptism. The heavens were opened to Jesus, and a voice said: "This is my Son, the beloved, whom I have approved." Whose voice was that? Jesus' own voice? Of course not! It was God's. Clearly, Jesus is God's Son, not God himself, as some people claim. **Matthew 3: 13-17; Luke 3:21-23; 1:34-36, 44; 2:10-14; John 1:32-34; Hebrews 10:5-9.**

♦ Why was Jesus no stranger to John?

♦ Since he had committed no sins, why was Jesus baptized?

♦ In view of what John knew about Jesus, why may he not have been surprised when God's spirit came upon Jesus?

Do You Show
Godlike Kindness?

CAN you remember the last time someone was truly kind to you? Surely, all of us appreciate the helpfulness, sympathy, and gentleness of a kind person.

Though often in short supply, kindness is not unknown in today's world. Salespersons are instructed to show it to their customers. Businessmen know its value in dealing with their clients. True, kindness is often shown with ulterior motives. Yet genuine human kindness does exist. Thus, when a married couple living a good distance away visited the husband's father who had been incapacitated by a stroke and was barely able to move, how refreshed they were to observe that the neighbors had already taken care of some necessary chores!

The Bible contains some outstanding examples of human kindness. While en route to Rome by ship, Julius, the army officer placed in charge of the apostle Paul, allowed his prisoner to visit and enjoy the care of friends at Sidon. Yes, Julius "treated Paul with human kindness." (Acts 27:3) Shortly thereafter, when a shipwreck occurred, the people of Malta showed all the 276 passengers and crew "extraordinary human kindness." In fact, Publius, "the principal man of the island," was notably hospitable.—Acts 28:1-10.

That all men, created in God's image, can reflect a measure of Jehovah's personality was indicated when the apostle Paul wrote: "Whenever people of the nations that do not have law do by nature the things of the law, these people, although not having law, are a law to themselves.

They are the very ones who demonstrate the matter of the law to be written in their hearts." (Romans 2:14, 15; Genesis 1:26) So some kindness is inherent in mankind. Yet we would rightly expect that true Christians would show a distinctly *godlike* kindness. What is the nature of such kindness? How does God exercise kindness? And how can we imitate him in displaying this fruit of his spirit?—Galatians 5:22.

Jehovah's Loving-Kindness

The Bible repeatedly extols God's loving-kindness. "Praise Jah, you people! Give thanks to Jehovah, for he is good; for his loving-kindness is to time indefinite," said the psalmist. (Psalm 106:1; 107:1) In the Hebrew Scriptures, the word used for "loving-kindness" refers to a quality that lovingly attaches itself to an object until the purpose is realized. Thus, out of his love for mankind, God has exercised loving-kindness with man's salvation in view. Otherwise, mankind would have perished long ago. Tolerating no wrongdoing, God expelled our first human parents, Adam and Eve, from the garden of Eden. Still, he showed loving-kindness by providing them with clothing, allowing them to bring forth children, and permitting them to live for a considerable time in spite of their rebellious acts.—Genesis 3:21–4:2; 5:4, 5.

In many ways, Jehovah has shown loving-kindness to Adam's sinful descendants. For instance, the apostle Paul could tell practicers of false religion in Lystra that God "did not leave himself without witness in that he did good, giving you rains from heaven and fruitful seasons, filling your hearts to the full with food and good cheer." (Acts 14:16, 17) Even though their worship was directed to a false god, Jehovah kindly provided for them richly in a material way.

Of much greater significance, however, was the loving-kindness God showed toward Adam's yet-unborn offspring. Through the promised "seed," Jehovah provided hope of deliverance from human sin and death. (Genesis 3:15; Romans 5:12) In spite of mankind's God-dishonoring record, God did not abandon mankind. Why, he even gave his most beloved and only-begotten Son as a ransom sacrifice in their behalf! (John 3:16) And in a further manifestation of "undeserved kindness," God has also arranged for some integrity-keeping humans to be joint heirs with Jesus Christ in the heavenly Kingdom that will bless all obedient mankind.—Romans 5:8, 15-17; 8:16, 17; Revelation 14:1-4.

Showing Godlike Kindness

How can imperfect humans show godlike kindness? Well, Jesus provided an example and guidelines that can help us to exercise such kindness. (1 Peter 2:21; Matthew 11:28-30) For instance, he indicated that we should be kind even to our enemies. Jesus said: "Continue to love your enemies and to do good and to lend without interest, not hoping for anything back; and your reward will be great, and you will be sons of the Most High, because he is kind toward the unthankful and wicked." (Luke 6:35) So if we would show the superior quality of godlike kindness, we will be kind not only to family members, friends, and Christian brothers but also to those who are unthankful and have shown themselves to be our enemies. This is not done to irritate them but to help them and to bring out the best in

them.—Galatians 6:10; Romans 12:20, 21.

Since our human inclination is to treat others as they treat us, we do well to remember Jehovah's reminder: "In loving-kindness I have taken delight, and not in sacrifice." (Hosea 6:6) Thus, if we wish to have Jehovah's favor, we must endeavor to display godlike kindness, or loving-kindness, in all our dealings with others. (Compare Micah 6:8.) But to demonstrate this godly quality, we need to imitate Jehovah in a specific way. What is that? Well, just as he kindly took the first steps to put us in good standing with him, so we should take the initiative in sharing Bible truths with others. Even if rebuffed at first, we must still exercise loving-kindness by endeavoring repeatedly to reach their hearts with the good news of God's Kingdom. How fine it is when this display of godlike kindness helps others to get on the road to life!—Matthew 7:13, 14.

How to Cultivate It

Cultivating godlike kindness is possible only by learning and acting in harmony with God's thoughts as expressed in the Bible. Yes, we must first gain an accurate knowledge of the truth. Paul commended Christians at Colossae and acknowledged that the truth had borne fruitage "from the day [they] heard and accurately knew the undeserved kindness of God in truth." (Colossians 1:5, 6) Yet, no Christian gets to the point where further progress cannot be made. Therefore, each one of us must "go on growing in the undeserved kindness and knowledge of our Lord and Savior Jesus Christ."—2 Peter 3:18.

Since kindness is part of the fruitage of God's holy spirit, Christians submitting to the influence of that spirit will be kind. In fact, Paul specifically connects godlike holiness with kindness, saying: "As God's chosen ones, holy and loved, clothe yourselves with the tender affections of compassion, kindness." (Colossians 3:12) So we must have God's holy spirit in order to display godlike kindness.

But how do we get Jehovah's spirit? By asking him for it—repeatedly. Jesus showed that if we humbly supplicate Jehovah for this precious gift, our heartfelt request will be granted. After mentioning the need to "keep on asking" and to "keep on seeking," Jesus said: "Therefore, if you, although being wicked, know how to give good gifts to your children, how much more so will the Father in heaven give holy spirit to those asking him!" (Luke 11:9-13) Indeed, by requesting Jehovah's spirit and specifically asking for his help in displaying greater kindness, we are assured of a favorable answer. (1 John 5:14, 15) Of course, our actions need to be consistent with our request for God's spirit.

Another aid in cultivating this quality is meditating on the expressions of Jehovah's kindness that we can observe around us. Concerning God, the psalmist said: "I shall certainly meditate on all your activity, and with your dealings I will concern myself." (Psalm 77:12) We do well to take note of and reflect on God's qualities as observed in everyday life. The beauties of creation, the delights of food and drink, the items we need for our comfort and pleasure, the joy that children bring —even the antics of animals—all bespeak God's kindness to mankind. Yes, a beautiful sunset, a colorful rainbow, a fine meal, or a treasured friendship can well remind us that God kindly provides many things for our enjoyment. Truly, "his invisible qualities [including kindness] are clearly seen from the world's creation onward, because they are perceived by the things made." (Romans 1:20) Meditation on such things is vital if we truly wish to imitate our great God of kindness.

Make It a Goal

It certainly is worth while to make it our goal to develop the quality of godlike kindness. Personal and family relationships are bound to improve where kindness is displayed. Kindness also attracts people to the Kingdom message. Many a skeptic has been moved to examine the truth because of the kindness shown by Jehovah's Witnesses in the ministry. Yes, kindness has brought out the best in those who might otherwise be hostile.

In the door-to-door ministry, one young Witness met a woman who curtly rebuffed her. Noting that the woman was ill, the sister asked if she could do anything for her. The woman coolly refused any assistance. But two weeks later the young sister stopped by to see the woman again and asked if she had been able to do any shopping for food since they had met. Since the woman had not been able to get food into her home, the sister insisted on going to the store for the needed items. Thereafter, this woman was much more cordial to Witnesses calling at her door—all of this because the sister had shown godlike kindness.

This most desirable quality has drawing power. Illustrating this are the observations of a young college graduate after going to the Kingdom Hall for the first time. At the hall, the Witnesses from humble backgrounds were concerned about how this woman would respond to them and their speech. But this educated woman did not recall failings they may have had. Rather, she remembered only that everyone was so kind to her, and she was impressed with the genuine interest they took in her. Moved by their example, she dedicated her life to God. Soon she was showing selfless interest in others as a regular pioneer and later as a member of the Bethel family.

Truly, godlike kindness is a most desirable quality. It is one that should be evident in all our dealings. Do you show it?

Insight on the News

Southern Baptist "Showdown"

Excitement ran high at a religious gathering in the Dallas Convention Center in June. Over 45,000 Baptist delegates met for what *The New York Times Magazine* called "a showdown between the fundamentalists and the more moderate factions for control of the presidency of the Southern Baptist Convention," the largest Protestant denomination in the United States. In the end, the fundamentalist incumbent, Charles Stanley, was elected over his more moderate rival, Winfred Moore. But the convention did little to quell the discord between church members.

While Southern Baptists believe that the Bible is inspired, the more moderate among them, whom fundamentalists call liberals, do not believe that the Scriptures are necessarily inerrant. The fundamentalists fear that the moderates are compromising traditional Baptist theology. On the other hand, the moderates resent the fact that their fundamentalist brothers do not adhere to a strict separation of Church and State but involve themselves in politics, as in lobbying for school prayer and for a ban on abortions. The differences between these factions are nowhere near being resolved. Thus the situation does not harmonize with the apostle Paul's exhortation that true Christians "speak in agreement" and "be fitly united in the same mind and in the same line of thought."—1 Corinthians 1:10.

Sports Violence

"Europe's soccer stadiums are increasingly coming to resemble gladiator pits." So observed *Time* magazine in a report on the tragic violence involving British and Italian soccer fans that resulted in 38 deaths at the European Cup finals in Brussels last May. Violence by fans is a growing problem in other parts of the world too. During May, Chinese fans in Peking rioted—smashing buses, overturning cars, and menacing foreigners—when their soccer team was eliminated from World Cup contention by Hong Kong.

Why do sports fans lose control? Authorities say it is because many sports enthusiasts are poor, bored, and ill-equipped to deal with defeat or humiliation. "But social class or economic considerations are not the main roots," says Dr. Jeffrey H. Goldstein, an expert on sports-related violence. "It's nationalism pure and simple. In an era of instant communications, people increasingly are making nationalist issues of international sporting events, and the people are abetted by the actions of the press, sports officials, politicians and the athletes themselves." Goldstein adds that to fans "international sporting events have become tests of the rightness or wrongness of ideology."

Although nationalism may spur many sports fans to violence, true Christians are neutral, peace-loving advocates of God's Kingdom. Moreover, they avoid getting caught up in the worldly competitive spirit.—John 17:16; Romans 12:18; Galatians 5:26.

Not 'Sticking to Their Role'

"One of the curious things about our very verbal political bishops is that they appear to have absolutely no sense of Christian priorities," writes columnist Paul Johnson in *The Daily Telegraph* of London. Church bishops spend too much time with political matters, he says, and ignore a far more significant problem. Says Johnson: "In both the United States and Britain, the biggest single cause of poverty is the one-parent family," often resulting from teenage immorality. "Yet oddly enough it is a long time since I have heard any clergyman, let alone a bishop, preach a sermon on the evils of fornication." If bishops "would only stick to their fundamental and traditional role as custodians of morality," he concludes, they could "have an important part to play in reducing economic hardship."

Johnson's comments bring to mind a situation in ancient Israel. Religious leaders at that time also failed to teach God's Word so that the people might "turn back from their bad way." Of such men, God said: "I am against the prophets, . . . the ones who are stealing away my words, each one from his companion." (Jeremiah 23:22, 30) Likewise, modern-day clergymen who fail to teach proper Christian morals, perhaps even misapplying Bible texts for political or other reasons, can expect to earn God's disfavor.—Compare Luke 11:52.

Ministerial Servants
A Blessing to Jehovah's People

> "Let these be tested as to fitness first, then let them serve as ministers, as they are free from accusation."—1 TIMOTHY 3:10.

JEHOVAH is "the happy God," and he wants his servants to be happy. (1 Timothy 1:11) To that end, he has provided elders and ministerial servants for the blessing of his people. These responsible men serve beneficial purposes and help to ensure the happiness, unity, and smooth operation of the Christian congregation. How grateful Jehovah's Witnesses are for the loving and helpful service rendered by these appointees within God's theocratic organization!

² Despite the vital contribution elders and ministerial servants make to the congregation, however, they are not to magnify their own importance. They must remember that Jesus Christ admonished his followers to be humble. He once told them: "Whoever will humble himself like this young child is the one that is the greatest in the kingdom of the heavens." (Matthew 18:4) And the disciple James wrote: "Humble yourselves in the eyes of Jehovah, and he will exalt you." (James 4:10; Romans 12:3) But having a humble attitude does not require that these men downplay the importance of their work as elders and ministerial servants. They can be humble and still take the lead in the service activities. Never should they lose sight of the beneficial purposes served by their activi-

ty, but they should always remember their obligation, both to Jehovah and to their Christian brothers, to do the best they can in fulfilling their duties.

³ United activity among Jehovah's Witnesses today can be compared to the unity in the human body. In fact, the apostle Paul likened the spiritual body of Christ to the human body made up of many members. Yet for mutual benefit, all members of the body work together. (1 Corinthians 12:12-31) And, surely, appointed elders and ministerial servants are a blessing to Jehovah's people, for these men further the unified operation of the Christian congregation today. (Compare Colossians 2: 18, 19.) Dedicated male members of the congregation who strive to support Jehovah's organizational arrangement by "reaching out for an office of overseer" are making a vital contribution to Christian unity and the advancement of Kingdom interests. (1 Timothy 3:1) But how does a Christian man qualify, in the first place, to become a ministerial servant?

"Tested as to Fitness First"

⁴ The apostle Paul told his co-worker Timothy what was required before men

---

1. Who help to ensure congregational happiness and unity?
2. What attitude should elders and ministerial servants have, but of what should they never lose sight?

3. United activity among Jehovah's Witnesses can be compared to what, and how can dedicated men promote such unity and the advancement of Kingdom interests?
4. (a) Why should prospective ministerial servants be "tested as to fitness first"? (b) These men should be willing to do what?

Elders and ministerial servants are a blessing to the congregation

could be appointed as ministerial servants. Among other things, Paul wrote: "Let these be tested as to fitness first, then let them serve as ministers, as they are free from accusation." (1 Timothy 3:10) This would prevent the appointing of unqualified men, those not meeting certain basic Scriptural requirements. It would also allow time to determine the motives of prospective ministerial servants. Surely, these men should not be motivated by a desire to gain prestige, for that would indicate a lack of humility. Rather, in recognition of the fact that a Christian's dedication to God is unconditional and all embracing, a brother should be willing to serve in any capacity in which Jehovah sees fit to use him in His organization. Yes, prospective ministerial servants should be as willing to serve as was faithful Isaiah, who said: "Here I am! Send me."—Isaiah 6:8.

⁵ "Ministerial servants should likewise be serious, not double-tongued, not giving themselves to a lot of wine, not greedy of dishonest gain," Paul explained. (1 Timothy 3:8) Although some ministerial servants may be comparatively young, they are not youths and must be "serious." They must have learned to view important matters seriously. (Compare Proverbs 22:15.) They must be reliable and conscientious, not men inclined to take responsibility lightly. Indeed, they should be dependable, taking their duties seriously. After all, what could be of more serious concern than sacred service to Jehovah? It is a matter of life and death —for them and for others. (Compare

5. (a) What requirements for ministerial servants are set out at 1 Timothy 3:8? (b) What does it mean to be "serious"? (c) Paul meant what in saying that ministerial servants must not be "double-tongued"?

1 Timothy 4:16.) Moreover, in saying that ministerial servants must not be "double-tongued," Paul meant that they were to be straightforward and truthful, not gossipy, hypocritical, or devious.—Proverbs 3:32.

⁶ Good balance is a *must* in the personal life of men who qualify to be ministerial servants. Paul obviously meant that they must shun drunkenness, greed, and dishonesty when he said that they should neither be "giving themselves to a lot of wine" nor be "greedy of dishonest gain." These Christian men must also avoid giving even the impression that they are excessively interested in pleasures or material things. They should always strive to put spiritual matters first in life. This will help them to maintain "a clean conscience" before fellow humans and, more importantly, in the eyes of God.—1 Timothy 3:8, 9.

⁷ The heavy responsibilities falling upon ministerial servants are not intended for youngsters. These men are spoken of in Scripture as being of such an age that they could be married and have a family. Under those circumstances, they would have to be "presiding in a fine manner over children and their own households." (1 Timothy 3:12) Does this mean that a young man would not become eligible to be a ministerial servant until he had first married and raised a family? No, not at all. In fact, his reluctance to rush into marriage without ample preparation or before finding a suitable baptized Christian partner may reveal a degree of maturity needed to take proper care of personal affairs and the far more serious congregational responsibilities.

⁸ Paul said that "men who minister in a fine manner are acquiring for themselves a fine standing and great freeness of speech in the faith in connection with Christ Jesus." (1 Timothy 3:13) One way they can show the required "great freeness of speech" is by taking an active part in preaching "this good news of the kingdom." (Matthew 24:14) They should realize that they share with the elders the responsibility for taking the lead in preaching from house to house and participating in other forms of the ministry. (Acts 5:42; 20:20, 21) As Satan's wicked system rapidly nears its end, the preaching activity takes on ever greater urgency. Ministerial servants should, therefore, keep the urgency of the Kingdom-preaching work before the congregation by setting an excellent personal example in the field ministry.

Helped by the Full-Time Ministry

⁹ In view of the urgency of our critical times, many Christian men and women have taken up the full-time ministry. Many, called pioneers, daily spend an average of between two and five hours in the preaching work, some of them as missionaries in foreign lands. Others serve full time at the Watch Tower Society's headquarters or in its branch offices around the earth. Their service is a source of joy and satisfaction to them and to those they serve. And in many cases experience in full-time service has helped men to develop the qualifications needed

6. What are some ways in which ministerial servants should manifest balance?
7. (a) Why can it be said that the responsibilities of ministerial servants are not intended for youngsters? (b) The fact of a ministerial servant's being single may reveal what about him?

8. In connection with 1 Timothy 3:13 and Matthew 24:14, what responsibility rests upon ministerial servants?
9. In view of the urgency of our times, what service have many Christians taken up?

to serve the congregation beneficially as ministerial servants.

¹⁰ One former ministerial servant, now an elder in a Berlin, Germany, congregation, says of the pioneer work he took up years ago as a young man: "I can say that it was a step I have never regretted. Jehovah has blessed me. My relationship with him has become more intimate." Yes, like thousands of others, this brother discovered that the full-time ministry can deepen a person's relationship with Jehovah and speed up progress toward Christian maturity.

¹¹ Another longtime pioneer explains how the full-time service helped him. "I quieted down and became more balanced as regards making hasty judgments," he says. "I was happier and became more flexible in dealing with different kinds of people." Are these not among the qualities needed by men desiring to serve as ministerial servants?

¹² Participating in the full-time ministry, if Scriptural responsibilities permit, can serve as a marvelous opportunity for Christian men to be "tested as to fitness first." Some can take up such ministry on a permanent basis, others from time to time. Younger people might do so during school vacations, and older ones during vacation periods or at other appropriate times throughout the year. Of course, participating in the full-time service calls for balance and careful planning. These abilities are needed by a ministerial servant and will help him to fulfill his duties. What duties?

10, 11. As indicated by personal expressions cited here, how may men desiring to be ministerial servants be benefited by full-time service?
12. (a) What opportunities are there to participate in the full-time ministry? (b) Participating in the full-time ministry calls for what abilities that would help a ministerial servant fulfill his duties?

Pioneer service is excellent training for those desiring to become ministerial servants or elders

Duties of Ministerial Servants

¹³ Although Acts 6:1-6 does not directly apply to the appointing of ministerial servants, what is said there does suggest the type of work or the nature of duties that normally would be assigned to ministerial servants. Not by instructing fellow believers but by distributing food, the "seven certified men" then chosen freed the apostles to 'devote themselves to prayer and to the ministry of the word.' By caring for similar duties today, ministerial servants provide the elders with more time for shepherding and teaching "the flock of God." —1 Peter 5:2, 3.

¹⁴ Regarding the duties of ministerial servants, the book *Organized to Accomplish Our Ministry* states: "One ministeri-

---

13. Acts 6:1-6 suggests what as to the type of work assigned to ministerial servants?
14. What varied duties may be assigned to ministerial servants?

al servant may be assigned to take care of the congregation literature, making it convenient for all of us to obtain the literature we need for our personal use and for field service. Another may care for the magazines in the congregation. Others are assigned duties to keep records such as for the congregation accounts or for the assigning of territory, or they are used to handle microphones, operate sound equipment, look after the platform or perhaps help the elders in other ways. There is much work to be done in maintaining the Kingdom Hall and keeping it clean, so ministerial servants are often called upon to assist in caring for such responsibilities. Ministerial servants are also assigned to serve as attendants, welcome new ones and help maintain order at congregation meetings."—Pages 57-8.

15 Could just any brother with practical ability perform such work? No, for the "certified men" chosen in first-century Jerusalem were "full of spirit and wisdom," or were "both practical and spiritually-minded." (Acts 6:3, *Phillips*) Even if they were already older men among Jehovah's people, they were assigned work similar to that now done by ministerial servants. So if present-day ministerial servants are to fulfill their duties effectively, they must be "both practical and spiritually-minded." While they are occupied with organizational details, their chief interest should be in serving *people* in spiritually beneficial ways.

16 Since ministerial servants must be spiritually minded, at times they can be used for work normally done by elders. *Organized to Accomplish Our Ministry*

(pages 58-9) explains: "If there are not enough elders to conduct the Congregation Book Studies, some of the more qualified ministerial servants are used as study conductors to care for assigned groups. They may be assigned to handle parts in the Service Meeting and the Theocratic Ministry School and to deliver public talks in the local congregation. Other privileges may be extended to some of the ministerial servants where there is particular need and they meet the requirements for the assignment.—Compare 1 Peter 4:10."

17 One of the "seven certified men" of Bible times was "Stephen, a man full of faith and holy spirit." (Acts 6:5) Before dying as a faithful martyr, Stephen gave a stirring testimony before the Jewish Sanhedrin. Read the account, and you will be convinced that he was spiritually minded, an outstanding witness receptive to the guidance of God's holy spirit and willing to give his life in Jehovah's service. (Acts 6:8–7:60) If you are a ministerial servant, do you take your congregational duties and field ministry as seriously as Stephen obviously took his responsibilities and his privilege to speak the truth?

How Are They Measuring Up?

18 Many ministerial servants are setting a fine example in Christian living, are caring for their congregational responsibilities very well, and are taking a good lead in the field ministry. Their work is greatly appreciated by fellow worshipers and will not be left unrewarded by Jehovah, for Hebrew Christians were assured: "God is not unrighteous so as to forget your work and the love you showed for his

15. (a) To serve effectively as a ministerial servant, what is needed besides practical ability? (b) Although ministerial servants look after various things, what should be their chief concern?
16. If there are not enough elders in a congregation, ministerial servants may be assigned what duties?

17. What kind of man was Stephen, and what question does this raise concerning ministerial servants?
18. What can be said about the work of many ministerial servants, and of what can they be assured?

name, in that you have ministered to the holy ones and continue ministering."—Hebrews 6:10.

¹⁹ However, each ministerial servant might well ask himself: How am I measuring up to Scriptural requirements? Do I really contribute to the unity of the congregation? Am I caring for my assigned duties properly and industriously? And am I setting a good example in the field ministry? Some ministerial servants have met with problems in measuring up to what is required of them. So let us discuss some of these problems. Doing so can help each ministerial servant to "prove what his own work is." (Galatians 6:4) It should also

increase the appreciation others have for the labors of love performed by these men who serve beneficial purposes among Jehovah's Witnesses and are a real blessing to God's people.

---

19. (a) What questions might each ministerial servant ask himself? (b) Why will it be beneficial to discuss problems experienced by some ministerial servants?

Can You Explain?

□ How are ministerial servants a blessing to Jehovah's people?

□ How can the full-time ministry help brothers who want to become ministerial servants?

□ Why must ministerial servants be "both practical and spiritually-minded"?

□ How was faithful Stephen a fine example for ministerial servants today?

Ministerial Servants
Maintain a Fine Standing!

"The men who minister in a fine manner are acquiring for themselves a fine standing and great freeness of speech in the faith in connection with Christ Jesus."—1 TIMOTHY 3:13.

MEN who now are ministerial servants have been "tested as to fitness first." (1 Timothy 3:10) But their appointment was not an end in itself. Their goal is to go on "acquiring for themselves a fine standing" by carrying out

their duties in "a fine manner." (1 Timothy 3:13) Each member of the united Christian congregation will want to support them in achieving this goal.

² The apostle Paul indicated that all members of the spiritual body of Christ benefit by working together and caring for

---

1. After his appointment as a ministerial servant, what should be a man's goal, and what should others in the congregation want to do?

---

2. How are members of the congregation affected by what is done by ministerial servants?

Ministerial servants must faithfully discharge their responsibilities in the disciple-making work and within the congregation

one another. (1 Corinthians 12:12-31) Similarly, when ministerial servants do their God-given work in "a fine manner," every member of the present-day Christian congregation is benefited. But when ministerial servants encounter problems that hinder them from fulfilling their duties properly, this may work a hardship on all members of the congregation.

³ All of Jehovah's people have the same fight, "a wrestling, not against blood and flesh, but . . . against the wicked spirit forces in the heavenly places." (Ephesians 6:12) Additionally, all of Jehovah's servants have a fight against their own imperfections and sinful tendencies. As a group, however, ministerial servants are faced with certain problems in a more pronounced way than are other groups of Jehovah's Witnesses. Helpful in illustrat-

ing this is a recent survey of over 320 congregations with 1,360 ministerial servants in one western European country.

Singleness and Marriage

⁴ Of the ministerial servants surveyed, slightly over 10 percent are still single. They thus enjoy freedom from certain responsibilities common to the nearly 90 percent who are married. But single brothers must be careful not to use this freedom simply in the pursuit of such personal things as excessive recreation or socializing. Nor should they allow the natural desire for marriage to take priority over everything else in life. (Matthew 6:33) Neither should they allow pressure from their married friends to force them into a hasty or unwise marriage. And, surely, Christians who care for one anoth-

3. (a) What problems are common to all of Jehovah's people? (b) What does a recent survey help to illustrate?

4. How should unmarried ministerial servants view their singleness, and what encouragement can others give them?

er will respect the single status of unmarried fellow believers and will encourage them to take advantage of their greater freedom to devote more time to theocratic pursuits, possibly by taking up the full-time ministry.

⁵ According to the aforementioned survey, about 62 percent of the ministerial servants are parents. For them, the danger of their hearts getting "weighed down" with the "anxieties of life" is greater than it is for single brothers. (Luke 21: 34-36) Thus, in recommending singleness, Paul said: "I want you to be free from anxiety. The unmarried man is anxious for the things of the Lord, how he may gain the Lord's approval. But the married man is anxious for the things of the world, how he may gain the approval of his wife, and he is divided. . . . He also that gives his virginity in marriage does well, but he that does not give it in marriage will do better."—1 Corinthians 7:32-38.

⁶ Although Jehovah's people do not believe that 'marriages are made in heaven,' they know that heavenly wisdom is needed to solve marital problems. (Psalm 19:7; Proverbs 3:5, 6) Hence, married ministerial servants need to follow the counsel of God's Word as closely as possible. They must strive for proper balance in fulfilling family responsibilities, and yet never use these as an excuse for neglecting their theocratic duties in the congregation. Among other things, a well-thought-out schedule is essential. Older and more experienced married couples may be able to offer younger ones helpful suggestions in this regard when called upon to do so.

---

5. What greater danger exists for married ministerial servants than for those who are single?
6. Married ministerial servants need to do what, and who may be able to offer helpful suggestions?

⁷ Support from his family is of great help to a married ministerial servant. Of course, family members who place excessive demands on his time and attention or are overly demanding in material ways can hinder his spiritual progress. But it is a blessing when his entire family supports his efforts to "minister in a fine manner." (1 Timothy 3:13) So how vital it is that *before* an unmarried ministerial servant becomes emotionally involved with a prospective marriage mate he try to determine whether she is likely to promote their spiritual progress!

Employment and Materialism

⁸ Eight out of every ten ministerial servants surveyed were under the age of 60. So in most cases they still do secular work to support themselves and their families. Nearly five of every ten of them are between 20 and 40 years of age—when men of the world normally get established in a job or career and strive to get ahead and become financially secure. If you are a ministerial servant in that age bracket, never underestimate the danger of developing worldly, materialistic attitudes that can weaken you spiritually. Rather, remember that Paul said: "Having sustenance and covering, we shall be content with these things." (1 Timothy 6:8) Jesus, too, gave fine counsel that can help all of us to combat materialism. Read it for yourself at Matthew 6:19-34.

⁹ You younger ministerial servants in

---

7. (a) How might the family of a married ministerial servant affect his efforts and spiritual progress? (b) Ministerial servants planning to get married would do well to keep what in mind?
8. (a) What possible danger do some ministerial servants face in connection with secular employment? (b) Meditation on what scriptures can help a person to combat materialism?
9. In harmony with Matthew 16:26, what is the course of wisdom for younger ministerial servants in particular?

particular, look at the "successful" men pursuing worldly careers or amassing wealth but leaving Jehovah out of their plans. (Compare Proverbs 16:3; 19:21.) Just how wise would it be to pattern yourselves after any unspiritual, materialistic individuals whose lives will soon be snuffed out during the "great tribulation"? (Matthew 24:21) What servant of Jehovah would trade places with them? "For," said Jesus, "what benefit will it be to a man if he gains the whole world but forfeits his soul?" (Matthew 16:26) Surely, the course of wisdom is to build a secure future with Jehovah's organization rather than a very insecure and *short one* with this dying world that is lying in Satan's power.—1 John 5:19.

Allegiance to God's Kingdom

10 Prophetically, it was said of Jehovah's Messianic King: "Your people will offer themselves willingly on the day of your military force. In the splendors of holiness, from the womb of the dawn, you have your company of young men just like dewdrops." (Psalm 110:3) This prophecy has been undergoing fulfillment since 1914, and those of the increasing "company of young men" realize that their first allegiance must be to God's Kingdom with the glorified Jesus Christ as King. So while these dedicated men, including ministerial servants, are in relative subjection to governmental "superior authorities," in any conflict of interests they "must obey God as ruler rather than men." (Romans 13:1; Acts 5:29) As Jesus said, his followers are "no part of the world." (John 15:19; 18:36) They remain neutral as to the political affairs of the nations, realizing that doing otherwise would make them traitors to God's Kingdom.

11 What if ministerial servants or others lose their employment or even their freedom because of maintaining Christian neutrality? (Isaiah 2:2-4; John 17:16) Then they know that their spiritual brothers and sisters will give them all the support possible spiritually, and, if necessary, materially. This is so because Jehovah's people lovingly care for one another. —Compare John 13:34, 35; 1 Corinthians 12:24, 25.

A Need for Greater Experience

12 Approximately one third of the ministerial servants surveyed have been Jehovah's Witnesses less than ten years. Obviously, these men have accepted the help and guidance of the more experienced members of the congregation. But 'acquiring a fine standing' would involve continuing to learn from others and gathering experience. It would also mean constantly setting personal goals and conscientiously striving to reach them. So if you earnestly desire to serve beneficial purposes as a ministerial servant or are reaching out for that privilege, have you set some personal goals? For example, why not decide to read through the entire Bible by a particular date or to be an auxiliary pioneer during certain months?

13 If you are young in years or experience, you can benefit from what is said at 1 Timothy 4:12-15. Although those words were directed to the young *overseer* Timothy, much of what Paul said there about speech and conduct would benefit any brother desiring to become a ministerial servant or who already serves in that ca-

---

10. As regards political affairs, what position is taken by the increasing "company of young men," including ministerial servants?

11. Brothers who suffer because of maintaining Christian neutrality can be certain of what?
12. 'Acquiring a fine standing' would include what?
13. What counsel given to Timothy would benefit a brother who wishes to become a ministerial servant or who now serves in that capacity?

Older ministerial servants can do much to help and encourage the congregation

pacity. The apostle wrote: "Let no man ever look down on your youth. On the contrary, become an example to the faithful ones in speaking, in conduct, in love, in faith, in chasteness. While I am coming, continue applying yourself to public reading, to exhortation, to teaching. Do not be neglecting the gift in you that was given you through a prediction and when the body of older men laid their hands upon you. Ponder over these things; be absorbed in them, that your advancement may be manifest to all persons." On what do you particularly need to work so that *"your* advancement may be manifest to all persons"? Prayerfully determine what you need to do, and then do it with Jehovah's help!

Coping With Discouragement

¹⁴ A great many ministerial servants no longer have to contend with problems

---

14, 15. (a) What Scriptural encouragement is there for ministerial servants who must contend with advanced age or poor health? (b) How can these men encourage others in the congregation?

unique to young men. They face advanced age or poor health, which can lead to discouragement. But those keeping strong spiritually can draw comfort from these words of Paul to fellow anointed Christians: "We do not give up, but even if the man we are outside is wasting away, certainly the man we are inside is being renewed from day to day. For though the tribulation is momentary and light, it works out for us a glory that is of more and more surpassing weight and is everlasting; while we keep our eyes, not on the things seen, but on the things unseen. For the things seen are temporary, but the things unseen are everlasting." (2 Corinthians 4:16-18) Jehovah's servants with earthly hopes also have very encouraging prospects—those of eternal life in an earthly paradise.—Luke 23:43; John 17:3.

¹⁵ So those ministerial servants who are unable to do as much as others because of poor health or advanced age have good reason to maintain a joyful and positive attitude. This mirrors appreciation for the truth and deep faith in things that are

everlasting. Such a fine spirit, coupled with humble service, will be of great benefit and encouragement to everyone in the congregation.

[16] If you are a ministerial servant, continue "reaching out for an office of overseer" by improving your teaching ability and spiritual qualities. (1 Timothy 3:1) But do not be discouraged if you are not quickly appointed as an elder. Remember that as a ministerial servant caring for your duties "in a fine manner" you are serving beneficial purposes and are a real asset to the congregation. It is a great privilege to serve in any way within Jehovah's organization and to help fellow believers carry out the Kingdom-preaching commission.—Matthew 24:14; 28:19, 20.

How Others Can Help

[17] Realizing the beneficial purposes served by ministerial servants, all of Jehovah's people should want to support their efforts. For example, it will be easier for such a man to continue 'ministering in a fine manner' if his wife and children are content with the necessities of life and do not demand many luxuries that would require that he spend extra effort in secular work.—1 Timothy 6:6-8.

[18] Elders can help ministerial servants by giving them any needed direction and counsel. And when improvement has been made, sincere commendation should be offered. Among other things, elders can accompany ministerial servants in the field ministry, assist them in preparing talks, and share with them their wealth of Christian experience. Apparently such interest and communication have sometimes been

neglected. For example, when asked about his low field service report, one ministerial servant told a circuit overseer: "Why do you ask? It has been low for years, but you are the first one ever to say anything about it." Elders who offer ministerial servants constructive, loving counsel and patiently help them with their problems often have the joy of seeing outstanding results.

[19] Actually, each member of the congregation can help the ministerial servants to maintain their fine standing. How? By cooperating with them and by showing heartfelt appreciation for their work. Even as all parts of the human body normally work together to maintain physical health, so all members of the congregation must cooperate to assure its good spiritual health. (Compare 1 Corinthians 12: 24, 25.) To that end, much is being done by hardworking ministerial servants who serve beneficial purposes and maintain a fine standing. May they, and all of Jehovah's loyal witnesses, look to a future of eternal happiness and unitedly continue to make the heart of "the happy God" rejoice.—1 Timothy 1:11; Proverbs 27:11.

16. Why should a ministerial servant not be discouraged if he is not appointed an elder?
17. How can a ministerial servant be helped by his wife and children?
18. (a) How can elders help ministerial servants? (b) Why is good communication vital between elders and ministerial servants?

19. How can each member of the congregation help the ministerial servants to maintain their fine standing?

Please Explain

☐ What problems may be faced by ministerial servants?

☐ What can the wives and children of ministerial servants do to help them?

☐ What can elders do to assist ministerial servants?

☐ What can each member of the congregation do to help ministerial servants?

Can You Enlarge Your Territory as a Pioneer?

JESUS CHRIST once said: "Also to other cities I must declare the good news of the kingdom of God, because for this I was sent forth." (Luke 4:43) Without question, Jesus was the foremost Kingdom proclaimer, a true pioneer in the sacred service of Jehovah.

Like Jesus, the apostle Paul was a full-time minister intensely interested in the evangelizing work. In fact, he had a keen desire to enlarge his ministerial territory. —Compare Romans 15:23, 24; 2 Corinthians 10:15, 16.

Undoubtedly with a similar spirit, many of Jehovah's modern-day witnesses have made themselves available to serve as missionaries in foreign lands. Other Christian ministers are serving where the need is great. And many more have found it possible to become pioneers, full-time preachers of the good news.

But what about you? If you are not now serving as a pioneer, can you enlarge your territory, so to speak, by becoming such a full-time Kingdom proclaimer?

Benefits of Pioneer Service

Zealous and effective pioneers are motivated not by self-interest but by love of God and the desire to help others. Such full-time ministers strongly feel the need to apply God's Word in their lives and are delighted that they can make room for full-time service. And there are benefits from doing so.

'Daily telling the good news of salvation by Jehovah' is one benefit of pioneer service. (Psalm 96:2) Indeed, regularly talking about God and his purposes is satisfying, especially because this helps others on the way to life. "There is no greater pleasure than that of studying the Bible with someone and seeing him become a worshiper of Jehovah," said a sister who has been in the pioneer service for 46 years.

Greater skill in handling 'the sword of the spirit, God's word,' is a benefit resulting from regular use of the Bible in the pioneer ministry. (Ephesians 6:17) Typical of expressions made by many pioneers is the following: "Apart from increasing my courage, pioneering helped me to become familiar with many Bible texts that had been committed to memory, ready for use."

The wholesome influence of pioneer service can also be felt in the congregation. Concerning this, one elder wrote: "What a difference it made! The congregation's pace changed. The tendency is to increase our participation in Jehovah's service more and more." Yes, others may be stimulated by the zealous example of pioneer ministers.

Greater confidence in Jehovah may well result from participation in the pioneer ministry. Of course, full-time ministers must overcome some problems. But one pioneer couple expressed their confidence in these words: "Thanks to Jehovah, we have never lacked anything. As pioneers we have become dependent on Jehovah and have seen how he provides help when we most need it."—Psalm 34:10; 37:25.

Blessings for Reaching Out

'Test me out, please, and see whether I shall not open the floodgates of the heavens and empty out upon you a blessing,' said Jehovah centuries ago. (Malachi 3:10) During the 1984 service year, the average number of pioneers worldwide was 258,936. And how Jehovah has blessed these full-time ministers!

For instance, consider blessings enjoyed by pioneers in the Amazon region of Brazil. Generally, boats are used to get to the widely scattered villages along the riverbanks. Some settlements are situated in riverbeds, the wooden houses being built on stilts to keep them above water during the flood season. These houses are connected by rough wooden walkways, at times quite precarious, especially for heavy persons. When the water is low, access is difficult but possible through the undergrowth or along the muddy riverbed. Traveling by light canoes can be quite an adventure, for these turn over at times. Add to all of this the problems resulting from malaria, typhoid fever, parasitic worms, intense heat, and insect infestation. Despite these difficulties, however, Jehovah's spirit helps our brothers to succeed in declaring the good

For pioneers in the Amazon region, canoes and large rowboats are the most common means of transportation

news in such territories.—Zechariah 4:6.

One pioneer sister serving in the Amazon region stated: "Our work was most gratifying." Citing a fine experience, she told of a return visit on a certain man who had previously accepted some of our literature. She had to travel two hours by boat, but on arriving she found the man roasting manioc flour in a huge oven. He could not interrupt the process without running the risk of burning the flour. So what could she do? Well, the pioneer asked her partner to keep turning the flour with the big wooden shovel. Thus the man had an opportunity to listen attentively while the pioneer demonstrated how to study the publication he had acquired.

Quite often, our brothers working in this region get up before daybreak so as to reach the homes of the people while it is still early. The pioneers then continue witnessing right through the day. And how richly Jehovah blesses them!—Proverbs 10:22.

Elsewhere in Brazil, too, pioneers are enjoying many blessings in Jehovah's service. For example, imagine the joy of a pioneer who was able to help a convict learn the truth. This man, once feared because of his violent temper, was serving a long prison sentence. Upon his becoming convinced of the truth, however, his personality was transformed to such an extent that the prison authorities were impressed and gave him permission to preach in the penitentiary. Now baptized, this man is on probation and conducts several home Bible studies.

This pioneer has also been able to help others in the same penitentiary. Concerning this work, he comments: "It is a reason for much happiness for me, because the seed I was able to sow has already germinated and produced fruitage." At least four men who have been released from prison now attend Christian meetings regularly. Four others are taking the truth seriously, and one of them is preparing for baptism.

The Territory Is Large

The continuing increase in the ranks of Jehovah's worshipers gives tangible evidence that God still has many people to gather throughout the worldwide territory. (Compare Acts 18:9, 10.) Can you have a greater share in this disciple-making work?

If you are not already pioneering, why not talk to those having success in full-time service? You, too, may be able to succeed as a pioneer. After prayerfully examining your circumstances, you may be able to enlarge your territory as a pioneer.

A Problem With Borrowing

"The problem with borrowing money is that as soon as one has, one inevitably begins to think of it as one's own. One becomes used to it, treats it like family and may even come to resent or lose sight of the fact that it must all someday leave to visit someone else. Borrowing is simple. Paying back is what hurts." So noted *Parade,* a Sunday newspaper magazine, regarding a psychological problem with borrowing money.

There is more to it, however, than the psychological factor. There is also the moral factor—the obligation to pay back what is borrowed. We do well, therefore, to keep in mind Jehovah's view of one who does not repay what he borrows. God's Word says: "The wicked one is borrowing and does not pay back."—Psalm 37:21.

A Unique Athenian Rock

TO THE WEST of Athens' famous Acropolis and separated from it by a small valley is an outcrop of limestone that the Greeks call the Areopagus. Its dimensions are not particularly impressive, measuring about 1,000 feet (300 m) long by a little over 400 feet (120 m) at its widest point and rising to a height of about 370 feet (115 m). What is unique about this rock is the extraordinary history, secular and Biblical, associated with it.

The name Areopagus literally means "Hill of Ares," or "Mars' Hill," Mars being the Roman equivalent of the Greek Ares, the god of war. According to legend, the first court hearing, on a bizarre murder case among the gods, was held here. Ares was on trial for killing the son of the sea god Poseidon. Thus the rock became important in the judicial and political affairs of ancient Athens. It eventually became the seat of the city's earliest court, which took on the name Court, or Council, of the Areopagus, or simply the Areopagus.

It is not certain just when the Court actually began. But by about the seventh century B.C.E., it wielded considerable power over all the affairs of the city, its members being elected from among the aristocratic and the wealthy, the elite of the people. As time went on, however, much of its power was transferred to the city magistrates and the popular court. Its jurisdiction was limited to homicide cases and religious and educational matters.

At the time of Pericles (c. 495-429 B.C.E.), for example, it was reported that the Areopagites were trying those who desecrated the "sacred olive trees" from which olive oil for sacred service was extracted. The Areopagites were considered the guardian and trustee of morals and religion, protecting the city from any undesirable "foreign deities." Interestingly, students of history will recall that the famous philosopher Socrates (470-399 B.C.E.) was condemned by the Athenian court for just such reasons: "corruption of the young" and "neglect of the gods whom the city worships and the practice of religious novelties."

When the Areopagus held sessions on homicide cases, they were generally conducted in the open air so that "the judges and the accuser might not be polluted by being brought under the same roof with the offender." The proceedings called for the accuser to be seated on a stone called Relentlessness and the accused on one called Outrage. Today, on top of the hill, one can see two white stones that are said to be the scene of the court. Hearings on other matters were probably held in the so-called Royal Gallery (Stoa Basileios) in the agora, or marketplace, situated in the valley below the Areopagus.

The best-known historical event to take place at the Areopagus, however, is the one recorded in the Bible in Acts chapter 17 —the apostle Paul's visit to Athens, where he gave his memorable speech "in the midst of the Areopagus."—Acts 17:22.

When Paul visited Athens, he was "irritated at beholding that the city was full of idols." This moved him to engage in many discussions with the people in the agora about "the good news of Jesus and the resurrection." Evidently this message piqued the curiosity of the people, especially the Epicurean and the Stoic philosophers, and they had Paul give a fuller account about the "foreign deities" and the "new teaching" at the Areopagus.—Acts 17:16-34.

Rising to the occasion, Paul courageously and vigorously defended the good news of Jesus. His speech is a masterpiece of logic and refutation; its impact remains as powerful today as when the Athenians first heard it. Today, there is a bronze plaque at the foot of the rock, on the western side, to commemorate the event. Paul's speech is engraved on it in large Greek uncials, or capital letters, for all to see. It is a silent witness not only to the long and unique history of the rock but also to the historical authenticity of the Bible.

Why Do You Want to Give a Bible Talk?

JESUS CHRIST often spoke to large crowds, and he surely was an effective speaker. In fact, after Jesus concluded his renowned Sermon on the Mount, "the effect was that the crowds were astounded at his way of teaching." (Matthew 7:28) There can be no doubt that the Son of God had the highest of motives and that his public discourses brought glory to his heavenly Father.—Compare John 12:46-50.

Public speaking was also one way that the good news was spread by Jesus' followers in the first century of our Common Era. For instance, at Corinth the apostle Paul "would give a talk in the synagogue every sabbath and would persuade Jews and Greeks." (Acts 18:1, 4) Moreover, Paul encouraged his co-worker Timothy with the words: "While I am coming, continue applying yourself to public reading, to exhortation, to teaching." (1 Timothy 4:13) So public reading and speaking, with noble motives, certainly had their place among Jehovah's loyal servants of the first century.

Yet, there is need for caution. When Herod, clad in royal raiment, began giving a public address, the assembled people started to shout: "A god's voice, and not a man's!" At that instant the angel of Jehovah struck Herod. Why? "Because he did not give the glory to God."—Acts 12:21-23.

Need for the Right Mental Attitude

Today, giving a public Bible talk surely is a very desirable privilege granted to mature Christian men. However, each minister would do well to examine his heart as to his motive. (Genesis 8:21; Jeremiah 17:9) Is he motivated by a desire to honor God and benefit fellow believers and others? Or does he wish to give such Bible talks because of the prominence associated with public speaking and his own desire to shine?

The right motive will manifest itself in various ways. For one thing, it will make us realize that only with the help of Jehovah's spirit can we do justice to the privilege of speaking God's truth from the public platform. Therefore, we will have an attitude similar to that of the apostle Peter, who said: "If anyone speaks, let him speak as it were the sacred pronouncements of God; if anyone ministers, let him minister as dependent on the strength that God supplies; so that in all things God may be glorified through Jesus Christ."—1 Peter 4:11.

Love must be the underlying reason for wanting to give a Bible talk. First of all, we must have love for Jehovah God, desiring to bring him honor and to share in the sanctifying of his holy name. Second, our motive should include love for our listeners, a sincere desire to instruct them and incite them to "holy acts of conduct and deeds of godly devotion."—2 Peter 3:11.

A sincere desire to upbuild our fellow believers and others should also be our motive for giving a public discourse. This will prevent us from attempting to 'tickle the ears' of our listeners by telling them only what they want to hear. (2 Timothy 4:3) The desire to upbuild others spiritually will also move us to refrain from telling jokes or saying things just to amuse our audiences or get them to laugh. Neither will we use flowery speech or make a display of worldly wisdom in an effort to impress our hearers. Rather, if we have the right motive in speaking publicly, we will follow the example of the apostle Paul, who gave 'a demonstration of spirit and power so that the faith of his hearers might be, not in men's wisdom, but in God's power.'—1 Corinthians 2:3-5.

Three Basic Elements

Giving a public Bible talk is a matter of mind and heart. Therefore, Christian speakers must have not only the right attitude but also something worth while to say. That requires the giving of thought to three basic elements. These are the Scriptures, facts, and logic.

In Our Next Issue

First, it must be remembered that the burden of a public Bible talk obviously is to be borne by the scriptures used by the speaker. If you are privileged to give such a talk, you should have a good knowledge of your subject and should be able to quote scriptures, read them well, and apply them properly. On the day of Pentecost, 33 C.E., the apostle Peter repeatedly referred to the Scriptures in support of his remarks. (Acts 2:14-41) The Beroeans were satisfied that Paul had based his remarks solidly on the Scriptures. (Acts 17:10, 11) And Apollos "demonstrated by the Scriptures that Jesus was the Christ," the long-looked-for Messiah.—Acts 18:28.

Of course, the Scriptural basis for a public talk is furnished in the outline provided by the Watch Tower Society. Yet, the speaker can use additional or parallel scriptures, provided they apply equally well and that this is not done excessively. In this regard, the Christian minister must be careful to keep up with the increasing spiritual light. For example, a speaker might incorrectly apply 1 Corinthians 2:9 to the future earthly Paradise, whereas the context (verses 7 and 10) shows that it applies to the deeper things of God's wisdom.

Second, there is the matter of facts used in support of remarks made by a public speaker. Care should be exercised so that the points presented are not open to legitimate question or challenge. Especially is care important if a point seems to be sensational. It is wise—and essential—to make certain that what is said really is factual. For this reason, it is always best to be able to refer to reliable sources of information in case certain statements are questioned. On the day of Pentecost, Peter pointed to well-known facts. So did the apostle Paul on the Areopagus, or Mars' Hill, in Athens.—Acts 2:22; 17:22, 23, 28.

Third, there is a definite need for logic. The Christian public speaker needs to reason with his listeners. Thus we read that Paul "began to reason in the synagogue with the Jews and the other people who worshiped God and every day in the marketplace with those who happened to be on hand." (Acts 17:17) In a public talk, the reasoning should be logical, simple, clear, easy to follow. Of great help in this regard is the use of connectives that show the relationship between what has been said and what follows it.

If you are privileged to be a public speaker, then be sure that you have the right mental attitude toward giving a Bible talk. Have love in your heart for your Creator and for your fellowman. Assemble and present scriptures and facts in a logical manner. Then this proverb will apply to you: "The tongue of the wise ones is a healing." (Proverbs 12:18) Moreover, giving fine Bible talks that honor God is one way to "save both yourself and those who listen to you."—1 Timothy 4:16.

Questions From Readers

■ How was Jerusalem "in slavery with her children," as the apostle Paul wrote in Galatians 4:25?

Primarily, Jerusalem and its people in Paul's day were in slavery to the Mosaic Law.

In Galatians chapter 4 the apostle showed that Christians in the new covenant had been purchased by Christ and thus were free. This contrasted with the situation of Jews under the Law covenant. Paul illustrated this with Abraham's wife (Sarah) and his concubine (Hagar), saying: "These women mean two covenants, the one from Mount Sinai, which brings forth children for slavery, and which is Hagar. Now this Hagar means Sinai, a mountain in Arabia [where Jehovah gave the Law to Israel through Moses], and she corresponds with the Jerusalem today, for she is in slavery with her children. But the Jerusalem above is free, and she is our mother."—Galatians 4:24-26.

When Paul said that the "women mean two covenants," he was simply speaking in an abbreviat-

ed style. Jehovah is not illustratively married to an impersonal covenant but to an organized people in the covenant. He had earlier considered Israel under the Law covenant to be like his wife. (Compare Isaiah 54:1, 6.) However, the free woman (Sarah) stood for the Jerusalem above, Jehovah's universal organization, which is as a wife to him.

But how could the Jews be considered to be in slavery to the Law, since it was perfect and was provided by God himself?

It is true that of itself 'the Law was holy, and the commandment was holy and righteous and good.' (Romans 7:12) But the imperfect Israelites under the Law could not keep it perfectly, much as they might try. (Romans 7:14-16) The apostle Peter referred to that fact when he asked the following question before the Christian governing body: "Why are you making a

test of God by imposing upon the neck of the disciples *a yoke* that neither our forefathers nor we were capable of bearing?" (Acts 15:10) Similarly, in Galatians 4:4, 5 Paul said that Christ came "that he might release by purchase those under law." Whoever would insist that Christians were obliged to 'observe days and months and seasons and years,' as prescribed by the Law, would cause slavery all over again.—Galatians 4:9, 10.

Of course, as pointed out on page 13 of *The Watchtower* of March 15, 1985, first-century Jews were slaves in a number of ways. They were politically in bondage to the Romans. They were slaves to sin. (John 8:34) And there were erroneous religious views to which they were bound. But the principal slavery to which Paul referred in Galatians 4:25 was the Jews' slavery to the Mosaic Law covenant, given at Sinai and represented by Abraham's slave concubine Hagar.

AMAZING FEATS OF MEMORY

A young child can remember more than you think. In a letter of thanks for the cassette tapes of *My Book of Bible Stories,* a mother from Arizona writes:

"Tonight my little four-year-old boy, Jamin, who can't read yet, quoted several Bible stories to my husband pretty much word for word. He has been listening to them every day for a few weeks. In fact, he has to have 'his tape' turned on to take his nap or go to bed. Before he went to bed tonight, my husband, Sid, was reading a Bible story to Jamin. I heard Sid chuckle.

Jamin had finished the story with him. He tried another but only said a couple of words before Jamin quoted it all. I suggested trying another story. Jamin did it again and again. Needless to say, we were both amazed."

October 1, 1985

The Watchtower

Announcing Jehovah's Kingdom

PEACE AND SECURITY
—From This Source?

The Watchtower®

Announcing Jehovah's Kingdom

October 1, 1985
Vol. 106, No. 19

In This Issue

THE PURPOSE OF "THE WATCHTOWER" is to exalt Jehovah God as the Sovereign of the universe. It keeps watch on world events as they fulfill Bible prophecy. It comforts all peoples with the good news that God's Kingdom will soon destroy those who oppress their fellowmen and that it will turn the earth into a paradise. It encourages faith in the now-reigning King, Jesus Christ, whose shed blood opens the way for mankind to gain eternal life. "The Watchtower," published by Jehovah's Witnesses continuously since 1879, is nonpolitical. It adheres to the Bible as its authority.

"WATCHTOWER" STUDIES FOR THE WEEKS

November 3: A "Disgusting Thing" Fails to Bring Peace. Page 8. Songs to Be Used: 168, 85.

November 10: Peace, Security, and the 'Image of the Beast.' Page 13. Songs to Be Used: 119, 139.

Average Printing Each Issue: 11,150,000

Now Published in 103 Languages

SEMIMONTHLY EDITIONS AVAILABLE BY MAIL
Afrikaans, Arabic, Cebuano, Chichewa, Chinese, Cibemba, Danish, Dutch,* Efik, English,* Finnish, French, German,* Greek, Hiligaynon, Igbo, Iloko, Italian,* Japanese,* Korean, Lingala, Malagasy, Maltese, Norwegian, Portuguese, Russian, Sepedi, Sesotho, Shona, Spanish,* Swahili, Swedish, Tagalog, Thai, Tswana, Xhosa, Yoruba, Zulu

MONTHLY EDITIONS AVAILABLE BY MAIL
Armenian, Bengali, Bicol, Bulgarian, Croatian, Czech, Ewe, Fijian, Ga, Greenlandic, Gujarati, Gun, Hausa, Hebrew, Hindi, Hiri Motu, Hungarian, Icelandic, Kannada, Kikuyu, Kiluba, Malayalam, Marathi, New Guinea Pidgin, Pangasinan, Papiamento, Polish, Rarotongan, Romanian, Samar-Leyte, Samoan, Sango, Serbian, Silozi, Sinhalese, Slovenian, Solomon Islands-Pidgin, Tahitian, Tamil, Telugu, Tshiluba, Tsonga, Turkish, Twi, Ukrainian, Urdu, Venda, Vietnamese
* Study articles also available in large-print edition.

The Bible translation used is the "New World Translation of the Holy Scriptures," unless otherwise indicated.

Twenty cents (U.S.) a copy

Watch Tower Society offices	Yearly subscription Semimonthly
America, U.S., Watchtower, Wallkill, N.Y. 12589	$4.00
Australia, Box 280, Ingleburn, N.S.W. 2565	A$7.00
Canada, Box 4100, Halton Hills (Georgetown), Ontario L7G 4Y4	$5.20
England, The Ridgeway, London NW7 1RN	£5.00
Ireland, 29A Jamestown Road, Finglas, Dublin 11	£5.00
New Zealand, 6-A Western Springs Rd., Auckland 3	$10.00
Nigeria, P.O. Box 194, Yaba, Lagos State	₦6.00
Philippines, P.O. Box 2044, Manila 2800	₱50.00
South Africa, Private Bag 2, Elandsfontein, 1406	R5,60

Remittances should be sent to the office in your country or to Watchtower, Wallkill, N.Y. 12589, U.S.A.

Changes of address should reach us 30 days before your moving date. Give us your old and new address (if possible, your old address label).

The Watchtower (ISSN 0043-1087) is published semimonthly for $4.00 (U.S.) per year by Watch Tower Bible and Tract Society of Pennsylvania, 25 Columbia Heights, Brooklyn, N.Y. 11201. Second-class postage paid at Brooklyn, N.Y., and at additional mailing offices.

Postmaster: Send address changes to Watchtower, **Wallkill, N.Y. 12589.**

Published by
Watch Tower Bible and Tract Society of Pennsylvania
25 Columbia Heights, Brooklyn, N.Y. 11201, U.S.A.
Frederick W. Franz, President

Peace and Security
—The Hope

"The General Assembly of the United Nations unanimously declared 1986 as the International Year of Peace. The Year will be solemnly proclaimed on 24 October 1985, the fortieth anniversary of the United Nations."

HOW do you view this official statement from the United Nations organization? Does it make you feel more confident about the future? Many would say that anything that holds out even the remotest chance of bringing peace is worth trying. So why not an "International Year of Peace"?

Certainly, such a "Year of Peace" would be in harmony with the goals of the founders of the United Nations organization. Back in 1944 the president of the United States declared: "We have been determined . . . to so organize the peace-loving nations that they may through unity of desire, unity of will, and unity of strength be in position to assure that no other would-be aggressor or conqueror shall even get started. That is why from the very beginning of the war, and paralleling our military plans, we have begun to lay the foundations for the general organization for the maintenance of peace and security."

Those ideals were shared by many. "For the United Nations to come into existence, it was necessary for a large body of persons to believe in the human capacity for good, and to feel that their hopes might be justified," says the book *Defeat of an Ideal* by Shirley Hazzard, who worked for a decade in the United Nations Secretariat.

The charter of the newborn organization expressed the hopes of its founders: "The Purposes of the United Nations are: 1. To maintain international peace and security . . . 2. To develop friendly relations among nations based on respect for the principle of equal rights and self-determination of peoples . . . 3. To achieve international cooperation in solving international problems." Could anything be wrong with such goals?

Admittedly, the United Nations had an impressive start. Weighty world issues were discussed. In 1948 an outstanding Universal Declaration of Human Rights was adopted. Valuable humanitarian work was initiated to alleviate poverty, hunger, sickness, and the plight of refugees. International standards were established, such as safety standards for ships and aircraft, health certificates for travelers to some regions, uniform postal rates, and the assignment of space on broadcast bands.

The United Nations was closely involved in the efforts to make peace in the India-Pakistan conflict of 1947-49. It even showed military muscle when soldiers under its flag went into Korea in 1950 and into the Congo (now Zaire) in 1960. There are still UN peace-keeping forces in Cyprus and the Middle East. Yes, in the last 40 years the United Nations has made its mark. More than 150 countries have shown that they recognize this by sending delegates to its distinctive headquarters in New York City, on the banks of the East River.

But to what extent has the United Nations fulfilled its basic mandate to "maintain international peace and security"? And what effect will the proclaimed "International Year of Peace" have?

Peace and Security
—From What Source?

WHILE the United Nations has performed valuable services in some fields, anyone who keeps up with the news has to admit that it has so far failed in the area of peace and security. This is openly admitted by the organization's most ardent advocates.

Thus, back in 1953, only eight years after its birth, Dag Hammarskjöld, then secretary-general, confessed: "Where our predecessors dreamed of a new heaven, our greatest hope is that we may be permitted to save the old earth." Twenty-six years later, C. William Maynes, a United States assistant secretary of state, was forced to admit: "The main purpose of the Security Council and the General Assembly was the maintenance of international peace and security. . . . You have evidence that the organization has failed in its central purpose."

How Relevant?

The truth is, most of the outstanding decisions affecting peace and security during the past 40 years have been made largely outside the United Nations. In 1982, Secretary-General Javier Pérez de Cuéllar bemoaned the fact that "this year, time after time we have seen the Organization set aside or rebuffed, for this reason or for that, in situations in which it should, and could, have played an important and constructive role." Why is this?

Some point to the organization's spectacular growth in membership as a reason. The 51 original members increased to more than 150, each with an equal vote in the General Assembly. Yet some of these nations are very small. Thus, the island nation of Saint Christopher and Nevis, the 158th nation to join the organization, has a population of fewer than 50,000, yet it has an equal vote with China, whose population is close to one billion. True, this arrangement gives smaller nations the opportunity to be heard; but it hardly encourages the larger powers to take the organization's decisions seriously.

A second problem is touched on by Shirley Hazzard: "Powers of compulsion were not invested in the United Nations Organization, except in so far as they might reside in the very members most likely to need compelling." In other words, the organization can make decisions, but for the most part it cannot enforce them. Weighty world problems are regularly discussed at length. Resolutions are solemnly passed—and then forgotten. In 1982 the UN secretary-general was moved to deplore the "lack of respect for its decisions by those to whom they are addressed."

These are organizational problems—and there are others mentioned by analysts. But there are deeper, more serious reasons why the United Nations has failed.

The Deeper Problems

"It then seemed possible to establish, as a first priority, a system for maintaining international peace and security under the provisions of the Charter," said Javier Pérez de Cuéllar, recalling the idealism of the founders of the organization. "What has happened to that majestic vision? It was soon clouded by the differences of the major Powers. . . . Moreover, the world turned out to be a more complex, far less orderly place than had been hoped."

In fact, there was never any chance that the United Nations would bring peace and security. The task was just too difficult. The secretary-general's comments remind us of the words of the prophet Jeremiah: "It does not belong to man who is walking even to direct his step." (Jeremiah 10:23) Humans, with their limited wisdom and abilities, will never be able to solve the problem of bringing peace and security for all.

The secretary-general said that the founders of the United Nations discovered the world to be "more complex" than they had hoped. There is a basic reason for this situation, and apparently they were not aware of it. But the apostle John explains it thus: "The whole world is lying in the power of the wicked one." (1 John 5:19) The Bible tells us that today "the wicked one," Satan, is causing "woe for the earth," "having great anger." (Revelation 12:12) The grim reality of Satan and his influence

The task of bringing peace is just too difficult for the United Nations

U.S. Army photo

foredoomed the United Nations' efforts to bring peace before the organization even got started.

Remember, too, that the United Nations organization is a child of this world and thus inherits its characteristics. The weaknesses, evils, and corruption that characterize the individual nations inevitably also exist in the United Nations. Alexander Solzhenitsyn was quoted as saying in 1972: "A quarter of a century ago, with great hopes from all mankind, the United Nations Organization was born. Alas, in an immoral world it too grew up immoral." The Bible warns: "'There is no peace,' Jehovah has said, 'for the wicked ones.'" (Isaiah 48:22) An "immoral" organization can never bring peace and security.

What About Peace and Security?

So, will the declaring of 1986 to be an "International Year of Peace" make any difference? That is highly unlikely, since the aforementioned problems are completely unsolvable by humans. The "Year of

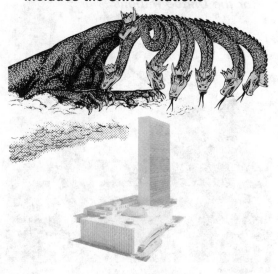

'The whole world lies in the power of the wicked one.' This includes the United Nations

dance of peace until the moon is no more." —Psalm 72:3, 7.

What ruler could possibly bring such lasting peace? David was pointing, not to a human organization, but to his God, Jehovah, as the one through whose authority this would happen. Was this mere wishful thinking? No. David's son Solomon relied on the same God, and during his reign, Jehovah showed His power in a typical way by bringing peace to Solomon's kingdom, situated as it was in one of the most war-torn regions on earth. Solomon was not a warrior-king, yet during his reign, "Judah and Israel continued to dwell in security, everyone under his own vine and under his own fig tree, from Dan [in the north] to Beer-sheba [in the south], all the days of Solomon."—1 Kings 4:25.

Of course, that peace did not last. The Israelites fell into the ways of the immoral world and lost their God-given security. Nevertheless, more than two centuries later, when the cruel Assyrians were engaged in a peace-through-terror campaign, the prophet Isaiah foretold the coming of the King that Solomon had foreshadowed. He wrote: "His name will be called Wonderful Counselor . . . *Prince of Peace*. To the abundance of the princely rule *and to peace* there will be no end."—Isaiah 9:6, 7.

Who is that "Prince of Peace"? More than 700 years after Isaiah, while the Roman world power was trying to enforce its version of international peace and security, that King appeared in David's country, Judea, in the person of Jesus Christ. He told his countrymen about God's Kingdom, of which he was to be the King. This Kingdom would be heavenly, thus able to solve the problems of Satan's influence and of man's innate inability to rule himself. Jesus' countrymen apparently preferred Roman rule and had Jesus judicially murdered. Nevertheless, as history clearly testifies, he was raised from the dead and

Peace" is no more likely to bring mankind closer to peace and security than the "Year of the Child" in 1979 improved the international lot of children or the "International Women's Year" in 1975 made the world a better place for women.

However, if mankind is to survive, it is obvious that *someone* has to do something about peace and security. Today, the nuclear-armed nations are in a position to destroy most life on earth. Sophisticated conventional weapons cause an appalling loss of life each year. Real peace seems further away than ever! If the United Nations has failed to solve these problems, who can?

A look at history suggests a hopeful answer. About 3,000 years ago King David, a Middle Eastern warrior-king, wrote about a future ruler who *would* succeed in bringing international peace. In a prayer for this ruler, David said: "Let the mountains carry peace to the people, also the hills, through righteousness. In his days the righteous one will sprout, and the abun-

ascended to heaven, awaiting God's due time for him to begin ruling as King of God's Kingdom.

In fact, fulfillment of prophecy marks our present day as the time for that great event. It was the birth of God's Kingdom in heaven and the subsequent casting of Satan to earth that led to Satan's "great anger" and his causing "woe for the earth." (Revelation 12:7-12) The result? Wars and other human distresses, as prophesied by Jesus himself. Earth has become the scene of "anguish of nations, not knowing the way out."—Luke 21:25, 26; Matthew 24: 3-13.

Man's Way or God's Way?

Jesus' prophecies, coming to us from almost 2,000 years ago, have provided a more accurate description of world conditions than the optimistic statements made at the birth of the United Nations 40 years ago. The failure of that organization to find a "way out" only serves to highlight the accuracy of the Bible's predictions. Truly, in the words of Isaiah, 'the very messengers of peace weep bitterly' in frustration at their failures.—Isaiah 33:7.

This highlights a final reason why the United Nations can never succeed in bringing peace to the earth. It is going about it in a way completely opposed to God's way. According to Jehovah's stated purposes, peace will come, not by a uniting of this world's nations, but by their being completely replaced by God's Kingdom. (Daniel 2:44) Dag Hammarskjöld said he was working to "save the old earth." If by this he meant the present world system comprised of independent political nations, then his hopes were doomed to failure from the outset. The fact is, the "old earth" has to give way to a new system. "The world is passing away." (1 John 2:17) Nothing can save it, not even a United Nations organization.

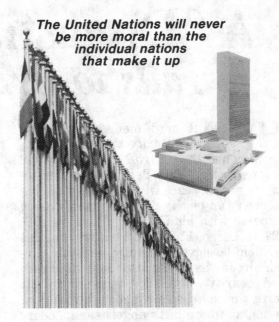

The United Nations will never be more moral than the individual nations that make it up

Given the nationalistic selfishness of the nations, there is only one realistic approach to bringing peace and security. God's Kingdom alone can bring the kind of peace that man has longed for since he was expelled from the garden of Eden. Here is one description of the security that will result from the Kingdom's activities: "[God] will wipe out every tear from their eyes, and death will be no more, neither will mourning nor outcry nor pain be anymore. The former things have passed away."—Revelation 21:4.

Does that promise sound unrealistic? In truth, it is the only hope we have, and the next issue of *The Watchtower* will discuss in greater depth why this is so. In the meantime, we would like to draw your attention to an important fact: The history of the United Nations has not yet ended. That organization has an important part to play in future events. We encourage you to read the next two articles, which discuss the future of the United Nations organization in the light of Bible prophecy.

A "Disgusting Thing"
Fails to Bring Peace

HOWEVER hard men try to bring peace and security through institutions such as the United Nations, they will never succeed. Why? Because mankind today is not at peace with God, and lasting security can be based only on man's being at peace with his Creator. (Psalm 46:1-9; 127:1; Isaiah 11:9; 57:21) How can this problem be solved? Happily, Jehovah himself already has the matter in hand. Peace and security will finally be brought to this earth through God's Kingdom by his Son, Jesus, at whose birth angels sang: "Glory in the heights above to God, and upon earth peace among men of goodwill." —Luke 2:14; Psalm 72:7.

² In the first century, Jesus announced God's Kingdom and offered peaceable ones the opportunity to become sons of God and corulers with him in that Kingdom. (Matthew 4:23; 5:9; Luke 12:32) The events that followed were very similar to events in our own century. Examining them will teach us much about the future course of man's "peace and security" organization, the United Nations.

The Jews Make a Choice

³ In Jesus' day, the Roman Empire ruled much of the earth and had its own ideas about peace and security. It had, by means of its legions, enforced the *Pax Romana* (Roman Peace) throughout much of the known world. But the *Pax Romana* could never be a permanent peace, because pagan Rome and its legions could never bring about a reconciliation between man and God. Hence, the Kingdom that Jesus announced was far superior.

⁴ Nevertheless, the majority of Jesus' fellow countrymen rejected God's Kingdom. (John 1:11; 7:47, 48; 9:22) Their rulers, viewing Jesus as a threat to national security, handed him over to be executed, insisting: "We have no king but Caesar." (John 11:48; 19:14, 15) Some Jews, however, and later many Gentiles, gladly recognized Jesus as God's chosen King. (Colossians 1:13-20) They preached about him in many lands, and Jerusalem became the center of an international association of Christians.—Acts 15:2; 1 Peter 5:9.

⁵ Despite the fact that the Jews had chosen Caesar over Christ, relations between Jerusalem and Rome soon deteriorated. Jewish Zealots conducted guerrilla campaigns against the empire until finally, in 66 C.E., open warfare erupted. Roman troops tried to restore *Pax Romana,* and soon Jerusalem was under siege. For Christians this was significant. Many years before, Jesus had warned: "When you see Jerusalem surrounded by encamped armies, then know that the deso-

---

1, 2. (a) Why will man never bring peace through organizations such as the United Nations? (b) How will God bring peace to the earth?
3. Who was trying to maintain international peace and security in Jesus' day, and why could this never succeed completely?

4. How did most Jews react to Jesus' preaching? Nevertheless, what gradually developed in the first century?
5, 6. (a) How did the relationship between the Jews and Rome develop? (b) What warning did Jesus give, and how did it save the lives of Christians in 70 C.E.?

"When you see Jerusalem surrounded by encamped armies . . . then let those in Judea begin fleeing to the mountains."—LUKE 21:20, 21.

lating of her has drawn near. Then let those in Judea begin fleeing to the mountains, and let those in the midst of her withdraw." (Luke 21:20, 21) Jerusalem was now surrounded, and the Christians waited for an opportunity to flee.

6 This came quickly. The Romans were undermining the temple wall, and many Jews were ready to surrender when the Roman commander, Cestius Gallus, unexpectedly withdrew his troops and left. The Zealots seized the opportunity to reorganize their defenses, but the Christians abandoned the doomed city. In 70 C.E., Roman legions were back, encamped around the walls of Jerusalem, and this time the city perished. How does this historical tragedy affect us? In this: Jesus' warning that saved his followers' lives also has meaning for us today.

More Than One Fulfillment

7 This warning was part of a long prophecy uttered by Jesus in response to an

7-9. (a) How do we know that Jesus' prophecy about the surrounding of Jerusalem by armies would have more than one fulfillment? (b) How does reading the book of Daniel with understanding support this?

important question. His followers had asked: "When will [the destruction of the Jewish temple] be, and what will be the sign of your presence and of the conclusion of the system of things?" In answer, Jesus gave a sign made up of many features, including the besieging of Jerusalem. (Matthew 24; Mark 13; Luke 21) In the years following Jesus' death, many of the features of this prophecy were fulfilled, culminating in the destruction of Jerusalem and the Jewish system of things in 70 C.E.—Matthew 24:7, 14; Acts 11:28; Colossians 1:23.

8 However, the disciples had also asked about Jesus' "presence," which the Bible associates with the end of a whole world system of things. (Daniel 2:44; Matthew 24:3, 21) Since Jesus' spiritual presence and the end of the worldwide system of things did not happen in the first century, a future, greater fulfillment of Jesus' prophecy could be expected, with those first-century events providing a pattern for the larger fulfillment. This would include a larger fulfillment of Jesus' warning about the destruction of Jerusalem.

9 This becomes more evident if we examine the way this warning was recorded in

the other two Bible books where it appears. In Matthew the besieging troops are described as "the disgusting thing that causes desolation, as spoken of through Daniel the prophet, standing in a holy place." (Matthew 24:15) In Mark's account "the disgusting thing" stands "where it ought not." (Mark 13:14) Matthew's account says that "the disgusting thing" was also mentioned in the book of Daniel. In fact, the expression "disgusting thing" appears three times in that book: once (in the plural) in Daniel 9:27 where it is part of a prophecy fulfilled when Jerusalem was destroyed in 70 C.E., and then, in Daniel 11:31 and Daniel 12:11. According to these latter two scriptures, a "disgusting thing" was to be set in place during "the time appointed," or "the time of the end." (Daniel 11:29; 12:9) We have been living in "the time of the end" since 1914; hence, Jesus' warning applies today too.—Matthew 24:15.

Christendom's Choice

10 In our century, events have followed a pattern similar to that of the first century. Today, as then, there is an empire dominating the world scene. The modern one is the Anglo-American world power, which tries hard to impose its own ideas about peace and security on mankind. In the first century, fleshly Israel rejected Jesus as God's anointed King. In 1914 Jesus' "presence" as Jehovah's enthroned King began. (Psalm 2:6; Revelation 11:15-18) But the nations, including those of Christendom, refused to acknowledge him. (Psalm 2:2, 3, 10, 11) In fact, they got involved in a vicious world war for international sovereignty. The religious leaders of Christendom—like the Jewish leaders—have taken the lead in rejecting Jesus. Since 1914 they have consistently

---

10, 11. How have events in our century resembled those in the first century?

acted in the political arena and have opposed the preaching of the good news of the Kingdom.—Mark 13:9.

11 Nevertheless, as in Jesus' day, many individuals today have gladly recognized Jehovah's King and have spread the good news of his Kingdom around the world. (Matthew 24:14) Over two and a half million of Jehovah's Witnesses now express loyalty to God's Kingdom. (Revelation 7:9, 10) Neutral as to this world's politics, they have full faith in Jehovah's arrangements for bringing peace and security. —John 17:15, 16; Ephesians 1:10.

"The Disgusting Thing" Today

12 What, then, is the modern "disgusting thing that causes desolation"? In the first century it was the Roman troops sent to reimpose *Pax Romana* in Jerusalem. In modern times, however, the nations that fought in World War I became disillusioned about the usefulness of all-out war in imposing peace and experimented with something new: an international organization to preserve world peace. This began life in 1919 as the League of Nations and still exists as the United Nations. Here is the modern "disgusting thing that causes desolation."

13 Interestingly, the Hebrew word translated "disgusting thing" in Daniel is *shiqquts'*. In the Bible, this word is used principally of idols and idolatry. (1 Kings 11:5, 7) With this in mind, read some comments by religious leaders about the League:

"What is this vision of a world-federation of humanity . . . if it be not of the Kingdom of God?" "The League of Nations is rooted in the Gospel." (Federal Council of the Churches

---

12. What is the modern-day "disgusting thing"?
13, 14. (a) What flattering statements have been made by Christendom about "the disgusting thing"? (b) Why was this idolatry, and where did it place "the disgusting thing"?

of Christ in America) "Every one of [the League of Nations'] objects and activities may be claimed as fulfilling the will of God as made known in the teaching of Jesus Christ." (Bishops of the Church of England) "The meeting therefore commends to the support and prayers of all Christian people the League of Nations as the only available instrument for attaining [peace on earth]." (General Body of Baptists, Congregationalists, and Presbyterians in Britain). "[The League of Nations] is the only organised effort which has been made to carry into effect the repeated wishes of the Holy See."—Cardinal Bourne, Archbishop of Westminster.

[14] When the nations not only rejected God's Kingdom but also established their own organization to bring peace, that was rebellion. When religious leaders of Christendom identified that organization with God's Kingdom and the Gospel, proclaiming it to be "the only available instrument" for bringing peace, that was idolatry. They were putting it in the position of God's Kingdom, "in a holy place." Certainly, it was "standing where it ought not." (Matthew 24:15; Mark 13:14) And religious leaders continue to support the League's successor, the United Nations, rather than point men to God's established Kingdom.

The Danger to Christendom

[15] Although Christendom's religions chose the League of Nations and its successor over God's Kingdom, their relations with the member nations of these organizations have deteriorated. This is similar to what happened between the Jews and Rome. Since 1945 the United Nations has included more and more countries that are either unchristian or antichristian, and this does not bode well for Christendom.

[16] Moreover, in many lands there is fric-

tion between Christendom's religions and the State. In Poland the Catholic Church is seen as an opponent of the regime there. In Northern Ireland and Lebanon, religions of Christendom have exacerbated the problems of peace and security. Additionally, Christendom's religions have produced some who, like the Jewish Zealots, encourage violence. Thus, the Protestant World Council of Churches has made donations to terrorist organizations, while Catholic priests fight in the jungles as guerrillas and serve in revolutionary governments.

[17] Time alone will reveal how far relations will deteriorate between Christendom's religions and the nations, but events in the first century have already foreshadowed how all of this will end. As Jesus foresaw, in the first century Rome's armies finally destroyed Jerusalem with much tribulation. True to the prophetic pattern, the nations along with the United Nations will attack and destroy "Jerusalem," that is, Christendom's religious structure.—Luke 21:20, 23.

Flee to the Mountains

[18] In the first century, after "the disgusting thing" appeared, Christians had the opportunity to flee. Jesus counseled them to do so instantly because they did not know how long that opportunity would last. (Mark 13:15, 16) In the same way,

> **When the religious leaders of Christendom identified the United Nations with God's Kingdom and the gospel, that was idolatry**

15, 16. How are relations developing between Christendom and the nations supporting "the disgusting thing"?

17. (a) What is modern-day Jerusalem? (b) What will finally happen to it?
18. What should meekhearted ones do when they discern that "the disgusting thing" is in place?

when meekhearted people today discern that "the disgusting thing" exists, they should immediately flee from the religious domain of Christendom. Every second they stay therein their spiritual lives are in danger, and who knows how long the opportunity to flee will be open to them?

19 Luke's gospel warned Christians of his day to flee when they saw "Jerusalem surrounded by encamped armies." As already noted, those armies came in 66 C.E., and the opportunity to flee arose that same year when Cestius Gallus withdrew his troops. After the Christians fled, war continued between the Jews and the Romans—although not around Jerusalem. Vespasian was sent by Emperor Nero to Palestine, and successful campaigns were conducted there in 67 and 68. Then Nero died, and Vespasian got involved in the Imperial succession. But after he was made emperor in 69 C.E., he sent his son Titus to finish the Judean war. In 70 C.E., Jerusalem was destroyed.

20 Christians, though, did not wait in Jerusalem to see all of that. As soon as they first saw the besieging armies, they knew the city was in deadly danger. Likewise today, the instrument of Christendom's destruction has appeared. Hence, *as soon as we discern the danger that Christendom is in,* we should 'flee to the mountains,' Jehovah's place of refuge with his theocratic organization. Other prophecies give no basis for believing that there will be a breathing space between the initial attack on Christendom and her final desolation. In truth, there will be no need for such a pause in hostilities. Meekhearted ones are wise to flee from Christendom now.

19, 20. (a) What did first-century Christians do when they saw Jerusalem surrounded by Roman armies? (b) What is represented today by "the mountains," and what should prompt meekhearted ones today to flee there?

Jerusalem and Christendom

21 Should we be surprised that in the first century "the disgusting thing" appeared just before the destruction of Jerusalem, whereas today it appeared right at the beginning of this world's time of the end? No. In each case, "the disgusting thing" appeared at the moment Jehovah wanted his people to flee. In the first century, Christians had to remain for a time in Jerusalem in order to preach there. (Acts 1:8) Only in 66 C.E., when destruction was imminent, did a "disgusting thing" appear, warning them to flee. But to be "in" modern-day Jerusalem means to be part of the religious domain of Christendom.* It is impossible to serve Jehovah acceptably in such a corrupt and apostate environment. Hence, early in this world's time of the end "the disgusting thing" appeared, warning Christians to flee. The

---

* A somewhat similar comparison could be made between the city of Babylon, from which the Jews fled in 537 B.C.E., and the modern Babylon the Great, from which Christians flee today.—Isaiah 52:11; Jeremiah 51:45; Revelation 18:4.

21. Why did "the disgusting thing" appear at the end of Jerusalem's time of the end, whereas in this century it appeared toward the beginning of this system's time of the end?

Do you remember?

□ Why must Jesus' prophecy about "the disgusting thing" have a modern-day fulfillment?

□ What is "the disgusting thing" today, and since when has it been in place?

□ What is the modern-day Jerusalem of Jesus' prophecy?

□ How does Luke 21:20, 21 help us to see the urgency of fleeing?

□ What are "the mountains" to which meekhearted ones flee?

flight out of Christendom is ongoing, each person having a warning to flee as soon as he discerns that "the disgusting thing" is in place.

²² We may ask, though, what leads to

22. What questions remain to be answered?

this most unexpected act, the destruction of Christendom by militarized elements from within the United Nations? When will it happen? And how can this possibly contribute to peace and security on our earth? We will discuss these questions in the next article.

Peace, Security, and the 'Image of the Beast'

"And he carried me away in the power of the spirit into a wilderness. And I caught sight of a woman sitting upon a scarlet-colored wild beast that was full of blasphemous names and that had seven heads and ten horns."—REVELATION 17:3.

THE apostle John saw this frightening beast in a divinely inspired vision. But John is not the only one to have seen it. In all likelihood, you, too, have seen it, or at least read about it in the newspapers. Did you recognize it?

² Of course, when we today see this beast, it does not have the appearance that John described. What John saw was symbolic of something that would exist on earth "in the Lord's day." (Revelation 1:10) Today we see its fulfillment. The repellent shape of the beast that John saw reflects Jehovah's view of what it represents—it is repugnant to Him! John had already witnessed in his vision Satan the Devil cast down to the

1. Why is John's vision of a seven-headed, ten-horned beast of concern to us?

2, 3. What series of creatures did John see in his vision?

earth "having great anger, knowing he has a short period of time." (Revelation 12:12) He had also seen the political systems of Satan's world represented as a monstrous beast with seven heads and ten horns ascending out of the "sea" of humanity. (Revelation 13:2; 17:15; Isaiah 57: 20; Luke 4:5, 6) This beast had authority over all mankind, and people were forced to submit to the 'mark of the beast' in their right hand or upon their forehead, signifying their support for it.—Revelation 13:7, 16, 17.

3 John had watched as men made an image of this beast. (Revelation 13:14, 15) It is this image that he saw in the above vision described in Revelation chapter 17. This seven-headed, ten-horned "image" will play an important part in future events; so it is vital for us to identify it. How can we do that?

The "Image" of the Beast Today

4 An angel gave John some information that helps us. He said: "The seven heads mean seven mountains, where the woman sits on top. And there are seven kings: five have fallen, one is, the other has not yet arrived, but when he does arrive he must remain a short while." (Revelation 17: 9, 10) The mention of "kings" and "mountains"—which in the Bible can often represent political powers—indicates that the heads of the beast represent governments. (Jeremiah 51:25) Which seven governments are involved?

5 Well, five had already fallen in John's day, one still existed, and one was to come. In Bible history, five major empires flourished, oppressed God's people, and then fell before John's day: Egypt, Assyria, Babylon, Medo-Persia, and Greece. When John was alive, the Roman

empire was in power. Centuries after John's death, the Roman empire passed from the scene as the dominant world power and was eventually replaced by the British empire. Soon this empire's western colonies gained independence and came to act closely with Britain to form the Anglo-American world power. This is the "king" that had "not yet arrived" in John's day. What was the relationship between the beast that John saw and the seven empires represented by its heads? "It is also itself an eighth king, but springs from the seven."—Revelation 17:11.

6 Remember, too, that the beast had ten horns. About these, the angel said: "The ten horns that you saw mean ten kings, who have not yet received a kingdom, but they do receive authority as kings one hour with the wild beast." (Revelation 17: 12) In the Bible, the number ten represents completeness as to things on earth. Therefore, these horns symbolize all the governmental powers earth wide that support the wild beast for a short time ("one hour") during "the Lord's day." They include the seventh world power, as well as the modern governments that have descended from the other six 'heads of the beast,' though these six are no longer world powers. These "kings" did not exist in John's day.* Now that they have gained authority, they "give their power and au-

---

* The political scene today is quite different from that of John's day. Very few member nations of the UN even existed back then. Hence, it is true to say that they had "not yet received a kingdom." There are a few exceptions, such as Egypt. But even in these lands, the power structure has changed so much over the centuries that the angel's comment is still true: The governments now in power had "not yet received a kingdom" in John's day.

4, 5. What did the heads of the visionary beast represent?

6. (a) What did the horns of the beast mean? (b) In what way had they "not yet received a kingdom"?

thority to the wild beast."—Revelation 17:13.

7 Do you recognize the beast now? Yes, it is the same as "the disgusting thing that causes desolation" that began as the League of Nations and that now exists as the United Nations. (Matthew 24:15; Daniel 12:11) How does this organization 'spring from the seven world powers'? In the sense that the whole beastlike organization, like an eighth power, is brought into existence by already existing governments, with the Anglo-American world power being its chief sponsor and supporter.

8 In addition, as the angel told John, all the "ten horns" give "power and authority to the wild beast." (Revelation 17:13) In fact, without support from the governments represented by the heads and the horns, the beast would be powerless. Why? Because it is merely an image. (Revelation 13:14) Like all images, it is powerless in itself. (Isaiah 44:14-17) Any life that it has comes from its supporters. (Revelation 13:15) At times some of these have taken decisive action through the United Nations, as, for example, during the Korean War.

9 Our identification of this beast is confirmed by some further details given by the angel: "The wild beast that you saw was, but is not, and yet is about to ascend out of the abyss, and it is to go off into destruction." (Revelation 17:8) This has already been fulfilled in part. The second world war effectively killed the League of Nations. In 1942, when Jehovah's Witnesses came to understand this prophecy clearly, it could be said of the League-

---

7, 8. (a) What is the beast that John saw, as described in Revelation chapter 17? (b) How is it related to the heads and the horns?
9. How is our identification of the beast confirmed?

> **Pope Paul VI saw in the United Nations "the reflection of the loving and transcendent design of God for the progress of the human family"**

beast: "It 'is not.'"* But in 1945 it 'ascended out of the abyss' as the United Nations organization. Will it succeed in its mission to bring peace and security? The prophecy says no. Rather, it is "to go off into destruction."

The Rider of the Beast

10 Did you notice something else about the beast? There was a "woman" riding it. She is identified as the worldwide empire of false religion, "Babylon the Great, the mother of the harlots and of the disgusting things of the earth." (Revelation 17: 3-5, 15) Have the world's religions 'ridden' both organizations, trying to guide their course? Yes, particularly the religions of Christendom.

11 For example, Dutch correspondent Pierre van Paassen described the "something akin to religious enthusiasm" of the representatives of the Protestant churches of America, Britain, and the Scandinavian countries who attended sessions of the League of Nations. In 1945 the Federal

---

* While World War II was escalating in all its fury, the president of the Watch Tower Society, on September 20, 1942, delivered to the New World Theocratic Convention of Jehovah's Witnesses the speech "Peace—Can It Last?" Therein, he showed from Revelation chapter 17 that, contrary to the expectation of many, World War II would not culminate in Armageddon. First the 'peace beast' must rise again from the abyss of inactivity to rule for a figurative "one hour" with the political powers.

10, 11. (a) Who was riding the beast in John's vision? (b) How has this feature of the vision been fulfilled in modern times?

Council of the Churches of Christ in America declared: "We are determined to work for the continued expansion of the curative and creative functions of the United Nations Organization." In 1965 Pope Paul VI declared that he saw in the organization "the reflection of the loving and transcendent design of God for the progress of the human family on earth—a reflection in which We see the message of the Gospel which is heavenly become earthly." Indeed, religious leaders have made that organization "full of blasphemous names."—Revelation 17:3; compare Matthew 24:15; Mark 13:14.

No Force for Peace

[12] The United Nations does not enjoy good relations with God's Kingdom. In fact, its supporters oppose that Kingdom. The angel told John: "[The ten horns] will battle with the Lamb, but, because he is Lord of lords and King of kings, the Lamb will conquer them. Also, those called and chosen and faithful with him will do so." (Revelation 17:14) True to the prophecy, the nations have persistently 'battled with the Lamb' throughout this time of the end, opposing and persecuting those who act as ambassadors of his Kingdom. The Lamb, though, is unconquerable, and so are his servants on earth who continue preaching the good news of God's Kingdom despite bannings, imprisonments, and even death.—Matthew 10:16-18; John 16:33; 1 John 5:4.

[13] In truth, the United Nations could never be a force for real peace. Its rider, "Babylon the Great," is one of the most wicked war makers in history, and she is "drunk with the blood of the holy ones and with the blood of the witnesses of Jesus." (Revelation 17:6) The wars of the nations who support that organization have soaked the earth in blood. (Matthew 24: 6, 7) And the power behind them, Satan the Devil, "the great dragon," is no peacemaker. (Revelation 12:9, 17; 13:2) Mankind will never enjoy security as long as these entities exist. They will have to be removed.

The Necessary Steps Toward Peace

[14] The first to go is false religion, in a most unexpected way. This is the way it happens: "The ten horns that you saw, and the wild beast, these will hate the harlot and will make her devastated and naked, and will eat up her fleshy parts and will completely burn her with fire." What a shock to mankind! (Revelation 17:16; 18: 9-19) It is the destructive, nationalistic "horns," prominent in the United Nations organization, that will devastate her. How remarkably this reminds us of Jesus' prophecy that "the disgusting thing" would desolate "Jerusalem"! (Mark 13: 14-20; Luke 21:20) However, while it is the nations that perform this execution, they are really carrying out God's judgment on "the great harlot," including Christendom. The result? False religion "will never be found again."—Revelation 17:1; 18:21.

[15] Jesus said that the destruction of Christendom would be the start of a "great tribulation such as has not occurred since the world's beginning until now, no, nor will occur again." (Matthew 24:15, 21) As the tribulation continues, God's Kingdom will execute judgment on

12. What has been the relationship of the United Nations organization's supporters and God's Kingdom?
13. Why could the United Nations never be a force for real peace?

14. (a) In John's vision, what happened to the rider of the beast? (b) How will this be fulfilled?
15, 16. (a) What is the "great tribulation"? (b) What will it result in? (c) How will Satan be prevented from ruining the peace prospects of mankind?

Peace lovers are urged to "get out of" Babylon the Great

all the political and commercial parts of Satan's organization. (Daniel 2:44) John now sees the King in action: "I saw the heaven opened, and, look! a white horse. And the one seated upon it is called Faithful and True, and he judges and carries on war in righteousness." Ranged against him are the political nations of the earth along with the 'image of the beast.' The result of the war? Once again, destruction for the peace destroyers!—Revelation 19: 11, 19-21.

16 That will leave just one great obstacle to peace: Satan the Devil himself. John goes on to describe the incapacitating of this great enemy of mankind: "I saw an angel coming down out of heaven with the key of the abyss and a great chain in his hand. And he seized the dragon, the original serpent, who is the Devil and Satan, and bound him for a thousand years." —Revelation 20:1-3.

A Time of Choice

17 What a time of changes for mankind! But while organizations and governments are being removed, what happens to individuals is largely a matter of their own choice. In an expression of love, Jehovah decreed: "In all the nations the good news has to be preached first," before the great tribulation. (Mark 13:10) Peace lovers are invited to "get out of" Babylon the Great. (Revelation 18:4) Those in Christendom are urged to 'flee to the mountains.' (Luke 21:21) Those who submit to God's Kingdom must avoid having 'the mark of the beast.' (Revelation 14:9-12; John 17: 15, 16) A great crowd of such righthearted ones will "come out of the great tribulation." (Revelation 7:9-14) In fact, no one necessarily has to perish along with Satan's system.—Proverbs 2:21, 22.

17. What steps should be taken now by individuals who desire to see real peace?

¹⁸ When will these earth-shaking events take place? Well, the "good news" is being heard around the world today. "The disgusting thing" is in place. (Matthew 24:14-16) In fact, the 'image of the beast,' already in the second stage of its existence, is now due to "go off into destruction." (Revelation 17:8) The fulfillment of the "sign" shows that we have been living in the time of Jesus' presence for 71 years, since 1914. (Matthew 24:3) Jesus said: "When you see all these things, know that he is near at the doors. Truly I say to you that this generation will by no means pass away until all these things occur." (Matthew 24:33, 34) Hence, the "great tribulation" must be very close. Can we be more precise than that? Not at this time.

¹⁹ The apostle Paul foretold: "Whenever it is that they are saying: 'Peace and security!' then sudden destruction is to be instantly upon them." (1 Thessalonians 5:3) So the great tribulation will be a shocking surprise to mankind in general. It will not, however, be a shock for Christians. They know that it is coming, and they follow Jesus' counsel: "Keep awake, then, all the time making supplication that you may succeed in escaping all these things that are destined to occur." —Luke 21:36.

²⁰ Nevertheless, Christians cannot say in advance exactly when the great tribulation will strike. Jehovah has not revealed "that day or the hour." (Mark 13:32; Matthew 24:42) Thus when, for example, the United Nations declares the year 1986 an "International Year of Peace," Christians watch the event with interest. But they cannot say in advance whether this will prove to be the fulfillment of

18, 19. (a) What can be said about *when* the great tribulation will break out? (b) How are Christians now preparing themselves for that time?
20. Why at this time can Christians not say when the great tribulation will come?

Paul's words quoted above. They are, though, grateful that Jehovah has enabled them to discern the significance of the 'image of the beast' and "the disgusting thing that causes desolation." Thus they see this organization the way Jehovah sees it and are not misled by its efforts to bring peace.

²¹ Those who do "keep awake" and submit themselves to God's Kingdom enjoy peace even now. Jehovah, "the God of peace," is with them and gives them "the peace of God that excels all thought." (Philippians 4:7, 9) Moreover, they look forward to the not-too-distant time when the whole earth will enjoy the fulfillment of Isaiah's beautiful prophecy: "The work of the true righteousness must become peace; and the service of the true righteousness, quietness and security to time indefinite. And my people must dwell in a peaceful abiding place and in residences of full confidence and in undisturbed resting-places." (Isaiah 32:16-18) This will be security on a worldwide scale. (Isaiah 11:9) And it will be *real* peace because Jehovah himself will be its author.

21. (a) What peace do Christians enjoy even now? (b) To what can they confidently look forward?

Do You Recall?

☐ What are some characteristics of the beast of Revelation 17?

☐ What does this beast represent?

☐ Why can this figurative beast never bring peace?

☐ How will God's Kingdom finally bring peace and security to mankind?

☐ How may individuals benefit from this knowledge?

My Ten Years in Spain's Military Prisons

As told by Fernando Marín

TEN years in prison in Franco's Spain —ten years that enriched my life. That might sound like a contradiction; yet that is true in my case. Not because those years were full of the comforts of life. On the contrary, there was all the cruel reality of a military prison. But along with all of that, there was also the real evidence, at times amazing, of divine protection. I can recall the events as if they happened yesterday.

I was raised a Catholic and had studied at Catholic schools in Barcelona. I grew up with a morbid fear of hellfire torment and purgatory. Then when I was 16 I studied the Bible with Jehovah's Witnesses, and those terrifying teachings were wiped from my mind. I saw clearly from the Bible that there is no immortal human soul. In that case, how could there be places of torment and purging for such? —Ezekiel 18:4, 20; Ecclesiastes 9:5, 6, 10.

In 1961, at the age of 18, I symbolized my dedication to God by baptism in Paris, France, at the first large convention that I attended. I was one of a small group of Spaniards who had been able to arrange the trip to France in spite of our poor economic situation and the ban on Jehovah's Witnesses in Spain at that time. Our preaching work was underground during most of the Franco era (1939-75).

I was so grateful to know Jehovah and his truth through Christ Jesus that my dedication was made without reservation. I wanted to be a full-time pioneer minister. My wish was fulfilled in February 1962. I have been in that service ever since—even when I was in prison. But why did I have to go to prison?

My First Big Test

In February of 1964, at the age of 21, I was drafted for military service. I was prepared for what was to come. For years, like other young men of my generation in the congregation, I had two goals in life —to be a full-time pioneer minister and to keep my integrity on the issue of Christian neutrality.—John 17:16; 18:36.

When I left home to go to the barracks, I went with an air of expectancy, with a kind of cold nervousness, but with my convictions very clear in mind. On my arrival at the local army quarters, I explained my position as a conscientious objector—something that was hardly understood at that time in Spain and certainly not tolerated. I was given a travel

Even in isolation, I had a constant reminder that I was not alone

pass and told to present myself at the barracks in Tenerife (Canary Islands) —over a thousand miles (1,600 km) from my home in Catalonia.

In Tenerife the military authorities thought I was mad. Who in his right mind would refuse to do military service under a Fascist dictatorship? I was assigned to a psychiatric hospital for treatment! Fortunately I was examined by a doctor who knew of the Witnesses, and I was thus saved from treatment that could have done permanent damage. They soon locked me up in a military prison. For how long would I be there? I had no idea, as there was no fixed sentence in those days for conscientious objectors.

During the years that followed, I came to know the inner emptiness of loneliness and the degradation of debased cell mates. I passed through life-threatening situations, and I was made tempting offers to break my integrity and neutrality. Slowly I came to realize that the small rectangle of a cell could also be a universe when one enjoys an intimate relationship with God. I developed an overwhelming trust in Jehovah as my God.—Psalm 23.

Solitary Confinement

From Tenerife I was sent to the dread military prison of San Francisco del Risco on the island of Las Palmas de Gran Canaria—dreaded because of the reputation of the prison commandant—a short, stocky, sadistic type who enjoyed beating up the prisoners personally. His nickname was *Pisamondongo* (Guts Treader).

I was put in solitary confinement, and all my belongings were removed, including my Bible. I was only briefly allowed out at night—to empty my latrine and to pick up my supper bowl. Yet, in all those months of solitary confinement I was never truly alone. (Psalm 145:18) Like missionary Harold King, who for years was in solitary confinement in China, I cultivated my relationship with Jehovah. (See *The Watchtower,* 1963, pages 437-42.)

One Sunday my meal included a slice of lemon. As I squeezed it onto the rice some drops fell on the red tile floor of my cell, leaving a slight stain. This gave me the idea of using lemon juice to inscribe a text on the cell floor. Once a week the meal included a slice of lemon. Thus, little by little, I was able to write across the floor of my cell: *"El nombre de mi Dios es Jehová."* ("The name of my God is Jehovah.") Those words were a constant reminder that I was not entirely alone. That simple truth at my feet triggered my mind to recall deeper truths about man's relationship to God. Later, using the wax from a candle, I polished the whole of the cell floor until it was smooth and shiny like a mirror.

What I Risked to Read the Bible

Brothers imprisoned in El Aaiún, in the Sahara, heard about my isolation and the fact that I was denied any Bible or Bible literature. By means of another prisoner who was being transferred, they managed to send some pages from a *Watchtower* magazine and a copy of one of the Gospels. The problem was, how could he get them to me while I was in solitary confinement?

That night when I went to empty my latrine a small package was dropped over the lavatory wall. I grabbed it like a starving man grasping bread. Back in my cell, I passed the night reading those pages again and again. It was the first literature speaking of Jehovah that I had seen in a year! Dawn came. With what ravishing hunger I had devoured those articles and Jesus' comforting words from the Gospel!

The following night, as I returned to my cell with my supper bowl in my hand, I saw the prison commandant, don Gregorio, waiting for me. He had a menacing look on his face and his short bull neck swelled with rage. In his hand were my magazine pages. My cache of precious Bible literature had been discovered! Using gross insults against Jehovah's name and threats of death, he called me over. I immediately offered an intense and silent prayer to Jehovah, asking that he help me to bear what was to follow with the dignity of a true Christian.

The commandant opened my cell door. I ran to the corner of the cell and tried to cover my vulnerable parts against the onslaught that I knew must come. Furious and screaming, with his eyes bloodshot, he hurled himself at me. The floor was highly polished. He slipped and fell on his face. Wild with rage, he tried to get up. As he did so, his eyes fell on the words written on the floor, *"El nombre de mi Dios es Jehová."* He was very superstitious. When he got to God's name, he said incredulously in a low tone, "Jehovah!" Then his voice rose as he began shouting again and again "Jehovah! Jehovah! . . . " Then, almost on all fours he fled from the cell! I was spared a thrashing, and he never bothered me again.

This experience strengthened my faith in Jehovah's protecting hand. Here I was totally alone and yet not abandoned. I was persecuted but not destroyed.—2 Corinthians 4:7-10.

A Congregation—In Prison

Eventually I was transferred to the prison of Santa Catalina, in Cádiz, where there were soon about a hundred brothers. We organized ourselves as a congregation, one of the largest in Spain at that time! We maintained our schedule of meetings and personal study and even repeated the circuit and district assembly programs right there in the prison.

It would have been easy to dramatize our situation, but our brothers and sisters on the outside were also facing tests of loyalty and integrity in their daily lives —in some cases tests that we did not have in prison. At least we did not feel cut off from Jehovah and his organization. His principles were vital to us, especially when psychological fatigue took over, and the days, which seemed endless, fell on us like the relentless blows of a hammer, crushing the flower of our youth. But we did not allow such despair to overcome us. —Psalm 71.

In our cramped surroundings, we had to maintain a good spirit of Christian coexistence, which was not always easy. Privacy was virtually impossible in communal cells even though we were separated from the other military prisoners. Unhappily, a case arose in our ranks of a gross moral sin. Action had to be taken to keep our congregation clean. The person was disfellowshipped. Yet he had to continue living with us—we could not put him out of the prison, nor did we want to ask to have him moved to the common prison

In Our Next Issue

- **Peace and Security —Through God's Kingdom**

- **The "Nation" That Feeds Famine-Stricken Millions**

- **How True Faith Can Help You**

The late Grant Suiter (center), member of the Governing Body of Jehovah's Witnesses, visited the military prison in Cádiz (left, translator Bernard Backhouse; right, Fernando Marin)

section because of the reproach it would cast on Jehovah and the rest of us. We were puzzled as to how to handle this embarrassing situation. An answer came from an unexpected source.

Through a Cupboard Door

At about that time we received a most welcome visit from Grant Suiter, a member of the Governing Body. He was allowed to see just one prisoner in the visitors' room. But we all wanted to see and hear him. How would it be possible? We had discovered in the workshop an unused door that led into our dormitory. It was hidden behind wallpaper. We decided to camouflage it completely by covering it with a backless cupboard. Thus one could step into the cupboard, open the door behind—and find oneself in a maze of tightly packed three-tier bunk beds!

When Brother Suiter was alone with me in the visiting room, I invited him to the workshop on the pretext of showing him some of our handiwork. Imagine his surprise at being asked to step into a cupboard—then to find himself in a dormitory with over a hundred brothers waiting to see him! We took a risk, but for us, starved for outside association, it was worth it. We could hardly believe that we had a member of the Governing Body actually in our midst.

We took the opportunity to explain our disfellowshipping problem to him. His an-

swer was clear: Jehovah's organization and principles cannot be subverted by man's rules and regulations. 'The organization is not in prison!' he said. Then he suggested, 'Why not speak to the commandant and ask to have the offender transferred?'

The commandant, the sarcastic type, usually scoffed at us. I explained to him, "We do not permit transgressors in our ranks. We must keep our organization clean." How did he react? As if he had understood some eternal principle that I had thought was beyond his ken, he tried to console me! I was flabbergasted! He said he would give orders immediately for the transgressor to be transferred and that he would not be readmitted to our section until our judicial committee requested it. He even praised our loyalty and respect for high principles.

Amnesty and Freedom

Our test in prison was not only the endless years of imprisonment but also the uncertainty—we never knew when we would get free, if ever. Why not? Because as each sentence was completed, we were put through the process again and given an even harsher sentence. One of the brothers was condemned to a total of 26 years in prison—all for refusing 18 months of military service! What sustained us during the long test? Prayer was one of the cornerstones of our integrity.

Rumors circulated from about 1972 onward that the Spanish government might grant amnesty to the conscientious objectors who had been so long in prison. A few days before the amnesty went into effect, 70 out of the 100 who were to be released applied for full-time pioneer service! That gives some idea of the elevated sense of Christian responsibility that we had developed over the years in prison. We did not see our new freedom as an excuse to live it up and make up for all we had apparently missed. Instead, we wanted to show Jehovah our gratitude for the protection we had enjoyed over the years. And it was no fleeting, emotional reaction—many of those brothers are still in the pioneer ranks! More than a dozen are in the circuit or district work, or in Bethel service, and that includes me and my wife Conchita.

Did I waste ten years of my life in prison? Integrity is never wasted. The combined record of integrity keeping of hundreds of faithful brothers imprisoned in Spain made Jehovah's name reach the highest circles of the government, parliament, and the Catholic Church. Even General Franco had to recognize this unusual body of unbending Christians. In 1970 Jehovah's Witnesses were granted legal recognition by his government.

In Spain's prisons we survived a long test of patience and endurance. But it was a unique opportunity for serious personal study of the Bible and for cultivating a close relationship with Jehovah. We did not waste those valuable years. That is why so many of us came out of prison much stronger spiritually than when we went in. Yes, for many years 'we were persecuted, but not left in the lurch; we were thrown down, but never destroyed.' —2 Corinthians 4:9.

"The Highest Service," "The Most Pleasant Life"

As a result of his deep study of the Christian Greek Scriptures, John Wycliffe, the courageous 14th-century Bible translator, came to an interesting conclusion about man's responsibility to the Almighty God. According to H. C. Conant's book *The English Bible,* Wycliffe concluded that *"the highest service to which man may attain on earth is to preach the word of God."* Some centuries later another Bible scholar, Matthew Henry, came to a similar conclusion. On his deathbed in 1714, he observed: *"A life spent in the service of God, and communion with him, is the most pleasant life that any one can live in this world."*

Well over two and a half million active Jehovah's Witnesses wholeheartedly concur! They experience this "most pleasant life." Why? Because they preach the good news of the Kingdom worldwide, thus obeying the exhortation: "Praise Jah, you people, . . . for it is pleasant."—Psalm 147:1.

Learning From Jesus' Temptations

IMMEDIATELY after his baptism, Jesus is led by God's spirit into the Judean wilderness. He has a lot to think about, for at his baptism "the heavens were opened up" so that he could discern heavenly things. Thus Jesus now fully remembers his life as a spirit son of God, including all the things God had spoken to him. Indeed, there is much for him to meditate on!

Jesus spends 40 days and 40 nights in the wilderness and eats nothing during this time. Then, when he is very hungry, the Devil approaches to tempt him, saying: "If you are a son of God, tell these stones to become loaves of bread." But Jesus knows it is wrong to use his miraculous powers to satisfy his personal desires. So he refuses to be tempted.

But the Devil does not give up. He tries another approach. He challenges Jesus to leap off the temple wall so that God's angels will rescue him. But Jesus is not tempted to make such a spectacular display. Quoting from the Scriptures, he shows that it is wrong to put God to the test in this way.

In a third temptation, the Devil shows Jesus all the kingdoms of the world in some miraculous way and says: "All these things I will give you if you fall down and do an act of worship to me." But again Jesus refuses to yield to temptation to do wrong, choosing to remain faithful to God.

We can learn from these temptations of Jesus. They show, for example, that the Devil is not a mere quality of evil, as some people claim, but that he is a real, invisible person. The temptation of Jesus also shows that all the world governments are the Devil's property. For how could the Devil's offer of them to Christ have been a real temptation if they were not really his?

And think of this: The Devil said he was willing to reward Jesus for one act of worship, even giving him *all the kingdoms of the world.* The Devil may well try to tempt us in a similar way, perhaps placing before us tantalizing opportunities to obtain worldly wealth, power, or position. But how wise we would be to follow Jesus' example by remaining faithful to God whatever the temptation may be! **Matthew 3:16; 4: 1-11; Mark 1:12, 13; Luke 4:1-13.**

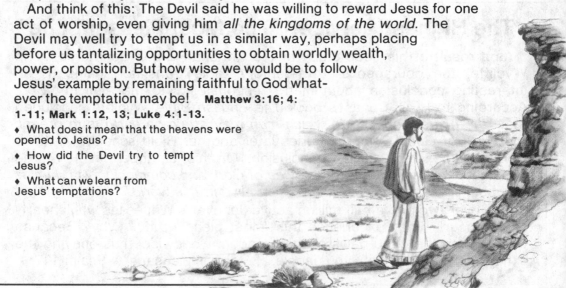

♦ What does it mean that the heavens were opened to Jesus?

♦ How did the Devil try to tempt Jesus?

♦ What can we learn from Jesus' temptations?

"Teach Me Goodness"

ONLY two persons responded when the elderly woman suddenly collapsed in the crowded subway car. The other passengers, their patience worn thin by rush-hour delays, saw her plight as another inconvenience. 'Can't somebody move that woman out of the way?' screamed one irate commuter. To their fellow passengers, the dying woman and the two riders desperately trying to revive her seemed to be no more than obstructions. Thus they were "repeatedly trampled."

Such scenes have been witnessed in many parts of the world. They dramatically underscore the Bible's prediction that "in the last days . . . men will be . . . without love of goodness." Christians, however, want to please Jehovah. They must "turn away" from individuals lacking goodness. (2 Timothy 3:1-5) But merely guarding our association is not enough. Goodness must be carefully cultivated as a fruit of God's spirit. (Galatians 5:22) But how? And what is goodness?

Goodness and Righteousness

Goodness is moral excellence and virtue, the quality or state of being good. But it is more than a passive state. When discussing the ransom provision, the apostle Paul said: "Hardly will anyone die for a righteous man; indeed, for the good man, perhaps, someone even dares to die. But God recommends his own love to us in that, while we were yet sinners, Christ died for us." (Romans 5:7, 8) Here goodness seemingly is contrasted with righteousness. But are they exact opposites?

No. Paul apparently had in mind the thought that righteousness involves conforming to a standard. In fact, righteousness has been associated with judgment. (Compare Revelation 19:11.) The "righteous" man is law abiding. He meets a criterion, fulfills a quota, but may do little beyond that. Thus he wins respect but not necessarily hearts. Few would be moved to die for him. However, the "good" man does more than fulfill obligations or avoid wrongdoing. His goodness motivates him to exert himself for others, to do things for them.

Those who exert themselves in doing good things for others prove to be real neighbors. Jesus' parable about the neighborly Samaritan illustrates this point. "Moved with pity," the Samaritan dressed the wounds of a beaten robbery victim, a Jew. Then this doer of good "mounted him upon his own beast and brought him to an inn and took care of him." (Luke 10:29-37) Is it any wonder, then, that some have called this illustration the parable of the *good* Samaritan?—Compare Matthew 12:35; 20:10-15; Luke 6:9, 33-36.

Goodness is not passive but is dynamically *active*. Recipients of the "good" person's kindness, generosity, and self-sacrifice might even be moved to die for him! So it is with good reason that the psalmist prayed: "Teach me goodness." (Psalm 119:66) But how does Jehovah do this?

Jehovah's Example of Goodness

Jehovah teaches us goodness by his own example. He is the very personification of goodness. When Moses asked to see God's glory, He said: "I myself shall cause all my goodness to pass before your face, and I will declare the name of Jehovah before you." How did this take place? Shortly thereafter, "Jehovah went passing by before his face and declaring: 'Jehovah, Jehovah, a God merciful and gracious, slow to anger and abundant in loving-kindness and truth, preserving loving-kindness for thousands, pardoning error and transgression and sin, but by no means will he give exemption from punishment.'"—Exodus 33:18, 19; 34:6, 7.

At that time Jehovah's goodness was highlighted in various ways. Prominent was his mercy and love of truth. Knowing mankind's imperfect state, Jehovah is considerate and patient toward those who really want to do what is right. Yet, he does not condone badness. Surely, then, we can benefit from meditating on the example Jehovah has set.

Jehovah has also manifested goodness through his creation. In fact, he was able to view his creative work as being "good." (Genesis 1:12, 18, 25, 31; Romans 1:20) God went beyond the bare minimum in equipping this planet to sustain life.

The generous supply of water to sustain life demonstrates Jehovah's goodness

"The pouring rain" is a good example of this. (Isaiah 55:10) With remarkable scientific accuracy, Elihu said that Jehovah "draws up the drops of water; they filter as rain for his mist, so that the clouds trickle, they drip upon mankind abundantly . . . He gives food in abundance." (Job 36:27-31) An estimated 132,000 million million gallons (500,000 million million liters) of water are involved daily in this cycle, the sun 'drawing' most of this water from the oceans.

According to a report in *The New York Times,* "researchers studying the dynamics of South America's tropical forest have produced scientific evidence showing with precision for the first time that a forest can return as much as 75 percent of the moisture it receives to the atmosphere." The report further indicated that "the amount of water a forest gathers can be returned to the air in large enough amounts to form new rain clouds." And, of course, rain is one of the vital factors in food production. Indeed, Jehovah has efficiently and abundantly provided for life on the earth. What goodness he has displayed in making all these provisions available even to thankless and unappreciative people.—Matthew 5:44, 45.

But an even more striking example of Jehovah's goodness is the way he has worked to fulfill his original purpose for humankind. (Genesis 1:28; 3:15; Romans 5:12) His goodness moved him to make a ransom provision for sinful mankind by giving "his only-begotten Son, in order that everyone exercising faith in him might not be destroyed but have everlasting life." (John 3:16; Romans 3:23, 24) Through God's Kingdom his goodness toward the honest hearted will soon be manifested in bringing about the end of this wicked system of things. (Daniel 2:44; Matthew 6:9, 10; 2 Peter 3:9, 10) And what goodness of God will be evident when this earth becomes a paradise under Kingdom rule!—Luke 23:43; 2 Peter 3:13; Revelation 21:1-5.

Imitate Jehovah's Goodness

Regular study of the Bible keeps Jehovah's perfect example of goodness constantly before us. In turn, this should move us to imitate his example. True, many necessary activities could interfere with studying the Scriptures regularly, among them cooking, cleaning, shopping, and household repairs. Yet, we must keep spiritual things in first place. Jesus Christ indicated this when visiting the home of Mary and Martha. While Martha busied herself with household duties, Mary sat at Jesus' feet and "kept listening to his word." When Martha sought Mary's help with the chores, Jesus said: "Martha, Martha, you are anxious and disturbed about many things. A few things, though, are needed, or just one. For her part, Mary chose the *good* portion, and it will not be taken away from her." You, too, can choose what is good by giving priority to such spiritual matters as personal and family study.—Luke 10:38-42.

Jehovah also teaches us goodness through the Christian congregation. There we associate with people who are "full of goodness." (Romans 15:14) Many experiences illustrate this. One witness of Jehovah (already a mother of two) recalled her amazement at learning she had given birth to triplets! 'How will we ever get to Christian meetings?' she wondered. 'How will we pay this hospital bill? How will we ever afford to feed and clothe five children?'

Soon, however, this woman had evidence that her Christian brothers and sisters are "full of goodness." "Upon arriving home," said she, "I found that several of my Christian sisters had cleaned our apartment. Further, the sisters arranged to have meals brought in and did the daily chores until I got my strength back." Many of the brothers contributed materially, one even sending anonymously $1,000! During the winter, though, this family ran up a considerable heating bill. So imagine this woman's anxiety when she received a telephone call from the fuel company. To her relief, however, she learned that a Christian sister had paid the bill! A notice to discontinue service intended for this struggling family had inadvertently been mailed to this fellow Witness, and goodness had moved her to help them.

Such goodness not only touches the heart but is also contagious. By Jehovah's Witnesses "I have been taught to love and to be kind," one former wife beater told his mate after she attended her first meeting. "That is why I don't beat you anymore."

Blessings of Learning Goodness

Even now we reap blessings from learning and loving goodness. Our association with our brothers and even with people of the world thus becomes more pleasant. (Proverbs 11:10; 1 Peter 3:13) Most important of all, if we endure suffering because of "doing good," "this is a thing agreeable with God." (1 Peter 2:20) In fact, our exercising faith and manifesting goodness will lead to our being protected during the "great tribulation" and ensures our entry into the New Order.—Hebrews 10:36-39; Matthew 24:21.

So allow Jehovah to teach you goodness. The rewards? Why, there will be "glory and honor and peace for everyone who works what is good"!—Romans 2:6-11.

Kingdom Proclaimers Report

Finding a Purpose in Life

IN THIS decadent, upside-down world a number of people are searching for a meaning and *purpose* in life. They ask: 'Why are we here? From where did we come? What does the future hold?' Many turn to God in search of answers, and he does not disappoint them. (Matthew 7:7, 8) Such was the experience of one woman in Greece. She says:

□ "I was 14 years old when I started wondering about man and his purpose in life. After a study of anthropology at school, I thought medicine would answer my questions, but I dismissed such thoughts when the origin of man could not be explained to me." She continues: "My thoughts turned to astrology, and I studied Eastern religions, such as Islam and the religion of Tibet. I began to apply the Lama's teaching in my life, then spiritism. When I contacted the spirits, I felt that I had found the truth. Western religions claimed to base their beliefs on the Bible, but since my religion teacher at school could not answer my questions from the Bible, I continued my spiritistic practices, astrojourneys, and hypnosis."

In 1982 this woman contacted Jehovah's Witnesses, but she relates: "Their explanation of the Bible was far too simple compared with the complex teachings I had learned. But something kept urging me to try the Bible. So out of sheer egotism I accepted a Bible study to prove the Witnesses wrong."

After studying the Bible with Jehovah's Witnesses for about a year, she explains: "Now I thank Jehovah with all my heart for helping me to learn the real truth. At last I am free from all the false theories and superstitions. The truth is so simple and easy to find in God's Word, the Bible. At last I have found the answers to my questions; now I know the origin of man and the purpose of life."

□ A 27-year-old Greek man who was originally involved with communism also found a purpose in life. He studied engineering in Germany, then returned to Greece and enlisted in the army. His experiences gradually convinced him that man was no longer in a position to solve his problems and to better his life. Before this man went to Germany, a Witness neighbor had talked to him about the Bible, and now he recalled those conversations. Hence, just a few months before being discharged from the army, he told his superior officer: "I no longer consider myself a soldier!" His family felt he had mental problems and forced him to visit psychiatrists. These gave him large doses of various medications, which affected him physically and mentally until he finally stopped using them.

He was found by two Witnesses in their door-to-door ministry and started to study the Bible with them. After bringing his life into harmony with Jehovah's requirements, he became an active proclaimer of the good news. In 1984 he attended the Memorial along with ten relatives he had invited.

Yes, he had found a purpose in life, and now he has the desire to serve Jehovah as a special pioneer. His hope is to gain eternal life in God's New Order of righteousness.—Isaiah 65: 17, 18.

School and Jehovah's Witnesses
—Are You Using It?

9-17-97

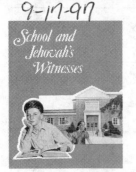

School and Jehovah's Witnesses

THE brochure *School and Jehovah's Witnesses* was provided to help school authorities understand why Witness youths do not share in certain school functions and programs. It also serves to help Jehovah's Witnesses explain why, as a result of their beliefs, they take the position that they do.

However, for the brochure to fulfill its stated purpose, *"to promote understanding and cooperation between Jehovah's Witnesses and school authorities,"* Witness families first need to study it themselves and then see that teachers receive a copy. Those who have put the *School* brochure to use have enjoyed fine results.

For example, on May 6, 1983, the Ministry of Education in the Bahamas sent out a circular that set out the morning assembly exercises for all schools. The last sentence in the circular stated: "Please note that no discretion is allowed in matters relating to National Symbols."

But, then, in the summer of 1983, the *School* brochure was released at the conventions of Jehovah's Witnesses and put to use in the Bahamas. Evidently as a direct result of such use, when a new circular was sent to the principals of schools on January 18, 1984, there was a complete reversal on the matter of national symbols. In the last paragraph under the heading "STUDENT PARTICIPATION IN PATRIOTIC ACTIVITIES IN SCHOOL," the circular said:

"Saluting the flag and the national anthem are intended to instill national pride and sense of patriotism in the people and the nation. As long as there are different nations, the flag and national anthems will have their place in organised society. Nevertheless, if a particular group has as one of the tenets of its religion that the singing of the national anthem and the saluting of the flag are pagan and therefore forbidden, then the constitution requires that they must be allowed the freedom so to teach and to think."

Appreciation by School Authorities

School authorities appreciate very much knowing how the beliefs of Jehovah's Witnesses affect their participation in school activities. A copy of the brochure was left with Mr. Andre Lemieux, the principal of the Chibougamau School Board in Quebec, Canada, and he later told the Witness who had provided it: "Your teaching requires that we exempt your children from holiday celebrations and we don't understand why, although they explain it to us. But with this brochure, we will understand your children much better and take your moral principles into consideration."

He then asked: "Would it be possible to have eight for all the schools, at least one for each school?" When told that this would be no problem, he said: "In that case, I will take 40 to start with." He added, "If every religion would explain its teaching, we would have fewer problems with the children. Thank you very much."

A Witness parent in the state of Kentucky in the United States explained that her children had a new principal, so she went to school to talk with him, taking along the *School* brochure. "He examined it closely," she noted, "and wanted to know if I could get any more. I was surprised when he asked for 25 more. He said that he would like to give one to each teacher."

This mother also talked with her children's teachers. They told her that they did not mind working with Witness children but that sometimes they could not understand the reasons for their actions. However, the mother wrote: "After reading the brochure, many of their questions were answered, and this has made school much easier for my children and other Witness children in the same school."

A mother from New York City writes that her 8-year-old twin daughters were having a problem making their teachers understand their beliefs.

"One particular teacher who teaches them music was very upset over matters of national songs and holidays," she said. "Our daughters tried to explain their stand to him and gave him the brochure." With what result? He thanked them, and later wrote them regarding the brochure:

"It sets out very clearly exactly what the Witnesses think about the various holidays and why they do not participate in them. Some of the reasons I knew before, but some of them I didn't. As a teacher I feel that the more that I am acquainted with the various religions of my students, the better I will be able to understand them."

Appreciation by Witness Youths

The brochure is especially appreciated by young ones. "Another benefit was my children's reactions," a mother from British Columbia, Canada, writes. "Being a mother with an unbelieving husband at times proves difficult when it comes to reinforcing Jehovah's view on holidays, flag, etc. But with the girls knowing that the teacher actually *expected* them to be different, the way was paved for them. They are coming home telling me of the times they have taken a stand, when before they were somewhat fearful. They have also related to me occasions where the teacher has quietly helped them out of situations with a kind word or two."

A number of young people have written to tell how the brochure has helped them. A youngster from Chicago, Illinois, told about a teacher that was pressuring her to run for homecoming queen. "The next day I brought the brochure," the girl said, "and as soon as she read the part on homecoming queen she said I didn't have to have any part in the contest. It was as easy as that."

A youth from Georgia, in the United States, explains that her teacher, to whom she gave the brochure, kindly excused her from participating in certain activities after reading it. "This brochure is very important to the young people in school," the youth wrote, "and I would like to thank you for it. It's nice to know the Society is thinking of the young people who have to face these problems."

The *School* brochure is indeed a fine instrument to help promote understanding and cooperation between Jehovah's Witnesses and school authorities. Are you using it?

Questions From Readers

■ The Bible says that Samson ripped apart a lion "just as someone tears a male kid in two." Does that mean that it was common for people back then to tear apart young goats?

No, this comment likely was but an illustration. It meant that with his bare hands Samson conquered the lion as easily as if it had been a mere defenseless young goat.

Samson, serving as judge in Israel, traveled to Timnah so as to find "an opportunity against the Philistines." Along the way, he met and may have been attacked by a roaring lion, a young, strong one. The historical record says that God's active force came upon Samson "so that he tore [the maned young lion] in two, just as someone tears a male kid in two, and there was nothing at all in his hand."—Judges 14:4-6.

Two other men of Bible record single-handedly killed lions, but only Samson is said to have done this with his bare hands. (1 Samuel 17:36; 2 Samuel 23:20) Moreover, he "tore it in two." If that meant that he tore apart the powerful jaws of the lion, conceivably some Israelites had enough strength to do the same to a young goat. But there is no evidence that they did such a thing, nor any reason why they would try. On the other hand, if Samson tore the lion 'limb from limb' in some fashion, it would be even more unlikely that the comment about the goat was anything but a simile. The point is that God's spirit gave Samson extraordinary physical strength. With such help a powerful, ferocious lion was no more formidable to unarmed Samson than a defenseless young goat would be to a normal man.

The dead lion's carcass was later involved in a riddle, giving rise to another case of God's empowering Samson, who on this occasion struck down 30 of the enemy.—Judges 14:8-19.

KIND ACTS BRING JOY

Earlier this year the following letter was received by the publishers of *The Watchtower*:

"Dear Sir:

"Last month in Philadelphia my teenage daughter had her wallet stolen from her backpack bookbag. Last week in the mail she received a package containing her wallet and her license and other important cards. The package was sent by someone who wished not to be identified, except that the package also contained a copy of your publication *The Watchtower*. Whoever did this act of brotherly love (from the city of brotherly love) had apparently found the wallet thrown away by the thief and went to some trouble and expense to return it to my daughter. My family and I are grateful to this kind person . . . It was a great way to 'witness,' especially to my teenagers (3 of them)."

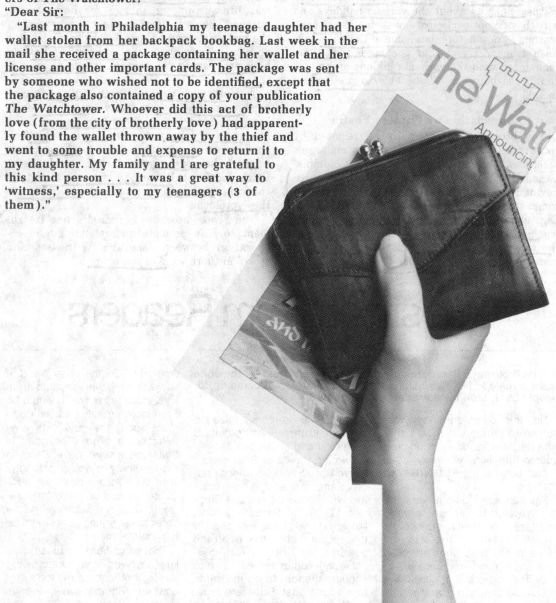

October 15, 1985

The Watchtower

Announcing Jehovah's Kingdom

PEACE AND SECURITY
—Through God's Kingdom

The Watchtower®
Announcing Jehovah's Kingdom

October 15, 1985
Vol. 106, No. 20

In This Issue

THE PURPOSE OF "THE WATCHTOWER" is to exalt Jehovah God as the Sovereign of the universe. It keeps watch on world events as they fulfill Bible prophecy. It comforts all peoples with the good news that God's Kingdom will soon destroy those who oppress their fellowmen and that it will turn the earth into a paradise. It encourages faith in the now-reigning King, Jesus Christ, whose shed blood opens the way for mankind to gain eternal life. "The Watchtower," published by Jehovah's Witnesses continuously since 1879, is nonpolitical. It adheres to the Bible as its authority.

"WATCHTOWER" STUDIES FOR THE WEEKS

November 17: The "Nation" That Fills Earth's Surface With Fruit. Page 10. Songs to Be Used: 49, 57.
November 24: The "Nation" That Feeds Famine-Stricken Millions. Page 15. Songs to Be Used: 31, 85.

Average Printing Each Issue: 11,150,000

Now Published in 103 Languages

SEMIMONTHLY EDITIONS AVAILABLE BY MAIL
Afrikaans, Arabic, Cebuano, Chichewa, Chinese, Cibemba, Danish, Dutch,* Efik, English,* Finnish, French, German,* Greek, Hiligaynon, Igbo, Iloko, Italian,* Japanese,* Korean, Lingala, Malagasy, Maltese, Norwegian, Portuguese, Russian, Sepedi, Sesotho, Shona, Spanish,* Swahili, Swedish, Tagalog, Thai, Tswana, Xhosa, Yoruba, Zulu

MONTHLY EDITIONS AVAILABLE BY MAIL
Armenian, Bengali, Bicol, Bulgarian, Croatian, Czech, Ewe, Fijian, Ga, Greenlandic, Gujarati, Gun, Hausa, Hebrew, Hindi, Hiri Motu, Hungarian, Icelandic, Kannada, Kikuyu, Kiluba, Malayalam, Marathi, New Guinea Pidgin, Pangasinan, Papiamento, Polish, Rarotongan, Romanian, Samar-Leyte, Samoan, Sango, Serbian, Silozi, Sinhalese, Slovenian, Solomon Islands-Pidgin, Tahitian, Tamil, Telugu, Tshiluba, Tsonga, Turkish, Twi, Ukrainian, Urdu, Venda, Vietnamese
* Study articles also available in large-print edition.

The Bible translation used is the "New World Translation of the Holy Scriptures," unless otherwise indicated.

Copyright © 1985 by Watch Tower Bible and Tract Society of Pennsylvania and International Bible Students Association. All rights reserved. Printed in U.S.A.

Twenty cents (U.S.) a copy

Watch Tower Society offices	Yearly subscription Semimonthly
America, U.S., Watchtower, Wallkill, N.Y. 12589	$4.00
Australia, Box 280, Ingleburn, N.S.W. 2565	A$7.00
Canada, Box 4100, Halton Hills (Georgetown), Ontario L7G 4Y4	$5.20
England, The Ridgeway, London NW7 1RN	£5.00
Ireland, 29A Jamestown Road, Finglas, Dublin 11	£5.00
New Zealand, 6-A Western Springs Rd., Auckland 3	$10.00
Nigeria, P.O. Box 194, Yaba, Lagos State	₦6.00
Philippines, P.O. Box 2044, Manila 2800	₱50.00
South Africa, Private Bag 2, Elandsfontein, 1406	R5,60

Remittances should be sent to the office in your country or to Watchtower, Wallkill, N.Y. 12589, U.S.A.

Changes of address should reach us 30 days before your moving date. Give us your old and new address (if possible, your old address label).

The Watchtower (ISSN 0043-1087) is published semimonthly for $4.00 (U.S.) per year by Watch Tower Bible and Tract Society of Pennsylvania, 25 Columbia Heights, Brooklyn, N.Y. 11201. Second-class postage paid at Brooklyn, N.Y., and at additional mailing offices.

Postmaster: Send address changes to Watchtower, *Wallkill, N.Y. 12589.*

Published by
Watch Tower Bible and Tract Society of Pennsylvania
25 Columbia Heights, Brooklyn, N.Y. 11201, U.S.A.
Frederick W. Franz, President

Peace and Security
—The Need

"War in the twentieth century has grown steadily more barbarous, more destructive, more debased in all its aspects. . . . The bombs dropped on Hiroshima and Nagasaki ended a war. They also made it wholly clear that we must never have another war. This is the lesson man and leaders everywhere must learn, and I believe that when they learn it they will find a way to lasting peace. There is no other choice."—Henry L. Stimson, "The Decision to Use the Atomic Bomb," *Harper's* Magazine, February 1947.

IT WAS just a year after the formation of the United Nations that Mr. Stimson, U.S. secretary of war from 1940-45, spoke the above words. Well, after almost 40 years, has man learned "the lesson"? Has the United Nations made it possible for you to enjoy life in "lasting peace"? Why, consider the high price mankind has paid for war and war preparation just since World War II.

THE HUMAN COST: What has been the human cost of wars since World War II, in the face of the United Nations' efforts to bring about peace? "Since the conflagration of World War II, there have been 105 major wars ([reckoned by] deaths of 1,000 or more per year) fought in 66 countries and territories. . . . The wars since 1945 have caused 16 million deaths, many more among civilians than among the armed forces involved. (The count, especially for civilians, is incomplete; no official records are kept for most wars.)"—*World Military and Social Expenditures 1983* by Ruth Sivard.

Peace and security actually are slipping farther away—the *frequency* of wars is on the rise. Explains Sivard: "In the 1950's the average [number of wars] was 9 a year; in the 60's, 11 a year; and in the 70's . . . , 14 a year."

THE PSYCHOLOGICAL COST: Ever since Hiroshima, man has lived in fear of nuclear war. Why, the few nuclear weapons of 1945 had grown to 50,000 worldwide by 1983. And still more are being produced! Obviously, as both the number of nuclear weapons and the nations possessing them increase, so does the risk of nuclear war. What, though, are the psychological effects of living in fear of nuclear war?

The book *Preparing for Nuclear War —The Psychological Effects* answers: "The effect of living in the shadow of nuclear weapons on the aspirations and behaviour of children and adults urgently needs further investigation . . . Here is a potentially vast, ongoing cost to our societies, compounding with interest as generations grow to maturity. What price the dreams of a child?"

Indeed, youths are particularly vulnerable to the lack of a secure future. A recent survey of Australian schoolchildren from 10 to 12 years of age produced comments such as: "When I grow up I think that there's going to be a war and everyone in Australia is going to die." "The world will be a wreck—there will be dead creatures everywhere, and the USA will get blown off the face of the earth." More than 70 percent of the children "mentioned nuclear war as a likely possibility." Social researchers fear that the lack of a secure future may be partly responsible for the let-me-live-today attitude of many youths, with the resulting search for kicks.

THE ECONOMIC COST: Before the mid-1930's, world military expenditures were about $4.5 billion (U.S.) per year. But in 1982 the figure had risen to $660 billion. And, as you know, it has kept on rising. To help put such costs in perspective, *World Military and Social Expenditures 1983* explains: "*Every minute* 30 children die for want of food and inexpensive vaccines and every minute the world's military budget absorbs $1.3 million of the public treasure." (Italics ours.) And now, in two more years, it has reached $2 million each minute.

When you consider the high price man has paid for war and war preparedness, one thing is certain: On his own, man has not found the "way to lasting peace." However, ask yourself: Is there a way to *worldwide* peace and security in our lifetime? From what source can it come? Should you look to the United Nations? If not, how will peace and security be achieved?

Peace and Security
—Through God's Kingdom

"**T**HE Purposes of the United Nations are: 1. To maintain international peace and security."—*Charter of the United Nations.*

This is a commendable ideal, to say the least. But as we have noted, the results of the last 40 years make it evident that the United Nations has not succeeded in 'maintaining international peace and security.' Nor will its declaring 1986 the "International Year of Peace" make any difference.*

There is only one way that lasting peace and security will be brought to this earth —*through God's Kingdom in the hands of*

---

* For a fuller discussion of why the United Nations has not succeeded, please see *The Watchtower* of October 1, 1985.

Jesus Christ. This is the real government in heaven for which Jesus taught his followers to pray. (Matthew 6:9, 10) But why will it succeed when the United Nations has failed? Put simply: God's Kingdom will succeed for the very reasons that the United Nations has not succeeded.

More Than Human Wisdom Needed

In our previous issue, we noted that one reason why the United Nations was doomed to failure is that God did not give man the wisdom or right to govern himself. (Jeremiah 10:23) Thus, no man-made organization, however well intentioned, can succeed in bringing peace and security.

In contrast, Jesus Christ, the appointed King of God's Kingdom, has always demonstrated *superhuman wisdom.* (Matthew 13:54) A prime example is his famous Sermon on the Mount. (Matthew, chapters 5 to 7) In it he explained how to find true happiness, settle quarrels, avoid sexual immorality, and have a secure future. Is it not reasonable that a ruler with such wisdom and understanding of human nature would know how to bring about peace and security?

More than that, Jesus' keen discernment was enhanced by his miraculous ability to see into men's hearts and to know their real motivation and inner reasonings. (Matthew 9:4; Mark 2:8) Consider what that means: One big obstacle to peace and security today is *distrust.* Not knowing the thinking and motivation of one another, men and nations often become distrustful. That distrust stands as a barrier to peace. But for the ruler who can "read men's hearts," that poses no problem at all.—John 2:25, *Knox.*

Removing the Superhuman Foes

Another major reason why the United Nations' efforts to bring peace were doomed was the influence of "the ruler of this world," Satan the Devil. (John 12:31) He and his demonic hordes know that they have only "a short period of time" before they are to be removed. Determined to cause "woe for the earth," they have stood in the way of peace by dividing mankind politically and nationally.—Revelation 12:9-12.

Who could remove such superhuman instigators of war? The Bible answers, Jesus Christ, the one referred to as Michael, who, with his angels, ousted Satan and his demons from the heavens. Thus we read: "I saw an angel [Jesus] coming down out of heaven with the key of the abyss and a great chain in his hand. And he seized the dragon, the original serpent, who is the Devil and Satan, and . . . he hurled him

Why the United Nations Has Failed:

☐ Human wisdom too limited (Jeremiah 10:23)

☐ Satan's influence dooms its efforts (Revelation 12:12)

☐ It is a child of this world and inherits its weaknesses (1 John 5:19)

☐ It is trying to save the "old earth," which is against God's purposes (1 John 2:17)

Why God's Kingdom Will Succeed:

☐ Its ruler has superhuman wisdom and can read men's hearts (John 2:25)

☐ It will remove the demonic instigators of war (Revelation 20:1-3)

☐ It is a "child" of God, and its ruler mirrors God's qualities (Revelation 12:5)

☐ It will establish a righteous "new earth" under a single heavenly government (Revelation 21:1)

into the abyss and shut it and sealed it over him." (Revelation 20:1-3) So Satan will be taken out of the way. Only then will it be possible to enjoy life in true peace and security.

A "Child" of God

Our previous issue noted a third reason why the United Nations could never bring peace and security: It is a child of this world and, as such, it inherits the weaknesses, evils, and corruption that characterize its member nations.

In refreshing contrast, the Kingdom that will bring peace and security is pictured in Revelation 12:5 as a "child" *of God.* Its ruler mirrors God's characteristics. Notice some of the endearing qualities manifested by its ruler, Jesus Christ: self-sacrificing love (John 15:12, 13); warmth and feeling (Matthew 9:10-13; Luke 7:36-48); humility (John 13:3-5,

12-17); compassion (Mark 6:30-34); sympathy (Hebrews 2:17, 18; 4:15); firmness for righteousness (Isaiah 11:4, 5). Would you not delight to submit yourself to such a Ruler?

In With the "New Earth"

A final reason why the United Nations could never succeed in bringing peace was indicated by the words of former Secretary-General Dag Hammarskjöld who, back in 1953, said: "Our greatest hope is that we may be permitted to save the old earth." If he had in mind preserving this worldwide system of things, then such efforts to save the "old earth" are doomed to failure. Why?

For one thing, this "old earth" is composed of man-made governments. Individual governments promote nationalism, which divides man; nationalism stresses the interests of one nation rather than seeking the overall welfare of all nations. This self-interest undermines any efforts of the United Nations to bring about peace. As an editorial in the British newspaper The Guardian noted: "Since none of the member nations is ready to sacrifice its own interests for the collective good, the prospects for reform are slim. The [United Nations General] Assembly's only real function is to serve as a kind of barometer of global opinion. Its agenda is full of issues that have been debated for years with little if any progress towards solution."

But there is a more compelling reason why the United Nations' efforts to save the "old earth" are futile: It is against God's purposes. How so? In God's eyes the "old earth" cannot be reformed. The time is nearing when God's stated purpose will be fulfilled. As the apostle John described it: "I saw a new heaven and a new earth; for the former heaven and the former earth had passed away." (Revelation 21:1)

In removing man-made governments, God's Kingdom will do away with divisive nationalism. In its place "a new earth," a righteously disposed human society, will thrive under a single heavenly government, God's Kingdom. Then, and only then, will mankind be able to enjoy genuine peace and security worldwide.

'Beating Swords Into Plowshares'

That this is a realistic hope is assured by the words of a Bible prophecy inscribed on a wall that is facing the United Nations. There it states: "They shall beat their swords into plowshares. And their spears into pruning hooks: nation shall not lift up sword against nation. Neither shall they learn war any more."—Quoted from Isaiah 2:4.

No, the United Nations has not succeeded in preventing the nations from 'lifting up sword' against one another. Nevertheless, there is a people who give living evidence that they have 'beaten their swords into plowshares.' They have demonstrated a unity that rises above racial and national barriers. No amount of pressure can force these Christian neutrals to "lift up sword" against their fellowman. Who are they? Jehovah's Witnesses.

Typical of their response when pressured to take part in the wars of the nations is what happened to one Witness in an African country that is rife with political terrorism.

To get recruits for their guerrilla army, a terrorist group in this country kidnaps men and then gives them a choice: Serve in the terrorist army or be shot. One day they kidnapped one of Jehovah's Witnesses. The leaders, who had been drinking, gave him the choice. Putting before him two beer bottles, they pointed to one and said that it represented the government, the other their terrorist group. 'Which one are you for?' they asked him. The Witness thought for a moment, and observing other beer bottles nearby, he picked one up and set it right between the two, stating: 'This is where I am.' He added: 'I am neutral, since I am for God's Kingdom.' After this, he was beaten several times. Then he was forced to do slave labor in the guerrilla camp, never knowing whether they would shoot him or not. After eight months, he escaped when government forces attacked the camp.

Jehovah's Witnesses have risked imprisonment, even death, rather than take part in the wars of the nations. Thus, in Nazi Germany thousands of them were put into concentration camps because they would not support the Nazi reign of terror. Hundreds of Witnesses were executed or died in the camps. Yet now, with the vicious Nazi government long since gone, Jehovah's Witnesses abound in Germany and around the globe.

But why are they able to 'beat swords into plowshares'? A clue can be found in the preamble to the UNESCO Charter, which says: "Since wars begin in the minds of men, it is in the minds of men that the defenses of peace must be constructed."

In line with that, regarding those who 'beat swords into plowshares,' Isaiah's prophecy says, "neither will they *learn war anymore.*" Rather, by the study and application of the Scriptures, they 'learn God's ways and walk in his paths.' (Isaiah 2:3, 4) With the help of his holy spirit, they 'make their minds over,' becoming peaceable.—Romans 12:2, 18.

God's Kingdom will establish "a new earth," a righteous human society, which will thrive under a single heavenly government

The clear evidence that Jehovah's Witnesses have 'beaten swords into plowshares' proves that living in peace and security is possible. Their present way of life demonstrates on a *small scale* what God's Kingdom through Christ will accomplish *earth wide* in the near future.

Does such a prospect appeal to you? Jehovah's Witnesses will gladly share with you the evidence that God's Kingdom will soon bring lasting peace and security. Why not get in touch with them locally or write to the publishers of this magazine? Learn more about how you can 'beat swords into plowshares' now, with the prospect of soon enjoying life in an entire world without war.

Jesus' First Disciples

AFTER 40 days in the wilderness, Jesus returns to John who had baptized him. As he approaches, John exclaims: "See, the Lamb of God that takes away the sin of the world! This is the one about whom I said, Behind me there comes a man who has advanced in front of me, because he existed before me." Although John is older than his cousin Jesus, John knows that Jesus existed before him as a spirit person in heaven.

The next day John is standing with two of his disciples. Again, as Jesus approaches, he says: "See, the Lamb of God!" At this, these two disciples of John the Baptizer follow Jesus. One of them is Andrew, and the other is evidently the very person who recorded these things, who was also named John. This John, according to indications, is also a cousin of Jesus, being a son of Mary's sister Salome.

Turning and seeing Andrew and John following him, Jesus asks: "What are you looking for?"

"Teacher," they ask, "where are you staying?"

"Come, and you will see," Jesus answers.

It is about four o'clock in the afternoon, and Andrew and John stay with Jesus the rest of that day. Afterward Andrew is so excited that he hurries to find his brother,

who is called Peter. "We have found the Messiah," he tells him. And he takes Peter to Jesus. Perhaps John at the same time finds his brother James and brings him to Jesus; yet, characteristically, John omits this personal information from his Gospel.

The next day, Jesus finds Philip and invites him: "Be my follower." Philip then finds Nathanael, who is also called Bartholomew, and says: "We have found the one of whom Moses, in the Law, and the Prophets wrote, Jesus, the son of Joseph, from Nazareth." Nathanael is doubtful. "Can anything good come out of Nazareth?" he asks.

"Come and see," Philip invites. When they come to Jesus, he says to Nathanael: "Before Philip called you, while you were under the fig tree, I saw you."

Nathanael is amazed. 'Teacher, you are the Son of God, you are King of Israel,' he answers.

Very soon after this, Jesus with his newly acquired disciples leaves the Jordan Valley and travels to Galilee. **John 1:29-51.**

♦ Who were the first disciples of Jesus?
♦ How was Peter, and perhaps James, introduced to Jesus?
♦ What convinced Nathanael that Jesus was the Son of God?

The "Nation" That Fills Earth's Surface With Fruit

"In the coming days Jacob will take root, Israel will put forth blossoms and actually sprout; and they will simply fill the surface of the productive land with produce."—ISAIAH 27:6.

CONCERNING the birth of the congregation of Christ's disciples as a "nation" in 33 C.E., the apostle Peter wrote these words shortly before the destruction of Jerusalem in the year 70 C.E.: "But you are 'a chosen race, a royal priesthood, a holy nation, a people for special possession, that you should declare abroad the excellencies' of the one that called you out of darkness into his wonderful light. For you were once not a people, but are now God's people; you were those who had not been shown mercy, but are now those who have been shown mercy." (1 Peter 2:9, 10) How gracious on God's part that was!

2 Today, 19 centuries after Peter wrote those words, there is still on earth a remnant of that spirit-begotten "nation." They are reduced now to less than ten thousand in number, according to the reports of the annual celebration of the Lord's Evening Meal. They are 'a people for Jehovah's special possession,' and as such they must declare abroad the excellencies of Jehovah God, who called them out of worldly "darkness into his wonderful light." This "light" has been shining especially since the end of "the times of the Gentiles," or "the appointed times of the nations," in the year 1914.* (Luke 21: 24, *King James Version; NW*) As the "special possession" of the Divine Giver of that wonderful light, they are prized by him. To him they are like a spiritual vineyard.

3 Here we recall what Jesus Christ said to his apostles, who represented all who would be his spirit-begotten followers: "I am the true vine, and my Father is the cultivator. Every branch in me not bearing fruit he takes away, and every one bearing fruit he cleans, that it may bear more fruit. You are already clean because of the word that I have spoken to you. Remain in union with me, and I in union with you. Just as the branch cannot bear fruit of itself unless it remains in the vine, in the same way neither can you, unless you remain in union with me. I am the vine, you are the branches. He that remains in union with me, and I in union with him, this one bears much fruit; because apart from me you can do nothing at all."—John 15:1-5.

---

1. How did the apostle Peter refer to the nation of spiritual Israel?

2, 3. As the special possession of Jehovah God, what obligation devolves upon spiritual Israel, and to what are they likened by Jesus Christ in John chapter 15?

* Interestingly, the *Oxford NIV Scofield Study Bible* (1984) comments on Luke 21:24: "The 'times of the Gentiles' began with the captivity of Judah under Nebuchadnezzar (2 Chr. 36:1-21). Since that time Jerusalem has been, as Christ said, 'trampled on by the Gentiles.'"

⁴ That comparison, or parable, made by Jesus Christ reminds us of Jehovah's words in Isaiah 27:2-4, where we read;

"In that day sing to her, you people: 'A vineyard of foaming wine! I, Jehovah, am safeguarding her. Every moment I shall water her. In order that no one may turn his attention against her, I shall safeguard her even night and day. There is no rage that I have.'"

The "vineyard of foaming wine" today on earth may be compared to the remnant of the branches in that symbolic "vine" in which the spirit-begotten Christians of the "holy nation" are productive members. Consequently, there rests upon them the obligation to bear much fruit. (John 15:5) According to Isaiah's prophecy, it was to be in the time of restoration of Jehovah's people to his favor that the song about the "vineyard of foaming wine" was to be sung. (Compare Isaiah 27:13.) This would locate the modern fulfillment of this glowing prophecy as going into effect with the postwar year of 1919, and the facts of history verify its fulfillment down till now. Today Jehovah has no "rage" against his people, neither against the remnant of his "holy nation," his "people for special possession," nor against the loyal Christians who look forward to eternal life on earth. Mercifully he has turned his favor to them, which accounts for their spiritual prosperity and fruitfulness.

⁵ This spiritual "nation," along with its hardworking associates, has been like a productive vineyard that has produced much "foaming wine." It is a spiritual wine that has made the heart of Jehovah and of man glad. (Judges 9:13) For this valid reason the people who have been gladdened by drinking this spiritual beverage can joyfully sing and can recount all that the Divine Cultivator of the "vineyard" has done for this symbolic "vineyard." Figuratively speaking, he has indeed 'watered' this "vineyard" for its constant refreshment, so that juicy, luscious fruit has been produced, with gladdening effect.

A Contrast—"The Vine of the Earth"

⁶ This has not been the case with what the last book of the Bible calls "the vine of the earth." Shortly, the divine command will be given to the heavenly executional forces: "Put your sharp sickle in and gather the clusters of the vine of the earth, because its grapes have become ripe." Then, as the prophetic Revelation goes on to show, "the angel thrust his sickle into the earth and gathered the vine of the earth, and he hurled it into the great winepress of the anger of God. And the winepress was trodden outside the city, and blood came out of the winepress as high up as the bridles of the horses, for a distance of a thousand six hundred furlongs." (Revelation 14:18-20) So it will happen to the governmental part of the Devil's visible organization on earth; it is something of which he is the cultivator, and it is in opposition to "the true vine" of which Jehovah God is the Cultivator. There will be no restoration of "the vine of the earth" at all!

⁷ However, this prophecy of Isaiah chapter 27 is really a prophecy of restoration, first of the nation of natural Israel and then of spiritual Israel in our own 20th century. This is evident from what the

---

4. (a) Jesus' illustration reminds us of what description in Isaiah chapter 27? (b) When does this prophecy have its modern fulfillment, and upon whom? (c) What attitude does God no longer have toward his people?
5. By what from this figurative vineyard have people been gladdened, and what can they recount about it?

6. What, however, will be the experience of "the vine of the earth," according to Revelation chapter 14?
7-9. What double fulfillment does Isaiah 27:7-13 have, and at what times?

prophecy says in verse 7 down to verse 13, with which the chapter closes. Those verses read:

⁸ "As with the stroke of one striking him does one have to strike him? Or as with the slaughter of his killed ones does he have to be killed? With a scare cry you will contend with her when sending her forth. He must expel her with his blast, a hard one in the day of the east wind. Therefore by this means the error of Jacob will be atoned for, and this is all the fruit when he takes away his sin, when he makes all the stones of the altar like chalkstones that have been pulverized, so that the sacred poles and the incense stands will not rise up. For the fortified city will be solitary, the pasture ground will be left to itself and abandoned like a wilderness. There the calf will graze, and there it will lie down; and he will actually consume her boughs. When her sprigs have dried up, women coming in will break them off, lighting them up. For it is not a people of keen understanding. That is why its Maker will show it no mercy, and its own Former will show it no favor.

⁹ "And it must occur in that day that Jehovah will beat off the fruit, from the flowing stream of the River to the torrent valley of Egypt, and so you yourselves will be picked up one after the other, O sons of Israel. And it must occur in that day that there will be a blowing on a great horn, and those who are perishing in the land of Assyria and those who are dispersed in the land of Egypt will certainly come and bow down to Jehovah in the holy mountain in Jerusalem."

¹⁰ In the days of this prophecy of Isaiah, Assyria had become the dominant world power in the earth, displacing the first of the series of seven world powers, although Egypt was still functioning but as a subsidiary power. The ten-tribe kingdom of Israel had broken away from the rule of the royal house of King David of the tribe of Judah. So it was against the city of Jerusalem that the king of Assyria came to demand its complete surrender, if it did not want to be destroyed. However, Jehovah fought for the kingdom of Judah and sent haughty King Sennacherib reeling back homeward in disgraceful defeat. —Isaiah, chapters 36 and 37.

¹¹ Hence, an emperor of a succeeding world power, the Babylonian World Power, was authorized to destroy the holy city of Jerusalem and its temple. According to Biblical indications, this occurred in the year 607 B.C.E., at the hand of Emperor Nebuchadnezzar. He was the one that carried off captives into the land of Babylonia, to spend 70 years of exile there. It was in view of the impending destruction of Jerusalem and the taking of exiles into Babylonian captivity for 70 years that the questions were properly raised:

"As with the stroke of one striking him [the nation of Israel] does one have to strike him?" (Isaiah 27:7)

As never before in its national history since 1513 B.C.E., God's nation was struck with a calamitous blow in 607 B.C.E., a stroke that almost spelled its destruction. Great was the mortality of the besieged city of Jerusalem. Yes, Jehovah saw that the need for this drastic action was vital, and it had to take place. He saw the dire need for contending with those who should have remained his friends, his own befriended ones, with whom he had entered into the Law covenant through the mediator Moses.

¹² Jehovah could thus ask further:

"Or as with the slaughter of his killed ones does

---

10. What world power was prominent in the time of Isaiah's prophecy, and how did it fare in its intended attack upon the capital of the kingdom of Judah?

11. By the emperor of what world power was the overthrow of the kingdom of Judah effected, and how does Isaiah 27 refer to this event?
12. So what question could Jehovah inspire the prophet Isaiah to ask with reference to Israel's experience, and thus what was the effect on Israel's relationship with Jehovah?

he [the nation of Israel, or Jacob] have to be killed?" (Isaiah 27:7)

Ah, yes, for now it had become necessary for Jehovah to contend with his once favored people, raising a frightful cry, a "scare cry," from the martial forces of the Babylonian World Power, the third in Bible history. Hence the divine statement:

"With a scare cry you will contend with her when sending her forth. He must expel her with his blast, a hard one in the day of the east wind [to indicate the direction from which the scary war cry would come]." (Isaiah 27:8)

Through the Babylonians, Jehovah dealt a severe blow in 607 B.C.E.

With such a preliminary he would send forth the unfaithful nation that had once been like a typical wife to him as his visible organization on earth. Now he was dismissing her from her God-given homeland and sending her off at the hands of the Babylonian captors to a distant land, as if temporarily divorced.—Compare Isaiah 50:1.

¹³ Now the time had come for the nation of Israel, or Jacob, to make atonement for its "error" by more costly means than animal sacrifices offered up on the altar of the temple in Jerusalem. This is what Jehovah prescribed in behalf of his wifelike organization, saying:

"Therefore by this means the error of Jacob will be atoned for, and this is all the fruit when he takes away his sin, when he makes all the stones of the altar like chalkstones that have been pulverized, so that the sacred poles and the incense stands will not rise up." (Isaiah 27:9)

What an expression of divine fury, or rage, the fulfillment of this prophecy would be, justifiably so! No more would the idolatrous sacred poles and the incense stands rise up again within his chastised nation.

¹⁴ Indicating the desolation that was to be brought upon this typical wifelike nation of ancient Israel, Jehovah adds:

"For the fortified city will be solitary, the pasture ground will be left to itself and abandoned like a wilderness."

The once populous land will be deserted, to become a mere grazing place for the time being.

"There the calf will graze, and there it will lie down; and he [Jehovah, by his agency] will actually consume her boughs. When her sprigs have dried up, women coming in will break them off, lighting them up [to burn]." (Isaiah 27:10, 11)

Thus Jehovah's typical wifelike nation would be reduced to mere fuel for the fire, for the feminine sex would without hardship be strong enough to avail themselves of what was left of it. What a sorry state to which to be reduced this would be for the typical wifelike organization of Israel!

---

13. How, according to Isaiah's prophecy, was the nation of Israel going to make atonement for its violation of God's covenant?

14. To what sort of desolation was the land of Israel to be reduced, and how was her development as a figurative tree to be dealt with?

But why would such crushing steps have to be taken by such a husbandlike Deity as Jehovah? Listen:

15 "For it is not a people of keen understanding. That is why its Maker will show it no mercy, and its own Former will show it no favor." (Isaiah 27:11)

With all the provision that Jehovah had made for the education and enlightenment of his wonderfully formed organization, the Israelites should have proved to be a people with great intelligence. They should have been sharp and discerning enough to see the vanity of idol worship, yes, discerning enough to see through the senselessness of idolatrous worship, practiced by the ignorant nations outside of covenant relationship with the one living and true God, Jehovah. But in view of the invisibility of their heavenly Maker and Former, they lost faith and chose to turn to visible man-made gods, to their own downfall. That was why further favor and divine mercy were withdrawn from such self-willed people.

---

15. In view of Jehovah's special treatment, what kind of people should the nation of Israel have proved to be, but why did they come to be like the idol-worshiping nations?

How Do You Answer?

□ When and how did natural Israel experience a "stroke," as foretold at Isaiah 27:7?

□ How did Israel "take root"? (Isaiah 27:2, 6)

□ Who in modern times are involved in the fulfillment of the prophecy in Isaiah chapter 27?

□ How have these become like a productive vineyard producing "foaming wine"?

Deliverance From Exile

16 So now, to restore them to his worship in their homeland, it would be necessary for Jehovah to turn his attention to the land of Babylonia through which the great "River," the Euphrates, flowed. He would give attention down southward even toward the land of Egypt, for in such localities his people had come to be exiled from him for their discipline. In this behalf Jehovah had to fulfill his next statement of purpose:

"And it must occur in that day that Jehovah will beat off the fruit, from the flowing stream of the River [Euphrates] to the torrent valley of Egypt [the wadi at the southwestern border of the Promised Land], and so you yourselves will be picked up one after the other, O sons of Israel."—Isaiah 27:12; compare Numbers 34: 2, 5.

17 In order for Jehovah to repatriate his people to their homeland of Judah, he would have to break off the exiled people like fruit, thus loosing them. This he effected by overturning the world power of Babylonia and ushering in the Medo-Persian Empire, the fourth world power of Bible history. The decree of the Persian emperor Cyrus the Great at the beginning of his reign was issued for the liberation of Jehovah's exiled people and for their return to the site of ancient Jerusalem to rebuild Jehovah's temple. This return came at the close of the 70 years of Jewish exile, in 537 B.C.E.—Isaiah 45:1-7.

18 The disciplined Israelites in Babylonia, and also in Assyria and Egypt, were Jehovah's property, and he was entitled to break them off like symbolic fruit from involuntary exile and dispersion and thus

---

16. In behalf of restoring his people, to what would Jehovah have to direct his attention?
17. How did Jehovah break off his people from their exiled state, and by what means?
18. What must have been the reaction of the exiles at the decree for their liberation?

to show them mercy, undeserved kindness. Oh, how those ancient Israelites must have rejoiced over that decree of Cyrus, and how zealous they must have displayed themselves in taking full advantage of the glorious opportunity afforded them! What, then, was there to be said about that auspicious "day"?

¹⁹ "And it must occur in that day that there will be a blowing on a great horn, and those who are perishing in the land of Assyria and those who are dispersed in the land of Egypt will certainly come and bow down to Jehovah in the holy mountain in Jerusalem." (Isaiah 27:13)

19. (a) To whom were the Israelites who were dispersed in Assyria and in Egypt foretold to bow down? (b) What would this mean respecting the worship of Jehovah at the original temple site, and this with overtones for what modern spiritual nation?

What else did that mean but the repopulating of the Promised Land and the rebuilding of the temple in Jerusalem, restored for the worship of the Former and Maker of the revived nation of Israel? This had to take place according to the earlier words of the prophet Isaiah set out in verse 6. The land of his repatriated people had to become a land teeming with inhabitants, unitedly engaged in his worship at his temple, even though this restored place of worship might not have the grandeur of the magnificent temple built by King Solomon. In this way it was to foreshadow the modern-day spiritual fulfillment involving "the Israel of God," in filling all "the productive land" with life-giving fruit, or "produce."—Galatians 6:16; Isaiah 27:6.

The "Nation" That Feeds Famine-Stricken Millions

THE billions of earth's population should be hungering for "food" that will nourish them for life unending here on earth, when the earth is converted into a global paradise. But to whom or where will they turn? The Republic of Israel is not attempting to fulfill the Bible prophecy in Isaiah 27:6 about filling the earth with "produce" for the lasting benefit of mankind.

² The nation of Israel in the first century of our Common Era lost its commission

1, 2. (a) What genuine need should be felt by earth's population? (b) To which people can we look in this regard?

to benefit all mankind. Thus it was merely to a small remnant of the natural Jews that the Messiah addressed his words: "All authority has been given me in heaven and on the earth. Go therefore and make disciples of people of all the nations, baptizing them in the name of the Father and of the Son and of the holy spirit . . . And, look! I am with you all the days until the conclusion of the system of things." (Matthew 28:18-20) But what about 19 centuries later? Who in our time have in mind the fulfillment of Isaiah 27:6? And how are you and your loved ones involved?

³ Even though we are decades removed from the specific events, we do well to examine briefly certain developments during the years of World War I. At that time Jehovah God had valid reason for feeling "rage" against the nations of Christendom because of their engaging in that bloodspilling conflict. (Compare Isaiah 27:4.) They did that rather than yield their national sovereignties to the Most High God when his Kingdom was set up in the heavens in 1914 in the hands of his glorified Son, Jesus Christ. They added fuel to his rage by persecuting the remnant of spiritual Israel, deliberately hindering these devoted Christian Bible Students from proclaiming freely his established Kingdom. But many of the remnant of spiritual Israel did, in fact, yield to the worldly pressures, thus coming short of their responsibility as chosen people taken out from this worldly system of things. They did not then see the issue of absolute neutrality toward the conflicts of this world, so they came under some bloodguilt, and for a time they merited a degree of God's "rage" too.

⁴ Had you lived back then, how do you think you would have reacted to those wartime pressures? You should consider such things, for by doing so you may firm up your resolve as to what you would do in the face of any future pressures. Back then it might have seemed to be a time to desist from Kingdom proclamation and to lie low. Many tended in that direction, feeling that they should simply wait for their early glorification to be with the enthroned Jesus Christ. (Luke 22:28-30) However, receiving some of Jehovah's "rage" was a disciplinary experience that

was not lost on true Christians of the period, and so it was not fruitless. It strengthened them for the oncoming work of declaring the day of vengeance of our God against the one whom the prophet Isaiah calls "Leviathan" in Isaiah 27:1, where we read:

⁵ "In that day Jehovah, with his hard and great and strong sword, will turn his attention to Leviathan, the gliding serpent, even to Leviathan, the crooked serpent, and he will certainly kill the sea monster that is in the sea."

Back in ancient times, Jehovah turned his attention to the captors of his people. As we have noted previously, that included the empire of Babylon, as well as Egypt and Assyria. (Isaiah 27:12, 13) Can you see a modern application of the symbolic words at Isaiah 27:1? In the period around World War I, God's people were not captive to any one nation or empire. But Jehovah did need to give attention to a symbolic Leviathan, namely, Satan the Devil. He glides in a wily manner through the sea of humanity and uses things on earth to endanger or obstruct God's servants.—Compare Revelation 17:15.

⁶ When in the year 1919 the remnant of spiritual Israel enthusiastically resumed their Kingdom preaching, it was the time for Jehovah to say:

"There is no rage that I have. Who will give me thornbushes and weeds in the battle? I will step on such. I will set such on fire at the same time."—Isaiah 27:4.

⁷ After the close of World War I, the League of Nations was set up in rejection of the Kingdom of God by Christ. We can liken this to "thornbushes and weeds"

---

3. Who in our century experienced God's "rage" mentioned in Isaiah 27:4?
4. How did God's "rage" affect his Christian servants, and what lesson might we learn from this?

5. In modern times, how has Jehovah turned his attention to "Leviathan" mentioned in Isaiah 27:1?
6, 7. (a) What in modern times became like "thornbushes and weeds"? (b) What can we expect regarding them in the future?

Some hope that humans will resolve the nuclear threat, but wise ones of all nations are 'taking hold of Jehovah's stronghold'

placed in the pathway of Jehovah God, as an obstruction or deterrent. Now the United Nations organization has replaced that League. By the United Nations the various member nations disclose their determination to hold out against the proclaimed Kingdom of Christ and their purpose to preserve their own world sovereignty. In "the war of the great day of God the Almighty" at Har-Magedon, he will figuratively step on all "thornbushes and weeds," crushing them and finally setting them on fire, as it were, to reduce them to mere ashes. He thus will demonstrate who really is the Universal Sovereign. You can, then, see that even if you were not alive among the anointed Christians back around World War I, you may be affected—for good or for bad—in the final results of events paralleling Isaiah 27:1.—Revelation 16:14-16; 17:1–18:4.

'Taking Hold of Jehovah's Stronghold'

8 The members of the United Nations are relying on their own strength and trusting in their man-made stronghold. Yet, their confidence in it has not been strong enough to deter them from inventing the most deadly of weapons, the ultimate of war weapons, the nuclear bomb. Likely, fear of reprisal by use of the nuclear bomb is what deters them, not the United Nations.

9 As we noted, though, what really threatens the continued existence of the nations is "the war of the great day of God the Almighty." What can the nations hope to do against God the Almighty, the One who put the awesome power within the nucleus of each atom of matter? You may well be convinced that the Creator is incomparably more powerful than the nations with all their weapons. Those who appreciate this fact—and Jehovah's Witnesses do—have only one recourse available. That is set forth in the further words of Jehovah:

8. On what do many nations today rely?
9, 10. Why is it wise for us to rely on another "stronghold"?

The increase in spiritually well-fed Christians is reflected in the expansion of branches of the Watch Tower Society

"Otherwise let him take hold of my stronghold, let him make peace with me; peace let him make with me." (Isaiah 27:5)

No human agency is the stronghold to which to resort for security or prevention of war on earth, and certainly not the stronghold for the families of the earth to flee to for keeping safe.

¹⁰ You likely know that many people today become emotionally involved with debates and movements concerned about nuclear weapons and disarmament. Sadly, that distracts them from the reality that the inevitable war of God the Almighty at Armageddon is what threatens destruction of all the nations. If you appreciate that reality, then the wise course for you involves turning to Jehovah. His "stronghold" is the thing upon which all safety seekers should take hold, namely, his own inexhaustible possession of strength. The entire organization of Satan the Devil will not be able to conquer the individual Christian who has taken hold of that "stronghold."

¹¹ Jehovah and his armies under the Captain, Jesus Christ, are now, as it were, on the march. While they are yet some distance away, the course that common sense, if not real wisdom, dictates is for a person to send, figuratively speaking, a peace mission ahead and to sue for peace in the face of overwhelming odds. The undefeatable Captain of Jehovah's hosts counseled such a course when he was down here on earth. (Luke 14:31-33) And if you examine closely what Jesus there said, you will see that he tied in our attitude toward our "belongings." Whether we live in an advanced and prosperous land or we live in a Third World country where it takes a real struggle to gain financial security, we should scrutinize our outlook. Ask yourself: Am I really putting my reliance on Jehovah's strength as my stronghold or letting "belongings" take the most prominent place? In this connection, please read Luke 12:15-21.

---

11. How can we apply Jesus' words at Luke 14:31-33 as we take hold of God's "stronghold"?

¹² Around the earth, many thousands of Jehovah's Witnesses have already turned unreservedly to Jehovah, seeking peace with him. Many are arranging their affairs to devote scores of hours each month to the disciple-making activity. Each one who truly exerts himself in serving Jehovah is in a position to experience the promised "peace of God" that surpasses all human thought and understanding. (Philippians 4:7) While there is still time, they keep helping others to enter into this peaceable arrangement of Jehovah of hosts. What place does such lifesaving work have in your life?

Filling "the Productive Land" with "Produce"

¹³ What was to be the world role of spiritual Israel after its being restored to divine favor following World War I? This is indicated for us in these heartening words of Isaiah 27:6:

"In the coming days Jacob will take root, Israel will put forth blossoms and actually sprout; and they will simply fill the surface of the productive land with produce."

Examine the reality of those words today. Doing so will give you added reason to become one of God's people or, if you already are, to become even more firmly resolved to remain among true worshipers no matter what tests or problems arise.

¹⁴ A situation such as prophesied in Isaiah 27:6 has increasingly been found among worshipers of Jehovah since the year 1919, when the first general convention of Jehovah's Witnesses was held at Cedar Point, Ohio. For example, it was not long after this that the Watch Tower Society began printing its new magazine, *The Golden Age,* now called *Awake!* It was as though spiritual Judah was then taking root.

¹⁵ Thus in the opening years of liberation and reinstatement in Jehovah's favor, true Christians began to blossom as "the planting of Jehovah." (Isaiah 61:3) In 1918, the final year of World War I, the astounding lecture "Millions Now Living May Never Die" was publicly delivered by J. F. Rutherford. With merely a small remnant of spirit-begotten disciples of the reigning King, Jesus Christ, left on earth to undertake the God-ordained work that then devolved upon them, was that an overestimation of matters?

¹⁶ How would Jehovah use such Christians to fill the surface of "the productive land with produce"? The remnant of spiritual Israel took the initiative, but what about the "produce" with which the productive land was to be filled? The remnant found the "produce," which included the good news of Jehovah's established Kingdom in the hands of Christ, so tasty and nourishing that they wanted to share it with their fellowmen. Jehovah had foretold that the little one would become a thousand and the small one a mighty nation, and this proved to be no miscalculation on God's part. (Isaiah 60:22) Soon the remnant of spiritual Israel was joined by "a great crowd" of "other sheep" of the Fine Shepherd, Jesus Christ.—Revelation 7:9-17; John 10:16.

¹⁷ You may be aware of the situation as to true Christianity today. The Watch Tower Society now has 94 branches all around

12. What evidence is there that many today are taking hold of Jehovah's strength?
13. What does Isaiah 27:6 indicate could be expected in our time?
14. How has Isaiah 27:6 found a fulfillment on God's people?

15. What thrilling prospect was presented to true worshipers starting in 1918?
16. (a) How did the remnant react to the prospects before them? (b) What "produce" did they rejoice in, and with what results?
17, 18. What can you attest to regarding 'filling the surface of the productive land with produce'?

the globe. The organized active congregations of Jehovah's Witnesses now number some 48,000, and these are to be found in 203 lands. To the true God goes all the credit for this, and these noteworthy developments stand in vindication of his infallible Word, whereas "the end," as foretold in Matthew 24:14, is not yet.

[18] Yes, there are nearly three million Christians working along with the Watch Tower Society around the globe. These millions are mainly those of Christ's "other sheep," who have long been carrying the brunt of the worldwide witnessing work, and 'the joy of Jehovah has been their strength, or stronghold.' (Nehemiah 8:10) Hence, each of us today has the opportunity to be well filled spiritually and to participate in 'filling the surface of the productive land with produce.'

[19] We can be sure that Jehovah will never permit the present "produce" of "the productive land," the field of activity of his Witnesses, to be destroyed. The work of his preaching Witnesses will never have been done in vain! The spiritual fruit, or "produce," as cultivated by true Chris-

---

19. What might you enjoy as to "the productive land," and how do you feel about that?

Can You Recall?

□ Why did true Christians feel Jehovah's "rage" earlier in this century, and what can we learn from this experience?

□ In contrast to the nations, how can we 'take hold of Jehovah as our stronghold'? (Isaiah 27:5)

□ How has "the productive land" been filled with "produce" in our time? (Isaiah 27:6)

□ What future fulfillment of Isaiah 27:1 can we confidently expect?

---

tians is for the feeding of all who want to avail themselves of it. This will include, in time, the billions of the human dead that are to be resurrected under the Millennial Reign of Jesus Christ. Imagine what that may mean for you in the future! In time, many natural Israelites of the past will be resurrected. Some of them may have been involved in the initial fulfillment of the prophecy in Isaiah chapter 27. Would it not be fascinating for you to be alive then, enabling you to explain how you participated in the larger, present-day 'filling of the productive land with produce'?—Compare Revelation 22:2, 3.

The Course of "Leviathan" Brought to an End

[20] Then the figurative Egypt, the present wicked system over which Satan the Devil has dominated as its god, will not exist. Jehovah will have turned his attention to the symbolic Leviathan, the gliding, crooked serpent that is in the midst of the sea of humanity. He and the nations, and even unions of nations, will be gone. He will not be around as a free, active corrupter of mankind for whom Jesus Christ died. (Isaiah 27:1) Yes, Satan the Devil will be abyssed throughout the Thousand Year Reign of Jesus Christ, the Son of David and the rightful Heir of the Kingdom. The 144,000 spiritual Israelites will be joint heirs in heaven with him, the figurative Lion of the tribe of Judah. (Romans 8:16, 17; Revelation 5:5, 9, 10; 7: 1-4) Jehovah God the Most High will have been vindicated forever as the Sovereign Lord of the universe. Jehovah's universal organization in heaven and on earth will joyously experience lasting peace and harmony. To endless time, even forevermore, Jehovah will rejoice over his unified universal organization.

---

20. What lies ahead for "Leviathan," and with what result respecting God's sovereignty?

Insight on the News

New World Translation Passes Examination

In times past, Bible readers of one religion were suspicious of translations made by another religious group. Such distrust is generally unwarranted, claims theologian C. Houtman in the scholarly *Nederlands Theologisch Tijdschrift* (Dutch Theological Magazine). After reviewing these translations, his opinion is that only rarely can passages be found that reflect "the translators' denominational or political and social viewpoint." While for the most part this is true, there are some cases in which Bible translators have let their religious bias show through their renderings. For example, some modern translators have completely eliminated the personal name of God from their works. Others have wrongly translated the word Gehenna as "hell fire." Yet, if someone deliberately changes or omits part of the contents of the Bible, he is on dangerous ground. As one Bible book warns: "If anyone takes anything away from the words of the scroll of this prophecy, God will take his portion away from the trees of life."—Revelation 22:19.

Rather than removing God's name from the Bible, the *New World Translation of the Holy Scriptures* has retained it —7,210 times. Copies of the Bible's original language text provide a basis for doing this. Interestingly, Houtman notes that on the point of translator bias "the *New World Translation* of the Jehovah's Witnesses can survive the scrutiny of criticism."

Man-Made Famine

African drought and famine have grabbed newspaper headlines for over a year. Yet the deadly toll has not been new to that continent. "Ethiopia's drought began in 1981," says researcher Lloyd Timberlake in *The Middle East* magazine. "Chad has suffered from drought for 10 years, Cape Verde for about 15. But the disaster response starts and stops, the timing based more on news reports than real human needs." Timberlake pins the major blame for Africa's food plight not on nature but on humans. He points to "unwise governments and foolish aid and development policies" as the chief culprits that have divided the key decision makers, who are urban officials, from country people, who are the sufferers.

Mankind's infliction of self-hurt is not new. About 3,000 years ago, Bible-writer King Solomon observed that "man has dominated man to his injury." (Ecclesiastes 8:9) Without consideration of godly principles, man's plans, including the providing of sufficient food for the hungry, will ultimately fail because of human selfishness or ignorance. How well the Bible sums up human wisdom compared to God's: "Many are the plans in the heart of a man, but the counsel of Jehovah is what will stand!"—Proverbs 19:21.

Heart Surgery on Children

Jehovah's Witnesses decline blood transfusions for religious reasons. 'Abstain from blood,' the Bible commands. (Acts 15: 20) Does this Scriptural position work a hardship in the health care of their children? No. For example, the article "Cardiac operation for congenital heart disease in children of Jehovah's Witnesses" in the June 1985 issue of *The Journal of Thoracic and Cardiovascular Surgery* concluded: "Cardiac operations and cardiopulmonary bypass can be safely performed in children without blood transfusion."

The article states: "Over a 20 year period ending June, 1983, 110 children of parents of the Jehovah's Witness faith, 6 months to 12 years of age, underwent operation for repair of congenital heart disease with the use of cardiopulmonary bypass at the Texas Heart Institute." Although the article did not provide statistics on the point, the surgeons stated that their impression was "that children of Jehovah's Witnesses usually do as well or better" than those transfused.

Interestingly, after listing things from which Christians are to abstain—including blood—the apostles and older Christians wrote: "If you carefully keep yourselves from these things, you will prosper. Good health to you!"—Acts 15:29.

How True Faith Can Help You

"ARE churches becoming irrelevant?" So asked free-lance writer Paul Fromm after attending the Sixth Assembly of the World Council of Churches held in 1983 at Vancouver, Canada. The reason for his question? The fact that this council had dwelt almost exclusively on politics. Said Fromm: "The mainline Protestant churches . . . have replaced the Gospel of Jesus Christ with the trendy gospel of leftist politics."

Religion's plunge into politics appears to be a desperate attempt to rekindle a waning interest in long-established religions. Reports from around the world indicate that faith in organized religion has indeed declined over the last few years.

This, however, does not surprise students of the Bible. Jesus prophesied that "because of the increasing of lawlessness the love of the greater number will cool off." (Matthew 24:12) As a result of this 'cooling off,' relatively few allow religion to have much influence in their lives, even if they do make an occasional trip to church for a wedding or a funeral.—Compare Luke 18:8.

But while faith in most organized religions leads to disappointment, Jesus observed: "Every good tree produces fine fruit, but every rotten tree produces worthless fruit; a good tree cannot bear worthless fruit, neither can a rotten tree produce fine fruit. Every tree not producing fine fruit gets cut down and thrown into the fire. Really, then, by their fruits you will recognize those men." (Matthew 7:17-20) Note that just as there is a form of worship that produces 'bad fruit,' there is a religious way of life that produces "fine fruit." The latter brings real benefits to the person of faith. What is such faith, and what are some of its benefits?

Basis for Faith

For millions, one's faith is something into which one is born. But for true Christians, faith is something that is acquired and cultivated. For them, faith is not "firm belief in something for which there is no proof," as one dictionary defines faith. On the contrary, the early Christian evangelist Paul wrote: "Faith is the assured expectation of things hoped for, the evident demonstration of realities though not beheld." (Hebrews 11:1) This means that our faith is based on reality.

For example, one approaching God "must believe that he *is*." (Hebrews 11:6) Many ridicule the idea that there is a God. 'Why believe in a God you cannot see?' they say. Yet the same ones have no trouble believing in television waves that are just as invisible. They, of course, can turn on their television sets and see the *results* of these invisible waves! Likewise with true Christians, our faith in God is not mere credulity or blind faith. Paul explains about God: "His invisible qualities are clearly seen from the world's creation onward, because they are perceived by the things made, even his eternal power and Godship, so that they are inexcusable."

(Romans 1:20) Though God is invisible, all around us there is abundant visible evidence of a Master Designer, a superhuman intellect, a Creator with unmatched power.

Our faith, though, must go beyond mere *belief* in God if it is really to benefit us. (James 2:19) We must also have faith in the Holy Bible as the Word of God. (John 17:17) This faith should be based, not on mere emotion or early religious training, but on a knowledge of the many features of the Scriptures that point to divine authorship. The Bible itself encourages its readers to "make sure of all things."—1 Thessalonians 5:21.

Television and radio waves are invisible. Yet their effects testify to their existence

How can you do this with regard to the Holy Scriptures? You might first consider the fact that the Bible is a series of writings by some 40 different servants of God. Though writing over a period of 1,600 years, the writers followed a common theme—God's Kingdom. Never did they contradict one another. Does not this indicate divine authorship? Also, the Bible shows remarkable accuracy in describing such things as the order of the appearance of living things on earth, a fact that is confirmed by modern science. (Genesis, chapter 1) Even more amazing is the fact that the Bible records *future* events! Some of the writers themselves confessed that they did not understand what they were writing; but what they wrote was truth, for they wrote under divine inspiration!—Daniel 12:8; 2 Peter 1:20, 21.

For many, however, the most persuasive reason to have faith in the Bible is that its counsel works! As you study and apply it, the Bible will exert a powerful motivating force for good in your life. This can help you to make changes that may amaze your friends and acquaintances. No wonder Paul said that "the word of God is alive and exerts power"! (Hebrews 4:12) True faith, therefore, has a rock-solid foundation. How, though, can you cultivate that faith?

Growing in Faith

A farmer plants his seed when the season and weather are right. Soon plants begin to sprout. With proper care they will grow to be strong and mature, blossoming and producing fruit. So it is with faith. When a person's heart is right and the seed of faith is planted, this faith must be cared for if it is to grow. What are some ways in which this can be done?

The Bible explains that faith is one of the nine fruits of the holy spirit. (Galatians 5:22, 23) And how does one receive God's spirit? Jesus said to listeners in his day: "If you, although being wicked, know

Prayer is one powerful means of building faith

truth expands, you are further moved to share your faith with others. Because "faith is not a possession of all people," this sharing of God's truth may expose you to attack or ridicule. (2 Thessalonians 3:2; 2 Peter 3: 3, 4) Still, so confident can you be about the basis for your faith that you will be able to declare, as did Paul: "I am not ashamed of the good news; it is, in fact, God's power for salvation to everyone having faith, to the Jew first and also to the Greek." (Romans 1:16) What a joy it is when someone responds to this message and the growth cycle begins all over again! God makes such growth possible. —1 Corinthians 3:5-9.

how to give good gifts to your children, how much more so will the Father in heaven give holy spirit to those asking him!" (Luke 11:13) So *ask* God for his spirit in prayer! Faith will develop as a natural result of having God's spirit.

It is also important to develop a close relationship with Jehovah God. That means making a conscientious study of his Word and endeavoring to follow it. The psalmist developed such a longing for God's Word and declared: "How I do love your law! All day long it is my concern." (Psalm 119:97) When you are truly concerned about following God's Word, you begin to take on the attributes of the Creator. God's spirit begins to bear fruitage in your life. No longer will you be attracted to wrongdoing, but God's spirit and a desire to maintain a happy relationship with God will turn you away from vile "works of the flesh."—Galatians 5: 16, 19-21; Psalm 15:1, 2.

As your appreciation for God and the

The Benefits of Faith

How, though, does faith *help* a person? Jesus Christ pointed to one long-term benefit at John 3:16: "God loved the world so much that he gave his only-begotten Son, in order that everyone exercising faith in him might not be destroyed but have *everlasting life.*" This alone is a marvelous reward for having faith. Faith in God's promise to reward his servants with everlasting life gives you a fresh perspective on life. The trials and problems of life no longer seem quite so important or overwhelming. You are freed from the philosophy "let us eat and drink, for tomorrow we are to die" that dominates this pleasure-mad world. (1 Corinthians 15:32) Even death no longer seems quite so frightening when you have firm faith in a resurrection.—Hebrews 2:15; Luke 12:4, 5.

Faith also helps one cope with economic stress. "What are we to eat?" and, "What are we to drink?" are real concerns for many today. Jesus, though, exhorted his followers to have faith in God's ability to provide. If you have such faith, you can "stop being anxious" over such things. (Matthew 6:25-34) Such faith spares you the pains that a pursuit of riches is sure to bring.—1 Timothy 6:10.

But what if a person has a serious problem and needs direction? People spend millions of dollars on self-help books and professional counseling. While the advice thus found may sometimes be helpful, a Christian's faith leads him to a far better source of aid. Says James: "So, if any one of you is lacking in wisdom, let him keep on asking God, for he gives generously to all and without reproaching; and it will be given him. But let him *keep on asking in faith,* not doubting at all, for he who doubts is like a wave of the sea driven by the wind and blown about." (James 1:5, 6) A Christian's faith is the guarantee that such divine aid will be provided. He has no hesitancy about approaching God in this way, for 'he has this freeness of speech and an approach with confidence through his faith in [Christ].'—Ephesians 3:12.

Admittedly, the direction God gives us can at times seem difficult—perhaps even impossible—to implement. Abraham, for example, received God's promise that he and his wife were to have a son. Considering the fact that their reproductive powers were 'dead,' attempting to have this child seemed futile. Yet, says Paul: "Although [Abraham] did not grow weak in faith, he considered his own body, now already deadened, as he was about one hundred years old, also the deadness of the womb of Sarah. But because of the promise of God he *did not waver* in a lack of faith, but became powerful by his faith, giving God glory and being fully convinced that what he had promised he was also able to do." (Romans 4:19-21) The reward for such faith? The blessing of having a son who would continue the line leading to the Messiah!

While God is not at this time performing such direct miracles, Christians today find that if they 'do not waver in a lack of faith,' they, too, can enjoy success when they apply God's direction. Said Jesus: "All things can be to one if one has faith." —Mark 9:23.

Safeguard Your Faith

Faith is therefore the key to enduring these trying times. But we must jealously safeguard it. If we allow our faith to weaken, we can find ourselves without direction in life. We can fall prey to the anxieties and problems that afflict mankind in general. So like Jesus' disciples, let us continually ask for more faith. (Luke 17:5) Let us regularly study God's Word and associate with people of like faith. (Romans 10:17) And let us zealously engage in the work Jesus assigned his followers to do, preaching the "good news of the kingdom."—Matthew 24:14.

The fact that this work is now being carried on in 203 lands should, in itself, build our faith, for this fact indicates that the prophesied "end" is near! Among these zealous preachers, Jehovah's Witnesses, we find people manifesting the fruits of God's spirit. They excel in faith, but also in love, joy, peace, long-suffering, kindness, goodness, mildness, and self-control. (Galatians 5:22, 23) They are living testimonies to the value of having faith, for it has enriched their personal lives, family relationships, and above all, their relationship with Jehovah God.

So in answer to Jesus' question, "When the Son of man arrives, will he really find the faith on the earth?" we can confidently say, Indeed he will! (Luke 18:8) May we prove to be among the many who daily demonstrate the value of a living faith!

Turkish Supreme Court Releases Jehovah's Witnesses

THERE was great joy among the 23 Jehovah's Witnesses released on June 14, 1985, after having spent a year in prison in Ankara. In 1984 they had been sentenced to terms ranging from four to six years by the State Security Court in Ankara. That court had found them guilty of violating article 163 of the penal code, which forbids religious activity aimed at 'changing the social, economic, political, or legal order of the state.' The court rejected their status as a religion. —See *The Watchtower,* April 1, 1985.

The verdict had been appealed, and on May 29, 1985, a hearing was granted before the Supreme Court of Turkey. At that hearing, a request was made to annul the verdict on the grounds that Jehovah's Witnesses are indeed a religious group and that there is no evidence for the crime charged.

Defense counsel pointed out that in all previous court cases in the country Jehovah's Witnesses had been acquitted of that same charge, and that all legal experts who had examined the activity of Jehovah's Witnesses over the past 20 years had never found any violation of the law. The attorneys also pointed out that the verdict was based on prejudiced and false information.

Court Decides

On June 19, 1985, the Supreme Court gave its unanimous decision. It annulled the verdict of the State Security Court and ordered the immediate release of the 23 Witnesses. The Court emphasized that under Turkey's constitution all religions have the same right to worship and to spread their beliefs, provided they do not interfere in the affairs of the State.

The Supreme Court pointed out that the accused had been convicted "just because of being . . . Jehovah's Witnesses." And that verdict had been based on the reports of two religiously prejudiced "experts." These had stated that Jehovah's Witnesses were "objectionable from the standpoint of religious unity and worship." But the Supreme Court showed that this was in no way evidence that the actions of the Witnesses violated article 163.

The Court concluded that Jehovah's Witnesses had not overstepped the boundary of religious freedom guaranteed by the constitution. The Court showed that therefore "a violation and misuse of freedom for evil purposes had not materialized."

This judgment is in harmony with the facts. It is also in harmony with the decision of the Supreme Court of Appeal in 1980. That court clearly stated that the activity of Jehovah's Witnesses is not subversive and does not constitute a danger to the country. It also said: "If one day the things occur which the accused ones believe and God's rule will be established over the world, a punishment of the accused ones because of such a belief will not prevent such events. But if their expectation is just a fancy idea and empty belief, their belief can in no way cause harm to our laical order of the State."

So all the accusations, as well as the information given by the two religiously prejudiced "experts," have been proved false. The nonpolitical and purely religious nature of the work of Jehovah's Witnesses has again been established.

Complete Acquittal Desired

Although the verdict has been annulled, the case has been turned over to the State Security Court for reexamination. It is hoped that this time the court will judge according to the facts and will totally acquit the accused ones of the charges.

Freedom-loving people all over the world will continue to watch for the outcome of this matter. They want to see if Jehovah's Witnesses will enjoy full freedom of worship. If this proves to be the case, then it can rightly be said that Turkey is endeavoring to live up to its claim that it is a democratic country.

Jehovah Has Done Great Things for Us

SOME seven years of de facto military government. War in the South Atlantic. Inflation of about 500 percent a year. Argentina has experienced all these things within the last decade.

Today, financial troubles have not subsided. But a republican government holds sway, and a war is not raging. So this land's 30 million inhabitants look to the future with increased optimism. Especially are some filled with surpassing happiness. Why? Because of the great things Jehovah God has been doing.

With divine blessing, about 55,000 witnesses of Jehovah are now spreading good news of great cheer in this South American country. It is this that has brought joy into the lives of so many inhabitants of Argentina.

The First Seeds Are Sown

The Kingdom-preaching work in this land had its start in 1924, when J. F. Rutherford (then president of the Watch Tower Society) sent Juan Muñiz here to care for Kingdom interests. About a year later, Carlos Ott arrived and began spreading the good news among the German-speaking population. Thus the first seeds of Kingdom truth were sown in Argentina.

By 1945 there were 363 Kingdom proclaimers in Argentina. The next year saw the arrival of missionaries, graduates of the Watchtower Bible School of Gilead. Brother Gwaenydd Hughes and Sister Ofelia Estrada, both Argentinean, were the first of a long list of Gilead graduates to serve in this country. Among them are Charles and Lorene Eisenhower, as well as Helen Wilson, all of whom arrived in 1948. After some 36 years, they are still active in Jehovah's service here. Helen Nichols, who also arrived in 1948, ended her earthly course in her missionary assignment at Tucumán in 1974.

The First Obstacles Arise

As our numbers increased, many young Witnesses of military age took their stand as Christian neutrals. (Isaiah 2:2-4; John 15:19) This brought opposition. Nevertheless, in 1950 the Watch Tower Society was legally recognized but only for a short time. Later that year, this recognition was withdrawn, and for the next 33 years Jehovah's Witnesses persevered without it.

Even under such difficult circumstanc-

es, however, the Kingdom-preaching work continued to expand. In 1974 the Governing Body of Jehovah's Witnesses decided that our journals *The Watchtower* and *Awake!* should be printed locally. So plans were made for the installation of the first rotary offset press ever to be used by the Society. The press itself came from France, a guillotine section (paper cutter) from Germany, and the stitcher portion from the United States. All of these were gifts made by the respective branches of the Society. Many difficulties had to be overcome before we could publish our first magazines in Argentina, but what joy we had when *The Watchtower* of April 15, 1975, rolled off the press!

Years Under Ban

In 1976 a new military government closed our Kingdom Halls. Our children were expelled from school, and throughout the land Jehovah's Witnesses were arrested for preaching the good news. The climax came on September 7, 1976, when the Society's printing establishment and offices were closed. Only the living quarters of the Bethel family remained open. All of this resulted from an order that 'absolutely prohibited the activity of Jehovah's Witnesses and the spreading and public exercise of their doctrines in the whole territory of the nation.'

In Our Next Issue

- ■ **Independence From God —Why Not?**

- ■ **Finding Joy in the Gift of Marriage**

- ■ **Modern Stewardship of God's Sacred Word**

Years of difficulty thus began. Yet, this was also a time of spiritual strengthening and enrichment. Never before had we received so much publicity in the secular press. The headlines themselves help to tell the story of what happened over a period of years: "Witnesses prisoners for repudiating the patriotic symbols"; "Expulsion of children from provincial primary schools"; "Readmission of scholar of Jehovah's Witnesses"; "Activities of Jehovah's Witnesses permitted."

In March 1979 the Supreme Court of Justice rendered a favorable decision in the case of *Juan Carlos Barros* vs. *National Council of Education*. Brother Barros' two sons, Paul and Hugh (seven and eight years old respectively), had been expelled from school for refusing to participate in a flag-raising ceremony. (Compare Exodus 20:4-6; Daniel 3:1, 16-18; 1 John 5:21.) The court decision said in part: "[Their] actions, merely passive in the case, . . . cannot be taken to constitute a rational manifestation of lack of respect for the patriotic symbols, but rather show an obedience to parental authority." Thus it was recognized that the religious position that the Witness children took in no way involved a lack of respect for Argentina's national symbols.

The rights of our youngsters were also upheld in the case of *Aurelio Francisco D'Aversa* vs. *the National Government*. The Teachers' Council had resolved to expel the D'Aversa child from all schools in the country, but when the case reached the Federal Court of Appeals, a favorable decision was handed down. It set some very interesting precedents. After mentioning that most of the country's citizens participate spontaneously in showing their feelings toward the national symbols, Judge Tonelli said: "On the other hand, it would be offensive to the conscience of the majority that has firmly

News headlines chronicle the problems under ban and finally the return of religious freedoms

established patriotic convictions to see someone, against his inward beliefs, obligated to show like feelings without sincerity." Judge Barletta recognized "the lack of facts that imply contempt, disrespect or public showing of such on the part of the pupil D'Aversa." The Supreme Court later confirmed this decision.

The ban placed on our work in 1976 apparently caused the decrease in the number of Jehovah's praisers from 33,503 that year to 31,846 in 1977. But once the brothers became accustomed to the new conditions, the Kingdom-preaching work again gained impetus.

In time, we even began to have small assemblies, first with only the elders and their wives present and later with all members of the congregations in attendance. These assemblies were held in the most unlikely places—in isolated rural areas, in sheds used for sheep shearing, and even in chicken coops. What happy days we had together enjoying spiritual instruction!

Even more important, we never missed an issue of *The Watchtower* for use in our weekly study. These magazines were printed on small offset presses at various places. All of this required much work and often put our brothers in danger of losing their freedom. At that time newspapers listed thousands of people who had vanished, but not one of Jehovah's Witnesses disappeared. Despite all the obstacles encountered, from 1977 to 1984 God's people saw an increase of 57 percent as more than 18,000 new Kingdom publishers joined their ranks.

Full Freedom Is Granted

Actually, our freedom came in two stages. First, on December 12, 1980, the de facto military regime lifted the ban. At that stage, our work was no longer prohibited, although it still was not legally recognized. Finally, the present government recognized the Association of Jehovah's Witnesses. This step was taken on March 9, 1984, by Dr. María T. de Morini, Undersecretary of Worship.

Behind us then were the long years of

Buenos Aires. This hall will accommodate 2,200 people. On the same property, there is also a farm that provides much of the food needed by the 78-member Bethel family.

The 1985 service year started off with a new peak of Kingdom proclaimers, reaching 51,962 in December. The number of congregations rose to 730. How happy we were when 135,379 gathered in 1985 to commemorate the Memorial of Christ's death! And in January 1985 we finished our series of nine "Kingdom Increase" District Conventions, with a total attendance of 97,167 people—17,000 more than the preceding year.

fighting for legal recognition. Our Kingdom Halls could be identified by signs for the first time. Why, the announcement of our legal inscription made us feel like 'those who were dreaming, and our tongue gave way to a joyful cry'! Truly, 'Jehovah had done a great thing for us.'—Compare Psalm 126:1, 2.

Rejoicing in Kingdom Increase

With legal recognition has come grand Kingdom increase. Because of this, plans were made for the construction of our first Assembly Hall. It was to be built near Moreno, some 25 miles (40 km) from

This increase made the branch facilities inadequate for our needs. We were able to buy a building complex, to be used for the factory and offices. On a neighboring lot, we plan to construct a ten-story building to house the Bethel family.

We hope that the new facilities will enable us to take good care of the Kingdom interests in Argentina. And we look to the future with optimism, thankful, indeed, for the great things Jehovah is doing for those who love him.

Questions From Readers

■ Are the remnant of the Lord's anointed on earth a part of Jehovah's heavenly, wifely organization, "Jerusalem above"?

Anointed ones on earth can be spoken of as the visible part of God's organization, his universal family of intelligent creatures.

As individuals who are "born again," they become spiritual sons of Jehovah. (John 3:3, 5; Romans 8:15-17) Jehovah is their Father. Yet they have also a "mother," for the apostle Paul wrote that "the Jerusalem above . . . is our mother." This must be a reference to a heavenly organization of loyal spirits whom Jehovah views as a figurative "wife." (Galatians 4:26) When anointed Christians receive their heavenly reward, they actually take their place in that heavenly organization.—Revelation 4:4; 14:1-5.

The anointed remnant on earth

are not yet literally a part of "Jerusalem above." But because of their unique position as spiritual sons with the prospect of heavenly life, and because they represent God's heavenly "wife," at times Jehovah includes them in a reflective way in directives, prophecies, promises, and words of comfort addressed to his wifely organization in heaven.

We can illustrate this with words involving ancient Israel. Through Isaiah, Jehovah described a woman in chains, in the dust, in need of waking up and shedding forth light. (Isaiah 51: 9, 14; 52:1, 2; 60:1) Those conditions have not existed among Jehovah's loyal spirit sons making up his heavenly "woman." However, they did exist in the nation of Israel. When the Israelites were released from captivity to Babylon in 537 B.C.E., they awakened, stood up from the dust, and began to reflect Jehovah's light. Rebuilt Jerusalem (standing for the nation) was like a wife who had been abandoned but who now had been reclaimed and was producing children, the Jews in the revived nation. (Isaiah 54:1-8; 60:1-22; 66:7-14) So the words in Isaiah about the situation of the "woman" (whose "husbandly owner" was Jehovah) took in the earthly nation representing her.

Now let us shift attention to the spiritual nation that God would accept once he (and his heavenly "woman") ceased using fleshly Israel. (Galatians 6:16) After being "barren" for many centuries, "Jerusalem above" began to produce spiritual sons. Jesus was the first one produced, in 29 C.E., to be followed by 144,000 others, beginning with the apostles and extending down to our time. (Galatians 4:21-31) For a brief period in the early part of this century, the remnant of spiritual Israelites gave in to pressures and came, as

it were, into captivity. Then, in 1919, they were brought out of Babylonish captivity as a newborn nation in a spiritual land. Thus, we can see that Isaiah's prophetic words regarding ancient Jerusalem find a parallel in spiritual Israel on earth.

Consider, too, Revelation 12: 1-17. At the end of the Gentile Times in 1914, God's heavenly "woman" produced the Kingdom government as a "male child." The debased Satan "grew wrathful at the woman." But his attack was not directly against God's wifely organization in heaven, to which

he no longer had access. Rather, Satan waged war "with the remaining ones of her seed" representing her here on earth.

Thus, as it was in the past with earthly Israel, so it is with spiritual Israel. The situation in "Jerusalem above" is reflected among her children on earth. In a practical sense, the commands, correction, comfort, and promises directed to Jehovah's heavenly woman, affect primarily those on the earth who represent her and who have the prospect of being part of God's heavenly organization.

■ Do those of the "great crowd" become part of Jehovah's universal organization?

Now, prior to the "great tribulation," all of Jehovah's Witnesses happily serve God in unity. (Matthew 24:21) There is no division over the fact that a small number are spirit anointed and look forward to going to heaven, while the majority have the hope of eternal life in an earthly paradise. As Jesus indicated, both the "sheep" and the "other sheep" become united in "one flock." (John 10:11, 16) Thus, Jehovah's present organization of servants is made up of those from both groups, with both destinies.

Jehovah foresaw that his woman would enjoy such prosperity. He indicated that people from all nations, those not spiritual Israelites, would be gathered in great numbers. (Isaiah 60: 1-22; 61:5-9) The book of Revelation describes "a great crowd, which no man was able to number, out of all nations and tribes and peoples and tongues, standing before the throne and before the Lamb." These are ones with

earthly hopes, not those of the spiritual nation of anointed ones who particularly represent Jehovah's universal organization today. Still, the "great crowd" stand before the throne of God and the Lamb in robes made white by washing in the Lamb's blood. What a fine standing they have even now!—Revelation 7:9-17.

These of the "great crowd" are also tested as to their integrity. Their continued faithfulness now and on through the Thousand Year Reign and the final test will result in Jehovah's declaring them righteous as perfect humans, along with resurrected ones who become part of Jesus' "other sheep." Being thus "set free from enslavement to corruption," they will enjoy "the glorious freedom of the children of God." (Romans 8:21) They then will be, as were originally Adam and Eve, the visible part of Jehovah's universal organization. They will be the perfect, intelligent offspring of Jehovah and his wifely organization in heaven.

"The More You Read It, the More You Like It"

"You Can Live Forever in Paradise on Earth is the book of books second only to the Bible," writes a reader from the Philippines. "You cannot help but like it with all your heart and soul. I've already read that book twice from cover to cover, yet I'm ever yearning to read it again. The more you read it, the more you like it. It's highly instructive. . . . The book, if applied, is enough to turn the world upside down."

You Can Live Forever in Paradise on Earth

November 1, 1985

The Watchtower

Announcing Jehovah's Kingdom

INDEPENDENCE FROM GOD– WHY NOT?

The Watchtower

Announcing Jehovah's Kingdom

November 1, 1985
Vol. 106, No. 21

In This Issue

THE PURPOSE OF "THE WATCHTOWER" is to exalt Jehovah God as the Sovereign of the universe. It keeps watch on world events as they fulfill Bible prophecy. It comforts all peoples with the good news that God's Kingdom will soon destroy those who oppress their fellowmen and that it will turn the earth into a paradise. It encourages faith in the now-reigning King, Jesus Christ, whose shed blood opens the way for mankind to gain eternal life. "The Watchtower," published by Jehovah's Witnesses continuously since 1879, is nonpolitical. It adheres to the Bible as its authority.

"WATCHTOWER" STUDIES FOR THE WEEKS

December 1: Finding Joy in the Gift of Marriage. Page 16. Songs to Be Used: 117, 89.

December 8: The Beauty of the Christian Personality. Page 21. Songs to Be Used: 22, 131.

Average Printing Each Issue: 11,150,000

Now Published in 103 Languages

SEMIMONTHLY EDITIONS AVAILABLE BY MAIL
Afrikaans, Arabic, Cebuano, Chichewa, Chinese, Cibemba, Danish, Dutch,* Efik, English,* Finnish, French, German,* Greek, Hiligaynon, Igbo, Iloko, Italian,* Japanese,* Korean, Lingala, Malagasy, Maltese, Norwegian, Portuguese, Russian, Sepedi, Sesotho, Shona, Spanish,* Swahili, Swedish, Tagalog, Thai, Tswana, Xhosa, Yoruba, Zulu

MONTHLY EDITIONS AVAILABLE BY MAIL
Armenian, Bengali, Bicol, Bulgarian, Croatian, Czech, Ewe, Fijian, Ga, Greenlandic, Gujarati, Gun, Hausa, Hebrew, Hindi, Hiri Motu, Hungarian, Icelandic, Kannada, Kikuyu, Kiluba, Malayalam, Marathi, New Guinea Pidgin, Pangasinan, Papiamento, Polish, Rarotongan, Romanian, Samar-Leyte, Samoan, Sango, Serbian, Silozi, Sinhalese, Slovenian, Solomon Islands-Pidgin, Tahitian, Tamil, Telugu, Tshiluba, Tsonga, Turkish, Twi, Ukrainian, Urdu, Venda, Vietnamese
* Study articles also available in large-print edition.

The Bible translation used is the "New World Translation of the Holy Scriptures," unless otherwise indicated.

Twenty cents (U.S.) a copy

Watch Tower Society offices	Yearly subscription Semimonthly
America, U.S., Watchtower, Wallkill, N.Y. 12589	$4.00
Australia, Box 280, Ingleburn, N.S.W. 2565	A$7.00
Canada, Box 4100, Halton Hills (Georgetown), Ontario L7G 4Y4	$5.20
England, The Ridgeway, London NW7 1RN	£5.00
Ireland, 29A Jamestown Road, Finglas, Dublin 11	£5.00
New Zealand, 6-A Western Springs Rd., Auckland 3	$10.00
Nigeria, P.O. Box 194, Yaba, Lagos State	₦6.00
Philippines, P.O. Box 2044, Manila 2800	₱50.00
South Africa, Private Bag 2, Elandsfontein, 1406	R5,60

Remittances should be sent to the office in your country or to Watchtower, Wallkill, N.Y. 12589, U.S.A.

Changes of address should reach us 30 days before your moving date. Give us your old and new address (if possible, your old address label).

The Watchtower (ISSN 0043-1087) is published semimonthly for $4.00 (U.S.) per year by Watch Tower Bible and Tract Society of Pennsylvania, 25 Columbia Heights, Brooklyn, N.Y. 11201. Second-class postage paid at Brooklyn, N.Y., and at additional mailing offices.

Postmaster: Send address changes to Watchtower, **Wallkill, N.Y. 12589.**

Published by
**Watch Tower Bible and Tract Society
of Pennsylvania**
25 Columbia Heights, Brooklyn, N.Y. 11201, U.S.A.
Frederick W. Franz, President

The Limits of Freedom

"None are more hopelessly enslaved than those who falsely believe they are free."—Goethe.

FREEDOM! What a ring that word has. But what does it mean to you? Does freedom mean that you have the inalienable right to do as you please, when or where you please, without regard for other people? Of course not! Limits are placed on your actions by lawmaking bodies to protect the rights and interests of others. Is this not vitally necessary when people live together as a community?

For example, you may have the freedom to travel, but you can operate your vehicle only within lawful limits. These limits, or laws, were established as a protection not only for others but also for you. Therefore, true freedom does not mean immunity from all restraint, discipline, and sacrifice; neither does it mean the absence of laws that are right and beneficial. Interestingly, *Black's Law Dictionary* defines freedom this way:

"The state of being free . . . without other check, hindrance, or prohibition than such as may be imposed by just and necessary laws and the duties of social life."

To enjoy freedom, we must live our lives within two boundaries—natural laws and moral laws.

Physical Laws Limit Man

It is impossible for any human to have total freedom even if he isolates himself on a tiny island in the middle of a vast ocean. The natural demands of his body and his dependence on the environment would impose limitations on his freedom. The Creator, Jehovah God, has established these natural boundaries and has established others by means of his laws and principles.—Acts 17:26-28.

God put in operation physical laws that keep the universe in marvelous harmony. These laws work for our good. For instance, do you feel tyrannized by God's natural law of gravity? Of course not! It is the necessary force that holds the universe together and keeps you from flying off the earth.

However, what if you deliberately were to ignore the law of gravity and jump from a one-hundred-foot cliff? You would fall to your death or else be severely injured. The result: not freedom but an increase in limitations. We cannot slight physical laws without paying a penalty. Yet, when we work within their limits, we reap the benefits.

Laws to Limit Behavior

About 300 years ago, the English philosopher John Locke summed up what you may have discovered about freedom and human law. He wrote: "Where there is no law there is no freedom. For liberty is to be free from restraint and violence from others, which cannot be where there is no law; and is not, as we are told, 'a liberty for every man to do what he lists [wishes].' For who could be free, when every other man's humour might domineer over him?"

How appropriate those words are when applied to human laws that limit harmful conduct! If man sees the need for law to govern social behavior, would not his Creator also have seen that need? Are we to think that God would cause physical laws to come into existence but leave mankind without laws to guide his conduct? Not at all.—Matthew 6:8.

The Creator's laws for mankind are written down and preserved so that we can know the best way to handle our affairs. (2 Timothy 3:16, 17) Of their quality, *The Bible in Living English* says: "Jehovah's instructions are unerring, life-restoring; Jehovah's lessons are trustworthy, enlightening simpletons; Jehovah's mandates are acceptable, gladdening hearts; Jehovah's commandment is honest, brightening eyes."—Psalm 19:7, 8.

A person trying to live free from all proper moral limits is like a ship that has lost both compass and rudder. Both are adrift and must find a safe course or face disastrous consequences. This, therefore, raises a serious question. Can we safely navigate our life independently from God?

Independence From God —Why Not?

"I'M LOOKING for excitement." "I'm sick and tired of being told what to do!" "Get off my back!" Expressions such as these may indicate a spirit of independence. Sometimes these words can even be heard coming from the lips of Christians.

How may Christians be infected by the spirit of independence, even independence from God? Usually it begins by adopting a distorted view of Jehovah God's requirements. (Psalm 73:2, 13, 14) They see God's laws as fun barriers, rather than as protectors of their enjoyment of life. The glitter and glamour of the ungodly world has fooled them into believing that they are missing out on pleasure. What about you? What are your feelings about independence from God?

An Age-Old Problem

The wanting of independence from God is not new. It is almost as old as man. The spirit of independence was introduced by Satan the Devil. He deceived the first woman, Eve, into thinking that she could be happier if she were only free from her Creator's guidance. Eve believed that such an independent course would open up for her many eye-opening experiences and pleasures withheld from her by God. —Genesis 3:1-5; Revelation 12:9.

With eyes blinded by her newly formed selfish desires, Eve appealed to her husband to join the rebellion. Adam chose independence from God too. The result: Sorrow replaced happiness. Sin, shame, sickness, pain, and death followed, not just for Adam and Eve but for all their offspring as well.—Genesis 3:6, 16-19; Romans 5:12.

The Bible records that angels, too, decided to follow the path of independence from God by seeking illicit pleasure with the 'good-looking daughters of men.' Did such an independent course bring genuine satisfaction? No. Rather, it produced so much gross immorality and violence that Jehovah determined to destroy that world of ungodly people. The independent angels became demons, who now promote this same destructive spirit of rebellion among mankind.—Genesis 6:1-7, 11; Ephesians 2:2; Jude 6-12.

The Need for Divine Guidance

The foregoing facts should help us appreciate a basic truth: In order to have a successful and delightful way of life, man must depend on God for guidance. That is one reason why the Bible says: "I well know, O Jehovah, that to earthling man his way does not belong. It does not belong to man who is walking even to direct his step." (Jeremiah 10:23) The ancient wise man Solomon recognized the danger of setting up personal standards for life independent of divine guidance. He wrote: "There exists a way that is upright before a man, but the ways of death are the end of it afterward."—Proverbs 14:12.

Let us illustrate this point in two ways. If all the commercial aircraft pilots ignored the directions given at airports and landed their airplanes at any time or location they pleased, how safe would air travel be? Or if a group of construction workers threw away the blueprints and each decided to do just as he fancied with his part of the construction, what type of building would result? We understand that standards must be followed if any orderly society is to exist.

No one is better qualified to provide these guidelines than the Creator of man, Jehovah. By reason of his Creatorship, Jehovah God, not the creature, man, has the absolute right to set the standards by which his intelligent creatures should live. He knows our limits; he knows exactly where the boundary line between happiness and sorrow lies. (Acts 17:26, 27) Time and time again, the experiences of life prove that God's way really works. It is the best way for us.

We do not have to guess what Jehovah's standards are; he kindly tells us in his Word, the Bible: "This book of the law should not depart from your mouth, and you must in an undertone read in it day and night, in order that you may take care to do according to all that is written in it; for then you will make your way successful and then you will act wisely." (Joshua 1:8) The apostle Paul explains how all-embracing God's standards are. He wrote at 2 Timothy 3:16, 17: "All Scripture is in-

What type of building would be constructed if each worker threw away the blueprints and built as he pleased?

human system of things imbued with the spirit of disobedience and extreme selfishness. (Ephesians 2:2; 1 John 2:15-17) And, of course, our own imperfections and deceptive heart-inclinations have to be fought. (Psalm 51:3-5; Jeremiah 17:9, 10) So to live without Jehovah's guidance makes about as much sense as it does to ride in a car without a steering wheel.

Jesus Christ is the best example of someone who appreciated divine guidance. Although perfect, he said of himself: "The Son cannot do a single thing of his own initiative, but only what he beholds the Father doing." (John 5:19) Jesus did not live to please himself. On another occasion he said: "I do nothing of myself: what the Father has taught me is what I preach; he who sent me is with me, and has not left me to myself, for I always do what pleases him." (John 8:28, 29, *The Jerusalem Bible*) Do you desire to be guided by the same standard Jesus Christ acknowledged? —1 Peter 2:21.

Value of Accepting Divine Guidance

Jehovah is "the happy God." (1 Timothy 1:11) He does not want to rob us of wholesome pleasure, excitement, or happiness. Think for a moment about the plainly stated words found at Romans 1:28-32. The results of independence from God bring only bad consequences, for the account states, according to *The New English Bible:*

spired of God and beneficial for teaching, for reproving, for setting things straight, for disciplining in righteousness, that the man of God may be fully competent, completely equipped for every good work."

Jehovah invites us to test his standards, 'to prove to ourselves the good and acceptable and perfect will of God.' (Romans 12:2) Of course, to do this properly, a thorough study of the Bible is necessary. Whether we are new to Bible study or have been studying God's Word for decades, the goal of gaining accurate knowledge and insight into God's will is important. If we fail to train our perceptive powers by using them, we will not keep Jehovah's guidelines in clear focus.—Hebrews 5:14.

To ignore God's standards is to invite disaster. There are just too many obstacles that a person has to cope with for him to succeed on the basis of his own understanding. First, a person has to contend with the subtle superhuman influences of Satan and his demons. (1 John 5:19; Revelation 12:12) Then there is the worldwide

"Thus, because they have not seen fit to acknowledge God, he has given them up to their own depraved reason. This leads them to break all rules of conduct. They are filled with every kind of injustice, mischief, rapacity, and malice; they are one mass of envy, murder, rivalry, treachery, and malevolence; whisperers and scandal-mongers, hateful to God, insolent, arrogant, and boastful; they invent new kinds of mischief, they show no loyalty to parents, no conscience, no fidelity to their plighted word; they are without natural affection and without pity. They know well enough the just decree of God, that those who behave like this deserve to die, and yet they do it; not only so, they actually applaud such practices."

On the other hand, those who choose to follow God's standards are encouraged to put away their old personality with its independent spirit and substitute for it a new Christlike one. The new personality includes becoming kind, tenderly compassionate, freely forgiving. (Ephesians 4: 20-32) And it is one that manifests the fruits of God's holy spirit: "love, joy, peace, long-suffering, kindness, goodness, faith, mildness, self-control."—Galatians 5:22, 23.

After taking a good look at both personalities, what sort of person are you? Which of the two would you prefer to see in your associates?

In addition, the Bible teaches that in the very near future all ungodly persons will suffer destruction at the hands of God. (2 Peter 3:7; 2 Thessalonians 1:7-9) Jesus Christ predicted that, just prior to this divine cleansing of the earth, people in general would be as indifferent to following God's standards as were the people in Noah's day. (Luke 17:26-30) So it is urgent that we gain full appreciation for the value of the guidelines that God has set. To survive, this is just as necessary for us today as it was for Noah in his day.

Therefore, independence from God does not bring real happiness; doing God's will does. Those submitting to Jehovah's guidance will be rewarded with everlasting life on an earth filled with people who have the Christlike personality.—Psalm 37:27-29.

"I Was Full of a Warm Feeling"

Burt lives in England. He spent six weeks in Australia, visiting his brother Eric and his wife who are Jehovah's Witnesses. Being of a different religion, Burt hesitated when his brother invited him to attend a meeting at the Kingdom Hall. But he was so surprised by the warm, friendly spirit with which he was greeted that, after his return to England, he wrote this letter of appreciation to the congregation:

"I must admit that I am not a Witness, being an active member of the Church of England, so it was with a certain amount of trepidation that I accompanied Eric and Joan to their Sunday worship.

"I need not have had any fears whatever. The welcome I received from almost the whole congregation was not only most brotherly and sincere but I was full of a warm feeling that, although a complete stranger, I was accepted, not so much as a visitor but as a welcome member of the congregation.

"While I did not fully understand your service and witness, I nevertheless took my leave at the end of the meeting feeling that I had benefited greatly from the experience and wondering why the love and sincerity that was evident during the whole service could not spread across this very troubled world of ours.

Yours very sincerely,
Burt B."

Jesus' First Miracle

JESUS and his newly acquired disciples have just left the Jordan Valley. It has been only a day or two since Andrew, Peter, John and perhaps James, Philip and Nathanael have become Jesus' first disciples.

They are now on their way home to the district of Galilee, where all of them originated. Their destination is Cana, the hometown of Nathanael, located in the hills not far from Nazareth where Jesus himself grew up. They have been invited to a wedding feast in Cana.

Jesus' mother, too, has come to the wedding. As a friend of the family of the ones getting married, Mary appears to have been involved in ministering to the needs of the many guests. So she is quick to note a shortage, which she reports to Jesus: "They have no wine."

When Mary thus, in effect, suggests that Jesus do something about the lack of wine, Jesus at first is reluctant. "What have I to do with you?" he asks. As God's appointed King, he is not to be directed in his activity by family or friends. So Mary wisely leaves the

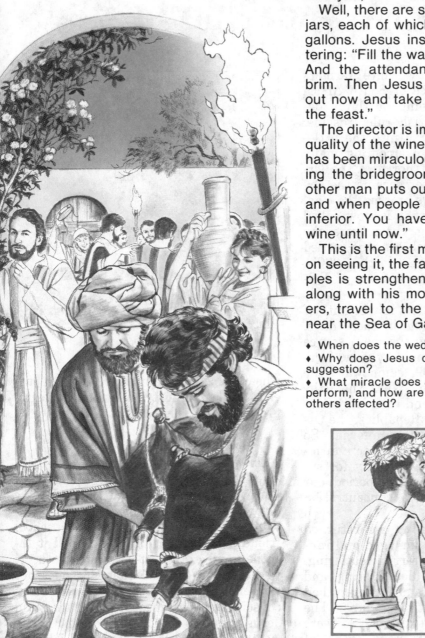

Jesus' Life and Ministry

matter in her son's hands, simply saying to those ministering: "Whatever he tells you, do."

Well, there are six large stone water jars, each of which can hold over ten gallons. Jesus instructs those ministering: "Fill the water jars with water." And the attendants fill them to the brim. Then Jesus says: "Draw some out now and take it to the director of the feast."

The director is impressed by the fine quality of the wine, not realizing that it has been miraculously produced. Calling the bridegroom, he says: "Every other man puts out the fine wine first, and when people are intoxicated, the inferior. You have reserved the fine wine until now."

This is the first miracle of Jesus, and on seeing it, the faith of his new disciples is strengthened. Afterward they, along with his mother and his brothers, travel to the city of Capernaum near the Sea of Galilee. **John 2:1-12.**

♦ When does the wedding in Cana occur?
♦ Why does Jesus object to his mother's suggestion?
♦ What miracle does Jesus perform, and how are others affected?

Determined to Be 'Steadfast and Unmovable'

As told by Paul Smit

IN THE 1830's many white farmers of the Cape Province of South Africa were very restless. Being of Dutch descent, they found British rule irksome. Thousands trekked north into the little-known interior. After overcoming many obstacles, some settled north of the Orange River in what later became the Orange Free State. Others crossed the Vaal River and settled in what is now called the Transvaal. Among them were my Afrikaans-speaking forebears who settled in the Northern Transvaal in the 1860's. I was born near the small town of Nylstroom in 1898.

The life-style of the few inhabitants of the area was very simple in those days. The plentiful game was the main source of livelihood, supplemented by some farm produce. Then, in 1899, came war—the South African, or Boer, War. The British had decided to extend their authority over the two Afrikaner Republics, the Orange Free State and the Transvaal. So for three years Briton and Boer ("farmer" in Afrikaans) fought bitterly for supremacy. In the course of this period, our family was interned in a concentration camp.

When hostilities ceased, we returned to find our farm badly damaged and ransacked. There had been terrible suffering. Thousands of men had died fighting, and thousands of women and children had expired in concentration camps. The country was poverty stricken. So were we. However, a government grant of wheat helped us to survive, and my parents worked industriously on the farm, growing vegetables and other produce.

The Truth Causes a "Cyclone"

Then came the memorable year 1915. As a schoolboy of 16, I received through the post a booklet entitled *What Say the Scriptures About Hell?* published by Jehovah's Witnesses of that time. A school friend, Abraham Stroh, and I read it together and agreed it was the truth. It was thrilling to learn that God does not torment people forever; the dead are unconscious, asleep in death, and awaiting Jesus' promise of a resurrection. (Ecclesiastes 9:5, 10; Ezekiel 18:4; John 5:

28, 29) We were enthused into action. Nylstroom became a centre of commotion, as if struck by a cyclone, as we two schoolboys made it known, positively and fearlessly, that the doctrines of the Dutch Reformed Church were false. The clergy, of course, were upset and denounced this "new religion" from their pulpits.

As a result, Abraham and I were no longer welcome at our friends' homes. Even my father threatened to put me out of the house. But my mother, a really sheeplike person, never said an unkind word. In time my dear old father, who had deep respect for the Bible, got used to the "new religion," and Witnesses were hospitably entertained in our home. In those early days, we knew nothing of the Society and relied entirely on Jehovah. Later, colporteurs (now called pioneers) visited us and brought us into contact with the Society and its office 1,000 miles (1,600 km) away in Cape Town. This led to my baptism in 1918.

Two years later I attended an assembly in Pretoria. Some 23 brothers and sisters were present, with Brother Ancketill, the Society's representative, presiding. How grand it was to be with fellow believers even though there were so few of us! The programme was composed mainly of doctrinal matters and "testimonies," or experiences, but was sufficiently stimulating for me to remain firm. I needed it.

A Disappointment—Then Blessings

The greatest shock of my life came when my close friend, Abraham, after leaving school and being employed by the local School Board, was later threatened with dismissal unless he gave up his religion. He did leave the truth and joined the Dutch Reformed Church. That left me, young and new in the truth, entirely alone in the Northern Transvaal. I shed many a tear over losing my companion, but I prayed without ceasing to Jehovah and was strengthened to be "steadfast, unmovable, always having plenty to do in the work of the Lord."—1 Corinthians 15:58.

Then came the early 1920's. Jehovah blessed my persistent efforts to live the truth to the best of my ability. I began to find "sheep" in my neighbourhood. The young son of a nearby farmer accepted the good news of the Kingdom, thus making up for my loss of a companion. This brother, Hannes Grobler, remained faithful until his recent death. I also started a study with a family of seven, the Vorsters, using the book *The Harp of God.**

Every Saturday I happily walked four miles (6.4 km) through the veld, or countryside, to conduct the study. The parents became baptised Witnesses and remained faithful until death.

In 1924, Brother George Phillips, who had recently arrived in South Africa to serve in the branch at Cape Town, made a visit to Nylstroom—a thrilling event for me. It began a close friendship and period of theocratic cooperation lasting until he finished his earthly course in 1982.

The local interest developed, and we soon had a fine group of 13 brothers and sisters—the first Witness group north of Pretoria. In time the message of the Kingdom radiated out into the vast area of the Northern Transvaal.

Problems and Progress in Pretoria

However, that same year my bank employers transferred me to Pretoria, where there was a small group of eight Bible

---

* Published by the Watch Tower Bible and Tract Society.

Students (Jehovah's Witnesses). But only one had a proper appreciation for theocratic matters, and he died soon after I arrived. The others—some were educated men—failed to appreciate the arrangement of the Society to organize the congregations for service, and two of them left.

Meanwhile, the "elder" of the group, in spite of the Society's disapproval, was writing a book with his own interpretation of the Scriptures. I personally appealed to him to abandon the idea. The climax came one Sunday morning. His book was already printed, and he brought some copies and asked the group to distribute it. I was shocked. I stood up and opposed his request. As a result, the "elder" and four or five others left the organization. This left only a dear old invalid sister, together with my wife and me. But we were determined to be 'steadfast and unmovable' and loyally support the Society. From then on, slowly but surely, Jehovah gave the increase.—1 Corinthians 3:6; 15:58.

In due time Jehovah added many more workers to the Pretoria Congregation. For example, in 1931 two black brothers came to our study centre and introduced themselves. After that, for some years it was my responsibility to serve both Europeans (whites) and Africans (blacks)—a rare privilege in South Africa. To help the African brothers, I conducted a group study in their own township, or separate residential area. I also used Brother Rutherford's recorded talks in the township. In addition to this, an African brother, Hamilton Kaphwitti Maseko, used to help me every Sunday evening to transmit these lectures by means of a powerful transcription machine on Church Square, the very heart of Pretoria.

With Jehovah giving the increase, an African congregation was formed. For many years, as city overseer, I arranged their special meetings. From small beginnings, the work among the Africans in Pretoria expanded to *16* congregations in the area by 1984.

A Wartime Ban

The outbreak of World War II in September 1939 brought tremendous suffering to many countries. South Africa, however, was an exception. Nevertheless, because of the world-shaking events, many South Africans awoke from their complacency and directed their minds to the fulfillment of Bible prophecy. As a result, there was an outstanding growth in Kingdom activity with a 50-percent increase in publishers for the 1941 service year. This aroused the ire of the churches, notably the Catholic Church, which accused the Society of being dangerous to the State. The Government then banned many of the Society's publications.

About that time, my wife Anna and I with our two children, Paul and Anelise, paid a visit to Nylstroom, where I had to give a talk. I took the opportunity to show the local brothers the feasibility of presenting our magazines on the street. I chose a position just outside the Magistrate's Court. Soon a Police Sergeant told me that I was doing an illegal work and must report to the Charge Office immediately. Nevertheless, since we had decided to work for an hour, I just carried on. Then a constable came to inform me that the Chief of Police was waiting for me. But I did not move. Another constable came with a similar message and got the same response. We completed the hour with good results, and then my family and I retired to a café for a cup of tea.

When I finally went to the Charge Office, I was asked what had happened to the literature. I explained that it had been distributed to the public. Later, the police came to my parents' farm where we were staying and took all the magazines they could find.

After discussing the matter with local brothers, we decided not to take the matter lying down. So the next week 30 of us were out in full force on the streets of Nylstroom, and the following week at Warmbad, 18 miles (29 km) south. Contrary to expectations, no one stopped us. Later, after considerable difficulty, all the publications not under ban were returned.

'Steadfast and Unmovable' Despite Old Age

My wife Anna gave me loyal support until she died in 1949. Since 1954, when I remarried, I have had the loyal support of my dear wife Maud. From an early age, the two children, Paul and Anelise, accompanied me in all features of Kingdom service. Both became pioneers on leaving home. Anelise and her husband, Jannie Muller, are still in that service. Paul later drifted away from the truth and pursued a university career, but in recent years he has renewed his association. My five grandchildren are Jehovah's Witnesses; two of them, together with their marriage mates, are serving full time in the ministry. I can strongly recommend that parents keep close to their children and, by precept and example, train them to love Jehovah and serve him wholesouled.—Deuteronomy 6:6, 7.

During 69 years of theocratic service, I have seen thrilling expansion. Back in 1931 there were five Kingdom proclaimers in the vicinity of Pretoria. Now there are over 1,500 associated with 26 congregations. All praise and honour for this belong to Jehovah! Now, at 86 years of age, health permitting, I still enjoy the challenge of house-to-house witnessing and offering the *Watchtower* and *Awake!* magazines on the street. Maud and I are determined to be 'steadfast and unmovable,' faithful to Jehovah, blessing his name forever and ever.

"I Want to Be an Uncompromising Christian"

After reading a book entitled *"Let Your Kingdom Come,"* published by the Watchtower Society, a young man in Zimbabwe was moved to write the following:

"I have been observing over the past few years that here in Zimbabwe it is you people, Jehovah's Witnesses, who are really trying to follow Christ's own example. I am a Seventh Day Adventist member, but it seems as if my Church in this country has lost the inspiration of the holy spirit. We are compromising with the world. For example, we believe, just as you do, that Christ was not born on the 25th [of] December, and yet our pastors tell us that we can celebrate Christmas as long as we keep in mind that Christ died for our sins. . . .

"Personally, I am sick and tired of professing to be a Christian while my way of life is contrary to Jesus' example. I want to be an uncompromising Christian . . . You are the only group, so far, that has managed to convince me of God's love and the power of His gospel, through your living and not only through speeches and writings. You are living and preaching the gospel while many, many people are preaching the gospel but not living it."

Kingdom Proclaimers Report

Conventioners Commended

"KEEP doing good, and you will have praise from it," said the apostle Paul at Romans 13:3. This proved true at last year's "Kingdom Increase" conventions in Brazil.

For example, after the convention in João Pessoa, the club director told the convention committee: "I congratulate you for the excellent way the assembly was held and for the fine behavior of you and your children. No other religious organization displays such good conduct. When we rent to you, we have no worries. The club doors are always open whenever you want to use our facilities."

Similar comments were heard from many others:

□ "I have worked for years with large crowds of people, but you are the best organized, the cleanest, and the most cooperative."—The administrator of the Maracanãzinho Stadium in Rio de Janeiro.

□ "I am really impressed with your movement. If Jesus Christ were to come now, I believe that the religion he would approve would be yours."—A fireman on duty at one of the Rio de Janeiro conventions.

□ "You don't bother us [policemen] a bit. I just wish that everyone was like you people. It would be marvelous. When I blow my whistle, I know that I'll be obeyed without any argument."—A traffic policeman assigned to the convention in Curitiba.

□ "We want to take this opportunity to congratulate you on your orderliness and marvelous, spontaneous discipline, and we wish you every success in future events, for which this Prefecture [Municipality] is always at your service."—A letter received by the convention overseer from the mayor's office in Santo André.

□ "There was a great contrast between your behavior and that of others who have used our hotel rooms. Your people kept all the installations clean and orderly, and their conduct revealed flawless respect for others."—A hotel manager in Novo Hamburgo.

□ "You folks must be well paid."—A bakery owner supplying bread for the convention in Sorocaba, after seeing how hard the brothers there worked. When he learned that they were all *unpaid*, volunteer workers, he returned to his bakery and brought his whole crew to the stadium to observe their diligence and dedication!

The Brazilian conventions even came to the attention of the news media. The *Tribuna da Bahia* gave this report: "With Bible in hand, looking in its verses for an explanation for human violence and deceit, the Witnesses do not discuss politics, do not interfere in social procedures, and know nothing about direct elections. Justification for this is in the fact that no matter who is the ruler, he will never be balanced, since only God can govern the world perfectly. . . . The basis for their faith is the coming of a new world that can be attained only by untiring study of the Bible and by changing evil habits to a pure heart."

Of course, Jehovah's Witnesses make no claim of being perfect but believe that God's Kingdom will bring in a perfect new order. They have, nevertheless, endeavored to apply the Bible's counsel at 1 Peter 2:12: "Maintain your conduct fine among the nations, that . . . they may as a result of your fine works of which they are eyewitnesses glorify God."

Christian conduct glorifies God

A Happy Day
for Japan's Missionaries

FRIDAY, May 17, 1985, was a spiritually sunny day for Japan's 76 missionaries. As the largest group in any one country, these missionaries after nearly 40 years are still actively spreading Bible truths. Excited about this once-a-year privilege of getting together, they made their way to the Ebina branch from their ten missionary homes scattered throughout the country. Some came from distant assignments in the traveling work.

Enthusiastic greetings and conversation among this happy group were interrupted at 1:00 p.m. The zone overseer called the meeting to order. As roll was called, each missionary told his country of origin, Gilead class number, and years in foreign service. How encouraging it was to see missionaries from as far back as the seventh class still active and faithful in their assignment after some 37 years! Following the presenting of information on the establishment of Gilead School in 1943, the zone overseer warmly commended the missionaries for learning the difficult Japanese language. Next, questions were entertained on improving the Bible educational service offered to the people of Japan. A lively exchange followed.

Experienced ministers told how they use the booklet *Look! I Am Making All Things New"* to give an overall view of the Bible's historical record and teachings. Regarding this discussion, one missionary summed up everyone's feelings like this: "It was so satisfying to know how much the brothers at headquarters care about helping the work here—just *knowing* that keeps us going." All the missionaries were overjoyed at being able to "share in the meeting" and, as they said, "express our needs for effectively carrying out the ministry that is so close to our hearts." One missionary appreciated that such interest on the part of Jehovah's organization truly "showed an effort to understand the situation" there. Another declared, "We were especially glad for the suggestion to prepare various presentations to cope with the problem of frequent territory coverage."

After this animated discussion, the missionaries were next treated to spiritually stimulating answers to Bible questions. Some said, "This presentation was reminiscent of Gilead days." Another noted: "It helped me to be determined really to dig into God's Word." All then adjourned to one of the dining rooms for refreshments and to get reacquainted with those from distant assignments. The evening was spent considering many interesting experiences as told by missionaries who shared in them. One involved a young woman who was moved to learn the truth because as a child she had observed the fine conduct of busy missionaries who lived near her home in Nagasaki. Today, both she and her husband are in the truth! Another told of a good Bible study that was started because the missionary had made "that one last call" at the end of the day.

Filled with renewed zeal and enthusiasm, the missionaries returned home to their assignments refreshed and grateful for the personal care extended to them by Jehovah through his loving organization. On the following Sunday, the zone overseer, A. D. Schroeder, addressed by telephone tie-in an audience of 174,959 assembled throughout Japan. As the climax to his talk, he released the Japanese edition of the 1,792-page *New World Translation of the Holy Scriptures —With References*—another fine new instrument for use by Japan's 102,206 Witnesses!

Finding Joy
in the Gift of Marriage

"What God has yoked together let no man put apart."—MATTHEW 19:6.

ARE those words familiar to you? They are no doubt familiar to millions of people in Christendom, who make up a large portion of the world's population, for they are the words of the Lord Jesus as he spoke to the religious Pharisees of his day. While the words may be familiar, what about the meaning of the statement of Jesus? Is the import of such advice followed by mankind in general? Let us see.

² In many lands today, there is very little regard on the part of the people for the marriage arrangement and for continuing that which God has yoked together. Divorce has reached what could be described as epidemic proportions in country after country. In lands where divorce is not legally permitted by the government, the picture is no brighter, for in such lands people often leave marriage mates and take up living with someone else. So the worthy advice of Jesus at Matthew 19:6 is not being heeded by millions of people in Christendom and elsewhere. Is this because the advice Jesus gave is bad, or is it because people do not listen when Jesus speaks, and they care little about the advice of Jesus in this regard?

³ The evidence is that a large percentage of people do not view marriage as a life-

1. What familiar words of Jesus are well known in Christendom, but what questions are there in connection therewith?
2-4. (a) What is the situation today in many lands as far as heeding Jesus' words at Matthew 19:6 is concerned? (b) What attitude is revealed by those who ignore the Bible's advice on the permanency of marriage?

time contract if it interferes with their own life-styles and desires. To such ones, a marriage need be only a temporary arrangement if it interferes with one's pursuits, likes, or dislikes. So it would almost seem that as easily as one sheds a coat or a hat, others shed a marriage mate, never thinking for a moment about the advice Jesus gave to those who enter into the marriage relationship.

4 With this everybody's-doing-it attitude so prevalent, those wishing to follow the secure advice of the Bible can be influenced in a manner that leads them away from the good teaching of God's Word. Fine counsel is given by the printed page and orally, but failure to heed the Bible's advice can lead to marriage problems. (Compare Psalm 19:7-11.) If we adopt the attitude that anything in marriage interfering with our life-style, our pleasures, our desires, can be changed by our not abiding by God's directions on marriage, then we are in danger. To have such an attitude brings us face to face with one of mankind's greatest problems, that of selfishness. For generally it is selfishness that lies at the root of marriage problems. Why do we say that?

The Role of Sin

5 Men and women, offspring of Adam and Eve, are born in sin and imperfection. This means that because of the inheritance of sin, man misses the mark and is lawless to one degree or another. (1 John 3:4) The apostle Paul spoke of the tremendous burden sin places upon mankind, for he found himself doing what he did not want to do and not doing what he should do. (Romans 7:15-20) Anyone deliberately breaking God's law is selfish. With some individuals it may be selfishness on a small scale, but with others it becomes the total way of life, and their selfishness becomes gross.

6 In the arrangement of marriage instituted by God, it is selfishness that is often at the root of a problem between marriage mates. The woman who wants to be waited on hand and foot, as the expression goes, as she may have been spoiled by her mother or father, is basically selfish. The man who wants to continue a life-style of singleness, that of always being with the "boys" after his marriage, is basically selfish. Think about all the ways in which husband and wife have differences, and you will see that selfishness is at the root of so many of the problems.

7 In striving to cope with the problems occurring in marriage, how does one overcome this inborn tendency toward selfishness? There are a number of things that can be done and which, when applied, can help a marriage that is foundering. But each partner in the marriage arrangement has to be willing to do his or her share. It is not a one-way street. Let us examine some of the factors involved.

Unselfishness in Marriage

8 Marriage is a sharing, meaning that neither marriage partner can take the other for granted and feel that only as long as one of the partners gives and the other takes will all be well. That will not work to the blessing of either. For example, the relatives on both sides have to be taken into consideration. This should not be allowed to become a sore point in the marriage arrangement, so that one's own parents or other relatives are taken into consideration and not those of one's mate. Where a family will spend vacations or other periods of relaxation should not al-

---

5. How does the apostle Paul at Romans 7:15-20 outline the problem we have as a result of being born in sin?

6, 7. What are two problems selfishness causes in marriage, leading us to what logical question?
8. How is marriage a sharing?

ways be one-sided decisions. Thoughtful concern shown in such matters will help make a marriage successful. Never take each other for granted but display unselfishness.—Philippians 2:4.

The Age Factor

9 Because of the prevailing view among many of this generation that if a marriage does not work out it can be terminated in divorce, many young people start out with that light view of the marriage arrangement. This can and does lead to breakups of many teenage marriages. It also leads to bringing many unwanted children into the world. These young ones often grow up never knowing what it is to have a mother and a father who deeply love and care for them.

10 How old should a person be before considering marriage? It would not be the course of wisdom to make rules on this score. Yet the Scriptures give good advice on what constitutes mental and spiritual maturity—the kind of maturity needed by those entering married life. Please read Galatians 5:22, 23, wherein you will find listed the fruitage of the spirit. Examine carefully each one of the fruits there mentioned. Those are the qualities that one needs to cultivate in life. It is not *after* marriage that a person should begin showing such qualities but long *before* in his daily life as a Christian.

11 For example, are you a person who is joyful in life, happy to be alive, serving the interests of the Kingdom of Christ? Are you at peace with others, promoting peaceful relations with them? Or are you contentious, given to fits of anger and abusive speech? Are you long-suffering, able to put up with the weaknesses of your brother or sister, mother or father? Or are you short-tempered and prone to anger if others do not immediately line up with what you want? Do you find that you show kindness to others in your dealings with them, being mild and doing good to them? Or are you selfish, egotistical, lacking in self-control, apt to fly off at others with the least provocation? Have you genuine love for others, wanting to help them, going out of your way, giving of yourself and your resources to bring happiness to others? Or do you want others to show love toward you, always giving to you from their resources?

12 It is correct to say that none of us have these qualities in a perfect way. However, the man or the woman who has been molded by some years of life, and who has had an opportunity to cultivate such spiritual qualities, is in a fine position to make a success of marriage—a much better position than that of the person who does not start trying to master these fruits of the spirit until after the marriage vows.—Compare 2 Peter 1:5-8.

13 Why not honestly examine yourself, your likes and dislikes? Do you not see that your appreciation for life has been enhanced by the passage of time? Did you have the same values at 13 that you had at 5, or the same values at 20 that you had at 13? Has your understanding and appreciation for life grown or lessened as you have gained greater experience over the years? Do you now, as an adult, look for the same qualities in people that you did

9. To what unfortunate results does a light view of marriage lead?
10. In what ways can Galatians 5:22, 23 be of help to those considering marriage?
11. What self-examination may be made by those contemplating marriage?

12. The man or the woman whose life has been molded prior to marriage holds what advantage?
13, 14. (a) What opportunity does the passage of time provide with regard to cultivating spiritual values? (b) What can parents do to assist their children?

as a child? Is it not often true that the "only" boy in a girl's life when she is 16 or 17 years old is long forgotten as she grows to womanhood and attaches greater importance to a man's godly traits and personality? Her view at 22 or 23 years of age will likely be centered more on the spiritual, mental, and emotional aspects of a man than on the physical characteristics. The same can be said for the young boy growing to manhood. His hopes and aspirations as far as a wife is concerned ripen as he matures. In his later years, as values change, what he will look for in a marriage mate is someone who is understanding and kind, who has ability to be a homemaker and a mother, and who has in her heart a deep-seated desire to please first her Creator, Jehovah, and to do his will. —Proverbs 31:10, 26, 27.

¹⁴ The point of the matter is that time changes a person's outlook on values. Therefore, rushing into matrimony at a young age is fraught with many dangers. It may not be possible to persuade two very young persons to wait for some time to pass before entering into a marriage. But parents, especially in the early years of their children's lives, can encourage them to think seriously about life, about being spiritually, emotionally, and mentally prepared for marriage before entering into a lifetime contract with another individual for better or for worse.

¹⁵ This is not to say that marrying when one is older is the total answer either. There can be problems then as well, especially if the attitude of selfishness is allowed to creep in and drive a wedge between two people. The mental, emotional, and spiritual needs of each one in the marriage bond must be taken into con-

Honest self-examination can reveal faults for us to remedy

sideration. Some Christians have allowed themselves to become deeply involved in secular work, to the exclusion of congregational activity, including attending meetings and sharing in the preaching and disciple-making work. Then they try to make up for what they feel is a lack in their lives by indulging in a lot of recreation. They seem to think that as long as they are occupied, their problems will somehow be solved for now, and then in the New Order of things they will get around to each other's needs emotionally, mentally, and spiritually. But life does not work that way. Paul's advice was that a man should care for his wife as he does for his own body. (Ephesians 5:28) That means giving attention *now* to the needs of his mate, even as he daily gives attention to his own needs. The same can be said for the woman.

---

15. Since late marriage is not always the answer to all problems, what counsel is provided about keeping the right outlook?

A Balanced Approach to Married Life

¹⁶ A balanced approach to life will assist in a balanced approach to marriage. The balanced person will realize that due to inherited selfish tendencies he must at all times work to overcome such blemishes. It is so easy never to think of the needs of others as coming before one's personal wants. The small child wants all the toys and generally, if not properly trained by the parents, will not share these with others. His selfishness will, in later years, stretch into other fields. Thus we often find the teenagers and young adults wanting things exclusively their own way, and in their quest for satisfying their wants, they are unconcerned that others may be hurt or suffer. In later adult years, such persons are always craving what *they* like, not caring in the least about the needs of others.

¹⁷ The balanced person will not deprive himself entirely, but he will manage his individual life so that others, too, are taken into consideration. He will ask what he can do to assist others, to give of himself and of what he has to benefit others. He will not insist on having his own way first, last, and always. The book of Proverbs says: "The generous soul will itself be made fat, and the one freely watering others will himself also be freely watered." —Proverbs 11:25.

¹⁸ Following such a course in single life will be most beneficial to a person later in married life. His or her mate will always be taken into consideration in any decisions made. Rather than thinking of marriage as an experiment or a temporary arrangement, such a person will look at marriage as the permanent arrangement Jehovah God had in mind when he joined the first human pair together in Eden. (Genesis 2:22-24) At every turn, efforts will be made to keep the marriage together, to help the mate, as both grow in appreciation for God and for each other.

In Summary

¹⁹ "What God has yoked together let no man put apart." Yes, those words of counsel by Jesus are filled with meaning for the true Christian. Marriage is no experimental arrangement that can be dropped if one finds the going difficult. We must constantly battle the imperfect flesh to keep the human tendency to selfishness in check and so gain God's approval. (Compare Romans 7:21-25.) To make a success of the marriage contract, both partners must learn to give and take, to provide

16-18. (a) Why is a balanced approach to life and marriage necessary, and how are we cautioned with regard to our wants and others' needs? (b) Why is it good to ponder on such matters before marriage?

19-21. (a) How can we make sure we will not view marriage as just an experimental arrangement? (b) What should be borne in mind by all persons, young or old, who seek genuine happiness in marriage?

In review, how would you answer the following?

☐ What attitudes toward marriage are to be avoided?

☐ How may mates cope with inborn tendencies toward sin?

☐ Why should youthful Christians not rush into marriage?

☐ What balanced approach to married life is recommended?

and be provided for, and never to take the other for granted.—Ephesians 5: 21-23, 28, 33.

20 And while no set age can be insisted upon as a rule of law for a person wanting to get married, beyond that which is set as the legal age by government, each one can certainly bear in mind the need to grow spiritually in harmony with Galatians 5:22, 23, in order to be a well-qualified marriage mate. Time does indeed change the outlook of a person. Hence, no one should rush into marriage. First, let each one cultivate the Christian personality so as to be properly prepared for the marriage yoke. And never forget that no one should put apart that which God has joined together.—Matthew 19:4-6.

21 By taking the balanced approach to life and then to marriage, one can find genuine joy and happiness in the arrangement ordained by Jehovah God himself for man and woman, as shown by the first marriage in Eden. (Proverbs 5:18) But just what can each one further do in life to prove himself or herself prepared to take on the role of husband or wife? Read, please, what follows on this matter as regards the personality of Christian men and women.

The Beauty
of the Christian Personality

"Put on the new personality which was created according to God's will in true righteousness and loyalty."—EPHESIANS 4:24.

THERE is a saying that 'beauty is in the eyes of the beholder,' meaning that beauty is relative. What is the beauty of a Christian man or a Christian woman? That is what we want to discuss now.

Defining Beauty in the Christian Man

2 Let us begin by considering the qualities that give a Christian man the pleasant appearance that will cause others to be pleased to be in his company. Physical qualities alone do not make a "man of God." (1 Timothy 6:11) A man's outward appearance, becoming as it may be, means little if he is empty-headed in his reasoning. If he is proud, rude, uncouth, and ignorant, he does not attract—he repels. If his manners show him to be unappreciative, he certainly can be a cause for stumbling to others. If he is only concerned with himself and how he looks or impresses others, he will not be the kind of person with whom others want to associate.

3 Rather, a man of God will have cultivated the qualities of justice, mercy, love,

---

1. What beauty do we here desire to describe?
2. Why do physical attributes alone fail to make a man of God?

3, 4. (a) What are some of the qualities of a man of God as exemplified by the man Jesus Christ? (b) How would you explain some of the characteristics of a man of God?

The spiritual man displays qualities that draw others to him

and kindness. Jesus Christ was not known for his perfect body but for his loyalty to principle and to truth. His way of teaching identified him as one who spoke with authority from God. (Matthew 7:28, 29; John 7:46) A man of God will not be corrupted by the desire for power or prominence. The advantages of a certain position cannot buy him. He is a man who possesses willpower. He loves humility and will not lie. He displays a wholesome fear of Jehovah. (Proverbs 22:4) These are some of the qualities that are to be found in a man of God.

⁴ A man of God has conscience, a good heart, and proper motive. (1 Timothy 1:5; Proverbs 4:23) He will not do things that violate his conscience, ignoring righteous principles. Having a good heart and proper motive, he will not use devious methods in his dealings with others. (Hebrews 13:18) He will not allow his good motives to be undermined by unclean conduct and actions. (Hosea 4:11) He consistently disciplines himself to keep his heart from becoming treacherous. In word and in deed he stands out as a man of principle. —Psalm 15:1, 2.

⁵ A man of God has compassion for others, is forgiving and kind. A compassionate man is a sympathetic man. He can show empathy and understanding when others have problems that are difficult to deal with and that bring anxiety. More than that, he can be forgiving when someone does him wrong. He can rise above the instinctive desire to repay injury for injury and reviling for reviling. Truly he fits the words of 1 Peter 3:8, 9. By bestowing a blessing rather than a cursing, he shows himself to be kind and in control of those baser desires that mark the petty man, the man without ability to be compassionate, forgiving, and kind to others.—Ephesians 4:31, 32.

⁶ Another outstanding quality marking a man of God is his generosity. And if married, he is a true husband and an honest father. In his capacity as a married person, the man of God has a tremendous opportunity to be an influence and pattern for good both for his wife and for his children. (Colossians 3:19, 21) In the matter of being generous, such a man follows the fine advice of the Lord Jesus Christ, who said: "Practice giving, and people will give to you. They will pour into your laps a fine measure, pressed down, shaken together and overflowing. For with the measure that you are measuring out, they will measure out to you in return." (Luke 6:38) In his family relationships, such a man will indeed care for those of his household. But he will also follow the fine

5. What role does compassion play in the life of a man of God?
6. (a) What other outstanding qualities of a man of God are there, and what do they mean? (b) What view will such a man's wife and children have of him?

admonition of Ephesians 4:28, to do "what is good work, that he may have something to distribute to someone in need." As a true husband, the man of God will keep fidelity in the marriage arrangement. His wife will be able to have complete trust and confidence in him as a man that truly is one with her in the marriage bond. (Proverbs 5:18, 19) Additionally, if there are children, he will show himself to be an honest father, not a cheater or dishonest in his dealings with others. Thus, he will inculcate the principles of honesty in his children. (Proverbs 4:1-5) What a fine example such a man is to the impressionable mind of his children! They will be able to look to him as a loyal man, an integrity keeper.—Proverbs 11:3, 4.

7 In this respect also, the man of God will watch that he and his family do not accumulate burdensome debts, knowing that these can lead to trying problems. This, of course, means he will not allow himself and his family to live beyond their means. He is a person who will count the cost before embarking on a particular course. (Luke 14:28-30) He can deny himself in the present time for the sake of the future and is able to give up the seen for the unseen, as it were. (Compare Hebrews 11:8-10.) Living in this way will help the man of God to maintain his Christian scruples in his everyday living.

8 In the lives of all mankind, due to sin and imperfection, it is necessary to face up to unpleasant circumstances at times. But the man of God will be courageous and principled in such situations, after the pattern set by Jesus. (John 16:33) In the strength of his God, Jehovah, he will face the difficult problems with courage, relying on Jehovah for help and guidance.—Proverbs 18:10.

9 A true man of God is the master of his

body. That is, he keeps his desires and passions under control, aware that his body is a proper servant but a very bad master. He remembers constantly the inspired words of the apostle Paul: "I pummel my body and lead it as a slave." (1 Corinthians 9:27) Therefore, he seeks always to cultivate that fruit "of the spirit . . . self-control," avoiding those things that would corrupt him. (Galatians 5:22, 23) He is wise in knowing that giving in to immoral thinking can lead to immoral action. Again, his reliance is on his God, Jehovah, and the strength He supplies.—Philippians 4:13.

10 And finally, the man of God can admit his mistakes, say he is sorry, express such sorrow to his marriage mate and to others he may offend or hurt in one way or another due to his imperfections. He can go to Jehovah and with a clean heart ask to be forgiven of his sins because he has asked his wife, his fellowman, his children, to forgive him. The ability to say, "I'm sorry, I was wrong" is indeed the mark of a real man, especially of a man of God.—Matthew 18:21, 22; Mark 11:25.

11 Would you not say that a man, a hus-

10, 11. (a) What redeeming quality is exhibited by a man of God when he makes errors in judgment? (b) What pattern will family heads follow with regard to family study?

In Our Next Issue

■ God's Kingdom
—Why We Need It

■ Can You Prepare Now
for Persecution?

■ Do Not Share in the
Sins of Others

---

7. What balanced view of indebtedness will be taken by the man of God?
8. How will such a man face unpleasant circumstances in his life?
9. How would you describe the moral life of a man seeking to please Jehovah?

A godly wife loves and is loved

thing about a woman of God: "Charm may be false, and prettiness may be vain; but the woman that fears Jehovah is the one that procures praise for herself." (Proverbs 31:30) How, then, does a woman acquire those qualities that endear her to her husband and children, or to others if she is single, and make her a person that others enjoy being near? To begin with, a woman of God is an openhearted person, meaning that she is generous, desirous of helping others in whatever ways she is able, materially or spiritually. When there are those in need, she is among the first to want to help, taking a genuine interest in the needs of others. But, of course, she balances such interest with the care and attention she, if married, must give to her own family.—Titus 2:3-5.

band, a father, of that caliber would have the help of Jehovah? (Psalm 54:4) Indeed, he would be equipped to cope with the problems that this modern world brings on all of us due to Satan's designs and purpose to wreck everything good, including marriage and the happy family unit. He would look after the spirituality of family members, leading them in regular study of God's Word and in prayer, after the pattern of faithful servants of God in Bible times.—Deuteronomy 11:18-21; Proverbs 7:1-3.

[12] But there is more to consider. There is also the role of the wife in coping with problems in the family. Let us now give our attention to those qualities she will want to cultivate in her life.—Proverbs 19:14.

Defining Beauty in the Christian Woman

[13] The book of Proverbs tells us some-

[14] Further, such a woman is humble-minded, not haughty; kind, not surly; tidy, not unkempt; sympathetic, not belligerent. And, if married, she strives to follow the counsel that the apostle gives at 1 Peter 3:1-5.

[15] Additionally, a woman of God is not worldly-wise, but she strives to cultivate spirituality. She is an earnest reader of the Bible and is interested in applying its principles in her life. (Psalm 119:66) This is not done in self-interest, only wanting knowledge for herself, but, rather, she has in mind sharing the good things she learns, both in the Christian ministry and in day-to-day contacts with neigh-

---

12. What important role will we next consider?
13, 14. What steps can a woman take to win the approval of Jehovah and, if she is married, of her family, and what was the apostle Peter's counsel at 1 Peter 3:1-5 to womankind?

---

15. (a) What goal should a woman of God have, and how may she attain it? (b) How is she supportive of her husband? (c) Why does she continue to be loved in the family circle?

bors, relatives, and friends. A Christian husband enjoys a wife with whom he can converse on spiritual matters, as his complement, someone who also appreciates spiritual things and wants to share with him in coming to know Jehovah better. (Proverbs 9:9, 10) So a woman of God is discerning and understanding. If married, she is aware of her role as her husband's complement. She is supportive of her husband in giving spiritual instruction to the children, especially when he is absent from the home. (Compare 2 Timothy 1:2, 5; 2 John 1, 2.) She will continue to be loving and loved in the family circle long after the beauty of youth may have faded. Her husband can count on her for good and just observations, sound opinions, and sincere encouragement, because she is amiable and sensible. (Proverbs 25:11) It was when Abigail acted with discernment and promptitude that David said: "Blessed be your sensibleness." —1 Samuel 25:32, 33.

16 The modest influence for good that a wife exercises in support of her husband will not be that of sharp, bitter, or sarcastic words. Favor is won by gracious looks, fitly spoken words, tender acts of love, industriousness, by gentle kindness and deep understanding. (Compare Proverbs 25:11; 31:10-28; 1 Thessalonians 2:7.) Meekness, faith, modesty, these are the things that win lasting dearness for the woman of God.—Psalm 37:11; Hebrews 11:11, 31, 35; Proverbs 11:2.

17 Another outstanding quality of a woman of God is her ability to show sympathy and affection. (Romans 12:10) Her fairest ornament is love, which will prevent her from being disagreeable in little things. How beautifully that love is described at 1 Corinthians 13:4-7. According to *The New English Bible,* it reads: "Love is patient; love is kind and envies no one. Love is never boastful, nor conceited, nor rude; never selfish, not quick to take offence. Love keeps no score of wrongs; does not gloat over other men's sins, but delights in the truth. There is nothing love cannot face; there is no limit to its faith, its hope, and its endurance."

What Are We?

18 The big question now is: Can each of us be identified as a Christian person, whether married or single? Are there areas wherein we can see the need to make further adjustments as we seek to be pleasing to Jehovah and to our fellowman? More than likely, any self-examination we undertake will show up areas in which we can improve. But what a joy it is to observe such improvement in ourselves and, more than that, to have others notice and comment on the changes we make because of our closely following the Word of God and its teachings! —2 Corinthians 13:5; 1 Timothy 4:15, 16.

19 In pursuing a life of singleness, a person can strive to cultivate these qualities. (1 Corinthians 7:32) And when the day may come that one decides to get married, such qualities will certainly serve well for the one who has cultivated them. Among those married, continued cultivation of Christian virtues will result in great happiness and joy. (Philippians 4:8, 9) Solving problems takes the effort of both partners in the marriage arrangement. Willingness to recognize and change one's disagreeable habits can con-

16. What kind of words and actions identify a woman of God?
17. Of what value is the quality of love to the woman of God?

18. What personal questions do each of us now face, and what will self-examination do?
19. How should we go about solving problems that we face in the pursuit of a peaceful, godly life?

Single Christians can cultivate the new personality for a full and joyful life

tribute greatly toward putting on a pleasing Christian personality. (Colossians 3: 8-10) Remember, too, the mark of a Christian man or a Christian woman is that ability to say, "I'm sorry, please forgive me." We all make mistakes. When we admit them, we give evidence of cultivating rich qualities of modesty and humility.—Micah 6:8; James 3:2.

²⁰ How appropriate are these words of Paul to the congregation in Colossae: "Then put on the garments that suit

God's chosen people, his own, his beloved: compassion, kindness, humility, gentleness, patience. Be forbearing with one another, and forgiving, where any of you has cause for complaint: you must forgive as the Lord forgave you. To crown all, there must be love, to bind all together and complete the whole. Let Christ's peace be arbiter in your hearts; to this peace you were called as members of a single body. And be filled with gratitude. Let the message of Christ dwell among you in all its richness. Instruct and admonish each other with the utmost wisdom. Sing thankfully in your hearts to God, with psalms and hymns and spiritual songs. Whatever you are doing, whether you speak or act, do everything in the name of the Lord Jesus, giving thanks to God the Father through him."—Colossians 3:12-17, *NEB*.

²¹ The fine examples in the Bible, and also in the Christian congregation in this 20th century, should be an encouragement to one and all to continue working on the new personality. (Ephesians 4:22-24) By doing this, we will become a blessing to all those with whom we associate. Moreover, many others to whom we take the Kingdom message will be impressed and encouraged, not only by our words but also by the zeal and good conduct that they see in the global family of Jehovah's Witnesses.—John 13:34, 35.

20. What appropriate words of the apostle Paul at Colossians 3:12-17 are helpful and fitting for all?

21. How can our conduct and activity encourage others?

In summary of the above, what would you say?
- ☐ What qualities are to be cultivated by the man of God?
- ☐ How will the Christian man care for his wife and family?
- ☐ The Christian woman is distinguished by what virtues?
- ☐ How may single persons build wisely for the future?

Modern Stewardship of God's Sacred Word

The New *Reference Bible*

JEHOVAH'S faithful servants in all ages have relied on the accurate recording and transmission of God's inspired written Word. During the 1,500 years that the nation of Israel was under the Law covenant, about 30 Israelite penmen were used to record God's Word in what became the 39 books of the Hebrew Scriptures. One of these penmen, Moses, indicated that these sacred 'revealed things' were entrusted to the Israelites as part of their divine education as God's "holy nation." (Deuteronomy 29:29; Exodus 19:6) Jesus alluded to the Jews as being the custodians of Scriptural knowledge when he said: "Salvation originates with the Jews." (John 4:22; Luke 11:52) Paul the apostle confirmed that the Jews "were entrusted with the sacred pronouncements of God."—Romans 3:2.

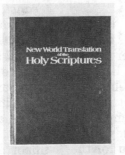

During the centuries preceding our Common Era, the Israelites were a literate people. Trained scribes among them produced scrolls containing highly accurate copies of the Sacred Scriptures that then existed, and these were widely distributed both in Palestine itself and among the Jews and proselytes scattered throughout the nations.—1 Chronicles 2:55; Acts 8: 4, 27, 28.

A significant event worthy of being noted in the Divine Record occurred in 29 C.E., when Jesus was baptized and became Jehovah's Anointed One, or Messiah. Thereafter, he proved to be the foremost publisher of sacred truth. (Matthew 4:4, 10, 17) Although Jesus personally did no Bible writing, his words were later written down on scrolls by his loyal disciples under inspiration of the holy spirit. (John 16:13) On the day of Pentecost of 33 C.E., after his resurrection and ascension, Jesus began to organize a new congregation made up of believing Israelites and proselytes. (Acts 2:1-11) Soon, Samaritans and Gentiles were invited to become part of it. Members of this growing international, yet united, congregation came to be called Christians and formed the new spiritual "Israel of God." (Galatians 6:16; Acts 11: 26) This new organization was entrusted with publishing spiritual truth, and Jesus called it "the faithful and discreet slave."—Matthew 24: 45-47; Luke 12:42-44.

In time, eight Jewish members of this congregation were inspired to produce an additional 27 books, this time writing mainly in Greek. (2 Peter 3:15, 16) Thus, the Divine Library's official catalog of Bible books increased to 66, penned by about 40 inspired natural Jews. Early Christians were eager to publish the Word of God, and Paul reports that in his day the good news had been "preached in all creation that is under heaven." (Colossians 1:23) Paul also explained that Christians were the new stewards entrusted with "the greatly diversified wisdom of God"—referring not only to the inspired books themselves but also to their message.—Ephesians 3:10.

Bible translator Edgar Goodspeed, in his book *Christianity Goes to Press* (1940), showed that this zeal to publish lasted well into the second century of our Common Era: "All this presents a picture of the early Christians quite unlike that usually offered by historians. They were to an unusual extent a book-buying and book-reading people. They were also a translating and publishing people. . . . [In 140 C.E.] Christian publishers . . . resorted to the leaf-book form, the codex, and found it so practical . . . and convenient that it became their characteristic book form."

What about spiritual Israel in our times? True to what Jesus said, his followers have been doing even greater works than he himself did. (John 14:12) Records show that from 1879 to 1984 Jehovah's modern-day witnesses have distributed more than 8.8 billion tracts, pamphlets, magazines, Bibles, and Bible study aids, all containing spiritual instruction for the world public.

In what other way has the modern "faithful and discreet slave," assisted since 1935 by "a great crowd" of "other sheep," acted as the modern steward of the Sacred Scriptures? (Revelation 7: 9, 10; John 10:16) Over the past hundred years, members of the anointed remnant have kept abreast of the discoveries of early Bible manuscripts. Eventually an anonymous committee of anointed Witnesses of Jehovah produced, between 1950 and 1960, the *New World Translation of the Holy Scriptures* in English. This was a completely new translation, untouched and unfettered by Christendom's religious traditions.

In this way the fine fabric of inspired words written thousands of years ago in languages not read by most people today was made available in a new, fresh way. The original printings of the *New World Translation* also contained helpful footnotes and appendixes, which the *New Catholic Encyclopedia* of 1967 described as "an impressive critical apparatus." In time, the *New World Translation* was made available in several other languages to facilitate accurate Bible study internationally.

At the "Kingdom Increase" District Conventions of Jehovah's Witnesses, held in the summer of 1984, a new edition of the *New World Translation* with references was released in English. This contains not only a revision of the *New World Translation* text but also 125,000 marginal, or cross, references, as an aid in Bible study. Additionally, there are more than 11,400 enlightening footnotes, containing vital textual information as well as alternate renderings, that make this *Reference Bible,* in effect, a multiversion translation. There are indexes of Bible and footnote words, and 43 Appendix sections giving important information about the transmission of the text and Bible authenticity. Truly, this new *Reference Bible* makes up-to-date Bible scholarship available to the student of the Sacred Scriptures.

Earth wide, the Watch Tower Society has a large staff of loyal, careful translators who are busy at this time preparing versions of the *Reference Bible* in other principal languages. As a person makes use of its several reference systems, he will enjoy learning why various Bible texts need to be rendered in certain ways so as to be accurate. Consider some examples.

The Name Jehovah

The value of the footnotes and the appendix sections in the *Reference Bible* is

make it sacred,* because on it he has been resting# from all his work that God has created for the purpose of making.△a

4 This is a history* of the heavens and the earth in the time of their being created, in the day that Jehovah# God△ made earth and heaven.b

5 Now there was as yet no bush of the field found in the earth and no vegetation of the field was as yet sprouting, because Jehovah God had not made it rainc upon the earth and there was no man to cultivate the ground. 6 But a mist*d would go up from the earth and it watered the entire surface of the ground.e

7 And Jehovah God proceeded to form the man out of dust*f from the groundg and to blow into his nostrils the breath of life,#h and the man came to be a

Ge 2:3* "And **make** it **sacred**." Or, "and proceeded to **sanctify** it (**treat** it **as holy**)." Heb., *wai·qad·desh' 'o·thoh'*; Lat., *et sanc·ti·fi·ca'vit il'lum.* See Ex 31:13 ftn. 3# Or, "he does rest (desist)." Heb., *sha·vath'*, perfect state. It shows the characteristic of an individual, namely, God, on the seventh day of his creative week. This rendering of *sha·vath'* agrees with the inspired writer's argument in Heb 4:3-11. See vs 2 ftn. 3△ "Making," that is, all definite things in heaven and earth. 4* Or, "These are the historical origins." Heb., *'el'leh thoh·ledhohth'*, "These are the begettings of"; Gr., *hau'te he bi'blos ge·ne'se·os*, "This is the book of origin (source)"; Lat., *i'stae ge·ne·ra·ti·o'nes*, "These are the generations." Compare Mt 1:1 ftn. 4# "Jehovah." Heb., יהוה (*YHWH*, here vowel-pointed as *Yehwah'*), meaning "He Causes to Become" (from Heb., הוה [*ha·wah'*, "to become"]); LXXA (Gr.), *Ky'ri·os*; Syr., *Mar·ya'*; Lat., *Do'mi·nus.* The first occurrence of God's distinctive personal name, יהוה (*YHWH*); these four Heb. letters are referred to as the Tetragrammaton. The divine name identifies Jehovah as the Purposer. Only the true God could rightly and authentically bear this name. See App 1A. 4△ "Jehovah God." Heb., *Yehwah' 'Elo·him'.*

	CHA
a	Ex 2
b	Isa 4
c	Mt 5
d	Job
e	Ps 1
f	Ge 3
	Ps 1
	Ec 3
	1Co
g	Job 3
	Isa 6
h	Ge 7
	Job 2
	Job 3
	Isa 4
	Ac 1

Second
a Eze 3
1Co
1Pe
b Ge 2
Ge 3
Isa 5
Eze
c Ge 1
Ps 1
Ro 9
d Ge 3
e Ge 2
Ge 3
f Ge 2
1Sa
g Ge 1
h Nu 1
i Ex 2
1Ch
Job 2
J Da 1
k Ge 1
Mic

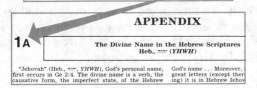

APPENDIX

1A

The Divine Name in the Hebrew Scriptures
Heb., יהוה (*YHWH*)

"Jehovah" (Heb., יהוה, *YHWH*), God's personal name, first occurs in Ge 2:4. The divine name is a verb, the causative form, the imperfect state, of the Hebrew

God's name . . . Moreover, great letters (except ther ing) it is in Hebrew Iehov

seen in connection with the divine name, Jehovah. This name first appears at Genesis 2:4, and here is what a footnote to that verse says: "The first occurrence of God's distinctive personal name, יהוה (*YHWH*); these four Heb[rew] letters are referred to as the Tetragrammaton. The divine name identifies Jehovah as the Purposer. Only the true God could rightly and authentically bear this name. See App 1A."

Turning to Appendix 1A, we find the title: "The Divine Name in the Hebrew Scriptures." Under this title, the appendix shows that the *New World Translation* renders YHWH as Jehovah all 6,827 times that it occurs in the traditional Hebrew text. It also adds 146 warranted restorations, making a grand total of 6,973 times that the name Jehovah appears from Genesis to Malachi. No other Bible translation gives this rightful place to Jehovah's name. That alone makes the *New World Translation* superior to all others.

People of the Nations Must Make Active Response

The *New World Translation* gives serious consideration to preserving verb forms so as to increase accurate understanding. For example, in Genesis 22:18 we read: "By means of your seed all nations of the earth will certainly bless themselves." There is an asterisk beside the phrase "will certainly bless themselves," referring us to a footnote that says: "The Heb[rew] verb is in the reflexive, or *hith·pa·'el'* form."

Most Bible translations render these words in a way similar to the *King James Version,* which says: "In thy seed shall all the nations of the earth *be blessed.*" Incorrectly, such renderings convey the idea that Jehovah's blessing will come automatically, whereas the Hebrew form here indicates that the people of the nations must "bless themselves." They must make the effort to meet Jehovah's requirements in order to receive his blessings through faith in the Messianic Seed, Jesus Christ.

This has great meaning for us today. Members of the "great crowd" must take positive steps in order to gain life. By means of actively exercising their faith in Jesus Christ, 'they wash their robes in the blood of the lamb.'—Revelation 7:14.

The Numbering of the Ten Commandments

The *New World Translation* footnotes give helpful information as to why differences exist between it and some other translations and why its renderings are reliable. For example, what is the proper way of dividing the text of the Ten Commandments? These commandments are found in the Bible in Exodus 20:1-17. In the *Reference Bible,* each separate commandment is written as a separate paragraph. Thus, the first commandment takes in verses 2 and 3. The second is covered in verses 4 to 6. The third is found in verse 7, and so forth. Not all would agree with this way of dividing the commandments. Hence, how do we know that it is correct?

A footnote to Exodus 20:17 gives this explanation: "This division of the Ten Commandments, vss 2-17, is the natural division. It agrees with the first-century C.E. Jewish historian Josephus . . . who divide[d] off vs 3 as the first commandment, vss 4-6 as the second commandment and vs 17, which forbids all covetousness, as the tenth commandment. Others, including Augustine, consider vss 3-6 as one commandment but divide vs 17 into two commandments, the ninth against coveting a fellowman's house and the tenth against coveting his living possessions . . . Augustine's division has been adopted by the Roman Catholic religious system." However, the *New World Translation* follows the "natural division" of Exodus chapter 20 as presented above. Thus the prohibition against making and bowing down to images receives due emphasis as the second commandment.

Added Portions From the *Septuagint*

In preparing the *New World Translation,* editions of the Greek *Septuagint,* the Syriac *Peshitta,* the Latin *Vulgate* and several other early manuscripts were examined. For example, observe Habakkuk 2:4. In the second half of this verse, the main text reads: "But as for the righteous one, by his faithfulness he will keep living." This represents what appears in the traditional Hebrew text. However, the footnote to these words indicates that the Greek *Septuagint* translation contains additional material not found in the Hebrew text: "If anyone shrinks back my soul . . . has no pleasure in him." This is of interest when we note that the apostle Paul quoted from Habakkuk 2:4, writing in his letter to the Hebrews: "'But my righteous one will live by reason of faith,' and, 'if he shrinks back, my soul has no pleasure in him.'" (Hebrews 10:38) Hence, Paul's quotation included the additional words found in the *Septuagint* version.

This reminds us of the fact that Paul and other writers of the inspired Christian Greek Scriptures often used the *Septuagint* version when quoting from earlier inspired writings. Since this version varies in some places from the traditional Hebrew text, their quotations sometimes contain material that is not found in the Hebrew text (as in the above example). In using this variant material, the Christian Bible writers made it part of the inspired record, and in such cases the footnotes in the *Reference Bible* are an invaluable aid in identifying the sources of quotations.

The above are only a few examples of the thousands of footnotes available in the Hebrew Scriptures section of the new *Reference Bible.* All these references support the accuracy and clarity of the *New World Translation* and its value in promoting Bible education. In the next issue of *The Watchtower,* interesting footnote information taken from the Christian Greek Scriptures, as found in the new *Reference Bible,* will be presented. Truly, there proves to be a modern stewardship of God's Sacred Word.

Questions From Readers

■ Does a "Declaration Pledging Faithfulness" in an existing marital relationship have the same permanence as a legalized marriage?

This has reference to the special arrangement granted only in those countries where divorce from a previous mate is not allowed under the law. Christians are appropriately interested in this matter, for God's Word shows how seriously he views the marital arrangement. In fact, the apostle Paul wrote: "Let marriage be honorable among all, and the marriage bed be without defilement, for God will judge fornicators and adulterers." (Hebrews 13:4) Hence, let us note the sort of situation giving rise to this question:

The truth finds a couple in a marital relationship that cannot be legalized, and yet Christian baptism is desired by one or both of the parties. The declaration is a pledge of faithfulness to this marital relationship until such time as it becomes possible to legalize the union according to the law of the land. *The Watchtower* of March 15, 1977, page 183, suggested how the declaration might be worded and stated: "Such declaration is viewed as no less binding than one made before a marriage officer representing a 'Caesar' government of the world."—See Jesus' words at Matthew 22:21.

However, what is the situation if "Caesar" changes the divorce law, as recently happened in Italy? Since it is now possible to obtain a divorce from a previous mate, the baptized Christian living in a marital relationship as covered by the "Declaration Pledging Faithfulness" must immediately take steps, according to the declaration, "to obtain legal recognition of this relationship." The first step would be to obtain a divorce from the previous mate. The next step would be to have the marriage with the present mate legalized. Even if the present mate is an unbeliever, that one would need to consent to this legalizing of the marriage. If the unbeliever refused to do so, the Christian mate would have to separate in order to maintain an approved standing in the congregation. The reason for this is that the "Declaration Pledging Faithfulness" can no longer be recognized by the congregation as valid, because a way has now been opened up for legal marriage.

However, when that way opens up and the two actually do get married, such legal marriage is binding permanently, in contrast to the "Declaration Pledging Faithfulness," which was a solemn interim arrangement.

U.S. Postal Service
STATEMENT OF OWNERSHIP, MANAGEMENT AND CIRCULATION
Required by 39 U.S.C. 3685

1A. TITLE OF PUBLICATION	1B. PUBLICATION NO.	2. DATE OF FILING
THE WATCHTOWER	6 6 8 5 8 0	Sept. 2, 1985

3. FREQUENCY OF ISSUE	3A. NO. OF ISSUES PUBLISHED ANNUALLY	3B. ANNUAL SUBSCRIPTION PRICE
Semimonthly	24	$4.00

4. COMPLETE MAILING ADDRESS OF KNOWN OFFICE OF PUBLICATION *(Street, City, County, State and ZIP+4 Code) (Not printers)*
117 Adams Street, Brooklyn, Kings, New York 11201

5. COMPLETE MAILING ADDRESS OF THE HEADQUARTERS OF GENERAL BUSINESS OFFICES OF THE PUBLISHER *(Not printer)*
25 Columbia Heights, Brooklyn, New York 11201

6. FULL NAMES AND COMPLETE MAILING ADDRESS OF PUBLISHER, EDITOR, AND MANAGING EDITOR *(This item MUST NOT be blank)*
PUBLISHER *(Name and Complete Mailing Address)*
Watch Tower Bible and Tract Society of Pennsylvania
117 Adams Street, Brooklyn, New York 11201
EDITOR *(Name and Complete Mailing Address)*
Same as "Publisher"
MANAGING EDITOR *(Name and Complete Mailing Address)*
By corporation - Same as "Publisher"

7. OWNER *(If owned by a corporation, its name and address must be stated and also immediately thereunder the names and addresses of stockholders owning or holding 1 percent or more of total amount of stock. If not owned by a corporation, the names and addresses of the individual owners must be given. If owned by a partnership or other unincorporated firm, its name and address, as well as that of each individual must be given. If the publication is published by a nonprofit organization, its name and address must be stated.) (Item must be completed.)*

FULL NAME	COMPLETE MAILING ADDRESS
Watch Tower Bible and Tract Society of Pennsylvania	25 Columbia Heights Brooklyn, New York 11201
No stockholders	

8. KNOWN BONDHOLDERS, MORTGAGEES, AND OTHER SECURITY HOLDERS OWNING OR HOLDING 1 PERCENT OR MORE OF TOTAL AMOUNT OF BONDS, MORTGAGES OR OTHER SECURITIES *(If there are none, so state)*

FULL NAME	COMPLETE MAILING ADDRESS
None	

9. FOR COMPLETION BY NONPROFIT ORGANIZATIONS AUTHORIZED TO MAIL AT SPECIAL RATES *(Section 423.12 DMM only)*
The purpose, function, and nonprofit status of this organization and the exempt status for Federal income tax purposes *(Check one)*
(1) [X] HAS NOT CHANGED DURING PRECEDING 12 MONTHS
(2) HAS CHANGED DURING PRECEDING 12 MONTHS *(If changed, publisher must submit explanation of change with this statement.)*

10. EXTENT AND NATURE OF CIRCULATION *(See instructions on reverse side)*	AVERAGE NO. COPIES EACH ISSUE DURING PRECEDING 12 MONTHS	ACTUAL NO. COPIES OF SINGLE ISSUE PUBLISHED NEAREST TO FILING DATE
A. TOTAL NO. COPIES *(Net Press Run)*	4,448,466	4,338,075
B. PAID AND/OR REQUESTED CIRCULATION		
1. Sales through dealers and carriers, street vendors and counter sales	3,591,752	3,513,016
2. Mail Subscription *(Paid and/or requested)*	841,239	813,743
C. TOTAL PAID AND/OR REQUESTED CIRCULATION *(Sum of 10B1 and 10B2)*	4,432,991	4,326,759
D. FREE DISTRIBUTION BY MAIL, CARRIER OR OTHER MEANS SAMPLES, COMPLIMENTARY, AND OTHER FREE COPIES	1	0
E. TOTAL DISTRIBUTION *(Sum of C and D)*	4,432,992	4,326,759
F. COPIES NOT DISTRIBUTED		
1. Office use, left over, unaccounted, spoiled after printing	15,474	11,316
2. Return from News Agents	None	None
G. TOTAL *(Sum of E, F1 and 2—should equal net press run shown in A)*	4,448,466	4,338,075

11. I certify that the statements made by me above are correct and complete
SIGNATURE AND TITLE OF EDITOR, PUBLISHER, BUSINESS MANAGER, OR OWNER
Director

PS Form 3526, July 1984 *(See instruction on reverse)*

How This Marriage Was Saved

"The application of the counsel in the book *Making Your Family Life Happy* saved my marriage," wrote an appreciative reader from South Africa. "Chapter five, 'A Wife Who Is Dearly Loved,' opened my eyes. I never imagined in my wildest dreams that I could unwittingly cause so many problems. Thank you very, very much. My marriage had been in most stormy parts of the sea, and now, after months, it is back in the quiet harbour of happiness."

Making Your
FAMILY LIFE
Happy

November 15, 1985

The Watchtower

Announcing Jehovah's Kingdom

Why Pray for

GOD'S KINGDOM?

The Watchtower®
Announcing Jehovah's Kingdom

November 15, 1985
Vol. 106, No. 22

In This Issue

Cover photo credits, see page 4.

THE PURPOSE OF "THE WATCHTOWER" is to exalt Jehovah God as the Sovereign of the universe. It keeps watch on world events as they fulfill Bible prophecy. It comforts all peoples with the good news that God's Kingdom will soon destroy those who oppress their fellowmen and that it will turn the earth into a paradise. It encourages faith in the now-reigning King, Jesus Christ, whose shed blood opens the way for mankind to gain eternal life. "The Watchtower," published by Jehovah's Witnesses continuously since 1879, is nonpolitical. It adheres to the Bible as its authority.

"WATCHTOWER" STUDIES FOR THE WEEKS

December 15: Can You Prepare Now for Persecution? Page 11. Songs to Be Used: 125, 107.

December 22: Do Not Share in the Sins of Others. Page 18. Songs to Be Used: 41, 191.

December 29: Elders, Take Your Shepherding Responsibilities Seriously. Page 23. Songs to Be Used: 156, 184.

Average Printing Each Issue: 11,150,000

Now Published in 103 Languages

SEMIMONTHLY EDITIONS AVAILABLE BY MAIL
Afrikaans, Arabic, Cebuano, Chichewa, Chinese, Cibemba, Danish, Dutch,* Efik, English,* Finnish, French, German,* Greek, Hiligaynon, Igbo, Iloko, Italian,* Japanese,* Korean, Lingala, Malagasy, Maltese, Norwegian, Portuguese, Russian, Sepedi, Sesotho, Shona, Spanish,* Swahili, Swedish, Tagalog, Thai, Tswana, Xhosa, Yoruba, Zulu

MONTHLY EDITIONS AVAILABLE BY MAIL
Armenian, Bengali, Bicol, Bulgarian, Croatian, Czech, Ewe, Fijian, Ga, Greenlandic, Gujarati, Gun, Hausa, Hebrew, Hindi, Hiri Motu, Hungarian, Icelandic, Kannada, Kikuyu, Kiluba, Malayalam, Marathi, New Guinea Pidgin, Pangasinan, Papiamento, Polish, Rarotongan, Romanian, Samar-Leyte, Samoan, Sango, Serbian, Silozi, Sinhalese, Slovenian, Solomon Islands-Pidgin, Tahitian, Tamil, Telugu, Tshiluba, Tsonga, Turkish, Twi, Ukrainian, Urdu, Venda, Vietnamese
* Study articles also available in large-print edition.

The Bible translation used is the "New World Translation of the Holy Scriptures," unless otherwise indicated.

Twenty cents (U.S.) a copy

Watch Tower Society offices	Yearly subscription Semimonthly
America, U.S., Watchtower, Wallkill, N.Y. 12589	$4.00
Australia, Box 280, Ingleburn, N.S.W. 2565	A$7.00
Canada, Box 4100, Halton Hills (Georgetown), Ontario L7G 4Y4	$5.20
England, The Ridgeway, London NW7 1RN	£5.00
Ireland, 29A Jamestown Road, Finglas, Dublin 11	£5.00
New Zealand, 6-A Western Springs Rd., Auckland 3	$15.00
Nigeria, P.O. Box 194, Yaba, Lagos State	₦6.00
Philippines, P.O. Box 2044, Manila 2800	₱50.00
South Africa, Private Bag 2, Elandsfontein, 1406	R5,60

Remittances should be sent to the office in your country or to Watchtower, Wallkill, N.Y. 12589, U.S.A.

Changes of address should reach us 30 days before your moving date. Give us your old and new address (if possible, your old address label).

The Watchtower (ISSN 0043-1087) is published semimonthly for $4.00 (U.S.) per year by Watch Tower Bible and Tract Society of Pennsylvania, 25 Columbia Heights, Brooklyn, N.Y. 11201. Second-class postage paid at Brooklyn, N.Y., and at additional mailing offices.

Postmaster: Send address changes to Watchtower, **Wallkill, N.Y. 12589.**

Published by
Watch Tower Bible and Tract Society of Pennsylvania
25 Columbia Heights, Brooklyn, N.Y. 11201, U.S.A.
Frederick W. Franz, President

Why Pray for God's Kingdom?

"OUR FATHER in the heavens, let your name be sanctified. Let your kingdom come. Let your will take place, as in heaven, also upon earth."—Matthew 6: 9, 10.

For almost 2,000 years, faithful Christians have used these words as a model for their own prayers to God. First spoken by Jesus Christ, it is known as the Lord's Prayer, or the Our Father.

Today, however, many no longer pray the Lord's Prayer. Rather than looking to God's Kingdom, they look to human gov-ernments, economic systems, scientific methods, or the United Nations to provide hope for the future. Do you do that? If so, are you being realistic?

The Problems

Some people regard today's civilization as the most prosperous in history. But it is in a precarious situation. Many forces threaten the future of civilization, even the future of life itself on earth. Consider just some of these threatening forces.

Nuclear Weapons

The total strength of such weapons currently existing is equivalent to more than three tons of TNT for every man, woman, and child on earth. In an article entitled "The Bomb —Beyond Control?" Canadian journalist David Lancashire noted that "with the growing sophistication of the weapons has come an increasing chance of accidental war by computer error." And he quoted a United Nations study as follows: "History indicates that once a particular type of weapon has been developed past the testing stage, it will generally be used. This has not been true of nuclear weapons, with two exceptions [at Hiroshima and Nagasaki], but there can be no assurance that it will remain so."

U.S. National Archives

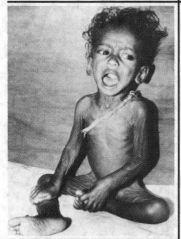

World Poverty

While some nations today have an extremely high standard of living, others are very, very poor. A writer in the magazine *New Scientist* felt that if the present inequalities continue, they will "inevitably lead to some sort of conflict." But even if they do not lead to conflict, these inequalities might bring disaster. How?

The poorer countries have huge debts. In 1981 correspondent John Madeley explained: "This has put the world banking and financial system nearer to the edge of a precipice than the banking world has previously wanted to admit. Unless there are immediate and fundamental reforms in the world economic system to give developing countries the chance to earn more, [there could be] even more defaults and reschedulings, setting off a chain reaction to collapse." (*World Press Review*) In various lands, the financial system remains in a precarious state.

WHO photo

Polluted Atmosphere

For a long time, mankind has been heedlessly pumping pollutants into the atmosphere. Now, according to the *Chicago Tribune,* "a growing number of scientists fear that, like a balloon stretched to the bursting point, the Earth's envelope of air has been pushed to the point where catastrophic changes may be in store. . . . Some of the disasters are already upon us and others are coming sooner than expected."

Polluted Water

Mankind has polluted the earth's water in various places. For instance, in the United States it is reported: "In Biscayne Bay, fish are turning into diseased monsters. In New Orleans, where 112 different chemicals have been found in the drinking water, the rate of cancer mortality is soaring. From coast to coast, people and animals alike are paying a fearful price for the continuing contamination of our fresh water, our sea water, and our tap water."—*New Times.*

These are just a few of the problems imperiling our future. Others include the depletion of energy sources, the population explosion, the destruction of forests, the spread of deserts, and the growing shortage of fresh water. It may be that *some* of the threats have been exaggerated. But do you honestly believe that all are exaggerations? And when considering all the problems, do you think that man has any chance of solving them? Yet if they are not solved, what future is there for the human race? And why are we plagued with so many seemingly insoluble problems?

Why the Problems?

Well, these problems demonstrate a basic truth: Man really cannot govern himself successfully. No human ruler has ever had the wisdom, the altruism, or the power to govern for the greatest good of everyone. The Bible tells us: "To earthling man his way does not belong. It does not belong to man who is walking even to direct his step." (Jeremiah 10:23) Man was not made to rule himself.

There is also another factor, one that many find it difficult to accept in this materialistic age. Rulership of mankind does not involve only humans. When Jesus was on earth, a superhuman creature, Satan, offered him rulership of all the kingdoms of the world. And later Jesus' follower Paul called Satan "the god of this system of things." (2 Corinthians 4:4; Matthew 4:8, 9) How can Satan be the ruler of this world, when so many no longer believe in him? Because most people —even if unknowingly—do not accept God's rulership and hence are furthering Satan's designs.—Matthew 12:30.

Satan's situation has worsened since Jesus' day. The Bible reveals that today Satan has "great anger, knowing he has a short period of time." (Revelation 12:12) Like Hitler at the end of the last world war, Satan is now desperate in his resolve to "rule or ruin." Since his long rule has been so unsuccessful, Satan the Devil is now clearly bent on ruining the human race. Is it not sobering to know that such a malevolent, powerful force exists? Especially is that so when we remember that all those stockpiled nuclear weapons seem to be "beyond [human] control"! But what does all of this have to do with God's Kingdom?

We Need the Kingdom

Since our problems are caused by man's inability to rule himself, and also by the baleful influence of a superhuman power, their solution clearly lies outside the human race. This is why we desperately need God's Kingdom. This Kingdom is a real government. But it is superhuman, heavenly, and has the power to overcome Satan. Being God's Kingdom, it also has the wisdom, altruism, and authority to make right decisions and rule successfully.

Hence, we can be happy that the Bible tells us: "In the days of those kings [modern-day rulers] the God of heaven will set up a kingdom that will never be brought to ruin. And the kingdom itself will not be passed on to any other people. It will crush and put an end to all these kingdoms, and it itself will stand to times indefinite." (Daniel 2:44) The King of that Kingdom is Jesus Christ, of whom it was said prophetically: "In his days the righteous one will sprout, and the abundance of peace until the moon is no more. And he will have subjects from sea to sea and from the River to the ends of the earth." —Psalm 72:7, 8.

Yes, God's Kingdom will solve mankind's problems. So why not search the Bible to find out what this Kingdom is and how you can even now be a subject of it. You, and all others of mankind, truly need this Kingdom. Jehovah's Witnesses stand ready to help you to learn about it.

Why Clothe Ourselves With Mildness?

IT IS admired and appreciated. It helps us to avoid strife. It is often mistaken for weakness, but it has far greater strength than steel. That is mildness!

In the Bible, mildness is associated with humility, meekness. The Greek term for it denotes meekness, 'mild and gentle friendliness; the opposite of roughness, bad temper, sudden anger, and brusqueness.' Yet, mildness is more readily demonstrated by actions than defined by words.

But why clothe ourselves with mildness? And how can it help us?

Why So Important

Christians should display mildness because this pleases Jehovah God. The Bible counsels us to walk "with complete lowliness of mind and mildness." Christian women are to put on "the incorruptible apparel of the quiet and mild spirit, which is of great value in the eyes of God." (Ephesians 4:1-3; 1 Peter 3:3, 4) And the apostle Paul fittingly urges fellow believers: "As God's chosen ones, holy and loved, clothe yourselves with the tender affections of compassion, kindness, lowliness of mind, *mildness,* and longsuffering."—Colossians 3:12.

Being clothed with mildness is beneficial because this protective covering can shield us from harm. By being clothed with mildness when a potentially explosive situation develops, we may be able to defuse the anger of the offended person and achieve peace. Indeed, "an answer, when mild, turns away rage." (Proverbs 15:1) Moreover, mildness helps us to cope with irksome everyday problems, relieves tense situations at work or in school, promotes peace and unity, and enables us to lead calmer, healthier, and happier lives. (Proverbs 14:30) So there are good reasons to clothe ourselves with mildness.

How It Can Be Done

Displaying mildness may seem difficult, but we can manifest this quality if that is our desire. Why? Well, for one thing, God created us in his image. (Genesis 1:26) Jehovah exemplifies mildness. His mildness is evident in the way he deals with sinful mankind. "He has not done to us even according to our sins; nor according to our errors has he brought upon us what we deserve."—Psalm 103:10.

Mildness is part of the fruitage of God's holy spirit. (Galatians 5:22, 23) If we sense a personal need for mildness, then, we can pray for the holy spirit that will help us to cultivate and display a mild attitude and manner.—Luke 11:13.

Since mildness is a product of God's spirit, it is an essential feature of the Christian personality. In effect, it must be part of the clothing that identifies us as Christians. Yes, we can and should 'clothe ourselves with mildness,' an endowment from Jehovah resulting from his spirit and blessing.

Mildness Is Practical

Jesus Christ, who is firm for righteousness, nevertheless displays mildness. He

pronounced mild-tempered ones happy. Jesus also taught the principle of 'turning the other cheek,' of not retaliating under provocation. (Matthew 5:5, 39; 21:5) Some say that this is impractical in today's competitive world. But it is a mistake to conclude that Christian mildness denotes cowardice or weakness of personality. Such mildness is blended with strong faith, love for Jehovah, and appreciation for his righteous ways. Hence, it has great strength.

Throughout Biblical history, God-fearing men and women provided fine examples of mildness. For instance, "Moses was by far the meekest [the most mild-tempered] of all the men who were upon the surface of the ground." (Numbers 12:3) But who would say that he had a weak personality or was a coward?

When contrasted with "the works of the flesh," mildness proves superior. (Gala-tians 5:19-23) For example, mildness is practical when contrasted with uncontrolled anger. The Roman poet Horace observed: "Anger is momentary madness, so control your passion or it will control you."

Acting "with a mildness that belongs to wisdom" means conducting ourselves in harmony with Jehovah's personality, dealings, and ways. (James 3:13) For instance, a man who qualifies to teach fellow believers needs to be gentle, peaceful, and calm, not harsh, arrogant, and opinionated. (1 Timothy 1:6, 7; 2 Timothy 2:24, 25) But mildness can also be of great help to us in other aspects of life.

How Mildness Helps in Daily Life

Mildness can help us if problems should arise with neighbors. It worked for Cathy. During a picnic with some friends at her home, one of the children climbed up on a neighbor's neat stack of firewood. The child tipped over part of the woodpile just as the neighbor was looking out his window. Infuriated, he charged outside, upbraiding the host family, the offending boy, and his parents. Instead of arguing, however, the hosts did what they could to allay their irate neighbor's anger. They answered in mildness. The next day, Cathy baked bread for her family and made two extra loaves for the neighbor and his wife. Well, this gesture of human kindness, without a word about the incident that had been handled with mildness, was all that was needed to ease the tension and restore good relations.

It has been said that a good supervisor takes less than his share of the credit when things go right and more than his share of the blame when things go wrong. Don, who directs a construction crew, follows that mild policy. It works for him. On one occasion the supervisor of a construction project became upset because of the way something was built. He demanded: "Who is responsible for this?" Although another worker had not followed Don's orders, Don answered: "It was my fault. I did not explain it clearly enough for my men to understand how it should be built." On the other hand, when others praise Don for a construction job well done, he responds: "These men deserve the credit." Because of Don's mild manner and strength of personality, he is loved and respected by his superiors and his men.

In Our Next Issue

- Are You Right With God?

- Do You Honor Jehovah With Your Valuable Things?

- 'Seek First the Kingdom' —Our Family Goal

These same principles apply when Jehovah's Witnesses visit their neighbors while engaging in the field ministry. Some people do not appreciate these visits and may even become angry. Yet, mildness helps the visiting Witnesses to avoid imputing bad motives to the householders or judging them harshly. Although Jehovah's Witnesses have good motives, did the call interrupt something the householder was enjoying? Did it wake him up? Mildness makes it possible to deal with such situations considerately.—1 Peter 3:15.

Similarly, if a person 'takes a false step before he is aware of it,' mildness helps Christian elders to maintain balance while counseling him. Their purpose is not to punish such a man but to "readjust" him, as when a doctor gently readjusts a bone that is out of joint. Indeed, those having spiritual qualifications must never forget that they should try to readjust the erring person "in a spirit of mildness."—Galatians 6:1.

Continue Pursuing Mildness

The quality of mildness may be likened to soil in which other fruits of God's spirit are more easily cultivated and maintained. If we are mild-tempered, we will readily yield to the guidance of Jehovah's spirit. And if we display mildness, God will bless us, for he loves the meek and mild-tempered.—Isaiah 29:18-21; 61:1.

People flocked to Jesus because he was "mild-tempered and lowly in heart." (Matthew 11:28, 29) That kind of disposition attracts honest-hearted people just as an inn with a glowing fireplace beckons weary travelers on a chilly night. A meek, mild person surely is a desirable associate. How fitting, then, that we pursue "mildness of temper"! (1 Timothy 6:11) Yes, let us clothe ourselves with mildness.

A New Theocratic Milestone in Korea

KEEPING pace with the rest of the world, the Kingdom-preaching work in Korea is moving forward by leaps and bounds. Just three years, almost to the day, after the branch building in Kongdo, Korea, was inaugurated, a new addition was dedicated on May 11, 1985.* It was another milestone in the theocratic history of Jehovah's Witnesses in Korea.

As seen in the picture, the new addition consists of a third floor on the office (the right section in the picture), two additional floors on the factory (the middle section), and an adjoining three-story Bethel home (the entire left section). The structures in the background are the existing Bethel home.

___
* For a report on the May 8, 1982, dedication, please see *The Watchtower* of September 15, 1982, pages 26-8.

But why the addition so soon? In 1982, when the new factory first went into operation, it was producing 380,000 *Watchtower* and *Awake!* magazines each month. This has now doubled to 760,000 each month. Clearly, the added factory space will be put to good use. To care for the increased production, there are now 86 staff members serving at the branch headquarters. The new home can more than accommodate the increase; there is now enough room for 120 members.

A. D. Schroeder, a member of the Governing Body of Jehovah's Witnesses in Brooklyn, New York, was on hand for the dedication program. Members of the Korean Branch Committee reported on the work in the field and gave details of the construction. All 2,199 present were filled with heartfelt thanks to Jehovah for his rich blessing.

Insight on the News

Argentina's Silent Church

"Blood taints church in Argentina," read the headline of the *National Catholic Reporter* of April 12, 1985. Incredibly, an estimated 10,000 to 30,000 citizens were abducted and killed without trial under Argentina's previous military government. Yet observers say that thousands of innocent lives could have been spared if the Catholic Church had protested. Instead, states the report, "the Argentine church—with a few heroic exceptions—was volubly silent throughout the seven-year terror," which ended when a civilian government took power in 1983. Worse, some members of the hierarchy collaborated with the military regime.

Why was the church silent? In part, because of fear of reprisals. But the newspaper cites another reason: "The episcopacy also embraced the military as a source of power." It was granted many privileges. Concludes the report: "The Argentine experience so closely resembles the performance of the Catholic church in Nazi Germany, it again raises the question of whether power is more important to the church than the Gospel imperative to be a witness to the truth."

This shows the folly of religion's currying the favor of political powers. It can lead to a compromise of principles. Interestingly, the book of Revelation condemns the linkage of Church and State when it describes the world empire of false religion as a harlot "with whom the kings of the earth committed fornication." (Revelation 17:2) No wonder Jesus told his followers that they were to be "no part of the world." —John 15:19.

"Inability to Feed Itself"

"It is impossible to travel in Africa today without being overwhelmed by military images," says the *Bulletin of the Atomic Scientists*. But the drain of money and manpower to sustain these armies contributes to famine, particularly when war breaks out. The *Bulletin* gives some examples: "In Ethiopia, Chad, Mozambique, Angola, the Sudan, and Uganda serious and often prolonged insurgencies, wars, or border conflicts have damaged infrastructure, destroyed crops, and deepened human suffering." States the report: "On a continent with such severe problems, including a fundamental inability to feed itself, the diversion of vast sums and significant manpower for military purposes is tragic."

Tragic indeed! Fittingly, the book of Revelation portrays these conditions symbolically. It describes a sword-wielding horseman on a fiery-colored horse, who "was granted to take peace away from the earth" by warfare. Then, immediately following, came a black horse with its rider announcing famine. (Revelation 6:3-6) The combination of war and famine in Africa is one example of this prophecy's fulfillment in our day. —See also Matthew 24:6-8.

"A Life of Drudgery"

"The traditional image of millionaires cavorting on the beaches of St Tropez, basking on the slopes of Aspen, driving their Cadillac or Rolls-Royce to the races or simply chewing a good cigar, is far from reality." So says *The Guardian Weekly* in a report of a recent study by Dr. Thomas Stanley of Georgia State University. "America's average millionaire is more than likely to live a life of drudgery." Why? Because he works longer hours than other people—typically 75 hours a week. "Most of the country's rich are simply ordinary small businessmen leading humdrum, hard lives." They save up money for retirement. But due to their exhausting work schedules, many die before they get to retire. Such men have little time for life's pleasures.

In contrast, a wise man of ancient times recommended: "Every man should eat and indeed drink and see good for all his hard work. It is the gift of God." (Ecclesiastes 3:12, 13) Instead of being drudgery, a man's work should be satisfying, enabling him to enjoy the wholesome, simple things that God provides. Wisely, then, true Christians shun the empty quest for wealth. They know that real contentment comes by 'storing up treasures in heaven, not on earth.'—Matthew 6: 19, 20.

Can You Prepare Now for Persecution?

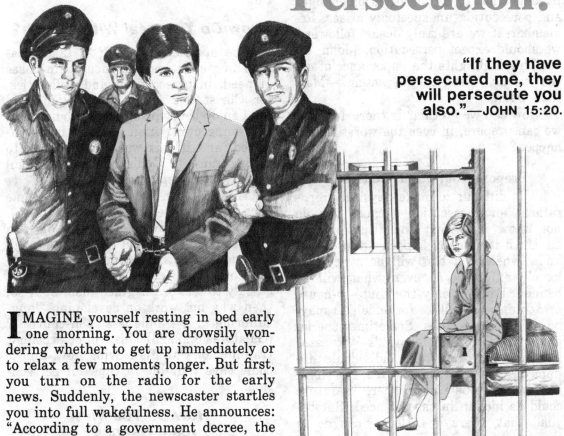

"If they have persecuted me, they will persecute you also."—JOHN 15:20.

IMAGINE yourself resting in bed early one morning. You are drowsily wondering whether to get up immediately or to relax a few moments longer. But first, you turn on the radio for the early news. Suddenly, the newscaster startles you into full wakefulness. He announces: "According to a government decree, the sect known as Jehovah's Witnesses has been banned throughout the country." No more relaxing for you!

² This, or something like it, has been the experience of Christians in some countries in modern times. Often, there have been warnings of what might happen. But sometimes the ban has been completely unexpected. Should this surprise us?

1, 2. What unexpected action have some governments taken against Jehovah's Witnesses?

³ Not really. Similar things happened in the first century. Remember how Jesus Christ, in the early spring of 33 C.E., rode into Jerusalem on an ass. The people joyfully acclaimed him, spreading their garments on the road ahead of him. But what happened a few days later? Jesus

---

3. What contrasting experiences did Jesus Christ have in 33 C.E.?

was on trial before Pontius Pilate, and a mob from that same city bloodthirstily yelled: "Let him be impaled! . . . Let him be impaled!" (Matthew 21:6-9; 27:22, 23) The situation had changed suddenly.

4 Hence, we should not be surprised if in some lands today the situation changes and persecution unexpectedly arises. Remember, if we are truly Jesus' followers, we should expect persecution. (John 15: 20) This highlights the importance of Jesus' words, "Keep on the watch."—Matthew 24:42.

5 How can we do this? Is there any way we can prepare, in case the worst should happen?

Prepare Your Mind and Heart

6 It is difficult to make physical preparations for persecution because you do not know just what the situation will be. Until it actually happens, you do not know whether a ban will be strictly or loosely enforced, or even what will be banned. Perhaps only the house-to-house preaching work will be forbidden, or maybe religious meetings. Sometimes the legal organization of Jehovah's Witnesses is dissolved, or certain individuals are immediately imprisoned. We can have in mind various places where literature could be hidden in case of need. But beyond that, there is little we can do in the way of physical preparation.

7 However, you *can* prepare your mind and heart, and this is far more important. Set your mind on why persecution is permitted and why you may be haled before

rulers. "For a witness," said Jesus. (Matthew 10:16-19) If your heart is fully prepared to stay faithful no matter what, Jehovah can reveal the wise way to act when the need arises. Hence, how can we prepare ourselves *spiritually* for persecution?

How Do You Deal With People?

8 The apostle Paul said: "I take pleasure in weaknesses, in insults, in cases of need, in persecutions and difficulties, for Christ." (2 Corinthians 12:10) Did Paul enjoy being insulted? Of course not. But persecution often involves being insulted, and if this was what it took to bring praise to God's name, then Paul was happy to endure it.

9 We, too, can be sure that at some time we will have to endure "insults . . . for Christ." We may be verbally, or even physically, abused. Will we endure? Well, how do we view ourselves now? Do we take ourselves very seriously and react quickly to real or imagined insults? If so, then why not work on developing "long-suffering, . . . mildness, self-control"? (Galatians 5:22, 23) This will be excellent training for Christian living now, and it could save your life in times of persecution.

How Do You View Field Service?

10 Often, the first thing restricted under a ban is the public preaching of the "good news." Yet preaching and disciple making are vital in these last days. How else will people learn about God's Kingdom?

---

4. As Jesus' followers, what treatment should we expect?
5. What questions now merit our consideration?
6, 7. (a) Why is it difficult to make physical preparations for persecution? (b) What far more important preparation for persecution can be made?

8. Why could Paul say that he 'took pleasure in insults'?
9. How can we now prepare to endure "insults . . . for Christ"?
10. What is the proper Scriptural reaction when our preaching work is banned?

Hence, the proper reaction to such a ban is the one expressed by the apostles, when the Jewish religious leaders tried to ban their preaching activity. (Acts 5:28, 29) Under ban, some avenues of preaching may be closed. But, somehow, the work has to be done. Would you have the strength to continue preaching under the pressure of persecution?

11 Well, how do you view the preaching work now? Do you permit small obstacles to interfere and make you irregular in the field service? If so, what would you do under a ban? Do you fear men now? Are you willing to preach from house to house on your own street? Are you afraid to work alone? In some lands, two people working together often draw too much attention. So, where it is safe to do so, why not work alone now from time to time? It will be good training.

12 Do you share in magazine street work? Do you have the courage and initiative to create opportunities for informal witnessing? Do you work business territories? Are you afraid to approach wealthy or influential people? If you only share in certain kinds of preaching, what will you do if, under ban, that kind of preaching is no longer possible?

13 Do you recognize that you have a weakness in some respect? Now is the time to work on it. Learn to rely on Jehovah and become more qualified as a minister. Then you will be better equipped to preach now and better prepared to persevere in times of persecution.

___

11, 12. How might you determine whether you would have the strength needed to continue preaching when persecuted?
13. What can you now do about your ministry so as to be better prepared to preach in times of persecution?

Are You Reliable?

14 Throughout the Christian Greek Scriptures, individuals are mentioned who were towers of strength in the congregation. For example, Onesiphorus courageously helped Paul when he was in prison in Rome. (2 Timothy 1:16) Phoebe was recommended because of her hard work in the congregation at Cenchreae. (Romans 16:1, 2) Such men and women must have been a fine stabilizing influence when persecution broke out. They 'stayed awake, stood firm in the faith, carried on as men, grew mighty.'—1 Corinthians 16:13.

15 All Christians, particularly elders, should try to make progress and become like the strong early Christians. (1 Timothy 4:15) Learn to keep confidential matters private and to make decisions based on Scriptural principles. Train yourself to discern Christian qualities in others so that you will know who will be reliable under pressure. Work, with Jehovah's strength, to become a pillar in your congregation, a person who helps others rather than one who always needs help. —Galatians 6:5.

How Do You Get Along With People?

16 The apostle Paul encouraged us: "Clothe yourselves with the tender affections of compassion, kindness, lowliness of mind, mildness, and long-suffering. Continue putting up with one another and forgiving one another freely." (Colossians 3:12, 13) Is this easy for you?

___

14, 15. (a) What kind of first-century Christians must have been a fine stabilizing influence when persecution broke out? (b) How can a present-day servant of Jehovah become like those strong early Christians?
16, 17. How can applying Colossians 3:12, 13 now help you to prepare for persecution?

Or do other people's imperfections irritate you unduly? Do you quickly take offense or get discouraged? If so, here is another field where preparation can be made.

¹⁷ In lands where meetings are banned, Christians regularly come together in small numbers. In such circumstances, their shortcomings become even more evident. So why not train yourself now to put up with others' weaknesses, just as they doubtless are putting up with yours? Do not be critical of others and thus greatly discourage them. Also, train yourself and your children to respect other people's property while attending Congregation Book Studies. Under persecution, such respect will promote peaceful relations.

Are You Inquisitive?

¹⁸ By nature, some of us are very inquisitive. We cannot bear not being "in the know." Are you like that? If so, consider this: Sometimes, when the work of Jehovah's Witnesses has been banned, the authorities try to discover their organizational arrangements and the names of responsible overseers. If you were one who knew these things, you could be subjected to physical abuse in an effort to force you to reveal them. And if you *did* reveal them, the work of your brothers could be seriously affected. Hence, sometimes it is safer to know only as much as you need to know and no more.

¹⁹ Can you train for that now? Yes. For example, if there is a judicial committee case in the congregation, individuals should be satisfied with whatever the elders see fit to say and not pry in order to find out any details. Wives and chil-

dren of elders should not try to pressure them into revealing confidential matters. In every way, we should learn not to 'meddle in what does not concern us.' —2 Thessalonians 3:11.

Are You a Bible Student?

²⁰ The Bible is the basis for a Christian's spiritual strength. It gives him answers to his most important questions and grants access to the wisdom of God himself. (2 Timothy 3:14-16) All Christians acknowledge this in principle, but what part does the Bible *really* play in your life? Do you study it regularly and allow it to guide you in everything you do?—Psalm 119:105.

²¹ Often, access to our Bible literature is severely restricted when the work is banned. Sometimes, even Bibles are hard to find. Under such circumstances, the holy spirit will remind you of things you have learned in times past. But it will not remind you of things you have not learned! Therefore, the more you study now, the more will be stored in your mind and heart for the holy spirit to bring out in times of need.—Mark 13:11.

Do You Pray?

²² This is an important question when we think of persecution. The Bible counsels: "Persevere in prayer." (Romans 12: 12) Prayer is direct communication with Jehovah God. Through it we can ask for the strength to endure difficulties and make right decisions, as well as build a personal relationship with Jehovah God. Even if opposers take away our literature, our Bibles, and our association with other Christians, they can never take away our

---

18. Why is it sometimes safer to know only what you need to know?
19. What can now help you to avoid revealing confidential matters when persecuted?

20, 21. How will diligent Bible study now help you if the work is banned?
22. How can 'persevering in prayer' prove helpful in preparing for persecution?

privilege of prayer. In the strongest prison, a Christian can get in touch with God. Taking full advantage of the privilege of prayer, then, is a fine way to prepare for whatever the future may hold.

Do You Trust Authority?

23 Building up this trust is also important. The elders in the congregation are a part of God's provision to protect us. Elders need to act in a way that deserves trust, and the rest of the congregation needs to learn to give them their trust. (Isaiah 32:1, 2; Hebrews 13:7, 17) Even more important, we should learn to trust "the faithful and discreet slave."—Matthew 24:45-47.

24 Enemies may spread lies about God's organization. (1 Timothy 4:1, 2) In one country, some Christians were misled to believe that the Governing Body of Jehovah's Witnesses had forsaken Christianity, whereas they themselves were still remaining faithful to it. A good way to prepare to resist attacks like this is to build a strong love for your brothers and learn to trust in Jehovah's arrangement of things.—1 John 3:11.

You Can Be Victorious

25 The aged apostle John, after suffering persecution, told us: "Everything that has been born from God conquers the world. And this is the conquest that has conquered the world, our faith." (1 John 5:4) You cannot conquer in your own strength. Satan and his world are stronger than you are. But they are not stronger than Jehovah God. Hence, if we obey God's commands, praying for his spirit

23. Why build up trust in the appointed elders and in "the faithful and discreet slave"?
24. What can be done to prepare to resist lying attacks by enemies of Jehovah's people?
25. What will help us to come off victorious when persecuted?

to uphold us and relying on him completely for strength to endure, then we can come off victorious.—Habakkuk 3: 13, 18; Revelation 15:2; 1 Corinthians 15:57.

26 In all lands, there are some Christians being persecuted, either by opposed marriage mates or in some other way. In some lands, all of God's servants are suffering because of the official acts of the local government. But even if, right now, you personally are not suffering opposition or unusual hardship, remember that it could happen at any time. Jesus said that persecution of Christians would be a part of the sign of the time of the end; hence, we should always expect it. (Matthew 24:9) So why not prepare for it now? Be determined that, whatever may lie ahead, your conduct will always bring praise to your heavenly Father, Jehovah God.—Proverbs 27:11.

26. Even if you are not now suffering persecution, what should you do?

What Are Your Answers?

☐ What kind of preparations for persecution can you now make?

☐ What can you now do to develop the strength needed to continue preaching when persecuted?

☐ How can applying Colossians 3: 12, 13 now be helpful when persecution occurs?

☐ Why build up your trust in the appointed elders and "the faithful and discreet slave"?

☐ How can you be a victor when persecuted?

Zeal for Jehovah's Worship

AFTER attending the wedding in Cana, Jesus travels to Capernaum, a city near the Sea of Galilee. With him are his disciples, his mother, and his brothers, who are James, Joseph, Simon, and Judas. Before making this trip, however, they may have stopped first at Jesus' home in Nazareth so that the family could pack the things they would need.

But why does Jesus go to Capernaum, rather than carry on his ministry in Cana, in Nazareth, or in some other place in the hills of Galilee? For one thing, Capernaum is more prominently situated and is evidently a larger city. Also, most of Jesus' newly acquired disciples live in or near Capernaum, so they will not have to leave their homes to receive training from him.

During his stay in Capernaum, Jesus performs marvelous works, as he himself testifies some months later. But soon Jesus and his companions are on the road again. It is spring, and they are on their way to Jerusalem to attend the Passover of 30 C.E. While there, his disciples see something about Jesus that they have perhaps not seen before.

According to God's Law, Israelites are required to make animal sacrifices. So, for their convenience,

merchants in Jerusalem sell animals or birds for this purpose. But they are selling right inside the temple, and they are cheating the people by charging them too much.

Filled with indignation, Jesus makes a whip of ropes and drives the sellers out. He pours out the coins of the money changers and overturns their tables. "Take these things away from here!" he cries out to those selling the doves. "Stop making the house of my Father a house of merchandise!"

When Jesus' disciples see this, they remember the prophecy about God's Son: "The zeal for your house will eat me up." But the Jews ask: "What sign have you to show us, since you are doing these things?" Jesus answers: "Break down this temple, and in three days I will raise it up."

The Jews assume that Jesus is talking about the literal temple, but he is talking about the temple of his body. And three years later his disciples remember this saying of his when he is raised from the dead. **John 2:12-22; Matthew 13:55; Luke 4:23.**

♦ After the wedding in Cana, to what places does Jesus travel?

♦ Why is Jesus indignant, and what does he do?

♦ What do Jesus' disciples recall on seeing his actions?

♦ What did Jesus say about "this temple," and what did he mean?

Do Not Share in the Sins of Others

"I have not sat with men of untruth; and with those who hide what they are I do not come in."—PSALM 26:4.

NINETEEN centuries ago, the disciple Jude had intended to write fellow believers about 'the salvation they held in common.' But he found it necessary to urge them to "put up a hard fight for the faith that was once for all time delivered to the holy ones." Why? Because certain "ungodly men" had slipped into the congregation and were "turning the undeserved kindness of our God into an excuse for loose conduct."—Jude 3, 4.

² How refreshing to discuss salvation held in common! Meditating on that message brings great satisfaction, and we rejoice when anticipating all the blessings of that salvation. Nevertheless, there are times when, rather than speaking about salvation, we are faced with the need to consider other serious matters. If not corrected, these can tear down our faith and cause us to lose out in the race for life. Even as Jude's warning against wrong conduct was strong and forceful, so Christians today must at times prayerfully consider Scriptural counsel that is direct, very much to the point.

Our Own Sins

³ The psalmist David said: "With error I was brought forth with birth pains, and in sin my mother conceived me." (Psalm 51:5) All of us have been born as sinners. (Romans 5:12) The apostle John wrote: "If we make the statement: 'We have no sin,' we are misleading ourselves and the truth is not in us." (1 John 1:8) As sinners, there are times when we need discipline so as to correct our course. Such discipline comes from Jehovah through his Word, the Bible, and his organization. His discipline corrects us and helps us to walk in uprightness before him. As the apostle Paul observed: "True, no discipline seems for the present to be joyous, but grievous; yet afterward to those who have been trained by it it yields peaceable fruit, namely, righteousness." (Hebrews 12:11) In view of the peaceable fruit of such discipline, we surely should receive it with gratitude.

⁴ Discipline from Jehovah may be given when we are just starting on a course that could lead to greater wrongdoing. (Galatians 6:1) At other times, the discipline may come after we have more fully entered into a wrong course. Such discipline may have to be severe, as when the apostle Paul strongly urged the Corinthians to take action against a fornicator in the congregation. (1 Corinthians 5:1-5) In either case, the discipline is given so that the wrongdoer might repent, turn around, and steer a steady course away from the

1. Why did Jude change his purpose in writing to fellow Christians?
2. Although it is refreshing to discuss salvation, at times what must we consider prayerfully?
3. Why do we need discipline, and how should it be received?

4. When may discipline be given, and what may be the effect of it?

sinful desires leading into serious wrong-doing. (Compare Acts 3:19.) Servants of Jehovah are grateful for such discipline, even as the rebuked individual in ancient Corinth benefited and apparently was restored to loving association with the congregation.—2 Corinthians 2:5-8.

⁵ The vast majority of those dedicated to Jehovah are very much aware of the need to walk in an upright manner before God. If they should become involved in serious sin, they quickly turn away from the bad course, go to the appointed elders, and give evidence of genuine repentance. (James 5:13-16) The fact that relatively few of Jehovah's Witnesses are disfellowshipped each year is evidence that they hate what is bad and desire to do what is good.—Psalm 34:14; 45:7.

The Sins of Others

⁶ Yet some who apparently love what is right seem to have allowed their hearts to deceive them, for they do not appear to hate what is bad. (Psalm 97:10; Amos 5:15) As a result, they get involved in doing sinful things and do not maintain the fight to do what is right. At times, they may go even further, seeking to involve others in their sinful course. How important that we reject such suggestions!—Compare Proverbs 1:10-15.

⁷ Sometimes those who apparently do not hate what is bad talk so smoothly that a yearning to do what is wrong may develop in the hearts of those listening to them. The encouragement may be to engage in immorality or in some action bordering on conduct disapproved by God. Or a person may be urged to become involved in a situation that is potentially dangerous in a spiritual way. Those thus trying to per-suade others may claim that Jehovah is a loving God who will be merciful when we sin. Such treachery of the heart can cause lasting damage. (Jeremiah 17:9; Jude 4) Surely, we should 'hold back our foot from their roadway'!—Proverbs 1:15.

Sharing in the Sins of Others

⁸ But suppose we realize that a suggested course of action is wrong? Does our rejecting it necessarily free us of further responsibility in the matter? If we know that those suggesting wrongdoing are engaging in it, what should we do?

⁹ Some who have knowledge of wrongdoing by others may be inclined to say nothing about it to those having the prime responsibility to keep the congregation clean. Why? Perhaps they do not want to be viewed as informers. Or, because of a false sense of loyalty, they may keep the matter quiet or may speak only to those who promise to keep it secret. This is very serious. Why? Because it can actually result in sharing in the sins of others.

¹⁰ The apostle John showed that it is possible to share in another person's sin. He wrote: "Everyone that pushes ahead and does not remain in the teaching of the Christ does not have God. . . . If anyone comes to you and does not bring this teaching, never receive him into your homes or say a greeting to him. For he that says a greeting to him is a sharer in his wicked works." (2 John 9-11) An apostate from "the teaching of the Christ" would not be a worthy associate, and by not even greeting him, the loyal Christian would avoid being a sharer in his wickedness.

---

5. Christians who become involved in serious sin usually do what?
6, 7. How do some wrongdoers try to influence others?

8. What questions require consideration?
9. Why may some fail to report wrongdoing by others, but why is this a serious matter?
10, 11. (a) What did the apostle John say about sharing in the sins of others? (b) If we have learned of wrongdoing by a member of the congregation, what might we ask ourselves?

The apostle John warned against sharing in the sins of others

¹¹ Since that is the case with an apostate, surely we would not want to become sharers in the wickedness of others whose immoral acts come to our attention. What, then, if we know that a member of the congregation has become a thief or a drunkard? If we fail to encourage that individual to seek Jehovah's forgiveness and confess his sin to the elders, are we entirely blameless? No, for we have a serious responsibility.

Cleanness and Protection Vital

¹² We must individually show concern for the spiritual cleanness of the congregation. How well this was emphasized when Jewish exiles were about to leave Babylon in the sixth century B.C.E.! The God-given command was: "Turn away, turn away, get out of there, touch nothing unclean; get out from the midst of [Babylon], keep yourselves clean, you who are carrying the utensils of Jehovah."—Isaiah 52:11.

---

12. Why show concern for the spiritual cleanness of the congregation?

¹³ We must also be concerned about protecting Jehovah's people from those who would seek to entice them into wrongdoing. The "ungodly men" of Jude's day sought to 'turn the undeserved kindness of God into an excuse for loose conduct,' but that loyal disciple acted to warn fellow believers and thus protect them. He reminded them of warning examples provided by unfaithful Israelites, the disobedient angels, and others. Read his divinely inspired letter, and you will see that loyal Christians cannot sit idly by when the cleanness of the congregation is threatened or God's people need protection from immoral persons having unclean motives.

¹⁴ Yet, suppose we have encouraged a wrongdoer to seek God's forgiveness and confess to the elders, but he keeps putting this off or sees no need to take these steps. Can we just drop the matter? Some might reason that they do not want to become involved. They may not want to risk losing the friendship of the erring one. And they may not want to be thought of as persons who betray a confidence by telling the elders. But this is faulty reasoning. The psalmist David said: "I have not sat with men of untruth; and with those who hide what they are I do not come in." (Psalm 26:4) Surely, then, we would not want to become accomplices of "those who hide what they are."

¹⁵ Therefore, after we have given the erring individual a reasonable amount of time to approach the elders about his wrongdoing, it is our responsibility before Jehovah not to be a sharer in his sin. We

---

13. How did Jude show that we must be concerned about protecting Jehovah's people from wrongdoers?
14. If a wrongdoer fails to confess to the elders, how can Psalm 26:4 help us to decide what to do?
15. How does Leviticus 5:1 show our responsibility after giving an erring individual a reasonable amount of time to approach the elders about his wrongdoing?

need to inform the responsible overseers that the person has revealed serious wrongdoing that merits their investigation. This would be in harmony with Leviticus 5:1, which says: "Now in case a soul sins in that he has heard public cursing and he is a witness or he has seen it or has come to know of it, if he does not report it, then he must answer for his error." Of course, we must avoid acting hastily on mere supposition of wrongdoing.

¹⁶ In today's world, covering over the wrongdoing of others is a general practice. Many are as mute as a stone wall when it comes to revealing the wrongdoing of others to those who should know about such actions. It requires strength of Christian personality to inform appointed elders of the serious sin of a fellow believer. But if we are to have Jehovah's favor, we must not let personal friendship blind us to the wrongdoing of another individual. Our relationship with God is of far greater importance than loyalty to a friend who is guilty of serious wrongdoing and refuses to reveal the matter to the appointed elders.

A Problem for All to Consider

¹⁷ The problem of sharing in the sins of others sometimes exists among certain youths in our midst. They may remain silent and refuse to tell those who should be informed when others do things that could detrimentally affect the congregation and could result in Jehovah's disfavor. Covering over the wrongdoing of others is quite common in the worldly school systems. But when this viewpoint spreads to the congregation, many problems may result. There have even been reports of young ones banding together to engage in wrong conduct while swearing one another to secrecy so that elders and parents will not learn about such activity. Yielding to pressure from peers and a desire to be accepted by the group has caused much heartache for these youths, their parents, and others in the congregation when the wrongdoing has been discovered. We must remember that there is nothing hidden that will not be revealed, and one of our primary responsibilities before Jehovah is to help to keep his organization clean. —Luke 8:17.

¹⁸ All servants of Jehovah should be very careful not to share in the sins of others. Some parents try to justify the wrong conduct of their children, endeavoring to shelter them. But Christian parents should not adopt the attitude that everyone is against their children when these younger ones do wrong. Instead, godly parents should help their erring offspring to receive, accept, and benefit from any needed discipline outlined in God's Word.

¹⁹ Christian married couples also need to be careful that they do not violate God's laws by covering over each other's serious sins. They should remember the case of Ananias and Sapphira, who conspired but unsuccessfully sought to cover over serious sin. (Acts 5:1-11) Elders must also be alert not to protect one another or ministerial servants if one of them has committed a serious sin that could result in disfellowshipping. They should follow the principle outlined by Paul, who wrote: "Never lay your hands hastily upon any

16. What is of far greater importance than loyalty to a friend who refuses to reveal his serious wrongdoing to the appointed elders?
17. What illustrates that certain youths among us need to guard against sharing in the sins of others?

18. Christian parents should do what if their children do wrong?
19. (a) Regarding serious sins, about what do Christian married couples need to be careful? (b) What must elders do if one of them or a ministerial servant should commit a serious sin?

man; neither be a sharer in the sins of others; preserve yourself chaste."—1 Timothy 5:22.

The Wisdom of Maintaining Blamelessness

20 Servants of Jehovah should neither share in nor imitate the bad ways of this world. In writing to Gaius, the apostle John said: "Beloved one, be an imitator, not of what is bad, but of what is good. He that does good originates with God. He that does bad has not seen God." (3 John 11) How good it is to be guided by the sure Word of God and thus do what is good! Rather than covering over or sharing in the gross sins of others, therefore, it should be our resolve to shine as illuminators, being blameless and innocent. (Philippians 2:14, 15) Each servant of God is responsible for keeping the congregation clean, while remaining unblemished personally. (2 Peter 3:14) But what if you are troubled about the propriety of what someone has done? You should feel free to speak with the elders and get direction as to the right course to follow.

21 Our love for Jehovah's organization should imitate the love of Jesus Christ for his spiritual bride, the congregation. He "loved the congregation and delivered up himself for it, that he might sanctify it, cleansing it with the bath of water by means of the word, that he might present the congregation to himself in its splendor, not having a spot or a wrinkle or any of such things, but that it should be holy and without blemish." (Ephesians 5:25-27) Similarly, our love for Jehovah's organization should move us to do what we can to keep it clean. Never may we do anything to dishonor God or his organization or condone the wrongdoing of others in the congregation. Rather, let us encourage wrongdoers to correct their conduct and seek the help of the elders. If they fail to do this within a reasonable amount of time, let us shoulder our responsibility to inform the appointed overseers. In this way, we will avoid becoming sharers in the sins of others and bearing some responsibility for their wrong conduct.

22 The salvation we hold in common is a treasure beyond compare. To attain it we must continue to walk before Jehovah in an upright way. Therefore, let us help one another to do so, never sharing in the sins of others. Jehovah has lovingly provided an organizational arrangement to assist us in these efforts, and in this regard appointed elders play an important role. But how do they imitate Jehovah and his Son, the Fine Shepherd? What assistance can elders give us on the roadway to life? The following article will answer these questions.

_____

20. Rather than covering over or sharing in the gross sins of others, what should we do?
21. (a) How is Christ's love for his congregation an example for us? (b) Regarding the wrongdoing of others, what responsibility should we shoulder?

_____

22. (a) To attain salvation, what must we do? (b) What questions remain for consideration?

Can You Recall?

□ How should you view discipline?

□ If a fellow believer tells you that he has committed a serious sin, what should you urge him to do?

□ What should you do if you know that a wrongdoer has not confessed his sin to the appointed elders?

□ Whether we are elders, marriage mates, or children, how can we avoid sharing in the sins of others?

Elders, Take Your Shepherding Responsibilities Seriously

"Shepherd the flock of God in your care."—1 PETER 5:2.

HOW appropriate it is that sheep should be used to symbolize humans favored by Jehovah God! Sheep are docile creatures that respond to the voice of their shepherd and readily follow him. God's sheeplike people similarly allow themselves to be led by the Fine Shepherd, Jesus Christ. They know him, respond to his voice, and joyfully accept his leadership. (John 10:11-16) Of course, without a good shepherd, literal sheep quickly become fearful and helpless. No wonder, then, that Jesus Christ felt pity for people who were "skinned and thrown about like sheep without a shepherd." —Matthew 9:36.

2 Jehovah God is deeply interested in the spiritual welfare of honest-hearted humans Scripturally designated as "sheep." For instance, through the prophet Ezekiel, God pronounced woe upon "the shepherds of Israel," the responsible men who fed themselves while neglecting the sheep. But Jehovah was not going to allow sheeplike ones to suffer without relief, for he said: "The lost one I shall search for, and the dispersed one I shall bring back, and the broken one I shall bandage and the ailing one I shall strengthen."—Ezekiel 34:2-16.

3 The Fine Shepherd, Jesus Christ, has similar concern for sheeplike ones. Before ascending to heaven, therefore, Jesus expressed his desire that the sheep receive proper care. He told the apostle Peter, 'Feed my lambs, shepherd my little sheep, feed my little sheep.' (John 21:15-17) And to assure continued loving attention to the sheep, Jesus gave "some as shepherds" to build up "the body of the Christ."—Ephesians 4:11, 12.

4 Since both God and Christ have such deep love and concern for the sheeplike ones, being an undershepherd of God's sheep is a very responsible assignment. Thus the apostle Paul urged the spirit-appointed "older men" of Ephesus to "shepherd the congregation of God," paying due attention to it. (Acts 20:17, 28) So how can appointed elders properly care for this responsibility?

Shepherds Receive Direction

5 The apostle Peter, who was expected to feed Jesus' sheep, told fellow overseers: "Shepherd the flock of God in your care, not under compulsion, but willingly; neither for love of dishonest gain, but eagerly; neither as lording it over those who are God's inheritance, but becoming examples to the flock." (1 Peter 5:1-3) Let us see how elders, appointed by holy spir-

---

1. Why is it so appropriate that sheep should be used to symbolize humans approved by God?
2. How did Jehovah view the sheeplike ones who suffered under the unloving "shepherds of Israel"?

3. How has Jesus Christ shown concern for the sheep?
4. The apostle Paul urged spirit-appointed "older men" to do what?
5. What counsel did Peter give fellow overseers?

it, can satisfactorily comply with this counsel.

⁶ Peter urged fellow elders: "Shepherd the flock of God in your care, not under compulsion, but willingly." Those privileged to serve as spiritual shepherds should not do so grudgingly, feeling compelled to care for the sheep. They should not feel coerced, as though this were some form of drudgery or as if others were prodding them to shepherd the flock. Rather, elders should serve with a willing spirit. (Compare Psalm 110:3.) When a person is willing to do good for others, he usually does so wholeheartedly, exerting himself and going out of his way to serve their interests. A willing elder gives freely of his time and energies. He knows that at times sheep may go astray, and he desires to help them, imitating God's concern for the sheeplike ones. Why, so great was Jehovah's concern for Israelites who went astray that his words were: "I have said, 'Here I am, here I am!' to a nation that was not calling upon my name"! —Isaiah 65:1.

⁷ Peter said that the shepherding work should be done "neither for love of dishonest gain, but eagerly." The appointed elders do not desire to be a burden to the sheep. That was the apostle Paul's attitude, for he told Christians in Thessalonica: "Certainly you bear in mind, brothers, our labor and toil. It was with working night and day, so as not to put an expensive burden upon any one of you, that we preached the good news of God to you." He also reminded them: "We did not behave disorderly among you nor did we eat food from anyone free. To the contrary, by labor and toil night and day we were working so as not to impose an expensive burden upon any one of you."—1 Thessalonians 2:9; 2 Thessalonians 3:7, 8.

⁸ Similarly, faithful shepherds of God's flock today do not covetously desire what the sheep have or try to make unjust profit at their expense. (Luke 12:13-15; Acts 20:33-35) Paul showed that those qualifying to be overseers 'must not be greedy of dishonest gain.' (Titus 1:7) Rather, they must serve eagerly, having enthusiastic interest in their work and seeking the advantage of the sheep entrusted to their care. (Philippians 2:4) In this way, these shepherds show unselfish concern for the sheep similar to that displayed by Jehovah God and his Son, Jesus Christ.

⁹ Peter also said that elders were to shepherd Jehovah's people "neither as lording it over those who are God's inheritance, but becoming examples to the flock." A loving shepherd is careful that he does not abuse his authority by having an air of superiority and lording it over the sheep. A proud spirit is unchristian and must be avoided by all those desiring to please Jehovah. Proverbs 21:4 says: "Haughty eyes and an arrogant heart, the lamp of the wicked ones, are sin." And Jesus told his followers: "You know that the rulers of the nations lord it over them and the great men wield authority over them. This is not the way among you; but whoever wants to become great among you must be your minister, and whoever wants to be first among you must be your slave." (Matthew 20:25-27) Indeed, elders must remember that those making up the flock are God's sheep and must not be dealt with in a harsh manner.

---

6. With what attitude should elders serve "the flock of God"?
7, 8. (a) What does it mean to carry out the shepherding work without love for dishonest gain? (b) Serving eagerly means doing what?

---

9. Why must a Christian shepherd 'not lord it over those who are God's inheritance'?

Like caring shepherds of ancient times, modern-day elders lovingly "shepherd the flock of God"

¹⁰ To the self-serving shepherds of Ezekiel's day, Jehovah said: "The sickened ones you have not strengthened, and the ailing one you have not healed, and the broken one you have not bandaged, and the dispersed one you have not brought back, and the lost one you have not sought to find, but with harshness you have had them in subjection, even with tyranny." God further said that the harsh shepherds had 'kept shoving all the sickened ones until these had been scattered.' (Ezekiel 34:4, 20, 21) But it is not that way with the loving shepherds of "the flock of God" today. They do not flaunt their authority and are careful not to stumble any of the sheep. (Compare Mark 9:42.) Rather, such elders provide loving help and encouragement. Moreover, they prayerfully rely on Jehovah and work hard to be fine examples "in speaking, in conduct, in love, in faith, in chasteness." (1 Timothy 4:12) Consequently, the sheep are contented and feel secure, knowing that they are being cared for by loving, God-fearing shepherds.

___

10. (a) What were some shepherds of the people doing in Ezekiel's day? (b) How are loyal overseers fine examples to the flock?

Dangers Face the Sheep

¹¹ Sheeplike persons today need to feel secure, reassured by the fine attention elders give to protecting the flock. (Isaiah 32:1, 2) This is especially so since Christians face many perils in these "critical times" marking "the last days." (2 Timothy 3:1-5) The psalmist David also faced dangers, but he could say: "Jehovah is my Shepherd. . . . Even though I walk in the valley of deep shadow, I fear nothing bad, for you are with me." (Psalm 23:1-4) Modern-day shepherds of God's flock should care so well for the sheep that, like David, these sheeplike ones feel very close to Jehovah. They should also feel secure as part of God's organization.

¹² One danger from which those of God's flock need protection is the present-day trend toward unprincipled, immoral conduct. Largely due to current forms of entertainment, whether through television or by other means, many people have developed a life-style directly in conflict

___

11. Why must modern-day shepherds care for God's flock so well that the sheep feel secure?
12. From what present-day trend do the sheep need to be protected, and how can elders be of help in this regard?

with the standards set forth in God's Word. Today, the anything-goes attitude of this world, with its gross sexual misconduct, needs to be counteracted by sound Scriptural counsel provided within the congregation. So shepherds of the flock must know well what the Bible teaches on matters of morality. Moreover, they should keep before the sheep their responsibility to remain clean for Jehovah's service.—Titus 2:13, 14.

¹³ There are also dangers from apostates. Remember that 19 centuries ago, certain "ungodly men" who were false teachers slipped into the congregation. They were dangerous "rocks hidden below water," false shepherds that fed themselves, animalistic men causing separations and lacking spirituality. The letter of Jude provides sound counsel that enables elders, and all the faithful, to "put up a hard fight for the faith." (Jude 3, 4, 12, 19) Unquestionably, elders must take a firm position with regard to any who seek to cause divisions, for Paul wrote: "Keep your eye on those who cause divisions and occasions for stumbling contrary to the teaching that you have learned, and avoid them." (Romans 16:17) Shepherds therefore have a responsibility to protect the flock from these or other 'wolves in sheep's covering.'—Matthew 7:15.

Helping the Sheep in Other Ways

¹⁴ Shepherding "the flock of God" may require helping the sheep with various problems that may arise within the congregation. At times, sheep may even begin contending with sheep. Because of small incidents, some may start to treat one another unkindly. These individuals may even slander one another and finally stop associating with their former companions in Jehovah's service, to their own great spiritual detriment.—Proverbs 18:1.

¹⁵ Spiritual shepherds must be very alert to help such fellow believers. For instance, the elders may need to point out how wrong it is to slander one another and how all loyal Christians must work to preserve the unity of the congregation. (Leviticus 19:16-18; Psalm 133:1-3; 1 Corinthians 1:10) Elders may be able to help by pointing to Paul's warning: "If . . . you keep on biting and devouring one another, look out that you do not get annihilated by one another."—Galatians 5:13-15; James 3:13-18.

¹⁶ Elders, remember that the Devil is going about "like a roaring lion, seeking to devour someone." (1 Peter 5:8) All true Christians have a fight, not against flesh and blood, but against wicked spirit forces. (Ephesians 6:10-13) Faithful shepherds certainly do not want the sheep to be overreached by Satan. So if some sheeplike ones begin to miss Christian meetings, caring elders ought to try to determine the reason and offer adequate spiritual help. Shepherds must know the appearance of the flock and be alert to any unhealthy trends in the congregation. (Proverbs 27:23) If they note some tendency to neglect the field ministry, to ignore personal study, or to become overly involved in recreational or materialistic pursuits, these responsible men must seek to remedy the situation. In imitation of Jehovah and the Fine Shepherd, Jesus Christ, elders caring for "the flock of God" appropriately offer personal assistance or,

---

13. (a) Against what danger does the letter of Jude provide sound counsel? (b) What position must elders take regarding apostates?
14, 15. How may elders be able to help fellow believers who treat one another unkindly?

---

16. What must elders do if they note any unhealthy trends in the congregation?

at times, provide needed counsel at meetings. (Galatians 6:1) In these and other ways, loving elders give evidence that they take their shepherding responsibilities seriously.—Acts 20:28.

Shepherding Is a Serious Matter

17 Shepherding "the flock of God" as an elder is an exacting work. The high standards to be met in order to qualify for such a privilege are clearly set out at 1 Timothy 3:1-7, Titus 1:5-9, and 1 Peter 5:1-4. Not just any brother can serve in this capacity, for only spiritual men can properly shoulder this responsibility. (1 Corinthians 2:6-16) Many men not now serving as elders could qualify for this privilege, but they must first 'reach out for an office of overseer.' They should be ardent students of God's Word so that they will have deep understanding of it. Indeed, they must show themselves worthy of recommendation because of meeting the Scriptural requirements for appointment as elders, suitable shepherds of "the flock of God."

18 Serving under Jehovah God is the head of the Christian congregation, the Fine Shepherd, Jesus Christ. (John 10:11; 1 Corinthians 11:3; Ephesians 5:22, 23) And how pleased Jesus must be to have undershepherds of the flock who properly lead and protect the sheep! These spiritual men meet the high Scriptural qualifications set for Christian elders. Moreover, they have the same deep concern for the sheep as that manifested by the apostle Paul, who wrote: "Besides those things [hardships and sufferings] of an external kind, there is what rushes in on me from day to day, the anxiety for all the congregations. Who is weak, and I am not weak?

Who is stumbled, and I am not incensed?" (2 Corinthians 11:23-29) Paul traveled extensively, and daily he experienced "anxiety for all the congregations," even as traveling overseers do today. Similarly, appointed elders in individual congregations experience anxiety for the sheep within the flock entrusted to their care as spiritual shepherds.

19 Shepherding "the flock of God" is hard work, but it is most rewarding. Therefore, shepherds of the flock, carefully guard your precious privilege. Care well for God's sheep. And may all sheeplike ones cooperate fully with the undershepherds appointed by holy spirit. "Be obedient to those who are taking the lead among you and be submissive," urged Paul, "for they are keeping watch over your souls as those who will render an account." (Hebrews 13:17) As all those wholeheartedly devoted to Jehovah work together unitedly, great spiritual blessings and benefits will continue to result from the faithful service of Christian elders who take their shepherding responsibilities seriously.

19. What will result as Hebrews 13:17 is applied and elders continue to take their shepherding responsibilities seriously?

17. What is required in order to qualify as an elder?
18. How did Paul feel about the congregations, and do others share his feeling?

Can You Explain?

□ Why should spiritual shepherds serve willingly?

□ Why must elders be free of the love of dishonest gain?

□ Why would it be wrong for elders to lord it over God's flock?

□ Why must overseers be examples to the flock?

□ What are some dangers from which shepherds need to protect "the flock of God"?

Spiritual Gems From the Christian Greek Scriptures

The New *Reference Bible*

IN THE *Watchtower* issue of November 1, 1985, consideration was given to the 1984 edition of the *New World Translation of the Holy Scriptures—With References*. It was shown that in this publication Jehovah's anointed remnant, loyal to their stewardship of the Holy Scriptures, have provided a faithful translation of the Bible as well as supportive references for use in a worldwide spiritual education program. The first article dealt mainly with the Hebrew Scriptures. This second article will consider how the *Reference Bible* offers further choice spiritual gems in the Christian Greek section of the Bible.

In its introduction (page 7, column 1, paragraph 4) the *Reference Bible* says: "Special care was taken in translating Hebrew and Greek verbs in order to capture the simplicity, warmth, character and forcefulness of the original expressions. An effort was made to preserve the flavor of the ancient Hebrew and Greek times, the people's way of thinking, reasoning and talking, their social dealings, etc." Let us see how this is so.

Verbs of Continuous Action

The writers of the Christian Greek Scriptures were careful and precise in their choice of words. This is demonstrated in the account of Jesus' Sermon on the Mount.

Several times in the original, a form of the verb is used that indicates continuous action, and this is faithfully represented in the translation. Thus, at Matthew 6:33 the *New World Translation* renders the opening words in this way: "Keep on, then, seeking first the kingdom." The footnote to the verse suggests an alternative rendering: "Or, 'Be you seeking.' . . . The verb form indicates continuous action."

Most other Bible translations ignore the continuous aspect of this verb. The *King James Version,* for example, renders it: "Seek ye first the kingdom." However, such a translation fails to capture the precision of Jesus' counsel. He did not imply that we should seek the Kingdom once or twice and then go on to other things. Rather, we should seek it continuously. It should always be first in our lives.

In Matthew 7:7 Jesus used this continuous form three times in this one verse, with emphatic meaning: *"Keep on asking,* and it will be given you; *keep on seeking,* and you will find; *keep on knocking,* and it will be opened to you." These careful Bible renderings provide gems of truth that sparkle with consistency.

Skillful Use of Negatives

The Bible writers were skillful in their use of negatives. Notice in the *New*

World Translation the careful rendering of Jesus' further counsel in the Sermon on the Mount. In Matthew 6:16 he is recorded as saying: "When you are fasting, *stop becoming sad-faced* like the hypocrites." Most other translations render this expression by a simple negative: "When ye fast, be not, as the hypocrites, of a sad countenance." (*KJ*) This rendering implies 'do not start looking sad.' However, the Bible writer used here a negative command in the present (continuous) tense. In Greek, that has a specific meaning. The action is currently going on and must cease. The *New World Translation* observes this fine point, which is ignored by most other translations. Note some further examples of such careful translation: *"Stop storing up* for yourselves treasures." (Matthew 6:19) *"Stop judging* that you may not be judged."—Matthew 7:1.

While considering the subject of negatives, notice the use of negative commands where the Bible writers used the aorist tense. In Greek, this tense indicates that the actions are prohibited at any given moment or time. Hence, Jesus told his hearers: "So, *never be anxious* [that is, do not be anxious at any moment] about the next day." (Matthew 6:34) Here again, most translations use some form of simple negative such as, "Do not be anxious." (*The New English Bible*) However, such a translation misses the full force of the original. The Bible's emphatic language is similarly preserved for us in the phrase: *"Never be anxious* and say, 'What are we to eat?'" (Matthew 6:31) These are a few jewels of careful translation.

Participate in Christian Activity

Often the alternative renderings of verbs that are found in the footnotes of the *Reference Bible* reveal new shades of meaning in a Bible verse. Take for example Paul's counsel to the Philippians found at Philippians 1:27: "Only *behave* in a manner worthy of the good news about the Christ." This is similar to the rendering found in other translations. For example, the *New International Version* reads: "Conduct yourselves in a manner worthy of the gospel of Christ." And *The New English Bible* says: "Let your conduct be worthy of the gospel of Christ." However, in the *Reference Bible* there is a footnote to the word "behave" that opens up a much deeper understanding of what that counsel would have meant to the Philippians. The footnote gives an alternative rendering of the word "behave": "Or, 'carry on as citizens.'"

The Greek word that is here translated "behave" is derived from a word meaning "citizen." The Philippians were to participate as "citizens" in declaring the good news. It must be remembered that Roman citizens generally took an active part in the affairs of the State, and Roman citizenship was highly prized—particularly, as in the case of Philippi, by cities outside Italy whose inhabitants had been granted citizenship by Rome. So, as the *Reference Bible* footnote helps us to understand, Paul is here telling Christians that they must not be inactive, merely nominal Christians. They must also participate in Christian activity, thereby proving themselves worthy of the good news. This deeper understanding is in harmony with Paul's later words to the Philippians: "As for us, our citizenship exists in the heavens."—Philippians 3:20.

Abraham "Attempted to Offer Up" Isaac

As observed previously, a clearer understanding is possible when the Greek verbs are carefully rendered into English. Consider the important text at Hebrews 11: 17. The *King James Version* renders this verse as follows: "Abraham when he was tried, *offered up* Isaac: and he . . . *offered up* his only begotten son." From that rendering, one would think that the verb "offered up" appeared in the same way in both instances in the Greek.

However, the Greek verb form differs in these two occurrences. In the first case, the verb "offer up" is in the perfect (completed) tense, whereas the second "offer up" is in the imperfect (past continuous) form. These verb tenses have many subtle meanings in Greek, and the *New World Translation* endeavors to bring them out by its rendering of the text: "Abraham, when he was tested, *as good as offered up* Isaac, and the man . . . *attempted to offer up* his only-begotten son." There is a footnote to the first occurrence of the verb that gives an alternative rendering: "Or, 'Abraham, when being tried, *has (as it were) offered.'*" And a footnote to the second verb suggests a second way that this verb in the imperfect form could be expressed: "Or, 'proceeded.'" Thus, the verse could read: "The man . . . *proceeded to offer up.*" In this way, the Greek verb indicates that the action was intended or attempted but not carried out to completion. This is in harmony with what actually happened. —Genesis 22:9-14.

The "Wall in Between"

The footnotes in the *Reference Bible* also provide helpful information taken from other works of Bible scholarship. Consider, for example, Paul's use of the term "wall in between," found at Ephesians 2:14. The *Reference Bible* footnote reads: "An allusion to the wall in the area of the temple that fenced off the unsanctified Gentile worshipers from entering the inner courtyards that were open only to the sanctified Jewish worshipers. According to the Mishnah (translated by Danby, 1950, p. 592), the stone barrier was called

'the Soreg.' This wall was said to be 1.3 m (4.3 ft) high. See App 9F."

Paul nicely argues in the context of Ephesians 2:14 that this "wall in between," the *Soreg* in Herod's temple of Jesus' day, pictured the prior legal separation between Jews and Gentiles by reason of the Law covenant made through Moses. But now this wall that separates, the Law covenant, has been put away because of Christ's sacrifice, which has sanctifying power to cleanse even Gentiles. (Colossians 2:13-15) Since 36 C.E., when believing Gentiles were joined to the congregation of Christian Jews, such Gentiles became anointed and sanctified ones as part of the spiritual "Israel of God." (Galatians 6:16) These Gentiles, now cleansed, were also a part of the heavenly sanctuary class, pictured by those who walked in the inner courtyards of the temple. No more were the Gentile Christians handicapped in their relationship to Jehovah by being confined to the outer courtyard known as the Court of the Gentiles.

Declaring the Good News "From House to House"

Many have criticized Jehovah's Witnesses for their global, effective house-to-house preaching work. Yet, there is a clear pattern set by the apostles and early Christians. In Acts 5:42, we read of their activity: "Every day in the temple and *from house to house* they continued without letup teaching and declaring the good news."

There is a comment in the footnote of the *Reference Bible* about the phrase "from house to house." Here is what it says: "Lit., 'according to **house.**' Gr[eek], *kat' oi′kon.* Here *ka·ta′* is used with the accusative sing[ular] in the distributive sense. R. C. H. Lenski, in his work *The Interpretation of The Acts of the Apostles,* Minneapolis (1961), made the following com-

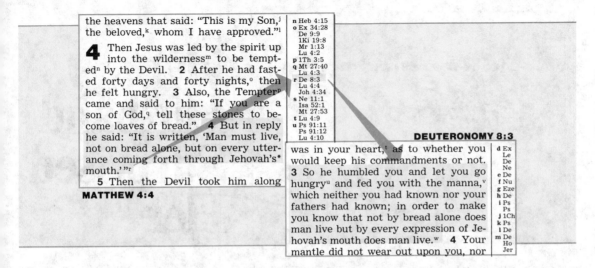

the heavens that said: "This is my Son,[j] the beloved,[k] whom I have approved."[l]

4 Then Jesus was led by the spirit up into the wilderness[m] to be tempted[n] by the Devil. **2** After he had fasted forty days and forty nights,[o] then he felt hungry. **3** Also, the Tempter[p] came and said to him: "If you are a son of God,[q] tell these stones to become loaves of bread." **4** But in reply he said: "It is written, 'Man must live, not on bread alone, but on every utterance coming forth through Jehovah's[*] mouth.'"[r]

5 Then the Devil took him along

MATTHEW 4:4

n	Heb 4:15
o	Ex 34:28
	De 9:9
	1Ki 19:8
	Mr 1:13
	Lu 4:2
p	1Th 3:5
q	Mt 27:40
	Lu 4:3
r	De 8:3
	Lu 4:4
	Joh 4:34
s	Ne 11:1
	Isa 52:1
	Mt 27:53
t	Lu 4:9
u	Ps 91:11
	Ps 91:12
	Lu 4:10

DEUTERONOMY 8:3

was in your heart,[t] as to whether you would keep his commandments or not. **3** So he humbled you and let you go hungry[u] and fed you with the manna,[v] which neither you had known nor your fathers had known; in order to make you know that not by bread alone does man live but by every expression of Jehovah's mouth does man live.[w] **4** Your mantle did not wear out upon you, nor

d	Ex
	Le
	De
	Ne
e	De
f	Nu
g	Eze
h	De
i	Ps
	Ps
j	1Ch
k	Ps
l	De
m	De
	Ho
	Jer

ment on Ac 5:42: 'Never for a moment did the apostles cease their blessed work. "Every day" they continued, and this openly "in the Temple" where the Sanhedrin and the Temple police could see and hear them, and, of course, also [*kat' oi'-kon*], which is distributive, "from house to house," and not merely adverbial, "at home."'"

Helpful Marginal References

When reading the Scriptures, one often finds that the Bible writer is quoting a passage from another part of the Scriptures or making an allusion to another passage in the Bible. In such cases, the *Reference Bible* can be very helpful. Its system of marginal references directs the student to other places where the subject is mentioned.

Consider Jesus' encounter with his Adversary, Satan, recorded at Matthew 4: 3-11. In verse 4 Jesus counters Satan's first temptation by saying: "It is written, 'Man must live, not on bread alone, but on every utterance coming forth through Jehovah's mouth.'" The reference indicates that Jesus was here quoting a scripture, found in our Bibles in Deuteronomy 8:3.

Satan presented Jesus with a second temptation, trying to support it by asserting: "It is written, 'He will give his angels a charge concerning you, and they will carry you on their hands, that you may at no time strike your foot against a stone.'" Where did Satan find those words? The marginal reference directs the student to Psalm 91:11, 12. Yes, Satan was quoting scripture, acting as "an angel of light." (2 Corinthians 11:14) Jesus replied, "Again it is written, 'You must not put Jehovah your God to the test.'" This also was a scripture quotation, but correctly applied. From where was it quoted? The marginal reference points us to Deuteronomy 6:16. When tempted for the third time, Jesus again quoted scripture. From where? From Deuteronomy 6:13, according to the marginal reference. Many other similarly helpful services are rendered by the 125,000 marginal references found in the *Reference Bible*.

From these samples one can see that the new *Reference Bible* heightens the beauty of the *New World Translation* by revealing its many accurate renderings of spiritual truths.

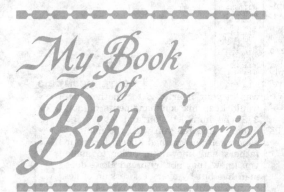

My Book of Bible Stories

Her Husband Surprised Her

When a telephone operator in Texas offered fellow employees the publication *My Book of Bible Stories,* showing them the beautiful illustrations and the valuable information, they accepted a total of 50 books. She explains what happened after one woman said she would like to have a copy.

"I'm sorry I asked you to bring that book," the woman said.

"Why?" I asked.

"I didn't know you were one of Jehovah's Witnesses," she answered, "and my husband hates you people."

"Oh, I'm sorry he feels that way," I replied. But noting that she was really impressed by the book, I said: "Please take it home and show it to him, and then if he doesn't want it, bring it back to me."

"OK," she said.

"The next night I met her, and she said, 'JoAnn, I'm so happy. I took the book home and put it on the dresser. I left to go grocery shopping. When I returned, my husband was sitting with the kids reading the book to them. He asked me where I got the book, and I told him from Jehovah's Witnesses. He said, "You know, it's really a good book. Look at all these pictures, and at the bottom of the page it shows where to find the information in the Bible."'"

December 1, 1985

The Watchtower

Announcing Jehovah's Kingdom

Are You
Right With God?

December 1, 1985
Vol. 106, No. 23

The Watchtower®
Announcing Jehovah's Kingdom

In This Issue

THE PURPOSE OF "THE WATCHTOWER" is to exalt Jehovah God as the Sovereign of the universe. It keeps watch on world events as they fulfill Bible prophecy. It comforts all peoples with the good news that God's Kingdom will soon destroy those who oppress their fellowmen and that it will turn the earth into a paradise. It encourages faith in the now-reigning King, Jesus Christ, whose shed blood opens the way for mankind to gain eternal life. "The Watchtower," published by Jehovah's Witnesses continuously since 1879, is nonpolitical. It adheres to the Bible as its authority.

"WATCHTOWER" STUDIES FOR THE WEEKS

January 5: Declared Righteous "for Life." Page 8.
Songs to Be Used: 11, 141.

January 12: Declared Righteous as a Friend of God.
Page 13. Songs to Be Used: 64, 142.

Average Printing Each Issue: 11,150,000

Now Published in 103 Languages

SEMIMONTHLY EDITIONS AVAILABLE BY MAIL
Afrikaans, Arabic, Cebuano, Chichewa, Chinese, Cibemba, Danish, Dutch,* Efik, English,* Finnish, French, German,* Greek, Hiligaynon, Igbo, Iloko, Italian,* Japanese,* Korean, Lingala, Malagasy, Maltese, Norwegian, Portuguese, Russian, Sepedi, Sesotho, Shona, Spanish,* Swahili, Swedish, Tagalog, Thai, Tswana, Xhosa, Yoruba, Zulu

MONTHLY EDITIONS AVAILABLE BY MAIL
Armenian, Bengali, Bicol, Bulgarian, Croatian, Czech, Ewe, Fijian, Ga, Greenlandic, Gujarati, Gun, Hausa, Hebrew, Hindi, Hiri Motu, Hungarian, Icelandic, Kannada, Kikuyu, Kiluba, Malayalam, Marathi, New Guinea Pidgin, Pangasinan, Papiamento, Polish, Rarotongan, Romanian, Samar-Leyte, Samoan, Sango, Serbian, Silozi, Sinhalese, Slovenian, Solomon Islands-Pidgin, Tahitian, Tamil, Telugu, Tshiluba, Tsonga, Turkish, Twi, Ukrainian, Urdu, Venda, Vietnamese
* Study articles also available in large-print edition.

The Bible translation used is the "New World Translation of the Holy Scriptures," unless otherwise indicated.

Twenty cents (U.S.) a copy

Watch Tower Society offices	Yearly subscription Semimonthly
America, U.S., Watchtower, Wallkill, N.Y. 12589	$4.00
Australia, Box 280, Ingleburn, N.S.W. 2565	A$7.00
Canada, Box 4100, Halton Hills (Georgetown), Ontario L7G 4Y4	$5.20
England, The Ridgeway, London NW7 1RN	£5.00
Ireland, 29A Jamestown Road, Finglas, Dublin 11	£5.00
New Zealand, 6-A Western Springs Rd., Auckland 3	$15.00
Nigeria, P.O. Box 194, Yaba, Lagos State	₦6.00
Philippines, P.O. Box 2044, Manila 2800	₱50.00
South Africa, Private Bag 2, Elandsfontein, 1406	R5,60

Remittances should be sent to the office in your country or to Watchtower, Wallkill, N.Y. 12589, U.S.A.

Changes of address should reach us 30 days before your moving date. Give us your old and new address (if possible, your old address label).

The Watchtower (ISSN 0043-1087) is published semimonthly for $4.00 (U.S.) per year by Watch Tower Bible and Tract Society of Pennsylvania, 25 Columbia Heights, Brooklyn, N.Y. 11201. Second-class postage paid at Brooklyn, N.Y., and at additional mailing offices.

Postmaster: Send address changes to Watchtower, **Wallkill, N.Y. 12589.**

Published by
**Watch Tower Bible and Tract Society
of Pennsylvania**
25 Columbia Heights, Brooklyn, N.Y. 11201, U.S.A.
Frederick W. Franz, President

Are You Right With God?

MANY people may see no point in that question. In their view, feeling right with oneself is more important. 'Do your own thing' is a popular maxim these days. 'Don't feel guilty' is another.

This is not just the viewpoint of a few youngsters imbued with the 'me-first' philosophy of life. For example, in France, where 82 percent of the population are baptized Catholics, a survey carried out in 1983 revealed that only 4 percent of the people accept the idea of sin. As to the United States, several years ago Dr. Karl Menninger, said to be the "father of American psychiatry," felt prompted to write a whole book on the subject *Whatever Became of Sin?* In it he wrote: "As a nation, we officially ceased 'sinning' some twenty years ago." The cover of the book stated: "The word 'sin' has almost disappeared from our vocabulary."

Indeed, the concept of sin is so obscure today that many people, even those claiming to be Christian, would have trouble explaining what sin really is.

Modern-Day Misgivings

In spite of this devaluation of the notion of sin, several recent developments on the world scene have set people thinking. One is the large number of abortions in many of the world's most developed countries. Some of these, although predominantly "Christian," have very liberal abortion laws. This glut of fetal killings has produced reactions that people who reject the concept of sin must find hard to explain.

Why, for example, should some women whose philosophy of life permits them to have an abortion have feelings of guilt afterward, even to the point of becoming psychologically ill? Yet, "studies show a high proportion of abortees to be maladjusted," even in communist Yugoslavia. (*The New Encyclopædia Britannica*) Professor Henri Baruk, member of the French Academy of Medicine, explains this phenomenon as being due to the violation of "a fundamental principle written in the heart of all people." Written by whom?

Another recent phenomenon that has set people thinking is the worldwide spread of sexually transmitted diseases. AIDS (Acquired Immune Deficiency Syndrome), with its high death rate, has triggered a wave of doubt and anguish among many people for whom promiscuous sex had supposedly brought liberation from outmoded taboos. The high price many are paying for their sexual "freedom" is causing some of them to wonder if, after all, they are not being punished. Punished by whom?

Such modern-day reminders that man cannot with impunity flout moral principles are making some thinking people reassess their opinions of sin and accountability to God.

The Churches and Sin

"The sin of this century is the loss of all sense of sin." Pope Pius XII made that forceful statement as early as 1946. Obviously, the situation has worsened since then. In his recent document on sin and confession, called "Reconciliation and

Penance," Pope John Paul II quoted those words of his predecessor and deplored what he called the eclipse of the concept of sin in today's secularized society.

The pope also reminded Catholic priests, and Catholics in general, that collective confession and absolution, as practiced in many Catholic churches today, is not good enough. He stated that individual confession is "the only ordinary and normal way" of observing the sacrament of penance. In Catholic dogma penance is associated with good works in reconciling the sinner with God.

Most Protestant churches deny the need for private confession to a priest. They hold that confession to God is sufficient for the forgiveness of sins, but some favor general confession and absolution at the "Communion service." Many Protestants believe that faith alone is necessary to be justified before God.

Such conflicting doctrines within the so-called Christian churches on the subject of confession, penance, and justification, or how to find a right standing before God, leave many people perplexed. They have a vague feeling that they should be doing something to get right with God, but they do not know how to go about it.

The following article will explain why we need to be put right with God, and it will examine the Catholic and Protestant viewpoints on "justification." Two other articles will explain what the Bible teaches on the subject of obtaining a righteous standing before God, and how this affects you.

Righteousness Before God—How?

"GOD 'e say 'im alrite." Such is apparently the way "justification" has been presented in a recent New Guinea Pidgin version of the "New Testament." As quaint as this may seem, it does express the basic idea behind the word translated in many English-language Bibles as "justification," or "declaration of righteousness," as expressed in Romans 5:16.

On the other hand, some people say: 'I lead a decent life. I do good to others when I can. I am prepared to meet my Maker.' They apparently understand justification to mean self-justification. According to the Bible, the doctrine of "justification" relates to the way *God* regards us and the way *he* deals with us. Jehovah is "the Creator." (Isaiah 40:28) He is "the Judge of all the earth." (Genesis 18:25) Nothing, therefore, could be more important than the way *he* considers us.

Why We Need to Be Put Right With God

The Bible says of Jehovah: "The Rock, perfect is his activity, for all his ways are justice. A God of faithfulness, with whom there is no injustice; righteous and upright is he." (Deuteronomy 32:4) He is the embodiment of righteousness. As the Creator and Life-Giver, he has the right to set the standard, or norm, for determining what is right and what is wrong. That which is in conformity with God's standard is righteous.

Thus, God sets the mark that his intelligent creatures must reach if they wish to live in harmony with their Creator. Missing that mark, or standard, is what the original languages of the Bible call sin. Sin is, therefore, unrighteousness. It is a failure to conform to God's definition of right and wrong. Consequently, sin is also a form of disorder, a form of lawlessness.—1 John 5:17; 3:4.

Jehovah "is a God, not of disorder, but of peace." (1 Corinthians 14:33) Originally, all his creatures in heaven and on earth were perfect. They were endowed with free will. (2 Corinthians 3:17) They enjoyed "the glorious freedom of the children of God." (Romans 8:21) As long as his righteous standards were respected, peace and order prevailed throughout the universe. Disorder intruded into the universe when, first in heaven, later on earth, some creatures became lawless before God, rejecting his right to rule over them. They deviated from God's standard of right and wrong. They missed the mark and thus made sinners of themselves.

This was the case with our first parents, Adam and Eve. (Genesis 3:1-6) "That is why . . . sin entered into the world and death through sin, and thus death spread to all men because they had all sinned." (Romans 5:12) Ever since their rebellion, sin has "ruled as king with death," because all Adam's descendants "have sinned and fall short" of God's righteous standard. (Romans 5:21; 3:23) Hence our need to be put right with God.

The Catholic View of "Justification"

This need for reconciliation with God is recognized by all the churches that claim to be Christian. However, the understanding of the way in which it is attained and of the Christian's standing before God differs in Catholic and Protestant doctrine.

As to Catholic dogma, *The Catholic Encyclopedia* states: "Justification denotes that change or transformation in the soul by which man is transferred from the state of original sin, in which as a child of Adam he was born, to that of grace and Divine sonship through Jesus Christ, the second Adam." *A Catholic Dictionary* further explains: "We confine ourselves here to the process by which adults are elevated from a state of death and sin to the favour and friendship of God; for with regard to infants the Church teaches that they are justified in baptism without any act of their own."

Briefly put, the Catholic Church teaches that "justification" is an act of God whereby a person who is baptized in the Catholic faith is really *made righteous* and *sanctified* by the gift of divine "grace." It also claims that such justification can be (1) increased by personal merit, or good works; (2) lost by mortal sin and by unbelief; (3) regained by the sacrament of penance. Within this arrangement, the justified Catholic must confess his sins to a priest and receive absolution. Any "temporal punishment" still due after absolution can be atoned for by good works or remitted by means of an "indulgence."*

The Protestant View

The abusive sale of indulgences in the early 16th century sparked the Protestant Reformation. Catholic monk Martin Luther attacked this practice in the 95 theses he posted on the door of the castle church in Wittenberg, Germany, in 1517. But, in reality, Luther's disagreement with official Catholic dogma went deeper than that. It embraced the church's entire doctrine of justification. Confirming this, *A Catholic Dictionary* states: "The difference of belief on the way by which sinners are justified before God formed the main subject of contention between Catholics and Protestants at the time of the Reformation. 'If this doctrine' (*i.e.* the doctrine of justification by faith alone) 'falls,' says Luther in his *Table Talk,* 'it is all over with us.'"

What, exactly, did Luther mean by 'justification by faith alone'? As a Catholic, Luther had learned that man's justifica-

---

* According to Catholic dogma, sin involves guilt and two kinds of punishment—eternal and temporal. Guilt and eternal punishment are remitted by means of the sacrament of penance. Temporal punishment must be atoned for in this life by good works and penitential practices, or in the next life in the fire of purgatory. An indulgence is a partial or a full (plenary) remission of temporal punishment by the application of the merits of Christ, Mary, and the "saints," that are stored up in the "Treasury of the Church." The "good works" required to obtain an indulgence can include a pilgrimage or the contributing of money to some "good" cause. In the past, money was thus raised for the Crusades and for the building of cathedrals, churches, and hospitals.

tion involves baptism, personal merit, and good works, as well as the sacrament of penance administered by a priest, who hears confession, grants absolution, and imposes compensatory works that can involve self-punishment.

In his efforts to find peace with God, Luther had expended all the resources of Roman dogma on justification, including fasting, prayers, and self-punishment, but to no avail. Unappeased, he read and reread the Psalms and Paul's letters, finally finding peace of mind by concluding that God justifies men, not because of their merits, good works, or penance, but solely because of their faith. He became so enthused by this thought of "justification by faith alone" that he added the word "alone" after the word "faith" in his German translation of Romans 3:28!*

Most of the Protestant churches basically adopted Luther's view of "justification by grace through faith." In fact, this had already been expressed by the French pre-Reformer Jacques Lefèvre d'Étaples. Summing up the difference between Catholic and Protestant views on justification, *A Catholic Dictionary* states: "Catholics regard justification as an act by which a man is really made just; Protestants, as one in which he is merely declared and reputed just, the merits of another—viz. Christ—being made over to his account."

Neither Catholic nor Protestant "Justification"

Catholic dogma goes beyond what the Bible teaches when it claims that "a man is *really* made just," or righteous, by the gift of divine grace bestowed at baptism. It is

---

* Luther also cast doubt on the canonicity of the letter of James, considering that his argumentation in chapter 2, that faith without works is dead, contradicts the apostle Paul's explanation of justification "apart from works." (Romans 4:6) He failed to recognize that Paul was speaking of works of the Jewish Law.—Romans 3:19, 20, 28.

not baptism that washes away original sin, but it is Christ's shed blood. (Romans 5:8, 9) There is a big difference between *really* being made righteous by God and being counted, or considered, as being righteous. (Romans 4:7, 8) Any honest Catholic, struggling in his fight against sin, knows that he has not *really* been made righteous. (Romans 7:14-19) If he were *really* righteous, he would have no sins to confess to a priest.

Furthermore, if Catholic dogma followed the Bible, the sin-conscious Catholic would confess his sins to God, asking forgiveness through Jesus Christ. (1 John 1:9–2:2) The intercession of a human priest at any stage of "justification" has no foundation in the Bible, no more than the accumulation of merits upon which the doctrine of indulgences is based.—Hebrews 7:26-28.

The Protestant concept of justification, as meaning a Christian's being declared righteous on the merits of Christ's sacrifice, is without a doubt nearer to what the Bible teaches. However, some Protestant churches teach "justification by faith alone," which, as we will later see, overlooks specific reasonings presented by the apostle Paul and by James. Those churches' spiritually smug attitude is summed up by the phrase "once saved, always saved." Some Protestants believe that it is sufficient to believe in Jesus to be saved and, therefore, that justification precedes baptism.

Further, certain Protestant churches, while teaching justification by faith, follow the French reformer John Calvin and teach personal predestination, thus denying the Biblical doctrine of free will. (Deuteronomy 30:19, 20) It can, therefore, be stated that neither the Catholic nor the Protestant concepts of justification are totally in harmony with the Bible.

> **THE BIBLE** teaches that man has free will and that Christ's ransom sacrifice opens up two hopes, one heavenly and the other earthly. Both hopes involve receiving a righteous standing before God

What Does the Bible Teach?

Yet the Bible definitely teaches the doctrine of "justification," or the way in which a human can be granted a righteous standing before God. We have earlier seen why we need to be put right with God, since we are all born, not as God's children, but as "children of wrath." (Ephesians 2:1-3) Whether God's wrath remains upon us or not depends upon our accepting or refusing his merciful provision for reconciliation with him, the holy, righteous God. (John 3:36) That loving provision is "the ransom paid by Christ Jesus."—Romans 3:23, 24.

The apostle Paul showed that Christ's ransom sacrifice opens up two hopes, one "upon the earth" and the other "in the heavens." He wrote: "God saw good for all fullness to dwell in him [Christ], and through him to reconcile again to himself all other things by making peace through the blood he shed on the torture stake, no matter whether they are the things upon the earth or the things in the heavens."—Colossians 1:19, 20.

To share in either of these two hopes, it is necessary to have a righteous standing before God, and this involves much more than merely "believing in Jesus." Just what is involved for Christians who have the heavenly hope and for those whose hope is to live forever in a paradise on earth will be considered in the following two articles. Please read on, and do not hesitate to ask the witness of Jehovah who supplied you with this magazine to discuss these articles with you, Bible in hand.

Declared Righteous *"for Life"*

"Through one act of justification the result . . . is a declaring of them righteous for life."—ROMANS 5:18.

"**H**APPY are those hungering and thirsting for righteousness, since they will be filled." (Matthew 5:6) Such thirst for righteousness will be fully satisfied not only for those to whom "the kingdom of the heavens belongs" but also for those who "will possess the earth." (Matthew 5:10; Psalm 37:29) Both classes share in the hope expressed by the apostle Peter when he wrote: "There are new heavens and a new earth that we are awaiting according to his [God's] promise, and in these righteousness is to dwell." (2 Peter 3:13) Yes, Jehovah God has prom-

ised a righteous new heavenly government, "the kingdom of the heavens," and a righteous "new earth," or human society in a paradise earth.

² But what exactly is to be understood by *righteous* new heavens and a *righteous* new earth? It means that both the new heavenly government and mankind on earth ruled by it must recognize God's standard of right and wrong. Jehovah is "the abiding place of righteousness." (Jeremiah 50:7) Righteousness is the very foundation of his sovereignty, or throne

---

1. Who are hungering and thirsting for righteousness, and how will their desire be fulfilled?

2. What relationship exists between Jehovah, righteousness, and our hope for a peaceful New Order?

position in the universe. (Job 37:23, 24; Psalm 89:14) For there to be peace in the universe, Jehovah's creatures have to recognize his right to establish the standards for what is righteous and for what is wicked. Conversely, our hope of a righteous New Order depends on Jehovah's abiding by his standards.—Psalm 145:17.

³ The question thus arises as to how the holy and righteous God Jehovah could have dealings with unrighteous sinners. (Compare Isaiah 59:2; Habakkuk 1:13.) How could he, while remaining faithful to his exalted standards of righteousness, choose from among sinners those who are to share in the righteous governmental "new heavens" and accept as his friends those who will be a part of the righteous "new earth"? To answer this, we must understand the Biblical doctrine of justification, or declaration of righteousness.

A Merciful Credit Arrangement

⁴ In the Scriptures, sins are likened to debts. (See Matthew 6:12, 14; 18:21-35; Luke 11:4.) All men are sinners and are, therefore, heavily in debt before God. "The wages sin pays is death." (Romans 6:23) Since they had been "sold under sin" by their forefather Adam, his descendants could do nothing to relieve themselves of this crushing debt. (Romans 7:14) Death of the debtor alone could wipe it out, "for he who has died has been acquitted from his sin." (Romans 6:7) No good works done during a sinner's lifetime could buy back what Adam lost, nor even give him a righteous standing before God.—Psalm 49:7, 9; Romans 3:20.

---

3. In view of Jehovah's absolute righteousness, what question comes to mind?
4. Why is fallen mankind heavily indebted to God, and why can we not relieve ourselves of this debt?

⁵ How could Jehovah provide relief for fallen mankind without compromising his own standards of righteousness? The answer highlights Jehovah's wisdom and undeserved kindness. The apostle Paul explains this beautifully in his letter to the Romans. He writes: "It is as a free gift that they [sinners] are being declared righteous by his undeserved kindness through the release by the ransom paid by Christ Jesus. God set him forth as an offering for propitiation through faith in his blood. This was in order to exhibit his own righteousness, because he was forgiving the sins that occurred in the past while God was exercising forbearance; so as to exhibit his own righteousness in this present season, that he might be righteous even when declaring righteous the man that has faith in Jesus."—Romans 3: 24-26.

⁶ By his undeserved kindness, Jehovah accepted Jesus' sacrifice in behalf of Adam's descendants. (1 Peter 2:24) It was an equivalent, or corresponding, sacrifice seeing that, as a perfect man, Jesus bought back what the perfect man Adam lost. (See Exodus 21:23; 1 Timothy 2:6.) Justice having been satisfied, Jehovah is lovingly willing to "wipe out," or 'blot out,' the sins charged against the account of "the man that has faith in Jesus." (Isaiah 44:22; Acts 3:19) If such a man remains faithful, not only does Jehovah refrain from 'reckoning to him his trespasses' but He actually credits righteousness to his account. (2 Corinthians 5:19) By means of this merciful credit arrangement, 'many have been constituted righteous.' (Ro-

---

5. How did Jehovah provide relief for sinful mankind while still respecting his perfect justice?
6. (a) How were Jehovah's standards of justice satisfied by Christ's sacrifice, and what is Jehovah thus willing to do? (b) How can God credit righteousness to the account of a person having faith?

mans 5:19) This is one aspect of justification, the act of God whereby a person is accounted guiltless. (Acts 13:38, 39) Who are the ones who have been justified, or declared righteous, during this system of things?

144,000 "Holy Ones"

⁷ Naturally, Christ himself needed no credit of righteousness, since he was *really* righteous. (1 Peter 3:18) Having proved faithful unto death as a perfect man ("the last Adam") and having sacrificed his right to life on earth, Jesus was resurrected by his Father, Jehovah. Jesus was "declared righteous in spirit," that is, pronounced fundamentally righteous on his own merit and raised as "a life-giving spirit." (1 Corinthians 15:45; 1 Timothy 3:16) By his sacrificial death, he provided the basis whereby Jehovah could credit righteousness to men and women of faith. —Romans 10:4.

⁸ Logically, those whom Jehovah chooses to make up the righteous "new heavens," or Kingdom government under the King Jesus Christ, are the first to benefit fully from this merciful arrangement in this system of things. The book of Daniel depicts the ceremony in the heavens by which Christ, the Son of man, receives "rulership and dignity and kingdom," so that "the peoples, national groups and languages [on earth] should all serve even him." Then Daniel shows that "the kingdom and the rulership" are also given to "the holy ones of the Supreme One," Jehovah.—Daniel 7:13, 14, 18, 27; compare Revelation 5:8-10.

⁹ The number of such "holy ones" chosen

---

7. In what way was Christ declared righteous, and what therefore became possible?
8, 9. (a) Who are the first ones to benefit by a credit of righteousness, and why? (b) Who make up the "new heavens," and over what will they rule?

to rule with the Lamb Jesus Christ on the heavenly Mount Zion is revealed as being 144,000, "bought from among mankind." (Revelation 14:1-5) These, together with Christ, make up the righteous "new heavens" of Jehovah's new system of things.

Counted Righteous—How and Why?

¹⁰ The Bible book that is doubtless the most explicit on God's declaring men righteous is Paul's letter to the Romans. Interestingly, he addressed this letter to those "called to be holy ones." (Romans 1: 1, 7) This explains why the doctrine of "justification," or declaration of righteousness, as outlined by Paul, is used in connection with the 144,000 "holy ones."

¹¹ The thrust of Paul's reasoning in Romans is that neither Jew nor Gentile can obtain a righteous standing before God by means of works, whether these be done to conform to the Mosaic Law or simply out of respect for instinctive moral law. (Romans 2:14, 15; 3:9, 10, 19, 20) Jew and Gentile alike can be declared righteous only on the basis of faith in Christ's ransom sacrifice. (Romans 3:22-24, 29, 30) However, the counsel in the closing chapters of Romans (12–15) shows that such faith must be backed up by godly works, as James also explains. (James 2:14-17) Such works simply prove that the justified Christian has the faith that is a prerequisite for justification by God.

¹² Still, for what impelling reason do Christians who are "called to be holy ones" need to be declared righteous? This is where the second aspect of justification

---

10. (a) Which Bible book is the most explicit on justification, and to whom was it written? (b) Who are principally involved in the Bible doctrine of justification?
11. What relationship is there between faith, works, and justification?
12, 13. (a) Why do the 144,000 "holy ones" need to be declared righteous? (b) What do they do with the life rights they receive?

There are two aspects to justification, or the declaration of righteousness:
(1) God's accounting that person guiltless
(2) God's declaring that person perfect and worthy of everlasting life on earth
The 144,000 anointed Christians are declared righteous in both respects. They sacrifice their human life rights and are begotten as spiritual "sons" called to become kings and priests with Christ in the "new heavens"

comes into account, namely, God's declaring a person worthy of life as His perfect human son. Due to the role they are called upon to play in the righteous "new heavens," the 144,000 must renounce and sacrifice forever any hope of life everlasting on earth. (Psalm 37:29; 115:16) In this sense they die a sacrificial death. They 'submit themselves to a death like Christ's.'—Philippians 3:8-11.

13 Now, in line with the principle set forth in the Mosaic Law, any sacrifice presented to Jehovah must be without defect. (Leviticus 22:21; Deuteronomy 15:21) The 144,000 "holy ones" are spoken of as "righteous ones who have been made perfect."—Hebrews 12:23.

Adopted as Spiritual Sons

14 While still living in the flesh, these "righteous ones" undergo a symbolic death. The apostle Paul explains: "Seeing that we died with reference to sin, how shall we keep on living any longer in it? Or do you not know that all of us who were baptized into Christ Jesus were baptized into his death? Therefore we were buried with him through our baptism into his death, in order that, just as Christ was

---

14, 15. (a) What change with reference to sin do the 144,000 undergo? (b) In what way are they raised up to "a newness of life"?

raised up from the dead through the glory of the Father, we also should likewise walk in a newness of life . . . because we know that our old personality was impaled with him, that our sinful body might be made inactive, that we should no longer go on being slaves to sin. For he who has died has been acquitted from his sin."—Romans 6:2-7.

15 During their human life, the 144,000 "holy ones," of whom only a small remnant remain on earth in this time of the end, 'die with reference to sin.' After their symbolic death, those "called to be holy ones" are raised up to "a newness of life." Having declared them righteous, Jehovah is in a position to beget them by his spirit to be his spiritual "children." They are "born again" and adopted as "God's sons." (John 3:3; Romans 8:9-16)* They become spiritual Israelites and are taken into the new covenant.—Jeremiah 31:31-34; Luke 22:20; Romans 9:6.

Heirs to Priesthood and Kingship

16 As adopted spiritual "sons" of God, the 144,000 "holy ones" also become

---

* For an in-depth discussion of being "born again," please see The Watchtower dated February 1, 1982, pages 18-29.

---

16. To what do the 144,000 "holy ones" become heirs?

'heirs.' (Galatians 4:5-7) Paul wrote to fellow spirit-begotten Christians: "If, then, we are children, we are also heirs: heirs indeed of God, but joint heirs with Christ, provided we suffer together that we may also be glorified together." (Romans 8:17) What is Christ's heritage? Jehovah has made him a King-Priest "according to the manner of Melchizedek forever." (Hebrews 6:19, 20; 7:1) As "joint heirs" with Christ, spirit-begotten Christians are also anointed by Jehovah as spiritual priests. (2 Corinthians 1:21; 1 Peter 2:9) Furthermore, one of the ultimate objects of their being declared righteous by Jehovah is for them later to "rule as kings in life through the one person, Jesus Christ."—Romans 5:17.

[17] While yet on earth, these anointed Christians, although declared righteous, still have to fight their sinful tendencies. (Romans 7:15-20) They need Christ's blood to cleanse them from their daily sins of imperfection. (1 John 1:7; 2:1, 2) When they remain faithful until the end of their earthly lives, they literally die and are resurrected "to an incorruptible and undefiled and unfading inheritance" as part of the righteous "new heavens."—1 Peter 1: 3, 4; 2 Peter 3:13.

"Waiting for the Revealing of the Sons of God"

[18] How does all of this affect those—far more numerous than the 144,000 spiritual "sons of God"—who hunger and thirst for righteousness but whose hope is to possess the earth? Of these, the apostle Paul writes: "For the eager expectation of the

creation is waiting for the revealing of the sons of God. For the creation was subjected to futility . . . on the basis of hope that the creation itself also will be set free from enslavement to corruption and have the glorious freedom of the children of God."—Romans 8:19-21.

[19] Such human "creation" whose hope is to live forever in a paradise earth are living in "eager expectation" of the time —now near—when the King Jesus Christ and the resurrected "sons of God" will be 'revealed' in destroying the present wicked system of things and thereafter ruling as kings and priests "for the thousand years." (Revelation 20:4, 6) During the Millennial Reign of Christ, human "creation itself also will be set free from enslavement to corruption."

[20] Just how humans living in the righteous "new earth" will finally attain to "the glorious freedom of the children of God," and how the Biblical doctrine of justification affects them even now, will be considered in the following article.

20. What will be considered in the following article?

17. (a) Although declared righteous, what do anointed Christians need to do daily? (b) How do they receive their reward?
18, 19. (a) What is human "creation" awaiting? (b) How will "the sons of God" be 'revealed,' and why is human "creation" living in eager expectation of this?

With regard to God's declaring men righteous—

☐ What does the Bible mean by righteous new heavens and a righteous new earth?

☐ Why does mankind need to be put right with Jehovah?

☐ How were Jehovah's standards of righteousness satisfied?

☐ Why are the 144,000 the first ones to be declared righteous, and what do they do with the life rights received?

☐ To what do the 144,000 become heirs with Christ?

Declared Righteous
as a Friend of God

"'Abraham put faith in Jehovah, and it was counted to him as righteousness,' and he came to be called 'Jehovah's friend.'"
—JAMES 2:23.

"**G**OD saw good for all fullness to dwell in him [Christ], and through him to reconcile again to himself all other things by making peace through the blood he shed on the torture stake, no matter whether they are the things upon the earth or the things in the heavens." (Colossians 1:19, 20) This divine purpose of reconciliation is moving to its climax.

2 "The things in the heavens" are not

1, 2. How are "things in the heavens" and "things upon the earth" being reconciled to God?

spirit creatures, for angels are not ransomed by Christ's blood. Rather, they are the humans bought with the Lamb's blood to be "a kingdom and priests" with Christ in the "new heavens." These have already been fully declared righteous through the blood of Christ. In addition, for some 50 years now, Jehovah has been making peace with "things upon the earth," those humans who will become a part of the righteous "new earth." (Revelation 5:9, 10; 2 Peter 3:13) This gathering of "all things together," both things earthly and things heavenly, "is according to his

[Jehovah's] good pleasure which he purposed in himself."—Ephesians 1:9, 10.

God's Purpose for His Son Adam

³ Adam was created a perfect, righteous, human son of God. (Luke 3:38) His righteousness was not credited, or imputed. It was inherent. From the standpoint of guiltlessness before Jehovah, Adam had no need to be "declared" righteous. As long as he submitted to God's legitimate rulership, he maintained a good standing before his Creator.

⁴ However, he had not yet proved himself to be an integrity keeper and had not yet been judged worthy of the right to everlasting life on earth. For that, he had to show, over a period of time, faithfulness to Jehovah and attachment to righteousness. Had he thus proved his integrity under test, he would have received the right to everlasting life on earth. It would have been as if God had declared, or gone on record as stating, that Adam merited endless life. In symbol of this, Jehovah no doubt would have led him to "the tree of life" and allowed him to eat of its fruit.—Genesis 2:9, 16, 17; 3:22.

⁵ But Adam failed when tested and thereby lost perfection, righteousness, and sonship for himself and his offspring. (Romans 5:12) Consequently, Adam's descendants were all born estranged from God, inherently unrighteous. (Ephesians 2:3; Romans 3:10) Thus, human creation "was subjected to futility" but "on the basis of hope," which hope of deliverance from sin and death was given immediately after the rebellion in Eden.—Romans 8:20, 21; Genesis 3:15.

3, 4. What was Adam's standing before God, but in what respect did he still need to be declared righteous?
5. (a) What did Adam lose for himself and for his offspring? (b) What hope of deliverance from sin and death did Jehovah give to human creation?

Declared Righteous Before Christ —How So?

⁶ Mankind's hope for deliverance from sin and death depended on the coming of the promised "seed," God's only-begotten Son. (John 3:16) Before Christ's sacrificial death, there was no way for men to obtain "acquittal and life," or "a declaring of them righteous for life." (Romans 5:18, *Revised Standard Version; New World Translation*) Nevertheless, even before Christ paid the ransom for man's deliverance, some men and women put faith in God's promise and backed up that faith by works. Because of this, Jehovah kindly pardoned their sin and accepted them as his servants. He lovingly accounted them relatively guiltless, when compared to the majority of mankind alienated from God. (Psalm 32:1, 2; Ephesians 2:12) He gave them a righteous standing, declaring them righteous to the extent that was appropriate at the time.

⁷ Thus, by faith Abel "had witness borne to him that he was righteous." (Hebrews 11:4) Noah "became an heir of the righteousness that is according to faith." (Hebrews 11:7) In spite of his failings, Job was said to be "blameless and upright." (Job 1:1, 22; 7:21) Phinehas showed zeal for pure worship, "and it came to be counted to him as righteousness." (Psalm 106:30, 31; Numbers 25: 1-13) "By faith" and by her works of kindness toward God's people, the non-Israelite harlot Rahab received a righteous standing, or was declared righteous.—Hebrews 11:31; James 2:25.

6, 7. (a) To what extent were some humans declared righteous before Christ's sacrificial death? (b) What are some examples of pre-Christian servants of Jehovah who received a righteous standing?

How Abraham
Was Accounted Righteous

8 The case of Abraham deserves particular attention. His being declared righteous is mentioned by two writers of the Christian Greek Scriptures, both of whom were writing to first-century Christians who were called to be a part of the 144,-000 members of spiritual Israel.—Romans 2:28, 29; 9:6; James 1:1; Revelation 7:4.

9 In his letter to the Romans, Paul argues that those "called to be holy ones" (1:7), both Jews and Gentiles (1:16, 17), are declared righteous "by faith apart from works of law." (3:28) To substantiate his argument, he opens a long explanation (4:1-22) and quotes Genesis 15:6 in saying: "Abraham exercised faith in Jehovah, and it was counted to him as righteousness." Then, in the concluding verses of chapter 4, Paul says that Jesus "was delivered up for the sake of our trespasses and was raised up for the sake of declaring us [that is, "the holy ones" (Romans 1:7)] righteous." "Us" cannot include Abraham, since he died long before

Christ's death and resurrection. Consequently, when, in the following chapters, Paul speaks of those who are to "rule as kings" and of their being declared righteous "for life" with a view to becoming "God's sons" and "joint heirs with Christ," he was obviously speaking of something quite different from God's attributing righteousness to Abraham. —Romans 5:17, 18; 8:14, 17, 28-33.

10 James also mentions Abraham as an example to prove that faith must be backed up by godly works. After stating that Abraham was declared righteous, quoting Genesis 15:6, James adds a comment that helps us to see the scope of Abraham's justification. He writes: "The scripture was fulfilled which says: 'Abraham put faith in Jehovah, and it was counted to him as righteousness,' *and he came to be called 'Jehovah's friend.'*" (James 2:20-23) Yes, due to his faith, Abraham was declared righteous *as a friend* of Jehovah, *not as a son with the right to perfect human life* or to kingship with Christ. Interestingly, in his *Synonyms of the Old Testament*, Robert Girdlestone wrote concerning Abraham's righteousness: "This righteousness was not *absolute, i.e.* such as would commend Abraham to God as a rightful claimant of the inheritance of sonship."

Jehovah's Book of Remembrance

11 The credit of relative righteousness to faithful men and women before Christ was a token of the real, or actual, righteousness and perfection associated with everlasting life that they may gain in God's new earth. In view of their life prospects, they may be viewed as having their names written in a book of remem-

---

8, 9. (a) Whose righteousness is the main topic of Paul's letter to the Romans? (b) In what respects does the declaration of righteousness of the "holy ones" go beyond that of Abraham?

---

10. How does James shed light on the scope of Abraham's being declared righteous?
11. Whose names are written in Jehovah's book of remembrance, and why?

In Our Next Issue

- Are You Grateful
  for What Jesus Did?

- Declare Abroad
  the Kingdom of God

- Self-Control
  —Vital for Christians

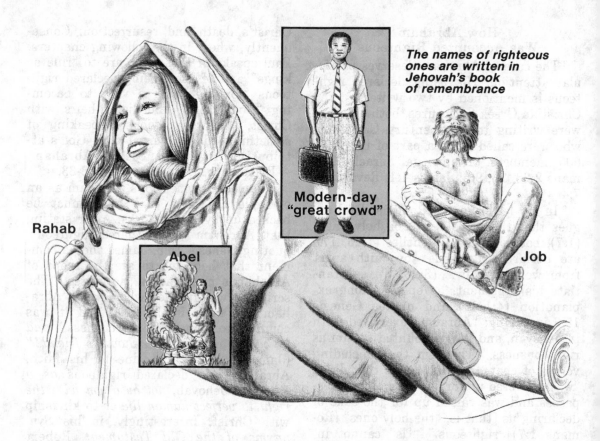

Rahab

Abel

Modern-day "great crowd"

The names of righteous ones are written in Jehovah's book of remembrance

Job

brance. (Compare Malachi 3:16; Exodus 32:32, 33.) It contains the names of those who are viewed by Jehovah as "righteous ones" who have demonstrated their faith by righteous works, and who are in line to receive everlasting life on earth. —Psalm 69:28; Habakkuk 2:4.

¹² However, such names are not yet written in Jehovah's "book of life." (Revelation 20:15) When such faithful men and women of the past come back on earth in 'the resurrection of the righteous,' they will no doubt accept with faith Jehovah's provision for life through Christ's ransom sacrifice. (Acts 24:15)

Thus they will become a part of Jesus' "other sheep," together with the "great crowd" who will have survived the "great tribulation." (John 10:16; Revelation 7: 9, 14) So doing, they will keep their names in Jehovah's book of remembrance.

Accounted Righteous as Friends for Survival

¹³ The Fine Shepherd, Jesus Christ, is now bringing in "other sheep" that are not of the "little flock" of 144,000 "holy ones" to whom the heavenly Kingdom is given. (Luke 12:32; Daniel 7:18) These "other sheep" listen to the voice of the

12. What will the "righteous" who are resurrected have to do to keep their names in Jehovah's book of remembrance?

13. Whom is the Fine Shepherd now bringing in, and how do they get inscribed in Jehovah's book of remembrance?

Fine Shepherd. (John 10:16) They exercise faith in Jehovah and in his Son. They dedicate their lives to Jehovah on the basis of Christ's ransom sacrifice. They are baptized "in the name of the Father and of the Son and of the holy spirit" and recognize the need to cultivate "the fruitage of the spirit." (Matthew 28:19, 20; Galatians 5:22, 23) Their names are written in Jehovah's book of remembrance.

¹⁴ These "other sheep" gathered in this time of the end will make up the "great crowd" whom the apostle John saw in vision, after he had seen the 144,000 members of spiritual Israel. (Revelation 7:4, 9) He described the "great crowd" as having "washed their robes and made them white in the blood of the Lamb." (Verse 14) Because of their faith in the Lamb's shed blood, a degree of righteousness is credited to them. This was depicted by their symbolic white robes. They have a clean standing before Jehovah, and "that is why" he allows them to 'render him sacred service day and night in his temple.' (Verse 15) Still, each day they must confess their sins to Jehovah and ask for forgiveness through Jesus Christ.—1 John 1:9–2:2.

¹⁵ That the "other sheep" are God's friends and even now have a relatively righteous standing before him is also made clear in Jesus' prophecy on 'the sign of his presence,' which includes the illustration of the sheep and the goats. Because the "sheep" do good to the remnant of Christ's 144,000 "brothers" still on earth, they are blessed by Jesus' Fa-

ther and are called "righteous ones." Like Abraham, they are accounted, or declared, righteous as friends of God. Their righteous standing will also mean survival for them when the "goats" depart into "everlasting cutting-off." (Matthew 24:3–25:46) They will "come out of the great tribulation" that will mark the end of the present wicked system of things.—Revelation 7:14.

Brought Up to Perfection

¹⁶ The "great crowd," who survive the "great tribulation," are not already declared righteous *for life*. We can see this from the fact that the chapter that mentions them goes on to say: "The Lamb, who is in the midst of the throne, will shepherd them, and *will guide them to fountains of waters of life*." (Revelation 7:17) So, even though God previously counted them as righteous compared to mankind in general and as his friends, they need additional help, or steps to be taken, so that they can be declared righteous *for life*.

¹⁷ During the Millennium, the enthroned Lamb, Christ Jesus, together with his 144,000 associate kings and priests, will apply a program of spiritual and physical "curing of the nations." (Revelation 22:1, 2) Such "nations" will be made up of the survivors of the great tribulation, any children born to them after Har-Magedon, and those who come back in the "resurrection of both the righteous and the unrighteous." (Acts 24:15) All who put faith in Christ's blood and accomplish appropriate "deeds" will even-

14. What gives the "other sheep" a clean standing before Jehovah, but for what do they need to ask God?
15. (a) How does the parable of the sheep and the goats show that the "other sheep" have a righteous standing with God? (b) To what extent are they declared righteous at the present time?

16. How do we know that the great crowd are not declared righteous for life before the "great tribulation"?
17. (a) What is meant by "the curing of the nations"? (b) Who will need to have their names inscribed in "the book of life"?

> **By faith in "the blood of the Lamb," the "other sheep" are given an approved standing before Jehovah and are thus declared righteous for friendship with him and for survival during the "great tribulation." They will attain to perfection by the end of the Millennium. After the final test they will be declared righteous *for life.***

tually have their names written in "the book of life."—Revelation 20:11-15.

¹⁸ By the end of Christ's Millennial Reign, those of earth's inhabitants who have shown that they accept Christ's ransom and will live by Jehovah's standards will have been raised to perfection. (Revelation 20:5) They will be as Adam was before he sinned. Like him, they will be tested as to their obedience.

"Glorious Freedom" as "Children of God"

¹⁹ Immediately after the Millennium, Christ will hand over to his Father a perfect human race. (1 Corinthians 15:28) "Satan will be let loose" for a decisive test of mankind. (Revelation 20:7, 8) The names of any who fail under test will not be "found written in the book of life." They will symbolically be "hurled into the lake of fire," which "means the second death."—Revelation 20:15; 21:8.

²⁰ Those who prove loyal to Jehovah will have their names indelibly written in the "book of life," as being perfect in integrity and worthy of the right to everlasting life on earth. Jehovah himself will

then declare them righteous in the complete sense. (Romans 8:33) They will have been justified to life eternal. God will adopt them as his earthly sons, and they will enter into the promised "glorious freedom of the children of God." (Romans 8:20, 21) Peace and harmony will have been restored to the universe. Reconciliation with God will be complete for "things upon the earth" and "things in the heavens." (Colossians 1:20) Jehovah's merciful arrangement of justification will have served its purpose. To the question, "Are you right with God?" every creature in heaven and on earth will be able to answer yes and add: "To the One sitting on the throne and to the Lamb be the blessing and the honor and the glory and the might forever and ever."—Revelation 5:13.

---

18. To what condition will earth's inhabitants have been raised by the end of the Millennium?
19. (a) What will occur immediately after the Millennium? (b) What will happen to those whose names are not found written in "the book of life"?
20. (a) Whom will Jehovah declare righteous for life, and why? (b) How will Jehovah's merciful arrangement of justification have served its purpose?

Concerning the standing of the "other sheep" before God—

☐ Why was Adam not declared righteous?

☐ To what extent were Abraham and other men and women before Christ declared righteous?

☐ Whose names were written in Jehovah's book of remembrance?

☐ To what extent do the "other sheep" have a righteous standing at the present time, and when will they be brought to perfection?

Kingdom Proclaimers Report

Love, the "Perfect Bond of Union"

LOVE among Christians is "a perfect bond of union," and when displayed it results in a worldwide brotherhood. (Colossians 3:14) This "perfect bond of union" is manifested by our brothers in Africa as they show love for one another and for Jehovah, the Giver and Sustainer of Life.—Psalm 36:9; Acts 17:28.

□ Because of the recent three-year drought in Zimbabwe, many areas were in a desperate condition. This, of course, affected our brothers who live in those areas. However, fellow Witnesses responded wonderfully to the call for help. In fact, so much clothing was donated that it was necessary to inform the brothers not to donate more until further notice. This, plus the aid given by the government, provided most of our brothers with the help they needed. "Those still in need are also being cared for," reports the Society's branch office.

This loving aid on the part of our brothers has not gone unnoticed. One unbelieving husband told his wife, who is a Witness: "While others are draining the people of all they have, you [Witnesses] are providing them with food and clothing." Favorable comments have been made by others also.

Love among Jehovah's Witnesses serves as "a perfect bond of union," and identifies them as true Christians.—John 13:35.

□ Another example of the

love and unity among Jehovah's people was seen at the "Kingdom Unity" District Convention held in Freetown, Sierra Leone. Delegates came to this convention from Guinea and Liberia, as well as from different parts of Sierra Leone. Two sessions ran simultaneously—one in English and Krio, the other in Kisi and French. The branch report describes the love and unity manifest on this occasion. It says:

"It was a thrilling moment when the Kisi- and French-speaking brothers joined the English session for the final song and prayer. Many shed tears of joy as they watched more than 400 delegates walk across the field to join them in unitedly worshiping Jehovah in song and prayer." It quotes one observer as saying: "Jehovah knows how to organize his people. What a clear demonstration of unity!"

This unity is emphasized when we consider that the ones gathered were from different tribes, and yet they met together in peace. It requires Jehovah's spirit to accomplish this. This unity was foretold in Revelation 7:9: "After these things I saw, and, look! a great crowd, which no man was able to number, out of all nations and tribes and peoples and tongues, standing before the throne and before the Lamb, dressed in white robes; and there were palm branches in their hands." Verse 10 of this same chapter shows the secret of this unity: "And they keep on crying with a loud voice, saying: 'Salvation we owe to our God, who is seated on the throne, and to the Lamb.'"

Do You Honor Jehovah With Your Valuable Things?

"Dear Brothers: How are you? I want to be a missionary when I grow up. Please use this dollar to help missionaries." So wrote three-year-old Shelley. Her childish scrawl was interpreted at the bottom of the letter by her mother.

More informally, Stephen wrote: "Dear Bible and Tract Society. I'm 8 years old. I live at 89 St. I hope you are having a fun time. I'm giving you one dollar for the Kingdom Hall fund. Send me a letter back soon."

WHY did these youngsters write to the Watchtower Society's headquarters? Because they wanted to honor Jehovah by using what they had in furtherance of his praise. They were following the Biblical injunction: "Honor Jehovah with your valuable things and with the first-fruits of all your produce."—Proverbs 3:9.

Certainly Jehovah is worthy of this honor. None can be compared to him. As Revelation 4:11 states: "You are worthy, Jehovah, even our God, to receive the glory and the honor and the power, because you created all things, and because of your will they existed and were created." Not only is it true that "by him we have life and move and exist," but he has provided the very best for us. (Acts 17:28) As the Bible writer James reminds us, God is the Giver of "every good gift and every perfect present."—James 1:17.

However, not all appreciate the need to praise and honor Jehovah. In fact, millions of people have not even learned his name! Many worship the things created "rather than the One who created." (Romans 1:25) Sincere-hearted ones need to

be enlightened. They need to know that Jehovah will soon swing into action. By means of the rulership of his Son, he will forever clear the earth of oppressors and their oppression, set things back in perfect balance, and restore Paradise and man's ability to live forever in perfect health. (Daniel 2:44; Revelation 21:1, 3, 4) Indeed, the very lives of those seeking righteousness depend on their taking in and acting on such knowledge.—Zephaniah 2:3; John 17:3.

Willingness and Appreciation Needed

Would you also like to share in this life-saving work? Much is involved in spreading the "good news" of that Kingdom to "all the inhabited earth." (Matthew 24:14) Willing workers have to be trained, equipped, and sent out to preach. How gratifying it is to see over 2,800,000 people now honoring Jehovah by preaching the Kingdom good news worldwide! Record numbers of these are doing so on a full-time basis, many even moving to areas where there is a greater need. Thousands of missionaries have already been sent to pioneer the preaching work in other lands, and more are continually being added to their ranks.

To oversee, maintain, and support all this activity requires a vast organization. New branch facilities and missionary homes around the globe have had to be built and expanded. Local places of worship—Kingdom Halls and Assembly Halls—are presently being constructed at an unprecedented rate. It is heartwarming to see how willingly Jehovah's people have responded, showing a readiness to use their all in Jehovah's service. (Psalm 110:3) But the foretold 'speeding up' of the ingathering work in these last days now calls for an intensified willingness to honor Jehovah with our valuable things. (Isaiah 60:22) What, then, is required of us?

Appreciation is one thing—appreciation for all that Jehovah has given us. Yes, our assets are actually gifts from Jehovah. "Indeed," asks the apostle Paul, "what do you have that you did not receive?" (1 Corinthians 4:7) And for what purpose has God given them to us? So that we can use such gifts in honoring him!—1 Peter 4: 10, 11.

These gifts include our physical, mental, spiritual, and material assets—yes, life itself. And how generous Jehovah has been to each one of us! What a fine example he has set in giving! Surely, having received so much of Jehovah's bounty should move us to show appreciation for such provisions. Are we thus not moved to honor him with what we have?

Perhaps you feel limited in what you can do. After all, not everyone can serve as a missionary in a distant land or devote himself to some other feature of full-time service. Nor do most of us have the ability or means to go and assist on construction projects. Individual circumstances also limit those who can devote their lives to serve at branch offices where vital publications, such as this magazine, are printed. Yet each of us can experience the greater happiness that comes from giving. (Acts 20:35) And all of us can use our lives and speech in ways that please God and bring honor and praise to him.—Colossians 3:23.

How It Can Be Done

Though of tender years, Shelley and Stephen found a way. They realized that their contribution to the Watchtower Society would be used for the furtherance of the worldwide preaching work. And their donation, regardless of the amount, was certainly appreciated. Stephen received his letter of acknowledgment. So did little Shelley. It is not the amount but the motive that counts, for to be acceptable a gift must be completely voluntary. (2 Corinthians 9:7) Jehovah is pleased with our contributions, whether large or small, when they represent our whole-souled devotion to him.—Luke 21:1-4.

Appreciation, then, is followed up with action. Have we taken stock of what valuable things we have that may be used for honoring God? Our lives, with whatever vigor and strength we have, are certainly precious and not to be wasted on vain pursuits. Do we spend as much time as we can in developing and strengthening a close, personal relationship with Jehovah? Do we honor him by proclaiming his name and message with our lips? (Hebrews 13: 15, 16) Young children are also a precious possession given by Jehovah. (Psalm 127:3) Do we encourage them toward dedicating their life in service to God?

Then there are our literal gold, silver, and other monetary assets. Contributions of such a nature support our local congregations, including the maintenance of the Kingdom Halls and Assembly Halls that serve as centers of Bible instruction and preaching activities in our communities. When sent to the Watchtower Society's headquarters or branch office in a particular country, these contributions help advance the worldwide Kingdom-preaching work. Such gifts can be earmarked for use in whatever avenue we wish. Young Shelley, with her goal of missionary service in mind, wanted to help missionaries. Stephen, hearing of the great need for hundreds of additional Kingdom Halls and the tremendous expense involved, wanted his donation added to the Society Kingdom Hall Fund. Others contribute toward special needs, such as providing relief in times of disaster.

Oftentimes, though, individuals prefer to let the branch office determine how the money will be spent, since those brothers know which need is the most pressing. One contributor wrote: "Please find enclosed check for the Society to use as they see fit in furthering the preaching work. We're very happy to see the fine increase due to the efforts of all of Jehovah's people with Jehovah's blessing on the work." Another letter said: "Recently, upon retirement, I was the recipient of a lump-sum distribution from the company I had worked for. It is the sincere desire of both my wife and myself that some of this money be put to use in furthering the Kingdom proclamation. So please find the enclosed check offered on behalf of us and our children. May Jehovah bless you as you determine how this money may best be used."

Jehovah is pleased to see such willingness to honor him with our valuable things. He continues with the promise: "Then your stores of supply will be filled with plenty; and with new wine your own press vats will overflow." As in ancient Israel, so today Jehovah abundantly rewards such a generous spirit. The use of one's valuable things in honoring him does not mean depletion of them but their being increased due to Jehovah's blessing on the giver!—Proverbs 3:9, 10.

What a privilege we have to be able to honor Jehovah and stand out as different "among a crooked and twisted generation"! And what a privilege is ours to be able to share in the Kingdom proclamation, the work he has assigned to be done before this wicked system of things ends. (Philippians 2:15; Matthew 24:14; 28: 19, 20) Soon the inspired vision will be fulfilled when "every creature," no matter where, will everlastingly ascribe honor, glory, and might to Jehovah. (Revelation 5:13; 7:12) By all means, let us even now honor Jehovah with our valuable things.

"Just How Is Your Work Financed?"

Many ask this question. They are surprised when Witnesses calling at their door do not solicit funds. Others are likewise amazed when, attending a Witness assembly or visiting a Kingdom Hall for the first time, they find that no collection is ever taken. How, then, is the witness work financed? The answer: through voluntary contributions from those who want to honor Jehovah with their valuable things. Following are some ways this is accomplished.

Gifts: Donations of money may be sent directly to the Watch Tower Bible and Tract Society of Pennsylvania, 25 Columbia Heights, Brooklyn, New York 11201, or in other countries to the Society's branch office located there. A brief letter stating that such is a donation should accompany these contributions. Property can also be donated.

Conditional Donation Arrangement: Money, stocks, bonds, and property can be given to the Society with the provision that, in cases of personal need, returns may be made to the donor. This method avoids the expense and uncertainties of probate of will, while ensuring that the Society receives the property in event of death.

Insurance: The Watch Tower Society may be named as the beneficiary of an insurance policy and should be thus informed. Likewise, bank savings accounts can also be placed in trust for the Society.

Wills: Property or money may be bequeathed to the Watch Tower Society by means of a legally executed will. A copy should be sent to the Society.

Further information or advice can be obtained by writing to the Watch Tower Bible and Tract Society, Office of the Secretary and Treasurer, 25 Columbia Heights, Brooklyn, New York 11201 or to any local branch office.

New Missionaries Strive for Real Success

SUNDAY, September 8, 1985, was a historic day for the 4,351 who crowded into the beautiful Jersey City Assembly Hall of Jehovah's Witnesses to witness the graduation of the 79th class of the Watchtower Bible School of Gilead.

The day was historic in that it witnessed the first use of the Assembly Hall after its official dedication. Then, too, it was the first time since 1970 that virtually the whole United States Bethel family had been together under one roof. This family, including workers at Brooklyn and the Society's farms, has come to number more than 3,500. With the completion of the Jersey City Assembly Hall, there is at last a facility that can hold them all.

The day was especially historic for the 24 young servants of Jehovah from ten different countries who made up the 79th class. They had spent the previous five months in an intensive Bible-study and missionary-preparation course. Now, in the words of Albert Schroeder, chairman for the day, they ceased to be Gilead students and became Gilead graduates.

In the air-conditioned comfort of the Assembly Hall, these 24 new missionaries were given a send-off that they will long remember. The chairman reminded them that at Gilead they had learned many facts. But Gilead had put the emphasis on something that was more important: spirituality. The chairman then introduced a number of speakers to address some final words to the graduates.

Carey Barber, a member of the Governing Body, spoke about the search for happiness. Solomon, he reminded the graduates, found that the pleasures of this world do not bring happiness. (Ecclesiastes 2:1-11, 17) Hence Jesus stressed the need for spiritual things in seeking happiness. (Matthew 5:3) Therefore, the graduates should follow Jesus' counsel. Then, even if their being missionaries involves giving up some fleshly comforts, they can still succeed.

The following speaker, John Booth, also of the Governing Body, reminded the audience that the older missionary Paul encouraged the younger missionary Timothy to keep on making progress in Christian conduct, personal study, and prayer. (1 Timothy 2:1, 8; 4:12-16) The new missionaries would need to make similar progress if they were to be successful. Then, the secretary-treasurer of the Society, Lyman Swingle, mentioned that recently he had asked missionaries in Brazil what counsel they would like to give new missionaries to help them succeed. "Tell them," he was urged, "that when they reach their assignments, they should keep on reading the Bible and doing Bible research."

David Olson, of the Service Department Committee, told the experience of a man who supervised part of the project that succeeded in putting a man on the moon. Later, this same man earned his living sweeping parking lots. He felt more of a success in his second career. Why? Because his new work allowed him time to serve Jehovah and care for his family. Truly, those who find delight in Jehovah, his law, and his service find real success. —Psalm 1:1-3.

Ulysses Glass, Gilead registrar, paid tribute to the graduates' seriousness and respectfulness. He noted the interest they had taken in their studies and their keen desire to come to a full understanding of matters. Such things, he said, would help them in their assignments. Gilead instructor Jack Redford added that the first year in their assignments would be a challenge. Nevertheless, to succeed they should work closely with other missionaries, be patient, and cultivate spiritual joy. —Ecclesiastes 7:8, 9.

The final speaker, Watchtower Society President Frederick Franz opened his talk with the words: "It was worth living for 92 years to be present at an occasion like this!" Then he told the graduates the history of how Gilead got started and urged them to stay faithful in their assignments.

After the talks, the students received their diplomas, and there was a break for refreshments. Then they gave comments on the current *Watchtower* study under the supervision of Dean Songer of the Factory Committee. And they delighted everyone with a presentation of experiences, music, and some skits that conveyed their joy at having been at Gilead and their determination to seek "the more important things." (Philippians 1:10) Finally, the graduates presented the timely drama: *Seek God's Righteousness for Survival.*

And so the historic day drew to a close. It was a day that will long be remembered by the students as they follow the advice they had heard and strive for real success in their missionary assignments.

Teaching Nicodemus

WHILE attending the Passover of 30 C.E., Jesus performs remarkable signs, or miracles. As a result, many people put their faith in him. Nicodemus, a member of the Sanhedrin, the Jewish high court, is impressed and wants to learn more. So he visits Jesus during the darkness of night, probably fearing that his reputation with other Jewish leaders will be damaged if he is seen.

"Rabbi," he says, "we know that you as a teacher have come from God; for no one can perform these signs that you perform unless God is with him." In reply, Jesus tells Nicodemus that in order to enter the Kingdom of God a person must be "born again."

Yet how can a person be born again? "He cannot enter into the womb of his mother a second time and be born, can he?" Nicodemus asks.

No, that is not what being born again means. "Unless anyone is born from

water and spirit," Jesus explains, "he cannot enter into the kingdom of God." When Jesus was baptized and holy spirit descended upon him, he was thus born "from water and spirit." By the accompanying declaration from heaven, 'This is my Son whom I have approved,' God announced that he had brought forth a spiritual son having the prospect of entering into the heavenly Kingdom. Later, at Pentecost 33 C.E., other baptized ones received holy spirit and were thus also born again as spiritual sons of God.

But the role of God's special human Son is vital. "Just as Moses lifted up the serpent in the wilderness," Jesus tells Nicodemus, "so the Son of man must be lifted up, that everyone believing in him may have everlasting life." Yes, as those Israelites bitten by poisonous snakes had to look at the copper serpent to be saved, so all humans need to exercise faith in God's Son to be saved from their dying condition.

Stressing Jehovah's loving role in this, Jesus next tells Nicodemus: "God loved the world so much that he gave his only-begotten Son, in order that everyone exercising faith in him might not be destroyed but have everlasting life." Thus, here in Jerusalem just six months after beginning his ministry, Jesus makes clear that he is Jehovah God's means for saving humankind. **John 2:23–3:21; Matthew 3:16, 17; Acts 2:1-4; Numbers 21:9.**

♦ What prompted Nicodemus' visit, and why did he come at night?

♦ What does it mean to be "born again"?

♦ How did Jesus illustrate his role in our salvation?

'Seek First the Kingdom'
—Our Family Goal

By Stan and Jim Woodburn

"THIS message has robbed me of a whole family!" Looking back on close to 50 years now, it is not difficult to understand the chagrin of our church minister. All seven of us Woodburns, brothers and sisters, in quick succession became Jehovah's Witnesses in Whitehaven, England.

It started when John Woodburn, my eldest brother, purchased two books, one of them *The Harp of God,* from Ida Eccles, a full-time minister (pioneer) who is still faithfully preaching in Blackpool. John immediately started to attend the Witnesses' meetings, and in 1936 three of us brothers, John, Tom, and myself, Stan, motored to Glasgow, Scotland, to hear the then president of the Watch Tower Society, J. F. Rutherford, speak on the subject of Armageddon. Although this was our first assembly, we joined the 70 volunteers called for to serve as ushers at Brother Rutherford's public talk.

Into Full-Time Service —And the War!

In 1937 a zealous 26-year-old brother arrived from Brooklyn headquarters to take over supervision of the London branch office. He was Brother A. D. Schroeder, now a member of the Governing Body of Jehovah's Witnesses. What a great encouragement he was to us younger ones who wanted to be full-time preachers! Early in 1939 three of us brothers, unattached and free of family responsibilities, accepted the call to pioneer.

The world scene was changing rapidly, and on September 3, 1939, came Britain's declaration of war against Germany. Pressure was on to stem the preaching work, and soon afterward we had to face the issue of Christian neutrality.

When I was called to face the tribunal as a conscientious objector, the jury of seven upheld my objection, and I was permitted to continue my ministry, much to the outspoken annoyance of the presiding judge. Tom also was exempted from military service. However, John, Jim, and Martin, another of my brothers, were not so fortunate. They all received prison terms.

We all had many thrilling experiences during those war years, and they were not without their amusing side. On one occasion a policeman put his head through the sound-car window to tell me that the villagers had reported that I was broadcasting and receiving messages from the Nazi enemy! But he soon saw for himself that the vehicle contained only a phonograph with amplification equipment, not even a radio receiver!

Jim, meanwhile, had moved south to Birmingham, in the industrial Midlands, where he received good training as a pioneer, visiting business houses while working alongside veteran preacher Albert Lloyd. The city suffered from the constant air raids, and the fine central Kingdom Hall was bombed. But the Kingdom preaching increased, and many congregations were formed in outlying districts.

Time after time, the brothers had good

reason to be thankful for protection as they went about the territory giving spiritual comfort to the people. And what a need there was! I can still vividly recall the very morning that war was declared. I was in a small Welsh village at the time, publicly playing the phonograph record "World's End." Groups of people quickly gathered and asked me for literature. In no time I had distributed 38 books! Little wonder that from 1939 to 1945 the number of Witnesses in the British Isles almost doubled, to reach a peak of 13,150 by the end of the war.

Parting of the Ways

Shortly after the war ended, I left England to attend the eighth class of the Watchtower Bible School of Gilead in New York, in the United States. Jim and Martin, now appointed as circuit overseers, continued their privileges in the British field. At my graduation in 1947, I was assigned to the British Isles as a district overseer, and for five years I travelled throughout the country, overseeing circuit assemblies almost every weekend. Between us, Jim, Martin, and I covered the whole country during those years.

But there was a parting of the ways for us in 1950 when Jim was called to the 15th class of Gilead. He graduated at the international Theocracy's Increase Assembly of Jehovah's Witnesses on July 30, 1950, with an assignment to serve in Ecuador, South America. He will now tell his part of the story.

Ecuador and the Missionary Field

Missionary life in Ecuador was a challenge. In spite of the difficult climate and different customs, we saw the influx of many new brothers and sisters. But it was not easy. For example, we had no funds to organize the first circuit assembly in Guayaquil. So we missionaries went out in the preaching work and pooled all the contributions we received for the literature placed. That gave us sufficient funds to cover the expenses for that assembly.

In 1959 I had a very happy change of assignment to La Libertad, where another missionary, Frances Kerr, already lived. She had picked up the pioneer spirit from her mother, who had pioneered from the year 1919. Frances and I had known each other for a while, and in 1959 we got married.

There were no Witnesses in La Libertad when the first missionaries arrived there, but in that section there are now three thriving congregations. Things moved quickly, and we had many different assignments, such as in Quito, Ambato, and Manta. During that period, we had the privilege of helping 147 new ones to serve

*Jim and Frances Woodburn
served as missionaries
in Ecuador*

Jehovah, and we were instrumental in strengthening many more.

Sickness and Back to England

After our 20 years of service there, Ecuador had truly become our home, but in 1971 we sadly returned to England since Frances needed specialized medical treatment. Nevertheless, I was determined to carry on in the full-time service and not to go back into secular work. Happily for us, there were many Spanish-speaking people in the Paddington area of London, and eventually we were able to form the first Spanish-speaking congregation in England.

London is always a challenge for Witnesses who desire to preach in the stores, offices, and hotels, where people of all nationalities are met. This was our assignment for six years. We covered a vast area of London, taking in Camden, Chelsea, Kensington, Mill Hill, Paddington, and Stepney. During that period we placed over 7,000 Bibles and Bible study aids. In one hotel the chef assembled the whole kitchen staff in the main dining room, and we were able to give a 15-minute talk. They were Spanish, Italian, and Portuguese, and many had never seen a Bible.

The response was truly wonderful.

One day, while visiting offices in London's business centre, I came to a well-known bank and, looking inside, I saw a tall man, well groomed and imposing in appearance. Negatively, I thought he would turn the message down; but I said a short prayer and approached him. Without a word, he walked over to his desk, pulled out a green Bible and a *Watchtower* and said, "I also am one of Jehovah's Witnesses." It was a lesson for me to remember—do not prejudge people.

Witnessing at Schools

We always had the desire to return to Ecuador, and when Frances was fully restored in health, we were able to do so in 1977. What a joy that was for us! Our first assignment was Santo Domingo de Los Colorados. While there, we started to explore another avenue of activity. One morning while preaching from house to house, we found that most people were not at home. But there were three schools in the territory where there was plenty of activity—why not visit them? We prayed about the matter and then went to the teachers with the two publications *Your Youth—Getting the Best out of It* and *Did Man Get Here by Evolution or by Creation?* The results were marvellous!

We found that teachers and students alike were very keen to study these two books. One schoolmaster, a Catholic priest, asked for a hundred copies of each to make sure that every student of three classes had a personal copy. In another high school, the director had studied both books

and was anxious that the students also should read them. There were over 3,000 students, so we had to go three times to reach all of them in their classrooms. We left over a thousand books there!

At another Catholic school, the principal, a priest from Spain, had read the *Evolution* book with appreciation, so he gave us permission to visit each classroom and give a brief talk. We placed every publication we had with the students, and we had to return. Then we learned that they had been asked to do research in the *Youth* book on the chapter dealing with drugs. Apparently drugs were a growing problem in that school. We placed over 400 books on that occasion.

Our next assignment was the city of Ambato, surrounded by snowcapped mountains. Here again, with good results we were able to visit a Catholic training college, as well as several more schools in the district. In one, we visited every classroom and left 438 *Youth* books. Some of the teachers were so enthusiastic about the book that they did most of the talking for us and read out all the chapter themes to the students. They told the students that they should really get a copy, instead of buying worthless books.

On looking back, we have had the joy of talking to thousands of students and hundreds of teachers, leaving with them over 11,000 Bible study aids. Some of these people lived way back in inaccessible jungle areas where no car can reach. Yes, there is still a great work to be done in Ecuador.

Time has flashed by, and now, following a bout of ill health, we are back in London. For more than four decades Jehovah has backed us up with his holy spirit. What an expression of his undeserved kindness that we have been able to use our lives in his service, from our youth on! (Ecclesiastes 12:1) But now, let Stan tell you the rest of the story.

Preaching in Ireland

In 1949 there was much opposition to the witness work in Ireland, which was then under the care of the Watch Tower Society's London office. As a result of our open-air Bible talks, the presiding minister of the Northern Ireland Baptist Church challenged Jehovah's Witnesses to a debate on "The Resurrection of the Lord Jesus Christ." The Society asked me as district overseer to take on this assignment. It was to be held in Portadown, where a small congregation was active.

The night of the debate saw the Town Hall packed to the doors. It appeared that the Baptists had hired it some hours previously for a prayer meeting. With a thousand people present from all over the area and some 70 clergy, Jehovah's Witnesses were outnumbered. The Baptist pastor only engaged in sentimental religious emotion, trying to whip the crowd into opposition. After two hours of debate, he refused to explain 1 Peter 3:18 and other texts that prove that Jesus was raised a spirit.

Finally, when I reminded them of Gamaliel's advice at Acts 5:34-39, that they might be fighting against God, the pastor lost his temper and cried out, "Shut your doors on them! It's not wrong to shut your doors on the Devil!" However, several in the audience could see who had the truth. Some of his flock resigned, and that weekend the small Portadown Congregation went out to the people and placed more literature than in all the previous six months! Now there is a large congregation there with a fine Kingdom Hall and many congregations in other nearby towns.

Maintaining the Pioneer Spirit

In 1952 I married Joyce Cattell, a member of the London Bethel family, and in 1957 we had the joyful surprise of a daughter, Jane. This event brought a change in our pattern of life. Reluctantly, I went out to find secular work. But in spite of this we still kept the Kingdom first in our lives and experienced the proof of David's expression in a favourite psalm: "I have placed Jehovah in front of me constantly. Because he is at my right hand, I shall not be made to totter."—Psalm 16:8.

During the ensuing years, we moved to several areas, serving where the need was greater and sharing in auxiliary pioneer service from time to time. Brothers kindly helped with jobs, but I resisted the temptation to make the pursuit of material riches my principal goal in life. Necessary work for providing needed accommodations was available as I searched for them. I am so happy that I retained this pioneer spirit.

To South Africa, Ireland, and Back to Britain

Having served in many locations throughout the British Isles, including the remote Outer Hebrides, we moved to South Africa in the late '60's. There we worked among the coloured population and were happy to share in the increase of a small group of 5 Witnesses, which grew to 61. (1 Corinthians 3:6-9) For health reasons we returned to Northern Ireland in 1974, where we served along the border area amid terrorist activity.

During a trip over the border in 1975 while delivering some goods in my part-time work, I was stopped on the road by three hooded terrorists who ordered me to get out of my car. Questioned as to who I was and what I was doing, I quickly stated, "I am one of Jehovah's Witnesses." After making certain that I was not a spy for the English cause, they released me, and I went on my way, grateful for Jehovah's protection.—Proverbs 18:10.

In 1977 we returned to England. Then, what a joyous privilege we received. At the age of 62 I was invited back into circuit work! By this time our 20-year-old daughter, Jane, was a regular pioneer and well able to look after herself. So we sold the few possessions we had, and after two years in the circuit ministry, I again had the responsibility of serving in the district work, overseeing the assemblies at the Manchester Assembly Hall in the north of England. Truly, Psalm 16 was again being experienced, as verse 6 so beautifully reads: "The measuring lines themselves have fallen for me in pleasant places. Really, my own possession has proved agreeable to me."

Now we are happily serving in circuit work in areas I served years ago. But, oh, the difference! Yes, we meet the faithful older brothers we knew then, but expansion of the Kingdom work has brought hundreds more along and many more congregations.

Although three of the original seven of the Woodburn family have now died, the rest of us—Beth, 80 years old, and Tom, now 78, along with Jim and me—continue to serve Jehovah. My brother Martin finished his course faithfully in 1973 after 34 years preaching full time, and Marie, his widow, is still active in Glasgow, Scotland.

What a privileged family we have been! Counting all the children and grandchildren, 35 of us dedicated our lives to Jehovah. The love and kindness of many dear brothers, along with the protective love and blessings of Jehovah himself, have proved to all of us that "seeking first the kingdom" is the truly safe and wise course for our day.—Matthew 6:33.

Questions From Readers

■ **Was the apostle Paul part of the Christian governing body?**

It is reasonable to conclude that Paul was a part of the Christian governing body in the first century.

The Bible provides only limited detail about the composition of the early governing body, most of the information being in Acts chapter 15. That account indicates that in 49 C.E. the group of men forming the governing body consisted of "the apostles and older men in Jerusalem." Who were these?—Acts 15:2, 4, 6.

James, the half brother of Jesus, presided at that meeting to discuss the question of whether Gentile converts to Christianity had to keep the Mosaic Law, including circumcision. The apostle Peter shared in that discussion. The account speaks of Judas (called Barsabbas) and Silas as "leading men among the brothers," but it does not specifically say that they were part of the governing body. (Acts 15: 7, 13, 22) The point is that the Bible does not give a complete list of names of those making up the governing body. Some have felt that Paul might not have been included since he was a

traveling missionary and since he brought the question from the congregation in Antioch of Syria.

It is true that Paul was not one of "the twelve" who had walked with Jesus, for Matthias had been selected to replace Judas Iscariot.* But neither was the disciple James, though he clearly was part of the governing body. (Acts 6:2; 1:15-26) Furthermore, Jesus appeared to Paul and designated him as 'a chosen vessel to bear His name to the nations.' Paul thus became "an apostle, neither from men nor through a man, but through Jesus Christ and God." He called himself "an apostle to the nations."—Acts 9: 3-6, 15; Galatians 1:1; Romans 11:13; 1 Corinthians 9:1; 15: 7, 8.

As further indication that Paul became part of the body of "apostles and older men" who directed the congregations, consider what he did under God's power. Paul wrote 14 books of the Christian Greek Scriptures. Peter equates the writings of "our beloved brother Paul" with "the rest

---

* By this time also the apostle James had been killed.—Acts 12:2.

---

of the Scriptures." (2 Peter 3: 15, 16) Paul took a significant lead in spreading Christianity, and he offered an abundance of direction to congregations. His inspired writings show that Paul sometimes settled issues himself. That is as might be expected back then with one of the governing body who was far away from the central body and faced with slow means of communication. (1 Corinthians 5:11-13; 7:10, 17) But at other times he brought matters before the entire body, as the account in Acts 15 illustrates.

To Titus, "Paul, a slave of God and an apostle of Jesus Christ," wrote: "I left you in Crete, that you might correct the things that were defective and might make appointments of older men in city after city, as I gave you orders." (Titus 1:1, 5) So while traveling, Paul certainly spoke for the central governing body.—Acts 16: 4, 5.

So, even though his assignment from the Lord involved extensive travels and consequent absences from some meetings of the central governing body, the evidence of how he was used by God and Christ indicates that Paul was part of that body.

'I Wish I Had Had It 70 Years Ago'

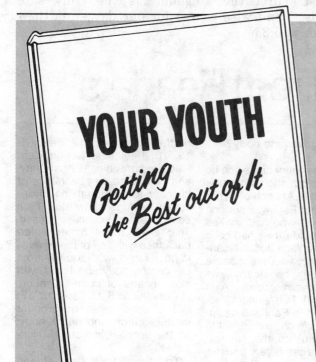

YOUR YOUTH
Getting the Best out of It

That is what an elderly woman said regarding the book *Your Youth—Getting the Best out of It*. She wrote: "Some time ago I ordered and received from you a copy of *Your Youth—Getting the Best out of It*. What a wonderful book! I wish I could have had something like it seventy years ago when I was a girl growing up! It is being used here, but now I am enclosing a check to you for four copies to be sent to my grandchildren who live far from me."

December 15, 1985

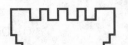

The Watchtower

Announcing Jehovah's Kingdom

Are You Grateful for What Jesus Did?

December 15, 1985
Vol. 106, No. 24

The Watchtower
Announcing Jehovah's Kingdom

THE PURPOSE OF "THE WATCHTOWER" is to exalt Jehovah God as the Sovereign of the universe. It keeps watch on world events as they fulfill Bible prophecy. It comforts all peoples with the good news that God's Kingdom will soon destroy those who oppress their fellowmen and that it will turn the earth into a paradise. It encourages faith in the now-reigning King, Jesus Christ, whose shed blood opens the way for mankind to gain eternal life. "The Watchtower," published by Jehovah's Witnesses continuously since 1879, is nonpolitical. It adheres to the Bible as its authority.

"WATCHTOWER" STUDIES FOR THE WEEKS

January 19: Declare Abroad the Kingdom of God. Page 10. Songs to Be Used: 148, 33.

January 26: Urgently Needed—More Harvest Workers! Page 16. Songs to Be Used: 223, 6.

Average Printing Each Issue: 11,150,000

Now Published in 103 Languages

SEMIMONTHLY EDITIONS AVAILABLE BY MAIL
Afrikaans, Arabic, Cebuano, Chichewa, Chinese, Cibemba, Danish, Dutch,* Efik, English,* Finnish, French, German,* Greek, Hiligaynon, Igbo, Iloko, Italian,* Japanese,* Korean, Lingala, Malagasy, Maltese, Norwegian, Portuguese, Russian, Sepedi, Sesotho, Shona, Spanish,* Swahili, Swedish, Tagalog, Thai, Tswana, Xhosa, Yoruba, Zulu

MONTHLY EDITIONS AVAILABLE BY MAIL
Armenian, Bengali, Bicol, Bulgarian, Croatian, Czech, Ewe, Fijian, Ga, Greenlandic, Gujarati, Gun, Hausa, Hebrew, Hindi, Hiri Motu, Hungarian, Icelandic, Kannada, Kikuyu, Kiluba, Malayalam, Marathi, New Guinea Pidgin, Pangasinan, Papiamento, Polish, Rarotongan, Romanian, Samar-Leyte, Samoan, Sango, Serbian, Silozi, Sinhalese, Slovenian, Solomon Islands-Pidgin, Tahitian, Tamil, Telugu, Tshiluba, Tsonga, Turkish, Twi, Ukrainian, Urdu, Venda, Vietnamese
* Study articles also available in large-print edition.

The Bible translation used is the "New World Translation of the Holy Scriptures," unless otherwise indicated.

Twenty cents (U.S.) a copy

Watch Tower Society offices	Yearly subscription Semimonthly
America, U.S., Watchtower, Wallkill, N.Y. 12589	$4.00
Australia, Box 280, Ingleburn, N.S.W. 2565	A$7.00
Canada, Box 4100, Halton Hills (Georgetown), Ontario L7G 4Y4	$5.20
England, The Ridgeway, London NW7 1RN	£5.00
Ireland, 29A Jamestown Road, Finglas, Dublin 11	£5.00
New Zealand, 6-A Western Springs Rd., Auckland 3	$15.00
Nigeria, P.O. Box 194, Yaba, Lagos State	₦6.00
Philippines, P.O. Box 2044, Manila 2800	₱50.00
South Africa, Private Bag 2, Elandsfontein, 1406	R5,60

Remittances should be sent to the office in your country or to Watchtower, Wallkill, N.Y. 12589, U.S.A.

Changes of address should reach us 30 days before your moving date. Give us your old and new address (if possible, your old address label).

The Watchtower (ISSN 0043-1087) is published semimonthly for $4.00 (U.S.) per year by Watch Tower Bible and Tract Society of Pennsylvania, 25 Columbia Heights, Brooklyn, N.Y. 11201. Second-class postage paid at Brooklyn, N.Y., and at additional mailing offices.

Postmaster: Send address changes to Watchtower, **Wallkill, N.Y. 12589.**

Published by
Watch Tower Bible and Tract Society of Pennsylvania
25 Columbia Heights, Brooklyn, N.Y. 11201, U.S.A.
Frederick W. Franz, President

Are You Grateful for What Jesus Did?

WHAT could be a more simple and direct way to express gratitude than by the words, "Thank you"? But not all who say, "Thank you" truly appreciate what they have received. Those words could be said for other reasons, such as a mere polite form of courtesy in response to another person's deed. Proper, yet mechanical.

However, upon receiving a gift, especially a prized one, genuine, heartfelt expressions of gratitude are most fitting. A gift can make us happy; it can fill a need. When it does both, the gift is of exceptional value. But if, thereafter, the gift is ignored or abused, then any expression of thanks was hollow. Therefore, appreciation, or lack of it, is often shown by how we feel about a gift and how we use it.

Mankind's Creator, Jehovah, gave us his most valuable possession, his Son, as a gift. John 3:16 says: "For God loved the world so much that he gave his only-begotten Son, in order that everyone exercising faith in him might not be destroyed but have everlasting life." That gift will make us happy and will fill our needs if we show genuine gratitude. Yet, since Jehovah is the Giver, why should you be grateful to Jesus?

What Jesus Did for You

'What did Jesus do for me?' you may ask. Even before you were born, Jesus did something for you. What was that? Jesus surrendered his heavenly, prehuman existence to be born as a human by means of the virgin Mary. (Luke 1:26-33) This was no little thing. Would you be willing to move away from a home of peace, security, and health, where you were surrounded by loyal friends, to reside in a place where strife, danger, and disease were constant, and foes were plotting your death? 'In no way,' most would answer. Yet, that is what Jesus did.—John 17:5; Philippians 2:5-8.

Because Jehovah God and not any human was his Father, Jesus was free from sin. (Luke 1:34, 35) Not once did he transgress in thought, word, or deed. In spite of the sinful conditions all around him and the opposition he had to face, he could say to his opposers: "Who of you convicts me of sin?" Not one could! As the apostle Peter expressed it: "He committed no sin, nor was deception found in his mouth." (John 8:46; 1 Peter 2:22) Based on these facts, let us illustrate further how this involves you.

Many people are squeamish about visiting the ill persons at a hospital, let alone living with them. Jesus was perfect in body, so he had perfect health. Still, he did not isolate himself from others, nor did he seek to live in a sterile environment. Rather, out of love, Jesus willingly ate, slept, and associated with diseased and dying mankind.—Matthew 15:30-37; Mark 1:40-42.

Then Jesus voluntarily gave up that perfect human existence for the benefit of mankind. Being perfect, he had the right to endless human life, and this he sacrificed to give us a grand opportunity. As he himself stated: "The Son of man came . . . to minister and to give his soul a ransom in exchange for many." (Matthew 20:28) His apostles gave like testimony regarding this: "We behold Jesus, who has been made a little lower than angels, . . . that he by God's undeserved kindness might taste death for every man." (Hebrews 2:9) Jesus' laying down his human life for mankind was the greatest possible expression of love any human could make. By it he provided the greatest gift that we as imperfect human creatures could possibly receive, namely, an opportunity for everlasting life.—John 3:16; 15:13.

'Jesus certainly has done much for me,' you may conclude, 'but how can I show that I am grateful?'

How You Can Show Gratitude for What Jesus Did

ACTIONS speak a louder "Thank you" than mere words. Therefore, if you appreciate what Jesus did for you, you will want to exercise faith in him as your Savior. In fact, it is only by doing so that you can hope to benefit from Jesus' sacrifice. Remember the expression "exercising faith," found at John 3:16? Well, that implies more than believing and giving mental assent to the fact that he died for you. It involves *acting* upon that belief too.

Heed the instructions Peter gave to his Jewish listeners shortly after Pentecost 33 C.E.: "Repent, therefore, and turn around so as to get your sins blotted out." (Acts 3:19) That indicates action of two sorts. On the one hand, we sincerely oppose the sinful tendencies of our minds and bodies. On the other hand, we plead with God for forgiveness of our sins on the basis of Jesus' sacrifice.—1 John 2: 1, 2.

Imitate Jesus' Example

Colin, who has been a baptized Christian for 24 years, was asked why he is grateful for what Jesus did. He replied: "I appreciate his ransom sacrifice, but it is his *example* that helps me the most. His life serves as a pattern for me to imitate."

If we are truly grateful, would we not want to follow Jesus' example of humility, subjection, and self-sacrificing love? If your lips respond, "Yes!" what do your attitude and actions answer? For instance, how would most people respond when faced with an assignment that will promote true worship but calls for humility and sacrifice on their part, such as scrubbing floors in a place used for Christian meetings? How would you react? Would you, out of appreciation for Jesus and his heavenly Father, be *willing* to accept an assignment that many would consider beneath them and too uncomfortable? Jesus humbled himself in performing a comparable service to others.—John 13:2-17; Philippians 2:7, 8.

Let us consider another example. Misunderstandings between people often lead to harsh words and hurt feelings. What would most do if they were in a room full of people that included someone who had deeply offended them? What would you do? Out of gratitude for Jesus and Jehovah, would you willingly take the first step to reconcile your differences with the offending party, doing so with a quiet and mild spirit? Jesus and his heavenly Father did so with sinful mankind.—Romans 5:6-10; 1 John 4:9-11.

In addition to giving up his heavenly glory to become a man and then laying down his earthly life as mankind's Redeemer, Jesus did humankind an incalculable service by his teaching. No other human so powerfully affected mankind for good as did Jesus Christ. He was a teacher without equal. He taught men regarding God's name, personality, purposes, and will for human creatures.—John 7:45, 46.

Among the outstanding examples of his teaching is the Sermon on the Mount. In it Jesus stated what has become known as the golden rule: "Always treat others as you would like them to treat you." (Matthew 7:12, *The New English Bible*) He also showed what the two greatest commandments of the Law were: 'To love Jehovah God with all your heart, soul, mind, and strength, and to love your neighbor as yourself.' (Mark 12:29-31) Not to be overlooked are his prophecies, the fulfillment of which so clearly shows where we are on God's timetable.—Matthew, chapters 24 and 25.

Jesus backed up his teaching by his course of action, giving us the ideal, the perfect, example to follow. He began his career by presenting himself entirely to do his Father's will and then symbolizing that by being baptized in water. God sent him to earth, primarily to bear witness to the truth. Just before Jesus died, he could say to his Father: "I have glorified you on the earth, having finished the work you have given me to do," and "I have made your name manifest to the men you gave me out of the world."—John 17:4, 6.

Jesus intended for others to imitate his example. This is apparent from his own words and those of others. "Come after me," and, "Come be my follower," said Jesus at Matthew 4:19 and 19:21. "Christ suffered for you, leaving you a model for you to follow his steps closely," and, "Become imitators of me, even as I am of Christ," wrote the apostles Peter and Paul.—1 Peter 2:21; 1 Corinthians 11:1.

To show gratitude for what Jesus Christ did for you as the Great Teacher and Exemplar, continue to familiarize yourself with his teachings. This requires regular study of God's Word, especially the Christian Greek Scriptures, in which Jesus'

Ways that you can show gratitude for Jesus

teachings are found. Since you will need help to understand and appreciate what you read, it would be wise to avail yourself of printed Bible study helps available for that very purpose.* Also, make a conscientious effort to apply what you learn in your everyday life. Yes, proper action is required. Jesus observed: "Not everyone saying to me, 'Lord, Lord,' will enter into the kingdom of the heavens, but the one *doing* the will of my Father who is in the heavens will."—Matthew 7:21; 4:17; Luke 4:17-21.

Put Worship of Jehovah First

Today more than 1,056,000,000 people claim to be Christian. But what little grat-

---

* We recommend, for example, *You Can Live Forever in Paradise on Earth,* published by the Watchtower Bible and Tract Society of New York, Inc.

itude most of them show for what Jesus did for them! Apparently, many feel that they are doing quite well if they go to church twice a year, on Christendom's major holidays. Or others will say, 'I love God because I believe in the Ten Commandments.' But how many obey them? That perfect law code, once binding upon the ancient nation of Israel, gave priority to the proper worship of Jehovah God, specifically by its first four commandments.—Exodus 20:1-11.

How many professed Christians are really following Jesus' example by applying the principles of the Ten Commandments in their daily life? Are they giving God their "exclusive devotion," as called for in the second commandment? Like Jesus, are they making manifest God's name in a proper way, which was the emphasis of the third commandment? True Christians not only are virtuous but also put the worship of Jehovah foremost in their lives.—Matthew 6:33.

Many such Christians are aware that assembling together is a part of God's worship. But have you ever considered regular attendance at Christian meetings to be a sign of gratefulness? The apostle Paul did. He reasons that way in the 10th chapter of his letter to the Hebrews. He also reveals the danger of indifference to Christian meetings. Such an attitude could cause a Christian to become discouraged and inactive in good deeds of faith. For some others, their appreciation for God's way of salvation through Christ could be shrinking. If this is true and their dwindling faith is not checked, it may lead to willful sin, even apostasy. This would amount to treating God's gift as something of "ordinary value," or as something common, an insult to both Jehovah and Jesus.—Hebrews 10:23-31.

Note Paul's warning concerning those who go beyond slighting meetings to actual rejection of God's gift for salvation. "Any man that has disregarded the law of Moses dies without compassion, upon the testimony of two or three. Of how much more severe a punishment, do you think, will the man be counted worthy who has trampled upon the Son of God and who has esteemed as of ordinary value the blood of the covenant by which he was sanctified, and who has outraged the spirit of undeserved kindness with contempt?" —Hebrews 10:28, 29.

The Law was God's gift through Moses. So Paul reminds his readers that if unrepentant violators of that divine Law received capital punishment, death, how much more deserving of punishment are those who contemptuously neglect God's greater gift through Jesus Christ, the Greater Moses. Those who desecrate the Son of God as their Savior and despise his sacrifice are in line for "the second death" —a severe punishment with no hope of a resurrection.—Revelation 21:8; Deuteronomy 13:6-10; 17:2-7.

Paul is also showing what an ingrate the willful sinner or apostate has become. Such a man has committed the ultimate insult in three ways. First, he "has trampled upon the Son of God." Either he now views Jesus as his enemy, for ancient conquerors trod on the necks of their conquered foes, or he looks upon Jesus with disdain, because men tread on what they despise. (Compare Matthew 7:6.) Second, he "has esteemed as of ordinary value the blood of the covenant by which he was sanctified." He scorns the means (Christ's blood) by which he was declared clean. He counts that blood, validating the new covenant, as of no more worth than the blood of imperfect men, as something not sacred. Third, he "has outraged the spirit of undeserved kindness with contempt." He has blasphemed God's active force, willfully opposing Jehovah's influence, saying it has no value and therefore is of no use to him.—Ephesians 4:30.

Such blatant acts of contempt can be avoided if we always prize God's gift for salvation. Christian meetings are a way by which we can maintain proper esteem. Since Jehovah and Jesus are present invisibly at these gatherings, grateful Christians will not snub them, as the apostates do, but rather do all they reasonably can to attend regularly.—Compare Malachi 3:16; Matthew 18:20.

Therefore, be grateful for what Jesus has done for you. Exercise genuine faith in his ransom sacrifice. Imitate his example in your dealings with others. Put first in your life the worship of his Father, Jehovah God. In this way you can say: "Thanks be to God for his indescribable free gift" of undeserved kindness through Jesus.—2 Corinthians 9:15.

John Decreases, Jesus Increases

FOLLOWING the Passover in the spring of 30 C.E., Jesus and his disciples leave Jerusalem. However, they do not return to their homes in Galilee but go into the country of Judea where they do baptizing. John the Baptizer has been doing the same work for about a year now, and he still has disciples associating with him.

Actually, Jesus does not do any baptizing himself, but his disciples do it under his direction. Their baptism has the same significance as that performed by John, it being a symbol of a Jew's repentance of sins against God's Law covenant. However, after his resurrection, Jesus instructs his disciples to do baptizing that is of different significance. Christian baptism is a symbol of a person's dedication to serve Jehovah God.

At this early point in Jesus' ministry, however, both John and he, although working separately, are teaching and baptizing repentant ones. But John's disciples become jealous and complain to him regarding Jesus: "Rabbi, . . . see, this one is baptizing and all are going to him."

Rather than being jealous, John rejoices in Jesus' success and also wants his disciples to rejoice. He reminds them: "You yourselves bear me witness that I said, I am not the Christ, but, I have been sent forth in advance of that one." Then he uses a beautiful illustration: "He that has the bride is the bridegroom. However, the friend of the bridegroom, when he stands and hears him, has a great deal of joy

on account of the voice of the bridegroom. Therefore this joy of mine has been made full."

John, as the friend of the Bridegroom, rejoiced some six months earlier when he introduced his disciples to Jesus. Certain ones of them became prospective members of Christ's heavenly bride class to be made up of Christians anointed with the spirit. John wants his present disciples also to follow Jesus, since his purpose is to prepare the way for Christ's successful ministry. As John explains: "That one must go on increasing, but I must go on decreasing."

Not long after this, John is arrested by King Herod. Herod has taken Herodias, the wife of Philip his brother, as his own, and when John publicly exposes his actions as improper, Herod has him put in prison. When Jesus hears about John's arrest, he leaves Judea with his disciples for Galilee. **John 3:22–4:3; Acts 19:4; Matthew 28:19; 2 Corinthians 11:2; Mark 1:14; 6:17-20.**

♦ What is the significance of baptisms done under Jesus' direction prior to his resurrection? And after his resurrection?

♦ How does John show that his disciples' complaint is unwarranted?

♦ Why is John put in prison?

Declare Abroad the Kingdom of God

"Let the dead bury their dead, but you go away and declare abroad the kingdom of God."—LUKE 9:60.

THE Kingdom of God—that was the most important interest in Jesus' life! It is the same today for all of us who are his true footstep followers. As Christians, we are striving to follow Jesus' steps closely by living according to the Bible. (1 Peter 2:21) But now, as we enter the year 1986, could it be that we need to reexamine our priorities in life? For instance, how would you explain Jesus' telling someone to "let the dead bury their dead"? Why do you think that Jesus then stressed the importance of declaring the Kingdom message, in contrast to what would seem to be appropriate family concerns? What do you say?

2 Long before Jesus used the expression "the kingdom of God," the psalmist David

1. What important questions are raised by Jesus' statement in Luke 9:60?

2. When did Jehovah's sovereignty start, and how enduring is it?

wrote under divine inspiration: "Jehovah himself has firmly established his throne in the very heavens; and over everything his own kingship has held domination." (Psalm 103:19) Jehovah's sovereignty started when he began his creation. The foundation of his throne can never be moved. His right to universal sovereignty can never be snatched away from him. Little wonder that a psalmist exhorts: "Declare among the nations his glory, . . . for Jehovah is great and very much to be praised"!—Psalm 96:3, 4; 109:21; Daniel 4:34, 35.

³ However, not all have continued to praise Jehovah. Satan, the first apostate, challenged the way that Jehovah had expressed and exercised His sovereignty toward His creatures on earth. (Genesis 3:1-5; Job 1:6-12; 2:1-5) As a result, on earth and later in heaven, some creatures became infected with Satan's rebellious attitude. Satan also influenced men to set up a series of human kingdoms. He has used these to challenge the rightness of God's rulership. (Revelation 13:1-6) To settle this issue of universal sovereignty, Jehovah purposed something unusual, as foretold at Daniel 2:44: "In the days of those kings the God of heaven will set up a kingdom that will never be brought to ruin. . . . It will crush and put an end to all these kingdoms, and it itself will stand to times indefinite."

Jehovah Becomes King Over Israel

⁴ It therefore now becomes clear that, although Jehovah's sovereignty dates from his commencing creation, he purposed to make a specific expression of his rulership to settle forever the question of the rightfulness of his sovereignty. This expression was the heavenly Messianic Kingdom. The earthly kingdom that Jehovah established over the nation of Israel served as a small-scale representation of this Kingdom "that will never be brought to ruin." Hence, when King David brought the ark of the covenant into the city of Jerusalem, he was able to sing exultantly: "Let the heavens rejoice, and let the earth be joyful, and let them say among the nations, 'Jehovah himself has become king!'" (1 Chronicles 16:31) Yes, in a special sense Jehovah had "become king" for all Israel. It was a time of great joy, and David wanted to declare abroad that wonderful event!

⁵ King David's shepherding background laid the basis for his being a unique king among kings. He was a shepherd-king. The psalmist describes David's being chosen by God for this position, saying: "[Jehovah] chose David his servant and took him from the pens of the flock . . . to be a shepherd over Jacob his people and over Israel his inheritance. And he began to shepherd them according to the integrity of his heart, and with the skillfulness of his hands he began leading them."—Psalm 78:70-72.

⁶ David's shepherding care for his people, his integrity of heart toward his God, and his skillfulness as a leader well qualified him to portray the coming Messiah, who was to be used in a special way to express Jehovah's universal kingship and to act as a loving Shepherd-King. This wonderful development in Jehovah's purposes was later foretold by the prophet Ezekiel: "I will raise up over [Israel] one shepherd, and he must feed them, even my servant David. . . . And I myself, Jehovah, will become their God, and my servant

---

3. (a) What events led up to a challenge of Jehovah's rulership? (b) How does God purpose to settle the issue of universal sovereignty?
4. In what sense could David say that "Jehovah himself has become king," and what did such an event call forth?

5, 6. (a) In what respect was David unique among kings? (b) Whom did David foreshadow, and in what respect?

Matthew left everything behind and followed Jesus

David a chieftain in the midst of them. I myself, Jehovah, have spoken."—Ezekiel 34:22-24.

The Foretold Shepherd-King Appears

⁷ The One foretold by Jehovah was his own Son, Jesus. Concerning him, the angel Gabriel told the virgin Mary: "Look! you will conceive in your womb and give birth to a son, and you are to call his name Jesus. This one will be great and will be called Son of the Most High; and Jehovah God will give him the throne of David his father, and he will rule as king over the house of Jacob forever, and there will be no end of his kingdom." (Luke 1: 31-33) What a wonderful expression of

---

7, 8. (a) How was the foretold Shepherd-King identified, and what did his appearance deserve? (b) For what purpose was Jesus "approved" by Jehovah?

Jehovah's kingship this was going to be! Surely, such a coming event would warrant the greatest worldwide declaration: "Jehovah himself has become king!"

⁸ Following Jesus' miraculous birth and his growth to manhood, he presented himself for baptism in the waters of the river Jordan. At that time God acknowledged Jesus as his Son by pouring out spirit upon him and saying: "You are my Son, the beloved; I have approved you." (Luke 3:22) For what was Jesus "approved"? Luke's account explains: "Jesus himself, when he commenced his work, was about thirty years old." (Luke 3:23; *Ref. Bi.* footnote: "Or, 'commenced [to teach].'") The *Revised Standard Version* and the *New International Version* say, "When he began his ministry." What was Jesus' "work," or "ministry"? What did he "teach"? The writer Matthew gives the

answer: "[Jesus] went around throughout the whole of Galilee, teaching in their synagogues and preaching the good news of the kingdom and curing every sort of disease and every sort of infirmity among the people."—Matthew 4:23.

⁹ Jesus devoted his life to 'declaring abroad the kingdom of God.' Like his forefather David, he demonstrated his integrity of heart by never compromising his allegiance to Jehovah's Kingdom. (Luke 9:60; 4:3-13; John 16:33) Jesus proved himself to be that "one shepherd" whom Jehovah had promised to raise up. He was happy to feed spiritually those whom the religious leaders had "skinned and thrown about like sheep without a shepherd." (Matthew 9:36) Regarding his skilled work of shepherding people and how it would gradually widen out in years to come, Jesus said: "I am the fine shepherd, and I know my sheep and my sheep know me . . . And I have other sheep, which are not of this fold; those also I must bring, and they will listen to my voice, and they will become one flock, one shepherd."—John 10:14, 16.

¹⁰ How did the Jews react to Jesus' invitation to become his sheeplike followers? Their reactions were varied. As we examine some of these reactions, consider what your response has been since coming in contact with the message of God's Kingdom.

"Be My Follower" —How Do You Respond?

¹¹ While Jesus was walking near the Sea of Galilee, he spotted Simon and his brother Andrew fishing. "Jesus said to them: 'Come after me, and I shall cause you to become fishers of men.' And at once they abandoned their nets and followed him. And after going a little farther he saw James the son of Zebedee and John his brother . . . and . . . he called them. In turn they left their father Zebedee in the boat with the hired men and went off after him." (Mark 1:16-20) The same positive reaction was shown by tax collector Levi, or Matthew. "[Jesus] said to him: 'Be my follower.' And leaving everything behind he rose up and went following him."—Luke 5:27, 28.

¹² However, not all reacted positively to Jesus' invitation, "Be my follower." Think of that man described in Luke chapter 9, whom Jesus met while traveling from one village to another. He said to Jesus: "I will follow you to wherever you may depart." Matthew's account indicates that this man was a scribe. The scribes were looked up to by the people and were called "Rabbi." Now notice Jesus' reply: "Foxes have dens and birds of heaven have roosts, but the Son of man has nowhere to lay down his head." (Luke 9:57, 58) Jesus was telling this man that he would have to rough it if he became His follower. The implication is that this man was too proud to accept this mode of life. The uncertainty of not knowing where he was going to spend the next night was too much for him to take.

¹³ Jesus said to another bystander: "Be my follower." But, in reply, he said to Jesus: "Permit me first to leave and bury my father." Note Jesus' reply: "Let the dead bury their dead, but you go away and declare abroad the kingdom of God."

---

9. In what respects was Jesus like his forefather David?
10. How can we learn from the varied reactions of the Jews to Jesus' invitation to follow him?
11. Describe the response of Simon, Andrew, James, John, and Matthew to Jesus' invitation, "Come after me."

---

12. What was the problem with the man who told Jesus: "I will follow you to wherever you may depart"?
13. Why did Jesus reply the way he did to another who could have become a follower?

(Luke 9:59, 60) This man's excuse did not imply that his father had already died. If he had died, it would have been very unlikely that the son would have been on that road listening to Jesus. No, it would appear from what the man said that he was bidding for time to await his father's death. He was not prepared to put the Kingdom of God first in his life immediately.—Matthew 6:33.

¹⁴ The record tells of a third man, who volunteered: "I will follow you, Lord; but first permit me to say good-bye to those in my household." This man was apparently asking for conditions to be attached to his becoming a follower of Jesus. He was, in effect, saying to Jesus: 'Look! I will be one of your followers, if . . . ' What was Jesus' answer? "No man that has put his hand to a plow and looks at the things behind is well fitted for the kingdom of God." (Luke 9:61, 62) When a plowman wants to turn over a straight furrow in the field, he must keep looking straight ahead. If he turns his head to look behind, that furrow will likely become crooked. He might even trip himself! So it is with Jesus' footstep followers; for them to look behind at this old system of things, even for a moment, is to court trouble, causing their feet to stumble and wander off the 'cramped road leading off into life.' —Matthew 7:14; see Luke 17:31-35.

¹⁵ Have you heard Jesus' invitation: "Be my follower"? What has been your response? Have you shown the same positive response as the disciples Simon, Andrew, James, John, and Matthew? Like those men, are you prepared to make any sacrifice needed in order to follow the Master's footsteps? If your answer is yes, then you will also enjoy the inestimable

privilege of sharing in declaring abroad the good news of God's Kingdom.

¹⁶ Before Jesus sent out his disciples to proclaim the Kingdom, he skillfully taught them how to do so by his own personal example. Following this, Jesus gave them detailed instructions on how to search out sheeplike ones in any given territory. Jesus' instructions are still applicable in this 20th century. Let us examine some of these as recorded in chapter 10 of Matthew's account.

Kingdom-Preaching Instructions

¹⁷ The theme of the disciples' message was to be the same as the one Jesus had been proclaiming: "As you go, preach, saying, 'The kingdom of the heavens has drawn near.'" (Matthew 10:7) However, that Kingdom has now been established in the heavens. Jehovah's Shepherd-King, Christ Jesus, now rules! Hence, the words of David now take on a greater meaning: "Let the heavens rejoice, and let the earth be joyful, and let them say among the nations, 'Jehovah himself has become king!'" (1 Chronicles 16:31) Today, not only are we privileged to support this special expression of Jehovah's universal kingship but we also have the joy of living in the time when the issue of Jehovah's sovereignty is to be settled for all time to come.

¹⁸ Matthew 10:8-10 describes the attitude of those sharing in the preaching work. God's Kingdom has to take first place in their life, physical needs are secondary. Why? Jesus says: "For the work-

---

14, 15. (a) What is indicated in the third man's request to Jesus? (b) What lesson can we today learn from Jesus' reply to this man?

16. How did Jesus prepare his disciples for sharing with him in preaching the good news?
17. Compare the substance of the Kingdom message preached in the first century with that of today.
18. What did Jesus emphasize to his followers in Matthew 10:8-10, and who can especially appreciate this today?

er deserves his food." Our heavenly Father will always take care of those who put their trust in him. And hundreds of thousands of full-time ministers of Jehovah's Witnesses today can testify to this fact.—Numbers 18:30, 31; Deuteronomy 25:4.

19 Jesus next instructs: "Into whatever city or village you enter, search out who in it is deserving, and stay there until you leave." (Matthew 10:11) Deserving of what? Deserving of the privilege of entertaining this servant of Jehovah and listening to the message of God's Kingdom. Of course, back then the disciples would probably have stayed in the home of that deserving person and used such as a base while they combed the rest of the territory to find other deserving ones. Today, Jehovah's Witnesses follow a similar procedure. They spend millions of hours and expend much effort in searching out deserving ones in various territories. Then, when these are found, the Witnesses have great happiness in revisiting those householders and explaining God's Word to them. Thus, today, Jesus is skillfully shepherding other sheeplike ones to his right side of favor.—Matthew 25:31-33.

20 "When you are entering into the house, greet the household; and if the house is deserving, let the peace you wish it come upon it." (Matthew 10:12, 13) "May this house have peace" was a common greeting in Jesus' day. (Luke 10:5) The angels sang at the time of Jesus' birth: "Glory in the heights above to God, and upon earth peace among men of goodwill." (Luke 2:14) A deserving household experienced this foretold peace by accepting the disciples' Kingdom message. Today, the Kingdom good news has the same effect. It brings people into peaceful relations with God through Jesus Christ, and it also brings peace among fellow believers.—2 Corinthians 5:20, 21; Philippians 4:7; Ephesians 4:3.

21 During the 1986 calendar year, the Kingdom Halls of Jehovah's Witnesses throughout the earth will be displaying the yeartext drawn from Luke 9:60: "Go . . . , declare abroad the kingdom of God." What a fine reminder and incentive this will be for all of God's true ministers to share regularly in preaching God's Kingdom! Yes, that Kingdom has been here since 1914! It is God's instrument in the hands of his Messianic King for crushing all of Satan's worldly kingdoms. No wonder, then, that the Kingdom of God should be of prime importance in the life of every one of Jehovah's Witnesses. We know that this means our salvation to life!—1 Timothy 4:16.

21. Why is the yeartext for 1986 so appropriate?

19. How is the searching out of deserving ones done today, and under whose direction?
20. How does a deserving household experience the peace wished upon it by the Kingdom preacher?

How Would You Answer?

□ How long-standing and secure is Jehovah's kingship?

□ What universal issue now needs to be settled?

□ What must all of Jesus' followers be prepared to do?

□ Why is the expression "Jehovah himself has become king" more meaningful today?

□ What purpose will be served by the 1986 yeartext?

Urgently Needed
—More Harvest Workers!

"The harvest, indeed, is great, but the workers are few. Therefore beg the Master of the harvest to send out workers into his harvest."—LUKE 10:2.

A S YOU read these words of Jesus, do you feel that they involve you? Since they were spoken over 19 centuries ago, you might be inclined to reason that they are no longer significant. Such a hasty conclusion would indeed be a mistake. To see the full import of Jesus' words, let us look back at what happened when the statement was first made, and then examine our own situation today.—Compare 1 Corinthians 10:11.

2 In 32 C.E., with the Festival of Booths past, only another six months remained before Jesus faced death on a torture stake. To help speed up the work of preaching, Jesus sent out 70 disciples "by twos in advance of him into every city and place to which he himself was going to come." They went off with Jesus' words ringing in their ears: "The harvest, indeed, is great, but the workers are few. Therefore beg the Master of the harvest to send out workers into his harvest."—Luke 10:1, 2.

A Great Harvest Results

3 What was the result of this increased

---

1. How might you reason regarding Jesus' words at Luke 10:2, but what would you be well advised to do?
2. What situation demanding urgent action faced Jesus in 32 C.E., and how did he handle it?

3. Describe some of the results of increased preaching during the last few months of Jesus' ministry.

preaching effort? We read: "Then the seventy returned with joy, saying: 'Lord, even the demons are made subject to us by the use of your name.'" What a marvelous display this was of God's power over the demons! Such a fine service report surely thrilled Jesus, for he said: "I began to behold Satan already fallen like lightning from heaven." (Luke 10:17, 18) Jesus knew that Satan and his demons were ultimately to be cast out of heaven following the birth of the Messianic Kingdom in the heavens. But while Jesus was yet on earth, this casting out of unseen demons by mere humans served as an added assurance to him of that coming joyful event. Jesus therefore spoke of this future fall of Satan from heaven as a certainty.—Revelation 12:5, 7-10.

⁴ The harvest Jesus spoke about was not one of grain or fruits but one of people, sheeplike people who would readily respond to the Kingdom message. Already the fruits of such a harvest were becoming manifest. However, the harvesting accomplished by Jesus and his followers in those few remaining months before Nisan 14, 33 C.E., was only the laying of the groundwork for a far greater harvest following Jesus' death and resurrection.—Compare Psalm 126:1, 2, 5, 6.

⁵ The time now was the day of Pentecost, 33 C.E. About 120 of Jesus' followers were met together in Jerusalem. "Suddenly there occurred from heaven a noise just like that of a rushing stiff breeze, and it filled the whole house in which they were sitting. . . . And they all became filled with holy spirit and started to speak with different tongues, just as the spirit was granting them to make utterance." This was the start of a phenomenal harvest! "On that day about three thousand souls were added." (Acts 1:15; 2:1-4, 41) "Day after day they were in constant attendance at the temple with one accord, . . . praising God and finding favor with all the people. At the same time Jehovah continued to join to them daily those being saved." (Acts 2:46, 47) Later we find: "Believers in the Lord kept on being added, multitudes both of men and of women." Still later: "The word of God went on growing, and the number of the disciples kept multiplying in Jerusalem very much; and a great crowd of priests began to be obedient to the faith."—Acts 5:14; 6:7.

⁶ Opposition to the Kingdom message now grew intense. Did this slow down the harvesting work? No, for "those who had been scattered went through the land declaring the good news of the word." Philip went to the city of Samaria; crowds listened to him eagerly; the demon possessed, the paralyzed, and the lame were all cured. No wonder that "there came to be a great deal of joy in that city."—Acts 8:1-8.

⁷ The resurrected Jesus had told his disciples: "You will be witnesses of me both in Jerusalem and in all Judea and Samaria and to the most distant part of the earth." (Acts 1:8) The vastness of the field of activity called for more workers—urgently! What a harvest of disciples was now to be expected! And it was already happening —all under the guidance of God's holy spirit. Following the conversion of the murderous-minded Saul, we have related for us: "Then, indeed, the congregation throughout the whole of Judea and Galilee and Samaria entered into a period of peace, being built up; and as it walked in the fear of Jehovah and in the comfort of the holy spirit it kept on multiplying." (Acts 9:31)

<hr/>

4. What was the purpose of the harvesting work done by Jesus and his disciples prior to Nisan 14, 33 C.E.?
5. What exciting events took place at Pentecost, 33 C.E., and how did these affect the harvest work to follow?

6. What effect did opposition to the preaching work have on Kingdom fruitage?
7. To what extent was Jesus' command to his disciples at Acts 1:8 finally carried out?

As the harvesting of sheeplike ones gained momentum, no doubt those early disciples constantly recalled Jesus' words: "Beg the Master of the harvest to send out workers into his harvest." Did Jehovah, "the Master of the harvest," answer that prayer? Indeed he did! Otherwise, how could it have been recorded: "The hope of that good news . . . was preached in all creation that is under heaven"?—Colossians 1:23.

Greater Urgency Today

8 Today, in the 1980's, the need for more harvest workers is greater than ever. Why? Because the scope of the world field is much greater. As a result, the crops to be reaped and gathered in are far more numerous. This is in harmony with what Jesus foretold. He said that his followers would do greater works than he had accomplished on earth, as far as the preaching of the good news was concerned.—John 14:12.

9 The sense of urgency in today's preaching work is highlighted in the dramatic setting described in a vision given to John, as recorded in Revelation chapter 7:1-3. There, "four angels standing upon the four corners of the earth" are seen "holding tight the four winds of the earth." How long is their grip on those "four winds" going to last? Only 'until after the sealing of the slaves of our God in their foreheads.' How long will that take? An indication is given by the fact that at the celebration of the Memorial on April 15, 1984, only 9,081 professed to be members of the 144,000. The anointed today are the last members of those described in Revelation 14:4 as being "bought from among mankind as firstfruits to God and to the Lamb." So it would appear that most of the "firstfruits" have been gathered in. But does the expression "firstfruits" mean that there are other fruits to follow? Why, of course! This was well symbolized by the abundant crops of other fruits gathered at the end of the Jewish agricultural year at the time of the Festival of Booths.—Deuteronomy 16:13-15.

10 Therefore it becomes clear that, as the harvest of the remnant of anointed ones drew to its close, another harvest ingathering was due to open up. Is this not reflected in what John next saw in vision? "After these things I saw, and, look! a great crowd, which no man was able to number, out of all nations and tribes and peoples and tongues." John was told: "These are the ones that come out of the great tribulation." (Revelation 7:9, 14) There is only a limited time left to complete the gathering of the "great crowd." Once those "four winds of the earth" are let loose, signaling the start of "the great tribulation," it will be too late! Can you not see the urgent need for more harvest workers to bring in the multitudes still to be found?

Thousands Now Responding

11 Jesus foretold this widening out of his harvesting work of sheeplike ones when he said: "And I have other sheep, which are not of this fold; those also I must bring, and they will listen to my voice, and they will become one flock, one shepherd." (John 10: 14, 16) Already there are more than 2,800,-000 of these "other sheep" who have actively identified themselves as belonging to that "one flock." Of that number, there were 179,421 who were baptized in the service

8. Why in the 1980's is the need greater than ever for more Kingdom workers?
9. (a) How is the urgency of today's preaching work emphasized in a vision of John, described in Revelation 7:1-3? (b) What significant conclusion can be drawn from the expression "firstfruits to God and to the Lamb" at Revelation 14:4?

10. What two harvestings have been in progress in modern times, and how does this fact underscore the urgent need for more harvest workers?
11. (a) To what extent are Jesus' "other sheep" sharing in the harvesting? (b) What is indicated by the attendance at the 1984 Memorial?

year of 1984! Yet, the attendance at the celebration of the Memorial was 7,416,974. What does this tell us? That there are many others who have heard the Shepherd's voice, but for one reason or another, they have not so far responded to Jesus' warm invitation: "Be my follower."—Luke 5:27.

¹² Where do you stand in relation to this vital harvesting work at the 'conclusion of this system of things'? (Matthew 13:39) Are you counted among the happy throngs of those who are now sharing in harvest joys? Or are you still an onlooker, mentally inclined to draw back from openly accepting the Fine Shepherd's invitation: "Be my follower"? Surely none today would want to make excuses like those three men in Luke chapter 9, discussed in our previous article. Think of what those three men missed out on—the joy of Kingdom service, including possibly a sharing in liberating some of those who were demon possessed!—Luke 9: 57-62; 10:17.

¹³ The apostle Paul said: "Without faith it is impossible to please [God] well." (Hebrews 11:6) Oh, yes, it does take faith on the part of everyone to put self-interest aside and willingly dedicate one's life to God as a harvest worker. For example, it may be that you have a serious health problem; perhaps some members of your family are violently opposed to Jehovah's Witnesses; maybe you feel that you are too old to make the needed changes in your life; on the other hand, you may consider yourself unable to face up to the peer pressure you experience at school. Whatever your circumstances may be, never forget that Jehovah understands your problems better than anyone else. Also, he is ready to draw close to you and to strengthen your resolve to serve him if only

you will take certain necessary steps yourself.—Psalm 103:13, 14; James 4:8.

Faith Moves 'Mountains'

¹⁴ Jesus said: "If you have faith the size of a mustard grain, you will say to this mountain, 'Transfer from here to there,' and it will transfer, and nothing will be impossible for you." This has been the personal experience of many of those hundreds of thousands who have responded to the call for more harvesters during the 1980's. Personal problems and difficulties that appeared mountainous to them at one time have been overcome with Jehovah's help. (Matthew 17:20; 19:26) Consider the following experiences:

¹⁵ A young man in California, U.S.A., was a polio victim, severely handicapped and sadly neglected by his family. Then one of Jehovah's Witnesses calling from house to house found him. A Bible study was started. But he was so shy that when the Witness arrived to conduct it, he would wheel his chair into a corner of the room and face the wall so that his face would not be seen. It took this young man months to overcome some of his problems. He did, however, and now he is a happy, baptized Witness.

¹⁶ A Catholic couple in Brazil were dissatisfied with their religion and eventually began studying the Bible with Jehovah's Witnesses. They felt that their spiritual needs were now being satisfied, but there was a big, a mountainous, problem: The husband, Antonio, was an inveterate smoker. He had smoked for 48 years, since he was seven years old! Over the years he had tried to break the habit but to no avail. This time, however, it was different, as Antonio relates: "Now I learned that if I wanted to

---

12. What important questions should we now ask ourselves?
13. How does faith play a vital part in your being a willing harvest worker?

14. Explain what Jesus meant by his words recorded at Matthew 17:20.
15, 16. Describe how a young man in the United States and a Catholic husband in Brazil overcame big problems standing in the way of their baptism.

please God and dedicate myself to do his will, I would have to quit. After much prayer, I was finally able to do so." How happy he was to be able to symbolize his dedication to Jehovah by water baptism! —Psalm 66:19; Mark 11:24.

[17] Demon possession of Jews was a problem that Jesus and his disciples continually encountered. The same evil influences are at work today, especially now that Satan and his demon forces have been hurled out of heaven down to this earth. (Revelation 12:7-9, 12, 17) In contrast with Christianity in its infancy, Jehovah has not given his people today the miraculous powers to cast out demons. However, the spiritual armor that he has provided for Christians can act as a protection against demon influence, and it can also be used as a means to free others from demonic control. (Ephesians 6:10-18) From Ghana comes this report: "By the determined efforts of the brothers, many are being freed from the grip of the demons." One Witness met a woman in the ministry, and as soon as a Bible discussion was begun, "the woman started weeping." What was the problem? The Witness related: 'A spirit possessed her, and whenever it did, it made her weep, and any money she happened to have on her vanished.' A regular Bible study helped her to break free from this demon harassment, enabling her to dedicate herself to Jehovah.—John 8:32.

[18] Problems like those described above might become so big in a person's mind that suicide is contemplated. Take the case of a young woman in New Zealand. The Witness who first called on her noticed that she was "uptight emotionally and obviously worked up over something." Later this person admitted that "she had been going to commit suicide and had decided to pray to God first to ask him to help her." At that point the Witness knocked on her door, so she really "thanked God for answering her prayer." Was this a coincidence? Then why do similar things happen so often? What did Jesus say? "When the Son of man arrives in his glory, and all the angels with him, . . . he will separate people one from another, just as a shepherd separates the sheep from the goats." (Matthew 25:31, 32; see also Revelation 14:6.) The angels are helping Jesus in the shepherding work, and they direct the Master's "fellow workers" to those who are crying to Him for help.—1 Corinthians 3:6, 9; see Acts 8:26-39; 16:9, 10.

[19] Today, no matter where we may be living, there are thousands of people who are burdened down and depressed with the same problems that many of Jehovah's people have already overcome. Some of them may be living just next door to you! They are urgently in need of help. Truly, as Jesus said: "The harvest, indeed, is great." We are begging the Master of the harvest now to send out more workers into his harvest during the year 1986. May your heart move you to respond to the call: Urgently Needed —More Harvest Workers!

19. What worldwide situation exists today, calling for what action on our part?

17. (a) What evil influence encountered by Jesus and his disciples is stronger than ever today? (b) How was demon possession dealt with by Jesus and his disciples in the first century, and how is it handled now?
18. What experience illustrates that angels are active in directing the preaching work?

Questions for Review

□ Who is the Master of the harvest?

□ What two harvests have been in progress?

□ What are the greater works that Jesus said his followers would do?

□ Why is faith needed by all harvest workers?

Self-Control
Vital for Christians

WHEN the police in a small town in New Mexico, U.S.A., responded to a report of a shooting, they found a young couple's kitchen spotted with blood and strewn with green beans. The woman of the home had suffered a flesh wound. Why? The alleged assailant, her companion, reportedly told the police: "Wouldn't you be mad if you had to eat green beans all the time?"

Hard to believe? Perhaps. Yet, for just such trifles people have even been killed. Such incidents are becoming more commonplace. To a large extent, this is due to a lack of self-control. Unable to control their emotions, people lash out in fits of anger—described by the apostle Paul as one of "the works of the flesh."—Galatians 5:19-21.

This increasing lack of self-control is part of the proof that we are living in the "critical times hard to deal with," "the last days" of this old, satanic system. Describing these days, Paul wrote that men (and women) would not be "open to any agreement, . . . *without self-control,* fierce." (2 Timothy 3:1, 3) Clearly, "the last days" are upon us, and they are becoming increasingly violent.

What are Christians to do in view of this? Paul urged them to combat "the works of the flesh" by developing the fruitage of God's spirit, including "self-control." (Galatians 5:19, 22, 23) What is self-control? Why does Paul recommend this? What are some of the benefits it brings?

Self-control has been defined as "restraint exercised over one's own impulses, emotions, or desires." Paul showed that such restraint helps to identify the true Christian. In fact, the exercise of self-control assists in developing the other fruits of God's spirit, such as peace, long-suffering, kindness, goodness, and mildness. It enables a Christian to persevere in serving God and in resisting the pressures from Satan, the world, and the imperfect flesh. Thus, Paul wrote the Galatians: "Keep walking by spirit and you will carry out no fleshly desire at all."—Galatians 5:16.

This is particularly necessary now since our days are marked by an increasing lack of self-control. For example, police in many lands find that more and more motorists are ignoring traffic laws. Such violations often produce angry shouting matches that can lead to fights. Why, one thoroughfare in Houston, Texas, has a stretch called "Altercation Avenue" because of the many fights that break out there. As another example, consider what has sometimes occurred as motorists have waited in line to buy gasoline. A lack of self-control has resulted in explosions of temper and even in murder as some motorists selfishly sought to cut in on the line to ensure getting the gasoline they wanted.

In these and similar pressure situations, the Christian must be sure not to be influenced by those who vent their anger on others. He should *always* be identified by self-control and mildness.

Benefits of Self-Control

Self-control brings many benefits, some of which are rather obvious. For example, God's Word condemns gluttony and drunkenness. (Proverbs 23:20, 21) The apostle Paul counsels: "Whether you are eating or drinking or doing anything else, do all things for God's glory." (1 Corinthians 10:31) Self-control helps us to comply, and this brings definite health benefits. However, overdrinking and gluttony are not only unhealthy but may even result in a Christian's being excluded from the Christian congregation. Hence, self-control in these areas helps a Christian to stay close to Jehovah.

Self-control also helps us to resist the permissive spirit of this world. (1 Corinthians 2:12) Today, fornication, homosexuality, adultery, and all types of sexual perversions are widely proclaimed to be acceptable, normal. However, Christian men and women resist such propaganda and fight to keep themselves clean in God's eyes. They know that "neither fornicators, nor idolaters, nor adulterers, nor men kept for unnatural purposes, nor men who lie with men . . . will inherit God's kingdom." (1 Corinthians 6:9, 10) Self-control makes it possible for them to resist contamination with immoral thinking that would suggest that such things are acceptable.

Wrong thinking spreads in various ways today but especially through entertainment, whether this be television, movies, music, stage plays, novels, or other media. The Christian must exercise self-control as to the *time* he spends enjoying entertainment, realizing that a person needs only so much entertainment to refresh himself, and after that point has been passed, entertainment becomes self-indulgent and a waste of time. He also has to use self-control as to the *type* of entertainment that he pursues, recognizing that much popular entertainment today highlights immoral attitudes, violent tendencies, or fascination with the occult. These things are not fit for Christians. —Ephesians 2:1-3.

Self-Control Results in Progress

Self-control is not just a protection. It also helps the Christian to make progress in spirituality and in his ministry. The apostle Peter stressed this when he wrote: "Supply to your faith virtue, to your virtue knowledge, to your knowledge self-control." These qualities, he said, along with endurance, godly devotion, brotherly affection, and love, "will prevent you from being either inactive or unfruitful regarding the accurate knowledge of our Lord Jesus Christ." (2 Peter 1:5-8) How does self-control help us to progress as Christian ministers?

The Christian usually spends much time each month telling others about the good news of God's Kingdom. (Matthew 24:14; 28:19, 20) However, some Christians may share in this activity only intermittently because of other demands made on their time or out of discouragement because of encountering a lack of interest. Such ones may possess an excellent knowledge of God's Word. However, instead of progressing, they retrogress, perhaps to the point of complete 'unfruitfulness.' What should they do?

'Supply to your knowledge self-control,' advised Peter. This may be self-control in connection with time devoted to recreation, social activity, or even secular work. Or the self-control may involve regularly strengthening oneself to persevere in spite of meeting up with apathy. This a person can cultivate by means of regular personal Bible study, as well as by attending Christian meetings.

Self-control also helps a Christian to make progress in his relationships with others. By cultivating self-control, he will enjoy more success in colaboring with others in the congregation, and a spirit of joy and peace will prevail. (Ephesians 4:3) Each one will, through self-control, seek not to become a cause of stumbling to others in the congregation.—Philippians 1:9, 10.

Self-control especially involves control of the tongue. This is essential if we are to avoid stumbling others. But this is not easy. The disciple James wrote: "If anyone does not stumble in word, this one is a perfect man." (James 3:2) James did, though, encourage all Christians to work at controlling their tongues, so that they could use them for blessing others. (James 3:5-12) Thus he wrote: "The fruit of righteousness has its seed sown under peaceful conditions for those who are making peace."—James 3:18.

Self-Control When Preaching

On occasion, a Christian in the preaching activity may meet a very uncontrolled individual. On such occasions the Christian must exercise strong self-control, staying calm and not retaliating in word or deed. One Christian woman set an astonishing example in this regard. At the third home she called on one Saturday morning, the householder opened the door and began shooting at her. The minister remained calm, however. "You shot me," she said. "Yes," replied the householder, "I shot you," and then continued shooting. The Witness reports: "I had two bullet holes in my coat, two in my bag and one in my foot. One bullet came between my feet. I felt powder burns on my legs as I was trying to get off her porch."

The Christian woman kept unusual control of herself in this trying situation. She prayed to Jehovah to help her to get to the next house and not fall on the way. She made it, negotiating the steps with the help of her hands. The householder answered her knock and, learning that she had been shot, very kindly took her inside. The woman and her older daughter, a nurse, gave first aid while another daughter called the police and the paramedics. The self-control of this Christian minister greatly impressed first the police, then the paramedics, the crowd that gathered, and finally the hospital staff.

True, most Christian ministers are not shot at. But they do often have to deal with individuals who are very upset and angry. They should remember that "an answer, when mild, turns away rage." (Proverbs 15:1) Jesus is their model. Of him, Peter wrote: "When he was being reviled, he did not go reviling in return.

In Our Next Issue

■ **The Mysterious Horsemen of the Apocalypse**

■ **Days Like "the Days of Noah"**

■ **Building for an Eternal Future**

When he was suffering, he did not go threatening, but kept on committing himself to the one who judges righteously." (1 Peter 2:23) Yes, self-control is an excellent recommendation for the Christian minister.

How to Cultivate Self-Control

Since self-control is a fruit of God's holy spirit, we need that spirit to develop it. As Paul wrote, "Keep walking by spirit." (Galatians 5:16, 22, 23) All Christians must be eager students of God's Word, itself a product of holy spirit. Regular study of that Word, and applying what we learn in our lives, will enable us to control our thoughts, to bring "every thought into captivity to make it obedient to the Christ." (2 Corinthians 10:5; Romans 12:2) Yes, it is vital for a Christian to learn to think as Jesus thinks and as Jehovah God thinks.

The heart, the seat of motivation, must also be constantly influenced by God's spirit since self-control means to control, or to restrain, one's emotions or desires, which spring from the heart. (Matthew 15:19) Remember, then, this good counsel: "More than all else that is to be guarded, safeguard your heart, for out of it are the sources of life." (Proverbs 4:23) Let God's spirit touch your heart as you learn Bible principles. Seek to memorize, if possible, Scriptural counsel that you can draw on when faced with trying situations.

Good association with fellow Christians also helps develop self-control. (Hebrews 10:23-25) The various meetings of the Christian congregation are designed to help all Christians to grow in Bible knowledge and in the ability to produce the fruitage of God's spirit. Additionally, seek out as associates those who are exemplary in the matter of self-control. Thus you, too, will be encouraged to develop this quality.—Proverbs 13:20; 27:17.

One thing that must never be neglected is regular communication with Jehovah through prayer. The Christian must constantly ask for his aid in cultivating self-control. Beg for his spirit to assist you. And if you find you have failed to exercise self-control in some matter, humbly and earnestly request Jehovah's forgiveness. Jesus taught us to pray: "Do not bring us into temptation." Paul encouraged Christians to "persevere in prayer." So, go to Jehovah "incessantly," asking for his help as you strive to cultivate self-control in your life.—Matthew 6:13; Romans 12:12; 1 Thessalonians 5:17.

What an excellent Christian quality self-control is! Continue to cultivate it. Those who do so have more self-respect. They enjoy greater peace and happiness in their family and congregational relationships, as well as better relationships with others in their daily lives. More importantly, self-control helps to ensure a good relationship with the Creator and serves to identify them as true Christian servants of their God, Jehovah.

For Your Study

This is the ninth article on "the fruitage of the spirit." You can find the other articles in this series in the *Watchtower* issues of March 15, June 15, July 1, August 1, September 15, October 1, October 15, and November 15, 1985. You may enjoy setting as a personal study project a review of this fine Scriptural information.

"The Word Was With God, and the Word Was . . . "?

FEW passages in the Bible have received more attention in the churches of Christendom than John 1:1. The way it reads in many Bible versions is similar to that of the *King James Version:* "In the beginning was the Word, and the Word was with God [ὁ θεός], and the Word was God [θεός]."

Many who accept the Trinity point to this passage in support of their doctrine. The verse, however, has been rendered differently in some translations, with the acknowledgment that the original Greek reveals a difference that is hidden in renderings such as the above.

In 1984 there appeared in English a translation from German of a commentary by scholar Ernst Haenchen (*Das Johannesevangelium. Ein Kommentar*). It renders John 1:1: "In the beginning was the Logos, and the Logos was with God, and divine [of the category divinity] was the Logos." —*John 1. A Commentary on the Gospel of John Chapters 1-6,* page 108, translated by Robert W. Funk.

When comparing Genesis 1:1 with the first verse of John's Gospel, this commentary observes: "John 1:1, however, tells of something that was in existence already in time primeval; astonishingly, it is not 'God.' . . . The Logos (we have no word in either German or English that corresponds to the range of meaning of the Greek term) is thereby elevated to such heights that it almost becomes offensive. The expression is made tolerable only by virtue of the continuation in 'and the Logos was in the presence of God,' viz., in intimate, personal union with God."

Does that sound as if scholar Haenchen discerned in the Greek some distinction between God and the Logos, or Word? The author's following words focus on the fact that in the original language no definite article is used with the word *the·os'*, or god, in the final phrase. The author explains:

"In order to avoid misunderstanding, it may be inserted here that θεός [*the·os'*] and ὁ θεός [*ho the·os'*] ('god, divine' and 'the God') were not the same thing in this period. Philo has therefore written: the λόγος [Logos] means only θεός ('divine') and not ὁ θεός ('God') since the logos is not God in the strict sense. . . . In a similar fashion, Origen, too, interprets: the Evangelist does not say that the logos is 'God,' but only that the logos is 'divine.' In fact, for the author of the hymn [in John 1:1], as for the Evangelist, only the Father was 'God' (ὁ θεός; cf. 17:3); 'the Son' was subordinate to him (cf. 14:28). But that is only hinted at in this passage because here the emphasis is on the proximity of the one to the other."

Then Haenchen observes: "It was quite possible in Jewish and Christian monotheism to speak of divine beings that existed alongside and under God but were not identical with him. Phil 2:6-10 proves that. In that passage Paul depicts just such a divine being, who later became man in Jesus Christ. . . . Thus, in both Philippians and John 1:1 it is not a matter of a dialectical relationship between two-in-one, but of a personal union of two entities." —Pages 109, 110.

Hence, rather than saying that the Logos (Jesus) was with God and was God, John 1:1 explains that the Logos was with the Almighty God and was divine, or was a god.

Insight on the News

"Being Given in Marriage"

Not only is marriage on the increase in the United States —up 16 percent from a decade ago—but so is its cost. The average outlay for a wedding and a reception (wedding feast) has skyrocketed past $6,000, with some so luxurious as to merit a $50,000-plus price tag. Is it any wonder that last year's wedding expenses rang up a bill of *$20 thousand million*—a growth of 152 percent since 1975? On what was the money spent? On just about everything "from rings and flowers to music, limousines, and honeymoon trips," reports *Fortune* magazine.

Weddings are to be joyous occasions. Yet, Jesus Christ pointed to an aspect of marriage as a characteristic of the generation that would live during 'his presence and the conclusion of this wicked system of things.' (Matthew 24:3, 34) He said: "Just as the days of Noah were, so the presence of the Son of man will be. For as they were in those days before the flood, eating and drinking, *men marrying and women being given in marriage,* until the day that Noah entered into the ark; and they took no note until the flood came and swept them all away, so the presence of the Son of man will be." (Matthew 24:37-39) Jesus did not mean that it is wrong for people living in "the last days" to marry. (2 Timothy 3:1) Rather, he warned that many would become so absorbed in marriage, which has now come to include extremely elaborate and costly weddings, that they would ignore the urgency of the times.

"Who Hid the Dead Sea Scrolls?"

Under that title, in *Biblical Archaeologist,* Norman Golb, professor of Hebrew and Judaeo-Arabic Studies at the University of Chicago, sets out to reveal who *really* hid the Dead Sea Scrolls. At the same time, he seeks to disprove a theory more than three decades old. In the spring of 1947, ancient Hebrew Scripture scrolls and non-Biblical texts were discovered in caves along the northwestern shore of the Dead Sea. That discovery was hailed as "the greatest find ever made in the field of biblical archaeology." The scrolls include the oldest known manuscripts of any books of the Bible and date back to the second century B.C.E.

Until now, scholars have attributed the manuscripts' origin to the Essenes, a Jewish religious sect. But Golb believes that subsequent discoveries of additional ancient Hebrew texts in Masada, Jericho, and elsewhere in the Judean desert point to Jerusalem as the place of the scrolls' origin. Not the Essenes but the Jews fleeing from the Roman armies between 66 and 70 C.E. "brought the bundles or sackfuls of texts from the capital to the desert caves for hiding," asserts Golb.

Regardless of further archaeological evidence that may be uncovered, the Biblical scrolls found in those caves underscore the purity of the Bible's text and Jehovah's ability to preserve his Word. "All flesh is like grass, and all its glory is like a blossom of grass; the grass becomes withered, and the flower falls off, but the saying of Jehovah endures forever," says 1 Peter 1:24, 25.

Godly Wisdom for World Leaders?

As world peace becomes more elusive, the ever-present threat of war continues to dominate the minds of world leaders. *Time* magazine reports that Soviet party leader Mikhail S. Gorbachev lamented: "Surely, God on high has not refused to give us enough wisdom to find ways to bring us an improvement . . . in relations between the two great nations on earth, nations on whom depends the very destiny of civilization." Similarly, when ending his controversial Durban speech on August 15, South African President P. W. Botha said out of concern for the peace of his nation: "We undertake to do all that man can possibly do. . . . I pray that Almighty God would grant us the wisdom and the strength to seek to fulfil His will."

It is interesting that noted governmental leaders speak of a need for godly wisdom in connection with their peacemaking efforts. However, according to the Bible, global peace and security will be realized only through God's Kingdom. (Daniel 2:44; compare Isaiah 9:6, 7.) Thus, only those who align themselves with this *heavenly* Kingdom can hope to find lasting peace.

An "Eight-Month Miracle" in Peru

THE crowd of 34,238 was exuberant. They had come from all over Peru, in fact, from many parts of the world, to attend the dedication of the beautiful new branch office of the Watch Tower Society in Lima. Their hearts were filled with excitement as they listened to the program detailing the construction, done in eight action-packed months—something quite unheard of in Peru for a project of this size.

Preliminary Preparations

The rapid expansion of true worship in Peru had resulted in the need for larger branch headquarters. A 1.8 hectare (4.4 a.) piece of property was bought in 1980. At first the land was used to grow fruits and vegetables for the branch workers.

Meanwhile, in view of the rapidly rising inflation rate, the Witnesses decided to start buying and storing up building materials, such as bricks, steel rods, fixtures, and tiles. A good supply of water was another essential. So why not dig a well? A crew of Witnesses started the job and dug by hand to a depth of 75 meters (246 ft). Then outside help was engaged to continue the project until water was struck 96 meters (315 ft) down.

Then early in February of 1984, three Witnesses in the United States provided a "fast-paced" plan. The proposed two-story building—including offices, 22 bedrooms, family room, dining room, laundry, and Kingdom Hall—could be put up in eight months they said. For Peru, that would amount to a modern-day miracle!

A Ready Organization

On March 25 a special kickoff meeting was held at the Society-owned assembly

Young and old shared in the work

site at Campoy to inform the local Witnesses of what was going to take place. Even though there were only 19,000 Kingdom publishers in all of Peru at the time, 26,500 people came to that meeting. The enthusiasm they then showed never waned throughout the project.

The work force was organized. Over 200 workers were drawn from the ranks of regular and special pioneers, and brothers with experience in convention organization were put in key positions. The congregations were assigned specific weekends to come and help.

To accommodate the full-time workers, the warehouse was converted into a huge dormitory. Mattresses were placed on top of cardboard cartons of literature. Showers and toilets were installed along the outside walls. Since this was the beginning of the winter season in Peru, the brothers learned to do a lively quickstep when taking their cold showers early in the morning. An excellent cafeteria was set up, with breakfast for all at 7:00 before work at 7:30. A half-hour's drive away at the Campoy assembly grounds, sisters took care of the laundry. A shoe-repair shop was also opened, as work shoes wore out quickly.

Help From Afar

A total of 145 brothers from North America came at various stages of the construction. Many of them had participated in Kingdom Hall building projects. As the work progressed and the need arose, concrete men, bricklayers, plumbers, and electricians arrived to do their part, completing it in two or three weeks and then returning to their home congregations. But a few stayed for the entire eight months.

These brothers came with their own tools and supplies to work alongside others whose language they could little understand. But sign language, facial expressions, and mispronounced words, along with the willingness to work together, got the points across and the job done.

Many Peruvian brothers lovingly opened their homes to accommodate these visitors. At 6:00 a.m. every working day, a 15-seat "gringo bus," as it affectionately came to be called, made the rounds to collect the guests and get them to the breakfast table at the work site. Members of the Peru Bethel family took part in this truly enjoyable work.

To care for spiritual needs, an English-language congregation was organized. A number of the visitors also did fine work in the field ministry, starting home Bible studies that continued after they left.

Public Interest Aroused

Hundreds of local brothers and sisters, young and old, came to the construction site on weekends to share in the work. It was encouraging to see sisters and small children having a share according to their ability. All this activity, of course, did not go unnoticed.

An engineer from a large construction company stopped by. Seeing the way the work was done, he asked, "How much do you have to pay them to get them to work like that?" Another observer inquired: "What makes your workers so cheerful?" A crew from a television station in Lima spent one whole afternoon filming and interviewing the different workers.

A Job Well Done

Was the building really completed in eight months? Yes, but never did the brothers feel they were being pressured into completing it in exactly that time. From the start, it was impressed upon all that what was desired was a well-built, sturdy structure that would truly represent Jehovah's people in a dignified way. If nine or ten months were needed to do such a job, then so be it.

With the willing local volunteers and experienced help from overseas, the work was finished right on target. On December 3, 1984, eight months and one week from the start, the Bethel family moved in.

The Big Day Arrived

January 27, 1985, was the eagerly awaited dedication day for the new branch building. M. G. Henschel, a member of the Governing Body of Jehovah's Witnesses, came from Brooklyn, New York, to serve as the principal speaker. Visitors from other lands and those who had worked full time on the building—about 500 in all—packed out the new Kingdom Hall and dining room. The Campoy assembly grounds were tied in by telephone wire.

In the morning, Brother Henschel delivered the dedication address in Spanish. The afternoon commenced with a special program at the Campoy assembly grounds. Then the entire crowd of 34,238 was invited to tour the new facilities. They rejoiced to see the "eight-month miracle," the physical evidence of Jehovah's blessing.

The building project has brought many blessings. Besides providing an up-to-date facility, working together for eight months proved to be invaluable. Christian unity was enhanced. Spiritual maturity was cultivated. The fine association at the meetings, at the meal tables, and especially at morning worship strengthened the bond of love among fellow Christians. Those who came from North America felt that the little bit of a "foreign assignment" did them a lot of good. Yes, the eight months of happy association and vigorous activity will long be remembered by all who had a share in the "miracle."
—Compare Haggai 1:7, 8.

Do You Remember?

How have you benefited from recent issues of *The Watchtower?* Why not test your memory with the following:

□ **How can parents today assist their children in developing godly devotion?**

Parents ought to be intensely concerned about their children's spiritual nourishment. They should teach them to do personal study at an early age. (2 Timothy 3:15) They should also make sure that each child has his own literature, prepares for the congregation meetings, and is urged to participate in them. The regular family study should provide knowledge in line with the children's specific needs.—8/15, pages 23, 24.

□ **What does it mean to 'walk with God' (Micah 6:8)?**

'Walking with God' means adopting a way of life that harmonizes with God's revealed will and purpose. (1 Corinthians 10:31) —9/1, page 5.

□ **Why did many of the kings of Judah fail to show complete confidence in Jehovah?**

Many of the kings of Judah fell into the snare of idolatry (2 Chronicles 25:14); some were trapped by making foreign alliances (2 Chronicles 16:1-3, 7; 28:16, 20); and still others were ensnared by haughtiness. (2 Chronicles 32:25, 26; Isaiah 39:1-7)—9/1, pages 29, 30.

□ **How can imperfect humans show godlike kindness?**

They can show the superior quality of godlike kindness by being kind not only to members of their own family but also to those around them who may be unthankful and have shown themselves to be enemies. (Luke 6:35) —9/15, page 11.

□ **What are some ways in which Jehovah has manifested goodness?**

Jehovah's goodness has been seen through his patient, merciful, and considerate attitude toward imperfect mankind (Exodus 34:6, 7); he has manifested goodness through his creation (Matthew 5:44, 45; Romans 1:20); it is also shown by the provision of a ransom for sinful mankind and by the Kingdom that will bring this earth to a paradise condition.—10/1, pages 27, 28.

□ **Why can the United Nations never succeed in bringing peace and security to this earth?**

God never gave man the wisdom and the right to govern himself. (Jeremiah 10:23) This world is under the influence of Satan the Devil. (John 12:31; Revelation 12:9-12) The United Nations inherits this world's weaknesses, evils, and corruption. The United Nations is trying to save this world that is opposed to God's purposes. (1 John 2:17; Revelation 21:1)—10/15, page 5.

□ **What is a very persuasive argument for having faith in the Bible?**

As a person studies the Bible and makes application thereof, it exerts a powerful motivating force for good in that one's life. (Hebrews 4:12)—10/15, page 23.

□ **What basic truth is highlighted in the Bible record of men and angels following the path of independence?**

The Bible shows that in order for man to have a successful and delightful way of life, he must be dependent on God for guidance. (Jeremiah 10:23; Proverbs 14: 12)—11/1, pages 4, 5.

□ **What is one important factor that can determine how old a person should be before considering marriage?**

The fruitage of God's spirit as described in Galatians 5:22, 23 should begin showing in that person's life long before marriage is contemplated. Hence, a determining factor would be, To what extent are these qualities already in evidence in the young person's life?—11/1, page 18.

□ **How can mildness act as a protective covering to shield us from harm?**

When faced with a potentially explosive situation, the anger of the offended person may be diffused by application of the proverb: "An answer, when mild, turns away rage." (Proverbs 15:1)—11/15, page 6.

□ **Can those having hope of everlasting life on earth be declared righteous even now?**

Those chosen by God for heavenly life must, even now, be declared righteous; perfect human life is imputed to them. (Romans 8:1) This is not necessary now for those who may live forever on earth. But such ones can now be declared righteous as friends of God, as was faithful Abraham. (James 2:21-23; Romans 4:1-4) After such ones achieve actual human perfection at the end of the Millennium and then pass the final test, they will be in position to be declared righteous for everlasting human life.—12/1, pages 10, 11, 17, 18.

SUBJECT INDEX FOR "THE WATCHTOWER" 1985

Indicating date of issue in which article appears

They Saw It on His Desk

An employee at the Milan airport in Italy laid on his desk a copy of the book *You Can Live Forever in Paradise on Earth*, leaving it open to the beautiful illustration on pages 12 and 13. As people came by they stopped and looked at the book, asking where they might get a copy. One pilot obtained the book, read it, and showed it to his crew. He returned and ordered 37 copies. A month later he asked for 48 more copies for other pilots and crew members. In time, the employee had supplied 120 books for others at the airport.